THE ENCHANTED WORLD

JOG ON, JOG ON

Jog on, jog on, the footpath way,
And merrily hent the stile-a:
A merry heart goes all the day,
Your sad tires in a mile-a.

WILLIAM SHAKESPEARE: *The Winter's Tale*

The Enchanted World

❖ ❖ ❖ ❖ ❖ ❖ ❖ ❖ ❖

THE GREATEST
FOLK & FAIRY TALES

Collector's Library Editions

This edition first published in 2008 by CRW Publishing Limited
69 Gloucester Crescent, London NW1 7EG
under the *Collector's Library Editions* imprint

ISBN   978 1 905716 46 3

2 4 6 8 10 9 7 5 3 1

Typeset in Great Britain by Antony Gray
Printed and bound in China by Imago

CONTENTS

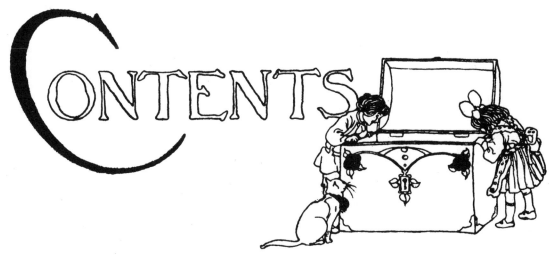

This compendium contains all the most familiar tales as well as several that are unusual. None of them
has been attributed to an author, country or date but they have been put in alphabetical order.
Dip in and enjoy some of the tales and characters that belong to the enchanted world.

Contents

SOME OF Aesop's Fables

The Goose that Laid the Golden Eggs

A man and his wife had the good fortune to possess a goose which laid a golden egg every day. Lucky though they were, they soon began to think they were not getting rich fast enough, and, imagining the bird must be made of gold inside, they decided to kill it in order to secure the whole store of precious metal at once. But when they cut it open they found it was just like any other goose. Thus, they neither got rich all at once, as they had hoped, nor enjoyed any longer the daily addition to their wealth.

Much wants more and loses all.

The Fox & the Grapes

A hungry fox saw some fine bunches of grapes hanging from a vine that was trained along a high trellis and did his best to reach them by jumping as high as he could into the air. But it was all in vain, for they were just out of reach: so he gave up trying, and walked away with an air of dignity and unconcern, remarking, 'I thought those grapes were ripe, but I see now they are quite sour.'

The Cat & the Mice

There was once a house that was overrun with mice. A cat heard of this, and said to herself, 'That's the place for me,' and off she went and took up her quarters in the house, and caught the mice one by one and ate them. At last the mice could stand it no longer, and they determined to take to their holes and stay there. 'That's awkward,' said the cat to herself: 'the only thing to do is to coax them out by a trick.' So she considered a while, and then climbed up the wall and let herself hang down by her hind legs from a peg, and pretended to be dead. By and by a mouse peeped out and saw the cat hanging there. 'Aha!' it cried, 'you're very clever, madam, no doubt: but you may turn yourself into a bag of meal hanging there, if you like, yet you won't catch us coming anywhere near you.'

If you are wise you won't be deceived by the innocent airs of those whom you have once found to be dangerous.

The Mischievous Dog

There was once a dog who used to snap at people and bite them without any provocation and he was a great nuisance to everyone who came to his master's house. So his master fastened a bell round his neck to warn people of his presence. The dog was very proud of the bell, and strutted about tinkling it with immense satisfaction. But an old dog came up to him and said, 'The fewer airs you give yourself the better, my friend. You don't think, do you, that your bell was given you as a reward of merit? On the contrary, it is a badge of disgrace.'

Notoriety is often mistaken for fame.

The Charcoal-Burner & the Fuller

There was once a charcoal-burner who lived and worked by himself. A fuller, however, happened to come and settle in the same neighbourhood; and the charcoal-burner, having made his acquaintance and finding he was an agreeable sort of fellow, asked him if he would come and share his house: 'We shall get to know one another better that way,' he said, 'and beside, our household expenses will be diminished.' The fuller thanked him, but replied, 'I couldn't think of it, sir: why, everything I take such pains to whiten would be blackened in no time by your charcoal.'

The Fox & the Crow

A crow was sitting on a branch of a tree with a piece of cheese in her beak when a fox observed her and set his wits to work to discover some way of getting the cheese. Coming and standing under the tree he looked up and said, 'What a noble bird I see above me! Her beauty is without equal, the hue of her plumage exquisite. If only her voice is as sweet as her looks are fair, she ought without doubt to be queen of the birds.' The crow was hugely flattered by this, and just to show the fox that she could sing she gave a loud caw. Down came the cheese, of course, and the fox, snatching it up, said, 'You have a voice, madam, I see: what you lack is wits.'

The Crab & His Mother

An old crab said to her son, 'Why do you walk sideways like that, my son? You ought to walk straight.' The young crab replied, 'Show me how, dear mother, and I'll follow your example.' The old crab tried, but tried in vain, and then saw how foolish she had been to find fault with her child.

Example is better than precept.

The Wolf & the Lamb

A wolf came upon a lamb straying from the flock, and felt some compunction about taking the life of so helpless a creature without some plausible excuse; so he cast about for a grievance and said at last, 'Last year, sirrah, you grossly insulted me.' 'That is impossible, sir,' bleated the lamb, 'for I wasn't born then.' 'Well,' retorted the wolf, 'you feed in my pastures.' 'That cannot be,' replied the lamb, 'for I have never yet tasted grass.' 'You drink from my spring, then,' continued the wolf. 'Indeed, sir,' said the poor lamb, 'I have never yet drunk anything but my mother's milk.' 'Well, anyhow,' said the wolf, 'I'm not going without my dinner': and he sprang upon the lamb and devoured it without more ado.

The Peacock & the Crane

A peacock taunted a crane with the dullness of her plumage. 'Look at my brilliant colours,' said he, 'and see how much finer they are than your poor feathers.' 'I am not denying,' replied the crane, 'that yours are far gayer than mine; but when it comes to flying I can soar into the clouds, whereas you are confined to the earth like any dunghill cock.'

The Cat & the Birds

A cat heard that the birds in an aviary were ailing. So he got himself up as a doctor, and, taking with him a set of the instruments proper to his profession, presented himself at the door, and inquired after the health of the birds. 'We shall do very well,' they replied, without letting him in, 'when we've seen the last of you.'

A villain may disguise himself, but he will not deceive the wise.

The Crow & the Pitcher

A thirsty crow found a pitcher with some water in it, but so little was there that, try as she might, she could not reach it with her beak, and it seemed as though  she would die of thirst within sight of the remedy. At last she hit upon a clever plan. She began dropping pebbles into the pitcher, and with each pebble the water rose a little higher until at last it reached the brim, and the knowing bird was enabled to quench her thirst.

Necessity is the mother of invention.

The Spendthrift & the Swallow

A spendthrift, who had wasted his fortune, and had nothing left but the clothes in which he stood, saw a swallow one fine day in early spring. Thinking that summer had come, and that he could now do without his coat, he went and sold it for what it would fetch. A change, however, took place in the weather, and there came a sharp frost which killed the unfortunate swallow. When the spendthrift saw its dead body he cried, 'Miserable bird! Thanks to you I am perishing of cold myself.'

One swallow does not make a summer.

The Mistress & Her Servants

A widow, thrifty and industrious, had two servants, whom she kept pretty hard at work. They were not allowed to lie long abed in the mornings, for the old lady had them up and doing as soon as the cock crew. They disliked intensely having to get up at such an hour, especially in wintertime, and they thought that if it were not for the cock waking up their mistress so horribly early, they could sleep longer. So they caught it and wrung its neck. But they weren't prepared for the consequences. For what happened was that their mistress, not hearing the cock crow as usual, waked them up earlier than ever, and set them to work in the middle of the night.

The North Wind & the Sun

A dispute arose between the North Wind and the Sun, each claiming that he was stronger than the other. At last they agreed to try their powers upon a traveller, to see which could soonest strip him of his cloak.

The North Wind had the first try, and gathering up all his force for the attack, he came whirling furiously down upon the man, and caught up his cloak as though he would wrest it from him by one single effort; but the harder he blew, the more closely the man wrapped it round himself. Then came the turn of the Sun. At first he beamed gently upon the traveller, who soon unclasped his cloak and walked on with it hanging loosely about his shoulders; then he shone forth in his full strength, and the man, before he had gone many steps, was glad to throw his cloak right off and complete his journey more lightly clad.

Persuasion is better than force.

The Thieves & the Cock

Some thieves broke into a house, and found nothing worth taking except a cock, which they seized and carried off with them. When they were preparing their supper, one of them caught up the cock, and was about to wring his neck, when he cried out for mercy and said, 'Pray do not kill me: you will find me a most useful bird, for I rouse honest men to their work in the morning by my crowing.' But the thief replied with some heat, 'Yes, I know you do, making it still harder for us to get a livelihood. Into the pot you go!'

The Ass & the Old Peasant

An old peasant was sitting in a meadow watching his ass, which was grazing close by, when all of a sudden he caught sight of armed men stealthily approaching. He jumped up in a moment, and begged the ass to fly with him as fast as he could, 'Or else,' said he, 'we shall both be captured by the enemy.' But the ass just looked round lazily and said, 'And if so, do you think they'll make me carry heavier loads than I have to now?' 'No,' said his master. 'Oh, well, then,' said the ass, 'I don't mind if they do take me, for I shan't be any worse off.'

The Dog in the Manger

A dog was lying in a manger on the hay which had been put there for the cattle, and when they came and tried to eat, he growled and snapped at them and wouldn't let them get at their food. 'What a selfish beast,' said one of them to his companions; 'he can't eat himself and yet he won't let those eat who can.'

The Goods & the Ills

There was a time in the youth of the world when goods and ills entered equally into the concerns of men, so that the goods did not prevail to make them altogether blessed, nor the ills to make them wholly miserable. But owing to the foolishness of mankind the ills multiplied greatly in number and increased in strength, until it seemed as though they would deprive the goods of all share in human affairs, and banish them from the earth. The latter, therefore, betook themselves to heaven and complained to Jupiter of the treatment they had received, at the same time praying him to grant them protection from the ills, and to advise them concerning the manner of their intercourse with men. Jupiter granted their request for protection, and decreed that for the future they should not go among men openly in a body, and so be liable to attack from the hostile ills, but singly and unobserved, and at infrequent and unexpected intervals. Hence it is that the earth is full of ills, for they come and go as they please and are never far away; while goods, alas! come one by one only, and have to travel all the way from heaven, so that they are very seldom seen.

The Boy & the Filberts

A boy put his hand into a jar of filberts, and grasped as many as his fist could possibly hold. But when he tried to pull it out again, he found he couldn't do so, for the neck of the jar was too small to allow of the passage of so large a handful. Unwilling to lose his nuts but unable to withdraw his hand, he burst into tears. A bystander, who saw where the trouble lay, said to him, 'Come, my boy, don't be so greedy: be content with half the amount, and you'll be able to get your hand out without difficulty.'

Do not attempt too much at once.

The Bear & the Fox

A bear was once bragging about his generous feelings, and saying how refined he was compared with other animals. (There is, in fact, a tradition that a bear will never touch a dead body.) A fox, who heard him talking in this strain, smiled and said, 'My friend, when you are hungry, I only wish you *would* confine your attention to the dead and leave the living alone.'

A hypocrite deceives no one but himself.

The Hare & the Tortoise

A hare was one day making fun of a tortoise for being so slow upon his feet. 'Wait a bit,' said the tortoise; 'I'll run a race with you, and I'll wager that I win.' 'Oh, well,' replied the hare, who was much amused at the idea, 'let's try and see'; and it was soon agreed that the fox should set a course for them, and be the judge. When the time came both started off together, but the hare was soon so far ahead that he thought he might as well have a rest: so down he lay and fell fast asleep. Meanwhile the tortoise kept plodding on, and in time reached the goal. At last the hare woke up with a start, and dashed on at his fastest, but only to find that the tortoise had already won the race.

Slow and steady wins the race.

The Man & the Image

A poor man had a wooden image of a god, to which he used to pray daily for riches. He did this for a long time, but remained as poor as ever, till one day he caught up the image in disgust and hurled it with all his strength against the wall. The force of the blow split open the head and a quantity of gold coins fell out upon the floor. The man gathered them up greedily, and said, 'Oh you old fraud, you! When I honoured you, you did me no good whatever, but no sooner do I treat you to insults and violence than you make a rich man of me!'

Hercules & the Wagoner

A wagoner was driving his team along a muddy lane with a full load behind them when the wheels of his wagon sank so deep in the mire that no efforts of his horses could move them. As he stood there, looking helplessly on, and calling loudly at intervals upon Hercules for assistance, the god himself appeared, and said to him, 'Put your shoulder to the wheel, man, and goad on your horses, and then you may call on Hercules to assist you. If you won't lift a finger to help yourself, you can't expect Hercules or anyone else to come to your aid.'

Heaven helps those who help themselves.

The Old Woman & the Wine-Jar

An old woman picked up an empty wine-jar which had once contained a rare and costly wine, and which still retained some traces of its exquisite bouquet. She raised it to her nose and sniffed at it again and again. 'Ah,' she cried, 'how delicious must have been the liquid which has left behind so ravishing a smell.'

Aladdin and the Wonderful Lamp

There once lived a poor tailor, who had a son called Aladdin, a careless, idle boy who would do nothing but play all day long in the streets with little idle boys like himself. This so grieved the father that he died; yet, in spite of his mother's tears and prayers, Aladdin did not mend his ways.

One day, when he was playing in the streets as usual, a stranger asked him his age, and if he were not the son of Mustapha the tailor. 'I am, sir,' replied Aladdin; 'but he died a long time ago.'

On this the stranger, who was a famous African magician, fell on his neck and kissed him, saying: 'I am your uncle, and knew you from your likeness to my brother. Go to your mother and tell her I am coming.'

Aladdin ran home, and told his mother of his newly found uncle.

'Indeed, child,' she said, 'your father had a brother, but I always thought he was dead.'

However, she prepared supper, and bade Aladdin seek his uncle, who came laden with wine and fruit. He presently fell down and kissed the place where Mustapha used to sit, bidding Aladdin's mother not to be surprised at not having seen him before, as he had been forty years out of the country. He then turned to Aladdin, and asked him his trade, at which the boy hung his head, while his mother burst into tears. On learning that Aladdin was idle and would learn no trade, he offered to take a shop for him and stock it with merchandise. Next day he bought Aladdin a fine suit of clothes, and took him all over the city, showing him the sights, and brought him home at nightfall to his mother, who was overjoyed to see her son so fine.

Next day the magician led Aladdin into some beautiful gardens a long way outside the city gates. They sat down by a fountain, and the magician pulled a cake from his girdle, which he divided between them. They then journeyed onwards till they almost reached the mountains. Aladdin was so tired that he begged to go back, but the magician beguiled him with pleasant stories, and led him on in spite of himself.

At last they came to two mountains divided by a narrow valley.

'We will go no farther,' said the false uncle. 'I will show you something wonderful; only do you gather up sticks while I kindle a fire.'

When it was lit the magician threw on it a powder he had about him, at the same time saying some magical words. The earth trembled a little and opened in front of them, disclosing a square flat stone with a brass ring in the middle to raise it by. Aladdin tried to run away, but the magician caught him and gave him a blow that knocked him down.

'What have I done, uncle?' he said piteously; whereupon the magician said more kindly: 'Fear nothing, but obey me. Beneath this stone lies a treasure which is to be yours, and no one else may touch it, so you must do exactly as I tell you.'

At the word treasure, Aladdin forgot his fears, and grasped the ring as he was told, saying the names of his father and grandfather. The stone came up quite easily and some steps appeared.

'Go down,' said the magician; 'at the foot of those steps you will find an open door leading into three large halls. Tuck up your gown and go through them without touching anything, or you will die instantly. These halls lead into a garden of fine fruit trees. Walk on till you come to a niche in a terrace where stands a lighted lamp. Pour out the oil it contains and bring it to me.'

He drew a ring from his finger and gave it to Aladdin, bidding him prosper.

Aladdin found everything as the magician had said, gathered some fruit off the trees, and, having got the lamp, arrived back at the mouth of the cave. The magician cried out in a great hurry: 'Make haste and give me the lamp.' This Aladdin refused to do until he was out of the cave. The magician flew into a terrible passion, and throwing some more powder on the fire, he said something, and the stone rolled back into its place.

The magician left Persia for ever, which plainly showed that he was no uncle of Aladdin's but a cunning magician who had read in his magic books of a wonderful lamp, which would make him the most powerful man in the world. Though he alone knew where to find it, he could only receive it from the hand of another. He had picked out the foolish Aladdin for this purpose, intending to get the lamp and kill him afterwards.

For two days Aladdin remained in the dark, crying and lamenting. At last he clasped his hands in prayer, and in so doing rubbed the ring, which the magician had forgotten to take from him. Immediately an enormous and frightful genie rose out of the earth, saying: 'What wouldst thou with me? I am the Slave of the Ring, and will obey thee in all things.'

Aladdin fearlessly replied: 'Deliver me from this place!' whereupon the earth opened, and he found himself outside. As soon as his eyes could bear the light he went home, but fainted on the threshold. When he came to himself he told his mother what had passed, and showed her the lamp and the fruits he had gathered in the garden, which were in reality precious stones. He then asked for some food.

'Alas! child,' she said, 'I have nothing in the house, but I have spun a little cotton and will go and sell it.'

Aladdin bade her keep her cotton, for he would sell the lamp instead. As it was very dirty she began to rub it, that it might fetch a higher price. Instantly a hideous genie appeared, and asked what she would have. She fainted away, but Aladdin, snatching the lamp, said boldly: 'Fetch me something to eat!'

The genie returned with a silver bowl, twelve silver plates containing rich meats, two silver cups, and two bottles of wine. Aladdin's mother, when she came to herself, said: 'Whence comes this splendid feast?'

'Ask not, but eat,' replied Aladdin.

So they sat at breakfast till it was dinner-time, and Aladdin and his mother talked about the lamp. She begged him to sell it, and have nothing to do with devils.

'No,' said Aladdin, 'since chance has made us aware of its virtues, we will use it and the ring like-

The Slave of the Ring appears to Aladdin

wise, which I shall always wear on my finger.' When they had eaten all the genie had brought, Aladdin sold one of the silver plates, and so on till none were left. He then had recourse to the genie, who gave him another set of plates, and thus they lived for many years.

One day Aladdin heard an order from the sultan proclaiming that everyone was to stay at home and close his shutters while the princess, his daughter, went to and from the bath. Aladdin was seized by a desire to see her face, which was very difficult, as she always went veiled. He hid himself behind the door of the bath, and peeped through a chink. The princess lifted her veil as she went in, and looked so beautiful that Aladdin fell in love with her at first sight. He went home so changed that his mother was frightened. He told her he loved the princess so deeply that he could not live without her, and meant to ask her in marriage of her father. His mother, on hearing this, burst out laughing, but Aladdin at last prevailed upon her to go before the sultan and carry his request. She fetched a napkin and laid in it the magic fruits from the enchanted garden, which sparkled and shone like the most beautiful jewels. She took these with her to please the sultan, and set out, trusting in the lamp. The grand-vizier and the lords of council had just gone in as she entered the hall and placed herself in front of the sultan. He, however, took no notice of her. She went every day for a week, and stood in the same place.

When the council broke up on the sixth day the sultan said to his vizier: 'I see a certain woman in the audience-chamber every day carrying something in a napkin. Call her next time, that I may find out what she wants.'

Next day, at a sign from the vizier, she went up to the foot of the throne, and remained kneeling till the sultan said to her: 'Rise, good woman, and tell me what you want.'

She hesitated, so the sultan sent away all but the vizier, and bade her speak freely, promising to forgive her beforehand for anything she might say. She then told him of her son's violent love for the princess.

'I prayed him to forget her,' she said, 'but in vain; he threatened to do some desperate deed if I refused to go and ask your majesty for the hand of the princess. Now I pray you to forgive not me alone, but my son Aladdin.'

The sultan asked her kindly what she had in the napkin, whereupon she unfolded the jewels and presented them.

He was thunderstruck, and turning to the vizier said: 'What sayest thou? Ought I not to bestow the princess on one who values her at such a price?'

The vizier, who wanted her for his own son, begged the sultan to withhold her for three months, in the course of which he hoped his son would contrive to make him a richer present. The sultan granted this, and told Aladdin's mother that, though he consented to the marriage, she must not appear before him again for three months.

Aladdin waited patiently for nearly three months, but after two had elapsed his mother, going into the city to buy oil, found everyone rejoicing, and asked what was going on.

'Do you not know,' was the answer, 'that the son of the grand-vizier is to marry the sultan's daughter tonight?'

Breathless, she ran and told Aladdin, who was overwhelmed at first, but presently bethought him of the lamp. He rubbed it, and the genie appeared, saying: 'What is thy will?'

Aladdin replied: 'The sultan, as thou knowest, has broken his promise to me, and the vizier's son is to have the princess. My command is that tonight you bring hither the bride and bride-groom.'

'Master, I obey,' said the genie.

Aladdin then went to his chamber, where, sure enough at midnight the genie transported the bed containing the vizier's son and the princess.

'Take this new-married man,' he said, 'and put him outside in the cold, and return at daybreak.'

Whereupon the genie took the vizier's son out of bed, leaving Aladdin with the princess.

'Fear nothing,' Aladdin said to her; 'you are my wife, promised to me by your unjust father, and no harm shall come to you.'

The princess was too frightened to speak, and passed the most miserable night of her life, while Aladdin lay down beside her and slept soundly. At the appointed hour the genie fetched in the shivering bridegroom, laid him in his place, and transported the bed back to the palace.

Presently the sultan came to wish his daughter good-morning. The unhappy vizier's son jumped up and hid himself, while the princess would not say a word, and was very sorrowful.

The sultan sent her mother to her, who said: 'How comes it, child, that you will not speak to your father? What has happened?'

The princess sighed deeply, and at last told her mother how, during the night, the bed had been carried into some strange house, and what had passed there. Her mother did not believe her in the least, but bade her rise and consider it an idle dream.

The following night exactly the same thing happened, and next morning, on the princess's refusing to speak, the sultan threatened to cut off her head. She then confessed all, bidding him ask the vizier's son if it were not so. The sultan told the vizier to ask his son, who owned the truth, adding that, dearly as he loved the princess, he had rather die than go through another such fearful night, and wished to be separated from her. His wish was granted, and there was an end of feasting and rejoicing.

When the three months were over, Aladdin sent his mother to remind the sultan of his promise. She stood in the same place as before, and the sultan, who had forgotten Aladdin, at once remembered him, and sent for her. On seeing her poverty the sultan felt less inclined than ever to keep his word, and asked the vizier's advice, who counselled him to set so high a value on the princess that no man living could come up to it.

The sultan then turned to Aladdin's mother, saying: 'Good woman, a sultan must remember his promises, and I will remember mine, but your son must first send me forty basins of gold, brimful with jewels, carried by forty black slaves, led by as many white ones, splendidly dressed. Tell him that I await his answer.' The mother of Aladdin bowed low and went home, thinking all was lost.

The eighty slaves, after kneeling before the sultan, stood in a half-circle round the throne with their arms crossed, while Aladdin's mother presented them to the sultan

She gave Aladdin the message, adding: 'He may wait long enough for your answer!'

'Not so long, mother, as you think,' her son replied. 'I would do a great deal more than that for the princess.'

He summoned the genie, and in a few moments the eighty slaves arrived, and filled up the small house and garden.

Aladdin made them set out to the palace, two and two, followed by his mother. They were so richly dressed, with such splendid jewels in their girdles, that everyone crowded to see them and the golden basins they carried on their heads.

They entered the palace, and, after kneeling before the sultan, stood in a half-circle round the throne with their arms crossed, while Aladdin's mother presented them to the sultan.

He hesitated no longer, but said: 'Good woman, return and tell your son that I wait for him with open arms.'

She lost no time in telling Aladdin, bidding him make haste. But Aladdin first called the genie. 'I would like a scented bath,' he said, 'a richly embroidered habit, a horse surpassing the sultan's, and twenty slaves to attend me. Besides this, six slaves, beautifully dressed, to wait on my mother; and lastly, ten thousand pieces of gold in ten purses.'

No sooner said than done. Aladdin mounted his horse and passed through the streets, the slaves strewing gold as they went. Those who had played with him in his childhood knew him not, he had grown so handsome.

When the sultan saw him he came down from his throne, embraced him, and led him into a hall where a feast was spread, intending to marry him to the princess that very day.

But Aladdin refused, saying, 'I must build a palace fit for her,' and took his leave.

Once home he said to the genie: 'Build me a palace of the finest marble, set with jasper, agate and other precious stones. In the middle you shall build me a large hall with a dome, its four walls of massy gold and silver, each side having six windows, whose lattices, all except one, which is to be left unfinished, must be set with diamonds and rubies. There must be stables and horses and grooms and slaves; go and see about it!'

The palace was finished by next day, and the genie carried him there and showed him all his orders faithfully carried out, even to the laying of a velvet carpet from Aladdin's palace to the sultan's. Aladdin's mother then dressed herself carefully, and walked to the palace with her slaves, while he followed her on horseback. The sultan sent musicians with trumpets and cymbals to meet them, so that the air resounded with music and cheers. She was taken to the princess, who saluted her and treated her with great honour. At night the princess said goodbye to her father, and set out on the carpet for Aladdin's palace, with his mother at her side, and followed by the hundred slaves. She was charmed at the sight of Aladdin, who ran to receive her.

'Princess,' he said, 'blame your beauty for my boldness if I have displeased you.'

She told him that, having seen him, she willingly obeyed her father in this matter. After the wedding had taken place Aladdin led her into the hall, where a feast was spread, and she supped with him, after which they danced till midnight.

Next day Aladdin invited the sultan to see the palace. On entering the hall with the four-and-twenty windows, with their rubies, diamonds, and emeralds, he cried: 'It is a world's wonder! There is only one thing that surprises me. Was it by accident that one window was left unfinished?'

'No, sir, by design,' returned Aladdin. 'I wished your majesty to have the glory of finishing this palace.'

The sultan was pleased, and sent for the best jewellers in the city. He showed them the unfinished window, and bade them fit it up like the others.

'Sir,' replied their spokesman, 'we cannot find jewels enough.'

The sultan had his own fetched, which they soon used, but to no purpose, for in a month's time the work was not half done. Aladdin, knowing that their task was vain, bade them undo their work and carry the jewels back, and the genie finished the window at his command. The sultan was surprised to receive his jewels again and visited Aladdin, who showed him the window finished. The sultan embraced him, the envious vizier meanwhile hinting that it was the work of enchantment.

Aladdin had won the hearts of the people by his gentle bearing. He was made captain of the sultan's armies, and won several battles for him, but remained modest and courteous as before, and lived thus in peace and content for several years.

But far away in Africa the magician remembered Aladdin, and by his magic arts discovered that Aladdin, instead of perishing miserably in the cave, had escaped, and had married a princess, with whom he was living in great honour and wealth. He knew that the poor tailor's son could only have accomplished this by means of the lamp, and travelled night and day till he reached the capital of China, bent on Aladdin's ruin. As he passed through the town he heard people talking everywhere about a marvellous palace.

'Forgive my ignorance,' he asked, 'what is this palace you speak of?'

'Have you not heard of Prince Aladdin's palace,' was the reply, 'the greatest wonder of the world? I will direct you if you have a mind to see it.'

The magician thanked him who spoke, and having seen the palace knew that it had been raised by the genie of the lamp, and became half mad with rage. He determined to get hold of the lamp, and again plunge Aladdin into the deepest poverty.

Unluckily, Aladdin had gone a-hunting for eight days, which gave the magician plenty of time. He bought a dozen copper lamps put them into a basket, and went to the palace, crying: 'New lamps for old!' followed by a jeering crowd.

The princess, sitting in the hall of four-and-twenty windows, sent a slave to find out what the noise was about. She came back laughing, so that the princess scolded her.

'Madam,' replied the slave, 'who can help laughing to see an old fool offering to exchange fine new lamps for old ones?'

Another slave, hearing this, said: 'There is an old one on the cornice there which he can have.'

Now this was the magic lamp, which Aladdin had left there, as he could not take it out hunting with him. The princess, not knowing its value, laughingly bade the slave take it and make the exchange.

She went and said to the magician: 'Give me a new lamp for this.'

He snatched it and bade the slave take her choice, amid the jeers of the crowd. Little he cared, but left off crying his lamps, and went out of the city gates to a lonely place, where he remained till nightfall, when he pulled out the lamp and rubbed it. The genie appeared, and at the magician's command carried him, together with the palace and the princess in it, to a lonely place in Africa.

Next morning the sultan looked out of the window towards Aladdin's palace and rubbed his eyes, for it was gone. He sent for the vizier, and asked what had become of the palace. The vizier looked out too, and was lost in astonishment. He again put it down to enchantment, and this time the sultan believed him, and sent thirty men on horseback to fetch Aladdin in chains. They met him riding home, bound him, and forced him to go with them on foot. The people, however, who loved him, followed, armed, to see that he came to no harm. He was carried before the sultan, who ordered the executioner to cut off his head. The executioner made Aladdin kneel down, bandaged his eyes, and raised his scimitar to strike.

At that instant the vizier, who saw that the crowd had forced their way into the courtyard and were scaling the walls to rescue Aladdin, called to the executioner to stay his hand. The people, indeed, looked so threatening that the sultan gave way and ordered Aladdin to be unbound, and pardoned him in the sight of the crowd.

Aladdin now begged to know what he had done.

'False wretch!' said the sultan, 'come hither,' and showed him from the window the place where his palace had stood.

Aladdin was so amazed that he could not say a word.

The magician snatched the lamp and bade the slave take her choice, amid the jeers of the crowd

'Where is my palace and my daughter?' demanded the sultan. 'For the first I am not so deeply concerned, but my daughter I must have, and you must find her or lose your head.'

Aladdin begged for forty days in which to find her, promising if he failed to return and suffer death at the sultan's pleasure. His prayer was granted, and he went forth sadly from the sultan's presence. For three days he wandered about like a madman, asking everyone what had become of his palace, but they only laughed and pitied him. He came to the banks of a river, and knelt down to say his prayers before throwing himself in. In so doing he rubbed the magic ring he still wore.

The genie he had seen in the cave appeared, and asked his will.

'Save my life, genie,' said Aladdin, 'and bring my palace back.'

'That is not in my power,' said the genie; 'I am only the slave of the ring; you must ask the slave of the lamp.'

'Even so,' said Aladdin; 'but thou canst take me to the palace, and set me down under my dear wife's window.' He at once found himself in Africa, under the window of the princess, and fell asleep out of sheer weariness.

He was awakened by the singing of the birds, and his heart was lighter. He saw plainly that all his misfortunes were owing to the loss of the lamp, and vainly wondered who had robbed him of it.

That morning the princess rose earlier than she had done since she had been carried into Africa by the magician, whose company she was forced to endure once a day. She, however, treated him so harshly that he dared not live there altogether. As she was dressing, one of her women looked out and saw Aladdin. The princess ran and opened the window, and at the noise she made Aladdin looked up. She called to him to come to her, and great was the joy of these lovers at seeing each other again.

After he had kissed her Aladdin said: 'I beg of you, princess, in God's name, before we speak of anything else, for your own sake and mine, tell me what has become of an old lamp I left on the cornice in the hall of four-and-twenty windows, when I went a-hunting.'

'Alas!' she said, 'I am the innocent cause of our sorrows,' and told him of the exchange of the lamp.

'Now I know,' cried Aladdin, 'that we have to thank the African magician for this! Where is the lamp?'

'He carries it about with him,' said the princess.

'I know, for he pulled it out of his breast to show me. He wishes me to break my faith with you and marry him, saying that you were beheaded by my father's command. He is forever speaking ill of you, but I only reply by my tears. If I persist, I doubt not that he will use violence.'

Aladdin comforted her, and left her for a while. He changed clothes with the first person he met in the town, and having bought a certain powder returned to the princess, who let him in by a little side door.

'Put on your most beautiful dress,' he said to her, 'and receive the magician with smiles, leading him to believe that you have forgotten me. Invite him to sup with you, and say you wish to taste the wine of his country. He will go for some, and while he is gone I will tell you what to do.'

She listened carefully to Aladdin, and when he left her arrayed herself gaily for the first time since she left China. She put on a girdle and headdress of diamonds, and seeing in a glass that she looked more beautiful than ever, received the magician, saying to his great amazement: 'I have made up my mind that Aladdin is dead, and that all my tears will not bring him back to me, so I am resolved to mourn no more, and have therefore invited you to sup with me; but I am tired of the wines of China, and would fain taste those of Africa.'

The magician flew to his cellar, and the princess put the powder Aladdin had given her in her cup. When he returned she asked him to drink her health in the wine of Africa, handing him her cup in exchange for his as a sign she was reconciled to him.

Before drinking the magician made her a speech

The death of the African magician

in praise of her beauty, but the princess cut him short saying: 'Let me drink first, and you shall say what you will afterwards.' She set her cup to her lips and kept it there, while the magician drained his to the dregs and fell back lifeless.

The princess then opened the door to Aladdin, and flung her arms round his neck, but Aladdin put her away, bidding her to leave him, as he had more to do. He then went to the dead magician, took the lamp out of the bosom of his garment, and bade the genie carry the palace and all in it back to China. This was done, and the princess in her chamber only felt two little shocks, and little thought she was at home again.

The sultan, who was sitting in his closet, mourning for his lost daughter, happened to look up, and rubbed his eyes, for there stood the palace as before! He hastened thither, and Aladdin received him in the hall of the four-and-twenty windows, with the princess at his side. Aladdin told him what had happened, and showed him the dead body of the magician, that he might believe. A ten days' feast was proclaimed, and it seemed as if Aladdin might now live the rest of his life in peace; but it was not to be.

The African magician had a younger brother, who was, if possible, more wicked and more cunning than himself. He travelled to China to avenge his brother's death, and went to visit a pious woman called Fatima, thinking she might be of use to him. He entered her cell and clapped a dagger to her breast, telling her to rise and do his bidding on pain of death. He changed clothes with her, coloured his face like hers, put on her veil and murdered her, that she might tell no tales. Then he went towards the palace of Aladdin, and all the people thinking he was the holy woman, gathered round him, kissing his hands and begging his blessing. When he got to the palace there was such a noise going on round him that the princess bade her slave look out of the window and ask what was the matter. The slave said it was the holy woman, curing people by her touch of their ailments, whereupon the princess, who had long desired to see Fatima, sent for her. On coming to the princess the magician offered up a prayer for her health and prosperity. When she had thanked him the princess made him sit by

her, and begged him to stay with her always. The false Fatima, who wished for nothing better, consented, but kept his veil down for fear of discovery. The princess showed him the hall, and asked him what he thought of it.

'It is truly beautiful,' said the false Fatima. 'In my mind it wants but one thing.'

'And what is that?' said the princess.

'If only a roc's egg,' replied he, 'were hung up from the middle of this dome, it would be the wonder of the world.'

After this the princess could think of nothing but a roc's egg, and when Aladdin returned from hunting he found her in a very ill humour. He begged to know what was amiss, and she told him that all her pleasure in the hall was spoilt for the want of a roc's egg hanging from the dome.

'It that is all,' replied Aladdin, 'you shall soon be happy.'

He left her and rubbed the lamp, and when the genie appeared commanded him to bring a roc's egg. The genie gave such a loud and terrible shriek that the hall shook.

'Wretch!' he cried, 'is it not enough that I have done everything for you, but you must command me to bring my master and hang him up in the midst of this dome? You and your wife and your palace deserve to be burnt to ashes; but this request does not come from you, but from the brother of the African magician whom you destroyed. He is now in your palace disguised as the holy woman – whom he murdered. He it was who put that wish into your wife's head. Take care of yourself, for he means to kill you.' So saying the genie disappeared.

Aladdin went back to the princess, saying his head ached, and requesting that the holy Fatima should be fetched to lay her hands on it. But when the magician came near, Aladdin, seizing his dagger, pierced him to the heart.

'What have you done?' cried the princess. 'You have killed the holy woman!'

'Not so,' replied Aladdin, 'but a wicked magician,' and told her of how she had been deceived.

After this Aladdin and his wife lived in peace. He succeeded the sultan when he died, and reigned for many years, leaving behind him a long line of kings.

Ali Baba and the Forty Thieves

In a town in Persia there dwelt two brothers, one named Cassim, the other Ali Baba. Cassim was married to a rich wife and lived in plenty, while Ali Baba had to maintain his wife and children by cutting wood in a neighbouring forest and selling it in the town. One day, when Ali Baba was in the forest, he saw a troop of men on horseback, coming towards him in a cloud of dust. He was afraid they were robbers, and climbed into a tree for safety. When they came up to him and dismounted, he counted forty of them. They unbridled their horses and tied them to trees. The finest man among them, whom Ali Baba took to be their captain, went a little way among some bushes, and said: 'Open, Sesame!' so plainly that Ali Baba heard him. A door opened in the rocks, and having made the troop go in, he followed them, and the door shut again of itself. They stayed some time inside, and Ali Baba, fearing they might come out and catch him, was forced to sit patiently in the tree. At last the door opened again, and the forty thieves came out. As the captain went in last he came out first, and made them all pass by him; he then closed the door, saying: 'Shut, Sesame!' Every man bridled his horse and mounted, the captain put himself at their head, and they returned as they came.

Then Ali Baba climbed down and went to the door concealed among the bushes, and said: 'Open, Sesame!' and it flew open. Ali Baba, who expected a dull, dismal place, was greatly surprised to find it large and well lighted, hollowed by the hand of man in the form of a vault, which received the light from an opening in the ceiling. He saw rich bales of merchandise – silk, stuff-brocades, all piled together, and gold and silver in heaps, and money in leather purses. He went in and the door shut behind him. He did not look at the silver, but brought out as many bags of gold as he thought his asses, which were browsing outside, could carry, loaded them with the bags, and hid it all with faggots. Using the words: 'Shut, Sesame!' he closed the door and went home.

Then he drove his asses into the yard, shut the gates, carried the money-bags to his wife, and emptied them out before her. He bade her keep the secret, and he would go and bury the gold. 'Let me first measure it,' said his wife. 'I will go and borrow a measure from someone, while you dig the hole.' So she ran to the wife of Cassim and borrowed a measure. Knowing Ali Baba's poverty, the sister was curious to find out what sort of grain his wife wished to measure, and artfully put some suet at the bottom of the measure. Ali Baba's wife

Ali Baba entered and was greatly surprised to find it large and well lighted

went home and set the measure on the heap of gold, and filled it and emptied it often, to her great content. She then carried it back to her sister, without noticing that a piece of gold was sticking to it, which Cassim's wife perceived directly her back was turned. She grew very curious, and said to Cassim when he came home: 'Cassim, your brother is richer than you. He does not count his money, he measures it.' He begged her to explain this riddle, which she did by showing him the piece of money and telling him where she found it. Then Cassim grew so envious that he could not sleep, and went to his brother in the morning before sunrise. 'Ali Baba,' he said, showing him the gold piece, 'you pretend to be poor and yet you measure gold.' By this Ali Baba perceived that through his wife's folly Cassim and his wife knew their secret, so he confessed all and offered Cassim a share. 'That I expect,' said Cassim; 'but I must know where to find the treasure, otherwise I will discover all, and you will lose all.' Ali Baba, more out of kindness than fear, told him of the cave, and the very words to use. Cassim left Ali Baba, meaning to be beforehand with him and get the treasure for himself. He rose early next morning, and set out with three mules loaded with great chests. He soon found the place, and the door in the rock. He said: 'Open, Sesame!' and the door opened and shut behind him. He could have feasted his eyes all day on the treasures, but he now hastened to gather together as much of it as possible; but when he was ready to go he could not remember what to say for thinking of his great riches. Instead of 'Sesame', he said: 'Open, Barley!' and the door remained fast. He named several different sorts of grain, all but the right one, and the door still stuck fast. He was so frightened at the danger he was in that he had as much forgotten the word as if he had never heard it.

About noon the robbers returned to their cave, and saw Cassim's mules roving about with great chests on their backs. This gave them the alarm; they drew their sabres, and went to the door, which opened on their captain's saying: 'Open, Sesame!' Cassim, who had heard the trampling of their horses' feet, resolved to sell his life dearly, so when the door opened he leaped out and threw the captain down. In vain, however, for the robbers with their sabres soon killed him. On entering the cave they saw all the bags laid ready, and could not imagine how anyone had got in without knowing their secret. They cut Cassim's body into four

quarters, and nailed them up inside the cave, in order to frighten anyone who should venture in, and went away in search of more treasure.

As night drew on Cassim's wife grew very uneasy, and ran to her brother-in-law, and told him where her husband had gone. Ali Baba did his best to comfort her, and set out to the forest in search of Cassim. The first thing he saw on entering the cave was his dead brother. Full of horror, he put the body on one of his asses, and bags of gold on the other two, and, covering all with some faggots, returned home. He drove the two asses laden with gold into his own yard, and led the other to Cassim's house. The door was opened by the slave Morgiana, whom he knew to be both brave and cunning. Unloading the ass, he said to her: 'This is the body of your master, who has been murdered, but whom we must bury as though he had died in his bed. I will speak with you again, but now tell your mistress I am come.' The wife of Cassim, on learning the fate of her husband, broke out into cries and tears, but Ali Baba offered to let her live with him and his wife if she would promise to keep his counsel and leave everything to Morgiana; whereupon she agreed, and dried her eyes.

Morgiana, meanwhile, sought an apothecary and asked him for some lozenges. 'My poor master,' she said, 'can neither eat nor speak, and no one knows what his distemper is.' She carried home the lozenges and returned next day weeping, and asked for an essence only given to those just about to die. Thus, in the evening, no one was surprised to hear the wretched shrieks and cries of Cassim's wife and Morgiana, telling everyone that Cassim was dead. The day after Morgiana went to an old cobbler near the gates of the town who opened his stall early, put a piece of gold in his hand, and bade him follow her with his needle and thread. Having bound his eyes with a handkerchief, she took him to the room where the body lay, pulled off the bandage, and bade him sew the quarters together, after which she covered his eyes again and led him home. Then they buried Cassim, and Morgiana his slave followed him to the grave, weeping and tearing her hair, while Cassim's wife stayed at home uttering lamentable cries. Next day Ali Baba took possession of the house and gave Cassim's shop to his eldest son.

The forty thieves, on their return to the cave, were much astonished to find Cassim's body gone and some of their money-bags. 'We are certainly discovered,' said the captain, 'and shall be undone

*One of you who is bold and artful must go into the city dressed as
a traveller, and discover whom we have killed*

if we cannot find out who it is that knows our secret. Two men must have known it; we have killed one, we must now find the other. To this end one of you who is bold and artful must go into the city dressed as a traveller, and discover whom we have killed, and whether men talk of the strange manner of his death. If the messenger fails he must lose his life, lest we be betrayed.' One of the thieves started up and offered to do this, and after the rest had highly commended him for his bravery he disguised himself, and happened to enter the town at daybreak, just by Baba Mustapha's stall. The thief bade him good-day, saying: 'Honest man, how can you possibly see to stitch at your age?' 'Old as I am,' replied the cobbler, 'I have very good eyes, and will you believe me when I tell you that I sewed a dead body together in a place where I had less light than I have now.' The robber was overjoyed at his good fortune, and, giving him a piece of gold, desired to be shown the house where he stitched up the dead body. At first Mustapha refused, saying that he had been blindfolded; but when the robber gave him another piece of gold he began to think he might remember the turnings if blindfolded as before. This means succeeded; the robber partly led him, and was partly guided by him, right to the house he sought, the door of which the robber marked with a piece of chalk. Then, well pleased,

he bade farewell to Baba Mustapha and returned to the forest. By and by Morgiana, going out, saw the mark the robber had made, quickly guessed that some mischief was brewing, and fetching a piece of chalk marked two or three doors on each side, without saying anything to her master or mistress.

The thief, meantime, told his comrades of his discovery. The captain thanked him, and bade him show him the house he had marked. But when they came to it they saw that five or six of the houses were chalked in the same manner. The guide was so confounded that he knew not which one to choose, and when they returned he was at once beheaded for having failed. Another robber was dispatched, and, having won over Baba Mustapha, marked the house in red chalk; but Morgiana being again too clever for them, the second messenger was put to death also. The captain now resolved to go himself, but, wiser than the others, he did not mark the house, but looked at it so closely that he could not fail to remember it. He returned, and ordered his men to go into the neighbouring villages and buy nineteen mules, and thirty-eight leather jars, all empty except one, which was to be full of oil. The captain put one of his men, fully armed, into each, rubbing the outside of the jars with oil from the full vessel.

24

Then the nineteen mules were loaded with thirty-seven robbers in jars, and the jar of oil, and reached the town by dusk. The captain stopped his mules in front of Ali Baba's house, and said to Ali Baba, who was sitting outside for coolness: 'I have brought some oil from a distance to sell at tomorrow's market, but it is now so late that I know not where to pass the night, unless you will do me the favour to take me in.' Though Ali Baba had seen the captain of the robbers in the forest, he did not recognise him in the disguise of an oil merchant. He bade him welcome, opened his gates for the mules to enter, and went to Morgiana to bid her prepare a bed and supper for his guest. He brought the stranger into his hall, and after they had supped went again to speak to Morgiana in the kitchen, while the captain went into the yard under pretence of seeing after his mules, but really to tell his men what to do. Beginning at the first jar and ending at the last, he said to each man: 'As soon as I throw some stones from the window of the chamber where I lie, cut the jars open with your knives and come out, and I will be with you in a

Then the nineteen mules were loaded with thirty-seven robbers in jars, and the jar of oil

trice.' He returned to the house, and Morgiana led him to his chamber. She then told Abdallah, her fellow-slave, to set on the pot to make some broth for her master, who had gone to bed. Meanwhile her lamp went out, and she had no more oil in the house. 'Do not be uneasy,' said Abdallah; 'go into the yard and take some out of one of those jars.' Morgiana thanked him for his advice, took the oil pot, and went into the yard. When she came to the first jar the robber inside said softly: 'Is it time?'

Any other slave but Morgiana, on finding a man in the jar instead of the oil she wanted, would have screamed and made a noise; but she, knowing the danger her master was in, bethought herself of a plan, and answered quietly: 'Not yet, but presently.' She went to all the jars, giving the same answer, till she came to the jar of oil. She now saw that her master, thinking to entertain an oil merchant, had let thirty-eight robbers into his house. She filled her oil pot, went back to the kitchen, and, having lit her lamp, went again to the oil jar and filled a large kettle full of oil. When it boiled she went and poured enough oil into every jar to stifle and kill the robber inside. When this brave deed was done she went back to the kitchen, put out the fire and the lamp, and waited to see what would happen.

In a quarter of an hour the captain of the robbers awoke, got up, and opened the window. As all seemed quiet, he threw down some little pebbles which hit the jars. He listened, and as none of his men seemed to stir he grew uneasy, and went down into the yard. On going to the first jar and saying, 'Are you asleep?' he smelt the hot boiled oil, and knew at once that his plot to murder Ali Baba and his household had been discovered. He found all the gang was dead, and, missing the oil out of the last jar, became aware of the manner of their death. He then forced the lock of a door leading into a garden, and climbing over several walls made his escape. Morgiana heard and saw all this, and, rejoicing at her success, went to bed and fell asleep.

At daybreak Ali Baba arose, and, seeing the oil jars still there, asked why the merchant had not gone with his mules. Morgiana bade him look in the first jar and see if there was any oil. Seeing a man, he started back in terror. 'Have no fear,' said Morgiana; 'the man cannot harm you: he is dead.' Ali Baba, when he had recovered somewhat from his astonishment, asked what had become of the merchant. 'Merchant!' said she, 'he is no more a merchant than I am!' and she told him the whole story, assuring him that it was a plot of the robbers

The captain returned to his lonely cave

of the forest, of whom only three were left, and that the white and red chalk marks had something to do with it. Ali Baba at once gave Morgiana her freedom, saying that he owed her his life. They then buried the bodies in Ali Baba's garden, while the mules were sold in the market by his slaves.

The captain returned to his lonely cave, which seemed frightful to him without his lost companions, and firmly resolved to avenge them by killing Ali Baba. He dressed himself carefully, and went into the town, where he took lodgings in an inn. In the course of a great many journeys to the forest he carried away many rich stuffs and much fine linen, and set up a shop opposite that of Ali Baba's son. He called himself Cogia Hassan, and as he was both civil and well dressed he soon made friends with Ali Baba's son, and through him with Ali Baba, whom he was continually asking to sup with him. Ali Baba, wishing to return his kindness, invited him into his house and received him smiling, thanking him for his kindness to his son. When the merchant was about to take his leave Ali Baba stopped him, saying: 'Where are you going, sir, in such haste? Will you not stay and sup with me?' The merchant refused, saying that he had a reason; and, on Ali Baba's asking him what that was, he replied: 'It is, sir, that I can eat no victuals that have any salt in them.' 'If that is all,' said Ali Baba, 'let me tell you that there shall be no salt in either the meat or the bread that we eat tonight.' He went to give this order to Morgiana, who was much surprised. 'Who is this man,' she said, 'who eats no salt with his meat?' 'He is an honest man, Morgiana,' returned her master; 'therefore do as I bid you.' But she could not

withstand a desire to see this strange man, so she helped Abdallah to carry up the dishes, and saw in a moment that Cogia Hassan was the robber captain, and carried a dagger under his garment. 'I am not surprised,' she said to herself, 'that this wicked man, who intends to kill my master, will eat no salt with him; but I will hinder his plans.'

She sent up the supper by Abdallah, while she made ready for one of the boldest acts that could be thought on. When the dessert had been served, Cogia Hassan was left alone with Ali Baba and his son, whom he thought to make drunk and then to murder. Morgiana, meanwhile, put on a headdress like a dancing-girl's, and clasped a girdle round her waist, from which hung a dagger with a silver hilt, and said to Abdallah: 'Take your tabor, and let us go and divert our master and his guest.' Abdallah took his tabor and played before Morgiana until they came to the door, where Abdallah stopped playing and Morgiana made a low courtesy. 'Come in, Morgiana,' said Ali Baba, 'and let Cogia Hassan see what you can do;' and, turning to Cogia Hassan, he said: 'She's my gifted housekeeper.' Cogia Hassan was by no means pleased, for he feared that his chance of killing Ali Baba was gone for the present; but he pretended great eagerness to see Morgiana, and Abdallah began to play and Morgiana to dance. After she had performed several dances she drew her dagger and made passes with it, sometimes pointing it at her own breast, sometimes at her master's, as if it were part of the dance. Suddenly, out of breath, she snatched the tabor from Abdallah with her left hand, and, holding the dagger in her right hand, held out the tabor to her master. Ali Baba and his son put a piece of gold into it, and Cogia Hassan, seeing that she was coming to him, pulled out his purse to make her a present, but while he was putting his hand into it Morgiana plunged the dagger into his heart.

'Unhappy girl!' cried Ali Baba and his son, 'what have you done to ruin us?'

'It was to preserve you, master, not to ruin you,' answered Morgiana. 'See here,' opening the false merchant's garment and showing the dagger; 'see what an enemy you have entertained! Remember, he would eat no salt with you, and what more would you have? Look at him! he is both the false oil merchant and the captain of the forty thieves.'

Ali Baba was so grateful to Morgiana for thus saving his life that he offered her to his son in marriage, who readily consented, and a few days after the wedding was celebrated with greatest splendour.

At the end of a year Ali Baba, hearing nothing of the two remaining robbers, judged they were dead, and set out to the cave. The door opened on his saying: 'Open, Sesame!' He went in, and saw that nobody had been there since the captain left it. He brought away as much gold as he could carry, and returned to town. He told his son the secret of the cave, which his son handed down in his turn, so the children and grandchildren of Ali Baba were rich to the end of their lives.

After she had performed several dances she drew her dagger and made passes with it,
sometimes pointing it at her own breast, sometimes at her master's, as if it were part of the dance

Ashputtel

The wife of a rich man fell sick; and when she felt that her end drew nigh, she called her only daughter to her bedside, and said, 'Always be a good girl, and I will look down from heaven and watch over you.'

Soon afterwards she shut her eyes and died, and was buried in the garden; and the little girl went every day to her grave and wept, and was always good and kind to all about her. And the snow fell and spread a beautiful white covering over the grave; but by the time the spring came, and the sun had melted it away again, her father had married another wife. This new wife had two daughters of her own that she brought home with her; they were fair in face but foul at heart, and it was now a sorry time for the poor little girl.

'What does the good-for-nothing want in the parlour?' said they; 'they who would eat bread should first earn it; away with the kitchen-maid!'

Then they took away her fine clothes, and gave her an old grey frock to put on, and laughed at her, and turned her into the kitchen. There she was forced to do hard work; to rise early before daylight to bring the water, to make the fire, to cook and to wash. Besides that, the sisters plagued her in all sorts of ways, and laughed at her. In the evening when she was tired, she had no bed to lie down on, but was made to lie by the hearth among the ashes; and as this, of course, made her always dusty and dirty, they called her Ashputtel.

It happened one day that the father was going to the fair, and he asked his wife's daughters what he should bring them.

'Fine clothes,' said the first.

'Pearls and diamonds,' cried the second.

'Now, child,' said he to his own daughter, 'what will you have?'

'The first twig, dear father, that brushes against your hat when you turn your face to come homewards,' said she.

Then he bought for the first two the fine clothes and pearls and diamonds they had asked for; and on his way home, as he rode through a green copse, a hazel twig brushed against him, and almost pushed off his hat: so he broke it off and brought it away; and when he got home he gave it to his daughter. Then she took it, and went to her mother's grave and planted it there; and cried so much that it was watered with her tears; and there it grew and became a fine tree. Three times every day she went to it and cried; and soon a little bird came and built its nest upon the tree, and talked with her, and watched over her, and brought her whatever she wished for.

Now it happened that the king of that land held a feast, which was to last three days; and out of those who came to it his son was to choose a bride for himself. Ashputtel's two sisters were asked to come, so they summoned her, and said, 'Now, comb our hair, brush our shoes and tie our sashes for us, for we are going to dance at the king's feast.'

Then she did as she was told; but when all was done she could not help crying, for she should so have liked to have gone with them to the ball; and at last she begged her stepmother very hard to let her go.

'You, Ashputtel!' said she; 'you who have nothing to wear, no clothes at all, and who cannot even dance – you want to go to the ball?' And when the girl kept on begging, she said at last, to get rid of her, 'I will throw this dishful of peas into the ash-heap, and if in two hours' time you have picked them all out, you shall go to the feast too.'

Then she threw the peas down among the ashes, but the little maiden ran out of the back door into the garden, and cried out:

> 'Hither, hither, through the sky,
> Turtle-doves and linnets, fly!
> Blackbird, thrush and chaffinch gay,
> Hither, hither, haste away!
> One and all come help me, quick!
> Haste ye, haste ye – pick, pick, pick!'

Then first came two white doves, flying in at the kitchen window; next came two turtle-doves; and after them came all the little birds under heaven, chirping and fluttering in, and they flew down into the ashes. And the little doves stooped their heads down and set to work, pick, pick, pick; and then the others began to pick, pick, pick; and among them all they soon picked out all the peas and put them into the dish, but left the ashes. Long before the end of the hour the work was quite done, and all flew out again at the windows.

Then Ashputtel brought the dish to her mother, overjoyed at the thought that now she should go to the ball. But the mother said, 'No, no! You slut, you have no clothes and cannot dance; you shall not go.' And when Ashputtel begged very hard to go, she said, 'If you can in one hour's time pick two of those dishes of peas out of the ashes, you shall go.' And thus she thought she should at least get rid of her. So she shook two dishes of peas into the ashes.

But the little maiden went out into the garden at the back of the house, and cried out as before:

'Hither, hither, through the sky,
Turtle-doves and linnets, fly!
Blackbird, thrush and chaffinch gay,
Hither, hither, haste away!
One and all come help me, quick!
Haste ye, haste ye – pick, pick, pick!'

Then first came two white doves in at the kitchen window; next came two turtle-doves; and after them came all the little birds under heaven, chirping and hopping about. And they flew down into the ashes; and the little doves put their heads down and set to work, pick, pick, pick; and then the others began pick, pick, pick; and they put all the peas into the dishes, and left all the ashes. Before half an hour's time all was done, and out they flew again. And then Ashputtel took the dishes to her mother, rejoicing to think that she should now go to the ball. But her mother said, 'It is all of no use, you cannot go; you have no clothes and cannot dance, and you would only put us to shame' – and off she went with her two daughters to the ball.

Now when all were gone, and nobody was left at home, Ashputtel went sorrowfully and sat down under the hazel tree and cried out:

'Shake, shake, hazel tree,
Gold and silver over me!'

Then her friend the bird flew out of the tree, and brought a gold and silver dress for her, and slippers of spangled silk; and she put them on, and followed her sisters to the feast. But they did not know her, and thought it must be some strange princess, she looked so fine and beautiful in her rich clothes; and they never once thought of Ashputtel, taking it for granted that she was safe at home in the dirt.

The king's son soon came up to her, and took her by the hand and danced with her, and no one else; and he never left her side, and when anyone else came to ask her to dance, he said, 'This lady is dancing with me.'

Thus they danced till a late hour of the night, and then she wanted to go home; and the king's son said, 'I shall escort you to your home;' for he wanted to see where the beautiful maiden lived. But she slipped away from him, unawares, and ran off towards home; and as the prince followed her, she jumped up into the pigeon-house and shut the door. Then he waited till her father came home, and told him that the unknown maiden, who had been at the feast, had hidden herself in the pigeon-house. But when they had broken open the door they found no one within; and as they came back into the house, Ashputtel was lying, as she always did, in her dirty frock by the ashes, and her dim little lamp was burning in the chimney. For she had run as quickly as she could through the pigeon-house and on to the hazel tree, and had there taken off her beautiful clothes, and put them beneath the tree, that the bird might carry them away, and had lain down again amid the ashes in her little grey frock.

The next day when the feast was again held, and her father, stepmother and sisters were gone, Ashputtel went to the hazel tree and said:

'Shake, shake, hazel tree,
Gold and silver over me!'

And the bird came and brought a still finer dress than the one she had worn the day before. And when she came in it to the ball, everyone wondered at her beauty; and the king's son, who was waiting for her, took her by the hand and danced with her; and when anyone asked her to dance, he said as before, 'This lady is dancing with me.'

When night came she wanted to go home, and the king's son followed her as before, that he might see into which house she went; but she sprang away from him all at once into the garden behind her father's house. In this garden stood a fine large pear tree full of ripe fruit; and Ashputtel, not knowing where to hide herself, jumped up into it without being seen. Then the king's son lost sight of her, and could not find out where she was gone, but waited till her father came home, and said to him, 'The unknown lady who danced with me has slipped away, and I think she must have sprung into the pear tree.' The father thought to himself, 'Can it be Ashputtel?' So he had an axe brought and they cut down the tree, but found no one upon it. And when they came back into the kitchen, there lay Ashputtel among the ashes; for she had slipped down on the other side of the tree, and carried her beautiful clothes back to the bird at the hazel tree, and then put on her little grey frock.

The third day, when her father and stepmother and sisters were gone, she went again into the garden and said:

'Shake, shake, hazel tree,
Gold and silver over me!'

Then her kind friend the bird brought a dress still finer than the former one, and slippers which were all of gold, so that when she came to the feast no one knew what to say for wonder at her beauty; and the king's son danced with nobody but her; and when anyone else asked her to dance, he said, 'This lady is my partner, sir.'

When night came she wanted to go home; and the king's son would go with her, and said to himself, 'I will not lose her this time;' but, somehow, she again slipped away from him, though in such a hurry that she dropped her left golden slipper upon the stairs.

The prince took the shoe, and went the next day to the king his father, and said, 'I will take for my wife the lady that this golden slipper fits.'

When night came she wanted to go home

*So the silly girl cut off her big toe, and
thus squeezed on the shoe*

Then both the sisters were overjoyed to hear it; for they had beautiful feet, and had no doubt that they could wear the golden slipper. The elder went first into the room where the slipper was, and wanted to try it on, and the mother stood by. But her big toe could not go into it, and the shoe was altogether much too small for her. Then the mother gave her a knife, and said, 'Never mind, cut it off; when you are queen you will not care about toes; you will not want to walk.' So the silly girl cut off her big toe, and thus squeezed on the shoe, and went to the king's son. Then he took her for his bride, and set her beside him on his horse, and rode away with her homewards.

But on their way home they had to pass by the hazel tree that Ashputtel had planted; and on the branch sat a little dove singing:

'Back again! back again! Look to the shoe!
The shoe is too small, and not made for you!
Prince! Prince! Look again for thy bride,
For she's not the true one that sits by thy side.'

Then the prince got down and looked at her foot; and he saw, by the blood that streamed from it, what a trick she had played on him. So he turned his horse round, and brought the false bride back to her home, and said, 'This is not the right bride; let the other sister try and put on the slipper.' Then she went into the room and got her foot into the shoe, all but the heel, which was too large. But her mother squeezed it in till the blood came, and took her to the king's son, and he set her as his bride by his side on his horse, and rode away with her.

But when they came to the hazel tree the little dove sat there still, and sang:

'Back again! back again! Look to the shoe!
The shoe is too small, and not made for you!
Prince! Prince! Look again for thy bride,
For she's not the true one that sits by thy side.'

Then he looked down, and saw that the blood streamed so much from the shoe, that her white stockings were quite red. So he turned his horse and brought her also back again. 'This is not the true bride,' said he to the father; 'have you no other daughters?'

'No,' said he; 'there is only a little dirty Ashputtel here, the child of my first wife; I am sure she cannot be the bride.' The prince told him to send for her. But the mother said, 'No, no, she is much too dirty; she will not dare to show herself.'

However, the prince would have her come; and she first washed her face and hands, and then went in and curtsied to him, and he handed her the golden slipper. Then she took her clumsy shoe off her left foot, and put on the golden slipper; and it fitted her as if it had been made for her. And when he drew near and looked at her face he knew her, and said, 'This is the right bride.'

But the stepmother and both the sisters were frightened, and turned pale with anger as he took Ashputtel on his horse and rode away with her. And when they came to the hazel tree, the white dove sang:

'Home! home! Look at the shoe!
Princess! The shoe was made for you!
Prince! Prince! Take home thy bride,
For she is the true one that sits by thy side!'

And when the dove had done its song, it came flying, and perched upon her right shoulder, and so went home with her.

The Ass, the Table and the Stick

A lad named Jack was once so unhappy at home through his father's ill-treatment, that he made up his mind to run away and seek his fortune in the wide world.

He ran, and he ran, till he could run no longer, and then he ran right up against a little old woman who was gathering sticks. He was too much out of breath to beg her pardon, but the woman was good-natured, and she said he seemed to be a likely lad, so she would take him to be her servant, and would pay him well. He agreed, for he was very hungry, and she brought him to her house in the wood, where he served her for twelve months and a day.

When the year had passed, she called him to her, and said she had good wages for him. So she presented him with an ass out of the stable, and he had but to pull Neddy's ears to make him begin at once to hee-haw! And when he brayed there dropped from his mouth silver sixpences, and half-crowns, and golden guineas.

The lad was well pleased with the wage he had received, and away he rode till he reached an inn. There he ordered the best of everything, and when the innkeeper refused to serve him without being paid beforehand, the boy went off to the stable, pulled the ass's ears and obtained his pocket full of money. The host had watched all this through a crack in the door, and when night came on he put an ass of his own in the place of the precious Neddy of the poor youth. So Jack, without knowing that any change had been made, rode away next morning to his father's house.

Now, I must tell you that near his home dwelt a poor widow with an only daughter. The lad and the maiden were fast friends and true loves; but when Jack asked his father's leave to marry the girl, 'Never till you have the money to keep her,' was the reply. 'I have that, father,' said the lad, and going to the ass he pulled its long ears; well, he pulled, and he pulled, till one of them came off in his

hand; but Neddy, though he hee-hawed and he hee-hawed let fall no half-crowns or guineas. The father picked up a hay-fork and beat his son out of the house. I promise you he ran. Ah! he ran and ran till he came bang against a door, and burst it open, and there he was in a joiner's shop. 'You're a likely lad,' said the joiner; 'serve me for twelve months and a day and I will pay you well.' So he agreed, and served the carpenter for a year and a day. 'Now,' said the master, 'I will give you your wage;' and he presented him with a table, telling him he had but to say, 'Table, be covered,' and at once it would be spread with lots to eat and drink.

Jack hitched the table on his back, and away he went with it till he came to the inn. 'Well, host,' shouted he, 'my dinner today, and that of the best.'

'Very sorry, but there is nothing in the house but ham and eggs.'

'Ham and eggs for me!' exclaimed Jack. 'I can do better than that. – Come, my table, be covered!'

At once the table was spread with turkey and sausages, roast mutton, potatoes, and greens. The publican opened his eyes, but he said nothing, not he.

That night he fetched down from his attic a table very like that of Jack, and exchanged the two. Jack, none the wiser, next morning hitched the worthless table on to his back and carried it home. 'Now, father, may I marry my lass?' he asked.

'Not unless you can keep her,' replied the father. 'Look here!' exclaimed Jack. 'Father, I have a table which does all my bidding.'

'Let me see it,' said the old man.

The lad set it in the middle of the room, and bade it be covered; but all in vain, the table remained bare. In a rage, the father caught the warming-pan down from the wall and warmed his son's back with it so that the boy fled howling from the house, and ran and ran till he came to a river and tumbled in. A man picked him out and bade him assist him in making a bridge over the river; and how do you think he was doing it? Why, by casting a tree across; so Jack climbed up to the top of the tree and threw his weight on it, so that when

the man had rooted the tree up, Jack and the tree-head dropped on the farther bank.

'Thank you,' said the man; 'and now for what you have done I will pay you;' so saying, he tore a branch from the tree, and fettled it up into a club with his knife. 'There,' exclaimed he; 'take this stick, and when you say to it, "Up stick and bang him," it will knock anyone down who angers you.'

The lad was overjoyed to get this stick – so away he went with it to the inn, and as soon as the publican, appeared, 'Up stick and bang him!' was his cry. At the word the cudgel flew from his hand and battered the old publican on the back, rapped his head, bruised his arms and tickled his ribs, till he fell groaning on the floor; still the stick belaboured the prostrate man, nor would Jack call it off till he had got back the stolen ass and table. Then he galloped home on the ass, with the table on his shoulders and the stick in his hand. When he arrived there he found his father was dead, so he brought his ass into the stable, and pulled its ears till he had filled the manger with money.

It was soon known through the town that Jack had returned rolling in wealth, and accordingly all the girls in the place set their caps at him. 'Now,' said Jack, 'I shall marry the richest lass in the place; so tomorrow do you all come in front of my house with your money in your aprons.'

Next morning the street was full of girls with aprons held out, and gold and silver in them; but Jack's own sweetheart was among them, and she had neither gold nor silver, nought but two copper pennies, that was all she had.

'Stand aside, lass,' said Jack to her, speaking roughly. 'Thou hast no silver nor gold – stand off from the rest.' She obeyed, and the tears ran down her cheeks, and filled her apron with diamonds.

'Up stick and bang them!' exclaimed Jack; whereupon the cudgel leaped up, and running along the line of girls, knocked them all on the head and left them senseless on the pavement. Jack took all their money and poured it into his truelove's lap. 'Now, lass,' he exclaimed, 'thou art the richest, and I shall marry thee.'

Beauty and the Beast

Once upon a time, in a very far-off country, there lived a merchant who had been so fortunate in all his undertakings that he was enormously rich. As he had, however, six sons and six daughters, he found that he needed every penny to let them all have everything they fancied, as they were accustomed to do.

But one day a most unexpected misfortune befell them. Their house caught fire and was speedily burnt to the ground, with all the splendid furniture, the books, pictures, gold, silver and precious goods it contained; and this was only the beginning of their troubles. Their father, who had until this moment prospered in all ways, suddenly lost every ship he had upon the sea, either by dint of pirates, shipwreck or fire. Then he heard that his clerks in distant countries, whom he trusted entirely, had proved unfaithful; and at last from great wealth he fell into the direst poverty.

All that he had left was a little house in a desolate place at least a hundred leagues from the town in which he had lived, and to this he was forced to retreat with his children, who were in despair at the idea of leading such a different life. Indeed, the daughters at first hoped that their friends, who had been so numerous while they were rich, would insist on their staying in their houses now they no longer possessed one. But they soon found that they were left alone, and that their former friends even attributed their misfortunes to their own extravagance, and showed no intention of offering them any help. So nothing was left for them but to take their departure to the cottage, which stood in the midst of a dark forest, and seemed to be the most dismal place upon the face of the earth. As they were too poor to have any servants, the girls had to work hard, like peasants, and the sons, for their part, cultivated the fields to earn their living. Roughly clothed, and living in the simplest way, the girls regretted unceasingly the luxuries and amusements of their former life; only the youngest tried to be brave and cheerful. She had been as sad as anyone when misfortune overtook her father, but, soon recovering her natural gaiety, she set to work to make the best of things, to amuse her father and brothers as well as she could and to try to persuade her sisters to join her in dancing and singing. But they would do nothing of the sort, and, because she was not as doleful as themselves, they declared that this miserable life was all she was fit for. But she was really far prettier and cleverer than they were; indeed, she was so lovely that she was always called Beauty. After two years, when they were all beginning to get used to their new life, something happened to disturb their tranquillity. Their father received the news that one of his ships, which he had believed to be lost, had come safely into port with a rich cargo. His sons and daughters at once thought that their poverty was at an end, and wanted to set out directly for the town; but their father, who was more prudent, begged them to wait a little, and, though it was harvest time, and he could ill be spared, determined to go himself first, to make enquiries. Only the youngest daughter had any doubt but that they would soon again be as rich as they were before, or at least rich enough to live comfortably in some town where they would find amusement and gay companions once more. So they all loaded their father with commissions for jewels and dresses which it would have taken a fortune to buy; only Beauty, feeling sure that it was of no use, did not ask for anything. Her father, noticing her silence, said: 'And what shall I bring for you, Beauty?'

'The only thing I wish for is to see you come home safely,' she answered.

But this only vexed her sisters, who fancied she was blaming them for having asked for such costly things. Her father, however, was pleased, but as he thought that at her age she certainly ought to like pretty presents, he told her to choose something.

'Well, dear father,' she said, 'as you insist upon it, I beg that you will bring me a rose. I have not seen one since we came here, and I love them so much.'

So the merchant set out and reached the town as quickly as possible, but only to find that his former companions, believing him to be dead, had divided between them the goods which the ship had brought; and after six months of trouble and expense he found himself as poor as when he started, having been able to recover only just enough to pay the cost of his journey. To make matters worse, he was obliged to leave the town in the most terrible weather, so that by the time he was within a few leagues of his home he was almost exhausted with cold and fatigue. Though he knew it would take some hours to get through the forest, he was so anxious to be at his journey's end that he resolved to go on; but night overtook him, and the deep snow and bitter frost made it impossible for his horse to carry him any farther. Not a house was to be seen; the only shelter he could get was the hollow trunk of a great tree, and there he crouched all the night, which seemed to him the longest he had ever known. In spite of his weariness the howling of the wolves kept him awake, and even when at last the day broke he was not much better off, for the falling snow had covered up every path, and he did not know which way to turn.

At length he made out some sort of track, and though at the beginning it was so rough and slippery that he fell down more than once, it presently became easier, and led him into an avenue of trees which ended in a splendid castle. It seemed to the merchant very strange that no snow had fallen in the avenue, which was entirely composed of orange trees, covered with flowers and fruit. When he reached the first court of the castle he saw before him a flight of agate steps, and went up them, and passed through several splendidly furnished rooms. The pleasant warmth of the air revived him, and he felt very hungry; but there seemed to be nobody in all this vast and splendid palace whom he could ask to give him something to assuage his hunger. Deep silence reigned everywhere, and at last, tired of roaming through empty rooms and galleries, he stopped in a room smaller than the rest, where a clear fire was burning and a couch was drawn up closely to it. Thinking that this must be prepared for someone who was expected, he sat down to wait till he should come, and very soon fell into a sweet sleep.

When his extreme hunger wakened him after several hours, he was still alone; but a little table, upon which was a good dinner, had been drawn up close to him, and, as he had eaten nothing for twenty-four hours, he lost no time in beginning his meal, hoping that he might soon have an opportunity of thanking his considerate entertainer, whoever that person might be. But no one appeared, and even after another long sleep, from which he awoke completely refreshed, there was no sign of anybody, though a fresh meal of dainty cakes and fruit was prepared upon the little table at his elbow. As he was naturally timid, the silence began to terrify him, and he resolved to search once more through all the rooms; but it was of no use. Not even a servant was to be seen; there was no sign of life in the palace! He began to wonder what he should do, and to amuse himself by pretending that all the treasures he saw were his own, and considering how he would divide them among his children. Then he went down into the garden, and though it was winter everywhere else, here the sun shone, and the birds sang, and the flowers bloomed, and the air was soft and sweet. The merchant, in ecstasies with all he saw and heard, said to himself: 'All this must be meant for me. I will go this minute and bring my children to share all these delights.'

In spite of being so cold and weary when he reached the castle, he had taken his horse to the stable and fed it. Now he thought he would saddle it for his homeward journey, and he turned down the path which led to the stable. This path had a hedge of roses on each side of it, and the merchant thought he had never seen or smelt such exquisite flowers. They reminded him of his promise to Beauty, and he stopped and had just gathered one to take to her when he was startled by a strange noise behind him. Turning round, he saw a frightful Beast, which seemed to be very angry and said, in a terrible voice: 'Who told you that you might gather my roses? Was it not enough that I allowed you to be in my palace and was kind to you? This is the way you show your gratitude, by stealing my flowers! But your insolence shall not go unpunished.' The merchant, terrified by these furious words, dropped the fatal rose, and, throwing himself on his knees, cried: 'Pardon me, noble sir. I am truly grateful to you for your hospitality, which was so magnificent that I could not imagine that you would be offended by my taking such a little thing as a rose.' But the Beast's anger was not lessened by this speech.

'You are very ready with excuses and flattery,' he cried; 'but that will not save you from the death you deserve.'

'Alas!' thought the merchant, 'if my daughter could only know what danger her rose has brought me into!'

And in despair he began to tell the Beast all his misfortunes, and the reason of his journey, not forgetting to mention Beauty's request.

'A king's ransom would hardly have procured all that my other daughters asked,' he said, 'but I thought that I might at least take Beauty her rose. I beg you to forgive me, for you see I meant no harm.'

The Beast considered for a moment, and then he said, in a less furious tone: 'I will forgive you on one condition – that is, that you will give me one of your daughters.'

'Ah!' cried the merchant, 'if I were cruel enough to buy my own life at the expense of one of my children's, what excuse could I invent to bring her here?'

'No excuse would be necessary,' answered the Beast. 'If she comes at all she must come willingly. On no other condition will I have her. See if any one of them is courageous enough and loves you well enough to come and save your life. You seem to be an honest man, so I will trust you to go home. I give you a month to see if any of your daughters will come back with you and stay here, to let you go free. If none of them is willing, you must come alone, after bidding them goodbye for ever, for then you will belong to me. And do not imagine that you can hide from me, for if you fail to keep your word I will come and fetch you!' added the Beast grimly.

The merchant accepted this proposal, though he did not really think any of his daughters could be persuaded to come. He promised to return at the time appointed, and then, anxious to escape from the presence of the Beast, he asked permission to set off at once. But the Beast answered that he could not go until next day.

'Then you will find a horse ready for you,' he said. 'Now go and eat your supper, and await my orders.'

The poor merchant, more dead than alive, went back to his room, where the most delicious supper was already served on the little table which was drawn up before a blazing fire. But he was too terrified to eat, and only tasted a few of the dishes, for fear the Beast should be angry if he did not

obey his orders. When he had finished he heard a great noise in the next room, which he knew meant that the Beast was coming. As he could do nothing to escape his visit, the only thing that remained was to seem as little afraid as possible; so when the Beast appeared and asked roughly if he had supped well, the merchant answered humbly that he had, thanks to his host's kindness. Then the Beast warned him to remember their agreement, and to prepare his daughter exactly for what she had to expect.

'Do not get up tomorrow,' he added, 'until you see the sun and hear a golden bell ring. Then you will find your breakfast waiting for you here, and the horse you are to ride will be ready in the court-yard. He will also bring you back again when you come with your daughter a month hence. Farewell. Take a rose to Beauty, and remember your promise!'

The merchant was only too glad when the Beast went away, and though he could not sleep for sadness, he lay down until the sun rose. Then, after a hasty breakfast, he went to gather Beauty's rose, and mounted his horse, which carried him off so swiftly that in an instant he had lost sight of the palace and was still wrapped in gloomy thoughts when it stopped before the door of the cottage.

His sons and daughters, who had been very uneasy at his long absence, rushed to meet him, eager to know the result of his journey, which, seeing him mounted upon a splendid horse and wrapped in a rich mantle, they supposed to be favourable. He hid the truth from them at first, only saying sadly to Beauty as he gave her the rose: 'Here is what you asked me to bring you; you little know what it has cost.'

But this excited their curiosity so greatly that presently he told them his adventures from beginning to end, and then they were all very unhappy. The girls lamented loudly over their lost hopes, and the sons declared that their father should not return to this terrible castle, and began to make plans for killing the Beast if it should come to fetch him. But he reminded them that he had promised to go back. Then the girls were very angry with Beauty, and said it was all her fault, and that if she had asked for something sensible this would never have happened, and complained bitterly that they should have to suffer for her folly.

Poor Beauty, much distressed, said to them: 'I have, indeed, caused this misfortune, but I assure you I did it innocently. Who could have guessed that to ask for a rose in the middle of summer would cause so much misery? But as I did the mischief it is only just that I should suffer for it. I will therefore go back with my father to keep his promise.'

At first nobody would hear of this arrangement, and her father and brothers, who loved her dearly, declared that nothing should make them let her go; but Beauty was firm. As the time drew near she divided all her little possessions between her sisters, and said goodbye to everything she loved, and when the fatal day came she encouraged and cheered her father as they mounted together the horse which had brought him back. It seemed to fly rather than gallop, but so smoothly that Beauty was not frightened; indeed, she would have enjoyed the journey if she had not feared what might happen to her at the end of it. Her father still tried to persuade her to go back, but in vain. While they were talking the night fell, and then, to their great surprise, wonderful coloured lights began to shine in all directions, and splendid fireworks blazed out before them; all the forest was illuminated by them, and even felt pleasantly warm, though it had been bitterly cold before. This lasted until they reached the avenue of orange trees, where were statues holding flaming torches, and when they got nearer to the palace they saw that it was illuminated from the roof to the ground, and music sounded softly from the courtyard. 'The Beast must be very hungry,' said Beauty, trying to laugh, 'if he makes all this rejoicing over the arrival of his prey.'

But, in spite of her anxiety, she could not help admiring all the wonderful things she saw.

The horse stopped at the foot of the flight of steps leading to the terrace, and when they had dismounted her father led her to the little room he had been in before, where they found a splendid fire burning, and the table daintily spread with a delicious supper.

The merchant knew that this was meant for them, and Beauty, who was rather less frightened now that she had passed through so many rooms and seen nothing of the Beast, was quite willing to begin, for her long ride had made her very hungry. But they had hardly finished their meal when the noise of the Beast's footsteps was heard approaching, and Beauty clung to her father in terror, which became all the greater when she saw how frightened he was. But when the Beast really appeared, though she trembled at the sight of him, she made a great effort to hide her terror, and saluted him respectfully.

This evidently pleased the Beast. After looking at her he said, in a tone that might have struck terror into the boldest heart, though he did not seem to be angry: 'Good-evening, old man. Good-evening, Beauty.'

The merchant was too terrified to reply, but Beauty answered sweetly: 'Good-evening, Beast.'

'Have you come willingly?' asked the Beast. 'Will you be content to stay here when your father goes away?'

Beauty answered bravely that she was quite prepared to stay.

'I am pleased with you,' said the Beast. 'As you have come of your own accord, you may stay. As for you, old man,' he added, turning to the merchant, 'at sunrise tomorrow you will take your departure. When the bell rings get up quickly and eat your breakfast, and you will find the same horse waiting to take you home; but remember that you must never expect to see my palace again.'

Then, turning to Beauty, he said: 'Take your father into the next room, and help him to choose everything you think your brothers and sisters would like to have. You will find two travelling-trunks there; fill them as full as you can. It is only just that you should send them something very precious as a remembrance of yourself.'

Then he went away, after saying, 'Goodbye, Beauty; goodbye, old man'; and though Beauty was beginning to think with great dismay of her father's departure, she was afraid to disobey the Beast's orders; and they went into the next room, which had shelves and cupboards all round it. They were greatly surprised at the riches it contained. There were splendid dresses fit for a queen, with all the ornaments that were to be worn with them; and when Beauty opened the cupboards she was quite dazzled by the gorgeous jewels that lay in heaps upon every shelf. After choosing a vast quantity, which she divided between her sisters – for she had made a heap of the wonderful dresses for each of them – she opened the last chest, which was full of gold.

'I think, father,' she said, 'that, as the gold will be more useful to you, we had better take out the other things again, and fill the trunks with it.' So they did this; but the more they put in the more room there seemed to be, and at last they put back all the jewels and dresses they had taken out, and Beauty even added as many more of the jewels as she could carry at once; and then the trunks were not too full, but they were so heavy that an elephant could not have carried them!

'The Beast was mocking us,' cried the merchant;

'he must have pretended to give us all these things, knowing that I could not carry them away.'

'Let us wait and see,' answered Beauty. 'I cannot believe that he meant to deceive us. All we can do is to fasten them up and leave them ready.'

So they did this and returned to the little room, where they slept until the bell rang at sunrise. Then, to their astonishment, they found breakfast ready. The merchant ate his with a good appetite, as the Beast's generosity made him believe that he might perhaps venture to come back soon and see Beauty. But she felt sure that her father was leaving her for ever, so she was very sad when the bell rang sharply for the second time, and warned them that the time had come for them to part. They went down into the courtyard, where two horses were waiting, one loaded with the two trunks, the other for him to ride. They were pawing the ground in their impatience to start, and the merchant was forced to bid Beauty a hasty farewell; and as soon as he was mounted he went off at such a pace that she lost sight of him in an instant. Then Beauty began to cry, and wandered sadly back to her own room. But she soon found that she was very sleepy, and as she had nothing better to do she lay down and instantly fell asleep. And then she dreamed that she was walking by a brook bordered with trees, and lamenting her sad fate, when a young prince, handsomer than anyone she had ever seen, and with a voice that went straight to her heart, came and said to her, 'Ah, Beauty! you are not so unfortunate as you suppose. Here you will be rewarded for all you have suffered elsewhere. Your every wish shall be gratified. Only try to find me out, no matter how I may be disguised, as I love you dearly, and in making me happy you will find your own happiness. Be as true-hearted as you are beautiful, and we shall have nothing left to wish for.'

'What can I do, Prince, to make you happy?' said Beauty.

'Only be grateful,' he answered, 'and do not trust too much to your eyes. And, above all, do not desert me until you have saved me from my cruel misery.'

After this she thought she found herself in a room with a stately and beautiful lady, who said to her: 'Dear Beauty, try not to regret all you have left behind you, for you are destined to a better fate. Only do not let yourself be deceived by appearances.'

Beauty found her dreams so interesting that she was in no hurry to awake, but presently the clock roused her by calling her name softly twelve times, and then she got up and found her dressing-table set out with everything she could possibly want; and when her toilet was finished she found dinner was waiting in the room next to hers. But dinner does not take very long when you are all by yourself, and very soon she sat down cosily in the corner of a sofa, and began to think about the charming prince she had seen in her dream.

'He said I could make him happy,' said Beauty to herself. 'It seems, then, that this horrible Beast keeps him a prisoner. How can I set him free? I wonder why they both told me not to trust to appearances? I don't understand it. But, after all, it was only a dream, so why should I trouble myself about it? I had better go and find something to do to amuse myself.' So she got up and began to explore some of the many rooms of the palace.

The first she entered was lined with mirrors, and Beauty saw herself reflected on every side, and thought she had never seen such a charming room. Then a bracelet which was hanging from a chandelier caught her eye, and on taking it down she was greatly surprised to find that it held a portrait of her unknown admirer, just as she had seen him in her dream. With great delight she slipped the bracelet on her arm, and went on into a gallery of pictures, where she soon found a portrait of the same handsome prince, as large as life, and so well painted that as she studied it he seemed to smile kindly at her. Tearing herself away from the portrait at last, she passed through into a room which contained every musical instrument under the sun, and here she amused herself for a long while in trying some of them, and singing until she was tired. The next room was a library, and she saw everything she had ever wanted to read, as well as everything she had read, and it seemed to her that a whole lifetime would not be enough even to read the names of the books, there were so many. By this time it was growing dusk, and wax candles in diamond and ruby candlesticks were beginning to light themselves in every room.

Beauty found her supper served just at the time she preferred to have it, but she did not see anyone or hear a sound, and, though her father had warned her that she would be alone, she began to find it rather dull.

But presently she heard the Beast coming, and wondered tremblingly if he meant to eat her up now.

However, as he did not seem at all ferocious, and only said gruffly: 'Good-evening, Beauty,' she answered cheerfully and managed to conceal her terror. Then the Beast asked her how she had been amusing herself, and she told him all the rooms she had seen.

Then he asked if she thought she could be happy in his palace; and Beauty answered that everything was so beautiful that she would be very hard to please if she could not be happy. And after about an hour's talk Beauty began to think that the Beast was not nearly so terrible as she had supposed at first. Then he got up to leave her, and said in his gruff voice: 'Do you love me, Beauty? Will you marry me?'

'Oh! what shall I say?' cried Beauty, for she was afraid to make the Beast angry by refusing.

'Say yes or no without fear,' he replied.

'Oh! no, Beast,' said Beauty hastily.

'Since you will not, good-night, Beauty,' he said.

And she answered, 'Good-night, Beast,' very glad to find that her refusal had not provoked him. And after he was gone she was very soon in bed and asleep, and dreaming of her unknown prince. She thought he came and said to her: 'Ah, Beauty! why are you so unkind to me? I fear I am fated to be unhappy for many a long day still.'

And then her dreams changed, but the charming prince figured in them all; and when morning came her first thought was to look at the portrait, and see if it was really like him, and she found that it certainly was.

This morning she decided to amuse herself in the garden, for the sun shone, and all the fountains were playing; but she was astonished to find that every place was familiar to her, and presently she came to the brook where the myrtle trees were growing where she had first met the prince in her dream, and that made her think more than ever that he must be kept a prisoner by the Beast. When she was tired she went back to the palace, and found a new room full of materials for every kind of work – ribbons to make into bows, and silks to work into flowers. Then there was an aviary full of rare birds, which were so tame that they flew to Beauty as soon as they saw her, and perched upon her shoulders and her head.

'Pretty little creatures,' she said, 'how I wish that your cage was nearer to my room, that I might often hear you sing!'

So saying she opened a door, and found, to her delight, that it led into her own room, though she had thought it was quite the other side of the palace.

There were more birds in a room farther on, parrots and cockatoos that could talk, and they greeted Beauty by name; indeed, she found them so entertaining that she took one or two back to her room, and they talked to her while she was at supper; after which the Beast paid her his usual visit, and asked her the same questions as before, and then with a gruff 'good-night' he took his departure, and Beauty went to bed to dream of her mysterious prince. The days passed swiftly in different amusements, and after a while Beauty found out another strange thing in the palace, which often pleased her when she was tired of being alone. There was one room which she had not noticed particularly; it was empty, except that under each of the windows stood a very comfortable chair; and the first time she had looked out of the window it had seemed to her that a black curtain prevented her from seeing anything outside. But the second time she went into the room, happening to be tired, she sat down in one of the chairs, and instantly the curtain was rolled aside, and a most amusing pantomime was acted before her: there were dances, and coloured lights, and music, and pretty dresses, and it was all so gay that Beauty was in ecstasies. After that she tried the other seven windows in turn, and there was some new and surprising entertainment to be seen from each of them, so that Beauty never could feel lonely any more.

Every evening after supper the Beast came to see her, and always before saying good-night asked her in his terrible voice: 'Beauty, will you marry me?' And it seemed to Beauty, now she understood him better, that when she said, 'No, Beast,' he went away quite sad.

But her happy dreams of the handsome young prince soon made her forget the poor Beast, and the only thing that at all disturbed her was to be constantly told to distrust appearances, to let her heart guide her, and not her eyes, and many other equally perplexing things, which, consider as she would, she could not understand.

So everything went on for a long time, until at last, happy as she was, Beauty began to long for the sight of her father and her brothers and sisters; and one night, seeing her look very sad, the Beast asked her what was the matter. Beauty had quite ceased to be afraid of him. Now she knew that he was really gentle in spite of his ferocious looks and his dreadful voice. So she answered that she was longing to see her home once more. Upon hearing this the Beast seemed sadly distressed, and cried miserably.

'Ah! Beauty, have you the heart to desert an

unhappy Beast like this? What more do you want to make you happy? Is it because you hate me that you want to escape?'

'No, dear Beast,' answered Beauty softly, 'I do not hate you, and I should be very sorry never to see you any more, but I long to see my father again. Only let me go for two months, and I promise to come back to you and stay for the rest of my life.'

The Beast, who had been sighing dolefully while she spoke, now replied: 'I cannot refuse you anything you ask, even though it should cost me my life. Take the four boxes you will find in the room next to your own, and fill them with everything you wish to take with you. But remember your promise and come back when the two months are over, or you may have cause to repent it, for if you do not come in good time you will find your faithful Beast dead. You will not need any chariot to bring you back. Only say goodbye to all your brothers and sisters the night before you come away, and when you have gone to bed turn this ring round upon your finger and say firmly: "I wish to go back to my palace and see my Beast again."'

As soon as Beauty was alone she hastened to fill the boxes with all the rare and precious things she saw about her, and only when she was tired of heaping things into them did they seem to be full.

Then she went to bed, but could hardly sleep for joy. And when at last she did begin to dream of her beloved prince she was grieved to see him stretched upon a grassy bank, sad and weary, and hardly like himself.

'What is the matter?' she cried.

He looked at her reproachfully, and said: 'How can you ask me, cruel one? Are you not leaving me to my death perhaps?'

'Ah! don't be so sorrowful,' cried Beauty; 'I am only going to assure my father that I am safe and happy. I have promised the Beast faithfully that I will come back, and he would die of grief if I did not keep my word!'

'What would that matter to you?' said the prince. 'Surely you would not care?'

'Indeed, I should be ungrateful if I did not care for such a kind Beast,' cried Beauty indignantly. 'I would die to save him from pain. I assure you it is not his fault that he is so ugly.'

Just then a strange sound woke her – someone was speaking not very far away; and opening her eyes she found herself in a room she had never seen before, which was certainly not nearly so

splendid as those she was used to in the Beast's palace. Where could she be? She got up and dressed hastily, and then saw that the boxes she had packed the night before were all in the room. While she was wondering by what magic the Beast had transported them and herself to this strange place she suddenly heard her father's voice, and rushed out and greeted him joyfully. Her brothers and sisters were all astonished at her appearance, as they had never expected to see her again, and there was no end to the questions they asked her. She had also much to hear about what had happened to them while she was away, and of her father's journey home. But when they heard that she had only come to be with them for a short time, and then must go back to the Beast's palace for ever, they lamented loudly. Then Beauty asked her father what he thought could be the meaning of her strange dreams, and why the prince constantly begged her not to trust to appearances. After much consideration, he answered: 'You tell me yourself that the Beast, frightful as he is, loves you dearly, and deserves your love and gratitude for his gentleness and kindness; I think the prince must mean you to understand that you ought to reward him by doing as he wishes you to, in spite of his ugliness.'

Beauty could not help seeing that this seemed very probable; still, when she thought of her dear prince who was so handsome, she did not feel at all inclined to marry the Beast. At any rate, for two months she need not decide, but could enjoy herself with her sisters. But though they were rich now, and lived in town again, and had plenty of acquaintances, Beauty found that nothing amused her very much; and she often thought of the palace, where she was so happy, especially as at home she never once dreamed of her dear prince, and she felt quite sad without him.

Then her sisters seemed to have got quite used to being without her, and even found her rather in the way, so she would not have been sorry when the two months were over but for her father and brothers, who begged her to stay, and seemed so grieved at the thought of her departure that she had not the courage to say goodbye to them. Every day when she got up she meant to say it at night, and when night came she put it off again, until at last she had a dismal dream which helped her to make up her mind. She thought she was wandering in a lonely path in the palace gardens, when she heard groans which seemed to come from some

Beauty and the Beast

bushes hiding the entrance of a cave, and running quickly to see what could be the matter, she found the Beast stretched out upon his side, apparently dying. He reproached her faintly with being the cause of his distress, and at the same moment a stately lady appeared, and said very gravely: 'Ah! Beauty, you are only just in time to save his life. See what happens when people do not keep their promises! If you had delayed one day more, you would have found him dead.'

Beauty was so terrified by this dream that the next morning she announced her intention of going back at once, and that very night she said goodbye to her father and all her brothers and sisters, and as soon as she was in bed she turned her ring round upon her finger, and said firmly, 'I wish to go back to my palace and see my Beast again,' as she had been told to do.

Then she fell asleep instantly, and only woke up to hear the clock saying 'Beauty, Beauty' twelve times in its musical voice, which told her at once that she was really in the palace once more. Everything was just as before, and her birds were so glad to see her! But Beauty thought she had never known such a long day, for she was so anxious to see the Beast again that she felt as if supper-time would never come.

But when it did come and no Beast appeared she was really frightened; so, after listening and waiting for a long time, she ran down into the garden to search for him. Up and down the paths and avenues ran poor Beauty, calling him in vain, for no one answered, and not a trace of him could she find; until at last, quite tired, she stopped for a minute's rest, and saw that she was standing opposite the shady path she had seen in her dream. She rushed down it, and, sure enough, there was the cave, and in it lay the Beast – asleep, as Beauty thought. Quite glad to have found him, she ran up and stroked his head, but, to her horror, he did not move or open his eyes.

'Oh! he is dead; and it is all my fault,' said Beauty, crying bitterly.

But then, looking at him again, she fancied he still breathed, and, hastily fetching some water from the nearest fountain, she sprinkled it over his face, and, to her great delight, he began to revive.

'Oh! Beast, how you frightened me!' she cried. 'I never knew how much I loved you until just now, when I feared I was too late to save your life.'

'Can you really love such an ugly creature as I am?' said the Beast faintly. 'Ah! Beauty, you only came just in time. I was dying because I thought you had forgotten your promise. But go back now and rest, I shall see you again by and by.'

Beauty, who had half expected that he would be angry with her, was reassured by his gentle voice, and went back to the palace, where supper was awaiting her; and afterwards the Beast came in as usual, and talked about the time she had spent with her father, asking if she had enjoyed herself, and if they had all been very glad to see her.

Beauty answered politely, and quite enjoyed telling him all that had happened to her. And when at last the time came for him to go, and he asked, as he had so often asked before, 'Beauty, will you marry me?'

She answered softly, 'Yes, dear Beast.'

As she spoke a blaze of light sprang up before the windows of the palace; fireworks crackled and guns banged, and across the avenue of orange trees, in letters all made of fireflies, was written: 'Long live the Prince and his Bride.'

Turning to ask the Beast what it could all mean, Beauty found that he had disappeared, and in his place stood her long-loved prince! At the same moment the wheels of a chariot were heard upon the terrace, and two ladies entered the room. One of them Beauty recognised as the stately lady she had seen in her dreams; the other was also so grand and queenly that Beauty hardly knew which to greet first.

But the one she already knew said to her companion: 'Well, Queen, this is Beauty, who has had the courage to rescue your son from the terrible enchantment. They love one another, and only your consent to their marriage is wanting to make them perfectly happy.'

'I consent with all my heart,' cried the Queen. 'How can I ever thank you enough, charming girl, for having restored my dear son to his natural form?'

And then she tenderly embraced Beauty and the prince, who had meanwhile been greeting the fairy and receiving her congratulations.

'Now,' said the fairy to Beauty, 'I suppose you would like me to send for all your brothers and sisters to dance at your wedding?'

And so she did, and the marriage was celebrated the very next day with the utmost splendour, and Beauty and the prince lived happily ever after.

Blue Beard

There was a man who had fine houses, both in town and country, a deal of silver and gold plate, embroidered furniture, and coaches gilded all over with gold. But this man was so unlucky as to have a blue beard, which made him so frightfully ugly that all the women and girls ran away from him.

One of his neighbours, a lady of quality, had two daughters who were perfect beauties. He desired of her one of them in marriage, leaving to her choice which of the two she would bestow on him. They would neither of them have him, and sent him backwards and forwards from one to the other, not being able to bear the thought of marrying a man who had a blue beard, and what besides gave them disgust and aversion was his having already been married to several wives, and nobody ever knew what became of them.

Blue Beard, to engage their affection, took them, with the lady their mother and three or four ladies of their acquaintance, with other young people of the neighbourhood, to one of his country seats, where they stayed a whole week.

There was nothing then to be seen but parties of pleasure, hunting, fishing, dancing, mirth and feasting. Nobody went to bed, but all passed the night in rallying and joking with each other. In short, everything succeeded so well that the younger daughter began to think the master of the house not to have a beard so very blue, and that he was a mighty civil gentleman.

As soon as they returned home, the marriage was concluded. About a month afterwards, Blue Beard told his wife that he was obliged to take a country journey for six weeks at least, about affairs of very great consequence, desiring her to divert herself in his absence, to send for her friends and acquaintances, to carry them into the country, if she pleased, and to make good cheer wherever she was.

'Here,' said he, 'are the keys of the two great wardrobes, wherein I have my best furniture; these are of my silver and gold plate, which is not every day in use; these open my strong boxes, which hold my money, both gold and silver; these my caskets of jewels; and this is the master-key to all my apartments. But for this little one here, it is the key of the closet at the end of the great gallery on the ground floor. Open them all; go into all and every one of them, except that little closet, which I forbid you, and forbid it in such a manner that, if you happen to open it, you may expect from me anger and resentment which will know no bounds.'

She promised to observe, very exactly, everything he had ordered, whereupon he, after having embraced her, got into his coach and proceeded on his journey.

She promised to observe, very exactly, everything he had ordered

Her neighbours and good friends did not wait to be sent for by the new married lady, so great was their impatience to see all the rich furniture of her house, not daring to come while her husband was there, because of his blue beard, which frightened them. They ran through all the rooms, closets and wardrobes, which were all so fine and rich that they seemed to surpass one another.

After that they went up into the two great rooms, where was the best and richest furniture; they could not sufficiently admire the number and beauty of the tapestries, beds, couches, cabinets, stands, tables and looking-glasses, in which you might see yourself from head to foot; some of them were framed with glass, others with silver, plain and gilded, the finest and most magnificent ever were seen.

They ceased not to extol and envy the happiness of their friend, who in the meantime in no way diverted herself in looking upon all these rich things, because of the impatience she had to go and open the closet on the ground floor. She was so much pressed by her curiosity that, without considering that it was very uncivil to leave her company, she went down a little back staircase, and with such excessive haste that she had twice or thrice like to have broken her neck.

They ran through all the rooms, closets and wardrobes,
which were all so fine and rich

Coming to the closet-door, she made a stop for some time, thinking upon her husband's orders, and considering what unhappiness might attend her if she was disobedient; but the temptation was so strong she could not overcome it. She then took the little key, and opened it, trembling, but could not at first see anything plainly, because the windows were shut. After some moments she began to perceive that the floor was all covered over with clotted blood, on which lay the bodies of several dead women, ranged against the walls. (These were all the wives whom Blue Beard had married and murdered, one after another.) She thought she should have died for fear, and the key, which she pulled out of the lock, fell out of her hand.

After having somewhat recovered from her surprise, she took up the key, locked the door and went upstairs into her chamber to compose herself; but she could not, she was so much frightened. Having observed that the key of the closet was stained with blood, she tried two or three times to wipe it off, but the blood would not come out; in vain did she wash it, and even rub it with soap and sand; the blood still remained, for the key was magical and she could never make it quite clean; when the blood was gone off from one side, it came again on the other.

Blue Beard returned from his journey the same evening, and said he had received letters upon the road, informing him that the affair he went about was ended to his advantage. His wife did all she could to convince him she was extremely glad of his speedy return.

Next morning he asked her for the keys, which she gave him, but with such a trembling hand that he easily guessed what had happened.

'What!' said he, 'is not the key of my closet among the rest?'

'I must certainly have left it above upon the table,' said she.

'Fail not to bring it to me presently,' said Blue Beard.

After several goings backwards and forwards she was forced to bring him the key. Blue Beard, having very attentively considered it, said to his wife,

'How comes this blood upon the key?'

'I do not know,' cried the poor woman, paler than death.

'You do not know!' replied Blue Beard. 'I very well know. You were resolved to go into the closet, were you not? Mighty well, madam; you shall go in, and take your place among the ladies you saw there.'

Upon this she threw herself at her husband's feet, and begged his pardon with all the signs of true repentance, vowing that she would never more be disobedient. She would have melted a rock, so beautiful and sorrowful was she; but Blue Beard had a heart harder than any rock!

'You must die, madam,' said he, 'and that presently.'

'Since I must die,' answered she (looking upon him with her eyes all bathed in tears), 'give me some little time to say my prayers.'

'I give you,' replied Blue Beard, 'half a quarter of an hour, but not one moment more.'

When she was alone she called out to her sister, and said to her: 'Sister Anne' (for that was her name), 'go up, I beg you, upon the top of the tower, and look if my brothers are not coming over; they promised me that they would come today, and if you see them, give them a sign to make haste.'

Her sister Anne went up upon the top of the tower, and the poor afflicted wife cried out from time to time: 'Anne, sister Anne, do you see anyone coming?'

And sister Anne said: 'I see nothing but the sun, which makes a dust, and the grass, which looks green.'

In the meanwhile Blue Beard, holding a great sabre in his hand, cried out as loud as he could bawl to his wife: 'Come down instantly, or I shall come up to you.'

'One moment longer, if you please,' said his wife, and then she cried out very softly, 'Anne, sister Anne, dost thou see anybody coming?'

And sister Anne answered: 'I see nothing but the sun, which makes a dust, and the grass, which is green.'

'Come down quickly,' cried Blue Beard, 'or I will come up to you.'

'God be praised,' replied the poor wife joyfully; 'they are my brothers.'

*They overtook him before he could get to the steps of the porch, when
they ran their swords through his body and left him dead*

'I am coming,' answered his wife; and then she cried, 'Anne, sister Anne, dost thou not see anyone coming?'

'I see,' replied sister Anne, 'a great dust, which comes on this side here.'

'Are they my brothers?'

'Alas! no, my dear sister, I see a flock of sheep.'

'Will you not come down?' cried Blue Beard

'One moment longer,' said his wife, and then she cried out: 'Anne, sister Anne, dost thou see nobody coming?'

'I see,' said she, 'two horsemen, but they are yet a great way off.'

'God be praised,' replied the poor wife joyfully; 'they are my brothers; I will make them a sign, as well as I can, for them to make haste.'

Then Blue Beard bawled out so loud that he made the whole house tremble. The distressed wife came down, and threw herself at his feet, all in tears, with her hair about her shoulders.

'This signifies nothing,' says Blue Beard; 'you must die'; then, taking hold of her hair with one hand, and lifting up the sword with the other, he was going to take off her head. The poor lady, turning about to him, and looking at him with

dying eyes, desired him to afford her one little moment to recollect herself.

'No, no,' said he, 'recommend thyself to God,' and was just ready to strike . . .

At this very instant there was such a loud knocking at the gate that Blue Beard made a sudden stop. The gate was opened, and presently entered two horsemen, who, dismounting and drawing their swords, ran directly to Blue Beard. He knew them to be his wife's brothers, one a dragoon, the other a musketeer, so that he ran away immediately to save himself; but the two brothers pursued so close that they overtook him before he could get to the steps of the porch, when they ran their swords through his body and left him dead. The poor wife was almost as dead as her husband, and had not strength enough to rise and welcome her brothers.

Blue Beard had no heirs, and so his wife became mistress of all his estate. She made use of one part of it to marry her sister Anne to a young gentleman who had loved her a long while; another part to buy captains' commissions for her brothers, and the rest to marry herself to a very worthy gentleman, who made her forget the ill time she had passed with Blue Beard.

The Blue Bird

Once upon a time there lived a king who was immensely rich. He had broad lands, and sacks overflowing with gold and silver; but he did not care a bit for all his riches, because the queen, his wife, was dead. He shut himself up in a little room and knocked his head against the walls for grief, until his courtiers were really afraid that he would hurt himself. So they hung featherbeds between the tapestry and the walls, and then he could go on knocking his head as long as it was any consolation to him without coming to much harm. All his subjects came to see him, and said whatever they thought would comfort him: some were grave, even gloomy with him; and some agreeable, even gay; but not one could make the least impression upon him. Indeed, he hardly seemed to hear what they said. At last came a lady who was wrapped in a black mantle, and seemed to be in the deepest grief. She wept and sobbed until even the king's attention was attracted; and when she said that, far from coming to try and diminish his grief, she, who had just lost a good husband, was come to add her tears to his, since she knew what he must be feeling, the king redoubled his lamentations. Then he told the sorrowful lady long stories about the good qualities of his departed queen, and she in her turn recounted all the virtues of her departed husband; and this passed the time so agreeably that the king quite forgot to thump his head against the featherbeds, and the lady did not need to wipe the tears from her great blue eyes as often as before. By degrees they came to talking about other things in which the king took an interest, and in a wonderfully short time the whole kingdom was astonished by the news that the king was married again to the sorrowful lady.

Now the king had one daughter, who was just fifteen years old. Her name was Fiordelisa, and she was the prettiest and most charming princess imaginable, always gay and merry. The new queen, who also had a daughter, very soon sent for her to come to the palace. Turritella, for that was her name, had been brought up by her godmother, the Fairy Mazilla, but in spite of all the care bestowed upon her, she was neither beautiful nor gracious. Indeed, when the queen saw how ill-tempered and ugly she appeared beside Fiordelisa she was in despair, and did everything in her power to turn the king against his own daughter, in the hope that he might take a fancy to Turritella. One day the king said that it was time Fiordelisa and Turritella were married, so he would give one of them to the first suitable prince who visited his court. The queen answered: 'My daughter certainly ought to be the first to be married; she is older than yours, and a thousand times more charming!'

The king, who hated disputes, said, 'Very well, it's no affair of mine, settle it your own way.'

Very soon after came the news that King Charming, who was the most handsome and magnificent prince in all the country round, was on his way to visit the king. As soon as the queen heard this, she set all her jewellers, tailors, weavers and embroiderers to work upon splendid dresses and ornaments for Turritella, but she told the king that Fiordelisa had no need of anything new, and the night before the young king was to arrive, she bribed her waiting woman to steal away all the princess's own dresses and jewels, so that when the day came, and Fiordelisa wished to adorn herself as became her high rank, not even a ribbon could she find.

However, as she easily guessed who had played her such a trick, she made no complaint, but sent to the merchants for some rich stuffs. But they said that the queen had expressly forbidden them to supply her with any, and they dared not disobey. So the princess had nothing left to put on but the little white frock she had been wearing the day before; and dressed in that, she went down when the time of the king's arrival came, and sat in a corner hoping to escape notice. The queen received her guest with great ceremony, and presented him to her daughter, who was gorgeously attired, but so much splendour only made her ugliness more noticeable, and the king, after one glance at her, looked the other way. The queen, however, only thought that he was bashful, and took pains to keep Turritella in full view. King Charming then asked if there was not another princess, called Fiordelisa.

'Yes,' said Turritella, pointing with her finger, 'there she is, trying to keep out of sight because she is not smart.'

At this Fiordelisa blushed, and looked so shy and so lovely, that the king was fairly astonished. He rose, and bowing low before her, said: 'Madam, your incomparable beauty needs no adornment.'

'Sire,' answered the princess, 'I assure you that I am not in the habit of wearing dresses as crumpled and untidy as this one, so I should have been better pleased if you had not seen me at all.'

'Impossible!' cried King Charming. 'Wherever such a marvellously beautiful princess appears I can look at nothing else.'

Here the queen broke in, saying sharply: 'I assure you, sire, that Fiordelisa is vain enough already. Pray make her no more flattering speeches.'

The king quite understood that she was not pleased, but that did not matter to him, so he admired Fiordelisa to his heart's content, and talked to her for three hours without stopping.

The queen was in despair, and so was Turritella, when they saw how much the king preferred Fiordelisa. They complained bitterly to her father, and begged and teased him, until he at last consented to have the princess shut up somewhere out of sight while King Charming's visit lasted. So that night, as she went to her room, she was seized by four masked figures, and carried up into the topmost room of a high tower, where they left her in the deepest dejection. She easily guessed that she was to be kept out of sight for fear the king should fall in love with her; but then, how disappointing that was, for she already liked him very much, and would have been quite willing to be chosen for his bride! As King Charming did not know what had happened to the princess, he looked forward impatiently to meeting her again, and he tried to talk about her with the courtiers who were placed in attendance on him. But by the queen's orders they would say nothing good of her, but declared that she was vain, capricious and bad-tempered; that she tormented her waiting-maids,

and that, in spite of all the money that the king gave her, she was so mean that she preferred to go about dressed like a poor shepherdess, rather than spend any of it. All these things vexed King Charming very much, and he was silent.

'It is true,' thought he, 'that she was very poorly dressed, but then she was so ashamed that it proves that she was not accustomed to be so. I cannot believe that with that lovely face she can be as ill-tempered and contemptible as they say. No, no, the queen must be jealous of her for the sake of that ugly daughter of hers, and so these evil reports are spread.'

The courtiers could not help seeing that what they had told the king did not please him, and one of them cunningly began to praise Fiordelisa, when he could talk to the king without being heard by the others.

King Charming thereupon became so cheerful, and interested in all he said, that it was easy to guess how much he admired the princess. So when the queen sent for the courtiers and questioned them about all they had found out, their report confirmed her worst fears. As to the poor Princess Fiordelisa, she cried all night without stopping.

'It would have been quite bad enough to be shut up in this gloomy tower before I had ever seen King Charming,' she said; 'but now when he is here, and they are all enjoying themselves with him, it is too unkind.'

The next day the queen sent King Charming splendid presents of jewels and rich stuffs, and among other things an ornament made expressly in honour of the approaching wedding. It was a heart cut out of one huge ruby, and was surrounded by several diamond arrows, and pierced by one. A golden true-lover's knot above the heart bore the motto, 'But one can wound me,' and the whole jewel was hung upon a chain of immense pearls. Never, since the world has been a world, had such a thing been made, and the king was quite amazed when it was presented to him. The page who brought it begged him to accept it from the princess, who chose him to be her knight.

'What!' cried he, 'does the lovely Princess Fiordelisa deign to think of me in this amiable and encouraging way?'

'You confuse the names, sire,' said the page hastily. 'I come on behalf of the Princess Turritella.'

'Oh, it is Turritella who wishes me to be her knight,' said the king coldly. 'I am sorry that I cannot accept the honour.' And he sent the splendid gifts back to the queen and Turritella, who were furiously angry at the contempt with which they were treated. As soon as he possibly could, King Charming went to see the king and queen, and as he entered the hall he looked for Fiordelisa, and every time anyone came in he started round to see who it was, and was altogether so uneasy and dissatisfied that the queen saw it plainly. But she would not take any notice, and talked of nothing but the entertainments she was planning. The prince answered at random, and presently asked if he was not to have the pleasure of seeing the Princess Fiordelisa.

'Sire,' answered the queen haughtily, 'her father has ordered that she shall not leave her own apartments until my daughter is married.'

'What can be the reason for keeping that lovely princess a prisoner?' cried the king in great indignation.

'That I do not know,' answered the queen; 'and even if I did, I might not feel bound to tell you.'

The king was terribly angry at being thwarted like this. He felt certain that Turritella was to blame for it, so casting a furious glance at her he abruptly took leave of the queen, and returned to his own apartments. There he said to a young squire whom he had brought with him: 'I would give all I have in the world to gain the goodwill of one of the princess's waiting-women, and obtain a moment's speech with Fiordelisa.'

'Nothing could be easier,' said the young squire; and he very soon made friends with one of the ladies, who told him that in the evening Fiordelisa would be at a little window which looked into the garden, where he could come and talk to her. Only, she said, he must take very great care not to be seen, as it would be as much as her place was worth to be caught helping King Charming to see the princess. The squire was delighted, and promised all she asked; but the moment he had run off to announce his success to the king, the false waiting-woman went and told the queen all that had passed. She at once determined that her own daughter should be at the little window; and she taught her so well all she was to say and do, that even the stupid Turritella could make no mistake.

The night was so dark that the king had not a chance of finding out the trick that was being played upon him, so he approached the window with the greatest delight, and said everything that he had been longing to say to Fiordelisa to persuade her of his love for her. Turritella answered as she had been taught, that she was very unhappy, and that there was no chance of her being better treated by the queen until her daughter was married. And then the king entreated her to marry him; and thereupon he drew his ring from his finger and put it upon Turritella's, and she answered him as well as she could. The king could not help thinking that she did not say exactly what he would have expected from his darling Fiordelisa, but he persuaded himself that the fear of being surprised by the queen was making her awkward and unnatural. He would not leave her until she had promised to see him again the next night, which Turritella did willingly enough. The queen was overjoyed at the success of her stratagem, and promised herself that all would now be as she wished; and sure enough, as soon as it was dark the following night the king came, bringing with him a chariot which had been given him by an Enchanter who was his friend. This chariot was drawn by flying frogs, and the king easily persuaded Turritella to come out and let him put her into it, then mounting beside her he cried triumphantly: 'Now, my princess, you are free; where will it please you that we shall hold our wedding?'

And Turritella, with her head muffled in her mantle, answered that the Fairy Mazilla was her godmother, and that she would like it to be at her castle. So the king told the frogs, who had the map of the whole world in their heads, and very soon he and Turritella were set down at the castle of the Fairy Mazilla. The king would certainly have found out his mistake the moment they stepped into the brilliantly lighted castle, but Turritella held her mantle more closely round her, and asked to see the Fairy by herself, and quickly told her all that had happened, and how she had succeeded in deceiving King Charming.

'Oho! my daughter,' said the Fairy, 'I see we have no easy task before us. He loves Fiordelisa so much that he will not be easily pacified. I feel sure he will defy us!' Meanwhile the king was waiting in a splendid room with diamond walls, so clear that he could see the Fairy and Turritella as they stood whispering together, and he was very much puzzled.

'Who can have betrayed us?' he said to himself. 'How comes our enemy here? She must be plotting to prevent our marriage. Why doesn't my lovely Fiordelisa make haste and come back to me?'

But it was worse than anything he had imagined

when the Fairy Mazilla entered, leading Turritella by the hand, and said to him, 'King Charming, here is the Princess Turritella to whom you have plighted your faith. Let us have the wedding at once.'

'I!' cried the king. 'I marry that little creature! What do you take me for? I have promised her nothing!'

'Say no more. Have you no respect for a Fairy?' cried she angrily.

'Yes, madam,' answered the king, 'I am prepared to respect you as much as a Fairy can be respected, if you will give me back my princess.'

'Am I not here?' interrupted Turritella. 'Here is the ring you gave me. With whom did you talk at the little window, if it was not with me?'

'What!' cried the king angrily, 'have I been altogether deceived and deluded? Where is my chariot? Not another moment will I stay here.'

'Oho,' said the Fairy, 'not so fast.' And she touched his feet, which instantly became as firmly fixed to the floor as if they had been nailed there.

'Oh! do whatever you like with me,' said the king; 'you may turn me to stone, but I will marry no one but Fiordelisa.'

And not another word would he say, though the Fairy scolded and threatened, and Turritella wept and raged for twenty days and twenty nights. At last the Fairy Mazilla said furiously (for she was quite tired out by his obstinacy), 'Choose whether you will marry my goddaughter, or do penance seven years for breaking your word to her.'

And then the king cried gaily: 'Pray do whatever you like with me, as long as you deliver me from this ugly scold!'

'Scold!' cried Turritella angrily. 'Who are you, I should like to know, that you dare to call me a scold? A miserable king who breaks his word, and goes about in a chariot drawn by croaking frogs out of a marsh!'

'Let us have no more of these insults,' cried the Fairy. 'Fly from that window, ungrateful king, and for seven years be a Blue Bird.' As she spoke the king's face altered, his arms turned to wings, his feet to little crooked black claws. In a moment he had a slender body like a bird, covered with shining blue feathers, his beak was like ivory, his eyes were bright as stars, and a crown of white feathers adorned his head.

As soon as the transformation was complete the king uttered a dolorous cry and fled through the open window, pursued by the mocking laughter of Turritella and the Fairy Mazilla. He flew on until he reached the thickest part of the wood, and there, perched upon a cypress tree, he bewailed his miserable fate. 'Alas! in seven years who knows what may happen to my darling Fiordelisa!' he said. 'Her cruel stepmother may have married her to someone else before I am myself again, and then what good will life be to me?'

In the meantime the Fairy Mazilla had sent Turritella back to the queen, who was all anxiety to know how the wedding had gone off. But when her daughter arrived and told her all that had happened she was terribly angry, and of course all her wrath fell upon Fiordelisa. 'She shall have cause to repent that the king admires her,' said the queen, nodding her head meaningly, and then she and Turritella went up to the little room in the tower where the princess was imprisoned. Fiordelisa was immensely surprised to see that Turritella was wearing a royal mantle and a diamond crown, and her heart sank when the queen said: 'My daughter is come to show you some of her wedding presents, for she is King Charming's bride, and they are the happiest pair in the world, he loves her to distraction.' All this time Turritella was spreading out lace, and jewels, and rich brocades, and ribbons before Fiordelisa's unwilling eyes, and taking good care to display King Charming's ring, which she wore upon her thumb. The princess recognised it as soon as her eyes fell upon it, and after that she could no longer doubt that he had indeed married Turritella. In despair she cried, 'Take away these miserable gauds! what pleasure has a wretched captive in the sight of them?' and then she fell insensible upon the floor, and the cruel queen laughed maliciously, and went away with Turritella, leaving her there without comfort or aid. That night the queen said to the king, that his daughter was so infatuated with King Charming, in spite of his never having shown any preference for her, that it was just as well she should stay in the tower until she came to her senses. To which he answered that it was her affair, and she could give what orders she pleased about the princess.

When the unhappy Fiordelisa recovered, and remembered all she had just heard, she began to cry bitterly, believing that King Charming was lost to her for ever, and all night long she sat at her open window sighing and lamenting; but when it was dawn she crept away into the darkest corner of her little room and sat there, too unhappy to care about anything. As soon as night came again she once more leaned out into the darkness and bewailed her miserable lot.

Now it happened that King Charming, or rather the Blue Bird, had been flying round the palace in the hope of seeing his beloved princess, but had not dared to go too near the windows for fear of being seen and recognised by Turritella. When night fell he had not succeeded in discovering where Fiordelisa was imprisoned, and, weary and sad, he perched upon a branch of a tall fir tree which grew close to the tower, and began to sing himself to sleep. But soon the sound of a soft voice lamenting attracted his attention, and listening intently he heard it say: 'Ah! cruel queen! what have I ever done to be imprisoned like this? And was I not unhappy enough before, that you must

needs come and taunt me with the happiness your daughter is enjoying now she is King Charming's bride?'

The Blue Bird, greatly surprised, waited impatiently for the dawn, and the moment it was light flew off to see who it could have been who spoke thus. But he found the window shut, and could see no one. The next night, however, he was on the watch, and by the clear moonlight he saw that the sorrowful lady at the window was Fiordelisa herself.

'My princess! have I found you at last?' said he, alighting close to her.

'Who is speaking to me?' cried the princess in great surprise.

'Only a moment since you mentioned my name,

and now you do not know me, Fiordelisa,' said he sadly. 'But no wonder, since I am nothing but a Blue Bird, and must remain one for seven years.'

'What! Little Blue Bird, are you really the powerful King Charming?' said the princess, caressing him.

'It is too true,' he answered. 'For being faithful to you I am thus punished. But believe me, if it were for twice as long I would bear it joyfully rather than give you up.'

'Oh! what are you telling me?' cried the princess. 'Has not your bride, Turritella, just visited me, wearing the royal mantle and the diamond crown you gave her? I cannot be mistaken, for I saw your ring upon her thumb.'

Then the Blue Bird was furiously angry, and told the princess all that had happened, how he had been deceived into carrying off Turritella, and how, for refusing to marry her, the Fairy Mazilla had condemned him to be a Blue Bird for seven years.

The princess was very happy when she heard how faithful her lover was, and would never have tired of hearing his loving speeches and explanations, but too soon the sun rose, and they had to part lest the Blue Bird should be discovered. After promising to come again to the princess's window as soon as it was dark, he flew away, and hid himself in a little hole in the fir tree, while Fiordelisa remained devoured by anxiety lest he should be caught in a trap, or eaten up by an eagle.

But the Blue Bird did not long stay in his hiding-place. He flew away, and away, until he came to his own palace, and got into it through a broken window, and there he found the cabinet where his jewels were kept, and chose out a splendid diamond ring as a present for the princess. By the time he got back, Fiordelisa was sitting waiting for him by the open window, and when he gave her the ring, she scolded him gently for having run such a risk to get it for her.

'Promise me that you will wear it always!' said the Blue Bird. And the princess promised on condition that he should come and see her in the day as well as by night. They talked all night long, and the next morning the Blue Bird flew off to his kingdom, and crept into his palace through the broken window, and chose from his treasures two bracelets, each cut out of a single emerald. When he presented them to the princess, she shook her head at him reproachfully, saying: 'Do you think I love you so little that I need all these gifts to remind me of you?'

And he answered: 'No, my princess; but I love you so much that I feel I cannot express it, try as I may. I only bring you these worthless trifles to show that I have not ceased to think of you, though I have been obliged to leave you for a time.' The following night he gave Fiordelisa a watch set in a single pearl. The princess laughed a little when she saw it, and said: 'You may well give me a watch, for since I have known you I have lost the power of measuring time. The hours you spend with me pass like minutes, and the hours that I drag through without you seem years to me.'

'Ah, princess, they cannot seem so long to you as they do to me!' he answered. Day by day he brought more beautiful things for the princess – diamonds, and rubies, and opals; and at night she decked herself with them to please him, but by day she hid them in her straw mattress. When the sun shone the Blue Bird, hidden in the tall fir tree, sang to her so sweetly that all the passers-by wondered, and said that the wood was inhabited by a spirit. And so two years slipped away, and still the princess was a prisoner, and Turritella was not married. The queen had offered her hand to all the neighbouring princes, but they always answered that they would marry Fiordelisa with pleasure, but not Turritella on any account. This displeased the queen terribly. 'Fiordelisa must be in league with them, to annoy me!' she said. 'Let us go and accuse her of it.'

So she and Turritella went up into the tower. Now it happened that it was nearly midnight, and Fiordelisa, all decked with jewels, was sitting at the window with the Blue Bird, and as the queen paused outside the door to listen she heard the princess and her lover singing together a little song he had just taught her. These were the words:

'Oh! what a luckless pair are we,
One in a prison, and one in a tree.
All our trouble and anguish came
From our faithfulness spoiling our
                              enemies' game.
But vainly they practise their cruel arts,
For nought can sever our two fond hearts.'

They sound melancholy perhaps, but the two voices sang them gaily enough, and the queen burst open the door, crying, 'Ah! my Turritella, there is some treachery going on here!'

As soon as she saw her, Fiordelisa, with great presence of mind, hastily shut her little window that the Blue Bird might have time to escape, and then turned to meet the queen, who overwhelmed her with a torrent of reproaches.

'Your intrigues are discovered, madam,' she said furiously; 'and you need not hope that your high rank will save you from the punishment you deserve.'

'And with whom do you accuse me of intriguing, madam?' said the princess. 'Have I not been your prisoner these two years, and whom have I seen except the gaolers sent by you?'

While she spoke the queen and Turritella were looking at her in the greatest surprise, perfectly dazzled by her beauty and the splendour of her jewels, and the queen said: 'If one may ask, madam, where did you get all these diamonds? Perhaps you mean to tell me that you have discovered a mine of them in the tower!'

'I certainly did find them here,' answered the princess.

'And pray,' said the queen, her wrath increasing every moment, 'for whose admiration are you decked out like this, since I have often seen you not half as fine on the most important occasions at court?'

'For my own,' answered Fiordelisa. 'You must admit that I have had plenty of time on my hands, so you cannot be surprised at my spending some of it in making myself smart.'

'That's all very fine,' said the queen suspiciously. 'I think I will look about, and see for myself.'

So she and Turritella began to search every corner of the little room, and when they came to the straw mattress out fell such a quantity of pearls, diamonds, rubies, opals, emeralds and sapphires that they were amazed, and could not tell what to think. But the queen resolved to hide somewhere a packet of false letters to prove that the princess had been conspiring with the king's enemies, and she chose the chimney as a good place. Fortunately for Fiordelisa this was exactly where the Blue Bird had perched himself, to keep an eye upon her proceedings, and try to avert danger from his beloved princess, and now he cried: 'Beware, Fiordelisa! Your false enemy is plotting against you.'

This strange voice so frightened the queen that she took the letter and went away hastily with Turritella, and they held a council to try and devise some means of finding out what Fairy or Enchanter was favouring the princess. At last they sent one of the queen's maids to wait upon Fiordelisa, and told her to pretend to be quite stupid, and to see and hear nothing, while she was really to watch the princess day and night, and keep the queen informed of all her doings.

Poor Fiordelisa, who guessed she was sent as a spy, was in despair, and cried bitterly that she dared not see her dear Blue Bird for fear that some evil might happen to him if he were discovered.

The days were so long, and the nights so dull, but for a whole month she never went near her little window lest he should fly to her as he used to do.

However, at last the spy, who had never taken her eyes off the princess day or night, was so overcome with weariness that she fell into a deep sleep, and as soon as the princess saw that, she flew to open her window and cried softly: 'Blue Bird, blue as the sky, Fly to me now, there's nobody by.'

And the Blue Bird, who had never ceased to flutter round within sight and hearing of her prison, came in an instant. They had so much to say, and were so overjoyed to meet once more, that it scarcely seemed to them five minutes before the sun rose, and the Blue Bird had to fly away.

But the next night the spy slept as soundly as before, so that the Blue Bird came, and he and the princess began to think they were perfectly safe, and to make all sorts of plans for being happy as they were before the queen's visit. But, alas! the third night the spy was not quite so sleepy, and when the princess opened her window and cried as usual: 'Blue Bird, blue as the sky, Fly to me now, there's nobody nigh,' she was wide awake in a moment, though she was sly enough to keep her eyes shut at first. But presently she heard voices, and peeping cautiously, she saw by the moonlight the most lovely blue bird in the world, who was talking to the princess, while she stroked and caressed it fondly.

The spy did not lose a single word of the conversation, and as soon as the day dawned, and the Blue Bird had reluctantly said goodbye to the princess, she rushed off to the queen, and told her all she had seen and heard.

Then the queen sent for Turritella, and they talked it over, and very soon came to the conclusion than this Blue Bird was no other than King Charming himself.

'Ah! that insolent princess!' cried the queen. 'To think that when we supposed her to be so miserable, she was all the while as happy as possible with that false king. But I know how we can avenge ourselves!'

So the spy was ordered to go back and pretend to

sleep as soundly as ever, and indeed she went to bed earlier than usual, and snored as naturally as possible, and the poor princess ran to the window and cried: 'Blue Bird, blue as the sky, Fly to me now, there's nobody by!'

But no bird came. All night long she called, and waited, and listened, but still there was no answer, for the cruel queen had caused the fir tree to be hung all over with knives, swords, razors, shears, billhooks and sickles, so that when the Blue Bird heard the princess call, and flew towards her, his wings were cut, and his little black feet clipped off, and, all pierced and stabbed in twenty places, he fell back bleeding into his hiding place in the tree, and lay there groaning and despairing, for he thought the princess must have been persuaded to betray him, to regain her liberty.

'Ah! Fiordelisa, can you indeed be so lovely and so faithless?' he sighed, 'then I may as well die at once!' And he turned over on his side and began to die. But it happened that his friend the Enchanter had been very much alarmed at seeing the frog chariot come back to him without King Charming, and had been round the world eight times seeking him, but without success. At the very moment when the king gave himself up to despair, he was passing through the wood for the eighth time, and called, as he had done all over the world: 'Charming! King Charming! Are you here?'

The king at once recognised his friend's voice, and answered very faintly: 'I am here.'

The Enchanter looked all round him, but could see nothing, and then the king said again: 'I am a Blue Bird.'

Then the Enchanter found him in an instant, and seeing his pitiable condition, ran hither and thither without a word, until he had collected a handful of magic herbs, with which, and a few incantations, he speedily made the king whole and sound again.

'Now,' said he, 'let me hear all about it. There must be a princess at the bottom of this.'

'There are two!' answered King Charming, with a wry smile.

And then he told the whole story, accusing Fiordelisa of having betrayed the secret of his visits to make her peace with the queen, and indeed saying a great many hard things about her fickleness and her deceitful beauty, and so on. The Enchanter quite agreed with him, and even went further, declaring that all princesses were alike, except perhaps in the matter of beauty, and advised him to have done with Fiordelisa, and forget all about her. But, somehow or other, this advice did not quite please the king.

'What is to be done next?' said the Enchanter, 'since you still have five years to remain a Blue Bird.'

'Take me to your palace,' answered the king; 'there you can at least keep me in a cage safe from cats and swords.'

'Well, that will be the best thing to do for the present,' said his friend. 'But I am not an Enchanter for nothing. I'm sure to have a brilliant idea for you before long.'

In the meantime Fiordelisa, quite in despair, sat at her window day and night calling her dear Blue Bird in vain, and imagining over and over again all the terrible things that could have happened to him, until she grew quite pale and thin. As for the queen and Turritella, they were triumphant; but their triumph was short, for the king, Fiordelisa's father, fell ill and died, and all the people rebelled against the queen and Turritella, and came in a body to the palace demanding Fiordelisa.

The queen came out upon the balcony with threats and haughty words, so that at last they lost their patience, and broke open the doors of the palace, one of which fell back upon the queen and killed her. Turritella fled to the Fairy Mazilla, and all the nobles of the kingdom fetched the princess Fiordelisa from her prison in the tower, and made her queen. Very soon, with all the care and attention they bestowed upon her, she recovered from the effects of her long captivity and looked more beautiful than ever, and was able to take counsel with her courtiers, and arrange for the governing of her kingdom during her absence. And then, taking a bagful of jewels, she set out all alone to look for the Blue Bird, without telling anyone where she was going.

Meanwhile, the Enchanter was taking care of King Charming, but as his power was not great enough to counteract the Fairy Mazilla's, he at last resolved to go and see if he could make any kind of terms with her for his friend; for you see, Fairies and Enchanters are cousins in a sort of way, after all; and after knowing one another for five or six hundred years and falling out, and making it up again pretty often, they understand one another well enough. So the Fairy Mazilla received him graciously. 'And what may you be wanting, Gossip?' said she.

'You can do a good turn for me if you will;' he answered. 'A king, who is a friend of mine, was unlucky enough to offend you –'

'Aha! I know who you mean,' interrupted the Fairy. 'I am sorry not to oblige you, Gossip, but he need expect no mercy from me unless he will marry my goddaughter, whom you see yonder looking so pretty and charming. Let him think over what I say.'

The Enchanter hadn't a word to say, for he thought Turritella really frightful, but he could not go away without making one more effort for his friend the king, who was really in great danger as long as he lived in a cage. Indeed, already he had met with several alarming accidents. Once the nail on which his cage was hung had given way, and his feathered majesty had suffered much from the fall, while Madam Puss, who happened to be in the room at the time, had given him a scratch in the eye which came very near blinding him. Another time they had forgotten to give him any water to drink, so that he was nearly dead with thirst; and the worst thing of all was that he was in danger of losing his kingdom, for he had been absent so long that all his subjects believed him to be dead. So considering all these things the Enchanter agreed with the Fairy Mazilla that she should restore the king to his natural form, and should take Turritella to stay in his palace for several months, and if, after the time was over, he still could not make up his mind to marry her, he should once more be changed into a Blue Bird.

Then the Fairy dressed Turritella in a magnificent gold and silver robe, and they mounted together upon a flying dragon, and very soon reached King Charming's palace, where he, too, had just been brought by his faithful friend the Enchanter.

Three strokes of the Fairy's wand restored his natural form, and he was as handsome and delightful as ever, but he considered that he paid dearly for his restoration when he caught sight of Turritella, and the mere idea of marrying her made him shudder.

Meanwhile, Queen Fiordelisa, disguised as a poor peasant girl, wearing a great straw hat that concealed her face, and carrying an old sack over her shoulder, had set out upon her weary journey, and had travelled far, sometimes by sea and sometimes by land; sometimes on foot, and sometimes on horseback, but not knowing which way to go. She feared all the time that every step she took was leading her farther from her lover. One day as she sat, quite tired and sad, on the bank of a little brook, cooling her white feet in the clear running water, and combing her long hair that glittered like gold in the sunshine, a little bent old woman passed by, leaning on a stick. She stopped, and said to Fiordelisa: 'What, my pretty child, are you all alone?'

'Indeed, good mother, I am too sad to care for company,' she answered; and the tears ran down her cheeks.

'Don't cry,' said the old woman, 'but tell me truly what is the matter. Perhaps I can help you.'

The queen told her willingly all that had happened, and how she was seeking the Blue Bird. Thereupon the little old woman suddenly stood up straight, and grew tall, and young, and beautiful, and said with a smile to the astonished Fiordelisa: 'Lovely queen, the king whom you seek is no longer a bird. My sister Mazilla has given his own form back to him, and he is in his own kingdom. Do not be afraid, you will reach him, and will prosper. Take these four eggs; if you break one when you are in any great difficulty, you will find aid.'

So saying, she disappeared, and Fiordelisa, feeling much encouraged, put the eggs into her bag and turned her steps towards Charming's kingdom. After walking on and on for eight days and eight nights, she came at long last to a tremendously high hill of polished ivory, so steep that it was impossible to get a foothold upon it. Fiordelisa tried a thousand times, and scrambled and slipped, but always in the end found herself exactly where she had started from. At last she sat down at the foot of it in despair, and then suddenly bethought herself of the eggs. Breaking one quickly, she found in it some little gold hooks, and with these fastened to her feet and hands, she mounted the ivory hill without further trouble, for the little hooks saved her from slipping. As soon as she reached the top a new difficulty presented itself, for all the other side, and indeed the whole valley, was one polished mirror, in which thousands and thousands of people were admiring their reflections. For this was a magic mirror, in which people saw themselves just as they wished to appear, and pilgrims came to it from the four corners of the world. But nobody had ever been able to reach the top of the hill, and when they saw Fiordelisa standing there, they raised a terrible outcry, declaring that if she set foot upon their

glass she would break it to pieces. The queen, not knowing what to do, for she saw it would be dangerous to try to go down, broke the second egg, and out came a chariot, drawn by two white doves, and Fiordelisa got into it, and was floated softly away. After a night and a day the doves alighted outside the gate of King Charming's kingdom. Here the queen got out of the chariot, and kissed the doves and thanked them, and then with a beating heart she walked into the town, asking the people she met where she could see the king. But they only laughed at her, crying: 'See the king? And pray, why do you want to see the king, my little kitchen-maid? You had better go and wash your face first, your eyes are not clear enough to see him!' For the queen had disguised herself, and pulled her hair down about her eyes, that no one might know her. As they would not tell her, she went on farther, and presently asked again, and this time the people answered that tomorrow she might see the king driving through the streets with the Princess Turritella, as it was said that at last he had consented to marry her. This was indeed terrible news to Fiordelisa. Had she come all this weary way only to find Turritella had succeeded in making King Charming forget her?

She was too tired and miserable to walk another step, so she sat down in a doorway and cried bitterly all night long. As soon as it was light she hastened to the palace, and after being sent away fifty times by the guards, she got in at last, and saw the thrones set in the great hall for the king and Turritella, who was already looked upon as queen.

Fiordelisa hid herself behind a marble pillar, and very soon saw Turritella make her appearance, richly dressed, but as ugly as ever, and with her came the king, more handsome and splendid even than Fiordelisa had remembered him. When Turritella had seated herself upon the throne, the queen approached her.

'Who are you, and how dare you come near my high-mightiness, upon my golden throne?' said Turritella, frowning fiercely at her.

'They call me the little kitchen-maid,' she replied, 'and I come to offer some precious things for sale,' and with that she searched in her old sack, and drew out the emerald bracelets King Charming had given her.

'Ho, ho!' said Turritella, those are pretty bits of glass. I suppose you would like five silver pieces for them.'

'Show them to someone who understands such things, madam,' answered the queen; 'after that we can decide upon the price.'

Turritella, who really loved King Charming as much as she could love anybody, and was always delighted to get a chance of talking to him, now showed him the bracelets, asking how much he considered them worth. As soon as he saw them he remembered those he had given to Fiordelisa, and turned very pale and sighed deeply, and fell into such sad thought that he quite forgot to answer her. Presently she asked him again, and then he said, with a great effort: 'I believe these bracelets are worth as much as my kingdom. I thought there was only one such pair in the world; but here, it seems, is another.'

Then Turritella went back to the queen, and asked her what was the lowest price she would take for them.

'More than you would find it easy to pay, madam,' answered she; 'but if you will manage for me to sleep one night in the Chamber of Echoes, I will give you the emeralds.'

'By all means, my little kitchen-maid,' said Turritella, highly delighted.

The king did not try to find out where the bracelets had come from, not because he did not want to know, but because the only way would have been to ask Turritella, and he disliked her so much that he never spoke to her if he could possibly avoid it. It was he who had told Fiordelisa about the Chamber of Echoes, when he was a Blue Bird. It was a little room below the king's own bed-chamber, and was so ingeniously built that the softest whisper in it was plainly heard in the king's room. Fiordelisa wanted to reproach him for his faithlessness, and could not imagine a better way than this. So when, by Turritella's orders, she was left there she began to weep and lament, and never ceased until daybreak.

The king's pages told Turritella, when she asked them, what a sobbing and sighing they had heard, and she asked Fiordelisa what it was all about. The queen answered that she often dreamed and talked aloud.

But by an unlucky chance the king heard nothing of all this, for he took a sleeping draught every night before he lay down, and did not wake up until the sun was high.

The queen passed the day in great disquietude.

'If he did hear me,' she said, 'could he remain so cruelly indifferent? But if he did not hear me, what can I do to get another chance? I have plenty of jewels, it is true, but nothing remarkable enough to catch Turritella's fancy.'

Just then she thought of the eggs, and broke one, out of which came a little carriage of polished steel ornamented with gold, drawn by six green mice. The coachman was a rose-coloured rat, the postilion a grey one, and the carriage was occupied by the tiniest and most charming figures, who could dance and do wonderful tricks. Fiordelisa clapped her hands and danced for joy when she saw this triumph of magic art, and as soon as it was evening, went to a shady garden-path down which she knew Turritella would pass, and then she made the mice gallop, and the tiny people show off their tricks, and sure enough Turritella came, and the moment she saw it all cried: 'Little kitchen-maid, little kitchen-maid, what will you take for your mouse-carriage?'

And the queen answered: 'Let me sleep once more in the Chamber of Echoes.'

'I won't refuse your request, poor creature,' said Turritella condescendingly.

And then she turned to her ladies and whispered 'The silly creature does not know how to profit by her chances; so much the better for me.'

When night came Fiordelisa said all the loving words she could think of, but alas! with no better success than before, for the king slept heavily after his draught. One of the pages said: 'This peasant girl must be crazy;' but another answered: 'Yet what she says sounds very sad and touching.'

As for Fiordelisa, she thought the king must have a very hard heart if he could hear how she grieved and yet pay her no attention. She had but one more chance, and on breaking the last egg she found to her great delight that it contained a more marvellous thing than ever. It was a pie made of six birds, cooked to perfection, and yet they were all alive, and singing and talking, and they answered questions and told fortunes in the most amusing way. Taking this treasure Fiordelisa once more set herself to wait in the great hall through which Turritella was sure to pass, and as she sat there one of the king's pages came by, and said to her: 'Well, little kitchen-maid, it is a good thing that the king always takes a sleeping draught, for if not he would be kept awake all night by your sighing and lamenting.'

Then Fiordelisa knew why the king had not heeded her, and taking a handful of pearls and diamonds out of her sack, she said, 'If you can promise me that tonight the king shall not have his sleeping draught, I will give you all these jewels.'

'Oh! I promise that willingly,' said the page.

At this moment Turritella appeared, and at the first sight of the savoury pie, with the pretty little birds all singing and chattering, she cried: 'That is

an admirable pie, little kitchen-maid. Pray what will you take for it?'

'The usual price,' she answered. 'To sleep once more in the Chamber of Echoes.'

'By all means, only give me the pie,' said the greedy Turritella. And when night was come, Queen Fiordelisa waited until she thought everybody in the palace would be asleep, and then began to lament as before.

The king asked an attendant the meaning of all this sobbing and sighing, and the page who had helped Fiordelisa heard him, and answered quickly: 'Find out the little kitchen-maid, and she will explain everything.'

Then the king in a great hurry sent for all his pages and said: 'If you can find the little kitchen-maid, bring her to me at once.'

'Nothing could be easier, sire,' they answered, 'for she is in the Chamber of Echoes.'

The king was much puzzled when he heard this. How could the lovely Princess Fiordelisa be a little kitchen-maid? or how could a little kitchen-maid have Fiordelisa's own voice? So he dressed hastily, and ran down a little secret staircase which led to the Chamber of Echoes. There, upon a heap of soft cushions, sat his lovely princess. She had laid aside all her ugly disguises and wore a white silken robe, and her golden hair shone in the soft lamplight. The king was overjoyed at the sight, and rushed to throw himself at her feet, and asked her a thousand questions without giving her time to answer one. Fiordelisa was equally happy to be with him once more, and nothing troubled them but the remembrance of the Fairy Mazilla. But at this moment in came the Enchanter, and with him a famous Fairy, the same in fact who had given Fiordelisa the eggs. After greeting the king and queen, they said that as they were united in wishing to help King Charming, the Fairy Mazilla had no longer any power against him, and he might marry Fiordelisa as soon as he pleased. The king's joy may be imagined, and as soon as it was day the news was spread through the palace, and everybody who saw Fiordelisa loved her directly. When Turritella heard what had happened she came running to the king, and when she saw Fiordelisa with him she was terribly angry, but before she could say a word the Enchanter and the Fairy changed her into a big brown owl, and she floated away out of one of the palace windows, hooting dismally. Then the wedding was held with great splendour, and King Charming and Queen Fiordelisa lived happily ever after.

The Boar with the Golden Bristles

Long, long ago, there were brave fighters and skilful hunters in Holland, but neither men nor women ever dreamed that food was to be got out of the ground, but only from the trees and bushes, such as berries, acorns and honey. They thought the crust of the earth was too hard to be broken up for seed, even if they knew what grain and bread were. They supposed that what nature provided in the forest was the only food for men. Besides this, they made their women do all the work and cook the acorns and brew the honey into mead, while they went out to fish and hunt and fight.

So the fairies took pity on the cold, northern people, who lived where it rained and snowed a great deal. They held a council and agreed that it was time to send down to the earth an animal, with tusks, to tear up the ground. Then the people would see the riches of the earth and learn what soil was. They would be blessed with farms and gardens, barns and stalls, hay and grain, horses and cattle, wheat and barley, pigs and clover.

Now there were powerful fairies, of a certain kind, who lived in a Happy Land far, far away, who had charge of everything in the air and water. One of them was named Fro, who became lord of the summer sunshine and warm showers, that make all things grow. It was in this bright region that the white elves lived.

It was a pretty custom in fairyland that when a fairy baby cut its first tooth, the mother's friends should make the little one some pretty present.

When Nerthus, the mother of the infant Fro, looked into its mouth and saw the little white thing that had come up through the baby's gums, she went in great glee and told the glad news to all the other fairies. It was a great event and she tried to guess what present her wonderful boy-baby should receive.

There was one giant-like fairy as strong as a polar bear, who agreed to get, for little Fro, a creature that could put his nose under the sod and root up the ground. In this way he would show men what the earth, just under its surface, contained, without their going into mines and caverns.

One day this giant fairy heard two stout dwarfs talking loudly in the region under the earth. They were boasting as to which could beat the other at the fire and bellows, for both were blacksmiths.

One was the king of the dwarfs, who made a bet that he could excel the other. So he set them to work as rivals, while a third dwarf worked the bellows. The dwarf-king threw some gold in the flames to melt; but, fearing he might not win the bet, he went away to get other fairies to help him. He told the bellows dwarf to keep on pumping air on the fire, no matter what might happen to him.

So when one giant fairy, in the form of a gadfly, flew at him, and bit him in the hand, the bellows-blower did not stop for the pain, but kept on until the fire roared loudly, making the cavern echo. Then all the gold melted in the fire and could be transformed. As soon as the dwarf-king came back, the bellows-blower took up the tongs and drew out of the fire a boar having golden bristles.

This fire-born golden boar had the power of travelling through the air as swiftly as a streak of lightning. It was named Gullin, or Golden, and was given to the fairy Fro, and he, when grown, used the wonderful creature as his steed. All the other good fairies and the elves rejoiced, because men on the earth would now be helped to do great things.

Even more wonderful to tell, this fire-born creature became the father of all the animals that have tusks and that roam in the woods. A tusk is a big tooth, of which the hardest and sharpest part grows, long and sharp, outside of the mouth, and it stays there, even when the mouth is shut.

When Gullin was not occupied, or being ridden by Fro on his errands over the world, he taught his sons, that is, the wild boars of the forest, how to root up the ground and make it soft for things to grow in. Then his master Fro sent the sunbeams and the warm showers to make the turned-up earth fruitful.

To do this, the wild boars were given two long tusks, as pointed as needles and sharp as knives. With one sweep of his head a boar could rip open a dog or a wolf, a bull or a bear, or furrow the earth like a ploughshare.

Now there were several cousins in the Tusk family. The elephant on land, and the walrus and narwhal in the seas; but none of these could plough ground, but because the boar's tusks grew out so long and were so sharp, and hooked at the end, it could tear open the earth's hard crust and root up the ground. This made a soil fit for tender plants to grow in, and even the wild flowers sprang up readily.

All this, when they first noticed it, was very wonderful to human beings. The children called one to the other to come and see the unusual sight. The little troughs, made first by the ripping of the boar's tusks, were widened by rooting with their snouts. These were welcomed by the birds, for they hopped into the lines thus made, to feed on the worms. So the birds, supposing that these little gutters in the ground were made especially for them, made great friends with the boars. They would even perch near by, or fly to their backs, and ride on them.

As for the men fathers, when they looked at the clods and the loose earth thus turned over, they found them to be very soft. So the women and girls were able to break them up with their sticks. Then the seeds, dropped by the birds that came flying back every springtime, from far-away lands, sprouted. It was noticed that new kinds of plants grew up, which had stalks. In the heads or ears of these were a hundredfold more seeds. When the children tasted them, they found, to their delight, that the little grains were good to eat. They swallowed them whole, they roasted them at the fire, or they pounded them with stones. Then they baked the meal thus made or made it into mush, eating it with honey.

For the first time people in the Dutch world had bread. When they added the honey, brought by the bees, they had sweet cakes with mead. Then, saving the seeds over from one summer to another, they in the springtime planted them in the little trenches made by the animal's tusks. Then the Dutch words for 'boar' and 'row' were put together, meaning boar row, and there issued, in time, our word 'furrow'.

The women were the first to become skilful in baking. In the beginning they used hot stones on which to lay the lump of meal, or flour and water, or the batter. Then having learned about yeast, which 'raised' the flour, that is, lifted it up, with gas and bubbles, they made real bread and cakes and baked them in the ovens which the men had made. When they put a slice of meat between upper and lower layers of bread, they called it 'broodje,' that is, little bread; or, sandwich. In time, instead of one kind of bread, or cake, they had a dozen or twenty different sorts, besides griddle cakes and waffles.

Now when the wise men of the mark, or neighbourhood, saw that the women did such wonderful things, they put their heads together and said one to the other: 'We are quite ready to confess that fairies and elves are smarter than we are. Our women, also, are certainly wonderful; but it will never do to let the boars think that they know more than we do. They did indeed teach us how to make furrows, and the birds brought us grain; but we are the greater, for we can hunt and kill the boars with our spears.

'Although they can tear up the sod and root in the ground with tusk and snout, they cannot make cakes, as our women can. So let us see if we cannot beat both the boars and birds, and even excel our women. We shall be more like the fairies, if we invent something that will outshine them all.'

So they thought and planned, and, little by little, they made the plough. First, with a sharp stick in their hands, the men scratched the surface of the ground into lines that were not very deep. Then they nailed plates of iron on those sticks. Next, they fixed this iron-shod wood in a frame to be pulled forward, and, by and by, they added handles. Men and women, harnessed together, pulled the plough. Indeed it was ages before they had oxen to do this heavy work for them. At last the perfect plough was seen. It had a knife in front to cut the clods, a coulter, a beam, a mould board and handles, and, after a while, a wheel to keep it straight. Then they set horses to draw it.

Fro the fairy was the owner, not only of the boar with the golden bristles, but also of the lightning-like horse, Sleipnir, that could gallop through fire and water with the speed of light. Fro also owned the magic ship, which could navigate both land and sea. It was so very elastic that it could be stretched out to carry a host of warriors over the seas to war, or fold up like a lady's handkerchief. With this flying vessel, Fro was able to move about like a cloud and also to change like them. He could also appear, or disappear, as he pleased, in one place or another.

By and by, the wild boars were all hunted to death and disappeared. Yet in one way, and a glorious one also, their name and fame were kept in men's memories. Brave knights had the boar's head painted on their shields and coats of arms. When the faith of the Prince of Peace made wars less frequent, the temples in honour of Fro were deserted, but the yule log and the revels, held to celebrate the passing of the Mother Night, in December, that is, the longest one of the year, were changed for the Christmas festival.

Then again, the memory of man's teacher of the plough was still kept green, for the boar was remembered as the giver, not only of nourishing meat, but of ideas for men's brains. Baked in the oven, and made delightful to the appetite, served on the dish, with its own savoury odours, and decorated with sprigs of rosemary, the boar's head was brought in for the great dinner, with the singing of Christmas carols.

The Boy Who Wanted More Cheese

Klaas Van Bommel was a Dutch boy, twelve years old, who lived where cows were plentiful. He was over five feet high, weighed a hundred pounds, and had rosy cheeks. His appetite was always good and his mother declared his stomach had no bottom. His hair was of a colour halfway between a carrot and a sweet potato. It was as thick as reeds in a swamp and was cut level, from under one ear to another.

Klaas stood in a pair of timber shoes, that made an awful rattle when he ran fast to catch a rabbit, or scuffed slowly along to school over the brick road of his village. In summer Klaas was dressed in a rough, blue-linen blouse. In winter he wore woollen breeches as wide as coffee bags. They were called bell trousers, and in shape were like a couple of cow-bells turned upwards. These were buttoned on to a thick warm jacket. Until he was five years old, Klaas was dressed like his sisters. Then, on his birthday, he had boy's clothes, with two pockets in them, of which he was proud enough.

Klaas was a farmer's boy. He had rye bread and fresh milk for breakfast. At dinner-time, beside cheese and bread, he was given a plate heaped with boiled potatoes. Into these he first plunged a fork and then dipped each round white ball into a bowl of hot melted butter. Very quickly then did potato and butter disappear 'down the red lane'. At supper, he had bread and skim milk, left after the cream had been taken off, with a saucer, to make butter. Twice a week the children enjoyed a bowl of bonnyclabber or curds, with a little brown sugar sprinkled on the top. But at every meal there was cheese, usually in thin slices, which the boy thought not thick enough. When Klaas went to bed he usually fell asleep as soon as his shock of yellow hair touched the pillow. In summertime he slept till the birds began to sing, at dawn. In winter, when the bed felt warm and Jack Frost was lively, he often heard the cows talking, in their way, before

he jumped out of his bag of straw, which served for a mattress. The Van Bommels were not rich, but everything was shining clean.

There was always plenty to eat at the Van Bommels' house. Stacks of rye bread, a yard long and thicker than a man's arm, stood on end in the corner of the cool, stone-lined basement. The loaves of dough were put in the oven once a week. Baking time was a great event at the Van Bommels' and no menfolk were allowed in the kitchen on that day, unless they were called in to help. As for the milk-pails and pans, filled or emptied, scrubbed or set in the sun every day to dry, and the cheeses, piled up in the pantry, they seemed sometimes enough to feed a small army.

But Klaas always wanted more cheese. In other ways, he was a good boy, obedient at home, always ready to work on the cow-farm, and diligent in school. But at the table he never had enough. Sometimes his father laughed and asked him if he had a well, or a cave, under his jacket.

Klaas had three younger sisters, Trintje, Anneke and Saartje; which is Dutch for Kate, Annie and Sallie. These, their fond mother, who loved them dearly, called her 'orange blossoms'; but when at dinner Klaas would keep on dipping his potatoes into the hot butter, while others were finished, his mother would laugh and call him her 'buttercup'. But always Klaas wanted more cheese. When unusually greedy, she twitted him as a boy 'worse than butter-and-eggs'; that is, as troublesome as the yellow and white plant, called toad-flax, is to the farmer – very pretty, but nothing but a weed.

One summer's evening, after a good scolding, which he deserved well, Klaas moped and, almost crying, went to bed in bad humour. He had teased each one of his sisters to give him her bit of cheese, and this, added to his own slice, made his stomach feel as heavy as lead.

Klaas's bed was up in the garret. When the house

was first built, one of the red tiles of the roof had been taken out and a sliding one, made of glass, was put in its place. In the morning, this gave the boy light to put on his clothes. At night, in fair weather, it supplied air to his room.

A gentle breeze was blowing from the pine woods on the sandy slope, not far away. So Klaas climbed up on the stool to sniff the sweet piny odours. He thought he saw lights dancing under the tree. One beam seemed to approach his roof hole, and coming nearer played round the chimney. Then it passed to and fro in front of him. It seemed to whisper in his ear, as it moved by. It looked very much as if a hundred fire-flies had united their cold light into one lamp. Then Klaas thought that the strange beams bore the shape of a lovely girl, but he only laughed at himself at the idea. Pretty soon, however, he thought the whisper became a voice. Again, he laughed, so heartily that he forgot his moping and the scolding his mother had given him. In fact, his eyes twinkled with delight, when the voice gave this invitation: 'There's plenty of cheese. Come with us.'

To make sure of it, the sleepy boy now rubbed his eyes and cocked his ears. Again, the light-bearer spoke to him: 'Come.'

Could it be? He had heard old people tell of the ladies of the wood, that whispered and warned travellers. In fact, he himself had often seen the 'fairies' ring' in the pine woods. To this, the flame-lady was inviting him.

Again and again the moving, cold light circled round the red-tile roof, which the moon, then rising and peeping over the chimneys, seemed to turn into silver plates. As the disc rose higher in the sky, he could hardly see the moving light that had looked like a lady; but the voice, no longer a whisper, as at first, was now even plainer: 'There's plenty of cheese. Come with us.'

'I'll see what it is, anyhow,' said Klaas, as he drew on his thick woollen stockings and prepared to go downstairs and out, without waking a soul. At the door he stepped into his wooden shoes. Just then the cat purred and rubbed up against his shins. He jumped, for he was scared; but looking down, for a moment, he saw the two balls of yellow fire in her head and knew what they were. Then he sped to the pine woods and towards the fairy ring.

What an odd sight! At first Klaas thought it was a circle of big fire-flies. Then he saw clearly that there were dozens of pretty creatures, hardly as large as dolls, but as lively as crickets. They were as full of light, as if lamps had wings. Hand in hand, they flitted and danced around the ring of grass, as if this was fun.

Hardly had Klaas got over his first surprise, than of a sudden he felt himself surrounded by the fairies. Some of the strongest among them had left the main party in the circle and come to him. He felt himself pulled by their dainty fingers. One of them, the loveliest of all, whispered in his ear: 'Come, you must dance with us.'

Then a dozen of the pretty creatures murmured in chorus: 'Plenty of cheese here. Plenty of cheese here. Come, come!'

Upon this, the heels of Klaas seemed as light as a feather. In a moment, with both hands clasped in those of the fairies, he was dancing in high glee. It was as much fun as if he were at the *kermis*, with a row of boys and girls, hand in hand, swinging along the streets, as Dutch maids and youth do, during *kermis* week.

Klaas had not time to look hard at the fairies, for he was too full of the fun. He danced and danced, all night and until the sky in the east began to turn, first grey and then rosy. Then he tumbled down, tired out, and fell asleep. His head lay on the inner curve of the fairy ring, with his feet in the centre.

Klaas felt very happy, for he had no sense of being tired, and he did not know he was asleep. He thought his fairy partners, who had danced with him, were now waiting on him to bring him cheeses. With a golden knife, they sliced them off and fed him out of their own hands. How good it tasted! He thought now he could, and would, eat all the cheese he had longed for all his life. There was no mother to scold him, or daddy to shake his finger at him. How delightful!

But by and by, he wanted to stop eating and rest a while. His jaws were tired. His stomach seemed to be loaded with cannon-balls. He gasped for breath.

But the fairies would not let him stop, for Dutch fairies never get tired. Flying out of the sky – from the north, south, east and west – they came, bringing cheeses. These they dropped down around him, until the piles of the round masses threatened first to enclose him as with a wall, and then to overtop him. There were the red balls from Edam, the pink and yellow spheres from Gouda, and the grey loaf-shaped ones from Leyden. Down through the vista of sand, from the pine woods, he looked, and oh, horrors! There were the tallest and strongest of the fairies rolling along the huge, round, flat cheeses from Friesland! Any one of these was as big as a cartwheel, and would feed a regiment. The fairies trundled the heavy discs along, as if they were playing with hoops. They shouted hilariously, as, with a pine stick, they beat them forward like boys at play. Farm cheese, factory cheese, Alkmaar cheese, and, to crown all, cheese from Limburg – which Klaas never could bear, because of its strong smell. Soon the cakes and balls were heaped so high around him that the boy, as he looked up, felt like a frog in a well. He groaned when he thought the high cheese walls were tottering to fall on him. Then he screamed, but the fairies thought he was making music. They, not being human, do not know how a boy feels.

At last, with a thick slice in one hand and a big hunk in the other, he could eat no more cheese; though the fairies, led by their queen, standing on one side or hovering over his head, still urged him to take more.

At this moment, while afraid that he would burst, Klaas saw the pile of cheeses, as big as a house, topple over. The heavy mass fell inwards upon him. With a scream of terror, he thought himself crushed as flat as a Friesland cheese.

But he wasn't! Waking up and rubbing his eyes, he saw the red sun rising on the sand-dunes. Birds were singing and the cocks were crowing all around him, in chorus, as if saluting him. Just then also the village clock chimed out the hour. He felt his clothes. They were wet with dew. He sat up to look around. There were no fairies, but in his mouth was a bunch of grass which he had been chewing lustily.

Klaas never would tell the story of his night with the fairies, nor has he yet settled the question of whether they left him because the cheese-house of his dream had fallen or because daylight had come.

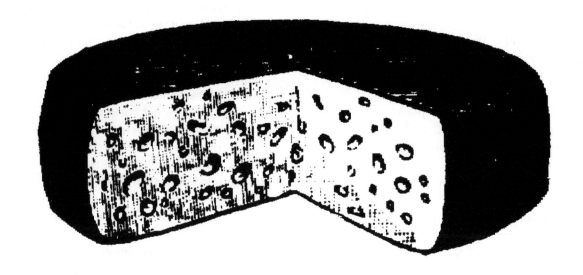

The Brother and Sister

The brother took his sister's hand and said to her, 'Since our mother died we have had no good days; our stepmother beats us every day, and if we go near her she kicks us away; we have nothing to eat but hard crusts of bread left over; the dog under the table fares better; he gets a good piece every now and then. If our mother only knew, how she would pity us! Come, let us go together out into the wide world!'

So they went, and journeyed the whole day through fields and meadows and stony places, and if it rained the sister said, 'The skies and we are weeping together.'

In the evening they came to a great wood, and they were so weary with hunger and their long journey, that they climbed up into a high tree and fell asleep.

The next morning, when they awoke, the sun was high in heaven and shone brightly through the leaves. Then said the brother, 'Sister, I am thirsty; if I only knew where to find a brook, that I might go and drink! I almost think that I hear one rushing.' So the brother got down and led his sister by the hand, and they went to seek the brook. But their wicked stepmother was a witch, and had known quite well that the two children had run away, and had sneaked after them, as only witches can, and had laid a spell on all the brooks in the forest. So when they found a little stream flowing smoothly over its pebbles, the brother was going to drink of it; but the sister heard how it said in its rushing,

'He a tiger will be who drinks of me,
Who drinks of me a tiger will be!'

Then the sister cried, 'Pray, dear brother, do not drink, or you will become a wild beast, and will tear me in pieces.'

So the brother refrained from drinking, though his thirst was great, and he said he would wait till he came to the next brook. When they came to a second brook the sister heard it say,

'He a wolf will be who drinks of me,
Who drinks of me a wolf will be!'

Then the sister cried, 'Pray, dear brother, do not drink, or you will be turned into a wolf, and will eat me up!'

So the brother refrained from drinking, and said, 'I will wait until we come to the next brook, and then I must drink, whatever you say; my thirst is so great.'

And when they came to the third brook the sister heard how in its rushing it said,

'Who drinks of me a fawn will be,
He a fawn will be who drinks of me!'

Then the sister said, 'O my brother, I pray drink not, or you will be turned into a fawn, and run away far from me.'

But he had already kneeled by the side of the brook and stooped and drunk of the water, and as the first drops passed his lips he became a fawn.

And the sister wept over her poor lost brother, and the fawn wept also, and stayed sadly beside her. At last the maiden said, 'Be comforted, dear fawn, indeed I will never leave you.'

Then she untied her golden girdle and bound it round the fawn's neck, and went and gathered rushes to make a soft cord, which she fastened to him; and then she led him on, and they went deeper into the forest. And when they had gone a long long way, they came at last to a little house, and the maiden looked inside, and as it was empty she thought, 'We might as well live here.'

And she fetched leaves and moss to make a soft bed for the fawn, and every morning she went out and gathered roots and berries and nuts for herself, and fresh grass for the fawn, who ate out of her hand with joy, frolicking round her. At night, when the sister was tired, and had said her prayers, she laid her head on the fawn's back, which served her for a pillow, and softly fell asleep. And if only the brother could have got back his own shape again, it would have been a charming life. So they lived a long while in the wilderness alone.

Now it happened that the king of that country held a great hunt in the forest. The blowing of the horns, the barking of the dogs and the lusty shouts of the huntsmen sounded through the wood, and the fawn heard them and was eager to be among them.

'Oh,' said he to his sister, 'do let me go to the hunt; I cannot stay behind any longer,' and begged so long that at last she consented.

'But mind,' said she to him, 'come back to me at night. I must lock my door against the wild hunters, so, in order that I may know you, you must knock and say, "Little sister, let me in," and unless I hear that I shall not unlock the door.'

Then the fawn sprang out, and felt glad and merry in the open air. The king and his huntsmen saw the beautiful animal, and began at once to pursue him, but they could not come within reach of him, for when they thought they were certain of him he sprang away over the bushes and disappeared. As soon as it was dark he went back to the little house, knocked at the door, and said, 'Little sister, let me in.'

Then the door was opened to him, and he went in, and rested the whole night long on his soft bed. The next morning the hunt began anew, and when the fawn heard the hunting-horns and the tally-ho of the huntsmen he could rest no longer, and said, 'Little sister, let me out, I must go.'

The sister opened the door and said, 'Now, mind you must come back at night and say the same words.'

When the king and his hunters saw the fawn with the golden collar again, they chased him closely, but he was too nimble and swift for them. This lasted the whole day, and at last the hunters surrounded him, and one of them wounded his foot a little, so that he was obliged to limp and to go slowly. Then a hunter slipped after him to the little house, and heard how he called out, 'Little sister, let me in,' and saw the door open and shut again after him directly. The hunter noticed all this carefully, went to the king, and told him all he had seen and heard.

Then said the king, 'Tomorrow we will hunt again.'

But the sister was very terrified when she saw that her fawn was wounded. She washed his foot, laid cooling leaves round it, and said, 'Lie down on your bed, dear fawn, and rest, that you may be soon well.' The wound was very slight, so that the fawn felt nothing of it the next morning. And when he heard the noise of the hunting outside, he said, 'I cannot stay in, I must go after them; I shall not be taken easily again!'

The sister began to weep, and said, 'I know you will be killed, and I left alone here in the forest, and forsaken of everybody. I cannot let you go!'

'Then I shall die here with longing,' answered the fawn; 'when I hear the sound of the horn I feel as if I should leap out of my skin.'

Then the sister, seeing there was no help for it, unlocked the door with a heavy heart, and the fawn bounded away into the forest, well and merry. When the king saw him, he said to his hunters, 'Now, follow him up all day long till the night comes, and see that you do him no hurt.'

So as soon as the sun had gone down, the king said to the huntsmen: 'Now, come and show me the little house in the wood.'

And when he got to the door he knocked at it, and cried, 'Little sister, let me in!'

Then the door opened, and the king went in, and there stood a maiden more beautiful than any he had seen before. The maiden shrieked out when she saw, instead of the fawn, a man standing there with a gold crown on his head. But the king looked kindly on her, took her by the hand, and said, 'Will you go with me to my castle, and be my dear wife?'

'Oh yes,' answered the maiden, 'but the fawn must come too. I could not leave him.'

And the king said, 'He shall remain with you as long as you live, and shall lack nothing.' Then the fawn came bounding in, and the sister tied the cord of rushes to him, and led him by her own hand out of the little house.

The king put the beautiful maiden on his horse, and carried her to his castle, where the wedding was held with great pomp; so she became his lady queen, and they lived together happily for a long while; the fawn was well tended and cherished, and he gambolled about the castle garden.

Now the wicked stepmother, whose fault it was that the children were driven out into the world, never dreamed but that the sister had been eaten up by wild beasts in the forest, and that the brother, in the likeness of a fawn, had been slain by the hunters. But when she heard that they were so happy, and that things had gone so well with them, jealousy and envy arose in her heart, and left her no peace, and her chief thought was how to bring misfortune upon them.

Her own daughter, who was as ugly as sin, and had only one eye, complained to her, and said, '*I* never had the chance of being a queen.'

'Never mind,' said the old woman, to satisfy her; 'when the time comes, I shall be at hand.'

After a while the queen brought a beautiful baby boy into the world, and that day the king was out hunting. The old witch took the shape of the bedchamber woman, and went into the room where the queen lay, and said to her, 'Come, the bath is ready; it will give you refreshment and new strength. Quick, or it will be cold.'

Her daughter was within call, so they carried the queen into the bathroom, and left her there. And in the bathroom they had made a great fire, so as to suffocate the beautiful young queen.

When that was managed, the old woman took her daughter, put a cap on her, and laid her in the bed in the queen's place, gave her also the queen's form and countenance, only she could not restore the lost eye. So, in order that the king might not remark it, she had to lie on the side where there was no eye. In the evening, when the king came home and heard that a little son was born to him, he rejoiced with all his heart, and was going at once to his dear wife's bedside to see how she did.

Then the old woman cried hastily, 'For your life, do not draw back the curtains to let in the light upon her; she must be kept quiet.' So the king went away, and never knew that a false queen was lying in the bed.

Now, when it was midnight, and everyone was asleep, the nurse, who was sitting by the cradle in the nursery and watching there alone, saw the door open, and the true queen come in. She took the child out of the cradle, laid it in her bosom, and fed it. Then she shook out its little pillow, put the child back again, and covered it with the coverlet. She did not forget the fawn either: she went to him where he lay in the corner, and stroked his back tenderly. Then she went in perfect silence out at the door, and the nurse next morning asked the watchmen if anyone had entered the castle during the night, but they said they had seen no one. And the queen came many nights, and never said a word; the nurse saw her always, but she did not dare speak of it to anyone.

After some time had gone by in this manner, the queen seemed to find voice, and said one night,

'My child and fawn twice more I come to see,
Twice more I come, and then the end must be.'

The nurse said nothing, but as soon as the queen had disappeared she went to the king and told him all.

The king said, 'Ah, heaven! what do I hear! I will myself watch by the child tomorrow night.'

So at evening he went into the nursery, and at midnight the queen appeared, and said,

'My child and fawn once more I come to see,
Once more I come, and then the end must be.'

And she tended the child, as she was accustomed to do, before she vanished. The king dared not speak to her, but he watched again the following night, and heard her say,

'My child and fawn this once I come to see,
This once I come, and now the end must be.'

Then the king could contain himself no longer, but rushed towards her, saying, 'You are no other than my dear wife!'

Then she answered, 'Yes, I am your dear wife,' and in that moment, by the grace of heaven, her life returned to her, and she was once more well and strong. Then she told the king the snare that the wicked witch and her daughter had laid for her. The king had them both brought to judgement, and sentence was passed upon them. The daughter was sent away into the wood, where she was devoured by the wild beasts, and the witch was burned, and ended miserably. And as soon as her body was in ashes the spell was removed from the fawn, and he took human shape again; and then the sister and brother lived happily together until the end.

The Bunyip

Long, long ago, far, far away on the other side of the world, some young men left the camp where they lived to get some food for their wives and children. The sun was hot, but they liked heat, and as they went they ran races and tried who could hurl his spear the farthest, or was cleverest in throwing a strange weapon called a boomerang, which always returns to the thrower. They did not get on very fast at this rate, but presently they reached a flat place that in time of flood was full of water, but was now, in the height of summer, only a set of pools, each surrounded with a fringe of plants, with bulrushes standing in the inside of all. In that country the people are fond of the roots of bulrushes, which they think as good as onions, and one of the young men said that they had better collect some of the roots and carry them back to the camp. It did not take them long to weave the tops of the willows into a basket, and they were just going to wade into the water and pull up the bulrush roots when a youth suddenly called out: 'After all, why should we waste our time in doing work that is only fit for women and children? Let them come and get the roots for themselves; but we will fish for eels and anything else we can get.'

This delighted the rest of the party, and they all began to arrange their fishing lines, made from the bark of the yellow mimosa, and to search for bait for their hooks. Most of them used worms, but one, who had put a piece of raw meat for dinner into his skin wallet, cut off a little bit and baited his line with it, unseen by his companions.

For a long time they cast patiently, without receiving a single bite; the sun had grown low in the sky, and it seemed as if they would have to go home empty-handed, not even with a basket of roots to show; when the youth, who had baited his hook with raw meat, suddenly saw his line disappear under the water. Something, a very heavy fish he supposed, was pulling so hard that he could hardly keep his feet, and for a few minutes it

seemed either as if he must let go or be dragged into the pool. He cried to his friends to help him, and at last, trembling with fright at what they were going to see, they managed between them to land on the bank a creature that was neither a calf nor a seal, but something of both, with a long, broad tail. They looked at each other with horror, cold shivers running down their spines; for though they had never beheld it, there was not a man amongst them who did not know what it was – the cub of the awful Bunyip!

All of a sudden the silence was broken by a low wail, answered by another from the other side of the pool, as the mother rose up from her den and came towards them, rage flashing from her horrible yellow eyes. 'Let it go! let it go!' whispered the young men to each other; but the captor declared that he had caught it, and was going to keep it. 'He had promised his sweetheart,' he said, 'that he would bring back enough meat for her father's house to feast on for three days, and though they could not eat the little Bunyip, her brothers and sisters should have it to play with.' So, flinging his spear at the mother to keep her back, he threw the little Bunyip on to his shoulders, and set out for the camp, never heeding the poor mother's cries of distress.

By this time it was getting near sunset, and the plain was in shadow, though the tops of the mountains were still quite bright. The youths had all ceased to be afraid, when they were startled by a low rushing sound behind them, and, looking round, saw that the pool was slowly rising, and the spot where they had landed the Bunyip was quite covered. 'What could it be?' they asked one of another; 'there was not a cloud in the sky, yet the water had risen higher already than they had ever known it do before.' For an instant they stood watching as if they were frozen, then they turned and ran with all their might, the man with the Bunyip running faster than all. When he reached a high peak overlooking all the plain he stopped to take breath, and turned to see if he was safe yet. Safe! why only the tops of the trees remained above that sea of water, and these were fast disappearing. They must run fast indeed if they were to escape. So on they flew, scarcely feeling the ground as they went, till they flung themselves on the ground before the holes scooped out of the earth where they had all been born. The old men were sitting in front, the children were playing, and the women chattering together, when the little Bunyip fell into their midst, and there was scarcely a child among them who did not know that something terrible was upon them. 'The water! the water!' gasped one of the young men; and there it was, slowly but steadily mounting the ridge itself. Parents and children clung together, as if by that means they could drive back the advancing flood; and the youth who had caused all this terrible catastrophe, seized his sweetheart, and cried: 'I will climb with you to the top of that tree, and there no waters can reach us.' But, as he spoke, something cold touched him, and quickly he glanced down at his feet. Then with a shudder he saw that they were feet no longer, but bird's claws. He looked at the girl he was clasping, and beheld a great black bird standing at his side; he turned to his friends, but a flock of great awkward flapping creatures stood in their place He put up his hands to cover his face, but they were no longer hands, only the ends of wings; and when he tried to speak, a noise such as he had never heard before seemed to come from his throat, which had suddenly become narrow and slender. Already the water had risen to his waist, and he found himself sitting easily upon it, while its surface reflected back the image of a black swan, one of many.

Never again did the swans become men; but they are still different from other swans, for in the night-time those who listen can hear them talk in a language that is certainly not swans' language; and there are even sounds of laughing and talking, unlike any noise made by the swans whom we know.

The little Bunyip was carried home by its mother, and after that the waters sank back to their own channels. The side of the pool where she lives is always shunned by everyone, as nobody knows when she may suddenly put out her head and draw him into her mighty jaws. But people say that underneath the black waters of the pool she has a house filled with beautiful things, such as mortals who dwell on the earth have no idea of. Though how they know I cannot tell you, as nobody has ever seen it.

Cap o' Rushes

Well, there was once a very rich gentleman, and he'd three daughters, and he thought he'd see how fond they were of him. So he says to the first, 'How much do you love me, my dear?'

'Why,' says she, 'as I love my life.'

'That's good,' says he.

So he says to the second, 'How much do *you* love me, my dear?'

'Why,' says she, 'better than all the world.'

'That's good,' says he.

So he says to the third, 'How much do *you* love me, my dear?'

'Why, I love you as fresh meat loves salt,' says she.

Well, he was that angry. 'You don't love me at all,' says he, 'and in my house you stay no more.' So he drove her out there and then, and shut the door in her face.

Well, she went away on and on till she came to a fen, and there she gathered a lot of rushes and made them into a kind of a sort of a cloak with a hood, to cover her from head to foot, and to hide her fine clothes. And then she went on and on till she came to a great house.

'Do you want a maid?' says she.

'No, we don't,' said they.

'I haven't nowhere to go,' says she; 'and I ask no wages, and do any sort of work,' says she.

'Well,' says they, 'if you like to wash the pots and scrape the saucepans you may stay,' said they.

So she stayed there and washed the pots and scraped the saucepans and did all the dirty work. And because she gave no name they called her 'Cap o' Rushes'.

Well, one day there was to be a great dance a little way off, and the servants were allowed to go and look on at the grand people. Cap o' Rushes said she was too tired to go, so she stayed at home.

But when they were gone she offed with her cap o' rushes, and cleaned herself, and went to the dance. And no one there was so finely dressed as she.

Well, who should be there but her master's son, and what should he do but fall in love with her the minute he set eyes on her. He wouldn't dance with anyone else.

But before the dance was done Cap o' Rushes slipped off, and away she went home. And when the other maids came back she was pretending to be asleep with her cap o' rushes on.

Well, next morning they said to her, 'You did miss a sight, Cap o' Rushes!'

'What was that?' says she.

'Why, the beautifullest lady you ever did see, dressed right gay and grand. The young master, he never took his eyes off her.'

'Well, I should have liked to have seen her,' says Cap o' Rushes.

'Well, there's to be another dance this evening, and perhaps she'll be there.'

But, come the evening, Cap o' Rushes said she was too tired to go with them. Howsoever, when they were gone, she offed with her cap o' rushes and cleaned herself, and away she went to the dance.

The master's son had been reckoning on seeing her, and he danced with no one else, and never took his eyes off her. But, before the dance was over, she slipped off, and home she went, and when the maids came back she, pretended to be asleep with her cap o' rushes on.

Next day they said to her again, 'Well, Cap o' Rushes, you should ha' been there to see the lady. There she was again, gay and grand, and the young master he never took his eyes off her.'

'Well, there,' says she, 'I should ha' liked to ha' seen her.'

'Well,' says they, 'there's a dance again this evening, and you must go with us, for she's sure to be there.'

Well, come the evening, Cap o' Rushes said she was too tired to go, and do what they would she stayed at home. But when they were gone she offed with her cap o' rushes and cleaned herself, and away she went to the dance.

The master's son was rarely glad when he saw her. He danced with none but her and never took his eyes off her. When she wouldn't tell him her name, nor where she came from, he gave her a ring and told her if he didn't see her again he should die.

Well, before the dance was over, off she slipped, and home she went, and when the maids came home she was pretending to be asleep with her cap o' rushes on.

Well, next day they says to her, 'There, Cap o' Rushes, you didn't come last night, and now you won't see the lady, for there's no more dances.'

'Well I should have rarely liked to have seen her,' says she.

The master's son he tried every way to find out where the lady was gone, but go where he might, and ask whom he might, he never heard anything about her. And he got worse and worse for the love of her till he had to keep his bed.

'Make some gruel for the young master,' they said to the cook. 'He's dying for the love of the lady.' The cook she had set about making it when Cap o' Rushes came in.

'What are you a-doing of?' says she.

'I'm going to make some gruel for the young master,' says the cook, 'for he's dying for love of the lady.'

'Let me make it,' says Cap o' Rushes.

Well, the cook wouldn't at first, but at last she said yes, and Cap o' Rushes made the gruel. And when she had made it she slipped the ring into it on the sly before the cook took it upstairs.

The young man he drank it and then he saw the ring at the bottom.

'Send for the cook,' says he.

So up she comes.

'Who made this gruel here?' says he.

'I did,' says the cook, for she was frightened.

And he looked at her, 'No, you didn't,' says he.

'Say who did it, and you shan't be harmed.'

'Well, then, 'twas Cap o' Rushes,' says she.

'Send Cap o' Rushes here,' says he.

So Cap o' Rushes came.

'Did you make my gruel?' says he.

'Yes, I did,' says she.

'Where did you get this ring?' says he.

'From him that gave it me,' says she.

'Who are you, then?' says the young man.

'I'll show you,' says she. And she offed with her cap o' rushes, and there she was in her beautiful clothes.

Well, the master's son he got well very soon, and they were to be married in a little time. It was to be a very grand wedding, and everyone was asked from far and near. And Cap o' Rushes' father was asked. But she still had never told anybody who she was. But before the wedding she went to the cook, and says she: 'I want you to dress every dish without a mite o' salt.'

'That'll be rare nasty,' says the cook.

'That doesn't signify,' says she.

'Very well,' says the cook.

Well, the wedding day came, and they were married. And after they were married all the company sat down to the dinner. When they began to eat the meat, it was so tasteless they couldn't eat it. But Cap o' Rushes' father he tried first one dish and then another, and then he burst out crying.

'What is the matter?' said the master's son to him.

'Oh!' says he, 'I had a daughter. And I asked her how much she loved me. And she said, "As much as fresh meat loves salt." And I turned her from my door, for I thought she didn't love me. And now I see she loved me best of all. And she may be dead for aught I know.'

'No, father, here she is!' says Cap o' Rushes. And she goes up to him and puts her arms round him.

And so they were happy ever after.

The Cat and the Mouse

The cat and the mouse play'd in the malt-house.

The cat bit the mouse's tail off.

'Pray, puss, give me my tail.'

'No,' says the cat, 'I'll not give you your tail, till you go to the cow, and fetch me some milk.'

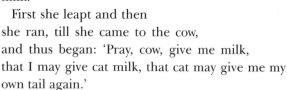

First she leapt and then she ran, till she came to the cow, and thus began: 'Pray, cow, give me milk, that I may give cat milk, that cat may give me my own tail again.'

'No,' said the cow, 'I will give you no milk, till you go to the farmer, and get me some hay.'

First she leapt, and then she ran, till she came to the farmer and thus began: 'Pray, farmer, give me hay, that I may give cow hay, that cow may give me milk, that I may give cat milk, that cat may give me my own tail again.'

'No,' says the farmer, 'I'll give you no hay, till you go to the butcher and fetch me some meat.'

First she leapt, and then she ran, till she came to the butcher, and thus began: 'Pray, butcher, give me meat, that I may give farmer meat, that farmer may give me hay, that I may give cow hay, that cow may give me milk, that I may give cat milk, that cat may give me my own tail again.'

'No,' says the butcher, 'I'll give you no meat, till you go to the baker and fetch me some bread.'

First she leapt and then she ran, till she came to the baker, and thus began: 'Pray, baker, give me bread, that I may give butcher bread, that butcher may give me meat, that I may give farmer meat, that farmer may give me hay, that I may give cow hay, that cow may give me milk, that I may give cat milk, that cat may give me my own tail again.'

'Yes,' says the baker, 'I'll give you some bread, But if you eat my meal, I'll cut off your head.'

Then the baker gave mouse bread, and mouse gave butcher bread, and butcher gave mouse meat, and mouse gave farmer meat, and farmer gave mouse hay, and mouse gave cow hay, and cow gave mouse milk, and mouse gave cat milk, and cat gave mouse her own tail again!

The Cat's Elopement

Once upon a time there lived a cat of marvellous beauty, with a coat as soft and shining as silk, and wise green eyes, that could see even in the dark. His name was Gon, and he belonged to a music teacher, who was so fond and proud of him that he would not have parted with him for anything in the world.

Now not far from the music master's house there dwelt a lady who possessed a most lovely little pussy cat called Koma. She was such a little dear altogether, and blinked her eyes so daintily, and ate her supper so tidily, and when she had finished she licked her pink nose so delicately with her little tongue, that her mistress was never tired of saying, 'Koma, Koma, what should I do without you?'

Well, it happened one day that these two, when out for an evening stroll, met under a cherry tree, and in one moment fell madly in love with each

other. Gon had long felt that it was time for him to find a wife, for all the ladies in the neighbourhood paid him so much attention that it made him quite shy; but he was not easy to please, and did not care about any of them. Now, before he had time to think, Cupid had entangled him in his net, and he was filled with love towards Koma. She fully returned his passion, but, like a woman, she saw the difficulties in the way, and consulted sadly with Gon as to the means of overcoming them. Gon entreated his master to set matters right by buying Koma, but her mistress would not part from her. Then the music master was asked to sell Gon to the lady, but he declined to listen to any such suggestion, so everything remained as before.

At length the love of the couple grew to such a pitch that they determined to please themselves, and to seek their fortunes together. So one moonlight night they stole away, and ventured out into an unknown world. All day long they marched bravely on through the sunshine, till they had left their homes far behind them, and towards evening they found themselves in a large park. The wanderers by this time were very hot and tired, and the grass looked very soft and inviting, and the trees cast cool deep shadows, when suddenly an ogre appeared in this paradise, in the shape of a big, big dog! He came springing towards them, showing all his teeth, and Koma shrieked, and rushed up a cherry tree. Gon, however, stood his ground boldly, and prepared to give battle, for he felt that Koma's eyes were upon him, and that he must not run away. But, alas! his courage would have availed him nothing had his enemy once touched him, for he was large and powerful, and very fierce. From her perch in the tree Koma saw it all, and screamed with all her might, hoping that someone would hear, and come to help. Luckily a servant of the princess to whom the park belonged was walking by, and he drove off the dog, and picking up the trembling Gon in his arms, carried him to his mistress.

So poor little Koma was left alone, while Gon was borne away full of trouble, not in the least knowing what to do. Even the attention paid him by the princess, who was delighted with his beauty and pretty ways, did not console him, but there was no use in fighting against fate, and he could only wait and see what would turn up.

The princess, Gon's new mistress, was so good and kind that everybody loved her, and she would have led a happy life, had it not been for a serpent who had fallen in love with her, and was constantly annoying her by his presence. Her servants had orders to drive him away as often as he appeared; but as they were careless, and the serpent very sly, it sometimes happened that he was able to slip past them, and to frighten the princess by appearing before her. One day she was seated in her room, playing on her favourite musical instrument, when she felt something gliding up her sash, and saw her enemy making his way to kiss her cheek. She shrieked and threw herself backwards, and Gon, who had been curled up on a stool at her feet, understood her terror, and with one bound seized the snake by his neck. He gave him one bite and one shake, and flung him on the ground, where he lay, never to worry the princess any more. Then she took Gon in her arms, and praised and caressed him, and saw that he had the nicest bits to eat, and the softest mats to lie on; and he would have had nothing in the world to wish for if only he could have seen Koma again.

Time passed on, and one morning Gon lay before the house door, basking in the sun. He looked lazily at the world stretched out before him, and saw in the distance a big ruffian of a cat teasing and ill-treating quite a little one. He jumped up, full of rage, and chased away the big cat, and then he turned to comfort the little one, when his heart nearly burst with joy to find that it was Koma. At first Koma did not know him again, he had grown so large and stately; but when it dawned upon her who it was, her happiness knew no bounds. And they rubbed their heads and their noses again and again, while their purring might have been heard a mile off.

Paw in paw they appeared before the princess, and told her the story of their life and its sorrows. The princess wept for sympathy, and promised that they should never more be parted, but should live with her to the end of their days. By and by the princess herself got married, and brought a prince to dwell in the palace in the park. And she told him all about her two cats, and how brave Gon had been, and how he had delivered her from her enemy the serpent.

And when the prince heard, he swore they should never leave them, but should go with the princess wherever she went. So it all fell out as the princess wished; and Gon and Koma had many children, and so had the princess, and they all played together, and were friends to the end of their lives.

The Cauld Lad of Hilton

At Hilton Hall,* long years ago, there lived a brownie that was the contrariest brownie you ever knew. At night, after the servants had gone to bed, it would turn everything topsy-turvy, put sugar in the salt-cellars, pepper into the beer, and was up to all kinds of pranks. It would throw the chairs down, put tables on their backs, rake out fires, and do as much mischief as could be. But sometimes it would be in a good temper.

'What's a brownie?' you say. Oh, it's a kind of a sort of a bogle, but it isn't so cruel as a redcap! What! you don't know what's a bogle or a redcap! Ah, me! what's the world a-coming to? Of course a brownie is a funny little thing, half man, half goblin, with pointed ears and a hairy hide. When you bury a treasure, you scatter over it blood drops of a newly slain kid or lamb, or, better still, bury the animal with the treasure, and a brownie will watch over it for you, and frighten everybody else away.

Where was I? Well, as I was a-saying, the brownie at Hilton Hall would play at mischief, but if the servants laid out for it a bowl of cream, or a knuckle cake spread with honey, it would clear away things for them, and make everything tidy in the kitchen.

One night, however, when the servants had stopped up late, they heard a noise in the kitchen, and, peeping in, saw the brownie swinging to and fro on the jack chain, and saying:

> 'Woe's me! woe's me!
> The acorn's not yet
> Fallen from the tree,
> That's to grow the wood,
> That's to make the cradle,
> That's to rock the bairn,
> That's to grow to the man,
> That's to set me free.
> Woe's me! woe's me!'

So they took pity on the poor brownie, and asked the nearest henwife what they should do to send it away. 'That's easy enough,' said the henwife, and told them that a brownie that's paid for its service, in aught that's not perishable, goes away at once. So they made a cloak of Lincoln green, with a hood to it, and put it by the hearth and watched. They saw the brownie come up, and seeing the hood and cloak, put them on, and frisk about, dancing on one leg and saying: 'I've taken your cloak, I've taken your hood; The Cauld Lad of Hilton will do no more good.'

And with that it vanished, and was never seen or heard of afterwards.

* The ruins of Hylton Castle near Sunderland in England are haunted by the ghost of a murdered stable-boy, known locally as the Cauld Lad of Hylton. The story goes that one night Baron Hylton caught his daughter in the arms of the stable-boy, Robert Skelton. The baron was so enraged that he killed the stable-boy and threw the body into a deep pond. Several months later, the body was recovered. The baron was tried for Skelton's murder, but was acquitted on the evidence of an old farm worker, who said that the baron had ordered the boy to remove a tool from the top shelf in the barn, and the boy had fallen, seriously wounding himself in the process; the baron had tended the wounds, but the boy had died. Soon afterwards, strange events began to occur in the castle.

Childe Rowland

Childe Rowland and his brothers twain
  Were playing at the ball,
And there was their sister Burd Ellen
  In the midst, among them all.

Childe Rowland kicked it with his foot
  And caught it with his knee;
At last as he plunged among them all
  O'er the church he made it flee.

Burd Ellen round about the aisle
  To seek the ball is gone,
But long they waited, and longer still,
  And she came not back again.

They sought her east, they sought her west,
  They sought her up and down,
And woe were the hearts of those brethren,
  For she was not to be found.

So at last her eldest brother went to the Warlock Merlin and told him all the case, and asked him if he knew where Burd Ellen was. 'The fair Burd Ellen,' said the Warlock Merlin, 'must have been carried off by the fairies, because she went round the church "widdershins" – the opposite way to the sun. She is now in the Dark Tower of the King of Elfland; it would take the boldest knight in Christendom to bring her back.'

'If it is possible to bring her back,' said her brother, 'I'll do it, or perish in the attempt.'

'Possible it is,' said the Warlock Merlin, 'but woe to the man or mother's son that attempts it, if he is not well taught beforehand what he is to do.'

The eldest brother of Burd Ellen was not to be put off, by any fear of danger, from attempting to get her back, so he begged the Warlock Merlin to tell him what he should do, and what he should not do, in going to seek his sister. And after he had been taught, and had repeated his lesson, he set out for Elfland.

But long they waited, and longer still,
  With doubt and muckle pain,
But woe were the hearts of his brethren,
  For he came not back again.

Then the second brother got tired and sick of waiting, and he went to the Warlock Merlin and

asked him the same as his brother. So he set out to find Burd Ellen.

> But long they waited, and longer still,
>   With muckle doubt and pain,
> And woe were his mother's and brother's heart,
>   For he came not back again.

And when they had waited and waited a good long time, Childe Rowland, the youngest of Burd Ellen's brothers, wished to go, and went to his mother, the good queen, to ask her to let him go. But she would not at first, for he was the last of her children she now had, and if he was lost, all would be lost. But he begged, and he begged, till at last the good queen let him go, and gave him his father's good brand that never struck in vain. And as she girt it round his waist, she said the spell that would give it victory.

So Childe Rowland said goodbye to the good queen, his mother, and went to the cave of the Warlock Merlin. 'Once more, and but once more,' he said to the Warlock, 'tell how man or mother's son may rescue Burd Ellen and her brothers twain.'

'Well, my son,' said the Warlock Merlin, 'there are but two things, simple they may seem, but hard they are to do. One thing to do, and one thing not to do. And the thing to do is this: after you have entered the land of Fairy, whoever speaks to you, till you meet the Burd Ellen, you must out with your father's brand and off with their head. And what you've not to do is this: bite no bit, and drink no drop, however hungry or thirsty you be; drink a drop, or bite a bit, while in Elfland you be, and never will you see Middle Earth again.'

So Childe Rowland said the two things over and over again, till he knew them by heart, and he thanked the Warlock Merlin and went on his way. And he went along, and along, and along, and still farther along, till he came to the horse-herd of the King of Elfland feeding his horses. These he knew by their fiery eyes, and knew that he was at last in the land of Fairy. 'Canst thou tell me,' said Childe Rowland to the horse-herd, 'where the King of Elfland's Dark Tower is?' 'I cannot tell thee,' said the horse-herd, 'but go on a little farther and thou wilt come to the cow-herd, and he, maybe, can tell thee.'

Then, without a word more, Childe Rowland drew the good brand that never struck in vain, and off went the horse-herd's head, and Childe Rowland went on farther, till he came to the cow-herd, and asked him the same question. 'I can't tell thee,' said he, 'but go on a little farther, and thou wilt come to the henwife, and she is sure to know.' Then Childe

Rowland out with his good brand, that never struck in vain, and off went the cow-herd's head. And he went on a little farther, till he came to an old woman in a grey cloak, and he asked her if she knew where the Dark Tower of the King of Elfland was. 'Go on a, little further,' said the henwife, 'till you come to a round green hill, surrounded with terrace-rings, from the bottom to the top; go round it three times, widdershins, and each time say:

> Open, door! open, door!
> And let me come in;

and the third time the door will open, and you may go in.' And Childe Rowland was just going on, when he remembered what he had to do; so he out with the good brand, that never struck in vain, and off went the henwife's head.

Then he went on, and on, and on, till he came to the round green hill with the terrace-rings from top to bottom, and he went round it three times, widdershins, saying each time:

> Open, door! open, door!
> And let me come in.

And the third time the door did open, and he went in, and it closed with a click, and Childe Rowland was left in the dark.

It was not exactly dark, but a kind of twilight or gloaming. There were neither windows nor candles, and he could not make out where the twilight came from, if not through the walls and roof. These were rough arches made of a transparent rock, encrusted with sheep-silver and rock spar and other bright stones. But though it was rock, the air was quite warm, as it always is in Elfland. So he went through this passage till at last he came to two wide and high folding-doors which stood ajar. And when he opened them, there he saw a most wonderful and glorious sight. A large and spacious hall, so large that it seemed to be as long, and as broad, as the green hill itself. The roof was supported by fine pillars, so large and lofty, that the pillars of a cathedral were as nothing to them. They were all of gold and silver, with fretted work, and between them and around them, wreaths of flowers, composed of what do you think? Why, of diamonds and emeralds and all manner of precious stones. And the very keystones of the arches had for ornaments clusters of diamonds and rubies and pearls and other precious stones. And all these arches met in the middle of the roof, and just there, hung by a gold chain, was an immense lamp made out of one great pearl, hollowed out and quite transparent. And in the middle of this was a, huge carbuncle, which kept spinning round and round, and this was what gave light by its rays to the whole hall, which seemed as if the setting sun was shining on it.

The hall was furnished in a manner equally grand, and at one end of it was a glorious couch of velvet, silk and gold, and there sat Burd Ellen, combing her golden hair with a silver comb. And when she saw Childe Rowland she stood up and said:

'God pity ye, poor luckless fool,
    What have ye here to do?
Hear ye this, my youngest brother,
    Why didn't ye bide at home?
Had you a hundred thousand lives
    Ye couldn't spare any a one.
But sit ye down; but woe, oh woe,
    That ever ye were born,
For come the King of Elfland in,
    Your fortune is forlorn.'

Then they sat down together, and Childe Rowland told her all that he had done, and she told him how their two brothers had reached the Dark Tower, but had been enchanted by the King of Elfland, and lay there entombed as if dead. And then after they had talked a little longer Childe Rowland began to feel hungry from his long travels, and told his sister Burd Ellen how hungry he was and asked for some food, forgetting all about the Warlock Merlin's warning.

Burd Ellen looked at Childe Rowland sadly, and shook her head, but she was under a spell, and could not warn him. So she rose up, and went out, and soon brought back a golden basin full of bread and milk. Childe Rowland was just going to raise it to his lips, when he looked at his sister and remembered why he had come all that way. So he dashed the bowl to the ground, and said: 'Not a sup will I swallow, nor a bit will I bite, till Burd Ellen is set free.'

Just at that moment they heard the noise of someone approaching, and a loud voice was heard saying:

'Fee, fi, fo, fum,
I smell the blood of a Christian man,
Be he dead, be he living, with my brand,
I'll dash his brains from his brain-pan.'

And then the folding-doors of the hall were burst open, and the King of Elfland rushed in.

'Strike then, bogle, if thou darest,' shouted out Childe Rowland, and rushed to meet him with his good brand that never yet did fail. They fought, and they fought, and they fought, till Childe Rowland beat the King of Elfland down on to his knees, and caused him to yield and beg for mercy. 'I grant thee mercy,' said Childe Rowland, 'if you release my sister from thy spells and raise my brothers to life and let us all go free.' 'I agree,' said the Elfin king, and rising up he went to a chest from which he took a phial filled with a blood-red liquor. With this he anointed the ears, eyelids, nostrils, lips and fingertips of the two brothers, and they sprang at once into life, and declared that their souls had been away, but had now returned. The Elfin king then said some words to Burd Ellen, and she was disenchanted, and they all four passed out of the hall, through the long passage, and turned their back on the Dark Tower, never to return again. And they reached home, and were restored to the good queen, their mother, and Burd Ellen never went round a church widdershins again.

The Story of Ciccu

Once upon a time there lived a man who had three sons. The eldest was called Peppe, the second Alfin and the youngest Ciccu. They were all very poor, and at last things got so bad that they really had not enough to eat. So the father called his sons, and said to them, ' My dear boys, I am too old to work any more, and there is nothing left for me but to beg in the streets.'

'No, no!' exclaimed his sons; 'that you shall never do. Rather, if it must be, would we do it ourselves. But we have thought of a better plan than that.'

'What is it?' asked the father.

'Well, we will take you into the forest, where you shall cut wood, and then we will bind it up in bundles and sell it in the town.' So their father let them do as they said, and they all made their way into the forest; and as the old man was weak from lack of food his sons took it in turns to carry him on their backs. Then they built a little hut where they might take shelter, and set to work. Every morning early the father cut his sticks, and the sons bound them in bundles and carried them to the town, bringing back the food the old man so much needed.

Some months passed in this way, and then the father suddenly fell ill, and knew that the time had come when he must die. He bade his sons fetch a lawyer, so that he might make his will, and when the man arrived he explained his wishes.

'I have,' said he, 'a little house in the village, and over it grows a fig-tree. The house I leave to my sons, who are to live in it together; the fig-tree I divide as follows. To my son Peppe I leave the branches. To my son Alfin I leave the trunk. To my son Ciccu I leave the fruit. Besides the house and tree, I have an old coverlet, which I leave to my eldest son. And an old purse, which I leave to my second son. And a horn, which I leave to my youngest son. And now farewell.'

Thus speaking, he laid himself down and died quietly. The brothers wept bitterly for their father,

whom they loved, and when they had buried him they began to talk over their future lives. 'What shall we do now?' said they. 'Shall we live in the wood or go back to the village?' And they made up their minds to stay where they were and continue to earn their living by selling firewood.

One very hot evening, after they had been working hard all day, they fell asleep under a tree in front of the hut. And as they slept there came by three fairies, who stopped to look at them.

'What fine fellows!' said one. 'Let us give them a present.'

'Yes, what shall it be?' asked another.

'This youth has a coverlet over him,' said the first fairy. 'When he wraps it round him, and wishes himself in any place, he will find himself there in an instant.'

Then said the second fairy: 'This youth has a purse in his hand. I will promise that it shall always give him as much gold as he asks for.'

Last came the turn of the third fairy. 'This one has a horn slung round him. When he blows at the small end the seas shall be covered with ships. And if he blows at the wide end they shall all be sunk in the waves.' So they vanished, without knowing that Ciccu had been awake and heard all they said.

The next day, when they were all cutting wood, he said to his brothers, 'That old coverlet and the purse are no use to you; I wish you would give them to me. I have a fancy for them, for the sake of old times.' Now Peppe and Alfin were very fond of Ciccu, and never refused him anything, so they let him have the coverlet and the purse without a word. When he had got them safely Ciccu went on, 'Dear brothers, I am tired of the forest. I want to live in the town, and work at some trade.'

'Oh Ciccu! stay with us,' they cried. 'We are very happy here; and who knows how we shall get on elsewhere?'

'We can always try,' answered Ciccu; 'and if times are bad we can come back here and take up

woodcutting.' So saying he picked up his bundle of sticks, and his brothers did the same.

But when they reached the town they found that the market was overstocked with firewood, and they did not sell enough to buy themselves a dinner, far less to get any food to carry home. They were wondering sadly what they should do when Ciccu said, 'Come with me to the inn and let us have something to eat.' They were so hungry by this time that they did not care much whether they paid for it or not, so they followed Ciccu, who gave his orders to the host. 'Bring us three dishes, the nicest that you have, and a good bottle of wine.'

'Ciccu! Ciccu!' whispered his brothers, horrified at this extravagance, 'are you mad? How do you ever mean to pay for it?'

'Let me alone,' replied Ciccu; 'I know what I am about.' And when they had finished their dinner Ciccu told the others to go on, and he would wait to pay the bill.

The brothers hurried on, without needing to be told twice, 'for,' thought they, 'he has no money, and of course there will be a row.'

When they were out of sight Ciccu asked the landlord how much he owed, and then said to his purse, 'Dear purse, give me, I pray you, six florins,' and instantly six florins were in the purse. Then he paid the bill and joined his brothers.

'How did you manage?' they asked.

'Never you mind,' answered he. 'I have paid every penny,' and no more would he say. But the other two were very uneasy, for they felt sure something must be wrong, and the sooner they parted company with Ciccu the better. Ciccu understood what they were thinking, and, drawing forty gold pieces from his pocket, he held out twenty to each, saying, 'Take these and turn them to good account. I am going away to seek my own fortune.' Then he embraced them, and struck down another road.

He wandered on for many days, till at length he came to the town where the king had his court. The first thing Ciccu did was to order himself some fine clothes, and then buy a grand house, just opposite the palace.

Next he locked his door, and ordered a shower of gold to cover the staircase, and when this was done, the door was flung wide open, and everyone came and peeped at the shining golden stairs. Lastly the rumour of these wonders reached the ears of the king, who left his palace to behold these splendours with his own eyes. And Ciccu received him with all respect, and showed him over the house.

When the king went home he told such stories of what he had seen that his wife and daughter declared that they must go and see them too. So the king sent to ask Ciccu's leave, and Ciccu answered that if the queen and the princess would be pleased to do him such great honour he would show them anything they wished. Now the princess was as beautiful as the sun, and when Ciccu looked upon her his heart went out to her, and he longed to have her to wife. The princess saw what was passing in his mind, and how she could make use of it to satisfy her curiosity as to the golden stairs; so she praised him and flattered him, and put cunning questions, till at length Ciccu's head was quite turned, and he told her the whole story of the fairies and their gifts. Then she begged him to lend her the purse for a few days, so that she could have one made like it, and so great was the love he had for her that he gave it to her at once.

The princess returned to the palace, taking with her the purse, which she had not the smallest intention of ever restoring to Ciccu. Very soon Ciccu had spent all the money he had by him, and could get no more without the help of his purse. Of course, he went at once to the king's daughter, and asked her if she had done with it, but she put him off with some excuse, and told him to come back next day. The next day it was the same thing, and the next, till a great rage filled Ciccu's heart instead of the love that had been there. And when night came he took in his hand a thick stick, wrapped himself in the coverlet, and wished himself in the chamber of the princess. The princess was asleep, but Ciccu seized her arm and pulled her out of bed, and beat her till she gave back the purse. Then he took up the coverlet, and wished he was safe in his own house.

No sooner had he gone than the princess hastened to her father and complained of her sufferings. Then the king rose up in a fury, and commanded Ciccu to be brought before him. 'You richly deserve death,' said he, 'but I will allow you to live if you will instantly hand over to me the coverlet, the purse and the horn.'

What could Ciccu do? Life was sweet, and he was in the power of the king; so he gave up silently his ill-gotten goods, and was as poor as when he was a boy.

While he was wondering how he was to live it suddenly came into his mind that this was the season for the figs to ripen, and he said to himself, 'I will go and see if the tree has borne well.' So he set off home, where his brothers still lived, and found them living very uncomfortably, for they had spent all their money, and did not know how to make any more. However, he was pleased to see that the fig-tree looked in splendid condition, and was full of fruit. He ran and fetched a basket, and was just feeling the figs, to make sure which of them were ripe, when his brother Peppe called to him, 'Stop! The figs of course are yours, but the branches they grow on are mine, and I forbid you to touch them.'

Ciccu did not answer, but set a ladder against the tree, so that he could reach the topmost branches, and had his foot already on the first rung when he heard the voice of his brother Alfin: 'Stop! the trunk belongs to me, and I forbid you to touch it!'

Then they began to quarrel violently, and there seemed no chance that they would ever cease, till one of them said, 'Let us go before a judge.' The others agreed, and when they had found a man whom they could trust, Ciccu told him the whole story.

'This is my verdict,' said the judge. 'The figs in truth belong to you, but you cannot pluck them without touching both the trunk and the branches. Therefore you must give your first basketful to your brother Peppe, as the price of his leave to put your ladder against the tree; and the second basketful to your brother Alfin, for leave to shake his boughs. The rest you can keep for yourself.'

And the brothers were contented, and returned home, saying one to the other, 'We will each of us send a basket of figs to the king. Perhaps he will give us something in return, and if he does we will divide it faithfully between us.' So the best figs were carefully packed in a basket, and Peppe set out with it to the castle.

On the road he met a little old man who stopped and said to him, 'What have you got there, my fine fellow?'

'What is that to you?' was the answer; 'mind your own business.' But the old man only repeated his question, and Peppe, to get rid of him, exclaimed in anger, 'Dirt.'

'Good,' replied the old man; 'dirt you have said, and dirt let it be.'

Peppe only tossed his head and went on his way till he got to the castle, where he knocked at the door. 'I have a basket of lovely figs for the king,' he said to the servant who opened it, 'if his majesty will be graciously pleased to accept them with my humble duty.'

The king loved figs, and ordered Peppe to be admitted to his presence, and a silver dish to be brought on which to put the figs. When Peppe uncovered his basket sure enough a layer of beautiful purple figs met the king's eyes, but underneath there was nothing but dirt. 'How dare you play me such a trick?' shrieked the king in a rage. 'Take him away, and give him fifty lashes.' This was done, and Peppe returned home, sore and angry, but determined to say nothing about his adventure. And when his brothers asked him what had happened he only answered, 'When we have all three been I will tell you.'

A few days after this more figs were ready for plucking, and Alfin in his turn set out for the palace. He had not gone far down the road before he met the old man, who asked him what he had in his basket.

'Horns,' answered Alfin, shortly.

'Good,' replied the old man; 'horns you have said, and horns let it be.'

When Alfin reached the castle he knocked at the door and said to the servant: 'Here is a basket of lovely figs, if his majesty will be good enough to accept them with my humble duty.'

The king commanded that Alfin should be admitted to his presence, and a silver dish to be brought on which to lay the figs. When the basket was uncovered some beautiful purple figs lay on the top, but underneath there was nothing but horns. Then the king was beside himself with passion, and screamed out, 'Is this a plot to mock me? Take him away, and give him a hundred and fifty lashes!' So Alfin went sadly home, but would not tell anything about his adventures, only saying grimly, 'Now it is Ciccu's turn.'

Ciccu had to wait a little before he gathered the last figs on the tree, and these were not nearly so good as the first set. However, he plucked them, as they had agreed, and set out for the king's palace. The old man was still on the road, and he came up and said to Ciccu, 'What've you got in that basket?'

'Figs for the king,' answered he.

'Let me have a peep,' and Ciccu lifted the lid. 'Oh, do give me one, I am so fond of figs,' begged the little man.

'I am afraid if I do that the hole will show,' replied Ciccu, but as he was very good-natured he gave him one. The old man ate it greedily and kept the stalk in his hand, and then asked for another and another and another till he had eaten half the basketful. 'But there are not enough left to take to the king,' murmured Ciccu.

'Don't be anxious,' said the old man, throwing the stalks back into the basket; 'just go on and carry the basket to the castle, and it will bring you luck.'

Ciccu did not much like it; however he went on his way, and with a trembling heart rang the castle bell. 'Here are some lovely figs for the king,' said he, 'if his majesty will graciously accept them with my humble duty.'

When the king was told that there was another man with a basket of figs he cried out, 'Oh, have him in, have him in! I suppose it is a wager!' But Ciccu uncovered the basket, and there lay a pile of beautiful ripe figs. And the king was delighted, and emptied them himself on the silver dish, and gave five florins to Ciccu, and offered besides to take him into his service. Ciccu accepted gratefully, but said he must first return home and give the five florins to his brothers.

When he got home Peppe spoke: 'Now we will see what we each have got from the king. I myself received from him fifty lashes.'

'And I a hundred and fifty,' added Alfin.

'And I five florins and some sweets, which you can divide between you, for the king has taken me into his service.' Then Ciccu went back to the court and served the king, and the king loved him.

The other two brothers heard that Ciccu had become quite an important person, and they grew envious, and thought how they could put him to shame. At last they came to the king and said to him, 'O king! your palace is beautiful indeed, but to be worthy of you it lacks one thing – the sword of the man eater.'

'How can I get it?' asked the king.

'Oh, Ciccu can get it for you; ask him.'

So the king sent for Ciccu and said to him, 'Ciccu, you must at any price manage to get the sword of the man eater.'

Ciccu was very much surprised at this sudden command, and he walked thoughtfully away to the stables and began to stroke his favourite horse, saying to himself, 'Ah, my pet, we must bid each other goodbye, for the king has sent me away to get the sword of the man eater.' Now this horse was not like other horses, for it was a talking horse, and knew a great deal about many things, so it answered, 'Fear nothing, and do as I tell you. Beg the king to give you fifty gold pieces and leave to ride me, and the rest will be easy.' Ciccu believed what the horse said, and prayed the king to grant him what he asked. Then the two friends set out, but the horse chose what roads he pleased, and directed Ciccu in everything.

It took them many days' hard riding before they reached the country where the man eater lived, and then the horse told Ciccu to stop a group of old women who were coming chattering through the wood, and offer them each a shilling if they would collect a number of mosquitoes and tie them up in a bag. When the bag was full Ciccu put it on his shoulder and stole into the house of the man eater (who had gone to look for his dinner) and let them all out in his bedroom. He himself hid carefully under the bed and waited. The man eater came in late, very tired with his long walk, and flung himself on the bed, placing his sword with its shining blade by his side. Scarcely had he lain down than the mosquitoes began to buzz about and bite him, and he rolled from side to side trying to catch them, which he never could do, though they always seemed to be close to his nose. He was so busy over the mosquitoes that he did not hear Ciccu steal softly out, or see him catch up the sword. But the horse heard and stood ready at the door, and as Ciccu came flying down the stairs and jumped on his back he sped away like the wind, and never stopped till they arrived at the king's palace.

The king had suffered much pain in his absence, thinking that if the man eater ate Ciccu, it would be all his fault. And he was so overjoyed to have him safe that he almost forgot the sword which he had sent him to bring. But the two brothers did not love Ciccu any better because he had succeeded when they hoped he would have failed, and one day they spoke to the king. 'It is all very well for Ciccu to have got possession of the sword, but it would have been far more to your majesty's honour if he had captured the man eater himself.' The king thought upon these words, and at last he said to Ciccu, 'Ciccu, I shall never rest until you bring me back the man eater himself. You may have any help you like, but somehow or other you must manage to do it.' Ciccu felt very much cast down at these words, and went to the stable to ask advice of his friend the horse. 'Fear nothing,' said the horse; 'just say you want me and fifty pieces of gold.' Ciccu did as he was bid, and the two set out together.

When they reached the country of the man eater, Ciccu made all the church bells toll and a proclamation to be made. 'Ciccu, the servant of the king, is dead.' The man eater soon heard what everyone was saying, and was glad in his heart, for he thought, 'Well, it is good news that the thief who stole my sword is dead.' But Ciccu bought an axe and a saw, and cut down a pine tree in the nearest wood, and began to hew it into planks.

'What are you doing in my wood?' asked the man eater, coming up.

'Noble lord,' answered Ciccu, 'I am making a coffin for the body of Ciccu, who is dead.'

'Don't be in a hurry,' answered the man eater, who of course did not know whom he was talking to, 'and perhaps I can help you;' and they set to work sawing and fitting, and very soon the coffin was finished.

Then Ciccu scratched his ear thoughtfully, and cried, 'Idiot that I am! I never took any measurements. How am I to know if it is big enough? But now I come to think of it, Ciccu was about your size. I wonder if you would be so good as just to put yourself in the coffin, and see if there is enough room.'

'Oh, delighted!' said the man eater, and laid himself at full length in the coffin. Ciccu clapped on the lid, put a strong cord round it, tied it fast on his horse, and rode back to the king. And when the king saw that he really had brought back the man eater, he commanded a huge iron chest to be brought, and locked the coffin up inside it.

Just about this time the queen died, and soon after the king thought he should like to marry again. He sought everywhere, but he could not hear of any princess that took his fancy. Then the two envious brothers came to him and said, 'O king! there is but one woman that is worthy of being your wife, and that is she who is the fairest in the whole world.'

'But where can I find her?' asked the king

'Oh, Ciccu will know, and he will bring her to you.'

Now the king had got so used to depending on Ciccu, that he really believed he could do everything. So he sent for him and said, 'Ciccu, unless within eight days you bring me the fairest in the whole world, I will have you hewn into a thousand pieces.' This mission seemed to Ciccu a hundred times worse than either of the others, and with tears in his eyes he took his way to the stables.

'Cheer up,' laughed the horse; 'tell the king you must have some bread and honey, and a purse of gold, and leave the rest to me.'

Ciccu did as he was bid, and they started at a gallop.

After they had ridden some way, they saw a swarm of bees lying on the ground, so hungry and weak that they were unable to fly. 'Get down, and give the poor things some honey,' said the horse, and Ciccu dismounted and did so. By and by they came to a stream, on the bank of which was a fish, flapping feebly about in its efforts to reach the water. 'Jump down, and throw the fish into the water; he will be useful to us,' and Ciccu did so. Farther along the hillside they saw an eagle whose leg was caught in a snare. 'Go and free that eagle from the snare; he will be useful to us;' and in a moment the eagle was soaring up into the sky.

At length they came to the castle where the fairest in the world lived with her parents. Then said the horse, 'You must get down and sit upon that stone, for I must enter the castle alone. Directly you see me come tearing by with the princess on my back, jump up behind, and hold her tight, so that she does not escape you. If you fail to do this, we are both lost.' Ciccu seated himself on the stone, and the horse went on to the courtyard of the castle, where he began to trot round in a graceful and elegant manner. Soon a crowd collected first to watch him and then to pat him, and the king and queen and princess came with the rest. The eyes of the fairest in the world brightened as she looked, and she sprang on the horse's saddle, crying, 'Oh, I really must ride him a little!' But the horse made one bound forward, and the princess was forced to hold tight by his mane, lest she should fall off. And as they dashed past the stone where Ciccu was waiting for them, he swung himself up and held her round the waist. As he put his arms round her waist, the fairest in the world unwound the veil from her head and cast it to the ground, and then she drew a ring from her finger and flung it into the stream. But she said nothing, and they rode on fast, fast.

The king of Ciccu's country was watching for them from the top of a tower, and when he saw in the distance a cloud of dust, he ran down to the steps so as to be ready to receive them. Bowing low before the fairest in the world, he spoke: 'Noble lady, will you do me the honour to become my wife?'

But she answered, 'That can only be when Ciccu brings me the veil that I let fall on my way here.'

And the king turned to Ciccu and said, 'Ciccu, if you do not find the veil at once, you shall lose your head.'

Ciccu, who by this time had hoped for a little peace, felt his heart sink at this fresh errand, and he went into the stable to complain to the faithful horse.

'It will be all right,' answered the horse when he had heard his tale; 'just take enough food for the day for both of us, and then get on my back.'

They rode back all the way they had come till they reached the place where they had found the eagle caught in the snare; then the horse bade Ciccu to call three times on the king of the birds, and when he replied, to beg him to fetch the veil which the fairest in the world had let fall.

'Wait a moment,' answered a voice that seemed to come from somewhere very high up indeed. 'An eagle is playing with it just now, but he will be here with it in an instant;' and a few minutes after there was a sound of wings, and an eagle came fluttering towards them with the veil in his beak. And Ciccu saw it was the very same eagle that he had freed from the snare. So he took the veil and rode back to the king.

Now the king was enchanted to see him so soon, and took the veil from Ciccu and flung it over the

princess, crying, 'Here is the veil you asked for, so I claim you for my wife.'

'Not so fast,' answered she. 'I can never be your wife till Ciccu puts on my finger the ring I threw into the stream. Ciccu, who was standing by expecting something of the sort, bowed his head when he heard her words, and went straight to the horse.

'Mount at once,' said the horse; 'this time it is very simple,' and he carried Ciccu to the banks of the little stream. 'Now, call three times on the emperor of the fishes, and beg him to restore you the ring that the princess dropped.

Ciccu did as the horse told him, and a voice was heard in answer that seemed to come from a very long way off. 'What is your will?' it asked; and Ciccu replied that he had been commanded to bring back the ring that the princess had flung away, as she rode past.

'A fish is playing with it just now,' replied the voice; 'however, you shall have it without delay.'

And sure enough, very soon a little fish was seen rising to the surface with the lost ring in his mouth. And Ciccu knew him to be the fish that he had saved from death, and he took the ring and rode back with it to the king.

'That is not enough,' exclaimed the princess when she saw the ring; 'before we can be man and wife, the oven must be heated for three days and three nights, and Ciccu must jump in.' And the king forgot how Ciccu had served him, and desired him to do as the princess had said.

This time Ciccu felt that no escape was possible, and he went to the horse and laid his hand on his neck. 'Now it is indeed goodbye, and there is no help to be got even from you,' and he told him what fate awaited him.

But the horse said, 'Oh, never lose heart, but jump on my back, and make me go till the foam flies in flecks all about me. Then get down, and scrape off the foam with a knife. This you must rub all over you, and when you are quite covered, you may suffer yourself to be cast into the oven, for the fire will not hurt you, nor anything else.' And Ciccu did exactly as the horse bade him, and went back to the king, and before the eyes of the fairest in the world he sprang into the oven.

And when the fairest in the world saw what he had done, love entered into her heart, and she said to the king, 'One thing more: before I can be your wife, you must jump into the oven as Ciccu has done.'

'Willingly,' replied the king, stooping over the oven. But on the brink he paused a moment and called to Ciccu, 'Tell me, Ciccu, how did you manage to prevent the fire burning you?'

Now Ciccu could not forgive his master, whom he had served so faithfully, for sending him to his death without a thought, so he answered, 'I rubbed myself over with fat, and I am not even singed.'

When he heard these words, the king, whose head was full of the princess, never stopped to enquire if they could be true, and smeared himself over with fat, and sprang into the oven. And in a moment the fire caught him, and he was burned up.

Then the fairest in the world held out her hand to Ciccu and smiled, saying, 'Now we will be man and wife.' So Ciccu married the fairest in the world, and became king of the country.

Cinderella

Once there was a gentleman who married, for his second wife, the proudest and most haughty woman that was ever seen. She had, by a former husband, two daughters of her own humour, who were, indeed, exactly like her in all things. He had likewise, by another wife, a young daughter, but of unparalleled goodness and sweetness of temper, which she took from her mother, who was the best creature in the world.

No sooner were the ceremonies of the wedding over but the stepmother began to show herself in her true colours. She could not bear the good qualities of this pretty girl, and the less because they made her own daughters appear the more odious. She employed her in the meanest work of the house: she scoured the dishes, tables, etc., and scrubbed madam's chamber, and those of her daughters; she lay up in a sorry garret, upon a wretched straw bed, while her sisters lay in fine rooms, with floors all inlaid, upon beds of the very newest fashion, and where they had looking-glasses so large that they might see themselves at their full length from head to foot.

The poor girl bore all patiently, and dared not tell her father, who would have sent her away; for his wife governed him entirely. When she had done her work, she used to go into the chimney-corner, and sit down among cinders and ashes, which made her commonly be called Cinderwench; but the younger sister, who was not so rude and uncivil as the elder, called her Cinderella. However, Cinderella, notwithstanding her mean apparel, was a hundred times handsomer than her sisters, though they were always dressed very richly.

It happened that the king's son gave a ball, and invited all persons of fashion to it. Our young misses were also invited, for they cut very grand figures among the quality. They were mightily delighted at this invitation, and wonderfully busy in choosing out such gowns, petticoats and head-clothes as might become them. This was a new trouble to Cinderella; for it was she who ironed her sisters' linen, and plaited their ruffles; they talked all day long of nothing but how they should be dressed.

'For my part,' said the elder, 'I will wear my red velvet suit with French trimming.'

'And I,' said the younger, 'shall have my usual petticoat; but then, to make amends for that, I will put on my gold-flowered manteau, and my diamond stomacher, which is far from being the most ordinary one in the world.'

They sent for the best tire-woman they could get to make up their headdresses and adjust their double pinners, and they had their red brushes and patches from Mademoiselle de la Poche.

Cinderella was likewise called up to them to be consulted in all these matters, for she had excellent notions, and advised them always for the best, nay, and offered her services to dress their heads, which they were very willing she should do. As she was doing this, they said to her: 'Cinderella, would you not be glad to go to the ball?'

'Alas!' said she, 'you only mock me; it is not for such as I am to go thither.'

'Thou art in the right of it,' replied they; 'it would make the people laugh to see a Cinderwench at a ball.'

Anyone but Cinderella would have dressed their heads awry, but she was very good, and dressed them perfectly well They were almost two days without eating, so much were they transported with joy. They broke above a dozen laces in trying to be laced up close, that they might have a fine slender shape, and they were continually at their looking-glasses. At last the happy day came; they went to court, and Cinderella followed them with her eyes as long as she could, and when she had lost sight of them, she fell a-crying.

Her godmother, who saw her all in tears, asked her what was the matter.

'I wish I could – I wish I could – ' she was not able to speak the rest, being interrupted by her tears and sobbing.

This godmother of hers, who was a fairy, said to her, 'Thou wishest thou couldst go to the ball; is it not so?'

'Y–es,' cried Cinderella, with a great sigh.

'Well,' said her godmother, 'be but a good girl, and I will contrive that thou shalt go.' Then she took her into her chamber, and said to her, 'Run into the garden, and bring me a pumpkin.'

Cinderella went immediately to gather the finest she could get, and brought it to her godmother, not being able to imagine how this pumpkin could make her go to the ball. Her godmother scooped out all the inside of it, having left nothing but the rind; which done, she struck it with her wand, and the pumpkin was instantly turned into a fine coach, gilded all over with gold.

She then went to look into her mousetrap, where she found six sleek mice, all alive, and ordered Cinderella to lift up a little the trap-door; then, giving each mouse, as it came out, a little tap with her wand, she turned every one into a fine horse, and altogether they made a very fine set of six horses of a beautiful mouse coloured dapple grey. Being at a loss for

Her godmother ordered Cinderella to lift up a little the trap-door

a coachman, Cinderella said, 'I will go and see if there is a rat in the rat-trap – we may make a coachman of him.'

'Thou art in the right,' replied her godmother; 'go and look.'

Cinderella brought the trap to her, and in it there were three huge rats. The fairy made choice of one of the three which had the largest beard, and, having touched him with her wand, she turned him into a fat, jolly coachman, who had the smartest whiskers eyes ever beheld. After that, she said to Cinderella: 'Go again into the garden, and you will find six lizards behind the watering-pot, bring them to me.'

She had no sooner done so but her godmother turned them into six footmen, who skipped up immediately behind the coach, with their liveries all bedaubed with gold and silver, and clung as close behind each other as if they had done nothing else their whole lives. The fairy then said to Cinderella: 'Well, you see here an equipage fit to go to the ball with; are you not pleased with it?'

'Oh! yes,' cried she; 'but must I go thither as I am, in these nasty rags?'

Her godmother only just touched her with her wand, and, at the same instant, her clothes were turned into cloth of gold and silver, all beset with jewels. This done, she gave her a pair of glass slippers, the prettiest in the whole world. Being thus decked out, Cinderella got up into her coach; but her godmother, above all things, commanded her not to stay till after midnight, telling her, at the same time, that if she stayed one moment longer, the coach would be a pumpkin again, her horses mice, her coachman a rat, her footmen lizards, and her clothes become just as they were before.

She promised her godmother she would not fail to leave the ball before midnight; and then away she drove, scarce able to contain herself for joy. The king's son, who was told that a great princess, whom nobody knew, was come, ran out to receive her; he gave her his hand as she alighted out of the coach, and led her into the ball, among all the company. There was immediately a profound silence, they left off dancing, and the violins ceased to play, so attentive was everyone to contemplate the singular beauties of the unknown newcomer. Nothing was then heard but a confused noise of: 'Ha! how handsome she is! Ha! how handsome she is!'

The king himself, old as he was, could not help watching her, and telling the queen softly that it was a long time since he had seen so beautiful and lovely a creature.

All the ladies were busied in considering her clothes and headdress, that they might have some made next day after the same pattern, provided they could meet with such fine material and as able hands to make them.

The king's son conducted her to the most honourable seat, and afterwards took her out to dance with him; she danced so very gracefully that they all more and more admired her. A fine collation was served up, whereof the young prince ate not a morsel, so intently was he busied in gazing on her.

She went and sat down by her sisters, showing them a thousand civilities, giving them part of the oranges and citrons which the prince had presented her with, which very much surprised them, for they did not know her. While Cinderella was thus amusing her sisters, she heard the clock strike eleven and three-quarters, whereupon she immediately made a curtsy to the company and hasted away as fast as she could.

When she got home she ran to seek out her godmother, and, after having thanked her, she said she could not but heartily wish she might go next day to the ball, because the king's son had desired her to.

As she was eagerly telling her godmother all that had passed at the ball, her two sisters knocked at the door, which Cinderella ran and opened.

'How long you have stayed!' cried she, gaping, rubbing her eyes and stretching herself as if she had been just waked out of her sleep; she had not, however, the least inclination to sleep, even now.

'If thou hadst been at the ball,' said one of her sisters, 'thou wouldst have marvelled indeed! There came thither the finest princess, the most beautiful ever was seen with mortal eyes; she showed us a thousand civilities, and gave us oranges and citrons.'

Cinderella seemed very indifferent in the matter; indeed, she asked them the name of that princess; but they told her they did not know it, and that the king's son was very uneasy on her account and would give all the world to know who she was. At this Cinderella, smiling, replied: 'She must, then, be very beautiful indeed; how happy you have been! Could not I see her? Ah! dear Miss Charlotte, do lend me your yellow suit of clothes which you wear every day.'

'Ay, to be sure!' cried Miss Charlotte; 'lend my clothes to such a dirty Cinderwench as thou art! I should be a fool.'

She left behind one of her glass slippers

Cinderella, indeed, expected well such answer, and was very glad of the refusal; for she would have been sadly put to it if her sister had lent her what she asked for jestingly.

The next day the two sisters were at the ball, and so was Cinderella, but dressed more magnificently than before. The king's son was always by her, and never ceased his compliments and kind speeches to her; to whom all this was so far from being tiresome that she quite forgot what her godmother had recommended to her; so that she, at last, counted the clock striking twelve when she took it to be no more than eleven; she then rose up and fled, as nimble as a deer. The prince followed, but could not overtake her. She left behind one of her glass slippers, which the prince took up most carefully. She got home but quite out of breath, and in her nasty old clothes, having nothing left her of all her finery but one of the little slippers, fellow to that she had dropped. The guards at the palace gate were asked if they had seen a princess go out. They said they had seen nobody go out but a young girl, very meanly dressed, who had more the air of a poor country wench than a gentlewoman.

When the two sisters returned from the ball Cinderella asked them if they had been well diverted, and if the fine lady had been there.

They told her: Yes, but that she hurried away immediately when it struck twelve, and with so much haste that she dropped one of her little glass slippers, the prettiest in the world, which the king's son had taken up; that he had done nothing but look at her all the time at the ball, and that most certainly he was very much in love with the beautiful person who owned the glass slipper.

What they said was very true; for a few days after the king's son caused it to be proclaimed, by sound of trumpet, that he would marry her whose foot the slipper would just fit. They whom he employed began to try it upon the princesses, then the duchesses and all the court, but in vain; it was brought to the two sisters, who did all they possibly could to thrust their foot into the slipper, but they could not effect it. Cinderella, who saw all this, and knew her slipper, said to them, laughing: 'Let me see if it will not fit me.'

Her sisters burst out a-laughing, and began to banter her. The gentleman who was sent to try the slipper looked earnestly at Cinderella, and, finding her very handsome, said it was but just that she should try, and that he had orders to let everyone make trial.

He obliged Cinderella to sit down, and, putting the slipper to her foot, he found it went on very easily, and fitted her as if it had been made of wax. The astonishment her two sisters were in was excessively great, but still abundantly greater when Cinderella pulled out of her pocket the other slipper, and put it on her other foot. Thereupon, in came her godmother, who, having touched with her wand Cinderella's clothes, made them richer and more magnificent than any of those she had before.

And now her two sisters found her to be that fine, beautiful lady whom they had seen at the ball. They threw themselves at her feet to beg pardon for all the ill-treatment they had made her undergo. Cinderella took them up, and, as she embraced them, cried that she forgave them with all her heart, and desired them always to love her.

She was conducted to the young prince, dressed as she was; he thought her more charming than ever, and, a few days after, married her. Cinderella, who was no less good than beautiful, gave her two sisters lodgings in the palace, and that very same day matched them with two great lords of the court.

Clever Gretel

There was once a cook named Gretel, who wore shoes with red heels, and when she walked out with them on, she turned herself this way and that, was quite happy and thought: 'You certainly are a pretty girl!' And when she came home, she drank, in her gladness of heart, a draught of wine, and as wine excites a desire to eat, she tasted the best of whatever she was cooking until she was satisfied, and said: 'The cook must know what the food is like.'

It came to pass that the master one day said to her: 'Gretel, there is a guest coming this evening; prepare me two fowls very daintily.'

'I will see to it, master,' answered Gretel. She killed two fowls, scalded them, plucked them, put them on the spit, and towards evening set them before the fire, that they might roast. The fowls began to turn brown, and were nearly ready, but the guest had not yet arrived. Then Gretel called out to her master: 'If the guest does not come, I must take the fowls away from the fire, but it will be a sin and a shame if they are not eaten the moment they are at their juiciest.'

The master said: 'I will run myself, and fetch the guest.'

When the master had turned his back, Gretel laid the spit with the fowls on one side, and thought: 'Standing so long by the fire there, makes one sweaty and thirsty; who knows when they will come? Meanwhile, I will run into the cellar, and take a drink.'

She ran down, filled a flagon, said: 'God bless it for you, Gretel,' and took a good drink; then thinking that wine should flow on, and should not be interrupted, she took yet another hearty draught.

Then she went and put the fowls over the fire again, basted them, and drove the spit merrily round. But as the roast meat smelt so good, Gretel thought: 'Something might be wrong, it ought to be tasted!' She touched it with her finger, and said: 'Ah! how good fowls are! It certainly is a sin and a shame that they are not eaten at the right time!' She ran to the window, to see if the master was coming with his guest, but she saw no one, and went back to the fowls and thought: 'One of the wings is burning! I had better take it off and eat it.' So she cut it off, ate it, and enjoyed it, and when she had done, she thought: 'The other must go down too, or else master will observe that something is missing.'

When the two wings were eaten, she went and looked for her master, and did not see him. It suddenly occurred to her: 'Who knows? They are perhaps not coming at all, and have turned in somewhere.' Then she said: 'Well, Gretel, enjoy yourself; one fowl has been cut into, take another drink, and eat it up entirely; when it is eaten you will have some peace; why should God's good gifts be spoilt?' So she ran into the cellar again and took an enormous drink, then ate up the one chicken in great glee. When one of the chickens was swallowed down, and still her master did not come, Gretel looked at the other and said: 'Where one is, the other should be likewise, the two go together; what's right for the one is right for the other; I think if I were to take another draught it would do me no harm.' So she took another hearty drink, and let the second chicken follow the first.

While she was making the most of it, her master came and cried: 'Hurry up, Gretel, the guest is coming directly after me!'

'Yes, sir, I will soon serve up,' answered Gretel.

Meantime the master looked to see that the table was properly laid, and took the great knife, wherewith he was going to carve the chickens, and sharpened it on the steps.

Presently the guest came, and knocked politely and courteously at the house-door. Gretel ran and looked to see who was there, and when she saw the

guest, she put her finger to her lips and said:
'Hush! Hush! Go away as quickly as you can; if my
master catches you it will be the worse for you; he
certainly did ask you to supper, but his intention
is to cut off your two ears. Just listen how he is
sharpening the knife for it!' The guest heard the
sharpening, and hurried down the steps again as
fast as he could.

Gretel was not idle; she ran screaming to her
master, and cried: 'You have invited a fine guest!'

'Why, Gretel? What do you mean by that?'

'Yes,' said she, 'he has taken the chickens, which I
was just going to serve up, off the dish, and has run
away with them!'

'That's a nice trick!' said her master, and
lamented the fine chickens. 'If he had but
left me one, so that something
remained for me to eat.' He
called to him to stop, but the
guest pretended not to hear.
Then he ran after him, with
the knife still in his hand,
crying: 'Just one, just one,'
meaning that the guest
should leave him just
one chicken, and not
take both. The guest,
however, thought no
otherwise than that
he was to give up one
of his ears, and ran as if
fire were burning under
him, in order to take
them both with him.

Clever Hans

The mother of Hans said: 'Whither away, Hans?'

Hans answered: 'To Gretel.'

'Behave well, Hans.'

'Oh, I'll behave well. Goodbye, mother.'

'Goodbye, Hans.'

Hans comes to Gretel. 'Good-day, Gretel.'

'Good-day, Hans. What do you bring that is good?'

'I bring nothing, I want to have something given me.'

Gretel presents Hans with a needle.

Hans says: 'Goodbye, Gretel.'

'Goodbye, Hans.'

Hans takes the needle, sticks it into a hay-cart, and follows the cart home.

'Good-evening, mother.'

'Good-evening, Hans. Where have you been?'

'With Gretel.'

'What did you take her?'

'Took nothing; had something given me.'

'What did Gretel give you?'

'Gave me a needle.'

'Where is the needle, Hans?'

'Stuck in the hay-cart.'

'That was ill done, Hans. You should have stuck the needle in your sleeve.'

'Never mind, I'll do better next time.'

'Whither away, Hans?'

'To Gretel, mother.'

'Behave well, Hans.'

'Oh, I'll behave well. Goodbye, mother.'

'Goodbye, Hans.'

Hans comes to Gretel. 'Good-day, Gretel.'

'Good-day, Hans. What do you bring that is good?'

'I bring nothing. I want to have something given to me.'

Gretel presents Hans with a knife.

'Goodbye, Gretel.'

'Goodbye, Hans.'

Hans takes the knife, sticks it in his sleeve, and goes home.

'Good-evening, mother.'

'Good-evening, Hans. Where have you been?'

'With Gretel.'

'What did you take her?'

'Took her nothing; she gave me something.'

'What did Gretel give you?'

'Gave me a knife.'

'Where is the knife, Hans?'

'Stuck in my sleeve.'

'That's ill done, Hans. You should have put the knife in your pocket.'

'Never mind, will do better next time.'

'Whither away, Hans?'

'To Gretel, mother.'

'Behave well, Hans.'

'Oh, I'll behave well. Goodbye, mother.'

'Goodbye, Hans.'

Hans comes to Gretel. 'Good-day, Gretel.'

'Good-day, Hans. What good thing do you bring?'

'I bring nothing, I want something given me.'

Gretel presents Hans with a young goat.

'Goodbye, Gretel.'

'Goodbye, Hans.'

Hans takes the goat, ties its legs, and puts it in his pocket. When he gets home it is suffocated.

'Good-evening, mother.'

'Good-evening, Hans. Where have you been?'

'With Gretel.'

'What did you take her?'

'Took nothing; she gave me something.'

'What did Gretel give you?'

'She gave me a goat.'

'Where is the goat, Hans?'

'Put it in my pocket.'

'That was ill done, Hans. You should have put a rope round the goat's neck.'

'Never mind, will do better next time.'

'Whither away, Hans?'

'To Gretel, mother.'

'Behave well, Hans.'

'Oh, I'll behave well. Goodbye, mother.'

'Goodbye, Hans.'

Hans comes to Gretel. 'Good-day, Gretel.'

'Good-day, Hans. What good thing do you bring?'

'I bring nothing, I want something given me.'

Gretel presents Hans with a piece of bacon.

'Goodbye, Gretel.'

'Goodbye, Hans.'

Hans takes the bacon, ties it to a rope, and drags it away behind him. The dogs come and devour the bacon. When he gets home, he has the rope in his hand, and there is no longer anything hanging on to it.

'Good-evening, mother.'

'Good-evening, Hans. Where have you been?'

'With Gretel.'

'What did you take her?'

'I took her nothing; she gave me something.'

'What did Gretel give you?'

'Gave me a bit of bacon.'

'Where is the bacon, Hans?'

'I tied it to a rope, brought it home, dogs took it.'

'That was ill done, Hans. You should have carried the bacon on your head.'

'Never mind, will do better next time.'

'Whither away, Hans?'

'To Gretel, mother.'

'Behave well, Hans.'

'I'll behave well. Goodbye, mother.'

'Goodbye, Hans.'

Hans comes to Gretel. 'Good-day, Gretel.'

'Good-day, Hans. What good thing do you bring?'

'I bring nothing, but would have something given.'

Gretel presents Hans with a calf.

'Goodbye, Gretel.'

'Goodbye, Hans.'

Hans takes the calf, puts it on his head, and the calf kicks his face.

'Good-evening, mother.'

'Good-evening, Hans. Where have you been?'

'With Gretel.'

'What did you take her?'

'I took nothing, but had something given me.'

'What did Gretel give you?'

'A calf.'

'Where is the calf, Hans?'

'I set it on my head and it kicked my face.'

'That was ill done, Hans. You should have led the calf, and put it in the stall.'

'Never mind, will do better next time.'

'Whither away, Hans?'

'To Gretel, mother.'

'Behave well, Hans.'

'I'll behave well. Goodbye, mother.'

'Goodbye, Hans.'

Hans comes to Gretel. 'Good-day, Gretel.'

'Good-day, Hans. What good thing do you bring?'

'I bring nothing, but would have something given.'

Gretel says to Hans: 'I will go with you.'

Hans takes Gretel, ties her to a rope, leads her to the rack, and binds her fast. Then Hans goes to his mother.

'Good-evening, mother.'

'Good-evening, Hans. Where have you been?'

'With Gretel.'

'What did you take her?'

'I took her nothing.'

'What did Gretel give you?'

'She gave me nothing. She came with me.'

'Where have you left Gretel?'

'I led her by the rope, tied her to the rack, and scattered some grass for her.'

'That was ill done, Hans, you should have cast friendly eyes on her.'

'Never mind, will do better.'

Hans went into the stable, cut out all the calves' and sheep's eyes, and threw them in Gretel's face. Then Gretel became angry, tore herself loose and ran away, and never became the bride of Hans.

Connla and the Fairy Maiden

Connla of the Fiery Hair was son of Conn of the Hundred Fights. One day as he stood by the side of his father on the height of Usna, he saw a maiden clad in strange attire coming towards him.

'Whence comest thou, maiden?' said Connla.

'I come from the Plains of the Ever Living,' she said, 'there where there is neither death nor sin. There we keep holiday always, nor need we help from any in our joy. And in all our pleasure we have no strife. And because we have our homes in the round green hills, men call us the Hill Folk.'

The king and all with him wondered much to hear a voice when they saw no one. For save Connla alone, none saw the fairy maiden.

'To whom art thou talking, my son?' said Conn the king.

Then the maiden answered, 'Connla speaks to a young, fair maid, whom neither death nor old age awaits. I love Connla, and now I call him away to the plain of pleasure, Moy Mell, where Boadag is king for aye, nor has there been complaint or sorrow in that land since he has held the kingship. Oh, come with me, Connla of the Fiery Hair, ruddy as the dawn with thy tawny skin. A fairy crown awaits thee to grace thy comely face and royal form. Come, and never shall thy comeliness fade, nor thy youth, till the last awful day of judgement.'

The king in fear at what the maiden said, which he heard though he could not see her, called aloud to his druid, Coran by name.

'Oh, Coran of the many spells,' he said, 'and of the cunning magic, I call upon thy aid. A task is upon me too great for all my skill and wit, greater than any laid upon me since I seized the kingship. A maiden unseen has met us, and by her power would take from me my dear, my comely son. If thou help not, he will be taken from thy king by woman's wiles and witchery.'

Then Coran the druid stood forth and chanted his spells towards the spot where the maiden's voice had been heard. And none heard her voice again, nor could Connla see her longer. Only as she vanished before the druid's mighty spell, she threw an apple to Connla.

For a whole month from that day Connla would take nothing, either to eat or to drink, save only from that apple. But as he ate it grew again and always kept whole. And all the while there grew within him a mighty yearning and longing after the maiden he had seen.

But when the last day of the month of waiting came, Connla stood by the side of the king his father on the plain of Arcomin, and again he saw the maiden come towards him, and again she spoke to him.

' 'Tis a glorious place, forsooth, that Connla holds among short-lived mortals awaiting the day of death. But now the folk of life, the ever-living ones, beg and bid thee come to Moy Mell, the plain of pleasure, for they have learnt to know thee, seeing thee in thy home among thy dear ones.'

When Conn the king heard the maiden's voice he called to his men aloud and said, 'Summon swift my druid Coran, for I see she has again this day the power of speech.'

Then the maiden said: 'Oh, mighty Conn, fighter of a hundred fights, the druid's power is little loved; it has little honour in the mighty land, peopled with so many of the upright. When the Law will come, it will do away with the druid's magic spells that come from the lips of the false black demon.'

Then Conn the king observed that since the maiden came Connla his son spoke to none that spake to him. So Conn of the hundred fights said to him, 'Is it to thy mind what the woman says, my son?'

' 'Tis hard upon me,' then said Connla; 'I love my own folk above all things; but yet, but yet a longing seizes me for the maiden.'

When the maiden heard this, she answered and said, 'The ocean is not so strong as the waves of thy longing. Come with me in my curragh, the gleaming, straight-gliding crystal canoe. Soon we can reach Boadag's realm. I see the bright sun sink, yet far as it is, we can reach it before dark. There is, too, another land worthy of thy journey, a land joyous to all that seek it. Only wives and maidens dwell there. If thou wilt, we can seek it and live there alone together in joy.'

When the maiden ceased to speak, Connla of the Fiery Hair rushed away from them and sprang into the curragh, the gleaming straight-gliding crystal canoe. And then they all, king and court, saw it glide away over the bright sea towards the setting sun. Away and away, till eye could see it no longer, and Connla and the fairy maiden went their way on the sea, and were no more seen, nor did any know where they came.

connla and the fairy maiden

The Story of Deirdre

There was a man in Ireland once who was called
Malcolm Harper. The man was a right good man,
and he had a goodly share of this world's goods.
He had a wife, but no family. What did Malcolm
hear but that a soothsayer had come home to the
place, and as the man was a right good man, he
wished that the soothsayer might come near them.
Whether it was that he was invited or that he came
of himself, the soothsayer came to the house of
Malcolm.

'Are you doing any soothsaying?' says Malcolm.

'Yes, I am doing a little. Are you in need of soothsaying?'

'Well, I do not mind taking soothsaying from you,
if you had soothsaying for me, and you would be
willing to do it.'

'Well, I will do soothsaying for you. What kind of
soothsaying do you want?'

'Well, the soothsaying I wanted was that you would
tell me my lot or what will happen to me, if you can
give me knowledge of it.'

'Well, I am going out, and when I return, I will
tell you.'

And the soothsayer went forth out of the house
and he was not long outside when he returned.

'Well,' said the soothsayer, 'I saw in my second
sight that it is on account of a daughter of yours
that the greatest amount of blood shall be shed
that has ever been shed in Erin since time and race
began. And the three most famous heroes that ever
were found will lose their heads on her account.'

After a time, a daughter was born to Malcolm; he
did not allow a living being to come to his house,
only himself and the nurse. He asked this woman,
'Will you yourself bring up the child to keep her in
hiding far away where eye will not see a sight of her
nor ear hear a word about her?'

The woman said she would, so Malcolm got three
men, and he took them away to a large mountain,
distant and far from reach, without the knowledge
or notice of anyone. He caused there a hillock,
round and green, to be dug out of the middle, and
the hole thus made to be covered carefully over so
that a little company could dwell there together.
This was done.

Deirdre and her foster-mother dwelt in the bothy
mid the hills without the knowledge or the suspicion of any living person about them and without
anything occurring, until Deirdre was sixteen years
of age. Deirdre grew like the white sapling, straight
and trim as the rash on the moss. She was the
creature of fairest form, of loveliest aspect, and of
gentlest nature that existed between earth and
heaven in all Ireland – whatever colour of hue she
had before, there was nobody that looked into her
face but she would blush fiery red over it.

The woman that had charge of her, gave Deirdre
every information and skill of which she herself
had knowledge and skill. There was not a blade of
grass growing from root, nor a bird singing in the
wood, nor a star shining from heaven but Deirdre
had a name for it. But one thing, she did not wish
her to have either part or parley with any single

living man of the rest of the world. But on a gloomy winter night, with black, scowling clouds, a hunter of game was wearily travelling the hills, and what happened but that he missed the trail of the hunt, and lost his course and companions. A drowsiness came upon the man as he wearily wandered over the hills, and he lay down by the side of the beautiful green knoll in which Deirdre lived, and he slept. The man was faint from hunger and wandering, and benumbed with cold, and a deep sleep fell upon him. When he lay down beside the green hill where Deirdre was, a troubled dream came to the man, and he thought that he enjoyed the warmth of a fairy broch, the fairies being inside playing music. The hunter shouted out in his dream, if there was anyone in the broch, to let him in for the Holy One's sake. Deirdre heard the voice and said to her foster mother, 'O foster-mother, what cry is that?' 'It is nothing at all, Deirdre – merely the birds of the air astray and seeking each other. But let them go past to the bosky glade. There is no shelter or house for them here.' 'Oh, foster-mother, the bird asked to get inside for the sake of the God of the Elements, and you yourself tell me that anything that is asked in His name we ought to do. If you will not allow the bird that is being benumbed with cold, and done to death with hunger, to be let in, I do not think much of your language or your faith. But since I give credence to your language and to your faith, which you taught me, I will myself let in the bird.' And Deirdre arose and drew the bolt from the leaf of the door, and she let in the hunter. She placed a seat in the place for sitting, food in the place for eating, and drink in the place for drinking for the man who came to the house. 'Oh, for this life and raiment, you man that came in, keep restraint on your tongue!' said the old woman. 'It is not a great thing for you to keep your mouth shut and your tongue quiet when you get a home and shelter of a hearth on a gloomy winter's night.' 'Well,' said the hunter, 'I may do that – keep my mouth shut and my tongue quiet, since I came to the house and received hospitality from you; but by the hand of thy father and grandfather, and by your own two hands, if some other of the people of the world saw this beauteous creature you have here hid away, they would not long leave her with you, I swear.'

'What men are these you refer to?' said Deirdre.

'Well, I will tell you, young woman,' said the hunter. 'They are Naois, son of Uisnech, and Allen and Arden his two brothers.'

'O foster-mother, what cry is that?'
'It is nothing at all, Deirdre – merely the birds
of the air astray and seeking each other.'

'What like are these men when seen, if we were to see them?' said Deirdre.

'Why, the aspect and form of the men when seen are these,' said the hunter: 'they have the colour of the raven on their hair, their skin like swan on the wave in whiteness, and their cheeks as the blood of the brindled red calf, and their speed and their leap are those of the salmon of the torrent and the deer of the grey mountainside. And Naois is head and shoulders over the rest of the people of Erin.'

'However they are,' said the nurse, 'be you off from here and take another road. In good sooth and certainty, little are my thanks for yourself or for her that let you in!'

The hunter went away, and went straight to the palace of King Connachar. He sent word into the king that he wished to speak to him if he pleased. The king answered the message and came out to speak to the man. 'What is the reason of your journey?' said the king to the hunter.

'I have only to tell you, O king,' said the hunter,

'that I saw the fairest creature that ever was born in Erin, and I came to tell you of it.'

'Who is this beauty and where is she to be seen, when she was not seen before till you saw her, if you did see her?'

'Well, I did see her,' said the hunter. 'But, if I did, no man else can see her unless he get directions from me as to where she is dwelling.'

'And will you direct me to where she dwells? And the reward of your directing me will be as good as the reward of your message,' said the king.

'Well, I will direct you, O king, although it is likely that this will not be what they want,' said the hunter.

Connachar, King of Ulster, sent for his nearest kinsmen, and he told them of his intent. Though early rose the song of the birds mid the rocky caves and the music of the birds in the grove, earlier than that did Connachar, King of Ulster, arise, with his little troop of dear friends, in the delightful twilight of the fresh and gentle May; the dew was heavy on each bush and flower and stem, as they went to bring Deirdre forth from the green knoll where she stayed. Many a youth was there, who had a lithe leaping and lissom step when they started, whose step was faint, failing and faltering when they reached the bothy on account of the length of the way and roughness of the road. 'Yonder, now, down in the bottom of the glen is the bothy where the woman dwells, but I will not go nearer than this to the old woman,' said the hunter.

Connachar with his band of kinsfolk went down to the green knoll where Deirdre dwelt and he knocked at the door of the bothy. The nurse replied, 'No less than a king's command and a king's army could put me out of my bothy tonight. And I should be obliged to you, were you to tell who it is that wants me to open my bothy door.' 'It is I, Connachar, King of Ulster.' When the poor woman heard who was at the door, she rose with haste and let in the king and all that could get in of his retinue.

When the king saw the woman that was before him that he had been in quest of, he thought he never saw in the course of the day nor in the dream of night a creature so fair as Deirdre and he gave his full heart's weight of love to her. Deirdre was raised on the topmost of the heroes' shoulders and she and her foster-mother were brought to the court of King Connachar of Ulster.

With the love that Connachar had for her, he wanted to marry Deirdre right off there and then,

if she would consent to marry him. But she said to him, 'I would be obliged to you if you will give me the respite of a year and a day.' He said, 'I will grant you that, hard though it is, if you will give me your unfailing promise that you will marry me at the year's end.' And she gave the promise. Connachar got for her a woman-teacher and merry modest maidens fair that would lie down and rise with her, that would play and speak with her. Deirdre was clever in maidenly duties and wifely understanding, and Connachar thought that he never saw with bodily eye a creature that pleased him more.

Deirdre and her women companions were one day out on the hillock behind the house enjoying the scene, and drinking in the sun's heat. What did they see coming but three men a-journeying. Deirdre was looking at the men that were coming, and wondering at them. When the men neared them, Deirdre remembered the language of the huntsman, and she said to herself that these were the three sons of Uisnech, and that this was Naois, he having what was above the bend of the two shoulders above the men of Erin all. The three brothers went past without taking any notice of them, without even glancing at the young girls on the hillock. What happened but that love for Naois struck the heart of Deirdre, so that she could not but follow after him. She girded up her raiment and went after the men that went past the base of the knoll, leaving her women attendants there. Allen and Arden had heard of the woman that Connachar, King of Ulster, had with him, and they thought that, if Naois, their brother, saw her, he would have her himself, more especially as she was not married to the king. They perceived the woman coming, and called on one another to hasten their step as they had a long distance to travel, and the dusk of night was coming on. They did so. She cried, 'Naois, son of Uisnech, will you leave me?' 'What piercing, shrill cry is that – the most melodious my ear ever heard, and the shrillest that ever struck my heart of all the cries I ever heard?' 'It is but the wail of the wave-swans of Connachar,' said his brothers. 'No! Yonder is a woman's cry of distress,' said Naois, and he swore he would not go farther until he saw from whom the cry came, and Naois turned back. Naois and Deirdre met, and Deirdre kissed Naois three times, and gave a kiss each to his brothers. With the confusion that she was in, Deirdre went into a crimson blaze of fire, and her colour came and went as rapidly as the movement of the aspen by the stream side. Naois thought he never saw a fairer creature, and Naois gave Deirdre the love that he never gave to thing, to vision, or to creature but to herself.

Then Naois placed Deirdre on the topmost height of his shoulder, and told his brothers to keep up their pace, and they kept up their pace. Naois thought that it would not be well for him to remain in Erin on account of the way in which Connachar, King of Ulster, his uncle's son, would turn against him because of the woman, though he had not married her; and he directed his steps to Alba, that is, Scotland. He reached the side of Loch Ness and made his habitation there. He could kill the salmon of the torrent from out his own door, and the deer of the grey gorge from out his window. Naois and Deirdre and Allen and Arden dwelt in a tower, and they were happy so long a time as they were there.

By this time the end of the period came at which Deirdre had to marry Connachar, King of Ulster. Connachar made up his mind to take Deirdre away by the sword whether she was married to Naois or not. So he prepared a great and gleeful feast. He sent word far and wide through Erin all to his kinspeople to come to the feast. Connachar thought to himself that Naois would not come though he should bid him; and the scheme that arose in his mind was to send for his father's brother, Ferchar Mae Ro, and to send him on an embassy to Naois. He did so; and Connachar said to Ferchar, 'Tell Naois, son of Uisnech, that I am setting forth a great and gleeful feast to my friends and kinspeople throughout the wide extent of Erin all, and that I shall not have rest by day nor sleep by night if he and Allen and Arden be not partakers of the feast.'

Ferchar Mae Ro and his three sons went on their journey, and reached the tower where Naois was dwelling by the side of Loch Etive. The sons of Uisnech gave a cordial kindly welcome to Ferchar Mae Ro and his three sons, and asked of him the news of Erin. 'The best news that I have for you,' said the hardy hero, 'is that Connachar, King of Ulster, is setting forth a great sumptuous feast to his friends and kinspeople throughout the wide extent of Erin all, and he has vowed by the earth beneath him, by the high heaven above him, and by the sun that wends to the west, that he will have no rest by day nor sleep by night if the sons of Uisnech, the sons of his own father's brother, will

not come back to the land of their home and the soil of their nativity, and to the feast likewise, and he has sent us on embassy to invite you.'

'We will go with you,' said Naois.

'We will,' said his brothers.

But Deirdre did not wish to go with Ferchar Mae Ro, and she tried every prayer to turn Naois from going with him. 'I saw a vision, Naois, and do you interpret it to me,' said Deirdre – then she sang:

'O Naois, son of Uisnech, hear
  What was shown in a dream to me:

There came three white doves out of the south
  Flying over the sea,
And drops of honey were in their mouth
  From the hive of the honey bee.

O Naois, son of Uisnech, hear
  What was shown in a dream to me:

I saw three grey hawks out of the south
  Come flying over the sea,
And the red red drops tthat were in their mouth
  They were dearer than life to me.'

Said Naois: 'It is nought but the fear of a woman's heart, and a dream of the night, Deirdre. The day that Connachar sent the invitation to his feast will be unlucky for us if we don't go, O Deirdre.'

'You will go there,' said Ferchar Mae Ro; 'and if Connachar show kindness to you, show ye kindness to him; and if he will display wrath towards you, display ye wrath towards him, and I and my three sons will be with you.'

'We will,' said Daring Drop.

'We will,' said Hardy Holly.

'We will,' said Fiallan the Fair.

'I have three sons, and they are three heroes, and in any harm or danger that may befall you, they will be with you, and I myself will be along with them.' And Ferchar Mae Ro gave his vow and his word in presence of his arms that, in any harm or danger that came in the way of the sons of Uisnech, he and his three sons would not leave head on live body in Erin, despite sword or helmet, spear or shield, blade or mail, be they ever so good.

Deirdre was unwilling to leave Alba, but she went with Naois. Deirdre wept tears in showers and she sang:

'Dear is the land, the land over there,
  Alba full of woods and lakes;
Bitter to my heart is leaving thee,
  But I go away with Naois.'

Ferchar Mae Ro did not stop till he got the sons of Uisnech away with him, despite the suspicion of Deirdre.

> The coracle was put to sea,
> The sail was hoisted to it;
> And the second morrow they arrived
> On the white shores of Erin.

As soon as the sons of Uisnech landed in Erin, Ferchar Mae Ro sent word to Connachar, King of Ulster, that the men whom he wanted were come, and let him now show kindness to them. 'Well,' said Connachar, 'I did not expect that the sons of Uisnech would come, though I sent for them, and I am not quite ready to receive them. But there is a house down yonder where I keep strangers, and let them go down to it today, and my house will be ready before them tomorrow.'

But he that was up in the palace felt it long that he was not getting word as to how matters were going on for those down in the house of the strangers. 'Go you, Gelban Grednach, son of Lochlin's king, go you down and bring me information as to whether her former hue and complexion are on Deirdre. If they be, I will take her out with edge of blade and point of sword, and if not, let Naois, son of Uisnech, have her for himself,' said Connachar.

Gelban, the cheering and charming son of Lochlin's king, went down to the place of the strangers, where the sons of Uisnech and Deirdre were staying. He looked in through the bicker-hole on the door-leaf. Now she that he gazed upon used to go into a crimson blaze of blushes when anyone looked at her. Naois looked at Deirdre and knew that someone was looking at her from the back of the door-leaf. He seized one of the dice on the table before him and fired it through the bicker-hole, and knocked the eye out of Gelban Grednach the cheerful and charming, right through the back of his head. Gelban returned back to the palace of King Connachar.

'You were cheerful, charming, going away, but you are cheerless, charmless, returning. What has happened to you, Gelban? But have you seen her, and are Deirdre's hue and complexion as before?' said Connachar.

'Well, I have seen Deirdre, and I saw her also truly, and while I was looking at her through the bicker-hole on the door, Naois, son of Uisnech, knocked out my eye with one of the dice in his hand. But of a truth and verity, although he put out even my eye, it were my desire still to remain looking at her with the other eye, were it not for the hurry you told me to be in,' said Gelban.

'That is true,' said Connachar. 'Let three hundred brave heroes go down to the abode of the strangers, and let them bring hither to me Deirdre, and kill the rest.'

Connachar ordered three hundred active heroes to go down to the abode of the strangers and to take Deirdre up with them and kill the rest. '

'The pursuit is coming,' said Deirdre.

'Yes, but I will myself go out and stop the pursuit,' said Naois.

'It is not you, but we that will go,' said Daring Drop and Hardy Holly and Fiallan the Fair; 'it is to us that our father entrusted your defence from harm and danger when he himself left for home.' And the gallant youths, full noble, full manly, full handsome, with beauteous brown locks, went forth girt with battle arms fit for fierce fight and clothed with combat dress for fierce contest fit, which was burnished, bright, brilliant, bladed, blazing, on which were many pictures of beasts and birds and creeping things, lions and lithe-limbed tigers, brown eagle and harrying hawk and adder fierce; and the young heroes laid low three-thirds of the company.

Connachar came out in haste and cried with wrath, 'Who is there on the floor of fight, slaughtering my men?'

'We, the three sons of Ferchar Mae Ro.'

'Well,' said the king, 'I will give a free bridge to your grandfather, a free bridge to your father, and a free bridge each to you three brothers, if you come over to my side tonight.'

'Well, Connachar, we will not accept that offer from you nor thank you for it. Greater by far do we prefer to go home to our father and tell the deeds of heroism we have done, than accept anything on these terms from you. Naois, son of Uisnech, and Allen and Arden are as nearly related to yourself as they are to us, though you are so keen to shed their blood, and you would shed our blood also, Connachar.' And the noble, manly, handsome youths with beauteous, brown locks returned inside. 'We are now,' said they, 'going home to tell our father that you are now safe from the hands of the king.' And the youths all fresh and tall and lithe and beautiful, went home to their father to tell that the sons of Uisnech were safe. This happened at the parting of the day and night in the morning twilight time, and Naois said they must go away, leave that house, and return to Alba.

Naois and Deirdre, Allan and Arden started to return to Alba. Word came to the king that the company he was in pursuit of were gone. The king then sent for Duanan Gacha Druid, the best magician he had, and he spoke to him as follows. 'Much wealth have I expended on you, Duanan Gacha Druid, to give schooling and learning and magic mystery to you. It will have been in vain if these people get away from me today without care, without consideration or regard for me, without chance of overtaking them, and without power to stop them.'

'Well, I will stop them,' said the magician. And the magician placed a wood before them through which no man could go, but the sons of Uisnech marched through the wood without halt or hesitation, and Deirdre held on to Naois's hand.

'What is the good of that? That will not do yet,' said Connachar. 'They are off without bending of their feet or stopping of their step, without heed or respect to me, and I am without power to keep up to them or opportunity to turn them back this night.'

'I will try another plan on them,' said the druid; and he placed before them a grey sea instead of a green plain. The three heroes stripped and tied their clothes behind their heads, and Naois placed Deirdre on the top of his shoulder.

They stretched their sides to the stream,
And sea and land were to them the same,
The rough grey ocean was the same
As meadow-land green and plain.

'Though that be good, O Duanan, it will not make the heroes return,' said Connachar; 'they are gone without regard for me, and without honour to me,

The three heroes stripped and tied their clothes behind their heads,
and Naois placed Deirdre on the top of his shoulder

and without power on my part to pursue them or to force them to return this night.'

'We shall try another method on them, since yon one did not stop them,' said the druid. And the druid froze the grey ridged sea into hard rocky knobs, the sharpness of sword being on the one edge and the poison power of adders on the other. Then Arden cried that he was getting tired, and nearly giving over. 'Come you, Arden, and sit on my right shoulder,' said Naois. Arden came and sat on Naois's shoulder. Arden was not long in this posture when he died; but though he was dead Naois would not let him go. Allen then cried out that he was getting faint and nigh-well giving up. When Naois heard his prayer, he gave forth the piercing sigh of death, and asked Allen to lay hold of him and he would bring him to land. Allen was not long when the weakness of death came on him and his hold failed. Naois looked around, and when he saw his two well-beloved brothers dead, he cared not whether he lived or died, and he gave forth the bitter sigh of death, and his heart burst.

'They are gone,' said Duanan Gacha Druid to the king, 'and I have done what you desired me. The sons of Uisnech are dead and they will trouble you no more; and you have your wife hale and whole to yourself.'

'Blessings for that upon you and may the good results accrue to me, Duanan. I count it no loss what I spent in the schooling and teaching of you. Now dry up the flood, and let me see if I can behold Deirdre,' said Connachar. And Duanan Gacha Druid dried up the flood from the plain and the three sons of Uisnech were lying together dead, without breath of life, side by side on the green meadow plain and Deirdre bending above showering down her tears.

Then Deirdre said this lament. 'Fair one, loved one, flower of beauty; beloved upright and strong; beloved noble and modest warrior. Fair one, blue-eyed, beloved of thy wife; lovely to me at the trysting-place came thy clear voice through the woods of Ireland. I cannot eat or smile henceforth. Break not today, my heart; soon enough shall I lie within my grave. Strong are the waves of sorrow, but stronger is sorrow's self, Connachar.'

The people then gathered round the heroes' bodies and asked Connachar what was to be done with the bodies. The order that he gave was that they should dig a pit and put the three brothers in it side by side.

Deirdre kept sitting on the brink of the grave, constantly asking the grave diggers to dig the pit wide and free. When the bodies of the brothers were put in the grave, Deirdre said:

'Come over hither, Naois, my love,
Let Arden close to Allen lie;
If the dead had any sense to feel,
Ye would have made a place for Deirdre.'

The men did as she told them. She jumped into the grave and lay down by Naois, and she was dead by his side.

The king ordered the body to be raised from out the grave and to be buried on the other side of the loch. It was done as the king bade, and the pit closed. Thereupon a fir shoot grew out of the grave of Deirdre and a fir shoot from the grave of Naois, and the two shoots united in a knot above the loch. The king ordered the shoots to be cut down, and this was done twice, until, at the third time, the wife whom the king had married caused him to stop this work of evil and his vengeance on the remains of the dead.

The Devoted Friend

One morning the old water-rat put his head out of his hole. He had bright beady eyes and stiff grey whiskers, and his tail was like a long bit of black indiarubber. The little ducks were swimming about in the pond, looking just like a lot of yellow canaries, and their mother, who was pure white with real red legs, was trying to teach them how to stand on their heads in the water.

'You will never be in the best society unless you can stand on your heads,' she kept saying to them; and every now and then she showed them how it was done. But the little ducks paid no attention to her. They were so young that they did not know what an advantage it is to be in society at all.

'What disobedient children!' cried the old water-rat, 'they really deserve to be drowned.'

'Nothing of the kind,' answered the duck, 'everyone must make a beginning, and parents cannot be too patient.'

'Ah! I know nothing about the feelings of parents,' said the water-rat. 'I am not a family man. In fact, I have never been married, and I never intend to be. Love is all very well in its way, but friendship is much higher. Indeed, I know of nothing in the world that is either nobler or rarer than a devoted friendship.'

'And what, pray, is your idea of the duties of a devoted friend?' asked a green linnet, who was sitting on a willow tree hard by, and had overheard the conversation.

'Yes, that is just what I want to know,' said the duck; and she swam away to the end of the pond, and stood upon her head, in order to give her children a good example.

'What a silly question!' cried the water-rat. 'I should expect my devoted friend to be devoted to me, of course.'

'And what would you do in return?' said the little bird, swinging upon a silver spray, and flapping his tiny wings.

'I don't understand you,' answered the water-rat.

'Let me tell you a story on the subject,' said the linnet.

'Is the story about me?' asked the water-rat. 'If so, I will listen to it, for I am extremely fond of fiction.'

'It is applicable to you,' answered the linnet and he flew down, and alighting upon the bank, he told the story of The Devoted Friend.

'Once upon a time,' said the linnet, 'there was an honest little fellow named Hans.'

'Was he very distinguished?' asked the water-rat.

'No,' answered the linnet, 'I don't think he was distinguished at all, except for his kind heart, and his funny, round, good-humoured face. He lived in a tiny cottage all by himself, and every day he worked in his garden. In all the countryside there was no garden so lovely as his. Sweet-williams grew there, and gilly-flowers, and shepherd's-purses, and fair-maids of France. There were damask roses and yellow roses, lilac crocuses and gold, purple violets and white. Columbine and ladysmock, marjoram and wild basil, the cowslip and the flower-de-luce, the daffodil and the clove-pink bloomed or blossomed in their proper order as the months went by, one flower taking another flower's place, so that there were always beautiful things to look at and pleasant odours to smell.

'Little Hans had a great many friends, but the most devoted friend of all was big Hugh the miller. Indeed, so devoted was the rich miller to little Hans, that he would never go by his garden without leaning over the wall and plucking a large nosegay, or a handful of sweet herbs, or filling his pockets with plums and cherries if it was the fruit season. "Real friends should have everything in common," the miller used to say, and little Hans nodded and smiled, and felt very proud of having a friend with such noble ideas.

'Sometimes, indeed, the neighbours thought it strange that the rich miller never gave little Hans anything in return, though he had a hundred sacks of flour stored away in his mill, and six milch cows, and a large flock of woolly sheep; but Hans never troubled his head about these things, and nothing gave him greater pleasure than to listen to all the wonderful things the miller used to say about the unselfishness of true friendship.

'So little Hans worked away in his garden. During the spring, the summer and the autumn he was very happy, but when the winter came, and he had no fruit or flowers to bring to the market, he suffered a good deal from cold and hunger, and often had to go to bed without any supper but a few dried pears or some hard nuts. In the winter, also, he was extremely lonely, as the miller never came to see him then.

' "There is no good in my going to see little Hans as long as the snow lasts," the miller used to say to his wife, "for when people are in trouble they should be left alone and not be bothered by visitors. That at least is my idea about friendship, and I am sure I am right. So I shall wait till the spring comes, and then I shall pay him a visit, and he will be able to give me a large basket of primroses, and that will make him so happy."

' "You are certainly very thoughtful about others," answered the wife, as she sat in her comfortable armchair by the big pinewood fire; "very thoughtful indeed. It is quite a treat to hear you talk about friendship. I am sure the clergyman himself could not say such beautiful things as you do, though he does live in a three-storeyed house and wear a gold ring on his little finger."

' "But could we not ask little Hans up here?" said the miller's youngest son. "If poor Hans is in trouble I will give him half my porridge, and show him my white rabbits."

' "What a silly boy you are!" cried the miller; "I really don't know what is the use of sending you to school. You seem not to learn anything. Why if little Hans came up here, and saw our warm fire, and our good supper, and our great cask of red wine, he might get envious, and envy is a most terrible thing, and would spoil anybody's nature. I certainly will not allow Hans's nature to be spoiled. I am his best friend, and I will always watch over him, and see that he is not led into any temptations. Besides, if Hans came here, he might ask me to let him have some flour on credit, and that I could not do. Flour is one thing, and friendship is another and they should not be confused. Why, the words are spelt differently, and mean quite different things. Everybody can see that."

' "How well you talk!" said the miller's wife, pouring herself out a large glass of warm ale; "really I feel quite drowsy. It is just like being in church."

' "Lots of people act well," answered the miller, "but very few people talk well, which shows that talking is much the more difficult thing of the two and much the finer thing also;" and he looked sternly across the table at his little son, who felt so ashamed of himself that he hung his head down, and grew quite scarlet and began to cry into his tea. However, he was so young that you must excuse him.'

'Is that the end of the story?' asked the water-rat.

'Certainly not,' answered the linnet, 'that is the beginning.'

'Then you are quite behind the age,' said the water-rat. 'Every good storyteller nowadays starts with the end, and then goes on to the beginning, and concludes with the middle. That is the new

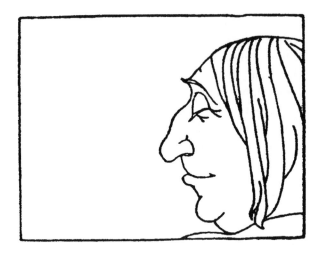

method. I heard all about it the other day from a critic who was walking round the pond with a young man. He spoke of the matter at great length, and I am sure he must have been right, for he had blue spectacles and a bald head and whenever the young man made any remark, he always answered "Pooh!" But pray go on with your story. I like the miller immensely. I have all kinds of beautiful sentiments myself, so there is a great sympathy between us.'

'Well,' said the linnet, hopping now on one leg and now on the other, 'as soon as the winter was over, and the primroses began to open their pale yellow stars, the miller said to his wife that he would go down and see little Hans.

' "Why, what a good heart you have!" cried his wife; "you are always thinking of others. And mind you take the big basket with you for the flowers.'

'So the miller tied the sails of the windmill together with a strong iron chain, and went down the hill with the basket on his arm.

' "Good-morning, little Hans," said the miller.

' "Good-morning," said Hans, leaning on his spade, and smiling from ear to ear.

' "And how have you been all the winter?" said the miller.

' "Well, really," cried Hans, "it is very good of you to ask, very good indeed. I am afraid I had rather a hard time of it, but now the spring has come, and I am quite happy, and all my flowers are doing well."

' "We often talked of you during the winter, Hans," said the miller, "and wondered how you were getting on.'

' "That was kind of you," said Hans; "I was half afraid you had forgotten me."

' "Hans, I am surprised at you," said the miller; "friendship never forgets. That is the wonderful thing about it, but I am afraid you don't understand the poetry of life. How lovely your primroses are looking, by the by!"

' "They are certainly very lovely," said Hans, "and it is a most lucky thing for me that I have so many. I am going to bring them into the market and sell them to the burgomaster's daughter, and buy back my wheelbarrow with the money."

' "Buy back your wheelbarrow? You don't mean to say you have sold it? What a very stupid thing to do!"

' "Well, the fact is," said Hans, "that I was obliged to. You see the winter was a very bad time for me and I really had no money at all to buy bread with. So I first sold the silver buttons off my Sunday coat, and then I sold my silver chain, and then I sold my big pipe, and at last I sold my wheelbarrow. But I am going to buy them all back again now.'

' "Hans," said the miller, "I will give you my wheelbarrow. It is not in very good repair; indeed, one side is gone, and there is something wrong with the wheel-spokes; but in spite of that I will give it to you. I know it is very generous of me, and a great many people would think me extremely foolish for parting with it, but I am not like the rest of the world. I think that generosity is the essence of friendship and, besides, I have got a new wheelbarrow for myself. Yes, you may set your mind at ease. I will give you my wheelbarrow."

' "Well, really, that is generous of you," said little Hans, and his funny round face glowed all over with pleasure. "I can easily put it in repair, as I have a plank of wood in the house."

' "A plank of wood!" said the miller, "why, that is just what I want for the roof of my barn. There is a very large hole in it, and the corn will all get damp if I don't stop it up. How lucky you mentioned it! It is quite remarkable how one good action always breeds another. I have given you my wheelbarrow, and now you are going to give me your plank. Of course, the wheelbarrow is worth far more than the plank, but true friendship never notices things like that. Pray get it at once, and I will set to work on my barn this very day."

' "Certainly," cried little Hans, and he ran into the shed and dragged the plank out.

' "It is not a very big plank," said the miller, looking at it, "and I am afraid that after I have mended my barn-roof there won't be any left for you to mend the wheelbarrow with; but, of course, that is not my fault. And now, as I have given you my wheelbarrow, I am sure you would like to give me some flowers in return. Here is the basket, and mind you fill it quite full."

' "Quite full?" said little Hans, rather sorrowfully, for it was really a very big basket, and he knew that if he filled it he would have no flowers left for the market, and he was very anxious to get his silver buttons back.

' "Well, really," answered the miller, "as I have given you my wheelbarrow, I don't think that it is much to ask you for a few flowers. I may be wrong but I should have thought that friendship, true friendship, was quite free from selfishness of any kind."

' "My dear friend, my best friend," cried little Hans, "you are welcome to all the flowers in my garden. I would much sooner have your good opinion than my silver buttons, any day,' and he ran and plucked all his pretty primroses, and filled the miller's basket.

' "Goodbye, little Hans," said the miller, and he went up the hill with the plank on his shoulder, and the big basket in his hand.

' "Goodbye," said little Hans, and he began to dig away quite merrily, he was so pleased about the wheelbarrow.

'The next day he was nailing up some honeysuckle against the porch, when he heard the miller's voice calling to him from the road. So he jumped off the ladder, and ran down the garden, and looked over the wall.

'There was the miller with a large sack of flour on his back.

' "Dear little Hans," said the miller, "would you mind carrying this sack of flour for me to market?"

' "Oh, I am so sorry," said Hans, "but I am really very busy today. I have got all my creepers to nail up, and all my flowers to water and all my grass to roll."

' "Well, really," said the miller, "I think that con-sidering that I am going to give you my wheel-barrow it is rather unfriendly of you to refuse."

' "Oh don't say that," cried little Hans, "I wouldn't be unfriendly for the whole world;" and he ran in for his cap, and trudged off with the big sack on his shoulders.

'It was a very hot day and the road was terribly dusty and before Hans had reached the sixth mile-stone he was so tired that he had to sit down and rest. However, he went on bravely, and at last he reached the market. After he had waited there for some time, he sold the sack of flour for a very good price, and then he returned home at once, for he was afraid that if he stopped too late he might meet some robbers on the way.

' "It has certainly been a hard day," said little Hans to himself as he was going to bed, "but I am glad I did not refuse the miller, for he is my best friend and, besides, he is going to give me his wheelbarrow."

'Early the next morning the miller came down to get the money for his sack of flour, but little Hans was so tired that he was still in bed.

' "Upon my word," said the miller, "you are very lazy. Really, considering that I am going to give you my wheelbarrow, I think you might work harder. Idleness is a great sin, and I certainly don't like any of my friends to be idle or sluggish. You must not mind my speaking quite plainly to you. Of course, I should not dream of doing so if I were not your friend. But what is the good of friendship if one cannot say exactly what one means? Anybody can say charming things and try to please and to flatter, but a true friend always says unpleasant things, and does not mind giving pain. Indeed, if he is a really true friend he prefers it, for he knows that then he is doing good."

' "I am very sorry," said little Hans, rubbing his eyes and pulling off his nightcap, "but I was so tired that I thought I would lie in bed for a little time, and listen to the birds singing. Do you know I always work better after hearing the birds sing?"

' "Well, I am glad of that," said the miller, clapping little Hans on the back, "for I want you to come up to the mill as soon as you are dressed and mend my barn-roof for me."

'Poor little Hans was very anxious to go and work in his garden, for his flowers had not been watered for two days, but he did not like to refuse the miller, as he was such a good friend to him.

' "Do you think it would be unfriendly of me if I said I was busy?" he enquired in a timid voice.

' "Well, really,' answered the miller, "I do not think it is much to ask of you, considering that I am going to give you my wheelbarrow; but, of course, if you refuse I will go and do it myself.'

' "Oh! on no account," cried little Hans; and he jumped out of bed, and dressed himself, and went up to the barn.

'He worked there all day long, till sunset, and at sunset the miller came to see how he was getting on.

' "Have you mended the hole in the roof yet, little Hans?" cried the miller in a cheery voice.

' "It is quite mended," answered little Hans, coming down the ladder.

' "Ah!" said the miller, "there is no work so delightful as the work one does for others."

' "It is certainly a great privilege to hear you talk," answered little Hans, sitting down and wiping his forehead, "a very great privilege. But I am afraid I shall never have such beautiful ideas as you have."

' "Oh! they will come to you," said the miller, "but you must take more pains. At present you have only the practice of friendship; some day you will have the theory also."

' "Do you really think I shall?" asked little Hans.

' "I have no doubt of it," answered the miller, "but now that you have mended the roof, you had better go home and rest, for I want you to drive my sheep to the mountain tomorrow."

'Poor little Hans was afraid to say anything to this, and early the next morning the miller brought his sheep round to the cottage, and Hans started off with them to the mountain. It took him the whole day to get there and back; and when he returned he was so tired that he went off to sleep in his chair, and did not wake up till it was broad daylight.

' "What a delightful time I shall have in my garden!" he said, and he went to work at once.

'But somehow he was never able to look after his flowers at all, for his friend the miller was always coming round and sending him off on long errands or getting him to help at the mill. Little Hans was very much distressed at times as he was afraid his flowers would think he had forgotten them, but he consoled himself by the reflection that the miller was his best friend. "Besides," he

used to say, "he is going to give me his wheelbarrow, and that is an act of pure generosity."

'So little Hans worked away for the miller, and the miller said all kinds of beautiful things about friendship, which Hans took down in a notebook, and used to read over at night, for he was a very good scholar.

'Now it happened that one evening little Hans was sitting by his fireside when a loud rap came at the door. It was a very wild night, and the wind was blowing and roaring round the house so terribly that at first he thought it was merely the storm. But a second rap came, and then a third, louder than any of the others.

' "It is some poor traveller," said little Hans to himself and he ran to the door.

'There stood the miller with a lantern in one hand and a big stick in the other.

' "Dear little Hans," cried the miller, "I am in great trouble. My little boy has fallen off a ladder and hurt himself, and I am going for the doctor. But he lives so far away, and it is such a bad night, that it has just occurred to me that it would be much better if you went instead of me. You know I am going to give you my wheelbarrow, and so it is only fair that you should do something for me in return.'

' "Certainly," cried little Hans, "I take it quite as a compliment your coming to me, and I will start off at once. But you must lend me your lantern, as the night is so dark that I am afraid I might fall into the ditch."

' "I am very sorry," answered the miller, "but it is my new lantern, and it would be a great loss to me if anything happened to it."

' "Well, never mind, I will do without it," cried little Hans, and he took down his great fur coat, and his warm scarlet cap, and tied a muffler round his throat, and started off. 'What a dreadful storm it was! The night was so black that little Hans could hardly see, and the wind was so strong that he could hardly stand.

However, he was very courageous, and after he had been walking about three hours, he arrived at the doctor's house, and knocked at the door.

' "Who is there?" cried the doctor, putting his head out of his bedroom window.

' "Little Hans, doctor."

' "What do you want, little Hans?"

' "The miller's son has fallen from a ladder, and has hurt himself, and the miller wants you to come at once."

' "All right!" said the doctor; and he ordered his horse, and his big boots, and his lantern, and came downstairs, and rode off in the direction of the miller's house, little Hans trudging behind him

'But the storm grew worse and worse, and the rain fell in torrents, and little Hans could not see where he was going, or keep up with the horse. At last he lost his way, and wandered off on the moor, which was a very dangerous place, as it was full of deep holes, and there poor little Hans was drowned. His body was found the next day by some goat-herds, floating in a great pool of water, and was brought back by them to the cottage.

'Everybody went to little Hans's funeral, as he was so popular, and the miller was the chief mourner.

' "As I was his best friend," said the miller, "it is only fair that I should have the best place,"
so he walked at the head of the procession in a long black cloak, and every now and then he wiped his eyes with a big pocket-handkerchief.

' "Little Hans is certainly a great loss to everyone," said the blacksmith, when the funeral was over, and they were all seated comfortably in the inn, drinking spiced wine and eating sweet cakes.

' "A great loss to me at any rate," answered the miller; "why, I had as good as given him my wheelbarrow,

and now I really don't know what to do with it. It is very much in my way at home, and it is in such bad repair that I could not get anything for it if I sold it. I will certainly take care not to give away anything again. One certainly suffers for being generous." '

'Well?' said the water-rat, after a long pause

'Well, that is the end,' said the linnet.

'What became of the miller?' asked the water-rat.

'Oh! I really don't know,' replied the linnet; 'and I am sure that I don't care.'

'It is quite evident then that you have no sympathy in your nature,' said the water-rat.

'I am afraid you don't quite see the moral of the story,' remarked the linnet.

'The what?' screamed the water-rat.

'The moral.'

'Do you mean to say that the story has a moral?'

'Certainly,' said the linnet.

'Well, really,' said the water-rat, in a very angry manner, 'I think you should have told me that before you began. If you had done so, I certainly would not have listened to you; in fact, I should have said "Pooh", like the critic. However, I can say it now;' so he shouted out 'Pooh' at the top of his voice, gave a whisk with his tail, and went back into his hole

'And how do you like the water-rat?' asked the duck, who came paddling up some minutes afterwards. 'He has a great many good points, but for my own part I have a mother's feelings and I can never look at a confirmed bachelor without the tears coming into my eyes.'

'I am rather afraid that I have annoyed him,' answered the linnet. 'The fact is that I told him a story with a moral.'

'Ah! that is always a very dangerous thing to do,' said the duck.

And I quite agree with her.

The History of Dick Whittington

Dick Whittington was a very little boy when his father and mother died; so little, indeed, that he never knew them, nor the place where he was born. He strolled about the country as ragged as a colt, till he met with a wagoner who was going to London, and who gave him leave to walk all the way by the side of his wagon without paying anything for his passage. This pleased little Whittington very much, as he wanted to see London badly, for he had heard that the streets were paved with gold, and he was willing to get a bushel of it; but how great was his disappointment, poor boy! when he saw the streets covered with dirt instead of gold, and found himself in a strange place, without a friend, without food and without money.

Though the wagoner was so charitable as to let him walk up by the side of the wagon for nothing, he took care not to know him when he came to town, and the poor boy was, in a little time, so cold and hungry that he wished himself in a good kitchen and by a warm fire in the country.

In his distress he asked charity of several people, and one of them bid him, 'Go to work for an idle rogue.'

'That I will,' said Whittington, 'with all my heart; I will work for you if you will let me.'

The man, who thought this savoured of wit and impertinence (though the poor lad intended only to show his readiness to work), gave him a blow with a stick which broke his head so that the blood ran down. In this situation, and fainting for want of food, he laid himself down at the door of one Mr Fitzwarren, a merchant, where the cook saw him, and, being an ill-natured hussy, ordered him to go about his business or she would scald him. At this time Mr Fitzwarren came from the Exchange, and began also to scold at the poor boy, bidding him to go to work.

Whittington answered that he should be glad to work if anybody would employ him, and that he should be able if he could get some victuals to eat,

for he had had nothing for three days, and he was a poor country boy, and knew nobody, and nobody would employ him.

He then endeavoured to get up, but he was so very weak that he fell down again, which excited so much compassion in the merchant that he ordered the servants to take him in and give him some meat and drink, and let him help the cook to do any dirty work that she had to set him about. People are too apt to reproach those who beg with being idle, but give themselves no concern to put them in the way of getting business to do, or considering whether they are able to do it, which is not charity.

But we return to Whittington, who could have lived happy in this worthy family had he not been bumped about by the cross cook, who must be always roasting and basting and who when the spit was idle employed her hands upon poor

'Turn again, Whittington, thrice Lord Mayor of London.'

Whittington! At last Miss Alice, his master's daughter, was informed of it, and then she took compassion on the poor boy, and made the servants treat him kindly.

Besides the crossness of the cook, Whittington had another difficulty to get over before he could be happy. He had, by order of his master, a flock-bed placed for him in a garret, where there was a number of rats and mice that often ran over the poor boy's nose and disturbed him in his sleep. After some time, however, a gentleman who came to his master's house gave Whittington a penny for brushing his shoes. This he put into his pocket, being determined to lay it out to the best advantage; and the next day, seeing a woman in the street with a cat under her arm, he ran up to know the price of it. The woman (as the cat was a good mouser) asked a deal of money for it, but on Whittington's telling her he had but a penny in the world, and that he wanted a cat badly, she let him have it.

This cat Whittington concealed in the garret, for fear she should be beat about by his mortal enemy the cook, and here she soon killed or frightened away the rats and mice, so that the poor boy could now sleep as sound as a top.

Soon after this the merchant, who had a ship ready to sail, called for his servants, as his custom was, in order that each of them might venture something to try their luck; and whatever they sent was to pay neither freight nor custom, for he thought justly that God Almighty would bless him the more for his readiness to let the poor partake of his fortune.

All the servants appeared but poor Whittington, who, having neither money nor goods, could not think of sending anything to try his luck; but his good friend Miss Alice, thinking his poverty kept him away, ordered him to be called.

She then offered to lay down something for him, but the merchant told his daughter that would not do, it must be something of his own. Upon which poor Whittington said he had nothing but a cat which he had bought for a penny that was given him. 'Fetch thy cat, boy,' said the merchant, 'and send her.' Whittington brought poor puss and delivered her to the captain, with tears in his eyes, for he said he should now be disturbed by the rats and mice as much as ever. All the company laughed at the adventure except Miss Alice, who pitied the poor boy, and gave him something to buy another cat.

While puss was beating the billows at sea, poor Whittington was severely beaten at home by his tyrannical mistress the cook, who used him so cruelly, and made such game of him for sending his cat to sea, that at last the poor boy determined to run away from his place, and having packed up the few things he had, he set out very early in the morning on All-Hallows day. He travelled through Holloway, which was then a village within sight of the great city, and at the foot of the steep hill that led up to the village of Highgate he sat down on a stone to consider what course he should take; but while he was thus ruminating, Bow bells, of which there were only six, began to ring; and he thought they seemed to say: 'Turn again, Whittington, thrice Lord Mayor of London.'

'Lord Mayor of London!' said he to himself, 'what would not one endure to be Lord Mayor of London, and ride in such a fine coach? Well, I'll go back again, and bear all the pummelling and ill-usage of Cicely rather than miss the opportunity of being Lord Mayor!' So home he went, and happily got into the house and about his business before Mrs Cicely made her appearance.

We must now follow Miss Puss to the coast of Africa. How perilous are voyages at sea, how uncertain the winds and the waves, and how many accidents attend a naval life!

The ship that had the cat on board was long beaten at sea, and at last, by contrary winds, driven on a part of the coast of Barbary which was in-habited by Moors unknown to the English. These people received our countrymen with civility, and therefore the captain, in order to trade with them, showed them the patterns of the goods he had on board, and sent some of them to the king of the country, who was so well pleased that he sent for the captain and the factor to come to his palace, which was about a mile from the sea. Here they were placed, according to the custom of the country, on rich carpets, flowered with gold and silver; and the king and queen being seated at the upper end of the room, dinner was brought in, which consisted of many dishes; but no sooner were the dishes put down but an amazing number of rats and mice came from all quarters and devoured all the meat in an instant.

The factor, in surprise, turned round to the nobles and asked if these vermin were not offensive. 'Oh! yes,' said they, 'very offensive; and the king would give half his treasure to be freed of them, for they not only destroy his dinner, as you see, but they assault him in his chamber, and even in bed, so that he is obliged to be watched while he is sleeping, for fear of them.'

The factor jumped for joy; he remembered poor Whittington and his cat, and told the king he had a creature on board the ship that would despatch all these vermin immediately. The king's heart heaved so high at the joy which this news gave him that his turban dropped off his head. 'Bring this creature to me,' said he; 'vermin are dreadful in a court, and if she will perform what you say I will load your ship with gold and jewels in exchange for her.' The factor, who knew his business, took this opportunity to set forth the merits of Miss Puss. He told his majesty that it would be inconvenient to part with her, as, when she was gone, the rats and mice might destroy the goods in the ship – but to oblige his majesty he would fetch her. 'Run, run,' said the queen; 'I am impatient to see the dear creature.'

Away flew the factor, while another dinner was providing, and returned with the cat just as the rats and mice were devouring that also. He immediately put down Miss Puss, who killed a great number of them.

The king rejoiced greatly to see his old enemies destroyed by so small a creature, and the queen was highly pleased, and desired the cat might be brought near that she might look at her. Upon which the factor called, 'Pussy, pussy, pussy!' and she came to him. He then presented her to the queen, who started back, and was afraid to touch a creature who had made such havoc among the rats and mice; however, when the factor stroked the cat and called, 'Pussy, pussy!' the queen also touched her and cried, 'Putty, putty!' for she had not learned English.

He then put her down on the queen's lap, where she, purring, played with her majesty's hand, and then sang herself to sleep.

The king, having seen the exploits of Miss Puss, bargained with the captain and factor for the whole ship's cargo, and then gave them ten times as much for the cat as all the rest amounted to. On which, taking leave of their majesties and other great personages at court, they sailed with a fair wind for England, whither we must now attend them.

The morn had scarcely dawned when Mr Fitz-warren arose to count over the cash and settle the business for that day. He had just entered the counting-house, and seated himself at the desk, when somebody came, tap, tap, at the door. 'Who's there?' said Mr Fitzwarren. 'A friend,' answered the other. 'What friend can come at this unseasonable time?' 'A real friend is never unseasonable,' answered the other. 'I come to bring you good news of your ship *Unicorn*.' The merchant bustled up in such a hurry that he forgot his gout; instantl opened the door, and who should be seen waiting but the captain and factor, with a cabinet of jewels, and a bill of lading, for which the merchant lifted up his eyes and thanked heaven for sending him such a prosperous voyage. Then they told him the adventures of the cat, and showed him the cabinet of jewels

going into the counting-house, saying the room was swept and his shoes were dirty and full of hob-nails. The merchant, however, made him come in, and ordered a chair to be set for him. Upon which, thinking they intended to make sport of him, as had been too often the case in the kitchen, he besought his master not to mock a poor simple fellow, who intended them no harm, but let him go about his business. The merchant, taking him by the hand, said: 'Indeed, Mr Whittington, I am in earnest with you, and sent for you to congratulate you on your great success. Your cat has procuredyou more money than I am worth in the world,

The king rejoiced greatly to see his old enemies destroyed by so small a creature

which they had brought for Mr Whittington. Upon which he cried out with great earnestness, but not in the most poetical manner:

'Go, send him in, and tell him of his fame,
And call him Mr Whittington by name.'

It is not our business to animadvert upon these lines; we are not critics, but historians. It is sufficient for us that they are the words of Mr Fitzwarren; and though it is beside our purpose, and perhaps not in our power to prove him a good poet, we shall soon convince the reader that he was a good man, which was a much better character; for when some who were present told him that this treasure was too much for such a poor boy as Whittington, he said: 'God forbid that I should deprive him of a penny; it is his own, and he shall have it to a farthing.' He then ordered Mr Whittington in, who was at this time cleaning the kitchen and would have excused himself from

and may you long enjoy it and be happy!'

At length, being shown the treasure, and convinced by them that all of it belonged to him, he fell upon his knees and thanked the Almighty for his providential care of such a poor and miserable creature. He then laid all the treasure at his master's feet, who refused to take any part of it, but told him he heartily rejoiced at his prosperity, and hoped the wealth he had acquired would be a comfort to him, and would make him happy. He then applied to his mistress, and to his good friend Miss Alice, who refused to take any part of the money, but told him she heartily rejoiced at his good success, and wished him all imaginable felicity. He then thanked the captain, factor and the ship's crew for the care they had taken of his cargo. He likewise distributed presents to all the servants in the house, not forgetting even his old enemy the cook, though she little deserved it.

After this Mr Fitzwarren advised Mr Whittington

to send for the necessary people and dress himself like a gentleman, and made him the offer of his house to live in till he could provide himself with a better.

Now it came to pass when Mr Whittington's face was washed, his hair curled, and he dressed in a rich suit of clothes, that he turned out a genteel young fellow; and, as wealth contributes much to give a man confidence, he in a little time dropped that sheepish behaviour which was principally occasioned by a depression of spirits, and soon grew a sprightly and good companion, insomuch that Miss Alice, who had formerly pitied him, now fell in love with him.

When her father perceived they had this good liking for each other he proposed a match between them, to which both parties cheerfully consented, and the Lord Mayor, Court of Aldermen, Sheriffs, the Company of Stationers, the Company of Mercers, the Royal Academy of Arts and a number of eminent merchants attended the ceremony, and were elegantly treated at an entertainment made for that purpose.

History further relates that they lived very happy, had several children and died at a good old age. Mr Whittington served as Sheriff of London and was three times Lord Mayor. In the last year of his mayoralty he entertained King Henry V, after his conquest of France, upon which occasion the king, in consideration of Whittington's merit, said: 'Never had prince such a subject;' which being told to Whittington at the table, he replied: 'Never had subject such a king.' His majesty conferred the honour of knighthood on him soon after.

Sir Richard many years before his death constantly fed a great number of poor citizens, built a church and a college to it, with a yearly allowance for poor scholars, and near it erected a hospital.

He also built Newgate for criminals, and gave liberally to ±St Bartholomew's Hospital and other public charities. And even to this day there stands a great and mighty hospital at the foot of Highgate Hill where he heard the bells summoning him to return to London. Also around that place are many reminders of the good and faithful cat that brought this tale to such a happy end.

The Donkey Cabbage

There was once a young hunter who went boldly into the forest. He had a merry and light heart, and as he went whistling along there came an ugly old woman, who said to him, 'Good-day, dear hunter! You are very merry and contented, but I suffer hunger and thirst, so give me a trifle.' The hunter was sorry for the poor old woman, and he felt in his pocket and gave her all he could spare. He was going on then, but the old woman stopped him and said, 'Listen, dear hunter, to what I say. Because of your kind heart I will make you a present. Go on your way, and in a short time you will come to a tree on which sit nine birds who have a cloak in their claws and are quarrelling over it. Then take aim with your gun and shoot in the middle of them; they will let the cloak fall, but one of the birds will be hit and will drop down dead. Take the cloak with you; it is a wishing-cloak, and when you throw it on your shoulders you have only to wish yourself at a certain place, and in the twinkling of an eye you will be there. Take the heart

out of the dead bird and swallow it whole, and early every morning when you get up you will find a gold piece under your pillow.'

The hunter thanked the wise woman, and thought to himself, 'These are splendid things she has promised me, if only they come to pass!' So he walked on about a hundred yards, and then he heard above him in the branches such a screaming and chirping that he looked up, and there he saw a heap of birds tearing a cloth with their beaks and feet, shrieking, tugging and fighting, as if each wanted it for himself. 'Well,' said the hunter, 'this is wonderful! It is just as the old woman said;' and he took his gun on his shoulder, pulled the trigger, and shot into the midst of them, so that their feathers flew about. Then the flock took flight with much screaming, but one fell dead, and the cloak fluttered down. Then the hunter did as the old woman had told him: he cut open the bird, found its heart, swallowed it, and took the cloak home with him. The next morning when he awoke he remembered the promise, and wanting to see if it had come true, he lifted up his pillow: there, indeed, sparkled the gold piece, and the next morning he found another, and so on every time he got up. He collected a heap of gold, but at last he thought to himself, 'What good is all my gold to me if I stay at home? I will travel and look a bit about me in the world.' So he took leave of his parents, slung his hunting knapsack and his gun round him, and journeyed into the world.

It happened that one day he went through a thick wood, and when he came to the end of it there lay in the plain before him a large castle. At one of the windows in it stood an old woman with a most beautiful maiden by her side, looking out. But the old woman was a witch, and she said to the girl, 'There comes one out of the wood who has a wonderful treasure in his body which we must manage to possess ourselves of, darling daughter; we have more right to it than he. He has a bird's

heart in him, and so every morning there lies a gold piece under his pillow.'

She told her how they could get hold of it, and how she was to coax it from him, and at last threatened her angrily, saying, 'And if you do not obey me, you shall repent it!'

When the hunter came nearer he saw the maiden, and said to himself, 'I have travelled so far now that I will rest, and turn into this beautiful castle; money I have in plenty.' But the real reason was that he had caught sight of the lovely face.

He went into the house, and was kindly received and hospitably entertained. It was not long before he was so much in love with the witch-maiden that he thought of nothing else, and only looked in her eyes, and whatever she wanted, that he gladly did. Then the old witch said, 'Now we must have the bird-heart; he will not feel when it is gone.' She prepared a drink, and when it was ready she poured it in a goblet and gave it to the maiden, who had to hand it to the hunter.

'Drink to me now, my dearest,' she said. Then he took the goblet, and when he had swallowed the drink the bird-heart came out of his mouth. The maiden had to get hold of it secretly and then swallow it herself, for the old witch wanted to have it. Thenceforward he found no more gold under his pillow, and it lay under the maiden's; but he was so much in love and so much bewitched that he thought of nothing except spending all his time with the maiden.

Then the old witch said, 'We have the bird-heart, but we must also get the wishing-cloak from him.'

The maiden answered, 'We will leave him that; he has already lost his wealth!'

The old witch grew angry, and said, 'Such a cloak is a wonderful thing, it is seldom to be had in the world, and have it I must and will.' She beat the maiden, and said that if she did not obey it would go ill with her.

So she did her mother's bidding, and, standing one day by the window, she looked away into the far distance as if she were very sad.

'Why are you standing there looking so sad?' asked the hunter.

'Alas, my love,' she replied, 'over there lies the granite mountain where the costly precious stones grow. I have a great longing to go there, so that when I think of it I am very sad. For who can fetch them? Only the birds who fly; a man, never.'

'If you have no other troubles,' said the hunter, 'that one I can easily remove from your heart.'

So he wrapped her round in his cloak and wished them away to the granite mountain, and in an instant there they were, sitting on it! The precious stones sparkled so brightly on all sides that it was a pleasure to see them, and they collected the most beautiful and costly together.

But now the old witch had through her caused the hunter's eyes to become heavy. He said to the maiden, 'We will sit down for a little while and rest; I am so tired that I can hardly stand on my feet.'

So they sat down, and he laid his head on her lap and fell asleep. As soon as he was sound asleep she unfastened the cloak from his shoulders, threw it on her own, left the granite and stones, and wished herself home again.

But when the hunter had finished his sleep and awoke, he found that his love had betrayed him and left him alone on the wild mountain. 'Oh,' said he, 'why is faithlessness so great in the world?' and he sat down in sorrow and trouble, not knowing what to do.

But the mountain belonged to fierce and huge giants, who lived on it and traded there, and he had not sat long before he saw three of them striding towards him. So he lay down as if he had fallen into a deep sleep.

The giants came up, and the first pushed him with his foot, and said, 'What sort of an earthworm is that?'

The second said, 'Crush him dead.'

But the third said contemptuously, 'It is not worth the trouble! Let him live; he cannot remain here, and if he goes higher up the mountain the clouds will take him and carry him off.'

Talking thus they went away. But the hunter had listened to their talk, and as soon as they had gone he rose and climbed to the summit. When he had sat there a little while a cloud swept by, and, seizing him, carried him away. It travelled for a time in the sky, and then it sank down and hovered over a large vegetable garden surrounded by walls, so that he came safely to the ground amidst cabbages of every sort. The hunter then looked about him, saying, 'If only I had something to eat! I am so hungry, and it will go badly with me in the future, for I see here not an apple or pear or fruit of any kind – nothing but cabbages everywhere.' At last he thought, 'At a pinch I can eat one; it does not taste particularly nice, but it will refresh me.'

So he looked about for a good head and ate it, but no sooner had he swallowed a couple of mouthfuls than he felt very strange, and found himself wonderfully changed. Four legs began to grow on him, a thick head and two long ears, and he saw with horror that he had changed into a donkey. But as he was still very hungry and this juicy salad tasted very good to his present nature, he went on eating with a still greater appetite. At last he got hold of another kind of cabbage, but scarcely had he swallowed it when he felt another change, and he once more regained his human form.

The hunter now lay down and slept off his weariness. When he awoke the next morning he broke off a head of the bad and a head of the good cabbage, thinking, 'This will help me to regain my own, and to punish faithlessness.' Then he put the heads in his pockets, climbed the wall, and started off to seek the castle of his love. When he had wandered about for a couple of days he found it quite easily. He then browned his face quickly, so that his own mother would not have known him,

and went into the castle, where he begged for a lodging.

'I am so tired,' he said, 'I can go no farther.'

The witch asked, 'Countryman, who are you, and what is your business?'

He answered, 'I am a messenger of the king, and have been sent to seek the finest salad that grows under the sun. I have been so lucky as to find it, and am bringing it with me; but the heat of the sun is so great that the tender cabbage threatens to grow soft, and I do not know if I shall be able to bring it any farther.'

When the old witch heard of the fine salad she wanted to eat it, and said, 'Dear countryman, just let me taste the wonderful salad.'

'Why not?' he answered; 'I have brought two heads with me, and will give you one.'

So saying, he opened his sack and gave her the bad one. The witch suspected no evil, and her

mouth watered so to taste the new dish that she went into the kitchen to prepare it herself. When it was ready she could not wait till it was served at the table, but she immediately took a couple of leaves and put them in her mouth. No sooner, however, had she swallowed them than she lost human form, and ran into the courtyard in the shape of a donkey.

Now the servant came into the kitchen, and when she saw the salad standing there ready cooked she was about to carry it up, but on the way, according to her old habit, she tasted it and ate a couple of leaves. Immediately the charm worked, and she became a donkey, and ran out to join the old witch, and the dish with the salad in it fell to the ground. In the meantime, the messenger was sitting with the lovely maiden, and as no one came with the salad, and she wanted very much to taste it, she said, 'I don't know where the salad is.'

Then thought the hunter, 'The cabbage must have already begun to work.' And he said, 'I will go to the kitchen and fetch it myself.'

When he came there he saw the two donkeys running about in the courtyard, but the salad was lying on the ground.

'That's all right,' said he; 'two have had their share!' And lifting the remaining leaves up, he laid them on the dish and brought them to the maiden.

'I am bringing you the delicious food my own self,' he said, 'so that you need not wait any longer.'

Then she ate, and, as the others had done, she at once lost her human form, and ran as a donkey into the yard.

When the hunter had washed his face, so that the changed ones might know him, he went into the yard, saying, 'Now you shall receive a reward for your faithlessness.'

He tied them all three with a rope, and drove them away till he came to a mill. He knocked at the window, and the miller put his head out and asked what he wanted.

'I have three tiresome animals,' he answered, 'which I don't want to keep any longer. If you will take them, give them food and stabling, and do as I tell you with them, I will pay you as much as you want.'

The miller replied, 'Why not? What shall I do with them?'

Then the hunter said he was to give to the old donkey, which was the witch, three beatings and one meal; to the younger one, which was the servant, one beating and three meals; and to the youngest one, which was the maiden, no beating and three meals; for he could not find it in his heart to let the maiden be beaten.

Then he went back into the castle, and he found there all that he wanted. After a couple of days the miller came and said that he must tell him that the old donkey which was to have three beatings and only one meal had died. 'The two others,' he added, 'are certainly not dead, and get their three meals every day, but they are so sad that they cannot last much longer.'

Then the hunter took pity on them, laid aside his anger, and told the miller to drive them back again. And when they came he gave them some of the good cabbage to eat, so that they became human again. Then the beautiful maiden fell on her knees before him, saying, 'Oh, my dearest, forgive me the ill I have done you! My mother compelled me to do it; it was against my will, for I love you dearly. Your wishing-cloak is hanging in a cupboard, and as for the bird-heart I will make a drink and give it back to you.'

But he changed his mind, and said, 'Keep it; it makes no difference, for I will take you to be my own dear true wife.'

And the wedding was celebrated, and they lived happy together till death.

THE YOUNG MAN GIVES THE DONKEYS TO THE MILLER

The Dragon of the North

Very long ago, as old people have told me, there lived a terrible monster, who came out of the North, and laid waste whole tracts of country, devouring both men and beasts; and this monster was so destructive that it was feared that unless help came no living creature would be left on the face of the earth. It had a body like an ox, and legs like a frog, two short forelegs and two long ones behind, and besides that it had a tail like a serpent, ten fathoms in length. When it moved it jumped like a frog, and with every spring it covered half a mile of ground. Fortunately its habit was to remain for several years in the same place, and not to move on till the whole neighbourhood was eaten up. Nothing could hunt it, because its whole body was covered with scales, which were harder than stone or metal; its two great eyes shone by night, and even by day, like the brightest lamps, and anyone who had the ill luck to look into those eyes became as it were bewitched, and was obliged to rush of his own accord into the monster's jaws. In this way the Dragon was able to feed upon both men and beasts without the least trouble to itself, as it needed not to move from the spot where it was lying. All the neighbouring kings had offered rich rewards to anyone who should be able to destroy the monster, either by force or enchantment, and many had tried their luck, but all had miserably failed. Once a great forest in which the Dragon lay had been set on fire; the forest was burnt down, but the fire did not do the monster the least harm. However, there was a tradition amongst the wise men of the country that the Dragon might be overcome by one who possessed King Solomon's signet-ring, upon which a secret writing was engraved. This inscription would enable anyone who was wise enough to interpret it to find out how the Dragon could be destroyed. Only no one knew where the ring was hidden, nor was there any sorcerer or learned man to be found who would be able to explain the inscription.

At last a young man, with a good heart and plenty of courage, set out to search for the ring. He took his way towards the sunrise, because he knew that all the wisdom of old time comes from the East. After some years he met with a famous Eastern magician, and asked for his advice in the matter. The magician answered: 'Mortal men have but little wisdom, and can give you no help, but the birds of the air would be better guides to you if you could learn their language. I can help you to understand it if you will stay with me a few days.'

The youth thankfully accepted the magician's offer, and said, 'I cannot now offer you any reward for your kindness, but should my undertaking succeed your trouble shall be richly repaid.'

Then the magician brewed a powerful potion out of nine sorts of herbs which he had gathered himself all alone by moonlight, and he gave the youth nine spoonfuls of it daily for three days, which made him able to understand the language of birds.

At parting the magician said to him, 'If you ever find King Solomon's ring and get possession of it, then come back to me, that I may explain the inscription on the ring to you, for there is no one else in the world who can do this.'

From that time the youth never felt lonely as he walked along; he always had company, because he understood the language of birds; and in this way he learned many things which mere human knowledge could never have taught him. But time went on, and he heard nothing about the ring. It happened one evening, when he was hot and tired with walking, and had sat down under a tree in a forest to eat his supper, that he saw two gaily-plumaged birds, that were strange to him, sitting at the top of the tree talking to one another about him. The first bird said: 'I know that wandering fool under the tree there, who has come so far without finding what he seeks. He is trying to find King Solomon's lost ring.'

The other bird answered, 'He will have to seek

help from the witch-maiden, who will doubtless be able to put him on the right track. If she has not got the ring herself, she knows well enough who has it.'

'But where is he to find the witch-maiden?' said the first bird. 'She has no settled dwelling, but is here today and gone tomorrow. He might as well try to catch the wind.'

The other replied, 'I do not know, certainly, where she is at present, but in three nights from now she will come to the spring to wash her face, as she does every month when the moon is full, in order that she may never grow old, nor wrinkled, but may always keep the bloom of youth.'

'Well,' said the first bird, 'the spring is not far from here. Shall we go and see how she does it?'

'Willingly, if you like,' said the other.

The youth immediately resolved to follow the birds to the spring, only two things made him uneasy: first, lest he might be asleep when the birds went, and secondly, lest he might lose sight of them, since he had not wings to carry him along so swiftly. He was too tired to keep awake all night, yet his anxiety prevented him from sleeping soundly, and when with the earliest dawn he looked up to the tree-top, he was glad to see his feathered companions still asleep with their heads under their wings. He ate his breakfast, and waited until the birds should start, but they did not leave the place all day. They hopped about from one tree to another looking for food, all day long until the evening, when they went back to their old perch to sleep. The next day the same thing happened, but on the third morning one bird said to the other, 'Today we must go to the spring to see the witch-maiden wash her face.' They remained on the tree till noon; then they flew away and went towards the south. The young man's heart beat with anxiety lest he should lose sight of his guides, but he managed to keep the birds in view until they again perched upon a tree. The young man ran after them until he was quite exhausted and out of breath, and after three short rests the birds at length reached a small open space in the forest, on the edge of which they placed themselves on the top of a high tree. When the youth had overtaken them, he saw that there was a clear spring in the middle of the space. He sat down at the foot of the tree upon which the birds were perched, and listened attentively to what they were saying to each other.

'The sun is not down yet,' said the first bird; 'we must wait yet awhile till the moon rises and the maiden comes to the spring. Do you think she will see that young man sitting under the tree?'

'Nothing is likely to escape her eyes, certainly not a young man, said the other bird. 'Will the youth have the sense not to let himself be caught in her toils?'

'We will wait,' said the first bird, 'and see how they get on together.'

The evening light had quite faded, and the full moon was already shining down upon the forest, when the young man heard a slight rustling sound. After a few moments there came out of the forest a maiden, gliding over the grass so lightly that her feet seemed scarcely to touch the ground till she stood beside the spring. The youth could not turn away his eyes from the maiden, for he had never in his life seen a woman so beautiful. Without seeming to notice anything, she went to the spring, looked up to the full moon, then knelt down and bathed her face nine times, then looked up to the moon again and walked nine times round the well, and as she walked she sang this song:

'Full-faced moon with light unshaded,
Let my beauty ne'er be faded.
Never let my cheek grow pale!
While the moon is waning nightly,
May the maiden bloom more brightly,
May her freshness never fail!'

Then she dried her face with her long hair, and was about to go away, when her eye suddenly fell upon the spot where the young man was sitting, and she turned towards the tree. The youth rose and stood waiting. Then the maiden said, 'You ought to have a heavy punishment because you have presumed to watch my secret doings in the moonlight. But I will forgive you this time, because you are a stranger and knew no better. But you must tell me truly who you are and how you came to this place, where no mortal has ever set foot before.'

The youth answered humbly: 'Forgive me, beautiful maiden, if I have unintentionally offended you. I chanced to come here after long wandering, and found a good place to sleep under this tree. At your coming I did not know what to do, but stayed where I was, because I thought my silent watching could not offend you.'

The maiden answered kindly, 'Come and spend this night with us. You will sleep better on a pillow than on damp moss.'

The youth hesitated for a little, but presently he heard the birds saying from the top of the tree, 'Go where she calls you, but take care to give no blood, or you will sell your soul.' So the youth went with her, and soon they reached a beautiful garden, where stood a splendid house, which glittered in the moonlight as if it was all built out of gold and silver. When the youth entered he found many splendid chambers, each one finer than the last. Hundreds of tapers burnt upon golden candlesticks, and shed a light like the brightest day. At length they reached a chamber where a table was spread with the most costly dishes. At the table were placed two chairs, one of silver, the other of gold. The maiden seated herself upon the golden chair, and offered the silver one to her companion. They were served by maidens dressed in white, whose feet made no sound as they moved about, and not a word was spoken during the meal. Afterwards the youth and the witch-maiden conversed pleasantly together, until a woman, dressed in red, came in to remind them that it was bedtime. The youth was now shown into another room, containing a silken bed with down cushions, where he slept delightfully, yet he seemed to hear a voice near his bed which repeated to him, 'Remember to give no blood!'

The next morning the maiden asked him whether he would not like to stay with her always in this beautiful place, and as he did not answer immediately, she continued: 'You see how I always remain young and beautiful, and I am under no one's orders, but can do just what I like, so that I have never thought of marrying before. But from the moment I saw you I took a fancy to you, so if you agree, we might be married and might live together like princes, because I have great riches.'

The youth could not but be tempted with the beautiful maiden's offer, but he remembered how the birds had called her the witch, and their warning always sounded in his ears. Therefore he answered cautiously, 'Do not be angry, dear maiden, if I do not decide immediately on this important matter. Give me a few days to consider before we come to an understanding.'

'Why not?' answered the maiden. 'Take some weeks to consider if you like, and take counsel with your own heart.' And to make the time pass pleasantly, she took the youth over every part of her beautiful dwelling, and showed him all her splendid treasures. But these treasures were all produced by enchantment, for the maiden could make anything she wished appear by the help of King Solomon's signet ring; only none of these things remained fixed; they passed away like the wind without leaving a trace behind. But the youth did not know this; he thought they were all real.

One day the maiden took him into a secret chamber, where a little gold box was standing on a silver table. Pointing to the box, she said, 'Here is my greatest treasure, whose like is not to be found in the whole world. It is a precious gold ring. When you marry me, I will give you this ring as a marriage gift, and it will make you the happiest of mortal men. But in order that our love may last for ever, you must give me for the ring three drops of blood from the little finger of your left hand.'

When the youth heard these words a cold shudder ran over him, for he remembered that his soul was at stake. He was cunning enough, however, to conceal his feelings and to make no direct answer, but he only asked the maiden, as if carelessly, what was remarkable about the ring?

She answered, 'No mortal is able entirely to understand the power of this ring, because no one thoroughly understands the secret signs engraved upon it. But even with my half-knowledge I can work great wonders. If I put the ring upon the little finger of my left hand, then I can fly like a bird through the air wherever I wish to go. If I put it on the third finger of my left hand I am invisible, and I can see everything that passes around me, though no one can see me. If I put the ring upon the middle finger of my left hand, then neither fire nor water nor any sharp weapon can hurt me. If I put it on the forefinger of my left hand, then I can with its help produce whatever I wish. I can in a single moment build houses or anything I desire. Finally, as long as I wear the ring on the thumb of my left hand, that hand is so strong that it can break down rocks and walls. Besides these, the ring has other secret signs which, as I said, no one can understand. No doubt it contains secrets of great importance. The ring formerly belonged to King Solomon, the wisest of kings, during whose reign the wisest men lived. But it is not known whether this ring was ever made by mortal hands: it is supposed that an angel gave it to the wise king.'

When the youth heard all this he determined to try and get possession of the ring, though he did not quite believe in all its wonderful gifts. He wished the maiden would let him have it in his hand, but he did not quite like to ask her to do so, and after a while she put it back into the box. A few days after they were again speaking of the magic ring, and the youth said, 'I do not think it possible that the ring can have all the power you say it has.'

Then the maiden opened the box and took the ring out, and it glittered as she held it like the clearest sunbeam. She put it on the middle finger of her left hand, and told the youth to take a knife and try as hard as he could to cut her with it, for he would not be able to hurt her. He was unwilling at first, but the maiden insisted. Then he tried, at first only in play, and then seriously, to strike her with the knife, but an invisible wall of iron seemed to be between them, and the maiden stood before him laughing and unhurt. Then she put the ring on her third finger, and in an instant she had vanished from his eyes. Presently she was beside him again laughing, and holding the ring between her fingers.

'Do let me try,' said the youth, 'whether I can do these wonderful things.'

The maiden, suspecting no treachery, gave him the magic ring.

The youth pretended to have forgotten what to do, and asked what finger he must put the ring on so that no sharp weapon could hurt him?'

'Oh, the middle finger of your left hand,' the maiden answered, laughing.

She took the knife and tried to strike the youth, and he even tried to cut himself with it, but found it impossible. Then he asked the maiden to show him how to split stones and rocks with the help of the ring. So she led him into a courtyard where stood a great boulder-stone. 'Now,' she said, 'put the ring upon the thumb of your left hand, and you will see how strong that hand has become. The youth did so, and found to his astonishment that with a single blow of his fist the stone flew into a thousand pieces. Then the youth bethought him that he who does not use his luck when he has it is a fool, and that this was a chance which once lost might never return. So while they stood laughing at the shattered stone he placed the ring, as if in play, upon the third finger of his left hand.

'Now,' said the maiden, 'you are invisible to me until you take the ring off again.'

But the youth had no mind to do that; on the contrary, he went farther off, then put the ring on the little finger of his left hand, and soared into the air like a bird.

When the maiden saw him flying away she thought at first that he was still in play, and cried, 'Come back, friend, for now you see I have told you the truth.' But the young man never came back.

Then the maiden saw she was deceived, and bitterly repented that she had ever trusted him with the ring.

The young man never halted in his flight until he reached the dwelling of the wise magician who had taught him the speech of birds. The magician was delighted to find that his search had been successful, and at once set to work to interpret the secret signs engraved upon the ring, but it took him seven weeks to make them out clearly. Then he gave the youth the following instructions how to overcome the Dragon of the North: 'You must have an iron horse cast, which must have little wheels under each foot. You must also be armed with a spear two fathoms long, which you will be able to wield by means of the magic ring upon your left thumb. The spear must be as thick in the middle as a large tree, and both its ends must be sharp. In the middle of the spear you must have two strong chains ten fathoms in length. As soon as the Dragon has made himself fast to the spear, which you must thrust through his jaws, you must spring quickly from the iron horse and fasten the ends of the chains firmly to the ground with iron stakes, so that he cannot get away from them. After two or three days the monster's strength will be so far exhausted that you will be able to come near him. Then you can put Solomon's ring upon your left thumb and give him the finishing stroke, but keep the ring on your third finger until you have come close to him, so that the monster cannot see you, else he might strike you dead with his long tail. But when all is done, take care you do not lose the ring, and that no one takes it from you by cunning.'

The young man thanked the magician for his directions, and promised, should they succeed, to reward him. But the magician answered, 'I have profited so much by the wisdom the ring has taught me that I desire no other reward.' Then they parted, and the youth quickly flew home through the air. After remaining in his own home for some weeks, he heard people say that the terrible Dragon of the North was not far off, and might shortly be expected in the country. The king announced publicly that he would give his daughter in marriage, as well as a large part of his kingdom, to whosoever should free the country from the monster. The youth then went to the king and told him that he had good hopes of subduing the Dragon, if the king would grant him all he desired for the purpose. The king willingly agreed, and the iron horse, the great spear and the chains were all prepared as the youth requested. When all was ready, it was found that the iron horse was so heavy that a hundred men could not move it from the spot, so the youth found there was nothing for it but to move it with his own strength by means of the magic ring. The Dragon was now so near that in a couple of springs he would be over the frontier. The youth now began to consider how he should act, for if he had to push the iron horse from behind he could not ride upon it as the sorcerer had said he must. But a raven unexpectedly gave him this advice: 'Ride upon the horse, and push the spear against the ground, as if you were pushing off a boat from the land.' The youth did so, and found that in this way he could easily move forwards. The Dragon had his monstrous jaws wide open, all ready for his expected prey. A few paces nearer, and man and horse would have been swallowed up by them! The youth trembled with horror, and his blood ran cold, yet he did not lose

his courage; but, holding the iron spear upright in his hand, he brought it down with all his might right through the monster's lower jaw. Then quick as lightning he sprang from his horse before the Dragon had time to shut his mouth. A fearful clap like thunder, which could be heard for miles around, now warned him that the Dragon's jaws had closed upon the spear. When the youth turned round he saw the point of the spear sticking up high above the Dragon's upper jaw, and knew that the other end must be fastened firmly to the ground; but the Dragon had got his teeth fixed in the iron horse, which was now useless. The youth now hastened to fasten down the chains to the ground by means of the enormous iron pegs which he had provided. The death struggle of the monster lasted three days and three nights; in his writhing he beat his tail so violently against the ground, that at ten miles' distance the earth trembled as if with an earthquake. When he at length lost power to move his tail, the youth with

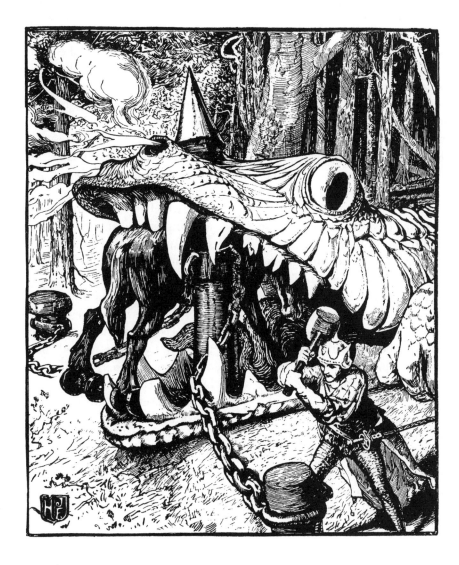

the help of the ring took up a stone which twenty ordinary men could not have moved, and beat the Dragon so hard about the head with it that very soon the monster lay lifeless before him.

You can fancy how great was the rejoicing when the news was spread abroad that the terrible monster was dead. His conqueror was received into the city with as much pomp as if he had been the mightiest of kings. The old king did not need to urge his daughter to marry the slayer of the Dragon; he found her already willing to bestow her hand upon this hero, who had done all alone what whole armies had tried in vain to do. In a few days a magnificent wedding was celebrated, at which the rejoicings lasted four whole weeks, for all the neighbouring kings had met together to thank the man who had freed the world from their common enemy. But everyone forgot amid the general joy that they ought to have buried the Dragon's monstrous body, for it began now to have such a bad smell that no one could live in the neighbourhood, and before long the whole air was poisoned, and a pestilence broke out which destroyed many hundreds of people. In this distress, the king's son-in-law resolved to seek help once more from the Eastern magician, to whom he at once travelled through the air like a bird by the help of the ring. But there is a proverb which says that ill-gotten gains never prosper, and the prince found that the stolen ring brought him ill-luck after all. The witch-maiden had never rested night nor day until she had found out where the ring was. As soon as she had discovered by means of magical arts that the prince in the form of a bird was on his way to the Eastern magician, she changed herself into an eagle and watched in the air until the bird she was waiting for came in sight, for she knew him at once by the ring which was hung round his neck by a ribbon. Then the eagle pounced upon the bird, and the moment she seized him in her talons she tore the ring from his neck before the man in bird's shape had time to prevent her. Then the eagle flew down to the earth with her prey, and the two stood face to face once more in human form.

'Now, villain, you are in my power!' cried the witch-maiden. 'I favoured you with my love, and you repaid me with treachery and theft. You stole my most precious jewel from me, and do you expect to live happily as the king's son-in-law? Now the tables are turned; you are in my power, and I will be revenged on you for your crimes.'

'Forgive me! forgive me!' cried the prince; 'I know too well how deeply I have wronged you, and most heartily do I repent it.'

The maiden answered, 'Your prayers and your repentance come too late, and if I were to spare you everyone would think me a fool. You have doubly wronged me; first you scorned my love, and then you stole my ring, and you must bear the punishment.'

With these words she put the ring upon her left thumb, lifted the young man with one hand, and walked away with him under her arm. This time she did not take him to a splendid palace, but to a deep cave in a rock, where there were chains hanging from the wall. The maiden now chained the young man's hands and feet so that he could not escape; then she said in an angry voice, 'Here you shall remain chained up until you die. I will bring you every day enough food to prevent you dying of hunger, but you need never hope for freedom any more.' With these words she left him.

The old king and his daughter waited anxiously for many weeks for the prince's return, but no news of him arrived. The king's daughter often dreamed that her husband was going through some great suffering: she therefore begged her father to summon all the enchanters and magicians, that they might try to find out where the prince was and how he could be set free. But the magicians, with all their arts, could find out nothing, except that he was still living and undergoing great suffering; but none could tell where he was to be found. At last a celebrated magician from Finland was brought before the king, who had found out that the king's son-in-law was imprisoned in the East, not by men, but by some more powerful being. The king now sent messengers to the East to look for his son-in-law, and they by good luck met with the old magician who had interpreted the signs on King Solomon's ring, and thus was possessed of more wisdom than anyone else in the world. The magician soon found out what he wished to know, and pointed out the place where the prince was imprisoned, but said: 'He is kept there by enchantment, and cannot be set free without my help. I will therefore go with you myself.'

So they all set out, guided by birds, and after some days came to the cave where the unfortunate prince had been chained up for nearly seven years. He recognised the magician immediately, but the old man did not know him, he had grown so thin. However, he undid the chains by the help of magic, and took care of the prince until he recovered and became strong enough to travel. When he reached home he found that the old king had died that morning, so that he was now raised to the throne. And now after his long suffering came prosperity, which lasted to the end of his life; but he never got back the magic ring, nor has it ever again been seen by mortal eyes.

Now, if *you* had been the prince, would you not rather have stayed with the pretty witch-maiden?

The Dream of Owen O'Mulready

There was a man long ago living near Ballaghad-ereen named Owen O'Mulready, who was a work-man for the gentleman of the place, and was a prosperous, quiet, contented man. There was no one but himself and his wife Margaret, and they had a nice little house and enough potatoes in the year, in addition to their share of wages, from their master. There wasn't a want or anxiety on Owen, except one desire, and that was to have a dream – for he had never had one.

One day when he was digging potatoes, his master – James Taafe – came out to his ridge, and they began talking, as was the custom with them. The talk fell on dreams, and said Owen that he would like better than anything if he could only have one.

'You'll have one tonight,' says his master, 'if you do as I tell you.'

'Musha, I'll do it, and welcome,' says Owen.

'Now,' says his master, 'when you go home tonight, draw the fire from the hearth, put it out, make your bed in its place and sleep there tonight, and you'll have enough of dreaming before the morning.'

Owen promised to do this. When, however, he began to draw the fire out, Margaret thought that he had lost his senses, so he explained everything James Taafe had said to him, had his own way, and they went to lie down together on the hearth.

Not long was Owen asleep when there came a knock at the door.

'Get up, Owen O'Mulready, and go with a letter from the master to America.'

Owen got up, and put his feet into his boots, saying to himself, 'It's late you come, messenger.'

He took the letter, and he went forward and never tarried till he came to the foot of Sliabh Charn, where he met a cow-boy, and he herding cows.

'The blessing of God be with you, Owen O'Mulready,' says the boy.

'The blessing of God and Mary be with you, my boy,' says Owen. 'Everyone knows me, and I don't know anyone at all.'

'Where are you going this time of night?' says the boy.

'I'm going to America, with a letter from the master; is this the right road?' says Owen.

'It is; keep straight to the west; but how are you going to get over the water?' says the boy.

'Time enough to think of that when I get to it,' replied Owen.

He went on the road again, till he came to the brink of the sea; there he saw a crane standing on one foot on the shore.

'The blessing of God be with you, Owen O'Mulready,' says the crane.

'The blessing of God and Mary be with you, Mrs Crane,' says Owen. 'Everybody knows me, and I don't know anyone.'

'What are you doing here?'

Owen told her his business, and that he didn't know how he'd get over the water.

'Leave your two feet on my two wings, and sit on my back, and I'll take you to the other side,' says the crane.

'What would I do if tiredness should come on you before we got over?' says Owen.

'Don't be afraid, I won't be tired or wearied till I fly over.'

Then Owen went on the back of the crane, and she arose over the sea and went forward, but she hadn't flown more than halfway, when she cried out, 'Owen O'Mulready get off me; I'm tired.'

'That you may be seven times worse this day twelve months, you rogue of a crane,' says Owen. 'I can't get off you now, so don't ask me.'

'I don't care,' replied the crane, 'if you'll rise off me a while till I'll take a rest.'

With that they saw threshers over their heads, and Owen shouted, 'Och! Thresher, thresher, leave down your flail at me, that I may give the crane a rest!'

The thresher left down the flail, but when Owen took a hold with his two hands, the crane went from him laughing and mocking.

'My share of misfortunes go with you!' said Owen.

'It's you've left me in a fix hanging between the heavens and the water in the middle of the great sea.'

It wasn't long till the thresher shouted to him to leave go the flail.

'I won't let it go,' said Owen. 'Shan't I be drowned?'

'If you don't let it go, I'll cut the whang.'

'I don't care,' says Owen; 'I have the flail;' and with that he looked away from him, and what should he see but a boat a long way off.

'O sailor, dear sailor, come, come; perhaps you'll take my lot of bones,' said Owen.

'Are we under you now?' says the sailor.

'Not yet, not yet,' says Owen.

'Fling down one of your shoes, till we see the way it falls,' says the captain.

Owen shook one foot, and down fell the shoe.

'Uill, uill, puil, uil liu – who is killing me?' came a scream from Margaret in the bed. 'Where are you, Owen?'

'I didn't know whether 'twas you were in it, Margaret.'

'Indeed, then it is,' says she, 'who else would it be?'

She got up and lit the candle. She found Owen halfway up the chimney, climbing by the hands on the crook, and he black with soot! He had one shoe on, but the point of the other had struck Margaret, and 'twas that which awoke her.

Owen came down off the crook and washed himself, and from that day on there was no envy on him ever to have a dream again.

Earl Mar's Daughter

One fine summer's day Earl Mar's daughter went into the castle garden, dancing and tripping along. And as she played and sported she would stop from time to time to listen to the music of the birds. After a while as she sat under the shade of a green oak tree she looked up and spied a sprightly dove sitting high up on one of its branches. She looked up and said: 'Coo-my-dove, my dear, come down to me and I will give you a golden cage. I'll take you home and pet you well, as well as any bird of them all.' Scarcely had she said these words when the dove flew down from the branch and settled on her shoulder, nestling up against her neck while she smoothed its feathers. Then she took it home to her own room.

The day was done and the night came on and Earl Mar's daughter was thinking of going to sleep when, turning round, she found at her side a handsome young man. She was startled, for the door had been locked for hours. But she was a brave girl and said: 'What are you doing here, young man, to come and startle me so? The door was barred these hours ago; how ever did you come here?'

'Hush! hush!' the young man whispered. 'I was that cooing dove that you coaxed from off the tree.'

'But who are you then?' she said quite low; 'and how came you to be changed into that dear little bird?'

'My name is Florentine, and my mother is a queen, and something more than a queen, for she knows magic and spells, and because I would not do as she wished she turned me into a dove by day, but at night her spells lose their power and I become a man again. Today I crossed the sea and saw you for the first time and I was glad to be a bird that I could come near you. Unless you love me, I shall never be happy more.'

'But if I love you,' says she, 'will you not fly away and leave me one of these fine days?'

'Never, never,' said the prince; 'be my wife and

I'll be yours for ever. By day a bird, by night a prince, I will always be by your side as a husband, dear.'

So they were married in secret and lived happily in the castle and no one knew that every night Coo-my-dove became Prince Florentine. And every year a little son came to them as bonny as bonny could be. But as each son was born Prince Florentine carried the little thing away on his back over the sea to where the queen his mother lived and left the little one with her.

Seven years passed thus and then a great trouble came to them. For the Earl Mar wished to marry his daughter to a noble of high degree who came wooing her. Her father pressed her sore but she said: 'Father dear, I do not wish to marry; I can be quite happy with Coo-my-dove here.'

Then her father got into a mighty rage and swore a great big oath, and said: 'Tomorrow, so sure as I live and eat, I'll twist that birdie's neck,' and out he stamped from her room.

'Oh, oh!' said Coo-my-dove; 'it's time that I was away,' and so he jumped upon the window-sill and in a moment was flying away. And he flew and he flew till he was over the deep, deep sea, and yet on he flew till he came to his mother's castle. Now the queen his mother was taking her walk abroad when she saw the pretty dove flying overhead and alighting on the castle walls.

'Here, dancers come and dance your jigs,' she called, 'and pipers, pipe you well, for here's my own Florentine, come back to me to stay for he's brought no bonny boy with him this time.'

'No, mother,' said Florentine, 'no dancers for me and no minstrels, for my dear wife, the mother of my seven boys, is to be wed tomorrow, and sad's the day for me.'

'What can I do, my son?' said the queen, 'tell me, and it shall be done if my magic has power to do it.'

'Well then, mother dear, turn the twenty-four

dancers and pipers into twenty-four grey herons, and let my seven sons become seven white swans, and let me be a goshawk and their leader.'

'Alas! alas! my son,' she said, 'that may not be; my magic reaches not so far. But perhaps my teacher, the spaewife of Ostree, may know better.' And away she hurries to the cave of Ostree, and after a while comes out as white as white can be and muttering over some burning herbs she brought out of the cave. Suddenly Coo-my-dove changed into a goshawk and around him flew twenty-four grey herons and above them flew seven cygnets.

Without a word or a goodbye off they flew over the deep blue sea which was tossing and moaning. They flew and they flew till they swooped down on Earl Mar's castle just as the wedding party were setting out for the church. First came the men-at-arms and then the bridegroom's friends, and then Earl Mar's men, and then the bridegroom, and lastly, pale and beautiful, Earl Mar's daughter herself. They moved down slowly to stately music till they came past the trees on which the birds were settling. A word from Prince Florentine, the goshawk, and they all rose into the air, herons beneath, cygnets above, and goshawk circling above all. The weddineers wondered at the sight when, swoop! the herons were down among them scattering the men-at-arms. The swanlets took charge of the bride while the goshawk dashed down and tied the bridegroom to a tree. Then the herons gathered themselves together into one featherbed and the cygnets

placed their mother upon them, and suddenly they all rose in the air bearing the bride away with them in safety towards Prince Florentine's home. Surely a wedding party was never so disturbed in this world. What could the weddineers do? They saw their pretty bride carried away and away till she and the herons and the swans and the goshawk disappeared, and that very day Prince Florentine brought Earl Mar's daughter to the castle of the queen his mother, who took the spell off him and they lived happy ever afterwards.

East of the Sun and West of the Moon

Once upon a time there was a poor husbandman who had many children and little to give them in the way either of food or clothing. They were all pretty, but the prettiest of all was the youngest daughter, who was so beautiful that there were no bounds to her beauty.

So once – it was late on a Thursday evening in autumn, and wild weather outside, terribly dark, and raining so heavily and blowing so hard that the walls of the cottage shook again – they were all sitting together by the fireside, each of them busy with something or other, when suddenly someone rapped three times against the window-pane.

The man went out to see what could be the matter, and when he got out there stood a great big white bear.

'Good-evening to you,' said the White Bear.

'Good-evening,' said the man.

'Will you give me your youngest daughter?' said the White Bear; 'if you will, you shall be as rich as you are now poor.'

Truly the man would have had no objection to be rich, but he thought to himself: 'I must first ask my daughter about this,' so he went in and told them that there was a great white bear outside who had faithfully promised to make them all rich if he might but have the youngest daughter.

She said no, and would not hear of it; so the man went out again, and settled with the White Bear that he should come again next Thursday evening, and get her answer. Then the man persuaded her, and talked so much to her about the wealth that they would have, and what a good thing it would be for herself, that at last she made up her mind to go, and washed and mended all her rags, made herself as smart as she could, and held herself in

Next Thursday evening the White Bear came to fetch her

130

readiness to set out. Little enough had she to take away with her.

Next Thursday evening the White Bear came to fetch her. She seated herself on his back with her bundle, and thus they departed. When they had gone a great part of the way, the White Bear said: 'Are you afraid?'

'No, that I am not,' said she.

'Keep tight hold of my fur, and then there is no danger,' said he.

And thus she rode far, far away, until they came to a great mountain. Then the White Bear knocked on it, and a door opened, and they went into a castle where there were many brilliantly lighted rooms which shone with gold and silver, likewise a large hall in which there was a well-spread table, and it was so magnificent that it would be hard to make anyone understand how splendid it was. The White Bear gave her a silver bell, and told her that when she needed anything she had but to ring this bell, and what she wanted would appear. So after she had eaten, and night was drawing near, she grew sleepy after her journey, and thought she would like to go to bed. She rang the bell, and scarcely had she touched it before she found herself in a chamber where a bed stood ready made for her, which was as pretty as anyone could wish to sleep in. It had pillows of silk, and curtains of silk fringed with gold, and everything that was in the room was of gold or silver, but when she had lain down and put out the light, a man came and lay down beside her, and behold it was the White Bear, who cast off the form of a beast during the night. She never saw him, however, for he always came after she had put out her light, and went away before daylight appeared.

So all went well and happily for a time, but then she began to be very sad and sorrowful, for all day long she had to go about alone; and she did so wish to go home to her father and mother and brothers and sisters. Then the White Bear asked what it was that she wanted, and she told him that it was so dull there in the mountain, and that she had to go about all alone, and that in her parents' house at home there were all her brothers and sisters, and it was because she could not go to them that she was so sorrowful.

'There might be a cure for that,' said the White Bear, 'if you would but promise me never to talk with your mother alone, but only when the others are there too; for she will take hold of your hand,' he said, 'and will want to lead you into a room to talk with you alone; but that you must by no means do, or you will bring great misery on both of us.'

So one Sunday the White Bear came and said that they could now set out to see her father and mother, and they journeyed thither, she sitting on his back, and they went a long, long way, and it took a long, long time; but at last they came to a large white farmhouse, and her brothers and sisters were running about outside it, playing, and it was so pretty that it was a pleasure to look at it.

'Your parents dwell here now,' said the White Bear; 'but do not forget what I said to you, or you will do much harm both to yourself and me.'

'No, indeed,' said she, 'I shall never forget;' and as soon as she was at home the White Bear turned round and went back again.

There were such rejoicings when she went in to her parents that it seemed as if they would never come to an end. Everyone thought that they could never be sufficiently grateful to her for all she had done for them. Now they had everything that they wanted, and everything was as good as it could be. They all asked her how she was getting on where she was. All was well with her too, she said; and she had everything that she could want. What other answers she gave I cannot say, but I am pretty sure that they did not learn much from her. But in the afternoon, after they had dined at midday, all happened just as the White Bear had said. Her mother wanted to talk with her alone in her own chamber. But she remembered what the White Bear had said, and would on no account go. 'What we have to say can surely be said at any time,' she answered. But somehow or other her mother at last persuaded her, and she was forced to tell the whole story. So she told how every night a man came and lay down beside her when the lights were all put out, and how she never saw him, because he always went away before it grew light in the morning, and how she continually went about in sadness, thinking how happy she would be if she could but see him, and how all day long she had to go about alone, and it was so dull and solitary. 'Oh!' cried the mother, in horror, 'you are very likely sleeping with a troll! But I will teach you a way to see him. You shall have a bit of one of my candles, which you can take away with you hidden in your breast. Look at him with that when he is asleep, but take care not to let any tallow drop upon him.'

So she took the candle, and hid it in her breast, and when evening drew near the White Bear came to fetch her away. When they had gone some distance on their way, the White Bear asked her if everything had not happened just as he had foretold, and she could not but own that it had. 'Then, if you have done what your mother wished,' said he, 'you have brought great misery on both of us.' 'No,' she said, 'I have not done anything at all.' So when she had reached home and had gone to bed it was just the same as it had been before, and a man came and lay down beside her, and late at night, when she could hear that he was sleeping, she got up and kindled a light, lit her candle, let her light shine on him, and saw him, and he was the handsomest prince that eyes had ever beheld, and she loved him so much that it seemed to her that she must die if she did not kiss him that very moment. So she did kiss him; but while she was doing it she let three drops of hot tallow fall upon his shirt, and he awoke. 'What have you done now?' said he; 'you have brought misery on both of us. If you had but held out for the space of one year I should have been free. I have a stepmother who has bewitched me so that I am a white bear by day and a man by night; but now all is at an end between you and me, and I must leave you, and go to her. She lives in a castle which lies east of the sun and west of the moon, and there too is a princess

She got up and kindled a light, lit her candle, let her light shine on him, and saw him, and he was the handsomest prince that eyes had ever beheld

with a nose which is three ells long, and she now is the one whom I must marry.'

She wept and lamented, but all in vain, for go he must. Then she asked him if she could not go with him. But no, that could not be. 'Can you tell me the way then, and I will seek you – that I may surely be allowed to do!'

'Yes, you may do that,' said he; 'but there is no way thither. It lies east of the sun and west of the moon, and never would you find your way there.'

When she awoke in the morning both the prince and the castle were gone, and she was lying on a small green patch in the midst of a dark, thick wood. By her side lay the selfsame bundle of rags which she had brought with her from her own home. So when she had rubbed the sleep out of her eyes, and wept till she was weary, she set out on her way, and thus she walked for many and many a long day, until at last she came to a great mountain. Outside it an aged woman was sitting, playing with a golden apple. The girl asked her if she knew the way to the prince who lived with his stepmother in the castle which lay east of the sun and west of the moon, and who was to marry a princess with a nose which was three ells long. 'How do you happen to know about him?' enquired the old woman; 'maybe you are she who ought to have had him.' 'Yes, indeed, I am,' she said. 'So it is you, then?' said the old woman; 'I know nothing about him but that he dwells in a castle which is east of the sun and west of the moon. You will be a long time in getting to it, if ever you get to it at all; but you shall have the loan of my horse, and then you can ride on it to an old woman who is a neighbour of mine: perhaps she can tell you about him. When you have got there you must just strike the horse beneath the left ear and bid it go home again; but you may take the golden apple with you.'

So the girl seated herself on the horse, and rode for a long, long way, and at last she came to the mountain, where an aged woman was sitting outside with a gold carding-comb. The girl asked her if she knew the way to the castle which lay east of the sun and west of the moon; but she said what the first old woman had said: 'I know nothing about it, but that it is east of the sun and west of the moon, and that you will be a long time in getting to it, if ever you get there at all; but you shall have the loan of my horse to an old woman who lives the nearest to me: perhaps she may know where the castle is, and when you have got to her you may just strike the horse beneath the left ear and bid it go home again.' Then she gave her the gold carding-comb, for it might, perhaps, be of use to her, she said.

So the girl seated herself on the horse, and rode a wearisome long way onward again, and after a very long time she came to a great mountain, where an aged woman was sitting, spinning at a golden spinning-wheel. Of this woman, too, she enquired if she knew the way to the prince, and where to find the castle which lay east of the sun and west of the moon. But it was only the same thing once again. 'Maybe it was you who should have had the prince,' said the old woman. 'Yes, indeed, I should have been the one,' said the girl. But this old crone knew the way no better than the others – it was east of the sun and west of the moon, she knew that, 'and you will be a long time in getting to it, if ever you get to it at all,' she said; 'but you may have the loan of my horse, and I think you had better ride to the East Wind, and ask him: perhaps he may know where the castle is, and will blow you thither. But when you have got to him you must just strike the horse beneath the left ear, and he will come home again.' And then she gave her the golden spinning-wheel, saying: 'Perhaps you may find that you have a use for it.'

The girl had to ride for a great many days, and for a long and wearisome time, before she got there; but at last she did arrive, and then she asked the East Wind if he could tell her the way to the prince who dwelt east of the sun and west of the moon. 'Well,' said the East Wind, 'I have heard tell of the prince, and of his castle, but I do not know the way to it, for I have never blown so far; but, if you like, I will go with you to my brother the West Wind: he may know that, for he is much stronger than I am. You may sit on my back, and then I can carry you there.' So she seated herself on his back, and they did go so swiftly! When they got there, the East Wind went in and said that the girl whom he had brought was the one who ought to have had the prince up at the castle which lay east of the sun and west of the moon, and that now she was travelling about to find him again, so he had come there with her, and would like to hear if the West Wind knew whereabouts the castle was. 'No,' said the West Wind; 'so far as that have I never blown; but if you like I will go with you to the South Wind, for he is much stronger than either of us, and he has roamed far and wide, and perhaps he can tell you what you want to know. You may seat yourself on my back, and then I will carry you to him.'

So she did this, and journeyed to the South

Wind, neither was she very long on the way. When they had got there, the West Wind asked him if he could tell her the way to the castle that lay east of the sun and west of the moon, for she was the girl who ought to marry the Prince who lived there. 'Oh, indeed!' said the South Wind, 'is that she? Well,' said he, 'I have wandered about a great deal in my time, and in all kinds of places, but I have never blown so far as that. If you like, however, I will go with you to my brother, the North Wind; he is the oldest and strongest of all of us, and if he does not know where it is no one in the whole world will be able to tell you. You may sit upon my back, and then I will carry you there.' So she seated herself on his back, and off he went from his house in great haste, and they were not long on the way. When they came near the North Wind's dwelling, he was so wild and frantic that they felt cold gusts a long while before they got there. 'What do you want?' he roared out from afar, and they froze as they heard. Said the South Wind: 'It is I, and this is she who should have had the prince who lives in the castle which lies east of the sun and west of the moon. And now she wishes to ask you if you have ever been there, and can tell her the way, for she would gladly find him again.'

'Yes,' said the North Wind, 'I know where it is. I once blew an aspen leaf there, but I was so tired that for many days afterwards I was not able to blow at all. However, if you really are anxious to go there, and are not afraid to go with me, I will take you on my back, and try if I can blow you there.'

'Get there I must,' said she; 'and if there is any way of going I will; and I have no fear, no matter how fast you go.'

'Very well then,' said the North Wind; 'but you must sleep here tonight, for if we are ever to get there we must have the day before us.'

The North Wind woke her betimes next morning, and puffed himself up, and made himself so big and so strong that it was frightful to see him, and away they went, high up through the air, as if they would not stop until they had reached the very end of the world. Down below there was such a storm! It blew down woods and houses, and when they were above the sea the ships were wrecked by hundreds. And thus they tore on and on, and a long time went by, and then yet more time passed, and still they were above the sea, and the North Wind grew tired, and more tired, and at last so utterly weary that he was scarcely able to blow any longer, and he sank and sank, lower and

'Art thou afraid?' said the North Wind. 'I have no fear,' said she; and it was true.

lower, until at last he went so low that the waves dashed against the heels of the poor girl he was carrying. 'Art thou afraid?' said the North Wind. 'I have no fear,' said she; and it was true. But they were not very, very far from land, and there was just enough strength left in the North Wind to enable him to throw her on to the shore, immediately under the windows of a castle which lay east of the sun and west of the moon; but then he was so weary and worn out that he was forced to rest for several days before he could go to his own home again.

Next morning she sat down beneath the walls of the castle to play with the golden apple, and the first person she saw was the maiden with the long nose, who was to have the prince. 'How much do you want for that gold apple of yours, girl?' said she, opening the window. 'It can't be bought either for gold or money,' answered the girl. 'If it cannot be bought either for gold or money, what will buy it? You may say what you please,' said the princess.

'Well, if I may go to the prince who is here, and be with him tonight, you shall have it,' said the girl who had come with the North Wind. 'You may do that,' said the princess, for she had made up her mind what she would do. So the princess got the golden apple, but when the girl went up to the prince's apartment that night he was asleep, for the princess had so contrived it. The poor girl called to him, and shook him, and between whiles she wept; but she could not wake him. In the morning, as soon as day dawned, in came the princess with the long nose, and drove her out again. In the daytime

she sat down once more beneath the windows of the castle, and began to card with her golden carding-comb; and then all happened as it had happened before. The princess asked her what she wanted for it, and she replied that it was not for sale, either for gold or money, but that if she could get leave to go to the prince, and be with him during the night, she should have it. But when she went up to the prince's room he was again asleep, and let her call him or shake him or weep as she would, he still slept on, and she could not put any life in him. When daylight came in the morning, the princess with the long nose came too, and once more drove her away. When day had quite come, the girl seated herself under the castle windows to spin with her golden spinning-wheel, and the princess with the long nose wanted to have that also. So she opened the window, and asked what she would take for it. The girl said what she had said on each of the former occasions – that it was not for sale either for gold or for money, but if she could get leave to go to the prince who lived there, and be with him during the night, she should have it.

'Yes,' said the princess, 'I will gladly consent to that.'

But in that place there were some Christian folk who had been carried off, and they had been sitting in the chamber which was next to that of the prince, and had heard how a woman had been in there who had wept and called on him two nights running, and they told the prince of this. So that evening, when the princess came once more with her sleeping-drink, he pretended to drink, but threw it away behind him, for he suspected that it was a sleeping-drink. So, when the girl went into the prince's room this time he was awake, and she had to tell him how she had come there. 'You have come just in time,' said the prince, 'for I should have been married tomorrow; but I will not have the long-nosed princess, and you alone can save me. I will say that I want to see what my bride can do, and bid her wash the shirt which has the three drops of tallow on it. This she will consent to do, for she does not know that it is you who let them fall on it; but no one can wash them out but one born of Christian folk: it cannot be done by one of a pack of trolls; and then I will say that no one shall ever be my bride but the woman who can do this, and I know that you can.' There was great joy and gladness between them all that night, and the next day, when the wedding was to take place, the prince said, 'I must see what my bride can do.'

That you may do,' said the stepmother.

'I have a fine shirt which I want to wear as my wedding shirt, but three drops of tallow have got upon it which I want to have washed off, and I have vowed to marry no one but the woman who is able to do it. If she cannot do that, she is not worth having.'

Well, that was a very small matter, they thought, and agreed to do it. The princess with the long nose began to wash as well as she could, but the more she washed and rubbed, the larger the spots grew. 'Ah! you can't wash at all,' said the old troll-hag, who was her mother. 'Give it to me.' But she too had not had the shirt very long in her hands before it looked worse still, and the more she washed it and rubbed it, the larger and blacker grew the spots.

So the other trolls had to come and wash, but the more they did, the blacker and uglier grew the shirt, until at length it was as black as if it had been up the chimney. 'Oh,' cried the prince, 'not one of you is good for anything at all! There is a beggar girl sitting outside the window, and I'll be bound that she can wash better than any of you! Come in, you girl there!' he cried. So she came in. 'Can you wash this shirt clean?' he cried. 'Oh! I don't know,' she said; 'but I will try.' And no sooner had she taken the shirt and dipped it in the water than it was white as driven snow, and even whiter than that. 'I will marry you,' said the prince. Then the old troll-hag flew into such a rage that she burst, and the princess with the long nose and all the little trolls must have burst too, for they have never been heard of since. The prince and his bride set free all the Christian folk who were imprisoned there, and took away with them all the gold and silver that they could carry, and moved far away from the castle which lay east of the sun and west of the moon.

The Elves and the Shoemaker

There was once a shoemaker, who worked very hard and was very honest, but still he could not earn enough to live upon; and at last all he had in the world was gone, save just leather enough to make one pair of shoes.

Then he cut his leather out, all ready to make up the next day, meaning to rise early in the morning to his work. His conscience was clear and his heart light amidst all his troubles; so he went peaceably to bed, left all his cares to heaven, and soon fell asleep. In the morning after he had said his prayers, he sat himself down to his work, but to his great wonder, there stood the shoes, all ready made, upon the table. The good man knew not what to say or think at such an odd thing happening. He looked at the workmanship; there was not one false stitch in the whole job; all was so neat and true, that it was quite a masterpiece.

The same day a customer came in, and the shoes suited him so well that he willingly paid a price higher than usual for them; and the poor shoemaker, with the money, bought leather enough to make two pairs more. In the evening he cut out the work, and went to bed early, that he might get up and begin

betimes next day; but he was saved all the trouble, for when he got up in the morning the work was done ready to his hand. Soon in came buyers, who paid him handsomely for his goods, so that he bought leather enough for four pair more. He cut out the work again overnight and found it done in the morning, as before; and so it went on for some time: what was got ready in the evening was always done by daybreak; and the good man soon became thriving and well off again.

One evening, about Christmastime, as he and his wife were sitting over the fire chatting together, he said to her, 'I should like to sit up and watch tonight, that we may see who it is that comes and does my work for me.' The wife liked the thought; so they left a light burning, and hid themselves in a corner of the room, behind a curtain that was hung up there, and watched what would happen.

As soon as it was midnight, there came in two little naked dwarfs; and they sat themselves upon the shoemaker's bench, took up all the work that was cut out, and began to ply with their little fingers, stitching and rapping and tapping away at such a rate, that the shoemaker was all wonder, and could not take his eyes off them. And on they went, till the job was quite done, and the shoes stood ready for use upon the table. This was long before daybreak; and then they bustled away as quick as lightning.

The next day the wife said to the shoemaker. 'These little wights have made us rich, and we ought to be thankful to them, and do them a good turn if we can. I am quite sorry to see them run about as they do; and indeed it is not very decent, for they have nothing upon their backs to keep off the cold. I'll tell you what: I will make each of them a shirt, and a coat and waistcoat, and a pair of pantaloons into the bargain; and do you make each of them a little pair of shoes.'

The thought pleased the good cobbler very much; and one evening, when all the things were ready, they laid them on the table, instead of the work that they usually cut out, and then went and hid themselves, to watch what the little elves would do.

About midnight in they came, dancing and skipping, hopped round the room, and then went to sit down to their work as usual; but when they saw the clothes lying for them, they laughed and chuckled, and seemed mightily delighted.

Then they dressed themselves in the twinkling of an eye, and danced and capered and sprang about, as merry as could be; till at last they danced out at the door, and away over the green. The good couple saw them no more; but everything went well with them from that time forward, as long as they lived.

The Story of the Emperor's New Clothes

Many years ago there lived an Emperor who was so fond of new clothes that he spent all his money on them in order to be beautifully dressed. He did not care about his soldiers, he did not care about the theatre; he only liked to go out walking to show off his new clothes. He had a coat for every hour of the day; and just as they say of a king, 'He is in the council-chamber,' they always said here, 'The Emperor is in the wardrobe.'

In the great city in which he lived there was always something going on; every day many strangers came there. One day two impostors arrived who gave themselves out as weavers, and said that they knew how to manufacture the most beautiful cloth imaginable. Not only were the texture and pattern uncommonly beautiful, but the clothes which were made of the stuff possessed this wonderful property that they were invisible to anyone who was not fit for his office, or who was unpardonably stupid.

'Those must indeed be splendid clothes,' thought the Emperor. 'If I had them on I could find out which men in my kingdom are unfit for the offices they hold; I could distinguish the wise from the stupid! Yes, this cloth must be woven for me at once.' And he gave both the impostors much money, so that they might begin their work.

They placed two weaving-looms, and began to make as if they were working, but they had not the least thing on the looms. They also demanded the finest silk and the best gold, which they put in their pockets, and worked at the empty looms till late into the night.

'I should like very much to know how far they have got on with the cloth,' thought the Emperor. But he remembered when he thought about it that whoever was stupid or not fit for his office would not be able to see it. Now he certainly believed that he had nothing to fear for himself, but he wanted first to send somebody else in order to see how he stood with regard to his office. Everybody in the whole town knew what a wonderful power the cloth had, and they were all curious to see how bad or how stupid their neighbour was.

'I will send my old and honoured minister to the weavers,' thought the Emperor. 'He can judge best what the cloth is like, for he has intellect, and no one understands his office better than he.'

Now the good old minister went into the hall where the two impostors sat working at the empty weaving-looms. 'Dear me!' thought the wise old minister, opening his eyes wide, 'I can see nothing!' But he did not say so.

Both the impostors begged him to be so kind as to step closer, and asked him what he thought of the beautiful texture and lovely colours. They pointed to the empty loom, and the poor old minister went forward rubbing his eyes; but he could see nothing, for there was nothing there.

'Dear, dear!' thought he, 'can I be stupid? I have never thought so, and nobody must know it! Can I be not fit for my office? No, I must certainly not say that I cannot see the cloth!'

'Have you nothing to say about it?' asked one of the men who was weaving.

'Oh, it is lovely, most lovely!' answered the old minister, looking through his spectacles. 'What a texture! What colours! Yes, I will tell the Emperor that it pleases me very much.'

'Now we are delighted at that,' said both the weavers, and thereupon they named the colours and explained the intricacies of the texture.

The old minister paid great attention, so that he could tell the same to the Emperor when he came back to him, which he did. The impostors now wanted more money, more silk and more gold to use in their weaving. They put it all in their own pockets, and there came

*One day two impostors arrived who gave themselves out as weavers, and said that
they knew how to manufacture the most beautiful cloth imaginable*

'Is it not a beautiful piece of cloth?' asked the two impostors

no threads on the loom, but they went on as they had done before, working at the empty loom. The Emperor soon sent another worthy statesman to see how the weaving was getting on, and whether the cloth would soon be finished. It was the same with him as the first one; he looked and looked, but because there was nothing on the empty loom he could see nothing. 'Is it not a beautiful piece of cloth?' asked the two impostors, and they pointed to and described the splendid material which was not there. 'Stupid I am not!' thought the man, 'so it must be my good office for which I am not fitted. It is strange, certainly, but no one must be allowed to notice it.' And so he praised the cloth which he did not see, and expressed to them his delight at the beautiful colours and the splendid texture. 'Yes, it is quite beautiful,' he said to the Emperor.

Everybody in the town was talking of the magnificent cloth.

Now the Emperor wanted to see it himself while it was still on the loom. With a great crowd of select followers, amongst whom were both the worthy statesmen who had already been there before, he went to the cunning impostors, who were now weaving with all their might, but without fibre or thread.

'Is it not splendid!' said both the old statesmen who had already been there. 'See, your majesty, what a texture! What colours!' And then they pointed to the empty loom, for they believed that the others could see the cloth quite well.

'What!' thought the Emperor, 'I can see nothing! This is indeed horrible! Am I stupid? Am I not fit to be Emperor? That were the most dreadful thing that could happen to me. Oh, it is very beautiful,' he said. 'It has my gracious approval.' And then he nodded pleasantly, and examined the empty loom, for he would not say that he could see nothing.

His whole court round him looked and looked, and saw no more than the others; but they said like the Emperor, 'Oh! it is beautiful!' And they advised him to wear these new and magnificent clothes for the first time at the great procession which was soon to take place. 'Splendid! Lovely! Most beautiful!' went from mouth to mouth; everyone seemed delighted over them, and the Emperor gave to the impostors the title of Court Weavers to the Emperor.

Throughout the whole of the night before the morning on which the procession was to take place, the impostors were up and were working by the light of over sixteen candles. The people could see

So the Emperor went along in the procession under the splendid canopy

that they were very busy making the Emperor's new clothes ready. They pretended they were taking the cloth from the loom, cut with huge scissors in the air, sewed with needles without thread, and then said at last, 'Now the clothes are finished!'

The Emperor came himself with his most distinguished knights, and each impostor held up his arm just as if he were holding something, and said, 'See! here are the breeches! Here is the coat! Here the cloak!' and so on.

'Spun clothes are so comfortable that one would imagine one had nothing on at all; but that is the beauty of it!'

'Yes,' said all the knights, but they could see nothing, for there was nothing there.

'Will it please your majesty graciously to take off your clothes,' said the impostors, 'then we will put on the new clothes, here before the mirror.'

The Emperor took off all his clothes, and the impostors placed themselves before him as if they were putting on each new item of clothing, and the Emperor turned and bent himself in front of the mirror.

'How beautifully they fit! How well they sit!' said everybody. 'What material! What colours! It is a gorgeous suit!'

'They are waiting outside with the canopy which your majesty is wont to have borne over you in the procession,' announced the master of the ceremonies.

'Look, I am ready,' said the Emperor. 'Doesn't it sit well!' And he turned himself again to the mirror to see if his finery was on all right.

The chamberlains who were used to carry the train put their hands near the floor as if they were lifting up the train; then they made as if they were holding something in the air. They would not have it noticed that they could see nothing.

So the Emperor went along in the procession under the splendid canopy, and all the people in the streets and at the windows said, 'How matchless are the Emperor's new clothes! That train fastened to his dress, how beautifully it hangs!'

No one wished it to be noticed that he could see nothing, for then he would have been unfit for his office, or else very stupid. None of the Emperor's clothes had met with such approval as these had.

'But he has nothing on!' said a little child at last.

'Just listen to the innocent child!' said the father, and each one whispered to his neighbour what the child had said.

'But he has nothing on!' the whole of the people called out at last.

This struck the Emperor, for it seemed to him as if they were right; but he thought to himself, 'I must go on with the procession now. And the chamberlains walked along still more uprightly, holding up the train which was not there at all.

Esben and the Witch

There was once a man who had twelve sons: the eleven eldest were both big and strong, but the twelfth, whose name was Esben, was only a little fellow. The eleven eldest went out with their father to field and forest, but Esben preferred to stay at home with his mother, and so he was never reckoned at all by the rest, but was a sort of outcast among them.

When the eleven had grown up to be men they decided to go out into the world to try their fortune, and they plagued their father to give them what they required for the journey. The father was not much in favour of this, for he was now old and weak, and could not well spare them from helping him with his work, but in the long run he had to give in. Each one of the eleven got a fine white horse and money for the journey, and so they said farewell to their father and their home, and rode away.

As for Esben, no one had ever thought about him; his brothers had not even said farewell to him.

After the eleven were gone Esben went to his father and said, 'Father, give me also a horse and money; I should also like to see round about me in the world.'

'You are a little fool,' said his father. 'If I could have let you go, and kept your eleven brothers at home, it would have been better for me in my old age.'

ESBEN

'Well, you will soon be rid of me at any rate,' said Esben.

As he could get no other horse, he went into the forest, broke off a branch, stripped the bark off it, so that it became still whiter than his brothers' horses, and, mounted on this, rode off after his eleven brothers.

The brothers rode on the whole day, and towards evening they came to a great forest, which they entered. Far within the wood they came to a little house, and knocked at the door. There came an old, ugly, bearded hag, and opened it, and they asked her whether all of them could get quarters for the night.

'Yes,' said the old, bearded hag, 'you shall all have quarters for the night, and, in addition, each of you shall have one of my daughters.'

The eleven brothers thought that they had come to very hospitable people. They were well attended to, and when they went to bed, each of them got one of the hag's daughters.

Esben had been coming along behind them, and had followed the same way, and had also found the same house in the forest. He slipped into this, without either the witch or her daughters noticing him, and hid himself under one of the beds. A little

before midnight he crept quietly out and wakened his brothers. He told these to change nightcaps with the witch's daughters. The brothers saw no reason for this, but, to get rid of Esben's persistence, they made the exchange, and slept soundly again.

When midnight came Esben heard the old witch come creeping along. She had a broad-bladed axe in her hand, and went over all the eleven beds. It was so dark that she could not see a hand's breadth before her, but she felt her way, and hacked the heads off all the sleepers who had the men's nightcaps on – and these were her own daughters. As soon as she had gone her way Esben wakened his brothers, and they hastily took their horses and rode off from the witch's house, glad that they had escaped so well. They quite forgot to thank Esben for what he had done for them.

When they had ridden onwards for some time they reached a king's palace, and enquired there whether they could be taken into service. Quite easily, they were told, if they would be stable men, otherwise the king had no use for them. They were quite ready for this, and got the task of looking after all the king's horses.

Long after them came Esben riding on his stick, and he also wanted to get a place in the palace, but no one had any use for him, and he was told that he could just go back the way he had come. However, he stayed there and occupied himself as best he could. He got his food, but nothing more, and by night he lay just where he could.

At this time there was in the palace a knight who was called Sir Red. He was very well liked by the king, but hated by everyone else, for he was wicked both in will and deed. This Sir Red became angry with the eleven brothers, because they would not always stand at attention for him, so he determined to avenge himself on them.

One day, therefore, he went to the king, and said that the eleven brothers who had come to the palace a little while ago, and served as stable men, could do a great deal more than they pretended. One day he had heard them say that if they liked they could get for the king a wonderful dove which had a feather of gold and a feather of silver time about. But they would not procure it unless they were threatened with death.

The king then had the eleven brothers called before him, and said to them, 'You have said that you can get me a dove which has feathers of gold and silver time about.'

All the eleven assured him that they had never said anything of the kind, and they did not believe that such a dove existed in the whole world.

'Take your own mind of it,' said the king; 'but if you don't get that dove within three days you shall lose your heads, the whole lot of you.'

With that the king let them go, and there was great grief among them; some wept and others lamented.

At that moment Esben came along, and, seeing their sorrowful looks, said to them, 'Hallo, what's the matter with you?'

'What good would it do to tell you, you little fool? You can't help us.'

'Oh, you don't know that,' answered Esben. 'I have helped you before.'

In the end they told him how unreasonable the king was, and how he had ordered them to get for him a dove with feathers of gold and silver time about.

'Give me a bag of peas,' said Esben, 'and I shall see what I can do for you.'

Esben got his bag of peas; then he took his white stick, and said,

'Fly quick, my little stick,
　Carry me across the stream.'

Straightway the stick carried him across the river and straight into the old witch's courtyard. Esben had noticed that she had such a dove; so when he arrived in the courtyard he shook the peas out of the bag, and the dove came fluttering down to pick them up. Esben caught it at once, put it into the bag, and hurried off before the witch caught sight of him; but the next moment she came running, and shouted after him, 'Hey! is that you, Esben?'

'Ye–e–s!'

'Is it you that has taken my dove?'

'Ye–e–s!'

'Was it you that made me kill my eleven daughters?'

'Ye–e–s!'

'Are you coming back again?'

'That may be,' said Esben.

'Then you'll catch it,' shouted the witch.

The stick carried Esben with the dove back to the king's palace, and his brothers were greatly delighted. The king thanked them many times for the dove, and gave them in return both silver and gold. At this Sir Red became still more embittered, and again thought of how to avenge himself on the brothers.

One day he went to the king and told him that the dove was by no means the best thing that the brothers could get for him; for one day he had heard them talking quietly among themselves, and they had said that they could procure a boar whose bristles were of gold and silver time about.

The king again summoned the brothers before him, and asked whether it was true that they had said that they could get for him a boar whose bristles were of gold and silver time about.

'No,' said the brothers; they had never said nor thought such a thing, and they did not believe that there was such a boar in the whole world.

'You must get me that boar within three days,' said the king, 'or it will cost you your heads.'

With that they had to go. This was still worse than before, they thought. Where could they get such a marvellous boar? They all went about hanging their heads; but when only one day remained of the three Esben came along. When he saw his brothers' sorrowful looks he cried, 'Hallo, what's the matter now?'

'Oh, what's the use of telling you?' said his brothers. 'You can't help us, at any rate.'

'Ah, you don't know that,' said Esben; 'I've helped you before.'

In the end they told him how Sir Red had stirred up the king against them, so that he had ordered them to get for him a boar with bristles of gold and silver time about.

'That's all right,' said Esben; 'give me a sack of malt, and it is not quite impossible that I may be able to help you.'

Esben got his sack of malt; then he took his little white stick, set himself upon it, and said,

'Fly quick, my little stick,
　Carry me across the stream.'

Off went the stick with him, and very soon he was again in the witch's courtyard. There he emptied out the malt, and next moment came the boar, of whose bristles half were gold and half were silver. Esben at once put it into his sack and hurried off before the witch should catch sight of him; but the next moment she came running, and shouted after him, 'Hey! is that you, Esben?'

'Ye–e–s!'

'Is it you that has taken my pretty boar?'

'Ye–e–s!'

'It was also you that took my dove?'

'Ye–e–s!'

'And it was you that made me kill my eleven daughters?'

'Ye–e–s!'

'Are you coming back again?'

'That may be,' said Esben.

'Then you'll catch it,' said the witch.

Esben was soon back at the palace with the boar, and his brothers scarcely knew which leg to stand on, so rejoiced were they that they were safe again. Not one of them, however, ever thought of thanking Esben for what he had done for them.

The king was still more rejoiced over the boar than he had been over the dove, and did not know what to give the brothers for it. At this Sir Red was again possessed with anger and envy, and again he went about and planned how to get the brothers into trouble.

One day he went again to the king and said, 'These eleven brothers have now procured the dove and the boar, but they can do much more than that; I know they have said that if they liked they could get for the king a lamp that can shine over seven kingdoms.'

'If they have said that,' said the king, 'they shall also be made to bring it to me. That would be a glorious lamp for me.'

Again the king sent a message to the brothers to come up to the palace. They went accordingly, although very unwillingly, for they suspected that Sir Red had fallen on some new plan to bring them into trouble.

As soon as they came before the king he said to them, 'You brothers have said that you could, if you liked, get for me a lamp that can shine over seven kingdoms. That lamp must be mine within three days, or it will cost you your lives.'

The brothers assured him that they had never said so, and they were sure that no such lamp existed, but their words were of no avail.

'The lamp!' said the king, 'or it will cost you your heads.'

The brothers were now in greater despair than ever. They did not know what to do, for such a lamp no one had ever heard of. But just as things looked their worst along came Esben.

'Something wrong again?' said he. 'What's the matter with you now?'

'Oh, it's no use telling you,' said they. 'You can't help us, at any rate.'

'Oh, you might at least tell me,' said Esben; 'I have helped you before.'

In the end they told him that the king had ordered them to bring him a lamp which could shine over seven kingdoms, but such a lamp no one had ever heard tell of.

'Give me a bushel of salt,' said Esben, 'and we shall see how matters go.'

He got his bushel of salt, and then mounted his little white stick, and said,

'Fly quick, my little stick,
Carry me across the stream.'

With that both he and his bushel of salt were over beside the witch's courtyard. But now matters were less easy, for he could not get inside the yard, as it was evening and the gate was locked. Finally he hit upon a plan; he got up on the roof and crept down the chimney.

He searched all round for the lamp, but could find it nowhere, for the witch always had it safely guarded, as it was one of her most precious treasures. When he became tired of searching for it, he crept into the baking-oven, intending to lie down there and sleep till morning; but just at that moment he heard the witch calling from her bed to the twelfth of her daughters, and telling her to make some porridge for her. She had grown hungry, and had taken such a fancy to some porridge. The daughter got out of bed, kindled the fire and put on a pot with water in it.

'You mustn't put any salt in the porridge, though,' cried the witch.

'No, neither will I,' said the daughter; but while she was away getting the meal Esben slipped out of the oven and emptied the whole bushel of salt into the pot. The daughter came back then and put in the meal, and after it had boiled a little she took it in to her mother. The witch took a spoonful and tasted it.

'Uh!' said she; 'didn't I tell you not to put any salt in it, and it's just as salt as the sea.'

HOW ESBEN STOLE THE WITCH'S LAMP

So the daughter had to go and make new porridge, and her mother warned her strictly not to put any salt in it. But now there was no water in the house, so she asked her mother to give her the lamp, so that she could go to the well for more.

'There you have it, then,' said the witch; 'but take good care of it.'

The daughter took the lamp which shone over seven kingdoms, and went out to the well for water, while Esben slipped out after her. When she was going to draw the water from the well she set the lamp down on a stone beside her. Esben watched his chance, seized the lamp, and gave her a push from behind, so that she plumped head first into the well. Then he made off with the lamp. But the witch got out of her bed and ran after him, crying:

'Hey! is that you again, Esben?'

'Ye–e–s!'

'Was it you that took my dove?'

'Ye–e–s!'

'Was it also you that took my boar?'

'Ye–e–s!'

'And it was you that made me kill my eleven daughters?'

'Ye–e–s!'

'And now you have taken my lamp, and drowned my twelfth daughter in the well?'

'Ye–e–s!'

'Are you coming back again?'

'That may be,' said Esben.

'Then you'll catch it,' said the witch.

It was only a minute before the stick had again landed Esben at the king's palace, and the brothers were then freed from their distress. The king gave them many fine presents, but Esben did not get even so much as thanks from them.

Never had Sir Red been so eaten up with envy as he was now, and he racked his brain day and night to find something quite impossible to demand from the brothers.

One day he went to the king and told him that the lamp the brothers had procured was good enough, but they could still get for him something that was far better. The king asked what that was.

'It is,' said Sir Red, 'the most beautiful coverlet that any mortal ever heard tell of. It also has the property that, when anyone touches it, it sounds so that it can be heard over eight kingdoms.'

'That must be a splendid coverlet,' said the king, and he at once sent for the brothers.

'You have said that you know of a coverlet, the most beautiful in the whole world, which sounds over eight kingdoms when anyone touches it. You shall procure it for me, or else lose your lives,' said he.

The brothers answered him that they had never said a word about such a coverlet, did not believe it existed, and that it was quite impossible for them to procure it. But the king would not hear a word; he drove them away, telling them that if they did not get it very soon it would cost them their heads.

Things looked very black again for the brothers, for they were sure there was no escape for them. The youngest of them, indeed, asked where Esben was, but the others said that that little fool could scarcely keep himself in clothes, and it was not to be expected that he could help them. Not one of them thought it worth while to look for Esben, but he soon came along of himself.

'Well, what's the matter now?' said he.

'Oh, what's the use of telling you?' said the brothers. 'You can't help us, at any rate.'

'Ah! who knows that?' said Esben. 'I have helped you before.'

In the end the brothers told him about the coverlet which, when one touched it, sounded so that it could be heard over eight kingdoms. Esben thought that this was the worst errand that he had had yet, but he could not do worse than fail, and so he would make the attempt.

He again took his little white stick, set himself on it, and said,

'Fly quick, my little stick,
Carry me across the stream.'

Next moment he was across the river and beside the witch's house. It was evening, and the door was locked, but he knew the way down the chimney. When he had got into the house, however, the worst yet remained to do, for the coverlet was on the bed in which the witch lay and slept. He slipped into the room without either her or her daughter wakening; but as soon as he touched the coverlet to take it, it sounded so that it could be heard over eight kingdoms. The witch awoke, sprang out of bed, and caught hold of Esben. He struggled with her, but could not free himself, and the witch called to her thirteenth daughter, 'Come and help me; we shall put him into the little dark room to be fattened. Ho, ho! now I have him!'

Esben was now put into a little dark hole, where he neither saw sun nor moon, and there he was fed on sweet milk and nut-kernels. The daughter had enough to do cracking nuts for him, and at the end of fourteen days she had only one tooth left in her mouth; she had broken all the rest with the nuts. In this time, however, she had taken a liking to Esben, and would willingly have set him free, but could not.

When some time had passed the witch told her daughter to go and cut a finger off Esben, so that she could see whether he was nearly fat enough yet. The daughter went and told Esben, and asked him what she should do. Esben told her to take an iron nail and wrap a piece of skin round it: she could then give her mother this to bite at.

The daughter did so, but when the witch bit it she cried, 'Uh! no, no! This is nothing but skin and bone; he must be fattened much longer yet.'

So Esben was fed for a while longer on sweet milk and nut-kernels, until one day the witch thought that now he must surely be fat enough, and told her daughter again to go and cut a finger off him.

HOW THE WITCH CAUGHT ESBEN

By this time Esben was tired of staying in the dark hole, so he told her to go and cut a teat off a cow, and give it to the witch to bite at. This the daughter did, and the witch cried, 'Ah! now he is fat – so fat that one can scarcely feel the bone in him. Now he shall be killed.'

Now this was just the very time that the witch had to go to Troms Church, where all the witches gather once every year, so she had no time to deal with Esben herself. She therefore told her daughter to heat up the big oven while she was away, take Esben out of his prison, and roast him in there before she came back. The daughter promised all this, and the witch went off on her journey.

The daughter then made the oven as hot as could be, and took Esben out of his prison in order to roast him. She brought the oven spade, and told Esben to seat himself on it, so that she could shoot him into the oven. Esben accordingly took his seat on it, but when she had got him to the mouth of the oven he spread his legs out wide, so that she could not get him pushed in.

'You mustn't sit like that,' said she.

'How then?' said Esben.

'You must cross your legs,' said the daughter; but Esben could not understand what she meant by this.

'Get out of the way,' said she, 'and I will show you how to place yourself.'

She seated herself on the oven spade, but no sooner had she done so than Esben laid hold of it, shot her into the oven, and fastened the door of it.

Then he ran and seized the coverlet, but as soon as he did so it sounded so that it could be heard over eight kingdoms, and the witch, who was at Troms Church, came flying home, and shouted, 'Hey! is that you again, Esben?'

'Ye–e–s!'

'It was you that made me kill my eleven daughters?'

'Ye–e–s!'

'And took my dove?'

'Ye–e–s!'

'And my beautiful boar?'

'Ye–e–s!'

'And drowned my twelfth daughter in the well, and took my lamp?'

'Ye–e–s!'

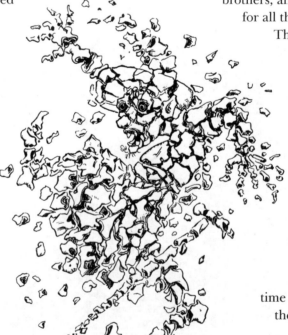

'And now you have roasted my thirteenth and last daughter in the oven, and taken my coverlet?'

'Ye–e–s!'

'Are you coming back again?'

'No, never again,' said Esben.

At this the witch became so furious that she sprang into numberless pieces of flint, and from this come all the flint stones that one finds about the country.

Esben had found again his little stick, which the witch had taken from him, so he said,

'Fly quick, my little stick,
Carry me across the stream.'

Next moment he was back at the king's palace. Here things were in a bad way, for the king had thrown all the eleven brothers into prison, and they were to be executed very shortly because they had not brought him the coverlet. Esben now went up to the king and gave him the coverlet, with which the king was greatly delighted. When he touched it it could be heard over eight kingdoms, and all the other kings sat and were angry because they had not one like it.

Esben also told how everything had happened, and how Sir Red had done the brothers all the ill he could devise because he was envious of them. The brothers were at once set at liberty, while Sir Red, for his wickedness, was hanged on the highest tree that could be found, and so he got the reward he deserved.

Much was made of Esben and his brothers, and these now thanked him for all that he had done for them. The twelve of them received as much gold and silver as they could carry, and betook themselves home to their old father. When he saw again his twelve sons, whom he had never expected to see more, he was so glad that he wept for joy. The brothers told him how much Esben had done, and how he had saved their lives, and from that time forward he was no longer the butt of the rest at home.

Fair, Brown and Trembling

King Hugh Curucha lived in Tir Conal, and he had three daughters, whose names were Fair, Brown and Trembling.

Fair and Brown had new dresses, and went to church every Sunday. Trembling was kept at home to do the cooking and work. They would not let her go out of the house at all; for she was more beautiful than the other two, and they were in dread she might marry before themselves.

They carried on in this way for seven years. At the end of seven years the son of the King of Emania fell in love with the eldest sister.

One Sunday morning, after the other two had gone to church, the old henwife came into the kitchen to Trembling, and said, 'It's at church you ought to be this day, instead of working here at home.'

'How could I go?' said Trembling. 'I have no clothes good enough to wear at church; and if my sisters were to see me there, they'd kill me for going out of the house.'

'I'll give you,' said the henwife, 'a finer dress than either of them has ever seen. And now tell me what dress will you have?'

'I'll have,' said Trembling, 'a dress as white as snow, and green shoes for my feet.'

Then the henwife put on the cloak of darkness, clipped a piece from the old clothes the young woman had on, and asked for the whitest robes in the world and the most beautiful that could be found, and a pair of green shoes.

That moment she had the robe and the shoes, and she brought them to Trembling, who put them on. When Trembling was dressed and ready, the henwife said, 'I have a honey-bird here to sit on your right shoulder, and a honey-finger to put on your left. At the door stands a milk-white mare, with a golden saddle for you to sit on, and a golden bridle to hold in your hand.'

Trembling sat on the golden saddle; and when she was ready to start, the henwife said, 'You must not go inside the door of the church, and the minute the people rise up at the end of Mass, do you make off, and ride home as fast as the mare will carry you.'

When Trembling came to the door of the church there was no one inside who could get a glimpse of her but was striving to know who she was; and when they saw her hurrying away at the end of Mass, they ran out to overtake her. But no use in their running; she was away before any man could come near her. From the minute she left the church till she got home, she overtook the wind before her, and outstripped the wind behind.

She came down at the door, went in, and found the henwife had dinner ready. She put off the white robes, and had on her old dress in a twinkling.

When the two sisters came home the henwife asked, 'Have you any news today from the church?'

'We have great news,' said they. 'We saw a wonderful grand lady at the church-door. The like of the robes she had we have never seen on woman before. It's little that was thought of our dresses beside what she had on; and there wasn't a man at the church, from the king to the beggar, but was trying to look at her and know who she was.'

The sisters would give no peace till they had two dresses like the robes of the strange lady; but honey-birds and honey-fingers were not to be found.

Next Sunday the two sisters went to church again, and left the youngest at home to cook the dinner.

After they had gone, the henwife came in and asked, 'Will you go to church today?'

'I would go,' said Trembling, 'if I could get the going.'

'What robe will you wear?' asked the henwife.

'The finest black satin that can be found, and red shoes for my feet.'

'What colour do you want the mare to be?'

'I want her to be so black and so glossy that I can see myself in her body.'

The henwife put on the cloak of darkness, and asked for the robes and the mare. That moment she had them. When Trembling was dressed, the henwife put the honey-bird on her right shoulder and the honey-finger on her left. The saddle on the mare was silver, and so was the bridle.

When Trembling sat in the saddle and was going away, the henwife ordered her strictly not to go inside the door of the church, but to rush away as soon as the people rose at the end of Mass, and hurry home on the mare before any man could stop her.

That Sunday the people were more astonished than ever, and gazed at her more than the first time; and all they were thinking of was to know who she was. But they had no chance; for the moment the people rose at the end of Mass she slipped from the church, was in the silver saddle, and home before a man could stop her or talk to her.

The henwife had the dinner ready. Trembling took off her satin robe, and had on her old clothes before her sisters got home.

'What news have you today?' asked the henwife of the sisters when they came from the church.

'Oh, we saw the grand strange lady again! And it's little that any man could think of our dresses after looking at the robes of satin that she had on! And all at church, from high to low, had their mouths open, gazing at her, and no man was looking at us.'

The two sisters gave neither rest nor peace till they got dresses as nearly like the strange lady's robes as they could find. Of course they were not so good; for the like of those robes could not be found in Erin.

When the third Sunday came, Fair and Brown went to church dressed in black satin. They left Trembling at home to work in the kitchen, and told her to be sure and have dinner ready when they came back.

After they had gone and were out of sight, the henwife came to the kitchen and said, 'Well, my dear, are you for church today?'

'I would go if I had a new dress to wear.'

'I'll get you any dress you ask for. What dress would you like?' asked the henwife.

'A dress red as a rose from the waist down, and white as snow from the waist up; a cape of green on my shoulders; and a hat on my head with a red, a white and a green feather in it; and shoes for my feet with the toes red, the middle white, and the backs and heels green.'

The henwife put on the cloak of darkness, wished for all these things, and had them. When Trembling was dressed, the henwife put the honey-bird on her right shoulder and the honey-finger on her left, and, placing the hat on her head, clipped a few hairs from one lock and a few from another with her scissors, and that moment the most beautiful golden hair was flowing down over the girl's shoulders. Then the henwife asked what kind of a mare she would ride. She said white, with blue and gold-coloured diamond-shaped spots all over her body, on her back a saddle of gold, and on her head a golden bridle.

The mare stood there before the door, and a bird sitting between her ears, which began to sing as soon as Trembling was in the saddle, and never stopped till she came home from the church.

The fame of the beautiful strange lady had gone out through the world, and all the princes and great men that were in it came to church that Sunday, each one hoping that it was himself would have her home with him after Mass.

The son of the King of Emania forgot all about the eldest sister, and remained outside the church, so as to catch the strange lady before she could hurry away.

The church was more crowded than ever before, and there were three times as many outside. There was such a throng before the church that Trembling could only come inside the gate.

As soon as the people were rising at the end of Mass, the lady slipped out through the gate, was in the golden saddle in an instant, and sweeping away ahead of the wind. But if she was, the Prince of Emania was at her side, and, seizing her by the foot, he ran with the mare for thirty perches, and never let go of the beautiful lady till the shoe was pulled from her foot, and he was left behind with it in his hand. She came home as fast as the mare could carry her, and was thinking all the time that the henwife would kill her for losing the shoe.

Seeing her so vexed and so changed in the face, the old woman asked, 'What's the trouble that's on you now?'

'Oh! I've lost one of the shoes off my feet,' said Trembling.

'Don't mind that; don't be vexed,' said the hen-wife. 'Maybe it's the best thing that ever happened to you.'

Then Trembling gave up all the things she had to the henwife, put on her old clothes, and went to work in the kitchen. When the sisters came home, the henwife asked, 'Have you any news from the church?'

'We have indeed,' said they, 'for we saw the grandest sight today. The strange lady came again, in grander array than before. On herself and the horse she rode were the finest colours of the world, and between the ears of the horse was a bird which never stopped singing from the time she came till she went away. The lady herself is the most beautiful woman ever seen by man in Erin.'

After Trembling had disappeared from the church, the son of the King of Emania said to the other kings' sons, 'I will have that lady for my own.'

They all said, 'You didn't win her just by taking the shoe off her foot; you'll have to win her by the point of the sword; you'll have to fight for her with us before you can call her your own.'

'Well,' said the son of the King of Emania, 'when I find the lady that shoe will fit, I'll fight for her, never fear, before I leave her to any of you.'

Then all the kings' sons were uneasy, and anxious to know who was she that lost the shoe; and they began to travel all over Erin to know could they find her. The Prince of Emania and all the others went in a great company together, and made the round of Erin; they went everywhere – north, south, east and west. They visited every place where a woman was to be found, and left not a house in the kingdom they did not search, to know could they find the woman the shoe would fit, not caring whether she was rich or poor, of high or low degree.

The Prince of Emania always kept the shoe; and when the young women saw it, they had great hopes, for it was of proper size, neither large nor small, and it would beat any man to know of what material it was made. One thought it would fit her if she cut a little from her great toe; and another, with too short a foot, put something in the tip of her stocking. But no use; they only spoiled their feet, and were curing them for months afterwards.

The two sisters, Fair and Brown, heard that the princes of the world were looking all over Erin for the woman that could wear the shoe, and every day they were talking of trying it on; and one day Trembling spoke up and said, 'Maybe it's my foot that the shoe will fit.'

'Oh, the breaking of the dog's foot on you! Why say so when you were at home every Sunday?'

They were that way waiting, and scolding the younger sister, till the princes were near the place. The day they were to come, the sisters put Trembling in a closet, and locked the door on her. When the company came to the house, the Prince of Emania gave the shoe to the sisters. But though they tried and tried, it would fit neither of them.

'Is there any other young woman in the house?' asked the prince.

'There is,' said Trembling, speaking up in the closet; 'I'm here.'

'Oh! We have her for nothing but to put out the ashes,' said the sisters.

But the prince and the others wouldn't leave the house till they had seen her; so the two sisters had to open the door. When Trembling came out, the shoe was given to her, and it fitted exactly.

The Prince of Emania looked at her and said, 'You are the woman the shoe fits, and you are the woman I took the shoe from.'

Then Trembling spoke up, and said, 'Do you stay here till I return.'

Then she went to the henwife's house. The old woman put on the cloak of darkness, got every-thing for her she had the first Sunday at church, and put her on the white mare in the same fashion. Then Trembling rode along the highway to the front of the house. All who saw her the first time said, 'This is the lady we saw at church.'

Then she went away a second time, and a second time came back on the black mare in the second dress which the henwife gave her. All who saw her the second Sunday said, 'That is the lady we saw at church.'

A third time she asked for a short absence, and soon came back on the third mare and in the third dress. All who saw her the third time said, 'That is the lady we saw at church.' Every man was satisfied, and knew that she was the woman.

Then all the princes and great men spoke up, and said to the son of the King of Emania, 'You'll have to fight now for her before we let her go with you.'

'I'm here before you, ready for combat,' answered the prince.

Then the son of the King of Lochlin stepped forth. The struggle began, and a terrible struggle it was. They fought for nine hours; and then the son of the King of Lochlin stopped, gave up his claim, and left the field. Next day the son of the King of Spain fought six hours, and yielded his claim. On the third day the son of the King of Nyerfói fought eight hours, and stopped. The fourth day the son of the King of Greece fought six hours, and stopped. On the fifth day no more strange princes wanted to fight; and all the sons of Kings in Erin said they would not fight with a man of their own land, that the strangers had had their chance, and, as no others came to claim the woman, she belonged of right to the son of the King of Emania.

The marriage-day was fixed, and the invitations were sent out. The wedding lasted for a year and a day. When the wedding was over, the king's son brought home the bride, and when the time came a son was born. The young woman sent for her elder sister, Fair, to be with her and care for her. One day, when Trembling was well, and when her husband was away hunting, the two sisters went out to walk; and when they came to the seaside, the eldest pushed the younger sister in. A great whale came and swallowed her.

The elder sister came home alone, and the husband asked, 'Where is your sister?'

'She has gone home to her father in Bally-shannon; now that I am well, I don't need her.'

'Well,' said the husband, looking at her, 'I'm in dread it's my wife that has gone.'

'Oh, no!' said she. 'It's my sister Fair that's gone.'

Since the sisters were very much alike, the prince was in doubt. That night he put his sword between them, and said, 'If you are my wife, this sword will get warm; if not, it will stay cold.'

In the morning when he rose up, the sword was as cold as when he put it there.

It happened, when the two sisters were walking by the seashore, that a little cowherd was down by the water minding cattle, and saw Fair push Trembling into the sea; and next day, when the tide came in, he saw the whale swim up and throw her out on the sand. When she was on the sand she said to the cowherd, 'When you go home in the evening with the cows, tell the master that my sister Fair pushed me into the sea yesterday; that a whale swallowed me, and then threw me out, but will come again and swallow me with the coming of the next tide; then he'll go out with the tide,

When the tide came in, the little cowherd saw the whale swim up and throw her out on the sand

and come again with tomorrow's tide, and throw me again on the strand. The whale will cast me out three times. I'm under the enchantment of this whale, and cannot leave the beach or escape myself. Unless my husband saves me before I'm swallowed the fourth time, I shall be lost. He must come and shoot the whale with a silver bullet when he turns on the broad of his back. Under the breast-fin of the whale is a reddish-brown spot. My husband must hit him in that spot, for it is the only place in which he can be killed.'

When the cowherd got home, the elder sister gave him a draught of oblivion, and he did not tell.

Next day he went again to the sea. The whale came and cast Trembling on shore again. She asked the boy, 'Did you tell the master what I told you to tell him?'

'I did not,' said he; 'I forgot.'

'How did you forget?' asked she.

'The woman of the house gave me a drink that made me forget.'

'Well, don't forget telling him this night; and if she gives you a drink, don't take it from her.'

As soon as the cowherd came home, the elder sister offered him a drink. He refused to take it till he had delivered his message and told all to the master. The third day the prince went down with his gun and a silver bullet in it. He was not long down when the whale came and threw Trembling upon the beach as the two days before. She had no power to speak to her husband till he had killed the whale. Then the whale went out, turned over once on the broad of his back, and showed the spot for a moment only. That moment the prince fired. He had but the one chance, and a short one at that; but he took it, and hit the spot, and the whale, mad with pain, made the sea all around red with blood, and died.

That minute Trembling was able to speak, and went home with her husband, who sent word to her father what his eldest daughter had done. The father came, and told him any death he chose to give her to give it. The prince told the father he would leave her life and death with himself. The father had her put out then on the sea in a barrel, with provisions in it for seven years.

In time Trembling had a second child, a daughter. The prince and she sent the cowherd to school, and trained him up as one of their own children, and said, 'If the little girl that is born to us now lives, no other man in the world will get her but him.'

The cowherd and the prince's daughter lived on till they were married. The mother said to her husband, 'You could not have saved me from the whale but for the little cowherd; on that account I don't grudge him my daughter.'

The son of the King of Emania and Trembling had fourteen children, and they lived happily till they both died of old age.

The Fairy

Once upon a time there was a widow who had two daughters. The elder was so much like her, both in looks and character, that whoever saw the daughter saw the mother. They were both so disagreeable and so proud that there was no living with them. The younger, who was the very picture of her father for sweetness of temper and virtue, was withal one of the most beautiful girls ever seen. As people naturally love their own likeness, this mother doted on her elder daughter, and at the same time had a great aversion for the younger. She made her eat in the kitchen and work continually.

Among other things, this unfortunate child had to go twice a day to draw water more than a mile and a half from the house, and bring home a pitcherful of it. One day, as she was at this fountain, there came to her a poor woman, who begged of her to let her drink.

One day, as she was at this fountain, there came to her a poor woman, who begged of her to let her drink

'Oh, yes, with all my heart, goody,' said this pretty little girl. Rinsing the pitcher at once, she took some of the clearest water from the fountain, and gave it to her, holding up the pitcher all the while, that she might drink the easier.

The good woman having drunk, said to her: 'You are so pretty, so good and courteous, that I cannot help giving you a gift.' For this was a fairy, who had taken the form of a poor country-woman, to see how far the civility and good manners of this pretty girl would go. 'I will give you for gift,' continued the fairy, 'that, at every word you speak, there shall come out of your mouth either a flower or a jewel.'

When this pretty girl returned, her mother scolded at her for staying so long at the fountain.

'I beg your pardon, mamma,' said the poor girl, 'for not making more haste.'

And in speaking these words there came out of her mouth two roses, two pearls and two large diamonds.

'What is it I see there?' said her mother, quite astonished. 'I think pearls and diamonds come out of the girl's mouth! How happens this, my child?'

This was the first time she had ever called her 'my child'.

The girl told her frankly all the matter, not without dropping out great numbers of diamonds.

'Truly,' cried the mother, 'I must send my own dear child thither. Fanny, look at what comes out of your sister's mouth when she speaks. Would you not be glad, my dear, to have the same gift? You have only to go and draw water out of the fountain, and when a poor woman asks you to let her drink, to give it to her very civilly.'

'I should like to see myself going to the fountain to draw water,' said this ill-bred minx.

'I insist you shall go,' said the mother, 'and that instantly.'

She went, but grumbled all the way, taking with her the best silver tankard in the house.

She no sooner reached the fountain than she saw coming out of the wood a magnificently dressed lady, who came up to her and asked to drink. This was the same fairy who had appeared to her sister, but she had now taken the disguise of a princess, to see how far this girl's rudeness would go.

'Am I come hither,' said the proud, ill-bred girl, 'to serve you with water, pray? I suppose this silver tankard was brought purely for your ladyship, was it? However, you may drink out of it, if you have a fancy.'

'You are scarcely polite,' answered the fairy, without anger. 'Well, then, since you are so disobliging, I give you for gift that at every word you speak there shall come out of your mouth a snake or a toad.'

So soon as her mother saw her coming, she cried out: 'Well, daughter?'

'Well, mother?' answered the unhappy girl, throwing out of her mouth a viper and a toad.

'Oh, mercy!' cried the mother, 'what is it I see? It is her sister who has caused all this, but she shall pay for it,' and immediately she ran to beat her. The poor child fled away from her, and went to hide herself in the forest nearby.

The king's son, who was returning from the chase, met her, and seeing her so beautiful, asked her what she did there alone and why she cried.

'Alas! sir, my mother has turned me out of doors.'

The king's son, who saw five or six pearls and as many diamonds come out of her mouth, desired her to tell him how that happened. She told him the whole story. The king's son fell in love with her, and, considering that such a gift was worth more than any marriage portion another bride could bring, conducted her to the palace of the king, his father, and there married her.

As for her sister, she made herself so much hated that her own mother turned her out of doors. The miserable girl, after wandering about and finding no one to take her in, went to a corner of the wood, and there died.

Fairy Ointment

Dame Goody was a nurse that looked after sick people, and minded babies. One night she was woken up at midnight, and when she went downstairs, she saw a strange squinny-eyed, little ugly old fellow, who asked her to come to his wife who was too ill to mind her baby. Dame Goody didn't like the look of the old fellow, but business is business; so she popped on her things, and went down to him. And when she got down to him, he whisked her up on to a large coal-black horse with fiery eyes, that stood at the door; and soon they were going at a rare pace, Dame Goody holding on to the old fellow like grim death.

They rode, and they rode, till at last they stopped before a cottage door. So they got down and went in and found the good woman abed with the children playing about; and the babe, a fine bouncing boy, beside her.

Dame Goody took the babe, which was as fine a baby boy as you'd wish to see. The mother, when she handed the baby to Dame Goody to mind, gave her a box of ointment, and told her to stroke the baby's eyes with it as soon as it opened them. After a while it began to open its eyes. Dame Goody saw that it had squinny eyes just like its father. So she took the box of ointment and stroked its two eyelids with it. But she couldn't help wondering what it was for, as she had never seen such a thing

Dame Goody saw that it had squinny eyes just like its father

done before. So she looked to see if the others were looking, and when they were not noticing she stroked her own right eyelid with the ointment.

No sooner had she done so than everything seemed changed about her. The cottage became elegantly furnished. The mother in the bed was a beautiful lady, dressed up in white silk. The little baby was still more beautiful than before, and its clothes were made of a sort of silvery gauze. Its little brothers and sisters around the bed were flat-nosed imps with pointed ears, who made faces at one another, and scratched their polls. Sometimes they would pull the sick lady's ears with their long and hairy paws. In fact, they were up to all kinds of mischief; and Dame Goody knew that she had got into a house of pixies. But she said nothing to nobody, and as soon as the lady was well enough to mind the baby, she asked the old fellow to take her back home. So he came round to the door with the coal-black horse with eyes of fire, and off they went as fast as before, or perhaps a little faster, till they came to Dame Goody's cottage, where the squinny-eyed old fellow lifted her down and left her, thanking her civilly enough, and paying her more than she had ever been paid before for such service.

Now next day happened to be market-day, and as Dame Goody had been away from home, she wanted many things in the house, and trudged off to get them at the market. As she was buying the things she wanted, who should she see but the squinny-eyed old fellow who had taken her on the coal-black horse. And what do you think he was doing? Why he went about from stall to stall taking up things from each, here some fruit, and there some eggs, and so on; and no one seemed to take any notice.

Now Dame Goody did not think it her business to interfere, but she thought she ought not to let so good a customer pass without speaking. So she ups to him and bobs a curtsey and said: 'Gooden, sir, I hopes as how your good lady and the little one are as well as – '

But she couldn't finish what she was a-saying, for the funny old fellow started back in surprise, and he says to her, says he: 'What! do you see me today?'

'See you,' says she, 'why, of course I do, as plain as the sun in the skies, and what's more,' says she, 'I see you are busy too, into the bargain.'

'Ah, you see too much,' said he; 'now, pray, with which eye do you see all this?'

'With the right eye to be sure,' said she, as proud as can be to find him out.

'The ointment! The ointment!' cried the old pixie thief. 'Take that for meddling with what don't concern you: you shall see me no more.' And with that he struck her on her right eye, and she couldn't see him any more; and, what was worse, she was blind on the right side from that hour till the day of her death.

The Fate of the Children of Lir

It happened that the five kings of Ireland met to determine who should have the head kingship over them, and King Lir of the Hill of the White Field expected surely he would be elected. When the nobles went into council together they chose for head king Dearg, son of Daghda, because his father had been so great a druid and he was the eldest of his father's sons. But Lir left the assembly of the kings and went home to the Hill of the White Field. The other kings would have followed after Lir to give him wounds of spear and wounds of sword for not yielding obedience to the man to whom they had given the overlordship. But Dearg the king would not hear of it and said, 'Rather let us bind him to us by the bonds of kinship, so that peace may dwell in the land. Send over to him for wife the choice of the three maidens of the fairest form and best repute in Erin, the three daughters of Oilell of Aran, my own three bosom-nurslings.'

So the messengers brought word to Lir that Dearg the king would give him a foster-child of his foster-children. Lir thought well of it, and set out next day with fifty chariots from the Hill of the White Field. And he came to the Lake of the Red Eye near Killaloe. And when Lir saw the three daughters of Oilell, Dearg the king said to him, 'Take thy choice of the maidens, Lir.'

'I know not,' said Lir, 'which is the choicest of them all; but the eldest of them is the noblest, it is she I had best take.'

'If so,' said Dearg the king, 'Ove is the eldest, and she shall be given to thee, if thou willest.'

So Lir and Ove were married and went back to the Hill of the White Field.

And after this there came to them twins, a son and a daughter, and they gave them for names Fingula and Aod. And two more sons came to them, Fiachra and Conn. When they came Ove died, and Lir mourned bitterly for her, and but for his great love for his children he would have died of his grief. And Dearg the king grieved for Lir and sent to him and said, 'We grieve for Ove for thy sake; but, that our friendship may not be rent asunder, I will give unto thee her sister, Oifa, for a wife.' So Lir agreed, and they were united, and he took her with him to his own house. And at first Oifa felt affection and honour for the children of Lir and her sister, and indeed everyone who saw the four children could not help giving them the love of his soul. Lir doted upon the children, and they always slept in beds in front of their father, who used to rise at early dawn every morning and lie down among his children. But thereupon the dart of jealousy passed into Oifa on account of this and she came to regard the children with hatred and enmity.

One day her chariot was yoked for her and she took with her the four children of Lir in it. Fingula was not willing to go with her on the journey, for she had dreamed a dream in the night warning her against Oifa: but she was not to avoid her fate. And when the chariot came to the Lake of the Oaks, Oifa said to the people, 'Kill the four children of Lir and I will give you your own reward of every kind in the world.' But they refused and told her it was an evil thought she had. Then she would have raised a sword herself to kill and destroy the children, but her own womanhood and her weakness prevented her; so she sent the children of Lir into the lake to bathe, and they did as Oifa told them. As soon as they were upon the lake she struck them with a druid's wand of spells and wizardry and put them into the forms of four beautiful, perfectly white swans, and she sang this song over them:

'Out with you upon the wild waves,
        children of the king!
Henceforth your cries shall be with
        the flocks of birds.'

And Fingula answered:

Oifa sent the children of Lir into the lake to bathe

'Thou witch! We know thee by thy right name!
Thou mayest drive us from wave to wave,
But sometimes we shall rest on the headlands;
We shall receive relief, but thou punishment.
Though our bodies may be upon the lake,
Our minds at least shall fly homewards.'

And again she spoke, 'Assign an end for the ruin and woe which thou hast brought upon us.'

Oifa laughed and said, 'Never shall ye be free until the woman from the south be united to the man from the north, until Lairgnen of Connaught wed Deoch of Munster; nor shall any have power to bring you out of these forms. Nine hundred years shall you wander over the lakes and streams of Erin. This only I will grant unto you: that you retain your own speech, and there shall be no music in the world equal to yours, the plaintive music you shall sing.' This she said because repentance seized her for the evil she had done.

And then she spake this lay:

'Away from me, ye children of Lir,
Henceforth the sport of the wild winds
Until Lairgnen and Deoch come together,
Until ye are on the north-west of Red Erin.

'A sword of treachery is through the heart of Lir,
Of Lir the mighty champion,
Yet though I have driven a sword
My victory cuts me to the heart.'

Then she turned her steeds and went on to the hall of Dearg the king. The nobles of the court asked her where were the children of Lir, and Oifa said, 'Lir will not trust them to Dearg the king.' But Dearg thought in his own mind that the woman had played some treachery upon them, and he accordingly sent messengers to the Hill of the White Field.

Lir asked the messengers, 'Wherefore are ye come?'

'To fetch thy children, Lir,' said they.

'Have they not reached you with Oifa?' said Lir.

'They have not,' said the messengers; 'and Oifa said it was you would not let the children go with her.'

Then was Lir melancholy and sad at heart, hearing these things, for he knew that Oifa had done wrong upon his children, and he set out towards the Lake of the Red Eye. And when the children of Lir saw him coming Fingula sang the lay:

> 'Welcome the cavalcade of steeds
> Approaching the Lake of the Red Eye,
> A company dread and magical
> Surely seek after us.

> 'Let us move to the shore, O Aod,
> Fiachra and comely Conn,
> No host under heaven can those horsemen be
> But King Lir with his mighty household.'

Now as she said this King Lir had come to the shores of the lake and heard the swans speaking with human voices. And he spoke to the swans and asked them who they were. Fingula answered and said, 'We are thy own children, ruined by thy wife, sister of our own mother, through her ill mind and her jealousy.' 'For how long is the spell to be upon you?' said Lir. 'None can relieve us till the woman from the south and the man from the north come together, till Lairgnen of Connaught wed Deoch of Munster.'

Then Lir and his people raised their shouts of grief, crying and lamentation, and they stayed by the shore of the lake listening to the wild music of the swans until the swans flew away, and King Lir went on to the hall of Dearg the king. He told Dearg the king what Oifa had done to his children. And Dearg put his power upon Oifa and bade her say what shape on earth she would think the worst of all. She said it would be in the form of an air-demon. 'It is into that form I shall put you,' said Dearg the king, and he struck her with a druid's wand of spells and wizardry and put her into the form of an air-demon. And she flew away at once, and she is still an air-demon, and shall be so for ever.

But the children of Lir continued to delight the Milesian clans with the very sweet fairy music of their songs, so that no delight was ever heard in Erin to compare with their music until the time came appointed for the leaving the Lake of the Red Eye.

As soon as they were upon the lake she struck them with a druid's wand of spells and wizardry and put them into the forms of four beautiful, perfectly white swans

Then Fingula sang this parting lay:

'Farewell to thee, Dearg the king,
Master of all druid's lore!
Farewell to thee, our father dear,
Lir of the Hill of the White Field!

'We go to pass the appointed time
Away and apart from the haunts of men
In the current of the Moyle.
Our garb shall be bitter and briny,

'Until Deoch come to Lairgnen.
So come, ye brothers of once ruddy cheeks;
Let us depart from this Lake of the Red Eye,
Let us separate in sorrow from the tribe that
has loved us.'

And then they took to flight, flying highly, lightly, aerially, till they reached the Moyle, between Erin and Albain.

The men of Erin were grieved at their leaving, and it was proclaimed throughout Erin that henceforth no swan should be killed. Then they stayed all solitary, all alone, filled with cold and grief and regret, until a thick tempest came upon them and Fingula said, 'Brothers, let us appoint a place to meet again if the power of the winds separate us.' And they said, 'Let us appoint to meet, O sister, at the Rock of the Seals.' Then the waves rose up and the thunder roared, the lightning flashed, the sweeping tempest passed over the sea, so that the children of Lir were scattered from each other over the great sea. There came, however, a placid calm after the great tempest and Fingula found herself alone, and she said this lay:

'Woe upon me that I am alive!
My wings are frozen to my sides.
O beloved three, O beloved three,
Who hid under the shelter of my feathers,
Until the dead come back to the living
I and the three shall never meet again!'

And she flew to the Lake of the Seals and soon saw Conn coming towards her with heavy step and drenched feathers, and Fiachra also, cold and wet and faint, and no word could they tell, so cold and faint were they: but she nestled them under her wings and said, 'If Aod could come to us now our happiness would be complete.' And soon they saw Aod coming towards them with dry head and preened feathers. Fingula put him under the feathers of her breast, and Fiachra under her right wing, and Conn under her left, and they made this lay:

'Bad was our stepmother with us,
She played her magic on us,
Sending us north on the sea
In the shapes of magical swans.

'Our bath upon the shore's ridge
Is the foam of the brine-crested tide,
Our share of the ale feast
Is the brine of the blue-crested sea.'

One day they saw a splendid cavalcade of pure white steeds coming towards them, and when they came near they were the two sons of Dearg the king who had been seeking for them to give them news of Dearg the king and Lir their father. 'They are well,' they said, 'and live together happy in all except that ye are not with them, and for not knowing where ye have gone since the day ye left the Lake of the Red Eye.'

'Happy are not we,' said Fingula, and she sang this song:

'Happy this night the household of Lir,
Abundant their meat and their wine.
But the children of Lir – what is their lot?
For bedclothes we have our feathers,
And as for our food and our wine –
The white sand and the bitter brine.
Fiachra's bed and Conn's place are
Under the cover of my wings on the Moyle,
Aod has the shelter of my breast,
And so side by side we rest.'

So the sons of Dearg the king came to the hall of Lir and told the king the condition of his children.

Then the time came for the children of Lir to fulfil their lot, and they flew in the current of the Moyle to the Bay of Erris, and remained there till the time of their fate, and then they flew to the Hill of the White Field and found all desolate and empty, with nothing but unroofed green raths and forests of nettles – no house, no fire, no dwelling-place. The four came close together, and they raised three shouts of lamentation aloud, and Fingula sang this lay:

'Uchone! It is bitterness to my heart
To see my father's place forlorn –
No hounds, no packs of dogs,
No women, and no valiant kings.

'No drinking-horns, no cups of wood,
No drinking in its lightsome halls.
Uchone! I see by the state of this house
That its lord our father lives no more.

'Much have we suffered in our wandering years,
By winds buffeted, by cold frozen;
Now has come the greatest of our pain –
There lives no man who knoweth us in
    the house where we were born.'

So the children of Lir flew away to the Glory Isle of Brandan the saint, and they settled upon the Lake of the Birds until the holy Patrick came to Erin and the holy Mac Howg came to Glory Isle.

And the first night he came to the island the children of Lir heard the voice of his bell ringing for matins, so that they started and leaped about in terror at hearing it; and her brothers left Fingula alone. 'What is it, beloved brothers?' said she. 'We know not what faint, fearful voice it is we have heard.' Then Fingula recited this lay:

'Listen to the cleric's bell,
Poise your wings and raise
Thanks to God for his coming,
Be grateful that you hear him.

'He shall free you from pain,
And bring you from the rocks and stones.
Ye comely children of Lir,
Listen to the bell of the cleric.'

And Mac Howg came down to the brink of the shore and said to them, 'Are ye the children of Lir?'

'We are indeed,' said they.

'Thanks be to God!' said the saint. 'It is for your sakes I have come to this isle beyond every other island in Erin. Come ye to land now and put your trust in me.'

So they came to land, and he made for them chains of bright white silver, and put a chain between Aod and Fingula and a chain between Conn and Fiachra.

It happened at this time that Lairgnen was Prince of Connaught and he was to wed Deoch the daughter of the King of Munster. She had heard the account of the birds and she became filled with love and affection for them, and she said she would not wed till she had the wondrous birds of Glory Isle. Lairgnen sent for them to the saint Mac Howg. But the saint would not give them, and both Lairgnen and Deoch went to Glory Isle. And Lairgnen went to seize the birds from the altar, but as soon as he had laid hands on them their feathery coats fell off, and the three sons of Lir became three withered bony old men, and Fingula, a lean withered old woman without blood or flesh. Lairgnen started at this and left the place hastily, but Fingula chanted this lay:

'Come and baptise us, O cleric,
Clear away our stains!
This day I see our grave –
Fiachra and Conn on each side,
And in my lap, between my two arms,
Place Aod, my beauteous brother.'

After this lay, the children of Lir were baptised. And they died, and were buried as Fingula had said, Fiachra and Conn on either side, and Aod before her face. A cairn was raised for them, and on it their names were written in runes. And that is the fate of the children of Lir.

The Field of Boliauns

One fine day in harvest – it was indeed Ladyday in harvest, that everybody knows to be one of the great holidays in the year – Tom Fitzpatrick was taking a ramble through the fields, and went along the sunny side of a hedge; when all of a sudden he heard a clacking sort of noise a little before him in the hedge. 'Dear me,' said Tom, 'but isn't it surprising to hear the stonechatters singing so late in the season?' So Tom stole on, going on the tops of his toes to try if he could get a sight of what was making the noise, to see if he was right in his guess. The noise stopped; but as Tom looked sharply through the bushes, what should he see in a nook of the hedge but a brown pitcher, that

What should he see in a nook of the hedge but a brown pitcher

might hold about a gallon and a half of liquor; and by and by a little wee teeny tiny bit of an old man, with a little *motty* of a cocked hat stuck upon the top of his head and a deeshy-daushy leather apron hanging before him, pulled out a little wooden stool, and stood up upon it, and dipped a little piggin into the pitcher, and took out the full of it, and put it beside the stool, and then sat down under the pitcher, and began to work at putting a heel-piece on a bit of a brogue just fit for himself.

'Well, by the powers,' said Tom to himself, 'I often heard tell of the leprechauns, and, to tell God's truth, I never rightly believed in them – but here's one of them in real earnest. If I go knowingly to work, I'm a made man. They say a body must never take their eyes off them, or they'll escape.'

Tom now stole on a little farther, with his eye fixed on the little man just as a cat does with a mouse. So when he got up quite close to him, 'God bless your work, neighbour,' said Tom.

The little man raised up his head and, 'Thank you kindly,' said he.

'I wonder you'd be working on the holiday!' said Tom.

'That's my own business, not yours,' was the reply.

'Well, maybe you'd be civil enough to tell us what you've got in the pitcher there?' said Tom.

'That I will, with pleasure,' said he; 'it's good beer.'

'Beer!' said Tom. 'Thunder and fire! Where did you get it?'

'Where did I get it, is it? Why, I made it. And what do you think I made it of?'

'Devil a one of me knows,' said Tom; 'but of malt, I suppose, what else?'

'There you're out. I made it of heath.'

'Of heath!' said Tom, bursting out laughing. 'Sure you don't think me to be such a fool as to believe that?'

'Do as you please,' said he, 'but what I tell you is the truth. Did you never hear tell of the Danes.'

'Well, what about *them*?' said Tom.

'Why, all the about them there is, is that when they were here they taught us to make beer out of the heath, and the secret's in my family ever since.'

'Will you give a body a taste of your beer?' said Tom.

'I'll tell you what it is, young man, it would be fitter for you to be looking after your father's property than to be bothering decent quiet people with your foolish questions. There now, while you're idling away your time here, there's the cows have broke into the oats, and are knocking the corn all about.'

Tom was taken so by surprise with this that he was just on the very point of turning round when he recollected himself; so, afraid that the like might happen again, he made a grab at the leprechaun, and caught him up in his hand; but in his hurry he overset the pitcher, and spilt all the beer, so that he could not get a taste of it to tell what sort it was. He then swore that he would kill him if he did not show him where his money was. Tom looked so wicked and so bloody-minded that the little man was quite frightened; so says he, 'Come along with me a couple of fields off; and I'll show you a crock of gold.'

So they went, and Tom held the leprechaun fast in his hand, and never took his eyes from off him, though they had to cross hedges and ditches, and a crooked bit of bog, till at last they came to a great field all full of boliauns, and the leprechaun pointed to a big boliaun, and says he, 'Dig under that boliaun, and you'll get the great crock all full of guineas.'

Tom in his hurry had never thought of bringing a spade with him, so he made up his mind to run home and fetch one; and that he might know the place again he took off one of his red garters, and tied it round the boliaun.

Then he said to the leprechaun, 'Swear ye'll not take that garter away from that boliaun.' And the leprechaun swore right away not to touch it.

'I suppose,' said the leprechaun, very civilly, 'you have no further occasion for me?'

'No,' says Tom; 'you may go away now, if you please, and God speed you, and may good luck attend you wherever you go.'

'Well, goodbye to you, Tom Fitzpatrick,' said the leprechaun; 'and much good may it do you when you get it.'

So Tom ran for dear life, till he came home and got a spade, and then away with him, as hard as he could go, back to the field of boliauns; but when he got there, lo and behold! Not a boliaun in the field but had a red garter, the very model of his own, tied about it; and as to digging up the whole field, that was all nonsense, for there were more than forty good Irish acres in it. So Tom came home again with his spade on his shoulder, a little cooler than he went, and many's the hearty curse he gave the leprechaun every time he thought of the neat turn he had served him.

The Fish and the Ring

Once upon a time, there was a mighty baron in the North Country who was a great magician that knew everything that would come to pass. So one day, when his little boy was four years old, he looked into the *Book of Fate* to see what would happen to him. And to his dismay, he found that his son would wed a lowly maid that had just been born in a house under the shadow of York Minster. Now the baron knew the father of the little girl was very, very poor, and he had five children already. So he called for his horse, and rode into York; and passed by the father's house, and saw him sitting by the door, sad and doleful. So he dismounted and went up to him and said: 'What is the matter, my good man?'

And the man said: 'Well, your honour, the fact is, I've five children already, and now a sixth's come, a little lass, and where to get the bread from to fill their mouths, that's more than I can say.'

'Don't be downhearted, my man,' said the baron. 'If that's your trouble, I can help you. I'll take away the last little one, and you won't have to bother about her.'

'Thank you kindly, sir,' said the man; and he went in and brought out the lass and gave her to the baron, who mounted his horse and rode away with her. And when he got by the bank of the River Ouse, he threw the little thing into the river, and rode off to his castle.

But the little lass didn't sink; her clothes kept her up for a time, and she floated, and she floated, till she was cast ashore just in front of a fisherman's hut. There the fisherman found her, and took pity on the poor little thing, and took her into his house, and she lived there till she was fifteen years old, and a fine handsome girl.

One day it happened that the baron went out hunting with some companions along the banks of the River Ouse, and stopped at the fisherman's hut to get a drink, and the girl came out to give it to them. They all noticed her beauty, and one of them said to the baron: 'You can read fates, baron, whom will she marry, d'ye think?'

'Oh! that's easy to guess,' said the baron; 'some yokel or other. But I'll cast her horoscope. Come here girl, and tell me on what day you were born?'

'I don't know, sir,' said the girl. 'I was picked up just here after having been brought down by the river about fifteen years ago.'

Then the baron knew who she was, and when they went away, he rode back and said to the girl: 'Hark ye, girl, I will make your fortune. Take this letter to my brother in Scarborough, and you will be settled for life.' And the girl took the letter and said she would go. Now this was what he had written in the letter:

Dear Brother – Take the bearer and put her to death immediately.
  Yours affectionately,
    Albert

So soon after the girl set out for Scarborough, and slept for the night at a little inn. Now that very night a band of robbers broke into the inn, and searched the girl, who had no money, and only the letter. So they opened this and read it, and thought it a shame. The captain of the robbers took a pen and paper and wrote this letter:

Dear Brother – Take the bearer and marry her to my son immediately.
  Yours affectionately,
    Albert

And then he gave it to the girl, bidding her begone. So she went on to the baron's brother at Scarborough, a noble knight, with whom the baron's son was staying. When she gave the letter to his brother, he gave orders for the wedding to be prepared at once, and they were married that very day.

Soon after, the baron himself came to his brother's castle, and what was his surprise to find that the very thing he had plotted against had

The captain of the robbers took a pen and paper and wrote a letter

come to pass. But he was not to be put off that way; and he took the girl out for a walk, as he said, along the cliffs. And when he got her all alone, he took her by the arms, and was going to throw her over. But she begged hard for her life. 'I have not done anything,' she said; 'if you will only spare me, I will do whatever you wish. I will never see you or your son again till you desire it.' Then the baron took off his gold ring and threw it into the sea, saying: 'Never let me see your face till you can show me that ring;' and he let her go.

The poor girl wandered on and on, till at last she came to a great noble's castle, and she asked to have some work given to her; and they made her the scullion girl of the castle, for she had been used to such work in the fisherman's hut.

Now one day, who should she see coming up to the noble's house but the baron and his brother and his son, her husband. She didn't know what to do; but thought they would not see her in the castle kitchen. So she went back to her work with a sigh, and set to cleaning a huge big fish that was to be boiled for their dinner. And, as she was cleaning it, she saw something shine inside it, and what do you think she found? Why, there was the baron's ring, the very one he had thrown over the cliff at Scarborough. She was right glad to see it, you may be sure. Then she cooked the fish as nicely as she could, and served it up.

Well, when the fish came on the table, the guests liked it so well that they asked the noble who cooked it. He said he didn't know, but called to his servants: 'Ho, there, send up the cook that cooked that fine fish.' So they went down to the kitchen and told the girl she was wanted in the hall. Then she washed and tidied herself and put the baron's gold ring on her thumb and went up into the hall.

When the banqueters saw such a young and beautiful cook they were surprised. But the baron was in a tower of a temper, and started up as if he would do her some violence. So the girl went up to him with her hand before her with the ring on it; and she put it down before him on the table. Then at last the baron saw that no one could fight against fate, and he handed her to a seat and announced to all the company that this was his son's true wife; and he took her and his son home to his castle; and they all lived as happy as could be ever afterwards.

The Fisherman and His Wife

There was once a fisherman who lived with his wife in a pigsty, close by the seaside. The fisherman used to go out fishing all day long, and one day, as he sat on the shore with his rod, looking at the sparkling waves and watching his line, all of a sudden his float was dragged away deep into the water, and in drawing it up he pulled out a great fish. But the fish said, 'Pray let me live! I am not a real fish; I am an enchanted prince. Put me in the water again, and let me go!'

'Oh, ho!' said the man, 'you need not make so many words about the matter; I will have nothing to do with a fish that can talk; so swim away, sir, as soon as you please!' Then he put him back into the water, and the fish darted straight down to the bottom, and left a long streak of blood behind him on the wave.

When the fisherman went home to his wife in the pigsty, he told her how he had caught a great fish, and how it had told him it was an enchanted prince, and how, on hearing it speak, he had let it go again. 'Did you not ask it for anything?' said the wife. 'We live very wretchedly here, in this nasty dirty pigsty; do go back and tell the fish we want a snug little cottage.'

The fisherman did not much like the business:

'We live very wretchedly here, in this nasty dirty pigsty;
do go back and tell the fish we want a snug little cottage.'

however, he went back to the seashore; and when he got there the water looked all yellow and green. And he stood at the water's edge, and said:

> 'O man of the sea!
> Hearken to me!
> My wife Ilsabill
> Will have her own will,
> And hath sent me to beg a boon of thee!'

Then the fish came swimming to him, and said, 'Well, what is her will? What does your wife want?'

'Ah!' said the fisherman, 'she says that when I had caught you, I ought to have asked you for something before I let you go; she does not like living any longer in the pigsty, and wants a snug little cottage.'

'Go home, then,' said the fish; 'she is in the cottage already!' So the man went home, and saw his wife standing at the door of a nice trim little cottage. 'Come in, come in!' said she. 'Is not this much better than the filthy pigsty we had?' And there was a parlour, and a bedchamber, and a kitchen; and behind the cottage there was a little garden, planted with all sorts of flowers and fruits; and there was a courtyard behind, full of ducks and chickens.

'Ah!' said the fisherman, 'how happily we shall live now!'

'We will try to do so, at least,' said his wife.

Everything went right for a week or two, and then Dame Ilsabill said, 'Husband, there is not nearly room enough for us in this cottage; the courtyard and the garden are a great deal too small; I should like to have a large stone castle to live in. Go to the fish again and tell him to give us a castle.'

'Wife,' said the fisherman, 'I don't like to go to him again, for perhaps he will be angry; we ought to be content with this pretty cottage to live in.'

'Nonsense!' said the wife; 'he will do it very willingly, I know; go along and try!'

The fisherman went, but his heart was very heavy: and when he came to the sea, it looked blue and gloomy, though it was very calm; and he went close to the edge of the waves, and said:

> 'O man of the sea!
> Hearken to me!
> My wife Ilsabill
> Will have her own will,
> And hath sent me to beg a boon of thee!'

'Well, what does she want now?' said the fish.

'Ah!' said the man, dolefully, 'my wife wants to live in a stone castle.'

'Go home, then,' said the fish; 'she is standing at the gate of it already.'

So away went the fisherman, and found his wife standing before the gate of a great castle. 'See,' said she, 'is not this grand?'

With that they went into the castle together, and found a great many servants there, and the rooms all richly furnished, and full of golden chairs and tables; and behind the castle was a garden, and around it was a park half a mile long, full of sheep, and goats, and hares, and deer; and in the courtyard were stables and cow-houses.

'Well,' said the man, 'now we will live cheerful and happy in this beautiful castle for the rest of our lives.'

'Perhaps we may,' said the wife; 'but let us sleep upon it, before we make up our minds to that.' So they went to bed.

The next morning when Dame Ilsabill awoke it was broad daylight, and she jogged the fisherman with her elbow, and said, 'Get up, husband, and bestir yourself, for we must be king of all the land.'

'Wife, wife,' said the man, 'why should we wish to be the king? I will not be king.'

'Then I will,' said she.

'But, wife,' said the fisherman, 'how can you be king – the fish cannot make you a king!'

'Husband,' said she, 'say no more about it, but go and try! I will be king.'

So the man went away quite sorrowful to think that his wife should want to be king. This time the sea looked a dark grey colour, and was overspread with curling waves with ridges of foam as he cried out:

> 'O man of the sea!
> Hearken to me!
> My wife Ilsabill
> Will have her own will,
> And hath sent me to beg a boon of thee!'

'Well, what would she have now?' said the fish.

'Alas!' said the poor man, 'my wife wants to be king.'

'Go home,' said the fish; 'she is king already.'

Then the fisherman went home; and as he came close to the palace he saw a troop of soldiers, and heard the sound of drums and trumpets. And when he went in he saw his wife sitting on a throne of gold and diamonds, with a golden crown upon her head; and on each side of her stood six fair maidens, each a head taller than the other. 'Well, wife,' said the fisherman, 'are you king?'

'Yes,' said she, 'I am king.'

And when he had looked at her for a long time, he said, 'Ah, wife! What a fine thing it is to be king! Now we shall never have anything more to wish for as long as we live.'

'I don't know how that may be,' said she; 'never is a long time. I am king, it is true; but I begin to be tired of that, and I think I should like to be emperor.'

'Alas, wife! Why should you wish to be emperor?' said the fisherman.

'Husband,' said she, 'go to the fish! I say I will be emperor.'

'Ah, wife!' replied the fisherman, 'the fish cannot make an emperor, I am sure, and I should not like to ask him for such a thing.'

'I am king,' said Ilsabill, 'and you are my slave; so go at once!'

So the fisherman was forced to go; and he muttered as he went along, 'This will come to no good, it is too much to ask; the fish will be tired at last, and then we shall be sorry for what we have done.'

He soon came to the seashore; and the water was quite black and muddy, and a mighty whirlwind blew over the waves and rolled them about, but he went as near as he could to the water's brink, and said:

> 'O man of the sea!
> Hearken to me!
> My wife Ilsabill
> Will have her own will,
> And hath sent me to beg a boon of thee!'

'What would she have now?' said the fish.

'Ah!' said the fisherman, 'she wants to be emperor.'

'Go home,' said the fish; 'she is emperor already.'

So he went home again; and as he came near he saw his wife Ilsabill sitting on a very lofty throne made of solid gold, with a great crown on her head full two yards high; and on each side of her stood her guards and attendants in a row, each one smaller than the other, from the tallest giant down to a little dwarf no bigger than my finger. And before her stood princes, and dukes, and earls; and the fisherman went up to her and said, 'Wife, are you emperor?'

'Yes,' said she, 'I am emperor.'

'Ah!' said the man, as he gazed upon her, 'what a fine thing it is to be emperor!'

'Husband,' said she, 'why should we stop at being emperor? I will be pope next.'

'O wife, wife!' said he, 'how can you be pope? There is but one pope at a time in Christendom.'

'Husband,' said she, 'I will be pope this very day.'

'But,' replied the husband, 'the fish cannot make you pope.'

'What nonsense!' said she; 'if he can make an emperor, he can make a pope. Go and try him.'

So the fisherman went. But when he came to the shore the wind was raging and the sea was tossed up and down in boiling waves, and the ships were in trouble, and rolled fearfully upon the tops of the billows. In the middle of the heavens there was a little piece of blue sky, but towards the south all was red, as if a fierce storm was rising. At this sight the fisherman was dreadfully frightened, and he trembled so that his knees knocked together, but still he went down near to the shore, and said:

> 'O man of the sea!
> Hearken to me!
> My wife Ilsabill
> Will have her own will,
> And hath sent me to beg a boon of thee!'

'What does she want now?' said the fish.

'Ah!' said the fisherman, 'my wife wants to be pope.'

'Go home,' said the fish; 'she is pope already.'

Then the fisherman went home, and found Ilsabill sitting on a throne that was two miles high. And she had three great crowns on her head, and around her stood all the pomp and power of the Church. And on each side of her were two rows of burning lights, of all sizes, the greatest as large as the highest and biggest tower in the world, and the least no larger than a small rush-light.

'Wife,' said the fisherman, as he looked at all this greatness, 'are you pope?'

'Yes,' said she, 'I am pope.'

'Well, wife,' replied he, 'it is a grand thing to be pope; and now you must be content, for you can be nothing greater.'

'I will think about that,' said the wife. Then they went to bed, but Dame Ilsabill could not sleep all night for thinking what she should be next. At last, just as she was falling asleep, morning broke and the sun rose. 'Ha!' thought she, as she woke up and looked at it through the window, 'after all I cannot prevent the sun rising.'

At this thought she was very angry, and wakened her husband, and said, 'Husband, go to the fish and tell him I must be lord of the sun and moon.'

The fisherman was half asleep, but the thought

frightened him so much that he started and fell out of bed. 'Alas, wife!' said he, 'can you not be content with being pope?'

'No,' said she, 'I am very uneasy as long as the sun and moon rise without my leave. Go to the fish at once!'

Then the man went shivering with fear; and as he was going down to the shore a dreadful storm arose, so that the trees and the very rocks shook. And all the heavens became black with stormy clouds, and the lightning played and the thunder rolled; and you might have seen in the sea great black waves, swelling up like mountains with crowns of white foam upon their heads. And the fisherman crept towards the sea, and cried out, as well as he could:

> 'O man of the sea!
> Hearken to me!
> My wife Ilsabill
> Will have her own will,
> And hath sent me to beg a boon of thee!'

'What does she want now?' said the fish.

'Ah!' said he, 'she wants to be lord of the sun and moon.'

'Go home,' said the fish, 'to your pigsty again.'

And there they live to this very day.

Then the man went shivering with fear; and as he was going down to the shore a dreadful storm arose

The Frog Prince

One fine evening, a young princess put on her bonnet and clogs, and went out to take a walk by herself in a wood; and when she came to a cool spring of water, that rose in the midst of it, she sat herself down to rest a while. Now she had a golden ball in her hand, which was her favourite plaything; and she was always tossing it up into the air, and catching it again as it fell. After a time she threw it up so high that she missed catching it as it fell, and the ball bounded away, and rolled along upon the ground, till at last it fell down into the spring. The princess looked into the spring after her ball, but it was very deep, so deep that she could not see the bottom of it. Then she began to bewail her loss, and said, 'Alas! if I could only get my ball again, I would give all my fine clothes and jewels, and everything that I have in the world.'

While she was speaking, a frog put his head out of the water, and said, 'Princess, why do you weep so bitterly?'

'Alas!' said she, 'what can you do for me, you nasty frog? My golden ball has fallen into the spring.'

The frog said, 'I want not your pearls, and jewels, and fine clothes; but if you will love me, and let me live with you and eat from off your golden plate and sleep upon your bed, I will bring you your ball again.'

'What nonsense,' thought the princess, 'this silly frog is talking! He can never even get out of the spring to visit me, though he may be able to get my ball for me, and therefore I will tell him he shall have what he asks.' So she said to the frog, 'Well, if you will bring me my ball, I will do all you ask.'

Then the frog put his head down, and dived deep under the water; and after a little while he came up again, with the ball in his mouth, and threw it on to the edge of the spring. As soon as the young princess saw her ball, she ran to pick it up; and she was so overjoyed to have it in her hand again, that she never thought of the frog, but ran home with it

as fast as she could. The frog called after her, 'Stay, princess, and take me with you as you said,' but she did not stop to hear a word.

The next day, just as the princess had sat down to dinner, she heard a strange noise – tap, tap – plash, plash – as if something was coming up the marble staircase, and soon afterwards there was a gentle knock at the door, and a little voice cried out and said:

'Open the door, my princess dear,
Open the door to thy true love here!
Remember the words that thou and I said
By the fountain cool, in the greenwood shade.'

Then the princess ran to the door and opened it, and there she saw the frog, whom she had quite forgotten. At this sight she was sadly frightened, and shutting the door as fast as she could came back to her seat. The king, her father, seeing that something had frightened her, asked her what was the matter. 'There is a nasty frog,' said she, 'at the door, that lifted my ball for me out of the spring last evening. I told him that he should live with me here, thinking that he could never get out of the spring; but there he is at the door, and he wants to come in.'

While she was speaking the frog knocked again at the door, and said:

'Open the door, my princess dear,
Open the door to thy true love here!
Remember the words that thou and I said
By the fountain cool, in the greenwood shade.'

Then the king said to the young princess, 'As you have given your word you must keep it; so go and let him in.' She did so, and the frog hopped into the room, and then straight on – tap, tap – plash, plash – from the bottom of the room to the top, till he came up close to the table where the princess sat. 'Pray lift me upon a chair,' said he to the princess, 'and let me sit next to you.' As soon as she had done this, the frog said, 'Put your plate nearer to me, that I may eat from it.' This she did, and when he had eaten as much as he could, he said, 'Now I am tired; carry me upstairs, and put me into your bed.' And the princess, though very unwilling, took him up in her hand, and put him upon the pillow of her own bed, where he slept all night long.

As soon as it was light he jumped up, hopped downstairs, and went out of the house. 'Now, then,' thought the princess, 'at last he is gone, and I shall be troubled with him no more.'

But she was mistaken; for when night came again she heard the same tapping at the door; and the frog came once more, and said:

'Open the door, my princess dear,
Open the door to thy true love here!
Remember the words that thou and I said
By the fountain cool, in the greenwood shade.'

And when the princess opened the door the frog came in, ate with her and slept upon her pillow as before, till the morning broke. And the third night he did the same.

But when the princess awoke on the following morning she was astonished to see, instead of the frog,

a handsome prince, gazing on her with the most beautiful eyes she had ever seen, and standing at the head of her bed.

He told her that he had been enchanted by a spiteful fairy, who had changed him into a frog; and that he had been fated so to abide till some princess should take him out of the spring, and let him eat from her plate, and sleep upon her bed for three nights. 'You,' said the prince, 'have broken his cruel charm, and now I have nothing to wish for but that you should go with me into my father's kingdom, where I will marry you, and love you as long as you live.'

The princess, you may be sure, was not long in giving her consent; and even as they spoke, a magnificent coach drove up, drawn by eight beautiful horses, decked with plumes of feathers and golden harness; and behind the coach rode the prince's servant, faithful Heinrich, who had bewailed the misfortunes of his dear master during his enchantment so long and so bitterly that his heart had well-nigh burst. They then took leave of the king, and got into the coach, and all set out, full of joy and merriment, for the prince's kingdom, which they reached safely; and there they lived happily a great many years.

And the princess, though very unwilling, took him up in her hand

172

The Frog Who Became an Emperor

Once upon a time there lived a very poor couple. A baby was on the way when the husband was forced to leave his home to find a living somewhere far away. Before he left, he embraced his wife fondly and gave her the last few silver pieces he had, saying, 'When the child is born, be it a boy or a girl, you must do all you can to bring it up. You and I are so poor that there is no hope for us now. But our child may be able to help us find a living.'

Three months after her husband's departure, the wife gave birth. The baby was neither a boy nor a little girl, but a frog!

The poor mother was heart-broken, and wept bitterly. 'Ah, an animal, not a child!' she cried. 'Our hopes for someone to care for us in our old age are gone! How can I ever face people again!' She thought at first she would do away with him, but she did not have the heart to do so. She wanted to bring him up, but was afraid of what the neighbours would say.

As she brooded over the matter, she remembered her husband's words before he went away, and she decided not to kill the child but always keep him hidden under the bed. In this way, no one knew she had given birth to a frog-child. But within two months, the frog-child had grown so big that he could no longer be kept under the bed. And one day, he suddenly spoke in a human voice.

'Mother,' he said, 'my father is coming back tonight. I am going to wait for him beside the road.' And sure enough, the husband did come home that very night.

'Have you seen your son?' the wife asked anxiously.

'Where? Where is my son?'

'He was waiting for you by the side of the road. Didn't you see him?'

'No! I saw no sign of anyone,' her husband answered, surprised. 'All I saw was an awful frog which gave me such a fright.'

'That frog was your son,' said the wife unhappily.

When the husband heard that his wife had given birth to a frog, he was grieved. 'Why did you tell him to meet me?' he said.

'What do you mean, tell him to meet you? He went without any telling from me. He suddenly said you were coming tonight and went out to meet you.'

'This is really extraordinary,' thought the husband, brightening up. 'No one knew I was coming. How could he have known?'

'Call him home, quickly,' he said aloud. 'He might catch cold outside.'

Just as the mother opened the door to do so, the frog came in. He hopped over to his father, who asked him, 'Was it you I met on the road?'

'Yes,' said the frog. 'I was waiting for you, father.'

'How did you know I was coming back tonight?'

'I know everything under heaven.'

The father and mother were amazed by his words and more amazed when he went on.

'Our country is in great peril,' he said solemnly. 'We are unable to resist the invaders. I want father to take me to the emperor, for I must save our country.'

'How can that be?' said the father. 'First, you have no horse. Secondly, you have no weapons, and thirdly, you have never been on a battlefield. How, then, do you propose to fight?'

The frog was very much in earnest. 'Only take me there,' he pleaded. 'I'll defeat the enemy, never fear.'

The father could not dissuade the frog, so he took his frog-son to the city to seek an audience with the emperor. After two days' journey, they arrived at the capital, where they saw the imperial decree displayed!

> The imperial capital is in danger. My country has been invaded. We are willing to marry our daughter to the man who can drive away the enemy.

The frog tore down the decree and with one gulp swallowed it. The soldier guarding the imperial decree was greatly alarmed. He could hardly imagine a frog accepting such a responsible duty. However, since the frog had swallowed the decree, he must be taken into the palace.

The emperor asked the frog if he had the means and ability to defeat the enemy. The frog replied,

'Yes, lord.' Then the emperor asked him how many men and horses he would need. 'Not a single horse or a single man,' answered the frog. 'All I need is a heap of hot, glowing embers.'

The emperor immediately commanded that a heap of hot, glowing embers be brought, and it was done. The heat was intense. The frog sat before the fire devouring the flames by the mouthful for three days and three nights. He ate till his belly was as big and round as a bladder full of fat. By now the city was in great danger, for the enemy was already clamouring at the walls. The emperor was terribly apprehensive, but the frog behaved as if nothing unusual was happening, and calmly went on swallowing fire and flame. Only after the third day had passed did he go to the top of the city wall and look at the situation. There, ringing the city, were thousands of soldiers and horses, as far as the eye could see.

'How, frog, are you going to drive back the enemy?' asked the emperor.

'Order your troops to stop plying their bows,' replied the frog, 'and open the city gate.'

The emperor turned pale with alarm when he heard these words.

'What! With the enemy at our very door! You tell me to open the gate! How dare you trifle with me?'

'Your imperial highness has bidden me to drive the enemy away,' said the frog. 'And that being so, you must heed my words.'

The emperor was helpless. He ordered the soldiers to stop bending their bows and lay down their arrows and throw open the gate.

As soon as the gate was open, the invaders poured in. The frog was above them in the gate tower and, as they passed underneath, he coolly and calmly spat fire down on them, searing countless men and horses. They fled back in disorder.

The emperor was overjoyed when he saw that the enemy was defeated. He made the frog a general and ordered that the victory should be celebrated for several days. But of the princess he said nothing, for he had not the slightest intention of letting his daughter marry a frog.

'Of course I cannot do such a thing!' he said to himself. Instead, he let it be known that it was the princess who refused. She must marry someone else, but whom? He did not know what to do. Anyone but a frog! Finally he ordained that her marriage should be decided by casting the Embroidered Ball.

Casting the Embroidered Ball! The news spread immediately throughout the whole country and within a few days the city was in a turmoil. Men from far and wide came to try their luck, and all manner of people flocked to the capital. The day came. The frog was present. He did not push his way into the mob but stood at the very edge of the crowded square.

A gaily festooned pavilion of a great height had been built. The emperor led the princess and her train of maids to their seats high up on the stand.

The moment arrived. The princess tossed the Embroidered Ball into the air, and down it gently floated. The masses in the square surged and roared like a raging sea. As one and all stretched eager hands to clutch the ball, the frog drew in a mighty breath and, like a whirling tornado, sucked the ball straight to him.

Now, surely, the princess will have to marry the frog! But the emperor was still unwilling to let this happen.

'An Embroidered Ball cast by a princess,' he declared, 'can only be seized by a human hand. No beast may do so.'

He told the princess to throw down a second ball.

This time a young, stalwart fellow caught the ball.

'This is the man!' cried the happy emperor. 'Here is the person fit to be my imperial son-in-law.'

A sumptuous feast was set to celebrate the occasion.

Can you guess who that young, stalwart fellow was? Of course it was the frog, now in the guise of a man.

Not till he was married to the princess did he change back again. By day he was a frog but at night he stripped off his green skin and was transformed into a fine, upstanding youth.

The princess could not keep it a secret and one day revealed it to her father, the emperor. He was startled but happy.

'At night,' he said to his son-in-law, 'you discard your outer garment, I hear, and become a handsome young man. Why do you wear that horrid frog-skin in the day?'

'Ah, sire,' replied the frog, 'this outer garment is priceless. When I wear it in winter, I am warm and cosy; and in summer, cool and fresh. It is proof against wind and rain. Not even the fiercest flame can set it alight. And as long as I wear it, I can live for thousands of years.'

'Let me try it on!' demanded the emperor.

'Yes, sire,' replied the frog and made haste to discard his skin.

The emperor smiled gleefully. He took off his dragon-embroidered robe and put on the frog-skin. But then he could not take it off again!

The frog put on the imperial robe and became the emperor. His father-in-law remained a frog for ever.

Frost

There was once an old man who had a wife and three daughters. The wife had no love for the eldest of the three, who was her stepdaughter, but was always scolding her. Moreover, she used to make her get up ever so early in the morning, and gave her all the work of the house to do. Before daybreak the girl would feed the cattle and give them to drink, fetch wood and water indoors, light the fire in the stove, give the room a wash, mend the dresses, and set everything in order.

Even then her stepmother was never satisfied, but would grumble away at Marfa, exclaiming: 'What a lazybones! what a slut! Why here's a brush not in its place, and there's something put wrong, and she's left the ashcan inside the house!'

The girl held her peace, and wept; she tried in every way to accommodate herself to her step-mother, and to be of service to her stepsisters. But they, following the example of their mother, were always insulting Marfa, quarrelling with her, and making her cry: that was even a pleasure to them! As for them, they lay in bed late, washed them-selves in water got ready for them, dried them-selves with a clean towel, and didn't sit down to work till after dinner.

Well, our girls grew and grew, until they grew up and were old enough to be married. The old man felt sorry for his eldest daughter, whom he loved because she was industrious and obedient, never was obstinate, always did as she was bid, and never uttered a word of contradiction. But he didn't know how he was to help her in her trouble. He was feeble, his wife was a scold, and her daughters were as obstinate as they were indolent.

Well, the old folks set to work to consider – the husband how he could get his daughters settled, the wife how she could get rid of the eldest one.

One day she says to him: 'I say, old man! let's get Marfa married.'

'Gladly,' says he, slinking off to the sleeping-place above the stove. But his wife called after him:

'Get up early tomorrow, old man, harness the mare to the sledge, and drive away with Marfa. And, Marfa, get your things together in a basket, and put on a clean shift; you're going away tomorrow on a visit.'

Poor Marfa was delighted to hear of such a piece of good luck as being invited on a visit, and she slept comfortably all night. Early next morning she got up, washed herself, prayed to God, got all her things together, packed them away in proper order, dressed herself in her best things, and looked something like a lass! – a bride fit for any place whatsoever!

Now it was wintertime, and out of doors was a rattling frost. Early in the morning, between daybreak and sunrise, the old man harnessed the mare to the sledge and led it up to the steps. Then he went indoors, sat down on the window-sill, and said: 'Now then! I've got everything ready.'

'Sit down to table and swallow your victuals!' replied the old woman.

The old man sat down to table, and made his daughter sit by his side. On the table stood a pannier; he took out a loaf, and cut bread for himself and his daughter. Meantime his wife served up a dish of old cabbage soup, and said: 'There, my pigeon, eat and be off; I've looked at you quite enough! Drive Marfa to her bride-groom, old man. And look here, old greybeard! drive straight along the road at first, and then turn off from the road to the right, you know, into the forest – right up to the big pine that stands on the hill, and there hand Marfa over to Frost.'

The old man opened his eyes wide, also his mouth, and stopped eating, and the girl began lamenting.

'Now then, what are you hanging your chaps and squealing about?' said her stepmother. 'Surely your bridegroom is a beauty, and he's that rich! Why, just see what a lot of things belong to him, the firs, the pine-tops and the birches, all in their robes of winter bark – ways and means that anyone might envy; and he himself a *bogatir*!'

The old man silently placed the things on the sledge, made his daughter put on a warm pelisse, and set off on the journey. After a time, he reached the forest, turned off from the road; and drove across the frozen snow. When he got into the depths of the forest, he stopped, made his daughter get out, laid her basket under the tall pine, and said: 'Sit here, and await the bridegroom. And mind you receive him as pleasantly as you can.'

Then he turned his horse round and drove off homewards.

The girl sat and shivered. The cold had pierced her through. She would fain have cried aloud, but she had not strength enough; only her teeth chattered. Suddenly she heard a sound. Not far off, Frost was cracking away on a fir. From fir to fir was he leaping, and snapping his fingers. Presently he appeared on that very pine under which the maiden was sitting and from above her head he cried: 'Art thou warm, maiden?'

'Warm, warm am I, dear Father Frost,' she replied.

Frost began to descend lower, all the more cracking and snapping his fingers. To the maiden said Frost: 'Art thou warm, maiden? Art thou warm, fair one?'

The girl could scarcely draw her breath, but still she replied: 'Warm am I, Frost dear: warm am I, father dear!'

Frost began cracking more than ever, and more loudly did he snap his fingers, and to the maiden he said: 'Art thou warm, maiden? Art thou warm, pretty one? Art thou warm, my darling?'

The girl was by this time numb with cold, and she could scarcely make herself heard as she replied: 'Oh! quite warm, Frost dearest!'

Then Frost took pity on the girl, wrapped her up in furs, and warmed her with blankets.

Next morning the old woman said to her husband: 'Drive out, old greybeard, and wake the young couple!'

The old man harnessed his horse and drove off. When he came to where his daughter was, he found she was alive and had got a good pelisse, a costly bridal veil and a pannier with rich gifts. He stowed everything away on the sledge without saying a word, took his seat on it with his daughter, and drove back. They reached home, and the daughter fell at her stepmother's feet. The old woman was thunderstruck when she saw the girl alive, and the new pelisse and the basket of linen.

'Ah, you wretch!' she cries. 'But you shan't trick me!'

Well, a little later the old woman says to her husband: 'Take my daughters, too, to their bridegroom. The presents he's made are nothing to what he'll give them.'

Well, early next morning the old woman gave her girls their breakfast, dressed them as befitted brides, and sent them off on their journey. In the same way as before the old man left the girls under the pine.

There the girls sat, and kept laughing and saying: 'Whatever is mother thinking of! All of a sudden to marry both of us off! As if there were no lads in our village, forsooth! Some rubbishy fellow may come, and goodness knows who he may be!'

The girls were wrapped up in pelisses, but for all that they felt the cold.

'I say, Prascovia! the frost's skinning me alive. Well, if our bridegroom doesn't come quick, we shall be frozen to death here!'

'Don't go talking nonsense, Mashka; as if suitors generally turned up in the forenoon. Why it's hardly dinner-time yet!'

'But I say, Prascovia! if only one comes, which of us will he take?'

'Not you, you stupid goose!'

'Then it will be you, I suppose!'

'Of course it will be me!'

'You, indeed! there now, have done talking stuff and treating people like fools!'

Meanwhile, Frost had numbed the girls' hands, so our damsels folded them under their dress, and then went on quarrelling as before.

'What, you fright! you sleepy-face! you abominable shrew! why, you don't know so much as how to begin weaving; and as to going on with it, you haven't an idea!'

'Aha, boaster! and what is it you know? Why, nothing at all except to go out to merry-makings and lick your lips there. We'll soon see which he'll take first!'

While the girls went on scolding like that, they began to freeze in downright earnest. Suddenly they both cried out at once: 'Whyever is he so long coming? Do you know, you've turned quite blue!'

Now, a good way off, Frost had begun cracking, snapping his fingers and leaping from fir to fir. To the girls it sounded as if someone was coming.

'Listen, Prascovia! He's coming at last, and with bells, too!'

'Get along with you! I won't listen; my skin is peeling with cold.'

'And yet you're still expecting to get married!'

Then they began blowing on their fingers.

Nearer and nearer came Frost. At length he appeared on the pine, above the heads of the girls, and said to them: 'Are ye warm, maidens? Are ye warm, pretty ones? Are ye warm, my darlings?'

'Oh, Frost, it's awfully cold! we're utterly perished! We're expecting a bridegroom, but the confounded fellow has disappeared.'

Frost slid lower down the tree, cracked away more, snapped his fingers oftener than before.

'Are ye warm, maidens? Are ye warm, pretty ones?'

'Get along with you! Are you blind that you can't see our hands and feet are quite dead?'

Still lower descended Frost, still more put forth his might, and said: 'Are ye warm, maidens?'

'Into the bottomless pit with you! Out of sight, accursed one!' cried the girls – and became lifeless forms.

Next morning the old woman said to her husband: 'Old man, go and get the sledge harnessed; put an armful of hay in it, and take some sheepskin wraps. I dare say the girls are half-dead with cold. There's a terrible frost outside! And, mind you, old greybeard, do it quickly!'

Before the old man could manage to get a bite he was out of doors and on his way. When he came to where his daughters were, he found them dead. So he lifted the girls on to the sledge, wrapped a blanket round them, and covered them up with a bark mat. The old woman saw him from afar, ran out to meet him, and called out ever so loud: 'Where are the girls?'

'In the sledge.'

The old woman lifted the mat, undid the blanket, and found the girls both dead.

Then, like a thunderstorm, she broke out against her husband, abusing him saying: 'What have you done, you old wretch? You have destroyed my daughters, the children of my own flesh and blood, my never-enough-to-be-gazed-on seedlings, my beautiful berries! I will thrash you with the tongs; I will give it you with the stove-rake.'

'That's enough, you old goose! You flattered yourself you were going to get riches, but your daughters were too stiff-necked. How was I to blame? it was you yourself would have it.'

The old woman was in a rage at first, and used bad language; but afterwards she made it up with her stepdaughter, and they all lived together peaceably, and thrived, and bore no malice. A neighbour made an offer of marriage, the wedding was celebrated, and Marfa is now living happily. The old man frightens his grandchildren with stories about Frost, and doesn't let them have their own way.

The Story of Gelert

It was somewhere about 1200, Prince Llewellyn had a castle at Aber, just abreast of us here; indeed, parts of the towers remain to this day. His consort was the Princess Joan; she was King John's daughter. Her coffin remains with us to this day. Llewellyn was a great hunter of wolves and foxes, for the hills of Carnarvonshire were infested with wolves in those days, after the young lambs.

Now the prince had several hunting-houses – sorts of farmhouses – and one of them was at the place now called Beth-Gelert, for the wolves were very thick there at this time. Now the prince used to travel from farmhouse to farmhouse with his family and friends, when going on these hunting parties.

One season they went hunting from Aber, and stopped at the house where Beth-Gelert is now – it's about fourteen miles away. The prince had all his hounds with him, but his favourite was Gelert, a hound who had never let off a wolf for six years.

The prince loved the dog like a child, and at the sound of his horn Gelert was always the first to come bounding up. There was company at the house, and one day they went hunting, leaving his wife and the child, in a big wooden cradle, behind him at the farmhouse.

The hunting party killed three or four wolves, and about two hours before the word passed for returning home, Llewellyn missed Gelert, and he asked his huntsmen: 'Where's Gelert? I don't see him.'

'Well, indeed, master, I've missed him this half-hour.'

And Llewellyn blew his horn, but no Gelert came at the sound.

Indeed, Gelert had got on to a wolf's track which led to the house.

The prince sounded the return, and they went home, the prince lamenting Gelert. 'He's sure to have been slain – he's sure to have been slain! since he did not answer the horn. Oh, my Gelert!' And they approached the house, and the prince went into the house, and saw Gelert lying by the over-turned cradle, and blood all about the room.

'What! hast thou slain my child?' said the prince, and ran his sword through the dog.

After that he lifted up the cradle to look for his child, and found the body of a big wolf underneath that Gelert had slain, and his child was safe. Gelert had capsized the cradle in the scuffle.

'Oh, Gelert! Oh, Gelert!' said the prince, 'my favourite hound, my favourite hound! Thou hast been slain by thy master's hand, and in death thou hast licked thy master's hand!' He patted the dog, but it was too late, and poor Gelert died licking his master's hand.

Next day they made a coffin, and had a regular funeral, the same as if it were a human being; all the servants in deep mourning, and everybody. They made him a grave, and the village was called after the dog, Beth-Gelert – Gelert's Grave; and the prince planted a tree, and put a gravestone of slate, though it was before the days of quarries. And they are to be seen to this day.

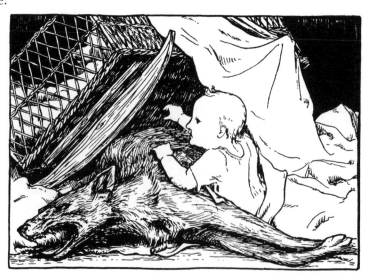

He lifted up the cradle and found the body of a big wolf that Gelert had slain, and his child who was safe

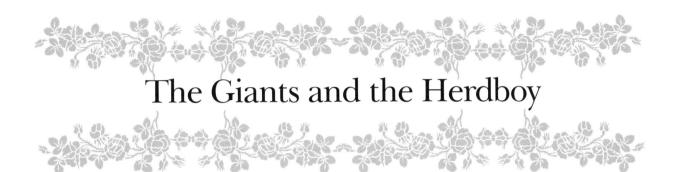

The Giants and the Herdboy

There was once upon a time a poor boy who had neither father nor mother. In order to gain a living he looked after the sheep of a great lord. Day and night he spent out in the open fields, and only when it was very wet and stormy did he take refuge in a little hut on the edge of a big forest. Now one night, when he was sitting on the grass beside his flocks, he heard not very far from him the sound as of someone crying. He rose up and followed the direction of the noise. To his dismay and astonishment he found a giant lying at the entrance of the wood; he was about to run off as fast as his legs could carry him, when the giant called out: 'Don't be afraid, I won't harm you. On the contrary, I will reward you handsomely if you will bind up my foot. I hurt it when I was trying to root up an oak tree.' The herdboy took off his shirt, and bound up the giant's wounded foot with it. Then the giant rose up and said, 'Now come and I will reward you. We are going to celebrate a marriage today, and I promise you we shall have plenty of fun. Come and enjoy yourself, but in order that my brothers mayn't see you, put this band round your waist and then you'll be invisible.' With these words he handed the herdboy a belt, and walking on in front he led him to a fountain where hundreds of giants and giantesses were assembled, preparing to hold a wedding. They danced and played different games till midnight; then one of the giants tore up a plant by its roots, and all the giants and giantesses made themselves so thin that they disappeared into the earth through the hole made by the uprooting of the plant. The wounded giant remained behind to the last and called out, 'Herdboy, where are you?' 'Here I am, close to you,' was the reply. 'Touch me,' said the giant, 'so that you too may come with us underground.' The herdboy did as he was told, and before he could have believed it possible he found himself in a big hall, where even the walls were made of pure gold. Then to his astonishment he saw that the hall was furnished with the tables and chairs that belonged to his master. In a few minutes the company began to eat and drink. The banquet was a very gorgeous one, and the poor youth fell to and ate and drank lustily. When he had eaten and drunk as much as he could he thought to himself, 'Why shouldn't I put a loaf of bread in my pocket? I shall be glad of it tomorrow.' So he seized a loaf when no one was looking and stowed it away under his tunic. No sooner had he done so than the wounded giant limped up to him and whispered softly, 'Herdboy, where are you?' 'Here I am,' replied the youth. 'Then hold on to me,' said the giant, 'so that I may lead you up above again.' So the herdboy held on to the giant, and in a few moments he found himself on the earth once more, but the giant had vanished. The herdboy returned to his sheep, and took off the magic belt which he hid carefully in his bag.

The next morning the lad felt hungry, and thought he would cut off a piece of the loaf he had carried away from the giants' wedding feast, and eat it. But although he tried with all his might, he couldn't cut off the smallest piece. Then in despair he bit the loaf, and what was his astonishment when a piece of gold fell out of his mouth and rolled at his feet. He bit the bread a second and third time, and each time a piece of gold fell out of his mouth; but the bread remained untouched. The herdboy was very much delighted over his stroke of good fortune, and, hiding the magic loaf in his bag, he hurried off to the nearest village to buy himself something to eat, and then returned to his sheep.

Now the lord whose sheep the herdboy looked after had a very lovely daughter, who always smiled and nodded to the youth when she walked with her father in his fields. For a long time the herdboy had made up his mind to prepare a surprise for this beautiful creature on her birthday. So when the day approached he put on his invisible belt, took a sack of gold pieces with him, and slipping into her room in the middle of the night, he placed the bag of gold beside her bed and returned to his sheep. The girl's joy was great and so was her parents' next day when they found the sack full of gold pieces. The herdboy was so pleased to think what pleasure he had given that the next night he placed another bag of gold beside the girl's bed. And this he continued to do for seven nights, and the girl and her parents made up their minds that it must be a good fairy who brought the gold every night. But one night they determined to watch, and see from their hiding place who the bringer of the sack of gold really was.

On the eighth night a fearful storm of wind and rain came on while the herdboy was on his way to bring the beautiful girl another bag of gold. Then for the first time he noticed, just as he reached his master's house, that he had forgotten the belt which made him invisible. He didn't like the idea of going back to his hut in the wind and wet, so he just stepped as he was into the girl's room, laid the

sack of gold beside her, and was turning to leave the room when his master confronted him and said, 'You young rogue, so you were going to steal the gold that a good fairy brings every night, were you?' The herdboy was so taken aback by his words that he stood trembling before him, and did not dare to explain his presence. Then his master spoke. 'As you have hitherto always behaved well in my service I will not send you to prison; but leave your place instantly and never let me see your face again.' So the herdboy went back to his hut, and taking his loaf and belt with him, he went to the nearest town. There he bought himself some fine clothes, and a beautiful coach with four horses, hired two servants, and drove back to his master. You may imagine how astonished he was to see his herdboy returning to him in this manner! Then the youth told him of the piece of good luck that had befallen him, and asked him for the hand of his beautiful daughter. This was readily granted, and the two lived in peace and happiness to the end of their lives.

There was once a man who travelled the land all over in search of a wife. He saw young and old, rich and poor, pretty and plain, and could not meet with one to his mind. At last he found a woman, young, fair and rich, who possessed a right arm of solid gold. He married her at once, and thought no man so fortunate as he was. They lived happily together, but, though he wished people to think otherwise, he was fonder of the golden arm than of all his wife's gifts besides.

At last she died. The husband put on the blackest black, and pulled the longest face at the funeral; but for all that he got up in the middle of the night, dug up the body and cut off the golden arm. He hurried home to hide his treasure, and thought no one would know.

The following night he put the golden arm under his pillow, and was just falling asleep, when the ghost of his dead wife glided into the room. Stalking up to the bedside, it drew the curtain, and looked at him reproachfully. Pretending not to be afraid, he spoke to the ghost, and said: 'What hast thou done with thy cheeks so red?'

'All withered and wasted away,' replied the ghost, in a hollow tone.

'What hast thou done with thy red rosy lips?'

'All withered and wasted away.'

'What hast thou done with thy golden hair?'

'All withered and wasted away.'

'What hast thou done with thy *golden arm*?'

'Thou hast it!'

The Golden Crab

Once upon a time there was a fisherman who had a wife and three children. Every morning he used to go out fishing, and whatever fish he caught he sold to the king. One day, among the other fishes, he caught a golden crab. When he came home he put all the fishes together into a great dish, but he kept the crab separate because it shone so beautifully, and placed it upon a high shelf in the cupboard. Now while the old woman, his wife, was cleaning the fish, and had tucked up her gown so that her feet were visible, she suddenly heard a voice, which said:

'Let down, let down thy petticoat
That lets thy feet be seen.'

She turned round in surprise, and then she saw the little creature, the golden crab.

'What! You can speak, can you, you ridiculous crab?' she said, for she was not quite pleased at the crab's remarks. Then she took him up and placed him on a dish.

When her husband came home and they sat down to dinner, they presently heard the crab's little voice saying, 'Give me some too.' They were all very much surprised, but they gave him something to eat. When the old man came to take away the plate which had contained the crab's dinner, he found it full of gold, and as the same thing happened every day he soon became very fond of the crab.

One day the crab said to the fisherman's wife, 'Go to the king and tell him I wish to marry his younger daughter.'

The old woman went to the castle accordingly, and laid the

matter before the king, who laughed a little at the notion of his daughter marrying a crab, but did not decline the proposal altogether, because he was a prudent monarch, and knew that the crab was likely to be a prince in disguise. He said, therefore, to the fisherman's wife, 'Go, old woman, and tell the crab I will give him my daughter if by tomorrow morning he can build a wall in front of my castle much higher than my tower, upon which all the flowers of the world must grow and bloom.'

The fisherman's wife went home and gave this message.

Then the crab gave her a golden rod, and said, 'Go and strike with this rod three times upon the ground on the place which the king showed you, and tomorrow morning the wall will be there.'

The old woman did so and went away again.

The next morning, when the king awoke, what do you think he saw? The wall stood there before his eyes, exactly as he had bespoken it! Then the old woman went back to the king and said to him, 'Your majesty's orders have been fulfilled.' 'That is all very well,' said the king, 'but I cannot give away my daughter until there stands in front of my palace a garden in which there are three fountains, of which the first must play gold, the second diamonds and the third brilliants.'

So the old woman had to strike again three times upon the ground with the rod, and the next morning the garden was there. The king now gave his consent, and the wedding was fixed for the very next day.

Then the crab said to the old fisherman, 'Now take this rod; go and knock with it on a certain mountain; then a black man will come out and ask you what you wish for. Answer him thus: "Your master, the king, has sent me to tell you that you must send him his golden garment that is like the sun." Make him give you, besides, the queenly robes of gold and precious stones which are like the flowery meadows, and bring them both to me. And bring me also the golden cushion.'

The old man went and did his errand. When he had brought the precious robes, the crab put on the golden garment and then crept upon the golden cushion, and in this way the fisherman carried him to the castle, where the crab presented the other garment to his bride. Now the ceremony took place, and when the married pair were alone together the crab made himself known to his young wife, and told her how he was the son of the greatest king in the world, and how he was enchanted, so that he became a crab by day and was a man only at night; and he could also change himself into an eagle as often as he wished. No sooner had he said this than he shook himself, and immediately became a handsome youth, but the next morning he was forced to creep back again into his crab-shell. And the same thing happened every day. But the princess's affection for the crab, and the polite attention with which she behaved to him, surprised the royal family very much. They suspected some secret, but though they spied and spied, they could not discover it. Thus a year passed away, and the princess had a son, whom she called Benjamin. But her mother still thought the whole matter very strange. At last she said to the king that he ought to ask his daughter whether she would not like to have another husband instead of the crab? But when the daughter was questioned she only answered: 'I am married to the crab, and him only will I have.'

Then the king said to her, 'I will appoint a tournament in your honour, and I will invite all the princes in the world to it, and if any one of them pleases you, you shall marry him.'

In the evening the princess told this to the crab, who said to her, 'Take this rod, go to the garden gate and knock with it, then a black man will come out and say to you, "Why have you called me, and what do you require of me?" Answer him thus: 'Your master the king has sent me hither to tell you to send him his golden armour and his steed and the silver apple." And bring them to me.'

The princess did so, and brought him what he desired.

The following evening the prince dressed himself for the tournament. Before he went he said to his wife, 'Now mind you do not say when you see me that I am the crab. For if you do this evil will come of it. Place yourself at the window with your sisters; I will ride by and throw you the silver apple. Take it in your hand, but if they ask you who I am, say that you do not know.' So saying, he kissed her, repeated his warning once more, and went away.

The princess went with her sisters to the window and looked on at the tournament. Presently her husband rode by and threw the apple up to her. She caught it in her hand and went with it to her room, and by and by her husband came back to her. But her father was much surprised that she did not seem to care about any of the princes; he therefore appointed a second tournament.

The crab then gave his wife the same directions as before, only this time the apple which she received from the black man was of gold. But before the prince went to the tournament he said to his wife, 'Now I know you will betray me today.'

But she swore to him that she would not tell who he was. He then repeated his warning and went away.

In the evening, while the princess, with her mother

The crab put on the golden garment and then crept upon the golden cushion, and in this way the fisherman carried him to the castle

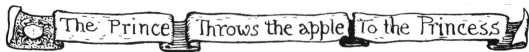

The Prince Throws the apple To the Princess

and sisters, was standing at the window, the prince suddenly galloped past on his steed and threw her the golden apple.

Then her mother flew into a passion, gave her a box on the ear, and cried out, 'Does not even that prince please you, you fool?'

The princess in her fright exclaimed, 'That is the crab himself!'

Her mother was still more angry because she had not been told sooner, ran into her daughter's room where the crab-shell was still lying, took it up and threw it into the fire. Then the poor princess cried bitterly, but it was of no use; her husband did not come back.

Now we must leave the princess and turn to the other persons in the story. One day an old man went to a stream to dip in a crust of bread which he was going to eat, when a dog came out of the water, snatched the bread from his hand, and ran away. The old man ran after him, but the dog reached a door, pushed it open, and ran in, the old man following him. He did not overtake the dog, but found himself above a staircase, which he descended. Then he saw before him a stately palace, and, entering, he found in a large hall a table set for twelve persons. He hid himself in the hall behind a great picture, that he might see what would happen. At noon he heard a great noise, so that he trembled with fear. When he took courage to look out from behind the picture, he saw twelve eagles flying in. At this sight his fear became still greater. The eagles flew to the basin of a fountain that was there and bathed themselves, when suddenly they were changed into twelve handsome youths. Now they seated themselves at the table, and one of them took up a goblet filled with wine, and said, 'A health to my father!' And another said, 'A health to my mother!' and so the healths went round. Then one of them said:

> 'A health to my dearest lady,
> Long may she live and well!
> But a curse on the cruel mother
> That burnt my golden shell!'

And so saying he wept bitterly. Then the youths rose from the table, went back to the great stone fountain, turned themselves into eagles again, and flew away.

Then the old man went away too, returned to the light of day, and went home. Soon after he heard that the princess was ill, and that the only thing that did her good was having stories told to her. He therefore went to the royal castle, obtained an audience of the princess, and told her about the strange things he had seen in the underground palace. No sooner had he finished than the princess asked him whether he could find the way to that palace.

'Yes,' he answered, 'certainly.'

And now she desired him to guide her thither at once. The old man did so, and when they came to the palace he hid her behind the great picture and advised her to keep quite still, and he placed himself behind the picture also. Presently the eagles came flying in, and changed themselves into young men, and in a moment the princess recognised her husband amongst them all, and tried to come out of her hiding-place; but the old man held her back. The youths seated themselves at the table; and now the prince said again, while he took up the cup of wine:

> 'A health to my dearest lady,
> Long may she live and well!
> But a curse on the cruel mother
> That burnt my golden shell!'

Then the princess could restrain herself no longer, but ran forward and threw her arms round her husband. And immediately he knew her again, and said: 'Do you remember how I told you that day that you would betray me? Now you see that I spoke the truth. But all that bad time is past. Now listen to me: I must still remain enchanted for three months. Will you stay here with me till that time is over?'

So the princess stayed with him, and said to the old man, 'Go back to the castle and tell my parents that I am staying here.'

Her parents were very much vexed when the old man came back and told them this, but as soon as the three months of the prince's enchantment were over, he ceased to be an eagle and became once more a man, and they returned home together. And then they lived happily, and we who hear the story are happier still.

The Golden Goose

There was a man who had three sons, the youngest of whom was called Simpleton and was despised, mocked and sneered at on every occasion.

It happened that the eldest wanted to go into the forest to hew wood, and before he went his mother gave him a beautiful sweet cake and a bottle of wine in order that he might not suffer from hunger or thirst.

When he entered the forest he met a little grey-haired old man who bade him good-day, and said: 'Do give me a piece of cake out of your pocket, and let me have a draught of your wine; I am so hungry and thirsty.'

But the clever son answered: 'If I give you my cake and wine, I shall have none for myself; be off with you,' and he left the little man standing and went on.

But when he began to hew down a tree, it was not long before he made a false stroke, and the axe cut him in the arm, so that he had to go home and have it bound up. And this was the little grey man's doing.

After this the second son went into the forest, and his mother gave him, like the eldest, a cake and a bottle of wine.

The little old grey man met him likewise, and asked him for a piece of cake and a drink of wine. But the second son, too, said sensibly enough: 'What I give you will be taken away from myself; be off!' and he left the little man standing and went on.

His punishment, however, was not delayed; when he had made a few blows at the tree he struck himself in the leg, so that he had to be carried home.

Then Simpleton said: 'Father, do let me go and cut wood.'

The father answered: 'Your brothers have hurt themselves with it; leave it alone, you do not understand anything about it.'

But Simpleton begged so long that at last he said: 'Just go then, you will get wiser by hurting yourself.' His mother gave him a cake made with water and baked in the cinders, and with it a bottle of sour beer.

When he came to the forest the little old grey man met him likewise, and greeting him, said: 'Give me a piece of your cake and a drink out of your bottle; I am so hungry and thirsty.'

Simpleton answered: 'I have only cinder-cake and sour beer; if that pleases you, we will sit down and eat.'

So they sat down, and when Simpleton pulled out his cinder-cake, it was a fine sweet cake, and the sour beer had become good wine.

So they ate and drank, and after that the little man said: 'Since you have a good heart, and are willing to divide what you have, I will give you good luck. There stands an old tree; cut it down, and you will find something at the roots.' Then the little man took leave of him.

Simpleton went and cut down the tree, and when it fell there was a goose sitting in the roots with feathers of pure gold. He lifted her up, and taking her with him, went to an inn where he thought he would stay the night.

You will find something at the roots

186

Now the host had three daughters, who saw the goose and were curious to know what such a wonderful bird might be, and would have liked to have one of its golden feathers.

The eldest thought: 'I shall soon find an opportunity of pulling out a feather,' and as soon as Simpleton had gone out she seized the goose by the wing, but her hand remained sticking fast to it.

The second came soon afterwards, thinking only of how she might get a feather for herself, but she had scarcely touched her sister than she was held fast.

At last the third also came with the like intent, and the others screamed out: 'Keep away; for goodness' sake, keep away!'

But she did not understand why she was to keep away. 'The others are there,' she thought, 'I may as well be there too,' and ran to them; but as soon as she had touched her sister, she remained sticking fast to her. So they had to spend the night with the goose.

The next morning Simpleton took the goose under his arm and set out, without troubling himself about the three girls who were hanging on to it. They were obliged to run after him continually, now left, now right, wherever his legs took him.

In the middle of the fields the parson met them, and when he saw the procession he said: 'For shame, you good-for-nothing girls, why are you running across the fields after this young man? Is that seemly?'

At the same time he seized the youngest by the hand in order to pull her away, but as soon as he touched her he likewise stuck fast, and was himself obliged to run behind.

Before long the sexton came by and saw his master, the parson, running behind three girls. He was astonished at this and called out: 'Hi! Your reverence, whither away so quickly? Do not forget that we have a christening today!' and running after him he took him by the sleeve, but was also held fast to it.

While the five were trotting thus, one behind the other, two labourers came with their hoes from the fields; the parson called out to them and begged that they would set him and the sexton free. But they had scarcely touched the sexton when they were held fast, and now there were seven of them running behind Simpleton and the goose.

Soon afterwards he came to a city, where a king ruled who had a daughter who was so serious that no one could make her laugh. So her father had put forth a decree that whosoever should be able to make her laugh should marry her.

When Simpleton heard this, he went with his goose and all her train before the king's daughter, and as soon as she saw the seven people running on and on, one behind the other, she began to laugh quite loudly and as if she would never stop. Thereupon Simpleton asked to have her for his wife; but the king did not want him for a son-in-law, and made all manner of excuses and said he must first produce a man who could drink a cellarful of wine.

Simpleton thought of the little grey man, who could certainly help him; so he went into the forest, and in the same place where he had felled the tree, he saw a man sitting, who had a very sorrowful face.

Simpleton asked him what he was taking to heart so sorely, and he answered: 'I have such a great thirst and cannot quench it; cold water I cannot stand, a barrel of wine I have just emptied, but that to me is like a drop on a hot stone!'

'There I can help you,' said Simpleton, 'just

come
with me
and you shall
be satisfied.' He led
him into the king's
cellar, and the man bent
over the huge barrels and
drank till his loins hurt, and before
the day was out he had emptied all the barrels.

Then Simpleton asked once more for his bride, but the king was vexed that such an ugly fellow, whom everyone called Simpleton, should take away his daughter, and he made a new condition; he must first find a man who could eat a whole mountain of bread.

Simpleton did not think long, but went straight into the forest, where in the same place there sat a man who was tying up his body with a strap, and making an awful face, and saying: 'I have eaten a whole ovenful of rolls, but what good is that when one has such a hunger as I? My stomach remains empty, and I must tie myself up if I am not to die of hunger.'

At this Simpleton was glad, and said: 'Get up and come with me; you shall eat yourself full.'

He led him to the king's palace where all the flour in the whole kingdom was collected, and from it he caused a huge mountain of bread to be baked.

The man from the forest stood before it, began to eat, and by the end of one day the whole mountain had vanished.

Then Simpleton for the third time asked for his bride; but the king again sought a way out, and ordered him to find a ship which could sail on land and on water.

'As soon as you come sailing back in it,' said he, 'you shall have my daughter for wife.'

Simpleton went straight into the forest, and there sat the little grey man to whom he had given his cake. When he heard what Simpleton wanted, he said: 'Since you have given me to eat and to drink, I will give you the ship; and I do all this because you once were kind to me.'

Then he gave him the ship which could sail on land and water, and when the king saw that, he could no longer prevent him from having his daughter.

The wedding was celebrated, and after the king's death, Simpleton inherited his kingdom and lived for a long time contentedly with his wife.

The Golden Harp

Morgan is one of the oldest names in Cymric land. It means one who lives near the sea. Every day, for centuries past, tens of thousands of Welsh folk have looked out on the great blue plain of salt water.

It is just as true, also, that there are all sorts of Morgans. One of these, named Taffy, was like nearly all Welshmen, in that he was very fond of singing. The trouble in his case, however, was that no one but himself loved to hear his voice, which was very disagreeable. Yet of the sounds which he himself made with voice or instrument he was an intense admirer. Nobody could persuade him that his music was poor and his voice rough. He always refused to improve.

Now in Wales, the bard, or poet who makes up his poetry or song as he goes along, is a very important person, and it is not well to offend one of these gentlemen. In French, they call such a person by a very long name – the *improvisateur*.

These poets have sharp tongues and often say hard things about people whom they do not like. If they used whetstones, or stropped their tongues on leather, as men do their razors, to give them a keener edge, their words could not cut more terribly.

Now, on one occasion, Taffy Morgan had offended one of these bards. It was while the poetic gentleman was passing by Taffy's house. He heard the jolly fellow inside singing, first at the top and then at the bottom of the scale. He would drop his voice down on the low notes and then again rise to the highest until it ended in a screech.

Someone on the street asked the poet how he liked the music which he had heard inside.

'Music?' replied the bard with a sneer. 'Is that what Morgan is trying? Why! I thought it was first the lowing of an aged cow, and then the yelping of a blind dog, unable to find its way. Do you call that music?'

The truth was that when the soloist had so filled himself with strong ale that his brain was fuddled, then it was hard to tell just what kind of a noise he was making. It took a wise man to discover the tune, if there was any.

One evening, when Morgan thought his singing unusually fine, and felt sorry that no one heard him, he heard a knock.

Instead of going to the door to enquire, or welcome the visitor, he yelled out 'Come in!'

The door opened and there stood three tired looking strangers. They appeared to be travellers. One of them said: 'Kind sir, we are weary and worn, and would be glad of a morsel of bread. If you can give us a little food, we shall not trouble you further.'

'Is that all?' said Morgan. 'See there the loaf and the cheese, with a knife beside them. Take what you want, and fill your bags. No man shall ever say that Taffy Morgan denied anyone food, when he had any himself.'

Whereupon the three travellers sat down and began to eat.

Meanwhile, without being invited to do so, their host began to sing for them.

Now the three travellers were fairies in disguise. They were journeying over the country, from cottage to cottage, visiting the people. They came to reward all who gave them a welcome and were kind to them, but to vex and play tricks upon those who were stingy, bad tempered or of sour disposition. Turning to Taffy before taking leave, one of them said: 'You have been good to us and we are grateful. Now what can we do for you? We have power to grant anything you may desire. Please tell us what you would like most.'

At this, Taffy looked hard in the faces of the three strangers, to see if one of them was the bard who had likened his voice in its ups and downs to a cow and a blind dog. Not seeing any familiar face, he plucked up his courage, and said: 'If you are not making fun of me, I'll take from you a harp. And, if I can have my wish in full, I want one that will play only lively tunes. No sad music for me!'

Here Morgan stopped. Again he searched their faces, to see if they were laughing at him and then proceeded.

'And something else, if I can have it; but it's really the same thing I am asking for.'

'Speak on, we are ready to do what you wish,' answered the leader.

'I want a harp, which, no matter how badly I may play, will sound out sweet and jolly music.'

'Say no more,' said the leader, who waved his hand. There was a flood of light, and, to Morgan's amazement, there stood on the floor a golden harp.

But where were the three travellers? They had disappeared in a flash.

Hardly able to believe his own eyes, it now dawned upon him that his visitors were fairies.

He sat down, behind the harp, and made ready to sweep the strings. He hardly knew whether or not he touched the instrument, but there rolled out volumes of lively music, as if the harp itself were mad. The tune was wild and such as would set the feet of young folks a-going, even in church.

As Taffy's fingers seemed every moment to become more skilful, the livelier the music increased, until the very dishes rattled on the cupboard, as if they wanted to join in. Even the chair looked as if about to dance.

Just then, Morgan's wife and some neighbours entered the house. Immediately, the whole party, one and all, began dancing in the jolliest way. For hours, they kept up the mad whirl. Yet all the while, Taffy seemed happier and the women the merrier.

No telegraph ever carried the news faster, all over the region, that Morgan had a wonderful harp. All the grass in front of the house was soon worn away by the crowds that came to hear and dance. As soon as Taffy touched the harp strings, the feet of everyone, young and old, began shuffling, nor could anyone stop, so long as Morgan played. Even very old, lame and one-legged people joined in. Several old women, whom nobody had ever prevailed upon to get out of their chairs, were cured of their rheumatism. Such unusual exercise was severe for them, but it seemed to be healthful.

A shrewd monk, the business manager of the monastery near by, wanted to buy Morgan's house, set up a sanatorium and advertise it as a holy place.

He hoped thus to draw pilgrims to it and get for it a great reputation as a healing place for the lame and the halt, the palsied and the rheumatic. Thus the monastery would be enriched and all the monks get fat.

But Taffy was a happy-go-lucky fellow, who cared little about money and would not sell; for, with his harp, he enjoyed both fun and fame.

One day, in the crowd that stood around his door waiting to begin to hop and whirl, Morgan espied the bard who had compared his voice to a cow and a cur. The bard had come to see whether the stories about the harp were true or not.

He found to his own discomfort what was the fact and the reality, which were not very convenient for him. As soon as the harp music began, his feet began to go up, and his legs to kick and whirl. The more Morgan played, the madder the dance and the wilder the antics of the crowd, and in these the bard had to join, for he could not help himself. Soon they all began to spin round and round on the flagstones fronting the door, as if crazy. They broke the paling of the garden fence. They came into the house and knocked over the chairs and sofa, even when they cracked their shins against the wood. They bumped their heads against the walls and ceiling, and some even scrambled over the roof and down again. The bard could no more stop his weary legs than could the other lunatics.

To Morgan his revenge was so sweet, that he kept on until the bard's legs snapped, and he fell down on top of people that had tumbled from shear weariness, because no more strength was left in them. Meanwhile, Morgan laughed until his jaws were tired and his stomach muscles ached.

But no sooner did he take his fingers off the strings, to rest them, than he opened his eyes in wonder; for in a flash the harp had disappeared.

He had made a bad use of the fairies' gift, and they were displeased. So both the monk and Morgan felt sorry.

Yet the grass grew again when the quondam harper and singer ceased desolating the air with his quavers. The air seemed sweeter to breathe, because of the silence.

However, the fairies kept on doing good to the people of goodwill, and today some of the sweetest singers in Wales come from the poorest homes.

The Golden Lion

There was once a rich merchant who had three sons, and when they were grown up the eldest said to him, 'Father, I wish to travel and see the world. I pray you let me.'

So the father ordered a beautiful ship to be fitted up, and the young man sailed away in it. After some weeks the vessel cast anchor before a large town, and the merchant's son went on shore.

The first thing he saw was a large notice written on a board saying that if any man could find the king's daughter within eight days he should have her to wife, but that if he tried and failed his head must be the forfeit.

A large notice written on a board

'Well,' thought the youth as he read this proclamation, 'that ought not to be a very difficult matter;' and he asked an audience of the king, and told him that he wished to seek for the princess.

'Certainly,' replied the king. 'You have the whole palace to search in; but remember, if you fail it will cost you your head.'

So saying, he commanded the doors to be thrown open, and food and drink to be set before the young man, who, after he had eaten, began to look for the princess. But though he visited every corner and chest and cupboard, she was not in any of them, and after eight days he gave it up and his head was cut off.

All this time his father and brothers had had no news of him, and were very anxious. At last the second son could bear it no longer, and said, 'Dear father, give me, I pray you, a large ship and some money, and let me go and seek for my brother.'

So another ship was fitted out, and the young man sailed away, and was blown by the wind into the same harbour where his brother had landed.

Now when he saw the first ship lying at anchor his heart beat high, and he said to himself, 'My brother cannot surely be far off,' and he ordered a boat and was put on shore.

As he jumped on to the pier his eye caught the notice about the princess, and he thought, 'He has undertaken to find her, and has certainly lost his head. I must try myself, and seek him as well as her. It cannot be such a very difficult matter.' But he fared no better than his brother, and in eight days his head was cut off.

So now there was only the youngest at home, and when the other two never came back he also begged for a ship that he might go in search of his lost brothers. And when the vessel started, a high wind arose, and blew him straight to the harbour where the notice was set.

'Oho!' said he, as he read, 'whoever can find the king's daughter shall have her to wife. It is quite clear now what has befallen my brothers. But in spite of that I think I must try my luck,' and he took the road to the castle.

On the way he met an old woman, who stopped and begged.

'Leave me in peace, old woman,' replied he.

'Oh, do not send me away empty,' she said. 'You are such a handsome young man you will surely not refuse an old woman a few pence.'

'I tell you, old woman, leave me alone.'

'You are in some trouble?' she asked. 'Tell me what it is, and perhaps I can help you.'

Then he told her how he had set his heart on finding the king's daughter.

'I can easily manage that for you as long as you have enough money.'

'Oh, as to that, I have plenty,' answered he.

'Well, you must take it to a goldsmith and get him to make it into a golden lion, with eyes of crystal; and inside it must have something that will enable it to play tunes. When it is ready bring it to me.'

The young man did as he was bid, and when the lion was made the old woman hid the youth in it, and brought it to the king, who was so delighted with it that he wanted to buy it. But she replied, 'It does not belong to me, and my master will not part from it at any price.'

'At any rate, leave it with me for a while,' said he; 'I should like to show it to my daughter.'

'Yes, I can do that,' answered the old woman; 'but tomorrow I must have it back again. And she went away.

The king watched her till she was quite out of sight, so as to make sure that she was not spying upon him; then he took the golden lion into his room and lifted some loose boards from the floor. Below the floor there was a staircase, which he went down till he reached a door at the foot. This he unlocked, and found himself in a narrow passage closed by another door, which he also opened. The young man, hidden in the golden lion, kept count of everything, and marked that there were in all seven doors. After they had all been unlocked the king entered a lovely hall, where the princess was amusing herself with eleven friends. All twelve girls wore the same clothes, and were as like each other as peas in a pod.

'What bad luck!' thought the youth. 'Even

All twelve girls wore the same clothes, and were as like each other as peas in a pod

supposing that I managed to find my way here again, I don't see how I could ever tell which was the princess.'

And he stared hard at the princess as she clapped her hands with joy and ran up to them, crying, 'Oh, do let us keep that delicious beast for tonight; it will make such a nice plaything.'

The king did not stay long, and when he left he handed over the lion to the maidens, who amused themselves with it for some time, till they got sleepy, and thought it was time to go to bed. But the princess took the lion into her own room and laid it on the floor.

She was just beginning to doze when she heard a voice quite close to her, which made her jump. 'O lovely princess, if you only knew what I have gone through to find you!' The princess jumped out of bed screaming, 'The lion! the lion!' but her friends thought it was a nightmare, and did not trouble themselves to get up.

'O lovely princess!' continued the voice, 'fear nothing! I am the son of a rich merchant, and desire above all things to have you for my wife. And in order to get to you I have hidden myself in this golden lion.'

'What use is that?' she asked. 'For if you cannot pick me out from among my companions you will still lose your head.'

'I look to you to help me,' he said. 'I have done so much for you that you might do this one thing for me.'

'Then listen to me. On the eighth day I will tie a white sash round my waist, and by that you will know me.'

The next morning the king came very early to fetch the lion, as the old woman was already at the palace asking for it. When they were safe from view she let the young man out, and he returned to the

king and told him that he wished to find the princess.

'Very good,' said the king, who by this time was almost tired of repeating the same words; 'but if you fail your head will be the forfeit.'

So the youth remained quietly in the castle, eating and looking at all the beautiful things around him, and every now and then pretending to be searching busily in all the closets and corners. On the eighth day he entered the room where the king was sitting. 'Take up the floor in this place,' he said. The king gave a cry, but stopped himself, and asked, 'What do you want the floor up for? There is nothing there.'

But as all his courtiers were watching him he did not like to make any more objections, and ordered the floor to be taken up, as the young man desired. The youth then want straight down the staircase till he reached the door; then he turned and demanded that the key should be brought. So the king was forced to unlock the door, and the next and the next and the next, till all seven were open, and they entered into the hall where the twelve maidens were standing all in a row, so like that none might tell them apart. But as he looked one of them silently drew a white sash from her pocket and slipped it round her waist, and the young man sprang to her and said, 'This is the princess, and I claim her for my wife.' And the king owned himself beaten, and commanded that the wedding feast should be held.

After eight days the bridal pair said farewell to the king, and set sail for the youth's own country, taking with them a whole shipload of treasures as the princess's dowry. But they did not forget the old woman who had brought about all their happiness, and they gave her enough money to make her comfortable to the end of her days.

Goldilocks and the Three Bears

Once upon a time there were three bears, who lived together in a house of their own, in a wood. One of them was a Little Wee Bear, and one was a Middle-sized Bear, and the other was a Great Big Bear. They had each a bowl for their porridge; a little bowl for the Little Wee Bear; and a middle-sized bowl for the Middle-sized Bear; and a great bowl for the Great Big Bear. And they had each a chair to sit in; a little chair for the Little Wee Bear; and a middle-sized chair for the Middle-sized Bear; and a great chair for the Great Big Bear. And they had each a bed to sleep in; a little bed for the Little Wee Bear; and a middle-sized bed for the Middle-sized Bear; and a great bed for the Great Big Bear.

One day, after they had made the porridge for their breakfast, and poured it into their porridge-bowls, they walked out into the wood while the porridge was cooling, that they might not burn their mouths by beginning too soon, for they were polite, well-brought-up bears. And while they were away a little girl called Goldilocks, who lived at the other side of the wood and had been sent on an errand by her mother, passed by the house, and looked in at the window. And then she peeped in at the keyhole, for she was not at all a well-brought-up little girl. Then seeing nobody in the house she lifted the latch. The door was not fastened, because the bears were good bears, who did nobody any harm, and never suspected that anybody would harm them. So Goldilocks opened the door and went in; and well pleased was she when she saw the porridge on the table. If she had been a well-brought-up little girl she would have waited till the bears came home, and then, perhaps, they would have asked her to breakfast; for they were good bears – a little rough or so, as the manner of bears is, but for all that very good-natured and hospitable. But she was an impudent, rude little girl, and so she set about helping herself.

First she tasted the porridge of the Great Big Bear, and that was too hot for her. Next she tasted the porridge of the Middle-sized Bear, but that was too cold for her. And then she went to the porridge of the Little Wee Bear, and tasted it, and that was neither too hot nor too cold, but just right, and she liked it so well that she ate it all up, every bit!

Then Goldilocks, who was tired, for she had been catching butterflies instead of running on her errand, sat down in the chair of the Great Big Bear, but that was too hard for her. And then she sat down in the chair of the Middle-sized Bear, and that was too soft for her. But when she sat down in the chair of the Little Wee Bear, that was neither too hard nor too soft, but just right. So she seated herself in it, and there she sat till the bottom of the chair came out, and down she came, plump upon the ground; and that made her very cross, for she was a bad-tempered little girl.

Now, being determined to rest, Goldilocks went upstairs into the bedchamber in which the Three Bears slept. And first she lay down upon the bed of the Great Big Bear, but that was too high at the head for her. And next she lay down upon the bed of the Middle-sized Bear, and that was too high at the foot for her. And then she lay down upon the bed of the Little Wee Bear, and that was neither too high at the head nor at the foot, but just right. So she covered herself up comfortably, and lay there till she fell fast asleep.

By this time the Three Bears thought their porridge would be cool enough for them to eat it properly; so they came home to breakfast. Now careless Goldilocks had left the spoon of the Great Big Bear standing in his porridge.

'Somebody has been at my porridge!' said the Great Big Bear in his great, rough, gruff voice.

Then the Middle-sized Bear looked at his porridge and saw the spoon was standing in it too.

'Somebody has been at my porridge!' said the Middle-sized Bear in his middle-sized voice.

Then the Little Wee Bear looked at his, and there was the spoon in the porridge-bowl, but the porridge was all gone!

'Somebody has been at my porridge and has finished it all up!' said the Little Wee Bear in his little wee voice.

Upon this the Three Bears, seeing that someone had entered their house, and eaten up the Little Wee Bear's breakfast, began to look about them. Now the careless Goldilocks had not put the hard cushion straight when she rose from the chair of the Great Big Bear.

'Somebody has ben sitting in my chair!' said the Great Big Bear in his great, rough, gruff voice.

And the careless Goldilocks had squatted down the soft cushion of the Middle-sized Bear.

'Somebody has ben sitting in my chair!' said the Middle-sized Bear in his middle-sized voice.

'Somebody has ben sitting in my chair and has sat the bottom through!' said the Little Wee Bear in his little wee voice.

Then the Three Bears thought they had better make further search in case it was a burglar, so they went upstairs into their bedchamber. Now Goldilocks had pulled the pillow of the Great Big Bear out of its place.

'Somebody has been lying in my bed!' said the Great Big Bear in his great, rough, gruff voice.

And Goldilocks had pulled the bolster of the Middle-sized Bear out of its place.

'Somebody has been lying in my bed!' said the Middle-sized Bear in his middle-sized voice.

But when the Little Wee Bear came to look at his bed, there was the bolster in its place!

And the pillow was in its place upon the bolster! And upon the pillow – ?

There was Goldilocks's yellow head – which was not in its place, for she had no business there.

'Somebody has been lying in my bed – and here she is still!' said the Little Wee Bear in his little wee voice.

Now Goldilocks had heard in her sleep the great, rough, gruff voice of the Great Big Bear; but she was so fast asleep that it was no more to her than the roaring of wind, or the rumbling of thunder. And she had heard the middle-sized voice of the Middle-sized Bear, but it was only as if she had heard someone speaking in a dream. But when she heard the little wee voice of the Little Wee Bear, it was so sharp, and so shrill, that it awakened her at once. Up she started, and when she saw the Three Bears on one side of the bed, she tumbled herself out at the other, and ran to the window. Now the window was open, because the bears, like good, tidy bears, as they were, always opened their bedchamber window when they got up in the morning. So naughty, frightened little Goldilocks jumped; and whether she broke her neck in the fall, or ran into the wood and was lost there, or found her way out of the wood and got whipped for being a bad girl and playing truant, no one can say. But the Three Bears never saw anything more of her.

'Somebody has been lying in my bed – and here she is still!'

The Goose Girl

The king of a great land died, and left his queen to take care of their only child. This child was a daughter, who was very beautiful; and her mother loved her dearly, and was very kind to her. And there was a good fairy too, who was fond of the princess, and helped her mother to watch over her. When she grew up, she was betrothed to a prince who lived a great way off; and as the time drew near for her to be married, she got ready to set off on her journey to his country. Then the queen her mother packed up a great many costly things: jewels, and gold, and silver; trinkets, and fine dresses, and in short everything that became a royal bride. And she gave her a waiting-maid to ride with her and give her into the bridegroom's hands; and each had a horse for the journey. Now the princess's horse was the fairy's gift, and it was called Falada, and could speak.

When the time came for them to set out, the fairy went into her bedchamber, and took a little knife, and cut off a lock of her hair, and gave it to the princess, and said, 'Take care of it, dear child; for it is a charm that may be of use to you on the road.' Then they all took a sorrowful leave of the princess; and she put the lock of hair into her bosom, got upon her horse, and set off on her journey to her bridegroom's kingdom.

One day, as they were riding along by a brook, the princess began to feel very thirsty: and she said to her maid, 'Pray get down and fetch me some water in my golden cup out of yonder brook, for I want to drink.'

'Nay,' said the maid, 'if you are thirsty, get off yourself, and stoop down by the water and drink; I shall not be your waiting-maid any longer.'

Then she was so thirsty that she got down, and knelt over the little brook, and drank; for she was frightened, and dared not bring out her golden cup; and she wept and said, 'Alas! what will become of me?'

And the lock answered her, and said:

'Alas! alas! if thy mother knew it,
    Sadly, sadly, would she rue it.'

But the princess was very gentle and meek, so she said nothing about her maid's ill behaviour, but got upon her horse again.

Then all rode farther on their journey, till the day grew so warm, and the sun so scorching, that the bride began to feel very thirsty again; and at last, when they came to a river, she forgot her maid's previous rude speech, and said, 'Pray get down, and fetch me some water to drink in my golden cup.'

But the maid answered her, and even spoke even more haughtily than before: 'Drink if you will, but I shall not be your waiting-maid.'

Then the princess was so thirsty that she got off her horse, and lay down, and held her head over the running stream, and cried and said, 'What will become of me?'

And the lock of hair answered her again:

'Alas! alas! if thy mother knew it,
    Sadly, sadly, would she rue it.'

And as she leaned down to drink, the lock of hair fell from her bosom, and floated away with the water.

Now she was so frightened that she did not see it; but her maid saw it, and was very glad, for she knew it was a charm; and she saw that the poor bride would be in her power, now that she had lost the hair.

So when the bride had done drinking, and would have got upon Falada again, the maid said, 'I shall ride upon Falada, and you may have my horse instead;' so she was forced to give up her horse, and soon afterwards to take off her royal clothes and put on her maid's shabby ones.

At last, as they drew near the end of their journey, this treacherous servant threatened to kill her mistress if she ever told anyone what had happened. But Falada saw it all, and marked it well.

Then the waiting-maid rode on upon Falada, and

the real bride rode upon the other horse, and they went on in this way till at last they came to the royal court. There was great joy at their coming, and the prince flew to meet them, and lifted the maid from her horse, thinking she was the one who was to be his wife; and she was led upstairs to the royal chamber; but the true princess was told to stay in the court below.

Now the old king happened just then to have nothing else to do; so he amused himself by sitting at his kitchen window, looking at what was going on; and he saw her in the courtyard. As she looked very pretty, and too delicate for a waiting-maid, he went up into the royal chamber to ask the bride who it was she had brought with her but had thus left standing in the court below.

'I brought her with me for the sake of her company on the road,' said she; 'pray give the girl some work to do, that she may not be idle.'

The old king could not for some time think of any work for her to do; but at last he said, 'I have a lad who takes care of my geese; she may go and help him.' Now the name of this lad that the real bride was to help in watching the king's geese was Curdken.

But the false bride said to the prince, 'Dear husband, pray do me one piece of kindness.'

'That I will,' said the prince.

'Then tell one of your slaughterers to cut off the head of the horse I rode upon, for it was very unruly, and plagued me sadly on the road.' But the truth was, she was very much afraid lest Falada should someday or other speak, and tell all she had done to the princess. She had her way, and the faithful Falada was killed; but when the true princess heard of it, she wept, and begged the man to nail up Falada's head in a large dark gateway of the city, through which she had to pass every morning and evening, that there she might still see him sometimes. Then the slaughterer said he would do as she wished; and cut off the head, and nailed it up in the dark gateway.

Early the next morning, as she and Curdken went out through the gate, she said sorrowfully: 'Falada, Falada, there thou hangest!' and the head answered:

She said sorrowfully: 'Falada, Falada, there thou hangest!'

'Bride, bride, there thou gangest!
Alas! alas! if thy mother knew it,
Sadly, sadly, would she rue it.'

Then they went out of the city, and drove the geese on. And when she came to the meadow, she sat down upon a bank there, and let down her waving locks of hair, which were all of pure silver; and when Curdken saw it glitter in the sun, he ran up, and would have pulled some of the locks out, but she cried:

'Blow, breezes, blow!
Let Curdken's hat go!
Blow, breezes, blow!
Let him after it go!
O'er hills, dales and rocks,
Away be it whirl'd,
Till the silvery locks
Are all comb'd and curl'd!

Then there came a wind so strong that it blew off Curdken's hat; and away it flew over the hills: and he was forced to turn and run after it. By the time he came back, she had done combing and curling her hair, and had put it up again safe. Then he was very angry and sulky, and would not speak to her at all; but they watched the geese until it grew dark in the evening, and then drove them homewards.

The next morning, as they were going through the dark gateway, the poor girl looked up at Falada's head, and cried: 'Falada, Falada, there thou hangest!' and the head answered:

'Bride, bride, there thou gangest!
Alas! alas! if they mother knew it,
Sadly, sadly, would she rue it.'

Then she drove on the geese, and sat down again in the meadow, and began to comb out her hair as before; and Curdken ran up to her, and wanted to take hold of it; but she cried out quickly:

'Blow, breezes, blow!
Let Curdken's hat go!
Blow, breezes, blow!
Let him after it go!
O'er hills, dales and rocks,
Away be it whirl'd,
Till the silvery locks
Are all comb'd and curl'd!

Then the wind came and blew away his hat; and off it flew a great way, over the hills and far away, so

that he had to run after it; and when he came back she had bound up her hair again, and all was safe. So they watched the geese till it grew dark.

In the evening, after they came home, Curdken went to the old king, and said, 'I cannot have that strange girl to help me to keep the geese any longer.'

'Why?' said the king.

'Because, instead of doing any good, she does nothing but tease me all day long.'

Then the king made him tell him what had happened. And Curdken said, 'When we go in the morning through the dark gateway with our flock of geese, she cries and talks with the head of a horse that hangs upon the wall, and says: 'Falada, Falada, there thou hangest!' and the head answers:

'Bride, bride, there thou gangest!
Alas! alas! if they mother knew it,
Sadly, sadly, would she rue it.'

And Curdken went on to tell the king what had happened upon the meadow where the geese fed: how his hat was blown away, and how he was forced to run after it, and to leave his flock of geese to themselves.

The old king told the boy to go out again the next day, and when morning came, he placed himself beside the dark gateway, and heard how she spoke to Falada, and how Falada answered. Then he went into the field, and hid himself in a bush by the meadow's side; and he soon saw with his own eyes how they drove the flock of geese; and how, after a little time, she let down her hair that glittered in the sun. And then he heard her say:

'Blow, breezes, blow!
Let Curdken's hat go!
Blow, breezes, blow!
Let him after it go!
O'er hills, dales and rocks,
Away be it whirl'd,
Till the silvery locks
Are all comb'd and curl'd!

And soon came a gale of wind, and carried away Curdken's hat, and away went Curdken after it, while the girl went on combing and curling her hair. All this the old king saw, and then he went home without being seen. When the little goose girl came back in the evening he called her aside, and asked her why she behaved as she did; she burst into tears, and said, 'That I must not tell you or any man, or I shall lose my life.'

But the old king begged so hard that she had no peace till she had told him all the tale, from beginning to end, word for word. And it was very lucky for her that she did so, for when she had done the king ordered royal clothes to be put upon her, and gazed on her with wonder, she was so beautiful. Then he called his son and told him that he had only a false bride, one who was merely a waiting-maid, while the true bride stood by. And the young king rejoiced when he saw her beauty, and heard how meek and patient she had been; and without saying anything to the false bride, the king ordered a great feast to be got ready for all his court. The bridegroom sat at the top, with the false princess on one side, and the true one on the other; but nobody recognised her, for her beauty was quite dazzling to their eyes; and she did not seem at all like the little goose girl, now that she had her brilliant dress on.

When they had eaten and drunk, and were very merry, the old king said he would tell them a tale. So he began, and told all the story of the princess, as if it was one that he had once heard; and he asked the true waiting-maid what she thought ought to be done to anyone who would behave thus.

'Nothing better,' said this false bride, 'than that she should be thrown into a cask stuck round with sharp nails, and that two white horses should be put to it, and should drag it from street to street till she was dead.'

'Thou art she!' said the old king; 'and as thou hast judged thyself, so shall it be done to thee.' And the young king was then married to his true wife, and they reigned over the kingdom in peace and happiness all their lives; and the good fairy came to see them, and restored the faithful Falada to life again.

The Great Red Dragon of Wales

Every old country that has won fame in history and built up a civilisation of its own, has a national flower. Besides this, some living creature, bird or beast, or, it may be, a fish is on its flag. In places of honour, it stands as the emblem of the nation; that is, of the people, apart from the land they live on. Besides flag and symbol, it has a motto. That of Wales is: 'Awake: It is light.'

Now because the glorious stories of Wales, Scotland and Ireland have been nearly lost in that of mighty England, men have at times almost forgotten about the leek, the thistle and the shamrock, which stand for the other three divisions of the British Isles.

Yet each of these peoples has a history as noble as that of which the rose and the lion are the emblems. Each has also its patron saint and civiliser. So we have beside St George, St David, St Andrew and St Patrick, all of them white-souled heroes. On the union flag, or standard of the United Kingdom, we see their three crosses.

The lion of England, the harp of Ireland, the thistle of Scotland and the Red Dragon of Wales represent the four peoples in the British Isles, each with its own speech, traditions and emblems; yet all in unity and in loyalty, none excelling the Welsh, whose symbol is the Red Dragon. In classic phrase, we talk of Albion, Scotia, Cymry and Hibernia.

But why red? Almost all the other dragons in the world are white, or yellow, green or purple, blue or pink. Why a fiery red colour like that of Mars?

Borne on the banners of the Welsh archers, who in old days won the Battles of Crecy and Agincourt, and now seen on the crests on the town halls and city flags, in heraldry, and in art, the Red Dragon is as rampant as when King Arthur sat with his Knights at the Round Table.

The Red Dragon has four three-toed claws, a long, barbed tongue, and tail ending like an arrow head. With its wide wings unfolded, it guards those ancient liberties which neither Saxon, nor Norman, nor German, nor kings on the throne, whether foolish or wise, have ever been able to take away. No people on earth combine so handsomely loyal freedom and the larger patriotism, or hold in purer loyalty to the union of hearts and hands in the British Empire, which the sovereign represents, as do the Welsh.

The Welsh are the oldest of the British peoples. They preserve the language of the Druids, bards and chiefs of primeval ages which go back and far beyond any royal line in Europe, while most of their fairy tales are pre-ancient and beyond the dating.

Why the Cymric dragon is red, is thus told, from times beyond human record.

It was in those early days, after the Romans in the south had left the island, and the Cymric king, Vortigern, was hard pressed by the Picts and Scots of the north. To his aid, he invited over from beyond the North Sea, or German Ocean, the tribes called the Long Knives, or Saxons, to help him.

But once on the big island, these friends became enemies and would not go back. They wanted to possess all Britain.

Vortigern thought this was treachery. Knowing that the Long Knives would soon attack him, he called his twelve wise men together for their advice. With one voice, they advised him to retreat westward behind the mountains into Cymry. There he must build a strong fortress and there defy his enemies.

So the Saxons, who were Germans, thought they had driven the Cymry beyond the western borders of the country which was later called England, and into what they named the foreign or Welsh parts. Centuries afterwards, this land received the name of Wales.

People in Europe spoke of Galatians, Wallachians,

Belgians, Walloons, Alsatians and others as 'Welsh'. They called the new fruit imported from Asia walnuts, but the names 'Wales' and 'Welsh' were unheard of until after the fifth century.

The place chosen for the fortified city of the Cymry was among the mountains. From all over his realm, the king sent for masons and carpenters and collected the materials for building. Then, a solemn invocation was made to the gods by the Druid priests. These grand-looking old men were robed in white, with long, snowy beards falling over their breasts, and they had milk-white oxen drawing their chariot. With a silver knife they cut the mistletoe from the tree-branch, hailing it as a sign of favour from God. Then with harp, music and song they dedicated the spot as a stronghold of the Cymric nation.

Then the king set the diggers to work. He promised a rich reward to those men of the pick and shovel who should dig the fastest and throw up the most dirt, so that the masons could, at the earliest moment, begin their part of the work.

But it all turned out differently from what the king expected. Some dragon, or powerful being underground, must have been offended by this invasion of his domain; for, the next morning, they saw that everything in the form of stone, timber, iron or tools, had disappeared during the night. It looked as if an earthquake had swallowed them all up.

Both king and seers, priests and bards, were greatly puzzled at this. However, not being able to account for it, and the Saxons likely to march on them at any time, the sovereign set the diggers at work and again collected more wood and stone.

This time, even the women helped, not only to cook the food, but to drag the logs and stones. They were even ready to cut off their beautiful long hair to make ropes, if necessary.

But in the morning, all had again disappeared, as if swept by a tempest. The ground was bare.

Nevertheless, all hands began again, for all hearts were united.

For the third time, the work proceeded. Yet when the sun rose next morning, there was not even a trace of either material or labour.

What was the matter? Had some dragon swallowed everything up?

Vortigern again summoned his twelve wise men, to meet in council and to enquire concerning the cause of the marvel and to decide what was to be done. After long deliberation, while all the work-men and people outside waited for their verdict, the wise men agreed upon a remedy.

Now in ancient times, it was a custom, all over the world, notably in China and Japan and among our ancestors, that when a new castle or bridge was to be built, they sacrificed a human being. This was done either by walling up the victim while alive, or by mixing his or her blood with the cement used in the walls. Often it was a virgin or a little child thus chosen by lot and made to die, the one for the many.

The idea was not only to ward off the anger of the spirits of the air, or to appease the dragons under ground, but also to make the workmen do their best work faithfully, so that the foundation should be sure and the edifice withstand the storm, the wind and the earthquake shocks.

So, nobody was surprised, or raised his eyebrows, or shook his head, or pursed up his lips, when the king announced that what the wise men declared must be done and that quickly. Nevertheless, many a mother hugged her darling more closely to her bosom, and fathers feared for their sons or daughters, lest one of these, their own, should be chosen as the victim to be slain.

King Vortigern had the long horn blown for perfect silence, and then he spoke: 'A child must be found who was born without a father. He must be brought here and be solemnly put to death. Then his blood will be sprinkled on the ground and the citadel will be built securely.'

Within an hour, swift runners were seen bounding over the Cymric hills. They were dispatched in search of a boy without a father, and a large reward was promised to the young man who found what was wanted. So into every part of the Cymric land, the searchers went.

One messenger noticed some boys playing ball. Two of them were quarrelling. Coming near, he heard one say to the other: 'Oh, you boy without a father, nothing good will ever happen to you.'

'This must be the one looked for,' said the royal messenger to himself. So he went up to the boy who had been thus twitted and spoke to him thus: 'Don't mind what he says.' Then he prophesied great things, if he would go along with him. The boy was only too glad to go, and the next day the lad was brought before King Vortigern.

The workmen and their wives and children, numbering thousands, had assembled for the solemn ceremony of dedicating the ground by shedding the boy's blood. In strained attention the people held their breath.

201

The boy asked the king: 'Why have your servants brought me to this place?'

Then the sovereign told him the reason, and the boy asked: 'Who instructed you to do this?'

'My wise men told me so to do, and even the sovereign of the land obeys his wise councillors.'

'Order them to come to me, your majesty,' pleaded the boy.

When the wise men appeared, the boy, in respectful manner, enquired of them thus: 'How was the secret of my life revealed to you? Please speak freely and declare who it was that discovered me to you.'

Turning to the king, the boy added: 'Pardon my boldness, your majesty. I shall soon reveal the whole matter to you, but I wish first to question your advisers. I want them to tell you what is the real cause, and reveal, if they can, what is hidden here underneath the ground.'

But the wise men were confounded. They could not tell and they fully confessed their ignorance.

The boy then said: 'There is a pool of water down below. Please order your men to dig for it.'

At once the spades were plied by strong hands, and in a few minutes the workmen saw their faces reflected, as in a looking glass. There was a pool of clear water there.

Turning to the wise men, the boy asked before all: 'Now tell me, what is in the pool?'

As ignorant as before, and now thoroughly ashamed, the wise men were silent.

'Your majesty, I can tell you, even if these men cannot. There are two vases in the pool.'

Two brave men leaped down into the pool. They felt around and brought up two vases, as the boy had said.

Again, the lad put a question to the wise men: 'What is in these vases?'

Once more, those who professed to know the secrets of the world, even to the demanding of the life of a human being, held their tongues.

'There is a tent in them,' said the boy. 'Separate them, and you will find it so.'

By the king's command, a soldier thrust in his hand and found a folded tent.

Again, while all wondered, the boy was in command of the situation. Everything seemed so reasonable that all were prompt and alert to serve him.

'What a splendid chief and general he would make to lead us against our enemies, the "Long Knives"!' whispered one soldier to another.

'What is in the tent?' asked the boy of the wise men.

Not one of the twelve knew what to say, and there was an almost painful silence.

'I will tell you, your majesty, and all here, what is in this tent. There are two serpents, one white and one red. Unfold the tent.'

With such a leader, no soldier was afraid, nor did a single person in the crowd draw back. Two stalwart fellows stepped forward to open the tent.

But now a few of the men and many of the women shrank back, while those that had babies, or little folk, snatched up their children, fearing lest the poisonous snakes might wriggle towards them.

The two serpents were coiled up and asleep, but they soon showed signs of waking, and their fiery, lidless eyes glared at the people.

'Now, your majesty, and all here, be you the witnesses of what will happen. Let the king and wise men look in the tent.'

At this moment, the serpents stretched themselves out at full length, while all fell back, giving them a wide circle to struggle in.

Then they reared their heads. With their glittering eyes flashing fire, they began to struggle with each other. The white one rose up first, threw the red one into the middle of the arena, and then pursued him to the edge of the round space.

Three times did the white serpent gain the victory over the red one.

But while the white serpent seemed to be gloating over the other for a final onset, the red one, gathering strength, erected its head and struck at the other.

The struggle went on for several minutes, but in the end the red serpent overcame the white, driving it first out of the circle, then from the tent, and into the pool, where it disappeared, while the victorious red one moved into the tent again.

When the tent flap was opened for all to see, nothing was visible except a red dragon; for the victorious serpent had turned into this great creature which combined in one new form the body and the powers of bird, beast, reptile and fish. It had wings to fly, the strongest animal strength, and could crawl, swim and live in either water or air, or on the earth. In its body was the sum total of all life.

Then, in the presence of all the assembly, the youth turned to the wise men to explain the meaning of what had happened. But not a word did they speak. In fact, their faces were full of shame before the great crowd.

'Now, your majesty, let me reveal to you the meaning of this mystery.'

'Speak on,' said the king, gratefully.

'This pool is the emblem of the world, and the tent is that of your kingdom. The two serpents are two dragons. The white serpent is the dragon of the Saxons, who now occupy several of the provinces and districts of Britain from sea to sea. But when they invade our soil our people will finally drive them back and hold fast for ever their beloved Cymric land. But you must choose another site on which to erect your castle.'

After this, whenever a castle was to be built no more human victims were doomed to death. All the twelve men, who had wanted to keep up the old cruel custom, were treated as deceivers of the people. By the king's orders, they were all put to death and buried before all the crowd.

Today, like so many who keep alive old and worn-out notions by means of deception and falsehood, these men are remembered only by the Twelve Mounds, which rise of the field hard by.

As for the boy, he became a great magician, or, as we in our age would call him, a man of science and wisdom, named Merlin. He lived long on the mountain, but when he went away with a friend, he placed all his treasures in a golden cauldron and hid them in a cave. He rolled a great stone over its mouth. Then with sod and earth he covered it all over so as to hide it from view. His purpose was to leave this his wealth for a leader, who, in some future generation, would use it for the benefit of his country, when most needed.

This special person will be a youth with yellow hair and blue eyes. When he comes to Denas, a bell will ring to invite him into the cave. The moment his foot is over the place, the stone of entrance will open of its own accord. Anyone else will be considered an intruder and it will not be possible for him to carry away the treasure.

The Greek Princess and the Young Gardener

There was once a king, but I didn't hear what country he was over, and he had one very beautiful daughter. Well, he was getting old and sickly, and the doctors found out that the finest medicine in the world for him was the apples of a tree that grew in the orchard just under his window. So you may be sure he had the tree well minded, and used to get the apples counted from the time they were the size of small marbles. One harvest, just as they were beginning to turn ripe, the king was awakened one night by the flapping of wings outside in the orchard; and when he looked out, what did he see but a bird among the branches of his tree. Its feathers were so bright that they made a light all round them, and the minute it saw the king in his nightcap and nightshirt it picked off an apple, and flew away. 'Oh, botheration to that thief of a gardener!' says the king. 'This is a nice way he's watching my precious fruit.'

He didn't sleep a wink the rest of the night; and as soon as anyone was stirring in the palace, he sent for the gardener, and abused him for his neglect.

'Please, your majesty,' says he, 'not another apple you shall lose! My three sons are the best shots at the bow and arrow in the kingdom, and they and myself will watch in turn every night.'

When the night came, the gardener's eldest son took his post in the garden, with his bow strung and his arrow between his fingers, and watched, and watched. But at the dead hour, the king, who was wide awake, heard the flapping of wings and ran to the window. There was the bright bird in the tree, and the boy fast asleep, sitting with his back to the wall, and his bow on his lap.

'Rise, you lazy thief!' says the king. 'There's the bird again, botheration to her!'

Up jumped the poor fellow; but while he was fumbling with the arrow and the string, away was the bird with the nicest apple on the tree. Well, to be sure, how the king fumed and fretted, and how he abused the gardener and the boy, and

what a twenty-four hours he spent till midnight came again!

He had his eye this time on the second son of the gardener; but though he was up and lively enough when the clock began to strike twelve, it wasn't done with the last clang when he saw him stretched like one dead on the long grass, and saw the bright bird again, and heard the flap of her wings, and saw her carry away the third apple. The poor fellow was woken by the roar of the king in his ears, and even was in time enough to let fly an arrow after the bird. He did not hit her, you may depend; and though the king was mad enough, he saw the poor fellows were under *pishtrogues*, and could not help it.

Well, he had some hopes out of the youngest, for he was a brave, active young fellow, that had everybody's good word. There he was ready, and there was the king watching him, and talking to him at the first stroke of twelve. At the last clang, the brightness coming before the bird lighted up the wall and the trees and the rushing of the wings was heard as it flew into the branches; but at the same instant the crack of the arrow on her side might be heard a quarter of a mile off. Down came the arrow and a large bright feather along with it, and away was the bird, with a screech that was enough to break the drum of your ear. She hadn't time to carry off an apple; and bedad, when the feather was thrown up into the king's room it was heavier than lead, and turned out to be the finest beaten gold.

Well, there was great *cooramuch* made about the youngest boy next day, and he watched night after night for a week, but not a mite of a bird or bird's feather was to be seen, and then the king told him to go home and sleep. Everyone admired the beauty of the gold feather beyond anything, but the king was fairly bewitched. He was turning it round and round, and rubbing it against his forehead and his nose the live-long day; and at last he proclaimed that he'd give his daughter and half his kingdom to whoever would bring him the bird with the gold feathers, dead or alive.

The gardener's eldest son had great conceit of himself, and away he went to look for the bird. In the afternoon he sat down under a tree to rest himself, and eat a bit of bread and cold meat that he had in his wallet, when up comes as fine a looking fox as you'd see in the burrow of Munfin. 'Musha, sir,' says he, 'would you spare a bit of that meat to a poor body that's hungry?'

'Well,' says the other, 'you must have the divil's own assurance, you common robber, to ask me such a question. Here's the answer,' and he let fly at the *moddhereen rua.*

The arrow scraped from his side up over his back, as if he was made of hammered iron, and stuck in a tree a couple of perches off.

'Foul play,' says the fox; 'but I respect your young brother, and will give a bit of advice. At nightfall you'll come into a village. One side of the street you'll see a large room lighted up, and filled with young men and women, dancing and drinking. The other side you'll see a house with no light, only from the fire in the front room, and no one near it but a man and his wife, and their child. Take a fool's advice, and get lodging there.' With that he curled his tail over his crupper, and trotted off.

The boy found things as the fox said, but *begonies* he chose the dancing and drinking, and there we'll leave him. In a week's time, when they got tired at home waiting for him, the second son said he'd try his fortune, and off he set. He was just as ill-natured and foolish as his brother, and the same thing happened to him. Well, when a week was over, away went the youngest of all, and as sure as the hearth-money, he sat under the same tree, and pulled out his bread and meat, and the same fox came up and saluted him. Well, the young fellow shared his dinner with the *moddhereen,* and he wasn't long beating about the bush, but told the other he knew all about his business.

'I'll help you,' says he, 'if I find you're biddable. So just at nightfall you'll come into a village . . . Goodbye till tomorrow.'

It was just as the fox said, but the boy took care not to go near dancer, drinker, fiddler or piper. He got welcome in the quiet house to supper and bed, and was on his journey next morning before the sun was the height of the trees.

He wasn't gone a quarter of a mile when he saw the fox coming out of a wood that was by the roadside.

'Good-morrow, fox,' says one.

'Good-morrow, sir,' says the other.

'Have you any notion how far you have to travel till you find the golden bird?'

'Dickens a notion have I – how could I?'

'Well, I have. She's in the King of Spain's palace, and that's a good two hundred miles off.'

'Oh, dear! We'll be a week going.'

'No, we won't. Sit down on my tail, and we'll soon make the road short.'

'Tail, indeed! That 'ud be the droll saddle, my poor *moddhereen.*'

'Do as I tell you, or I'll leave you to yourself.'

Well, rather than vex him he sat down on the tail that was spread out level like a wing, and away they went like thought. They overtook the wind that was before them, and the wind that came after didn't overtake them. In the afternoon, they stopped in a wood near the King of Spain's palace, and there they stayed till nightfall.

'Now,' says the fox, 'I'll go before you to make the minds of the guards easy, and you'll have nothing to do but go from lighted hall to another lighted hall till you find the golden bird in the last. If you have a head on you, you'll bring herself and her cage outside the door, and no one then can lay hands on her or you. If you haven't a head I can't help you, nor no one else.' So he went over to the gates.

In a quarter of an hour the boy followed, and in the first hall he passed he saw a score of armed guards standing upright, but all dead asleep. In the next he saw a dozen, and in the next half a dozen, and in the next three, and in the room beyond that there was no guard at all, nor lamp, nor candle, but it was as bright as day; for there was the golden bird in a common wood and wire cage, and on the table were the three apples turned into solid gold.

On the same table was the most lovely golden cage eye ever beheld, and it entered the boy's head that it would be a thousand pities not to put the precious bird into it, the common cage was so unfit for her. Maybe he thought of the money it was worth; anyhow he made the exchange, and he had soon good reason to be sorry for it. The instant the shoulder of the bird's wing touched the golden wires, she let such a squawk out of her as was enough to break all the panes of glass in the windows, and at the same minute the three men, and the half-dozen, and the dozen, and the score men, woke up and clattered their swords and spears, and surrounded the poor boy, and jibed, and cursed, and swore at him, till he didn't know whether it was his foot or his head he was standing on. They called the king, and told him what happened, and he put on a very grim face. 'It's on a gibbet you ought to be this moment,' says he, 'but I'll give you a chance of your life, and of the golden bird, too. I lay you under prohibitions, and restrictions, and death, and destruction, to go and bring me the King of Morocco's bay filly that outruns the wind and leaps over the walls of castle-bawns. When you fetch her into the bawn of this palace, you may get the golden bird and liberty to go where you please.'

Out passed the boy, very downhearted, but as he went along, who should come out of a brake but the fox again.

'Ah, my friend,' says he, 'I was right when I suspected you hadn't a head on you; but I won't rub your hair again' the grain. Get on my tail again, and when we come to the King of Morocco's palace, we'll see what we can do.'

So away they went like thought. The wind that was before them they would overtake; the wind that was behind them would not overtake them.

Well, the nightfall came on them in a wood near the palace, and says the fox, 'I'll go and make things easy for you at the stables, and when you are leading out the filly, don't let her touch the door, nor doorposts, nor anything but the ground, and that with her hoofs; and if you haven't a head on you once you are in the stable, you'll be worse off than before.'

The bird let such a squawk out of her as was enough to break all the panes of glass in the windows

So the boy delayed for a quarter of an hour, and then he went into the big bawn of the palace. There were two rows of armed men reaching from the gate to the stable, and every man was in the depth of deep sleep, and through them went the boy till he got into the stable. There was the filly, as handsome a beast as ever stretched leg, and there was one stableboy with a currycomb in his hand, and another with a bridle, and another with a sieve of oats, and another with an armful of hay, and all as if they were cut out of stone. The filly was the only live thing in the place except himself. She had a common wood and leather saddle on her back, but a golden saddle with the nicest work on it was hung from the post, and he thought it the greatest pity not to put it in place of the other. Well, I believe there was some *pishtrogues* over it for a saddle; anyhow, he took off the other, and put the gold one in its place.

Out came a squeal from the filly's throat when she felt the strange article that might be heard from Tombrick to Bunclody, and all as ready were the armed men and the stableboys to run and surround the *omadhan* of a boy, and the King of Morocco was soon there along with the rest, with a face on him as black as the sole of your foot. After he stood enjoying the abuse the poor boy got from everybody for some time, he says to him, 'You deserve high hanging for your impudence, but I'll give you a chance for your life and the filly, too. I lay on you all sorts of prohibitions, and restrictions, and death, and destruction, to go and bring me Princess Golden Locks, the King of Greece's daughter. When you deliver her into my hand, you may have the "daughter of the wind", and welcome. Come in and take your supper and your rest, and be off at the flight of night.'

The poor boy was down in the mouth, you may suppose, as he was walking away next morning, and very much ashamed when the fox looked up in his face after coming out of the wood.

'What a thing it is,' says he, 'not to have a head when a body wants it most; and here we have a fine long journey before us to the King of Greece's palace. The worse luck now, the same always. Here, get on my tail, and we'll be making the road shorter.'

So he sat on the fox's tail, and swift as thought they went. The wind that was before them they would overtake it, the wind that was behind them would not overtake them, and in the evening they were eating their bread and cold meat in the wood near the castle.

'Now,' says the fox, when they were done, 'I'll go before you to make things easy. Follow me in a quarter of an hour. Don't let Princess Golden Locks touch the jambs of the doors with her hands, or hair, or clothes, and if you're asked any favour, mind how you answer. Once she's outside the door, no one can take her from you.'

Into the palace walked the boy at the proper time, and there were the score, and the dozen, and the half-dozen, and the three guards all standing up or leaning on their arms, and all dead asleep, and in the farthest room of all was the Princess Golden Locks, as lovely as Venus herself. She was asleep in one chair, and her father, the King of Greece, in another. He stood before her for ever so long with the love sinking deeper into his heart every minute, till at last he went down on one knee, and took her darling white hand in his hand, and kissed it.

When she opened her eyes, she was a little frightened, but I believe not very angry, for the boy, as I call him, was a fine handsome young fellow, and all the respect and love that ever you could think of was in his face. She asked him what he wanted, and he stammered, and blushed, and began his story six times, before she understood it.

'And would you give me up to that ugly black King of Morocco?' says she.

'I am obliged to do so,' says he, 'by prohibitions, and restrictions, and death, and destruction, but I'll have his life and free you, or lose my own. If I can't get you for my wife, my days on the earth will be short.'

'Well,' says she, 'let me take leave of my father at any rate.'

'Ah, I can't do that,' says he, 'or they'd all waken, and myself would be put to death, or sent to some task worse than any I got yet.'

But she asked leave at any rate to kiss the old man; that wouldn't waken him, and then she'd go. How could he refuse her, and his heart tied up in every curl of her hair? But, bedad, the moment her lips touched her father's, he let a cry, and everyone of the score, the dozen guards woke up, and clashed their arms, and were going to make *gibbets* of the foolish boy.

But the king ordered them to hold their hands, till he'd found out what it was all about, and when he heard the boy's story he gave him a chance for his life.

'There is,' says he, 'a great heap of clay in front of the palace that won't let the sun shine on the walls in the middle of summer. Everyone that ever worked at it found two shovelfuls added to it for every one they threw away. Remove it, and I'll let my daughter go with you. If you're the man I suspect you to be, I think she'll be in no danger of being wife to that yellow *Molott*.'

Early next morning was the boy tackled to his work, and for every shovelful he flung away two came back on him, and at last he could hardly get out of the heap that gathered round him. Well, the poor fellow scrambled out some way, and sat down on a sod, and he'd have cried only for the shame of it. He began at it in ever so many places, and one was still worse than the other, and in the heel of the evening, when he was sitting with his head between his hands, who should be standing before him but the fox.

'Well, my poor fellow,' says he, 'you're low enough. Go in: I won't say anything to add to your trouble. Take your supper and your rest: tomorrow will be a new day.'

'How is the work going off?' says the king, when they were at supper.

'Faith, your majesty,' says the poor boy, 'it's not going off, but coming on it is. I suppose you'll have the trouble of digging me out at sunset tomorrow, and waking me.'

'I hope not,' says the princess, with a smile on her kind face; and the boy was as happy as anything the rest of the evening.

He was wakened up next morning with voices shouting, and bugles blowing, and drums beating, and such a hullabaloo he never heard in his life before. He ran out to see what was the matter, and there, where the heap of clay was the evening before, were soldiers, and servants, and lords, and ladies, dancing like mad for joy that it was gone.

'Ah, my poor fox!' says he to himself. 'This is your work.'

Well, there was little delay about his return. The king was going to send a great retinue with the princess and himself, but he wouldn't let him take the trouble.

'I have a friend,' says he, 'that will bring us both to the King of Morocco's palace in a day, devil fly away with him!'

There was great crying when she was parting from her father.

'Ah!' says he, 'what a lonesome life I'll have now! Your poor brother in the power of that wicked witch, and kept away from us, and now you taken from me in my old age!'

Well, they both were walking on through the wood, and he telling her how much he loved her; out walked the fox from behind a brake, and in a short time he and she were sitting on the brush, and holding one another fast for fear of slipping off, and away they went like thought. The wind that was before them they would overtake it, and in the evening he and she were in the big bawn of the King of Morocco's castle.

'Well,' says he to the boy, 'you've done your duty well; bring out the bay filly. I'd give the full of the bawn of such fillies, if I had them, for this handsome princess. Get on your steed, and here is a good purse of guineas for the road.'

'Thank you,' says he. 'I suppose you'll let me shake hands with the princess before I start.'

'Yes, indeed, and welcome.'

Well, he was some little time about the handshaking, and before it was over he had her fixed snug behind him; and while you could count three, he and she and the filly were through all the guards, and a hundred perches away. On they went, and next morning they were in the wood near the King of Spain's palace, and there was the fox before them.

'Leave your princess here with me,' says he, 'and go and get the golden bird and the three apples. If you don't bring us back the filly along with the bird, I must carry you both home myself.'

Well, when the King of Spain saw the boy and the filly in the bawn, he ordered the golden bird and the golden cage and the golden apples be brought out and handed to him, and was very thankful and very glad of his prize. But the boy could not part with the nice beast without petting it and rubbing it; and while no one was expecting such a thing, he was up on its back, and through the guards, and a hundred perches away, and he wasn't long till he came to where he left his princess and the fox.

They hurried away till they were safe out of the King of Spain's land, and then they went on easier; and if I was to tell you all the loving things they said to one another, the story wouldn't be over till morning. When they were passing the village of the dance house, they found his two brothers begging and they brought them along. When they came to where the fox appeared first, he begged the young man to cut off his head and his tail. He would not do it for him; he shivered at the very thought, but the eldest brother was ready enough. The head and tail vanished with the blows, and the body changed into the finest young man you could see, and who was he but the princess's brother that was bewitched. Whatever joy they had before, they had twice as much now, and when they arrived at the palace bonfires were set blazing, oxes roasting and puncheons of wine put out on the lawn. The young Prince of Greece was married to the king's daughter, and the prince's sister to the gardener's son.

He and she went a shorter way back to her father's house, with many attendants, and the king was o glad of the golden bird and the golden apples, that he had sent a wagon full of gold and a wagon full of silver along with them.

Guleesh

There was once a boy in the County Mayo; Guleesh was his name. There was the finest rath a little way off from the gable of the house, and he was often in the habit of seating himself on the fine grass bank that was running round it. One night he stood, half leaning against the gable of the house, and looking up into the sky, and watching the beautiful white moon over his head. After he had been standing that way for a couple of hours, he said to himself, 'My bitter grief is that I am not gone away out of this place altogether. I'd sooner be any place in the world than here. Och, it's well for you, white moon,' says he, 'that's turning round, turning round, as you please yourself, and no man can stay your course. I wish I was the same as you.'

Hardly was the word out of his mouth when he heard a great noise coming like the sound of many people running together, and talking, and laughing, and making sport, and the sound went by him like a whirl of wind, and he was listening to it going into the rath. 'Musha, by my soul,' says he, 'but ye're merry enough, and I'll follow ye.'

What was in it but the fairy host, though he did not know at first that it was they who were in it, but he followed them into the rath. It's there he heard the *fulparnee* and the *folpornee*, the *rap-lay-hoota* and the *roolya-boolya* that they had there, and every man of them crying out as loud as he could, 'My horse, and bridle, and saddle! My horse, and bridle, and saddle!'

'By my hand,' said Guleesh, 'my boy, that's not bad. I'll imitate ye,' and he cried out as well as they, 'My horse, and bridle, and saddle! My horse, and bridle, and saddle!' And on the moment there was a fine horse with a bridle of gold, and a saddle of silver standing before him. He leaped up on it, and the moment he was on its back he saw clearly that the rath was full of horses, and of little people going riding on them.

Said a man of them to him, 'Are you coming with us tonight, Guleesh?'

'I am surely,' said Guleesh.

'If you are, come along,' said the little man, and out they went all together, riding like the wind, faster than the fastest horse ever you saw a-hunting, and faster than the fox and the hounds at his tail.

The cold winter's wind that was before them, they overtook her, and the cold winter's wind that was behind them, she did not overtake them. And stop nor stay of that full race did they make none, until they came to the brink of the sea.

Then every one of them said, 'Hie over cap! Hie over cap!' and that moment they were up in the air, and before Guleesh had time to remember where he was, they were down on dry land again, and were going like the wind.

At last they stood still, and a man of them said to Guleesh, 'Guleesh, do you know where you are now?'

'Not an idea,' says Guleesh.

'You're in France, Guleesh,' said he. 'The daughter of the King of France is to be married tonight, the handsomest woman that the sun ever saw, and we must do our best to bring her with us, if we're only able to carry her off; and you must come with us that we may be able to put the young girl up behind you on the horse, when we'll be bringing her away, for it's not lawful for us to put her sitting behind ourselves. But you're flesh and blood, and she can take a good grip of you, so that she won't fall off the horse. Are you satisfied, Guleesh, and will you do what we're telling you?'

'Why shouldn't I be satisfied?' said Guleesh. 'I'm satisfied, surely, and anything that ye will tell me to do I'll do it without doubt.'

They got off their horses there, and a man of them said a word that Guleesh did not understand, and on the moment they were lifted up, and Guleesh found himself and his companions in the palace. There was a great feast going on there, and there was not a nobleman or a gentleman in the kingdom but was gathered there, dressed in silk and satin, and gold and silver, and the night was as bright as the day with all the lamps and candles that were lit, and Guleesh had to shut his two eyes at the brightness. When he opened them again and looked from him, he thought he never saw anything as fine as all he saw there. There were a hundred tables spread out, and their fill of meat and drink on each table of them, flesh-meat, and cakes and sweetmeats, and wine and ale, and every drink that ever a man saw. The musicians were at the two ends of the hall, and they were playing the sweetest music that ever a man's ear heard, and there were young women and fine youths in the middle of the hall, dancing and turning, and going round so quickly and so lightly, that it put a *soorawn* in Guleesh's head to be looking at them. There were more there playing tricks, and more making fun and laughing, for such a feast as there was that day had not been in France for twenty years, because the old king had no children alive but only the one daughter, and she was to be married to the son of another king that night. Three days the feast was going on, and the third night she was to be married, and that was the night that Guleesh and the sheehogues came, hoping, if they could, to carry off with them the king's young daughter.

Guleesh and his companions were standing together at the head of the hall, where there was a fine altar dressed up, and two bishops behind it waiting to marry the girl, as soon as the right time should come. Now nobody could see the sheehogues, for they said a word as they came in that made them all invisible, as if they had not been in it at all.

'Tell me which of them is the king's daughter,' said Guleesh, when he was becoming a little used to the noise and the light.

'Don't you see her there away from you?' said the little man that he was talking to.

Guleesh looked where the little man was pointing with his finger, and there he saw the loveliest woman that was, he thought, upon the ridge of the world. The rose and the lily were fighting together in her face, and one could not tell which of them got the victory. Her arms and hands were like the lime, her mouth as red as a strawberry when it is ripe, her foot was as small and as light as another one's hand, her form was smooth and slender, and her hair was falling down from her head in buckles of gold. Her garments and dress were woven with gold and silver, and the bright stone that was in the ring on her hand was as shining as the sun.

Guleesh was nearly blinded with all the loveliness and beauty that was in her; but when he looked again, he saw that she was crying, and that there was the trace of tears in her eyes. 'It can't be,' said Guleesh, 'that there's grief on her, when everybody round her is so full of sport and merriment.'

'Musha, then, she is grieved,' said the little man; 'for it's against her own will she's marrying, and she has no love for the husband she is to marry. The king was going to give her to him three years ago, when she was only fifteen, but she said she was too young, and requested him to leave her as she was yet. The king gave her a year's grace, and when that year was up he gave her another year's grace, and then another; but a week or a day he would not give her longer, and she is eighteen years old tonight, and it's time for her to marry; but, indeed,' says he, and he crooked his mouth in an ugly way – 'indeed, it's no king's son she'll marry, if I can help it.'

Guleesh pitied the handsome young lady greatly when he heard that, and he was heartbroken to think that it would be necessary for her to marry a man she did not like, or, what was worse, to take a nasty sheehogue for a husband. However, he did not say a word, though he could not help giving many a curse to the ill-luck that was laid out for himself, to be helping the people that were to snatch her away from her home and from her father.

He began thinking, then, what it was he ought to do to save her, but he could think of nothing. 'Oh! If I could only give her some help and relief,' said he, 'I wouldn't care whether I were alive or dead; but I see nothing that I can do for her.'

He was looking on when the king's son came up to her and asked her for a kiss, but she turned her head away from him. Guleesh had double pity for her then, when he saw the lad taking her by the soft white hand, and drawing her out to dance. They went round in the dance near where Guleesh was, and he could plainly see that there were tears in her eyes.

When the dancing was over, the old king, her father, and her mother the queen, came up and said that this was the right time to marry her, that the bishop was ready, and it was time to put the wedding ring on her and give her to her husband.

The king took the youth by the hand, and the queen took her daughter, and they went up together to the altar, with the lords and great people following them.

When they came near the altar, and were no more than about four yards from it, the little sheehogue stretched out his foot before the girl, and she fell.

Before she was able to rise again he threw something that was in his hand upon her, said a couple of words, and upon the moment the maiden was gone from amongst them. Nobody could see her, for that word made her invisible. The little *maneen* seized her and raised her up behind Guleesh, and the king nor no one else saw them, but out with them through the hall till they came to the door.

Oro! Dear Mary! It's there the pity was, and the trouble, and the crying, and the wonder, and the searching, and the *rookawn*, when that lady disappeared from their eyes and without their seeing what did it. Out of the door of the palace they went, without being stopped or hindered, for nobody saw them, and, 'My horse, my bridle, and saddle!' says every man of them. 'My horse, my bridle, and saddle!' says Guleesh; and on the moment the horse was standing ready caparisoned before him. 'Now, jump up, Guleesh,' said the little man, 'and put the lady behind you, and we will be going; the morning is not far off from us now.'

Guleesh raised her up on the horse's back, and leaped up himself before her, and, 'Rise, horse,' said he; and his horse, and the other horses with him, went in a full race until they came to the sea.

'Hie over cap!' said every man of them.

'Hie over cap!' said Guleesh; and on the moment the horse rose under him, and cut a leap in the clouds, and came down in Erin.

They did not stop there, but went of a race to the place where was Guleesh's house and the rath. And when they came as far as that, Guleesh turned and caught the young girl in his two arms, and leaped off the horse.

'I call and cross you to myself, in the name of God!' said he; and on the spot, before the word was out of his mouth, the horse fell down, and what was in it but the beam of a plough, of which they had made a horse; and every other horse they had, it was that way they made it. Some of them were riding on an old besom, and some on a broken stick, and more on a bohalawn or a hemlock-stalk.

The good people called out together when they heard what Guleesh said, 'Oh! Guleesh, you clown, you thief, that no good may happen to you, why did you play that trick on us?'

But they had no power at all to carry off the girl, after Guleesh had consecrated her to himself.

'Oh! Guleesh, isn't that a nice turn you did us,

'Now, jump up, Guleesh,' said the little man, 'and put the lady behind you,
and we will be going; the morning is not far off from us now.'

and we so kind to you? What good have we now out of our journey to France. Never mind yet, you clown, but you'll pay us another time for this. Believe us, you'll repent it.'

'He'll have no good to get out of the young girl,' said the little man that was talking to him in the palace before that, and as he said the word he moved over to her and struck her a slap on the side of the head. 'Now,' says he, 'she'll be without talk any more; now, Guleesh, what good will she be to you when she'll be dumb? It's time for us to go – but you'll remember us, Guleesh!'

When he said that he stretched out his two hands, and before Guleesh was able to give an answer, he and the rest of them were gone into the rath out of his sight, and he saw them no more.

He turned to the young woman and said to her, 'Thanks be to God, they're gone. Would you not sooner stay with me than with them?' She gave him no answer. 'There's trouble and grief on her yet,' said Guleesh in his own mind, and he spoke to her again, 'I am afraid that you must spend this night in my father's house, lady, and if there is anything that I can do for you, tell me, and I'll be your servant.'

The beautiful girl remained silent, but there were tears in her eyes, and her face was white and red after each other.

'Lady,' said Guleesh, 'tell me what you would like me to do now. I never belonged at all to that lot of sheehogues who carried you away with them. I am the son of an honest farmer, and I went with them without knowing it. If I'll be able to send you back to your father I'll do it, and I pray you make any use of me now that you may wish.'

He looked into her face, and he saw the mouth moving as if she was going to speak, but there came no word from it.

'It cannot be,' said Guleesh, 'that you are dumb. Did I not hear you speaking to the king's son in the palace tonight? Or has that devil made you really dumb, when he struck his nasty hand on your jaw?'

The girl raised her white smooth hand, and laid her finger on her tongue, to show him that she had lost her voice and power of speech, and the tears ran out of her two eyes like streams, and Guleesh's own eyes were not dry, for as rough as he was on the outside he had a soft heart, and could not stand the sight of the young girl, and she in that unhappy plight.

He began thinking with himself what he ought to do, and he did not like to bring her home with himself to his father's house, for he knew well that they would not believe him, that he had been in France and brought back with him the King of France's daughter, and he was afraid they might make a mock of the young lady or insult her.

As he was doubting what he ought to do, and hesitating, he chanced to remember the priest. 'Glory be to God,' said he, 'I know now what I'll do; I'll bring her to the priest's house, and he won't refuse me to keep the lady and care for her.' He turned to the lady again and told her that he was loth to take her to his father's house, but that there was an excellent priest very friendly to himself, who would take good care of her, if she wished to remain in his house; but that if there was any other place she would rather go, he said he would bring her to it.

She bent her head, to show him she was obliged, and gave him to understand that she was ready to follow him to any place he was going. 'We will go to the priest's house, then,' said he; 'he is under an obligation to me, and will do anything I ask him.'

They went together accordingly to the priest's house, and the sun was just rising when they came to the door. Guleesh beat it hard, and as early as it was the priest was up, and opened the door himself. He wondered when he saw Guleesh and the girl, for he was certain that it was coming wanting to be married they were.

'Guleesh, Guleesh, isn't it the nice boy you are that you can't wait till ten o'clock or till twelve, but that you must be coming to me at this hour, looking for marriage, you and your sweetheart? You ought to know that I can't marry you at such a time, or, at all events, can't marry you lawfully. But, Guleesh!' said he, suddenly, as he looked again at the young girl, 'in the name of God, who have you here? Who is she, or how did you get her?'

'Father,' said Guleesh, 'you can marry me, or anybody else, if you wish; but it's not looking for marriage I came to you now, but to ask you, if you please, to give a lodging in your house to this young lady.'

The priest looked at him as though he had ten heads on him; but without putting any other question to him, he desired him to come in, himself and the maiden, and when they came in, he shut the door, brought them into the parlour, and put them sitting.

'Now, Guleesh,' said he, 'tell me truly who is this young lady, and whether you're out of your senses really, or are only making a joke of me.'

'I'm not telling a word of lie, nor making a joke of you,' said Guleesh; 'but it was from the palace of the King of France I carried off this lady, and she is the daughter of the King of France.'

He began his story then, and told the whole to the priest, and the priest was so much surprised that he could not help calling out at times, or clapping his hands together.

When Guleesh said from what he saw he thought the girl was not satisfied with the marriage that was going to take place in the palace before he and the sheehogues broke it up, there came a red blush into the girl's cheek, and he was more certain than ever that she had sooner be as she was – badly as she was – than be the married wife of the man she hated. When Guleesh said that he would be very thankful to the priest if he would keep her in his own house, the kind man said he would do that as long as Guleesh pleased, but that he did not know what they ought to do with her, because they had no means of sending her back to her father again.

Guleesh answered that he was uneasy about the same thing, and that he saw nothing to do but to keep quiet until they should find some opportunity of doing something better. They made it up then between themselves that the priest should let on that it was his brother's daughter he had, who was come on a visit to him from another county, and that he should tell everybody that she was dumb, and do his best to keep everyone away from her. They told the young girl what it was they intended to do, and she showed by her eyes that she was obliged to them.

Guleesh went home then, and when his people asked him where he had been, he said that he had been asleep at the foot of the ditch, and had passed the night there.

There was great wonderment on the priest's neighbours at the girl who came so suddenly to his house without anyone knowing where she was from, or what business she had there. Some of the people said that everything was not as it ought to be, and others, that Guleesh was not like the same man that was in it before, and that it was a great story, how he was drawing every day to the priest's house, and that the priest had a wish and a respect for him, a thing they could not clear up at all.

That was true for them, indeed, for it was seldom the day went by but Guleesh would go to the priest's house and have a talk with him, and as often as he would come he used to hope to find the young lady well again, and with leave to speak; but,

alas, she remained dumb and silent, without relief or cure. Since she had no other means of talking, she carried on a sort of conversation between herself and himself, by moving her hand and fingers, winking her eyes, opening and shutting her mouth, laughing or smiling, and a thousand other signs, so that it was not long before they understood each other very well. Guleesh was always thinking how he should send her back to her father; but there was no one to go with her, and he himself did not know what road to go, for he had never been out of his own country before the night he brought her away with him. Nor had the priest any better knowledge than he; but when Guleesh asked him, he wrote three or four letters to the King of France, and gave them to buyers and sellers of wares, who used to be going from place to place across the sea; but they all went astray, and never a one came to the king's hand.

This was the way they were for many months, and Guleesh was falling deeper and deeper in love with her every day, and it was plain to himself and the priest that she liked him. The boy feared greatly at last, lest the king should really hear where his daughter was, and take her back from himself, and he besought the priest to write no more, but to leave the matter to God.

So they passed the time for a year, until there came a day when Guleesh was lying by himself on the grass, on the last day of the last month in autumn, and he was thinking over again in his own mind of everything that had happened to him from the day that he went with the sheehogues across the sea. He remember then, suddenly, that it was one November night that he was standing at the gable of the house, when the whirlwind came, and the sheehogues in it, and he said to himself, 'We have November night again today, and I'll stand in the same place I was last year, until I see if the good people come again. Perhaps I might see or hear something that would be useful to me, and might bring back her talk again to Mary' – that was the name himself and the priest called the king's daughter, for neither of them knew her right name. He told his intention to the priest, and the priest gave him his blessing.

Guleesh accordingly went to the old rath when the night was darkening, and he stood with his bent elbow leaning on a grey old flag, waiting till the middle of the night should come. The moon rose slowly, and it was like a knob of fire behind him; and there was a white fog which was raised up over the fields of grass and all damp places, through the coolness of the night after the warmth of the day. The night was calm as is a lake when there is not a breath of wind to move a wave on it, and there was no sound to be heard but the *cronawn* of the insects that would go by from time to time, or the hoarse sudden scream of the wild geese, as they passed from lake to lake, half a mile up in the air over his head; or the sharp whistle of the golden and green plover, rising and lying, lying and rising, as they do on a calm night. There were a thousand thousand bright stars shining over his head, and there was a little frost out, which left the grass under his foot white and crisp.

He stood there for an hour, for two hours, for three hours, and the frost increased greatly, so that he heard the breaking of the *traneens* under his foot as often as he moved. He was thinking, in his own mind, at last, that the sheehogues would not come that night, and that it was as good for him to return back again, when he heard a sound far away from him, coming towards him, and he recognised what it was at the first moment. The sound increased, and at first it was like the beating of waves on a stony shore, and then it was like the falling of a great waterfall, and at last it was like a loud storm in the tops of the trees, and then the whirlwind burst into the rath all of a rout, and the sheehogues were in it.

It all went by him so suddenly that he lost his breath with it, but he came to himself on the spot, and put an ear on himself, listening to what they would say.

Scarcely had they gathered into the rath till they all began shouting, and screaming, and talking amongst themselves; and then each one of them cried out, 'My horse and bridle, and saddle! My horse, and bridle, and saddle!' and Guleesh took courage, and called out as loudly as any of them, 'My horse, and bridle, and saddle! My horse and bridle, and saddle!' But before the word was well out of his mouth, another man cried out, 'Ora! Guleesh, my boy, are you here with us again? How are you getting on with your woman? There's no use in your calling for your horse tonight. I'll go bail you won't play such a trick on us again. It was a good trick you played on us last year!'

'It was,' said another man; 'he won't do it again.'

'Isn't he a prime lad, the same lad! To take a woman with him that never said as much to him as, "How do you do?" since this time last year!' says the third man.

'Perhaps he likes to be looking at her,' said another voice.

'And if the *omadawn* only knew that there's a herb growing up by his own door and if he were to boil it and give it to her she'd be well,' said another voice.

'That's true for you.'

'He is an *omadawn*.'

'Don't bother your head with him; we'll be going.'

'We'll leave the *bodach* as he is.'

And with that they rose up into the air, and out with them with one *roolya-boolya* the way they came; and they left poor Guleesh standing where they found him, and the two eyes going out of his head, looking after them and wondering.

He did not stand long till he returned back, and he thinking in his own mind on all he saw and heard, and wondering whether there was really a herb at his own door that would bring back the talk to the king's daughter. 'It can't be,' says he to himself, 'that they would tell it to me, if there was any virtue in it; but perhaps the sheehogue didn't observe himself when he let the word slip out of his mouth. I'll search well as soon as the sun rises, whether there's any plant growing beside the house except thistles and dockings.'

He went home, and as tired as he was he did not sleep a wink until the sun rose on the morrow. He got up then, and it was the first thing he did to go out and search well through the grass round about the house, trying could he get any herb that he did not recognise. And, indeed, he was not long searching till he observed a large strange herb that was growing up just by the gable of the house.

He went over to it, and observed it closely, and saw that there were seven little branches coming out of the stalk, and seven leaves growing on every one of them; and that there was a white sap in the leaves. 'It's very wonderful,' said he to himself, 'that I never noticed this herb before. If there's any virtue in a herb at all, it ought to be in such a strange one as this.'

He drew out his knife, cut the plant, and carried it into his own house; stripped the leaves off it and cut up the stalk; and there came a thick, white juice out of it, as there comes out of the sow-thistle when it is bruised, except that the juice was more like oil.

He put it in a little pot and a little water in it, and laid it on the fire until the water was boiling, and then he took a cup, filled it half up with the juice, and put it to his own mouth. It came into his head then that perhaps it was poison that was in it, and that the good people were only tempting him that he might kill himself with that trick, or put the girl to death without meaning it. He put down the cup again, raised a couple of drops on the top of his finger, and put it to his mouth. It was not bitter, and, indeed, had a sweet, agreeable taste. He grew bolder then, and drank the full of a thimble of it, and then as much again, and he never stopped till he had half the cup drunk. He fell asleep after that, and did not wake till it was night, and there was great hunger and great thirst on him.

He had to wait, then, till the day rose; but he determined, as soon as he should wake in the morning, that he would go to the king's daughter and give her a drink of the juice of the herb.

As soon as he got up in the morning, he went over to the priest's house with the drink in his hand, and he never felt himself so bold and valiant, and spirited and light, as he was that day, and he was quite certain that it was the drink he drank which made him so hearty.

When he came to the house, he found the priest and the young lady within, and they were wondering greatly why he had not visited them for two days.

He told them all his news, and said that he was certain that there was great power in that herb, and that it would do the lady no hurt, for he had tried it himself and got good from it, and then he made her taste it, for he vowed and swore that there was no harm in it.

Guleesh handed her the cup, and she drank half of it, and then fell back on her bed and a heavy sleep came on her, and she never woke out of that sleep till the day on the morrow.

Guleesh and the priest sat up the entire night with her, waiting till she should awake, and they between hope and unhope, between expectation of saving her and fear of hurting her.

She awoke at last when the sun had gone half its way through the heavens. She rubbed her eyes and looked like a person who did not know where she was. She was like one astonished when she saw Guleesh and the priest in the same room with her, and she sat up doing her best to collect her thoughts.

The two men were in great anxiety waiting to see would she speak, or would she not speak, and when they remained silent for a couple of minutes, the priest said to her, 'Did you sleep well, Mary?'

And she answered him, 'I slept, thank you.'

No sooner did Guleesh hear her talking than he put a shout of joy out of him, and ran over to her and fell on his two knees, and said, 'A thousand thanks to God, who has given you back the talk; lady of my heart, speak again to me.'

The lady answered him that she understood it was he who boiled that drink for her, and gave it to her; that she was obliged to him from her heart for all the kindness he had showed her since the day she first came to Ireland, and that he might be certain that she never would forget it.

Guleesh was ready to die with satisfaction and delight. Then they brought her food, and she ate with a good appetite, and was merry and joyous, and never left off talking with the priest while she was eating.

After that Guleesh went home to his house, and stretched himself on the bed and fell asleep again, for the force of the herb was not all spent, and he passed another day and a night sleeping. When he woke up he went back to the priest's house, and found that the young lady was in the same state, and that she was asleep almost since the time that he left the house.

He went into her chamber with the priest, and they remained watching beside her till she awoke the second time, and she had her talk as well as ever, and Guleesh was greatly rejoiced. The priest put food on the table again, and they ate together, and Guleesh used after that to come to the house from day to day, and the friendship that was between him and the king's daughter increased, because she had no one to speak to except Guleesh and the priest, and she liked Guleesh best.

So they married one another, and that was the fine wedding they had, and if I were to be there then, I would not be here now; but I heard it from a birdeen that there was neither cark nor care, sickness nor sorrow, mishap nor misfortune on them till the hour of their death, and may the same be with me, and with us all!

Hans in Luck

Some men are born to good luck: all they do or try to do comes right, all that falls to them is so much gain, all their geese are swans, all their cards are trumps – toss them which way you will, they will always, like poor puss, alight upon their legs, and only move on so much the faster. The world may very likely not always think of them as they think of themselves, but what care they for the world? What can it know about the matter?

One of these lucky beings was neighbour Hans. Seven long years he had worked hard for his master. At last he said, 'Master, my time is up; I must go home and see my poor mother once more; so pray pay me my wages and let me go.'

And the master said, 'You have been a faithful and good servant, Hans, so your pay shall be handsome.' Then he gave him a lump of silver as big as his head.

Hans took out his pocket-handkerchief, put the piece of silver into it, threw it over his shoulder, and set off on his road homewards. As he went lazily on, dragging one foot after another, a man came in sight, trotting gaily along on a capital horse. 'Ah!' said Hans aloud, 'what a fine thing it is to ride on horseback! There he sits as easy and happy as if he was at home, in the chair by his fireside; he trips against no stones, saves shoe-leather and gets where he's going he hardly knows how.'

Hans did not speak softly so the horseman heard it all. 'Well, friend, why do you go on foot then?' he asked.

'Ah!' said Hans, 'I have this load to carry: to be sure it is silver, but it is so heavy that I can't hold up my head, and I can tell you it hurts my shoulder sadly.'

'What do you say of making an exchange?' said the horseman. 'I will give you my horse, and you shall give me the silver; which will save you a great deal of trouble in carrying such a heavy load about with you.'

'With all my heart,' said Hans: 'but as you are so kind to me, I must tell you one thing – you will have a weary task to draw that silver about with you.'

Undeterred, the horseman got off, took the silver, helped Hans up, gave him the bridle into one hand and the whip into the other, and said, 'When you want to go very fast, smack your lips loudly together, and cry "Jip!" '

Hans was delighted as he sat on the horse, drew himself up, squared his elbows, turned out his toes, cracked his whip, and rode merrily off, one minute whistling a merry tune, and another singing,

> 'No care and no sorrow,
> A fig for the morrow!
> We'll laugh and be merry,
> Sing neigh down derry!'

After a time he thought he should like to go a little faster, so he smacked his lips and cried 'Jip!' Away went the horse at full gallop; and before Hans knew what he was about, he was thrown off, and lay on his back by the roadside. His horse would have run off, if a shepherd who was coming by, driving a cow, had not stopped it. Hans soon came to himself, and got upon his legs again, sadly vexed, and said to the shepherd, 'This riding is no joke for a man who has the luck to get upon a beast like this that stumbles and flings him off as if it would break his neck. However, I'm off now once and for all! I like your cow now a great deal better than this smart beast that played me this trick, and has spoiled my best coat, as you see, in this puddle; which, by the by, smells not very like a nosegay. One can walk along at one's leisure behind that cow – keep good company, and have milk, butter and cheese every day into the bargain. What would I give to have such a prize!'

'Well,' said the shepherd, 'if you are so fond of her, I will change my cow for your horse; I like to do good to my neighbours, even though I lose by it myself.'

'Done!' said Hans, merrily. 'What a noble heart that good man has!' thought he. Then the shepherd jumped upon the horse, wished Hans and the cow good-morning, and away he rode.

Hans brushed his coat, wiped his face and hands, rested a while, and then drove off his cow quietly, and thought his bargain a very lucky one. 'If I have only a piece of bread (and I certainly shall always be able to get that), I can, whenever I like, eat my butter and cheese with it; and when I am thirsty I can milk my cow and drink the milk: who could wish for more?' When he came to an inn, he halted, ate up all his bread, and gave away his last penny for a glass of beer. When he had rested himself he set off again, driving his cow towards his mother's village. But the heat grew greater as soon as noon came on, till at last, as he found himself on a wide heath that would take him more than an hour to cross, he began to be so hot and parched that his tongue cleaved to the roof of his mouth. 'I can find a cure for this,' thought he; 'now I will milk my cow and quench my thirst': so he tied her to the stump of a tree, and held his leathern cap to milk into; but not a drop was to be had. Who would have thought that this cow, which was to bring him milk and butter and cheese, was all the time utterly dry? Hans had not even considered the possibility.

While he was trying his luck in milking, and managing the matter very clumsily, the uneasy beast began to think him very troublesome; and at last she gave him such a kick on the head that she knocked him down; and there he lay a long while senseless. Luckily a butcher soon came by, pushing a pig in a wheelbarrow.

'What is the matter with you, my man?' said the butcher, as he helped him up.

Hans told him what had happened, how he was dry, and wanted to milk his cow, but found the cow was dry too. Then the butcher gave him a flask of ale, saying, 'There, drink and refresh yourself; your cow will give you no milk: don't you see she is an old beast, good for nothing but the slaughter-house?'

'Alas, alas!' said Hans, 'who would have thought it? What a shame to take my horse, and give me only a dry cow! If I kill her, what will she be good for? I hate cow-beef; it is not tender enough for me. If she were a pig now – like that fat gentleman you are wheeling along at his ease – one could do something with her; she would at any rate make sausages.'

Luckily a butcher soon came by, pushing a pig in a wheelbarrow.

'Well,' said the butcher, 'I don't like to say no, when one is asked to do a kind, neighbourly thing. To please you I will change, and give you my fine fat pig for the cow.'

'Heaven reward you for your kindness and self-denial!' said Hans, as he gave the butcher the cow; and taking the pig off the wheelbarrow, drove it away, holding it by the string that was tied to its leg.

So on he jogged, and all seemed now to go right with him: he had met with some misfortunes, to be sure; but he was now well repaid for all. How could it be otherwise with such a travelling companion as he had at last got?

The next man he met was a countryman carrying a fine white goose. The countryman stopped to ask him the time; this led to further chat; and Hans told him all his luck, how he had had so many good bargains, and how all the world had seemed to be smiling with him. The countryman then began to tell his tale, and said he was going to take the goose to a christening. 'Feel,' said he, 'how heavy it is, and yet it is only eight weeks old. Whoever roasts and eats it will find plenty of fat upon it, it has lived so well!'

'You're right,' said Hans, as he weighed it in his hands; 'but if you talk of fat, my pig is no trifle.'

Meantime the countryman began to look grave, and shook his head. 'Hark ye,' said he, 'my worthy friend, you seem a good sort of fellow, so I can't help doing you a kind turn. Your pig may get you into a scrape. In the village I just came from, the squire has had a pig stolen out of his sty. I was dreadfully afraid when I saw you that you had got the squire's pig. If you have, and they catch you, it will be a bad job for you. The least they will do will be to throw you into the horse-pond. Can you swim?'

Poor Hans was sadly frightened. 'Good man,' cried he, 'pray get me out of this scrape. I know nothing of where the pig was either bred or born; but he may have been the squire's for aught I can tell: you know this country better than I do, take my pig and give me the goose.'

'I ought to have something into the bargain,' said the countryman; 'give a fat goose for a pig, indeed! 'Tis not everyone would do so much for you as that. However, I will not be hard upon you, as you are in trouble.'

Then he took the string in his hand, and drove off the pig by a side path, while Hans went on the way homewards free from care. 'After all,' thought he, 'that chap is pretty well taken in. I don't care whose pig it is, but wherever it came from, in this it has been a very good friend to me. I have much the best of the bargain. First there will be a capital roast; then the fat will find me in goose-grease for six months; and then there are all the beautiful white feathers. I will put them into my pillow, and then I am sure I shall sleep soundly without rocking. How happy my mother will be! Talk of a pig, indeed! Give me a fine fat goose.'

As he came to the next village, he saw a scissor-grinder with his wheel, working and singing,

'O'er hill and o'er dale,
So happy I roam;
Work light and live well,
All the world is my home;
Then who so blithe, so merry as I?'

Hans stood looking on for a while, and at last said, 'You must be well off, master grinder! You seem so happy at your work.'

'Yes,' said the other, 'mine is a golden trade; a good grinder never puts his hand into his pocket without finding money in it – but where did you get that beautiful goose?'

'I did not buy it, I gave a pig for it.'

'And where did you get the pig?'

'I gave a cow for it.'

'And the cow?'

'I gave a horse for it.'

'And the horse?'

'I gave a lump of silver as big as my head for it.'

'And the silver?'

'Oh! I worked hard for that seven long years.'

'You have thrived well in the world hitherto,' said the grinder; 'now if you could find money in your pocket whenever you put your hand in it, your fortune would be made.'

'Very true, but how is that to be managed?'

'How? Why, you must turn grinder like myself,' said the other; 'you only want a grindstone; the rest will come of itself. Here is one that is but little the worse for wear. I would not ask more than the value of your goose for it – will you buy?'

'How can you ask?' said Hans. 'I should be the happiest man in the world, if I could have money whenever I put my hand in my pocket: what could I want more? There's the goose.'

'Now,' said the grinder, as he gave him a common rough stone that lay by his side, 'this is a most capital stone; do but work it well enough, and you can make an old nail cut with it.'

Hans took the stone, and went his way with a light heart; his eyes sparkled for joy, and he said to himself, 'Surely I must have been born in a lucky hour; everything I could want or wish for comes of itself. People are so kind; they seem really to think I do them a favour in letting them make me rich, and giving me good bargains.'

Meantime he began to be tired, and hungry too, for he had given away his last penny in his joy at getting the cow.

At last he could go no farther, for the stone tired him sadly, and he dragged himself to the side of a river, that he might take a drink of water, and rest a while. He laid the stone carefully by his side on the bank: but, as he stooped down to drink, he forgot it, pushed it a little, and down it rolled, plump into the stream.

For a while he watched it sinking in the deep clear water – then sprang up and danced for joy, and again fell upon his knees and thanked heaven, with tears in his eyes, for its kindness in taking away his only plague, the ugly heavy stone.

'How happy am I!' cried he; 'nobody was ever so lucky as I.' Then up he got with a light heart, free from all his troubles, and walked on till he reached his mother's house, and told her how very easy the road to good luck was.

Hans, the Mermaid's Son

In a village there once lived a smith called Basmus, who was in a very poor way. He was still a young man, and a strong handsome fellow to boot, but he had many little children and there was little to be earned by his trade. He was, however, a diligent and hard-working man, and when he had no work in the smithy he was out at sea fishing or gathering wreckage on the shore.

It happened one time that he had gone out to fish in good weather, all alone in a little boat, but he did not come home that day, nor the following one, so that all believed he had perished out at sea. On the third day, however, Basmus came to shore again and had his boat full of fish, so big and fat that no one had ever seen their like. There was nothing the matter with him, and he complained

neither of hunger or thirst. He had got into a fog, he said, and could not find land again. What he did not tell, however, was where he had been all the time; that only came out six years later, when people got to know that he had been caught by a mermaid out on the deep sea, and had been her guest during the three days that he was missing. From that time forth he went out no more to fish; nor, indeed, did he require to do so, for whenever he went down to the shore it never failed that some wreckage was washed up, and in it all kinds of valuable things. In those days everyone took what they found and got leave to keep it, so that the smith grew more prosperous day by day.

When seven years had passed since the smith went out to sea, it happened one morning, as he

stood in the smithy, mending a plough, that a handsome young lad came in to him and said, 'Good-day, father; my mother the mermaid sends her greetings, and says that she has had me for six years now, and you can keep me for as long.'

He was a strange enough boy to be six years old, for he looked as if he were eighteen, and was even bigger and stronger than lads commonly are at that age.

'Will you have a bite of bread?' said the smith.

'Oh, yes,' said Hans, for that was his name.

The smith then told his wife to cut a piece of bread for him. She did so, and the boy swallowed it at one mouthful and went out again to the smithy to his father.

'Have you got all you can eat?' said the smith.

'No,' said Hans, 'that was just a little bit.'

The smith went into the house and took a whole loaf, which he cut into two slices and put butter and cheese between them, and this he gave to Hans. In a while the boy came out to the smithy again.

'Well, have you got as much as you can eat?' said the smith.

'No, not nearly,' said Hans; 'I must try to find a better place than this, for I can see that I shall never get my fill here.'

Hans wished to set off at once, as soon as his father would make a staff for him of such a kind as he wanted.

'It must be of iron,' said he, 'and cut out for heavy duty.'

The smith brought him an iron rod as thick as an ordinary staff, but Hans took it and twisted it round his finger, so that wouldn't do. Then the smith came dragging one as thick as a wagon-pole, but Hans bent it over his knee and broke it like a straw. The smith then had to collect all the iron he had, and Hans held it while his father forged for him a staff, which was heavier than the anvil. When Hans had got this he said, 'Many thanks, father; now I have got my inheritance.' With this he set off into the country, and the smith was very pleased to be rid of that son, before he ate him out of house and home.

Hans first arrived at a large estate, and it so happened that the squire himself was standing outside the farmyard.

'Where are you going?' said the squire.

'I am looking for a place,' said Hans, 'where they have need of strong fellows, and can give them plenty to eat.'

'Well,' said the squire, 'I generally have twenty-four men at this time of the year, but I have only twelve just now, so I can easily take you on.'

'Very well,' said Hans, 'I shall easily do twelve men's work, but then I must also have as much to eat as the twelve would.'

All this was agreed to, and the squire took Hans into the kitchen, and told the servant girls that the new man was to have as much food as the other twelve. It was arranged that he should have a pot to himself, and he could then use the ladle to take his food with.

It was in the evening that Hans arrived there, so he did nothing more that day than eat his supper – a big pot of buckwheat porridge, which he cleaned to the bottom and was then so far satisfied that he said he could sleep on that, so he went off to bed. He slept both well and long, and all the rest were up and at their work while he was still sleeping soundly. The squire was also on foot, for he was curious to see how the new man would behave who was both to eat and work for twelve.

But as yet there was no Hans to be seen, and the sun was already high in the heavens, so the squire himself went and called on him.

'Get up, Hans,' he cried; 'you are sleeping too long.'

Hans woke up and rubbed his eyes. 'Yes, that's true,' he said, 'I must get up and have my breakfast.'

So he rose and dressed himself, and went into the kitchen, where he got his pot of porridge; he swallowed all of this, and then asked what work he was to have.

He was to thresh that day, said the squire; the other twelve men were already busy at it. There were twelve threshing-floors, and the twelve men were at work on six of them – two on each. Hans must thresh by himself all that was lying upon the other six floors. He went out to the barn and got hold of a flail. Then he looked to see how the others did it and did the same, but at the first stroke he smashed the flail in pieces. There were several flails hanging there, and Hans took them, one after the other, but they all went the same way, every one flying in splinters at the first stroke. He then looked round for something else to work with, and found a pair of strong beams lying near. Next he caught sight of a horse-hide nailed up on the barn-door. With the beams he made a flail, using the skin to tie them together. The one beam he used as a handle, and the other to strike with, and now that was all right. But the barn was too low, there was no room to swing the flail, and the floors were too small. Hans, however, found a remedy for this – he simply lifted the whole roof off the barn, and set it down in the field beside. He then emptied down all the corn that he could lay his hands on and threshed away. He went through one lot after another, and it was all the same to him what he got hold of, so before midday he had threshed all the squire's grain, his rye and wheat and barley and oats, all mixed through each other. When he was finished with this, he lifted the roof up on the barn again, like setting a lid on a box, and went in and told the squire that the job was done.

The squire opened his eyes at this announcement; and came out to see if it was really true. It was true, sure enough, but he was scarcely delighted with the mixed grain that he got from all his crops. However, when he saw the flail that Hans had used, and learned how he had made room for himself to swing it, he was so afraid of the strong fellow, that he dared not say anything, except that it was a good thing he had got it threshed; but it had still to be cleaned.

'What does that mean?' asked Hans.

It was explained to him that the corn and the chaff had to be separated; as yet both were lying in one heap, right up to the roof. Hans began to take up a little and sift it in his hands, but he soon saw that this would never do. He soon thought of a plan, however; he opened both barn-doors, and then lay down at one end and blew, so that all the chaff flew out and lay like a sandbank at the other end of the barn, and the grain was as clean as it could be. Then he reported to the squire that that job also was done. The squire said that that was well; there was nothing more for him to do that day. Off went Hans to the kitchen, and got as much as he could eat; then he went and took a midday nap which lasted till supper-time.

Meanwhile the squire was quite miserable, and made his moan to his wife, saying that she must help him to find some means of getting rid of this strong fellow, for he durst not give him his marching orders. She sent for the steward, and it was arranged that next day all the men should go to the forest for firewood, and that they should make a bargain among them that the one who came home last with his load should be hanged. They thought they could easily manage that it would be Hans who would lose his life, for the others would be early on the road, while Hans would certainly oversleep himself. In the evening, therefore, the men sat and

talked together, saying that next morning they must set out early for the forest, and as they had a hard day's work and a long journey before them, they would, for their amusement, make a compact, that whichever of them came home last with his load should lose his life on the gallows. So Hans had no objections to make.

Long before the sun was up next morning, all the twelve men were on foot. They took all the best horses and carts, and drove off to the forest. Hans, however, lay and slept on, and the squire said, 'Just let him lie.'

At last, Hans thought it was time to have his breakfast, so he got up and put on his clothes. He took plenty of time at his breakfast, and then went out to get his horse and cart ready. The others had taken everything that was any good, so that he had difficulty in scraping together four wheels of different sizes and fixing them to an old cart, and he could find no other horses than a pair of old hacks. He did not know where it lay, but he followed the track of the other carts, and in that way came to it all right. On coming to the gate leading into the forest, he was unfortunate enough to break it in pieces, so he took a huge stone that was lying on the field, seven ells long and seven ells broad, and set this in the gap, then he went on and joined the others. These laughed at him heartily, for they had laboured as hard as they could since daybreak, and had helped each other to fell trees and put them on the carts, so that all of these were now loaded except one.

Hans got hold of a woodman's axe and proceeded to fell a tree, but he destroyed the edge and broke the shaft at the first blow. He therefore laid down the axe, put his arms round the tree, and pulled it up by the roots. This he threw upon his cart, and then another and another, and thus he went on while all the others forgot their work, and stood with open mouths, gazing at this strange woodcraft. All at once they began to hurry; the last cart was loaded, and they whipped up their horses, so as to be the first to arrive home.

When Hans had finished his work, he again put his old hacks into the cart, but they could not move it from the spot. He was annoyed at this, and took them out again, twisted a rope round the cart, and all the trees, lifted the whole affair on his back, and set off home, leading the horses behind him by the rein. When he reached the gate, he found the whole row of carts standing there, unable to get any farther for the stone which lay in the gap.

'What!' said Hans, 'can twelve men not move that stone?' With that he lifted it and threw it out of the way, and went on with his burden on his back, and the horses behind him, and arrived at the farm long before any of the others. The squire was walking about there, looking and looking, for he was very curious to know what had happened. Finally, he caught sight of Hans coming along in this fashion, and was so frightened that he did not know what to do, but he shut the gate and put on the bar. When Hans reached the gate of the court-yard, he laid down the trees and hammered at it, but no one came to open it. He then took the trees and tossed them over the barn into the yard, and the cart after them, so that every wheel flew off in a different direction.

When the squire saw this, he thought to himself, 'The horses will come the same way if I don't open the gate,' so he did this.

'Good day, master,' said Hans, and put the horses into the stable, and went into the kitchen, to get something to eat. At length the other men came home with their loads. When they came in, Hans said to them, 'Do you remember the bargain we made last night? Which of you is it that's going to be hanged?' 'Oh,' said they, 'that was only a joke; it didn't mean anything.' 'Oh well, it doesn't matter,' said Hans, and there was no more about it.

The squire, however, and his wife and the steward, had much to say to each other about the terrible man they had got, and all were agreed that they must get rid of him in some way or other. The steward said that he would manage this all right. Next morning they were to clean the well, and they would make use of that opportunity. They would get him down into the well, and then have a big millstone ready to throw down on top of him – that would settle him. After that they could just fill in the well, and then escape being at any expense for his funeral. Both the squire and his wife thought this a splendid idea, and went about rejoicing at the thought that now they would get rid of Hans.

But Hans was hard to kill, as we shall see. He slept long next morning, as he always did, and finally, as he would not waken by himself, the squire had to go and call him. 'Get up, Hans, you are sleeping too long,' he cried. Hans woke up and rubbed his eyes. 'That's so,' said he, 'I shall rise and have my breakfast.' He got up then and dressed himself, while the breakfast stood waiting for him. When he had finished the whole of this, he asked what he was to do that day. He was told to

help the other men to clean out the well. That was all right, and he went out and found the other men waiting for him. To these he said that they could choose whichever task they liked – either to go down into the well and fill the buckets while he pulled them up, or pull them up, and he alone would go down to the bottom of the well. They answered that they would rather stay above-ground, as there would be no room for so many of them down in the well.

Hans therefore went down alone, and began to clean out the well, but the men had arranged how they were to act, and immediately each of them seized a stone from a heap of huge blocks, and threw it down on top of him, thinking to kill him with these. Hans, however, gave no more heed to this than to shout up to them to keep the hens away from the well, for they were scraping gravel down on the top of him.

They then saw that they could not kill him with little stones, but they had still the big one left. The whole twelve of them set to work with poles and rollers and rolled the big millstone to the brink of the well. It was with the greatest difficulty that they got it thrown down there, and now they had no doubt that he had got all that he wanted. But the stone happened to fall so luckily that his head went right through the hole in the middle of the mill-stone, so that it sat round his neck like a priest's collar. At this, Hans would stay down no longer. He came out of the well, with the millstone round his neck, and went straight to the squire and com-plained that the other men were trying to make a fool of him. He would not be their priest, he said; he had too little learning for that. Saying this, he bent down his head and shook the stone off, so that it crushed one of the squire's big toes.

The squire went limping in to his wife, and the steward was sent for. He was told that he must devise some plan for getting rid of this terrible person. The scheme he had devised before had been of no use, and now good counsel was scarce.

'Oh, no,' said the steward, 'there are good enough ways yet. The squire can send him this evening to fish in Devil Moss Lake: he will never escape alive from there, for no one can go there by night for Old Eric.'

That was a grand idea, both the squire and his wife thought, and so he limped out again to Hans, and said that he would punish his men for having tried to make a fool of him. Meanwhile, Hans could do a little job where he would be free from these rascals. He should go out on the lake and fish there that night, and would then be free from all work on the following day.

'All right,' said Hans; 'I am well content with that, but I must have something with me to eat – a baking of bread, a cask of butter, a barrel of ale and a keg of brandy. I can't do with less than that.'

The squire said that he could easily get all that, so Hans got all of these tied up together, hung them over his shoulder on his good staff, and tramped away to Devil Moss Lake.

There he got into the boat, rowed out upon the lake, and got everything ready to fish. As he now lay out there in the middle of the lake, and it was pretty late in the evening, he thought he would have something to eat first, before starting to work. Just as he was at his busiest with this, Old Eric rose out of the lake, caught him by the scruff of the neck, whipped him out of the boat, and dragged him down to the bottom. It was a lucky thing that Hans

had his walking-stick with him that day, and had just time to catch hold of it when he felt Old Eric's claws in his neck, so when they got down to the bottom he said, 'Stop now, just wait a little; here is solid ground.' With that he caught Old Eric by the back of the neck with one hand, and hammered away on his back with the staff, till he beat him out as flat as a pancake. Old Eric then began to lament and howl, begging him just to let him go, and he would never come back to the lake again.

'No, my good fellow,' said Hans, 'you won't get off until you promise to bring all the fish in the lake up to the squire's courtyard, before tomorrow morning.'

Old Eric eagerly promised this, if Hans would only let him go; so Hans rowed ashore, ate up the rest of his provisions, and went home to bed.

Next morning, when the squire rose and opened his front door, the fish came tumbling into the porch, and the whole yard was crammed full of

them. He ran in again to his wife, for he could never devise anything himself, and said to her, 'What shall we do with him now? Old Eric hasn't taken him. I am certain that all the fish are out of the lake, for the yard is just filled with them.'

'Yes, that's a bad business,' said she; 'you must see if you can't get him sent to Purgatory, to demand tribute.' The squire therefore made his way to the men's quarters, to speak to Hans, and it took him all his time to push his way along the walls, under the eaves, on account of the fish that filled the yard. He thanked Hans for having fished so well, and said that now he had an errand for him, which he could only give to a trusty servant, and that was to journey to Purgatory, and demand three years tribute, which, he said, was owing to him from that quarter.

'Willingly,' said Hans; 'but what road do I go to get there?'

The squire stood, and did not know what to say, and had first to go in to his wife to ask her.

'Oh, what a fool you are!' said she. 'Can't you direct him straight forward, south through the wood? Whether he gets there or not, we shall be quit of him.'

Out goes the squire again to Hans.

'The way lies straight forward, south through the wood,' said he.

Hans then must have his provisions for the journey: two bakings of bread, two casks of butter, two barrels of ale and two kegs of brandy. He tied all these up together, and got them on his shoulder, hanging from his stout walking-stick, and off he tramped southward.

After he had got through the wood, there was more than one road, and he was in doubt which of them was the right one, so he sat down and opened up his bundle of provisions. He found he had left his knife at home, but by good chance, there was a plough lying close at hand, so he took the coulter of this to cut the bread with. As he sat there and took his bite, a man came riding past him.

'Where are you from?' said Hans.

'From Purgatory,' said the man.

'Then stop and wait a little,' said Hans; but the man was in a hurry, and would not stop, so Hans ran after him and caught the horse by the tail. This

brought it down on its hind legs, and the man went flying over its head into a ditch. 'Just wait a little,' said Hans; 'I am going the same way.' He got his provisions tied up again, and laid them on the horse's back; then he took hold of the reins and said to the man, 'We two can go along together on foot.'

As they went on their way Hans told the stranger both about the errand he had on hand and the fun he had had with Old Eric. The other said but little but he was well acquainted with the way, and it was no long time before they arrived at the gate. There both horse and rider disappeared, and Hans was left alone outside. 'They will come and let me in presently,' he thought to himself; but no one came. He hammered at the gate; still no one appeared. Then he got tired of waiting, and smashed at the gate with his staff until he knocked it in pieces and got inside. A whole troop of little demons came down upon him and asked what he wanted. His master's compliments, said Hans, and he wanted three years' tribute. At this they howled at him, and were about to lay hold of him and drag him off; but when they had got some raps from his walking-stick they let go again, howled still louder than before, and ran in to Old Eric, who was still in bed, after his adventure in the lake. They told him that a messenger had come from the squire at Devil Moss to demand three years' tribute. He had knocked the gate to pieces and bruised their arms and legs with his iron staff.

'Give him three years'! give him ten!' shouted Old Eric, 'only don't let him come near me.'

So all the little demons came dragging so much silver and gold that it was something awful. Hans filled his bundle with gold and silver coins, put it on his neck, and tramped back to his master, who was scared beyond all measure at seeing him again.

But Hans was also tired of service now. Of all the gold and silver he brought with him he let the squire keep one half, and he was glad enough, both for the money and at getting rid of Hans. The other half he took home to his father the smith in Furreby. To him also he said, 'Farewell;' he was now tired of living on shore among mortal men, and preferred to go home again to his mother. Since that time no one has ever again seen Hans, the mermaid's son.

Hansel and Gretel

Hard by a great forest dwelt a poor woodcutter with his wife and the two children of his former marriage. The boy was called Hansel and the girl Gretel. He earned very little, and once when a great famine fell on the land, he could no longer procure even daily bread. Now, when he thought over this by night in his bed, and tossed about in his anxiety, he groaned and said to his wife: 'What is to become of us? How are we to feed our poor children when we no longer have anything even for ourselves?'

'I'll tell you what, husband,' answered the woman, 'early tomorrow morning we will take the children out into the forest to where it is the thickest; there we will light a fire for them, and give each of them one last piece of bread, and then we will go to our work and leave them alone. They will not find the way home again, and we shall be rid of them.'

'No, wife,' said the man, 'I will not do that; how can I bear to leave my children alone in the forest? The wild animals would soon come and tear them to pieces.'

'Oh, you fool!' said she; 'then we must all four die of hunger; you may as well plane the planks for our coffins,' and she left him no peace until he consented.

'But I feel very sorry for the poor children, all the same,' said the man.

The two children had also not been able to sleep for hunger and had heard what their stepmother had said to their father. Gretel wept bitter tears, and said to Hansel: 'Now all is over with us.'

'Be quiet, Gretel,' said Hansel, 'do not distress yourself, I will soon find a way to help us.' And when the old folk had fallen asleep, he got up, put on his little coat, opened the door below and crept outside.

The moon shone brightly, and the white pebbles which lay in front of the house glittered like real silver pennies. Hansel stooped and stuffed the little pocket of his coat with as many as he could get in. Then he went back and said to Gretel: 'Be comforted, dear little sister, and sleep in peace, God will not forsake us,' and he lay down again in his bed.

When day dawned, but before the sun had risen, the woman came and awoke the two children, saying: 'Get up, you sluggards! we are going into the forest to fetch wood.' She gave each a little piece of bread, and said: 'There is something for your dinner, but do not eat it up before then, for you will get nothing else.'

The moon shone brightly, and the white pebbles which lay in front of the house glittered like real silver pennies

Gretel took the bread under her apron, as Hansel had the pebbles in his pocket. Then they all set out together on the way to the forest. When they had walked a short time, Hansel stood still and peeped back at the house, and did so again and again. His father said: 'Hansel, what are you looking at there and staying behind for? Pay attention, and do not forget how to use your legs.'

'Ah, father,' said Hansel, 'I am looking at my little white cat; she is sitting up on the roof, and wants to say goodbye to me.'

The wife said: 'Fool, that is not your little cat, that is the morning sun which is shining on the chimney.'

Hansel, however, had not been looking back at the cat, but had been constantly throwing one of the white pebble-stones out of his pocket on the road.

When they had reached the middle of the forest, the father said: 'Now, children, pile up some wood, and I will light a fire that you may not be cold.'

Hansel and Gretel gathered brushwood together, as high as a little hill. The brushwood was lighted, and when the flames were burning very high, the woman said: 'Now, children, lay yourselves down by the fire and rest; we will go into the forest and cut some wood. When we have done, we will come back and fetch you away.'

Hansel and Gretel sat by the fire, and when noon came, each ate a little piece of bread, and as they heard the strokes of the wood-axe they believed that their father was near. It was not the axe, however, but a branch which he had fastened to a withered tree which the wind was blowing backwards and forwards. And as they had been sitting such a long time, their eyes closed with fatigue, and they fell fast asleep. When at last they awoke, it was already dark night.

Gretel began to cry and said: 'How are we to get out of the forest now?'

But Hansel comforted her and said: 'Just wait a little, until the moon has risen, and then we will soon find the way.'

And when the full moon had risen, Hansel took his little sister by the hand, and followed the pebbles which shone like newly-coined silver pieces, and showed them the way.

They walked the whole night long, and by break of day came once more to their father's house. They knocked at the door, and when the woman opened it and saw that it was Hansel and Gretel, she said: 'You naughty children, why have you slept so long in the forest? We thought you were never coming back at all!' The father, however, rejoiced, for it had cut him to the heart to leave them behind alone.

Not long afterwards, there was once more great dearth throughout the land, and the children heard their mother saying at night to their father: 'Everything is eaten again, we have one half-loaf left, and that is the end. The children must go, we will take them farther into the wood, so that they will not find their way out again; there is no other means of saving ourselves!' The man's heart was heavy, and he thought: 'It would be better for me to share the last mouthful with my children.' The woman, however, would listen to nothing that he had to say, but scolded and reproached him. He who says A must say B likewise, and as he had yielded the first time, he had to do so a second time also.

The children, however, were still awake and had heard the conversation. When the old folk were asleep, Hansel again got up, and wanted to go out and pick up pebbles as he had done before, but the woman had locked the door, and Hansel could not get out. Nevertheless he comforted his little sister, and said: 'Do not cry, Gretel, go to sleep quietly, the good God will help us.'

Early in the morning came the woman, and took the children out of their beds. Their piece of bread was given to them, but it was still smaller than the time before. On the way into the forest Hansel crumbled his in his pocket, and often stood still and threw a morsel on the ground.

'Hansel, why do you stop and look round?' said the father. 'Come on, do.'

'I am looking back at my little pigeon which is sitting on the roof and wants to say goodbye to me,' answered Hansel.

'Fool!' said the woman, 'that is not your little pigeon, that is the morning sun that is shining on the chimney.'

Hansel, however, little by little, threw all the crumbs on the path.

The woman led the children still deeper into the forest, where they had never in their lives been before. Then a great fire was again made, and the mother said: 'Just sit there, you children, and when you are tired you may sleep a little; we are going into the forest to cut wood, and in the evening when we are done, we will come and fetch you away.'

When it was noon, Gretel shared her piece of bread with Hansel, who had scattered his by the way. Then they fell asleep and evening passed, but no one came to the poor children. They did not awake until it was dark night, and Hansel comforted his little sister and said: 'Just wait, Gretel, until the moon rises, and then we shall see the crumbs of bread which I have strewn about; they will show us our way home again.'

When the moon came they set out, but they found no crumbs, for the many thousands of birds which fly about in the woods and fields had picked them all up. Hansel said to Gretel: 'We shall soon find the way,' but they did not find it. They walked the whole night and all the next day too, from morning till evening, but they did not get out of the forest, and they were very hungry for they had had nothing to eat but two or three berries which grew on the ground. And as they were so weary that their legs would carry them no longer, they lay down beneath a tree and fell asleep.

It was now three mornings since they had left their father's house. They began to walk again, but they always came deeper into the forest, and if help did not come soon, they must die of hunger and weariness. When it was midday, they saw a beautiful snow-white bird sitting on a bough, which sang so delightfully that they stood still and listened to it. And when its song was over, it spread its wings and flew away before them, and they followed it until they reached a little house, on the roof of which it alighted; and when they approached the little house they saw that it was built of bread and covered with cakes, but that the windows were of clear sugar. 'We will set to work on that,' said Hansel, 'and have a good meal. I will eat a bit of the roof, and you Gretel, can eat some of the window, it will taste sweet.' Hansel reached up and broke off a little of the roof to try how it tasted, and Gretel leant against the window and nibbled at the panes. Then a soft voice cried from the parlour: 'Nibble, nibble, gnaw. Who is nibbling at my little house?'

The children answered: 'The wind, the wind, the heaven-born wind,' and went on eating without disturbing themselves. Hansel, who liked the taste of the roof, tore down a great piece of it, and Gretel pushed out the whole of one round windowpane and sat down on the ground to enjoy it.

Suddenly the door opened, and a woman as old as the hills, who supported herself on crutches, came hobbling out. Hansel and Gretel were so terribly frightened that they let fall what they had in their hands. The old woman, however, nodded her head, and said: 'Oh, you dear children, who

has brought you here? Do come in, and stay with me. No harm shall come to you.'

She took them both by the hand, and led them into her little house. Then good food was set before them, milk and pancakes, with sugar, apples and nuts. Afterwards two pretty little beds were covered with clean white linen, and Hansel and Gretel lay down in them, and thought they were in heaven.

The old woman had only pretended to be so kind; she was in reality a wicked witch, who lay in wait for children, and had only built the little house of bread in order to entice them there. When a child fell into her power, she killed it, cooked and ate it, and that was a feast day with her. Witches have red eyes, and cannot see far, but they have a keen sense of smell like the beasts, and are aware when human beings draw near. When Hansel and Gretel came into her neighbourhood, she laughed with malice, and said mockingly: 'I have them, they shall not escape me!'

Early in the morning before the children were awake, she was already up, and when she saw both of them sleeping and looking so pretty, with their plump and rosy cheeks, she muttered to herself: 'That will be a dainty mouthful!' Then she seized Hansel with her shrivelled hand, carried him into a little stable, and locked him in behind a grated door. Scream as he might, it would not help him. Then she went to Gretel, shook her till she awoke, and cried: 'Get up, lazy thing, fetch some water, and cook something good for your brother; he is in the stable outside, and is to be made fat. When he is fat, I will eat him.' Gretel began to weep bitterly, but it was all in vain, for she was forced to do what the wicked witch commanded.

And now the best food was cooked for poor Hansel, but Gretel got nothing but crab-shells. Every morning the woman crept to the little stable, and cried: 'Hansel, stretch out your finger that I may feel if you will soon be fat.' Hansel, however, stretched out a little bone to her, and the old woman, who had dim eyes, could not see it, and thought it was Hansel's finger, and was astonished that there was no way of fattening him.

When four weeks had gone by, and Hansel still remained thin, she was seized with impatience and would not wait any longer. 'Now, then, Gretel,' she cried to the girl, 'stir yourself, and bring some water. Let Hansel be fat or lean, tomorrow I will kill him, and cook him.'

Ah, how the poor little sister did lament when she had to fetch the water, and how her tears did flow

*'Hansel, stretch out your finger that I may
feel if you will soon be fat.'*

down her cheeks! 'Dear God, do help us,' she cried.
'If the wild beasts in the forest had but devoured us,
we should at any rate have died together.'

'Just keep your noise to yourself,' said the old
woman, 'it won't help you at all.'

Early in the morning, Gretel had to go out and
hang up the cauldron with the water, and light the
fire.

'We will bake first,' said the old woman, 'I have
already heated the oven, and kneaded the dough.'
She pushed poor Gretel out to the oven, from
which flames of fire were already darting. 'Creep
in,' said the witch, 'and see if it is properly heated,
so that we can put the bread in.'

Once Gretel was inside, she intended to shut the
oven and let her bake in it, and then she would eat
her, too. But Gretel saw what she had in mind, and
said: 'I do not know how I am to do it; how do I
get in?'

'Silly goose,' said the old woman. 'The door is big

enough; just look, I can get in myself!' and she
crept up and thrust her head into the oven. Then
Gretel gave her a push that drove her far into it,
and shut the iron door, and fastened the bolt. Oh!
Then she began to howl quite horribly, but Gretel
ran away and the wicked witch was miserably burnt
to death.

Gretel, however, ran like lightning to Hansel,
opened his little stable, and cried: 'Hansel, we are
saved! The old witch is dead!' Then Hansel sprang
like a bird from its cage when the door is opened.
How they did rejoice and embrace each other, and
dance about and kiss each other! And as they had
no longer any need to fear her, they went into
the witch's house, and in every corner there stood
chests full of pearls and jewels. 'These are far
better than pebbles!' said Hansel, and thrust into
his pocket whatever could be got in, and Gretel
said: 'I, too, will take something home with me,'
and filled her pinafore full. 'But now we must be
off,' said Hansel, 'that we may get out of the witch's
forest.'

When they had walked for two hours, they came
to a great stretch of water. 'We cannot cross,' said
Hansel, 'I see no foot-plank, and no bridge.'

'And there is alas no ferry,' answered Gretel; 'but
a white duck is swimming there: if I ask her, she will
help us over.' Then she cried:

'Little duck, little duck, dost thou see,
  Hansel and Gretel are waiting for thee?
  There's never a plank or bridge in sight,
  Take us across on thy back so white.'

The duck came to them, and Hansel seated
himself on its back, and told his sister to sit by him.
'No,' replied Gretel, 'that will be too heavy for the
little duck; she shall take us across one after the
other.' The good little duck did so, and when they
were once safely across and had walked for a short
time, the forest seemed to be more and more
familiar to them, and at length they saw from afar
their father's house.

Then they began to run, rushed into the parlour
and threw themselves round their father's neck.
The man had not known one happy hour since he
had left the children in the forest; and the woman,
who had been so cruel, was dead.

Gretel emptied her pinafore so that quantities of
pearls and precious stones ran about the room, and
Hansel threw one handful after another out of his
pocket to add to them. Then all anxiety was at an
end, and they lived together in perfect happiness.

The Happy Prince

High above the city, on a tall column, stood the statue of the Happy Prince. He was gilded all over with thin leaves of fine gold, for eyes he had two bright sapphires, and a large red ruby glowed on his sword-hilt.

He was very much admired indeed. 'He is as beautiful as a weathercock,' remarked one of the town councillors who wished to gain a reputation for having artistic tastes; 'only not quite so useful,' he added, fearing lest people should think him unpractical, which he really was not.

'Why can't you be like the Happy Prince?' asked a sensible mother of her little boy who was crying for the moon. 'The Happy Prince never dreams of crying for anything.'

'I am glad there is someone in the world who is quite happy,' muttered a disappointed man as he gazed at the wonderful statue.

'He looks just like an angel,' said the charity children as they came out of the cathedral in their bright scarlet cloaks and their clean white pinafores.

'How do you know?' said the mathematical master, 'you have never seen one.'

'Ah! but we have, in our dreams,' answered the children; and the mathematical master frowned and looked very severe, for he did not approve of children dreaming.

One night there flew over the city a little swallow. His friends had gone away to Egypt six weeks before, but he had stayed behind, for he was in love with the most beautiful reed. He had met her early in the spring as he was flying down the river after a big yellow moth, and had been so attracted by her slender waist that he had stopped to talk to her.

'Shall I love you?' said the swallow, who liked to come to the point at once, and the reed made him a low bow. So he flew round and round her, touching the water with his wings, and making silver ripples. This was his courtship, and it lasted all through the summer.

'It is a ridiculous attachment,' twittered the other swallows, 'she has no money, and far too many relations,' and indeed the river was quite full of reeds. Then, when the autumn came they all flew away.

After they had gone he felt lonely, and began to tire of his lady-love. 'She has no conversation,' he said, 'and I am afraid that she is a coquette, for she is always flirting with the wind.' And certainly, whenever the wind blew, the reed made the most graceful curtseys. 'I admit that she is domestic,' he continued, 'but I love travelling, and my wife, consequently, should love travelling also.'

'Will you come away with me?' he said finally to her, but the reed shook her head, she was so attached to her home. 'You have been trifling with me,' he cried. 'I am off to the Pyramids. Goodbye!' and he flew away.

All day long he flew, and at night-time he arrived at the city. 'Where shall I put up?' he said; 'I hope the town has made preparations.'

Then he saw the statue on the tall column.

'I will put up there,' he cried; 'it is a fine position, with plenty of fresh air.' So he alighted just between the feet of the Happy Prince.

'I have a golden bedroom,' he said softly to himself as he looked round, and he prepared to go to sleep; but just as he was putting his head under his wing a large drop of water fell on him. 'What a curious thing!' he cried; 'there is not a single cloud in the sky, the stars are quite clear and bright, and yet it is raining. The climate in the north of Europe is really dreadful. The reed used to like the rain, but that was merely her selfishness.'

Then another drop fell.

'What is the use of a statue if it cannot keep the rain off?' he said. 'I must look for a good chimney-pot,' and he determined to fly away.

But before he had opened his wings, a third drop fell, and he looked up, and saw – Ah! what did he see?

The eyes of the Happy Prince were filled with tears, and tears were running down his golden cheeks. His face was so beautiful in the moonlight that the little swallow was filled with pity.

'Who are you?' he said.

'I am the Happy Prince.'

'Why are you weeping then?' asked the swallow; 'you have quite drenched me.'

'When I was alive and had a human heart,' answered the statue, 'I did not know what tears were, for I lived in the Palace of Sans-Souci, where sorrow is not allowed to enter. In the daytime I played with my companions in the garden, and in the evening I led the dance in the great hall. Round the garden ran a very lofty wall, but I never cared to ask what lay beyond it, everything about me was so beautiful. My courtiers called me the Happy Prince, and happy indeed I was, if pleasure be happiness. So I lived, and so I died. And now that I am dead they have set me up here so high that I can see all the ugliness and all the misery of my city, and though my heart is made of lead yet I cannot choose but weep.'

'What! is he not solid gold?' said the swallow to

himself. He was too polite to make any personal remarks out loud.

'Far away,' continued the statue in a low musical voice, 'far away in a little street there is a poor house. One of the windows is open, and through it I can see a woman seated at a table. Her face is thin and worn and she has coarse, red hands, all pricked by the needle, for she is a seamstress. She is embroidering passion-flowers on a satin gown for the loveliest of the queen's maids-of-honour to wear at the next court-ball. In a bed in the corner of the room her little boy is lying ill. He has a fever and is asking for oranges. His mother has nothing to give him but river water, so he is crying. Swallow, swallow, little swallow, will you not bring her the ruby out of my sword-hilt? My feet are fastened to this pedestal and I cannot move.'

'I am waited for in Egypt,' said the swallow. 'My friends are flying up and down the Nile, and talking to the large lotus-flowers. Soon they will go to sleep in the tomb of the great king. The king is there himself in his painted coffin. He is wrapped in yellow linen, and embalmed with spices. Round his neck is a chain of pale green jade, and his hands are like withered leaves.'

'Swallow, swallow, little swallow,' said the prince, 'will you not stay with me for one night, and be my messenger? The boy is so thirsty, and the mother so sad.'

'I don't think I like boys,' answered the swallow. 'Last summer, when I was staying on the river there were two rude boys, the miller's sons, who were always throwing stones at me. They never hit me, of course; we swallows fly far too well for that, and besides, I come of a family famous for its agility; but still, it was a mark of disrespect.'

But the Happy Prince looked so sad that the little swallow was sorry. 'It is very cold here,' he said, 'but I will stay with you for one night, and be your messenger.'

'Thank you, little swallow,' said the prince.

So the swallow picked out the great ruby from the prince's sword, and flew away with it in his beak over the roofs of the town.

He passed by the cathedral tower, where the white marble angels were sculptured. He passed by the palace and heard the sound of dancing. A beautiful girl came out on the balcony with her lover. 'How wonderful the stars are,' he said to her, 'and how wonderful is the power of love!'

'I hope my dress will be ready in time for the state ball,' she answered; 'I have ordered passion-flowers to be embroidered on it: but the seamstresses are so lazy.'

He passed over the river, and saw the lanterns hanging from the masts of the ships. He passed over the ghetto, and saw the old Jews bargaining with each other, and weighing out money in copper scales. At last he came to the poor house and looked in. The boy was tossing feverishly on his bed, and the mother had fallen asleep, she was so tired. In he hopped, and laid the great ruby on the table beside the woman's thimble. Then he flew gently round the bed, fanning the boy's forehead with his wings. 'How cool I feel!' said the boy, 'I must be getting better,' and he sank into a delicious slumber.

Then the swallow flew back to the Happy Prince, and told him what he had done. 'It is curious,' he remarked, 'but I feel quite warm now, although it is so cold.'

'That is because you have done a good action,' said the prince. And the little swallow began to think, and then he fell asleep. Thinking always made him sleepy.

When day broke he flew down to the river and had a bath. 'What a remarkable phenomenon!' said the professor of ornithology as he was passing over the bridge. 'A swallow in winter!' And he wrote a long letter about it to the local newspaper. Everyone quoted it, it was full of so many words that they could not understand.

'Tonight I go to Egypt,' said the swallow, and he was in high spirits at the prospect. He visited all the public monuments, and sat a long time on top of the church steeple. Wherever he went the sparrows chirruped, and said to each other, 'What a distinguished stranger!' so he enjoyed himself very much.

When the moon rose he flew back to the Happy Prince. 'Have you any commissions for Egypt?' he cried; 'I am just starting.'

'Swallow, swallow, little swallow,' said the prince, 'will you not stay with me one night longer?'

'I am waited for in Egypt,' answered the swallow. 'Tomorrow my friends will fly up to the Second Cataract. The river-horse couches there among the bulrushes, and on a great granite throne sits the god Memnon. All night long he watches the stars, and when the morning star shines he utters one cry of joy and then he is silent. At noon the yellow lions come down to the water's edge to drink. They have eyes like green beryls, and their roar is louder than the roar of the cataract.'

'Swallow, swallow, little swallow,' said the prince, 'far away across the city I see a young man in a garret. He is leaning over a desk covered with papers, and in a tumbler by his side there is a bunch of withered violets. His hair is brown and crisp, and his lips are red as a pomegranate, and he has large and dreamy eyes. He is trying to finish a play for the director of the theatre, but he is too cold to write any more. There is no fire in the grate, and hunger has made him faint.'

'I will wait with you one night longer,' said the swallow, who really had a good heart. 'Shall I take him another ruby?'

'Alas! I have no ruby now,' said the prince, 'my eyes are all that I have left. They are made of rare sapphires, which were brought out of India a thousand years ago. Pluck out one of them and take it to him. He will sell it to the jeweller, and buy firewood, and finish his play.'

'Dear prince,' said the swallow, 'I cannot do that,' and he began to weep.

'Swallow, swallow, little swallow,' said the prince, 'do as I command you.'

So the swallow plucked out the prince's eye, and flew away to the student's garret. It was easy enough to get in, as there was a hole in the roof. Through this he darted, and came into the room. The young man had his head buried in his hands, so he did not hear the flutter of the bird's wings, and when he looked up he found the beautiful sapphire lying on the withered violets.

'I am beginning to be appreciated,' he cried; 'this is from some great admirer. Now I can finish my play,' and he looked quite happy.

The next day the swallow flew down to the harbour. He sat on the mast of a large vessel and watched the sailors hauling big chests out of the hold with ropes. 'Heave a-hoy!' they shouted as each chest came up. 'I am going to Egypt!' cried the swallow, but nobody minded, and when the moon rose he flew back to the Happy Prince.

'I am come to bid you goodbye,' he cried.

'Swallow, swallow, little swallow,' said the prince, 'will you not stay with me one night longer?'

'It is winter,' answered the swallow, 'and the chill snow will soon be here. In Egypt the sun is warm on the green palm trees, and the crocodiles lie in the mud and look lazily about them. My companions are building a nest in the Temple of Baalbec, and the pink and white doves are watching them, and cooing to each other. Dear prince, I must leave you, but I will never forget you, and next spring I will bring you back two beautiful jewels in place of those you have given away. The ruby shall be redder than a red rose and the sapphire shall be as blue as the great sea.'

'In the square below,' said the Happy Prince, 'there stands a little matchgirl. She has let her matches fall in the gutter, and they are all spoiled. Her father will beat her if she does not bring home some money, and she is crying. She has no shoes or stockings, and her little head is bare. Pluck out my other eye, and give it to her, and her father will not beat her.'

'I will stay with you one night longer,' said the swallow, 'but I cannot pluck out your eye. You would be quite blind then.'

'Swallow, swallow, little swallow,' said the prince, 'do as I command you.'

So he plucked out the prince's other eye, and darted down with it. He swooped past the matchgirl, and slipped the jewel into the palm of her hand. 'What a lovely bit of glass!' cried the little girl: and she ran home, laughing.

Then the swallow came back to the prince. 'You are blind now,' he said, 'so I will stay with you always.'

'No, little swallow,' said the poor prince, 'you must go away to Egypt.'

'I will stay with you always,' said the swallow and he slept at the prince's feet.

All the next day he sat on the prince's shoulder and told him stories of what he had seen in strange lands. He told him of the red ibises, who stand in long rows on the banks of the Nile, and catch goldfish in their beaks; of the Sphinx, who is as old as the world itself, and lives in the desert, and knows everything; of the merchants, who walk slowly by the side of their camels and carry amber beads in their hands; of the King of the Mountains of the Moon, who is as black as ebony, and worships a large crystal; of the great green snake that sleeps in a palm tree, and has twenty priests to feed it with honey-cakes; and of the pygmies who sail over a big lake on large flat leaves and are always at war with the butterflies.

'Dear little swallow,' said the prince, 'you tell me of marvellous things, but more marvellous than anything is the suffering of men and of women. There is no mystery so great as Misery. Fly over my city, little swallow, and tell me what you see there.'

So the swallow flew over the great city, and saw the rich making merry in their beautiful houses, while the beggars were sitting at the gates. He flew into dark lanes, and saw the white faces of starving children looking out listlessly at the black streets. Under the archway of a bridge two little boys were lying in one another's arms to try and keep themselves warm. 'How hungry we are!' they said. 'You must not lie here,' shouted the watchman, and they wandered out into the rain.

Then he flew back and told the prince what he had seen.

'I am covered with fine gold,' said the prince, 'you must take it off, leaf by leaf, and give it to my poor; the living always think that gold can make them happy.'

Leaf after leaf of the fine gold the swallow picked off, till the Happy Prince looked quite dull and grey. Leaf after leaf of the fine gold he brought to the poor, and the children's faces grew rosier, and they laughed and played games in the street. 'We have bread now!' they cried.

Then the snow came, and after the snow came the frost. The streets looked as if they were made of silver, they were so bright and glistening; long icicles like crystal daggers hung down from the eaves of the houses, everybody went about in furs, and the little boys wore scarlet caps and skated on the ice.

The poor little swallow grew colder and colder but he would not leave the prince, he loved him too well. He picked up crumbs outside the baker's door when the baker was not looking, and tried to keep himself warm by flapping his wings.

But at last he knew that he was going to die. He had just enough strength to fly up to the prince's shoulder once more. 'Goodbye, dear prince!' he murmured, 'will you let me kiss your hand?'

'I am glad that you are going to Egypt at last, little swallow,' said the prince, 'you have stayed too long here; but you must kiss me on the lips, for I love you.'

'It is not to Egypt that I am going,' said the swallow. 'I am going to the House of Death. Death is the brother of Sleep, is he not?'

And he kissed the Happy Prince on the lips, and fell down dead at his feet.

At that moment a curious crack sounded inside the statue, as if something had broken. The fact is that the leaden heart had snapped right in two. It certainly was a dreadfully hard frost.

Early the next morning the mayor was walking in the square below in company with the town councillors. As they passed the column he looked up at the statue: 'Dear me! how shabby the Happy Prince looks!' he said.

'How shabby, indeed!' cried the town councillors who always agreed with the mayor; and they went up to look at it.

'The ruby has fallen out of his sword, his eyes are gone, and he is golden no longer,' said the mayor: 'in fact he is little better than a beggar!'

'Little better than a beggar,' said the town councillors.

'And here is actually a dead bird at his feet!' continued the mayor. 'We really must issue a proclamation that birds are not to be allowed to die here.' And the town clerk made a note of the suggestion.

So they pulled down the statue of the Happy Prince. 'As he is no longer beautiful he is no longer useful,' said the art professor at the university.

Then they melted the statue in a furnace, and the mayor held a meeting of the corporation to decide what was to be done with the metal. 'We must have another statue, of course,' he said, 'and it shall be a statue of myself.'

'Of myself,' said each of the town councillors, and they quarrelled. When I last heard of them they were quarrelling still.

'What a strange thing!' said the overseer of the workmen at the foundry. 'This broken lead heart will not melt in the furnace. We must throw it away.' So they threw it on a dust-heap where the dead swallow was also lying.

'Bring me the two most precious things in the city,' said God to one of His angels; and the angel brought Him the leaden heart and the dead bird.

'You have rightly chosen,' said God, 'for in my garden of Paradise this little bird shall sing for evermore, and in my city of gold the Happy Prince shall praise me.'

Henny-Penny

One day Henny-penny was picking up corn in the cornyard when – whack! – something hit her upon the head. 'Goodness gracious me!' said Henny-penny; 'the sky's a-going to fall; I must go and tell the king.'

So she went along and she went along and she went along till she met Cocky-locky. 'Where are you going, Henny-penny?' says Cocky-locky. 'Oh! I'm going to tell the king the sky's a-falling,' says Henny-penny. 'May I come with you?' says Cocky-locky. 'Certainly,' says Henny-penny. So Henny-penny and Cocky-locky went to tell the king the sky was falling.

They went along, and they went along, and they went along, till they met Ducky-daddles. 'Where are you going to, Henny-penny and Cocky-locky?' says Ducky-daddles. 'Oh! we're going to tell the king the sky's a-falling,' said Henny-penny and Cocky-locky. 'May I come with you?' says Ducky-daddles. 'Certainly,' said Henny-penny and Cocky-locky. So Henny-penny, Cocky-locky and Ducky-daddles went to tell the king the sky was a-falling.

So they went along, and they went along, and they went along, till they met Goosey-poosey, 'Where are you going to, Henny-penny, Cocky-locky and Ducky-daddles?' said Goosey-poosey. 'Oh! we're going to tell the king the sky's a-falling,' said Henny-penny and Cocky-locky and Ducky-daddles. 'May I come with you,' said Goosey-poosey. 'Certainly,' said Henny-penny, Cocky-locky and Ducky-daddles. So Henny-penny, Cocky-locky, Ducky-daddles and Goosey-poosey went to tell the king the sky was a-falling.

So they went along, and they went along, and they went along, till they met Turkey-lurkey. 'Where are you going, Henny-penny, Cocky-locky, Ducky-daddles, and Goosey-poosey?' says Turkey-lurkey. 'Oh! we're going to tell the king the sky's a-falling,' said Henny-penny, Cocky-locky, Ducky-daddles and Goosey-poosey. 'May I come with you?

Henny-penny, Cocky-locky, Ducky-daddles and Goosey-poosey?' said Turkey-lurkey. 'Why, certainly, Turkey-lurkey,' said Henny-penny, Cocky-locky, Ducky-daddles, and Goosey-poosey. So Henny-penny, Cocky-locky, Ducky-daddles, Goosey-poosey and Turkey-lurkey all went to tell the king the sky was a-falling.

So they went along, and they went along, and they went along, till they met Foxy-woxy, and Foxy-woxy said to Henny-penny, Cocky-locky, Ducky-daddles, Goosey-poosey and Turkey-lurkey: 'Where are you going, Henny-penny, Cocky-locky, Ducky-daddles, Goosey-poosey, and Turkey-lurkey?' And Henny-penny, Cocky-locky, Ducky-daddles, Goosey-poosey, and Turkey-lurkey said to Foxy-woxy: 'We're going to tell the king the sky's a-falling.' 'Oh! but this is not the way to the king, Henny-penny, Cocky-locky, Ducky-daddles, Goosey-poosey and Turkey-lurkey,' says Foxy-woxy; 'I know the proper way; shall I show it you?' 'Why certainly, Foxy-woxy,' said Henny-penny, Cocky-locky, Ducky-daddles, Goosey-poosey, and Turkey-lurkey. So Henny-penny, Cocky-locky, Ducky-daddles, Goosey-poosey, Turkey-lurkey, and Foxy-woxy all went to tell the king the sky was a-falling. So they went along, and they went along, and they went along, till they came to a narrow and dark hole.

Now this was the door of Foxy-woxy's cave. But Foxy-woxy said to Henny-penny, Cocky-locky, Ducky-daddles, Goosey-poosey, and Turkey-lurkey:

'This is the short way to the king's palace; you'll soon get there if you follow me. I will go first and you come after, Henny-penny, Cocky-locky, Ducky daddles, Goosey-poosey and Turkey-lurkey.' 'Why of course, certainly, without doubt, why not?' said Henny-Penny, Cocky-locky, Ducky-daddles, Goosey-poosey and Turkey-lurkey.

So Foxy-woxy went into his cave, and he didn't go very far but turned round to wait for Henny-penny, Cocky-locky, Ducky-daddles, Goosey-poosey and Turkey-lurkey. So first of all Turkey-lurkey went through the dark hole into the cave. He hadn't got far when, 'Hrumph,' Foxy-woxy snapped off Turkey-lurkey's head and threw his body over his left shoulder. Then Goosey-poosey went in, and, 'Hrumph,' off went her head and Goosey-poosey was thrown beside Turkey-lurkey. Then Ducky-daddles waddled down, and, 'Hrumph,' snapped Foxy-woxy, and Ducky-daddles' head was off and Ducky-daddles was thrown alongside Turkey-lurkey and Goosey-poosey. Then Cocky-locky strutted down into the cave and he hadn't gone far when, 'Snap, Hrumph!' went Foxy-woxy and Cocky-locky was thrown alongside of Turkey-lurkey, Goosey-poosey and Ducky-daddles.

But Foxy-woxy had made two bites at Cocky-locky, and when the first snap only hurt Cocky-locky, but didn't kill him, he called out to Henny-penny. So she turned tail and ran back home, so she never told the king the sky was a-falling.

The Horned Women

A rich woman sat up late one night carding and preparing wool, while all the family and servants were asleep. Suddenly a knock was given at the door, and a voice called, 'Open! Open!'

'Who is there?' said the woman of the house.

'I am the Witch of One Horn,' was answered.

The mistress, supposing that one of her neighbours had called and required assistance, opened the door, and a woman entered, having in her hand a pair of wool-carders, and bearing a horn on her forehead, as if growing there. She sat down by the fire in silence, and began to card the wool with violent haste. Suddenly she paused, and said aloud, 'Where are the women? They delay too long.'

Then a second knock came to the door, and a voice called as before, 'Open! Open!'

The mistress felt herself obliged to rise and open to the call, and immediately a second witch entered, having two horns on her forehead and in her hand a wheel for spinning wool.

'Give me place,' she said; 'I am the Witch of the Two Horns,' and she began to spin as quick as lightning.

And so the knocks went on, and the call was heard and the witches entered, until at last twelve women sat round the fire – the first with one horn, the last with twelve horns.

And they carded the thread, and turned their spinning wheels, and wound and wove, all singing together an ancient rhyme, but no word did they speak to the mistress of the house. Strange to hear, and frightful to look upon, were these twelve

women, with their horns and their wheels; and the mistress felt near to death, and she tried to rise that she might call for help, but she could not move, nor could she utter a word or a cry, for the spell of the witches was upon her.

Then one of them called to her in Irish, and said, 'Rise, woman, and make us a cake.'

Then the mistress searched for a vessel to bring water from the well that she might mix the meal and make the cake, but she could find none.

And they said to her, 'Take a sieve and bring water in it.'

And she took the sieve and went to the well; but the water poured from it, and she could fetch none for the cake, and she sat down by the well and wept.

Then a voice came by her and said, 'Take yellow clay and moss, and bind them together, and plaster the sieve so that it will hold.'

This she did, and the sieve held the water for the cake; and the voice said again, 'Return, and when thou comest to the north angle of the house, cry aloud three times and say, "The mountain of the Fenian women and the sky over it is all on fire." '

And she did so.

When the witches inside heard the call, a great and terrible cry broke from their lips, and they rushed forth with wild lamentations and shrieks, and fled away to Slievenamon, where was their chief abode. But the Spirit of the Well bade the mistress of the house to enter and prepare her home against the enchantments of the witches if they returned.

And first, to break their spells, she sprinkled the water in which she had washed her child's feet, the feet-water, outside the door on the threshold; secondly, she took the cake which in her absence the witches had made of meal mixed with the blood drawn from the sleeping family, and she broke the cake in bits, and placed a bit in the mouth of each sleeper, and they were restored; and she took the cloth they had woven, and placed it half in and half out of the chest with the padlock; and lastly, she secured the door with a great crossbeam fastened in the jambs, so that the witches could not enter, and having done these things she waited.

Not long were the witches in coming back, and they raged and called for vengeance.

'Open! Open!' they screamed. 'Open, feet-water!'

'I cannot,' said the feet-water; 'I am scattered on the ground, and my path is down to the lough.'

'Open, open, wood and trees and beam!' they cried to the door.

'I cannot,' said the door, 'for the beam is fixed in the jambs and I have no power to move.'

'Open, open, cake that we have made and mingled with blood!' they cried again.

'I cannot,' said the cake, 'for I am broken and bruised, and my blood is on the lips of the sleeping children.'

Then the witches rushed through the air with great cries, and fled back to Slievenamon, uttering strange curses on the Spirit of the Well, who had wished their ruin; but the woman and the house were left in peace, and a mantle dropped by one of the witches in her flight was kept hung up by the mistress in memory of that night; and this mantle was kept by the same family from generation to generation for five hundred years after.

How Jack Went to Seek His Fortune

Once on a time there was a boy named Jack, and one morning he started to go and seek his fortune.

He hadn't gone very far before he met a cat.

'Where are you going, Jack?' said the cat.

'I am going to seek my fortune.'

'May I go with you?'

'Yes,' said Jack, 'the more the merrier.'

So on they went, jiggelty-jolt, jiggelty-jolt.

They went a little farther and they met a dog.

'Where are you going, Jack?' said the dog.

'I am going to seek my fortune.'

'May I go with you?'

'Yes,' said Jack, 'the more the merrier.'

So on they went, jiggelty-jolt, jiggelty-jolt. They went a little farther and they met a goat.

'Where are you going, Jack?' said the goat.

'I am going to seek my fortune.'

'May I go with you?'

'Yes,' said Jack, 'the more the merrier.'

So on they went, jiggelty-jolt, jiggelty-jolt.

They went a little farther and they met a bull.

'Where are you going, Jack?' said the bull.

'I am going to seek my fortune.'

'May I go with you?'

'Yes,' said Jack, 'the more the merrier.'

So on they went, jiggelty-jolt, jiggelty-jolt.

They went a little farther and they met a rooster.

'Where are you going, Jack?' said the rooster.

'I am going to seek my fortune.'

'May I go with you?'

'Yes,' said Jack, 'the more the merrier.'

So on they went, jiggelty-jolt, jiggelty-jolt.

Well, they went on till it was about dark, and they began to think of some place where they could spend the night. About this time they came in sight of a house, and Jack told them to keep still while he went up and looked in through the window. And there were some robbers counting over their money. Then Jack went back and told them to wait till he gave the word, and then to make all the noise they could. So when they were all ready Jack gave the word, and the cat mewed, and the dog barked, and the goat bleated, and the bull bellowed, and the rooster crowed, and all together they made such a dreadful noise that it frightened the robbers all away.

And then they went in and took possession of the house. Jack was afraid the robbers would come back in the night, and so when it came time to go to bed he put the cat in the rocking-chair, and he put the dog under the table, and he put the goat upstairs, and he put the bull down in the cellar, and the rooster flew up on to the roof, and Jack went to bed.

By and by the robbers saw it was all dark and they sent one man back to the house to look after their money. Before long he came back in a great fright and told them his story.

'I went back to the house,' said he, 'and went in and tried to sit down in the rocking-chair, and there was an old woman knitting, and she stuck her knitting-needles into me.' That was the cat, you know.

'I went to the table to look after the money and there was a shoemaker under the table, and he stuck his awl into me.' That was the dog, you know.

'I started to go upstairs, and there was a man up there threshing, and he knocked me down with his flail.' That was the goat, you know.

'I started to go down into the cellar, and there was a man down there chopping wood, and he knocked me over with his axe.' That was the bull, you know.

'But I shouldn't have minded all that if it hadn't been for that little fellow on top of the house, who kept a-hollering, "Chuck him up to me–e! Chuck him up to me–e!" ' Of course that was the cock-a-doodle-do.

How Six Men Travelled the Wide World

There was once upon a time a man who understood all sorts of arts; he served in the war, and bore himself bravely and well; but when the war was over, he got his discharge, and set out on his travels with pay of only three farthings in his pocket. 'Wait,' he said; 'that does not please me; only let me find the right people, and the king shall yet give me all the treasures of his kingdom.' He strode angrily into the forest, and there he saw a man standing who had uprooted six trees as if they were straws. He said to him, 'Will you be my servant and travel with me?'

'Yes,' he answered; 'but first of all I will take this little bundle of sticks home to my mother,' and he took one of the trees and wound it round the other five, raised the bundle on his shoulders and bore it off. Then he came back and went with his master, who said, 'We two ought to be able to travel through the wide world!' And when they had gone a little way they came upon a hunter, who was on his knees, his gun on his shoulder, aiming at something. The master said to him, 'Hunter, what are you aiming at?'

He answered, 'Two miles from this place sits a fly on a branch of an oak; I want to shoot out its left eye.'

'Oh, go with me,' said the man; 'if we three are together we shall easily travel through the wide world.'

The hunter agreed and went with him, and they came to seven windmills whose sails were going round quite fast, and yet there was not a breath of wind, nor was a leaf moving. The man said, 'I don't know what is turning those windmills; there is not the slightest breeze blowing.' So he walked on with his servants, and when they had gone two miles they saw a man sitting on a tree, holding one of his nostrils and blowing out of the other.

'Fellow, what are you puffing at up there?' asked the man.

He replied, 'Two miles from this place are standing seven windmills; see, I am blowing to drive them round.'

'Oh, go with me,' said the man; 'if we four are together we shall easily travel through the wide world.'

So the blower got down and went with him, and after a time they saw a man who was standing on one leg, and had unstrapped the other and laid it near him. Then said the master, 'You have made yourself very comfortable to rest!'

'I am a runner,' answered he; 'and so that I shall not go too quickly, I have unstrapped one leg; when I run with two legs, I go faster than a bird flies.'

'Oh, go with me; if we five are together, we shall easily travel through the wide world.' So he went with him; and, not long afterwards, they met a man who wore a little hat, but he had it slouched over one ear.

'Manners, manners!' said the master to him; 'don't hang your hat over one ear; you look like a madman!'

'I dare not,' said the other, 'for if I were to put my hat on straight, there would come such a frost that the very birds in the sky would freeze and fall dead on the earth.'

'Oh, go with me,' said the master; 'if we six are together, we shall easily travel through the wide world.

Now the six came to a town in which the king had proclaimed that whoever should run with his daughter in a race, and win, should become her husband; but if he lost, he must lose his head. This was reported to the man, who declared he would compete, 'but,' he said, 'I shall let my servant run for me.'

The king replied, 'Then both your heads must be staked, and your head and his must be guaranteed for the winner.'

When this was agreed upon and settled, the man strapped on the runner's other leg, saying to him, 'Now be nimble, and see that we win!' It was arranged that whoever should first bring water out of a stream a long way off should be the victor. Then the runner got a pitcher, and the king's daughter another, and they began to run at the same time; but in a moment, when the king's daughter was only just a little way off, no spectator could see the runner, and it seemed as if the wind had whistled past. In a short time he reached the stream, filled his pitcher with water, and turned round again. But, half way home, a great drowsiness came over him; he put down his pitcher, lay down and fell asleep. He had, however, put a horse's skull, which was lying on the ground, for his pillow, so that he should not be too comfortable and might soon wake up.

In the meantime the king's daughter, who could also run well, as well as an ordinary man could, reached the stream, and hastened back with her pitcher full of water. When she saw the runner lying there asleep, she was delighted, and said, 'My enemy is given into my hands!' She emptied his pitcher and ran on.

Everything now would have been lost, if by good luck the hunter had not been standing on the castle tower and seen everything with his sharp eyes.

'Ah,' said he, 'the king's daughter shall not overreach us;' and, loading his gun, he shot so cleverly, that he shot away the horse's skull from under the runner's head, without its hurting him. Then the runner awoke, jumped up, and saw that his pitcher was empty and the king's daughter far ahead. But he did not lose courage, and ran back to the stream with his pitcher, filled it once more with water, and was home ten minutes before the king's daughter arrived.

'Look,' said he, 'I have only just exercised my legs; that was nothing of a run.'

But the king was angry, and his daughter even more so, that she should be carried away by a common, discharged soldier. They consulted together how they could destroy both him and his companions.

'Then,' said the king to her, 'I have found a way.

· MY · ENEMY · IS · GIVEN · INTO · MY · HANDS ·

Don't be frightened; they shall not come home again.'
He said to them, 'You must now make merry together,
and eat and drink,' and he led them into a room which
had a floor of iron; the doors were also of iron, and the
windows were barred with iron. In the room was a table
spread with delicious food. The king said to them, 'Go in
and enjoy yourselves,' and as soon as they were inside he
had the doors shut and bolted. Then he made the cook
come, and ordered him to keep up a large fire under the
room until the iron was red-hot. The cook did so, and the
six sitting round the table felt it grow very warm, and
they thought this was

because of their good fare; but when the heat became still greater and they wanted to go out, but found the doors and windows fastened, then they knew that the king meant them harm and was trying to suffocate them.

'But he shall not succeed,' cried he of the little hat, 'I will make a frost come which shall make the fire ashamed and die out!' So he put his hat on straight, and at once there came such a frost that all the heat disappeared and the food on the dishes began to freeze. When a couple of hours had passed, and the king thought they must be quite dead from the heat, he had the doors opened and went in himself to see.

But when the doors were opened, there stood all six, alive and well, saying they were glad they could come out to warm themselves, for the great cold in the room had frozen all the food hard in the dishes. Then the king went angrily to the cook, and scolded him, and asked him why he had not done what he was told.

But the cook answered, 'There is heat enough there; see for yourself.' Then the king saw a huge fire burning under the iron room, and understood that he could do no harm to the six in this way. The king now began again to think how he could free himself from his unwelcome guests. He commanded the master to come before him, and said, 'If you will take gold, and give up your right to my daughter, you shall have as much as you like.'

'Oh, yes, your majesty,' answered he, 'give me as much as my servant can carry, and I will give up your daughter.'

The king was delighted, and the man said, 'I will come and fetch it in fourteen days.'

Then he called all the tailors in the kingdom together, and made them sit down for fourteen days sewing at a sack. When it was finished, he made the strong man who had uprooted the trees take the sack on his shoulder and go with him to the king. Then the king said, 'What a powerful fellow that is, carrying that bale of linen as large as a house on his shoulder!' and he was much frightened, and thought 'What a lot of gold he will make away with!' Then he had a ton of gold brought, which sixteen of the strongest men had to carry; but the strong man seized it with one hand and put it in the sack, saying, 'Why don't you bring me more? That scarcely covers the bottom!' Then the king had to send again and again to fetch his treasures, which the strong man shoved into the sack, and the sack was only half full.

'Bring more,' he cried, 'these crumbs don't fill it.' So seven thousand wagons of the gold of the whole kingdom were driven up; these the strong man shoved into the sack, oxen and all.

'I will no longer be particular,' he said, 'and will take what comes, so that the sack shall be full.'

When everything was put in and there was not yet enough, he said, 'I will make an end of this; it is easy to fasten a sack when it is not full.' Then he threw it on his back and went with his companions.

Now, when the king saw how a single man was carrying away the wealth of the whole country he was very angry, and made his cavalry mount and pursue the six to bring back the strong man with the sack. Two regiments soon overtook them, and called to them, 'You are prisoners! lay down the sack of gold or you shall be cut down.'

'What do you say?' said the blower, 'we are prisoners? Before that, you shall dance in the air!' And he held one nostril and blew with the other at the two regiments; they were separated and blown away in the blue sky over the mountains, one this way and the other that. A sergeant-major cried for mercy, saying he had nine wounds, and was a brave fellow, and did not deserve this disgrace. So the blower let him off, and he came down without hurt. Then he said to him, 'Now go home to the king, and say that if he sends any more cavalry I will blow them all into the air.'

When the king received the message, he said, 'Let the fellows go; they are bewitched.' Then the six brought the treasure home, shared it among themselves, and lived contentedly till the end of their days.

How the Raja's Son Won Princess Labam

In a country there was a Raja who had an only son who every day went out to hunt. One day the Rani, his mother, said to him, 'You can hunt wherever you like on these three sides; but you must never go to the fourth side.' This she said because she knew if he went on the fourth side he would hear of the beautiful Princess Labam, and that then he would leave his father and mother and seek for the princess.

The young prince listened to his mother, and obeyed her for some time; but one day, when he was hunting on the three sides where he was allowed to go, he remembered what she had said to him about the fourth side, and he determined to go and see why she had forbidden him to hunt on that side. When he got there, he found himself in a jungle, and nothing in the jungle but a quantity of parrots, who lived in it. The young Raja shot at some of them, and at once they all flew away up to the sky. All, that is, but one, and this was their Raja, who was called Hiraman parrot.

When Hiraman parrot found himself left alone, he called out to the other parrots, 'Don't fly away and leave me alone when the Raja's son shoots. If you desert me like this, I will tell the Princess Labam.'

Then the parrots all flew back to their Raja, chattering. The prince was greatly surprised, and said, 'Why, these birds can talk!' Then he said to the parrots, 'Who is the Princess Labam? Where does she live?' But the parrots would not tell him where she lived. 'You can never get to the Princess Labam's country.' That is all they would say.

The prince grew very sad when they would not tell him anything more; and he threw his gun away, and went home. When he got home, he would not speak or eat, but lay on his bed for four or five days, and seemed very ill.

At last he told his father and mother that he wanted to go and see the Princess Labam. 'I must go,' he said; 'I must see what she is like. Tell me where her country is.'

'We do not know where it is,' answered his father and mother.

'Then I must go and look for it,' said the prince.

'No, no,' they said, 'you must not leave us. You are our only son. Stay with us. You will never find the Princess Labam.'

'I must try and find her,' said the prince. 'Perhaps God will show me the way. If I live and I find her, I will come back to you; but perhaps I shall die, and then I shall never see you again. Still I must go.'

So they had to let him go, though they cried very much at parting with him. His father gave him fine clothes to wear, and a fine horse. And he took his gun, and his bow and arrows, and a great many other weapons, 'For,' he said, 'I may want them.' His father, too, gave him plenty of rupees.

Then he himself got his horse all ready for the journey, and he said goodbye to his father and mother; and his mother took her handkerchief and wrapped some sweetmeats in it, and gave it to her son. 'My child,' she said to him, 'when you are hungry eat some of these sweetmeats.'

He then set out on his journey, and rode on and on till he came to a jungle in which were a tank and shady trees. He bathed himself and his horse in the tank, and then sat down under a tree. 'Now,' he said to himself, 'I will eat some of the sweetmeats my mother gave me, and I will drink some water, and then I will continue my journey.' He opened his handkerchief, and took out a sweetmeat. He found an ant in it. He took out another. There was an ant in that one too. So he laid the two sweetmeats on the ground, and he took out another, and another, and another, until he had taken them all out; but in each he found an ant. 'Never mind,' he said, 'I won't eat the sweetmeats; the ants shall eat them.' Then the Ant-Raja came and stood before him and said, 'You have been good to us. If ever you are in trouble, think of me and we will come to you.'

The Raja's son thanked him, mounted his horse

243

and continued his journey. He rode on and on until he came to another jungle, and there he saw a tiger who had a thorn in his foot, and was roaring loudly from the pain.

'Why do you roar like that?' said the young Raja. 'What is the matter with you?'

'I have had a thorn in my foot for twelve years,' answered the tiger, 'and it hurts me so; that is why I roar.'

'Well,' said the Raja's son, 'I will take it out for you. But perhaps, as you are a tiger, when I have made you well, you will eat me?'

'Oh, no,' said the tiger, 'I won't eat you. Do make me well.'

Then the prince took a little knife from his pocket, and cut the thorn out of the tiger's foot; but when he cut, the tiger roared louder than ever – so loud that his wife heard him in the next jungle, and came bounding along to see what was the matter. The tiger saw her coming, and hid the prince in the jungle, so that she should not see him.

'What man hurt you that you roared so loud?' said the wife. 'No one hurt me,' answered the husband; 'but a Raja's son came and took the thorn out of my foot.'

'Where is he? Show him to me,' said his wife.

'If you promise not to kill him, I will call him,' said the tiger.

'I won't kill him; only let me see him,' answered his wife.

Then the tiger called the Raja's son, and when he came the tiger and his wife made him a great many salaams. Then they gave him a good dinner, and he stayed with them for three days. Every day he looked at the tiger's foot, and the third day it was quite healed. Then he said goodbye to the tigers, and the tiger said to him, 'If ever you are in trouble, think of me, and we will come to you.'

The Raja's son rode on and on till he came to a third jungle. Here he found four fakirs whose teacher and master had died, and had left four things – a bed, which carried whoever sat on it whithersoever he wished to go; a bag, that gave its owner whatever he wanted, jewels, food or clothes; a stone bowl that gave its owner as much water as he wanted, no matter how far he might be from a tank; and a stick and rope, to which its owner had only to say, if anyone came to make war on him, 'Stick, beat as many men and soldiers as are here,' and the stick would beat them and the rope would tie them up.

The four fakirs were quarrelling over these four things. One said, 'I want this;' another said, 'You cannot have it, for I want it;' and so on.

The Raja's son said to them, 'Do not quarrel for these things. I will shoot four arrows in four different directions. Whichever of you gets to my first arrow, shall have the first thing – the bed. Whosoever gets to the second arrow, shall have the second thing – the bag. He who gets to the third arrow, shall have the third thing – the bowl. And he who gets to the fourth arrow, shall have the last things – the stick and rope.' To this they agreed, and the prince shot off his first arrow. Away raced the fakirs to get it. When they brought it back to him he shot off the second, and when they had found and brought it to him he shot off his third, and when they had brought him the third he shot off the fourth.

While they were away looking for the fourth arrow the Raja's son let his horse loose in the jungle, and sat on the bed, taking the bowl, the stick and rope, and the bag with him. Then he said, 'Bed, I wish to go to the Princess Labam's country.' The little bed instantly rose up into the air and began to fly, and it flew and flew till it came to the Princess Labam's country, where it settled on the ground. The Raja's son asked some men he saw, 'Whose country is this?'

'The Princess Labam's country,' they answered. Then the prince went on till he came to a house where he saw an old woman.

'Who are you?' she said. 'Where do you come from?'

'I come from a far country,' he said; 'do let me stay with you tonight.'

'No,' she answered, 'I cannot let you stay with me; for our king has ordered that men from other countries may not stay in his country. You cannot stay in my house.'

'You are my aunty,' said the prince; 'let me remain with you for this one night. You see it is evening, and if I go into the jungle, then the wild beasts will eat me.'

'Well,' said the old woman, 'you may stay here tonight; but tomorrow morning you must go away, for if the king hears you have passed the night in my house, he will have me seized and put into prison.'

Then she took him into her house, and the Raja's son was very glad. The old woman began preparing dinner, but he stopped her. 'Aunty,' he said, 'I will give you food.' He put his hand into his bag, saying, 'Bag, I want some dinner,' and the bag gave him instantly a delicious dinner, served up on two gold plates. The old woman and the Raja's son then dined together.

When they had finished eating, the old woman said, 'Now I will fetch some water.'

'Don't go,' said the prince. 'You shall have plenty of water directly.' So he took his bowl and said to it, 'Bowl, I want some water,' and then it filled with water. When it was full, the prince cried out, 'Stop, bowl,' and the bowl stopped filling. 'See, aunty,' he said, 'with this bowl I can always get as much water as I want.'

By this time night had come. 'Aunty,' said the Raja's son, 'why don't you light a lamp?'

'There is no need,' she said. 'Our king has forbidden the people in his country to light any lamps; for, as soon as it is dark, his daughter, the Princess Labam, comes and sits on her roof, and she shines so that she lights up all the country and our houses, and we can see to do our work as if it were day.'

When it was quite black night the princess got up. She dressed herself in her rich clothes and jewels, and rolled up her hair, and across her head she put a band of diamonds and pearls. Then she shone like the moon, and her beauty made night day. She came out of her room, and sat on the roof of her palace. In the daytime she never came out of her house; she only came out at night. All the people in her father's country then went about their work and finished it.

The Raja's son watched the princess quietly, and was very happy. He said to himself, 'How lovely she is!'

At midnight, when everybody had gone to bed, the princess came down from her roof, and went to her room; and when she was in bed and asleep, the Raja's son got up softly, and sat on his bed. 'Bed,' he said to it, 'I want to go to the Princess Labam's bedroom.' So the little bed carried him to the room where she lay fast asleep.

The young Raja took his bag and said, 'I want a great deal of betel-leaf,' and it at once gave him quantities of betel-leaf. This he laid near the princess's bed, and then his little bed carried him back to the old woman's house.

Next morning all the princess's servants found the betel-leaf, and began to eat it. 'Where did you get all that betel-leaf?' asked the princess.

'We found it near your bed,' answered the servants. Nobody knew the prince had come in the night and put it all there.

In the morning the old woman came to the Raja's son. 'Now it is morning,' she said, 'and you must go; for if the king finds out all I have done for you, he will seize me.'

'I am ill today, dear aunty,' said the prince; 'do let me stay till tomorrow morning.'

'Good,' said the old woman. So he stayed, and they took their dinner out of the bag, and the bowl gave them water.

When night came the princess got up and sat on her roof, and at twelve o'clock, when everyone was in bed, she went to her bedroom, and was soon fast asleep. Then the Raja's son sat on his bed, and it carried him to the princess. He took his bag and said, 'Bag, I want a most lovely shawl.' It gave him a splendid shawl, and he spread it over the princess as she lay asleep. Then he went back to the old woman's house and slept till morning.

In the morning, when the princess saw the shawl she was delighted. 'See, mother,' she said; 'Khuda must have given me this shawl, it is so beautiful.' Her mother was very glad too.

'Yes, my child,' she said; 'Khuda must have given you this splendid shawl.'

When it was morning the old woman said to the Raja's son, 'Now you must really go.'

'Aunty,' he answered, 'I am not well enough yet. Let me stay a few days longer. I will remain hidden in your house, so that no one may see me.' So the old woman let him stay.

When it was black night, the princess put on her lovely clothes and jewels and sat on her roof. At midnight she went to her room and went to sleep. Then the Raja's son sat on his bed and flew to her bedroom. There he said to his bag, 'Bag, I want a very, very beautiful ring.' The bag gave him a glorious ring. Then he took the Princess Labam's hand gently to put on the ring, and she started up very much frightened.

'Who are you?' she said to the prince. 'Where do you come from? Why do you come to my room?'

'Do not be afraid, princess,' he said; 'I am no thief. I am a great Raja's son. Hiraman parrot, who lives in the jungle where I went to hunt, told me your name, and then I left my father and mother, and came to see you.'

'Well,' said the princess, 'as you are the son of such a great Raja, I will not have you killed, and I will tell my father and mother that I wish to marry you.'

The prince then returned to the old woman's house; and when morning came the princess said to her mother, 'The son of a great Raja has come to this country, and I wish to marry him.' Her mother told this to the king.

'Good,' said the king; 'but if this Raja's son wishes to marry my daughter, he must first do whatever I bid him. If he fails I will kill him. I will give him eighty pounds weight of mustard seed, and out of this he must crush the oil in one day. If he cannot do this he shall die.'

In the morning the Raja's son told the old woman that he intended to marry the princess. 'Oh,' said the old woman, 'go away from this country, and do not think of marrying her. A great many Rajas and Rajas' sons have come here to marry her, and her father has had them all killed. He says whoever wishes to marry his daughter must first do whatever he bids him. If he can, then he shall marry the princess; if he cannot, the king will have him killed. But no one can do the things the king tells him to do; so all the Rajas and Rajas' sons who have tried have been put to death. You will be killed too, if you try. Do go away.' But the prince would not listen to anything she said.

The king sent for the prince to the old woman's house, and his servants brought the Raja's son to the king's courthouse. There the king gave him eighty pounds of mustard seed, and told him to crush all the oil out of it that day, and bring it next morning to him to the courthouse. 'Whoever wishes to marry my daughter,' he said to the prince, 'must first do all I tell him. If he cannot, then I have him killed. So if you cannot crush all the oil out of this mustard seed, you will die.'

The prince was very sorry when he heard this. 'How can I crush the oil out of all this mustard seed in one day?' he said to himself; 'and if I do not, the king will kill me.' He took the mustard seed to the old woman's house, and did not know what to do. At last he remembered the Ant-Raja, and the moment he did so, the Ant-Raja and his ants came to him. 'Why do you look so sad?' said the Ant-Raja.

The prince showed him the mustard seed, and said to him, 'How can I crush the oil out of all this mustard seed in one day? And if I do not take the oil to the king tomorrow morning, he will kill me.'

'Be happy,' said the Ant-Raja; 'lie down and sleep; we will crush all the oil out for you during the day, and tomorrow morning you shall take it to the king.' The Raja's son lay down and slept, and the ants crushed out the oil for him. The prince was very glad when he saw the oil.

The next morning he took it to the courthouse to the king. But the king said, 'You cannot yet marry my daughter. If you wish to do so, you must first fight with my two demons and kill them.' The king a long time ago had caught two demons, and then, as he did not know what to do with them, he had shut them up in a cage. He was afraid to let them loose for fear they would eat up all the people in his country; and he did not know how to kill them. So all the kings and kings' sons who wanted to marry the Princess Labam had to fight with these demons; 'for,' said the king to himself, 'perhaps the demons may be killed, and then I shall be rid of them.'

When he heard of the demons the Raja's son was very sad. 'What can I do?' he said to himself. 'How can I fight with these two demons?' Then he thought of his tiger: and the tiger and his wife came to him and said, 'Why are you so sad?' The Raja's son answered, 'The king has ordered me to fight with his two demons and kill them. How can I do this?' 'Do not be frightened,' said the tiger. 'Be happy. I and my wife will fight with them for you.'

Then the Raja's son took out of his bag two splendid coats. They were all gold and silver, and covered with pearls and diamonds. These he put on the tigers to make them beautiful, and he took them to the king, and said to him, 'May these tigers fight your demons for me?' 'Yes,' said the king, who did not care in the least who killed his demons, provided they were killed. 'Then call your demons,' said the Raja's son, 'and these tigers will fight them.' The king did so, and the tigers and the demons fought and fought until the tigers had killed the demons.

'That is good,' said the king. 'But you must do something else before I give you my daughter. Up in the sky I have a kettledrum. You must go and beat it. If you cannot do this, I will kill you.'

The Raja's son thought of his little bed; so he went to the old woman's house and sat on his bed. 'Little bed,' he said, 'up in the sky is the king's kettledrum. I want to go to it.' The bed flew up with him, and the Raja's son beat the drum, and the king heard him. Still, when he came down, the king would not give him his daughter. 'You have,' he said to the prince, 'done the three things I told you to do; but you must do one thing more.' 'If I can, I will,' said the Raja's son.

Then the king showed him the trunk of a tree that was lying near his courthouse. It was a very, very thick trunk. He gave the prince a wax hatchet, and said, 'Tomorrow morning you must cut this trunk in two with this wax hatchet.'

The Raja's son went back to the old woman's house. He was very sad, and thought that now the Raja would certainly kill him. 'I had his oil crushed out by the ants,' he said to himself. 'I had his demons killed by the tigers. My bed helped me to beat his kettledrum. But now what can I do? How can I cut that thick tree-trunk in two with a wax hatchet?'

At night he went on his bed to see the princess. 'Tomorrow,' he said to her, 'your father will kill me.' 'Why?' asked the princess.

'He has told me to cut a thick tree-trunk in two with a wax hatchet. How can I ever do that?' said the Raja's son. 'Do not be afraid,' said the princess; 'do as I bid you, and you will cut it in two quite easily.'

Then she pulled out a hair from her head, and gave it to the prince.

'Tomorrow,' she said, 'when no one is near you, you must say to the tree-trunk, 'The Princess Labam commands you to let yourself be cut in two by this hair.' Then stretch the hair down the edge of the wax hatchet's blade.'

The prince next day did exactly as the princess had told him; and the minute the hair that was stretched down the edge of the hatchet-blade touched the tree-trunk it split into two pieces.

The king said, 'Now you can marry my daughter.' Then the wedding took place. All the Rajas and kings of the countries round were asked to come to it, and there were great rejoicings. After a few days the prince's son said to his wife, 'Let us go to my father's country.' The Princess Labam's father gave them a quantity of camels and horses and rupees and servants, and they travelled in great state to the prince's country, where they lived happily.

The prince always kept his bag, bowl, bed and stick; only, as no one ever came to make war on him, he never needed to use the stick.

How to Tell a True Princess

There was once upon a time a prince who wanted to marry a princess, but she must be a true princess. So he travelled through the whole world to find one, but there was always something against each. There were plenty of princesses, but he could not find out if they were true princesses. In every case there was some little defect, which showed the genuine article was not yet found. So he came home again in very low spirits, for he had wanted very much to have a true princess. One night there was a dreadful storm; it thundered and lightened and the rain streamed down in torrents. It was fearful! There was a knocking heard at the palace gate, and the old king went to open it.

There stood a princess outside the gate; but oh, in what a sad plight she was from the rain and the storm! The water was running down from her hair and her dress into the points of her shoes and out at the heels again. And yet she said she was a true princess!

'Well, we shall soon find out!' thought the old queen. But she said nothing, and went into the sleeping-room, took off all the bedclothes, and laid a pea on the base of the bed. Then she put twenty mattresses on top of the pea, and twenty eiderdown quilts on the top of the mattresses. And this was the bed in which the princess was to sleep.

The next morning she was asked how she had slept.

'Oh, very badly!' said the princess. 'I scarcely closed my eyes all night! I am sure I don't know what was in the bed. I lay on something so hard that my whole body is black and blue. It is dreadful!'

Now they perceived that she was a true princess, because she had felt the pea through the twenty mattresses and the twenty eiderdown quilts.

No one but a true princess could be so sensitive.

So the prince married her, for now he knew that at last he had got hold of a true princess. And the pea was put into the Royal Museum, where it is still to be seen if no one has stolen it. Now this is a true story.

'I scarcely closed my eyes all night!'

Hudden and Dudden and Donald O'Neary

There was once upon a time two farmers, and their names were Hudden and Dudden. They had poultry in their yards, sheep on the uplands, and scores of cattle in the meadowland alongside the river. But for all that they weren't happy. For just between their two farms there lived a poor man by the name of Donald O'Neary. He had a hovel over his head and a strip of grass that was barely enough to keep his one cow, Daisy, from starving, and, though she did her best, it was but seldom that Donald got a drink of milk or a roll of butter from Daisy. You would think there was little here to make Hudden and Dudden jealous, but so it is, the more one has the more one wants, and Donald's neighbours lay awake of nights scheming how they might get hold of his little strip of grassland. Daisy, poor thing, they never thought of; she was just a bag of bones.

One day Hudden met Dudden, and they were soon grumbling as usual, and all to the tune of, 'If only we could get that vagabond Donald O'Neary out of the country.'

'Let's kill Daisy,' said Hudden at last; 'if that doesn't make him clear out, nothing will.'

No sooner said than agreed, and it wasn't dark before Hudden and Dudden crept up to the little shed where lay poor Daisy trying her best to chew the cud, though she hadn't had as much grass in the day as would cover your hand. And when Donald came to see if Daisy was all snug for the night, the poor beast had only time to lick his hand once before she died.

Well, Donald was a shrewd fellow, and downhearted though he was, began to think if he could get any good out of Daisy's death. He thought and he thought, and the next day you could have seen him trudging off early to the fair, Daisy's hide over his shoulder, every penny he had jingling in his pockets. Just before he got to the fair, he made several slits in the hide, put a penny in each slit, walked into the best inn of the town as bold as if it belonged to him, and, hanging the hide up to a nail in the wall, sat down.

'Some of your best whiskey,' says he to the landlord. But the landlord didn't like his looks. 'Is it fearing I won't pay you, you are?' says Donald.

'Why I have a hide here that gives me all the money I want.' And with that he hit it a whack with his stick and out hopped a penny. The landlord opened his eyes, as you may fancy.

'What'll you take for that hide?'

'It's not for sale, my good man.'

'Will you take a gold piece?'

'It's not for sale, I tell you. Hasn't it kept me and mine for years?' and with that Donald hit the hide another whack and out jumped a second penny.

Well, the long and the short of it was that Donald let the hide go, and that very evening, who but he should walk up to Hudden's door?

'Good-evening, Hudden. Will you lend me your best pair of scales?'

Hudden stared and Hudden scratched his head, but he lent the scales.

When Donald was safe at home, he pulled out his pocketful of bright gold and began to weigh each piece in the scales. But Hudden had put a lump of butter at the bottom, and so the last piece of gold stuck fast to the scales when he took them back to Hudden.

If Hudden had stared before, he stared ten times more now, and no sooner was Donald's back turned, than he was off as hard as he could pelt to Dudden's.

'Let's kill Daisy,' said Hudden at last; 'if that doesn't make him clear out, nothing will.'

'Good-evening, Dudden. That vagabond, bad luck to him – '

'You mean Donald O'Neary?'

'And who else should I mean? He's back here weighing out sackfuls of gold.'

'How do you know that?'

'Here are my scales that he borrowed, and here's a gold piece still sticking to them.'

Off they went together, and they came to Donald's door. Donald had finished making the last pile of ten gold pieces. And he couldn't finish because a piece had stuck to the scales.

In they walked without an 'If you please' or 'By your leave'.

'Well, I never!' That was all they could say.

'Good-evening, Hudden; good-evening, Dudden. Ah! You thought you had played me a fine trick, but you never did me a better turn in all your lives. When I found poor Daisy dead, I thought to myself, "Well, her hide may fetch something"; and it did. Hides are worth their weight in gold in the market just now.'

Hudden nudged Dudden, and Dudden winked at Hudden.

'Good-evening, Donald O'Neary.'

'Good-evening, kind friends.'

The next day there wasn't a cow or a calf that belonged to Hudden or Dudden but her hide was going to the fair in Hudden's biggest cart drawn by Dudden's strongest pair of horses.

When they came to the fair, each one took a hide over his arm, and there they were walking through the fair, bawling out at the top of their voices, 'Hides to sell! Hides to sell!'

Out came the tanner.

'How much for your hides, my good men?'

'Their weight in gold.'

'It's early in the day to come out of the tavern.' That was all the tanner said, and back he went to his yard.

'Hides to sell! Fine fresh hides to sell!'

Out came the cobbler.

'How much for your hides, my men?'

'Their weight in gold.'

'Is it making game of me you are! Take that for your pains,' and the cobbler dealt Hudden a blow that made him stagger.

Up the people came running from one end of the fair to the other. 'What's the matter? What's the matter?' cried they.

'Here are a couple of vagabonds selling hides for their weight in gold,' said the cobbler.

'Hold 'em fast; hold 'em fast!' bawled the inn-keeper, who was the last to come up, he was so fat.

'Good-evening, Hudden; good-evening, Dudden.'

'I'll wager it's one of the rogues who tricked me out of thirty gold pieces yesterday for a wretched hide.'

It was more kicks than halfpence that Hudden and Dudden got before they were well on their way home again, and they didn't run the slower because all the dogs of the town were at their heels.

Well, as you may fancy, if they loved Donald little before, they loved him less now.

'What's the matter, friends?' said he, as he saw them tearing along, their hats knocked in, and their coats torn off, and their faces black and blue. 'Is it fighting you've been? Or mayhap you met the police, in luck to them?'

'We'll police you, you vagabond. It's mighty smart you thought yourself, deluding us with your lying tales.'

'Who deluded you? Didn't you see the gold with your own two eyes?'

But it was no use talking. Pay for it he must, and should. There was a meal-sack handy, and into it Hudden and Dudden popped Donald O'Neary, tied him up tight, ran a pole through the knot, and off they started for the Brown Lake of the Bog, each with a pole-end on his shoulder, and Donald O'Neary between.

But the Brown Lake was far, the road was dusty, Hudden and Dudden were sore and weary and parched with thirst. There was an inn by the roadside.

'Let's go in,' said Hudden; 'I'm dead beat. It's heavy he is for the little he had to eat.'

If Hudden was willing, so was Dudden. As for Donald, you may be sure his leave wasn't asked, but he was lumped down at the inn door for all the world as if he had been a sack of potatoes.

'Sit still, you vagabond,' said Dudden; 'if we don't mind waiting, you needn't.'

Donald held his peace, but after a while he heard the glasses clink, and Hudden singing away at the top of his voice.

'I won't have her, I tell you; I won't have her!' said Donald. But nobody heeded what he said.

'I won't have her, I tell you; I won't have her!' said Donald, and this time he said it louder; but nobody heeded what he said.

'I won't have her, I tell you; I won't have her!' said Donald; and this time he said it as loud as he could.

'And who won't you have, may I be so bold as to ask?' said a farmer, who had just come up with a drove of cattle and was turning in for a glass.

'It's the king's daughter. They are bothering the life out of me to marry her.'

'You're the lucky fellow. I'd give something to be in your shoes.'

'Do you see that now! Wouldn't it be a fine thing for a farmer to be marrying a princess, all dressed in gold and jewels?'

'Jewels, do you say? Ah, now, couldn't you take me with you?'

'Well, you're an honest fellow, and as I don't care for the king's daughter, though she's as beautiful as the day, and is covered with jewels from top to toe, you shall have her. Just undo the cord, and let me out; they tied me up tight, as they knew I'd run away from her.'

Out crawled Donald, in crept the farmer.

'Now lie still, and don't mind the shaking; it's only rumbling over the palace steps you'll be. And maybe they'll abuse you for a vagabond, who won't have the king's daughter; but you needn't mind that. Ah! It's a deal I'm giving up for you, sure as it is that I don't care for the princess.'

'Take my cattle in exchange,' said the farmer; and you may guess it wasn't long before Donald was at their tails driving them homewards.

Out came Hudden and Dudden, and the one took one end of the pole, and the other the other.

'I'm thinking he's heavier,' said Hudden.

'Ah, never mind,' said Dudden; 'it's only a step now to the Brown Lake.'

'I'll have her now! I'll have her now!' bawled the farmer, from inside the sack.

'By my faith, and you shall though,' said Hudden, and he laid his stick across the sack.

'I'll have her! I'll have her!' bawled the farmer, louder than ever.

'Well, here you are,' said Dudden, for they were now come to the Brown Lake, and, unslinging the sack, they pitched it plump into the lake.

'You'll not be playing your tricks on us any longer,' said Hudden.

'True for you,' said Dudden. 'Ah, Donald, my boy, it was an ill day when you borrowed my scales.'

Off they went, with a light step and an easy heart, but when they were near home, who should they see but Donald O'Neary, and all around him the cows were grazing, and the calves were kicking up their heels and butting their heads together.

'Is it you, Donald?' said Dudden. 'Faith, you've been quicker than we have.'

'True for you, Dudden, and let me thank you kindly; the turn was good, if the will was ill. You'll have heard, like me, that the Brown Lake leads to the Land of Promise. I always put it down as lies, but it is just as true as my word. Look at the cattle.'

Hudden stared, and Dudden gaped; but they couldn't get over the cattle; fine fat cattle they were too.

'It's only the worst I could bring up with me,' said Donald O'Neary; 'the others were so fat, there was no driving them. Faith, too, it's little wonder they didn't care to leave, with grass as far as you could see, and as sweet and juicy as fresh butter.'

'Ah, now, Donald, we haven't always been friends,' said Dudden, 'but, as I was just saying, you were ever a decent lad, and you'll show us the way, won't you?'

'I don't see that I'm called upon to do that; there is a power more cattle down there. Why shouldn't I have them all to myself?'

'Faith, they may well say, the richer you get, the harder the heart. You always were a neighbourly lad, Donald. You wouldn't wish to keep the luck all to yourself?'

'True for you, Hudden, though 'tis a bad example you set me. But I'll not be thinking of old times. There is plenty for all there, so come along with me.'

Off they trudged, with a light heart and an eager step. When they came to the Brown Lake, the sky was full of little white clouds, and, if the sky was full, the lake was as full.

'Ah now! Look, there they are,' cried Donald, as he pointed to the clouds in the lake.

'Where? Where?' cried Hudden, and, 'Don't be greedy!' cried Dudden, as he jumped his hardest to be up first with the fat cattle. But if he jumped first, Hudden wasn't long behind.

They never came back. Maybe they got too fat, like the cattle. As for Donald O'Neary, he had cattle and sheep all his days to his heart's content.

The Invisible Prince

Once upon a time there lived a Fairy who had power over the earth, the sea, fire and the air; and this Fairy had four sons. The eldest, who was quick and lively, with a vivid imagination, she made Lord of Fire, which was in her opinion the noblest of all the elements. To the second son, whose wisdom and prudence made amends for his being rather dull, she gave the government of the earth. The third was wild and savage, and of monstrous stature and the Fairy, his mother, who was ashamed of his defects, hoped to hide them by creating him King of the Seas. The youngest, who was the slave of his passions and of a very uncertain temper, became Prince of the Air.

Being the youngest, he was naturally his mother's favourite; but this did not blind her to his weaknesses, and she foresaw that someday he would suffer much pain through falling in love. So she thought the best thing she could do was to bring him up with a horror of women; and, to her great delight, she saw this dislike only increased as he grew older. From his earliest childhood he heard nothing but stories of princes who had fallen into all sorts of troubles through love; and she drew such terrible pictures of poor little Cupid that the young man had no difficulty in believing that he was the root of all evil.

All the time that this wise mother could spare from filling her son with hatred for all womenkind she passed in giving him a love of the pleasures of the chase, which henceforth became his chief joy. For his amusement she had made a new forest, planted with the most splendid trees, and turned loose in it every animal that could be found in any of the four quarters of the globe. In the midst of this forest she built a palace which had not its equal for beauty in the whole world, and then she considered that she had done enough to make any prince happy.

Now it is all very well to abuse the God of Love, but a man cannot struggle against his fate. In his secret heart the prince got tired of his mother's constant talk on this subject; and when one day she quitted the palace to attend to some business, begging him never to go beyond the grounds, he at once jumped at the chance of disobeying her.

Left to himself the prince soon forgot the wise counsels of his mother, and feeling very much bored with his own company, he ordered some of the spirits of the air to carry him to the court of a neighbouring sovereign. This kingdom was situated in the Island of Roses, where the climate is so delicious that the grass is always green and the flowers always sweet. The waves, instead of beating on the rocks, seemed to die gently on the shore; clusters of golden bushes covered the land, and the vines were bent low with grapes.

The king of this island had a daughter named Rosalie, who was more lovely than any girl in the whole world. No sooner had the eyes of the Prince of the Air rested on her than he forgot all the terrible woes which had been prophesied to him ever since he was born, for in one single moment the plans of years are often upset. He instantly began to think how best to make himself happy, and the shortest way that occurred to him was to have Rosalie carried off by his attendant spirits.

It is easy to imagine the feelings of the king when he found that his daughter had vanished. He wept her loss night and day, and his only comfort was to talk over it with a young and unknown prince, who had just arrived at the court. Alas! he did not know what a deep interest the stranger had in Rosalie, for he too had seen her, and had fallen a victim to her charms.

One day the king, more sorrowful than usual, was walking sadly along the seashore, when after a long silence the unknown prince, who was his only companion, suddenly spoke. 'There is no evil without a remedy,' he said to the unhappy father; 'and if you will promise me your daughter in marriage, I will undertake to bring her back to you.'

'You are trying to soothe me by vain promises,' answered the king. 'Did I not see her caught up into the air, in spite of cries which would have softened the heart of anyone but the barbarian who has robbed me of her? The unfortunate girl is pining away in some unknown land, where perhaps no foot of man has ever trod, and I shall see her no more. But go, generous stranger; bring back Rosalie if you can, and live happy with her ever after in this country, of which I now declare you heir.'

Although the stranger's name and rank were unknown to Rosalie's father, he was really the son of the King of the Golden Isle, which had for capital a city that extended from one sea to another. The walls, washed by the quiet waters, were covered with gold, which made one think of the yellow sands. Above them was a rampart of orange and lemon trees, and all the streets were paved with gold.

The king of this beautiful island had one son, for whom a life of adventure had been foretold at his birth. This so frightened his father and mother that in order to comfort them a Fairy, who happened to be present at the time, produced a little pebble which she told them to keep for the prince till he grew up, as by putting it in his mouth he would become invisible, as long as he did not try to speak, for if he did the stone would lose all its virtue. In this way the good fairy hoped that the prince would be protected against all dangers.

No sooner did the prince begin to grow out of boyhood than he longed to see if the other countries of the world were as splendid as the one in which he lived. So, under pretence of visiting some small islands that belonged to his father, he set out. But a frightful storm drove his ship on to unknown shores, where most of his followers were put to death by the savages, and the prince himself only managed to escape by making use of his magic pebble. By this means he passed through the midst of them unseen, and wandered on till he reached the coast, where he re-embarked on board his ship.

The first land he sighted was the Island of Roses, and he went at once to the court of the king, Rosalie's father. The moment his eyes beheld the princess, he fell in love with her like everyone else.

He had already spent several months in this condition when the Prince of the Air whirled her away, to the grief and despair of every man on the island. But sad though everybody was, the Prince of the Golden Isle was perfectly inconsolable, and he passed both days and nights in bemoaning his loss.

'Alas!' he cried; 'shall I never see my lovely princess again?' Who knows where she may be, and what fairy may have her in his keeping? I am only a man, but I am strong in my love, and I will seek the whole world through till I find her.'

So saying, he left the court, and made ready for his journey.

He travelled many weary days without hearing a single word of the lost princess, till one morning, as he was walking through a thick forest, he suddenly perceived a magnificent palace standing at the end of a pine avenue, and his heart bounded to think that he might be gazing on Rosalie's prison. He hastened his steps, and quickly arrived at the gate of the palace, which was formed of a single agate. The gate swung open to let him through, and he next passed successively three courts, surrounded by deep ditches filled with running water, with birds of brilliant plumage flying about the banks. Everything around was rare and beautiful, but the prince scarcely raised his eyes to all these wonders. He thought only of the princess and where he should find her, but in vain he opened every door and searched in every corner; he neither saw Rosalie nor anyone else. At last there was no place left for him to search but a little wood, which contained in the centre a sort of hall built entirely of orange trees, with four small rooms opening out of the corners. Three of these were empty except for statues and wonderful things, but in the fourth the Invisible prince caught sight of Rosalie. His joy at beholding her again was, however, somewhat lessened by seeing that the Prince of the Air was kneeling at her feet, and pleading his own cause. But it was in vain that he implored her to listen; she only shook her head. 'No,' was all she would say; 'you snatched me from my father whom I loved, and all the splendour in the world can never console me. Go! I can never feel anything towards you but hate and contempt.' With these words she turned away and entered her own apartments.

Unknown to herself the Invisible prince had followed her, but fearing to be discovered by the princess in the presence of others, he made up his mind to wait quietly till dark; and employed the long hours in writing a poem to the princess, which he laid on the bed beside her. This done, he thought of nothing but how best to deliver Rosalie, and he resolved to take advantage of a visit which the Prince of the Air paid every year to his mother and brothers in order to strike the blow.

One day Rosalie was sitting alone in her room thinking of her troubles when she suddenly saw a pen get up from off the desk and begin to write all by itself on a sheet of white paper. As she did not know that it was guided by an invisible hand she was very much astonished, and the moment that the pen had ceased to move she instantly went over to the table, where she found some lovely verses, telling her that another shared her distresses, whatever they might be, and loved her with all his heart; and that he would never rest until he had delivered her from the hands of the man she hated. Thus encouraged, she told him all her story, and of the arrival of a young stranger in her father's palace, whose looks had so charmed her that since that day she had thought of no one else. At these words the prince could contain himself no longer. He took the pebble from his mouth, and flung himself at Rosalie's feet.

When they had got over the first rapture of meeting they began to make plans to escape from the power of the Prince of the Air. But this did not prove easy, for the magic stone would only serve for one person at a time, and in order to save Rosalie the Prince of the Golden Isle would have to expose himself to the fury of his enemy. But Rosalie would not hear of this.

'No, prince,' she said; 'since you are here this island no longer feels a prison. Besides, you are under the protection of a Fairy, who always visits your father's court at this season. Go instantly and seek her, and when she is found implore the gift of another stone with similar powers. Once you have that, there will be no further difficulty in the way of escape.'

The Prince of the Air returned a few days later from his mother's palace, but the Invisible prince had already set out. He had, however, entirely forgotten the road by which he had come, and lost himself for so long in the forest, that when at last he reached home the Fairy had already left, and, in spite of all his grief, there was nothing for it but to wait till the Fairy's next visit, and allow Rosalie to suffer three months longer. This thought drove him to despair, and he had almost made up his mind to return to the place of her captivity, when one day, as he was strolling along an alley in the woods, he saw a huge oak open its trunk, and out of it step two princes in earnest conversation. As our hero had the magic stone in his mouth they imagined themselves alone, and did not lower their voices.

'What!' said one, 'are you always going to allow yourself to be tormented by a passion which can never end happily, and in your whole kingdom can you find nothing else to satisfy you?'

'What is the use,' replied the other, 'of being Prince of the Gnomes, and having a mother who is queen over all the four elements, if I cannot win the love of the Princess Argentine? From the moment that I first saw her, sitting in the forest surrounded by flowers, I have never ceased to think of her night and day, and, although I love her, I am quite convinced that she will never care for me. You know that I have in my palace the cabinets of the years. In the first, great mirrors reflect the past; in the second, we contemplate the present; in the third, the future can be read. It was here that I fled after I had gazed on the Princess Argentine, but instead of love I only saw scorn and contempt. Think how great must be my devotion, when, in spite of my fate, I still love on!'

Now the Prince of the Golden Isle was enchanted with this conversation, for the Princess Argentine was his sister, and he hoped, by means of her influence over the Prince of the Gnomes, to obtain from his brother the release of Rosalie. So he joyfully returned to his father's palace, where he found his friend the Fairy, who at once presented him with a magic pebble like his own. As may be imagined, he lost no time in setting out to deliver Rosalie, and travelled so fast that he soon arrived at the forest, in the midst of which she lay a captive. But though he found the palace he did not find Rosalie. He hunted high and low, but there was no sign of her, and his despair was so great that he was ready, a thousand times over, to take his own life. At last he remembered the conversation of the two princes about the cabinets of the years, and knew that if he could manage to reach the oak tree, he would be certain to discover what had become of Rosalie. Happily, he soon found out the secret of

the passage and entered the cabinet of the present, where he saw reflected in the mirrors the unfortunate Rosalie, sitting on the floor of a castle weeping bitterly and surrounded by genii who never left her night or day.

This sight only increased the misery of the prince, for he did not know where the castle was, nor how to set about finding it. However, he resolved to seek the whole world through till he came to the right place. He began by setting sail in a favourable wind, but his bad luck followed him even on the sea. He had scarcely lost sight of the land when a violent storm arose, and after several hours of beating about, the vessel was driven on to some rocks, on which it dashed itself to bits. The prince was fortunate enough to be able to lay hold of a floating spar, and contrived to keep himself afloat; and, after a long struggle with the winds and waves, he was cast upon a strange island. But what was his surprise, on reaching the shore, to hear sounds of the most heart-rending distress, mingled with the sweetest songs which had ever charmed him! His curiosity was instantly roused, and he advanced cautiously till he saw two huge dragons guarding the gate of a wood. They were terrible indeed to look upon. Their bodies were covered with glittering scales; their curly tails extended far over the land; flames darted from their mouths and noses, and their eyes would have made the bravest shudder; but as the prince was invisible and they did not see him, he slipped past them into the wood. He found himself at once in a labyrinth, and wandered about for a long time without meeting anyone; in fact, the only sight he saw was a circle of human hands, sticking out of the ground above the wrist, each with a bracelet of gold, on which a name was written. The farther he advanced in the labyrinth the more curious he became, till he was stopped by two corpses lying in the midst of a cypress alley, each with a scarlet cord round his neck and a bracelet on his arm; on these bracelets were engraved their own names, and those of two princesses.

The invisible prince recognised these dead men as kings of two large islands near his own home, but the names of the princesses were unknown to

In·the·labyrinth·of·Despair

him. He grieved for their unhappy fate, and at once proceeded to bury them; but no sooner had he laid them in their graves, than their hands started up through the earth and remained sticking up like those of their fellows.

The prince went on his way, thinking about this strange adventure, when suddenly at the turn of the walk he perceived a tall man whose face was the picture of misery, holding in his hands a silken cord of the exact colour of those round the necks of the dead men. A few steps farther this man came up with another as miserable to the full as he himself; they silently embraced, and then without a word passed the cords round their throats, and fell dead side by side. In vain the prince rushed to their assistance and strove to undo the cords. He could not loosen them; so he buried them like the others and continued his path.

He felt, however, that great prudence was necessary, or he himself might become the victim of some enchantment; and he was thankful to slip past the dragons, and enter a beautiful park, with clear streams and sweet flowers, and a crowd of men and maidens. But he could not forget the terrible things he had seen, and hoped eagerly for a clue to the mystery. Noticing two young people talking together, he drew near thinking that he might get some explanation of what puzzled him. And so he did.

'You swear,' said the prince, 'that you will love me till you die, but I fear your faithless heart, and I feel that I shall soon have to seek the Fairy Despair, ruler of half this island. She carries off the lovers who have been cast away by their mistresses, and wish to have done with life. She places them in a labyrinth where they are condemned to walk for ever, with a bracelet on their arms and a cord round their necks, unless they meet another as miserable as themselves. Then the cord is pulled and they lie where they fall, till they are buried by the first passer-by. Terrible as this death would be,' added the prince, 'it would be sweeter than life if I had lost your love.'

The sight of all these happy lovers only made the prince grieve the more, and he wandered along the seashore spending his days; but one day he was sitting on a rock bewailing his fate, and the impossibility of leaving the island, when all in a moment the sea appeared to raise itself nearly to the skies, and the caves echoed with hideous screams. As he looked a woman rose from the depths of the sea, flying madly before a furious giant. The cries she uttered softened the heart of the prince; he took the stone from his mouth, and drawing his sword he rushed after the giant, so as to give the lady time to escape. But hardly had he come within reach of the enemy, than the giant touched him with a ring that he held in his hand, and the prince remained immovable where he stood. The giant then hastily rejoined his prey, and, seizing her in his arms, he plunged her into the sea. Then he sent some tritons to bind chains about the Prince of the Golden Isle, and he too felt himself borne to the depths of the ocean, and without the hope of ever again seeing his princess.

Now the giant whom the prince had so rashly attacked was the Lord of the Sea, and the third son of the Queen of the Elements, and he had touched the youth with a magic ring which enabled a mortal to live under water. So the Prince of the Golden Isle found, when bound in chains by the tritons, he was carried through the homes of strange monsters and past immense seaweed forests, till he reached a vast sandy space, surrounded by huge rocks. On the tallest of the rocks sat the giant as on a throne.

'Rash mortal,' said he, when the prince was dragged before him, 'you have deserved death, but you shall live only to suffer more cruelly. Go, and add to the number of those whom it is my pleasure to torture.'

At these words the unhappy prince found himself tied to a rock; but he was not alone in his misfortunes, for all round him were chained princes and princesses, whom the giant had made captive. Indeed, it was his chief delight to create a storm, in order to add to the list of his prisoners.

As his hands were fastened, it was impossible for the Prince of the Golden Isle to make use of his magic stone, and he passed his nights and days dreaming of Rosalie. But at last the time came when the giant took it into his head to amuse himself by arranging fights between some of his captives. Lots were drawn, and one fell upon our prince, whose chains were immediately loosened. The moment he was set free, he snatched up his stone, and became invisible.

The astonishment of the giant at the sudden disappearance of the prince may well be imagined. He ordered all the passages to be watched, but it was too late, for the prince had already glided between two rocks. He wandered for a long while through the forests, where he met nothing but fearful monsters; he climbed rock after rock, steered his way from tree to tree, till at length he arrived at the edge of the sea, at the foot of a mountain that he remembered to have seen in the cabinet of the present, where Rosalie was held captive.

Filled with joy, he made his way to the top of the mountain which pierced the clouds, and there he found a palace. He entered, and in the middle of a long gallery he discovered a crystal room, in the midst of which sat Rosalie, guarded night and day by genii. There was no door anywhere, nor any window. At this sight the prince became more puzzled than ever, for he did not know how he was to warn Rosalie of his return. Yet it broke his heart to see her weeping from dawn till dark.

One day, as Rosalie was walking up and down her room, she was surprised to see that the crystal which served for a wall had grown cloudy, as if someone had breathed on it, and, what was more, wherever she moved the brightness of the crystal always became clouded. This was enough to cause the princess to suspect that her lover had returned. In order to set the Prince of the Air's mind at rest she began being very gracious to him, so that when she begged that her captivity might be a little lightened she should not be refused. At first the only favour she asked was to be allowed to walk for one hour every day up and down the long gallery. This was granted, and the Invisible prince speedily took the opportunity of handing her the stone, which she at once slipped into her mouth. No words can paint the fury of her captor at her disappearance. He ordered the spirits of the air to fly through all space, and to bring back Rosalie wherever she might be. They instantly flew off to obey his commands, and spread themselves over the whole earth.

Meantime Rosalie and the Invisible prince had reached, hand in hand, a door of the gallery which led through a terrace into the gardens. In silence they glided along, and thought themselves already safe, when a furious monster dashed itself by accident against Rosalie and the Invisible prince, and in her fright she let go his hand. No one can speak as long as he is invisible, and besides, they knew that the spirits were all around them, and at the slightest sound they would be recognised; so all they could do was to feel about in the hope that their hands might once more meet.

But, alas! the joy of liberty lasted but a short time. The princess, having wandered in vain up and down the forest, stopped at last on the edge of a fountain. As she walked she wrote on the trees: 'If ever the prince, my lover, comes this way, let him know that it is here I dwell, and that I sit daily on the edge of this fountain, mingling my tears with its waters.'

These words were read by one of the genii, who repeated them to his master. The Prince of the Air, in his turn making himself invisible, was led to the fountain, and waited for Rosalie. When she drew near he held out his hand, which she grasped eagerly, taking it for that of her lover; and, seizing his opportunity, the prince passed a cord round her arms, and throwing off his invisibility cried to his spirits to drag her into the lowest pit.

It was at this moment that the Invisible prince appeared, and at the sight of the Prince of the Genii mounting into the air, holding a silken cord, he guessed instantly that he was carrying off Rosalie.

He felt so overwhelmed by despair that he thought for an instant of putting an end to his life. 'Can I survive my misfortunes?' he cried. 'I fancied I had come to an end of my troubles, and now they are worse than ever. What will become of me? Never can I discover the place where this monster will hide Rosalie.'

The unhappy youth had determined to let himself die, and indeed his sorrow alone was enough to kill him, when the thought that by means of the cabinets of the years he might find out where the princess was imprisoned gave him a little ray of comfort. So he continued to walk on through the forest, and after some hours he arrived at the gate of a temple, guarded by two huge lions. Being invisible, he was able to enter unharmed. In the middle of the temple was an altar, on which lay a book, and behind the altar hung a great curtain. The prince approached the altar and opened the book, which contained the names of all the lovers in the world: and in it he read that Rosalie had been carried off by the Prince of the Air to an abyss which had no entrance except the one that lay by way of the Fountain of Gold.

Now, as the prince had not the smallest idea where this fountain was to be found, it might be thought that he was not much nearer Rosalie than before. This was not, however, the view taken by the prince.

'Though every step that I take may perhaps lead me farther from her,' he said to himself, 'I am still thankful to know that she is alive somewhere.'

On leaving the temple the Invisible prince saw six paths lying before him, each of which led through the wood. He was hesitating which to choose, when he suddenly beheld two people coming towards him, down the track which lay most to his right. They turned out to be the Prince Gnome and his friend, and the sudden desire to get some news of his sister, Princess Argentine, caused the Invisible prince to follow them and to listen to their conversation.

'Do you think,' the Prince Gnome was saying, 'do you think that I would not break my chains if I could? I know that the Princess Argentine will never love me, yet each day I feel her dearer still. And as if this were not enough, I have the horror of feeling that she probably loves another. So I have resolved to put myself out of my pain by means of the Golden Fountain. A single drop of its water falling on the sand around will trace the name of my rival for her heart. I dread the test, and yet this very dread convinces me of my misfortune.'

It instantly wrote the name of Prince Flame, his brother

It may be imagined that after listening to these words the Invisible prince followed Prince Gnome like his shadow, and after walking some time they arrived at the Golden Fountain. The unhappy lover stooped down with a sigh, and dipping his finger in the water let fall a drop on the sand. It instantly wrote the name of Prince Flame, his brother. The shock of this discovery was so real, that Prince Gnome sank fainting into the arms of his friend.

Meanwhile the Invisible prince was turning over in his mind how he could best deliver Rosalie. As, since he had been touched by the giant's ring, he had the power to live in the water as well as on land, he at once dived into the fountain. He perceived in one corner a door leading into the mountain, and at the foot of the mountain was a high rock on which was fixed an iron ring with a cord attached. The prince promptly guessed that the cord was used to chain the princess, and drew his sword and cut it. In a moment he felt the princess's hand in his, for she had always kept her magic pebble in her mouth, in spite of the prayers and entreaties of the Prince of the Air to make herself visible.

So hand in hand the Invisible Prince and Rosalie crossed the mountain; but as the princess had no power of living under water, she could not pass the Golden Fountain. Speechless and invisible they clung together on the brink, trembling at the frightful tempest the Prince of the Air had raised in his fury. The storm had already lasted many days when tremendous heat began to make itself felt. The lightning flashed, the thunder rattled, fire bolts fell from heaven, burning up the forests and even the fields of corn. In one instant the very streams were dried up, and the prince, seizing his opportunity, carried the princess over the Golden Fountain.

It took them a long time still to reach the Golden Isle, but at last they got there, and we may be quite sure they never wanted to leave it any more.

Jack and His Comrades

Once there was a poor widow, as often there has been, and she had one son. A very scarce summer came, and they didn't know how they'd live till the new potatoes would be fit for eating. So Jack said to his mother one evening, 'Mother, bake my cake, and kill my hen, till I go seek my fortune; and if I meet it, never fear but I'll soon be back to share it with you.'

So she did as he asked her, and he set out at break of day on his journey. His mother came along with him to the yard gate, and says she, 'Jack, which would you rather have, half the cake and half the hen with my blessing, or the whole of 'em with my curse?'

'Oh dear, mother,' says Jack, 'why do you ax me that question? Sure you know I wouldn't have your curse whatever came along with it.'

'Well, then, Jack,' says she, 'here's the whole lot of 'em, with my thousand blessings along with them.' So she stood on the yard fence and blessed him as far as her eyes could see him.

Well, he went along and along till he was tired, and ne'er a farmer's house he went into wanted a boy. At last his road led by the side of a bog, and there was a poor ass up to his shoulders near a big bunch of grass he was striving to come at.

'Ah, then, Jack,' says he, 'help me out or I'll be drowned.'

'Never say't twice,' says Jack, and he pitched in big stones and sods into the bog, till the ass got good ground under him.

'Thank you, Jack,' says he, when he was out on the hard road; 'I'll do as much for you another time. Where are you going?'

'Faith, I'm going to seek my fortune till harvest comes in, God bless it!'

'And if you like,' says the ass, 'I'll go along with you; who knows what luck we may have!'

'With all my heart; it's getting late, let us be jogging.'

Well, they were going through a village, and a whole army of gossoons were hunting a poor dog with a kettle tied to his tail. He ran up to Jack for protection, and the ass let such a roar out of him that the little thieves took to their heels as if the divil was after them.

'More power to you, Jack,' says the dog. 'I'm much obleeged to you; where is the baste and yourself going?'

'We're going to seek our fortune till harvest comes in.'

'And wouldn't I be proud to go with you!' says the dog. 'And get rid of them ill-conducted boys; purshuin' to 'em.'

'Well, well, throw your tail over your arm, and come along.'

They got outside the town, and sat down under an old wall, and Jack pulled out his bread and meat, and shared with the dog; and the ass made his dinner on a bunch of thistles. While they were eating and chatting, what should come by but a poor half-starved cat, and the caterwauling he gave out of him would make your heart ache.

'You look as if you saw the tops of nine houses since breakfast,' says Jack; 'here's a bone and something on it.'

'May your child never know a hungry belly!' says Tom. 'It's myself that's in need of your kindness. May I be so bold as to ask where yez are all going?'

'We're going to seek out fortune till the harvest comes in, and you may join us if you like.'

'And that I'll do with a heart and a half,' says the cat, 'and thank'ee for asking me.'

Off they set again, and just as the shadows of the trees were three times as long as themselves, they heard a great cackling in a field inside the road, and out over the ditch jumped a fox with a fine black cock in his mouth.

'Oh, you anointed villain!' says the ass, roaring like thunder.

'At him, good dog!' says Jack, and the word wasn't out of his mouth when Coley was in full sweep after the Red Dog. Reynard dropped his prize like a hot potato, and was off like a shot, and the poor cock came back fluttering and trembling to Jack and his comrades.

'Oh my dear naybours!' says he. 'Wasn't it the height o' luck that threw you in my way! I won't forget your kindness if ever I find you in hardship; and where in the world are you all going?'

'We're going to seek our fortune till the harvest comes in; you may join our party if you like, and sit on Neddy's crupper when your legs and wings are tired.'

Well, the march began again, and just as the sun was gone down they looked around, and there was neither cabin nor farmhouse in sight.

'Well, well,' says Jack, 'the worse luck now the better another time, and it's only a summer night after all. We'll go into the wood, and make our bed on the long grass.'

No sooner said than done. Jack stretched himself on a bunch of dry grass, the ass lay near him, the dog and cat lay in the ass's warm lap, and the cock went to roost in the next tree.

Well, the soundness of deep sleep was over them all, when the cock took a notion of crowing.

'Bother you, Black Cock!' says the ass. 'You disturbed me from as nice a wisp of hay as ever I tasted. What's the matter?'

'It's daybreak that's the matter: don't you see light yonder?'

'I see a light indeed,' says Jack, 'but it's from a candle it's coming, and not from the sun. As you've roused us we may as well go over, and ask for lodging.'

So they all shook themselves, and went on through grass, and rocks, and briars, till they got down into a hollow, and there was the light coming through the shadow, and along with it came singing, and laughing, and cursing.

'Easy, boys!' says Jack. 'Walk on your tippy toes till we see what sort of people we have to deal with.'

So they crept near the window, and there they saw six robbers inside, with pistols, and blunderbushes, and cutlashes, sitting at a table, eating roast beef and pork, and drinking mulled beer, and wine, and whiskey punch.

'Wasn't that a fine haul we made at the Lord of Dunlavin's!' says one ugly-looking thief with his mouth full. 'And it's little we'd get only for the honest porter! Here's his purty health!'

'The porter's purty health!' cried out every one of them, and Jack bent his finger at his comrades.

'Close your ranks, my men,' says he in a whisper, 'and let everyone mind the word of command.'

So the ass put his fore-hoofs on the sill of the window, the dog got on the ass's head, the cat on the dog's head, and the cock on the cat's head. Then Jack made a sign, and they all sang out like mad.

'Hee-haw, hee-haw!' roared the ass; 'Bow-wow!' barked the dog; 'Miaow-miaow!' cried the cat; 'Cock-a-doodle-doo!' crowed the cock.

'Level your pistols!' cried Jack, 'and make smithereens of 'em. Don't leave a mother's son of 'em alive; present, fire!'

With that they gave another halloo, and smashed every pane in the window. The robbers were frightened out of their lives. They blew out the candles, threw down the table, and skelped out at the back door as if they were in earnest, and never drew rein till they were in the very heart of the wood.

Jack and his party got into the room, closed the shutters, lighted the candles, and ate and drank till hunger and thirst were gone. Then they lay down to rest – Jack in the bed, the ass in the stable, the dog on the mat, the cat by the fire, and the cock on the perch.

At first the robbers were very glad to find themselves safe in the thick wood, but they soon began to get vexed.

'This damp grass is very different from our warm room,' says one.

'I was obliged to drop a fine pig's foot,' says another.

'I didn't get a tayspoonful of my last tumbler,' says another.

'And the Lord of Dunlavin's gold and silver all left behind!' says the last.

'I think I'll venture back,' says the captain, 'and see if we can recover anything.'

'That's a good boy!' said they all, and away he went.

The lights were all out, and so he groped his way

261

to the fire, and there the cat flew in his face, and tore him with teeth and claws. He let a roar out of him, and made for the room door, to look for a candle inside. He trod on the dog's tail, and for that he got the marks of his teeth in his arms, and legs, and thighs.

'Thousand murders!' cried he; 'I wish I was out of this unlucky house.'

When he got to the street door, the cock dropped down upon him with his claws and bill, and what the cat and dog did to him was only a flay-bite to what he got from the cock.

'Oh, tattheration to you all, you unfeeling vaga-bones!' says he, when he recovered his breath; and he staggered and spun round and round till he reeled into the stable, back foremost, but the ass received him with a kick on the broadest part of his small clothes, and laid him comfortably on the dunghill.

When he came to himself, he scratched his head, and began to think what happened him; and as soon as he found that his legs were able to carry him, he crawled away, dragging one foot after another, till he reached the wood.

'Well, well,' cried them all, when he came within hearing, 'any chance of our property?'

'You may say chance,' says he, 'and it's itself is the poor chance all out. Ah, will any of you pull a bed of dry grass for me? All the sticking-plaster in Enniscorthy will be too little for the cuts and bruises I have on me. Ah, if you only knew what I have gone through for you! When I got to the kitchen fire, looking for a sod of lighted turf, what should be there but an old woman carding flax, and you may see the marks she left on my face with the cards. I made to the room door as fast as I could, and who should I stumble over but a cobbler and his seat, and if he did not work at me with his awls and his pinchers you may call me a rogue. Well, I got away from him somehow, but when I was passing through the door, it must be the divel himself that pounced down on me with his claws and his teeth, that were equal to sixpenny nails, and his wings – ill luck he in his road! Well, at last I reached the stable, and there, by way of salute, I got a pelt from a sledgehammer that sent me half a mile off. If you don't believe me, I'll give you leave to go and judge for yourselves.'

'Oh, my poor captain,' says they, 'we believe you to the nines. Catch us, indeed, going within a hen's race of that unlucky cabin!'

Well, before the sun shook his doublet next morning, Jack and his comrades were up and about. They made a hearty breakfast on what was left the night before, and then they all agreed to set off to the castle of the Lord of Dunlavin, and give him back all his gold and silver. Jack put it all in the two ends of a sack and laid it across Neddy's back, and all took the road in their hands. Away they went, through bogs, up hills, down dales, and sometimes along the yellow high road, till they came to the hall door of the Lord of Dunlavin, and who should be there, airing his powdered head, his white stockings and his red breeches, but the thief of a porter.

He gave a cross look to the visitors, and says he to Jack, 'What do you want here, my fine fellow? There isn't room for you all.'

'We want,' says Jack, 'what I'm sure you haven't to give us – and that is, common civility.'

'Come, be off, you lazy strollers!' says he. 'While a cat 'ud be licking her ear, or I'll let the dogs at you.'

'Would you tell a body,' says the cock that was perched on the ass's head, 'who was it that opened the door for the robbers the other night?'

Ah! Maybe the porter's red face didn't turn the colour of his frill, and the Lord of Dunlavin and his pretty daughter, that were standing at the parlour window unknownst to the porter, put out their heads.

'I'd be glad, Barney,' says the master, 'to hear your answer to the gentleman with the red comb on him.'

'Ah, my lord, don't believe the rascal; sure I didn't open the door to the six robbers.'

'And how did you know there were six, you poor innocent?' said the lord.

'Never mind, sir,' says Jack, 'all your gold and silver is there in that sack, and I don't think you will begrudge us our supper and bed after our long march from the wood of Athsalach.'

'Begrudge, indeed! Not one of you will ever see a poor day if I can help it.'

So all were welcomed to their heart's content, and the ass and the dog and the cock got the best posts in the farmyard, and the cat took possession of the kitchen. The lord took Jack in hand, dressed him from top to toe in broadcloth, and frills as white as snow, and turnpumps, and put a watch in his fob. When they sat down to dinner, the lady of the house said Jack had the air of a born gentleman about him, and the lord said he'd make him his steward. Jack brought his mother, and settled her comfortably near the castle, and all were as happy as you please.

Jack and His Golden Snuff Box

Once upon a time, and a very good time it was, though it was neither in my time nor in your time nor in anyone else's time, there was an old man and an old woman, and they had one son, and they lived in a great forest. And their son never saw any other people in his life, but he knew that there were some more in the world besides his own father and mother, because he had lots of books, and he used to read every day about them. And when he read about some pretty young women, he used to go mad to see some of them; till one day, when his father was out cutting wood, he told his mother that he wished to go away to look for his living in some other country, and to see some other people besides them two. And he said, 'I see nothing at all here but great trees around me; and if I stay here, maybe I shall go mad before I see anything.' The young man's father was out all this time, when this talk was going on between him and his poor old mother.

The old woman begins by saying to her son before leaving, 'Well, well, my poor boy, if you want to go, it's better for you to go, and God be with you.' (The old woman thought it was for the best when she said that.) 'But stop a bit before you go. Which would you like best for me to make you, a little cake and bless you, or a big cake and curse you?' 'Dear, dear!' said he, 'make me a big cake. Maybe I shall be hungry on the road.' The old woman made the big cake, and she went on top of the house, and she cursed him as far as she could see him.

He presently meets with his father, and the old man says to him: 'Where are you going, my poor boy?' The son told the father the same tale as he told his mother. 'Well,' says his father, 'I'm sorry to see you going away, but if you've made up your mind to go, it's better for you to go.'

The poor lad had not gone far, when his father called him back; then the old man drew out of his pocket a golden snuffbox, and said to him: 'Here, take this little box, and put it in your pocket, and be sure not to open it till you are near your death.' And away went poor Jack upon his road, and walked till he was tired and hungry, for he had eaten all his cake upon the road; and by this time night was upon him, so he could hardly see his way ahead before him. He could see some light a long way, and he made for it, and found the back door and knocked at it, till one of the maidservants came and asked him what he wanted. He said that night was on him, and he wanted to get some place to sleep. The maidservant called him in to the fire, and gave him plenty to eat, good meat and bread and beer; and as he was eating his food by the fire, there came the young lady to look at him, and she loved him well and he loved her. And the young lady ran to tell her father, and said there was a pretty young man in the back kitchen; and immediately the gentleman came to him, and questioned him, and asked what work he could do. Jack said, the silly fellow, that he could do anything. (He meant that he could do any foolish bit of work that would be wanted about the house.)

'Well,' says the gentleman to him, 'if you can do anything, at eight o'clock in the morning I must have a great lake and some of the largest man-of-war vessels sailing before my mansion, and one of the largest vessels must fire a royal salute, and the last round must break the leg of the bed where my young daughter is sleeping. And if you don't do that, you will have to forfeit your life.'

'All right,' said Jack; and away he went to his bed, and said his prayers quietly, and slept till it was near eight o'clock, and he had hardly any time to think what he was to do, till all of a sudden he remembered about the little golden box that his father gave him. And he said to himself: 'Well, well, I never was so near my death as I am now;' and then he felt in his pocket, and drew the little box out. And when he opened it, out there hopped three little red men, and asked Jack: 'What is your will with us?' 'Well,' said Jack, 'I want a great lake and some of the largest man-of-war vessels in the world before this mansion, and one of the largest vessels to fire a royal salute, and the last round to break one of the legs of the bed where this young lady is sleeping.' 'All right,' said the little men; 'go to sleep.'

Jack had hardly time to bring the words out of his mouth, to tell the little men what to do, but what it struck eight o'clock, and Bang! Bang! went one of the largest man-of-war vessels; and it made Jack jump out of bed to look through the window; and I can assure you it was a wonderful sight for him to see, after being so long with his father and mother living in a wood.

In no time Jack dressed himself, and said his prayers, and came down laughing; for he was proud, he was, because the thing was done so well. The gentleman comes to him, and says to him: 'Well, my young man, I must say that you are very clever indeed. Come and have some breakfast.' And the gentleman tells him, 'Now there are two more things you have to do, and then you shall have my daughter in marriage.' Jack gets his breakfast, and has a good squint at the young lady, and also she at him.

The other thing that the gentleman told him to do was to fell all the great trees for miles around by eight o'clock in the morning; and, to make my long story short, it was done, and it pleased the gentleman well. The gentleman said to him: 'The other thing you have to do' – and it was the last thing – 'you must get me a great castle standing on twelve golden pillars; and there must come regiments of soldiers and go through their drill. At eight o'clock the commanding officer must say, "Shoulder up." ' 'All right,' said Jack; when the third and last morning came the third great feat was finished, and he had the young daughter in marriage. But, oh dear! there is worse to come yet.

The gentleman now makes a large hunting party, and invites all the gentlemen around the country to it, and to see the castle as well. And by this time Jack has a beautiful horse and a scarlet dress to go with it. On that morning his valet, when putting Jack's clothes by after he had changed to go a-hunting, put his hand in one of Jack's waistcoat-pockets, and pulled out the little golden snuffbox, as poor Jack left behind in a mistake. And that man opened the little box, and there hopped out the three little red men, and asked him what he wanted with them. 'Well,' said the valet to them, 'I want this castle to be moved from this place far and far across the sea.' 'All right,' said the little red men to him; 'do you wish to go with it?' 'Yes,' said he. 'Well,

There hopped out the three little red men, and asked him what he wanted with them

get up,' said they to him; and away they went far and far over the great sea.

Now the grand hunting party comes back, and the castle upon the twelve golden pillars had disappeared, to the great disappointment of those gentlemen as did not see it before. That poor silly Jack is threatened with having his beautiful young wife taken from him, for cheating them in the way he did. But the gentleman at last makes an agreement with him, and he is to have a twelve-months and a day to look for it; and off he goes with a good horse and money in his pocket.

Now poor Jack goes in search of his missing castle, over hills, dales, valleys and mountains, through woolly woods and sheep-walks, farther than I can tell you or ever intend to tell you, until at last he comes up to the place where lives the king of all the little mice in the world. There was one of the little mice on sentry at the front gate going up to the palace, and he tried to stop Jack from going in. He asked the little mouse: 'Where does the king live? I should like to see him.' This one sent another with him to show him the place; and when the king saw him, he called him in. And the king questioned him, and asked him where he was going. Well, Jack told him all the truth – that he had lost the great castle, and was going to look for it, and he had a whole twelvemonths and a day to find it. And Jack asked him whether he knew anything about it; and the king said: 'No, but I am the king of all the little mice in the world, and I will call them all up in the morning, and maybe they have seen something of it.'

Then Jack got a good meal and bed, and in the morning he and the king went on to the fields; and the king called all the mice together, and asked them whether they had seen the great beautiful castle standing on golden pillars. And all the little mice said, No, there was none of them had seen it. The old king said to him that he had two brothers: 'One is the king of all the frogs; and my other brother, who is the oldest, he is the king of all the birds in the world. And if you go there, maybe they know something about the missing castle.' The king said to him: 'Leave your horse here with me till you come back, and take one of my best horses under you, and give this cake to my brother; he will know then who you got it from. Mind and tell him I am well, and should like dearly to see him.' And then the king and Jack shook hands together.

And when Jack was going through the gates, the little mouse asked him, should he go with him; and

Jack said to him: 'No, I shall get myself into trouble with the king.' And the little thing told him: 'It will be better for you to let me go with you; maybe I shall do some good to you sometime without you knowing it.' 'Jump up, then.' And the little mouse ran up the horse's leg, and made it dance; and Jack put the mouse in his pocket.

Now Jack, after wishing good-morning to the king and pocketing the little mouse which was on sentry, trudged on his way; and such a long way he had to go and this was his first day. At last he found the place; and there was one of the frogs on sentry, and gun upon his shoulder, and he tried to hinder Jack from going in; but when Jack said to him that he wanted to see the king, he allowed him to pass; and Jack made up to the door. The king came out, and asked him his business; and Jack told him all from beginning to end. 'Well, well, come in.' He gets good entertainment that night; and in the morning the king made such a funny sound, and collected all the frogs in the world. And he asked them, did they know or see anything of a castle that stood upon twelve golden pillars; and they all made a curious sound, *Kro-kro, kro-kro*, and said, No.

Jack had to take another horse, and a cake to this king's brother, who is the king of all the fowls of the air; and as Jack was going through the gates, the little frog that was on sentry asked Jack should he go with him. Jack refused him for a bit; but at last he told him to jump up, and Jack put him in his other waistcoat pocket. And away he went again on his great long journey; it was three times as long this time as it was the first day; however, he found the place, and there was a fine bird on sentry. And Jack passed him, and he never said a word to him; and he talked with the king, and told him everything, all about the castle. 'Well,' said the king to him, 'you shall know in the morning from my birds, whether they know anything or not.' Jack put up his horse in the stable, and then went to bed, after having something to eat. And when he got up in the morning the king and he went on to some field, and there the king made some funny noise, and there came all the fowls that were in all the world. And the king asked them: 'Did you see the fine castle?' and all the birds answered: 'No'. 'Well,' said the king, 'where is the great bird?' They had to wait then for a long time for the eagle to make his appearance, when at last he came all in a perspiration, after sending two little birds high up in the sky to whistle on him to make all the haste he possibly could. The king asked the great bird: 'Did you see the great castle?' and the bird said: 'Yes, I came from there where it now is.' 'Well,' says the king to him; 'this young gentleman has lost it, and you must go with him back to it; but stop till you get a bit of something to eat first.'

They killed a calf, and sent the best part of it to feed the eagle on his journey over the seas, for he had to carry Jack on his back. Now when they came in sight of the castle, they did not know what to do to get the little golden box. Well, the little mouse said to them: 'Leave me down, and I will get the little box for you.' So the mouse stole into the castle, and got hold of the box; and when he was coming down the stairs, it fell down, and he was very near being caught. He came running out with it, laughing his best. 'Have you got it?' Jack said to him; he said: 'Yes;' and off they went back again, and left the castle behind.

As they were all of them (Jack, mouse, frog and eagle) passing over the great sea, they fell to quarrelling about who was to get the little box, till down it slipped into the water. (It was by them looking at it and handing it from one hand to the other that they dropped the little box to the bottom of the sea.) 'Well, well,' said the frog, 'I knew that I would have to do something, so you had better let me go down in the water.' And they let him go, and he was down for three days and three nights; and up he comes, and shows his nose and little mouth out of the water; and all of them asked him, 'Did you get it? and he told them, 'No.' 'Well, what are you doing there, then?' 'Nothing

at all,' he said, 'only I want my full breath;' and the poor little frog went down the second time, and he was down for a day and a night, and up he brings it.

And away they did go, after being there four days and nights; and after a long tug over seas and mountains, they arrived at the palace of the old king, who is the master of all the birds in the world. And the king is very proud to see them, and has a hearty welcome and a long conversation. Jack opens the little box, and told the little men to go back and to bring the castle here to them; 'and all of you make as much haste back again as you possibly can.'

The three little men went off; and when they came near the castle they were afraid to go to it till the gentleman and lady and all the servants were gone out to some dance. And there was no one left behind there only the cook and another maid with her; and the little red men asked them which would they rather – go, or stop behind? and they both said: 'I will go with you;' and the little men told them to run upstairs quick. They were no sooner up and in one of the drawing-rooms than here comes just in sight the gentleman and lady and all the servants; but it was too late. Off the castle went at full speed, with the women laughing at them through the window, while they made motions for them to stop, but all to no purpose. They were nine days on their journey, in which they did try to

The eagle flew over the seas with Jack on his back

keep the Sunday holy, when one of the little men turned to be the priest, the other the clerk, and the third presided at the organ, and the women were the singers, for they had a grand chapel in the castle already. Very remarkable, there was a discord made in the music, and one of the little men ran up one of the organ-pipes to see where the bad sound came from; when he found out, it only happened to be that the two women were laughing at the little red man stretching his little legs full length on the bass pipes, also his two arms at the same time, with his little red nightcap, which he never forgot to wear; and what they never witnessed before could not help calling forth some good merriment while they were on the face of the deep. And poor thing! through them not paying proper attention, they very near came to danger, as the castle was once very near sinking in the middle of the sea.

At length, after a merry journey, they came again to Jack and the king. The king was quite struck with the sight of the castle; and going up the golden stairs, went to see the inside.

The king was very much pleased with the castle, but poor Jack's time of a twelvemonths and a day was drawing to a close; and he, wishing to go home to his young wife, gives orders to the three little men to get ready by the next morning at eight o'clock to be off to the next brother, and to stop there for one night; also to proceed from there to the last or the youngest brother, the master of all the mice in the world, in such place where the castle shall be left under his care until it's sent for. Jack takes a farewell of the king, and thanks him very much for his hospitality.

Away went Jack and his castle again, and stopped one night in that place; and away they went again to the third place, and there left the castle under his care. As Jack had to leave the castle behind, he had to take to his own horse, which he left there when he first started.

Now poor Jack leaves his castle behind and faces towards home; and after having so much merriment with the three brothers every night, Jack became sleepy on horseback, and would have lost the road if it was not for the little men a-guiding him. At last he arrived weary and tired, and they did not seem to receive him with any kindness whatever, because he had not found the stolen castle; and to make it worse, he was disappointed in not seeing his young and beautiful wife to come and meet him, through being hindered by her parents. But that did not last long. Jack put full power on and dispatched the little men off to bring the castle from there, and they soon got there.

Jack shook hands with the king, and returned many thanks for his kingly kindness in minding the castle for him; and then Jack instructed the little men to spur up and put speed on. And off they went, and were not long before they reached their journey's end, when out comes the young wife to meet him with a fine lump of a young son, and they all lived happy ever afterwards.

Jack and His Master

A poor woman had three sons. The eldest and second eldest were cunning clever fellows, but they called the youngest Jack the Fool, because they thought he was no better than a simpleton. The eldest got tired of staying at home, and said he'd go look for service. He stayed away a whole year, and then came back one day, dragging one foot after the other, and a poor wizened face on him, and he as cross as two sticks. When he was rested and got something to eat, he told them how he got service with the Grey Churl of the Townland of Mischance, and that the agreement was, whoever would first say he was sorry for his bargain, should get an inch wide of the skin of his back, from shoulder to hips, taken off. If it was the master, he should also pay double wages; if it was the servant, he should get no wages at all. 'But the thief,' says he, 'gave me so little to eat, and kept me so hard at work, that flesh and blood couldn't stand it; and when he asked me once, when I was in a passion, if I was sorry for my bargain, I was mad enough to say I was, and here I am disabled for life.'

Vexed enough were the poor mother and brothers; and the second eldest said on the spot he'd go and take service with the Grey Churl, and punish him by all the annoyance he'd give him till he'd make him say he was sorry for his agreement. 'Oh, won't I be glad to see the skin coming off the old villain's back!' said he. All they could say had no effect: he started off for the Townland of Mischance, and in a twelvemonth he was back just as miserable and helpless as his brother.

All the poor mother could say didn't prevent Jack the Fool from starting to see if he was able to regulate the Grey Churl. He agreed with him for a year for twenty pounds, and the terms were the same.

'Now, Jack,' said the Grey Churl, 'if you refuse to do anything you are able to do, you must lose a month's wages.'

'I'm satisfied,' said Jack; 'and if you stop me from doing a thing after telling me to do it, you are to give me an additional month's wages.'

'I am satisfied,' says the master.

'Or if you blame me for obeying your orders, you must give the same.'

'I am satisfied,' said the master again.

The first day that Jack served he was fed very poorly, and was worked to the saddleskirts. Next day he came in just before the dinner was sent up to the parlour. They were taking the goose off the spit, but well becomes Jack, he whips a knife off the dresser and cuts off one side of the breast, one leg and thigh and one wing and fell to. In came the master, and began to abuse him for his assurance. 'Oh, you know, master, you're to feed me, and wherever the goose goes won't have to be filled again till supper. Are you sorry for our agreement?'

The master was going to cry out he was, but he bethought himself in time. 'Oh no, not at all,' said he.

'That's well,' said Jack.

Next day Jack was to go clamp turf on the bog. They weren't sorry to have him away from the kitchen at dinner-time. He didn't find his breakfast very heavy on his stomach; so he said to the mistress, 'I think, ma'am, it will be better for me to get my dinner now, and not lose time coming home from the bog.'

'That's true, Jack,' said she. So she brought out a good cake, and a print of butter, and a bottle of milk, thinking he'd take them away to the bog. But Jack kept his seat, and never drew rein till bread, butter and milk went down the red lane.

'Now, mistress,' said he, 'I'll be earlier at my work tomorrow if I sleep comfortably on the sheltery side of a pile of peat on dry grass, and'll not be coming here and going back. So you may as well give me my supper, and be done with the day's trouble.' She gave him that, thinking he'd take it to the bog; but he fell to on the spot, and did not leave a single scrap; and the mistress was a little astonished.

He called to speak to the master in the haggard, and said he, 'What are servants asked to do in this country after eating their supper?'

'Nothing at all, but to go to bed.'

'Oh, very well, sir.' He went up on the stable-loft, stripped and lay down, and someone that saw him told the master. He came up.

'Jack, you anointed scoundrel, what do you mean?'

'To go to sleep, master. The mistress, God bless her, is after giving me my breakfast, dinner and supper, and yourself told me that bed was the next thing. Do you blame me, sir?'

'Yes, you rascal, I do.'

'Hand me out one pound thirteen and four-pence, if you please, sir.'

'One divel and thirteen imps, you tinker! What for?'

'Oh, I see, you've forgot your bargain. Are you sorry for it?'

'Oh, ye – no, I mean. I'll give you the money after your nap.'

Next morning early, Jack asked how he'd be employed that day. 'You are to be holding the plough in that fallow, outside the paddock.' The master went over about nine o'clock to see what kind of a ploughman was Jack, and what did he see but the little boy driving the bastes, and the sock and coulter of the plough skimming along the sod, and Jack pulling ding-dong again' the horses.

'What are you doing, you contrary thief?' said the master.

'An' ain't I strivin' to hold this divel of a plough, as you told me; but that ounkrawn of a boy keeps whipping on the bastes in spite of all I say; will you speak to him?'

'No, but I'll speak to you. Didn't you know, you bosthoon, that when I said "holding the plough", I meant reddening the ground.'

'Faith, an' if you did, I wish you had said so. Do you blame me for what I have done?'

The master caught himself in time, but he was so stomached, he said nothing.

'Go on and redden the ground now, you knave, as other ploughmen do.'

'An' are you sorry for our agreement?'

'Oh, not at all, not at all!'

Jack ploughed away like a good workman all the rest of the day.

In a day or two the master bade him go and mind the cows in a field that had half of it under young corn. 'Be sure, particularly,' said he, 'to keep Browney from the wheat; while she's out of mischief there's no fear of the rest.'

About noon, he went to see how Jack was doing his duty, and what did he find but Jack asleep with his face to the sod, Browney grazing near a thorn tree, one end of a long rope round her horns, and the other end round the tree, and the rest of the beasts all trampling and eating the green wheat. Down came the switch on Jack.

'Jack, you vagabone, do you see what the cows are at?'

'And do you blame me, master?'

'To be sure, you lazy sluggard, I do!'

'Hand me out one pound thirteen and four-pence, master. You said if I only kept Browney out of mischief, the rest would do no harm. There she is as harmless as a lamb. Are you sorry for hiring me, master?'

'To be – that is, not at all. I'll give you your money when you go to dinner. Now, understand me; don't let a cow go out of the field nor into the wheat the rest of the day.'

'Never fear, master!' and neither did he. But the Grey Churl would rather than a great deal he had not hired him.

The next day three heifers were missing, and the master bade Jack go in search of them.

'Where will I look for them?' said Jack.

'Oh, every place likely and unlikely for them all to be in.'

The Churl was getting very exact in his words. When he was coming into the bawn at dinner-time, what work did he find Jack at but pulling armfuls of the thatch off the roof, and peeping into the holes he was making?

'What are you doing there, you rascal?'

'Sure, I'm looking for the heifers, poor things!'

'What would bring them there?'

'I don't think anything could bring them in it; but I looked first into the likely places, that is, the cow-houses and the pastures and the fields next 'em, and now I'm looking in the unlikeliest place I can think of. Maybe it's not pleasing to you it is?'

'And to be sure it isn't pleasing to me, you aggravating goose-cap!'

'Please, sir, hand me one pound thirteen and four-pence before you sit down to your dinner. I'm afraid it's sorrow that's on you for hiring me at all?'

'May the div – oh no; I'm not sorry. Will you begin, if you please, and put in the thatch again, just as if you were doing it for your mother's cabin?'

'Oh, faith I will, sir, with a heart and a half;' and

by the time the farmer came out from his dinner, Jack had the roof better than it was before, for he made the boy give him new straw.

Says the master when he came out, 'Go, Jack, and look for the heifers, and bring them home.'

'And where will I look for 'em?'

'Go and search for them as if they were your own.' The heifers were all in the paddock before sunset.

Next morning, says the master, 'Jack, the path across the bog to the pasture is very bad; the sheep are sinking in it every step; go and make the sheep's feet a good path.' About an hour after he came to the edge of the bog, and what did he find Jack at but sharpening a carving knife, and the sheep standing or grazing round.

'Is this the way you are mending the path, Jack?' said he.

'Everything must have a beginning, master,' said Jack, 'and a thing well begun is half done. I am sharpening the knife, and I'll have the feet off every sheep in the flock while you'd be blessing yourself.'

'Feet off my sheep, you anointed rogue! And what would you be taking their feet off for?'

'An' sure to mend the path as you told me. Says you, "Jack, make a path with the feet of the sheep."'

'Oh, you fool, I meant make good the path for the sheep's feet.'

'It's a pity you didn't say so, master. Hand me out one pound thirteen and fourpence if you don't like me to finish my job.'

'Divel do you good with your one pound thirteen and fourpence!'

'It's better pray than curse, master. Maybe you're sorry for your bargain?'

'And to be sure I am – not yet, anyway.'

The next night the master was going to a wedding; and says he to Jack, before he set out, 'I'll leave at midnight, and I wish you to come and be with me home, for fear I might be overtaken with the drink. If you're

there before, you may throw a sheep's eye at me, and I'll be sure to see that they'll give you something for yourself.'

About eleven o'clock, while the master was in great spirits, he felt something clammy hit him on the cheek. It fell beside his tumbler, and when he looked at it what was it but the eye of a sheep? Well, he couldn't imagine who threw it at him, or why it was thrown at him. After a little he got a blow on the other cheek, and still it was by another sheep's eye. Well, he was very vexed, but he thought better to say nothing. In two minutes more, when he was opening his mouth to take a sup, another sheep's eye was slapped into it. He sputtered it out, and cried, 'Man o' the house, isn't it a great shame for you to have anyone in the room that would do such a nasty thing?'

'Master,' says Jack, 'don't blame the honest man. Sure it's only myself that was throwin' them sheep's eyes at you, to remind you I was here, and that I wanted to drink the bride and bridegroom's health. You know yourself bade me.'

'I know that you are a great rascal; and where did you get the eyes?'

'An' where would I get em' but from the heads of your own sheep? Would you have me meddle with the bastes of any neighbour, who might put me in the Stone Jug for it?'

'Sorrow on me that ever I had the bad luck to meet with you.'

'You're all witness,' said Jack, 'that my master says he is sorry for having met with me. My time is up. Master, hand me over double wages, and come into the next room, and lay yourself out like a man that has some decency in him, till I take a strip of skin an inch broad from your shoulder to your hip.'

Everyone shouted out against that; but, says Jack, 'You didn't hinder him when he took the same strips from the backs of my two brothers, and sent them home in that state, and penniless, to their poor mother.'

When the company heard the rights of the business, they were only too eager to see the job done. The master bawled and roared, but there was no help at hand. He was stripped to his hips, and laid on the floor in the next room, and Jack had the carving knife in his hand ready to begin.

'Now, you cruel old villain,' said he, giving the knife a couple of scrapes along the floor, 'I'll make you an offer. Give me, along with my double wages, two hundred guineas to support my poor brothers, and I'll do without the strap.'

'No!' said he. 'I'll let you skin me from head to foot first.'

'Here goes then,' said Jack with a grin, but the first little scar he gave, the Churl roared out, 'Stop your hand; I'll give the money.'

'Now, neighbours,' said Jack, 'you mustn't think worse of me than I deserve. I wouldn't have the heart to take an eye out of a rat itself; I got half a dozen of them from the butcher, and only used three of them.'

So all came again into the other room, and Jack was made to sit down, and everybody drank his health, and he drank everybody's health at one offer. And six stout fellows saw himself and the master home, and waited in the parlour while he went up and brought down the two hundred guineas, and double wages for Jack himself. When he got home, he brought the summer along with him to the poor mother and the disabled brothers; and he was no more Jack the Fool in the people's mouths, but 'Skin-Churl Jack'.

Jack and the Beanstalk

There was once upon a time a poor widow who had an only son named Jack, and a cow named Milky-white. And all they had to live on was the milk the cow gave every morning which they carried to the market and sold. But one morning Milky-white gave no milk and they didn't know what to do.

'What shall we do, what shall we do?' said the widow, wringing her hands.

'Cheer up, mother, I'll go and get work somewhere,' said Jack.

'We've tried that before, and nobody would take you,' said his mother; 'we must sell Milky-white and with the money do something – start a shop or something.'

'All right, mother,' says Jack; 'it's market-day today, and I'll soon sell Milky-white, and then we'll see what we can do.'

So he took the cow's halter in his hand, and off he starts. He hadn't gone far when he met a funny-looking old man who said to him: 'Good-morning, Jack.'

'Good-morning to you,' said Jack, and wondered how he knew his name.

'Well, Jack, and where are you off to?' said the man.

'I'm going to market to sell our cow here.'

'Oh, you look the proper sort of chap to sell cows,' said the man; 'I wonder if you know how many beans make five.'

'Two in each hand and one in your mouth,' says Jack, as sharp as a needle.

'Right you are,' said the man, 'and here they are the very beans themselves,' he went on pulling out of his pocket a number of strange-looking beans. 'As you are so sharp,' says he, 'I don't mind doing a swop with you – your cow for these beans.'

'Walker!' says Jack; 'wouldn't you like it?'

'Ah! you don't know what these beans are,' said the man; 'if you plant them overnight, by morning they grow right up to the sky.'

'Really?' says Jack; 'you don't say so.'

'Yes, that is so, and if it doesn't turn out to be true you can have your cow back.'

'Right,' says Jack, and hands him over Milky-white's halter and pockets the beans.

Back goes Jack home, and as he hadn't gone very far it wasn't dusk by the time he got to his door.

'What back, Jack?' said his mother; 'I see you haven't got Milky-white, so you've sold her. How much did you get for her?'

'You'll never guess, mother,' says Jack.

'No, you don't say so. Good boy! Five pounds, ten, fifteen, no, it can't be twenty.'

'I told you you couldn't guess, what do you say to these beans; they're magical, plant them overnight and – '

'What!' says Jack's mother, 'have you been such a fool, such a dolt, such an idiot, as to give away my Milky-white, the best milker in the parish, and prime beef to boot, for a set of paltry beans. Take that! Take that! Take that! And as for your precious

'Right,' says Jack, and hands him over Milky-white's halter and pockets the beans

beans here they go out of the window. And now off with you to bed. Not a sup shall you drink, and not a bite shall you swallow this very night.'

So Jack went upstairs to his little room in the attic, and sad and sorry he was, to be sure, as much for his mother's sake, as for the loss of his supper.

At last he dropped off to sleep.

When he woke up, the room looked so funny. The sun was shining into part of it, and yet all the rest was quite dark and shady. So Jack jumped up and dressed himself and went to the window. And what do you think he saw? why, the beans his mother had thrown out of the window into the garden had sprung up into a big beanstalk which went up and up and up till it reached the sky. So the man spoke truth after all.

The beanstalk grew up quite close past Jack's window, so all he had to do was to open it and give a jump on to the beanstalk which was made like a big plaited ladder. So Jack climbed and he climbed and he climbed and he climbed and he climbed and he climbed and he climbed till at last he reached the sky. And when he got there he found a long broad road going as straight as a dart. So he walked along and he walked along and he walked along till he came to a great big tall house, and on the doorstep there was a great big tall woman.

'Good-morning, mum,' says Jack, quite polite-like. 'Could you be so kind as to give me some breakfast?' For he hadn't had anything to eat, you know, the night before and was as hungry as a hunter.

'It's breakfast you want, is it?' says the great big tall woman, 'it's breakfast you'll be if you don't move off from here. My man is an ogre and there's nothing he likes better than boys broiled on toast. You'd better be moving on or he'll soon be coming.'

'Oh! please mum, do give me something to eat, mum. I've had nothing to eat since yesterday morning, really and truly, mum,' says Jack. 'I may as well be broiled as die of hunger.'

Well, the ogre's wife wasn't such a bad sort, after all. So she took Jack into the kitchen, and gave him a hunk of bread and cheese and a jug of milk. But Jack hadn't half finished these when thump! thump! thump! the whole house began to tremble with the noise of someone coming.

'Goodness gracious me! It's my old man,' said the ogre's wife, 'what on earth shall I do? Here, come quick and jump in here.' And she bundled Jack into the oven just as the ogre came in.

He was a big one, to be sure. At his belt he had

three calves strung up by the heels, and he unhooked them and threw them down on the table and said: 'Here, wife, broil me a couple of these for breakfast. Ah what's this I smell? Fee, fi, fo, fum! I smell the blood of an Englishman. Be he alive, or be he dead, I'll grind his bones to make my bread.'

'Nonsense, dear,' said his wife, 'you're dreaming. Or perhaps you smell the scraps of that little boy you liked so much for yesterday's dinner. Here, go you and have a wash and tidy up, and by the time you come back your breakfast'll be ready for you.'

So the ogre went off, and Jack was just going to jump out of the oven and run off when the woman stopped him. 'Wait till he's asleep,' says she; 'he always has a snooze after breakfast.'

Well, the ogre had his breakfast, and after that he goes to a big chest and takes out of it a couple of bags of gold and sits down counting the pieces till at last his head began to nod and he began to snore till the whole house shook again.

Then Jack crept out on tiptoe from his oven, and as he was passing the ogre he took one of the bags of gold under his arm, and off he pelters till he came to the beanstalk, and then he threw down the bag of gold which of course fell into his mother's garden, and then he climbed down and climbed down till at last he got home and told his mother and showed her the gold and said: 'Well, mother, wasn't I right about the beans. They are really magical, you see.'

So they lived on the bag of gold for some time, but at last they came to the end of it. So Jack made up his mind to try his luck once more up at the top of the beanstalk. So one fine morning he got up early, and got on to the beanstalk, and he climbed and he climbed and he climbed and he climbed and he climbed and he climbed till at last he got on the road again and came to the great big tall house he had been to before. There, sure enough, was the great big tall woman a-standing on the doorstep.

'Good-morning, mum,' says Jack, as bold as brass, 'could you be so good as to give me something to eat?'

'Go away, my boy,' said the big, tall woman, 'or else my man will eat you up for breakfast. But aren't you the youngster who came here once before? Do you know, that very day, my man missed one of his bags of gold.'

'That's strange, mum,' says Jack. 'I dare say I could tell you something about that but I'm so hungry I can't speak till I've had something to eat.'

His head began to nod and he began to snore till the whole house shook again

Well the big tall woman was that curious that she took him in and gave him something to eat. But he had scarcely begun munching it as slowly as he could when thump! thump! thump! they heard the giant's footstep, and his wife hid Jack away in the oven.

All happened as it did before. In came the ogre as he did before, said: 'Fee, fi, fo, fum!' and had his breakfast off three broiled oxen. Then he said: 'Wife, bring me the hen that lays the golden eggs.' So she brought it, and the ogre said: 'Lay,' and it laid an egg all of gold. And then the ogre began to nod his head, and to snore till the house shook.

Then Jack crept out of the oven on tiptoe and caught hold of the golden hen, and was off before you could say 'Jack Robinson'. But this time the hen gave a cackle which woke the ogre, and just as Jack got out of the house he heard him calling: 'Wife, wife, what have you done with my golden hen?'

And the wife said: 'Why, my dear?'

But that was all Jack heard, for he rushed off to the beanstalk and climbed down like a house on fire. And when he got home he showed his mother the wonderful hen and said, 'Lay,' to it; and it laid a golden egg every time he said, 'Lay.'

Well, Jack was not content, and it wasn't very long before he determined to have another try at his luck up there at the top of the beanstalk. So one fine morning, he got up early, and went on to the beanstalk, and he climbed and he climbed and he

climbed and he climbed till he got to the top. But this time he knew better than to go straight to the ogre's house. And when he got near it he waited behind a bush till he saw the ogre's wife come out with a pail to get some water, and then he crept into the house and got into the copper. He hadn't been there long when he heard thump! thump! thump! as before, and in came the ogre and his wife.

'Fee, fi, fo, fum! I smell the blood of an Englishman,' cried out the ogre; 'I smell him, wife, I smell him.'

'Do you, my dearie?' says the ogre's wife. 'Then if it's that little rogue that stole your gold and the hen that laid the golden eggs he's sure to have got into the oven.' And they both rushed to the oven. But Jack wasn't there, luckily, and the ogre's wife said: 'There you are again with your Fee, fi, fo, fum!. Why of course it's the laddie you caught last night that I've broiled for your breakfast. How forgetful I am, and how careless you are not to tell the difference between a live un and a dead un.'

So the ogre sat down to the breakfast and ate it, but every now and then he would mutter: 'Well, I could have sworn – ' and he'd get up and search the larder and the cupboards, and everything, only luckily he didn't think of the copper.

After breakfast was over, the ogre called out: 'Wife, wife, bring me my golden harp.' So she brought it and put it on the table before him. Then

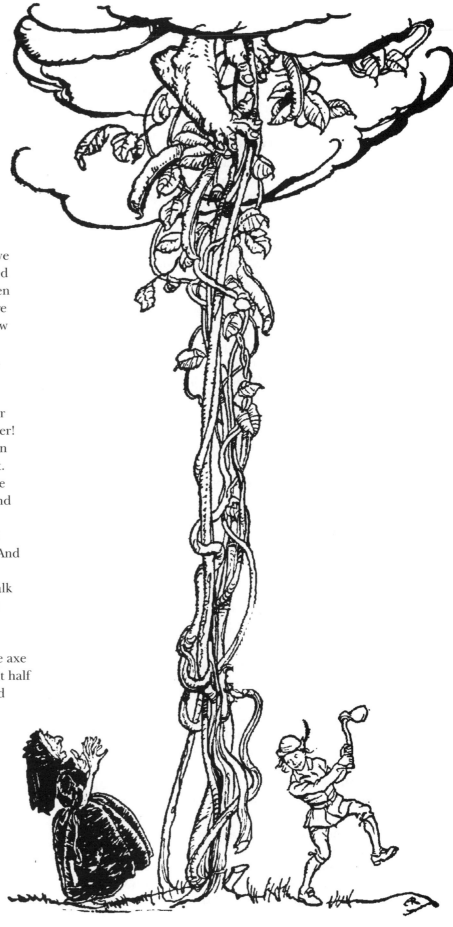

he said: 'Sing!' and the golden harp sang most beautifully. And it went on singing till the ogre fell asleep, and commenced to snore like thunder.

Then Jack lifted up the copper-lid very quietly and got down like a mouse and crept on hands and knees till he got to the table; then he got up and caught hold of the golden harp and dashed with it towards the door. But the harp called out quite loud: 'Master! Master!' and the ogre woke up just in time to see Jack running off with his harp.

Jack ran as fast as he could, and the ogre came rushing after, and would soon have caught him, only Jack had a start and dodged him a bit and knew where he was going. When he got to the beanstalk the ogre was not more than twenty yards away when suddenly he saw Jack disappear, and when he got up to the end of the road he saw Jack underneath, climbing down for dear life. Well, the ogre didn't like trusting himself to such a ladder, and he stood and waited, so Jack got another start. But just then the harp cried out: 'Master! master!' and the ogre swung himself down on to the beanstalk which shook with his weight. Down climbs Jack, and after him climbed the ogre. By this time Jack had climbed down and climbed down and climbed down till he was very nearly home. So he called out: 'Mother! mother! bring me an axe, bring me an axe.' And his mother came rushing out with the axe in her hand, but when she came to the beanstalk she stood stock still with fright for there she saw the ogre just coming down below the clouds.

But Jack jumped down and got hold of the axe and gave a chop at the beanstalk which cut it half in two. The ogre felt the beanstalk shake and quiver so he stopped to see what was the matter. Then Jack gave another chop with the axe, and the beanstalk was cut in two and began to topple over. Then the ogre fell down and broke his crown, and the beanstalk came toppling after.

Then Jack showed his mother his golden harp, and what with showing that and selling the golden eggs, Jack and his mother became very rich, and he married a great princess, and they lived happy ever after.

Jack Hannaford

There was an old soldier who had been long in the wars – so long, that he was quite out-at-elbows, and he did not know where to go to find a living. So he walked up moors, down glens, till at last he came to a farm, from which the good man had gone away to market. The wife of the farmer was a very foolish woman, who had been a widow when he married her; the farmer was foolish enough, too, and it is hard to say which of the two was the more foolish. When you've heard my tale you may decide.

Now before the farmer goes to market says he to his wife: 'Here is ten pounds all in gold; take care of it till I come home.' If the man had not been a fool he would never have given the money to his wife to keep. Well, off he went in his cart to market, and the wife said to herself: 'I will keep the ten pounds quite safe from thieves;' so she tied it up in a rag, and she put the rag up the parlour chimney.

'There,' said she, 'no thieves will ever find it now, that is quite sure.'

Jack Hannaford, the old soldier, came and rapped at the door.

'Who is there?' asked the wife.

'Jack Hannaford.'

'Where do you come from?'

'Paradise.'

'Lord a' mercy! and maybe you've seen my old man there,' alluding to her former husband.

'Yes, I have.'

'And how was he a-doing?' asked the goody.

'But middling; he cobbles old shoes, and he has nothing but cabbage for victuals.'

'Deary me!' exclaimed the woman. 'Didn't he send a message to me?'

'Yes, he did,' replied Jack Hannaford. 'He said that he was out of leather, and his pockets were empty, so you were to send him a few shillings to buy a fresh stock of leather.'

'He shall have them, bless his poor soul!' And away went the wife to the parlour chimney, and she pulled the rag with the ten pounds in it from the chimney, and she gave the whole sum to the soldier, telling him that her old man was to use as much as he wanted, and to send back the rest.

It was not long that Jack waited after receiving the money; he went off as fast as he could walk.

Presently the farmer came home and asked for his money. The wife told him that she had sent it by a soldier to her former husband in Paradise, to buy him leather for cobbling the shoes of the saints and angels of heaven. The farmer was very angry, and he swore that he had never met with such a fool as his wife. But the wife said that her husband was a greater fool for letting her have the money.

There was no time to waste words; so the farmer mounted his horse and rode off after Jack Hannaford. The old soldier heard the horse's hoofs clattering on the road behind him, so he knew it must be the farmer pursuing him. He lay down on the ground, and shading his eyes with one hand, looked up into the sky, and pointed heavenwards with the other hand.

'What are you about there?' asked the farmer, pulling up.

'Lord save you!' exclaimed Jack. 'I've seen a rare sight.'

'What was that?'

'A man going straight up into the sky, as if he were walking on a road.'

'Can you see him still?'

'Yes, I can.'

'Where?'

'Get off your horse and lie down.'

'If you will hold the horse.'

Jack did so readily.

'I cannot see him,' said the farmer.

'Shade your eyes with your hand, and you'll soon see a man flying away from you.'

Sure enough he did so, for Jack leaped on the horse, and rode away with it. The farmer walked home without his horse.

'You are a bigger fool than I am,' said the wife; 'for I did only one foolish thing, and you have done two.'

Jack the Cunning Thief

There was a poor farmer who had three sons, and on the same day the three boys went to seek their fortune. The eldest two were sensible, industrious young men; the youngest never did much at home that was any use. He loved to be setting snares for rabbits and tracking hares in the snow, and inventing all sorts of funny tricks to annoy people at first and then set them laughing.

The three parted at crossroads, and Jack took the lonesomest. The day turned out rainy, and he was wet and weary, you may depend, at nightfall, when he came to a lonesome house a little off the road.

'What do you want?' said a blear-eyed old woman, that was sitting at the fire.

'My supper and a bed to be sure,' said he.

'You can't get it,' said she.

'What's to hinder me?' said he.

'The owners of the house is,' said she: 'six honest men that does be out mostly till three or four o'clock in the morning, and if they find you here they'll skin you alive at the very least.'

'Well, I think,' said Jack, 'that their very most couldn't be much worse. Come, give me something out of the cupboard, for here I'll stay. Skinning is not much worse than catching your death of cold in a ditch or under a tree such a night as this.'

Begonins she got afraid, and gave him a good supper; and when he was going to bed he said if she let any of the six honest men disturb him when they came home she'd sup sorrow for it. When he awoke in the morning, there were six ugly-looking spalpeens standing round his bed. He leaned on his elbow, and looked at them with great contempt.

'Who are you,' said the chief, 'and what's your business?'

'My name,' says he, 'is Master Thief, and my business just now is to find apprentices and workmen. If I find you any good, maybe I'll give you a few lessons.'

Bedad they were a little cowed, and says the head man, 'Well, get up, and after breakfast, we'll see who is to be the master, and who the journeyman.'

They were just done breakfast, when what should they see but a farmer driving a fine large goat to market. 'Will any of you,' says Jack, 'undertake to steal that goat from the owner before he gets out of the wood, and that without the smallest violence?'

'I couldn't do it,' says one; and, 'I couldn't do it,' says another.

'I'm your master,' says Jack, 'and I'll do it.'

He slipped out, went through the trees to where there was a bend in the road, and laid down his right brogue in the very middle of it. Then he ran on to another bend, and laid down his left brogue and went and hid himself.

When the farmer sees the first brogue, he says to himself, 'That would be worth something if it had the fellow, but it is worth nothing by itself.'

He goes on till he comes to the second brogue.

'What a fool I was,' says he, 'not to pick up the other! I'll go back for it.'

So he tied the goat to a sapling in the hedge, and returned for the brogue. But Jack, who was behind a tree had it already on his foot, and when the man was beyond the bend he picked up the other and loosened the goat, and led him off through the wood.

Ochone! The poor man couldn't find the first brogue, and when he came back he couldn't find the second, nor neither his goat.

'*Mile mollacht!*' says he. 'What will I do after promising Johanna to buy her a shawl. I must only go and drive another beast to the market unknownst. I'd never hear the last of it if Joan found out what a fool I had made of myself.'

The thieves were in great admiration at Jack, and wanted him to tell them how he had hoodwinked the farmer, but he wouldn't tell them.

By and by, they see the poor man driving a fine fat wether the same way.

'Who'll steal that wether,' says Jack, 'before it's out of the wood, and no roughness used?'

'I couldn't,' says one; and, 'I couldn't,' says another.

'I'll try,' says Jack. 'Give me a good rope.'

The poor farmer was jogging along and

thinking of his misfortune, when he sees a man hanging from the bough of a tree. 'Lord save us!' says he. 'The corpse wasn't there an hour ago.' He went on about half a quarter of a mile, and there was another corpse again hanging over the road. 'God between us and harm,' said he, 'am I in my right senses?' There was another turn about the same distance, and just beyond it the third corpse was hanging. 'Oh, murdher!' said he. 'I'm beside myself. What would bring three hung men so near one another? I must be mad. I'll go back and see if the others are there still.'

He tied the wether to a sapling, and back he went. But when he was round the bend, down came the corpse, and loosened the wether, and drove it home through the wood to the robbers' house. You all may think how the poor farmer felt when he could find no one dead or alive, going or coming, nor his wether, nor the rope that fastened him. 'Oh, misfortunate day!' cried he. 'What'll Joan say to me now? My morning gone, and the goat and wether lost! I must sell something to make the price of the shawl. Well, the fat bullock is in the nearest field. She won't see me taking it.'

Well, the robbers were nothing if not surprised when Jack came into the bawn with the wether! 'If you do another trick like this,' said the captain, 'I'll resign the command to you.'

They soon saw the farmer going by again, driving a fat bullock this time.

'Who'll bring that fat bullock here,' says Jack, 'and use no violence?'

'I couldn't,' says one; and, 'I couldn't,' says another.

'I'll try,' says Jack, and away he went into the wood.

The farmer was about the spot where he saw the first brogue, when he heard the bleating of a goat off at his right in the wood.

He cocked his ears, and the next thing he heard was the maaing of a sheep.

'Blood alive!' says he. 'Maybe these are my own that I lost.' There was more bleating and more maaing. 'There they are as sure as a gun,' says he, and he tied his bullock to a sapling that grew in the hedge, and away he went into the wood. When he got near the place where the cries came from, he heard them a little before him, and on he followed them. At last, when he was about half a mile from the spot where he tied the beast, the cries stopped altogether. After searching and searching till he was tired, he returned for his bullock; but there wasn't the ghost of a bullock there, nor anywhere else that he searched.

This time, when the thieves saw Jack and his prize coming into the bawn, they couldn't help shouting out, 'Jack must be our chief.' So there was nothing but feasting and drinking hand to fist the rest of the day. Before they went to bed, they showed Jack the cave where their money was hid, and all their disguises in another cave, and swore obedience to him.

One morning, when they were at breakfast, about a week after, said they to Jack, 'Will you mind the house for us today while we are at the fair of Mochurry? We hadn't a spree for ever so long: you must get your turn whenever you like.'

'Never say't twice,' says Jack, and off they went.

After they were gone says Jack to the wicked housekeeper, 'Do these fellows ever make you a present?'

'Ah, catch them at it! Indeed, and they don't, purshuin to 'em.'

'Well, come along with me, and I'll make you a rich woman.'

He took her to the treasure cave; and while she was in raptures, gazing at the heaps of gold and silver, Jack filled his pockets as full as they could hold, put more into a little bag, and walked out, locking the door on the old hag, and leaving the key in the lock. He then put on a rich suit of clothes, took the goat, and the wether, and the bullock, and drove them before him to the farmer's house.

Joan and her husband were at the door, and when they saw the animals, they clapped their hands and laughed for joy.

'Do you know who owns them bastes, neighbours?'

'We certainly do! Sure they're ours.'

He took the wicked housekeeper to the treasure cave

'I found them straying in the wood. Is that bag with ten guineas in it that's hung round the goat's neck yours?'

'Faith, it isn't.'

'Well, you may as well keep it for a godsend! I don't want it.'

'Heaven be in your road, good gentleman!'

Jack travelled on till he came to his father's house in the dusk of the evening. He went in. 'God save all here!'

'God save you kindly, sir!'

'Could I have a night's lodging here?'

'Oh, sir, our place isn't fit for the likes of a gentleman such as you.'

'Oh, father, don't you know your own son?'

Well, they opened their eyes, and it was only a strife to see who'd have him in their arms first.

'But, Jack my boy, where did you get the fine clothes?'

'Oh, you may as well ask me where I got all this money!' said he, emptying his pockets on the table.

Well, they got in a great fright, but when he told them his adventures, they were easier in mind, and all went to bed in great content.

'Father,' says Jack, next morning, 'go over to the landlord, and tell him I wish to be married to his daughter.'

'Faith, I'm afraid he'll only set the dogs at me. If he asks me how you made your money, what'll I say?'

'Tell him I am a master thief, and that there is no one equal to me in the three kingdoms; that I am worth a thousand pounds, and all taken from the biggest rogues unhanged. Speak to him when the young lady is by.'

'It's a droll message you're sending me on. I'm afraid it won't end well.'

The old man came back in two hours.

'Well, what news?'

'Droll news, enough. The lady didn't seem a bit unwilling. I suppose it's not the first time you spoke to her; and the squire laughed, and said you would have to steal the goose off o' the spit in his kitchen next Sunday, and he'd see about it.'

'Oh! That won't be hard, anyway.'

Next Sunday, after the people came from early Mass, the squire and all his people were in the kitchen, and the goose turning before the fire. The kitchen door opened, and a miserable old beggarman with a big wallet on his back put in his head.

'Would the mistress have anything for me when dinner is over, your honour?'

'To be sure. We have no room here for you just now; sit in the porch for a while.'

'God bless your honour's family, and yourself!'

Soon someone that was sitting near the window cried out, 'Oh, sir, there's a big hare scampering like the divil round the bawn. Will we run out and pin him?'

'Pin a hare indeed! Much chance you'd have; sit where you are.'

That hare made his escape into the garden, but Jack that was in the beggar's clothes soon let another out of the bag.

'Oh, master, there he is still pegging round. He can't make his escape. Let us have a chase. The hall door is locked on the inside, and Mr Jack can't get in.'

'Stay quiet, I tell you.'

In a few minutes he shouted out again that the hare was there still, but it was the third that Jack was just after giving its liberty. Well, by the laws, they couldn't be kept in any longer. Out pegged every mother's son of them, and the squire after them.

'Will I turn the spit, your honour, while they're catching the *hareyeen*?' says the beggar.

'Do, and don't let anyone in for your life.'

'Faith, an' I won't, you may depend on it.'

The third hare got away after the others, and when they all came back from the hunt, there was neither beggar nor goose in the kitchen.

'Purshuin' to you, Jack,' says the landlord, 'you've come over me this time.'

Well, while they were thinking of making out another dinner, a messenger came from Jack's father to beg that the squire, and the mistress, and the young lady would step across the fields, and take share of what God sent. There was no dirty mean pride about the family, and they walked over, and got a dinner with roast turkey, and roast beef, and their own roast goose; and the squire had like to burst his waistcoat with laughing at the trick, and Jack's good clothes and good manners did not take away any liking the young lady had for him already.

While they were taking their punch at the old oak table in the nice clean little parlour with the sanded floor, says the squire, 'You can't be sure of my daughter, Jack, unless you steal away my six horses from under the six men that will be watching them tomorrow night in the stable.'

'I'll do more than that,' says Jack, 'for a pleasant look from the young lady;' and the young lady's cheeks turned as red as fire.

Monday night the six horses were in their stalls, and a man on every horse, and a good glass of whiskey under every man's waistcoat, and the door was left wide open for Jack. They were merry enough for a long time, and joked and sang, and were pitying the poor fellow. But the small hours crept on, and the whiskey lost its power, and they began to shiver and wish it was morning. A miserable old colliach, with half a dozen bags round her, and a beard half an inch long on her chin came to the door.

'Ah, then, tendher-hearted Christians,' says she, 'would you let me in, and allow me a wisp of straw in the corner; the life will be froze out of me, if you don't give me shelter.'

Well, they didn't see any harm in that, and she made herself as snug as she could, and they soon saw her pull out a big black bottle, and take a sup. She coughed and smacked her lips, and seemed a little more comfortable, and the men couldn't take their eyes off her.

'Indeed,' says she, 'I'd offer you a drop of this, only you might think it too free-making.'

'Oh, hang all impedent pride,' says one, 'we'll take it, and thankee.'

So she gave them the bottle, and they passed it round, and the last man had the manners to leave half a glass in the bottom for the old woman. They all thanked her, and said it was the best drop ever passed their tongue.

'In throth,' said she, 'it's myself that's glad to show how I value your kindness in giving me shelter; I'm not without another *buideal*, and you may pass it round while myself finishes what the dasent man left me.'

Well, what they drank out of the other bottle only gave them a relish for more, and by the time the last man got to the bottom, the first man was dead asleep in the saddle, for the second bottle had a sleepy posset mixed with the whiskey. The beggar woman lifted each man down, and laid him in the manger, or under the manger, snug and sausty, drew a stocking over every horse's hoof, and led them away without any noise to one of Jack's father's outhouses. The first thing the squire saw next morning was Jack riding up the avenue, and five horses stepping after the one he rode.

'Confound you, Jack!' says he. 'And confound the numskulls that let you outwit them!'

He went out to the stable, and didn't the poor fellows look very sorry for themselves, when they could be woke up in earnest!

'After all,' says the squire, when they were sitting at breakfast, 'it was no great thing to outwit such ninnyhammers. I'll be riding out on the common from one to three today, and if you can outwit me of the beast I'll be riding, I'll say you deserve to be my son-in-law.'

'I'd do more than that,' says Jack, 'for the honour, if there was no love at all in the matter,' and the young lady held up her saucer before her face.

Well, the squire kept riding about and riding about till he was tired, and no sign of Jack. He was thinking of going home at last, when what should he see but one of his servants running from the house as if he was mad.

'Oh masther, masther,' says he, as far as he could be heard, 'fly home if you wish to see the poor mistress alive! I'm running for the surgeon. She fell down two flights of stairs, and her neck, or her hips, or both her arms are broke, and she's speechless, and it's a mercy if you find the breath in her. Fly as fast as the baste will carry you.'

'But hadn't you better take the horse? It's a mile and a half to the surgeon's.'

'Oh, anything you like, master. Oh, alas, puir misthress, that I should ever see the day! And your purty body disfigured as it is!'

'Here, stop your noise, and be off like wildfire. Oh, my darling, my darling, isn't this a trial?'

He tore home like a fury, and wondered to see no stir outside, and when he flew into the hall, and from that to the parlour, his wife and daughter that were sewing at the table screeched out at the rush he made, and the wild look that was on his face.

'Oh, my darling!' said he, when he could speak. 'How's this? Are you hurt? Didn't you fall down the stairs? What happened at all? Tell me!'

'Why, nothing at all happened, thank God, since you rode out; where did you leave the horse?'

Well, no one could describe the state he was in for about a quarter of an hour, between joy for his wife and anger with Jack, and *sharoose* for being tricked. He saw the beast coming up the avenue, and a little gossoon in the saddle with his feet in the stirrup leathers. The servant didn't make his appearance for a week; but what did he care with Jack's ten golden guineas in his pocket.

Jack didn't show his nose till next morning, and it was a queer reception he met.

'That was all foul play you gave,' says the squire. 'I'll never forgive you for the shock you gave me. But then I am so happy ever since, that I think I'll give you only one trial more. If you will take away the sheet from under my wife and myself tonight, the marriage may take place tomorrow.'

'We'll try,' says Jack, 'but if you keep my bride from me any longer, I'll steal her away if she was minded by fiery dragons.'

When the squire and his wife were in bed, and the moon shining in through the window, he saw a head rising over the sill to have a peep, and then bobbing down again.

'That's Jack,' says the squire; 'I'll astonish him a bit,' says the squire, pointing a gun at the lower pane.

'Oh Lord, my dear!' says the wife. 'Sure, you wouldn't shoot the brave fellow?'

'Indeed, an' I wouldn't for a kingdom; there's nothing but powder in it.'

Up went the head, bang went the gun, down dropped the body, and a great thud was heard on the gravel walk.

'Oh, Lord,' says the lady, 'poor Jack is killed or disabled for life.'

'I hope not,' says the squire, and down the stairs he ran. He never minded to shut the door, but opened the gate and ran into the garden. His wife heard his voice at the room door, before he could be under the window and back, as she thought.

'Wife, wife,' says he from the door, 'the sheet, the sheet! He is not killed, I hope, but he is bleeding like a pig. I must wipe it away as well as I can, and get someone to carry him in with me.' She pulled it off the bed, and threw it to him. Down he ran like lightning, and he had hardly time to be in the garden, when he was back, and this time he came back in his shirt, as he went out.

'High hanging to you, Jack,' says he, 'for an arrant rogue!'

'Arrant rogue?' says she. 'Isn't the poor fellow all cut and bruised?'

'I didn't much care if he was. What do you think was bobbing up and down at the window, and sossed down so heavy on the walk? A man's clothes stuffed with straw, and a couple of stones.'

'And what did you want with the sheet just now to wipe his blood, if he was only a man of straw?'

'Sheet, woman! I wanted no sheet.'

'Well, whether you wanted it or not, I threw it to you, and you standing outside o' the door.'

'Oh, Jack, Jack, you terrible tinker!' says the squire. 'There's no use in striving with you. We must do without the sheet for one night. We'll have the marriage tomorrow to get ourselves out of trouble.'

So married they were, and Jack turned out a real good husband. And the squire and his lady were never tired of praising their son-in-law, 'Jack the Cunning Thief'.

Jack the Giant Killer

When good King Arthur reigned with Guinevere his queen, there lived, near the Land's End in Cornwall, a farmer who had one only son called Jack. Now Jack was brisk and ready; of such a lively wit that none nor nothing could worst him.

In those days, the Mount of St Michael in Cornwall was the fastness of a hugeous giant whose name was Cormoran.

He was full eighteen feet in height, some three yards about his middle, of a grim fierce face, and he was the terror of all the countryside. He lived in a cave amidst the rocky Mount, and when he desired victuals he would wade across the tides to the mainland and furnish himself forth with all that came in his way. The poor folk and the rich folk alike ran out of their houses and hid themselves when they heard the swish-swash of his big feet in the water; for if he saw them, he would think nothing of broiling half a dozen or so of them for breakfast. As it was, he seized their cattle by the score, carrying off half a dozen fat oxen on his back at a time, and hanging sheep and pigs to his waistbelt like bunches of dip-candles. Now this had gone on for long years, and the poor folk of Cornwall were in despair, for none could put an end to the giant Cormoran.

It so happened that one market day Jack, then quite a young lad, found the town upside down over some new exploit of the giant's. Women were weeping, men were cursing, and the magistrates were sitting in council over what was to be done. But none could suggest a plan. Then Jack, blithe and gay, went up to the magistrates, and with a fine courtesy – for he was ever polite – asked them what reward would be given to him who killed the giant Cormoran?

'The treasures of the giant's cave,' quoth they.

'Every whit of it?' quoth Jack, who was never to be done.

'To the last farthing,' quoth they.

'Then will I undertake the task,' said Jack, and forthwith set about the business.

It was wintertime, and having got himself a horn, a pickaxe and a shovel, he went over to the Mount in the dark evening, set to work, and before dawn he had dug a pit no less than twenty-two feet deep and nigh as big across. This he covered with long thin sticks and straw, sprinkling a little loose mould over all to make it look like solid ground. So, just as dawn was breaking, he planted himself fair and square on the side of the pit that was farthest from the giant's cave, raised the horn to his lips, and with full blast sounded: 'Tantivy! Tantivy! Tantivy!' just as he would have done had he been hunting a fox.

Of course this woke the giant, who rushed in a rage out of his cave, and seeing little Jack, fair and square blowing away at his horn, as calm and cool as may be, he became still more angry, and made for the disturber of his rest, bawling out, 'I'll teach you to wake a giant, you little whippersnapper. You shall pay dearly for your tantivys. I'll take you and broil you whole for break –'

He had only got as far as this when crash – he fell into the pit! So there was a break indeed; such a one that it caused the very foundations of the Mount to shake.

But Jack shook with laughter. 'Ho, ho!' he cried, 'how about breakfast now, sir giant? Will you have me broiled or baked? And will no diet serve you but poor little Jack? Faith! I've got you in Lob's pound now! You're in the stocks for bad behaviour, and I'll plague you as I like. Would I had rotten eggs; but this will do as well.' And with that he up with his pickaxe and dealt the giant Cormoran such a most weighty knock on the very crown of his head, that he killed him on the spot.

Whereupon Jack calmly filled the pit with earth

again and went to search the cave, where he found much treasure.

Now when the magistrates heard of Jack's great exploit, they proclaimed that henceforth he should be known as Jack the Giant Killer. And they presented him with a sword and belt, on which these words were embroidered in gold:

> Here's the valiant Cornishman,
> Who slew the giant Cormoran.

*   *   *

Of course the news of Jack's victory soon spread over all England, so that another giant named Blunderbore, who lived to the north, hearing of it, vowed if ever he came across Jack he would be revenged upon him. Now this giant Blunderbore was lord of an enchanted castle that stood in the middle of a lonesome forest.

It so happened that Jack, about four months after he had killed Cormoran, had occasion to journey into Wales, and on the road he passed this forest. Weary with walking, and finding a pleasant fountain by the wayside, he lay down to rest and was soon fast asleep.

Now the giant Blunderbore, coming to the well for water, found Jack sleeping, and knew by the lines embroidered on his belt that here was the far-famed giant killer. Rejoiced at his luck, the giant, without more ado, lifted Jack to his shoulder and began to carry him through the wood to the enchanted castle.

But the rustling of the boughs awakened Jack, who, finding himself already in the clutches of the giant, was terrified; nor was his alarm decreased by seeing the courtyard of the castle all strewn with men's bones.

'Yours will be with them ere long,' said Blunderbore as he locked poor Jack into an immense chamber above the castle gateway. It had a high-pitched, beamed roof, and one window that looked down the road. Here poor Jack was to stay while Blunderbore went to fetch his brother-giant, who lived in the same wood, so that he might share in the feast.

Now, after a time, Jack, watching through the window, saw the two giants tramping hastily down the road, eager for their dinner.

'Now,' quoth Jack to himself, 'my death or my deliverance is at hand.' For he had thought out a plan. In one corner of the room he had seen two strong cords. These he took, and making a

cunning noose at the end of each, he hung them out of the window, and as the giants were unlocking the iron door of the gate managed to slip them over their heads without their noticing it. Then, quick as thought, he tied the other ends to a beam, so that as the giants moved on the nooses tightened and throttled them until they grew black in the face. Seeing this, Jack slid down the ropes, and drawing his sword, slew them both.

So, taking the keys of the castle, he unlocked all the doors and set free three beauteous ladies who, tied by the hair of their heads, he found almost starved to death.

'Sweet ladies,' quoth Jack kneeling on one knee – for he was ever polite – 'here are the keys of this enchanted castle. I have destroyed the giant Blunderbore and his brutish brother, and thus have restored to you your liberty. These keys should bring you all else you require.'

So saying he proceeded on his journey to Wales.

*   *   *

He travelled as fast as he could; perhaps too fast, for, losing his way he found himself benighted and far from any habitation. He wandered on always in hopes, until on entering a narrow valley he came on a very large, dreary-looking house standing alone. Being anxious for shelter he went up to the door and knocked. You may imagine his surprise and alarm when the summons was answered by a giant with two heads. But though this monster's look was exceedingly fierce, his manners were quite polite. The truth was that he was a Welsh giant, and as such double-faced and smooth, given to gaining his malicious ends by show of false friendship.

So he welcomed Jack heartily in a strong Welsh accent, and prepared a bedroom for him, where he was left with kind wishes for a good rest. Jack, however, was too tired to sleep well, and as he lay awake, he overheard his host muttering to himself in the next room. Having very keen ears he was able to make out these words or something like them:

> 'Though here you lodge with me this night,
> You shall not see the morning light.
> My club shall dash your brains outright.'

'Say'st thou so!' quoth Jack to himself, starting up at once. 'So that is your Welsh trick, is it? But I will be even with you.' Then, leaving his bed, he laid a big billet of wood among the blankets and, taking one of these to keep himself warm, made himself snug in a corner of the room, pretending to snore, so as to make Mr Giant think he was asleep.

And sure enough, after a little time in came the monster on tiptoe as if treading on eggs, and carrying a big club. Then – Whack! Whack! Whack!

Jack could hear the bed being belaboured until the giant, thinking every bone of his guest's body must be broken, stole out of the room again; whereupon Jack went calmly to bed once more and slept soundly! Next morning the giant couldn't believe his eyes when he saw Jack coming down the stairs fresh and hearty.

'Odds splutter hur nails!' he cried astonished. 'Did ye sleep well? Was there not nothing felt in the night?'

'Oh,' replied Jack, laughing in his sleeve, 'I think a rat did come and give me a few flaps of his tail.'

On this the giant was dumbfoundered, and led Jack to breakfast, bringing him a bowl which held at least four gallons of hasty-pudding, and bidding him, as a man of such mettle, eat the lot. Now Jack when travelling wore under his cloak a leathern bag to carry his things withal; so, quick as thought, he hitched this round in front with the opening just under his chin; thus, as he ate, he could slip the best part of the pudding into it without the giant's being any the wiser. So they sat down to breakfast, the giant gobbling down his own measure of hasty-pudding, while Jack made away with his.

'See,' says crafty Jack when he had finished. 'I'll show you a trick worth two of yours,' and with that he up with a carving-knife and ripping up the leathern bag out fell all the hasty-pudding on the floor!

'Odds splutter hur nails!' cried the giant, not to be outdone. 'Hur can do that hurself!' Whereupon he seized the carving-knife, and ripping open his own belly fell down dead.

Thus was Jack quit of the Welsh giant.

*　　*　　*

Whereupon he seized the carving-knife, and ripping open his own belly fell down dead

Now it so happened that in those days when gallant knights were always seeking adventures, King Arthur's only son, a very valiant prince, begged of his father a large sum of money to enable him to journey to Wales, and there strive to set free a certain beautiful lady who was possessed by seven evil spirits. In vain the king denied him; so at last he gave way and the prince set out with two horses, one of which he rode, the other he had laden with gold pieces. Now after some days' journey the prince came to a market-town in Wales where there was a great commotion. On asking the reason for it he was told that, according to law, the corpse of a very generous man had been arrested on its way to the grave, because, in life, it had owed large sums to the moneylenders.

'That is a cruel law,' said the young prince. 'Go, bury the dead in peace, and let the creditors come to my lodgings; I will pay the debts of the dead.'

So the creditors came, but they were so numerous that by evening the prince had but twopence left for himself, and could not go farther on his journey.

Now it so happened that Jack the Giant Killer on his way to Wales passed through the town, and, hearing of the prince's plight, was so taken with his kindness and generosity that he determined to be the prince's servant. So this was agreed upon, and next morning, after Jack had paid the reckoning with his last farthing, the two set out together. But as they were leaving the town, an old woman ran after the prince and called out, 'Justice! Justice! The dead man owed me twopence these seven years. Pay me as well as the others.'

And the prince, kind and generous, put his hand to his pocket and gave the old woman the two-pence that was left to him. So now they had not a penny between them, and when the sun grew low the prince said: 'Jack! Since we have no money, how are we to get a night's lodging?'

Then Jack replied, 'We shall do well enough, master; for within two or three miles of this place there lives a huge and monstrous giant with three heads who can fight four hundred men in armour and make them fly from him like chaff before the wind.'

'And what good will that be to us?' quoth the prince. 'He will for sure chop us up in a mouthful.'

'Nay,' said Jack, laughing. 'Let me go and prepare the way for you. By all accounts this giant is a dolt. Mayhap I may manage better than that.'

So the prince remained where he was, and Jack pricked his steed at full speed till he came to the giant's castle, at the gate of which he knocked so loud that he made the neighbouring hills resound.

On this the giant roared from within in a voice like thunder: 'Who's there?'

Then said Jack as bold as brass, 'None but your poor cousin Jack.'

'Cousin Jack!' quoth the giant astounded. 'And what news with my poor cousin Jack?' For, see you, he was quite taken aback; so Jack made haste to reassure him.

'Dear coz, heavy news, God wot!'

'Heavy news,' echoed the giant, half afraid. 'God wot no heavy news can come to me. Have I not three heads? Can I not fight five hundred men in armour? Can I not make them fly like chaff before the wind?'

'True,' replied crafty Jack, 'but I came to warn you because the great King Arthur's son with a thousand men in armour is on his way to kill you.'

At this the giant began to shiver and to shake. 'Ah! Cousin Jack! Kind cousin Jack! This is heavy news indeed,' quoth he. 'Tell me, what am I to do?'

'Hide yourself in the vault,' says crafty Jack, 'and I will lock and bolt and bar you in, and keep the key till the prince has gone. So you will be safe.'

Then the giant made haste and ran down into the vault and Jack locked and bolted and barred him in. Then, having him thus secure, he went and fetched his master, and the two made themselves heartily merry over what the giant was to have had for supper, while the miserable monster shivered and shook with fright in the underground vault.

Well, after a good night's rest Jack woke his master in early morn, and having furnished him well with gold and silver from the giant's treasure, bade him

Then the giant made haste and ran down into the vault and Jack locked and bolted and barred him in

ride three miles forward on his journey. So when Jack judged that the prince was pretty well out of the smell of the giant, he took the key and let his prisoner out. He was half dead with cold and damp, but very grateful; and he begged Jack to let him know what he would be given as a reward for saving the giant's life and castle from destruction, and he should have it.

'You're very welcome,' said Jack, who always had his eyes about him. 'All I want is the old coat and cap, together with the rusty old sword and slippers which are at your bed-head.'

When the giant heard this he sighed, and shook his head. 'You don't know what you are asking,' quoth he. 'They are the most precious things I possess, but as I have promised, you must have them. The coat will make you invisible, the cap will tell you all you want to know, the sword will cut asunder whatever you strike, and the slippers will take you wherever you want to go in the twinkling of an eye!'

So Jack, overjoyed, rode away with the coat and cap, the sword and the slippers, and soon overtook his master; and they rode on together until they reached the castle where the beautiful lady lived whom the prince sought.

Now she was very beautiful, for all she was possessed of seven devils, and when she heard the prince sought her as a suitor, she smiled and ordered a splendid banquet to be prepared for his reception. And she sat on his right hand, and plied him with food and drink.

And when the repast was over she took out her own handkerchief and wiped his lips gently, and said with a smile: 'I have a task for you, my lord! You must show me that kerchief tomorrow morning or lose your head.'

And with that she put the handkerchief in her bosom and said, 'Good-night!'

The prince was in despair, but Jack said nothing till his master was in bed. Then he put on the old cap he had got from the giant, and lo! in a minute he knew all that he wanted to know. So, in the dead of the night, when the beautiful lady called on one of her familiar spirits to carry her to Lucifer himself, Jack was beforehand with her, and putting on his coat of darkness and his slippers of swiftness, was there as soon as she was. And when she gave the handkerchief to the Devil, bidding him keep it safe, and he put it away on a high shelf, Jack just up and nipped it away in a trice!

So the next morning when the beauteous

enchanted lady looked to see the prince crestfallen, he just made a fine bow and presented her with the handkerchief.

At first she was terribly disappointed, but as the day drew on, she ordered another and still more splendid repast to be got ready. And this time when the repast was over, she kissed the prince full on the lips and said: 'I have a task for you, my lover. Show me tomorrow morning the last lips I kiss tonight or you lose your head.'

Then the prince, who by this time was head over ears in love, said tenderly, 'If you will kiss none but mine, I will.'

Now the beauteous lady for all she was possessed by seven devils could not but see that the prince was a very handsome young man; so she blushed a little, and said: 'That is neither here nor there: you must show me them, or death is your portion.'

So the prince went to his bed, sorrowful as before; but Jack put on the cap of knowledge and knew in a moment all he wanted to know.

Thus when, in the dead of the night, the beauteous lady called on her familiar spirit to take her to Lucifer himself, Jack in his coat of darkness and his shoes of swiftness was there before her.

'Thou hast betrayed me once,' said the beauteous lady to Lucifer, frowning, 'by letting go my handkerchief. Now will I give thee something none can steal, and so best the prince, king's son though he be.'

With that she kissed the loathly demon full on the lips, and left him. Whereupon Jack, with one blow of the rusty sword of strength, cut off Lucifer's head and, hiding it under his coat of darkness, brought it back to his master.

Thus next morning when the beauteous lady, with malice in her beautiful eyes, asked the prince to show her the lips she had last kissed, he pulled out the demon's head by the horns. On that the seven devils, which possessed the poor lady, gave seven dreadful shrieks and left her. Thus the enchantment being broken, she appeared in all her perfect beauty and goodness.

So she and the prince were married the very next morning. After which they journeyed back to the court of King Arthur, where Jack the Giant Killer, for his many exploits, was made one of the Knights of the Round Table.

*   *   *

This, however, did not satisfy our hero, who was soon on the road again searching for giants. Now he had not gone far when he came upon one, seated on a huge block of timber near the entrance to a dark cave. He was a most terrific giant. His goggle eyes were as coals of fire, his countenance was grim and gruesome; his cheeks, like huge flitches of bacon, were covered with a stubbly beard, the bristles of which resembled rods of iron wire, while the locks of hair that fell on his brawny shoulders showed like curled snakes or hissing adders. He held a knotted iron club, and breathed so heavily you could hear him a mile away. Nothing daunted by this fearsome sight, Jack alighted from his horse and putting on his coat of darkness went close up to the giant and said softly: 'Hallo! is that you? It will not be long before I have you fast by your beard.'

A giant seated on a huge block of timber near the entrance to a dark cave

So saying he made a cut with the sword of strength at the giant's head, but, somehow, missing his aim, cut off the nose instead, clean as a whistle! My goodness! How the giant roared! It was like claps of thunder, and he began to lay about him with the knotted iron club, like one possessed. But Jack in his coat of darkness easily dodged the blows, and running in behind, drove the sword up to the hilt into the giant's back, so that he fell stone dead.

Jack then cut off the head and sent it to King Arthur by a wagoner whom he hired for the purpose. After which he began to search the giant's cave to find his treasure. He passed through many windings and turnings until he came to a huge hall paved and roofed with freestone. At the upper end of this was an immense fireplace where hung an iron cauldron, the like of which, for size, Jack had never seen before. It was boiling and gave out a savoury steam; while beside it, on the right hand, stood a big massive table set out with huge platters and mugs. Here it was that the giants used to dine. Going a little farther he came upon a sort of window barred with iron, and looking within beheld a vast number of miserable captives.

'Alas! Alack!' they cried on seeing him. 'Art come, young man, to join us in this dreadful prison?'

'That depends,' quoth Jack; 'but first tell me wherefore you are thus held imprisoned?'

'Through no fault,' they cried at once. 'We are captives of the cruel giants and are kept here and well nourished until such time as the monsters desire a feast. Then they choose the fattest and sup off them.'

On hearing this Jack straightway unlocked the door of the prison and set the poor fellows free. Then, searching the giants' coffers, he divided the gold and silver equally amongst the captives as some redress for their sufferings, and taking them to a neighbouring castle gave them a right good feast.

*   *   *

Now as they were all making merry over their deliverance, and praising Jack's prowess, a messenger arrived to say that one Thunderdell, a huge giant with two heads, having heard of the death of his kinsman was on his way from the northern dales to be revenged, and was already within a mile or two of the castle, the country folk with their flocks and herds flying before him like chaff before the wind.

Now the castle with its gardens stood on a small island that was surrounded by a moat twenty feet wide and thirty feet deep, having very steep sides. And this moat was spanned by a drawbridge. This, without a moment's delay, Jack ordered should be sawn on both sides at the middle, so as to leave only one plank uncut over which he in his invisible coat of darkness passed swiftly to meet his enemy, bearing in his hand the wonderful sword of strength.

Now though the giant could not, of course, see Jack, he could smell him, for giants have keen noses. Therefore Thunderdell cried out in a voice like his name:

> 'Fee, fi, fo, fum!
> I smell the blood of an Englishman.
> Be he alive, or be he dead,
> I'll grind his bones to make my bread!'

'Is that so?' quoth Jack, cheerful as ever. 'Then art thou a monstrous miller for sure!'

On this the giant peering round everywhere for a glimpse of his foe, shouted out: 'Art thou, indeed, the villain who hath killed so many of my kinsmen? Then, indeed, will I tear thee to pieces with my teeth, suck thy blood, and grind thy bones to powder.'

'Thou'lt have to catch me first,' quoth Jack, laughing, and throwing off his coat of darkness and putting on his slippers of swiftness he began nimbly

to
lead the
giant a pretty
dance, he leaping and
doubling light as a feather, the
monster following heavily like a walking
tower, so that the very foundations of the earth
seemed to shake at every step. At this game the onlookers nearly split their sides with laughter, until Jack, judging there had been enough of it, made for the drawbridge, ran neatly over the single plank, and reaching the other side waited in teasing fashion for his adversary.

On came the giant at full speed, foaming at the mouth with rage, and flourishing his club. But when he came to the middle of the bridge his great weight, of course, broke the plank, and there he was fallen headlong into the moat, rolling and wallowing like a whale, plunging from place to place yet unable to get out and be revenged.

The spectators greeted his efforts with roars of laughter, and Jack himself was at first too overcome with merriment to do more than scoff. At last,

however, he went for a rope, cast it over the giant's two heads, and so with the help of a team of horses drew them shorewards, where two blows from the sword of strength settled the matter.

*   *   *

After some time spent in mirth and pastimes, Jack began once more to grow restless, and taking leave of his companions set out for fresh adventures.

He travelled far and fast, through woods, and vales, and hills, till at last he came, late at night, on a lonesome house set at the foot of a high mountain.

He knocked at the door, and it was opened by an old man whose head was white as snow.

'Father,' said Jack, ever courteous, 'can you lodge a benighted traveller?'

'Ay, that will I, and welcome to my poor cottage,' replied the old man.

Whereupon Jack came in, and after supper they sat together chatting in friendly fashion. Then it was that the old man, seeing by Jack's belt that he was the famous Giant Killer, spoke in this wise: 'My son! You are the great conqueror of evil monsters. Now close by there lives one well worthy of your prowess. On the top of yonder high hill is an enchanted castle kept by a giant named Galligantua, who, by the help of a wicked old magician, inveigles many beautiful ladies and valiant knights into the castle, where they are transformed into all sorts of birds and beasts, yea, even into fishes and insects. There they live pitiably in confinement; but most of all do I grieve for a duke's daughter whom they kidnapped in her father's garden, bringing her hither in a burning chariot drawn by fiery dragons. Her form is that of a white hind; and though many valiant knights have tried their utmost to break the spell and work her deliverance, none have succeeded; for, see you, at the entrance to the castle are two dreadful griffins who destroy everyone who attempts to pass them by.'

Now Jack bethought him of the coat of darkness which had served him so well before, and he put on the cap of knowledge, and in an instant he knew what had to be done. Then the very next morning, at dawn-time, Jack arose and put on his invisible coat and his slippers of swiftness. And in the twinkling of an eye there he was on the top of the mountain! And there were the two griffins guarding the castle gates – horrible creatures with forked tails and tongues.

But they could not see him because of the coat of darkness, so he passed them by unharmed.

And hung to the doors of the gateway he found a golden trumpet on a silver chain, and beneath it was engraved in red lettering:

Whoever shall this trumpet blow
Will cause the giant's overthrow.
The black enchantment he will break,
And gladness out of sadness make.

No sooner had Jack read these words than he put the horn to his lips and blew a loud 'Tantivy! Tantivy! Tantivy!'

Now at the very first note the castle trembled to its vast foundations, and before he had finished the measure, both the giant and the magician were biting their thumbs and tearing their hair, knowing that their wickedness must now come to an end. But the giant showed fight and took up his club to defend himself; whereupon Jack, with one clean cut of the sword of strength, severed his head from his body, and would doubtless have done the same to the magician, but that the latter was a coward, and, calling up a whirlwind, was swept away by it into the air, nor has he ever been seen or heard of since. The enchantments being thus broken, all the valiant knights and beautiful ladies who had been transformed into birds and beasts and fishes and reptiles and insects returned to their proper shapes, including the duke's daughter, who, from being a white hind, showed as the most beauteous maiden upon whom the sun ever shone. Now, no sooner had this occurred than the whole castle vanished away in a cloud of smoke, and from that moment giants vanished also from the land.

So Jack, when he had presented the head of Galligantua to King Arthur, together with all the lords and ladies he had delivered from enchantment, found he had nothing more to do. So as a reward for past services King Arthur bestowed the hand of the duke's daughter upon honest Jack the Giant Killer. So married they were, and the whole kingdom was filled with joy at their wedding. Furthermore, the king bestowed on Jack a noble castle with a magnificent estate belonging thereto, whereon he, his lady and their children lived in great joy and content for the rest of their days.

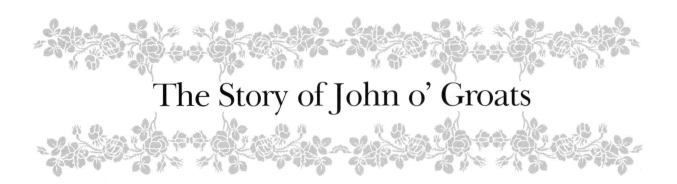

The Story of John o' Groats

He was an old seaman, with weather-beaten face and black eyes, that had looked upon many lands and many sights.

'Well, indeed, I'll tell you about Johnny Groats as it was told to me one night in the trades,' he said, blowing a whiff of smoke from his wheezy pipe.

'Well, in olden times there was a rich lord, who owned all the property looking on to the Pentlands – an awful place in bad weather; indeed, in any weather.

'He was a lone man, for his wife was dead and his son had turned out to be a rake and a spendthrift, spending all his substance upon harlots and entertainments.

'Now this lord had a factor, by name John o' Scales, a stingy, cunning man, who robbed his master all he could during the week, and prayed hard for forgiveness on the Sabbath.

'The lord, who was getting very old, was much grieved on account of his son's behaviour. "He'll spend everything when I am gone, and the estates will go into other hands," the old man said to himself.'

*   *   *

'One fine morning in summer the factor received orders to build a hut by the sea, and plant bushes and trees round about it. "But don't make the door to fit close; leave the space of a foot at the bottom, so the leaves can blow in, for I want the hut to shoot sea-fowl as they flight, and it is cold standing on the bare ground," said the old man.

'The factor carried out his master's instructions, but not without suspicion of ulterior motives on his master's part. However, when he saw my lord shooting the birds and stuffing many of them his suspicions were allayed, and the factor thought that, after all, though his master wanted the hut for flight-shooting, still he must be getting softening of the brain, for it was very eccentric that he should take up this new hobby in his old age.

'So the old lord was never disturbed in his hut by curious and ill-timed visits.

'After a time the lord died, and was laid with his fathers, the prodigal inheriting the property.

'The old castle was then the scene of perpetual feastings and card parties, so that in a few years the property was heavily mortgaged, the old factor advancing the money.

'Things went apace, until one day the factor informed the young spendthrift that he had spent everything, and the estates were no longer his, so he gave him a few pounds, and turned him out.

'When the news spread round the countryside his old friends began to drop off, until at last the spendthrift found every door closed against him.

'When he had spent his last penny, the prodigal thought of the key which his father had given him, saying, "When you have spent everything, take this key, and go to the hut."

'But he had lost the key long before. Nevertheless, he went to the hut. It had a deserted appearance, being overgrown with moss and lichens.

'He managed to squeeze himself under the door, and when he stood up he saw a rope, with a noose, hanging from the centre of the roof. Pursuing his investigations, he found a parchment nailed to the back of the door, and in one corner stood an old three-legged stool. There was nothing else in the damp, mouldy room, so he began to read the parchment.

' "Thou art come to beggary; end thy miserable existence, for it is thy father's wish," he read.

'He was dazed, and looked from the parchment to the rope, and from the rope to the parchment, saying to himself: "Well, I have come to that, I must follow my father's wish."

'So he got the stool and put it under the noose, and standing upon it, adjusted the rope with trembling fingers round his neck; then he said, hoarsely: "Father, I do thy bidding," and he kicked the stool from under him.

'Immediately he heard a crash, and found himself lying upon the leaves, with a feeling that his neck had been jerked off. However, he soon recovered, and, taking the noose from his neck, he looked up and saw an open trap-door in the ceiling. Placing the stool beneath the opening, he got on to it, lifted himself through the trap-door and found himself in a loft; a parchment was nailed to the wall facing him, and on the parchment was written, "This has been prepared, for your end was foreseen, and your foolish father buried three chests of gold one foot below the surface of the floor of the hut. Go and take it and buy back your estate: marry, and beget an heir."

' "Good God! is this a ghastly joke?" said the prodigal. But the words looked truthful; so he tore down the parchment, dropped through the trap-door, shut it, and readjusted the rope. He left the hut and borrowed a pick and shovel, and returning to the hut, he began to dig, and found one chest full of gold. When he made this discovery he closed the chest, filled in the hole, and spread leaves over the spot. He then ran off to his father's best friend, and told him of his good luck. They then called in two other friends, and consulted together how the old lord's wish was best to be carried out. "I'll tell you," said his father's oldest friend. "Mr John o' Scales gives a great dinner party once a month, and three of us here are invited as usual. You must come in in the middle of dinner in your ordinary beggar clothes and beg humbly for some food, when he will give orders to have you turned out. Then you must begin to call him a liar and a thief, and accuse him of robbing your father and yourself of your inheritance. You'll see he'll get angry, and offer to let you have it back."

'So the prodigal dug up the chests, and carted the money away in canvas bags, storing it at his friend's house.'

*   *   *

'When the night of the dinner party came, the prodigal drove up to the castle in a cart filled with canvas bags. Jumping off his seat by the driver, he went into the feast in his beggar's clothes, and going up to the host, he begged humbly for some food.

' "Go from this house! What business have you here?" asked the host.

'Most of the gentlemen and ladies began to frown upon him, and murmur against him, as he walked to the lady of the house and begged her to give him some food; but she replied: ' "Oh, thou spendthrift! thou fool of fools! if all fools were hanged, as they ought to be, you'd be the first."

'Then the beggar's countenance changed, a deep flush of anger overspread his features, and drawing himself up to his full height, he said, with solemn voice, addressing the host: ' "Thou hast robbed my father all the days of his life, and thou hast robbed the orphan. May the curse of God be upon you!"

'The host grew furious; then he looked ashamed, and shouted angrily: ' "Bring me £40,000, and you shall have your estate back. I never robbed you, but you lost your inheritance by your own follies."

' "Gentlemen," said the beggar, "I take you all to witness that this thief says I can have my estate back for £40,000."

'The people murmured, and the three friends said: "We are witnesses."

'The beggar ran out into the night, and returned with a man laden with sacks, and they began to count out £40,000 upon a side-table, where a haunch of venison still smoked.

'When they had counted out the money, the beggar said: ' "There is your £40,000; sign this receipt."

'The amazed factor drew back, but the three friends said: ' "You must sign; you are a gentleman of your word, of course."

'Mechanically John o' Scales signed the paper.

' "And now," said the former beggar, "leave my house at once, with your wife – you coward! you cur! You robbed my father, and then cheated me when I was a spendthrift. Begone, and may your name be accursed in the land!"

'And the son turned all out except his three friends.

'In a few months he married the daughter of one of his friends; but he never gambled again, only entertaining his three friends and their families, who came and went as they liked.

'And from that day John o' Scales was called John o' Groats.'

Johnny-Cake

Once upon a time there was an old man, and an old woman, and a little boy. One morning the old woman made a Johnny-Cake, and put it in the oven to bake. 'You watch the Johnny-Cake while your father and I go out to work in the garden.' So the old man and the old woman went out and began to hoe potatoes, and left the little boy to tend the oven. But he didn't watch it all the time, and all of a sudden he heard a noise, and he looked up and the oven door popped open, and out of the oven jumped Johnny-Cake, and went rolling along end over end, towards the open door of the house. The little boy ran to shut the door, but Johnny-Cake was too quick for him and rolled through the door, down the steps, and out into the road long before the little boy could catch him. The little boy ran after him as fast as he could clip it, crying out to his father and mother, who heard the uproar, and threw down their hoes and gave chase too. But Johnny-Cake outran all three a long way, and was soon out of sight, while they had to sit down, all out of breath, on a bank to rest.

On went Johnny-Cake, and by and by he came to two well-diggers who looked up from their work and called out: 'Where ye going, Johnny-Cake?'

He said: 'I've outrun an old man, and an old woman, and a little boy, and I can outrun you too—o—o!'

'Ye can, can ye? we'll see about that?' said they; and they threw down their picks and ran after him, but couldn't catch up with him, and soon they had to sit down by the roadside to rest.

On ran Johnny-Cake, and by and by he came to two ditch-diggers who were digging a ditch. 'Where

ye going, Johnny-Cake?' said they. He said: 'I've outrun an old man, and an old woman, and a little boy, and two well-diggers, and I can outrun you too–o–o!'

'Ye can, can ye? we'll see about that!' said they; and they threw down their spades, and ran after him too. But Johnny-Cake soon outstripped them also, and seeing they could never catch him, they gave up the chase and sat down to rest.

On went Johnny-Cake, and by and by he came to a bear. The bear said: 'Where are ye going, Johnny-Cake?'

He said: 'I've outrun an old man, and an old woman, and a little boy, and two well-diggers, and two ditch-diggers, and I can outrun you too–o–o!'

'Ye can, can ye?' growled the bear, 'we'll see about that!' and he trotted as fast as his legs could carry him after Johnny-Cake, who never stopped to look behind him. Before long the bear was left so far behind that he saw he might as well give up the hunt first as last, so he stretched himself out by the roadside to rest.

On went Johnny-Cake, and by and by he came to a wolf. The wolf said: 'Where ye going, Johnny-

Cake?' He said: 'I've outrun an old man, and an old woman, and a little boy, and two well-diggers, and two ditch-diggers, and a bear, and I can outrun you too–o–o!'

'Ye can, can ye?' snarled the wolf, 'we'll see about that!' And he set into a gallop after Johnny-Cake, who went on and on so fast that the wolf too saw there was no hope of overtaking him, and he too lay down to rest.

On went Johnny-Cake, and by and by he came to a fox that lay quietly in a corner of the fence. The fox called out in a sharp voice, but without getting up: 'Where ye going Johnny-Cake?'

He said: 'I've outrun an old man, and an old woman, and a little boy, and two well-diggers, and two ditch-diggers, a bear, and a wolf, and I can outrun you too–o–o!'

The fox said: 'I can't quite hear you, Johnny-Cake, won't you come a little closer?' turning his head a little to one side.

Johnny-Cake stopped his race for the first time, and went a little closer, and called out in a very loud voice 'I've outrun an old man, and an old woman, and a little boy, and two well-diggers, and two ditch-diggers, and a bear, and a wolf, and I can outrun you too–o–o!'

'Can't quite hear you; won't you come a *little* closer?' said the fox in a feeble voice, as he stretched out his neck towards Johnny-Cake, and put one paw behind his ear.

Johnny-Cake came up close, and leaning towards the fox screamed out 'I've outrun an old man, and an old woman, and a little boy, and two well-diggers, and two ditch-diggers, and a bear, and a wolf, and I can outrun you too–o–o!'

'You can, can you?' yelped the fox, and he snapped up the Johnny-Cake in his sharp teeth in the twinkling of an eye.

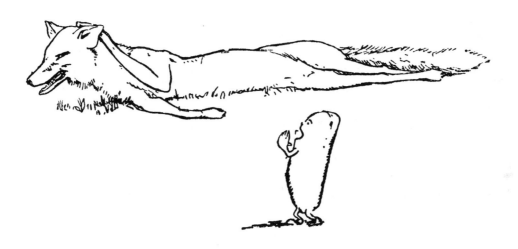

Kate Crackernuts

Once upon a time there was a king and a queen, as in many lands have been. The king had a daughter, Anne, and the queen had one named Kate, but Anne was far bonnier than the queen's daughter, though they loved one another like real sisters. The queen was jealous of the king's daughter being bonnier than her own, and cast about to spoil her beauty. So she took counsel of the henwife, who told her to send the lassie to her next morning fasting.

So next morning early, the queen said to Anne, 'Go, my dear, to the henwife in the glen, and ask her for some eggs.' So Anne set out, but as she passed through the kitchen she saw a crust, and she took and munched it as she went along.

When she came to the henwife's she asked for eggs, as she had been told to do; the henwife said to her, 'Lift the lid off that pot there and see.' The lassie did so, but nothing happened. 'Go home to your stepmother and tell her to keep her larder door better locked,' said the henwife. So she went home to the queen and told her what the henwife had said. The queen knew from this that the lassie had had something to eat, so watched the next morning and sent her away fasting; but the princess saw some country-folk picking peas by the roadside, and being very kind she spoke to them and took a handful of the peas, which she ate by the way.

When she came to the henwife's, she said, 'Lift the lid off the pot and you'll see.' So Anne lifted the lid but nothing happened. Then the henwife was rare angry and said to Anne, 'Tell your stepmother the pot won't boil if the fire's away.' So Anne went home and told the queen.

The third day the queen goes along with the girl herself to the henwife. Now, this time, when Anne lifted the lid off the pot, off falls her own pretty head, and on jumps a sheep's head.

So the queen was now quite satisfied, and went back home.

Her own daughter, Kate, however, took a fine linen cloth and wrapped it round her sister's head and took her by the hand and they both went out to seek their fortune. They went on, and they went on, and they went on, till they came to a castle. Kate knocked at the door and asked for a night's lodging for herself and a sick sister. They went in and found it was a king's castle, who had two sons, and one of them was sickening away to death and no one could find out what ailed him. And the curious thing was that whoever watched him at night was never seen any more. So the king had offered a peck of silver to anyone who would stop up with him. Now Katie was a very brave girl, so she offered to sit up with him.

Till midnight all goes well. As twelve o'clock strikes, however, the sick prince rises, dresses himself and slips downstairs. Kate followed, but he didn't seem to notice her. The prince went to the stable, saddled his horse, called his hound, jumped into the saddle, and Kate leapt lightly up behind him. Away rode the prince and Kate through the greenwood, Kate, as they pass, plucking nuts from the trees and filling her apron with them. They rode on and on till they came to a green hill. The prince here drew bridle and spoke, 'Open, open, green hill, and let the young prince in with his horse and his hound,' and Kate added, 'and his lady him behind.'

Immediately the green hill opened and they passed in. The prince entered a magnificent hall, brightly lighted up, and many beautiful fairies surrounded the prince and led him off to the dance. Meanwhile, Kate, without being noticed, hid herself behind the door. There she sees the prince dancing, and dancing, and dancing, till he could dance no longer and fell upon a couch. Then the fairies would fan him till he could rise again and go on dancing.

At last the cock crew, and the prince made all haste to get on horseback; Kate jumped up behind, and home they rode. When the morning sun rose they came in and found Kate sitting down by the fire and cracking her nuts. Kate said the prince had a good night; but she would not sit up another night unless she was to get a peck of gold. The second night passed as the first had done. The prince got up at midnight and rode away to the green hill and the fairy ball, and Kate went with him, gathering nuts as they rode through the forest. This time she did not watch the prince, for she knew he would dance, and dance, and dance. But she sees a fairy baby playing with a wand, and overhears one of the fairies say: 'Three strokes of that wand would make Kate's sick sister as bonnie as ever she was.' So Kate rolled nuts to the fairy baby, and rolled nuts till the baby toddled after the nuts and let fall the wand, and Kate took it up and put it in her apron. And at cockcrow they rode home as before, and the moment Kate got home to her room she rushed and touched Anne three times with the wand, and the nasty sheep's head fell off and she was her own pretty self again. The third night Kate consented to watch, only if she should marry the sick prince. All went on as on the first two nights. This time the fairy baby was playing with a birdie; Kate heard one of the fairies say: 'Three bites of that birdie would make the sick prince as well as ever he was.' Kate rolled all the nuts she had to the fairy baby till the birdie was dropped, and Kate put it in her apron.

At cockcrow they set off again, but instead of cracking her nuts as she used to do, this time Kate plucked the feathers off and cooked the birdie. Soon there arose a very savoury smell. 'Oh!' said the sick prince, 'I wish I had a bite of that birdie,' so Kate gave him a bite of the birdie, and he rose up on his elbow. By and by he cried out again: 'Oh, if I had another bite of that birdie!' so Kate gave him another bite, and he sat up on his bed. Then he said again: 'Oh! if I only had a third bite of that birdie!' So Kate gave him a third bite, and he rose quite well, dressed himself, and sat down by the fire, and when the folk came in next morning they found Kate and the young prince cracking nuts together. Meanwhile his brother had seen Annie and had fallen in love with her, as everybody did who saw her sweet pretty face. So the sick son married the well sister, and the well son married the sick sister, and they all lived happy and died happy, and never drank out of a dry cappie.

Meanwhile, Kate, without being noticed, hid herself behind the door

The Story of King Frost

There was once upon a time a peasant-woman who had a daughter and a stepdaughter. The daughter had her own way in everything, and whatever she did was right in her mother's eyes; but the poor stepdaughter had a hard time. Let her do what she would, she was always blamed, and got small thanks for all the trouble she took; nothing was right, everything wrong; and yet, if the truth were known, the girl was worth her weight in gold – she was so unselfish and good-hearted. But her step-mother did not like her, and the poor girl's days were spent in weeping; for it was impossible to live peacefully with the woman. The wicked shrew was determined to get rid of the girl by fair means or foul, and kept saying to her father: 'Send her away, old man; send her away – anywhere so that my eyes shan't be plagued any longer by the sight of her, or my ears tormented by the sound of her voice. Send her out into the fields, and let the cutting frost do for her.'

In vain did the poor old father weep and implore her pity; she was firm, and he dared not gainsay her. So he placed his daughter in a sledge, not even daring to give her a horse-cloth to keep herself warm with, and drove her out on to the bare, open fields, where he kissed her and left her, driving home as fast as he could, that he might not witness her miserable death.

Deserted by her father, the poor girl sat down under a fir tree at the edge of the forest and began to weep silently. Suddenly she heard a faint sound: it was King Frost springing from tree to tree, and cracking his fingers as he went. At length he reached the fir tree beneath which she was sitting, and with a crisp crackling sound he alighted beside her, and looked at her lovely face.

'Well, maiden,' he snapped out, 'do you know who I am? I am King Frost, king of the red-noses.'

'All hail to you, great king!' answered the girl, in a gentle, trembling voice. 'Have you come to take me?'

'Are you warm, maiden?' he replied.

'Quite warm, King Frost,' she answered, though she shivered as she spoke.

Then King Frost stooped down, and bent over the girl, and the crackling sound grew louder, and the air seemed to be full of knives and darts; and again he asked: 'Maiden, are you warm? Are you warm, you beautiful girl?'

And though her breath was almost frozen on her lips, she whispered gently, 'Quite warm, King Frost.'

Then King Frost gnashed his teeth, and cracked his fingers, and his eyes sparkled, and the crackling, crisp sound was louder than ever, and for the last time he asked her: 'Maiden, are you still warm? Are you still warm, little love?'

And the poor girl was so stiff and numb that she could just gasp, 'Still warm, O king!'

Now her gentle, courteous words and her un-complaining ways touched King Frost, and he had pity on her, and he wrapped her up in furs, and covered her with blankets, and he fetched a great box, in which were beautiful jewels and a rich robe embroidered in gold and silver. And she put it on, and looked more lovely than ever, and King Frost stepped with her into his sledge, with six white horses.

In the meantime the wicked stepmother was waiting at home for news of the girl's death, and preparing pancakes for the funeral feast. And she said to her husband: 'Old man, you had better go out into the fields and find your daughter's body and bury her.' Just as the old man was leaving the house the little dog under the table began to bark, saying:

'*Your* daughter shall live to be your delight;
Her daughter shall die this very night.'

'Hold your tongue, you foolish beast!' scolded the woman. 'There's a pancake for you, but you must say:

"*Her* daughter shall have much silver and gold;
His daughter is frozen quite stiff and cold." '

But the doggie ate up the pancake and barked, saying:

'*His* daughter shall wear a crown on her head;
Her daughter shall die unwooed, unwed.'

Then the old woman tried to coax the doggie with more pancakes and to terrify it with blows, but he barked on, always repeating the same words. And suddenly the door creaked and flew open, and a great heavy chest was pushed in, and behind it came the stepdaughter, radiant and beautiful, in a dress all glittering with silver and gold. For a moment the stepmother's eyes were dazzled. Then she called to her husband: 'Old man, yoke the horses at once into the sledge, and take my daughter to the same field and leave her on the same spot exactly;' and so the old man took the girl and left her beneath the same tree where he had parted from his daughter. In a few minutes King Frost came past, and, looking at the girl, he said: 'Are you warm, maiden?'

'What a blind old fool you must be to ask such a question!' she answered angrily. 'Can't you see that my hands and feet are nearly frozen?'

Then King Frost sprang to and fro in front of her, questioning her, and getting only rude, rough words in reply, till at last he got very angry, and cracked his fingers, and gnashed his teeth, and froze her to death.

But in the hut her mother was waiting for her return, and as she grew impatient she said to her husband: 'Get out the horses, old man, to go and fetch her home; but see that you are careful not to upset the sledge and lose the chest.'

But the doggie beneath the table began to bark, saying:

'Your daughter is frozen quite stiff and cold,
And shall never have a chest full of gold.'

'Don't tell such wicked lies!' scolded the woman. 'There's a cake for you; now say: '*Her* daughter shall marry a mighty king.'

At that moment the door flew open, and she rushed out to meet her daughter, and as she took her frozen body in her arms she too was chilled to death.

"MAIDEN ARE YOU WARM?"

King O'Toole and His Goose

Och, I thought all the world, far and near, had heerd o' King O'Toole – well, well, but the darkness of mankind is untellible! Well, sir, you must know, as you didn't hear it afore, that there was a king, called King O'Toole, who was a fine old king in the old ancient times, long ago; and it was he that owned the churches in the early days. The king, you see, was the right sort; he was the real boy, and loved sport as he loved his life, and hunting in particular; and from the rising o' the sun, up he got, and away he went over the mountains after the deer; and fine times they were.

Well, it was all mighty good, as long as the king had his health; but, you see, in course of time the king grew old, by raison he was stiff in his limbs, and when he got stricken in years, his heart failed him, and he was lost entirely for want o' diversion, because he couldn't go a-hunting no longer; and, by dad, the poor king was obliged at last to get a goose to divert him. Oh, you may laugh, if you like, but it's truth I'm telling you; and the way the goose diverted him was this-a-way: You see, the goose used to swim across the lake, and go diving for trout, and catch fish on a Friday for the king, and flew every other day round about the lake, diverting the poor king. All went on mighty well

The goose got stricken in years like her master

until, by dad, the goose got stricken in years like her master, and couldn't divert him no longer, and then it was that the poor king was lost entirely. The king was walkin' one mornin' by the edge of the lake, lamentin' his cruel fate, and thinking of drowning himself, that could get no diversion in life, when all of a sudden, turning round the corner, who should he meet but a mighty decent young man coming up to him.

'God save you,' says the king to the young man.

'God save you kindly, King O'Toole,' says the young man.

'True for you,' says the king. 'I am King O'Toole. Prince and plennypennytinchery of these parts. But how came ye to know that?'

'Oh, never mind,' says St Kavin.

You see it was St Kavin, sure enough – the saint himself in disguise, and nobody else. 'Oh, never mind,' says he, 'I know more than that. May I make bold to ask how is your goose, King O'Toole?'

'Blur-an-agers, how came ye to know about my goose?' says the king.

'Oh, no matter; I was given to understand it,' says St Kavin.

After some more talk the king says, 'What are you?'

'I'm an honest man,' says St Kavin.

'Well, honest man,' says the king, 'and how is it you make your money so aisy?'

'By makin' old things as good as new,' says St Kavin.

'Is it a tinker you are?' says the king.

'No,' says the saint; 'I'm no tinker by trade, King O'Toole; I've a better trade than a tinker,' says he. 'What would you say,' says he, 'if I made your old goose as good as new?'

My dear, at the word of making his goose as good as new, you'd think the poor old king's eyes were ready to jump out of his head. With that the king whistled, and down came the poor goose, just like a hound, waddling up to the poor cripple, her master, and as like him as two peas. The minute the saint clapped his eyes on the goose, 'I'll do the job for you,' says he, 'King O'Toole.'

'By *Jaminee!*' says King O'Toole. 'If you do, I'll say you're the cleverest fellow in the seven parishes.'

'Oh, by dad,' says St Kavin, 'you must say more nor that – my horn's not so soft all out,' says he, 'as to repair your old goose for nothing; what'll you gi' me if I do the job for you?' says St Kavin.

'I'll give you whatever you ask,' says the king; 'isn't that fair?'

'Divil a fairer,' says the saint; 'that's the way to do business. Now,' says he, 'this is the bargain I'll make with you, King O'Toole: will you gi' me all the ground the goose flies over, the first offer, after I make her as good as new?'

'I will,' says the king.

'You won't go back o' your word?' says St Kavin.

'Honour bright!' says King O'Toole, holding out his fist.

'Honour bright!' says St Kavin, back agin, 'it's a bargain. Come here!' says he to the poor old goose, 'come here, you unfortunate ould cripple, and it's I that'll make you the sporting bird.' With that, my dear, he took up the goose by the two wings – 'Criss o' my cross an you,' says he, markin' her to grace with the blessed sign at the same minute – and throwing her up in the air. 'Whew,' says he, jist givin' her a blast to help her; and with that, my jewel, she took to her heels, flyin' like one o' the eagles themselves, and cutting as many capers as a swallow before a shower of rain.

Well, my dear, it was a beautiful sight to see the king standing with his mouth open, looking at his poor old goose flying as light as a lark, and better than ever she was; and when she lit at his feet, he patted her on the head, and, '*Ma vourneen,*' says he, 'but you are the *darlint* o' the world.'

'And what do you say to me,' says St Kavin, 'for making her the like?'

'By Jabers,' says the king, 'I say nothing beats the art o' man, barring the bees.'

'And do you say no more nor that?' says St Kavin.

'And that I'm beholden to you,' says the king.

'But will you gi'e all the ground the goose flew over?' says St Kavin.

'I will,' says King O'Toole, 'and you're welcome to it,' says he, 'though it's the last acre I have to give.'

'But you'll keep your word true?' says the saint.

'As true as the sun,' says the king.

'It's well for you, King O'Toole, that you said that word,' says he; 'for if you didn't say that word, the devil the bit o' your goose would ever fly agin.'

When the king was as good as his word, St Kavin was pleased with him, and then it was that he made himself known to the king. 'And,' says he, 'King O'Toole, you're a decent man, for I only came here to try you. You don't know me,' says he, 'because I'm disguised.'

'Musha! Then,' says the king, 'who are you?'

'I'm St Kavin,' said the saint, blessing himself.

'Oh, queen of heaven!' says the king, making the sign of the cross between his eyes, and falling down on his knees before the saint. 'Is it the great St Kavin,' says he, 'that I've been discoursing with all this time without knowing it,' says he, 'all as one as if he was a lump of a gossoon? – and so you're a saint?' says the king.

'I am,' says St Kavin.

'By Jabers, I thought I was only talking to a dacent boy,' says the king.

'Well, you know the difference now,' says the saint. 'I'm St Kavin,' says he, 'the greatest of all the saints.'

And so the king had his goose as good as new, to divert him as long as he lived and the saint supported him after he came into his property, as I told you, until the day of his death – and that was soon after; for the poor goose thought he was catching a trout one Friday; but, my jewel, it was a mistake he made – and instead of a trout, it was a thieving horse-eel; and instead of the goose killing a trout for the king's supper, by dad, the eel killed the king's goose – and small blame to him; but he didn't ate her, because he darn't ate what St Kavin had laid his blessed hands on.

The King of the Golden Mountain

There was once a merchant who had only one child, a son, who was very young and barely able to run alone. He had two richly laden ships then making a voyage upon the seas, in which he had embarked all his wealth, in the hope of making great gains, but news came that both were lost. Thus from being a rich man he became all at once so very poor that nothing was left to him but one small plot of land; and there he often went in an evening to take his walk, and ease his mind of a little of his trouble.

One day, as he was roaming along in a brown study, thinking with no great comfort on what he had been and what he now was and was likely to be, all of a sudden there stood before him a little, rough-looking, black dwarf. 'Prithee, friend, why so sorrowful?' said he to the merchant; 'what is it you take so deeply to heart?'

'If you would do me any good I would willingly tell you,' said the merchant.

'Who knows but I may?' said the little man. 'Tell me what ails you, and perhaps you will find I may be of some use.'

Then the merchant told him how all his wealth was gone to the bottom of the sea, and how he had nothing left but that little plot of land.

'Oh, trouble not yourself about that,' said the dwarf; 'only undertake to bring me here, twelve years hence, whatever meets you first on your going home, and I will give you as much as you please.'

The merchant thought this was no great thing to ask; that it would most likely be his dog or his cat, or something of that sort, but forgot his little boy Heinel; so he agreed to the bargain, and signed and sealed the bond to do what was asked of him.

But as he drew near home, his little boy was so glad to see him that he crept behind him, and laid fast hold of his legs, and looked up in his face and laughed.

Then the father started, trembling with fear and horror, and saw what it was that he had bound himself to do; but as no gold was come, he made himself easy by thinking that it was only a joke that the dwarf was playing him, and that, at any rate, when the money came, he should see the bearer, and would not take it in.

About a month afterwards he went upstairs into a lumber-room to look for some old iron, that he might sell it and raise a little money; and there, instead of his iron, he saw a large pile of gold lying on the floor.

At the sight of this he was overjoyed, and forgetting all about his son, went into trade again, and became a richer merchant than before.

Meantime little Heinel grew up, and as the end of the twelve years drew near the merchant began to call to mind his bond, and became very sad and thoughtful; so that care and sorrow were written upon his face.

The boy one day asked what was the matter, but his father would not tell for some time; at last, however, he said that he had, without knowing it, sold him for gold to a little, ugly-looking, black dwarf, and that the twelve years were coming round when he must keep his word.

Then Heinel said, 'Father, give yourself very little trouble about that; I shall be too much for the little man.'

When the time came, the father and son went out together to the place agreed upon, and the son drew a circle on the ground and set himself and his father in the middle of it. The little black dwarf soon came, and walked round and round about the circle, but could not find any way to get into it, and he either could not or dared not jump over it.

At last the boy said to him. 'Have you anything to say to us, my friend? What do you want?' Now Heinel had found a friend in a good fairy, that was fond of him and had told him what to do; for this fairy knew what good luck was in store for him.

'Have you brought me what you said you would?' said the dwarf to the merchant.

When the time came, they went to the place agreed upon, and the son drew a circle on the ground and set himself and his father in the middle of it

The old man held his tongue, but Heinel said again, 'What do you want here?'

The dwarf said, 'I come to talk with your father, not with you.'

'You have cheated and taken in my father,' said the son; 'pray give him up his bond at once.'

'Fair and softly,' said the little old man; 'right is right; I have paid my money, and your father has had it, and spent it; so be so good as to let me have what I paid it for.'

'You must have my consent to that first,' said Heinel, 'so please to step in here, and let us talk.'

The old man grinned, and showed his teeth, as if he should have been very glad to get into the circle if he could. Then at last, after a long talk, they came to terms. Heinel agreed that his father must give him up, and that so far the dwarf should have his way; but, on the other hand, the fairy had told Heinel what fortune was in store for him if he followed his own course; and he did not choose to be given up to his humpbacked friend, who seemed so anxious for his company.

So, to make a sort of drawn battle of the matter, it was settled that Heinel should be put into an open

boat that lay on the seashore hard by; that the father should push him off with his own hand, and that he should thus be set adrift, and left to the bad or good luck of wind and weather. Then he took leave of his father, and set himself in the boat, but before it got far off a wave struck it, and it fell with one side low in the water, so the merchant thought that poor Heinel was lost, and went home very sorrowful, while the dwarf went his way, thinking that at any rate he had had his revenge.

The boat, however, did not sink, for the good fairy took care of her friend, and soon raised the boat up again, and it went safely on. The young man sat safe within, till at length it ran ashore upon an unknown land. As he jumped upon the shore he saw before him a beautiful castle, but empty and dreary within, for it was enchanted. 'Here,' said he to himself, 'must I find the prize the good fairy told me of.' So he searched the whole palace through, till at last he found a white snake, lying coiled up on a cushion in one of the chambers.

Now the white snake was an enchanted princess; and she was very glad to see him, and said, 'Are you at last come to set me free? Twelve long years have I waited here for the fairy to bring you hither as she promised, for you alone can save me. This night twelve men will come: their faces will be black, and they will be dressed in chain armour. They will ask what you do here, but give no answer; and let them do what they will – beat, whip, pinch, prick or torment you – bear all; only speak not a word, and at twelve o'clock they must go away. The second night twelve others will come; and the third night twenty-four, who will even cut off your head; but at the twelfth hour of that night their power will be gone, and I shall be free, and will come and bring you the Water of Life, and will wash you with it, and bring you back to life and health.' And all came to pass as she had said; Heinel bore all, and spoke not a word; and the third night the princess came, and fell on his neck and kissed him. Joy and gladness filled the castle, the wedding was celebrated, and he was crowned King of the Golden Mountain.

They lived together very happily, and the queen had a son. And thus eight years had passed over their heads, when the king thought of his father; and he began to long to see him once again. But the queen was against his going, and said, 'I know well that misfortunes will come upon us if you go.' However, he gave her no rest till she agreed. At his going away she gave him a wishing-ring, and said, 'Take this ring, and put it on your finger; whatever you wish it will bring you; only promise never to make use of it to bring me hence to your father's house.' Then he said he would do what she asked, and put the ring on his finger, and wished himself near the town where his father lived.

Heinel found himself at the gates in a moment; but the guards would not let him go in, because he was so strangely clad. So he went up to a neighbouring hill, where a shepherd dwelt, and borrowed his old smock, and thus passed unknown into the town. When he came to his father's house, he said he was his son; but the merchant would not believe him, and said he had had but one son, his poor Heinel, who he knew was long since dead; and as he was only dressed like a poor shepherd, he would not even give him anything to eat. The king, however, still vowed that he was his son, and said, 'Is there no mark by which you would know that I am really your son?'

'Yes,' said his mother, 'our Heinel had a mark like a raspberry on his right arm.' Then he showed them the mark, and they knew that what he had said was true.

He next told them how he was King of the Golden Mountain, and was married to a princess, and had a son seven years old.

But the merchant said, 'That can never be true; he must be a fine king truly who travels about in a shepherd's smock!'

At this the son was vexed; and forgetting his word, turned his ring and wished for his queen and son. In an instant they stood before him; but the queen wept, and said he had broken his word, and bad luck would follow. He did all he could to soothe her, and she at last seemed to be appeased; but she was not so in truth, and was only thinking how she should punish him.

One day he took her to walk with him out of the town, and showed her the spot where the boat was set adrift upon the wide waters. Then he sat himself down, and said, 'I am very much tired; sit by me, I will rest my head in your lap, and sleep a while.' As soon as he had fallen asleep, however, she drew the ring from his finger, and crept softly away, and wished herself and her son at home in their kingdom. And when he awoke he found himself alone, and saw that the ring was gone from his finger. 'I can never go back to my father's house,' said he; 'they would say I am a sorcerer. I will journey forth into the world, till I come again to my kingdom.'

So saying he set out and travelled till he came to a hill where three giants were sharing their father's goods; and as they saw him pass they cried out and said, 'Little men have sharp wits; he shall part the goods between us.' Now there was a sword that cut off an enemy's head whenever the wearer gave the words, 'Heads off!'; a cloak that made the owner invisible, or gave him any form he pleased; and a pair of boots that carried the wearer wherever he wished. Heinel said they must first let him try these wonderful things, then he might know how to set a value upon them. Then they gave him the cloak, and he wished himself a fly, and in a moment he was a fly. 'The cloak is very well,' said he; 'now give me the sword.'

'No,' said they; 'not unless you undertake not to say, "Heads off!" for if you do we are all dead men.' So they gave it him, charging him to try it on a tree. He next asked for the boots also; and the moment he had all three in his power, he wished himself at the Golden Mountain; and there he was at once. So the giants were left behind with no goods to share or quarrel about.

As Heinel came near his castle he heard the sound of merry music; and the people around told him that his queen was about to marry another husband. Then he threw his cloak around him, and passed through the castle hall, and placed himself by the side of the queen, where no one saw him. But when anything to eat was put upon her plate, he took it away and ate it himself; and when a glass of wine was handed to her, he took it and drank it; and thus, though they kept on giving her meat and drink, her plate and cup were always empty.

Upon this, fear and remorse came over her, and she went into her chamber alone, and sat there weeping; and he followed her there. 'Alas!' said she to herself, 'was I not once set free? Why then does this enchantment still seem to bind me?'

'False and fickle one!' said he. 'One indeed came who set thee free, and he is now near thee again; but how have you used him? Ought he to have had such treatment from thee?'

Then he went out and sent away the company, and said the wedding was at an end now that he had come back to his kingdom. But the princes, peers and great men mocked at him. However, he would enter into no parley with them, but only asked them if they would go in peace or not. Then they turned upon him and tried to seize him; but he drew his sword. 'Heads off!' cried he; and with the word the traitors' heads fell before him, and Heinel was once more King of the Golden Mountain.

The King Who Would Have a Beautiful Wife

Fifty years ago there lived a king who was very anxious to get married; but, as he was quite determined that his wife should be as beautiful as the sun, the thing was not so easy as it seemed, for no maiden came up to his standard. Then he ordered a trusty servant to search through the length and breadth of the land till he found a girl fair enough to be queen, and if he had the good luck to discover one he was to bring her back with him.

The servant set out at once on his journey, and sought high and low – in castles and cottages; but though pretty maidens were plentiful as blackberries, he felt sure that none of them would please the king.

One day he had wandered far and wide, and was feeling very tired and thirsty. By the roadside stood a tiny little house, and here he knocked and asked for a cup of water. Now in this house dwelt two sisters, and one was eighty and the other ninety years old. They were very poor, and earned their living by spinning. This had kept their hands very soft and white, like the hands of a girl, and when the water was passed through the lattice, and the servant saw the small, delicate fingers, he said to himself: 'A maiden must indeed be lovely if she has a hand like that.' And he made haste back, and told the king.

'Go back at once,' said his majesty, 'and try to get a sight of her.'

The faithful servant departed on his errand without losing any time, and again he knocked at the door of the little house and begged for some water. As before, the old woman did not open the door, but passed the water through the lattice.

'Do you live here alone?' asked the man.

'No,' replied she, 'my sister lives with me. We are poor girls, and have to work for our bread.'

'How old are you?'

'I am fifteen, and she is twenty.'

Then the servant went back to the king, and told him all he knew. And his majesty answered: 'I will have the fifteen-year-old one. Go and bring her here.'

The servant returned a third time to the little house and knocked at the door. In reply to his knock the lattice window was pushed open, and a voice enquired what it was he wanted.

'The king has desired me to bring back the younger of you to become his queen,' he replied.

'Tell his majesty I am ready to do his bidding, but since my birth no ray of light has fallen upon my face. If it should ever do so I shall instantly grow black. Therefore beg, I pray you, his most gracious majesty to send this evening a shut carriage, and I will return in it to the castle.'

When the king heard this he ordered his great golden carriage to be prepared, and in it to be placed some magnificent robes; and the old woman wrapped herself in a thick veil, and was driven to the castle.

The king was eagerly awaiting her, and when she arrived he begged her politely to raise her veil and let him see her face.

But she answered: 'Here the tapers are too bright and the light too strong. Would you have me turn black under your very eyes?'

And the king believed her words, and the marriage took place without the veil being once lifted. Afterwards, when they were alone, he raised the corner, and knew for the first time that he had wedded a wrinkled old woman. And, in a furious burst of anger, he dashed open the window and flung her out. But, luckily for her, her clothes caught on a nail in the wall, and kept her hanging between heaven and earth.

While she was thus suspended, expecting every moment to be dashed to the ground, four fairies happened to pass by.

'Look, sisters,' cried one, 'surely that is the old woman that the king sent for. Shall we wish that her clothes may give way, and that she should be dashed to the ground?'

'Oh no! no!' exclaimed another. 'Let us wish her something good. I myself will wish her youth.'

'And I beauty.'

'And I wisdom.'

'And I a tender heart.'

So spake the fairies, and went their way, leaving the most beautiful maiden in the world behind them.

The next morning when the king looked from his window he saw this lovely creature hanging on the nail. 'Ah! what have I done? Surely I must have been blind last night!'

And he ordered long ladders to be brought and the maiden to be rescued. Then he fell on his knees before her, and prayed her to forgive him, and a great feast was made in her honour.

Some days after came the ninety-year-old sister to the palace and asked for the queen.

'Who is that hideous old witch?' said the king.

'Oh, an old neighbour of mine, who is half silly,' she replied.

But the old woman looked at her steadily, and knew her again, and said: 'How have you managed to grow so young and beautiful? I should like to be young and beautiful too.'

This question she repeated the whole day long, till at length the queen lost patience and said: 'I had my old head cut off, and this new head grew in its place.'

Then the old woman went to a barber, and spoke to him, saying, 'I will give you all you ask if you will only cut off my head, so that I may become young and lovely.'

'But, my good woman, if I do that you will die!'

But the old woman would listen to nothing; and at last the barber took out his knife and struck the first blow at her neck. 'Ah!' she shrieked as she felt the pain. 'Il faut souffrir pour etre belle,' said the barber, who had been in France. And at the second blow her head rolled off, and the old woman was dead for good and all

The Lad with the Goatskin

Long ago, a poor widow woman lived down near the iron forge, by Enniscorth, and she was so poor she had no clothes to put on her son; so she used to fix him in the ash-hole, near the fire, and pile the warm ashes about him; and according as he grew up, she sunk the pit deeper. At last, by hook or by crook, she got a goatskin, and fastened it round his waist, and he felt quite grand, and took a walk down the street.

So she says to him next morning, 'Tom, you thief, you've never done any good yet, and you six foot high and past nineteen – take that rope and bring me a faggot from the wood.'

'Never say't twice, mother,' says Tom. 'Here goes.'

When he had it gathered and tied, what should come up but a big giant, nine foot high, and made a lick of a club at him. Tom jumped to one side, and picked up a ram-pike; and the first crack he gave the big fellow, he made him kiss the clod.

'If you have e'er a prayer,' says Tom, 'now's the time to say it, before I make fragments of you.'

'I have no prayers,' says the giant, 'but if you spare my life I'll give you that club; and as long as you keep from sin, you'll win every battle you ever fight with it.'

Tom made no bones about letting him off; and as soon as he got the club in his hands, he sat down on the bresna, and gave it a tap with the kippeen, and says, 'Faggot, I had great trouble gathering you, and ran the risk of my life for you, the least you can do is to carry me home.' And sure enough, the wind o' the word was all it wanted. It went off through the wood, groaning and crackling, till it came to the widow's door.

Well, when the sticks were all burned, Tom was sent off again to pick more; and this time he had to fight with a giant that had two heads on him. Tom had a little more trouble with him – that's all; and the prayers he said was to give Tom a fife, that nobody could help dancing to when he was playing it. Begonies, he made the big faggot dance home, with himself sitting on it. The next giant was a beautiful boy with three heads on him. He had neither prayers nor catechism no more nor the others; and so he gave Tom a bottle of green ointment, that wouldn't let you be burned, nor scalded, nor wounded. 'And now,' says he, 'there's no more of us. You may come and gather sticks here till little Lunacy Day in Harvest, without giant or fairy-man to disturb you.'

Well, now, Tom was prouder nor ten paycocks, and used to take a walk down the street in the heel of the evening; but some o' the little boys had no more manners than if they were Dublin jackeens, and put out their tongues at Tom's club and Tom's goatskin. He didn't like that at all, but it would be mean to give one of them a clout. At last, what should come through the town but a kind of a bellman, only it's a big bugle he had, and a huntsman's cap on his head, and a kind of a painted shirt. So this – he wasn't a bellman, and I don't know what to call him – bugle-man, maybe, proclaimed that the king of Dublin's daughter was so melancholy that she didn't give a laugh for seven years, and that her father would grant her in marriage to whoever could make her laugh three times.

'That's the very thing for me to try,' says Tom; and so, without burning any more daylight, he kissed his mother, curled his club at the little boys, and off he set along the yalla highroad to the town of Dublin.

At last Tom came to one of the city gates, and the guards laughed and cursed at him instead of letting him in. Tom stood it all for a little time, but at last one of them – out of fun, as he said – drove his bayonet half an inch or so into his side. Tom did nothing but take the fellow by the scruff o' the neck and the waistband of his corduroys and fling him into the canal. Some ran to pull the fellow out, and others to let manners into the vulgarian with their swords and daggers; but a tap from his club sent them headlong into the moat or down on the stones, and they were soon begging him to stay his hands.

So at last one of them was glad enough to show Tom the way to the palace-yard; and there was the king, and the queen, and the princess, in a gallery, looking at all sorts of wrestling, and sword-playing, and long-dances, and mumming, all to please the princess; but not a smile came over her handsome face.

Well, they all stopped when they saw the young giant, with his boy's face, and long black hair, and his short curly beard – for his poor mother couldn't afford to buy razors – and his great strong arms, and bare legs, and no covering but the goatskin that reached from his waist to his knees. But an envious wizened bit of a fellow, with a red head, that wished to be married to the princess, and didn't like how she opened her eyes at Tom, came forward, and asked his business very snappishly.

'My business,' says Tom, says he, 'is to make the beautiful princess, God bless her, laugh three times.'

'Do you see all them merry fellows and skilful swordsmen,' says the other, 'that could eat you up with a grain of salt, and not a mother's soul of 'em ever got a laugh from her these seven years?'

So the fellows gathered round Tom, and the bad man aggravated him till he told them he didn't care a pinch o' snuff for the whole bilin' of 'em; let 'em come on, six at a time, and try what they could do.

The king, who was too far off to hear what they were saying, asked what did the stranger want.

'He wants,' says the red-headed fellow, 'to make hares of your best men.'

'Oh!' says the king. 'If that's the way, let one of 'em turn out and try his mettle.'

So one stood forward, with sword and pot-lid, and made a cut at Tom. He struck the fellow's elbow with the club, and up over their heads flew the sword, and down went the owner of it on the gravel from a thump he got on the helmet. Another took his place, and another, and another, and then half a dozen at once, and Tom sent swords, helmets, shields and bodies rolling over and over, and themselves bawling out that they were kilt, and disabled, and damaged, and rubbing their poor elbows and hips, and limping away. Tom contrived not to kill anyone; and the princess was so amused, that she let a great sweet laugh out of her that was heard over all the yard.

'King of Dublin,' says Tom, 'I've a third part of your daughter.'

And the king didn't know whether he was glad or sorry, and all the blood in the princess's heart run into her cheeks.

So there was no more fighting that day, and Tom was invited to dine with the royal family. Next day, Redhead told Tom of a wolf, the size of a yearling heifer, that used to be serenading about the walls, and eating people and cattle; and said what a pleasure it would give the king to have it killed.

'With all my heart,' says Tom. 'Send a jackeen to show me where he lives, and we'll see how he behaves to a stranger.'

The princess was not well pleased, for Tom looked a different person with fine clothes and a nice green birredh over his long curly hair; and besides, he'd got one laugh out of her. However, the king gave his consent; and in an hour and a half the horrible wolf was walking into the palace-yard, and Tom a step or two behind, with his club on his shoulder, just as a shepherd would be walking after a pet lamb.

The king and queen and princess were safe up in their gallery, but the officers and people of the court that were padrowling about the great bawn, when they saw the big baste coming in, gave themselves up, and began to make for doors and gates; and the wolf licked his chops, as if he was saying, 'Wouldn't I enjoy a breakfast off a couple of yez!'

The king shouted out, 'O Tom with the Goatskin, take away that terrible wolf, and you must have all my daughter.'

But Tom didn't mind him a bit. He pulled out his flute and began to play like vengeance; and dickens a man or boy in the yard but began shovelling away heel and toe, and the wolf himself was obliged to get on his hind legs and dance 'Tatther Jack Walsh' along with the rest. A good deal of the people got inside, and shut the doors, the way the hairy fellow wouldn't pin them; but Tom kept playing, and the outsiders kept dancing and shouting, and the wolf kept dancing and roaring with the pain his legs were giving him; and all the time he had his eyes on Redhead, who was shut out along with the rest. Wherever Redhead went, the wolf followed, and kept one eye on him and the other on Tom, to see if he would give him leave to eat him. But Tom shook his head, and never stopped the tune, and Redhead never stopped dancing and bawling, and the wolf dancing and roaring, one leg up and

the other down, and he ready to drop out of his standing from fair tiresomeness.

When the princess saw that there was no fear of anyone being kilt, she was so divarted by the stew that Redhead was in that she gave another great laugh; and well become Tom, out he cried, 'King of Dublin, I have two parts of your daughter.'

'Oh, two parts or all,' says the king, 'put away that divel of a wolf, and we'll see about it.'

So Tom put his flute in his pocket, and says he to the baste that was sittin' on his currabingo ready to faint, 'Walk off to your mountain, my fine fellow, and live like a respectable baste; and if ever I find you come within seven miles of any town, I'll – '

He said no more, but spit in his fist, and gave a flourish of his club. It was all the poor divel of a wolf wanted: he put his tail between his legs, and took to his pumps without looking at man or mortal, and neither sun, moon or stars ever saw him in sight of Dublin again.

At dinner everyone laughed but the foxy fellow; and sure enough he was laying out how he'd settle poor Tom next day.

'Well, to be sure!' says he. 'King of Dublin, you are in luck. There's the Danes moidhering us to no end. Deuce run to Lusk wid 'em! And if anyone can save us from 'em, it is this gentleman with the goatskin. There is a flail hangin' on the collar-beam in hell, and neither Dane nor devil can stand before it.'

'So,' says Tom to the king, 'will you let me have the other part of the princess if I bring you the flail?'

'No, no,' says the princess. 'I'd rather never be your wife than see you in that danger.'

But Redhead whispered and nudged Tom about how shabby it would look to renegue on the adventure. So he asked which way he was to go, and Redhead directed him.

Well, he travelled and travelled, till he came in sight of the walls of hell; and, bedad, before he knocked at the gates, he rubbed himself all over with the greenish ointment. When he knocked, a hundred little imps popped their heads out through the bars, and axed him what he wanted.

'I want to speak to the big divel of all,' says Tom. 'Open the gate.'

It wasn't long till the gate was thrune open, and the Ould Boy received Tom with bows and scrapes, and axed his business.

'My business isn't much,' says Tom. 'I only came for the loan of that flail that I see hanging on the collar-beam, for the King of Dublin to give a thrashing to the Danes.'

'Well,' says the other, 'the Danes is much better customers to me; but since you walked so far, I won't refuse. Hand that flail,' says he to a young imp; and he winked the far-off eye at the same time. So, while some were barring the gates, the young devil climbed up, and took down the flail that had the handstaff and booltheen both made out of red-hot iron. The little vagabond was grinning to think how it would burn the hands o' Tom, but the dickens a burn it made on him, no more nor if it was a good oak sapling.

'Thankee,' says Tom. 'Now would you open the gate for a body, and I'll give you no more trouble.'

'Oh, tramp!' says Ould Nick. 'Is that the way? It is easier getting inside them gates than getting out again. Take that tool from him, and give him a dose of the oil of stirrup.'

So one fellow put out his claws to seize on the flail, but Tom gave him such a welt of it on the side of the head that he broke off one of his horns, and made him roar like a devil as

307

he was. Well, they rushed at Tom, but he gave them, little and big, such a thrashing as they didn't forget for a while. At last says the ould thief of all, rubbing his elbow, 'Let the fool out; and woe to whoever lets him in again, great or small.'

So out marched Tom, and away with him, without minding the shouting and cursing they kept up at him from the tops of the walls; and when he got home to the big bawn of the palace, there never was such running and racing as to see himself and the flail. When he had his story told, he laid down the flail on the stone steps, and bid no one for their lives to touch it. If the king, and queen, and princess, made much of him before, they made ten times more of him now; but Redhead, the mean scruffhound, stole over, and thought to catch hold of the flail to make an end of him. His fingers had hardly touched it when he let a roar out of him as if heaven and earth were coming together, and kept flinging his arms about and dancing so that it was pitiful to look at him. Tom ran at him as soon as he could rise, caught his hands in his own two, and rubbed them this way and that, and the burning pain left them before you could reckon one. Well the poor fellow, between the pain that was only just gone and the comfort he was in, had the comicalest face that you ever see, it was such a mixtherum-gatherum of laughing and crying. Everybody burst out a-laughing – the princess could not stop no more than the rest; and then says Tom, 'Now, ma'am, if there were fifty parts of you, I hope you'll give me them all.'

Well, the princess looked at her father, and by my word, she came over to Tom, and put her two delicate hands into his two rough ones, and I wish it was myself was in his shoes that day!

Tom would not bring the flail into the palace. You may be sure no other body went near it; and when the early risers were passing next morning, they found two long clefts in the stone where it was after burning itself an opening downwards, nobody could tell how far. But a messenger came in at noon, and said that the Danes were so frightened when they heard of the flail coming into Dublin, that they got into their ships and sailed away.

Well, I suppose, before they were married, Tom got some man, like Pat Mara of Tomenine, to learn him the 'principles of politeness', fluxions, gunnery and fortification, decimal fractions, practice and the rule of three direct, so that he'd be able to keep up a conversation with the royal family. Whether he ever lost his time learning them sciences, I'm not sure, but it's as sure as fate that his mother never more saw any want till the end of her days.

The Laidly Worm of Spindlestone Heugh

In Bamborough Castle once lived a king who had a fair wife and two children, a son named Childe Wynd and a daughter named Margaret. Childe Wynd went forth to seek his fortune, and soon after he had gone the queen his mother died. The king mourned her long and faithfully, but one day while he was hunting he came across a lady of great beauty, and became so much in love with her that he determined to marry her. So he sent word home that he was going to bring a new queen to Bamborough Castle.

Princess Margaret was not very glad to hear of her mother's place being taken, but she did not repine but did her father's bidding, and at the appointed day came down to the castle gate with the keys all ready to hand over to her stepmother. Soon the procession drew near, and the new queen came towards Princess Margaret, who bowed low and handed her the keys of the castle. She stood there with blushing cheeks and eye on the ground, and said: 'Oh welcome, father dear, to your halls and bowers, and welcome to you my new mother, for all that's here is yours,' and again she offered the keys. One of the king's knights, who had escorted the new queen, cried out in admiration: 'Surely this northern princess is the loveliest of her kind.' At that the new queen flushed up and cried out: 'At least your courtesy might have excepted me,' and then she muttered below her breath: 'I'll soon put an end to her beauty.'

That same night the queen, who was a noted witch, stole down to a lonely dungeon wherein she did her magic, and with spells three times three and with passes nine times nine she cast Princess Margaret under her spell. And this was her spell:

'I weird ye to be a Laidly Worm,
And restored shall ye never be,
Until Childe Wynd, the king's own son,
Come to the Heugh and thrice kiss thee;
Until the world comes to an end,
Restored shall ye never be.'

So Lady Margaret went to bed a beauteous maiden, and rose up a Laidly Worm. And when her maidens came in to dress her in the morning they found coiled up on the bed a dreadful dragon, which uncoiled itself and came towards them. But they ran away shrieking, and the Laidly Worm crawled and crept, and crept and crawled, till it reached the Heugh or rock of the Spindlestone, round which it coiled itself, and lay there basking with its terrible snout in the air.

The Laidly Worm crawled and crept, and crept and crawled, till it reached the Heugh or rock of the Spindlestone, round which it coiled itself

Soon the country round about had reason to know of the Laidly Worm of Spindlestone Heugh. For hunger drove the monster out from its cave and it used to devour everything it could come across. So at last they went to a mighty warlock and asked him what they should do. Then he consulted his works and his familiar, and told them: 'The Laidly Worm is really the Princess Margaret and it is hunger that drives her forth to do such deeds. Put aside for her seven kine, and each day as the sun goes down, carry every drop of milk they yield to the stone trough at the foot of the Heugh, and the Laidly Worm will trouble the country no longer. But if ye would that she be restored to her natural shape, and that she who bespelled her be rightly punished, send over the seas for her brother, Childe Wynd.'

All was done as the warlock advised, the Laidly Worm lived on the milk of the seven kine, and the country was troubled no longer. But when Childe Wynd heard the news, he swore a mighty oath to rescue his sister and revenge her on her cruel step-mother. And three-and-thirty of his men took the oath with him. Then they set to work and built a long ship, and its keel they made of the rowan tree. And when all was ready, they out with their oars and pulled sheer for Bamborough Keep.

But as they got near the keep, the stepmother felt by her magic power that something was being wrought against her, so she summoned her familiar imps and said: 'Childe Wynd is coming over the seas; he must never land. Raise storms, or bore the hull, but nohow must he touch shore.' Then the imps went forth to meet Childe Wynd's ship, but when they got near, they found they had no power over the ship, for its keel was made of the rowan tree. So back they came to the queen witch, who knew not what to do. She ordered her men-at-arms to resist Childe Wynd if he should land near them, and by her spells she caused the Laidly Worm to wait by the entrance of the harbour.

As the ship came near, the Worm unfolded its coils, and dipping into the sea, caught hold of the ship of Childe Wynd, and kept it off the shore. Three times Childe Wynd urged his men on to row bravely and strong, but each time the Laidly Worm kept it off the shore. Then Childe Wynd ordered the ship to be put about, and the witch-queen thought he had given up the attempt. But instead of that, he only rounded the next point and landed safe and sound in Budle Creek, and then, with sword drawn and bow bent, rushed up followed by his men to fight the terrible Worm that had kept him from landing.

But the moment Childe Wynd had landed, the witch-queen's power over the Laidly Worm had gone, and she went back to her bower all alone, not an imp, nor a man-at-arms to help her, for she knew her hour was come. So when Childe Wynd came rushing up to the Laidly Worm it made no attempt to stop him or hurt him, but just as he was going to raise his sword to slay it, the voice of his own sister Margaret came from its jaws saying:

> 'Oh, quit your sword, unbend your bow,
> And give me kisses three;
> For though I am a poisonous worm,
> No harm I'll do to thee.'

Childe Wynd stayed his hand, but he did not know if some witchery were not in it. Then said the Laidly Worm again:

> 'Oh, quit your sword, unbend your bow,
> And give me kisses three,
> If I'm not won ere set of sun,
> Won never shall I be.'

Then Childe Wynd went up to the Laidly Worm and kissed it once; but no change came over it. Then Childe Wynd kissed it once more; but yet no change came over it. For a third time he kissed the loathsome thing, and with a hiss and a roar the Laidly Worm reared back and before Childe Wynd stood his sister Margaret. He wrapped his cloak about her, and then went up to the castle with her. When he reached the keep, he went off to the witch-queen's bower, and when he saw her, he touched her with a twig of a rowan tree. No sooner had he touched her than she shrivelled up and shrivelled up, till she became a huge ugly toad, with bold staring eyes and a horrible hiss. She croaked and she hissed, and then hopped away down the castle steps, and Childe Wynd took his father's place as king, and they all lived happy afterwards. But to this day, the loathsome toad is seen at times, haunting the neighbourhood of Bamborough Keep, and the wicked witch-queen is that Laidly Toad.

Lazy Jack

Once upon a time there was a boy whose name was Jack, and he lived with his mother on a common. They were very poor, and the old woman got her living by spinning, but Jack was so lazy that he would do nothing but bask in the sun in the hot weather, and sit by the corner of the hearth in the wintertime. So they called him Lazy Jack. His mother could not get him to do anything for her, and at last told him, one Monday, that if he did not begin to work for his porridge she would turn him out to get his living as he could.

This roused Jack, and he went out and hired himself for the next day to a neighbouring farmer for a penny; but as he was coming home, never having had any money before, he lost it in passing over a brook. 'You stupid boy,' said his mother, 'you should have put it in your pocket.' 'I'll do so another time,' replied Jack.

On Wednesday, Jack went out again and hired himself to a cow-keeper, who gave him a jar of milk for his day's work. Jack took the jar and put it into the large pocket of his jacket, spilling it all, long before he got home. 'Dear me!' said the old woman; 'you should have carried it on your head.' 'I'll do so another time,' said Jack.

So on Thursday, Jack hired himself again to a farmer, who agreed to give him a cream cheese for his services. In the evening Jack took the cheese, and went home with it on his head. By the time he got home the cheese was all spoilt, part of it being lost, and part matted with his hair. 'You stupid lout,' said his mother, 'you should have carried it very carefully in your hands.' 'I'll do so another time,' replied Jack.

On Friday, Lazy Jack again went out, and hired himself to a baker, who would give him nothing for his work but a large tom-cat. Jack took the cat, and began carrying it very carefully in his hands, but in a short time pussy scratched him so much that he was compelled to let it go. When he got home, his mother said to him, 'You silly fellow, you should have tied it with a string, and dragged it along after you.' 'I'll do so another time,' said Jack.

So on Saturday, Jack hired himself to a butcher, who rewarded him by the handsome present of a shoulder of mutton. Jack took the mutton, tied it to a string, and trailed it along after him in the dirt, so that by the time he had got home the meat was completely spoilt. His mother was this time quite out of patience with him, for the next day was Sunday, and she was obliged to make do with cabbage for her dinner. 'You ninney-hammer,' said she to her son; 'you should have carried it on your shoulder.' 'I'll do so another time,' replied Jack.

On the next Monday, Lazy Jack went once more, and hired himself to a cattle-keeper, who gave him a donkey for his trouble. Jack found it hard to hoist the donkey on his shoulders, but at last he did it, and began walking slowly home with his prize. Now it happened that in the course of his journey there lived a rich man with his only daughter, a beautiful girl, but deaf and dumb. Now she had never laughed in her life, and the doctors said she would never speak till somebody made her laugh. This young lady happened to be looking out of the window when Jack was passing with the donkey on his shoulders, with the legs sticking up in the air, and the sight was so comical and strange that she burst out into a great fit of laughter, and immediately recovered her speech and hearing. Her father was overjoyed, and fulfilled his promise by marrying her to Lazy Jack, who was thus made a rich gentleman. They lived in a large house, and Jack's mother lived with them in great happiness until she died.

The Little Mermaid

Far out at sea the water is as blue as the bluest cornflower, and as clear as the clearest crystal; but it is very deep, too deep for any cable to fathom, and if many steeples were piled on the top of one another they would not reach from the bed of the sea to the surface of the water. It is down there that the mermen live.

Now don't imagine that there are only bare white sands at the bottom; oh no! the most wonderful trees and plants grow there, with such flexible stalks and leaves that at the slightest motion of the water they move just as if they were alive. All the fish, big and little, glide among the branches just as, up here, birds glide through the air. The palace of the merman king lies in the very deepest part; its walls are of coral and the long pointed windows of the clearest amber, but the roof is made of mussel shells which open and shut with the lapping of the water. This has a lovely effect, for there are gleaming pearls in every shell, any one of which would be the pride of a queen's crown.

The merman king had been for many years a widower, but his old mother kept house for him; she was a clever woman, but so proud of her noble birth that she wore twelve oysters on her tail, while the other grandees were only allowed six. Otherwise she was worthy of all praise, especially because she was so fond of the little mermaid princesses, her grandchildren. They were six beautiful children, but the youngest was the prettiest of all, her skin was as soft and delicate as a rose leaf, her eyes as blue as the deepest sea, but like all the others she had no feet, and instead of legs she had a fish's tail.

All the livelong day they used to play in the palace in the great halls, where living flowers grew out of the walls. When the great amber windows were thrown open the fish swam in, just as the swallows fly into our rooms when we open the windows, but the fish swam right up to the little princesses, ate out of their hands and allowed themselves to be patted.

Outside the palace was a large garden, with fiery red and deep blue trees, the fruit of which shone like gold, while the flowers glowed like fire on their ceaselessly waving stalks. The ground was of the finest sand, but it was of a blue phosphorescent tint. Everything was bathed in a wondrous blue light down there; you might more readily have supposed yourself to be high up in the air, with only the sky above and below you, than that you were at the bottom of the ocean. In a dead calm you could just catch a glimpse of the sun like a purple flower with a stream of light radiating from its calyx.

Each little princess had her own little plot of garden, where she could dig and plant just as she liked. One made her flower-bed in the shape of a whale, another thought it nice to have hers like a little mermaid; but the youngest made hers quite round like the sun, and she would only have flowers of a rosy hue like its beams. She was a curious child, quiet and thoughtful, and while the other sisters decked out their gardens with all kinds of extraordinary objects which they got from wrecks, she would have nothing besides the rosy flowers like the sun up above, except a statue of a beautiful boy. It was hewn out of the purest white marble and had gone to the bottom from some wreck. By the statue she planted a rosy red weeping willow which grew splendidly, and the fresh delicate branches hung round and over it, till they almost touched the blue sand where the shadows showed violet, and were ever moving like the branches. It looked as if the leaves and the roots were playfully interchanging kisses.

Nothing gave her greater pleasure than to hear about the world of human beings up above; she made her old grandmother tell her all that she knew about ships and towns, people and animals. But above all it seemed strangely beautiful to her that up on the earth the flowers were scented, for they were not so at the bottom of the sea; also that the woods were green, and that the fish which were to be seen among the branches could sing so loudly and sweetly that it was a delight to listen to them. You see the grandmother called little birds fish, or the mermaids would not have understood her, as they had never seen a bird.

'When you are fifteen,' said the grandmother, 'you will be allowed to rise up from the sea and sit on the rocks in the moonlight, and look at the big ships sailing by, and you will also see woods and towns.'

One of the sisters would be fifteen in the following year, but the others – well, they were each one year younger than the other, so that the youngest had five whole years to wait before she would be allowed to come up from the bottom, to see what things were like on earth. But each one promised the others to give a full account of all that she had seen, and found most wonderful on the first day. Their grandmother could never tell them enough, for there were so many things about which they wanted information.

None of them was so full of longings as the youngest, the very one who had the longest time to wait, and who was so quiet and dreamy. Many a night she stood by the open windows and looked up through the dark blue water which the fish were lashing with their tails and fins. She could see the moon and the stars, it is true, their light was pale but they looked much bigger through the water than they do to our eyes. When she saw a dark shadow glide between her and them, she knew that it was either a whale swimming above her, or else a ship laden with human beings. I am certain they never dreamt that a lovely little mermaid was standing down below, stretching up her white hands towards the keel.

The eldest princess had now reached her fifteenth birthday, and was to venture above the water. When she came back she had hundreds of things to tell them, but the most delightful of all, she said, was to lie in the moonlight, on a sandbank in a calm sea, and to gaze at the large town close to the shore, where the lights twinkled like hundreds of stars; to listen to music and the noise and bustle of carriages and people, to see the many church towers and spires, and to hear the bells ringing; and just because she could not go on shore she longed for that most of all.

Oh! how eagerly the youngest sister listened, and when, later in the evening, she stood at the open window and looked up through the dark-blue water, she thought of the big town with all its noise and bustle, and fancied that she could even hear the church bells ringing.

The year after, the second sister was allowed to mount up through the water and swim about wherever she liked. The sun was just going down when she reached the surface, the most beautiful sight, she thought, that she had ever seen. The whole sky had looked like gold, she said, and as for the clouds! well, their beauty was beyond description, they floated in red and violet splendour over her head, and far faster than they went, a flock of wild swans flew like a long white veil over the water towards the setting sun; she swam towards it, but it sank and all the rosy light on clouds and water faded away.

The year after that the third sister went up, and being much the most venturesome of them all, swam up a broad river which ran into the sea. She saw beautiful green, vine-clad hills; palaces and country seats peeping through splendid woods. She heard the birds singing, and the sun was so hot that she was often obliged to dive, to cool her burning face. In a tiny bay she found a troop of little children running about naked and paddling in the water; she wanted to play with them, but they were frightened and ran away. Then a little black animal came up, it was a dog, but she had never seen one before; it barked so furiously at her that she was frightened and made for the open sea. She could never forget the beautiful woods, the green hills and the lovely children who could swim in the water although they had no fishes' tails

The fourth sister was not so brave, she stayed in the remotest part of the ocean, and, according to her account, that was the most beautiful spot. You could see for miles and miles around you, and the sky above was like a great glass dome. She had seen ships, but only far away, so that they looked like seagulls. There were grotesque dolphins turning somersaults, and gigantic whales squirting water through their nostrils like hundreds of fountains on every side.

Now the fifth sister's turn came. Her birthday fell in the winter, so that she saw sights that the others had not seen on their first trips. The sea looked quite green, and large icebergs were floating about, each one of which looked like a pearl, she said, but was much bigger than the church towers built by men. They took the most wonderful shapes, and sparkled like diamonds. She had seated herself on one of the largest, and all the passing ships sheered of in alarm when they saw her sitting there with her long hair streaming loose in the wind.

In the evening the sky became overcast with dark clouds; it thundered and lightning flashed, and the huge icebergs glittering in the bright lightning were lifted high into the air by the black waves. All the ships shortened sail, and there was fear and trembling on every side, but she sat quietly on her floating iceberg watching the blue lightning dart in zigzags down on to the shining sea.

The first time any of the sisters rose above the water she was delighted by the novelties and beauties she saw; but once grown up, and at liberty to go where she liked, she became indifferent and longed for her home; in the course of a month or so they all said that after all their own home in the deep was best, it was so cosy there.

Many an evening the five sisters interlacing their arms would rise above the water together. They had lovely voices, much clearer than any mortal, and when a storm was rising, and they expected ships to be wrecked, they would sing in the most seductive strains of the wonders of the deep, bidding the sea-farers have no fear of them. But the sailors could not understand the words, they thought it was the voice of the storm; nor could it be theirs to see this Elysium of the deep, for when the ship sank they were drowned, and only reached the merman's palace in death. When the elder sisters rose up in this manner, arm in arm, in the evening, the youngest remained behind quite alone, looking after them as if she must weep, but mermaids have no tears and so they suffer all the more.

'Oh! if I were only fifteen!' she said, 'I know how fond I shall be of the world above, and of the mortals who dwell there.'

At last her fifteenth birthday came.

'Now we shall have you off our hands,' said her grandmother, the old queen dowager. 'Come now, let me adorn you like your other sisters!' and she put a wreath of white lilies round her hair, but every petal of the flowers was half a pearl; then the old queen had eight oysters fixed on to the princess's tail to show her high rank.

'But it hurts so!' said the little mermaid.

'You must endure the pain for the sake of the finery!' said her grandmother.

But oh! how gladly would she have shaken off all this splendour, and laid aside the heavy wreath. Her red flowers in her garden suited her much better, but she did not dare to make any alteration. 'Goodbye,' she said, and mounted as lightly and airily as a bubble through the water.

The sun had just set when her head rose above the water, but the clouds were still lighted up with a rosy and golden splendour, and the evening star sparkled in the soft pink sky, the air was mild and fresh, and the sea as calm as a millpond. A big three-masted ship lay close by with only a single sail set, for there was not a breath of wind, and the sailors were sitting about the rigging, on the cross trees and at the mastheads. There was music and singing on board, and as the evening closed in, hundreds of gaily coloured lanterns were lighted – they looked like the flags of all nations waving in the air. The little mermaid swam right up to the cabin windows, and every time she was lifted by the swell she could see through the transparent panes crowds of gaily dressed people. The handsomest of them all was the young prince with large dark eyes; he could not be much more than sixteen, and all these festivities were in honour of his birthday. The sailors danced on deck, and when the prince appeared among them hundreds of rockets were let off making it as light as day, and frightening the little mermaid so much that she had to dive under the water. She soon ventured up again, and it was just as if all the stars of heaven were falling in showers round about her. She had never seen such magic fires. Great suns whirled round, gorgeous fire-fish hung in the blue air, and all was reflected in the calm and glassy sea. It was so light on board the ship that every little rope could be seen, and the people still better. Oh! how handsome the prince was, how he laughed and smiled as he greeted his guests, while the music rang out in the quiet night.

It got quite late, but the little mermaid could not take her eyes off the ship and the beautiful prince. The coloured lanterns were put out, no more rockets were sent up, and the cannon had ceased its thunder, but deep down in the sea there was a dull murmuring and moaning sound. Meanwhile she was rocked up and down on the waves, so that she could look into the cabin; but the ship got more and more way on, sail after sail was filled by the wind, the waves grew stronger, great clouds gathered, and lightning forked in the distance. Oh, there was going to be a fearful storm! and soon the sailors had to shorten sail. The great ship rocked and rolled as she dashed over the angry sea, the black waves rose like mountains, high enough to overwhelm her, but she dived like a swan through them and rose again and again on their towering crests. The little mermaid thought it a most amusing race, but not so the sailors. The ship creaked and groaned, the mighty timbers bulged and bent under the heavy blows, the water broke over the decks, snapping the main mast like a reed, she heeled over on her side and the water rushed into the hold.

Now the little mermaid saw that they were in danger and she had for her own sake to beware of the floating beams and wreckage. One moment it was so pitch dark that she could not see at all, but when the lightning flashed it became so light that she could see all on board. Every man was looking out for his own safety as best he could, but she more particularly followed the young prince with her eyes, and when the ship went down she saw him sink in the deep sea. At first she was quite delighted, for now he was coming to be with her, but then she remembered that human beings could not live under water, and that only if he were dead

could he go to her father's palace. No! he must not die; so she swam towards him all among the drifting beams and planks, quite forgetting that they might crush her. She dived deep down under the water, and came up again through the waves, and at last reached the young prince just as he was becoming unable to swim any farther in the stormy sea. His limbs were numbed, his beautiful eyes were closed, and he must have died if the little mermaid had not come to the rescue. She held his head above the water and let the waves drive them whithersoever they would.

By daybreak all the storm was over, of the ship not a trace was to be seen; the sun rose from the water in radiant brilliance and his rosy beams seemed to cast a glow of life into the prince's cheeks, but his eyes remained closed. The mermaid kissed his fair and lofty brow, and stroked back the dripping hair; it seemed to her that he was like the marble statue in her little garden, she kissed him again and longed that he might live.

At last she saw dry land before her, high blue mountains on whose summits the white snow glistened as if a flock of swans had settled there; down by the shore were beautiful green woods, and in the foreground a church or temple, she did not quite know which, but it was a building of some sort. Lemon and orange trees grew in the garden and lofty palms stood by the gate. At this point the sea formed a little bay where the water was quite calm, but very deep, right up to the cliffs; at their foot was a strip of fine white sand to which she swam with the beautiful prince, and laid him down on it, taking great care that his head should rest high up in the warm sunshine.

The bells now began to ring in the great white building and a number of young maidens came into the garden. Then the little mermaid swam further off behind some high rocks and covered her hair and breast with foam, so that no one should see her little face, and then she watched to see who would discover the poor prince.

It was not long before one of the maidens came up to him; at first she seemed quite frightened, but only for a moment, and then she fetched several others, and the mermaid saw that the prince was coming to life, and that he smiled at all those around him, though he had never smiled at her; you see he did not know that she had saved him; she felt so sad that when he was led away into the great building she dived sorrowfully into the water and made her way home to her father's palace.

Always silent and thoughtful, she became more so now than ever. Her sisters often asked her what she had seen on her first visit to the surface, but she never would tell them anything.

Many an evening and many a morning she would rise to the place where she had left the prince. She saw the fruit in the garden ripen, and then gathered, she saw the snow melt on the mountain-tops, but she never saw the prince, so she always went home still sadder than before. At home her only consolation was to sit in her little garden with her arms twined round the handsome marble statue which reminded her of the prince. It was all in gloomy shade now, as she had ceased to tend her flowers and the garden had become a neglected wilderness of long stalks and leaves entangled with the branches of the tree.

At last she could not bear it any longer, so she told one of her sisters, and from her it soon spread to the others, but to no one else except to one or two other mermaids who only told their dearest friends. One of these knew all about the prince, she had also seen the festivities on the ship; she knew where he came from and where his kingdom was situated.

'Come, little sister!' said the other princesses, and, throwing their arms round each other's shoulders, they rose from the water in a long line, just in front of the prince's palace.

It was built of light yellow glistening stone, with great marble staircases, one of which led into the garden. Magnificent gilded cupolas rose above the roof, and the spaces between the columns which encircled the building were filled with lifelike marble statues. Through the clear glass of the lofty windows you could see gorgeous halls adorned with costly silken hangings, and the pictures on the walls were a sight worth seeing. In the midst of the central hall a large fountain played, throwing its jets of spray upwards to a glass dome in the roof, through which the sunbeams lighted up the water and the beautiful plants which grew in the great basin.

She knew now where he lived and often used to go there in the evenings and by night over the water; she swam much nearer the land than any of the others dared, she even ventured right up the narrow channel under the splendid marble terrace which threw a long shadow over the water. She used to sit here looking at the young prince who thought he was quite alone in the clear moonlight.

She saw him many an evening sailing about in his beautiful boat, with flags waving and music playing; she used to peep through the green rushes, and if the wind happened to catch her long silvery veil and anyone saw it, they only thought it was a swan flapping its wings.

Many a night she heard the fishermen, who were fishing by torchlight, talking over the good deeds of the young prince; and she was happy to think that she had saved his life when he was drifting about on the waves, half dead, and she could not forget how closely his head had pressed her breast, and how passionately she had kissed him; but he knew nothing of all this, and never saw her even in his dreams.

She became fonder and fonder of mankind, and longed more and more to be able to live among them; their world seemed so infinitely bigger than hers; with their ships they could scour the ocean, they could ascend the mountains high above the clouds, and their wooded, grass-grown lands extended farther than her eye could reach. There was so much that she wanted to know, but her sisters could not give an answer to all her questions, so she asked her old grandmother who knew the upper world well, and rightly called it the country above the sea.

'If men are not drowned,' asked the little mermaid, 'do they live for ever. Do they not die as we do down here in the sea?'

'Yes,' said the old lady, 'they have to die too, and their lifetime is even shorter than ours. We may live here for three hundred years, but when we cease to exist we become mere foam on the water and do not have so much as a grave among our dear ones. We have no immortal souls, we have no future life, we are just like the green seaweed, which once cut down can never revive again! Men, on the other hand, have a soul which lives for ever, lives after the body has become dust; it rises through the clear air, up to the shining stars! Just as we rise from the water to see the land of mortals, so they rise up to unknown beautiful regions which we shall never see.'

'Why have we no immortal souls?' asked the little mermaid sadly. 'I would give all my three hundred years to be a human being for one day, and afterwards to have a share in the heavenly kingdom.'

'You must not be thinking about that,' said the grandmother, 'we are much better off and happier than human beings.'

'Then I shall have to die and to float as foam on the water, and never hear the music of the waves or see the beautiful flowers or the red sun! Is there nothing I can do to gain an immortal soul?'

'No,' said the grandmother; 'only if a human being so loved you that you were more to him than father or mother, if all his thoughts and all his love were so centred in you that he would let the priest join your hands and would vow to be faithful to you here, and to all eternity; then your body would become infused with his soul. Thus and only thus, could you gain a share in the felicity of mankind. He would give you a soul while yet keeping his own. But that can never happen! That which is your greatest beauty in the sea, your fish's tail, is thought hideous up on earth, so little do they understand about it; to be pretty there you must have two clumsy supports which they call legs!'

Then the little mermaid sighed and looked sadly at her fish's tail.

'Let us be happy,' said the grandmother; 'we will hop and skip during our three hundred years of life, it is surely a long enough time, and after it is over, we shall rest all the better in the foamy deep. There is to be a court ball tonight.'

This was a much more splendid affair than we ever see on earth. The walls and the ceiling of the great ballroom were of thick but transparent glass. Several hundreds of colossal mussel shells, rose-red and grass-green, were ranged in order round the sides holding blue lights, which illuminated the whole room and shone through the walls, so that the sea outside was quite lit up. You could see countless fish, great and small, swimming towards the glass walls, some with shining scales of crimson hue, while others were golden and silvery. In the middle of the room was a broad stream of running water, and on this the mermaids and mermen danced to their own beautiful singing. No earthly beings have such lovely voices. The little mermaid sang more sweetly than any of them and they all applauded her. For a moment she felt glad at heart, for she knew that she had the finest voice either in the sea or on land. But she soon began to think again about the upper world; she could not forget

the handsome prince and her sorrow in not possessing, like him, an immortal soul. Therefore she stole out of her father's palace, and while all within was joy and merriment, she sat sadly in her little garden. Suddenly she heard the sound of a horn through the water, and she thought, 'Now he is out sailing up there; he whom I love more than father or mother, he to whom my thoughts cling and to whose hands I am ready to commit the happiness of my life. I will dare anything to win him and to gain an immortal soul! While my sisters are dancing in my father's palace, I will go to the sea witch of whom I have always been very much afraid, she will perhaps be able to advise and help me!'

Thereupon the little mermaid left the garden and went towards the roaring whirlpools at the back of which the witch lived. She had never been that way before; no flowers grew there, no seaweed, only the bare grey sands stretched towards the whirlpools, which like rushing mill-wheels swirled round, dragging everything that came within reach down to the depths. She had to pass between these boiling eddies to reach the witch's domain, and for a long way the only path led over warm bubbling mud, which the witch called her 'peat bog'. Her house stood behind this in the midst of a weird forest. All the trees and bushes were polyps, half animal and half plant; they looked like hundred-headed snakes growing out of the sand: the branches were long slimy arms, with tentacles like wriggling worms, every joint of which from the root to the outermost tip was in constant motion. They wound themselves tightly round whatever they could lay hold of and never let it escape. The little mermaid standing outside was quite frightened, her heart beat fast with terror and she nearly turned back; but then she remembered the prince and the immortal soul of mankind and took courage. She bound her long flowing hair tightly round her head, so that the polyps should not seize her by it, folded her hands over her breast, and darted like a fish through the water, in between the hideous polyps which stretched out their sensitive arms and tentacles towards her. She could see that every one of them had something or other, which they had grasped with their hundred arms, and which they held as if in iron bands. The bleached bones of men who had perished at sea and sunk below peeped forth from the arms of some, while others clutched rudders and sea chests, or the skeleton of some land animal; and most horrible of all, a little mermaid whom they had caught and suffocated. Then she came to a large opening in the wood where the ground was all slimy and where some huge fat water snakes were gambolling about. In the middle of this opening was a house built of the bones of the wrecked; there sat the witch, letting a toad eat out of her mouth, just as mortals let a little canary eat sugar. She called the hideous water-snakes her little chickens, and allowed them to crawl about on her unsightly bosom.

'I know very well what you have come here for,' said the witch. 'It is very foolish of you! All the same you shall have your way, because it will lead you into misfortune, my fine princess. You want to get rid of your fish's tail, and instead to have two stumps to walk about upon like human beings, so that the young prince may fall in love with you, and that you may win him and an immortal soul.' Saying this, she gave such a loud hideous laugh that the toad and the snakes fell to the ground and wriggled about there.

'You are just in the nick of time,' said the witch. 'After sunrise tomorrow I should not be able to help you until another year had run its course. I will make you a potion, and before sunrise you must swim ashore with it, seat yourself on the beach and drink it; then your tail will divide and shrivel up to what men call beautiful legs; but it hurts, it is as if a sharp sword were running through you. All who see you will say that you are the most beautiful child of man they have ever seen. You will keep your gliding gait, no dancer will rival you, but every step you take will be as if you were treading upon sharp knives, so sharp as to draw blood. If you are willing to suffer all this I am ready to help you!'

'Yes!' said the little princess with a trembling voice, thinking of the prince and of winning an undying soul.

'But remember,' said the witch, 'when once you have received a human form, you can never be a mermaid again, you will never again be able to dive down through the water to your sisters and to your father's palace. And if you do not succeed in winning the prince's love, so that for your sake he will forget father and mother, cleave to you with his whole heart, let the priest join your hands and make you man and wife, you will gain no immortal soul! The first morning after his marriage with another your heart will break, and you will turn into foam of the sea.'

'I will do it,' said the little mermaid as pale as death.

'But you will have to pay me, too,' said the witch, 'and it is no trifle that I demand. You have the most beautiful voice of any at the bottom of the sea, and I dare say that you think you will fascinate him with it, but you must give me that voice. I will have the best you possess in return for my precious potion! I have to mingle my own blood with it so as to make it as sharp as a two-edged sword.'

'But if you take my voice,' said the little mermaid, 'what have I left?'

'Your beautiful form,' said the witch, 'your gliding gait, and your speaking eyes, with these you ought surely to be able to bewitch a human heart. Well! have you lost courage? Put out your little tongue and I will cut it off in payment for the powerful draught.'

'Let it be done,' said the little mermaid, and

the witch put on her cauldron to brew the magic potion. 'There is nothing like cleanliness,' said she, as she scoured the pot with a bundle of snakes; then she punctured her breast and let the black blood drop into the cauldron, and the steam took the most weird shapes, enough to frighten anyone. Every moment the witch threw new ingredients into the pot, and when it boiled the bubbling was like the sound of crocodiles weeping. At last the potion was ready and it looked like the clearest water.

'There it is,' said the witch, and thereupon she cut off the tongue of the little mermaid, who was dumb now and could neither sing nor speak.

'If the polyps should seize you, when you go back through my wood,' said the witch, 'just drop a single drop of this liquid on them, and their arms and fingers will burst into a thousand pieces.' But the little mermaid had no need to do this, for at the mere sight of the bright liquid which sparkled in her hand like a shining star, they drew back in terror. So she soon got past the wood, the bog and the eddying whirlpools

She saw her father's palace, the lights were all out in the great ballroom, and no doubt all the household was asleep, but she did not dare to go in now that she was dumb and about to leave her home for ever. She felt as if her heart would break with grief. She stole into the garden and plucked a flower from each of her sister's plots, wafted with her hand countless kisses towards the palace, and then rose up through the dark blue water.

The sun had not risen when she came in sight of the prince's palace and landed at the beautiful marble steps. The moon was shining bright and clear. The little mermaid drank the burning, stinging draught, and it was like a sharp, two-edged sword running through her tender frame; she fainted away and lay as if she were dead. When the sun rose on the sea she woke up and became conscious of a sharp pang but just in front of her stood the handsome young prince, fixing his coal-black eyes on her; she cast hers down and saw that her fish's tail was gone, and that she had the prettiest little white legs any maiden could desire, but she was quite naked, so she wrapped her long thick hair around her. The prince asked who she was and how she came there; she looked at him tenderly and with a sad expression in her dark blue eyes, but could not speak. Then he took her by the hand and led her into the palace. Every step she took was, as the witch had warned her beforehand,

as if she were treading on sharp knives and spikes but she bore it gladly; led by the prince she moved as lightly as a bubble, and he and everyone else marvelled at her graceful gliding gait.

Clothed in the costliest silks and muslins she was the greatest beauty in the palace, but she was dumb and could neither sing nor speak. Beautiful slaves clad in silks and gold came forward and sang to the prince and his royal parents; one of them sang better than all the others, and the prince clapped his hands and smiled at her; that made the little mermaid very sad, for she knew that she used to sing far better herself. She thought, 'Oh! if he only knew that for the sake of being with him I had given up my voice for ever!' Now the slaves began to perform, graceful and undulating dances to enchanting music; thereupon the little mermaid lifting her beautiful white arms and raising herself on tiptoe glided on the floor with a grace which none of the other dancers had yet attained. With every motion her grace and beauty became more apparent, and her eyes appealed more deeply to the heart than the songs of the slaves. Everyone was delighted with it, especially the prince, who called her his little foundling, and she danced on and on, notwithstanding that every time her foot touched the ground it was like treading on sharp knives. The prince said that she should always be near him, and she was allowed to sleep outside his door on a velvet cushion.

He had a man's dress made for her, so that she could ride about with him. They used to ride through scented woods, where the green branches brushed her shoulders, and little birds sang among the fresh leaves. She climbed up the highest mountains with the prince, and although her delicate feet bled so that others saw it, she only laughed and followed him until they saw the clouds sailing below them like a flock of birds, taking flight to distant lands.

At home in the prince's palace, when at night the others were asleep, she used to go out on to the marble steps; it cooled her burning feet to stand in the cold sea water, and at such times she used to think of those she had left in the deep.

One night her sisters came arm in arm; they sang so sorrowfully as they swam on the water that she beckoned to them and they recognised her, and told her how she had grieved them all. After that they visited her every night, and one night she saw, a long way out, her old grandmother (who for many years had not been above the water), and

the merman king with his crown on his head; they stretched out their hands towards her, but did not venture so close to land as her sisters.

Day by day she became dearer to the prince, he loved her as one loves a good sweet child, but it never entered his head to make her his queen; yet unless she became his wife she would never win an everlasting soul, but on his wedding morning would turn to sea foam.

'Am I not dearer to you than any of them?' the little mermaid's eyes seemed to say when he took her in his arms and kissed her beautiful brow.

'Yes, you are the dearest one to me,' said the prince, 'for you have the best heart of them all, and you are fondest of me; you are also like a young girl I once saw, but whom I never expect to see again. I was on board a ship which was wrecked, I was driven on shore by the waves close to a holy temple where several young girls were ministering at a service; the youngest of them found me on the beach and saved my life; I saw her but twice. She was the only person I could love in this world, but you are like her, you almost drive her image out of my heart. She belongs to the holy temple, and therefore by good fortune you have been sent to me, we will never part!'

'Alas! he does not know that it was I who saved his life,' thought the little mermaid. 'I bore him over the sea to the wood, where the temple stands. I sat behind the foam and watched to see if anyone would come. I saw the pretty girl he loves better than me.' And the mermaid heaved a bitter sigh, for she could not weep.

'The girl belongs to the holy temple, he has said, she will never return to the world, they will never meet again, I am here with him, I see him every day. Yes, I will tend him, love him, and give up my life to him.'

But now the rumour ran that the prince was to be married to the beautiful daughter of a neighbouring king, and for that reason was fitting out a splendid ship. It was given out that the prince was going on a voyage to see the adjoining countries, but it was without doubt to see the king's daughter; he was to have a great suite with him, but the little mermaid shook her head and laughed; she knew the prince's intentions much better than any of the others. 'I must take this voyage,' he had said to her; 'I must go and see the beautiful princess; my parents demand that, but they will never force me to bring her home as my bride; I can never love her! She will not be like the

lovely girl in the temple whom you resemble. If ever I had to choose a bride it would sooner be you with your speaking eyes, my sweet, dumb foundling!' And he kissed her rosy mouth, played with her long hair, and laid his head upon her heart, which already dreamt of human joys and an immortal soul.

'You are not frightened of the sea, I suppose, my dumb child?' he said, as they stood on the proud ship which was to carry them to the country of the neighbouring king; and he told her about storms and calms, about curious fish in the deep, and the marvels seen by divers; and she smiled at his tales, for she knew all about the bottom of the sea much better than anyone else.

At night, in the moonlight, when all were asleep, except the steersman who stood at the helm, she sat at the side of the ship trying to pierce the clear water with her eyes, and fancied she saw her father's palace, and above it her old grandmother with her silver crown on her head, looking up through the cross-currents towards the keel of the ship. Then her sisters rose above the water, they gazed sadly at her, wringing their white hands; she beckoned to them, smiled, and was about to tell them that all was going well and happily with her, when the cabin boy approached, and the sisters dived down, but he supposed that the white objects he had seen were nothing but flecks of foam.

The next morning the ship entered the harbour of the neighbouring king's magnificent city. The church bells rang and trumpets were sounded from every lofty tower, while the soldiers paraded with flags flying and glittering bayonets. There was a fête every day, there was a succession of balls and receptions followed one after the other; but the princess was not yet present, she was being brought up a long way off, in a holy temple they said, and was learning all the royal virtues. At last she came. The little mermaid stood eager to see her beauty, and she was obliged to confess that a lovelier creature she had never beheld. Her complexion was exquisitely pure and delicate, and her trustful eyes of the deepest blue shone through their dark lashes.

'It is you,' said the prince, 'you who saved me when I lay almost lifeless on the beach!' And he clasped his blushing bride to his heart. 'Oh! I am too happy!' he exclaimed to the little mermaid. 'A greater joy than I had dared to hope for has come to pass. You will rejoice at my joy, for you love me better than anyone.' Then the little mermaid kissed his hand, and felt as if her heart were broken already.

His wedding morn would bring death to her and change her to foam.

All the church bells pealed and heralds rode through the town proclaiming the nuptials. Upon every altar throughout the land fragrant oil was burnt in costly silver lamps. Amidst the swinging of censers by the priests, the bride and bridegroom joined hands and received the bishop's blessing. The little mermaid dressed in silk and gold stood holding the bride's train, but her ears were deaf to the festal strains; her eyes saw nothing of the sacred ceremony; she was thinking of her coming death and of all that she had lost in this world.

That same evening the bride and bridegroom embarked, amidst the roar of cannon and the waving of banners. A royal tent of purple and gold softly cushioned was raised amidships where the bridal pair were to repose during the calm cool night.

The sails swelled in the wind and the ship skimmed lightly and almost without motion over the transparent sea.

At dusk lanterns of many colours were lighted and the sailors danced merrily on deck. The little mermaid could not help thinking of the first time she came up from the sea and saw the same splendour and gaiety; and she now threw herself among the dancers, whirling, as a swallow skims through the air when pursued. The onlookers cheered her in amazement, never had she danced so divinely; her delicate feet pained her as if they were cut with knives, but she did not feel it, for the pain at her heart was much sharper. She knew that it was the last night that she would breathe the same air as he, and would look upon the mighty deep, and the blue starry heavens; an endless night without thought and without dreams awaited her, who neither had a soul, nor could win one. The joy and revelry on board lasted till long past midnight; she went on laughing and dancing with the thought of death all the time in her heart. The prince caressed his lovely bride and she played with his raven locks, and with their arms entwined they retired to the gorgeous tent. All became hushed and still on board the ship, only the steersman stood at the helm; the little mermaid laid her white arms on the gunwale and looked eastwards for the pink-tinted dawn; the first sunbeam, she knew, would be her death. Then she saw her sisters rise from the water, they were as

pale as she was, their beautiful long hair no longer floated on the breeze, for it had been cut off.

'We have given it to the witch to obtain her help, so that you may not die tonight! She has given us a knife, here it is, look how sharp it is! Before the sun rises, you must plunge it into the prince's heart, and when his warm blood sprinkles your feet they will join together and grow into a tail, and you will once more be a mermaid; you will be able to come down into the water to us, and to live out your three hundred years before you are turned into dead, salt, sea-foam. Make haste! You or he must die before sunrise! Our old grandmother is so full of grief that her white hair has fallen off as ours fell under the witch's scissors. Slay the prince and come back to us! Quick! Quick! Do you not see the rosy streak in the sky? In a few moments the sun will rise and then you must die!' Saying this they heaved a wondrous deep sigh and sank among the waves.

The little mermaid drew aside the purple curtain from the tent and looked at the beautiful bride asleep with her head on the prince's breast; she bent over him and kissed his fair brow, looked at the sky where the dawn was spreading fast; looked at the sharp knife, and again fixed her eyes on the prince who, in his dream, called his bride by name; yes! she alone was in his thoughts! – For a moment the knife quivered in her grasp, then she threw it far out among the waves now rosy in the morning light and where it fell the water bubbled up like drops of blood.

Once more she looked at the prince, with her eyes already dimmed by death, then dashed overboard and fell, her body dissolving into foam.

Now the sun rose from the sea and with its kindly beams warmed the deadly cold foam, so that the little mermaid did not feel the chill of death. She saw the bright sun and above her floated hundreds of beauteous ethereal beings through which she could see the white ship and the rosy heavens; their voices were melodious but so spirit-like that no human ear could hear them, any more than an earthly eye could see their forms. Light as bubbles they floated through the air without the aid of wings. The little mermaid perceived that she had a form like theirs, it gradually took shape out of the foam. 'To whom am I coming?' said she, and her voice sounded like that of the other beings, so unearthly in its beauty that no music of ours could reproduce it.

'To the daughters of the air!' answered the others, 'a mermaid has no undying soul, and can never gain one without winning the love of a human being. Her eternal life must depend upon an unknown power. Nor have the daughters of the air an everlasting soul, but by their own good deeds they may create one for themselves. We fly to the tropics where mankind is the victim of hot and pestilent winds, there we bring cooling breezes. We diffuse the scent of flowers all around, and bring refreshment and healing in our train. When, for three hundred years, we have laboured to do all the good in our power we gain an undying soul and take a part in the everlasting joys of mankind. You, poor little mermaid, have with your whole heart struggled for the same thing that we have struggled for. You have suffered and endured, raised yourself to the spirit world of the air; and now, by your own good deeds, you may, in the course of three hundred years, work out for yourself an undying soul.'

Then the little mermaid lifted her transparent arms towards God's sun, and for the first time shed tears.

On board ship all was again life and bustle; she saw the prince with his lovely bride searching for her, they looked sadly at the bubbling foam, as if they knew that she had thrown herself into the waves. Unseen she kissed the bride on her brow, smiled at the prince and rose aloft with the other spirits of the air to the rosy clouds which sailed above. 'In three hundred years we shall thus float into Paradise.'

'We might reach it sooner,' whispered one. 'Unseen we flit into those homes of men where there are children, and for every day that we find a good child who gives pleasure to its parents and deserves their love, God shortens our time of probation. The child does not know that when we fly through the room, and when we smile with pleasure at it, one year of our three hundred is taken away. But if we see a naughty or badly disposed child, we cannot help shedding tears of sorrow, and every tear adds a day to the time of our probation.'

Little One-Eye, Little Two-Eyes and Little Three-Eyes

There was once a woman who had three daughters, of whom the eldest was called Little One-Eye, because she had only one eye in the middle of her forehead; and the second, Little Two-Eyes, because she had two eyes like other people; and the youngest, Little Three-Eyes, because she had three eyes, and *her* third eye was also in the middle of her forehead. But because Little Two-Eyes did not look any different from other children, her sisters and mother could not bear her. They would say to her, 'You with your two eyes are no better than common folk; you don't belong to us.' They pushed her here, and threw her wretched clothes there, and gave her to eat only what they left, and they were as unkind to her as ever they could be.

It happened one day that Little Two-Eyes had to go out into the fields to take care of the goat, but she was still quite hungry because her sisters had given her so little to eat. So she sat down in the meadow and began to cry, and she cried so much that two little brooks ran out of her eyes. But when she looked up once in her grief there stood a woman beside her who asked, 'Little Two-Eyes, what are you crying for?' Little Two-Eyes answered, 'Have I not reason to cry? Because I have two eyes like other people, my sisters and my mother cannot bear me; they push me out of one corner into another, and give me nothing to eat except what they leave. Today they have given me so little that I am still quite hungry.' Then the wise woman said, 'Little Two-Eyes, dry your eyes, and I will tell you something so that you need never be hungry again. Only say to your goat, "Little goat, bleat. Little table, appear," and a beautifully spread table will stand before you, with the most delicious food on it, so that you can eat as much as you want. And when you have had enough and don't want the little table any more, you have only to say, "Little goat, bleat. Little table, away," and then it will vanish.' Then the wise woman went away.

So Little Two-Eyes thought, 'I must try at once if

what she has told me is true, for I am more hungry than ever'; and she said, 'Little goat, bleat. Little table appear,' and scarcely had she uttered the words, when there stood a little table before her covered with a white cloth, on which were arranged a plate, with a knife and fork and a silver spoon, and the most beautiful dishes, which were smoking hot, as if they had just come out of the kitchen. Then Little Two-Eyes said the shortest grace she knew, and set to work and made a good dinner. And when she had had enough, she said, as the wise woman had told her, 'Little goat, bleat. Little table, away,' and immediately the table and all that was on it disappeared again. 'That is a splendid way of housekeeping,' thought Little Two-Eyes, and she was quite happy and contented.

In the evening, when she went home with her goat, she found a little earthenware dish with the food that her sisters had thrown to her, but she did not touch it. The next day she went out again with her goat, and left the few scraps which were given her. The first and second times her sisters did not notice this, but when it happened continually, they remarked it and said, 'Something is the matter with Little Two-Eyes, for she always leaves her food now, and she used to gobble up all that was given her. She must have found other means of getting food.' So in order to get at the truth, Little One-Eye was told to go out with Little Two-Eyes when she drove the goat to pasture, and to notice particularly what

she got there, and whether anyone brought her food and drink.

Now when Little Two-Eyes was setting out, Little One-Eye came up to her and said, 'I will go into the field with you and see if you take good care of the goat, and if you drive him properly to get grass.' But Little Two-Eyes saw what Little One-Eye had in her mind, and she drove the goat into the long grass and said, 'Come, Little One-Eye, we will sit down here, and I will sing you something.'

Little One-Eye sat down, and as she was very much tired by the long walk to which she was not used, and by the hot day, and as Little Two-Eyes went on singing, 'Little One-Eye, are you awake? Little One-Eye, are you asleep?' she shut her one eye and fell asleep. When Little Two-Eyes saw that Little One-Eye was asleep and could find out nothing, she said, 'Little goat, bleat. Little table, appear,' and sat down at her table and ate and drank as much as she wanted.

Then she said again, 'Little goat, bleat. Little table, away,' and in the twinkling of an eye all had vanished.

Little Two-Eyes then woke Little One-Eye and said, 'Little One-Eye, you meant to watch, and, instead, you went to sleep; in the meantime the goat might have run far and wide. Come, we will go home.' So they went home, and Little Two-Eyes again left her little dish untouched, and Little One-Eye could not tell her mother why she would not eat, and said as an excuse, 'I was so sleepy out-of-doors.'

The next day the mother said to Little Three-Eyes, 'This time you shall go with Little Two-Eyes and watch whether she eats anything out in the fields, and whether anyone brings her food and drink, for eat and drink she must secretly.' So Little Three-Eyes went to Little Two-Eyes and said, 'I will go with you and see if you take good care of the goat, and if you drive him properly to get grass.' But Little Two-Eyes knew what Little Three-Eyes had in her mind, and she drove the goat out into the tall grass and said, 'We will sit down here, Little Three-Eyes, and I will sing you something.' Little Three-Eyes sat down; she was tired by the walk and the hot day, and Little Two-Eyes sang the same little song again: 'Little Three-Eyes, are you awake?' but instead of singing as she ought to have done, 'Little Three-Eyes, are you asleep?' she sang, without thinking, 'Little *Two*-Eyes, are you asleep?'

She went on singing, 'Little Three-Eyes, are you awake? Little *Two*-Eyes, are you asleep?' so that the two eyes of Little Three-Eyes fell asleep, but the third, which was not spoken to in the little rhyme, did not fall asleep. Of course Little Three-Eyes shut that eye also out of cunning, to look as if she were asleep, but it was blinking and could see everything quite well.

And when Little Two-Eyes thought that Little Three-Eyes was sound asleep, she said her rhyme, 'Little goat, bleat. Little table, appear,' and ate and drank to her heart's content, and then made the table go away again, by saying, 'Little goat, bleat. Little table, away.'

But Little Three-Eyes had seen everything. Then Little Two-Eyes came to her, and woke her and said, 'Well, Little Three-Eyes, have you been asleep? You watch well! Come, we will go home.' When they reached home, Little Two-Eyes did not eat again, and Little Three-Eyes said to the mother, 'I know now why that proud thing eats nothing. When she says to the goat in the field, "Little goat, bleat. Little table, appear," a table stands before her, spread with the best food, much better than we have; and when she has had enough, she says, "Little goat, bleat. Little table, away," and everything disappears again. I saw it all exactly. She made two of my eyes go to sleep with a little rhyme, but the one in my forehead remained awake, luckily!'

Then the envious mother cried out, 'Will you fare better than we do? you shall not have the chance to do so again!' and she fetched a knife, and killed the goat.

When Little Two-Eyes saw this, she went out full of grief, and sat down in the meadow and wept bitter tears. Then again the wise woman stood before her, and said, 'Little Two-Eyes, what are you crying for?' 'Have I not reason to cry?' she answered. 'The goat, which when I said the little rhyme, spread the table so beautifully, my mother has killed, and now I must suffer hunger and want again.' The wise woman said, 'Little Two-Eyes, I will give you a good piece of advice. Ask your sisters to give you the heart of the dead goat, and bury it in the earth before the house-door; that will bring you good luck.' Then she disappeared, and Little Two-Eyes went home, and said to her sisters, 'Dear sisters, do give me something of my goat; I ask nothing better than its heart.' Then they laughed and said, 'You can have that if you want nothing more.' And Little Two-Eyes took the heart and buried it in the evening when all was quiet, as the wise woman had told her, before the house-door. The next morning when they all awoke and came to the house-door, there stood a most wonderful tree, which had leaves of silver and fruit of gold growing on it – you never saw anything more lovely and gorgeous in your life! But they did not know how the tree had grown up in the night; only Little Two-Eyes knew that it had sprung from the heart of the goat, for it was standing just where she had buried it in the ground. Then the mother said to Little One-Eye, 'Climb up, my child, and break us off the fruit from the tree.' Little One-Eye climbed up, but just when she was going to take hold of one of the golden apples the bough sprang out of her hands; and this happened every time, so that she could not break off a single apple, however hard she tried. Then the mother said, 'Little Three-Eyes, do you climb up; you with your three eyes can see round better than Little One-Eye.' So Little One-Eye slid down, and Little Three-Eyes climbed up; but she was not any more successful; look round as she might, the golden apples bent themselves back. At last the mother got impatient and climbed up herself, but she was even less successful than Little One-Eye and Little Three-Eyes in catching hold of the fruit, and only grasped at the empty air. Then Little Two-Eyes said, 'I will just try once, perhaps I shall succeed better.' The sisters called out, 'You with your two eyes will no doubt succeed!' But Little Two-Eyes climbed up, and the golden apples did not jump away from her, but behaved quite properly, so that she could pluck them off, one after the other, and brought a whole apron-full down with her. The mother took them from her, and, instead of behaving better to poor Little Two-Eyes, as they ought to have done, they were jealous that she only could reach the fruit and behaved still more unkindly to her.

It happened one day that when they were all standing together by the tree a young knight came riding along. 'Be quick, Little Two-Eyes,' cried the two sisters, 'creep under this, so that you shall not disgrace us,' and they put over poor Little Two-Eyes as quickly as possible an empty cask, which was standing close to the tree, and they pushed the golden apples which she had broken off under with her. When the knight, who was a very handsome young man, rode up, he wondered to see the marvellous tree of gold and silver, and said to the two sisters, 'Whose is this beautiful tree? Whoever will give me a twig of it shall have whatever she wants.' Then Little One-Eye and Little Three-Eyes answered that the tree belonged to them, and that they would certainly break him off a twig. They gave themselves a great deal of trouble, but in vain; the twigs and fruit bent back every time from their hands. Then the knight said, 'It is very strange that the tree should belong to you, and yet that you have not the power to break anything from it!' But they would have that the tree was theirs; and while they were saying this, Little Two-Eyes rolled a couple of golden apples from under the cask, so that they lay at the knight's feet, for she was angry with Little One-Eye and Little Three-Eyes for not speaking the truth. When the knight saw the apples he was astonished, and asked where they came from. Little One-Eye and Little Three-Eyes answered that they had another sister, but she could not be seen because she had only two eyes, like ordinary people. But the knight demanded to see her, and called out, 'Little Two-Eyes, come forth.' Then Little Two-Eyes came out from under the cask quite happily, and the knight was astonished at her great beauty, and said, 'Little Two-Eyes, I am sure you can break me off a twig from the tree.' 'Yes,' answered Little Two-Eyes, 'I can, for the tree is mine.' So she climbed up and broke off a small branch with its silver leaves and golden fruit without any trouble, and gave it to the knight. Then he said, 'Little Two-Eyes, what shall I give you for this?' 'Ah,' answered Little Two-Eyes, 'I suffer hunger and thirst, want and sorrow, from early morning till late in the evening; if you would take me with you, and free me from this, I should be happy!' Then the knight lifted Little Two-Eyes on his horse, and took her home to his father's castle. There he gave her beautiful clothes, and food and drink, and because he loved her so much he married her, and the wedding was celebrated with great joy.

When the handsome knight carried Little Two-Eyes away with him, the two sisters envied her good luck at first. 'But the wonderful tree is still with us, after all,' they thought, 'and although we cannot break any fruit from it, everyone will stop and look at it, and will come to us and praise it; who knows whether *we* may not reap a harvest from it?' But the next morning the tree had flown, and their hopes with it; and when Little Two-Eyes looked out of her window there it stood underneath, to her great delight. Little Two-Eyes lived happily for a long time. Once two poor women came to the castle to beg alms. Then Little Two-Eyes looked at then and recognised both her sisters, Little One-Eye and Little Three-Eyes, who had become so poor that they came to beg bread at her door. But Little Two-Eyes bade them welcome, and was so good to them that they both repented from their hearts of having been so unkind to their sister.

Little Red Riding Hood

Once upon a time there lived in a certain village a little country girl, the prettiest creature was ever seen. Her mother was excessively fond of her; and her grandmother doted on her still more. This good woman had made for her a little red riding hood; which became the girl so extremely well that everybody called her Little Red Riding Hood.

One day her mother, having made some custards, said to her: 'Go, my dear, and see how thy grandmama does, for I hear she has been very ill; carry her a custard, and this little pot of butter.'

Little Red Riding Hood set out immediately to go to her grandmother, who lived in another village.

As she was going through the wood, she met with Gaffer Wolf, who had a very great mind to eat her up, but he dared not, because of some woodcutters hard by in the forest. He asked her whither she was going. The poor child, who did not know that it was dangerous to stay and hear a wolf talk, said to him: 'I am going to see my grandmama and carry her a custard and a little pot of butter from my mama.'

'Does she live far off?' asked the Wolf.

'Oh! ay,' answered Little Red Riding Hood; 'it is beyond that mill you see there, at the first house in the village.'

'Well,' said the Wolf, 'and I'll go and see her too. I'll go this way and you go that, and we shall see who will be there soonest.'

The Wolf began to run as fast as he could, taking the nearest way, and the little girl went by that farthest about, diverting herself in gathering nuts, running after butterflies, and making nosegays of such little flowers as she met with. The Wolf was not long before he got to the old woman's house. He knocked at the door – tap, tap.

'Who's there?'

'Your grandchild, Little Red Riding Hood,' replied the Wolf, counterfeiting her voice; 'who has brought you a custard and a little pot of butter sent you by mama.'

The good grandmother, who was in bed, because she was somewhat ill, cried out: 'Pull the bobbin, and the latch will go up.'

The Wolf pulled the bobbin, and the door opened, and then presently he fell upon the good woman and ate her up in a moment, for it was above three days that he had not touched a bit. He then shut the door and went into the grandmother's bed, expecting Little Red Riding Hood, who came some time afterwards and knocked at the door – tap, tap.

'Who's there?'

Little Red Riding Hood, hearing the big voice of the Wolf, was at first afraid; but believing her grandmother had got a cold and was hoarse, answered: ''Tis your grandchild, Little Red Riding Hood, who has brought you a custard and a little pot of butter mama sends you.'

The Wolf cried out to her, softening his voice as much as he could: 'Pull the bobbin, and the latch will go up.'

Little Red Riding Hood pulled the bobbin, and the door opened.

The Wolf, seeing her come in, said to her, hiding himself under the bedclothes: 'Put the custard and the little pot of butter upon the stool, and come and talk with me.'

Little Red Riding Hood went over to the bed, where, being greatly amazed to see how her grandmother looked in her nightclothes, she said to her: 'Grandmama, what great arms you have got!'

'That is the better to hug thee, my dear.'

'Grandmama, what great legs you have got!'
'That is to run the better, my child.'
'Grandmama, what great ears you have got!'
'That is to hear the better, my child.'
'Grandmama, what great eyes you have got!'
'It is to see the better, my child.'
'Grandmama, what great teeth you have got!'
'That is to eat you up.'

And, saying these words, this wicked wolf fell upon Little Red Riding Hood, and ate her all up.

The Magpie's Nest

Once upon a time when pigs spoke rhyme
And monkeys chewed tobacco,
And hens took snuff to make them tough,
And ducks went quack, quack, quack, O!

All the birds of the air came to the magpie and asked her to teach them how to build nests. For the magpie is the cleverest bird of all at building nests. So she put all the birds round her and began to show them how to do it. First of all she took some mud and made a sort of round cake with it.

'Oh, that's how it's done,' said the thrush; and away it flew, and so that's how thrushes build their nests.

Then the magpie took some twigs and arranged them round in the mud.

'Now I know all about it,' says the blackbird, and off he flew; and that's how the blackbirds make their nests to this very day.

Then the magpie put another layer of mud over the twigs.

'Oh that's quite obvious,' said the wise owl, and away it flew; and owls have never made better nests since.

After this the magpie took some twigs and twined them round the outside.

'The very thing!' said the sparrow, and off be went; so sparrows make rather slovenly nests to this day.

Well, then Madge Magpie took some feathers and stuff and lined the nest very comfortably with it.

'That suits me,' cried the starling, and off it flew; and very comfortable nests have starlings.

So it went on, every bird taking away some knowledge of how to build nests, but none of them waiting to the end. Meanwhile Madge Magpie went on working and working without looking up till the only bird that remained was the turtle-dove, and that hadn't paid any attention all along, but only kept on saying its silly cry, 'Take two, Taffy, take two–o–o–o.'

At last the magpie heard this just as she was putting a twig across. So she said: 'One's enough.' But the turtle-dove kept on saying: 'Take two, Taffy, take two–o–o–o.' Then the magpie got angry and said: 'One's enough I tell you.' Still the turtle-dove cried: 'Take two, Taffy, take two–o–o–o.' At last, and at last, the magpie looked up and saw nobody near her but the silly turtle-dove, and then she got rare angry and flew away and refused to tell the birds how to build nests again. And that is why different birds build their nests differently.

Maiden Bright-Eye

Once, upon a time there was a man and his wife who had two children, a boy and a girl. The wife died, and the man married again. His new wife had an only daughter, who was both ugly and untidy, whereas her stepdaughter was a beautiful girl, and was known as Maiden Bright-Eye. Her stepmother was very cruel to her on this account; she had always to do the hardest work, and got very little to eat, and no attention paid to her; but to her own daughter she was all that was good. She was spared from all the hardest of the housework, and had always the prettiest clothes to wear.

Maiden Bright-Eye had also to watch the sheep, but of course it would never do to let her go idle and enjoy herself too much at this work, so she had to pull heather while she was out on the moors with them. Her stepmother gave her pancakes to take with her for her dinner, but she had mixed the flour with ashes, and made them just as bad as she could.

The little girl came out on the moor and began to pull heather on the side of a little mound, but next minute a little fellow with a red cap on his head popped up out of the mound and said: 'Who's that pulling the roof off my house?'

'Oh, it's me, a poor little girl,' said she; 'my mother sent me out here, and told me to pull heather. If you will be good to me I will give you a bit of my dinner.'

The little fellow was quite willing, and she gave him the bigger share of her pancakes. They were not particularly good, but when one is hungry anything tastes well.

After he had got them all eaten he said to her: 'Now, I shall give you three wishes, for you are a very nice little girl; but I will choose the wishes for you. You are beautiful, and much more beautiful shall you be; yes, so lovely that there will not be your like in the world. The next wish shall be that every time you open your mouth a gold coin shall fall out of it, and your voice shall be like the most beautiful music. The third wish shall be that you may be married to the young king, and become the queen of the country. At the same time I shall give you a cap, which you must carefully keep, for it can save you, if you ever are in danger of your life, if you just put it on your head.

Maiden Bright-Eye thanked the little bergman ever so often, and drove home her sheep in the evening. By that time she had grown so beautiful that her people could scarcely recognise her. Her stepmother asked her how it had come about that she had grown so beautiful. She told the whole story – for she always told the truth – that a little man had come to her out on the moor and had given her all this beauty. She did not tell, however, that she had given him a share of her dinner.

The stepmother thought to herself, 'If one can become so beautiful by going out there, my own daughter shall also be sent, for she can well stand being made a little prettier.'

Next morning she baked for her the finest cakes, and dressed her prettily to go out with the sheep. But she was afraid to go away there without having a stick to defend herself with if anything should come near her.

She was not very much inclined for pulling the heather, as she never was in the habit of doing any work, but she was only a minute or so at it when up came the same little fellow with the red cap, and said: 'Who's that pulling the roof off my house?'

'What's that to you?' said she.

'Well, if you will give me a bit of your dinner, I won't do you any mischief,' said he.

'I will give you something else in place of my dinner,' said she. 'I can easily eat it myself; but if you will have something you can have a whack of my stick,' and with that she raised it in the air and struck the bergman over the head with it.

'What a wicked little girl you are!' said he; 'but you shall be none the better of this. I shall give you three wishes, and choose them for you. First, I shall say, "Ugly are you, but you shall become so ugly that there will not be an uglier one on earth." Next I shall wish that every time you open your mouth a big toad may fall out of it, and your voice shall be like the roaring of a bull. In the third place I shall wish for you a violent death.'

The girl went home in the evening, and when her mother saw her she was as vexed as she could be, and with good reason, too; but it was still worse when she saw the toads fall out of her mouth and heard her voice.

Now we must hear something about the stepson. He had gone out into the world to look about him, and took service in the king's palace. About this time he got permission to go home and see his sister, and when he saw how lovely and beautiful she was, he was so pleased and delighted that when he came back to the king's palace everyone there wanted to know what he was always so happy about. He told them that it was because he had such a lovely sister at home.

At last it came to the ears of the king what the brother said about his sister, and, besides that, the report of her beauty spread far and wide, so that the youth was summoned before the king, who asked him if everything was true that was told about the girl. He said it was quite true, for he had seen her beauty with his own eyes, and had heard with his own ears how sweetly she could sing and what a lovely voice she had.

The king then took a great desire for her, and ordered her brother to go home and bring her back with him, for he trusted no one better to accomplish that errand. He got a ship, and everything else that he required, and sailed home for his sister. As soon as the stepmother heard what his errand was she at once said to herself, 'This will never come about if I can do anything to hinder it. She must not be allowed to come to such honour.'

She then got a dress made for her own daughter, like the finest robe for a queen, and she had a mask prepared and put upon her face, so that she looked quite pretty, and gave her strict orders not to take it off until the king had promised to wed her.

The brother now set sail with his two sisters, for the stepmother pretended that the ugly one wanted to see the other a bit on her way. But when they got out to sea, and Maiden Bright-Eye came up on deck, the sister did as her mother had instructed her – she gave her a push and made her fall into the water. When the brother learned what had happened he was greatly distressed, and did not know what to do. He could not bring himself to tell the truth about what had happened, nor did he expect that the king would believe it. In the long run he decided to hold on his way, and let things go as they liked. What he had expected happened – the king received his sister and wedded her at once, but repented it after the first night, as he could scarcely put down his foot in the morning for all the toads that were about the room, and when he saw her real face he was so enraged against the brother that he had him thrown into a pit full of serpents. He was so angry, not merely because he had been deceived, but because he could not get rid of the ugly wretch that was now tied to him for life.

Now we shall hear a little about Maiden Bright-Eye. When she fell into the water she was fortunate enough to get the bergman's cap put on her head, for now she was in danger of her life, and she was at once transformed into a duck. The duck swam away after the ship, and came to the king's palace on the next evening. There it waddled up the drain, and so into the kitchen, where her little dog lay on the hearthstone; it could not bear to stay in the fine chambers along with the ugly sister, and had taken refuge down here. The duck hopped up till it could talk to the dog.

'Good-evening,' it said.

'Thanks, Maiden Bright-Eye,' said the dog.

'Where is my brother?'

'He is in the serpent-pit.'

'Where is my wicked sister?'

'She is with the noble king.'

'Alas! alas! I am here this evening, and shall be for two evenings yet, and then I shall never come again.'

When it had said this the duck waddled off again. Several of the servant girls heard the conversation, and were greatly surprised at it, and thought that it would be worth while to catch the bird next evening and see into the matter a little more closely. They had heard it say that it would come again.

Next evening it appeared as it had said, and a great many were present to see it. It came waddling in by the drain, and went up to the dog, which was lying on the hearthstone.

'Good-evening,' it said.

'Thanks, Maiden Bright-Eye,' said the dog.

'Where is my brother?'

'He is in the serpent-pit.'

'Where is my wicked sister?'

'She is with the noble king.'

'Alas! alas! I am here this evening, and shall be for one evening yet, and then I shall never come again.'

After this it slipped out, and no one could get hold of it. But the king's cook thought to himself, 'I shall see if I can't get hold of you tomorrow evening.'

On the third evening the duck again came waddling in by the drain, and up to the dog on the hearthstone.

'Good-evening,' it said.

'Thanks, Maiden Bright-Eye,' said the dog.

'Where is my brother?'

'He is in the serpent-pit.'

'Where is my wicked sister?'

'She is with the noble king.'

'Alas! alas! now I shall never come again.'

With this it slipped out again, but in the meantime the cook had posted himself at the outer end of the drain with a net, which he threw over it as it came out. In this way he caught it, and came in to the others with the most beautiful duck they had ever seen – with so many golden feathers on it that everyone marvelled. No one, however, knew what was to be done with it; but after what they had heard they knew that there was something uncommon about it, so they took good care of it. At this time the brother in the serpent-pit dreamed that his right sister had come swimming to the king's palace in the shape of a duck, and that she could not regain her own form until her beak was cut off. He got this dream told to someone, so that the king at last came to hear of it, and had him taken up out of the pit and brought before him. The king then asked him if he could produce to him his sister as beautiful as he had formerly described her. The brother said he could if they would bring him the duck and a knife.

Both of them were brought to him, and he said, 'I wonder how you would look if I were to cut the point off your beak.'

With this he cut a piece off the beak, and there came a voice which said, 'Oh, oh, you cut my little finger!'

Next moment Maiden Bright-Eye stood there, as lovely and beautiful as he had seen her when he was at home. This was his sister, he said; and the whole story now came out of how the other had behaved to her. The wicked sister was put into a barrel with spikes round it which was dragged off by six wild horses, and so she came to her end. But the king was delighted with Maiden Bright-Eye, and immediately made her his queen, while her brother became his prime minister.

The Man Without a Heart

Once upon a time there were seven brothers, who were orphans, and had no sister. Therefore they were obliged to do all their own housework. This they did not like at all; so after much deliberation they decided to get married. There were, unfortunately, no young girls to be found in the place where they lived; but the elder brothers agreed to go out into the world and seek for brides, promising to bring back a very pretty wife for the youngest also if he would meanwhile stay at home and take care of the house. He consented willingly, and the six young men set off in good spirits.

On their way they came to a small cottage standing quite by itself in a wood; and before the door stood an old, old man, who accosted the brothers saying, 'Hallo, you young fellows! Whither away so fast and cheerily?'

'We are going to find bonny brides for ourselves, and one for our youngest brother at home,' they replied.

'Oh! dear youths,' said the old man, 'I am terribly lonely here; pray bring a bride for me also; only remember, she must be young and pretty.'

'What does a shrivelled old grey thing like that want with a pretty young bride?' thought the brothers, and went on their way.

Presently they came to a town where were seven sisters, as young and as lovely as anyone could wish. Each brother chose one, and the youngest they kept for their brother at home. Then the whole party set out on the return journey, and again their path led through the wood and past the old man's cottage.

There he stood before the door, and cried: 'Oh! you fine fellows, what a charming bride you have brought me!'

'She is not for you,' said the young men. 'She is for our youngest brother, as we promised.'

'What!' said the old man, 'promised! I'll make you eat your promises!' And with that he took his magic wand, and, murmuring a charm, he touched both brothers and brides, and immediately they were turned into grey stones.

Only the youngest sister he had not bewitched. He took her into the cottage, and from that time she was obliged to keep house for him. She was not very unhappy, but one thought troubled her. What if the old man should die and leave her here alone in the solitary cottage deep in the heart of the wood! She would be as 'terribly lonely' as he had formerly been.

One day she told him of her fear.

'Don't be anxious,' he said. 'You need neither fear my death nor desire it, for I have no heart in my breast! However, if I should die, you will find my wand above the door, and with it you can set free your sisters and their lovers. Then you will surely have company enough.'

'Where in all the world do you keep your heart, if not in your breast?' asked the girl.

'Do you want to know everything?' her husband said. 'Well, if you must know, my heart is in the bed-cover.'

When the old man had gone out about his business his bride passed her time in embroidering beautiful flowers on the bed quilt to make his heart happy. The old man was much amused. He laughed, and said to her: 'You are a good child, but I was only joking. My heart is really in – in – '

'Now where is it, dear husband?'

'It is in the doorway,' he replied.

Next day, while he was out, the girl decorated the door with gay feathers and fresh flowers, and hung garlands upon it. And on his return the old fellow asked what it all meant.

'I did it to show my love for your heart,' said the girl.

And again the old man smiled, saying, 'You are a dear child, but my heart is not in the doorway.'

Then the poor young bride was very vexed, and said, 'Ah, my dear! you really have a heart some-where, so you may die and leave me all alone.'

The old man did his best to comfort her by repeating all he had said before, but she begged him afresh to tell her truly where his heart was and at last he told her.

'Far, far from here,' said he, 'in a lonely spot, stands a great church, as old as old can be. Its doors are of iron, and round it runs a deep moat, spanned by no bridge. Within that church is a bird which flies up and down; it never eats, and never drinks, and never dies. No one can catch it, and while that bird lives so shall I, for in it is my heart.'

It made the little bride quite sad to think she could do nothing to show her love for the old man's heart. She used to think about it as she sat all alone during the long days, for her husband was almost always out.

One day a young traveller came by the house, and seeing such a pretty girl he wished her, 'Good-day.'

She returned his greeting, and as he drew near she asked him whence he came and where he was going.

'Alas!' sighed the youth, 'I am very sorrowful. I had six brothers, who went away to find brides for themselves and one for me; but they have never come home, so now I am going to look for them.'

'Oh, good friend,' said the girl, 'you need go no farther. Come, sit down, eat and drink, and after-wards I'll tell you all about it.'

She gave him food, and when he had finished his meal, she told him how his brothers had come to the town where she lived with her sisters, how they had each chosen a bride, and, taking herself with them, had started for home. She wept as she told

how the others were turned to stone while she was kept as the old man's bride. She left out nothing, even telling him the story of her husband's heart.

When the young man heard this he said: 'I shall go in search of the bird. It may be that God will help me to find and catch it.'

'Yes, do go,' she said; 'it will be a good deed, for then you can set your brothers and my sisters free.' Then she hid the young man, for it was now late, and her husband would soon be home.

Next morning, when the old man had gone out, she prepared a supply of provisions for her guest, and sent him off on his travels, wishing him good luck and success.

He walked on and on till he thought it must be time for breakfast; so he opened his knapsack, and was delighted to find such a store of good things. 'What a feast!' he exclaimed; 'will anyone come and share it?'

'Moo-oo,' sounded close behind him, and looking round he saw a great red ox, which said, 'I have much pleasure in accepting your kind invitation.'

'I'm delighted to see you. Pray help yourself. All I have is at your service,' said the hospitable youth. And the ox lay down comfortably, licking his lips, and made a hearty meal.

'Many thanks to you,' said the animal as it rose up. 'When you are in danger or necessity call me, even if only by a thought,' and it disappeared among the bushes.

The young man packed up all the food that was left, and wandered on till the shortening shadows and his own hunger warned him that it was mid-day. He laid the cloth on the ground and spread out his provisions, saying: 'Dinner is ready, and anyone who wishes to share it is welcome.'

Then there was a great rustling in the under-growth, and out ran a wild boar, grunting, 'Umph, umph, umph; someone said dinner was ready. Was it you? and did you mean me to come?'

'By all means. Help yourself to what I have,' said the young traveller. And the two enjoyed their meal together.

Afterwards the boar got up, saying, 'Thank you; when in need you be you must quickly call for me,' and he trotted off.

For a long time the youth walked on. By evening he was miles away. He felt hungry again, and, having still some provisions left, thought he had better make ready his supper. When it was all spread out he cried as before, 'Anyone who cares to share my meal is welcome.'

He heard a sound overhead like the flapping of wings, and a shadow was cast upon the ground. Then a huge griffin appeared, saying: 'I heard someone giving an invitation to eat; is there anything for me?'

'Why not?' said the youth. 'Come down and take all you want. There won't be much left after this.'

So the griffin alighted and ate his fill, saying, as he flew away, 'Call me if you need me.'

'What a hurry he was in!' the youth said to himself. 'He might have been able to direct me to the church, for I shall never find it alone.'

He gathered up his things, and started to walk a little farther before resting. He had not gone far when all of a sudden he saw the church!

He soon came to it, or rather to the wide and deep moat which surrounded it without a single bridge by which to cross.

It was too late to attempt anything now; and, besides, the poor youth was very tired, so he lay down on the ground and fell fast asleep.

Next morning, when he awoke, he began to wish himself over the moat; and the thought occurred to him that if only the red ox were there, and thirsty enough to drink up all the water in the moat, he might walk across it dry shod.

Scarcely had the thought crossed his brain before the ox appeared and began to drink up the water.

The grateful youth hastened across as soon as the moat was dry, but found it impossible to penetrate the thick walls and strong iron doors of the church.

'I believe that big boar would be of more use here than I am,' he thought, and lo! at the wish the wild boar came and began to push hard against the wall. He managed to loosen one stone with his tusks, and, having made a beginning, stone after stone was poked out till he had made quite a large hole, big enough to let a man go through.

The young man quickly entered the church, and saw a bird flying about, but he could not catch it.

'Oh!' he exclaimed, 'if only the griffin were here, he would soon catch it.'

At these words the griffin appeared, and, seizing the bird, gave it to the youth, who carried it off carefully, while the griffin flew away.

The young man hurried home as fast as possible, and reached the cottage before evening. He told his story to the little bride, who, after giving him some food and drink, hid him with his bird beneath the bed.

Presently the old man came home, and complained of feeling ill. Nothing, he said, would go well with him any more: his 'heart bird' was caught.

The youth under the bed heard this, and thought, 'This old fellow has done me no particular harm, but then he has bewitched my brothers and their brides, and has kept my bride for himself, and that is certainly bad enough.'

So he pinched the bird, and the old man cried, 'Ah! I feel death gripping me! Child, I am dying!'

With these words the old man fell from his chair. The youth, not knowing what he had done, had squeezed the bird and at the same time killed the old man.

Out crept the young man from under the bed, and the girl took the magic wand (which she found where the old man had told her), and, touching the twelve grey stones, transformed them at once into the six brothers and their brides.

Then there was great joy, and kissing and embracing. And there lay the old man, quite dead, and no magic wand could restore him to life, even had they wished it.

After that they all went away and were married, and lived many years happily together.

The Master Cat or Puss in Boots

There was a miller who left no more estate to the three sons he had than his mill, his ass and his cat. The partition was soon made. Neither scrivener nor attorney was sent for. They would soon have eaten up all the poor patrimony. The eldest had the mill, the second the ass and the youngest nothing but the cat. The poor young fellow was quite comfortless at having so poor a lot.

'My brothers,' said he, 'may get their living handsomely enough by joining their stocks together; but for my part, when I have eaten up my cat, and made me a muff of his skin, I must die of hunger.'

The cat, who heard all this, but made as if he did not, said to him with a grave and serious air: 'Do not thus afflict yourself, my good master. You have nothing else to do but to give me a bag and get a pair of boots made for me that I may scamper through the dirt and the brambles, and you shall see that you have not so bad a portion in me as you imagine.'

The cat's master did not build very much upon what he said. He had often seen him play a great many cunning tricks to catch rats and mice, as when he used to hang by the heels or hide himself in the meal and make as if he were dead; so that he did not altogether despair of his affording him some help in his miserable condition. When the cat had what he asked for he booted himself very gallantly, and putting his bag about his neck, he held the strings of it in his two forepaws and went into a warren where was great abundance of rabbits. He put bran and sow-thistle into his bag, and stretching out at length, as if he had been dead, he waited for some young rabbits, not yet acquainted with the deceits of the world, to come and rummage his bag for what he had put into it.

Scarce was he lain down but he had what he wanted. A rash and foolish young rabbit jumped into his bag, and Monsieur Puss, immediately drawing close the strings, took and killed him without pity. Proud of his prey, he went with it to the palace and asked to speak with his majesty. He was shown upstairs into the king's apartment, and, making a low reverence, said to him: 'I have brought you, sir, a rabbit of the warren, which my noble lord the Marquis of Carabas' (for that was the title which puss was pleased to give his master) 'has commanded me to present to your majesty from him.'

'Tell thy master,' said the king, 'that I thank him and that he does me a great deal of pleasure.'

Another time he went and hid himself among some standing corn, holding still his bag open, and when a brace of partridges ran into it he drew the strings and so caught them both. He went and made a present of these to the king, as he had done before of the rabbit which he took in the warren. The king, in like manner, received the partridges with great pleasure, and ordered him some money for drink.

The cat continued for two or three months thus to carry his majesty, from time to time, game of his master's taking. One day in particular, when he knew for certain that he was to take the air along the riverside, with his daughter, the most beautiful princess in the world, he said to his master: 'If you will follow my advice your fortune is made. You have nothing else to do but go and wash yourself in the river, in that part I shall show you, and leave the rest to me.'

The Marquis of Carabas did what the cat advised him to, without knowing why or wherefore. While he was washing, the king passed by, and the cat began to cry out: 'Help! help! My Lord Marquis of Carabas is going to be drowned.'

At this noise the king put his head out of the coach-window, and, finding it was the cat who had so often brought him such good game, he commanded his guards to run immediately to the assistance of his lordship the Marquis of Carabas. While they were drawing the poor marquis out of the river, the cat came up to the coach and told the king that, while his master was washing, there

'Help! help! My Lord Marquis of Carabas is going to be drowned.'

came by some rogues, who went off with his clothes, though he had cried out: 'Thieves! thieves!' several times, as loud as he could.

This cunning cat had hidden them under a great stone. The king immediately commanded the officers of his wardrobe to run and fetch one of his best suits for the Lord Marquis of Carabas.

The king received him with many compliments, and as the fine clothes he had given him extremely set off his good mien (for he was well made and very handsome in his person), the king's daughter took a secret inclination to him, and the Marquis of Carabas had no sooner cast her two or three respectful and somewhat tender glances but she fell in love with him to distraction. The king would needs have him come into the coach and take part in the airing. The cat, quite overjoyed to see his project begin to succeed, marched on before, and, meeting with some countrymen, who were mowing a meadow, he said to them: 'Good people, you who are mowing, if you do not tell the king that the meadow you mow belongs to my Lord Marquis of Carabas, you shall be chopped as small as herbs for the pot.'

The king did not fail asking of the mowers to whom the meadow they were mowing belonged.

'To my Lord Marquis of Carabas,' answered they altogether, for the cat's threats had made them terribly afraid.

'You see, sir,' said the marquis, 'this is a meadow which never fails to yield a plentiful harvest every year.'

The Master Cat, who went still on before, met with some reapers, and said to them: 'Good people, you who are reaping, if you do not tell the king that all this corn belongs to the Marquis of Carabas, you shall be chopped as small as herbs for the pot.'

The king, who passed by a moment after, would

'Good people, you who are mowing, if you do not tell the king that the meadow you mow belongs to my Lord Marquis of Carabas, you shall be chopped as small as herbs for the pot.'

needs know to whom all that corn, which he then saw, did belong.

'To my Lord Marquis of Carabas,' replied the reapers, and the king was very well pleased with it, as well as the marquis, whom he congratulated thereupon. The Master Cat, who went always before, said the same words to all he met, and the king was astonished at the vast estates of my Lord Marquis of Carabas.

Monsieur Puss came at last to a stately castle, the master of which was an ogre, the richest had ever been known; for all the lands which the king had then gone over belonged to this castle. The cat, who had taken care to inform himself who this ogre was and what he could do, asked to speak with him, saying he could not pass so near his castle without having the honour of paying his respects to him.

The ogre received him as civilly as an ogre could do, and made him sit down.

'I have been assured,' said the cat, 'that you have the gift of being able to change yourself into all sorts of creatures you have a mind to; you can, for example, transform yourself into a lion, or an elephant, and the like.'

'That is true,' answered the ogre very briskly; 'and to convince you, you shall see me now become a lion.'

Puss was so sadly terrified at the sight of a lion so near him that he immediately got into the roof gutter, not without abundance of trouble and danger, because of his boots, which were of no use at all to him in walking upon the tiles. A little while after, when Puss saw that the ogre had resumed his natural form, he came down, and owned he had been very much frightened.

'I have been, moreover, informed,' said the cat, 'but I know not how to believe it, that you have also the power to take on you the shape of the smallest

'Impossible!' cried the ogre; 'you shall see that presently.'

animals; for example, to change yourself into a rat or a mouse; but I must own to you I take this to be impossible.'

'Impossible!' cried the ogre; 'you shall see that presently.'

And at the same time he changed himself into a mouse, and began to run about the floor. Puss no sooner perceived this but he fell upon him and ate him up.

Meanwhile the king, who saw, as he passed, this fine castle of the ogre's, had a mind to go into it. Puss, who heard the noise of his majesty's coach passing over the drawbridge, ran out, and said to the king: 'Your majesty is welcome to this castle of my Lord Marquis of Carabas.'

'What! my Lord Marquis,' cried the king, 'and does this castle also belong to you? There can be nothing finer than this court with all the stately buildings around it; let us go in, if you please.'

The marquis gave his hand to the princess, and followed the king, who went first. They passed into a spacious hall, where they found a magnificent collation, which the ogre had prepared for his friends, who were that very day to visit him, but dared not enter, knowing the king was there. His majesty was perfectly charmed with the good qualities of my Lord Marquis of Carabas, as was his daughter, who had fallen violently in love with him, and, seeing the vast estate he possessed, said to him, after having drunk five or six glasses: 'It will be owing to yourself only, my Lord Marquis, if you are not my son-in-law.'

The marquis, making several low bows, accepted the honour which his majesty conferred upon him, and forthwith, that very same day, married the princess.

Puss became a great lord, and never ran after mice any more, except for his diversion.

Master of All Masters

A girl once went to the fair to hire herself for servant. At last a funny-looking old gentleman engaged her, and took her home to his house. When she got there, he told her that he had something to teach her, for that in his house he had his own names for things.

He said to her: 'What will you call me?'

'Master or mister, or whatever you please, sir,' says she.

He said: 'You must call me "Master of All Masters". And what would you call this?' pointing to his bed.

'Bed or couch, or whatever you please, sir.'

'No, that's my "barnacle". And what do you call these?' said he pointing to his pantaloons.

'Breeches or trousers, or whatever you please, sir.'

'You must call them "squibs and crackers". And what would you call her?' pointing to the cat.

'Cat or kit, or whatever you please, sir.'

'You must call her "white-faced simminy". And this now,' showing the fire, 'what would you call this?'

'Fire or flame, or whatever you please, sir.'

'You must call it "hot cockalorum", and what this?' he went on, pointing to the water.

'Water or wet, or whatever you please, sir.'

'No, "pondalorum" is its name. And what do you call all this?' asked he, as he pointed to the house.

'House or cottage, or whatever you please, sir.'

'You must call it "high-topper mountain".'

That very night the servant woke her master up in a fright and said: 'Master of All Masters, get out of your barnacle and put on your squibs and crackers. For white-faced simminy has got a spark of hot cockalorum on her tail, and unless you get some pondalorum, high-topper mountain will be all on hot cockalorum.' . . . That's all.

The Story of the McAndrew Family

A long time ago, in the County Mayo, there lived a rich man of the name of McAndrew. He owned cows and horses without number, not to mention ducks and geese and pigs; and his land extended as far as the eye could reach on the four sides of you.

McAndrew was a lucky man, the neighbours all said; but as for himself, when he looked on his seven big sons growing up like weeds and with scarcely any more sense, he felt sore enough, for of all the stupid omadhauns the seven McAndrew brothers were the stupidest.

When the youngest grew to be a man, the father built a house for each of them, and gave every one a piece of land and a few cows, hoping to make men of them before he died, for, as the old man said, 'While God spares my life, I'll be able to have an eye to them, and maybe they will learn from experience.'

The seven young McAndrews were happy enough. Their fields were green, their cows were fat and sleek, and they thought they would never see a poor day.

All went well for a time, and the day of the fair of Killalla was as fine a day as ever shone in Ireland, when the whole seven got ready to be off, bright and early, in the morning.

Each one of them drove before him three fine cows, and a finer herd, when they were all together, was never seen in the country far or near.

Now, there was a smart farmer, named O'Toole, whose fields were nearing on the McAndrews', and he had many a time set his heart on the fine cattle belonging to his easy-going neighbours; so when he saw them passing with their twenty-one cows he went out and hailed them.

'Where are ye going to, this fine morning?'

'It's to the fair of Killalla we're going, to sell these fine cows our father gave us,' they all answered together.

'And are ye going to sell cows that the evil eye has long been set on? Oh, Con and Shamus, I would never belave it of ye, even if that spalpeen of a Pat would do such a thing; anyone would think that the spirit of the good mother that bore ye would stretch out a hand and kape ye from committing such a mortal sin.'

This O'Toole said to the three eldest, who stood trembling, while the four younger ones stuck their knuckles into their eyes and began to cry.

'Oh, indade, Mr O'Toole, we never knew that the cows were under the evil eye. How did ye find it out? Oh, sorra the day when such a fine lot of cattle should go to the bad,' answered Con.

'Indade ye may well ask it, whin it's meself that was always a good neighbour and kept watch on auld Judy, the witch, when she used to stand over there laughing at the ravens flying over the cows. Do ye mind the time yer father spoke ugly to her down by the crossroads? She never forgot it, and now yer twenty-one fine cows will never be worth the hides on their backs.'

'Worra, worra, worra,' roared the seven McAndrews, so loud that pretty Katie O'Toole bobbed her head out of the window, and the hindermost cows began to caper like mad.

'The spell has come upon them!' cried Shamus. 'Oh! What'll we do? What'll we do?'

'Hould yer whist, man alive,' said O'Toole. 'I'm a good neighbour, as I said before, so to give ye a lift in the world I'll take the risk on meself and buy the cows from ye for the price of their hides. Sure no harm can be done to the hides for making leather, so I'll give ye a shilling apiece, and that's better than nothing. Twenty-one bright shillings going to the fair may make yer fortune.'

It seemed neck or nothing with the McAndrews, and they accepted the offer, thanking O'Toole for his generosity, and helped him drive the cows into his field. Then they set off for the fair.

They had never been in a fair before, and when they saw the fine sights they forgot all about the cows, and only remembered that they had each a shilling to spend.

Everyone knew the McAndrews, and soon a crowd gathered round them, praising their fine looks and telling them what a fine father they had to give them so much money, so that the seven omadhauns lost their heads entirely, and treated right and left until there wasn't a farthing left of the twenty-one shillings. Then they staggered home a little the worse for the fine whiskey they drank with the boys.

It was a sorry day for old McAndrew when his seven sons came home without a penny of the price of their twenty-one fine cows, and he vowed he'd never give them any more.

So one day passed with another, and the seven young McAndrews were as happy as could be until the fine old father fell sick and died.

The eldest son came in for all the father had, so he felt like a lord. To see him strut and swagger was a sight to make a grum growdy laugh.

One day, to show how fine he could be, he dressed in his best, and with a purse filled with gold pieces started off for the market town.

When he got there, in he walked to a public house, and called for the best of everything, and to make a fine fellow of himself he tripled the price of everything to the landlord. As soon as he got through his eye suddenly caught sight of a little keg, all gilded over to look like gold, that hung outside the door for a sign. Con had never heeded it before, and he asked the landlord what it was.

Now the landlord, like many another, had it in mind that he might as well get all he could out of a McAndrew, and he answered quickly, 'You stupid omadhaun, don't you know what that is? It's a mare's egg.'

'And will a foal come out of it?'

'Of course; what a question to ask a dacent man!'

'I niver saw one before,' said the amazed McAndrew.

'Well, ye see one now, Con, and take a good look at it.'

'Will ye sell it?'

'Och, Con McAndrew, do ye think I want to sell that fine egg afther kaping it so long hung up there before the sun – when it is ready to hatch out a foal that will be worth twenty good guineas to me?'

'I'll give ye twenty guineas for it,' answered Con.

'Thin it's a bargain,' said the landlord; and he took down the keg and handed it to Con, who handed out the twenty guineas, all the money he had.

'Be careful of it, and carry it as aisy as ye can, and when ye get home hang it up in the sun.'

Con promised, and set off home with his prize.

Near the rise of a hill he met his brothers.

'What have ye, Con?'

'The most wonderful thing in the world – a mare's egg.'

'Faith, what is it like?' asked Pat, taking it from Con.

'Go aisy, can't ye? It's very careful ye have to be.'

But the brothers took no heed to Con, and before one could say, 'whist', away rolled the keg down the hill, while all seven ran after it; but before anyone could catch it, it rolled into a clump of bushes, and in an instant out hopped a hare.

'Bedad, there's the foal,' cried Con, and all seven gave chase; but there was no use trying to catch a hare.

'That's the foinest foal that ever was, if he was five year old the devil himself could not catch him,' Con said; and with that the seven omadhauns gave up the chase and went quietly home.

As I said before, everyone had it in mind to get all he could out of the McAndrews.

Everyone said, 'One man might as well have it as another, for they're bound to spend every penny they have.'

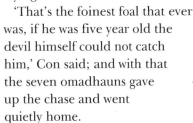

So their money dwindled away; then a fine horse would go for a few bits of glass they took for precious stones, and by and by a couple of pigs or a pair of fine geese for a bit of ribbon to tie on a hat; and at last their land began to go.

One day Shamus was sitting by his fireplace warming himself, and to make a good fire he threw on a big heap of turf so that by and by it got roaring hot, and instead of feeling chilly as he had before, Shamus got as hot as a spare rib on a spit. Just then in came his youngest brother.

'That's a great fire ye have here, Shamus.'

'It is, indade, and too near it is to me; run like a good boy to Giblin, the mason, and see if he can't move the chimney to the other side of the room.'

The youngest McAndrew did as he was bid, and soon in came Giblin, the mason.

'Ye're in a sad plight, Shamus, roasting alive; what can I do for ye?'

'Can ye move the chimney over beyant?'

'Faith, I can, but ye will have to move a bit; just go out for a walk with yer brother, and the job will be done when ye come back.'

Shamus did as he was bid, and Giblin took the chair the omadhaun was sitting on and moved it away from the fire, and then sat down for a quiet laugh for himself and to consider on the price he'd charge for the job.

When Shamus came back, Giblin led him to the chair, saying, 'Now, isn't that a great deal better?'

'Ye're a fine man, Giblin, and ye did it without making a bit of dirt; what'll I give ye for so fine a job?'

'If ye wouldn't mind, I'd like the meadow field nearing on mine. It's little enough for a job like that.'

'It's yours and welcome, Giblin;' and without another word the deed was drawn.

That was the finest of the McAndrew fields, and the only pasture land left to Shamus.

It was not long before it came about that first one and then another lost the house he lived in, until all had to live together in the father's old place.

O'Toole and Giblin had encroached field by field, and there was nothing left but the old house and a strip of garden that none of them knew how to till.

It was hard times for the seven McAndrews, but they were happy and contented as long as they had enough to eat, and that they had surely, for the wives of the men who got away all their fine lands and cattle, had sore hearts when they saw their men enriched at the expense of the omadhauns,

and every day, unbeknown to their husbands, they carried them meat and drink.

O'Toole and Giblin now had their avaricious eyes set on the house and garden, and they were on the watch for a chance to clutch them, when luck, or something worse, threw the chance in the way of O'Toole.

He was returning from town one day just in the cool of the afternoon, when he spied the seven brothers by the roadside, sitting in a circle facing each other.

'What may ye be doing here instead of earning yer salt, ye seven big sturks?'

'We're in a bad fix, Mr O'Toole,' answered Pat. 'We can't get up.'

'What's to hinder ye from getting up? I'd like to know.'

'Don't ye see our feet are all here together in the middle, and not for the life of us can we each tell our own. You see if one of us gets up he don't know what pair of feet to take with him.'

O'Toole was never so ready to laugh before in his life, but he thought, 'Now's me chance to get the house and garden before Giblin, the mason, comes round;' so he looked very grave and said, 'I suppose it is hard to tell one man's feet from another's when they're all there in a heap, but I think I can help you as I have many a time before. It would be a sorry day for ye if ye did not have me for a neighbour. What will ye give me if I help you find yer feet?'

'Anything, anything we have, so that we can get up from here,' answered the whole seven together.

'Will ye give me the house and garden?'

'Indade we will; what good is a house and garden, if we have to sit here all the rest of our lives?'

'Then it's a bargain,' said O'Toole; and with that he went over to the side of the road and pulled a good stout rod. Then he commenced to belabour the poor McAndrews over their heads, their feet, their shoulders, and any place he could get in a stroke, until with screeches of pain they all jumped up, everyone finding his own feet, and away they ran.

So O'Toole got the last of the property of the McAndrews, and there was nothing left for them but to go and beg.

The Mighty Monster Afang

After the Cymric folk, that is, the people we call Welsh, had come up from Cornwall into their new land, they began to cut down the trees, to build towns and to have fields and gardens. Soon they made the landscape smile with pleasant homes, rich farms and playing children.

They trained vines and made flowers grow. The young folks made pets of the wild animals' cubs, which their fathers and big brothers brought home from hunting. Old men took rushes and reeds and wove them into cages for song birds to live in.

While they were draining the swamps and bogs, they drove out the monsters that had made their lair in these wet places. These terrible creatures liked to poison people with their bad breath, and even ate up very little boys and girls, when they strayed away from home.

So all the face of the open country between the forests became very pretty to look at. The whole of Cymric land, which then extended from the northern Grampian Hills to Cornwall, and from the Irish Sea, past their big fort, afterwards called London, even to the edge of the German Ocean, became a delightful place to live in.

The lowlands and the rivers, in which the tide rose and fell daily, were especially attractive. This was chiefly because of the many bright flowers growing there; while the yellow gorse and the pink heather made the hills look as lovely as a young girl's face. Besides this, the Cymric maidens were the prettiest ever, and the lads were all brave and healthy; while both of these knew how to sing often and well.

Now there was a great monster named the Afang, that lived in a big bog, hidden among the high hills and inside of a dark, rough forest.

This ugly creature had an iron-clad back and a long tail that could wrap itself around a mountain. It had four front legs, with big knees that were bent up like a grasshopper's, but were covered with scales like armour. These were as hard as steel, and bulged out at the thighs. Along its back, was a ridge of horns, like spines, and higher than an alligator's. Against such a tough hide, when the hunters shot their darts and hurled their javelins, these weapons fell down to the ground, like harmless pins.

On this monster's head, were big ears, halfway between those of a jackass and an elephant. Its eyes were as green as leeks, and were round, but scalloped on the edges, like squashes, while they were as big as pumpkins.

The Afang's face was much like a monkey's, or a gorilla's, with long straggling grey hairs around its cheeks like those of a walrus. It always looked as if a napkin as big as a bath towel would be necessary to keep its mouth clean. Yet even then, it slobbered a good deal, so that no nice fairy liked to be near the monster.

When the Afang growled, the bushes shook and the oak leaves trembled on the branches, as if a strong wind was blowing.

But after its dinner, when it had swallowed down a man, or two calves, or four sheep, or a fat heifer, or three goats, its body swelled up like a balloon. Then it usually rolled over, lay along the ground, or in the soft mud, and felt very stupid and sleepy, for a long while.

All around its lair lay wagon-loads of the bones of the creatures, girls, women, men, boys, cows, and occasionally a donkey, which it had devoured.

But when the Afang was ravenously hungry and could not get these animals and when fat girls and careless boys were scarce, it would live on birds, beasts and fishes. Although it was very fond of cows and sheep, yet the wool and hair of these animals stuck in its big teeth, so it often felt very miserable and its usually bad temper grew worse. Then, like a beaver, it would cut down a tree, sharpen it to a point and pick its teeth until its mouth was clean.

Yet it seemed all the more hungry and eager for fresh human victims to eat, especially juicy maidens – just as children like cake more than bread.

The Cymric men were not surprised at this, for they knew that girls were very sweet and they almost worshipped women. So they learned to guard their daughters and wives. They saw that to do such things as eating up people was in the nature of the beast, which could never be taught good manners.

But what made them mad beyond measure was the trick which the monster often played upon them by breaking the river banks, and the dykes which with great toil they had built to protect their crops. Then the waters overflowed all their farms, ruined their gardens and spoiled their cow houses and stables.

This sort of mischief the Afang liked to play, especially about the time when the oat and barley crops were ripe and ready to be gathered to make cakes and flummery (that is sour oat-jelly, or pap). So it often happened that the children had to do without their cookies and porridge during the winter. Sometimes the floods rose so high as to wash away the houses and float the cradles. Even those with little babies in them were often seen on the raging waters and went dancing on the waves down the river to the sea.

Once in a while, a mother cat and all her kittens were seen mewing for help, or a lady dog howling piteously. Often it happened that both puppies and kittens were drowned.

So, whether for men or mothers, pussies or puppies, the Cymric men thought the time had come to stop this monster's mischief. It was bad enough that people should be eaten up, but to have all their crops ruined and animals drowned, so that they had to go hungry all winter, with only a little fried fish, and no turnips, was too much for human patience. There were too many weeping mothers and sorrowful fathers, and squalling brats and animals whining for something to eat.

Besides, if all the oats were washed away, how could their wives make flummery, without which no Cymric man is ever happy? And where would they get seed for another year's sowing? And if there were no cows, how could the babies or kitties live, or any grown-up persons get buttermilk?

Someone may ask, why did not some brave man shoot the Afang with a poisoned arrow, or drive a spear into him under the arms, where the flesh was tender, or cut off his head with a sharp sword?

The trouble was just here. There were plenty of brave fellows ready to fight the monster, but nothing made of iron could pierce that hide of his. This was like armour, or one of the steel battleships of our day, and the Afang always spat out fire or poison breath down the road, up which a man was coming, long before the brave fellow could get near him. Nothing would do, but to go up into his lair, and drag him out.

But what man or company of men was strong enough to do this, when a dozen giants in a gang, with ropes as thick as a ship's hawser, could hardly tackle the job?

Nevertheless, in what neither man nor giant could do, a pretty maiden might succeed. True, she must be brave also, for how could she not know that if hungry the Afang might eat her up?

However, one valiant damsel, of great beauty, who had lots of perfumery and plenty of pretty clothes, volunteered to bind the monster in his lair. She said, 'I'm not afraid.' Her sweetheart was named Gadern, and he was a young and strong hunter. He talked over the matter with her and they two resolved to act together.

Gadern went all over the country, summoning the farmers to bring their ox teams and log chains. Then he set the blacksmiths to work, forging new and especially heavy ones, made of the best native iron, from the mines for which Wales is still famous.

Meanwhile, the lovely maiden arrayed herself in her prettiest clothes, dressed her hair in the most enticing way, hanging a white blossom on each side, over her ears, and placing one flower also at her neck.

When she had perfumed her garments, she sallied forth and up the lake where the big bog and the waters were and where the monster hid himself.

While the maiden was still quite a distance away, the terrible Afang, scenting his visitor from afar, came rushing out of his lair. When she was very near, he reared his head high in the air, expecting to pounce on her with his iron-clad claws and at one swallow make a breakfast of the girl.

But the odours of her perfumes were so sweet that he forgot what he had thought to do. Moreover, when he looked at her, he was so taken with her unusual beauty, that he flopped at once on his forefeet. Then he behaved just like a lovelorn beau, when his best girl comes near. He ties his necktie and pulls down his coat and brushes off the collar. So the Afang began to spruce up. It was real fun to see how a monster behaves when smitten with love for a pretty girl. He had no idea how funny he was.

The girl was not at all afraid, but smoothed the monster's back, stroked and played with his big moustaches and tickled his neck until the Afang's throat actually gurgled with a laugh. Pretty soon he guffawed, for he was so delighted.

When he did this, the people down in the valley thought it was thunder, though the sky was clear and blue.

The maiden tickled his chin, and even put up his whiskers in curl papers. Then she stroked his neck, so that his eyes closed. Soon she had gently lulled him to slumber, by singing a cradle song, which her mother had taught her. This she did so softly, and sweetly, that in a few minutes, with its head in her lap, the monster was sound asleep and even began to snore.

Then, quietly, from their hiding places in the bushes, Gadern and his men crawled out. When near the dreaded Afang, they stood up and sneaked forward, very softly on tiptoe. They had wrapped the links of the chain in grass and leaves, so that no clanking was heard. They also held the oxen's yokes, so that nothing could rattle or make any noise. Slowly but surely they passed the chain over its body, in the middle, besides binding the brute securely between its fore and hind legs.

All this time, the monster slept on, for the girl kept on crooning her melody.

When the forty yoke of oxen were all harnessed together, the drovers cracked all their whips at once, so that it sounded like a clap of thunder and the whole team began to pull together.

Then the Afang woke up with a start.

The sudden jerk roused the monster to wrath, and its bellowing was terrible. It rolled round and round, and dug its four sets of toes, each with three claws, every one as big as a plowshare, into the ground. It tried hard to crawl into its lair, or slip into the lake.

Finding that neither was possible, the Afang looked about for some big tree to wrap its tail around. But all his writhings and plungings were of no use. The drovers plied their whips and the oxen kept on with one long pull together and forward. They strained so hard, that one of them dropped its eye out. This formed a pool, and to this day they call it the Pool of the Ox's Eye. It never dries up or overflows, though the water in it rises and falls as regularly as the tides.

For miles over the mountains the sturdy oxen hauled the monster. The pass over which they toiled and strained so hard is still named the Pass of the Oxen's Slope. When going downhill, the work of dragging the Afang was easier.

In a great hole in the ground, big enough to be a pond, they dumped the carcass of the Afang, and soon a little lake was formed. This uncanny bit of water is called the Lake of the Green Well. It is considered dangerous for man or beast to go too near it. Birds do not like to fly over the surface, and when sheep tumble in, they sink to the bottom at once.

If the bones of the Afang still lie at the bottom, they must have sunk very deep, for the monster had no more power to get out or to break the river banks. The farmers no longer had to worry about the creature, and they hardly ever think of the old story now, except when a sheep is lost.

As for Gadern and his brave and lovely sweetheart, they were married and lived long and happily. Their descendants, in the thirty-seventh generation, are proud of the grand exploit of their ancestors, while all the farmers honour his memory and bless the name of the lovely girl that put the monster to sleep.

Morraha

Morraha rose in the morning and washed his hands and face, and said his prayers, and ate his food; and he asked God to prosper the day for him. So he went down to the brink of the sea, and he saw a currach, short and green, coming towards him; and in it there was but one youthful champion, and he was playing hurly from prow to stern of the currach. He had a hurl of gold and a ball of silver; and he stopped not till the currach was in on the shore; and he drew her up on the green grass, and put fastenings on her for a year and a day, whether he should be there all that time or should only be on land for an hour by the clock. And Morraha saluted the young man courteously; and the other saluted him in the same fashion, and asked him would he play a game of cards with him; and Morraha said that he had not the wherewithal; and the other answered that he was never without a candle or the making of it; and he put his hand in his pocket and drew out a table and two chairs and a pack of cards, and they sat down on the chairs and went to card-playing. The first game Morraha won, and the Slender Red Champion bade him make his claim; and he asked that the land above him should be filled with stock of sheep in the morning. It was well; and he played no second game, but home he went.

The next day Morraha went to the brink of the sea, and the young man came in the currach and asked him would he play cards; they played, and Morraha won. The young man bade him make his claim; and he asked that the land above should be filled with cattle in the morning. It was well; and he played no other game, but went home.

On the third morning Morraha went to the brink of the sea, and he saw the young man coming. He drew up his boat on the shore and asked him would he play cards. They played, and Morraha won the game; and the young man bade him give his claim. And he said he would have a castle and a wife, the finest and fairest in the world; and they were his. It was well; and the Red Champion went away.

On the fourth day his wife asked him how he had found her. And he told her. 'And I am going out,' said he, 'to play again today.'

'I forbid you to go again to him. If you have won so much, you will lose more; have no more to do with him.'

But he went against her will, and he saw the currach coming; and the Red Champion was driving his balls from end to end of the currach; he had balls of silver and a hurl of gold, and he stopped not till he drew his boat on the shore, and made her fast for a year and a day. Morraha and he saluted each other; and he asked Morraha if he would play a game of cards, and they played, and he won. Morraha said to him, 'Give your claim now.'

Said he, 'You will hear it too soon. I lay on you bonds of the art of the druid, not to sleep two nights in one house, nor finish a second meal at the one table, till you bring me the sword of light and news of the death of Anshgayliacht.'

He went home to his wife and sat down in a chair, and gave a groan, and the chair broke in pieces.

'That is the groan of the son of a king under spells,' said his wife; 'and you had better have taken my counsel than that the spells should be on you.'

He told her he had to bring news of the death of Anshgayliacht and the sword of light to the Slender Red Champion.

'Go out,' said she, 'in the morning of the morrow, and take the bridle in the window, and shake it; and whatever beast, handsome or ugly, puts its head in it, take that one with you. Do not speak a word to her till she speaks to you; and take with you three pint bottles of ale and three sixpenny loaves, and do the thing she tells you; and when she runs to my father's land, on a height above the castle, she will shake herself, and the bells will ring, and my father will say, "Brown Allree is in the land. And if the son of a king or queen is there, bring him to me on your shoulders; but if it is the son of a poor man, let him come no farther." '

He rose in the morning, and took the bridle that was in the window, and went out and shook it; and Brown Allree came and put her head in it. He took the three loaves and three bottles of ale, and went riding; and when he was riding she bent her head down to take hold of her feet with her mouth, in hopes he would speak in ignorance; but he spoke not a word during the time, and the mare at last spoke to him, and told him to dismount and give her her dinner. He gave her the sixpenny loaf toasted, and a bottle of ale to drink.

'Sit up now riding, and take good heed of yourself: there are three miles of fire I have to clear at a leap.'

She cleared the three miles of fire at a leap, and asked if he were still riding, and he said he was. Then they went on, and she told him to dismount and give her a meal; and he did so, and gave her a sixpenny loaf and a bottle; she consumed them and said to him there were before them three miles of hill covered with steel thistles, and that she must clear it. She cleared the hill with a leap, and she asked him if he were still riding, and he said he was. They went on, and she went not far before she told him to give her a meal, and he gave her the bread and the bottleful. She went over three miles of sea with a leap, and she came then to the land of the King of France; she went up on a height above the castle, and she shook herself and neighed, and the bells rang; and the king said that it was Brown Allree was in the land.

'Go out,' said he; 'and if it is the son of a king or queen, carry him in on your shoulders; if it is not, leave him there.'

They went out; and the stars of the son of a king were on his breast; they lifted him high on their shoulders and bore him into the king. They passed the night cheerfully, playing and drinking, with sport and with diversion, till the whiteness of the day came upon the morrow morning.

Then the young king told the cause of his journey, and he asked the queen to give him counsel and good luck, and she told him everything he was to do.

'Go now,' said she, 'and take with you the best mare in the stable, and go to the door of Rough Niall of the Speckled Rock, and knock, and call on him to give you news of the death of Anshgayliacht

and the sword of light: and let the horse's back be to the door, and apply the spurs, and away with you.'

In the morning he did so, and he took the best horse from the stable and rode to the door of Niall, and turned the horse's back to the door, and demanded news of the death of Anshgayliacht and the sword of light; then he applied the spurs, and away with him. Niall followed him hard, and, as he was passing the gate, cut the horse in two. His wife was there with a dish of puddings and flesh, and she threw it in his eyes and blinded him, and said, 'Fool! Whatever kind of man it is that's mocking you, isn't that a fine condition you have got your father's horse into?'

On the morning of the next day Morraha rose, and took another horse from the stable, and went again to the door of Niall, and knocked and demanded news of the death of Anshgayliacht and the sword of light, and applied the spurs to the horse and away with him. Niall followed, and as Morraha was passing the gate, cut the horse in two and took half the saddle with him; but his wife met him and threw flesh in his eyes and blinded him.

On the third day, Morraha went again to the door of Niall; and Niall followed him, and as he was passing the gate, cut away the saddle from under him and the clothes from his back. Then his wife said to Niall, 'The fool that's mocking you is out yonder in the little currach, going home; and take good heed to yourself, and don't sleep one wink for three days.'

For three days the little currach kept in sight, but then Niall's wife came to him and said, 'Sleep as much as you want now. He is gone.'

He went to sleep, and there was heavy sleep on him, and Morraha went in and took hold of the sword that was on the bed at his head. And the sword thought to draw itself out of the hand of Morraha; but it failed. Then it gave a cry, and it wakened Niall, and Niall said it was a rude and rough thing to come into his house like that; and said Morraha to him, 'Leave your much talking, or I will cut the head off you. Tell me the news of the death of Anshgayliacht.'

'Oh, you can have my head.'

'But your head is no good to me; tell me the story.'

'Oh,' said Niall's wife, 'you must get the story.'

'Well,' said Niall, 'let us sit down together till I tell the story. I thought no one would ever get it; but now it will be heard by all.'

The Story

When I was growing up, my mother taught me the language of the birds; and when I got married, I used to be listening to their conversation; and I would be laughing; and my wife would be asking me what was the reason of my laughing, but I did not like to tell her, as women are always asking questions. We went out walking one fine morning, and the birds were arguing with one another. One of them said to another, 'Why should you be comparing yourself with me, when there is not a king nor knight that does not come to look at my tree?'

'What advantage has your tree over mine, on which there are three rods of magic mastery growing?'

When I heard them arguing, and knew that the rods were there, I began to laugh.

'Oh,' asked my wife, 'why are you always laughing? I believe it is at myself you are jesting, and I'll walk with you no more.'

'Oh, it is not about you I am laughing. It is because I understand the language of the birds.'

Then I had to tell her what the birds were saying to one another; and she was greatly delighted, and she asked me to go home, and she gave orders to the cook to have breakfast ready at six o'clock in the morning. I did not know why she was going out early, and breakfast was ready in the morning at the hour she appointed. She asked me to go out walking. I went with her. She went to the tree, and asked me to cut a rod for her.

'Oh, I will not cut it. Are we not better without it?'

'I will not leave this until I get the rod, to see if there is any good in it.'

I cut the rod and gave it to her. She turned from me and struck a blow on a stone, and changed it; and she struck a second blow on me, and made of me a black raven, and she went home and left me after her. I thought she would come back; she did not come, and I had to go into a tree till morning. In the morning, at six o'clock, there was a bellman out, proclaiming that everyone who killed a raven would get a fourpenny-bit. At last you could not find man or boy without a gun, nor, if you were to walk three miles, a raven that was not killed. I had to make a nest in the top of the parlour chimney, and hide myself all day till night came, and go out to pick up a bit to support me, till I spent a month. Here she is herself to say if it is a lie I am telling.

'It is not,' said she.

Then I saw her out walking. I went up to her, and I thought she would turn me back to my own shape, and she struck me with the rod and made of me an old white horse, and she ordered me to be put to a cart with a man, to draw stones from morning till night. I was worse off then. She spread abroad a report that I had died suddenly in my bed, and prepared a coffin, and waked and buried me. Then she had no trouble. But when I got tired I began to kill everyone who came near me, and I used to go into the haggard every night and destroy the stacks of corn; and when a man came near me in the morning I would follow him till I broke his bones. Everyone got afraid of me. When she saw I was doing mischief she came to meet me, and I thought she would change me. And she did change me, and made a fox of me. When I saw she was doing me every sort of damage I went away from her. I knew there was a badger's hole in the garden, and I went there till night came, and I made great slaughter among the geese and ducks. There she is herself to say if I am telling a lie.

'Oh! You are telling nothing but the truth, only less than the truth.'

When she had enough of my killing the fowl she came out into the garden, for she knew I was in the badger's hole. She came to me and made me a wolf. I had to be off, and go to an island, where no

She struck a second blow on me, and made of me a black raven

one at all would see me, and now and then I used to be killing sheep, for there were not many of them, and I was afraid of being seen and hunted; and so I passed a year, till a shepherd saw me among the sheep and a pursuit was made after me. And when the dogs came near me there was no place for me to escape to from them; but I recognised the sign of the king among the men, and I made for him, and the king cried out to stop the hounds. I took a leap upon the front of the king's saddle, and the woman behind cried out, 'My king and my lord, kill him or he will kill you!'

'Oh! He will not kill me. He knew me; he must be pardoned.'

The king took me home with him, and gave orders I should be well cared for. I was so wise, when I got food, I would not eat one morsel until I got a knife and fork. The man told the king, and the king came to see if it was true, and I got a knife and fork, and I took the knife in one paw and the fork in the other, and I bowed to the king. The king gave orders to bring him drink, and it came; and the king filled a glass of wine and gave it to me.

I took hold of it in my paw and drank it, and thanked the king.

'On my honour,' said he, 'it is some king or other has lost him, when he came on the island; and I will keep him, as he is trained; and perhaps he will serve us yet.'

And this is the sort of king he was – a king who had not a child living. Eight sons were born to him and three daughters, and they were stolen the same night they were born. No matter what guard was placed over them, the child would be gone in the morning. A twelfth child now came to the queen, and the king took me with him to watch the baby. The women were not satisfied with me.

'Oh,' said the king, 'what was all your watching ever good for? One that was born to me I have not; I will leave this one in the dog's care, and he will not let it go.'

A coupling was put between me and the cradle, and when everyone went to sleep I was watching till the person woke who attended in the daytime; but I was there only two nights; when it was near the day, I saw a hand coming down through the chimney, and the hand was so big that it took round the child altogether, and thought to take him away. I caught hold of the hand above the wrist, and as I was fastened to the cradle, I did not let go my hold till I cut the hand from the wrist,

and there was a howl from the person without. I laid the hand in the cradle with the child, and as I was tired I fell asleep; and when I awoke, I had neither child nor hand; and I began to howl, and the king heard me, and he cried out that something was wrong with me, and he sent servants to see what was the matter with me, and when the messenger came he saw me covered with blood, and he could not see the child; and he went to the king and told him the child was not to be got. The king came and saw the cradle coloured with the blood, and he cried out, 'Where has the child gone?' and everyone said it was the dog had eaten it.

The king said, 'It is not: loose him, and he will get the pursuit himself.'

When I was loosed, I found the scent of the blood till I came to a door of the room in which the child was. I went back to the king and took hold of him, and went back again and began to tear at the door. The king followed me and asked for the key. The servant said it was in the room of the stranger woman. The king caused search to be made for her, and she was not to be found. 'I will break the door,' said the king, 'as I can't get the key.' The king broke the door, and I went in, and went to the

I saw a hand coming down the chimney, and the hand was so big that it took round the child altogether

trunk, and the king asked for a key to unlock it. He got no key, and he broke the lock. When he opened the trunk, the child and the hand were stretched side by side, and the child was asleep. The king took the hand and ordered a woman to come for the child, and he showed the hand to everyone in the house. But the stranger woman was gone, and she did not see the king – and here she is herself to say if I am telling lies of her.

'Oh, it's nothing but the truth you have!'

The king did not allow me to be tied any more. He said there was nothing so much to wonder at as that I cut the hand off, as I was tied.

The child was growing till he was a year old. He was beginning to walk, and no one cared for him more than I did. He was growing till he was three, and he was running out every minute; so the king ordered a silver chain to be put between me and the child, that he might not go away from me. I was out with him in the garden every day, and the king was as proud as the world of the child. He would be watching him everywhere we went, till the child grew so wise that he would loose the chain and get off. But one day that he loosed it I failed to find him; and I ran into the house and searched the house, but there was no getting him for me. The king cried to go out and find the child, that had got loose from the dog. They went searching for him, but could not find him. When they failed altogether to find him, there remained no more favour with the king towards me, and everyone disliked me, and I grew weak, for I did not get a

morsel to eat half the time. When summer came, I said I would try and go home to my own country. I went away one fine morning, and I went swimming, and God helped me till I came home. I went into the garden, for I knew there was a place in the garden where I could hide myself, for fear my wife should see me. In the morning I saw her out walking, and the child with her, held by the hand. I pushed out to see the child, and as he was looking about him everywhere, he saw me and called out, 'I see my shaggy papa. Oh!' said he. 'Oh, my heart's love, my shaggy papa, come here till I see you!'

I was afraid the woman would see me, as she was asking the child where he saw me, and he said I was up in a tree; and the more the child called me, the more I hid myself. The woman took the child home with her, but I knew he would be up early in the morning.

I went to the parlour-window, and the child was within, and he playing. When he saw me he cried out, 'Oh! My heart's love, come here till I see you, shaggy papa.' I broke the window and went in, and he began to kiss me. I saw the rod in front of the chimney, and I jumped up at the rod and knocked it down. 'Oh! My heart's love, no one would give me the pretty rod,' said he. I hoped he would strike me with the rod, but he did not. When I saw the time was short I raised my paw, and I gave him a scratch below the knee. 'Oh! You naughty, dirty, shaggy papa, you have hurt me so much, I'll give you a blow of the rod.' He struck me a light blow, and so I came back to my own shape again. When he saw a man standing before him he gave a cry, and I took him up in my arms. The servants heard the child. A maid came into see what was the matter with him. When she saw me she gave a cry out of her, and she said, 'Oh, if the master isn't come to life again!'

Another came in, and said it was he really. When the mistress heard of it, she came to see with her own eyes, for she would not believe I was there; and when she saw me she said she'd drown herself. But I said to her, 'If you yourself will keep the secret, no living man will ever get the story from me until I lose my head.' Here she is herself to say if I am telling the truth.

'Oh, it's nothing but truth you are telling.'

When I saw I was in a man's shape, I said I would take the child back to his father and mother, as I knew the grief they were in after him. I got a ship, and took the child with me; and as I journeyed I came to land on an island, and I saw not a living soul on it, only a castle dark and gloomy. I went in to see was there anyone in it. There was no one but an old hag, tall and frightful, and she asked me, 'What sort of person are you?' I heard someone groaning in another room, and I said I was a doctor, and I asked her what ailed the person who was groaning.

'Oh,' said she, 'it is my son, whose hand has been bitten from his wrist by a dog.'

I knew then that it was he who had taken the child from me, and I said I would cure him if I got a good reward.

'I have nothing; but there are eight young lads and three young women, as handsome as anyone ever laid eyes on, and if you cure him I will give you them.'

'Tell me first in what place his hand was cut from him?'

'Oh, it was out in another country, twelve years ago.'

'Show me the way, that I may see him.'

She brought me into a room, so that I saw him, and his arm was swelled up to the shoulder. He asked me if I would cure him; and I said I would cure him if he would give me the reward his mother promised.

'Oh, I will give it; but cure me.'

'Well, bring them out to me.'

The hag brought them out of the room. I said I should burn the flesh that was on his arm. When I looked on him he was howling with pain. I said that I would not leave him in pain long. The wretch had only one eye in his forehead. I took a bar of iron, and put it in the fire till it was red, and I said to the hag, 'He will be howling at first, but will fall asleep presently, and do not wake him till he has slept as much as he wants. I will close the door when I am going out.' I took the bar with me, and I stood over him, and I turned it across through his eye as far as I could. He began to bellow, and tried to catch me, but I was out and away, having closed the door. The hag asked me, 'Why is he bellowing?'

'Oh, he will be quiet presently, and will sleep for a good while, and I'll come again to have a look at him; but bring me out the young men and the young women.'

I took them with me, and I said to her, 'Tell me where you got them.'

'My son brought them with him, and they are all the children of one king.'

I was well satisfied, and I had no wish for delay to get myself free from the hag, so I took them on board the ship, and the child I had myself. I thought the king might leave me the child I nursed myself; but when I came to land, and all those young people with me, the king and queen were out walking. The king was very aged, and the queen aged likewise. When I came to converse with them, and the twelve with me, the king and queen began to cry. I asked, 'Why are you crying?'

'It is for good cause I am crying. As many children as these I should have, and now I am withered, grey, at the end of my life, and I have not one at all.'

I told him all I went through, and I gave him the child in his hand, and I said, 'These are your other children who were stolen from you, whom I am giving to you safe. They are gently reared.'

When the king heard who they were he smothered them with kisses and drowned them with tears, and dried them with fine cloths silken and the hair of his own head, and so also did their mother, and great was his welcome for me, as it was I who found them all. The king said to me, 'I will give you the last child, as it is you who have earned him best; but you must come to my court every year, and the child with you, and I will share with you my possessions.

'I have enough of my own, and after my death I will leave them to the child.'

I spent a time, till my visit was over, and I told the king all the troubles I went through, only I said nothing about my wife. And now you have the story.

And now when you go home, and the Slender Red Champion asks you for news of the death of Anshgayliacht and for the sword of light, tell him the way in which his brother was killed, and say you have the sword; and he will ask the sword from you. Say you to him, 'If I promised to bring it to you, I did not promise to bring it for you;' and then throw the sword into the air and it will come back to me.

*   *   *

Morraha went home, and he told the story of the death of Anshgayliacht to the Slender Red Champion, 'And here,' said he, 'is the sword.' The Slender Red Champion asked for the sword; but he said, 'If I promised to bring it to you, I did not promise to bring it for you;' and he threw it into the air and it returned to Blue Niall.

Mouse and Mouser

The Mouse went to visit the Cat, and found her sitting behind the hall door, spinning.

MOUSE

What are you doing, my lady, my lady,
What are you doing, my lady?

CAT (*sharply*)

I'm spinning old breeches, good body, good body
I'm spinning old breeches, good body.

MOUSE

Long may you wear them, my lady, my lady,
Long may you wear them, my lady.

CAT (*gruffly*)

I'll wear' em and tear 'em, good body, good body.
I'll wear 'em and tear 'em, good body.

MOUSE

I was sweeping my room, my lady, my lady,
I was sweeping my room, my lady.

CAT

The cleaner you'd be, good body, good body,
The cleaner you'd be, good body.

MOUSE

I found a silver sixpence, my lady, my lady,
I found a silver sixpence, my lady.

CAT

The richer you were, good body, good body,
The richer you were, good body.

MOUSE

I went to the market, my lady, my lady,
I went to the market, my lady.

CAT

The farther you went, good body, good body
The farther you went, good body.

MOUSE

I bought me a pudding, my lady, my lady,
I bought me a pudding, my lady.

CAT (*snarling*)

The more meat you had, good body, good body,
The more meat you had, good body.

MOUSE

I put it in the window to cool, my lady,
I put it in the window to cool.

CAT (*sharply*)

The faster you'd eat it, good body, good body,
The faster you'd eat it, good body.

MOUSE (*timidly*)

The cat came and ate it, my lady, my lady,
The cat came and ate it, my lady.

CAT (*pouncingly*)

And I'll eat you, good body, good body,
And I'll eat you, good body.

(*Springs upon the mouse and kills it.*)

Mr Fox

Lady Mary was young and Lady Mary was fair. She had two brothers, and more lovers than she could count. But of them all, the bravest and most gallant was a Mr Fox, whom she met when she was down at her father's country-house. No one knew who Mr Fox was; but he was certainly brave, and surely rich, and of all her lovers, Lady Mary cared for him alone. At last it was agreed upon between them that they should be married. Lady Mary asked Mr Fox where they should live, and he described to her his castle, and where it was; but, strange to say, did not ask her or her brothers to come and see it.

So one day, near the wedding day, when her brothers were out, and Mr Fox was away for a day or two on business, as he said, Lady Mary set out for Mr Fox's castle. And after many searchings, she came at last to it, and a fine strong house it was, with high walls and a deep moat. And when she came up to the gateway she saw written on it:

BE BOLD, BE BOLD.

But as the gate was open, she went through it, and found no one there. So she went up to the doorway, and over it she found written:

BE BOLD, BE BOLD, BUT NOT TOO BOLD.

Still she went on till she came into the hall, and went up the broad stairs till she came to a door in the gallery, over which was written:

BE BOLD, BE BOLD, BUT NOT TOO BOLD, LEST YOUR HEART'S BLOOD SHOULD RUN COLD.

But Lady Mary was a brave one, she was, and she opened the door, and what do you think she saw? Why, bodies and skeletons of beautiful young ladies all stained with blood. So Lady Mary thought it was

Lady Mary rushed downtairs, and hid herself behind a cask,
just in time, as Mr Fox came in with the poor young lady who seemed to be fainting

high time to get out of that horrid place, and she closed the door, went through the gallery, and was just going down the stairs, and out of the hall, when who should she see through the window but Mr Fox dragging a beautiful young lady along from the gateway to the door. Lady Mary rushed downtairs, and hid herself behind a cask, just in time, as Mr Fox came in with the poor young lady who seemed to be fainting. Just as he got near Lady Mary, Mr Fox saw a diamond ring glittering on the finger of the young lady he was dragging, and he tried to pull it off. But it was tightly fixed, and would not come off, so Mr Fox cursed and swore, and drew his sword, raised it, and brought it down upon the hand of the poor lady. The sword cut off the hand, which jumped up into the air, and fell of all places in the world into Lady Mary's lap. Mr Fox looked about a bit, but did not think of looking behind the cask, so at last he went on, dragging the young lady up the stairs into the Bloody Chamber.

As soon as she heard him pass through the gallery, Lady Mary crept out of the door, down through the gateway, and ran home as fast as she could.

Now it happened that the very next day the marriage contract of Lady Mary and Mr Fox was to be signed, and there was a splendid breakfast before that. And when Mr Fox was seated at table opposite Lady Mary, he looked at her. 'How pale you are this morning, my dear.' 'Yes,' said she, 'I had a bad night's rest last night. I had horrible dreams.' 'Dreams go by contraries,' said Mr Fox; 'but tell us your dream, and your sweet voice will make the time pass till the happy hour comes.'

'I dreamed,' said Lady Mary, 'that I went yester-morn to your castle, and I found it in the woods, with high walls, and a deep moat, and over the gateway was written:

BE BOLD, BE BOLD.

'But it is not so, nor it was not so,' said Mr Fox.

'And when I came to the doorway over it was written:

BE BOLD, BE BOLD, BUT NOT TOO BOLD.

'It is not so, nor it was not so,' said Mr Fox.

'And then I went upstairs, and came to a gallery, at the end of which was a door, on which was written:

BE BOLD, BE BOLD, BUT NOT TOO BOLD, LEST YOUR HEART'S BLOOD SHOULD RUN COLD.

'It is not so, nor it was not so,' said Mr Fox.

'And then – and then I opened the door, and the room was filled with bodies and skeletons of poor dead women, all stained with their blood.'

'It is not so, nor it was not so. And God forbid it should be so,' said Mr Fox.

'I then dreamed that I rushed down the gallery, and just as I was going down the stairs, I saw you, Mr Fox, coming up to the hall door, dragging after you a poor young lady, rich and beautiful.'

'It is not so, nor it was not so. And God forbid it should be so,' said Mr Fox.

'I rushed downstairs, just in time to hide myself behind a cask, when you, Mr Fox, came in dragging the young lady by the arm. And, as you passed me, Mr Fox, I thought I saw you try and get off her diamond ring, and when you could not, Mr Fox, it seemed to me in my dream, that you out with your sword and hacked off the poor lady's hand to get the ring.'

'It is not so, nor it was not so. And God forbid it should be so,' said Mr Fox, and was going to say something else as he rose from his seat, when Lady Mary cried out: 'But it is so, and it was so. Here's hand and ring I have to show,' and pulled out the lady's hand from her dress, and pointed it straight at Mr Fox.

At once her brothers and her friends drew their swords and cut Mr Fox into a thousand pieces.

'But it is so, and it was so. Here's hand and ring I have to show.'

Mr Miacca

Tommy Grimes was sometimes a good boy and sometimes a bad boy; and when he was a bad boy, he was a very bad boy. Now his mother used to say to him: 'Tommy, Tommy, be a good boy, and don't go out of the street, or else Mr Miacca will take you.' But still when he was a bad boy he would go out of the street; and one day, sure enough, he had scarcely got round the corner, when Mr Miacca did catch him and popped him into a bag upside down, and took him off to his house.

When Mr Miacca got Tommy inside, he pulled him out of the bag and set him down, and felt his arms and legs. 'You're rather tough,' says he; 'but you're all I've got for supper, and you'll not taste bad boiled. But body o' me, I've forgot the herbs, and it's bitter you'll taste without herbs. Sally! Here, I say, Sally!' and he called Mrs Miacca.

So Mrs Miacca came out of another room and said: 'What d'ye want, my dear?'

'Oh, here's a little boy for supper,' said Mr Miacca, 'and I've forgot the herbs. Mind him, will ye, while I go for them.'

'All right, my love,' says Mrs Miacca, and off he goes.

Then Tommy Grimes said to Mrs Miacca: 'Does Mr Miacca always have little boys for supper?'

'Mostly, my dear,' said Mrs Miacca, 'if little boys are bad enough, and get in his way.'

'And don't you have anything else but boy-meat? No pudding?' asked Tommy.

'Ah, I loves pudding,' says Mrs Miacca. 'But it's not often the likes of me gets pudding.'

'Why, my mother is making a pudding this very day,' said Tommy Grimes, 'and I am sure she'd give you some, if I ask her. Shall I run and get some?'

'Now, that's a thoughtful boy,' said Mrs Miacca, 'only don't be long and be sure to be back for supper.'

So off Tommy pelters, and right glad he was to get off so cheap; and for many a long day he was as good as good could be, and never went round the corner of the street. But he couldn't always be good; and one day he went round the corner, and as luck would have it, he hadn't scarcely got round it when Mr Miacca grabbed him up, popped him in his bag, and took him home.

When he got him there, Mr Miacca dropped him out; and when he saw him, he said: 'Ah, you're the youngster what served me and my missus that shabby trick, leaving us without any supper. Well, you shan't do it again. I'll watch over you myself. Here, get under the sofa, and I'll set on it and watch the pot boil for you.'

So poor Tommy Grimes had to creep under the sofa, and Mr Miacca sat on it and waited for the pot to boil. And they waited, and they waited, but still the pot didn't boil, till at last Mr Miacca got tired of waiting, and he said: 'Here, you under there, I'm not going to wait any longer; put out your leg, and I'll stop your giving us the slip.'

So Tommy put out a leg, and Mr Miacca got a chopper, and chopped it off, and pops it in the pot.

Suddenly he calls out: 'Sally, my dear, Sally!' and nobody answered. So he went into the next room to look for Mrs Miacca, and while he was there, Tommy crept out from under the sofa and ran out of the door. For it was a leg of the sofa that he had put out. So Tommy Grimes ran home, and he never went round the corner again till he was old enough to go alone.

Mr Vinegar

Mr and Mrs Vinegar lived in a vinegar bottle. Now, one day, when Mr Vinegar was away from home, Mrs Vinegar, who was a very good housewife, was busily sweeping her house, when an unlucky thump of the broom brought the whole house clitter-clatter, clitter-clatter, about her ears. In an agony of grief she rushed forth to meet her husband.

On seeing him she exclaimed, 'Oh, Mr Vinegar, Mr Vinegar, we are ruined. I have knocked the house down, and it is all to pieces!' Mr Vinegar then said: 'My dear, let us see what can be done. Here is the door; I will take it on my back, and we will go forth to seek our fortune.'

They walked all that day, and at nightfall entered a thick forest. They were both very, very tired, and Mr Vinegar said: 'My love, I will climb up into a tree, drag up the door, and you shall follow.' He accordingly did so, and they both stretched their weary limbs on the door, and fell fast asleep.

In the middle of the night Mr Vinegar was disturbed by the sound of voices underneath, and to his horror and dismay found that it was a band of thieves met to divide their booty.

'Here, Jack,' said one, 'here's five pounds for you; here, Bill, here's ten pounds for you; here, Bob, here's three pounds for you.'

Mr Vinegar could listen no longer; his terror was so great that he trembled and trembled, and shook down the door on their heads. Away scampered the thieves, but Mr Vinegar dared not quit his retreat till broad daylight.

He then scrambled out of the tree, and went to lift up the door. And what did he see but a number of golden guineas. 'Come down, Mrs Vinegar,' he cried; 'come down, I say; our fortune's made, our fortune's made! Come down, I say.' Mrs Vinegar got down as fast as she could, and when she saw the money she jumped for joy. 'Now, my dear,' said she, 'I'll tell you what you shall do. There is a fair at the neighbouring town; you shall take these forty guineas and buy a cow. I can make butter and cheese, which you shall sell at market, and we shall then be able to live very comfortably.'

Mr Vinegar joyfully agrees, takes the money, and off he goes to the fair. When he arrived, he walked up and down, and at length saw a beautiful red cow. It was an excellent milker, and perfect in every way. 'Oh,' thought Mr Vinegar, 'if I had but that cow, I should be the happiest, man alive.' So he offers the forty guineas for the cow, and the owner said that, as he was a friend, he'd oblige him. So the bargain was made, and he got the cow and he drove it backwards and forwards to show it.

By and by he saw a man playing the bagpipes – Tweedle-dum tweedle-dee. The children followed him about, and he appeared to be pocketing money on all sides. 'Well,' thought Mr Vinegar, 'if I had but that beautiful instrument I should be the happiest man alive – my fortune would be made.'

So he went up to the man. 'Friend,' says he, 'what

a beautiful instrument that is, and what a deal of money you must make.' 'Why, yes,' said the man, 'I make a great deal of money, to be sure, and it is a wonderful instrument.' 'Oh!' cried Mr Vinegar, 'how I should like to possess it!' 'Well,' said the man, 'as you are a friend, I don't much mind parting with it; you shall have it for that red cow.' 'Done!' said the delighted Mr Vinegar. So the beautiful red cow was given for the bagpipes.

He walked up and down with his purchase; but it was in vain he tried to play a tune, and instead of pocketing pence, the boys followed him hooting, laughing and pelting.

Poor Mr Vinegar, his fingers grew very cold, and, just as he was leaving the town, he met a man with a fine thick pair of gloves. 'Oh, my fingers are so very cold,' said Mr Vinegar to himself. 'Now if I had but those beautiful gloves I should be the happiest man alive.' He went up to the man, and said to him, 'Friend, you seem to have a capital pair of gloves there.' 'Yes, truly,' cried the man; 'and my hands are as warm as possible this cold November day.' 'Well,' said Mr Vinegar, 'I should like to have them.'. 'What will you give?' said the man; 'as you are a friend, I don't much mind letting you have them for those bagpipes.' 'Done!' cried Mr Vinegar. He put on the gloves, and felt perfectly happy as he trudged homewards.

At last he grew very tired, and just then saw a man coming towards him with a good stick in his hand.

'Oh,' said Mr Vinegar, 'that I had but that stick! I should then be the happiest man alive.' He said to the man: 'Friend! what a rare good stick you have got.' 'Yes,' said the man; 'I have used it for many a long mile, and a good friend it has been; but if

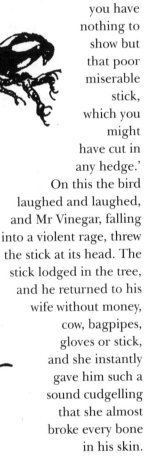

you have a fancy for it, as you are a friend, I don't mind giving it to you for that pair of gloves.' Mr Vinegar's hands were so warm, and his legs so tired, that he gladly made the exchange.

As he drew near to the wood where he had left his wife, he heard a parrot on a tree calling out his name: 'Mr Vinegar, you foolish man, you blockhead, you simpleton; you went to the fair, and laid out all your money in buying a cow. Not content with that, you changed it for bagpipes, on which you could not play, and which were not worth one-tenth of the money. You fool, you – you had no sooner got the bagpipes than you changed them for the gloves, which were not worth one-quarter of the bagpipes; and when you had got the gloves, you changed them for a poor miserable stick; and now for your forty guineas, cow, bagpipes and gloves, you have nothing to show but that poor miserable stick, which you might have cut in any hedge.' On this the bird laughed and laughed, and Mr Vinegar, falling into a violent rage, threw the stick at its head. The stick lodged in the tree, and he returned to his wife without money, cow, bagpipes, gloves or stick, and she instantly gave him such a sound cudgelling that she almost broke every bone in his skin.

Munachar and Manachar

There once lived a Munachar and a Manachar, a long time ago, and it is a long time since it was, and if they were alive now they would not be alive then. They went out together to pick raspberries, and as many as Munachar used to pick Manachar used to eat. Munachar said he must go and look for a rod to make a gad to hang Manachar, who ate his raspberries every one; and he came to the rod. 'What news the day?' said the rod. 'It is my own news that I'm seeking. Going looking for a rod, a rod to make a gad, a gad to hang Manachar, who ate my raspberries every one.'

'You will not get me,' said the rod, 'until you get an axe to cut me.' He came to the axe. 'What news today?' said the axe. 'It's my own news I'm seeking. Going looking for an axe, an axe to cut a rod, a rod to make a gad, a gad to hang Manachar who ate my raspberries every one.'

'You will not get me,' said the axe, 'until you get a flag to edge me.' He came to the flag. 'What news today?' says the flag. 'It's my own news I'm seeking. Going looking for a flag, flag to edge axe, axe to cut a rod, a rod to make a gad, a gad to hang Manachar, who ate my raspberries every one.'

'You will not get me,' says the flag, 'till you get water to wet me.' He came to the water. 'What news today?' says the water. 'It's my own

news that I'm seeking. Going looking for water, water to wet flag to edge axe, axe to cut a rod, a rod to make a gad, a gad to hang Manachar, who ate my raspberries every one.'

'You will not get me,' said the water, 'until you get a deer who will swim me.' He came to the deer. 'What news today?' says the deer. 'It's my own news I'm seeking. Going looking for a deer, deer to swim water, water to wet flag, flag to edge axe, axe to cut a rod, a rod to make a gad, a gad to hang Manachar, who ate my raspberries every one.'

'You will not get me,' said the deer, 'until you get a hound who will hunt me.' He came to the hound. 'What news today?' says the hound. 'It's my own news I'm seeking. Going looking for a hound, hound to hunt deer, deer to swim water, water to wet flag, flag to edge axe, axe to cut a rod, a rod to make a gad, a gad to hang Manachar, who ate my raspberries every one.'

'You will not get me,' said the hound, 'until you get a bit of butter to put in my claw.' He came to the butter. 'What news today?' says the butter. 'It's my own news I'm seeking. Going looking for butter, butter to go in claw of hound, hound to hunt deer, deer to swim water, water to wet flag, flag to edge axe, axe to cut a rod, a rod to make a gad, a gad to hang Manachar, who ate my raspberries every one.'

'You will not get me,' said the butter, 'until you get a cat who shall scrape me.' He came to the cat. 'What news today?' said the cat. 'It's my own news I'm seeking. Going looking for a cat, cat to scrape butter, butter to go in claw of hound, hound to hunt deer, deer to swim water, water to wet flag, flag to edge axe, axe to cut a rod, a rod to make a gad, gad to hang Manachar, who ate my raspberries every one.'

'You will not get me,' said the cat, 'until you will get milk which you will give me.' He came to the cow. 'What news today?' said the cow. It's my own news I'm seeking. Going looking for a cow, cow to give me milk, milk I will give to the cat, cat to scrape butter, butter to go in claw of hound, hound to hunt deer, deer to swim water, water to wet flag, flag to edge axe, axe to cut a rod, a rod to make a gad, a gad to hang Manachar, who ate my raspberries every one.'

'You will not get any milk from me,' said the cow, 'until you bring me a whisp of straw from those threshers yonder.' He came to the threshers. 'What news today?' said the threshers. 'It's my own news I'm seeking. Going looking for a whisp of straw from ye to give to the cow, the cow to give me milk, milk I will give to the cat, cat to scrape butter, butter to go in claw of hound, hound to hunt deer, deer to swim water, water to wet flag, flag to edge axe, axe to cut a rod, a rod to make a gad, a gad to hang Manachar, who ate my raspberries every one.'

You will not get any whisp of straw from us,' said the threshers, 'until you bring us the makings of a cake from the miller over yonder.' He came to the miller. 'What news today?' said the miller. 'It's my own news I'm seeking. Going looking for the makings of a cake which I will give to the threshers, the threshers to give me a whisp of straw, the whisp of straw I will give to the cow, the cow to give me milk, milk I will give to the cat, cat to scrape butter, butter to go in claw of hound, hound to hunt deer, deer to swim water, water to wet flag, flag to edge axe, axe to cut a rod, a rod to make a gad, a gad to hang Manachar, who ate my raspberries every one.'

'You will not get any makings of a cake from me,' said the miller, 'till you bring me the full of that

sieve of water from the river over there.' He took the sieve in his hand and went over to the river, but as often as ever he would stoop and fill it with water, the moment he raised it the water would run out of it again, and sure, if he had been there from that day till this, he never could have filled it.

A crow went flying by him, over his head. 'Daub! Daub!' said the crow. 'My blessings on ye, then,' said Munachar, 'but it's the good advice you have,' and he took the red clay and the daub that was by the brink, and he rubbed it to the bottom of the sieve, until all the holes were filled, and then the sieve held the water, and he brought the water to the miller, and the miller gave him the makings of a cake, and he gave the makings of the cake to the threshers, and the threshers gave him a whisp of straw, and he gave the whisp of straw to the cow, and the cow gave him milk, the milk he gave to the cat, the cat scraped the butter, the butter went into the claw of the hound, the hound hunted the deer, the deer swam the water, the water wet the flag, the flag sharpened the axe, the axe cut the rod, and the rod made a gad, and when he had it ready to hang Manachar he found that Manachar had burst.

The Nightingale and the Rose

'She said that she would dance with me if I brought her red roses,' cried the young student, 'but in all my garden there is no red rose.'

From her nest in the holm-oak tree the nightingale heard him, and she looked out through the leaves and wondered.

'No red rose in all my garden!' he cried, and his beautiful eyes filled with tears. 'Ah, on what little things does happiness depend! I have read all that the wise men have written, and all the secrets of philosophy are mine, yet for want of a red rose is my life made wretched.'

'Here at last is a true lover,' said the nightingale. 'Night after night have I sung of him, though I knew him not; night after night have I told his story to the stars and now I see him. His hair is dark as the hyacinth-blossom, and his lips are red as the rose of his desire; but passion has made his face like pale ivory, and sorrow has set her seal upon his brow.'

'The prince gives a ball tomorrow night,' murmured the young student, 'and my love will be of the company. If I bring her a red rose she will dance with me till dawn. If I bring her a red rose, I shall hold her in my arms, and she will lean her head upon my shoulder, and her hand will be clasped in mine. But there is no red rose in my garden, so I shall sit lonely, and she will pass me by. She will have no heed of me, and my heart will break.'

'Here, indeed, is the true lover,' said the nightingale. 'What I sing of, he suffers; what is joy to me, to him is pain. Surely love is a wonderful thing. It is more precious than emeralds, and dearer than fine opals. Pearls and pomegranates cannot buy it, nor is it set forth in the market-place. It may not be purchased from the merchants, nor can it be weighed out in the balance for gold.'

'The musicians will sit in their gallery,' said the young student, 'and play upon their stringed instruments, and my love will dance to the sound of the harp and the violin. She will dance so lightly that her feet will not touch the floor, and the courtiers in their gay dresses will throng round her. But with me she will not dance, for I have no red rose to give her;' and he flung himself down on the grass, and buried his face in his hands, and wept.

'Why is he weeping?' asked a little green lizard as he ran past him with his tail in the air.

'Why, indeed!' said a butterfly, who was fluttering about after a sunbeam.

'Why, indeed?' whispered a daisy to his neighbour, in a soft, low voice.

'He is weeping for a red rose,' said the nightingale.

'For a red rose?' they cried; 'how very ridiculous!' and the little lizard, who was something of a cynic, laughed outright.

But the nightingale understood the secret of the student's sorrow, and she sat silent in the oak tree, and thought about the mystery of love.

Suddenly she spread her brown wings for flight, and soared into the air. She passed through the grove like a shadow and like a shadow she sailed across the garden.

In the centre of the grass-plot was standing a beautiful rose tree, and when she saw it she flew over to it, and lit upon a spray.

'Give me a red rose,' she cried, 'and I will sing you my sweetest song.'

But the tree shook its head. 'My roses are white,' it answered; 'as white as the foam of the sea, and whiter than the snow upon the mountain. But go to my brother who grows round the old sundial, and perhaps he will give you what you want.'

So the nightingale flew over to the rose tree that was growing round the old sundial.

'Give me a red rose,' she cried, 'and I will sing you my sweetest song.'

But the tree shook its head. 'My roses are yellow,' it answered; 'as yellow as the hair of the mermaiden who sits upon an amber throne, and yellower than the daffodil that blooms in the meadow before the mower comes with his scythe. But go to my brother who grows beneath the student's window, and perhaps he will give you what you want."

So the nightingale flew over to the rose tree that was growing beneath the student's window.

'Give me a red rose,' she cried, 'and I will sing you my sweetest song.'

But the tree shook its head.

'My roses are red,' it answered, 'as red as the feet of the dove and redder than the great fans of coral that wave and wave in the ocean-cavern. But the winter has chilled my veins, and the frost has nipped my buds, and the storm has broken my branches, and I shall have no roses at all this year.'

'One red rose is all I want,' cried the nightingale, 'only one red rose! Is there no way by which I can get it?'

'There is a way,' answered the tree; 'but it is so terrible that I dare not tell it to you.'

'Tell it to me,' said the nightingale, 'I am not afraid.'

'If you want a red rose,' said the tree, 'you must build it out of music by moonlight, and stain it with your own heart's-blood. You must sing to me with your breast against a thorn. All night long you must sing to me, and the thorn must pierce your heart, and your life-blood must flow into my veins and become mine.'

'Death is a great price to pay for a red rose,' cried the nightingale, 'and life is very dear to all. It is pleasant to sit in the greenwood, and to watch the sun in his chariot of gold, and the moon in her chariot of pearl. Sweet is the scent of the hawthorn, and sweet are the bluebells that hide in the valley, and the heather that blows on the hill. Yet love is better than life and what is the heart of a bird compared to the heart of a man?'

So she spread her brown wings for flight, and soared into the air. She swept over the garden like a shadow, and like a shadow she sailed through the grove.

The young student was still lying on the grass, where she had left him, and the tears were not yet dry in his beautiful eyes.

'Be happy,' cried the nightingale, 'be happy; you shall have your red rose. I will build it out of music by moonlight, and stain it with my own heart's-blood. All that I ask of you in return is that you will be a true lover, for Love is wiser than Philosophy, though he is wise, and mightier than Power, though he is mighty. Flame-coloured are his wings, and coloured like flame is his body. His lips are sweet as honey, and his breath is like frankincense.'

The student looked up from the grass, and listened, but he could not understand what the nightingale was saying to him, for he only knew the things that are written down in books.

But the oak tree understood, and felt sad for he was very fond of the little nightingale who had built her nest in his branches.

'Sing me one last song,' he whispered. 'I shall feel lonely when you are gone.'

So the nightingale sang to the oak tree, and her voice was like water bubbling from a silver jar.

When she had finished her song, the student got up, and pulled a notebook and a lead-pencil out of his pocket.

'She has form,' he said to himself, as he walked away through the grove – 'that cannot be denied to her; but has she got feeling? I am afraid not. In fact, she is like most artists; she is all style without any sincerity. She would not sacrifice herself for others. She thinks merely of music, and everybody knows that the arts are selfish. Still, it must be admitted that she has some beautiful notes in her voice. What a pity it is that they do not mean anything, or do any practical good!' And he went into his room, and lay down on his little pallet-bed, and began to think of his love; and, after a time, he fell asleep.

And when the moon shone in the heavens the nightingale flew to the rose tree, and set her breast against the thorn. All night long she sang, with her breast against the thorn, and the cold crystal moon leaned down and listened. All night long she sang, and the thorn went deeper and deeper into her breast, and her lifeblood ebbed away from her.

She sang first of the birth of love in the heart of a boy and a girl. And on the topmost spray of the rose tree there blossomed a marvellous rose, petal following petal, as song followed song. Pale was it, at first, as the mist that hangs over the river – pale as the feet of the morning, and silver as the wings of the dawn. As the shadow of a rose in a mirror of silver, as the shadow of a rose in a water-pool, so was the rose that blossomed on the topmost spray of the tree.

But the tree cried to the nightingale to press closer against the thorn. 'Press closer, little nightingale,' cried the tree, 'or the day will come before the rose is finished.'

So the nightingale pressed closer against the thorn and louder and louder grew her song, for she sang of the birth of passion in the soul of a man and a maid.

And a delicate flush of pink came into the leaves of the rose, like the flush in the face of the bridegroom when he kisses the lips of the bride. But the thorn had not yet reached her heart, so the rose's heart remained white, for only a nightingale's heart's-blood can crimson the heart of a rose.

And the tree cried to the nightingale to press closer against the thorn. 'Press closer, little nightingale,' cried the tree, 'or the day will come before the rose is finished.'

So the nightingale pressed closer against the thorn, and the thorn touched her heart, and a fierce pang of pain shot through her. Bitter, bitter was the pain, and wilder and wilder grew her song,

for she sang of the love that is perfected by death, of the love that dies not in the tomb.

And the marvellous rose became crimson, like the rose of the eastern sky. Crimson was the girdle of petals, and crimson as a ruby was the heart.

But the nightingale's voice grew fainter, and her little wings began to beat, and a film came over her eyes. Fainter and fainter grew her song, and she felt something choking her in her throat.

Then she gave one last burst of music. The white moon heard it, and she forgot the dawn, and lingered on in the sky. The red rose heard it, and it trembled all over with ecstasy, and opened its petals to the cold morning air. Echo bore it to her purple cavern in the hills, and woke the sleeping shepherds from their dreams. It floated through the reeds of the river, and they carried its message to the sea.

'Look, look!' cried the tree, 'the rose is finished now;' but the nightingale made no answer, for she was lying dead in the long grass, with the thorn in her heart.

And at noon the student opened his window and looked out.

'Why what a wonderful piece of luck,' he cried; 'here is a red rose! I have never seen any rose like it in all my life. It is so beautiful that I am sure it has a long Latin name;' and he leaned down and plucked it.

Then he put on his hat, and ran up to the professor's house with the rose in his hand.

The daughter of the professor was sitting in the doorway winding blue silk on a reel, and her little dog was lying at her feet.

'You said that you would dance with me if I brought you a red rose,' cried the student. 'Here is the reddest rose in all the world. You will wear it tonight next your heart, and as we dance together it will tell you how I love you.'

But the girl frowned.

'I am afraid it will not go with my dress,' she answered; 'and, besides, the chamberlain's nephew has sent me some real jewels, and everybody knows that jewels cost far more than flowers.'

'Well, upon my word, you are very ungrateful,' said the student angrily; and he threw the rose into the street, where it fell into the gutter, and a cartwheel went over it.

'Ungrateful!' said the girl. 'I tell you what, you are very rude; and, after all, who are you? Only a student. Why, I don't believe you have even got silver buckles to your shoes as the chamberlain's nephew has;' and she got up from her chair and went into the house.

'What a silly thing love is!' said the student as he walked away. 'It is not half as useful as logic, for it does not prove anything, and it is always telling one of things that are not going to happen, and making one believe things that are not true. In fact, it is quite unpractical, and, as in this age to be practical is everything, I shall go back to philosophy and study metaphysics.'

So he returned to his room and pulled out a great dusty book, and began to read.

Nix Nought Nothing

There once lived a king and a queen as many a one has been. They were long married and had no children; but at last a baby boy came to the queen when the king was away in the far countries. The queen would not christen the boy till the king came back, and she said, 'We will just call him Nix Nought Nothing until his father comes home.' But it was long before he came home, and the boy had grown a nice little laddie. At length the king was on his way back; but he had a big river to cross, and there was a whirlpool, and he could not get over the water. But a giant came up to him, and said, 'I'll carry you over.' But the king said: 'What's your pay?' 'Oh, give me Nix, Nought, Nothing, and I will carry you over the water on my back.' The king had never heard that his son was called Nix Nought Nothing, and so he said: 'Oh, I'll give you that and my thanks into the bargain.' When the king got home again, he was very happy to see his wife again, and his young son. She told him that she had not given the child any name, but just Nix Nought Nothing, until he should come home again himself. The poor king was in a terrible case. He said: 'What have I done? I promised to give the giant who carried me over the river on his back Nix Nought Nothing.' The king and the queen were sad and sorry, but they said: 'When the giant comes we will give him the henwife's boy; he will never know the difference.' The next day the giant came to claim the king's promise, and they sent for the henwife's boy, and the giant went away with the boy on his back. He travelled till he came to a big stone, and there he sat down to rest. He said, 'Hidge, Hodge, on my back, what time of day is that?'

The poor little boy said: 'It is the time that my mother, the henwife, takes up the eggs for the queen's breakfast.'

The giant was very angry, and dashed the boy's head on the stone and killed him.

So he went back in a tower of a temper and this time they gave him the gardener's boy. He went off with him on his back till they got to the stone again when the giant sat down to rest. And he said: 'Hidge, Hodge, on my back, what time of day do you make that?'

The gardener's boy said: 'Sure it's the time that my mother takes up the vegetables for the queen's dinner.' Then the giant was right wild and dashed his brains out on the stone.

Then the giant went back to the king's house in a terrible temper and said he would destroy them all if they did not give him Nix Nought Nothing this time. They had to do it; and when he came to the big stone, the giant said: 'What time of day is that?' Nix Nought Nothing said: 'It is the time that my father the king will be sitting down to supper.' The giant said: 'I've got the right one now;' and took Nix Nought Nothing to his own house and brought him up till he was a man.

The giant had a bonny daughter, and she and the lad grew very fond of each other. The giant said one day to Nix Nought Nothing: 'I've work for you tomorrow. There is a stable seven miles long and seven miles broad, and it has not been cleaned for seven years, and you must clean it tomorrow, or I will have you for my supper.'

The giant's daughter went out next morning with the lad's breakfast, and found him in a terrible state, for always as he cleaned out a bit, it just fell in again. The giant's daughter said she would help him, and she called all the beasts in the field and all the fowls of the air and in a minute they all came and carried away everything that was in the stable and made it all clean before the giant came home. He said: 'Shame on the wit that helped you; but I have a worse job for you tomorrow.' Then he said to Nix Nought Nothing: 'There's a lake seven miles long and seven miles deep and seven miles broad, and you must drain it tomorrow by nightfall, or else I'll have you for my supper.' Nix Nought Nothing began early next morning and tried to lave the water with his pail, but the lake was never getting any less, and he didn't know what to do; but the giant's daughter called on all the fish in the sea to come and drink the water, and very soon they drank it dry. When the giant saw the work done he was in a rage, and said: 'I've a worse job for you tomorrow; there is a tree, seven miles high, and no branch on it till you get to the top, and there is a nest with seven eggs in it, and you must bring down all the eggs without breaking one, or else I'll have you for my supper.' At first the giant's daughter did not know how to help Nix Nought Nothing; but she cut off first her fingers and then her toes, and made steps of them, and he climbed the tree and got all the eggs safe till he came just to the bottom, and then one was broken. So they determined to run away together and after the giant's daughter had tidied up her hair a bit and got her magic flask they set out together as fast as they could run. And they hadn't got but three fields away when they looked back and saw the giant walking along at top speed after them. 'Quick, quick,' called out the giant's daughter, 'take my comb from my hair and throw it down.' Nix Nought Nothing took her comb from her hair and threw it down, and out of every one of its prongs there sprang up a fine thick briar in the way of the giant. You may be sure it took him a long time to work his way through the briars and by the time he was well through Nix Nought

Nothing and his sweetheart had run on a tidy step away from him. But he soon came along after them and was just like to catch 'em up when the giant's daughter called out to Nix Nought Nothing, 'Take my hair dagger and throw it down, quick, quick.' So Nix Nought Nothing threw down the hair dagger and out of it grew as quick as lightning a thick hedge of sharp razors placed criss-cross. The giant had to tread very cautiously to get through all this and meanwhile the young lovers ran on, and on, and on, till they were nearly out of sight. But at last the giant was through, and it wasn't long before he was like to catch them up. But just as he was stretching out his hand to catch Nix Nought Nothing his daughter took out her magic flask and dashed it on the ground. And as it broke out of it welled a big, big wave that grew, and that grew, till it reached the giant's waist, and then his neck, and when it got to his head, he was drowned dead, and dead, and dead indeed. So he goes out of the story.

But Nix Nought Nothing fled on till where do you think they came to? Why, to near the castle of Nix Nought Nothing's father and mother. But the giant's daughter was so weary that she couldn't move a step farther. So Nix Nought Nothing told her to wait there while he went and found out a lodging for the night. And he went on towards the lights of the castle, and on the way he came to the

The giant's daughter called on all the fish in the sea to come and drink the water, and very soon they drank it dry

cottage of the henwife whose boy had had his brains dashed out by the giant. Now she knew Nix Nought Nothing in a moment, and hated him because he was the cause of her son's death. So when he asked his way to the castle she put a spell upon him, and when he got to the castle, no sooner was he let in than he fell down dead asleep upon a chair in the hall. The king and queen tried all they could do to wake him up, but all in vain. So the king promised that if any lady could wake him up she should marry him. Meanwhile the giant's daughter was waiting and waiting for him to come back. And she went up into a tree to watch for him. The gardener's daughter, going to draw water in the well, saw the shadow of the lady in the water and thought it was herself, and said: 'If I'm so bonny, if I'm so brave, why do you send me to draw water?' So she threw down her pail and went to see if she could wed the sleeping stranger. And she went to the henwife, who taught her an unspelling catch which would keep Nix Nought Nothing awake as long as the gardener's daughter liked. So she went up to the castle and sang her catch and Nix Nought Nothing was wakened for a bit and they promised to wed him to the gardener's daughter. Meanwhile the gardener went down to draw water from the well and saw the shadow of the lady in the

water. So he looks up and finds her, and he brought the lady from the tree, and led her into his house. And he told her that a stranger was to marry his daughter, and took her up to the castle and showed her the man: and it was Nix Nought Nothing asleep in a chair. And she saw him, and cried to him: 'Waken, waken, and speak to me!' But he would not waken, and soon she cried: 'I cleaned the stable, I laved the lake and I climbed the tree, and all for the love of thee, and thou wilt not waken and speak to me.' The king and the queen heard this, and came to the bonny young lady, and she said: 'I cannot get Nix Nought Nothing to speak to me for all that I can do.'

Then were they greatly astonished when she spoke of Nix Nought Nothing, and asked where he was, and she said: 'He that sits there in the chair.' Then they ran to him and kissed him and called him their own dear son; so they called for the gardener's daughter and made her sing her charm, and he wakened, and told them all that the giant's daughter had done for him, and of all her kindness. Then they took her in their arms and kissed her, and said she should now be their daughter, for their son should marry her. But they sent for the henwife and put her to death. And they lived happy all their days.

The Nixy

There was once upon a time a miller who was very well off, and had as much money and as many goods as he knew what to do with. But sorrow comes in the night, and the miller all of a sudden became so poor that at last he could hardly call the mill in which he sat his own. He wandered about all day full of despair and misery, and when he lay down at night he could get no rest, but lay awake sunk in sorrowful thoughts.

One morning he rose up before dawn and went outside, for he thought his heart would be lighter in the open air. As he wandered up and down on the banks of the millpond he heard a rustling in the water, and when he looked near he saw a white woman rising up from the waves.

He realised at once that this could be none other than the nixy of the millpond, and in his terror he didn't know if he should fly away or remain where he was. While he hesitated the nixy spoke, called him by his name, and asked him why he was so sad.

When the miller heard how friendly her tone was, he plucked up heart and told her how rich and prosperous he had been all his life hitherto, but now he didn't know what he was to do for want and misery.

Then the nixy spoke comforting words to him, and promised that she would make him richer and more prosperous than he had ever been in his life before if he would give her in return the youngest thing in his house.

The miller thought she must mean one of his puppies or kittens, so promised the nixy at once what she asked and returned to his mill full of hope. On the threshold he was greeted by a servant with the news that his wife had just given birth to a boy.

The poor miller was much horrified by these tidings, and went in to his wife with a heavy heart to tell her and his relations of the fatal bargain he had just struck with the nixy. 'I would gladly give up all the good fortune she promised me,' he said, 'if I could only save my child.' But no one could think of any advice to give him, beyond taking care that the child never went near the millpond.

So the boy thrived and grew big, and in the meantime all prospered with the miller, and in a few years he was richer than he had ever been before. But all the same he did not enjoy his good fortune, for he could not forget his compact with the nixy, and he knew that sooner or later she would demand his fulfilment of it. But year after year went by, and the boy grew up and became a great hunter, and the lord of the land took him into his service, for he was as smart and bold a hunter as you would wish to see. In a short time he married a pretty young wife, and lived with her in great peace and happiness.

One day when he was out hunting a hare sprang up at his feet, and ran for some way in front of him in the open field. The hunter pursued it hotly for some time, and at last shot it dead. Then he proceeded to skin it, never noticing that he was close to the millpond, which from childhood up he had been taught to avoid. He soon finished the skinning, and went to the water to wash the blood off his hands. He had hardly dipped them in the pond when the nixy rose up in the water, and seizing him in her wet arms she dragged him down with her under the waves.

When the hunter did not come home in the evening his wife grew very anxious, and when his game bag was found close to the millpond she guessed at once what had befallen him. She was nearly beside herself with grief, and roamed round and round the pond calling on her husband without ceasing. At last, worn out with sorrow and fatigue, she fell asleep and dreamt that she was wandering along a flowery meadow when she came to a hut where she found an old witch who promised to restore her husband to her.

When she awoke next morning she determined to set out and find the witch; so she wandered on for many a day, and at last she reached the flowery

meadow and found the hut where the old witch lived. The poor wife told her all that had happened and how she had been told in a dream of the witch's power to help her.

The witch counselled her to go to the pond the first time there was a full moon, and to comb her black hair with a golden comb, and then to place the comb on the bank. The hunter's wife gave the witch a handsome present, thanked her heartily, and returned home.

Time dragged heavily till the time of the full moon, but it passed at last, and as soon as it rose the young wife went to the pond, combed her black hair with a golden comb, and when she had finished, placed the comb on the bank; then she

watched the water impatiently. Soon she heard a rushing sound, and a big wave rose suddenly and swept the comb off the bank, and a minute after the head of her husband rose from the pond and gazed sadly at her. But immediately another wave came, and the head sank back into the water without having said a word. The pond lay still and motionless, glittering in the moonshine, and the hunter's wife was not a bit better off than she had been before.

In despair she wandered about for days and nights, and at last, worn out by fatigue, she sank once more into a deep sleep, and dreamt exactly the same dream about the old witch. So next morning she went again to the flowery meadow

and sought the witch in her hut, and told her of her grief. The old woman counselled her to go to the millpond the next full moon and play upon a golden flute, and then to lay the flute on the bank.

As soon as the moon was again full the hunter's wife went to the millpond, played on a golden flute, and when she had finished placed it on the bank. Then a rushing sound was heard, and a wave swept the flute off the bank, and soon the head of the hunter appeared and rose up higher and higher till he was half out of the water. Then he gazed sadly at his wife and stretched out his arms towards her. But another rushing wave arose and dragged him under once more. The hunter's wife, who had stood on the bank full of joy and hope, sank into despair when she saw her husband snatched away again before her eyes.

But for her comfort she dreamt the same dream a third time, and betook herself once more to the old witch's hut in the flowery meadow. This time the old woman told her to go the next full moon to the millpond, and to spin there with a golden spinning-wheel, and then to leave the spinning-wheel on the bank.

The hunter's wife did as she was advised, and the first night the moon was full she sat and spun with a golden spinning-wheel, and then left the wheel on the bank. In a few minutes a rushing sound was heard in the waters, and a wave swept the spinning-wheel from the bank. Immediately the head of the hunter rose up from the pond, getting higher and higher each moment, till at length he stepped on to the bank and fell on his wife's neck.

But the waters of the pond rose up suddenly, overflowed the bank where the couple stood, and dragged them under the flood. In her despair the young wife called on the old witch to help her, and in a moment the hunter was turned into a frog and his wife into a toad. But they were not able to remain together, for the water tore them apart, and when the flood was over they both resumed their own shapes again, but the hunter and the hunter's wife found themselves each in a strange country, and neither knew what had become of the other.

The hunter determined to become a shepherd, and his wife too became a shepherdess. So they herded their sheep for many years in solitude and sadness.

Now it happened once that the shepherd came to the country where the shepherdess lived. The neighbourhood pleased him, and he saw that the pasture was rich and suitable for his flocks. So he brought his sheep there, and herded them as before. The shepherd and shepherdess became great friends, but they did not recognise each other in the least.

But one evening when the moon was full they sat together watching their flocks, and the shepherd played upon his flute. Then the shepherdess thought of that evening when she had sat at the full moon by the millpond and had played on the golden flute; the recollection was too much for her, and she burst into tears. The shepherd asked her why she was crying, and left her no peace till she told him all her story. Then the scales fell from the shepherd's eyes, and he recognised his wife, and she him. So they returned joyfully to their own home, and lived in peace and happiness ever after.

The Ogre of Rashomon

Long, long ago in Kyoto, the people of the city were terrified by accounts of a dreadful ogre, who, it was said, haunted the Gate of Rashomon at twilight and seized whoever passed by. The missing victims were never seen again, so it was whispered that the ogre was a horrible cannibal, who not only killed the unhappy victims but ate them also. Now everybody in the town and neighbourhood was in great fear, and no one durst venture out after sunset near the Gate of Rashomon.

Now at this time there lived in Kyoto a general named Raiko, who had made himself famous for his brave deeds. Some time before this he had made the country ring with his name, for he had attacked Oeyama, where a band of ogres lived with their chief and instead of wine drank the blood of human beings. He had routed them all and cut off the head of the chief monster.

This brave warrior was always followed by a band of faithful knights. In this band there were five knights of great valour. One evening as the five knights sat at a feast quaffing sake in their rice bowls and eating all kinds of fish, raw and stewed and broiled, and toasting each other's healths and exploits, the first knight, Hojo, said to the others: 'Have you all heard the rumour that every evening after sunset there comes an ogre to the Gate of Rashomon, and that he seizes all who pass by?'

The second knight, Watanabe, answered him, saying: 'Do not talk such nonsense! All the ogres were killed by our chief Raiko at Oeyama! It cannot be true, because even if any ogres did escape from that great killing they would not dare to show themselves in this city, for they know that our brave master would at once attack them if he knew that any of them were still alive!'

'Then do you disbelieve what I say, and think that I am telling you a falsehood?'

'No, I do not think that you are telling a lie,' said Watanabe; 'but you have heard some old woman's story which is not worth believing.'

'Then the best plan is to prove what I say, by going there yourself and finding out yourself whether it is true or not,' said Hojo.

Watanabe, the second knight, could not bear the thought that his companion should believe he was afraid, so he answered quickly: 'Of course, I will go at once and find out for myself!'

So Watanabe at once got ready to go – he buckled on his long sword and put on a coat of armour, and tied on his large helmet. When he was ready to start he said to the others: 'Give me something so that I can prove I have been there!'

Then one of the men got a roll of writing paper and his box of indian ink and brushes, and the four comrades wrote their names on a piece of paper.

'I will take this,' said Watanabe, 'and put it on the Gate of Rashomon, so tomorrow morning you can all go and look at it. I may be able to catch an ogre or two by then!' and he mounted his horse and rode off gallantly.

It was a very dark night, and there was neither moon nor star to light Watanabe on his way. To make the darkness worse a storm came on, the rain fell heavily and the wind howled like wolves in the mountains. Any ordinary man would have trembled at the thought of going out of doors, but Watanabe was a brave warrior and dauntless, and his honour and word were at stake; so he sped on into the night, while his companions listened to the sound of his horse's hoofs dying away in the distance, then shut the sliding shutters close and gathered round the charcoal fire and wondered what would happen – and whether their comrade would encounter one of those horrible Oni.

At last Watanabe reached the Gate of Rashomon, but peer as he might through the darkness he could see no sign of an ogre.

'It is just as I thought,' said Watanabe to himself; 'there are certainly no ogres here; it is only an old woman's story. I will stick this paper on the gate so that the others can see I have been here when they come tomorrow, and then I will take my way home and laugh at them all.'

He fastened the piece of paper, signed by all his four companions, on the gate, and then turned his horse's head towards home.

As he did so he became aware that someone was behind him, and at the same time a voice called out to him to wait. Then his helmet was seized from the back. 'Who are you?' said Watanabe fearlessly. He then put out his hand and groped around to find out who or what it was that held him by the helmet. As he did so he touched something that felt like an arm – it was covered with hair and as big round as the trunk of a tree!

Watanabe knew at once that this was the arm of an ogre, so he drew his sword and cut at it fiercely.

There was a loud yell of pain, and then the ogre dashed in front of the warrior.

Watanabe's eyes grew large with wonder, for he saw that the ogre was taller than the great gate, his eyes were flashing like mirrors in the sunlight, his huge mouth was wide open, and as the monster breathed, flames of fire shot out of his mouth.

The ogre thought to terrify his foe, but Watanabe never flinched. He attacked the ogre with all his strength, and thus they fought face to face for a long time. At last the ogre, finding that he could neither frighten nor beat Watanabe and that he might himself be beaten, took to flight. But Watanabe, determined not to let the monster escape, put spurs to his horse and gave chase.

But though the knight rode very fast the ogre ran faster, and to his disappointment he found himself unable to overtake the monster, who was gradually lost to sight.

Watanabe returned to the gate where the fierce fight had taken place, and got down from his horse. As he did so he stumbled upon something lying on the ground.

Stooping to pick it up he found that it was one of the ogre's huge arms which he must have slashed off in the fight. His joy was great at having secured such a prize, for this was the best of all proofs of his adventure with the ogre. So he took it up carefully and carried it home as a trophy of his victory.

When he got back, he showed the arm to his comrades, who one and all called him the hero of their band and gave him a great feast. His wonderful deed was soon noised abroad in Kyoto, and people from far and near came to see the ogre's arm.

Watanabe now began to grow uneasy as to how he should keep the arm in safety, for he knew that the ogre to whom it belonged was still alive. He felt sure that one day or other, as soon as the ogre got over his scare, he would come to try to get his arm back again. Watanabe therefore had a box made of the strongest wood and banded with iron. In this he placed the arm, and then he sealed down the heavy lid, refusing to open it for anyone. He kept the box in his own room and took charge of it himself, never allowing it out of his sight.

Now one night he heard someone knocking at the porch, asking for admittance. When the servant went to the door to see who it was, there was only an old woman, very respectable in appearance. On being asked who she was and what was her business, the old woman replied with a smile that she had been nurse to the master of the house when he was a little baby. If the lord of the house were at home she begged to be allowed to see him. The servant left the old woman at the door and went to tell his master that his old nurse had come to see him. Watanabe thought it strange that she should come at that time of night, but at the thought of his old nurse, who had been like a foster-mother to him and whom he had not seen for a long time, a very tender feeling sprang up for her in his heart. He ordered the servant to show her in.

The old woman was ushered into the room, and after the customary bows and greetings were over, she said: 'Master, the report of your brave fight with the ogre at the Gate of Rashomon is so widely known that even your poor old nurse has heard of it. Is it really true, what everyone says, that you cut off one of the ogre's arms? If you did, your deed is highly to be praised!'

'I was very disappointed,' said Watanabe, 'that I was not able take the monster captive, which was what I wished to do, instead of only cutting off an arm!'

'I am very proud to think,' answered the old woman, 'that my master was so brave as to dare to cut off an ogre's arm. There is nothing that can be compared to your courage. Before I die it is the great wish of my life to see this arm,' she added pleadingly.

'No,' said Watanabe. 'I am sorry, but I cannot grant your request.'

'But why?' asked the old woman.

'Because,' replied Watanabe, 'ogres are very revengeful creatures, and if I open the box there is no telling but that the ogre may suddenly appear and carry off his arm. I have had a box made on purpose with a very strong lid, and in this box I keep the ogre's arm secure; and I never show it to anyone, whatever happens.'

'Your precaution is very reasonable,' said the old woman. 'But I am your old nurse, so surely you will not refuse to show *me* the arm. I have only just heard of your brave act, and not being able to wait till the morning I came at once to ask you to show it to me.'

Watanabe was very troubled at the old woman's pleading, but he still persisted in refusing. Then the old woman said: 'Do you suspect me of being a spy sent by the ogre?'

'No, of course I do not suspect you of being the ogre's spy, for you are my old nurse,' answered Watanabe.

'Then you cannot surely refuse to show me the arm any longer?' entreated the old woman; 'for it is the great wish of my heart to see for once in my life the arm of an ogre!'

Watanabe could not hold out in his refusal any longer, so he gave in at last, saying: 'Then I will show you the ogre's arm, since you so earnestly wish to see it. Come, follow me!' and he led the way to his own room, the old woman following.

When they were both in the room Watanabe shut the door carefully, and then going towards a big box which stood in a corner of the room, he took off the heavy lid. He then called to the old woman to come near and look in, for he never took the arm out of the box.

'What is it like? Let me have a good look at it,' said the old nurse, with a joyful face.

She came nearer and nearer, as if she were afraid, till she stood right against the box. Suddenly she plunged her hand into the box and seized the arm, crying with a exultant voice which made the room shake: 'Oh, joy! I have got my arm back again!'

And from an old woman she was suddenly transformed into the towering figure of the frightful ogre!

Watanabe sprang back and was unable to move for a moment, so great was his astonishment; but recognising the ogre who had attacked him at the Gate of Rashomon, he determined with his usual courage to put an end to him this time. He seized his sword, drew it out of its sheath in a flash, and tried to cut the ogre down.

So quick was Watanabe that the creature had a narrow escape. But the ogre sprang up to the ceiling, and bursting through the roof, disappeared in the mist and clouds.

In this way the ogre escaped with his arm. The knight gnashed his teeth with disappointment, but that was all he could do. He waited in patience for another opportunity to dispatch the ogre. But the latter was afraid of Watanabe's great strength and daring, and never troubled Kyoto again. So once more the people of the city were able to go out without fear even at night, and the brave deeds of Watanabe have never been forgotten!

The Old Man and the Fairies

Many years ago the Welsh mountains were full of fairies. People used to go by moonlight to see them dancing, for they knew where they would dance by seeing green rings in the grass.

There was an old man living in those days who used to frequent the fairs that were held across the mountains. One day he was crossing the mountains to a fair, and when he got to a lonely valley he sat down, for he was tired, and he dropped off to sleep, and his bag fell down by his side. When he was sound asleep the fairies came and carried him off, bag and all, and took him under the earth, and when he awoke he found himself in a great palace of gold, full of fairies dancing and singing. And they took him and showed him everything, the splendid gold room and gardens, and they kept dancing round him until he fell asleep.

When he was asleep they carried him back to the same spot where they had found him, and when he awoke he thought he had

been dreaming, so he looked for his bag, and got hold of it, but he could hardly lift it. When he opened it he found it was nearly filled with gold.

He managed to pick it up, and turning round, he went home.

When he got home, his wife Kaddy said: 'What's to do, why haven't you been to the fair?'

'I've got something here,' he said, and showed his wife the gold.

'Why, where did you get that?'

But he wouldn't tell her. Since she was curious, like all women, she kept worrying him all night – for he'd put the money in a box under the bed – so he told her about the fairies.

Next morning, when he awoke, he thought he'd go to the fair and buy a lot of things, and he went to the box to get some of the gold, but found it full of cockleshells.

The Old Woman and Her Pig

An old woman was sweeping her house, and she found a little crooked sixpence. 'What,' said she, 'shall I do with this little sixpence? I will go to market, and buy a little pig.'

As she was coming home, she came to a stile: but the piggy wouldn't go over the stile.

She went a little further, and she met a dog. So she said to the dog: 'Dog! bite pig; piggy won't go over the stile; and I shan't get home tonight.' But the dog wouldn't.

She went a little farther, and she met a stick. So she said: 'Stick! stick! beat dog! dog won't bite pig; piggy won't get over the stile; and I shan't get home tonight.' But the stick wouldn't.

She went a little farther, and she met a fire. So she said: 'Fire! fire! burn stick; stick won't beat dog; dog won't bite pig; piggy won't get over the stile; and I shan't get home tonight.' But the fire wouldn't.

She went a little farther, and she met some water. So she said: 'Water, water! quench fire; fire won't burn stick; stick won't beat dog; dog won't bite pig; piggy won't get over the stile; and I shan't get home tonight.' But the water wouldn't.

She went a little farther, and she met an ox. So she said: 'Ox! ox! drink water; water won't quench fire; fire won't burn stick; stick won't beat dog; dog won't bite pig; piggy won't get over the stile; and I shan't get home tonight.' But the ox wouldn't.

She went a little farther, and she met a butcher. So she said: 'Butcher! butcher! kill ox; ox won't drink water; water won't quench fire; fire won't burn stick; stick won't beat dog; dog won't bite pig; piggy won't get over the stile; and I shan't get home tonight.' But the butcher wouldn't.

She went a little farther, and she met a rope. So she said: 'Rope! rope! hang butcher; butcher won't kill ox; ox won't drink water; water won't quench fire; fire won't burn stick; stick won't beat dog; dog won't bite pig; piggy won't get over the stile; and I shan't get home tonight.' But the rope wouldn't.

She went a little farther, and she met a rat. So she said: 'Rat! rat! gnaw rope; rope won't hang butcher; butcher won't kill ox; ox won't drink water; water won't quench fire; fire won't burn stick; stick won't beat dog; dog won't bite pig; piggy won't get over

the stile; and I shan't get home tonight.' But the rat wouldn't.

She went a little farther, and she met a cat. So she said: 'Cat! cat! kill rat; rat won't gnaw rope; rope won't hang butcher; butcher won't kill ox; ox won't drink water; water won't quench fire; fire won't burn stick; stick won't beat dog; dog won't bite pig; piggy won't get over the stile; and I shan't get home tonight.' But the cat said to her, 'If you will go to yonder cow, and fetch me a saucer of milk, I will kill the rat.' So away went the old woman to the cow.

But the cow said to her: 'If you will go to yonder hay-stack, and fetch me a handful of hay, I'll give you the milk.' So away went the old woman to the haystack and she brought the hay to the cow.

As soon as the cow had eaten the hay, she gave the old woman the milk; and away she went with it in a saucer to the cat.

As soon as the cat had lapped up the milk, the cat began to kill the rat; the rat began to gnaw the rope; the rope began to hang the butcher; the butcher began to kill the ox; the ox began to drink the water; the water began to quench the fire; the fire began to burn the stick; the stick began to beat the dog; the dog began to bite the pig; the little pig in a fright jumped over the stile, and so the old woman got home that night.

Paddy O'Kelly and the Weasel

A long time ago there was once a man of the name of Paddy O'Kelly, living near Tuam, in the county Galway. He rose up one morning early, and he did not know what time of day it was, for there was fine light coming from the moon. He wanted to go to the fair of Cauher-na-mart to sell a *sturk* of an ass that he had.

He had not gone more than three miles of the road when a great darkness came on, and a shower began falling. He saw a large house among trees about five hundred yards in from the road, and he said to himself that he would go to that house till the shower would be over. When he got to the house he found the door open before him, and in with him. He saw a large room to his left, and a fine fire in the grate. He sat down on a stool that was beside the wall, and had begun falling asleep, when he saw a big weasel coming to the fire with something yellow in her mouth, which she dropped on the hearth-stone, and then she went away. She soon came back again with the same thing in her mouth, and he saw that it was a guinea she had. She dropped it on the hearth-stone, and went away again. She was coming and going, until there was a great heap of guineas on the hearth. But at last, when she got her gone, Paddy rose up, thrust all the gold she had gathered into his pockets, and out with him.

He had not gone far till he heard the weasel coming after him, and she screeching as loud as a bagpipes. She went before Paddy and got on the road, and she was twisting herself backwards and forwards, and trying to get a hold of his throat. Paddy had a good oak stick, and he kept her from him, until two men came up who were going to the same fair, and one of them had a good dog, and it routed the weasel into a hole in the wall.

Paddy went to the fair, and instead of coming home with the money he got for his old ass, as he thought would be the way with him in the morning, he went and bought a horse with some of the money he took from the weasel, and he came home riding. When he came to the place where the dog had routed the weasel into the hole in the wall, she came out before him, gave a leap, and caught the horse by the throat. The horse made off, and Paddy could not stop him, till at last he gave a leap into a big drain that was full up with water and black mud, and he was drowning and choking as fast as he could, until men who were coming from Galway came up and drove away the weasel.

Paddy brought the horse home with him, and put him into the cow's byre and fell asleep.

Next morning, the day on the morrow, Paddy rose up early, and went out to give his horse hay and oats. When he got to the door he saw the weasel coming out of the byre and she covered with blood.

'My seven thousand curses on you,' said Paddy, 'but I'm afraid you've done harm.'

He went in and found the horse, a pair of milch cows and two calves dead. He came out and set a dog he had after the weasel. The dog got a hold of her, and she got a hold of the dog. The dog was a good one, but he was forced to loose his hold of her before Paddy could come up. He kept his eye on her, however, all through, until he saw her creeping into a little hovel that was on the brink of a lake. Paddy came running, and when he got to the little hut he gave the dog a shake to rouse him up and put anger on him, and then he sent him in. When the dog went in he began barking. Paddy went in after him, and saw an old hag in the corner. He asked her if she had seen a weasel coming in there.

'I did not,' said she. 'I'm all destroyed with a plague of sickness, and if you don't go out quick, you'll catch it from me.'

While Paddy and the hag were talking, the dog kept moving in all the time, till at last he gave a leap and caught the hag by the throat. She screeched and said, 'Paddy Kelly, take off your dog, and I'll make you a rich man.'

Paddy made the dog loose his hold, and said, 'Tell me who you are, or why did you kill my horse and my cows?'

'And why did you bring away my gold that I was gathering for five hundred years throughout the hills and hollows of the world?'

'I thought you were a weasel,' said Paddy, 'or I wouldn't touch your gold; and another thing,' says he, 'if you're for five hundred years in this world, it's time for you to go to rest now.'

'I committed a great crime in my youth,' said the hag, 'and now I am to be released from my sufferings if you can pay twenty pounds for a hundred and three-score masses for me.'

'Where's the money?' said Paddy.

'Go and dig under a bush that's over a little well in the corner of that field there without, and you'll get a pot filled with gold. Pay the twenty pounds for the masses, and yourself shall have the rest. When you'll lift the flag off the pot, you'll see a big black dog coming out; but don't be afraid before him; he is a son of mine. When you get the gold, buy the house in which you saw me at first. You'll get it cheap, for it has the name of there being a ghost in it. My son will be down in the cellar. He'll do you no harm, but he'll be a good friend to you. I shall be dead a month from this day, and when you get me dead, put a coal under this little hut and burn it. Don't tell a living soul anything about me – and the luck will be on you.'

'What is your name?' said Paddy.

'Mary Kerwan,' said the hag.

Paddy went home, and when the darkness of the night came on, he took with him a spade and went to the bush that was in the corner of the field, and began digging. It was not long till he found the pot, and when he took the flag off of it a big black dog leaped out, and off and away with him, and Paddy's dog after him.

Paddy brought home the gold, and hid it in the cowhouse, and in the morning he went to the priest and paid for the hundred and three-score masses to be said for Mary Kerwan.. About a month after that he went to the fair of Galway, and bought a pair of cows, a horse and a dozen sheep. The neighbours did not know where he had got all the money; they said that he had a share with the good people.

One day Paddy dressed himself, and went to the gentleman who owned the large house where he first saw the weasel, and asked to buy the house of him, and the land that was round about.

'You can have the house without paying any rent at all; but there is a ghost in it, and I wouldn't like you to go to live in it without my telling you. But I couldn't part with the land without getting a hundred pounds more than you have to offer me.'

'Perhaps I have as much as you have, yourself,' said Paddy. 'I'll be here tomorrow with the money, if you're ready to give me possession.'

'I'll be ready,' said the gentleman.

Paddy went home and told his wife that he had bought a large house and a holding of land.

'Where did you get the money?' says his wife.

'Isn't it all one to you where I got it?' says Paddy.

The day on the morrow Paddy went to the gentleman, gave him the money, and got possession of the house and land; and the gentleman left him the furniture and everything that was in the house, into the bargain.

Paddy remained in the house that night, and when darkness came he went down to the cellar, and he saw a little man with his two legs spread on a barrel.

'God save you, honest man,' says he to Paddy.

'The same to you,' says Paddy.

'Don't be afraid of me, at all,' says the little man. 'I'll be a friend to you, if you are able to keep a secret.'

'I am able, indeed; I kept your mother's secret, and I'll keep yours as well.'

'Maybe you're thirsty?' said the little man.

'I'm not free from it,' said Paddy.

The little man put a hand in his bosom and drew out a gold goblet. He gave it to Paddy, and said, 'Draw wine out of that barrel under me.'

Paddy drew the full up of the goblet, and handed it to the little man.

'Drink yourself first,' says he.

Paddy drank, drew another goblet, and handed it to the little man, and he drank it.

'Fill up and drink again,' said the little man. 'I have a mind to be merry tonight.'

The pair of them sat there drinking until they were half drunk. Then the little man gave a leap down to the floor, and said to Paddy, 'Don't you like music?'

'I do, surely,' said Paddy, 'and I'm a good dancer, too.'

'Lift up the big flag over there in the corner, and you'll get my pipes under it.'

Paddy lifted the flag, got the pipes, and gave them to the little man. He squeezed the pipes on him, and began playing melodious music. Paddy began dancing till he was tired. Then they had another drink, and the little man said, 'Do as my mother told you, and I'll show you great riches. You can bring your wife in here, but don't tell her that I'm there, and she won't see me. Any time at all that ale or wine are wanting, come here and draw. Farewell, now; go to sleep, and come again to me tomorrow night.'

Paddy went to bed, and it wasn't long till he fell asleep.

On the morning of the day on the morrow, Paddy went home, and brought his wife and children to the big house, and they were very comfortable. That night Paddy went down to the cellar; the little man welcomed him and asked him did he wish to dance?

'Not till I get a drink,' said Paddy.

'Drink your fill,' said the little man. 'That barrel will never be empty as long as you live.'

Paddy drank the full of the goblet, and gave a drink to the little man. Then the little man said to him,

'I am going to the Fortress of the Fairies tonight, to play music for the good people, and if you come with me you'll see fine fun. I'll give you a horse that you never saw the like of him before.'

'I'll go with you, and welcome,' said Paddy; 'but what excuse will I make to my wife?'

'I'll bring you away from her side without her knowing it when you are both asleep together, and I'll bring you back to her the same way,' said the little man.

'I'm obedient,' says Paddy. 'We'll have another drink before I leave you.'

He drank drink after drink, till he was half drunk, and he went to bed with his wife.

When he awoke he found himself riding on a broom near Doon-na-shee, and the little man riding on another besom by his side. When they came as far as the green hill of the Doon, the little man said a couple of words that Paddy did not understand. The green hill opened, and the pair went into a fine chamber.

Paddy never saw before a gathering like that which was in the Doon. The whole place was full up of little people, men and women, young and old. They all welcomed little Donal – that was the name of the piper – and Paddy O'Kelly. The king and queen of the fairies came up to them, and said, 'We are all going on a visit tonight to Cnoc Matha, to the high king and queen of our people.'

They all rose up then and went out. There were horses ready for each one of them, and the coash-t'ya bower for the king and queen. The king and queen got into the coach, each man leaped on his own horse, and be certain that Paddy was not behind. The piper went out before them, and began playing them music, and then off and away with them. It was not long till they came to Cnoc Matha. The hill opened, and the king of the fairy host passed in. Finvara and Nuala were there, the arch-king and queen of the fairy host of Connacht, and thousands of little persons. Finvara came up and said, 'We are going to play a hurling match tonight against the fairy host of Munster, and unless we beat them our fame is gone for ever. The match is to be fought out on Moytura, under Slieve Belgadaun.'

The Connacht host cried out, 'We are all ready, and we have no doubt but we'll beat them.'

'Out with ye all,' cried the high king; 'the men of the hill of Nephin will be on the ground before us.'

They all went out, and little Donal and twelve pipers more before them, playing melodious music. When they came to Moytura, the fairy host of Munster and the fairy men of the hill of Nephin were there before them. Now it is necessary for the fairy host to have two live men beside them when they are fighting or at a hurling match, and that was the reason that little Donal took Paddy O'Kelly with him. There was a man they called the 'Yellow Stongirya' with the fairy host of Munster, from Ennis, in the County Clare.

It was not long till the two hosts took sides, the ball was thrown up between them and the fun began in earnest.

They were hurling away, and the pipers playing music, until Paddy O'Kelly saw the host of Munster getting the strong hand, and he began helping the fairy host of Connacht. The Stongirya came up and he made at Paddy O'Kelly, but Paddy turned him head over heels. From hurling the two hosts began at fighting, but it was not long until the host of Connacht beat the other host. Then the host of Munster made flying beetles of themselves, and they began eating every green thing that they came up to. They were destroying the country before them until they came as far as Cong. Then there rose up thousands of doves out of the hole, and they swallowed down the beetles. That hole has no other name until this day but Pull-na-gullam, the doves' hole.

When the fairy host of Connacht won their battle, they came back to Cnoc Matha joyous enough, and the king Finvara gave Paddy O'Kelly a purse of gold, and the little piper brought him home, and put him into bed beside his wife, and left him sleeping there.

A month went by after that without anything worth mentioning, until one night Paddy went down to the cellar, and the little man said to him, 'My mother is dead; burn the house over her.'

'It is true for you,' said Paddy. 'She told me that she hadn't but a month to be in the world, and the month was up yesterday.'

On the next morning of the next day Paddy went to the hut and he found the hag dead. He put a coal under the hut and burned it. He came home and told the little man that the hag was burnt. The little man gave him a purse and said to him, 'This purse will never be empty as long as you are alive. Now, you will never see me more; but have a loving remembrance of the weasel. She was the beginning and the prime cause of your riches.' Then he went away and Paddy never saw him again.

Paddy O'Kelly and his wife lived for years after this in the large house, and when he died he left great wealth behind him, and a large family to spend it.

There now is the story for you, from the first word to the last, as I heard it from my grandmother.

The Pied Piper of Hamelin

1

Hamelin Town's in Brunswick,
    By famous Hanover city;
The River Weser, deep and wide,
Washes its wall on the southern side;
A pleasanter spot you never spied;
    But, when begins my ditty,
Almost five hundred years ago,
To see the townsfolk suffer so
    From vermin, was a pity.

2

Rats!
They fought the dogs and killed the cats,
    And bit the babies in the cradles,
And ate the cheeses out of the vats,
    And licked the soup from the cooks' own ladles,
Split open the kegs of salted sprats,
Made nests inside men's Sunday hats,
And even spoiled the women's chats
        By drowning their speaking
        With shrieking and squeaking
In fifty different sharps and flats.

3

At last the people in a body
    To the Town Hall came flocking:
' 'Tis clear,' cried they, 'our Mayor's a noddy;
    And as for our Corporation – shocking
To think we buy gowns lined with ermine
For dolts that can't or won't determine
What's best to rid us of our vermin!
You hope, because you're old and obese,
To find in the furry civic robe ease?
Rouse up, sirs! Give your brains a racking
To find the remedy we're lacking,
Or, sure as fate, we'll send you packing!'
At this the Mayor and Corporation
Quaked with a mighty consternation.

4

An hour they sat in council,
    At length the Mayor broke silence:
'For a guilder I'd my ermine gown sell,
    I wish I were a mile hence!
It's easy to bid one rack one's brain –
I'm sure my poor head aches again,
I've scratched it so, and all in vain.
Oh for a trap, a trap, a trap!'
Just as he said this, what should hap
At the chamber door but a gentle tap?
'Bless us,' cried the Mayor, 'what's that?'
(With the Corporation as he sat,
Looking little though wondrous fat;
Nor brighter was his eye, nor moister
Than a too-long-opened oyster,
Save when at noon his paunch grew mutinous
For a plate of turtle green and glutinous.)
'Only a scraping of shoes on the mat?
Anything like the sound of a rat
Makes my heart go pit-a-pat!'

5

'Come in!' – the Mayor cried, looking bigger:
And in did come the strangest figure!
His queer long coat from heel to head
Was half of yellow and half of red,
And he himself was tall and thin,
With sharp blue eyes, each like a pin,
And light loose hair, yet swarthy skin,
No tuft on cheek nor beard on chin,
But lips where smiles went out and in;
There was no guessing his kith and kin:
And nobody could enough admire
The tall man and his quaint attire.
Quoth one: 'It's as my great-grandsire,
Starting up at the Trump of Doom's tone,
Had walked this way from his painted
                tombstone!'

6

He advanced to the council-table:
And, 'Please your honours,' said he, 'I'm able,
By means of a secret charm, to draw
   All creatures living beneath the sun,
   That creep or swim or fly or run,
After me so as you never saw!
And I chiefly use my charm
On creatures that do people harm,
The mole and toad and newt and viper;
And people call me the Pied Piper.'
(And here they noticed round his neck
   A scarf of red and yellow stripe,
To match with his coat of the self-same cheque;
   And at the scarf's end hung a pipe;
And his fingers, they noticed, were ever straying
As if impatient to be playing
Upon this pipe, as low it dangled
Over his vesture so old-fangled.)
'Yet,' said he, 'poor piper as I am,
In Tartary I freed the Cham,
   Last June, from his huge swarms of gnats;
I eased in Asia the Nizam
   Of a monstrous brood of vampyre-bats:
And as for what your brain bewilders,
   If I can rid your town of rats
Will you give me a thousand guilders?'
'One? fifty thousand!' – was the exclamation
Of the astonished Mayor and Corporation.

7

Into the street the Piper stept,
   Smiling first a little smile,
As if he knew what magic slept
   In his quiet pipe the while;
Then, like a musical adept,
To blow the pipe his lips he wrinkled,
And green and blue his sharp eyes twinkled,
Like a candle-flame where salt is sprinkled;
And ere three shrill notes the pipe uttered,
You heard as if an army muttered;
And the muttering grew to a grumbling;
And the grumbling grew to a mighty rumbling;
And out of the houses the rats came tumbling.
Great rats, small rats, lean rats, brawny rats,
Brown rats, black rats, grey rats, tawny rats,
Grave old plodders, gay young friskers,
   Fathers, mothers, uncles, cousins,
Cocking tails and pricking whiskers,

   Families by tens and dozens,
Brothers, sisters, husbands, wives –
Followed the Piper for their lives.
From street to street he piped advancing,
And step for step they followed dancing,
Until they came to the River Weser,
   Wherein all plunged and perished!
   Save one who, stout as Julius Cæsar,
Swam across and lived to carry
   (As he, the manuscript he cherished)
To Rat-land home his commentary:
Which was, 'At the first shrill notes of the pipe,
I heard a sound as of scraping tripe,
And putting apples, wondrous ripe,
Into a cider-press's gripe:
And a moving away of pickle-tub-boards,
And a leaving ajar of conserve-cupboards,
And a drawing the corks of train-oil-flasks,
And a breaking the hoops of butter-casks:
And it seemed as if a voice
   (Sweeter far than by harp or by psaltery
Is breathed) called out, "Oh rats, rejoice!
   The world is grown to one vast dry-saltery!
So munch on, crunch on, take your nuncheon,
Breakfast, supper, dinner, luncheon!"

And just as a bulky sugar-puncheon,
All ready staved, like a great sun shone
Glorious scarce an inch before me,
Just as methought it said, "Come, bore me!"
– I found the Weser rolling o'er me.'

8

You should have heard the Hamelin people
Ringing the bells till they rocked the steeple.
'Go,' cried the Mayor, 'and get long poles,
Poke out the nests and block up the holes!
Consult with carpenters and builders,
And leave in our town not even a trace
Of the rats!' – when suddenly, up the face
Of the Piper perked in the market-place,
With a, 'First, if you please, my thousand
                                  guilders!'

9

A thousand guilders! The Mayor looked blue;
So did the Corporation too.
For council dinners made rare havoc
With Claret, Moselle, Vin-de-Grave, Hock;
And half the money would replenish
Their cellar's biggest butt with Rhenish.
To pay this sum to a wandering fellow
With a gipsy coat of red and yellow!
'Beside,' quoth the Mayor with a knowing wink,
'Our business was done at the river's brink;
We saw with our eyes the vermin sink,
And what's dead can't come to life, I think.
So, friend, we're not the folks to shrink
From the duty of giving you something for drink,
And a matter of money to put in your poke;
But as for the guilders, what we spoke
Of them, as you very well know, was in joke.
Beside, our losses have made us thrifty.
A thousand guilders! Come, take fifty!'

10

The Piper's face fell, and he cried,
'No trifling! I can't wait, beside!
I've promised to visit by dinner-time
Bagdat, and accept the prime
Of the head-cook's pottage, all he's rich in,
For having left, in the Caliph's kitchen,
Of a nest of scorpions no survivor:
With him I proved no bargain-driver,
With you, don't think I'll bate a stiver!
And folks who put me in a passion
'May find me pipe after another fashion.'

11

'How?' cried the Mayor, 'd'ye think I brook
Being worse treated than a cook?
Insulted by a lazy ribald
With idle pipe and vesture piebald?
You threaten us, fellow? Do your worst,
Blow your pipe there till you burst!'

12

Once more he stept into the street
   And to his lips again
   Laid his long pipe of smooth straight cane;
And ere he blew three notes (such sweet
Soft notes as yet musician's cunning
   Never gave the enraptured air),
There was a rustling that seemed like a bustling
Of merry crowds justling at pitching and
                              hustling,
Small feet were pattering, wooden shoes
                              clattering,
Little hands clapping and little tongues
                              chattering,
And, like fowls in a farmyard when barley
                           is scattering,
Out came the children running.
All the little boys and girls,
With rosy cheeks and flaxen curls,
And sparkling eyes and teeth like pearls,
Tripping and skipping, ran merrily after
The wonderful music with shouting and
                             laughter.

13

The Mayor was dumb, and the Council stood
As if they were changed into blocks of wood,
Unable to move a step or cry
To the children merrily skipping by –
Could only follow with the eye
That joyous crowd at the Piper's back.
But how the Mayor was on the rack,
And the wretched Council's bosoms beat,
As the Piper turned from the High Street
To where the Weser rolled its waters
Right in the way of their sons and daughters.
However he turned from South to West,
And to Koppelberg Hill his steps addressed,
And after him the children pressed;
Great was the joy in every breast,
'He never can cross that mighty top!
He's forced to let the piping drop,
And we shall see our children stop!'

When, lo, as they reached the mountainside,
A wondrous portal opened wide,
As if a cavern was suddenly hollowed;
And the Piper advanced and the childeren
                         followed,
And when all were in to the very last,
The door in the mountainside shut fast.
Did I say, all? No! One was lame,
  And could not dance the whole of the way;
And in after years, if you would blame
  His sadness, he was used to say,
'It's dull in our town since my playmates left!
I can't forget that I'm bereft
Of all the pleasant sights they see,
Which the Piper also promised me.
For he led us, he said, to a joyous land,
Joining the town and just at hand,
Where waters gushed and fruit trees grew
And flowers put forth a fairer hue,
And everything was strange and new;
The sparrows were brighter than peacocks
                         here,
And their dogs outran our fallow deer,
And honey-bees had lost their stings,
And horses were born with eagles' wings:
And just as I became assured
My lame foot would be speedily cured,
The music stopped and I stood still,
And found myself outside the hill,
Left alone against my will,
To go now limping as before,
And never hear of that country more!'

14

Alas, alas for Hamelin!
  There came into many a burgher's pate
  A text which says that heaven's gate
  Opes to the rich at as easy rate
As the needle's eye takes a camel in!
The mayor sent East, West, North and South,
To offer the Piper, by word of mouth,
  Wherever it was men's lot to find him,
Silver and gold to his heart's content,
If he'd only return the way he went,
  And bring the children behind him.
But when they saw 'twas a lost endeavour,
And Piper and dancers were gone for ever,
They made a decree that lawyers never
  Should think their records dated duly
If, after the day of the month and year,

These words did not as well appear,
'And so long after what happened here
  On the Twenty-second of July,
Thirteen hundred and seventy-six:'
And the better in memory to fix
The place of the children's last retreat,
They called it the Pied Piper's Street –
Where anyone playing on pipe or tabor
Was sure for the future to lose his labour.
Nor suffered they hostelry or tavern
  To shock with mirth a street so solemn;
But opposite the place of the cavern
  They wrote the story on a column,
And on the great church-window painted
The same, to make the world acquainted
How their children were stolen away,
And there it stands to this very day.
And I must not omit to say
That in Transylvania there's a tribe
Of alien people who ascribe
The outlandish ways and dress,
On which their neighbours lay such stress,
To their fathers and mothers having risen
Out of some subterraneous prison
Into which they were trepanned
Long time ago in a mignty band
Out of Hamelin town in Brunswick land,
But how or wny, they don't understand.

15

So, Willy, let me and you be wipers
Of scores out with all men – especially pipers!
And, whether they pipe us free from rats or
                         from mice,
If we've promised them aught, let us keep
                         our promise!

Pinocchio

CHAPTER 1

*How it came to pass that Master Cherry the carpenter found
a piece of wood that laughed and cried like a child.*

There was once upon a time . . .

A king!' my little readers will instantly exclaim.

No, children, you are wrong. There was once
upon a time a piece of wood.

This wood was not valuable: it was only a common
log like those that are burnt in winter in the stoves
and fireplaces to make a cheerful blaze and warm
the rooms.

I cannot say how it came about, but the fact is that
one fine day this piece of wood was lying in the shop
of an old carpenter of the name of Master Antonio.
He was, however, called by everybody Master
Cherry, on account of the end of his nose, which
was always as red and polished as a ripe cherry.

No sooner had Master Cherry set eyes on the
piece of wood than his face beamed with delight;
and, rubbing his hands together with satisfaction,
he said softly to himself: 'This wood has come at
the right moment; it will just do to make the leg of
a little table.'

Having said this he immediately took a sharp axe
with which to remove the bark and the rough
surface. Just, however, as he was going to give the
first stroke he remained with his arm suspended
in the air, for he heard a very small voice saying
imploringly, 'Do not strike me so hard!'

Picture to yourselves the astonishment of good
old Master Cherry!

He turned his terrified eyes all round the room
to try and discover where the little voice could
possibly have come from, but he saw nobody! He
looked under the bench – nobody; he looked into a
cupboard that was always shut – nobody; he looked
into a basket of shavings and sawdust – nobody;
he even opened the door of the shop and gave a

glance into the street – and still nobody. Who, then,
could it be?

'I see how it is,' he said, laughing and scratching
his wig; 'evidently that little voice was all my
imagination. Let us set to work again.'

And taking up the axe he struck a tremendous
blow on the piece of wood.

'Oh! oh! you have hurt me!' cried the same little
voice dolefully.

This time Master Cherry was petrified. His eyes
started out of his head with fright, his mouth
remained open, and his tongue hung out almost to
the end of his chin, like a mask on a fountain. As
soon as he had recovered the use of his speech, he
began to say, stuttering and trembling with fear:
'But where on earth can that little voice have come
from that said, Oh! oh!? . . . Here there is certainly
not a living soul. Is it possible that this piece of
wood can have learnt to cry and to lament like a

child? I cannot believe it. This piece of wood, here it is; a log for fuel like all the others, and thrown on the fire it would about suffice to boil a saucepan of beans . . . How then? Can anyone be hidden inside it? If anyone is hidden inside, so much the worse for him. I will settle him at once.'

So saying, he seized the poor piece of wood and commenced beating it without mercy against the walls of the room.

Then he stopped to listen if he could hear any little voice lamenting. He waited two minutes – nothing; five minutes – nothing; ten minutes – still nothing!

'I see how it is,' he then said, forcing himself to laugh and pushing up his wig; 'evidently the little voice that said Oh! oh! was all my imagination! Let us set to work again.'

But as all the same he was in a great fright, he tried to sing to give himself a little courage.

Putting the axe aside he took his plane, to plane and polish the bit of wood; but whilst he was running it up and down he heard the same little voice say, laughing: 'Have done! you are tickling me all over!'

This time poor Master Cherry fell down as if he had been struck by lightning. When he at last opened his eyes he found himself seated on the floor.

His face was quite changed, even the end of his nose, instead of being crimson, as it was nearly always, had become blue from fright.

CHAPTER 2

Master Cherry makes a present of the piece of wood to his friend Geppetto, who takes it to make for himself a wonderful puppet that shall know how to dance, and to fence, and to leap like an acrobat.

At that moment someone knocked at the door.

'Come in,' said the carpenter, without having the strength to rise to his feet.

A lively little old man immediately walked into the shop. His name was Geppetto, but when the boys of the neighbourhood wished to put him in a passion they called him by the nickname of Polendina, because his yellow wig greatly resembled a pudding made of Indian corn.

Geppetto was very fiery. Woe to him who called him Polendina! He became furious, and there was no holding him.

'Good-day, Master Antonio,' said Geppetto; 'what are you doing there on the floor?'

'I am teaching the alphabet to the ants.'

'Much good may that do you.'

'What has brought you to me, neighbour Geppetto?'

'My legs. But to say the truth, Master Antonio, I am come to ask a favour of you.'

'Here I am, ready to serve you,' replied the carpenter, getting on to his knees.

'This morning an idea came into my head.'

'Let us hear it.'

'I thought I would make a beautiful wooden puppet; but a wonderful puppet that should know how to dance, to fence, and to leap like an acrobat. With this puppet I would travel about the world to earn a piece of bread and a glass of wine. What do you think of it?'

'Bravo, Polendina!' exclaimed the same little voice, and it was impossible to say where it came from.

Hearing himself called Polendina, Geppetto became as red as a turkey-cock from rage, and turning to the carpenter he said in a fury: 'Why do you insult me?'

'Who insults you?'

'You called me Polendina!'

'It was not I!'

'Would you have it, then, that it was I? It was you, I say!'

'No!'

'Yes!'

'No!'

'Yes!'

And becoming more and more angry, from words they came to blows, and flying at each other they bit, and fought, and scratched manfully.

When the fight was over Master Antonio was in possession of Geppetto's yellow wig, and Geppetto discovered that the grey wig belonging to the carpenter had remained between his teeth.

'Give me back my wig,' screamed Master Antonio.

'And you, return me mine, and let us make friends.'

The two old men having each recovered his own wig shook hands, and swore that they would remain friends to the end of their lives.

'Well then, neighbour Geppetto,' said the carpenter, to prove that peace was made, 'what is the favour that you wish of me?'

'I want a little wood to make my puppet; will you give me some?'

CHAPTER 3

Geppetto having returned home begins at once to make a puppet, to which he gives the name of Pinocchio. The first tricks played by the puppet.

Geppetto lived in a small ground-floor room that was only lighted from the staircase. The furniture could not have been simpler – a bad chair, a poor bed and a broken-down table. At the end of the room there was a fireplace with a lighted fire; but the fire was painted, and by the fire was a painted saucepan that was boiling cheerfully, and sending out a cloud of smoke that looked exactly like real smoke.

As soon as he reached home Geppetto took his tools and set to work to cut out and model his puppet.

'What name shall I give him?' he said to himself; 'I think I will call him Pinocchio. It is a name that will bring him luck. I once knew a whole family so called. There was Pinocchio the father, Pinocchia the mother, and Pinocchi the children, and all of them did well. The richest of them was a beggar.'

Having found a name for his puppet he began to work in good earnest, and he first made his hair, then his forehead, and then his eyes.

Master Antonio was delighted, and he immediately went to the bench and fetched the piece of wood that had caused him so much fear. But just as he was going to give it to his friend the piece of wood gave a shake, and wriggling violently out of his hands struck with all its force against the dried-up shins of poor Geppetto.

'Ah! is that the courteous way in which you make your presents, Master Antonio? You have almost lamed me!'

'I swear to you that it was not I!'

'Then you would have it that it was I?'

'The wood is entirely to blame!'

'I know that it was the wood; but it was you that hit my legs with it!'

'I did not hit you with it!'

'Liar!'

'Geppetto, don't insult me or I will call you Polendina!'

'Ass!'

'Polendina!'

'Donkey!'

'Polendina!'

'Baboon!'

'Polendina!'

On hearing himself called Polendina for the third time Geppetto, blind with rage, fell upon the carpenter and they fought desperately.

When the battle was over, Master Antonio had two more scratches on his nose, and his adversary had two buttons too little on his waistcoat. Their accounts being thus squared they shook hands, and swore to remain good friends for the rest of their lives.

Geppetto carried off his fine piece of wood and, thanking Master Antonio, returned limping to his house.

The eyes being finished, imagine his astonishment when he perceived that they moved and looked fixedly at him.

Geppetto seeing himself stared at by those two wooden eyes took it almost in bad part, and said in an angry voice: 'Wicked wooden eyes, why do you look at me?'

No one answered.

He then proceeded to carve the nose; but no sooner had he made it than it began to grow. And it grew, and grew, and grew, until in a few minutes it had become an immense nose that seemed as if it would never end.

Poor Geppetto tired himself out with cutting it off; but the more he cut and shortened it, the longer did that impertinent nose become!

The mouth was not even completed when it began to laugh and deride him.

'Stop laughing!' said Geppetto, provoked; but he might as well have spoken to the wall.

'Stop laughing, I say!' he roared in a threatening tone.

The mouth then ceased laughing, but put out its tongue as far as it would go.

Geppetto, not to spoil his handiwork, pretended not to see, and continued his labours. After the mouth he fashioned the chin, then the throat, then the shoulders, the stomach, the arms and the hands.

The hands were scarcely finished when Geppetto felt his wig snatched from his head. He turned round, and what did he see? He saw his yellow wig in the puppet's hand.

'Pinocchio! . . . Give me back my wig instantly!'

But Pinocchio, instead of returning it, put it on his own head, and was in consequence nearly smothered.

Geppetto at this insolent and derisive behaviour felt sadder and more melancholy than he had ever been in his life before; and turning to Pinocchio he said to him: 'You young rascal! You are not yet completed, and you are already beginning to show want of respect to your father! That is bad, my boy, very bad!'

And he dried a tear.

The legs and the feet remained to be done.

When Geppetto had finished the feet he received a kick on the point of his nose.

'I deserve it!' he said to himself; 'I should have thought of it sooner! Now it is too late!'

He then took the puppet under the arms and placed him on the floor to teach him to walk.

Pinocchio's legs were stiff and he could not move, but Geppetto led him by the hand and showed him how to put one foot before the other.

When his legs became flexible Pinocchio began to walk by himself and to run about the room; until, having gone out of the house door, he jumped into the street and escaped.

Poor Geppetto rushed after him but was not able to overtake him, for that rascal Pinocchio leapt in front of him like a hare, and knocking his wooden feet together against the pavement made as much clatter as twenty pairs of peasants' clogs.

'Stop him! stop him!' shouted Geppetto; but the people in the street, seeing a wooden puppet running like a racehorse, stood still in astonishment to look at it, and laughed, and laughed, and laughed, until it beats description.

At last, as good luck would have it, a *carabiniere* arrived who, hearing the uproar, imagined that a colt had escaped from his master. Planting himself courageously with his legs apart in the middle of the road, he waited with the determined purpose of stopping him, and thus preventing the chance of worse disasters.

When Pinocchio, still at some distance, saw the *carabiniere* barricading the whole street, he endeavoured to take him by surprise and to pass between his legs. But he failed signally.

The *carabiniere* without disturbing himself in the least caught him cleverly by the nose – it was an immense nose of ridiculous proportions that seemed made on purpose to be laid hold of by *carabinieri* – and consigned him to Geppetto.

Wishing to punish him, Geppetto intended to pull his ears at once. But imagine his feelings when he could not succeed in finding them. And do you know the reason? It was that, in his hurry to model him, he had forgotten to make them.

He then took him by the collar, and as he was leading him away he said to him, shaking his head threateningly: 'We will go home at once, and as soon as we arrive we will regulate our accounts, never doubt it.'

At this announcement Pinocchio threw himself on the ground and would not take another step. In the meanwhile a crowd of idlers and inquisitive people began to assemble and to make a ring round them.

Some of them said one thing, some another.

'Poor puppet!' said several, 'he is right not to wish to return home! Who knows how Geppetto, that bad old man, will beat him! . . . '

And the others added maliciously: 'Geppetto seems a good man! but with boys he is a regular tyrant! If that poor puppet is left in his hands he is quite capable of tearing him in pieces! . . . '

It ended in so much being said and done that the *carabiniere* at last set Pinocchio at liberty and conducted Geppetto to prison. The poor man, not being ready with words to defend himself, cried like a calf, and as he was being led away to prison sobbed out: 'Wretched boy! And to think how I have laboured to make him a well-conducted puppet! But it serves me right! I should have thought of it sooner!'

What happened afterwards is a story that really is past all belief, but I will relate it to you in the following chapters.

CHAPTER 4

The story of Pinocchio and the Talking-Cricket, from which we see that naughty boys cannot endure to be corrected by those who know more than they do.

Well then, children, I must tell you that whilst poor Geppetto was being taken to prison for no fault of his, that imp Pinocchio, finding himself free from the clutches of the *carabiniere*, ran off as fast as his legs could carry him. That he might reach home the quicker he rushed across the fields, and in his mad hurry he jumped high banks, thorn hedges, and ditches full of water, exactly as a kid or a leveret would have done if pursued by hunters.

Having arrived at the house he found the street door ajar. He pushed it open, went in, and having secured the latch threw himself seated on the ground and gave a great sigh of satisfaction.

But his satisfaction did not last long, for he heard some one in the room who was saying: 'Cri-cri-cri!'

'Who calls me?' said Pinocchio in a fright.

'It is I!'

Pinocchio turned round and saw a big cricket crawling slowly up the wall.

'Tell me, Cricket, who may you be?'

'I am the Talking-Cricket, and I have lived in this room a hundred years and more.'

'Now, however, this room is mine,' said the puppet, 'and if you would do me a pleasure go away at once, without even turning round.'

'I will not go,' answered the Cricket, 'until I have told you a great truth.'

'Tell it me, then, and be quick about it.'

'Woe to those boys who rebel against their parents, and run away capriciously from home. They will never come to any good in the world, and sooner or later they will repent bitterly.'

'Sing away, Cricket, as you please, and as long as you please. For me, I have made up my mind to run away tomorrow at daybreak, because if I remain I shall not escape the fate of all other boys; I shall be sent to school and shall be made to study either by love or by force. To tell you in confidence, I have no wish to learn; it is much more amusing to run after butterflies, or to climb trees and to take the young birds out of their nests.'

'Poor little goose! But do you not know that in that way you will grow up a perfect donkey, and that everyone will make game of you?'

'Hold your tongue, you wicked ill-omened croaker!' shouted Pinocchio.

But the Cricket, who was patient and philosophical, instead of becoming angry at this impertinence, continued in the same tone: 'But if you do not wish to go to school why not at least learn a trade, if only to enable you to earn honestly a piece of bread!'

'Do you want me to tell you?' replied Pinocchio, who was beginning to lose patience. 'Amongst all the trades in the world there is only one that really takes my fancy.'

'And that trade – what is it?'

'It is to eat, drink, sleep, and amuse myself, and to lead a vagabond life from morning to night.'

'As a rule,' said the Talking-Cricket with the same composure, 'all those who follow that trade end almost always either in a hospital or in prison.'

'Take care, you wicked ill-omened croaker! Woe to you if I fly into a passion!'

'Poor Pinocchio! I really pity you!'

'Why do you pity me?'

'Because you are a puppet and, what is worse, because you have a wooden head.'

At these last words Pinocchio jumped up in a rage, and snatching a wooden hammer from the bench he threw it at the Talking-Cricket.

Perhaps he never meant to hit him; but unfortunately it struck him exactly on the head, so that the poor Cricket had scarcely breath to cry a last cri–cri–cri before being obliged to remain dried up and flattened against the wall.

CHAPTER 5

Pinocchio is hungry and searches for an egg to make himself an omelette; but just at the most interesting moment the omelette flies out of the window.

Night was coming on, and Pinocchio, remembering that he had eaten nothing all day, began to feel a gnawing in his stomach that very much resembled appetite.

But appetite with boys travels quickly, and in fact after a few minutes his appetite had become hunger,

and in no time his hunger became ravenous – a hunger that was really quite insupportable.

Poor Pinocchio ran quickly to the fireplace where a saucepan was boiling, and was going to take off the lid to see what was in it, but the saucepan was only painted on the wall. You can imagine his feelings. His nose, which was already long, became longer by at least three fingers.

He then began to run about the room, searching in the drawers and in every imaginable place, in hopes of finding a bit of bread. If it was only a bit of dry bread, a crust, a bone left by a dog, a little mouldy pudding of Indian corn, a fish bone, a cherry stone – in fact anything that he could gnaw. But he could find nothing, nothing at all, absolutely nothing.

And in the meanwhile his hunger grew and grew; and poor Pinocchio had no other relief than yawning, and his yawns were so tremendous that sometimes his mouth almost reached his ears. And after he had yawned he spluttered, and felt as if he was going to faint.

Then he began to cry desperately, and he said: 'The Talking-Cricket was right. I did wrong to rebel against my papa and to run away from home . . . If my papa was here I should not now be dying of yawning! Oh! what a dreadful illness hunger is!'

Just then he thought he saw something in the dust-heap – something round and white that looked like a hen's egg. To give a spring and seize hold of it was the affair of a moment. It was indeed an egg.

Pinocchio's joy beats description; it can only be imagined. Almost believing it must be a dream he kept turning the egg over in his hands, feeling it and kissing it. And as he kissed it he said: 'And now, how shall I cook it? Shall I make an omelette? . . . No, it would be better to cook it in a saucer! . . . Or would it not be more savoury to fry it in the frying-pan? Or shall I simply boil it? No, the quickest way of all is to cook it in a saucer: I am in such a hurry to eat it!'

Without loss of time he placed an earthenware

saucer on a brazier full of red-hot embers. Into the saucer instead of oil or butter he poured a little water; and when the water began to smoke, tac! . . . he broke the eggshell over it that the contents might drop in. But instead of the white and the yolk a little chicken popped out very gay and polite. Making a beautiful courtesy it said to him: 'A thousand thanks, Master Pinocchio, for saving me the trouble of breaking the shell. Adieu until we meet again. Keep well, and my best compliments to all at home!'

Thus saying it spread its wings, darted through the open window, and flying away was lost to sight.

The poor puppet stood as if he had been bewitched, with his eyes fixed, his mouth open, and the eggshell in his hand. Recovering, however, from his first stupefaction, he began to cry and scream, and to stamp his feet on the floor in desperation, and amidst his sobs he said: 'Ah! indeed the Talking-Cricket was right. If I had not run away from home, and if my papa was here, I should not now be dying of hunger! Oh! what a dreadful illness hunger is! . . . '

And as his stomach cried out more than ever and he did not know how to quiet it, he thought he would leave the house and make an excursion in the neighbourhood in hopes of finding some charitable person who would give him a piece of bread.

CHAPTER 6

Pinocchio falls asleep with his feet on the brazier, and wakes in the morning to find them burnt off.

It was a wild and stormy winter's night. The thunder was tremendous and the lightning so vivid that the sky seemed on fire. A bitter blusterous wind whistled angrily, and raising clouds of dust swept over the country, causing the trees to creak and groan as it passed.

Pinocchio had a great fear of thunder, but hunger was stronger than fear. He therefore closed the house door and made a rush for the village, which he reached in a hundred bounds, with his tongue hanging out and panting for breath, like a dog after game.

But he found it all dark and deserted. The shops were closed, the windows shut, and there was not so much as a dog in the street. It seemed the land of the dead.

Pinocchio, urged by desperation and hunger, laid hold of the bell of a house and began to peal it with all his might, saying to himself: 'That will bring somebody.'

And so it did. A little old man appeared at a window with a nightcap on his head, and called to him angrily: 'What do you want at such an hour?'

'Would you be kind enough to give me a little bread?'

'Wait there, I will be back directly,' said the little old man, thinking he had to do with one of those rascally boys who amuse themselves at night by ringing the house bells to rouse respectable people who are sleeping quietly.

After half a minute the window was again opened, and the voice of the same little old man shouted to Pinocchio: 'Come underneath and hold out your cap.'

Pinocchio pulled off his cap; but just as he held it out an enormous basin of water was poured down on him, watering him from head to foot as if he had been a pot of dried-up geraniums.

He returned home like a wet chicken quite exhausted with fatigue and hunger; and having no longer strength to stand, he sat down and rested his damp and muddy feet on a brazier full of burning embers.

And then he fell asleep; and whilst he slept his feet, which were wooden, took fire, and little by little they burnt away and became cinders.

Pinocchio continued to sleep and to snore as if his feet belonged to someone else. At last about daybreak he awoke because someone was knocking at the door.

'Who is there?' he asked, yawning and rubbing his eyes.

'It is I!' answered a voice.

And the voice was Geppetto's voice.

CHAPTER 7

Geppetto returns home, makes the puppet new feet, and gives him the breakfast that the poor man had brought for himself.

Poor Pinocchio, whose eyes were still half shut from sleep, had not as yet discovered that his feet were burnt off. The moment, therefore, that he heard his father's voice he slipped off his stool to run and open the door; but after stumbling two or three times he fell his whole length on the floor.

And the noise he made in falling was as if a sack of wooden ladles had been thrown from a fifth storey.

'Open the door!' shouted Geppetto from the street.

'Dear papa, I cannot,' answered the puppet, crying and rolling about on the ground.

'Why cannot you?'

'Because my feet have been eaten.'

'And who has eaten your feet?'

'The cat,' said Pinocchio, seeing the cat, who was amusing herself by making some shavings dance with her forepaws.

'Open the door, I tell you!' repeated Geppetto. 'If you don't, when I get into the house you shall have the cat from me!'

'I cannot stand up, believe me. Oh, poor me! poor me! I shall have to walk on my knees for the rest of my life! . . . '

Geppetto, believing that all this lamentation was only another of the puppet's tricks, thought of a means of putting an end to it, and climbing up the wall he got in at the window.

He was very angry, and at first he did nothing but scold; but when he saw his Pinocchio lying on the ground and really without feet he was quite overcome. He took him in his arms and began to kiss and caress him and to say a thousand endearing things to him, and as the big tears ran down his cheeks, he said, sobbing: 'My little Pinocchio! how did you manage to burn your feet?'

'I don't know, papa, but believe me it has been an infernal night that I shall remember as long as I live. It thundered and lightened, and I was very hungry, and then the Talking-Cricket said to me: "It serves you right; you have been wicked and you deserve it," and I said to him: "Take care, Cricket!" and he said: "You are a puppet and you have a wooden head," and I threw the handle of a hammer at him, and he died, but the fault was his, for I didn't wish to kill him, and the proof of it is that I put an earthenware saucer on a brazier of burning embers, but a chicken flew out and said: "Adieu until we meet again, and many compliments to all at home": and I got still more hungry, for which reason that little old man in a nightcap opening the window said to me: "Come underneath and hold out your hat,' and poured a basinful of water on my head, because asking for a little bread isn't a disgrace, is it? and I returned home at once, and because I was always very hungry I put my feet on the brazier to dry them, and then you returned, and I found they were burnt off, and I am always hungry, but I have no longer any feet! Ih! Ih! Ih! Ih! . . . ' And poor Pinocchio began to cry and to roar so loudly that he was heard five miles off.

Geppetto, who from all this jumbled account had only understood one thing, which was that the puppet was dying of hunger, drew from his pocket three pears, and giving them to him said: 'These three pears were intended for my breakfast; but I will give them to you willingly. Eat them, and I hope they will do you good.'

'If you wish me to eat them, be kind enough to peel them for me.'

'Peel them?' said Geppetto, astonished. 'I should never have thought, my boy, that you were so dainty and fastidious. That is bad! In this world we should accustom ourselves from childhood to like and to eat everything, for there is no saying to what we may be brought. There are so many chances! . . . '

'You are no doubt right,' interrupted Pinocchio, 'but I will never eat fruit that has not been peeled. I cannot bear rind.'

So that good Geppetto fetched a knife, and arming himself with patience peeled the three pears, and put the rind on a corner of the table.

Having eaten the first pear in two mouthfuls, Pinocchio was about to throw away the core; but Geppetto caught hold of his arm and said to him: 'Do not throw it away; in this world everything may be of use.'

'But core I am determined I will not eat,' shouted the puppet, turning upon him like a viper.

'Who knows! there are so many chances! . . . ' repeated Geppetto without losing his temper.

And so the three cores, instead of being thrown out of the window, were placed on the corner of the table together with the three rinds.

Having eaten, or rather having devoured the three pears, Pinocchio yawned tremendously, and then said in a fretful tone: 'I am as hungry as ever!'

'But, my boy, I have nothing more to give you!'

'Nothing, really nothing?'

'I have only the rind and the cores of the three pears.'

'One must have patience!' said Pinocchio; 'if there is nothing else I will eat a rind.'

And he began to chew it. At first he made a wry face; but then one after another he quickly disposed of the rinds; and after the rinds even the cores, and when he had eaten up everything he clapped his hands on his sides in his satisfaction, and said joyfully: 'Ah! now I feel comfortable.'

'You see now,' observed Geppetto, 'that I was right when I said to you that it did not do to accustom ourselves to be too particular or too dainty in our tastes. We can never know, my dear boy, what may happen to us. There are so many chances! . . . '

CHAPTER 8

*Geppetto makes Pinocchio new feet, and sells his
own coat to buy him a spelling-book.*

No sooner had the puppet appeased his hunger than he began to cry and to grumble because he wanted a pair of new feet.

But Geppetto, to punish him for his naughtiness, allowed him to cry and to despair for half the day. He then said to him: 'Why should I make you new feet? To enable you, perhaps, to escape again from home?'

'I promise you,' said the puppet, sobbing, 'that for the future I will be good.'

'All boys,' replied Geppetto, 'when they are bent upon obtaining something, say the same thing.'

'I promise you that I will go to school, and that I will study and earn a good character.'

'All boys, when they are bent on obtaining something, repeat the same story.'

'But I am not like other boys! I am better than all of them and I always speak the truth. I promise you, papa, that I will learn a trade, and that I will be the consolation and the staff of your old age.'

Geppetto, although he put on a severe face, had his eyes full of tears and his heart big with sorrow at seeing his poor Pinocchio in such a pitiable state. He did not say another word, but taking his tools and two small pieces of well-seasoned wood he set to work with great diligence.

In less than an hour the feet were finished: two little feet – swift, well-knit and nervous. They might have been modelled by an artist of genius.

Geppetto then said to the puppet: 'Shut your eyes and go to sleep!'

And Pinocchio shut his eyes and pretended to be asleep.

And whilst he pretended to sleep, Geppetto, with a little glue which he had melted in an eggshell, fastened his feet in their place, and it was so well done that not even a trace could be seen of where they were joined.

No sooner had the puppet discovered that he had feet than he jumped down from the table on which he was lying, and began to spring and to cut a thousand capers about the room, as if he had gone mad with the greatness of his delight.

'To reward you for what you have done for me,' said Pinocchio to his father, 'I will go to school at once.'

'Good boy.'

'But to go to school I shall want some clothes.' Geppetto, who was poor, and who had not so much as a farthing in his pocket, then made him a little dress of flowered paper, a pair of shoes from the bark of a tree, and a cap of the crumb of bread.

Pinocchio ran immediately to look at himself in a crock of water, and he was so pleased with his appearance that he said, strutting about like a peacock: 'I look quite like a gentleman!'

'Yes indeed,' answered Geppetto, 'for bear in mind that it is not fine clothes that make the gentleman, but rather clean clothes.'

'By the by,' added the puppet, 'to go to school I am still in want – indeed I am without the best thing, and the most important.'

'And what is it?'

'I have no spelling-book.'

'You are right: but what shall we do to get one?'

'It is quite easy. We have only to go to the bookseller's and buy it.'

'And the money?'

'I have got none.'

'No more have I,' added the good old man very sadly.

And Pinocchio, although he was a very merry boy, became sad also; because poverty, when it is real poverty, is understood by everybody – even by boys.

'Well, patience!' exclaimed Geppetto, all at once rising to his feet, and putting on his old fustian coat, all patched and darned, he ran out of the house.

He returned shortly, holding in his hand a spelling-book for Pinocchio, but the old coat was gone. The poor man was in his shirt sleeves, and out of doors it was snowing.

'And the coat, papa?'

'I have sold it.'

'Why did you sell it?'

'Because I found it too hot.'

Pinocchio understood this answer in an instant, and unable to restrain the impulse of his good heart he sprang up, and throwing his arms round Geppetto's neck he began kissing him again and again.

CHAPTER 9

Pinocchio sells his spelling-book that he may go and see a puppet-show.

As soon as it had done snowing Pinocchio set out for school with his fine spelling-book under his arm. As he went along he began to imagine a thousand things in his little brain, and to build a thousand castles in the air, one more beautiful than the other.

And talking to himself he said: 'Today at school I will learn to read at once; then tomorrow I will begin to write, and the day after tomorrow to cipher. Then with my acquirements I will earn a

great deal of money, and with the first money I have in my pocket I will immediately buy for my papa a beautiful new cloth coat. But what am I saying? Cloth, indeed! It shall be all made of gold and silver, and it shall have diamond buttons. That poor man really deserves it; for to buy me books and have me taught he has remained in his shirt sleeves . . . And in this cold! It is only fathers who are capable of such sacrifices! . . .'

Whilst he was saying this with great emotion he thought that he heard music in the distance that sounded like fifes and the beating of a big drum: fi-fi-fi, fi-fi-fi, zum, zum, zum, zum.

He stopped and listened. The sounds came from the end of a cross street that led to a little village on the seashore.

'What can that music be? What a pity that I have to go to school, or else . . .'

And he remained irresolute. It was, however, necessary to come to a decision. Should he go to school? or should he go after the fifes?

'Today I will go and hear the fifes, and tomorrow I will go to school,' finally decided the young scapegrace, shrugging his shoulders.

The more he ran the nearer came the sounds of the fifes and the beating of the big drum: fi-fi-fi, zum, zum, zum, zum.

At last he found himself in the middle of a square quite full of people, who were all crowding round a building made of wood and canvas, and painted a thousand colours.

'What is that building?' asked Pinocchio, turning to a little boy who belonged to the place.

'Read the placard – it is all written – and then you will know.'

'I would read it willingly, but it so happens that today I don't know how to read.'

'Bravo, blockhead! Then I will read it to you. The writing on that placard in those letters red as fire is:

GREAT PUPPET THEATRE.'

'Has the play begun long?'

'It is beginning now.'

'How much does it cost to go in?'

'Twopence.'

Pinocchio, who was in a fever of curiosity, lost all control of himself, and without any shame, he said to the little boy to whom he was talking: 'Would you lend me twopence until tomorrow?'

'I would lend them to you willingly,' said the other, taking him off, 'but it so happens that today I cannot give them to you.'

'I will sell you my jacket for twopence!' the puppet then said to him.

'What do you think that I could do with a jacket of flowered paper? If there was rain and it got wet, it would be impossible to get it off my back.'

'Will you buy my shoes?'

'They would only be of use to light the fire.'

'How much will you give me for my cap?'

'That would be a wonderful acquisition indeed! A cap of breadcrumb! There would be a risk of the mice coming to eat it whilst it was on my head.'

Pinocchio was on thorns. He was on the point of making another offer, but he had not the courage. He hesitated, felt irresolute and remorseful. At last he said: 'Will you give me twopence for this new spelling-book?'

'I am a boy and I don't buy from boys,' replied his little interlocutor, who had much more sense than he had.

'I will buy the spelling-book for twopence,' called out a hawker of old clothes, who had been listening to the conversation.

And the book was sold there and then. And to think that poor Geppetto had remained at home trembling with cold in his shirt sleeves that he might buy his son a spelling-book!

CHAPTER 10

The puppets recognise their brother Pinocchio, and receive him with delight; but at that moment their master, Fire-Eater, makes his appearance and Pinocchio is in danger of coming to a bad end.

When Pinocchio came into the little puppet theatre, an incident occurred that almost produced a revolution.

I must tell you that the curtain was drawn up, and the play had already begun.

On the stage Harlequin and Punchinello were as usual quarrelling with each other, and threatening every moment to come to blows.

The audience, all attention, laughed till they were ill as they listened to the bickerings of these two puppets, who gesticulated and abused each other so naturally that they might have been two reasonable beings, and two persons of the world.

All at once Harlequin stopped short, and turning to the public he pointed with his hand to someone far down in the pit, and exclaimed in a dramatic tone: 'Gods of the firmament! do I dream, or am I awake? But surely that is Pinocchio! . . . '

'It is indeed Pinocchio!' cried Punchinello.

'It is indeed himself!' screamed Miss Rose, peeping from behind the scenes.

'It is Pinocchio! it is Pinocchio!' shouted all the puppets in chorus, leaping from all sides on to the stage. 'It is Pinocchio! It is our brother Pinocchio! Long live Pinocchio! . . . '

'Pinocchio, come up here to me,' cried Harlequin, 'and throw yourself into the arms of your wooden brothers!'

At this affectionate invitation Pinocchio made a leap from the end of the pit into the reserved seats; another leap landed him on the head of the leader of the orchestra, and he then sprang upon the stage.

The embraces, the hugs, the friendly pinches, and the demonstrations of warm brotherly

the ground. I need only say that he trod upon it when he walked. His mouth was as big as an oven, and his eyes were like two lanterns of red glass with lights burning inside them. He carried a large whip made of snakes and foxes' tails twisted together, which he cracked constantly.

At his unexpected appearance there was a profound silence: no one dared to breathe. A fly might have been heard in the stillness. The poor puppets of both sexes trembled like so many leaves.

'Why have you come to raise a disturbance in my theatre?' asked the showman of Pinocchio, in the gruff voice of a hobgoblin suffering from a severe cold in the head.

'Believe me, honoured sir, that it was not my fault! . . .'

'That is enough! Tonight we will settle our accounts.'

As soon as the play was over the showman went into the kitchen where a fine sheep, preparing for his supper, was turning slowly on the spit in front of the fire. As there was not enough wood to finish roasting and browning it, he called Harlequin and Punchinello, and said to them: 'Bring that puppet here: you will find him hanging on a nail. It seems to me that he is made of very dry wood, and I am sure that if he was thrown on the fire he would make a beautiful blaze for the roast.'

At first Harlequin and Punchinello hesitated; but, appalled by a severe glance from their master, they obeyed. In a short time they returned to the kitchen carrying poor Pinocchio who was wriggling like an eel taken out of water, and screaming desperately: 'Papa! papa! save me! I will not die, I will not die!'

affection that Pinocchio received from the excited crowd of actors and actresses of the puppet dramatic company beat description.

The sight was doubtless a moving one, but the public in the pit, finding that the play was stopped, became impatient, and began to shout: 'We will have the play – go on with the play!'

It was all breath thrown away. The puppets, instead of continuing the recital, redoubled their noise and outcries, and putting Pinocchio on their shoulders they carried him in triumph before the footlights.

At that moment out came the showman. He was very big, and so ugly that the sight of him was enough to frighten anyone. His beard was as black as ink, and so long that it reached from his chin to

CHAPTER 11

Fire-Eater sneezes and pardons Pinocchio,
who then saves the life of his friend Harlequin.

The showman Fire-Eater – for that was his name – looked, I must say, a terrible man, especially with his black beard that covered his chest and legs like an apron. On the whole, however, he had not a bad heart. In proof of this, when he saw poor Pinocchio brought before him, struggling and screaming, 'I will not die, I will not die!' he was quite moved and felt very sorry for him. He tried to hold out, but after a little he could stand it no longer and he sneezed violently. When he heard the sneeze, Harlequin, who up to that moment had been in the

'Thank you! All the same, some compassion is due to me, for as you see I have no more wood with which to finish roasting my mutton, and to tell you the truth, under the circumstances you would have been of great use to me! However, I have had pity on you, so I must have patience. Instead of you will burn under the spit one of the puppets belonging to my company. Ho there, gendarmes!'

deepest affliction, and bowed down like a weeping willow, became quite cheerful, and leaning towards Pinocchio he whispered to him softly: 'Good news, brother. The showman has sneezed, and that is a sign that he pities you, and consequently you are saved.'

For you must know that whilst most men, when they feel compassion for somebody, either weep or at least pretend to dry their eyes, Fire-Eater, on the contrary, whenever he was really overcome, had the habit of sneezing.

After he had sneezed, the showman, still acting the ruffian, shouted to Pinocchio: 'Have done crying! Your lamentations have given me a pain in my stomach . . . I feel a spasm, that almost . . . Etci! etci!' and he sneezed again twice.

'Bless you!' said Pinocchio.

'Thank you! And your papa and your mama, are they still alive?' asked Fire-Eater.

'Papa, yes; my mama I have never known.'

'Who can say what a sorrow it would be for your poor old father if I was to have you thrown amongst those burning coals! Poor old man! I feel compassion for him! . . . Etci! etci! etci!' and he sneezed again three times.

'Bless you!' said Pinocchio.

At this call two wooden gendarmes immediately appeared. They were very long and very thin, and had on cocked hats, and held unsheathed swords in their hands.

The showman said to them in a hoarse voice: 'Take Harlequin, bind him securely, and then throw him on the fire to burn. I am determined that my mutton shall be well roasted.'

Only imagine that poor Harlequin! His terror was so great that his legs bent under him, and he fell with his face on the ground.

At this agonising sight Pinocchio, weeping bitterly, threw himself at the showman's feet, and bathing his long beard with his tears he began to say in a supplicating voice: 'Have pity, Sir Fire-Eater! . . .'

'Here there are no sirs,' the showman answered severely.

'Have pity, Sir Knight! . . .'

'Here there are no knights!'

'Have pity, Commander! . . .'

'Here there are no commanders!'

'Have pity, Excellence! . . .'

Upon hearing himself called Excellence the showman began to smile, became at once kinder and more tractable. Turning to Pinocchio he asked: 'Well, what do you want from me?'

'I implore you to pardon poor Harlequin.'

'For him there can be no pardon. As I have spared you, he must be put on the fire, for I am determined that my mutton shall be well roasted.'

'In that case,' cried Pinocchio proudly, rising and throwing away his cap of breadcrumb – 'in that case I know my duty. Come on, gendarmes! Bind me and throw me amongst the flames. No, it is not just that poor Harlequin, my true friend, should die for me! . . .'

These words, pronounced in a loud heroic voice, made all the puppets who were present cry. Even the gendarmes, although they were made of wood, wept like two newly-born lambs.

Fire-Eater at first remained as hard and unmoved as ice, but little by little he began to melt and to sneeze. And having sneezed four or five times, he opened his arms affectionately, and said to Pinocchio: 'You are a good, brave boy! Come here and give me a kiss.'

Pinocchio ran at once, and climbing like a squirrel up the showman's beard he deposited a hearty kiss on the point of his nose.

'Then the pardon is granted?' asked poor Harlequin in a faint voice that was scarcely audible.

'The pardon is granted!' answered Fire-Eater; he then added, sighing and shaking his head: 'I must have patience! Tonight I shall have to resign myself to eat the mutton half raw; but another time, woe to him who chances! . . .'

At the news of the pardon the puppets all ran to the stage, and having lighted the lamps and chandeliers as if for a full-dress performance, they began to leap and to dance merrily. At dawn they were still dancing.

CHAPTER 12

The showman, Fire-Eater, makes Pinocchio a present of five gold pieces to take home to his father, Geppetto; but Pinocchio instead allows himself to be taken in by the Fox and the Cat, and goes with them.

The following day Fire-Eater called Pinocchio on one side and asked him: 'What is your father's name?'

'Geppetto.'

'And what trade does he follow?'

'He is a beggar.'

'Does he gain much?'

'Gain much? Why, he has never a penny in his pocket. Only think, to buy a spelling-book for me to go to school he was obliged to sell the only coat he had to wear – a coat that, between patches and darns, was not fit to be seen.'

'Poor devil! I feel almost sorry for him! Here are five gold pieces. Go at once and take them to him with my compliments.'

You can easily understand that Pinocchio thanked the showman a thousand times. He embraced all the puppets of the company one by one, even to the gendarmes, and beside himself with delight set out to return home.

But he had not gone far when he met on the road a Fox lame of one foot, and a Cat blind of both eyes, who were going along helping each other, like good companions in misfortune. The Fox, who was lame, walked leaning on the Cat, and the Cat, who was blind, was guided by the Fox.

'Good-day, Pinocchio,' said the Fox, accosting him politely.

'How do you come to know my name?' asked the puppet.

'I know your father well.'

'Where did you see him?'

'I saw him yesterday at the door of his house.'

'And what was he doing?'

'He was in his shirt sleeves and shivering with cold.'

'Poor papa! But that is over; for the future he shall shiver no more!'

'Why?'

'Because I am become a gentleman.'

'A gentleman – you!' said the Fox, and he began to laugh rudely and scornfully. The Cat also began to laugh, but to conceal it she combed her whiskers with her forepaws.

'There is little to laugh at,' cried Pinocchio angrily. 'I am really sorry to make your mouths water, but if you know anything about it, you can see that these here are five gold pieces.'

And he pulled out the money that Fire-Eater had made him a present of.

At the sympathetic ring of the money the Fox, with an involuntary movement, stretched out the paw that had seemed crippled, and the Cat opened wide two eyes that looked like two green lanterns. It is true that she shut them again, and so quickly that Pinocchio observed nothing.

'And now,' asked the Fox, 'what are you going to do with all that money?'

'First of all,' answered the puppet, 'I intend to buy a new coat for my papa, made of gold and silver, and with diamond buttons; and then I will buy a spelling-book for myself.'

'For yourself?'

'Yes indeed: for I wish to go to school to study in earnest.'

'Look at me!' said the Fox. 'Through my foolish passion for study I have lost a leg.'

'Look at me!' said the Cat. 'Through my foolish passion for study I have lost the sight of both my eyes.'

At that moment a white Blackbird, that was perched on the hedge by the road, began his usual song, and said: 'Pinocchio, don't listen to the advice of bad companions: if you do you will repent it! . . . '

Poor Blackbird! If only he had not spoken! The Cat, with a great leap, sprang upon him, and without even giving him time to say Oh! ate him in a mouthful, feathers and all.

Having eaten him and cleaned her mouth she shut her eyes again and feigned blindness as before.

'Poor Blackbird!' said Pinocchio to the Cat, 'why did you treat him so badly?'

'I did it to give him a lesson. He will learn another time not to meddle in other people's conversation.'

They had gone almost halfway when the Fox, halting suddenly, said to the puppet: 'Would you like to double your money?'

'In what way?'

'Would you like to make out of your five miserable sovereigns, a hundred, a thousand, two thousand?'

'I should think so! but in what way?'

'The way is easy enough. Instead of returning home you must go with us.'

'And where do you wish to take me?'

'To the land of the Owls.'

Pinocchio reflected a moment, and then he said resolutely: 'No, I will not go. I am already close to the house, and I will return home to my papa who is waiting for me. Who can tell how often the poor old man must have sighed yesterday when I did not come back! I have indeed been a bad son, and the Talking-Cricket was right when he said: "Disobedient boys never come to any good in the world." I have found it to my cost, for many misfortunes have happened to me. Even yesterday in Fire-Eater's house I ran the risk . . . Oh! it makes me shudder only to think of it!'

'Well, then,' said the Fox, 'you are quite decided to go home? Go, then, and so much the worse for you.'

'So much the worse for you!' repeated the Cat.

'Think well of it, Pinocchio, for you are giving a kick to fortune.'

'To fortune!' repeated the Cat.

'Between today and tomorrow your five sovereigns would have become two thousand.'

'Two thousand!' repeated the Cat.

'But how is it possible that they could have become so many?' asked Pinocchio, remaining with his mouth open from astonishment.

'I will explain it to you at once,' said the Fox. 'You

must know that in the land of the Owls there is a sacred field called by everybody the Field of Miracles. In this field you must dig a little hole, and you put into it, we will say, one gold sovereign. You then cover up the hole with a little earth: you must water it with two pails of water from the fountain, then sprinkle it with two pinches of salt, and when night comes you can go quietly to bed. In the meanwhile, during the night, the gold piece will grow and flower, and in the morning when you get up and return to the field, what do you find? You find a beautiful tree laden with as many gold sovereigns as a fine ear of corn has grains in the month of June.'

'So that,' said Pinocchio, more and more bewildered, 'supposing I buried my five sovereigns in that field, how many should I find there the following morning?'

'That is an exceedingly easy calculation,' replied the Fox, 'a calculation that you can make on the ends of your fingers. Put that every sovereign gives you an increase of five hundred, multiply five hundred by five, and the following morning will find you with two thousand five hundred shining gold pieces in your pocket.'

'Oh! how delightful!' cried Pinocchio, dancing for joy. 'As soon as ever I have obtained those sovereigns, I will keep two thousand for myself, and the other five hundred I will make a present of to you two.'

'A present to us?' cried the Fox with indignation and appearing much offended. 'What are you dreaming of?'

'What are you dreaming of?' repeated the Cat.

'We do not work,' said the Fox, 'for dirty interest: we work solely to enrich others.'

'Others!' repeated the Cat.

'What good people!' thought Pinocchio to himself: and forgetting there and then his papa, the new coat, the spelling-book, and all his good resolutions, he said to the Fox and the Cat: 'Let us be off at once. I will go with you.'

CHAPTER 13

The Inn of the Red Crawfish

They walked, and walked, and walked, until at last, towards evening, they arrived dead tired at the Inn of the Red Crawfish.

'Let us stop here a little,' said the Fox, 'that we may have something to eat and rest ourselves for an hour or two. We will start again at midnight, so as to arrive at the Field of Miracles by dawn tomorrow morning.'

Having gone into the inn they all three sat down to table: but none of them had any appetite.

The Cat, who was suffering from indigestion and feeling seriously indisposed, could only eat thirty-five mullet with tomato sauce, and four portions of tripe with Parmesan cheese; and because she thought the tripe was not seasoned enough, she asked three times for the butter and grated cheese!

The Fox would also willingly have picked a little, but as his doctor had ordered him a strict diet, he was forced to content himself simply with a hare dressed with a sweet-and-sour sauce, and garnished lightly with fat chickens and early pullets. After the hare he sent for a made dish of partridges, rabbits, frogs, lizards and other delicacies; he could not touch anything else. He had such a disgust to food, he said, that he could put nothing to his lips.

The one who ate the least was Pinocchio. He asked for some walnuts and a hunch of bread, and left everything on his plate. The poor boy, whose thoughts were continually fixed on the Field of Miracles, had got in anticipation an indigestion of gold pieces.

When they had supped, the Fox said to the host: 'Give us two good rooms, one for Mr Pinocchio, and the other for me and my companion. We will snatch a little sleep before we leave. Remember, however, that at midnight we wish to be called to continue our journey.'

'Yes, gentlemen,' answered the host, and he winked at the Fox and the Cat, as much as to say: 'I know what you are up to. We understand one another!'

No sooner had Pinocchio got into bed than he fell asleep at once and began to dream. And he dreamt that he was in the middle of a field, and the field was full of shrubs covered with clusters of gold sovereigns, and as they swung in the wind they went zin, zin, zin, almost as if they would say: 'Let

who will, come and take us.' But when Pinocchio was at the most interesting moment, that is, just as he was stretching out his hand to pick handfuls of those beautiful gold pieces and to put them in his pocket, he was suddenly wakened by three violent blows on the door of his room.

It was the host who had come to tell him that midnight had struck.

'Are my companions ready?' asked the puppet.

'Ready! Why, they left two hours ago.'

'Why were they in such a hurry?'

'Because the Cat had received a message to say that her eldest kitten was ill with chilblains on his feet, and was in danger of death.'

'Did they pay for the supper?'

'What are you thinking of? They are much too well educated to dream of offering such an insult to a gentleman like you.'

'What a pity! It is an insult that would have given me so much pleasure!' said Pinocchio, scratching his head. He then asked: 'And where did my good friends say they would wait for me?'

'At the Field of Miracles, tomorrow morning at daybreak.'

Pinocchio paid a sovereign for his supper and that of his companions, and then left.

Outside the inn it was so pitch dark that he had almost to grope his way, for it was impossible to see a hand's breadth in front of him. In the adjacent country not a leaf moved. Only some night-birds flying across the road from one hedge to the other brushed Pinocchio's nose with their wings as they passed, which caused him so much terror that, springing back, he shouted: 'Who goes there?' and the echo in the surrounding hills repeated in the distance: 'Who goes there? Who goes there? Who goes there?'

As he was walking along he saw a little insect shining dimly on the trunk of a tree, like a night-light in a lamp of transparent china.

'Who are you?' asked Pinocchio.

'I am the ghost of the Talking-Cricket,' answered the insect in a low voice, so weak and faint that it seemed to come from the other world.

'What do you want with me?' said the puppet.

'I want to give you some advice. Go back, and take the four sovereigns that you have left to your poor father, who is weeping and in despair because you have never returned to him.'

'By tomorrow my papa will be a gentleman, for these four sovereigns will have become two thousand.'

'Don't trust, my boy, to those who promise to make you rich in a day. Usually they are either mad or rogues! Give ear to me, and go back.'

'On the contrary, I am determined to go on.'

'The hour is late!'

'I am determined to go on.'

'The night is dark!'

'I am determined to go on.'

'The road is dangerous!'

'I am determined to go on.'

'Remember that boys who are bent on following their caprices, and will have their own way, sooner or later repent it.'

'Always the same stories. Good-night, Cricket.'

'Good-night, Pinocchio, and may Heaven preserve you from dangers and from assassins.'

No sooner had he said these words than the Talking-Cricket vanished suddenly like a light that has been blown out, and the road became darker than ever.

CHAPTER 14

Pinocchio, because he would not heed the good counsels of the Talking-Cricket, falls amongst assassins.

'Really,' said the puppet to himself as he resumed his journey, 'how unfortunate we poor boys are. Everybody scolds us, everybody admonishes us, everybody gives us good advice. To let them talk, they would all take it into their heads to be our fathers and our masters – all: even the Talking-Cricket. See now; because I don't choose to listen to that tiresome Cricket, who knows, according to him, how many misfortunes are to happen to me! I am even to meet with assassins! That is, however, of little consequence, for I don't believe in assassins –

I have never believed in them. For me, I think that assassins have been invented purposely by papas to frighten boys who want to go out at night. Besides, supposing I was to come across them here in the road, do you imagine they would frighten me? not the least in the world. I should go to meet them and cry: "Gentlemen assassins, what do you want with me? Remember that with me there is no joking. Therefore go about your business and be quiet!" At this speech, said in a determined tone, those poor assassins – I think I see them – would run away like the wind. If, however, they were so badly educated as not to run away, why, then, I would run away myself, and there would be an end of it . . .'

But Pinocchio had not time to finish his reasoning, for at that moment he thought that he heard a slight rustle of leaves behind him.

He turned to look, and saw in the gloom two evil-looking black figures completely enveloped in charcoal sacks. They were running after him on tiptoe, and making great leaps like two phantoms.

'Here they are in reality!' he said to himself, and not knowing where to hide his gold pieces he put them in his mouth precisely under his tongue.

Then he tried to escape. But he had not gone a step when he felt himself seized by the arm, and heard two horrid sepulchral voices saying to him: 'Your money or your life!'

Pinocchio, not being able to answer in words, owing to the money that was in his mouth, made a thousand low bows and a thousand pantomimes. He tried thus to make the two muffled figures, whose eyes were only visible through the holes in their sacks, understand that he was a poor puppet, and that he had not as much as a false farthing in his pocket.

'Come now! Less nonsense and out with the money!' cried the two brigands threateningly.

And the puppet made a gesture with his hands to signify: 'I have got none.'

'Deliver up your money or you are dead,' said the taller of the brigands.

'Dead!' repeated the other.

'And after we have killed you, we will also kill your father.'

'Also your father!'

'No, no, no, not my poor papa!' cried Pinocchio in a despairing tone; and as he said it, the sovereigns clinked in his mouth.

'Ah! you rascal! Then you have hidden your money under your tongue! Spit it out at once!'

But Pinocchio was obdurate.

'Ah! you pretend to be deaf, do you? Wait a moment, leave it to us to find a means to make you spit it out.'

And one of them seized the puppet by the end of his nose and the other took him by the chin and they began to pull brutally, the one up and the other down, to constrain him to open his mouth. But it was all to no purpose. Pinocchio's mouth seemed to be nailed and riveted together.

Then the shorter assassin drew out an ugly knife and tried to force it between his lips like a lever or chisel. But Pinocchio, as quick as lightning, caught his hand with his teeth, and with one bite bit it clean off and spat it out. Imagine his astonishment when instead of a hand he perceived that he had spat a cat's paw on to the ground.

Encouraged by this first victory he used his nails to such purpose that he succeeded in liberating himself from his assailants, and jumping the hedge by the roadside he began to fly across country. The assassins ran after him like two dogs chasing a hare: and the one who had lost a paw ran on one leg, and no one ever knew how it was done.

After a race of some miles Pinocchio could do no more. Giving himself up for lost he climbed the stem of a very high pine tree and seated himself in the topmost branches. The assassins attempted to climb after him, but when they had reached half-way up the stem they slid down again, and arrived on the ground with the skin grazed from their hands and knees.

But they were not to be beaten by so little; collecting a quantity of dry wood they piled it beneath the pine and set fire to it. In less time than it takes to tell, the pine began to burn and to flame like a candle blown by the wind. Pinocchio, seeing that the flames were mounting higher every instant, and not wishing to end his life like a roasted pigeon, made a stupendous leap from the top of the tree and started afresh across the fields and vineyards. The assassins followed him, and kept behind him without once giving in.

The day began to break and they were still pursuing him. Suddenly Pinocchio found his way barred by a wide deep ditch full of dirty water the colour of coffee. What was he to do? 'One! two! three!' cried the puppet, and making a rush, he sprang to the other side. The assassins also jumped, but not having measured the distance properly – splash, splash! . . . they fell into the very middle of the ditch. Pinocchio, who heard the plunge and the splashing of the water, shouted out, laughing, and without stopping: 'A fine bath to you, gentleman assassins.'

And he felt convinced that they were drowned, until, turning to look, he perceived that on the contrary they were both running after him, still enveloped in their sacks, with the water dripping from them as if they had been two hollow baskets.

CHAPTER 15

The assassins pursue Pinocchio; and having overtaken him hang him from a branch of the Big Oak.

At this sight the puppet's courage failed him, and he was on the point of throwing himself on the ground and giving himself over for lost. Turning, however, his eyes in every direction, he saw at some distance, standing out amidst the dark green of the trees, a small house as white as snow.

'If I had only breath to reach that house,' he said to himself, 'perhaps I should be saved.'

And without delaying an instant, he recommenced running for his life through the wood, and the assassins after him.

At last, after a desperate race of nearly two hours, he arrived quite breathless at the door of the house, and knocked.

No one answered.

He knocked again with great violence, for he heard the sound of steps approaching him, and the heavy panting of his persecutors. The same silence.

Seeing that knocking was useless he began in desperation to kick and pummel the door with all his might. The window then opened and a beautiful Child appeared at it. She had blue hair and a face as white as a waxen image; her eyes were closed and her hands were crossed on her breast. Without moving her lips in the least, she said in a voice that seemed to come from the other world: 'In this house there is no one. They are all dead.'

'Then at least open the door for me yourself,' shouted Pinocchio, crying and imploring.

'I am dead also.'

'Dead? then what are you doing there at the window?'

'I am waiting for the bier to come to carry me away.'

Having said this she immediately disappeared, and the window was closed again without the slightest noise.

'Oh! beautiful Child with blue hair,' cried Pinocchio, 'open the door for pity's sake! Have compassion on a poor boy pursued by assas – '

But he could not finish the word, for he felt himself seized by the collar, and the same two horrible voices said to him threateningly: 'You shall not escape from us again!'

The puppet, seeing death staring him in the face, was taken with such a violent fit of trembling that the joints of his wooden legs began to creak, and the sovereigns hidden under his tongue to clink.

'Now then,' demanded the assassins, 'will you open your mouth, yes or no? Ah! no answer . . . Leave it to us: this time we will force you to open it! . . . '

And drawing out two long horrid knives as sharp as razors, clash . . . they attempted to stab him twice.

But the puppet, luckily for him, was made of very hard wood; the knives therefore broke into a thousand pieces, and the assassins were left with the handles in their hands staring at each other.

'I see what we must do,' said one of them. 'He must be hung! let us hang him!'

'Let us hang him!' repeated the other.

Without loss of time they tied his arms behind him, passed a running noose round his throat, and then hanged him from the branch of a tree called the Big Oak.

They then sat down on the grass and waited for his last struggle. But at the end of three hours the puppet's eyes were still open, his mouth closed, and he was kicking more than ever.

Losing patience they turned to Pinocchio and said in a bantering tone: 'Goodbye till tomorrow. Let us hope that when we return you will be polite enough to allow yourself to be found quite dead, and with your mouth wide open.'

And they walked off.

In the meantime a tempestuous northerly wind began to blow and roar angrily, and it beat the poor puppet as he hung from side to side, making him swing violently like the clatter of a bell ringing for a wedding. And the swinging gave him atrocious spasms, and the running noose, becoming still tighter round his throat, took away his breath.

Little by little his eyes began to grow dim, but although he felt that death was near he still continued to hope that some charitable person would come to his assistance before it was too late. But when, after waiting and waiting, he found that no one came, absolutely no one, then he remembered his poor father, and thinking he was dying, he stammered out: 'Oh, papa! papa! if only you were here!'

His breath failed him and he could say no more. He shut his eyes, opened his mouth, stretched his legs, gave a long shudder, and hung stiff and insensible.

CHAPTER 16

The beautiful Child with blue hair has the puppet taken down: has him put to bed and calls in three doctors to know if he is alive or dead.

Whilst poor Pinocchio, suspended from a branch of the Big Oak, was apparently more dead than alive, the beautiful Child with blue hair came again to the window. When she saw the unhappy puppet hanging by his throat, and dancing up and down in the gusts of the north wind, she was moved by compassion. Striking her hands together she made three little claps.

At this signal there came the sound of the sweep of wings flying rapidly, and a large Falcon flew on to the window-sill.

'What are your orders, gracious Fairy?' he asked, inclining his beak in sign of reverence – for I must tell you that the Child with blue hair was no more and no less than a beautiful Fairy, who for more than a thousand years had lived in the wood.

'Do you see that puppet dangling from a branch of the Big Oak?'

'I see him.'

'Very well. Fly there at once: with your strong beak break the knot that keeps him suspended in the air, and lay him gently on the grass at the foot of the tree.'

The Falcon flew away, and after two minutes he returned, saying: 'I have done as you commanded.'

'And how did you find him?'

'To see him he appeared dead, but he cannot really be quite dead, for I had no sooner loosened the running noose that tightened his throat than, giving a sigh, he muttered in a faint voice: "Now I feel better!" '

The Fairy then striking her hands together made two little claps, and a magnificent Poodle appeared, walking upright on his hind-legs exactly as if he had been a man.

He was in the full-dress livery of a coachman. On his head he had a three-cornered cap braided with gold, his curly white wig came down on to his shoulders, he had a chocolate-coloured waistcoat with diamond buttons, and two large pockets to contain the bones that his mistress gave him at dinner. He had besides a pair of short crimson velvet breeches, silk stockings, cut-down shoes, and hanging behind him a species of umbrella-case made of blue satin, to put his tail into when the weather was rainy.

'Be quick, Medoro, like a good dog!' said the Fairy to the Poodle. 'Have the most beautiful carriage in my coach-house put to, and take the road to the wood. When you come to the Big Oak you will find a poor puppet stretched on the grass half dead. Pick him up gently, and lay him flat on the cushions of the carriage and bring him here to me. Have you understood?'

The Poodle, to show that he had understood, shook the case of blue satin three or four times, and ran off like a racehorse.

Shortly afterwards a beautiful little carriage came out of the coach-house. The cushions were stuffed with canary feathers, and it was lined in the inside with whipped cream, custard and Savoy biscuits. The little carriage was drawn by a hundred pairs of white mice, and the Poodle, seated on the coach-box, cracked his whip from side to side like a driver when he is afraid that he is behind time.

A quarter of an hour had not passed when the carriage returned. The Fairy, who was waiting at the door of the house, took the poor puppet in her arms, and carried him into a little room that was wainscoted with mother-of-pearl, and sent at once to summon the most famous doctors in the neighbourhood.

The doctors came immediately one after the other: namely a Crow, an Owl and a Talking-Cricket.

'I wish to know from you gentlemen,' said the Fairy, turning to the three doctors who were assembled round Pinocchio's bed – 'I wish to know from you gentlemen, if this unfortunate puppet is alive or dead! . . .'

At this request the Crow, advancing first, felt Pinocchio's pulse; he then felt his nose, and then the little toe of his foot: and having done this carefully, he pronounced solemnly the following words: 'To my belief the puppet is already quite dead; but if unfortunately he should not be dead, then it would be a sign that he is still alive!'

'I regret,' said the Owl, 'to be obliged to contradict the Crow, my illustrious friend and colleague; but in my opinion the puppet is still alive: but if unfortunately he should not be alive, then it would be a sign that he is dead indeed!'

'And you – have you nothing to say?' asked the Fairy of the Talking-Cricket.

'In my opinion the wisest thing a prudent doctor can do, when he does not know what he is talking about, is to be silent. For the rest, that puppet there has a face that is not new to me. I have known him for some time! . . .'

Pinocchio, who up to that moment had lain immovable, like a real piece of wood, was seized with a fit of convulsive trembling that shook the whole bed.

'That puppet there,' continued the Talking-Cricket, 'is a confirmed rogue . . .'

Pinocchio opened his eyes, but shut them again immediately.

'He is a ragamuffin, a do-nothing, a vagabond . . .'

Pinocchio hid his face beneath the clothes.

'That puppet there is a disobedient son who will make his poor father die of a broken heart!'

At that instant a suffocated sound of sobs and crying was heard in the room. Imagine everybody's astonishment when, having raised the sheets a little, it was discovered that the sounds came from Pinocchio.

'When the dead person cries, it is a sign that he is on the road to recovery,' said the Crow solemnly.

'I grieve to contradict my illustrious friend and colleague,' added the Owl; 'but for me, when the dead person cries, it is a sign that he is sorry to die.'

CHAPTER 17

Pinocchio eats the sugar, but will not take his medicine: when, however, he sees the grave-diggers, who have arrived to carry him away, he takes it. He then tells a lie, and as a punishment his nose grows longer.

As soon as the three doctors had left the room the Fairy approached Pinocchio, and having touched his forehead she perceived that he was in a high fever that was not to be trifled with.

She therefore dissolved a certain white powder in half a tumbler of water, and offering it to the puppet, she said to him lovingly: 'Drink it, and in a few days you will be cured.'

Pinocchio looked at the tumbler, made a wry face, and then asked in a plaintive voice: 'Is it sweet or bitter?'

'It is bitter, but it will do you good.'

'If it is bitter, I will not take it.'

'Listen to me: drink it.'

'I don't like anything bitter.'

'Drink it, and when you have drunk it I will give you a lump of sugar to take away the taste.'

'Where is the lump of sugar?'

'Here it is,' said the Fairy, taking a piece from a gold sugar-basin.

'Give me first the lump of sugar, and then I will drink that bad bitter water . . .'

'Do you promise me?'

'Yes . . .'

The Fairy gave him the sugar, and Pinocchio, having crunched it up and swallowed it in a second, said, licking his lips: 'It would be a fine thing if sugar was medicine! . . . I would take it every day.'

'Now keep your promise and drink these few drops of water, which will restore you to health.'

Pinocchio took the tumbler unwillingly in his hand and put the point of his nose to it; he then approached it to his lips; he then again put his nose to it, and at last said: 'It is too bitter! too bitter! I cannot drink it.'

'How can you tell that, when you have not even tasted it?'

'I can imagine it! I know it from the smell. I want first another lump of sugar . . . and then I will drink it! . . .'

The Fairy then, with all the patience of a good mama, put another lump of sugar in his mouth, and then again presented the tumbler to him.

'I cannot drink it so!' said the puppet, making a thousand grimaces.

'Why?'

'Because that pillow that is down there on my feet bothers me.'

The Fairy removed the pillow.

'It is useless. Even so I cannot drink it . . .'

'What is the matter now?'

'The door of the room, which is half open, bothers me.'

The Fairy went and closed the door.

'In short,' cried Pinocchio, bursting into tears, 'I will not drink that bitter water – no, no, no!'

'My boy, you will repent it.'

'I don't care.'

'Your illness is serious.'

'I don't care.'

'The fever in a few hours will carry you into the other world.'

'I don't care.'

'Are you not afraid of death?'

'I am not in the least afraid! I would rather die than drink that bitter medicine.'

At that moment the door of the room flew open, and four rabbits as black as ink entered carrying on their shoulders a little bier.

'What do you want with me?' cried Pinocchio, sitting up in bed in a great fright.

'We are come to take you,' said the biggest rabbit.

'To take me? . . . But I am not yet dead! . . .'

'No, not yet: but you have only a few minutes to live, as you have refused the medicine that would have cured you of the fever.'

'Oh, Fairy, Fairy!' the puppet then began to scream, 'give me the tumbler at once . . . be quick, for pity's sake, for I will not die – no . . . I will not die . . .'

And taking the tumbler in both hands he emptied it at a draught.

'We must have patience!' said the rabbits; 'this time we have made our journey in vain.' And taking the little bier again on their shoulders they left the room, grumbling and murmuring between their teeth.

In fact, a few minutes afterwards Pinocchio jumped down from the bed quite well: because you must know that wooden puppets have the privilege of being seldom ill and of being cured very quickly.

The Fairy, seeing him running and rushing about the room as gay and as lively as a young cock, said to him: 'Then my medicine has really done you good?'

'Good, I should think so! It has restored me to life!'

'Then why on earth did you require so much persuasion to take it?'

'Because you see that we boys are all like that! We are more afraid of medicine than of the illness.'

'Disgraceful! Boys ought to know that a good remedy taken in time may save them from a serious illness, and perhaps even from death . . .'

'Oh! but another time I shall not require so much persuasion. I shall remember those black rabbits with the bier on their shoulders . . . and then I shall immediately take the tumbler in my hand and down it will go!'

'Now come here to me, and tell me how it came about that you fell into the hands of those assassins.'

'It came about that the showman Fire-Eater gave me some gold pieces and said to me: "Go, and take them to your father!" and instead I met on the road a Fox and a Cat, two very respectable persons, who said to me: "Would you like those pieces of gold to become a thousand or two? Come with us and we will take you to the Field of Miracles," and I said: "Let us go." And they said: "Let us stop at the Inn of the Red Crawfish," and after midnight they left. And when I awoke I found that they were no longer there, because they had gone away. Then I began to travel by night, for you cannot imagine how dark it was, and on that account I met on the road two assassins in charcoal sacks who said to me: "Out with your money," and I said to them: "I have got none," because I had hidden the four gold pieces in my mouth, and one of the assassins tried to put his hand in my mouth, and I bit his hand off and spat it out, but instead of a hand I spat out a cat's paw. And the assassins ran after me,

and I ran, and ran, until at last they caught me, and tied me by the neck to a tree in this wood, and said to me: "Tomorrow we shall return here, and then you will be dead with your mouth open, and we shall be able to carry off the pieces of gold that you have hidden under your tongue." '

'And the four pieces – where have you put them?' asked the Fairy.

'I have lost them!' said Pinocchio; but he was telling a lie, for he had them in his pocket.

He had scarcely told the lie when his nose, which was already long, grew at once two fingers longer.

'And where did you lose them?'

'In the wood near here.'

At this second lie his nose went on growing.

'If you have lost them in the wood near here,' said the Fairy, 'we will look for them, and we shall find them: because everything that is lost in that wood is always found.'

'Ah! now I remember all about it,' replied the puppet, getting quite confused; 'I didn't lose the four gold pieces, I swallowed them inadvertently whilst I was drinking your medicine.'

At this third lie his nose grew to such an extraordinary length that poor Pinocchio could not move in any direction. If he turned to one side he struck his nose against the bed or the window-panes, if he turned to the other he struck it against the walls or the door, if he raised his head a little he ran the risk of sticking it into one of the Fairy's eyes.

And the Fairy looked at him and laughed.

'What are you laughing at?' asked the puppet, very confused and anxious at finding his nose growing so prodigiously.

'I am laughing at the lie you have told.'

'And how can you possibly know that I have told a lie?'

'Lies, my dear boy, are found out immediately, because they are of two sorts. There are lies that have short legs, and lies that have long noses. Your lie, as it happens, is one of those that have a long nose.'

Pinocchio, not knowing where to hide himself for shame, tried to run out of the room; but he did not succeed, for his nose had increased so much that it could no longer pass through the door.

CHAPTER 18

Pinocchio meets again the Fox and the Cat, and goes with them to bury his money in the Field of Miracles.

The Fairy, as you can imagine, allowed the puppet to cry and to roar for a good half-hour over his nose, which could no longer pass through the door of the room. This she did to give him a severe lesson, and to correct him of the disgraceful fault of telling lies – the most disgraceful fault that a boy can have. But when she saw him quite disfigured, and his eyes swollen out of his head from weeping, she felt full of compassion for him. She therefore beat her hands together, and at that signal a thousand large birds called Woodpeckers flew in at the window. They immediately perched on Pinocchio's nose, and began to peck at it with such zeal that in a few minutes his enormous and ridiculous nose was reduced to its usual dimensions.

'What a good Fairy you are,' said the puppet, drying his eyes, 'and how much I love you!'

'I love you also,' answered the Fairy; 'and if you will remain with me, you shall be my little brother and I will be your good little sister . . .'

'I would remain willingly . . . but my poor papa?'

'I have thought of everything. I have already let your father know, and he will be here tonight.'

'Really?' shouted Pinocchio, jumping for joy. 'Then, little Fairy, if you consent, I should like to go and meet him. I am so anxious to give a kiss to that poor old man, who has suffered so much on my account, that I am counting the minutes.'

'Go, then, but be careful not to lose yourself. Take the road through the wood and I am sure that you will meet him.'

Pinocchio set out; and as soon as he was in the wood he began to run like a kid. But when he had reached a certain spot, almost in front of the Big Oak, he stopped, because he thought that he heard people amongst the bushes. In fact, two persons came out on to the road. Can you guess who they were? . . . His two travelling companions, the Fox and the Cat, with whom he had supped at the Inn of the Red Crawfish.

'Why, here is our dear Pinocchio!' cried the Fox, kissing and embracing him. 'How come you to be here?'

'How come you to be here?' repeated the Cat.

'It is a long story,' answered the puppet, 'which I will tell you when I have time. But do you know that the other night, when you left me alone at the inn, I met with assassins on the road . . . '

'Assassins! . . . Oh, poor Pinocchio! And what did they want?'

'They wanted to rob me of my gold pieces.'

'Villains! . . . ' said the Fox.

'Infamous villains!' repeated the Cat.

'But I ran away from them,' continued the puppet, 'and they followed me: and at last they overtook me and hung me from a branch of that oak tree . . . '

And Pinocchio pointed to the Big Oak, which was two steps from them.

'Is it possible to hear of anything more dreadful?' said the Fox. 'In what a world we are condemned to live! Where can respectable people like us find a safe refuge?'

Whilst they were thus talking Pinocchio observed that the Cat was lame of her front right leg, for in fact she had lost her paw with all its claws. He therefore asked her: 'What have you done with your paw?'

The Cat tried to answer but became confused. Therefore the Fox said immediately: 'My friend is too modest, and that is why she doesn't speak. I will answer for her. I must tell you that an hour ago we met an old wolf on the road, almost fainting from want of food, who asked alms of us. Not having so much as a fish-bone to give him, what did my friend, who has really the heart of a Caesar, do? She bit off one of her fore paws, and threw it to that poor beast that he might appease his hunger.'

And the Fox, in relating this, dried a tear.

Pinocchio was also touched, and approaching the Cat he whispered into her ear: 'If all cats resembled you, how fortunate the mice would be!'

'And now, what are you doing here?' asked the Fox of the puppet.

'I am waiting for my papa, whom I expect to arrive every moment.'

'And your gold pieces?'

'I have got them in my pocket, all but one that I spent at the Inn of the Red Crawfish.'

'And to think that, instead of four pieces, by tomorrow they might become one or two thousand! Why do you not listen to my advice? why will you not go and bury them in the Field of Miracles?'

'Today it is impossible: I will go another day.'

'Another day it will be too late!' said the Fox.

'Why?'

'Because the field has been bought by a gentleman, and after tomorrow no one will be allowed to bury money there.'

'How far off is the Field of Miracles?'

'Not two miles. Will you come with us? In half an hour you will be there. You can bury your money at once, and in a few minutes you will collect two thousand, and this evening you will return with your pockets full. Will you come with us?'

Pinocchio thought of the good Fairy, old Geppetto, and the warnings of the Talking-Cricket, and he hesitated a little before answering. He ended, however, by doing as all boys do who have not a grain of sense and who have no heart – he ended by giving his head a little shake, and saying to the Fox and the Cat: 'Let us go: I will come with you.'

And they went.

After having walked half the day they reached a town that was called Trap for Blockheads. As soon as Pinocchio entered this town, he saw that the streets were crowded with dogs who had lost their coats and who were yawning from hunger, shorn sheep trembling with cold, cocks without combs or crests who were begging for a grain of Indian corn, large butterflies who could no longer fly because they had sold their beautiful coloured wings, peacocks who had no tails and were ashamed to be seen, and pheasants who went scratching about in a subdued fashion, mourning for their brilliant gold and silver feathers gone for ever.

In the midst of this crowd of beggars and shamefaced creatures, some lordly carriage passed from time to time containing a Fox, or a thieving Magpie, or some other ravenous bird of prey.

'And where is the Field of Miracles?' asked Pinocchio.

'It is here, not two steps from us.'

They crossed the town, and having gone beyond the walls they came to a solitary field which to look at resembled all other fields.

'We are arrived,' said the Fox to the puppet. 'Now stoop down and dig with your hands a little hole in the ground and put your gold pieces into it.'

Pinocchio obeyed. He dug a hole, put into it the four gold pieces that he had left, and then filled up the hole with a little earth.

'Now, then,' said the Fox, go to that canal close to us, fetch a can of water, and water the ground where you have sown them.'

Pinocchio went to the canal, and as he had no can he took off one of his old shoes, and filling it with water he watered the ground over the hole.

He then asked: 'Is there anything else to be done?'

'Nothing else,' answered the Fox. 'We can now go away. You can return in about twenty minutes, and you will find a shrub already pushing through the ground, with its branches quite loaded with money.'

The poor puppet, beside himself with joy, thanked the Fox and the Cat a thousand times, and promised them a beautiful present.

'We wish for no presents,' answered the two rascals. 'It is enough for us to have taught you the way to enrich yourself without undergoing hard work, and we are as happy as folk out for a holiday.'

Thus saying they took leave of Pinocchio, and, wishing him a good harvest, went about their business.

CHAPTER 19

Pinocchio is robbed of his money, and as a punishment he is sent to prison for four months.

The puppet returned to the town and began to count the minutes one by one; and when he thought that it must be time he took the road leading to the Field of Miracles.

And as he walked along with hurried steps his heart beat fast, tic, tac, tic, tac, like a drawing-room clock when it is really going well. Meanwhile he was thinking to himself: 'And if instead of a thousand gold pieces, I was to find on the branches of the tree two thousand? . . . And instead of two thousand supposing I found five thousand? and instead of five thousand that I found a hundred thousand? Oh! what a fine gentleman I should then become! . . . I would have a beautiful palace, a thousand little wooden horses and a thousand stables to amuse myself with, a cellar full of currant-wine and sweet syrups, and a library quite full of candies, tarts, plum-cakes, macaroons and biscuits with cream.'

Whilst he was building these castles in the air he had arrived in the neighbourhood of the field, and he stopped to look if by chance he could perceive a tree with its branches laden with money: but he saw nothing. He advanced another hundred steps – nothing; he entered the field . . . he went right up to the little hole where he had buried his sovereigns – and nothing. He then became very thoughtful, and forgetting the rules of society and good manners he took his hands out of his pockets and gave his head a long scratch.

At that moment he heard an explosion of laughter close to him, and looking up he saw a large Parrot perched on a tree, who was preening the few feathers he had left.

'Why are you laughing?' asked Pinocchio in an angry voice.

'I am laughing because in preening my feathers I tickled myself under my wings.'

The puppet did not answer, but went to the canal, filled the same old shoe with water and proceeded to water the earth that covered his gold pieces.

Whilst he was thus occupied another laugh, and still more impertinent than the first, rang out in the silence of that solitary place.

'Oh yes,' shouted Pinocchio in a rage, 'may I know, you ill-educated Parrot, what you are laughing at?'

'I am laughing at those simpletons who believe in all the foolish things that are told them, and who allow themselves to be entrapped by those who are more cunning than they are.'

'Are you perhaps speaking of me?'

'Yes, I am speaking of you, poor Pinocchio – of you who are simple enough to believe that money can be sown and gathered in fields in the same way as beans and gourds. I also believed it once, and today I am suffering for it. Today – but it is too late – I have at last learnt that to put a few pennies honestly together it is necessary to know how to earn them, either by the work of our own hands or by the cleverness of our own brains.'

'I don't understand you,' said the puppet, who was already trembling with fear.

'Have patience! I will explain myself better,' rejoined the Parrot. 'You must know, then, that whilst you were in the town the Fox and the Cat returned to the field: they took the buried money and then fled like the wind. And now he that catches them will be clever.'

Pinocchio remained with his mouth open, and not choosing to believe the Parrot's words he began with his hands and nails to dig up the earth that he had watered. And he dug, and dug, and dug, and made such a deep hole that a rick of straw might have stood upright in it: but the money was no longer there.

He rushed back to the town in a state of desperation, and went at once to the Courts of Justice to denounce the two knaves who had robbed him to the judge.

The judge was a big ape of the gorilla tribe – an old ape respectable for his age, his white beard, but especially for his gold spectacles without glass that he was always obliged to wear, on account of an inflammation of the eyes that had tormented him for many years.

Pinocchio related in the presence of the judge all the particulars of the infamous fraud of which he had been the victim. He gave the names, the surnames, and other details, of the two rascals, and ended by demanding justice.

The judge listened with great benignity; took a lively interest in the story; was much touched and moved; and when the puppet had nothing further to say he stretched out his hand and rang a bell.

At this summons two mastiffs immediately appeared dressed as gendarmes. The judge then, pointing to Pinocchio, said to them: 'That poor devil has been robbed of four gold pieces; take him up, and put him immediately into prison.'

The puppet was petrified on hearing this unexpected sentence, and tried to protest; but the gendarmes, to avoid losing time, stopped his mouth, and carried him off to the lock-up.

And there he remained for four months – four long months – and he would have remained longer still if a fortunate chance had not released him. For I must tell you that the young Emperor who reigned over the town of Trap for Blockheads, having won a splendid victory over his enemies, ordered great public rejoicings. There were illuminations, fireworks, horse races and velocipede races, and as a further sign of triumph he commanded that the prisons should be opened and all the prisoners liberated.

'If the others are to be let out of prison, I will go also,' said Pinocchio to the jailor.

'No, not you,' said the jailor, 'because you do not belong to the fortunate class.'

'I beg your pardon,' replied Pinocchio, 'I am also a criminal.'

'In that case you are perfectly right,' said the jailor; and taking off his hat and bowing to him respectfully he opened the prison doors and let him escape.

CHAPTER 20

Liberated from prison, he starts to return to the Fairy's house;
but on the road he meets with a horrible Serpent, and
afterwards he is caught in a trap.

You can imagine Pinocchio's joy when he found himself free. Without stopping to take breath he immediately left the town and took the road that led to the Fairy's house.

On account of the rainy weather the road had become a marsh into which he sank knee-deep. But the puppet would not give in. Tormented by the desire of seeing his father and his little sister with blue hair again he ran and leapt like a grey-hound, and as he ran he was splashed with mud from head to foot. And he said to himself as he went along: 'How many misfortunes have happened to me . . . and I deserved them! for I am an obstinate, passionate puppet . . . I am always bent upon having my own way, without listening to those who wish me well, and who have a thousand times more sense than I have! . . . But from this time forth I am determined to change and to become orderly and obedient . . . For at last I have seen that disobedient boys come to no good and gain nothing. And will my papa have waited for me? Shall I find him at the Fairy's house! Poor man, it is so long since I last saw him: I am dying to embrace him, and to cover him with kisses! And will the Fairy forgive me my bad conduct to her? . . . To think of all the kindness and loving care I received from her . . . to think that if I am now alive I owe it to her! . . . Would it be possible to find a more ungrateful boy, or one with less heart than I have! . . . '

Whilst he was saying this he stopped suddenly, frightened to death, and made four steps back-wards.

What had he seen?

He had seen an immense Serpent stretched across the road. Its skin was green and it had red eyes, and a pointed tail that was smoking like a chimney.

It would be impossible to imagine the puppet's terror. He walked away to a safe distance, and sitting down on a heap of stones waited until the Serpent should have gone about its business and had left the road clear.

He waited an hour; two hours; three hours; but the Serpent was always there, and even from a distance he could see the red light of his fiery eyes and the column of smoke that ascended from the end of his tail.

At last Pinocchio, trying to feel courageous, approached to within a few steps, and said to the Serpent in a little, soft, insinuating voice: 'Excuse me, Sir Serpent, but would you be so good as to move a little to one side, just enough to allow me to pass?'

He might as well have spoken to the wall. Nobody moved.

He began again in the same soft voice: 'You must know, Sir Serpent, that I am on my way home, where my father is waiting for me, and it is such a long time since I saw him last! . . . Will you therefore allow me to continue my road?'

He waited for a sign in answer to this request, but there was none: in fact the Serpent, who up to that moment had been sprightly and full of life, became motionless and almost rigid. He shut his eyes and his tail ceased smoking.

'Can he really be dead?' said Pinocchio, rubbing his hands with delight; and he determined to jump over him and reach the other side of the road. But just as he was going to leap, the Serpent raised himself suddenly on end, like a spring set in motion; and the puppet, drawing back, in his terror caught his feet and fell to the ground.

And he fell so awkwardly that his head stuck in the mud and his legs went into the air.

At the sight of the puppet kicking violently with his head in the mud the Serpent went into con-vulsions of laughter, and he laughed, and laughed, and laughed, until from the violence of his laughter he broke a blood-vessel in his chest and died. And that time he was really dead.

Pinocchio then set off running in hopes that he should reach the Fairy's house before dark. But before long he began to suffer so dreadfully from hunger that he could not bear it, and he jumped into a field by the wayside intending to pick some bunches of muscatel grapes. Oh, that he had never done it!

He had scarcely reached the vines when crack . . . his legs were caught between two cutting iron bars, and he became so giddy with pain that stars of every colour danced before his eyes.

The poor puppet had been taken in a trap put there to capture some big polecats who were the scourge of the poultry-yards in the neighbourhood.

CHAPTER 21

Pinocchio is taken by a peasant, who obliges him to fill the place of his watchdog in the poultry-yard.

Pinocchio as you can imagine, began to cry and scream: but his tears and groans were useless, for there was not a house to be seen, and not a living soul passed down the road.

At last night came on.

Partly from the pain of the trap that cut his legs, and a little from fear at finding himself alone in the dark in the midst of the fields, the puppet was on the point of fainting. Just at that moment he saw a Firefly flitting over his head. He called to it and

said: 'Oh, little Firefly, will you have pity on me and liberate me from this torture?'

'Poor boy!' said the Firefly, stopping and looking at him with compassion, 'but how could your legs have been caught by those sharp irons?'

'I came into the field to pick two bunches of these muscatel grapes, and . . . '

'But were the grapes yours?'

'No . . . '

'Then who taught you to carry off other people's property?'

'I was so hungry . . . '

'Hunger, my boy, is not a good reason for appropriating what does not belong to us.'

'That is true, that is true!' said Pinocchio, crying. 'I will never do it again.'

At this moment their conversation was interrupted by a slight sound of approaching footsteps. It was the owner of the field coming on tiptoe to see if one of the polecats that ate his chickens during the night had been caught in his trap.

His astonishment was great when, having brought out his lantern from under his coat, he perceived that instead of a polecat a boy had been taken.

'Ah, little thief!' said the angry peasant, 'then it is you who carries off my chickens?'

'No, it is not I; indeed it is not!' cried Pinocchio, sobbing. 'I only came into the field to take two bunches of grapes!'

'He who steals grapes is quite capable of stealing chickens. Leave it to me, I will give you a lesson that you will not forget in a hurry.'

Opening the trap he seized the puppet by the collar, and carried him to his house as if he had been a young lamb.

When he reached the yard in front of the house he threw him roughly on the ground, and putting his foot on his neck he said to him: 'It is late, and I want to go to bed; we will settle our accounts tomorrow. In the meanwhile, as the dog who kept guard at night died today, you shall take his place at once. You shall be my watchdog.'

And taking a great collar covered with brass knobs he strapped it tightly round his throat that he might not be able to draw his head out of it. A heavy chain attached to the collar was fastened to the wall.

'If it should rain tonight,' he then said to him, 'you can go and lie down in the kennel; the straw that has served as a bed for my poor dog for the last four years is still there. If unfortunately robbers should come, remember to keep your ears pricked and to bark.'

After giving him this last injunction the man went into the house, shut the door, and put up the chain.

Poor Pinocchio remained lying on the ground more dead than alive from the effects of cold, hunger and fear. From time to time he put his hands angrily to the collar that tightened round his throat and said, crying: 'It serves me right! Decidedly it serves me right! I was determined to be a vagabond and a good-for-nothing . . . I would listen to bad companions, and that is why I always meet with misfortunes. If I had been a good little boy as so many are; if I had been willing to learn and to work; if I had remained at home with my poor papa, I should not now be in the midst of the fields and obliged to be the watchdog to a peasant's house. Oh, if I could be born again! But now it is too late, and I must have patience!'

Relieved by this little outburst, which came straight from his heart, he went into the dog-kennel and fell asleep.

CHAPTER 22

Pinocchio discovers the robbers, and as a reward for his fidelity is set at liberty.

He had been sleeping heavily for about two hours when, towards midnight, he was roused by a whispering of strange voices that seemed to come from the courtyard. Putting the point of his nose out of the kennel he saw four little beasts with dark fur, that looked like cats, standing consulting together. But they were not cats; they were polecats – carnivorous little animals, especially greedy for eggs and young chickens. One of the polecats, leaving his companions, came to the opening of the kennel and said in a low voice: 'Good-evening, Melampo.'

'My name is not Melampo,' answered the puppet.

'Oh! then who are you?'

'I am Pinocchio.'

'And what are you doing here?'

'I am acting as watchdog.'

'Then where is Melampo? Where is the old dog who lived in this kennel?'

'He died this morning.'

'Is he dead? Poor beast! He was so good. But judging you by your face I should say that you were also a good dog.'

'I beg your pardon, I am not a dog.'

'Not a dog? Then what are you?'

'I am a puppet.'

'And you are acting as watchdog?'

'That is only too true – as a punishment.'

'Well, then, I will offer you the same conditions that we made with the deceased Melampo, and I am sure you will be satisfied with them.'

'What are these conditions?'

'One night in every week you are to permit us to

visit this poultry-yard as we have hitherto done, and to carry off eight chickens. Of these chickens seven are to be eaten by us, and one we will give to you, on the express understanding, however, that you pretend to be asleep, and that it never enters your head to bark and to wake the peasant.'

'Did Melampo act in this manner?' asked Pinocchio.

'Certainly, and we were always on the best terms with him. Sleep quietly, and rest assured that before we go we will leave by the kennel a beautiful chicken ready plucked for your breakfast tomorrow. Have we understood each other clearly?'

'Only too clearly! . . . ' answered Pinocchio, and he shook his head threateningly as much as to say: 'You shall hear of this shortly!'

The four polecats thinking themselves safe repaired to the poultry-yard, which was close to the kennel, and having opened the wooden gate with their teeth and claws, they slipped in one by one. But they had only just passed through when they heard the gate shut behind them with great violence.

It was Pinocchio who had shut it; and for greater security he put a large stone against it to keep it closed.

He then began to bark, and he barked exactly like a watchdog: bow-wow, bow-wow.

Hearing the barking the peasant jumped out of bed, and taking his gun he came to the window and asked: 'What is the matter?'

'There are robbers!' answered Pinocchio.

'Where are they?'

'In the poultry-yard.'

'I will come down directly.'

In fact, in less time than it takes to say Amen, the peasant came down. He rushed into the poultry-yard, caught the polecats, and having put them into a sack, he said to them in a tone of great satisfaction: 'At last you have fallen into my hands! I might punish you, but I am not so cruel. I will content myself instead by carrying you in the morning to the innkeeper of the neighbouring village, who will skin and cook you as hares with a sweet-and-sour sauce. It is an honour that you don't deserve, but generous people like me don't consider such trifles! . . . '

He then approached Pinocchio and began to caress him, and amongst other things he asked him: 'How did you manage to discover the four thieves? To think that Melampo, my faithful Melampo, never found out anything!'

The puppet might then have told him the whole story; he might have informed him of the disgraceful conditions that had been made between the dog and the polecats; but he remembered that the dog was dead, and he thought to himself: 'What is the good of accusing the dead? The dead are dead, and the best thing to be done is to leave them in peace!'

'When the thieves got into the yard were you asleep or awake?' the peasant went on to ask him.

'I was asleep,' answered Pinocchio, 'but the polecats woke me with their chatter, and one of them came to the kennel and said to me: "If you promise not to bark, and not to wake the master, we will make you a present of a fine chicken ready plucked!" To think that they should have had the audacity to make such a proposal to me! For although I am a puppet, possessing perhaps nearly all the faults in the world, there is one that I certainly will never be guilty of, that of making terms with, and sharing in the gains of, dishonest people!'

'Well said, my boy!' cried the peasant, slapping him on the shoulder. 'Such sentiments do you honour: and as a proof of my gratitude I will at once set you at liberty, and you may return home.'

And he removed the dog's collar.

CHAPTER 23

Pinocchio mourns the death of the beautiful Child with the blue hair. He then meets with a Pigeon who flies with him to the seashore, and there he throws himself into the water to go to the assistance of his father Geppetto.

As soon as Pinocchio was released from the heavy and humiliating weight of the dog-collar he started off across the fields, and never stopped until he had reached the high road that led to the Fairy's house. There he turned and looked down into the plain beneath. He could see distinctly with his naked eye the wood where he had been so unfortunate as to meet with the Fox and the Cat; he could see amongst the trees the top of the Big Oak from which he had been hung; but although he looked in every direction the little house belonging to the beautiful Child with the blue hair was nowhere visible.

Seized with a sad presentiment he began to run with all the strength he had left, and in a few minutes he reached the field where the little white house had once stood. But the little white house was no longer there. He saw instead a marble stone, on which were engraved these sad words:

HERE LIES THE CHILD WITH THE BLUE HAIR
WHO DIED FROM SORROW BECAUSE SHE WAS
ABANDONED BY HER LITTLE BROTHER
PINOCCHIO

I leave you to imagine the puppet's feelings when he had with difficulty spelt out this epitaph. He fell with his face on the ground and, covering the tombstone with a thousand kisses, burst into an agony of tears. He cried all night, and when morning came he was still crying although he had no tears left, and his sobs and lamentations were so acute and heart-breaking that they roused the echoes in the surrounding hills.

And as he wept he said: 'Oh, little Fairy, why did you die? Why did not I die instead of you, I who am so wicked, whilst you were so good? . . . And my papa? Where can he be? Oh, little Fairy, tell me where I can find him, for I want to remain with him always and never to leave him again, never again! Oh, little Fairy, tell me that it is not true that you are dead! . . . If you really love me . . . if you really love your little brother, come to life again . . . come to life as you were before! . . . Does it not grieve you to see me alone and abandoned by everybody? . . . If assassins come they will hang me again from the branch of a tree . . . and then I should die indeed. What do you imagine that I can do here alone in the world? Now that I have lost you and my papa, who will give me food? Where shall I go to sleep at night? Who will make me a new jacket? Oh, it would be better, a hundred times better, that I should die also! Yes, I want to die . . . ih! ih! ih!'

And in his despair he tried to tear his hair, but, being made of wood, he could not even have the satisfaction of sticking his fingers into it.

Just then a large Pigeon flew over his head, and stopping with distended wings called down to him from a great height: 'Tell me, child, what are you doing there?'

'Don't you see? I am crying!' said Pinocchio, raising his head towards the voice and rubbing his eyes with his jacket.

'Tell me,' continued the Pigeon, 'amongst your companions, do you happen to know a puppet who is called Pinocchio?'

'Pinocchio? . . . Did you say Pinocchio?' repeated the puppet, jumping quickly to his feet. 'I am Pinocchio!'

The Pigeon at this answer descended rapidly to the ground. He was larger than a turkey.

'Do you also know Geppetto?' he asked.

'Do I know him! He is my poor papa! Has he perhaps spoken to you of me? Will you take me to him? Is he still alive? Answer me for pity's sake: is he still alive?'

'I left him three days ago on the seashore.'

'What was he doing?'

'He was building a little boat for himself, to cross the ocean. For more than three months that poor man has been going all round the world looking for you. Not having succeeded in finding you he has now taken it into his head to go to the distant countries of the New World in search of you.'

'How far is it from here to the shore?' asked Pinocchio breathlessly.

'More than six hundred miles.'

'Six hundred miles? Oh, beautiful Pigeon, what a fine thing it would be to have your wings!'

'If you wish to go, I will carry you there.'

'How?'

'Astride on my back. Do you weigh much?'

'I weigh next to nothing. I am as light as a feather.'

And without waiting for more Pinocchio jumped at once on the Pigeon's back, and putting a leg on each side of him, as men do on horseback, he exclaimed joyfully: 'Gallop, gallop, my little horse, for I am anxious to arrive quickly!'

The Pigeon took flight, and in a few minutes had soared so high that they almost touched the clouds. Finding himself at such an immense height the puppet had the curiosity to turn and look down; but his head spun round, and he became so frightened that to save himself from the danger of falling he wound his arms tightly round the neck of his feathered steed.

They flew all day. Towards evening the Pigeon said: 'I am very thirsty!'

'And I am very hungry!' rejoined Pinocchio.

'Let us stop at that dovecot for a few minutes; and then we will continue our journey that we may reach the seashore by dawn tomorrow.'

They went into a deserted dovecot, where they found nothing but a basin full of water and a basket full of vetch.

The puppet had never in his life been able to eat vetch: according to him it made him sick and revolted him. That evening, however, he ate to repletion, and when he had nearly emptied the basket he turned to the Pigeon and said to him: 'I never could have believed that vetch was so good!'

'Be assured, my boy,' replied the Pigeon, 'that when hunger is real, and there is nothing else to eat, even vetch becomes delicious. Hunger knows neither caprice nor greediness.'

Having quickly finished their little meal they recommenced their journey and flew away. The following morning they reached the seashore.

The Pigeon placed Pinocchio on the ground, and not wishing to be troubled with thanks for having done a good action, flew quickly away and disappeared.

The shore was crowded with people who were looking out to sea, shouting and gesticulating.

'What has happened?' asked Pinocchio of an old woman.

'A poor father who has lost his son has gone away in a boat to search for him on the other side of the water, and today the sea is tempestuous and the little boat is in danger of sinking.'

'Where is the little boat?'

'It is out there in a line with my finger,' said the old woman, pointing to a little boat which, seen at that distance, looked like a nutshell with a very little man in it.

Pinocchio fixed his eyes on it, and after looking attentively he gave a piercing scream, crying: 'It is my papa! it is my papa!'

The boat meanwhile, beaten by the fury of the waves, at one moment disappeared in the trough of the sea, and the next came again to the surface. Pinocchio, standing on the top of a high rock, kept calling to his father by name, and making every kind of signal to him with his hands, his handkerchief and his cap.

And although he was so far off, Geppetto appeared to recognise his son, for he also took off his cap and waved it, and tried by gestures to make him understand that he would have returned if it had been possible, but that the sea was so tempestuous that he could not use his oars or approach the shore.

Suddenly a tremendous wave rose and the boat disappeared. They waited, hoping it would come again to the surface, but it was seen no more.

'Poor man!' said the fishermen who were assembled on the shore, and murmuring a prayer they turned to go home.

Just then they heard a desperate cry, and looking back they saw a little boy who exclaimed, as he jumped from a rock into the sea: 'I will save my papa!'

Pinocchio, being made of wood, floated easily and he swam like a fish. At one moment they saw him disappear under the water, carried down by the fury of the waves; and next he reappeared struggling with a leg or an arm. At last they lost sight of him, and he was seen no more.

'Poor boy!' said the fishermen who were collected on the shore, and murmuring a prayer they returned home.

CHAPTER 24

Pinocchio arrives at the island of the 'Industrious Bees',
and finds the Fairy again.

Pinocchio, hoping to be in time to help his father, swam the whole night.

And what a horrible night it was! The rain came down in torrents, it hailed, the thunder was frightful, and the flashes of lightning made it as light as day.

Towards morning he saw a long strip of land not far off. It was an island in the midst of the sea.

He tried his utmost to reach the shore: but it was all in vain. The waves, racing and tumbling over each other, knocked him about as if he had been a stick or a wisp of straw. At last, fortunately for him, a billow rolled up with such fury and impetuosity that he was lifted up and thrown violently far on to the sands.

He fell with such force that, as he struck the ground, his ribs and all his joints cracked, but he comforted himself, saying: 'This time also I have made a wonderful escape!'

Little by little the sky cleared, the sun shone out in all his splendour, and the sea became as quiet and smooth as oil.

The puppet put his clothes in the sun to dry, and began to look in every direction in hopes of seeing on the vast expanse of water a little boat with a little man in it. But although he looked and looked, he could see nothing but the sky, and the sea, and the sail of some ship, but so far away that it seemed no bigger than a fly.

'If I only knew what this island was called!' he said to himself. 'If I only knew whether it was inhabited by civilised people – I mean, by people who have not got the bad habit of hanging boys from the branches of the trees. But whom can I ask? Is there nobody? . . . '

This idea of finding himself alone, alone, all alone, in the midst of this great uninhabited country, made him so melancholy that he was just beginning to cry. But at that moment, at a short distance from the shore, he saw a big fish swimming by; it was going quietly on its own business with its head out of the water.

Not knowing its name the puppet called to it in a loud voice to make himself heard: 'Eh, Sir Fish, will you permit me a word with you?'

'Two if you like,' answered the fish, who was a Dolphin, and so polite that few similar are to be found in any sea in the world.

'Will you be kind enough to tell me if there are villages in this island where it would be possible to obtain something to eat, without running the danger of being eaten?'

'Certainly there are,' replied the Dolphin. 'Indeed you will find one at a short distance from here.'

'And what road must I take to go there?'

'You must take that path to your left and follow your nose. You cannot make a mistake.'

'Will you tell me another thing? You who swim about the sea all day and all night, have you by chance met a little boat with my papa in it?'

'And who is your papa?'

'He is the best papa in the world, whilst it would be difficult to find a worse son than I am.'

'During the terrible storm last night,' answered the Dolphin, 'the little boat must have gone to the bottom.'

'And my papa?'

'He must have been swallowed by the terrible Dogfish who for some days past has been spreading devastation and ruin in our waters.'

'Is this Dogfish very big?' asked Pinocchio, who was already beginning to quake with fear.

'Big! . . . ' replied the Dolphin. 'That you may form some idea of his size, I need only tell you that he is bigger than a five-storeyed house, and that his mouth is so enormous and so deep that a railway train with its smoking engine could pass easily down his throat.'

'Mercy upon us!' exclaimed the terrified puppet; and putting on his clothes with the greatest haste he said to the Dolphin: 'Goodbye, Sir Fish: excuse the trouble I have given you, and many thanks for your politeness.'

He then took the path that had been pointed out to him and began to walk fast – so fast, indeed, that he was almost running. And at the slightest noise he turned to look behind him, fearing that he might see the terrible Dogfish with a railway train in its mouth following him.

After a walk of half an hour he reached a little village called the Village of the Industrious Bees.

The road was alive with people running here and there to attend to their business: all were at work, all had something to do. You could not have found an idler or a vagabond, not even if you had searched for him with a lighted lamp.

'Ah!' said that lazy Pinocchio at once, 'I see that this village will never suit me! I wasn't born to work!'

In the meanwhile he was tormented by hunger, for he had eaten nothing for twenty-four hours – not even vetch. What was he to do?

There were only two ways by which he could obtain food – either by asking for a little work, or by begging for a halfpenny or for a mouthful of bread.

He was ashamed to beg, for his father had always preached to him that no one had a right to beg except the aged and the infirm. The really poor in this world, deserving of compassion and assistance, are only those who from age or sickness are no longer able to earn their own bread with the labour of their hands. It is the duty of everyone else to work; and if they will not work, so much the worse for them if they suffer from hunger.

At that moment a man came down the road, tired and panting for breath. He was dragging alone, with fatigue and difficulty, two carts full of charcoal.

Pinocchio, judging by his face that he was a kind man, approached him, and casting down his eyes with shame he said to him in a low voice: 'Would you have the charity to give me a halfpenny, for I am dying of hunger?'

'You shall have not only a halfpenny,' said the man, 'but I will give you twopence, provided that you help me to drag home these two carts of charcoal.'

'I am surprised at you!' answered the puppet in a tone of offence. 'Let me tell you that I am not accustomed to do the work of a donkey: I have never drawn a cart!'

'So much the better for you,' answered the man. 'Then, my boy, if you are really dying of hunger, eat two fine slices of your pride, and be careful not to get indigestion.'

A few minutes afterwards a mason passed down the road carrying on his shoulders a basket of lime.

'Would you have the charity, good man, to give a halfpenny to a poor boy who is yawning for want of food?'

'Willingly,' answered the man. 'Come with me and carry the lime, and instead of a halfpenny I will give you five.'

'But the lime is heavy,' objected Pinocchio, 'and I don't want to tire myself.'

'If you don't want to tire yourself, then, my boy, amuse yourself with yawning, and much good may it do you.'

In less than half an hour twenty other people went by; and Pinocchio asked charity of them all, but they all answered: 'Are you not ashamed to beg? Instead of idling about the roads, go and look for a little work and learn to earn your bread.'

At last a nice little woman carrying two cans of water came by.

'Will you let me drink a little water out of one of your cans?' asked Pinocchio, who was burning with thirst.

'Drink, my boy, if you wish it!' said the little woman, setting down the two cans.

Pinocchio drank like a fish, and as he dried his mouth he mumbled: 'I have quenched my thirst. If I could only appease my hunger! . . .'

The good woman hearing these words said at once: 'If you will help me to carry home these two cans of water, I will give you a fine piece of bread.'

Pinocchio looked at the cans and answered neither yes nor no.

'And besides the bread you shall have a nice dish of cauliflower dressed with oil and vinegar,' added the good woman.

Pinocchio gave another look at the cans, and answered neither yes nor no.

'And after the cauliflower I will give you a beautiful bonbon full of syrup.'

The temptation of this last dainty was so great that Pinocchio could resist no longer, and with an air of decision he said: 'I must have patience! I will carry one of the cans to your house.'

The can was heavy, and the puppet, not being strong enough to carry it in his hand, had to resign himself to carry it on his head.

When they reached the house the good little woman made Pinocchio sit down at a small table already laid, and she placed before him the bread, the cauliflower and the bonbon.

Pinocchio did not eat, he devoured. His stomach was like an apartment that had been left empty and uninhabited for five months.

When his ravenous hunger was somewhat appeased he raised his head to thank his benefactress; but he had no sooner looked at her than he gave a prolonged Oh–h–h! of astonishment, and continued staring at her, with wide open eyes, his fork in the air, and his mouth full of bread and cauliflower, as if he had been bewitched.

'What has surprised you so much?' asked the good woman, laughing.

'It is . . . ' answered the puppet, 'it is . . . it is . . . that you are like . . . that you remind me . . . yes, yes, yes, the same voice . . . the same eyes . . . the same hair . . . yes, yes, yes . . . you also have blue hair . . . as she had . . . Oh little Fairy! . . . tell me that it is you, really you! . . . Do not make me cry any more! If you knew . . . I have cried so much, I have suffered so much . . . '

And throwing himself at her feet on the floor, Pinocchio embraced the knees of the mysterious little woman and began to cry bitterly.

CHAPTER 25

Pinocchio promises the Fairy to be good and studious,
for he is quite sick of being a puppet and wishes
to become an exemplary boy.

At first the good little woman maintained that she was not the little Fairy with blue hair; but seeing that she was found out, and not wishing to continue the comedy any longer, she ended by making herself known, and she said to Pinocchio: 'You little rogue! how did you ever discover who I was?'

'It was my great affection for you that told me.'

'Do you remember? You left me a child, and now that you have found me again I am a woman – a woman almost old enough to be your mama.'

'I am delighted at that, for now, instead of calling you little sister, I will call you mama. I have wished for such a long time to have a mama like other boys! . . . But how did you manage to grow so fast?'

'That is a secret.'

'Teach it to me, for I should also like to grow. Don't you see? I always remain no bigger than a ninepin.'

'But you cannot grow,' replied the Fairy.

'Why?'

'Because puppets never grow. They are born puppets, live puppets and die puppets.'

'Oh, I am sick of being a puppet!' cried Pinocchio, giving himself a slap. 'It is time that I became a man . . . '

'And you will become one, if you know how to deserve it.'

'Not really? And what can I do to deserve it?'

'A very easy thing: by learning to be a good boy.'

'And you think I am not?'

'You are quite the contrary. Good boys are obedient, and you . . . '

'And I never obey.'

'Good boys like to learn and to work, and you . . . '

'And I instead lead an idle vagabond life the year through.'

'Good boys always speak the truth . . . '

'And I always tell lies.'

'Good boys go willingly to school . . . '

'And school gives me pain all over my body. But from today I will change my life.'

'Do you promise me?'

'I promise you. I will become a good little boy,

and I will be the consolation of my papa . . . Where is my poor papa at this moment?'

'I do not know.'

'Shall I ever have the happiness of seeing him again and kissing him?'

'I think so; indeed I am sure of it.'

At this answer Pinocchio was so delighted that he took the Fairy's hands and began to kiss them with such fervour that he seemed beside himself. Then raising his face and looking at her lovingly, he asked: 'Tell me, little mama: then it was not true that you were dead?'

'It seems not,' said the Fairy, smiling.

'If you only knew the sorrow I felt and the tightening of my throat when I read, "here lies . . . " '

'I know it, and it is on that account that I have forgiven you. I saw from the sincerity of your grief that you had a good heart; and when boys have good hearts, even if they are scamps and have got bad habits, there is always something to hope for: that is, there is always hope that they will turn to better ways. That is why I came to look for you here. I will be your mama . . . '

'Oh, how delightful!' shouted Pinocchio, jumping for joy.

'You must obey me and do everything that I bid you.'

'Willingly, willingly, willingly!'

'Tomorrow,' rejoined the Fairy, 'you will begin to go to school.'

Pinocchio became at once a little less joyful.

'Then you must choose an art, or a trade, according to your own wishes.'

Pinocchio became very grave.

'What are you muttering between your teeth?' asked the Fairy in an angry voice.

'I was saying,' moaned the puppet in a low voice, 'that it seemed to me too late for me to go to school now . . . '

'No, sir. Keep it in mind that it is never too late to learn and to instruct ourselves.'

'But I do not wish to follow either an art or a trade.'

'Why?'

'Because it tires me to work.'

'My boy,' said the Fairy, 'those who talk in that way end almost always either in prison or in the hospital. Let me tell you that every man, whether he is born rich or poor, is obliged to do something in this world – to occupy himself, to work. Woe to those who lead slothful lives. Sloth is a dreadful illness and must be cured at once, in childhood. If not, when we are old it can never be cured.'

Pinocchio was touched by these words, and lifting his head quickly he said to the Fairy: 'I will study, I will work, I will do all that you tell me, for indeed I have become weary of being a puppet, and I wish at any price to become a boy. You promised me that I should, did you not?'

'I did promise you, and it now depends upon yourself.'

CHAPTER 26

Pinocchio accompanies his schoolfellows to the seashore to see the terrible Dogfish.

The following day Pinocchio went to the government school.

Imagine the delight of all the little rogues when they saw a puppet walk into their school! They set up a roar of laughter that never ended. They played him all sorts of tricks. One boy carried off his cap, another pulled his jacket behind; one tried to give him a pair of inky moustachios just under his nose, and another attempted to tie strings to his feet and hands to make him dance.

For a short time Pinocchio pretended not to care and got on as well as he could; but at last, losing all patience, he turned to those who were teasing him most and making game of him, and said to them, looking very angry: 'Beware, boys: I am not come here to be your buffoon. I respect others, and I intend to be respected.'

'Well said, boaster! You have spoken like a book!' howled the young rascals, convulsed with mad laughter; and one of them, more impertinent than the others, stretched out his hand intending to seize the puppet by the end of his nose.

But he was not in time, for Pinocchio stuck his leg out from under the table and gave him a great kick on his shins.

'Oh, what hard feet!' roared the boy, rubbing he bruise that the puppet had given him.

'And what elbows! . . . even harder than his feet!' said another, who for his rude tricks had received a blow in the stomach.

But nevertheless the kick and the blow acquired at once for Pinocchio the sympathy and the esteem of all the boys in the school. They all made friends with him and liked him heartily.

And even the master praised him, for he found him attentive, studious and intelligent – always the first to come to school, and the last to leave when school was over.

But he had one fault: he made too many friends; and amongst them were several young rascals well known for their dislike of study and love of mischief.

The master warned him every day, and even the good Fairy never failed to tell him, and to repeat constantly: 'Take care, Pinocchio! Those bad schoolfellows of yours will end sooner or later by making you lose all love of study, and perhaps even they may bring upon you some great misfortune.'

'There is no fear of that!' answered the puppet, shrugging his shoulders and touching his forehead as much as to say: 'There is so much sense here!'

Now it happened that one fine day, as he was on his way to school, he met several of his usual companions who, coming up to him, asked: 'Have you heard the great news?'

'No.'

'In the sea near here a Dogfish has appeared as big as a mountain.'

'Not really? Can it be the same Dogfish that was there when my poor papa was drowned?'

'We are going to the shore to see him. Will you come with us?'

'No; I am going to school.'

'What matters school? We can go to school tomorrow. Whether we have a lesson more or a lesson less, we shall always remain the same donkeys.'

'But what will the master say?'

'The master may say what he likes. He is paid on purpose to grumble all day.'

'And my mama? . . .'

'Mamas know nothing,' answered those bad little boys.

'Do you know what I will do?' said Pinocchio. 'I have reasons for wishing to see the Dogfish, but I will go and see him when school is over.'

'Poor donkey!' exclaimed one of the number. 'Do you suppose that a fish of that size will wait your convenience? As soon as he is tired of being here he will start for another place, and then it will be too late.'

'How long does it take from here to the shore?' asked the puppet.

'We can be there and back in an hour.'

'Then away!' shouted Pinocchio, 'and he who runs fastest is the best!'

Having thus been given the signal to start, the boys, with their books and copybooks under their arms, rushed off across the fields, and Pinocchio was always the first – he seemed to have wings to his feet.

From time to time he turned to jeer at his companions, who were some distance behind, and seeing them panting for breath, covered with dust and their tongues hanging out of their mouths, he laughed heartily. The unfortunate boy little knew what terrors and horrible disasters he was going to meet with!

CHAPTER 27

Great fight between Pinocchio and his companions. One of them is wounded, and Pinocchio is arrested by the gendarmes.

When he arrived on the shore Pinocchio looked out to sea; but he saw no Dogfish. The sea was as smooth as a great crystal mirror.

'Where is the Dogfish?' he asked, turning to his companions.

'He must have gone to have his breakfast,' said one of them, laughing.

'Or he has thrown himself on to his bed to have a little nap,' added another, laughing still louder.

From their absurd answers and silly laughter Pinocchio perceived that his companions had been making a fool of him in inducing him to believe a tale with no truth in it. Taking it very badly he said to them angrily: 'And now may I ask what fun you could find in deceiving me with the story of the Dogfish?'

'Oh, it was great fun!' answered the little rascals in chorus.

'And in what did it consist?'

'In making you miss school, and persuading you to come with us. Are you not ashamed of being always so punctual and so diligent with your lessons? Are you not ashamed of studying so hard?'

'And if I study hard what concern is it of yours?'

'It concerns us excessively, because it makes us appear in a bad light to the master.'

'Why?'

'Because boys who study make those who, like us, have no wish to learn seem worse by comparison. And that is too bad. We too have our pride!'

'Then what must I do to please you?'

'You must follow our example and hate school, lessons and the master – our three greatest enemies.'

'And if I wish to continue my studies?'

'In that case we will have nothing more to do with you, and at the first opportunity we will make you pay for it.'

'Really,' said the puppet, shaking his head, 'you make me inclined to laugh.'

'Eh, Pinocchio!' shouted the biggest of the boys, confronting him. 'None of your superior airs: don't come here to crow over us! . . . for if you are not afraid of us, we are not afraid of you. Remember that you are one against seven of us.'

'Seven, like the seven deadly sins,' said Pinocchio with a shout of laughter.

'Listen to him! He has insulted us all! He called us the seven deadly sins!'

'Pinocchio! beg pardon . . . or it will be the worse for you!'

'Cuckoo!' sang the puppet, putting his forefinger to the end of his nose scoffingly.

'Pinocchio! it will end badly!'

'Cuckoo!'

'You will get as many blows as a donkey!'

'Cuckoo!'

'You will return home with a broken nose!'

'Cuckoo!'

'Ah, you shall have the cuckoo from me!' said the most courageous of the boys. 'Take that to begin with, and keep it for your supper tonight.'

And so saying he gave him a blow on the head with his fist.

But it was give and take; for the puppet, as was to be expected, immediately returned the blow, and the fight in a moment became general and desperate.

Pinocchio, although he was one alone, defended himself like a hero. He used his feet, which were of the hardest wood, to such purpose that he kept his enemies at a respectful distance. Wherever they touched they left a bruise by way of reminder.

The boys, becoming furious at not being able to measure themselves hand to hand with the puppet, had recourse to other weapons. Loosening their satchels they commenced throwing their school-books at him – grammars, dictionaries, spelling-books, geography books, and other scholastic works. But Pinocchio was quick and had sharp eyes, and always managed to duck in time, so that the books passed over his head and all fell into the sea.

Imagine the astonishment of the fish! Thinking that the books were something to eat they all arrived in shoals, but having tasted a page or two, or a frontispiece, they spat it quickly out and made a wry face that seemed to say: 'It isn't food for us; we are accustomed to something much better!'

The battle meantime had become fiercer than ever, when a big Crab, who had come out of the water and had climbed slowly up on to the shore, called out in a hoarse voice that sounded like a trumpet with a bad cold: 'Have done with that, you young ruffians, for you are nothing else! These hand-to-hand fights between boys seldom finish well. Some disaster is sure to happen! . . . '

Poor Crab! He might as well have preached to the wind. Even that young rascal Pinocchio, turning round, looked at him mockingly and said rudely: 'Hold your tongue, you tiresome crab! You had better suck some liquorice lozenges to cure that cold in your throat. Or better still, go to bed and try to get a reaction!'

Just then the boys, who had no more books of their own to throw, spied at a little distance the satchel that belonged to Pinocchio, and took possession of it in less time than it takes to tell.

Amongst the books there was one bound in strong cardboard with the back and points of parchment. It was a *Treatise on Arithmetic*. I leave you to imagine if it was big or not!

One of the boys seized this volume, and aiming at Pinocchio's head threw it at him with all the force he could muster. But instead of hitting the puppet it struck one of his companions on the temple, who, turning as white as a sheet, said only: 'Oh, mother, help . . . I am dying! . . . ' and fell his whole length on the sand. Thinking he was dead the terrified boys ran off as hard as their legs could carry them, and in a few minutes they were out of sight.

But Pinocchio remained. Although from grief and fright he was more dead than alive, nevertheless he ran and soaked his handkerchief in the sea and began to bathe the temples of his poor schoolfellow. Crying bitterly in his despair he kept calling him by name and saying to him: 'Eugene! . . . my poor Eugene! . . . open your eyes and look at me! . . . why do you not answer? I did not do it, indeed it was not I that hurt you so! believe me, it was not! Open your eyes, Eugene . . . If you keep your eyes shut I shall die too . . . Oh! what shall I do? how shall I ever return home? How can I ever have the courage to go back to my good mama? What will become of me? . . . Where can I fly to? . . . Oh! how much better it would have been, a thousand times better, if I had only gone to school! . . . Why did I listen to my companions? they have been my ruin. The master said to me, and my mama repeated it often: "Beware of bad companions!" But I am obstinate . . . a wilful fool . . . I let them talk and then I always take my own way! and I have to suffer for it. And so, ever since I have been in the world, I have never had a happy quarter of an hour. Oh dear! what will become of me, what will become of me, what will become of me? . . . '

And Pinocchio began to cry and sob, and to strike his head with his fists, and to call poor Eugene by his name. Suddenly he heard the sound of approaching footsteps.

He turned and saw two *carabinieri*.

'What are you doing there lying on the ground?' they asked Pinocchio.

'I am helping my schoolfellow.'

'Has he been hurt?'

'So it seems.'

'Hurt indeed!' said one of the *carabinieri*, stooping down and examining Eugene closely. 'This boy has been wounded in the temple. Who wounded him?'

'Not I,' stammered the puppet breathlessly.

'If it was not you, who then did it?'

'Not I,' repeated Pinocchio.

'And with what was he wounded?'

'With this book.' And the puppet picked up from the ground the *Treatise on Arithmetic*, bound in cardboard and parchment, and showed it to the *carabiniere*.

'And to whom does this book belong?'

'To me.'

'That is enough: nothing more is wanted. Get up and come with us at once.'

'But I . . .'

'Come along with us!'

'But I am innocent . . .'

'Come along with us!'

Before they left, the *carabinieri* called some fishermen, who were passing at that moment near the shore in their boat, and said to them: 'We give this boy who has been wounded

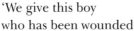

in the head into your charge. Carry him to your house and nurse him. Tomorrow we will come and see him.'

They then turned to Pinocchio, and having placed him between them they said to him in a commanding voice: 'Forward! and walk quickly! or it will be the worse for you.'

Without requiring it to be repeated, the puppet set out along the road leading to the village. But the poor little devil hardly knew where he was. He thought he must be dreaming, and what a dreadful dream! He was beside himself. He saw double; his legs shook; his tongue clung to the roof of his mouth, and he could not utter a word. And yet in the midst of his stupefaction and apathy his heart was pierced by a cruel thorn – the thought that he would have to pass under the windows of the good Fairy's house between the *carabinieri*. He would rather have died.

They had already reached the village when a gust of wind blew Pinocchio's cap off his head and carried it ten yards off.

'Will you permit me,' said the puppet to the *carabinieri*, 'to go and get my cap?'

'Go, then; but be quick about it.'

The puppet went and picked up his cap . . . but instead of putting it on his head he took it between his teeth and began to run as hard as he could towards the seashore.

The *carabinieri*, thinking it would be difficult to overtake him, sent after him a large mastiff who had won the first prize at all the dog-races. Pinocchio ran, but the dog ran faster. The people came to their windows and crowded into the street in their anxiety to see the end of the desperate race. But they could not satisfy their curiosity, for Pinocchio and the dog raised such clouds of dust that in a few minutes nothing could be seen of either of them.

CHAPTER 28

Pinocchio is in danger of being fried in a frying-pan like a fish.

There came a moment in this desperate race – a terrible moment when Pinocchio thought himself lost; for you must know that Alidoro – for so the mastiff was called – had run so swiftly that he had nearly come up with him.

The puppet could hear the panting of the dreadful beast close behind him; there was not a hand's breadth between them, he could even feel the dog's hot breath.

Fortunately the shore was close and the sea but few steps off.

As soon as he reached the sands the puppet made a wonderful leap – a frog could have done no better – and plunged into the water.

Alidoro, on the contrary, wished to stop himself; but carried away by the impetus of the race he also went into the sea. The unfortunate dog could not swim, but he made great efforts to keep himself afloat with his paws; but the more he struggled the farther he sank head downwards under the water.

When he rose to the surface again his eyes were rolling with terror, and he barked out: 'I am drowning! I am drowning!'

'Drown!' shouted Pinocchio from a distance, seeing himself safe from all danger.

'Help me, dear Pinocchio! . . . save me from death! . . .'

At that agonising cry the puppet, who had in reality an excellent heart, was moved with compassion, and turning to the dog, he said: 'But if I save your life, will you promise to give me no further annoyance, and not to run after me?'

'I promise! I promise! Be quick, for pity's sake, for if you delay another half-minute I shall be dead.'

Pinocchio hesitated, but remembering that his father had often told him that a good action is never lost, he swam to Alidoro, and taking hold of his tail with both hands brought him safe and sound on to the dry sand of the beach.

The poor dog could not stand. He had drunk, against his will, so much salt water that he was like a balloon. The puppet, however, not wishing to trust him too far, thought it more prudent to jump again into the water. When he had swum some distance from the shore he called out to the friend he had rescued: 'Goodbye, Alidoro; a good journey to you, and take my compliments to all at home.'

'Goodbye, Pinocchio,' answered the dog; 'a thousand thanks for having saved my life. You have done me a great service, and in this world what is given is returned. If an occasion offers I shall not forget it.'

Pinocchio swam on, keeping always near the land. At last he thought that he had reached a safe place. Giving a look along the shore he saw amongst the rocks a kind of cave from which a cloud of smoke was ascending.

'In that cave,' he said to himself, 'there must be a fire. So much the better. I will go and dry and warm myself, and then? . . . and then we shall see.'

Having taken this resolution he approached the rocks; but as he was going to climb up, he felt something under the water that rose higher and higher and carried him into the air. He tried to escape, but it was too late, for to his extreme surprise he found himself enclosed in a great net, together with a swarm of fish of every size and shape, who were flapping and struggling like so many despairing souls.

At the same moment a fisherman came out of the cave; he was so ugly, so horribly ugly, that he looked like a sea monster. Instead of hair his head was covered with a thick bush of

green grass, his skin was green, his eyes were green, his long beard that came down to the ground was also green. He had the appearance of an immense lizard standing on its hind-paws.

When the fisherman had drawn his net out of the sea, he exclaimed with great satisfaction: 'Thank heaven! Again today I shall have a splendid feast of fish!'

'What a mercy that I am not a fish!' said Pinocchio to himself, regaining a little courage.

The net full of fish was carried into the cave, which was dark and smoky. In the middle of the cave a large frying-pan full of oil was frying, and sending out a smell of mushrooms that was suffocating.

'Now we will see what fish we have taken!' said the green fisherman; and putting into the net an enormous hand, so out of all proportion that it looked like a baker's shovel, he pulled out a handful of mullet.

'These mullet are good!' he said, looking at them and smelling them complacently. And after he had smelt them he threw them into a pan without water. He repeated the same operation many times; and as he drew out the fish, his mouth watered and he said, chuckling to himself: 'What good whiting! . . . What exquisite sardines! . . . These soles are delicious! . . . And these crabs excellent! . . . What dear little anchovies! . . .' I need not tell you that the whiting, the sardines, the soles, the crabs and the anchovies were all thrown promiscuously into the pan to keep company with the mullet. The last to remain in the net was Pinocchio. No sooner had the fisherman taken him out than he opened his big green eyes with astonishment, and cried, half-frightened: 'What species of fish is this? Fish of this kind I never remember to have eaten!' And he looked at him again attentively, and having examined him well all over, he ended by saying: 'I know: he must be a crawfish.'

Pinocchio, mortified at being mistaken for a crawfish, said in an angry voice: 'A crawfish indeed! do you take me for a crawfish? what treatment! Let me tell you that I am a puppet.'

'A puppet?' replied the fisherman. 'To tell the truth, a puppet is quite a new fish for me. All the better! I shall eat you with greater pleasure.'

'Eat me! but will you understand that I am not a fish? Do you hear that I talk and reason as you do?'

'That is quite true,' said the fisherman; 'and as I see that you are a fish possessed of the talent of talking and reasoning as I do, I will treat you with all the attention that is your due.'

'And this attention? . . .'

'In token of my friendship and particular regard, I will leave you the choice of how you would like to be cooked. Would you like to be fried in the frying-pan, or would you prefer to be stewed with tomato sauce?'

'To tell the truth,' answered Pinocchio, 'if I am to choose, I should prefer to be set at liberty and to return home.'

'You are joking! Do you imagine that I would lose the opportunity of tasting such a rare fish? It is not every day, I assure you, that a puppet fish is caught in these waters. Leave it to me. I will fry you in the frying-pan with the other fish, and you will be quite satisfied. It is always consolation to be fried in company.'

At this speech the unhappy Pinocchio began to cry and scream and to implore for mercy; and he said, sobbing: 'How much better it would have been if I had gone to school! . . . I would listen to my companions and now I am paying for it! Ih! . . . Ih! . . . Ih! . . .'

And he wriggled like an eel, and made indescribable efforts to slip out of the clutches of the green fisherman. But it was useless: the fisherman took a long strip of rush, and having bound his hands and feet as if he had been a sausage, he threw him into the pan with the other fish.

He then fetched a wooden bowl full of flour and began to flour them each in turn, and as soon as they were ready he threw them into the frying-pan.

The first to dance in the boiling oil were the poor whiting; the crabs followed, then the sardines, then the soles, then the anchovies, and at last it was Pinocchio's turn. Seeing himself so near death, and such a horrible death, he was so frightened, and trembled so violently, that he had neither voice nor breath left for further entreaties.

But the poor boy implored with his eyes! The green fisherman, however, without caring in the least, plunged him five or six times in the flour, until he was white from head to foot, and looked like a puppet made of plaster.

He then took him by the head, and . . .

CHAPTER 29

He returns to the Fairy's house. She promises him that the following day he shall cease to be a puppet and shall become a boy. Grand breakfast of coffee and milk to celebrate this great event.

Just as the fisherman was on the point of throwing Pinocchio into the frying-pan a large dog entered the cave, enticed there by the strong and savoury odour of fried fish.

'Get out!' shouted the fisherman threateningly, holding the floured puppet in his hand.

But the poor dog, who was as hungry as a wolf, whined and wagged his tail as much as to say: 'Give me a mouthful of fish and I will leave you in peace.'

'Get out, I tell you!' repeated the fisherman, and he stretched out his leg to give him a kick.

But the dog, who, when he was really hungry, would not stand trifling, turned upon him, growling and showing his terrible tusks.

At that moment a little feeble voice was heard saying entreatingly: 'Save me, Alidoro! If you do not save me I shall be fried! . . .'

The dog recognised Pinocchio's voice, and to his extreme surprise perceived that it proceeded from the floured bundle that the fisherman held in his hand.

So what do you think he did? He made a spring, seized the bundle in his mouth, and holding it gently between his teeth he rushed out of the cave and was gone like a flash of lightning.

The fisherman, furious at seeing a fish he was so anxious to eat snatched from him, ran after the dog; but he had not gone many steps when he was taken with a fit of coughing and had to give it up.

Alidoro, when he had reached the path that led to the village, stopped, and put his friend Pinocchio gently on the ground.

'How much I have to thank you for!' said the puppet.

'There is no necessity,' replied the dog. 'You saved me and I have now returned it. You know that we must all help each other in this world.'

'But how came you to the cave?'

'I was lying on the shore more dead than alive when the wind brought to me the smell of fried fish. The smell excited my appetite, and I followed it up. If I had arrived a second later . . .'

'Do not mention it!' groaned Pinocchio, who was still trembling with fright. 'Do not mention it! If you had arrived a second later I should by this time have been fried, eaten and digested. Brrr! . . . it makes me shudder only to think of it!'

Alidoro, laughing, extended his right paw to the puppet, who shook it heartily in token of great friendship, and they then separated.

The dog took the road home; and Pinocchio, left alone, went to a cottage not far off, and said to a little old man who was warming himself in the sun: 'Tell me, good man, do you know anything of a poor boy called Eugene who was wounded in the head?'

'The boy was brought by some fishermen to this cottage, and now . . .'

'And now he is dead!' interrupted Pinocchio with great sorrow.

'No, he is alive, and has returned to his home.'

'Not really? not really?' cried the puppet, dancing with delight. 'Then the wound was not serious?'

'It might have been very serious and even fatal,' answered the little old man, 'for they threw a thick book bound in cardboard at his head.'

'And who threw it at him?'

'One of his schoolfellows, a certain Pinocchio . . .'

'And who is this Pinocchio?' asked the puppet, pretending ignorance.

'They say that he is a bad boy, a vagabond, a regular good-for-nothing . . .'

'Calumnies! all calumnies!'

'Do you know this Pinocchio?'

'By sight!' answered the puppet.

'And what is your opinion of him?' asked the little man.

'He seems to me to be a very good boy, anxious to learn, and obedient and affectionate to his father and family . . .'

Whilst the puppet was firing off all these lies, he touched his nose and perceived that it had lengthened more than a hand. Very much alarmed he began to cry out: 'Don't believe, good man, what I have been telling you. I know Pinocchio very well, and I can assure you that he is really a very bad boy, disobedient and idle, who instead of going to school runs off with his companions to amuse himself.'

He had hardly finished speaking when his nose became shorter and returned to the same size that it was before.

'And why are you all covered with white?' asked the old man suddenly.

'I will tell you . . . Without observing it I rubbed myself against a wall which had been freshly whitewashed,' answered the puppet, ashamed to confess that he had been floured like a fish prepared for the frying-pan.

'And what have you done with your jacket, your trousers, and your cap?'

'I met with robbers who took them from me. Tell me, good old man, could you perhaps give me some clothes to return home in?'

'My boy, as to clothes, I have nothing but a little sack in which I keep beans. If you wish for it, take it; there it is.'

Pinocchio did not wait to be told twice. He took the sack at once, and with a pair of scissors he cut a hole at the end and at each side, and put it on like a shirt. And with this slight clothing he set off for the village.

But as he went he did not feel at all comfortable – so little so, indeed, that for a step forward he took another backwards, and he said, talking to himself: 'How shall I ever present myself to my good little Fairy? What will she say when she sees me? . . . Will she forgive me this second escapade? . . . I bet that she will not forgive me! Oh, I am sure that she will not forgive me! . . . And it serves me right, for I am a rascal. I am always promising to correct myself, and I never keep my word! . . .'

When he reached the village it was night and very dark. A storm had come on, and as the rain was coming down in torrents he went straight to the

Fairy's house, resolved to knock at the door, and hoping to be let in.

But when he was there his courage failed him, and instead of knocking he ran away some twenty paces. He returned to the door a second time, but could not make up his mind; he came back a third time, still he dared not; the fourth time he laid hold of the knocker and, trembling, gave a little knock.

He waited and waited. At last, after half an hour had passed, a window on the top floor was opened – the house was four storeys high – and Pinocchio saw a big Snail with a lighted candle on her head looking out. She called to him: 'Who is there at this hour?'

'Is the Fairy at home?' asked the puppet.

'The Fairy is asleep and must not be awakened; but who are you?'

'It is I!'

'Who is I?'

'Pinocchio.'

'And who is Pinocchio?'

'The puppet who lives in the Fairy's house.'

'Ah, I understand!' said the Snail. 'Wait for me there. I will come down and open the door directly.'

'Be quick, for pity's sake, for I am dying of cold.'

'My boy, I am a snail, and snails are never in a hurry.'

An hour passed, and then two, and the door was not opened. Pinocchio, who was wet through and trembling from cold and fear, at last took courage and knocked again, and this time he knocked louder.

At this second knock a window on the lower storey opened, and the same Snail appeared at it.

'Beautiful little Snail,' cried Pinocchio from the street, 'I have been waiting for two hours! And two hours on such a bad night seem longer than two years. Be quick, for pity's sake.'

'My boy,' answered the calm, phlegmatic little animal – 'my boy, I am a snail, and snails are never in a hurry.'

And the window was shut again.

Shortly afterwards midnight struck; then one o'clock, then two o'clock, and the door remained still closed.

Pinocchio at last, losing all patience, seized the knocker in a rage, intending to give a blow that would resound through the house. But the knocker, which was iron, turned suddenly into an eel, and slipping out of his hands disappeared in the stream of water that ran down the middle of the street.

'Ah! is that it?' shouted Pinocchio, blind with rage. 'Since the knocker has disappeared, I will kick instead with all my might.'

And drawing a little back he gave a tremendous kick against the house door. The blow was indeed so violent that his foot went through the wood and stuck; and when he tried to draw it back again it was trouble thrown away, for it remained fixed like a nail that has been hammered down.

Think of poor Pinocchio! He was obliged to spend the remainder of the night with one foot on the ground and the other in the air.

The following morning at daybreak the door was at last opened. That clever little Snail had taken only nine hours to come down from the fourth storey to the house door. It is evident that her exertions must have been great.

'What are you doing with your foot stuck in the door?' she asked the puppet, laughing.

'It was an accident. Do try, beautiful little Snail, if you cannot release me from this torture.'

'My boy, that is the work of a carpenter, and I have never been a carpenter.'

'Beg the Fairy from me! . . .'

'The Fairy is asleep and must not be wakened.'

'But what do you suppose that I can do all day nailed to this door?'

'Amuse yourself by counting the ants that pass down the street.'

'Bring me at least something to eat, for I am quite exhausted.'

'At once,' said the Snail.

In fact, after three hours and a half she returned to Pinocchio carrying a silver tray on her head. The tray contained a loaf of bread, a roast chicken, and four ripe apricots.

'Here is the breakfast that the Fairy has sent you,' said the Snail.

The puppet felt very much comforted at the sight of these good things. But when he began to eat them, what was his disgust at making the discovery that the bread was plaster, the chicken cardboard and the four apricots painted alabaster.

He wanted to cry. In his desperation he tried to throw away the tray and all that was on it; but instead, either from grief or exhaustion, he fainted away.

When he came to himself he found that he was lying on a sofa, and the Fairy was beside him.

'I will pardon you once more,' the Fairy said, 'but woe to you if you behave badly a third time!'

Pinocchio promised, and swore that he would study, and that for the future he would always conduct himself well.

And he kept his word for the remainder of the year. Indeed, at the examinations before the holidays, he had the honour of being the first in the school, and his behaviour in general was so satisfactory and praiseworthy that the Fairy was very much pleased, and said to him: 'Tomorrow your wish shall be gratified.'

'And that is?'

'Tomorrow you shall cease to be a wooden puppet, and you shall become a boy.'

No one who had not witnessed it could ever imagine Pinocchio's joy at this long-sighed-for good fortune. All his schoolfellows were to be invited for the following day to a grand breakfast at the Fairy's house that they might celebrate together the great event. The Fairy had prepared two hundred cups of coffee and milk, and four hundred rolls cut and buttered on each side. The day promised to be most happy and delightful, but . . .

Unfortunately in the lives of puppets there is always a 'but' that spoils everything.

CHAPTER 30

Pinocchio, instead of becoming a boy, starts secretly with his friend Candlewick for the Land of Boobies.

Pinocchio, as was natural, asked the Fairy's permission to go round the town to make the invitations; and the Fairy said to him: 'Go if you like and invite your companions for the breakfast tomorrow, but remember to return home before dark. Have you understood?'

'I promise to be back in an hour,' answered the puppet.

'Take care, Pinocchio! Boys are always very ready to promise; but generally they are little given to keep their word.'

'But I am not like other boys. When I say a thing, I do it.'

'We shall see. If you are disobedient, so much the worse for you.'

'Why?'

'Because boys who do not listen to the advice of those who know more than they do always meet with some misfortune or other.'

'I have experienced that,' said Pinocchio. 'But I shall never make that mistake again.'

'We shall see if that is true.'

Without saying more the puppet took leave of his good Fairy, who was like a mama to him, and went out of the house singing and dancing.

In less than an hour all his friends were invited. Some accepted at once heartily; others at first required pressing; but when they heard that the rolls to be eaten with the coffee were to be buttered on both sides, they ended by saying: 'We will come also, to do you a pleasure.'

Now I must tell you that amongst Pinocchio's friends and schoolfellows there was one that he greatly preferred and was very fond of. This boy's name was Romeo; but he always went by the nickname of Candlewick, because he was so thin, straight and bright, like the new wick of a little nightlight.

Candlewick was the laziest and the naughtiest boy in the school; but Pinocchio was devoted to him. He had indeed gone at once to his house to invite him to the breakfast, but he had not found him. He returned a second time, but Candlewick was not there. He went a third time, but it was in vain. Where could he search for him? He looked here, there and everywhere, and at last he saw him hiding in the porch of a peasant's cottage.

'What are you doing there?' asked Pinocchio, coming up to him.

'I am waiting for midnight, to start . . .'

'Why, where are you going?'

'Very far, very far, very far away.'

'And I have been three times to your house to look for you.'

'What did you want with me?'

'Do you not know the great event? Have you not heard of my good fortune?'

'What is it?'

'Tomorrow I cease to be a puppet, and become a boy like you, and like all the other boys.'

'Much good may it do you.'

'Tomorrow, therefore, I expect you to breakfast at my house.'

'But I tell you that I am going away tonight.'

'At what o'clock?'

'In a short time.'

'And where are you going?'

'I am going to live in a country . . . the most delightful country in the world: a real land of Cocagne! . . .'

'And how is it called?'

'It is called the Land of Boobies. Why do you not come too?'

'I? No, never!'

'You are wrong, Pinocchio. Believe me, if you do not come you will repent it. Where could you find a better country for us boys? There are no schools there; there are no masters; there are no books. In that delightful land nobody ever studies. On Thursday there is never school; and every week consists of six Thursdays and one Sunday. Only think, the holidays begin on the 1st of January and finish on the last day of December. That is the country for me! That is what all civilised countries should be like!'

'But how are the days spent in the Land of Boobies?'

'They are spent in play and amusement from morning till night. When night comes you go to bed, and recommence the same life in the morning. What do you think of it?'

'Hum! . . . ' said Pinocchio; and he shook his head slightly as much as to say, 'That is a life that I also would willingly lead.'

'Well, will you go with me? Yes or no? Resolve quickly.'

'No, no, no, and again no. I promised my good Fairy to become a well-conducted boy, and I will keep my word. And as I see that the sun is setting I must leave you at once and run away. Goodbye, and a pleasant journey to you.'

'Where are you rushing off to in such a hurry?'

'Home. My good Fairy wishes me to be back before dark.'

'Wait another two minutes.'

'It will make me too late.'

'Only two minutes.'

'And if the Fairy scolds me?'

'Let her scold. When she has scolded well she will hold her tongue,' said that rascal Candlewick.

'And what are you going to do? Are you going alone or with companions?'

'Alone? We shall be more than a hundred boys.'

'And do you make the journey on foot?'

'A coach will pass by shortly which is to take me to that happy country.'

'What would I not give for the coach to pass by now!'

'Why?'

'That I might see you all start together.'

'Stay here a little longer and you will see us.'

'No, no, I must go home.'

'Wait another two minutes.'

'I have already delayed too long. The Fairy will be anxious about me.'

'Poor Fairy! Is she afraid that the bats will eat you?'

'But now,' continued Pinocchio, 'are you really sure that there are no schools in that country?'

'Not even the shadow of one.'

'And no masters either?'

'Not one.'

'And no one is ever made to study?'

'Never, never, never!'

'What a delightful country!' said Pinocchio, his mouth watering. 'What a delightful country! I have never been there, but I can quite imagine it . . .'

'Why will you not come also?'

'It is useless to tempt me. I promised my good Fairy to become a sensible boy, and I will not break my word.'

'Goodbye, then, and give my compliments to all the boys at the gymnasiums, and also to those at the lyceums, if you meet them in the street.'

'Goodbye, Candlewick: a pleasant journey to you, amuse yourself, and think sometimes of your friends.'

Thus saying the puppet made two steps to go, but then stopped, and turning to his friend he enquired: 'But are you quite certain that in that country all the weeks consist of six Thursdays and one Sunday?'

'Most certain.'

'But do you know for certain that the holidays begin on the 1st of January and finish on the last day of December?'

'Assuredly.'

'What a delightful country!' repeated Pinocchio, looking enchanted. Then, with a resolute air, he added in a great hurry: 'This time really goodbye, and a pleasant journey to you.'

'Goodbye.'

'When do you start?'

'Shortly.'

'What a pity! If really it wanted only an hour to the time of your start, I should be almost tempted to wait.'

'And the Fairy?'

'It is already late . . . If I return home an hour sooner or an hour later it will be all the same.'

'Poor Pinocchio! And if the Fairy scolds you?'

'I must have patience! I will let her scold. When she has scolded well she will hold her tongue.'

In the meantime night had come on and it was quite dark. Suddenly they saw in the distance a small light moving . . . and they heard a noise of talking, and the sound of a trumpet, but so small and feeble that it resembled the hum of a mosquito.

'Here it is!' shouted Candlewick, jumping to his feet.

'What is it?' asked Pinocchio in a whisper.

'It is the coach coming to take me. Now will you come, yes or no?'

'But is it really true,' asked the puppet, 'that in that country boys are never obliged to study?'

'Never, never, never!'

'What a delightful country! . . . What a delightful country! . . . What a delightful country!'

CHAPTER 31

After five months' residence in the land of Cocagne, Pinocchio, to his great astonishment, grows a beautiful pair of donkey's ears, and he becomes a little donkey, tail and all.

At last the coach arrived; and it arrived without making the slightest noise, for its wheels were bound round with tow and rags.

It was drawn by twelve pairs of donkeys, all the same size but of different colours.

Some were grey, some white, some brindled like pepper and salt, and others had large stripes of yellow and blue.

But the most extraordinary thing was this: the twelve pairs, that is, the twenty-four donkeys, instead of being shod like other beasts of burden, had on their feet men's boots made of white kid.

And the coachman? . . .

Picture to yourself a little man broader than he was long, flabby and greasy like a lump of butter, with a small round face like an orange, a little mouth that was always laughing, and a soft caressing voice like a cat when she is trying to insinuate herself into the good graces of the mistress of the house.

All the boys as soon as they saw him fell in love with him, and vied with each other in taking places in his coach to be conducted to the true land of Cocagne, known on the geographical map by the seducing name of the Land of Boobies.

The coach was in fact quite full of boys between

eight and twelve years old, heaped one upon another like herrings in a barrel. They were uncomfortable, packed close together and could hardly breathe: but nobody said Oh! – nobody grumbled. The consolation of knowing that in a few hours they would reach a country where there were no books, no schools and no masters made them so happy and resigned that they felt neither fatigue nor inconvenience, neither hunger, nor thirst, nor want of sleep.

As soon as the coach had drawn up the little man turned to Candlewick, and with a thousand smirks and grimaces said to him, smiling: 'Tell me, my fine boy, would you also like to go to that fortunate country?'

'I certainly wish to go.'

'But I must warn you, my dear child, that there is not a place left in the coach. You can see for yourself that it is quite full . . .'

'No matter,' replied Candlewick; 'if there is no place inside, I will manage to sit on the springs.'

And giving a leap he seated himself astride on the springs.'

'And you, my love! . . . ' said the little man, turning in a flattering manner to Pinocchio, 'what do you intend to do? Are you coming with us, or are you going to remain behind?'

'I remain behind,' answered Pinocchio. 'I am going home. I intend to study and to earn a good character at school, as all well-conducted boys do.'

'Much good may it do you!'

'Pinocchio!' called out Candlewick, 'listen to me! Come with us and we shall have such fun.'

'No, no, no!'

'Come with us, and we shall have such fun,' cried four other voices from the inside of the coach.

'Come with us, and we shall have such fun,' shouted in chorus a hundred voices from the inside of the coach.

'But if I come with you, what will my good Fairy say?' said the puppet, who was beginning to yield.

'Do not trouble your head with melancholy thoughts. Consider only that we are going to a country where we shall be at liberty to run riot from morning till night.'

Pinocchio did not answer; but he sighed; he sighed again; he sighed for the third time, and he said finally: 'Make a little room for me, for I am coming too.'

'The places are all full,' replied the little man; 'but to show you how welcome you are, you shall have my seat on the box . . .'

'And you? . . . '

'Oh, I will go on foot.'

'No, indeed, I could not allow that. I would rather mount one of these donkeys,' cried Pinocchio.

Approaching the right-hand donkey of the first pair he attempted to mount him, but the animal turned on him, and giving him a great blow in the stomach rolled him over with his legs in the air.

You can imagine the impertinent and immoderate laughter of all the boys who witnessed this scene.

But the little man did not laugh. He approached the rebellious donkey and, pretending to give him a kiss, bit off half of his ear.

Pinocchio in the meantime had got up from the ground in a fury, and with a spring he seated himself on the poor animal's back. And he sprang so well that the boys stopped laughing and began to shout: 'Hurrah, Pinocchio!' and they clapped their hands and applauded him as if they would never finish.

But the donkey suddenly kicked up its hind-legs, and backing violently threw the poor puppet into the middle of the road on to a heap of stones.

The roars of laughter recommenced: but the little man, instead of laughing, felt such affection for the restive ass that he kissed him again, and as he did so he bit half of his other ear clean off. He then said to the puppet: 'Mount him now without fear. That little donkey had got some whim into his head; but I whispered two little words into his ears which have, I hope, made him gentle and reasonable.'

Pinocchio mounted, and the coach started. Whilst the donkeys were galloping and the coach was rattling over the stones of the high road, the puppet thought that he heard a low voice that was scarcely intelligible saying to him: 'Poor fool! you would follow your own way, but you will repent it!'

Pinocchio, feeling almost frightened, looked from side to side to try and discover where these words could come from: but he saw nobody. The donkeys galloped, the coach rattled, the boys inside slept, Candlewick snored liked a dormouse, and the little man seated on the box sang between his teeth:

> During the night all sleep,
> But I sleep never . . .

After they had gone another mile, Pinocchio heard the same little low voice saying to him: 'Bear it in mind, simpleton! Boys who refuse to study, and turn their backs upon books, schools and masters to pass their time in play and amusement, sooner or later come to a bad end . . . I know it by experience . . . and I can tell you. A day will come when you will weep as I am weeping now . . . but then it will be too late!'

On hearing these words whispered very softly the puppet, more frightened than ever, sprang down from the back of his donkey and went and took hold of his mouth.

Imagine his surprise when he found that the donkey was crying . . . and he was crying like a boy!

'Eh! Sir Coachman,' cried Pinocchio to the little man, 'here is an extraordinary thing! This donkey is crying.'

'Let him cry; he will laugh when he is a bridegroom.'

'But have you by chance taught him to talk?'

'No; but he spent three years in a company of learned dogs, and he learnt to mutter a few words.'

'Poor beast!'

'Come, come,' said the little man, 'don't let us waste time in seeing a donkey cry. Mount him, and let us go on: the night is cold and the road is long.'

Pinocchio obeyed without another word. In the morning about daybreak they arrived safely in the Land of Boobies.

It was a country unlike any other country in the world. The population was composed entirely of boys. The oldest were fourteen, and the youngest scarcely eight years old. In the streets there was such merriment, noise and shouting that it was enough to turn anybody's head. There were troops of boys everywhere. Some were playing with nuts, some with battledores, some with balls. Some rode velocipedes, others wooden horses. A party were playing at hide and seek, a few were chasing each other. Boys dressed in straw were eating lighted tow; some were reciting, some singing, some leaping. Some were amusing themselves with walking on their hands with their feet in the air; others were trundling hoops, or strutting about dressed as generals, wearing leaf helmets and commanding a squadron of cardboard soldiers. Some were laughing, some shouting, some were calling out; others clapped their hands, or whistled, or clucked like a hen who has just laid an egg. To sum it all up, it was such a pandemonium, such a bedlam, such an uproar, that not to be deafened it would have been necessary to stuff one's ears with cotton wool. In every square, canvas theatres had been erected, and they were crowded with boys from morning till evening. On the walls of the houses there were inscriptions written in charcoal: 'Long live playthings; We will have no more schools; Down with arithmetic'; and similar other fine sentiments, all in bad spelling.

Pinocchio, Candlewick and the other boys who had made the journey with the little man, had scarcely set foot in the town before they were in the thick of the tumult, and I need not tell you that in a few minutes they had made acquaintance with everybody. Where could happier or more contented boys be found?

In the midst of continual games and every variety of amusement, the hours, the days and the weeks passed like lightning.

'Oh, what a delightful life!' said Pinocchio, whenever by chance he met Candlewick.

'See, then, if I was not right?' replied the other. 'And to think that you did not want to come! To think that you had taken it into your head to return home to your Fairy, and to lose your time in studying! . . . If you are at this moment free from the bother of books and school, you must acknowledge that you owe it to me, to my advice and to my persuasion. It is only friends who know how to render such great services.'

'It is true, Candlewick! If I am now a really happy boy, it is all your doing. But do you know what the master used to say when he talked to me of you? He always said to me: "Do not associate with that rascal Candlewick, for he is a bad companion, and will only lead you into mischief!" '

'Poor master!' replied the other, shaking his head. 'I know only too well that he disliked me, and amused himself by calumniating me; but I am generous and I forgive him!'

'Noble soul!' said Pinocchio, embracing his friend affectionately, and kissing him between the eyes.

This delightful life had gone on for five months. The days had been entirely spent in play and amusement, without a thought of books or school, when one morning Pinocchio awoke to a most disagreeable surprise that put him into a very bad humour.

CHAPTER 32

Pinocchio gets donkey's ears; and then he becomes
a real little donkey and begins to bray.

What was this surprise?

I will tell you, my dear little readers. The surprise was that Pinocchio when he awoke scratched his head; and in scratching his head he discovered . . . Can you guess in the least what he discovered?

He discovered to his great astonishment that his ears had grown to a great length.

You know that the puppet from his birth had always had very small ears – so small that they were not visible to the naked eye. You can imagine then what he felt when he found that during the night his ears had become so long that they seemed like two brooms.

He went at once in search of a glass that he might look at himself, but not being able to find one he filled the basin of his washing-stand with water, and he saw reflected what he certainly would never have wished to see. He saw his head embellished with a magnificent pair of donkey's ears!

Only think of poor Pinocchio's sorrow, shame and despair!

He began to cry and roar, and he beat his head against the wall; but the more he cried the longer his ears grew: they grew, and grew, and became hairy towards the points.

At the sound of his loud outcries a beautiful little Marmot that lived on the first floor came into the room. Seeing the puppet in such grief she asked earnestly: 'What has happened to you, my dear fellow-lodger?'

'I am ill, my dear little Marmot, very ill . . . and of an illness that frightens me. Do you understand counting a pulse?'

'A little.'

'Then feel and see if by chance I have got fever.'

The little Marmot raised her right forepaw; and after having felt Pinocchio's pulse she said to him, sighing: 'My friend, I am grieved to be obliged to give you bad news!'

'What is it?'

'You have got a very bad fever!'

'What fever is it?'

'It is donkey fever.'

'That is a fever that I do not understand,' said the puppet, but he understood it only too well.

'Then I will explain it to you,' said the Marmot. 'You must know that in two or three hours you will be no longer a puppet, or a boy . . . '

'Then what shall I be?'

'In two or three hours you will become really and truly a little donkey, like those that draw carts and carry cabbages and salad to market.'

'Oh! unfortunate that I am! unfortunate that I am!' cried Pinocchio, seizing his two ears with his hands, and pulling them and tearing them furiously as if they had been someone else's ears.

'My dear boy,' said the Marmot, by way of consoling him, 'what can you do to prevent it? It is destiny. It is written in the decrees of wisdom that all boys who are lazy, and who take a dislike to books, to schools and to masters, and who pass their time in amusement, games and diversions, must end sooner or later by becoming transformed into so many little donkeys.'

'But is it really so?' asked the puppet, sobbing.

'It is indeed only too true! And tears are now useless. You should have thought of it sooner!'

'But it was not my fault: believe me, little Marmot, the fault was all Candlewick's!'

'And who is this Candlewick?'

'One of my schoolfellows. I wanted to return home. I wanted to be obedient. I wished to study and to earn a good character . . . but Candlewick said to me: "Why should you bother yourself by studying? Why should you go to school? Come with us instead to the Land of Boobies: there we shall none of us have to learn: there we shall amuse ourselves from morning to night, and we shall always be merry." '

'And why did you follow the advice of that false friend? of that bad companion?'

'Why? . . . Because, my dear little Marmot, I am a puppet with no sense . . . and with no heart. Ah! if I had had the least heart I should never have left that good Fairy who loved me like a mama, and who had done so much for me! . . . and I should be no longer a puppet . . . for I should by this time have become a little boy like so many others! But if I meet Candlewick, woe to him! He shall hear what I think of him!'

And he turned to go out. But when he reached the door he remembered his donkey's ears, and feeling ashamed to show them in public, what do you think he did? He took a big cotton cap, and putting it on his head he pulled it well down over the point of his nose.

He then set out, and went everywhere in search of Candlewick. He looked for him in the streets, in the squares, in the little theatres, in every possible place; but he could not find him. He enquired for him of everybody he met, but no one had seen him.

He then went to seek him at his house; and having reached the door he knocked.

'Who is there?' asked Candlewick from within.

'It is I!' answered the puppet.

'Wait a moment and I will let you in.'

After half an hour the door was opened, and imagine Pinocchio's feelings when upon going into the room he saw his friend Candlewick with a big cotton cap on his head which came down over his nose.

At the sight of the cap Pinocchio felt almost consoled, and thought to himself: 'Has my friend got the same illness that I have? Is he also suffering from donkey fever?'

And pretending to have observed nothing he asked him, smiling: 'How are you, my dear Candlewick?'

'Very well; as well as a mouse in a Parmesan cheese.'

'Are you saying that seriously?'

'Why should I tell you a lie?'

'Excuse me; but why, then, do you keep that cotton cap on your head which covers up your ears?'

'The doctor ordered me to wear it because I have hurt this knee. And you, dear puppet, why have you got on that cotton cap pulled down over your nose?'

'The doctor prescribed it because I have grazed my foot.'

'Oh, poor Pinocchio! . . . '

'Oh, poor Candlewick! . . . '

After these words a long silence followed, during which the two friends did nothing but look mockingly at each other.

At last the puppet said in a soft mellifluous voice to his companion: 'Satisfy my curiosity, my dear Candlewick: have you ever suffered from disease of the ears?'

'Never! . . . And you?'

'Never! Only since this morning one of my ears aches.'

'Mine is also paining me.'

'You also? . . . And which of your ears hurts you?'

'Both of them. And you?'

'Both of them. Can we have got the same illness?'

'I fear so.'

'Will you do me a kindness, Candlewick?'

'Willingly! With all my heart.'

'Will you let me see your ears?'

'Why not? But first, my dear Pinocchio, I should like to see yours.'

'No: you must be the first.'

'No, dear! First you and then I!'

'Well,' said the puppet, 'let us come to an agreement like good friends.'

'Let us hear it.'

'We will both take off our caps at the same moment. Do you agree?'

'I agree.'

'Then attention!'

And Pinocchio began to count in a loud voice: 'One! Two! Three!'

At the word three! the two boys took off their caps and threw them into the air.

And then a scene followed that would seem incredible if it was not true. That is, that when Pinocchio and Candlewick discovered that they were both struck with the same misfortune, instead of feeling full of mortification and grief, they began to prick their ungainly ears and to make a thousand antics, and they ended by going into bursts of laughter.

And they laughed, and laughed, and laughed, until they had to hold themselves together. But in the midst of their merriment, Candlewick suddenly stopped, staggered, and changing colour, said to his friend: 'Help, help, Pinocchio!'

'What is the matter with you?'

'Alas, I cannot any longer stand upright.'

'No more can I,' exclaimed Pinocchio, tottering and beginning to cry.

And whilst they were talking they both doubled up and began to run round the room on their hands and feet. And as they ran, their hands became hoofs, their faces lengthened into muzzles, and their backs became covered with a light grey hairy coat sprinkled with black.

But do you know what was the worst moment for these two wretched boys? The worst and the most humiliating moment was when their tails grew. Vanquished by shame and sorrow they wept and lamented their fate.

Oh, if they had but been wiser! But instead of sighs and lamentations they could only bray like asses; and they brayed loudly and said in chorus: 'J–a, j–a, j–a.'

Whilst this was going on someone knocked at the door, and a voice on the outside said: 'Open the door! I am the little man, I am the coachman, who brought you to this country. Open at once, or it will be the worse for you!'

CHAPTER 33

Pinocchio, having become a genuine little donkey, is taken to be sold, and is bought by the director of a company of buffoons to be taught to dance, and to jump through hoops; but one evening he lames himself, and then he is bought by a man who purposes to make a drum of his skin.

Finding that the door remained shut the little man burst it open with a violent kick, and coming into the room he said to Pinocchio and Candlewick with his usual little laugh: 'Well done, boys! You brayed well, and I recognised you by your voices. That is why I am here.'

At these words the two little donkeys were quite stupefied, and stood with their heads down, their ears lowered, and their tails between their legs.

At first the little man stroked and caressed them; then taking out a currycomb he currycombed them well. And when by this process he had polished them till they shone like two mirrors, he put a halter round their necks and led them to the marketplace, in hopes of selling them and making a good profit.

And indeed buyers were not wanting. Candlewick was bought by a peasant whose donkey had died the previous day. Pinocchio was sold to the director of a company of buffoons and tightrope dancers, who bought him that he might teach him to leap and to dance with the other animals belonging to the company.

And now, my little readers, you will have understood the fine trade that little man pursued. The wicked little monster, who had a face all milk and honey, made frequent journeys round the world with his coach. As he went along he collected, with promises and flattery, all the idle boys who had taken an aversion to books and school. As soon as his coach was full he conducted them to the Land of Boobies, that they might pass their time in games, in uproar and in amusement. When these poor deluded boys, from continual play and no study, had become so many little donkeys, he took possession of them with great delight and satisfaction, and carried them off to the fairs and markets to be sold. And in this way he had in a few years made heaps of money and had become a millionaire.

What became of Candlewick I do not know; but I do know that Pinocchio from the very first day had to endure a very hard, laborious life.

When he was put into his stall his master filled the manger with straw; but Pinocchio, having tried a mouthful, spat it out again.

Then his master, grumbling, filled the manger with hay; but neither did the hay please him.

'Ah!' exclaimed his master in a passion. 'Does not hay please you either? Leave it to me, my fine donkey; if you are so full of caprices I will find a way to cure you!'

And by way of correcting him he struck his legs with his whip.

Pinocchio began to cry and to bray with pain, and he said, braying: 'J–a, j–a, I cannot digest straw!'

'Then eat hay!' said his master, who understood perfectly the asinine dialect.

'J–a, j–a, hay gives me a pain in my stomach.'

'Do you mean to pretend that a little donkey like you must be kept on breast of chicken and capons in jelly?' asked his master, getting more and more angry and whipping him again.

At this second whipping Pinocchio prudently held his tongue and said nothing more.

The stable was then shut and Pinocchio was left alone. He had not eaten for many hours, and he began to yawn from hunger. And when he yawned he opened a mouth that seemed as wide as an oven.

At last, finding nothing else in the manger, he resigned himself and chewed a little hay; and after he had chewed it well, he shut his eyes and swallowed it.

'This hay is not bad,' he said to himself; 'but how much better it would have been if I had gone on with my studies! . . . Instead of hay I might now be eating a hunch of new bread and a fine slice of sausage! But I must have patience! . . .'

The next morning when he woke he looked in the manger for a little more hay; but he found none, for he had eaten it all during the night.

Then he took a mouthful of chopped straw; but whilst he was chewing it he had to acknowledge that the taste of chopped straw did not in the least resemble a savoury dish of macaroni or rice.

'But I must have patience!' he repeated as he went on chewing. 'May my example serve at least as a warning to all disobedient boys who do not want to study. Patience! . . . patience! . . .'

'Patience indeed!' shouted his master, coming at that moment into the stable. 'Do you think, my little donkey, that I bought you only to give you food and drink? I bought you to make you work, and that you might earn money for me. Up, then, at once! you must come with me into the circus, and there I will teach you to jump through hoops, to go through frames of paper head foremost, to dance waltzes and polkas, and to stand upright on your hind legs.'

Poor Pinocchio, either by love or by force, had to learn all these fine things. But it took him three months before he had learnt them, and he got many a whipping that nearly took off his skin.

At last a day came when his master was able to announce that he would give a really extraordinary

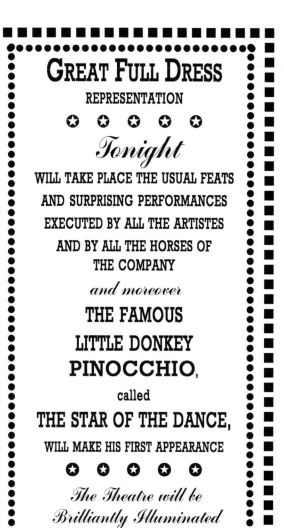

GREAT FULL DRESS
REPRESENTATION
✪ ✪ ✪ ✪ ✪
Tonight
WILL TAKE PLACE THE USUAL FEATS
AND SURPRISING PERFORMANCES
EXECUTED BY ALL THE ARTISTES
AND BY ALL THE HORSES OF
THE COMPANY
and moreover
**THE FAMOUS
LITTLE DONKEY
PINOCCHIO,**
called
THE STAR OF THE DANCE,
WILL MAKE HIS FIRST APPEARANCE
✪ ✪ ✪ ✪ ✪
*The Theatre will be
Brilliantly Illuminated*

representation and many-coloured placards were stuck on the street corners.

On that evening, as you may imagine, an hour before the play was to begin the theatre was crammed.

There was not a place to be had either in the pit or the stalls, or in the boxes even, by paying its weight in gold.

The benches round the circus were crowded with children and with boys of all ages, who were in a fever of impatience to see the famous little donkey Pinocchio dance.

When the first part of the performance was over, the director of the company, dressed in a black coat, white shorts, and big leather boots that came above his knees, presented himself to the public, and after making a profound bow he began with much solemnity the following ridiculous speech:

'Respectable public, ladies and gentlemen! The humble undersigned being a passer-by in this illustrious city, I have wished to procure for myself the honour, not to say the pleasure, of presenting to this intelligent and distinguished audience a celebrated little donkey, who has already had the honour of dancing in the presence of His Majesty the Emperor of all the principal Courts of Europe.

'And thanking you, I beg of you to help us with your inspiring presence and to be indulgent to us.'

This speech was received with much laughter and applause; but the applause redoubled and became tumultuous when the little donkey Pinocchio made his appearance in the middle of the circus. He was decked out for the occasion. He had a new bridle of polished leather with brass buckles and studs, and two white camelias in his ears. His mane was divided and curled, and each curl was tied with a bow of coloured ribbon. He had a girth of gold and silver round his body, and his tail was plaited with amaranth and blue velvet ribbons. He was, in fact, a little donkey to fall in love with!

The director, in presenting him to the public, added these few words: 'My respectable auditors! I am not here to tell you falsehoods of the great difficulties that I have overcome in understanding and subjugating this mammifer, whilst he was grazing at liberty amongst the mountains in the plains of the torrid zone. I beg you will observe the wild rolling of his eyes. Every means having been tried in vain to tame him, and to accustom him to the life of domestic quadrupeds, I was often forced to have recourse to the convincing argument of the whip. But all my goodness to him, instead of gaining his affections, has, on the contrary, increased his viciousness. However, following the system of Gall, I discovered in his cranium a bony cartilage that the Faculty of Medicine in Paris has itself recognised as the regenerating bulb of the hair, and of dance. For this reason I have not only taught him to dance, but also to jump through hoops and through frames covered with paper. Admire him, and then pass your opinion on him! But before taking my leave of you, permit me, ladies and gentlemen, to invite you to the daily performance that will take place tomorrow evening; but in the apotheosis that the weather should threaten rain, the performance will be postponed till tomorrow morning at eleven antemeridian of postmeridian.'

Here the director made another profound bow; and then turning to Pinocchio, he said: 'Courage, Pinocchio! before you begin your feats make your bow to this distinguished audience – ladies, gentlemen and children.'

Pinocchio obeyed, and bent both his knees till they touched the ground, and remained kneeling until the director, cracking his whip, shouted to him: 'At a foot's pace!'

Then the little donkey raised himself on his four legs and began to walk round the theatre, keeping at a foot's pace.

After a little the director cried: 'Trot!' and Pinocchio, obeying the order, changed to a trot.

'Gallop!' and Pinocchio broke into a gallop.

'Full gallop!' and Pinocchio went full gallop. But whilst he was going full speed like a racehorse, the director, raising his arm in the air, fired off a pistol.

At the shot the little donkey, pretending to be wounded, fell his whole length on the boards, as if he was really dying.

As he got up again, amidst an outburst of applause, shouts and loud clapping of hands, he naturally raised his head and looked up . . . and he saw in one of the boxes a beautiful lady who wore round her neck a thick gold chain from which hung a medallion. On the medallion was painted the portrait of a puppet.

'That is my portrait! . . . that lady is the Fairy!' said Pinocchio to himself, recognising her immediately; and overcome with delight he tried to cry: 'Oh, my little Fairy! Oh, my little Fairy!'

But instead of these words a bray came from his throat, so sonorous and so prolonged that all the spectators laughed, and more especially all the children who were in the theatre.

Then the director, to give him a lesson, and to make him understand that it is not good manners to bray before the public, gave him a blow on his nose with the handle of his whip.

The poor little donkey put his tongue out an inch, and licked his nose for at least five minutes, thinking perhaps that it would ease the pain he felt. But what was his despair when, looking up a second time, he saw that the box was empty and that the Fairy had disappeared! . . .

He thought he was going to die: his eyes filled with tears and he began to weep. Nobody, however, noticed it, and least of all the director who, cracking his whip, shouted: 'Courage, Pinocchio! Now let the audience see how gracefully you can jump through the hoops.'

Pinocchio tried two or three times, but each time that he came in front of the hoop, instead of going through it, he found it easier to go under it. At last he made a leap and went through it; but his right leg unfortunately caught in the hoop, and that caused him to fall to the ground doubled up in a heap on the other side.

When he got up he was lame, and it was only with great difficulty that he managed to return to the stable.

'Bring out Pinocchio! We want the little donkey! Bring out the little donkey!' shouted all the boys in the theatre, touched and sorry for the sad accident.

But the little donkey was seen no more that evening.

The following morning the veterinary, that is, the doctor of animals, paid him a visit, and declared that he would remain lame for life.

The director then said to the stable-boy: 'What do you suppose I can do with a lame donkey? He would eat food without earning it. Take him to the market and sell him.'

When they reached the market a purchaser was found at once. He asked the stable-boy: 'How much do you want for that lame donkey?'

'Twenty francs.'

'I will give you twenty pence. Don't suppose that I am buying him to make use of; I am buying him solely for his skin. I see that his skin is very hard, and I intend to make a drum with it for the band of my village.'

I leave it to my readers to imagine poor Pinocchio's feelings when he heard that he was destined to become a drum!

As soon as the purchaser had paid his twenty pence he conducted the little donkey to the seashore. He then put a stone round his neck, and tying a rope, the end of which he held in his hand, round his leg, he gave him a sudden push and threw him into the water.

Pinocchio, weighed down by the stone, went at once to the bottom; and his owner, keeping tight hold of the cord, sat down quietly on a piece of rock to wait until the little donkey was drowned, intending then to skin him.

CHAPTER 34

Pinocchio, having been thrown into the sea, is eaten by the fish and becomes a puppet as he was before. Whilst he is swimming away to save his life he is swallowed by the terrible Dogfish.

After Pinocchio had been fifty minutes under the water, his purchaser said aloud to himself: 'My poor little lame donkey must by this time be quite drowned. I will therefore pull him out of the water, and I will make a fine drum of his skin.'

And he began to haul in the rope that he had tied to the donkey's leg; and he hauled, and hauled, and hauled, until at last . . . what do you think appeared above the water? Instead of a little dead donkey he saw a live puppet, who was wriggling like an eel.

Seeing this wooden puppet the poor man thought he was dreaming, and, struck dumb with astonishment, he remained with his mouth open and his eyes starting out of his head.

Having somewhat recovered from his first stupefaction, he asked in a quavering voice: 'And the little donkey that I threw into the sea? What has become of him?'

'I am the little donkey!' said Pinocchio, laughing.

'You?'

'I.'

'Ah, you young scamp! Do you dare to make game of me?'

'To make game of you? Quite the contrary, my dear master; I am speaking seriously.'

'But how can you, who, but a short time ago, were a little donkey, have become a wooden puppet, only from having been left in the water?'

'It must have been the effect of sea-water. The sea makes extraordinary changes.'

'Beware, puppet, beware! . . . Don't imagine that you can amuse yourself at my expense. Woe to you, if I lose patience! . . .'

'Well, master, do you wish to know the true story? If you will set my leg free I will tell it you.'

The good man, who was curious to hear the true story, immediately untied the knot that kept him bound; and Pinocchio, finding himself as free as a bird in the air, commenced as follows: 'You must know that I was once a puppet as I am now, and I

was on the point of becoming a boy like the many that there are in the world. But instead, induced by my dislike of study and the advice of bad companions, I ran away from home . . . and one fine day when I awoke I found myself changed into a donkey with long ears . . . and a long tail! What a disgrace it was to me! – a disgrace, dear master, that the blessed St Anthony would not inflict even upon you! Taken to the market to be sold, I was bought by the director of an equestrian company, who took it into his head to make a famous dancer of me, and a famous leaper through hoops. But one night during a performance I had a bad fall in the circus and lamed both my legs. Then the director, not knowing what to do with a lame donkey, sent me to be sold, and you were the purchaser!'

'Only too true! And I paid twenty pence for you. And now who will give me back my poor pennies?'

'And why did you buy me? You bought me to make a drum of my skin! . . . a drum!'

'Only too true! And now where shall I find another skin?'

'Don't despair, master. There are such a number of little donkeys in the world!'

'Tell me, you impertinent rascal, does your story end here?'

'No,' answered the puppet; 'I have another two words to say and then I shall have finished. After you had bought me you brought me to this place to kill me; but then, yielding to a feeling of compassion, you preferred to tie a stone round my neck and to throw me into the sea. This humane feeling does you great honour, and I shall always be grateful to you for it. But nevertheless, dear master, this time you made your calculations without considering the Fairy!'

'And who is this Fairy?'

'She is my mama, and she resembles all other good mamas who care for their children, and who never lose sight of them, but help them lovingly, even when, on account of their foolishness and evil conduct, they deserve to be abandoned and left to themselves. Well, then, the good Fairy, as soon as she saw that I was in danger of drowning, sent immediately an immense shoal of fish, who, believing me really to be a little dead donkey, began to eat me. And what mouthfuls they took! I should never have thought that fish were greedier than boys! . . . Some ate my ears, some my muzzle, others my neck and mane, some the skin of my legs, some my coat . . . and amongst them there was a little fish so polite that he even condescended to eat my tail.'

'From this time forth,' said his purchaser, horrified, 'I swear that I will never touch fish. It would be too dreadful to open a mullet, or a fried whiting, and to find inside a donkey's tail!'

'I agree with you,' said the puppet, laughing. 'However, I must tell you that when the fish had finished eating the donkey's hide that covered me from head to foot, they naturally reached the bone – or rather the wood, for as you see I am made of the hardest wood. But after giving a few bites they soon discovered that I was not a morsel for their teeth, and, disgusted with such indigestible food, they went off, some in one direction and some in another, without so much as saying thank you to me. And now, at last, I have told you how it was that when you pulled up the rope you found a live puppet instead of a dead donkey.'

'I laugh at your story,' cried the man in a rage. 'I know only that I spent twenty pence to buy you, and I will have my money back. Shall I tell you what I will do? I will take you back to the market and I will sell you by weight as seasoned wood for lighting fires.'

'Sell me if you like; I am content,' said Pinocchio.

But as he said it he made a spring and plunged into the water. Swimming gaily away from the shore he called to his poor owner: 'Goodbye, master; if you should be in want of a skin to make a drum, remember me.'

And he laughed and went on swimming; and after a while he turned again and shouted louder: 'Goodbye, master; if you should be in want of a little well-seasoned wood for lighting the fire, remember me.'

In the twinkling of an eye he had swum so far off that he was scarcely visible. All that could be seen of him was a little black speck on the surface of the sea that from time to time lifted its legs out of the water and leapt and capered like a dolphin enjoying himself.

Whilst Pinocchio was swimming he knew not whither, he saw in the midst of the sea a rock that seemed to be made of white marble, and on the summit there stood a beautiful little goat who bleated lovingly and made signs to him to approach.

But the most singular thing was this. The little goat's hair, instead of being white or black, or a mixture of two colours as is usual with other goats, was blue, and of a very vivid blue, greatly resembling the hair of the beautiful Child.

I leave you to imagine how rapidly poor Pinocchio's heart began to beat. He swam with redoubled strength and energy towards the white rock; and he was already halfway when he saw, rising up out of the water and coming to meet him, the horrible head of a sea-monster. His wide-open cavernous mouth and his three rows of enormous teeth would have been terrifying to look at even in a picture.

And do you know what this sea-monster was?

This sea-monster was neither more nor less than that gigantic Dogfish who has been mentioned many times in this story, and who, for his slaughter and for his insatiable voracity, had been named the 'Attila of fish and fishermen'.

Only think of poor Pinocchio's terror at the sight of the monster. He tried to avoid it, to change his direction; he tried to escape; but that immense wide-open mouth came towards him with the velocity of an arrow.

'Be quick, Pinocchio, for pity's sake,' cried the beautiful little goat, bleating.

And Pinocchio swam desperately with his arms, his chest, his legs and his feet.

'Quick, Pinocchio, the monster is close upon you! . . .'

And Pinocchio swam quicker than ever, and flew on with the rapidity of a ball from a gun. He had nearly reached the rock, and the little goat, leaning over towards the sea, had stretched out her forelegs to help him out of the water!

But it was too late! The monster had overtaken him, and, drawing in his breath, he sucked in the poor puppet as he would have sucked a hen's egg; and he swallowed him with such violence and avidity that Pinocchio, in falling into the Dogfish's stomach, received such a blow that he remained unconscious for a quarter of an hour afterwards.

When he came to himself again after the shock he could not in the least imagine in what world he was. All round him it was quite dark, and the darkness was so black and so profound that it seemed to him that he had fallen head downwards into an inkstand full of ink. He listened, but he could hear no noise; only from time to time great gusts of wind blew in his face. At first he could not understand where the wind came from, but at last he discovered that it came out of the monster's lungs. For you must know that the Dogfish suffered very much from asthma, and when he breathed it was exactly as if a north wind was blowing: Pinocchio at first tried to keep up his courage; but when he had one proof after another that he was really shut up in the body of this sea-monster he began to cry and scream and to sob out: 'Help! help! Oh, how unfortunate I am! Will nobody come to save me?'

'Who do you think could save you, unhappy wretch?' said a voice in the dark that sounded like a guitar out of tune.

'Who is speaking?' asked Pinocchio, frozen with terror.

'It is I! I am a poor Tunny who was swallowed by the Dogfish at the same time that you were. And what fish are you?'

'I have nothing in common with fish. I am a puppet.'

'Then if you are not a fish, why did you let yourself be swallowed by the monster?'

'I didn't let myself be swallowed: it was the monster swallowed me! And now, what are we to do here in the dark?'

'Resign ourselves and wait until the Dogfish has digested us both.'

'But I do not want to be digested!' howled Pinocchio, beginning to cry again.

'Neither do I want to be digested,' added the Tunny; 'but I am enough of a philosopher to console myself by thinking that when one is born a Tunny it is more dignified to die in the water than in oil.'

'That is all nonsense!' cried Pinocchio.

'It is my opinion,' replied the Tunny; 'and opinions, so say the political Tunnies, ought to be respected.'

'To sum it all up . . . I want to get away from here, I want to escape.'

'Escape if you are able!'

'Is this Dogfish who has swallowed us very big?' asked the puppet.

'Big! Why, only imagine, his body is two miles long without counting his tail.'

Whilst they were holding this conversation in the dark, Pinocchio thought that he saw a light a long way off.

'What is that little light I see in the distance?' he asked.

'It is most likely some companion in misfortune who is waiting like us to be digested.'

'I will go and find him. Do you not think that it may by chance be some old fish who perhaps could show us how to escape?'

'I hope it may be so with all my heart, dear puppet.'

'Goodbye, Tunny.'

'Goodbye, puppet, and good fortune attend you.'

'Where shall we meet again?'

'Who can say? . . . It is better not even to think of it!'

CHAPTER 35

Pinocchio finds in the body of the Dogfish . . . whom does he find? Read this chapter and you will know.

Pinocchio, having taken leave of his friend the Tunny, began to grope his way in the dark through the body of the Dogfish, taking a step at a time in the direction of the light that he saw shining dimly at a great distance.

The farther he advanced the brighter became the light; and he walked and walked until at last he reached it: and when he reached it . . . what did he find? I will give you a thousand guesses. He found a little table spread out, and on it a lighted candle stuck into a green glass bottle, and seated at the table was a little old man. He was eating some live fish, and they were so very much alive that whilst he was eating them they sometimes even jumped out of his mouth.

At this sight Pinocchio was filled with such great and unexpected joy that he became almost delirious. He wanted to laugh, he wanted to cry, he wanted to say a thousand things, and instead he could only stammer out a few confused and broken words. At last he succeeded in uttering, a cry of joy, and opening his arms he threw them round the little old man's neck, and began to shout: 'Oh, my

dear papa! I have found you at last! I will never leave you more, never more, never more!'

'Then my eyes tell me true?' said the little old man, rubbing his eyes; 'then you are really my dear Pinocchio?'

'Yes, yes, I am Pinocchio, really Pinocchio! And you have quite forgiven me, have you not? Oh, my dear papa, how good you are! . . . and to think that I, on the contrary . . . Oh! but if you only knew what misfortunes have been poured on my head, and all that has befallen me! Only imagine, the day that you, poor dear papa, sold your coat to buy me a spelling-book that I might go to school, I escaped to see the puppet-show, and the showman wanted to put me on the fire that I might roast his mutton, and he was the same that afterwards gave me five gold pieces to take them to you, but I met the Fox and the Cat, who took me to the Inn of the Red Crawfish, where they ate like wolves, and I left by myself in the middle of the night, and I encountered assassins who ran after me, and I ran away, and they followed, and I ran, and they always followed me, and I ran, until they hung me from a branch of a Big Oak, and the beautiful Child with blue hair sent a little carriage to fetch me, and the doctors when they had seen me said immediately, "If he is not dead, it is a proof that he is still alive" – and then by chance I told a lie, and my nose began to grow until I could no longer get through the door of the room, for which reason I went with the Fox and the Cat to bury the four gold pieces, for one I had spent at the inn, and the Parrot began to laugh, and instead of two thousand gold pieces I found none left, for which reason the judge when he heard that I had been robbed had me immediately put in prison to content the robbers, and then when I was coming away I saw a beautiful bunch of grapes in a field, and I was caught in a trap, and the peasant, who was quite right, put a dog-collar round my neck that I might guard the poultry-yard, and acknowledging my innocence let me go, and the Serpent with the smoking tail began to laugh and broke a blood-vessel in his chest, and so I returned to the house of the beautiful Child who was dead, and the Pigeon, seeing that I was crying, said to me, "I have seen your father who was building a little boat to go in search of you," and I said to him, "Oh! if I had also wings," and he said to me, "Do you want to go to your father?" and I said, "Without doubt! but who will take me to him?" and he said to me, "I will take you," and I said to him, "How?" and he said to me, "Get on my back," and so we flew all night, and then in the morning all the fishermen who were looking out to sea said to me, "There is a poor man in a boat who is on the point of being drowned," and I recognised you at once, even at that distance, for my heart told me, and I made signs to you to return to land . . . '

'I also recognised you,' said Geppetto, 'and I would willingly have returned to the shore: but what was I to do! The sea was tremendous, and a great wave upset my boat. Then a horrible Dogfish who was near, as soon as he saw me in the water, came towards me, and putting out his tongue took hold of me, and swallowed me as if I had been a little Bologna tart.'

'And how long have you been shut up here?' asked Pinocchio.

'Since that day – it must be nearly two years ago: two years, my dear Pinocchio, that have seemed to me like two centuries!'

'And how have you managed to live? And where did you get the candle? And the matches to light it? Who gave them to you?'

'Stop, and I will tell you everything. You must know, then, that in the same storm in which my boat was upset a merchant vessel foundered. The sailors were all saved, but the vessel went to the bottom, and the Dogfish, who had that day an excellent appetite, after he had swallowed me, swallowed also the vessel . . . '

'How?'

'He swallowed it in one mouthful, and the only thing that he spat out was the mainmast, that had stuck between his teeth like a fish-bone. Fortunately for me the vessel was laden with preserved meat in tins, biscuit, bottles of wine, dried raisins, cheese, coffee, sugar, candles and boxes of wax matches. With this providential supply I have been able to live for two years. But I have arrived at the end of my resources: there is nothing left in the larder, and this candle that you see burning is the last that remains . . . '

'And after that?'

'After that, dear boy, we shall both remain in the dark.'

'Then, dear little papa,' said Pinocchio, 'there is no time to lose. We must think of escaping . . . '

'Of escaping? . . . and how?'

'We must escape through the mouth of the Dog-fish, throw ourselves into the sea and swim away.'

'You talk well; but, dear Pinocchio, I don't know how to swim.'

'What does that matter? . . . I am a good swimmer, and you can get on my shoulders and I will carry you safely to shore.'

'All illusions, my boy!' replied Geppetto, shaking his head, with a melancholy smile. 'Do you suppose it possible that a puppet like you, scarcely a metre high, could have the strength to swim with me on his shoulders!'

'Try it and you will see!'

Without another word Pinocchio took the candle in his hand, and going in front to light the way, he said to his father: 'Follow me, and don't be afraid.'

And they walked for some time and traversed the body and the stomach of the Dogfish. But when they had arrived at the point where the monster's big throat began, they thought it better to stop to give a good look round and to choose the best moment for escaping.

Now I must tell you that the Dogfish, being very old, and suffering from asthma and palpitation of the heart, was obliged to sleep with his mouth open. Pinocchio, therefore, having approached the entrance to his throat, upon looking up could see beyond the enormous gaping mouth a large piece of starry sky and beautiful moonlight.

'This is the moment to escape,' he whispered, turning to his father; 'the Dogfish is sleeping like a dormouse, the sea is calm, and it is as light as day. Follow me, dear papa, and in a short time we shall be in safety.'

They immediately climbed up the throat of the sea-monster, and having reached his immense mouth they began to walk on tiptoe down his tongue.

Before taking the final leap the puppet said to his father: 'Get on my shoulders and put your arms tight round my neck. I will take care of the rest.'

As soon as Geppetto was firmly settled on his son's shoulders, Pinocchio, feeling sure of himself, threw himself into the water and began to swim. The sea was as smooth as oil, the moon shone brilliantly and the Dogfish was sleeping so profoundly that even a cannonade would have failed to wake him.

CHAPTER 36

Pinocchio at last ceases to be a puppet and becomes a boy.

Whilst Pinocchio was swimming quickly towards the shore he discovered that his father, who was on his shoulders with his legs in the water, was trembling as violently as if the poor man had got an attack of ague fever.

Was he trembling from cold or from fear? . . . Perhaps a little from both the one and the other. But Pinocchio, thinking that it was from fear, said to comfort him: 'Courage, papa! In a few minutes we shall be safely on shore.'

'But where is this blessed shore?' asked the little old man, becoming still more frightened, and screwing up his eyes as tailors do when they wish to thread a needle. 'I have been looking in every direction and I see nothing but the sky and the sea.'

'But I see the shore as well,' said the puppet. 'You must know that I am like a cat: I see better by night than by day.'

Poor Pinocchio was making a pretence of being in good spirits, but in reality . . . in reality he was beginning to feel discouraged: his strength was failing, he was gasping and panting for breath . . . he could do no more, and the shore was still far off.

He swam until he had no breath left; then he turned his head to Geppetto and said in broken words: 'Papa . . . help me . . . I am dying!'

The father and son were on the point of drowning when they heard a voice like a guitar out of tune saying: 'Who is it that is dying?'

'It is I, and my poor father!'

'I know that voice! You are Pinocchio!'

'Precisely: and you?'

'I am the Tunny, your prison companion in the body of the Dogfish.'

'And how did you manage to escape?'

'I followed your example. You showed me the road, and I escaped after you.'

'Tunny, you have arrived at the right moment! I implore you to help us, or we are lost.'

'Willingly and with all my heart. You must, both of you, take hold of my tail and leave me to guide you. I will take you on shore in four minutes.'

Geppetto and Pinocchio, as I need not tell you, accepted the offer at once; but instead of holding on by his tail they thought it would be more comfortable to get on the Tunny's back.

Having reached the shore Pinocchio sprang first on land that he might help his father to do the same. He then turned to the Tunny, and said to him in a voice full of emotion: 'My friend, you have saved my papa's life. I can find no words with which to thank you properly. Permit me at least to give you a kiss as a sign of my eternal gratitude! . . . '

The Tunny put his head out of the water, and Pinocchio, kneeling on the ground, kissed him tenderly on the mouth. At this spontaneous proof of warm affection, the poor Tunny, who was not accustomed to it, felt extremely touched, and, ashamed to let himself be seen crying like a child, he plunged under the water and disappeared.

By this time the day had dawned. Pinocchio then offering his arm to Geppetto, who had scarcely breath to stand, said to him: 'Lean on my arm, dear papa, and let us go. We will walk very slowly like the ants, and when we are tired we can rest by the wayside.'

'And where shall we go?' asked Geppetto.

'In search of some house or cottage, where they will give us for charity a mouthful of bread, and a little straw to serve as a bed.'

They had not gone a hundred yards when they saw by the roadside two villainous-looking individuals begging.

They were the Cat and the Fox, but they were scarcely recognisable. Fancy! the Cat had so long feigned blindness that she had become blind in reality, and the Fox, old, mangy, and with one side paralysed, had not even his tail left. That sneaking thief having fallen into the most squalid misery, one fine day had found himself obliged to sell his beautiful tail to a travelling pedlar, who bought it to drive away flies.

'Oh, Pinocchio!' cried the Fox, 'give a little in charity to two poor infirm people.'

'Infirm people,' repeated the Cat.

'Begone, impostors!' answered the puppet. 'You took me in once, but you will never catch me again.'

'Believe me, Pinocchio, we are now poor and unfortunate indeed!'

'If you are poor, you deserve it. Recollect the proverb: "Stolen money never fructifies." Begone, impostors!'

And thus saying Pinocchio and Geppetto went their way in peace. When they had gone another hundred yards they saw, at the end of a path in the middle of the fields, a nice little straw hut with a roof of tiles and bricks.

'That hut must be inhabited by someone,' said Pinocchio. 'Let us go and knock at the door.'

They went and knocked.

'Who is there?' said a little voice from within.

'We are a poor father and son without bread and without a roof,' answered the puppet.

'Turn the key and the door will open,' said the same little voice.

Pinocchio turned the key and the door opened. They went in and looked here, there and everywhere, but could see no one.

'Oh! where is the master of the house?' said Pinocchio, much surprised.

'Here I am, up here!'

The father and son looked immediately up to the ceiling, and there on a beam they saw the Talking-Cricket.

'Oh, my dear little Cricket!' said Pinocchio, bowing politely to him.

'Ah! now you call me your "dear little Cricket". But do you remember the time when you threw the handle of a hammer at me, to drive me from your house?'

'You are right, Cricket! Drive me away also . . . throw the handle of a hammer at me; but have pity on my poor papa . . . '

'I will have pity on both father and son, but I wished to remind you of the ill treatment I received from you, to teach you that in this world, when it is possible, we should show courtesy to everybody if we wish it to be extended to us in our hour of need.'

'You are right, Cricket, you are right, and I will bear in mind the lesson you have given me. But tell me how you managed to buy this beautiful hut.'

'This hut was given to me yesterday by a goat whose wool was of a beautiful blue colour.'

'And where has the goat gone?' asked Pinocchio with lively curiosity.

'I do not know.'

'And when will it come back?'

'It will never come back. It went away yesterday in great grief and, bleating, it seemed to say: "Poor Pinocchio . . . I shall never see him more . . . by this time the Dogfish must have devoured him! . . . " '

'Did it really say that? . . . Then it was she! . . . it was she! . . . it was my dear little Fairy . . . ' exclaimed Pinocchio, crying and sobbing.

When he had cried for some time he dried his eyes, and prepared a comfortable bed of straw for Geppetto to lie down upon. Then he asked the Cricket: 'Tell me, little Cricket, where can I find a tumbler of milk for my poor papa?'

'Three fields off from here there lives a gardener called Giangio who keeps cows. Go to him and you will get the milk you are in want of.'

Pinocchio ran all the way to Giangio's house; and the gardener asked him: 'How much milk do you want?'

'I want a tumblerful.'

'A tumbler of milk costs a halfpenny. Begin by giving me the halfpenny.'

'I have not even a farthing,' replied Pinocchio, grieved and mortified.

'That is bad, puppet,' answered the gardener. 'If you have not even a farthing, I have not even a drop of milk.'

'I must have patience!' said Pinocchio, and he turned to go.

'Wait a little,' said Giangio. 'We can come to an arrangement together. Will you undertake to turn the pumping machine?'

'What is the pumping machine?'

'It is a wooden pole which serves to draw up the water from the cistern to water the vegetables.'

'You can try me . . . '

'Well, then, if you will draw a hundred buckets of water, I will give you in compensation a tumbler of milk.'

'It is a bargain.'

Giangio then led Pinocchio to the kitchen garden and taught him how to turn the pumping machine. Pinocchio immediately began to work; but before he had drawn up the hundred buckets of water the perspiration was pouring from his head to his feet. Never before had he undergone such fatigue.

'Up till now,' said the gardener, 'the labour of turning the pumping machine was performed by my little donkey; but the poor animal is dying.'

'Will you take me to see him?' said Pinocchio.

'Willingly.'

When Pinocchio went into the stable he saw a beautiful little donkey stretched on the straw, worn out from hunger and overwork. After looking at him earnestly he said to himself, much troubled: 'I am sure I know this little donkey! His face is not new to me.'

And bending over him he asked him in asinine language: 'Who are you?'

At this question the little donkey opened his dying eyes, and answered in broken words in the same language: 'I am . . . Can . . . dle . . . wick . . . '

And having again closed his eyes he expired.

'Oh, poor Candlewick!' said Pinocchio in a low voice; and taking a handful of straw he dried a tear that was rolling down his face.

'Do you grieve for a donkey that cost you nothing?' said the gardener. 'What must it be to me who bought him for ready money?'

'I must tell you . . . he was my friend!'

'Your friend?'

'One of my schoolfellows! . . .'

'How?' shouted Giangio, laughing loudly. 'How? had you donkeys for schoolfellows? . . . I can imagine what wonderful studies you must have made!'

The puppet, who felt much mortified at these words, did not answer; but taking his tumbler of milk, still quite warm, he returned to the hut.

And from that day for more than five months he continued to get up at daybreak every morning to go and turn the pumping machine, to earn the tumbler of milk that was of such benefit to his father in his bad state of health. Nor was he satisfied with this; for during the time that he had over he learnt to make hampers and baskets of rushes, and with the money he obtained by selling them he was able with great economy to provide for all the daily expenses. Amongst other things he constructed an elegant little wheelchair, in which he could take his father out on fine days to breathe a mouthful of fresh air.

By his industry, ingenuity, and his anxiety to work and to overcome difficulties, he not only succeeded in maintaining his father, who continued infirm, in comfort, but he also contrived to put aside forty pence to buy himself a new coat.

One morning he said to his father: 'I am going to the neighbouring market to buy myself a jacket, a cap and a pair of shoes. When I return,' he added, laughing, 'I shall be so well dressed that you will take me for a fine gentleman.'

And leaving the house he began to run merrily and happily along. All at once he heard himself called by name, and turning round he saw a big Snail crawling out from the hedge.

'Do you not know me?' asked the Snail.

'It seems to me . . . and yet I am not sure . . .'

'Do you not remember the Snail who was lady's-maid to the Fairy with blue hair? Do you not remember the time when I came downstairs to let you in, and you were caught by your foot which you had stuck through the house door?'

'I remember it all,' shouted Pinocchio. 'Tell me quickly, my beautiful little Snail, where have you left my good Fairy? What is she doing? has she forgiven me? does she still remember me? does she still wish me well? is she far from here? can I go and see her?'

To all these rapid, breathless questions the Snail replied in her usual phlegmatic manner: 'My dear Pinocchio, the poor Fairy is lying in bed at the hospital!'

'At the hospital?'

'It is only too true. Overtaken by a thousand misfortunes she has fallen seriously ill, and she has not even enough to buy herself a mouthful of bread.'

'Is it really so? . . . Oh, what sorrow you have given me! Oh, poor Fairy! poor Fairy! poor Fairy! If I had a million I would run and carry it to her . . . but I have only forty pence . . . here they are: I was going to buy a new coat. Take them, Snail, and carry them at once to my good Fairy.'

'And your new coat? . . .'

'What matters my new coat? I would sell even these rags that I have got on to be able to help her. Go, Snail, and be quick; and in two days return to this place, for I hope I shall then be able to give you some more money. Up to this time I have worked to maintain my papa; from today I will work five hours more that I may also maintain my good mama. Goodbye, Snail, I shall expect you in two days.'

The Snail, contrary to her usual habits, began to run like a lizard in a hot August sun.

That evening Pinocchio, instead of going to bed at ten o'clock, sat up till midnight had struck; and instead of making eight baskets of rushes he made sixteen.

Then he went to bed and fell asleep. And whilst he slept he thought that he saw the Fairy smiling and beautiful, who, after having kissed him, said to him: 'Well done, Pinocchio! To reward you for your good heart I will forgive you for all that is past. Boys who minister tenderly to their parents, and assist them in their misery and infirmities, are deserving of great praise and affection, even if they cannot be cited as examples of obedience and good behaviour. Try and do better in the future and you will be happy.'

At this moment his dream ended, and Pinocchio opened his eyes and awoke.

But imagine his astonishment when upon awakening he discovered that he was no longer a wooden puppet, but that he had become instead a boy, like all other boys. He gave a glance round and saw that the straw walls of the hut had disappeared, and that he was in a pretty little room furnished and arranged with a simplicity that was almost elegance. Jumping out of bed he found a new suit of clothes ready for him, a new cap and a pair of new leather boots that fitted him beautifully.

He was hardly dressed when he naturally put his hands in his pockets, and pulled out a little ivory purse on which these words were written: 'The Fairy with blue hair returns the forty pence to her dear Pinocchio, and thanks him for his good heart.' He opened the purse, and instead of forty copper pennies he saw forty shining gold pieces fresh from the mint.

He then went and looked at himself in the glass, and he thought he was someone else. For he no longer saw the usual reflection of a wooden puppet; he was greeted instead by the image of a bright intelligent boy with chestnut hair, blue eyes, and looking as happy and joyful as if it were the Easter holidays.

In the midst of all these wonders succeeding each other Pinocchio felt quite bewildered, and he could not tell if he was really awake or if he was dreaming with his eyes open.

'Where can my papa be?' he exclaimed suddenly, and going into the next room he found old Geppetto quite well, lively and in good humour, just as he had been formerly. He had already resumed his trade of wood-carving, and he was designing a rich and beautiful frame of leaves, flowers and the heads of animals.

'Satisfy my curiosity, dear papa,' said Pinocchio, throwing his arms round his neck and covering him with kisses; 'how can this sudden change be accounted for?'

'This sudden change in our home is all your doing,' answered Geppetto.

'How my doing?'

'Because when boys who have behaved badly turn over a new leaf and become good, they have the power of bringing content and happiness to their families.'

'And where has the old wooden Pinocchio hidden himself?'

'There he is,' answered Geppetto, and he pointed to a big puppet leaning against a chair, with its head on one side, its arms dangling, and its legs so crossed and bent that it was really a miracle that it remained standing.

Pinocchio turned and looked at it; and after he had looked

at it for a short time, he said to himself with

great complacency: 'How ridiculous I was

when I was a puppet! and how glad I am

that I have become a *well-behaved*

LITTLE BOY.'

The Story of Pretty Goldilocks

Once upon a time there was a princess who was the prettiest creature in the world. And because she was so beautiful, and because her hair was like the finest gold, and waved and rippled nearly to the ground, she was called Pretty Goldilocks. She always wore a crown of flowers, and her dresses were embroidered with diamonds and pearls, and everybody who saw her fell in love with her.

Now one of her neighbours was a young king who was not married. He was very rich and handsome, and when he heard all that was said about Pretty Goldilocks, though he had never seen her, he fell so deeply in love with her that he could neither eat nor drink. So he resolved to send an ambassador to ask her in marriage. He had a splendid carriage made for his ambassador, and gave him more than a hundred horses and a hundred servants, and told him to be sure and bring the princess back with him. After he had started nothing else was talked of at court, and the king felt so sure that the princess would consent that he set his people to work at pretty dresses and splendid furniture, that they might be ready by the time she came. Meanwhile, the ambassador arrived at the princess's palace and delivered his little message, but whether she happened to be cross that day, or whether the compliment did not please her, is not known. She only answered that she was very much obliged to the king, but she had no wish to be married. The ambassador set off sadly on his homeward way, bringing all the king's presents back with him, for the princess was too well brought up to accept the pearls and diamonds when she would not accept the king, so she had only kept twenty-five English pins that he might not be vexed.

When the ambassador reached the city, where the king was waiting impatiently, everybody was very much annoyed with him for not bringing the princess, and the king cried like a baby, and nobody could console him. Now there was at the court a young man, who was more clever and handsome than anyone else. He was called Charming, and everyone loved him, excepting a few envious people who were angry at his being the king's favourite and knowing all the state secrets. He happened one day to be with some people who were speaking of the ambassador's return and saying that his going to the princess had not done much good, when Charming said rashly: 'If the king had sent me to the Princess Goldilocks I am sure she would have come back with me.'

His enemies at once went to the king and said: 'You will hardly believe, sire, what Charming has the audacity to say – that if *he* had been sent to the Princess Goldilocks she would certainly have come back with him. He seems to think that he is so much handsomer than you that the princess would have fallen in love with him and followed him willingly.' The king was very angry when he heard this.

'Ha, ha!' said he; 'does he laugh at my unhappiness, and think himself more fascinating than I am? Go, and let him be shut up in my great tower to die of hunger.'

So the king's guards went to fetch Charming, who had thought no more of his rash speech, and carried him off to prison with great cruelty. The poor prisoner had only a little straw for his bed, and but for a little stream of water which flowed through the tower he would have died of thirst.

One day when he was in despair he said to himself: 'How can I have offended the king? I am his most faithful subject, and have done nothing against him.'

The king chanced to be passing the tower and recognised the voice of his former favourite. He stopped to listen in spite of Charming's enemies, who tried to persuade him to have nothing more to do with the traitor. But the king said: 'Be quiet, I wish to hear what he says.'

And then he opened the tower door and called to

Charming, who came very sadly and kissed the king's hand, saying: 'What have I done, sire, to deserve this cruel treatment?'

'You mocked me and my ambassador,' said the king, 'and you said that if I had sent you for the Princess Goldilocks you would certainly have brought her back.'

'It is quite true, sire,' replied Charming; 'I should have drawn such a picture of you, and represented your good qualities in such a way, that I am certain the princess would have found you irresistible. But I cannot see what there is in that to make you angry.'

The king could not see any cause for anger either when the matter was presented to him in this light, and he began to frown very fiercely at the courtiers who had so misrepresented his favourite.

So he took Charming back to the palace with him, and after seeing that he had a very good supper he said to him: 'You know that I love Pretty Goldilocks as much as ever, her refusal has not made any difference to me; but I don't know how to make her change her mind; I really should like to send you, to see if you can persuade her to marry me.'

Charming replied that he was perfectly willing to go, and would set out the very next day.

'But you must wait till I can get a grand escort for you,' said the king. But Charming said that he only wanted a good horse to ride, and the king, who was delighted at his being ready to start so promptly, gave him letters to the princess, and bade him good speed. It was on a Monday morning that he set out all alone upon his errand, thinking of nothing but how he could persuade the Princess Goldilocks to marry the king. He had a writing-book in his pocket, and whenever any happy thought struck him he dismounted from his horse and sat down under the trees to put it into the harangue which he was preparing for the princess, before he forgot it.

One day when he had started at the very earliest dawn, and was riding over a great meadow, he suddenly had a capital idea, and, springing from his horse, he sat down under a willow tree which grew by a little river. When he had written it down he was looking round him, pleased to find himself in such a pretty place, when all at once he saw a great golden carp lying gasping and exhausted upon the grass. In leaping after little flies she had thrown herself high upon the bank, where she had lain till she was nearly dead. Charming had pity upon her, and, though he couldn't help thinking that she would have been very nice for dinner, he picked her up gently and put her back into the water. As soon as Dame Carp felt the refreshing coolness of the water she sank down joyfully to the bottom of the river, then, swimming up to the bank

He had a writing-book in his pocket, and whenever any happy thought struck him
he dismounted from his horse and sat down under the trees

quite boldly, she said: 'I thank you, Charming, for the kindness you have done me. You have saved my life; one day I will repay you.' So saying, she sank down into the water again, leaving Charming greatly astonished at her politeness.

Another day, as he journeyed on, he saw a raven in great distress. The poor bird was closely pursued by an eagle, which would soon have eaten it up, had not Charming quickly fitted an arrow to his bow and shot the eagle dead. The raven perched upon a tree very joyfully.

'Charming,' said he, 'it was very generous of you to rescue a poor raven; I am not ungrateful, some day I will repay you.'

Charming thought it was very nice of the raven to say so, and went on his way.

Before the sun rose he found himself in a thick wood where it was too dark for him to see his path, and here he heard an owl crying as if it were in despair.

'Hark!' said he, 'that must be an owl in great trouble, I am sure it has gone into a snare'; and he began to hunt about, and presently found a great net which some bird-catchers had spread the night before.

'What a pity it is that men do nothing but torment and persecute poor creatures which never do them any harm!' said he, and he took out his knife and cut the cords of the net, and the owl flitted away into the darkness, but then turning, with one flicker of her wings, she came back to Charming and said: 'It does not need many words to tell you how great a service you have done me. I was caught; in a few minutes the fowlers would have been here – without your help, I should have been killed. I am grateful, and one day I will repay you.'

These three adventures were the only ones of any consequence that befell Charming upon his journey, and he made all the haste he could to reach the palace of the Princess Goldilocks.

When he arrived he thought everything he saw delightful and magnificent. Diamonds were as plentiful as pebbles, and the gold and silver, the beautiful dresses, the sweetmeats and pretty things that were everywhere quite amazed him; he thought to himself: 'If the princess consents to leave all this, and come with me to marry the king, he may think himself lucky!'

Then he dressed himself carefully in rich brocade, with scarlet and white plumes, and threw a splendid embroidered scarf over his shoulder,

and, looking as gay and as graceful as possible, he presented himself at the door of the palace, carrying in his arm a tiny pretty dog which he had bought on the way. The guards saluted him respectfully, and a messenger was sent to the princess to announce the arrival of Charming as ambassador of her neighbour the king.

'Charming,' said the princess, 'the name promises well; I have no doubt that he is good-looking and fascinates everybody.'

'Indeed he does, madam,' said all her maids of honour in one breath. 'We saw him from the window of the garret where we were spinning flax, and we could do nothing but look at him as long as he was in sight.'

'Well to be sure,' said the princess, 'that's how you amuse yourselves, is it? Looking at strangers out of the window! Be quick and give me my blue satin embroidered dress, and comb out my golden hair. Let somebody make me fresh garlands of flowers, and give me my high-heeled shoes and my fan, and tell them to sweep my great hall and my throne, for I want everyone to say I am really "Pretty Goldilocks".'

You can imagine how all her maids scurried this way and that to make the princess ready, and how in their haste they knocked their heads together and hindered each other, till she thought they would never have done. However, at last they led her into the gallery of mirrors that she might assure herself that nothing was lacking in her appearance, and then she mounted her throne of gold, ebony and ivory, while her ladies took their guitars and began to sing softly. Then Charming was led in, and was so struck with astonishment and admiration that at first not a word could he say. But presently he took courage and delivered his harangue, bravely ending by begging the princess to spare him the disappointment of going back without her.

'Sir Charming,' answered she, 'all the reasons you have given me are very good ones, and I assure you that I should have more pleasure in obliging you than anyone else, but you must know that a month ago as I was walking by the river with my ladies I took off my glove, and as I did so a ring that I was wearing slipped off my finger and rolled into the water. As I valued it more than my kingdom, you may imagine how vexed I was at losing it, and I vowed never to listen to any proposal of marriage unless the ambassador first brought me back my ring. So now you know what is expected of you, for

*'So now you know what is expected of you, for if you talked for fifteen days and fifteen
nights you could not make me change my mind.'*

if you talked for fifteen days and fifteen nights you
could not make me change my mind.'

Charming was very much surprised by this
answer, but he bowed low to the princess, and
begged her to accept the embroidered scarf and
the tiny dog he had brought with him. But she
answered that she did not want any presents, and
that he was to remember what she had just told
him. When he got back to his lodging he went to
bed without eating any supper, and his little dog,
who was called Frisk, couldn't eat any either, but
came and lay down close to him. All night
Charming sighed and lamented.

'How am I to find a ring that fell into the river a
month ago?' said he. 'It is useless to try; the
princess must have told me to do it on purpose,
knowing it was impossible.' And then he sighed
again.

Frisk heard him and said: 'My dear master, don't
despair; the luck may change, you are too good not
to be happy. Let us go down to the river as soon as
it is light.'

But Charming only gave him two little pats and
said nothing, and very soon he fell asleep.

At the first glimmer of dawn Frisk began to jump
about, and when he had waked Charming they
went out together, first into the garden, and then
down to the river's brink, where they wandered up

and down. Charming was thinking sadly of having
to go back unsuccessful when he heard someone
calling: 'Charming, Charming!' He looked all
about him and thought he must be dreaming, as he
could not see anybody. Then he walked on and the
voice called again: 'Charming, Charming!'

'Who calls me?' said he. Frisk, who was very small
and could look closely into the water, cried out: 'I
see a golden carp coming.' And sure enough there
was the great carp, who said to Charming: 'You
saved my life in the meadow by the willow tree, and
I promised that I would repay you. Take this, it is
Princess Goldilocks' ring.' Charming took the ring
out of Dame Carp's mouth, thanking her a
thousand times, and he and tiny Frisk went straight
to the palace, where someone told the princess that
he was asking to see her.

'Ah! poor fellow,' said she, 'he must have come to
say goodbye, finding it impossible to do as I asked.'

So in came Charming, who presented her with
the ring and said: 'Madam, I have done your
bidding. Will it please you to marry my master?'
When the princess saw her ring brought back to
her unhurt she was so astonished that she thought
she must be dreaming.

'Truly, Charming,' said she, 'you must be the
favourite of some fairy, or you could never have
found it.'

'Madam,' answered he, 'I was helped by nothing but my desire to obey your wishes.'

'Since you are so kind,' said she, 'perhaps you will do me another service, for till it is done I will never be married. There is a prince not far from here whose name is Galifron, who once wanted to marry me, but when I refused he uttered the most terrible threats against me, and vowed that he would lay waste my country. But what could I do? I could not marry a frightful giant as tall as a tower, who eats up people as a monkey eats chestnuts, and who talks so loud that anybody who has to listen to him becomes quite deaf. Nevertheless, he does not cease to persecute me and to kill my subjects. So before I can listen to your proposal you must kill him and bring me his head.'

Charming was rather dismayed at this command, but he answered: 'Very well, princess, I will fight this Galifron; I believe that he will kill me, but at any rate I shall die in your defence.'

Then the princess was frightened and said everything she could think of to prevent Charming from fighting the giant, but it was of no use, and he went out to arm himself suitably; and then, taking little Frisk with him, he mounted his horse and set out for Galifron's country. Everyone he met told him what a terrible giant Galifron was, and that nobody dared go near him; and the more he heard, the more frightened he grew. Frisk tried to encourage him by saying: 'While you are fighting the giant, dear master, I will go and bite his heels, and when he stoops down to look at me you can kill him.'

Charming praised his little dog's plan, but knew that this help would not do much good.

At last he drew near the giant's castle, and saw to his horror that every path that led to it was strewn with bones. Before long he saw Galifron coming. His head was higher than the tallest trees, and he sang in a terrible voice:

'Bring out your little boys and girls,
Pray do not stay to do their curls,
For I shall eat so very many,
I shall not know if they have any.'

Thereupon Charming sang out as loud as he could to the same tune:

'Come out and meet the valiant Charming,
Who finds you not at all alarming;
Although he is not very tall,
He's big enough to make you fall.'

The rhymes were not very correct, but you see he had made them up so quickly that it is a miracle that they were not worse; especially as he was horribly frightened all the time. When Galifron heard these words he looked all about him, and saw Charming standing, sword in hand. This put the giant into a terrible rage, and he aimed a blow at Charming with his huge iron club, which would certainly have killed him if it had reached him, but at that instant a raven perched upon the giant's head, and, pecking with its strong beak and beating with its great wings, so confused and blinded him that all his blows fell harmlessly upon the air, and Charming, rushing in, gave him several strokes with his sharp sword so that he fell to the ground. Whereupon, Charming cut off his head before he knew anything about it, and the raven from a tree close by croaked out: 'You see I have not forgotten the good turn you did me in killing the eagle. Today I think I have fulfilled my promise of repaying you.'

'Indeed, I owe you more gratitude than you ever owed me,' replied Charming.

And then he mounted his horse and rode off with Galifron's head.

When he reached the city the people ran after him in crowds, crying: 'Behold the brave Charming, who has killed the giant!' And their shouts reached the princess's ear, but she dared not ask what was happening, for fear she should hear that Charming had been killed. But very soon he arrived at the palace with the giant's head, of which she was still terrified, though it could no longer do her any harm.

'Princess,' said Charming, 'I have killed your enemy; I hope you will now consent to marry the king my master.'

'Oh dear! no,' said the princess, 'not until you have brought me some water from the Gloomy Cavern.

'Not far from here there is a deep cave, the entrance to which is guarded by two dragons with fiery eyes, who will not allow anyone to pass them. When you get into the cavern you will find an immense hole, which you must go down, and it is full of toads and snakes; at the bottom of this hole there is another little cave, in which rises the Fountain of Health and Beauty. It is some of this water that I really must have: everything it touches becomes wonderful. The beautiful things will always remain beautiful, and the ugly things become lovely. If one is young one never grows old, and if one is old one becomes young. You see,

Charming, I could not leave my kingdom without taking some of it with me.'

'Princess,' said he, 'you at least can never need this water, but I am an unhappy ambassador, whose death you desire. Where you send me I will go, though I know I shall never return.'

And, as the Princess Goldilocks showed no sign of relenting, he started with his little dog for the Gloomy Cavern. Everyone he met on the way said: 'What a pity that a handsome young man should throw away his life so carelessly! He is going to the cavern alone, though if he had a hundred men with him he could not succeed. Why does the princess ask impossibilities?' Charming said nothing, but he was very sad. When he was near the top of a hill he dismounted to let his horse graze, while Frisk amused himself by chasing flies. Charming knew he could not be far from the Gloomy Cavern, and on looking about him he saw a black hideous rock from which came a thick smoke, followed in a moment by one of the dragons with fire blazing from his mouth and eyes. His body was yellow and green, and his claws scarlet, and his tail was so long that it lay in a hundred coils. Frisk was so terrified at the sight of it that he did not know where to hide. Charming, quite determined to get the water or die, now drew his sword, and, taking the crystal flask which Pretty Goldilocks had given him to fill, said to Frisk: 'I feel sure that I shall never come back from this expedition; when I am dead, go to the princess and tell her that her errand has cost me my life. Then find the king my master, and relate all my adventures to him.'

As he spoke he heard a voice calling: 'Charming, Charming!'

'Who calls me?' said he; then he saw an owl sitting in a hollow tree, who said to him: 'You saved my life when I was caught in the net, now I can repay you. Trust me with the flask, for I know all the ways of the Gloomy Cavern, and can fill it from the Fountain of Beauty.' Charming was only too glad to give her the flask, and she flitted into the cavern, quite unnoticed by the dragon, and after some time returned with the flask, filled to the very brim with sparkling water. Charming thanked her with all his heart, and joyfully hastened back to the town.

He went straight to the palace and gave the flask to the princess, who had no further objection to make. So she thanked Charming, and ordered that preparations should be made for her departure, and they soon set out together. The princess found Charming such an agreeable companion that she

After some time the owl returned with the flask, filled to the very brim with sparkling water

sometimes said to him: 'Why didn't we stay where we were? I could have made you king, and we should have been so happy!'

But Charming only answered: 'I could not have done anything that would have vexed my master so much, even for a kingdom, or to please you, though I think you are as beautiful as the sun.'

At last they reached the king's great city, and he came out to meet the princess, bringing magnificent presents, and the marriage was celebrated with great rejoicings. But Goldilocks was so fond of Charming that she could not be happy unless he was near her, and she was always singing his praises.

'If it hadn't been for Charming,' she said to the king, 'I should never have come here; you ought to be very much obliged to him, for he did the most impossible things and got me water from the Fountain of Beauty, so I can never grow old, and shall get prettier every year.'

Then Charming's enemies said to the king: 'It is a wonder that you are not jealous: the queen thinks there is nobody in the world like Charming. As if anybody you had sent could not have done just as much!'

'It is quite true, now I come to think of it,' said

the king. 'Let him be chained hand and foot, and thrown into the tower.'

So they took Charming, and as a reward for having served the king so faithfully he was shut up in the tower, where he only saw the jailer, who brought him a piece of black bread and a pitcher of water every day.

However, little Frisk came to console him, and told him all the news.

When Pretty Goldilocks heard what had happened, she threw herself at the king's feet and begged him to set Charming free, but the more she cried, the more angry he was, and at last she saw that it was useless to say any more; but it made her very sad. Then the king took it into his head that perhaps he was not handsome enough to please the Princess Goldilocks, and he thought he would bathe his face with the water from the Fountain of Beauty, which was in the flask on a shelf in the princess's room, where she had placed it that she might see it often. Now it happened that one of the princess's ladies in chasing a spider had knocked the flask off the shelf and broken it, and every drop of the water had been spilt. Not knowing what to do, she had hastily swept away the pieces of crystal, and then remembered that in the king's room she had seen a flask of exactly the same shape, also filled with sparkling water. So, without saying a word, she fetched it and stood it upon the queen's shelf.

Now the water in this flask was what was used in the kingdom for getting rid of troublesome people. Instead of having their heads cut off in the usual way, their faces were bathed with the water, and they instantly fell asleep and never woke up any more. So, when the king, thinking to improve his beauty, took the flask and sprinkled the water upon his face, *he* fell asleep, and nobody could wake him.

Little Frisk was the first to hear the news, and he ran to tell Charming, who sent him to beg the princess not to forget the poor prisoner. All the palace was in confusion on account of the king's death, but tiny Frisk made his way through the crowd to the princess's side, and said: 'Madam, do not forget poor Charming.'

Then she remembered all he had done for her, and without saying a word to anyone went straight to the tower, and with her own hands took off Charming's chains. Then, putting a golden crown upon his head, and the royal mantle upon his shoulders, she said: 'Come, faithful Charming, I make you king, and will take you for my husband.'

Charming, once more free and happy, fell at her feet and thanked her for her gracious words.

Everybody was delighted that he should be king, and the wedding, which took place at once, was the prettiest that can be imagined, and Prince Charming and Princess Goldilocks lived happily ever after.

Without saying a word to anyone, the princess went straight to the tower,
and with her own hands took off Charming's chains

The Prince and the Fakir

There was once upon a time a king who had no children. Now this king went and lay down to rest at a place where four roads met, so that everyone who passed had to step over him.

At last a fakir came along, and he said to the king, 'Man, why are you lying here?'

He replied, 'Fakir, a thousand men have come and passed by; you pass on too.'

But the fakir said, 'Who are you, man?'

The king replied, 'I am a king, fakir. Of goods and gold I have no lack, but I have lived long and have no children. So I have come here to lie at the crossroads. My sins and offences have been very many, so I have come and am lying here that men may pass over me, and perchance my sins may be forgiven me, and God may be merciful, and I may have a son.'

The fakir answered him, 'Oh king! If you have children, what will you give me?'

'Whatever you ask, fakir,' answered the king.

The fakir said, 'Of goods and gold I have no lack, but I will say a prayer for you, and you will have two sons; one of those sons will be mine.'

Then he took out two sweetmeats and handed them to the king, and said, 'King! take these two sweetmeats and give them to your wives; give them to the wives you love best.'

The king took the sweetmeats and put them in his bosom.

Then the fakir said, 'King! in a year I will return, and of the two sons who will be born to you one is mine and one yours.'

The king said, 'Well, I agree.'

Then the fakir went on his way, and the king came home and gave one sweetmeat to each of his two wives. After some time two sons were born to the king. Then what did the king do but place those two sons in an underground room, which he had built in the earth.

Some time passed, and one day the fakir appeared, and said, 'King! bring me those sons of yours!'

What did the king do but bring two slave-girls' sons and present them to the fakir. While the fakir was sitting there the king's sons were sitting down below in their cellar eating their food. Just then a hungry ant had carried away a grain of rice from their food, and was going along with it to her children. Another stronger ant came up and attacked her in order to get this grain of rice. The first ant said, 'O ant, why do you drag this away from me? I have long been lame in my feet, and I have got just one grain, and am carrying it to my children. The king's sons are sitting in the cellar eating their food; you go and fetch a grain from there; why should you take mine from me?' On this the second ant let go and did not rob the first, but went off to where the king's sons were eating their food.

On hearing this the fakir said, 'King! these are not your sons; go and bring those children who are eating their food in the cellar.'

Then the king went and brought his own sons. The fakir chose the elder son and took him away, and set off with him on his journey, When he got home he told the king's son to go out to gather fuel.

So the king's son went out to gather cow-dung, and when he had collected some he brought it in.

Then the fakir looked at the king's son and put on a great pot, and said, 'Come round here, my pupil.'

But the king's son said, 'Master first, and pupil after.'

The fakir told him to come once, he told him twice, he told him three times, and each time the king's son answered, 'Master first, and pupil after.'

Then the fakir made a dash at the king's son, thinking to catch him and throw him into the caldron. There were about a hundred gallons of oil in this caldron, and the fire was burning beneath it.

Then the king's son, lifting the fakir, gave him a jerk and threw him into the caldron, and he was burnt, and became roast meat. He then saw a key of the fakir's lying there; he took this key and opened the door of the fakir's house. Now many men were locked up in this house; two horses were standing there in a hut of the fakir's; two greyhounds were tied up there; two simurgs were imprisoned, and two tigers also stood there. So the king's son let all the creatures go, and took them out of the house, and they all returned thanks to God. Next he let out all the men who were in prison. He took away with him the two horses, and he took away the two tigers, and he took away the two hounds, and he took away the two simurgs, and with them he set out for another country.

As he went along the road he saw above him a bald man, grazing a herd of calves, and this bald man called out to him, 'Fellow! can you fight at all?'

The king's son replied, 'When I was little I could fight a bit, and now, if anyone wants to fight, I am not so unmanly as to turn my back. Come, I will fight you.'

The bald man said, 'If I throw you, you shall be my slave; and if you throw me, I will be your slave.' So they got ready and began to fight, and the king's son threw him.

On this the king's son said, 'I will leave my beasts here, my simurgs, tigers, and dogs, and horses; they will all stay here while I go to the city to see the sights. I appoint the tiger as guard over my property. And as you are my slave, you, too, must stay here with my belongings.' So the king's son started off to the city to see the sights, and arrived at a pool.

He saw that it was a pleasant pool, and thought he would stop and bathe there, and therewith he began to strip off his clothes.

Now the king's daughter, who was sitting on the roof of the palace, saw his royal marks, and she said, 'This man is a king; when I marry, I will marry him and no other.' So she said to her father, 'My father; I wish to marry.'

'Good,' said her father.

Then the king made a proclamation: 'Let all men, great and small, attend today in the hall of audience, for the king's daughter will today take a husband.'

All the men of the land assembled, and the traveller prince also came, dressed in the fakir's clothes, saying to himself, 'I must see this ceremony today.' He went in and sat down.

The king's daughter came out and sat in the balcony, and cast her glance round all the assembly. She noticed that the traveller prince was sitting in the assembly in fakir's attire.

The princess said to her handmaiden, 'Take this dish of henna, go to that traveller dressed like a fakir, and sprinkle scent on him from the dish.'

The handmaiden obeyed the princess's order, went to him and sprinkled the scent over him.

Then the people said, 'The slave-girl has made a mistake.'

But she replied, 'The slave-girl has made no mistake, 'tis her mistress has made the mistake.'

On this the king married his daughter to the fakir, who was really no fakir, but a prince.

What fate had decreed came to pass in that country, and they were married. But the king of that city became very sad in his heart, because when so many chiefs and nobles were sitting there his daughter had chosen none of them, but had chosen that fakir; but he kept these thoughts concealed in his heart.

One day the traveller prince said, 'Let all the king's sons-in-law come out with me today to hunt.'

People said, 'What is this fakir that he should go a-hunting?'

However, they all set out for the hunt, and fixed their meeting-place at a certain pool.

The newly married prince went to his tigers, and told his tigers and hounds to kill and bring in a great number of gazelles and hog-deer and markhor. Instantly they killed and brought in a great number. Then taking with him these spoils of the chase, the prince came to the pool settled on as a meeting-place. The other princes, sons-in-law of the king of that city, also assembled there; but they had brought in no game, and the new prince had brought a great deal. Thence they returned home to the town, and went to the king their father-in-law, to present their game.

Now that king had no son. Then the new prince told him that in fact he, too, was a prince. At this the king, his father-in-law, was greatly delighted and took him by the hand and embraced him. He seated him by himself, saying, 'O prince, I return thanks that you have come here and become my son-in-law; I am very happy at this, and I make over my kingdom to you.'

Prince Featherhead &
the Princess Celandine

Once upon a time there lived a king and queen who were the best creatures in the world, and so kind-hearted that they could not bear to see their subjects want for anything. The consequence was that they gradually gave away all their treasures, till they positively had nothing left to live upon; and this coming to the ears of their neighbour, King Bruin, he promptly raised a large army and marched into their country. The poor king, having no means of defending his kingdom, was forced to disguise himself with a false beard, and, carrying his only son, the little Prince Featherhead, in his arms, and accompanied only by the queen, to make the best of his way into the wild country. They were lucky enough to escape the soldiers of King Bruin, and at last, after unheard-of fatigues and adventures, they found themselves in a charming green valley, through which flowed a stream clear as crystal and overshadowed by beautiful trees. As they looked round them with delight, a voice said suddenly: 'Fish, and see what you will catch.' Now the king had always loved fishing, and never went anywhere without a fish-hook or two in his pocket, so he drew one out hastily, and the queen lent him her girdle to fasten it to, and it had hardly touched the water before it caught a big fish, which made them an excellent meal – and not before they needed it, for they had found nothing until then but a few wild berries and roots. They thought that for the present they could not do better than stay in this delightful place, and the king set to work, and soon built a

bower of branches to shelter them; and when it was finished the queen was so charmed with it that she declared nothing was lacking to complete her happiness but a flock of sheep, which she and the little prince might tend while the king fished. They soon found that the fish were not only abundant and easily caught, but also very beautiful, with glittering scales of every imaginable hue; and before long the king discovered that he could teach them to talk and whistle better than any parrot. Then he determined to carry some to the nearest town and try to sell them; and as no one had ever before seen any like them the people flocked about him eagerly and bought all he had caught, so that presently not a house in the city was considered complete without a crystal bowl full of fish, and the king's customers were very particular about having them to match the rest of the furniture, and gave him a vast amount of trouble in choosing them. However, the money he obtained in this way enabled him to buy the queen her flock of sheep, as well as many of the other things which go to make life pleasant, so that they never once regretted their lost kingdom. Now it happened that the Fairy of the Beech-Woods lived in the lovely valley to which chance had led the poor fugitives, and it was she who had, in pity for their forlorn condition, sent the king such good luck to his fishing, and generally taken them under her protection. This she was all the more inclined to do as she loved children, and little Prince Featherhead, who never cried and grew prettier day by day, quite won her heart. She made the acquaintance of the king and the queen without at first letting them know that she was a fairy, and they soon took a great fancy to her, and even trusted her with the precious prince, whom she carried off to her palace, where she regaled him with cakes and tarts and every other good thing. This was the way she chose of making him fond of her; but afterwards, as he grew older, she spared no pains in educating and training him as a prince should be trained. But unfortunately, in spite of all her care, he grew so vain and frivolous that he quitted his peaceful country life in disgust, and rushed eagerly after all the foolish gaieties of the neighbouring town, where his handsome face and charming manners speedily made him popular. The king and queen deeply regretted this alteration in their son, but did not know how to mend matters, since the good old fairy had made him so self-willed.

Just at this time the Fairy of the Beech-Woods received a visit from an old friend of hers called Saradine, who rushed into her house so breathless with rage that she could hardly speak.

'Dear, dear! what is the matter?' said the Fairy of the Beech-Woods soothingly.

'The matter!' cried Saradine. 'You shall soon hear all about it. You know that, not content with endowing Celandine, Princess of the Summer Islands, with everything she could desire to make her charming, I actually took the trouble to bring her up myself; and now what does she do but come to me with more coaxings and caresses than usual to beg a favour. And what do you suppose this favour turns out to be – when I have been cajoled into promising to grant it? Nothing more nor less than a request that I will take back all my gifts – "since," says my young madam, "if I have the good fortune to please you, how am I to know that it is really I, myself? And that's how it will be all my life long, whenever I meet anybody. You see what a weariness my life will be to me under these circumstances, and yet I assure you I am not ungrateful to you for all your kindness!" I did all I could,' continued Saradine, 'to make her think better of it, but in vain; so after going through the usual ceremony for taking back my gifts, I'm come to you for a little peace and quietness. But, after all, I have not taken anything of consequence from this provoking Celandine. Nature had already made her so pretty, and given her such a ready wit of her own, that she will do perfectly well without me. However, I thought she deserved a little lesson, so to begin with I have whisked her off into the desert, and there left her!'

'What! all alone, and without any means of existence?' cried the kind-hearted old fairy. 'You had better hand her over to me. I don't think so

very badly of her after all. I'll just cure her vanity by making her love someone better than herself. Really, when I come to consider of it, I declare the little minx has shown more spirit and originality in the matter than one expects of a princess.'

Saradine willingly consented to this arrangement, and the old fairy's first care was to smooth away all the difficulties which surrounded the princess, and lead her by the mossy path overhung with trees to the bower of the king and queen, who still pursued their peaceful life in the valley.

They were immensely surprised at her appearance, but her charming face, and the deplorably ragged condition to which the thorns and briers had reduced her once elegant attire, speedily won their compassion; they recognised her as a companion in misfortune, and the queen welcomed her heartily, and begged her to share their simple repast. Celandine gracefully accepted their hospitality, and soon told them what had happened to her. The king was charmed with her spirit, while the queen thought she had indeed been daring thus to go against the fairy's wishes.

'Since it has ended in my meeting you,' said the princess, 'I cannot regret the step I have taken, and if you will let me stay with you, I shall be perfectly happy.'

The king and queen were only too delighted to have this charming princess to supply the place of Prince Featherhead, whom they saw but seldom, since the fairy had provided him with a palace in the neighbouring town, where he lived in the greatest luxury, and did nothing but amuse himself from morning to night. So Celandine stayed, and helped the queen to keep house, and very soon they loved her dearly. When the Fairy of the Beech-Woods came to them, they presented the princess to her, and told her story, little thinking that the fairy knew more about Celandine than they did. The old fairy was equally delighted with her, and often invited her to visit her leafy palace, which was the most enchanting place that could be imagined, and full of treasures. Often she would say to the princess, when showing her some wonderful thing: 'This will do for a wedding gift some day.' And Celandine could not help thinking that it was to her that the fairy meant to give the two blue wax-torches which burned without ever getting smaller, or the diamond from which more diamonds were continually growing, or the boat that sailed under water, or whatever beautiful or wonderful thing they might happen to be looking at. It is true that

she never said so positively, but she certainly allowed the princess to believe it, because she thought a little disappointment would be good for her. But the person she really relied upon for curing Celandine of her vanity was Prince Featherhead. The old fairy was not at all pleased with the way he had been going on for some time, but her heart was so soft towards him that she was unwilling to take him away from the pleasures he loved, except by offering him something better, which is not the most effectual mode of correction, though it is without doubt the most agreeable.

However, she did not even hint to the princess that Featherhead was anything but absolutely perfect, and talked of him so much that when at last she announced that he was coming to visit her, Celandine made up her mind that this delightful prince would be certain to fall in love with her at once, and was quite pleased at the idea. The old fairy thought so too, but as this was not at all what she wished, she took care to throw such an enchantment over the princess that she appeared to Featherhead quite ugly and awkward, though to everyone else she looked just as usual. So when he arrived at the leafy palace, more handsome and fascinating even than ever she had been led to expect, he hardly so much as glanced at the princess, but bestowed all his attention upon the old fairy, to whom he seemed to have a hundred things to say. The princess was immensely astonished at his indifference, and put on a cold and offended air, which, however, he did not seem to observe. Then as a last resource she exerted all her wit and gaiety to amuse him, but with no better success, for he was of an age to be more attracted by beauty than by anything else, and though he responded politely enough, it was evident that his thoughts were elsewhere. Celandine was deeply mortified, since for her part the prince pleased her very well, and for the first time she bitterly regretted the fairy gifts she had been anxious to get rid of. Prince Featherhead was almost equally puzzled, for he had heard nothing from the king and queen but the praises of this charming princess, and the fact that they had spoken of her as so very beautiful only confirmed his opinion that people who live in the country have no taste. He talked to them of his charming acquaintances in the town, the beauties he had admired, did admire, or thought he was going to admire, until Celandine, who heard it all, was ready to cry with vexation. The fairy too was quite shocked at his conceit, and hit upon a plan for curing him of it. She sent to him by an unknown messenger a portrait of Princess Celandine as she really was, with this inscription: 'All this beauty and sweetness, with a loving heart and a great kingdom, might have been yours but for your well-known fickleness.'

This message made a great impression upon the prince, but not so much as the portrait. He positively could not tear his eyes away from it, and exclaimed aloud that never, never had he seen anything so lovely and so graceful. Then he began to think that it was too absurd that he, the fascinating Featherhead, should fall in love with a portrait; and, to drive away the recollections of its haunting eyes, he rushed back to the town; but somehow everything seemed changed. The beauties no longer pleased him, their witty speeches had ceased to amuse; and indeed, for their parts, they found the prince far less amiable than of yore, and were not sorry when he declared that, after all, a country life suited him best, and went back to the leafy palace. Meanwhile, the

Princess Celandine had been finding the time pass but slowly with the king and queen, and was only too pleased when Featherhead reappeared. She at once noticed the change in him, and was deeply curious to find the reason of it. Far from avoiding her, he now sought her company and seemed to take pleasure in talking to her, and yet the princess did not for a moment flatter herself with the idea that he was in love with her, though it did not take her long to decide that he certainly loved someone. But one day the princess, wandering sadly by the river, spied Prince Featherhead fast asleep in the shade of a tree, and stole nearer to enjoy the delight of gazing at his dear face unobserved. Judge of her astonishment when she saw that he was holding in his hand a portrait of herself! In vain did she puzzle over the apparent contradictoriness of his behaviour. Why did he cherish her portrait while he was so fatally indifferent to herself? At last she found an opportunity of asking him the name of the princess whose picture he carried about with him always.

'Alas! how can I tell you?' replied he. 'Why should

you not?' said the princess timidly. 'Surely there is nothing to prevent you.'

'Nothing to prevent me!' repeated he, 'when my utmost efforts have failed to discover the lovely original. Should I be so sad if I could but find her? But I do not even know her name.'

More surprised than ever, the princess asked to be allowed to see the portrait, and after examining it for a few minutes returned it, remarking shyly that at least the original had every cause to be satisfied with it.

'That means that you consider it flattering,' said the prince severely. 'Really, Celandine, I thought better of you, and should have expected you to be above such contemptible jealousy. But all women are alike!'

'Indeed, I meant only that it was a good likeness,' said the princess meekly.

'Then you know the original,' cried the prince, throwing himself on his knees beside her. 'Pray tell me at once who it is, and don't keep me in suspense!'

'Oh! don't you see that it is meant for me?' cried Celandine.

The prince sprang to his feet, hardly able to refrain from telling her that she must be blinded by vanity to suppose she resembled the lovely portrait even in the slightest degree; and after gazing at her for an instant with icy surprise, turned and left her without another word, and in a few hours quitted the leafy palace altogether.

Now the princess was indeed unhappy, and could no longer bear to stay in a place where she had been so cruelly disdained. So, without even bidding farewell to the king and queen, she left the valley behind her, and wandered sadly away, not caring whither. After walking until she was weary, she saw before her a tiny house, and turned her slow steps towards it. The nearer she approached the more miserable it appeared, and at length she saw a little old woman sitting upon the doorstep, who said grimly: 'Here comes one of these fine beggars who are too idle to do anything but run about the country!'

'Alas! madam,' said Celandine, with tears in her pretty eyes, 'a sad fate forces me to ask you for shelter.'

'Didn't I tell you what it would be?' growled the old hag. 'From shelter we shall proceed to supper, and from supper money to take us on our way. Upon my word, if I could be sure of finding some-one every day whose head was as soft as his heart,

I wouldn't wish for a more agreeable life myself! But I have worked hard to build my house and secure a morsel to eat, and I suppose you think that I am to give away everything to the first passer-by who chooses to ask for it. Not at all! I wager that a fine lady like you has more money than I have. I must search her, and see if it is not so,' she added, hobbling towards Celandine with the aid of her stick.

'Alas! madam,' replied the princess, 'I only wish I had. I would give it to you with all the pleasure in life.'

'But you are very smartly dressed for the kind of life you lead,' continued the old woman.

'What!' cried the princess, 'do you think I am come to beg of you?'

'I don't know about that,' answered she; 'but at any rate you don't seem to have come to bring me anything. But what is it that you do want? Shelter? Well, that does not cost much; but after that comes supper, and that I can't hear of. Oh dear no! Why, at your age one is always ready to eat; and now you have been walking, and I suppose you are ravenous?'

'Indeed no, madam,' answered the poor princess, 'I am too sad to be hungry.'

'Oh, well! if you will promise to go on being sad, you may stay for the night,' said the old woman mockingly.

Thereupon she made the princess sit down beside her, and began fingering her silken robe, while she muttered, 'Lace on top, lace underneath! This must have cost you a pretty penny! It would have been better to save enough to feed yourself, and not come begging to those who want all they have for themselves. Pray, what may you have paid for these fine clothes?'

'Alas! madam,' answered the princess, 'I did not buy them, and I know nothing about money.'

'What do you know, if I may ask?' said the old dame.

'Not much; but indeed I am very unhappy,' cried Celandine, bursting into tears, 'and if my services are any good to you –'

'Services!' interrupted the hag crossly. 'One has to pay for services, and I am not above doing my own work.'

'Madam, I will serve you for nothing,' said the poor princess, whose spirits were sinking lower and lower. 'I will do anything you please; all I wish is to live quietly in this lonely spot.'

'Oh! I know you are only trying to take me in,'

'Lace on top, lace underneath! This must have cost you a pretty penny!'

answered she; 'and if I do let you serve me, is it fitting that you should be so much better dressed than I am? If I keep you, will you give me your clothes and wear some that I will provide you with? It is true that I am getting old and may want someone to take care of me someday.'

'Oh! for pity's sake, do what you please with my clothes,' cried poor Celandine miserably.

And the old woman hobbled off with great alacrity, and fetched a little bundle containing a wretched dress, such as the princess had never even seen before, and nimbly skipped round, helping her to put it on instead of her own rich robe, with many exclamations of: 'Saints! – what a magnificent lining! And the width of it! It will make me four dresses at least. Why, child, I wonder you could walk under such a weight, and certainly in my house you would not have had room to turn round.'

So saying, she folded up the robe, and put it by with great care, while she remarked to Celandine:

'That dress of mine certainly suits you to a marvel; be sure you take great care of it.'

When supper-time came she went into the house, declining all the princess's offers of assistance, and shortly afterwards brought out a very small dish, saying: 'Now let us sup.'

Whereupon she handed Celandine a small piece of black bread and uncovered the dish, which contained two dried plums.

'We will have one between us,' continued the old dame; 'and as you are the visitor, you shall have the half which contains the stone; but be very careful that you don't swallow it, for I keep them against the winter, and you have no idea what a good fire they make. Now, you take my advice – which won't cost you anything – and remember that it is always more economical to buy fruit with stones on this account.'

Celandine, absorbed in her own sad thoughts, did not even hear this prudent counsel, and quite forgot to eat her share of the plum, which delighted the old woman, who put it by carefully for her breakfast, saying: 'I am very much pleased with you, and if you go on as you have begun, we shall do very well, and I can teach you many useful things which people don't generally know. For instance, look at my house! It is built entirely of the seeds of all the pears I have eaten in my life. Now, most people throw them away, and that only shows what a number of things are wasted for want of a little patience and ingenuity.'

But Celandine did not find it possible to be interested in this and similar pieces of advice. And the old woman soon sent her to bed, for fear the night air might give her an appetite. She passed a sleepless night; but in the morning the old dame remarked: 'I heard how well you slept. After such a night you cannot want any breakfast; so while I do my household tasks you had better stay in bed, since the more one sleeps the less one need eat; and as it is market-day I will go to town and buy a pennyworth of bread for the week's eating.'

And so she chattered on, but poor Celandine did not hear or heed her; she wandered out into the desolate country to think over her sad fate. However, the good Fairy of the Beech-Woods did not want her to be starved, so she sent her unlooked-for relief in the shape of a beautiful white cow, which followed her back to the tiny house. When the old woman saw it her joy knew no bounds.

'Now we can have milk and cheese and butter!' cried she. 'Ah! how good milk is! What a pity it is so ruinously expensive!' So they made a little shelter of branches for the beautiful creature, which was quite gentle, and followed Celandine about like a dog when she took it out every day to graze. One morning as she sat by a little brook, thinking sadly, she suddenly saw a young stranger approaching, and got up quickly, intending to avoid him. But Prince Featherhead, for it was he, perceiving her at the same moment, rushed towards her with every

demonstration of joy: for he had recognised her, not as the Celandine whom he had slighted, but as the lovely princess whom he had sought vainly for so long. The fact was that the Fairy of the Beech-Woods, thinking she had been punished enough, had withdrawn the enchantment from her, and transferred it to Featherhead, thereby in an instant depriving him of the good looks which had done so much towards making him the fickle creature he was. Throwing himself down at the princess's feet, he implored her to stay, and at least speak to him, and she at last consented, but only because he seemed to wish it so very much. After that he came every day in the hope of meeting her again, and often expressed his delight at being with her. But one day, when he had been begging Celandine to love him, she confided to him that it was quite impossible, since her heart was already entirely occupied by another.

'I have,' said she, 'the unhappiness of loving a prince who is fickle, frivolous, proud and incapable of caring for anyone but himself, who has been spoilt by flattery, and, to crown all, who does not love me.'

'But,' cried Prince Featherhead, 'surely you cannot care for so contemptible and worthless a creature as that.'

'Alas! but I do care,' answered the princess, weeping.

'But where can his eyes be,' said the prince, 'that your beauty makes no impression upon him? As for me, since I have possessed your portrait I have wandered over the whole world to find you, and, now we have met, I see that you are ten times lovelier than I could have imagined, and I would give all I own to win your love.'

'My portrait?' cried Celandine with sudden interest. 'Is it possible that Prince Featherhead can have parted with it?'

'He would part with his life sooner, lovely

princess,' answered he; 'I can assure you of that, for I am Prince Featherhead.'

At the same moment the Fairy of the Beech-Woods took away the enchantment, and the happy princess recognised her lover, now truly hers, for the trials they had both undergone had so changed and improved them that they were capable of a real love for each other. You may imagine how perfectly happy they were, and how much they had to hear and to tell. But at length it was time to go back to the little house, and as they went along Celandine remembered for the first time what a ragged old dress she was wearing, and what an odd appearance she must present. But the prince declared that it became her vastly, and that he thought it most picturesque. When they reached the house the old woman received them very crossly.

'I declare,' said she, 'that it's perfectly true: wherever there is a girl you may be sure that a young man will appear before long! But don't imagine that I'm going to have you here – not a bit of it, be off with you, my fine fellow!'

Prince Featherhead was inclined to be angry at this uncivil reception, but he was really too happy to care much, so he only demanded, on Celandine's behalf, that the old dame should give her back her own attire, that she might go away suitably dressed.

This request roused her to fury, since she had counted upon the princess's fine robes to clothe her for the rest of her life, so that it was some time before the prince could make himself heard to explain that he was willing to pay for them. The sight of a handful of gold pieces somewhat mollified her, however, and after making them both promise faithfully that on no consideration would they ask for the gold back again, she took the princess into the house and grudgingly doled out to her just enough of her gay attire to make her presentable, while the rest she pretended to have lost. After this they found that they were very hungry, for one cannot live on love, any more than on air, and then the old woman's lamentations were louder than before. 'What!' she cried, 'feed people who were as happy as all that! Why, it was simply ruinous!'

But as the prince began to look angry, she, with many sighs and mutterings, brought out a morsel of bread, a bowl of milk and six plums, with which the lovers were well content: for as long as they could look at one another they really did not know what they were eating. It seemed as if they would go on for ever with their reminiscences, the prince telling how he had wandered all over the world from beauty to beauty, always to be disappointed when he found that no one resembled the portrait; the princess wondering how it was he could have been so long with her and yet never have recognised her, and over and over again pardoning him for his cold and haughty behaviour to her.

'For,' she said, 'you see, Featherhead, I love you, and love makes everything right! But we cannot stay here,' she added; 'what are we to do?'

The prince thought they had better find their way to the Fairy of the Beech-Woods and put themselves once more under her protection, and they had hardly agreed upon this course when two little chariots wreathed with jasmine and honeysuckle suddenly appeared, and, stepping into them, they were whirled away to the leafy palace. Just before they lost sight of the little house they heard loud cries and lamentations from the miserly old dame, and, looking round, perceived that the beautiful cow was vanishing in spite of her frantic efforts to hold it fast. And they afterwards heard that she spent the rest of her life in trying to put the handful of gold the prince had thrown to her into her money-bag. For the fairy, as a punishment for her avarice, caused it to slip out again as fast as she dropped it in.

The Fairy of the Beech-Woods ran to welcome the prince and princess with open arms, only too delighted to find them so much improved that she could, with a clear conscience, begin to spoil them again. Very soon the Fairy Saradine also arrived, bringing the king and queen with her. Princess Celandine implored her pardon, which she graciously gave; indeed the princess was so charming she could refuse her nothing. She also restored to her the Summer Islands, and promised her protection in all things. The Fairy of the Beech-Woods then informed the king and queen that their subjects had chased King Bruin from the throne, and were waiting to welcome them back again; but they at once abdicated in favour of Prince Featherhead, declaring that nothing could induce them to forsake their peaceful life, and the fairies undertook to see the prince and princess established in their beautiful kingdoms. Their marriage took place the next day, and they lived happily ever afterwards, for Celandine was never vain and Featherhead was never fickle any more.

Prince Ring

Once upon a time there was a king and his queen in their kingdom. They had one daughter, who was called Ingiborg, and one son, whose name was Ring. He was less fond of adventures than men of rank usually were in those days, and was not famous for strength or feats of arms. When he was twelve years old, one fine winter day he rode into the forest along with his men to enjoy himself. They went on a long way, until they caught sight of a hind with a gold ring on its horns. The prince was eager to catch it, if possible, so they gave chase and rode on without stopping until all the horses began to founder beneath them. At last the prince's horse gave way too, and then there came over them a darkness so black that they could no longer see the hind. By this time they were far away from any house, and thought it was high time to be making their way home again, but they found they had got lost now. At first they all kept together, but soon each began to think that he knew the right way best; so they separated, and all went in different directions.

The prince, too, had got lost like the rest, and wandered on for a time until he came to a little clearing in the forest, not far from the sea, where he saw a woman sitting on a chair and a big barrel standing beside her. The prince went up to her and saluted her politely, and she received him very graciously. He looked down into the barrel then, and saw lying at the bottom an unusually beautiful gold ring, which pleased him so much that he could not take his eyes off it. The woman saw this, and said that he might have it if he would take the trouble to get it; for which the prince thanked her, and said it was at least worth trying. So he leaned over into the barrel, which did not seem very deep, and thought he would easily reach the ring; but the more he stretched down after it the deeper grew the barrel. As he was thus bending down into it the woman suddenly rose up and pushed him in head first, saying that now he could take up his quarters

there. Then she fixed the top on the barrel and threw it out into the sea.

The prince thought himself in a bad plight now, as he felt the barrel floating out from the land and tossing about on the waves. How many days he spent thus he could not tell, but at last he felt

that the barrel was knocking against rocks, at which he was a little cheered, thinking it was probably land and not merely a reef in the sea. Being something of a swimmer, he at last made up his mind to kick the bottom out of the barrel, and having done so he was able to get on shore, for the rocks by the sea were smooth and level; but overhead there were high cliffs. It seemed difficult to get up these, but he went along the foot of them for a little, making frequent efforts to climb up, and at last he succeeded.

Having got to the top, he looked round about him and saw that he was on an island, which was

covered with forest, with apples growing, and altogether pleasant as far as the land was concerned. After he had been there several days, he one day heard a great noise in the forest, which made him terribly afraid, so that he ran to hide himself among the trees. Then he saw a giant approaching, dragging a sledge loaded with wood, and making straight for him, so that he could see nothing for it but to lie down just where he was. When the giant came across him, he stood still and looked at the prince for a little; then he took him up in his arms and carried him home to his house, and was exceedingly kind to him. He gave him to his wife, saying he had found this child in the wood, and she could have him to help her in the house. The old woman was greatly pleased, and began to fondle the prince with the utmost delight. He stayed there with them, and was very willing and obedient to them in everything, while they grew kinder to him every day.

One day the giant took him round and showed him all his rooms except the parlour; this made the prince curious to have a look into it, thinking there must be some very rare treasure there. So one day, when the giant had gone into the forest, he tried to get into the parlour, and managed to get the door open halfway. Then he saw that some living creature moved inside and ran along the floor towards him and said something, which made him so frightened that he sprang back from the door and shut it again. As soon as the fright began to pass off he tried it again, for he thought it would be interesting to hear what it said; but things went just as before with him. He then got angry with himself, and, summoning up all his courage, tried it a third time, and opened the door of the room and stood firm. Then he saw that it was a big dog, which spoke to him and said: 'Choose me, Prince Ring.'

The prince went away rather afraid, thinking to himself that it was no great treasure after all; but all the same what it had said to him stuck in his mind.

It is not said how long the prince stayed with the giant, but one day the latter came to him and said he would now take him over to the mainland out of the island, for he himself had no long time to live. He also thanked him for his good service, and told him to choose some one of his possessions, for he would get whatever he wanted. Ring thanked him heartily, and said there was no need to pay him for his services, they were so little worth; but if he did wish to give him anything, he would choose what was in the parlour. The giant was taken by surprise,

and said: 'There, you chose my old woman's right hand; but I must not break my word.'

Upon this he went to get the dog, which came running with signs of great delight; but the prince was so much afraid of it that it was all he could do to keep from showing his alarm.

After this the giant accompanied him down to the sea, where he saw a stone boat which was just big enough to hold the two of them and the dog. On reaching the mainland the giant took a friendly farewell of Ring, and told him he might take possession of all that was in the island after he and his wife died, which would happen within two weeks from that time. The prince thanked him for this and for all his other kindnesses, and the giant returned home, while Ring went up some distance from the sea; but he did not know what land he had come to, and was afraid to speak to the dog. After he had walked on in silence for a time the dog spoke to him and said: 'You don't seem to have much curiosity, seeing you never ask my name.'

The prince then forced himself to ask, 'What is your name?'

'You had best call me Snati-Snati,' said the dog. 'Now we are coming to a king's seat, and you must ask the king to keep us all winter, and to give you a little room for both of us.'

The prince now began to be less afraid of the dog. They came to the king and asked him to keep them all the winter, to which he agreed. When the king's men saw the dog they began to laugh at it, and make as if they would tease it; but when the prince saw this he advised them not to do it, or they might have the worst of it. They replied that they didn't care a bit what he thought.

After Ring had been with the king for some days the latter began to think there was a great deal in him, and esteemed him more than the others. The king, however, had a counsellor called Red, who became very jealous when he saw how much the king esteemed Ring; and one day he talked to him, and said he could not understand why he had so good an opinion of this stranger, who had not yet shown himself superior to other men in anything. The king replied that it was only a short time since he had come there. Red then asked him to send them both to cut down wood next morning, and see which of them could do most work. Snati-Snati heard this and told it to Ring, advising him to ask the king for two axes, so that he might have one in reserve if the first one got broken. Next morning the king asked Ring and Red to go and cut down trees for him, and both agreed. Ring got the two axes, and each went his own way; but when the prince had got out into the wood Snati took one of the axes and began to hew along with him. In the evening the king came to look over their day's work, as Red had proposed, and found that Ring's wood-heap was more than twice as big.

'I suspected,' said the king, 'that Ring was not quite useless; never have I seen such a day's work.'

Ring was now in far greater esteem with the king than before, and Red was all the more discontented. One day he came to the king and said, 'If Ring is such a mighty man, I think you might ask him to kill the wild oxen in the wood here, and flay them the same day, and bring you the horns and the hides in the evening.'

'Don't you think that a desperate errand?' said the king, 'seeing they are so dangerous, and no one has ever yet ventured to go against them?'

Red answered that he had only one life to lose, and it would be interesting to see how brave he was; besides, the king would have good reason to ennoble him if he overcame them. The king at last allowed himself, though rather unwillingly, to be won over by Red's persistency, and one day asked Ring to go and kill the oxen that were in the wood for him, and bring their horns and hides to him in the evening. Not knowing how dangerous the oxen were, Ring was quite ready, and went off at once, to the great delight of Red, who was now sure of his death.

As soon as Ring came in sight of the oxen they came bellowing to meet him; one of them was tremendously big, the other rather less. Ring grew terribly afraid.

'How do you like them?' asked Snati.

'Not well at all,' said the prince.

'We can do nothing else,' said Snati, 'than attack them, if it is to go well; you will go against the little one, and I shall take the other.'

With this Snati leapt at the big one, and was not long in bringing him down. Meanwhile the prince went against the other with fear and trembling, and by the time Snati came to help him the ox had nearly got him under, but Snati was not slow in helping his master to kill it.

Each of them then began to flay their own ox, but Ring was only half through by the time Snati had finished his. In the evening, after they had finished this task, the prince thought himself unfit to carry all the horns and both the hides, so Snati told him to lay them all on his back until they got to the palace gate.

The prince agreed, and laid everything on the dog except the skin of the smaller ox, which he staggered along with himself. At the palace gate he left everything lying, went before the king, and asked him to come that length with him, and there handed over to him the hides and horns of the oxen. The king was greatly surprised at his valour, and said he knew no one like him, and thanked him heartily for what he had done.

After this the king set Ring next to himself, and all esteemed him highly, and held him to be a great hero; nor could Red any longer say anything against him, though he grew still more determined to destroy him. One day a good idea came into his head. He came to the king and said he had something to say to him.

'What is that?' said the king.

Red said that he had just remembered the gold cloak, gold chessboard and bright gold piece that the king had lost about a year before.

'Don't remind me of them!' said the king.

Red, however, went on to say that, since Ring was such a mighty man that he could do everything, it had occurred to him to advise the king to ask him to search for these treasures, and come back with them before Christmas; in return the king should promise him his daughter.

The king replied that he thought it altogether unbecoming to propose such a thing to Ring, seeing that he could not tell him where the things were; but Red pretended not to hear the king's excuses, and went on talking about it until the king gave in to him. One day, a month or so before Christmas, the king spoke to Ring, saying that he wished to ask a great favour of him.

'What is that?' said Ring.

'It is this,' said the king: 'that you find for me my gold cloak, my gold chessboard and my bright gold piece that were stolen from me about a year ago. If you can bring them to me before Christmas I will give you my daughter in marriage.'

'Where am I to look for them, then?' said Ring.

'That you must find out for yourself,' said the king: 'I don't know.'

Ring now left the king, and was very silent, for he saw he was in a great difficulty: but, on the other hand, he thought it was excellent to have such a chance of winning the king's daughter. Snati noticed that his master was at a loss, and said to him that he should not disregard what the king had asked him to do; but he would have to act upon his advice, otherwise he would get into great difficulties. The prince assented to this, and began to prepare for the journey.

After he had taken leave of the king, and was setting out on the search, Snati said to him, 'Now you must first of all go about the neighbourhood, and gather as much salt as ever you can.' The prince did so, and gathered so much salt that he could hardly carry it; but Snati said, 'Throw it on my back,' which he accordingly did, and the dog then ran on before the prince, until they came to the foot of a steep cliff.

'We must go up here,' said Snati.

'I don't think that will be child's play,' said the prince.

'Hold fast by my tail,' said Snati; and in this way he pulled Ring up on to the lowest shelf of the rock. The prince began to get giddy, but up went Snati on to the second shelf. Ring was nearly swooning by this time, but Snati made a third effort and reached the top of the cliff, where the prince fell down in a faint. After a little, however, he recovered again, and they went a short distance along a level plain, until they came to a cave. This was on Christmas Eve. They went up above the cave, and found a window in it, through which they looked, and saw four trolls lying asleep beside the fire, over which a large porridge-pot was hanging.

'Now you must empty all the salt into the porridge-pot,' said Snati.

Ring did so, and soon the trolls wakened up. The old hag, who was the most frightful of them all, went first to taste the porridge.

'How comes this?' she said; 'the porridge is salt! I got the milk by witchcraft yesterday out of four kingdoms, and now it is salt!'

All the others then came to taste the porridge, and thought it nice, but after they had finished it the old hag grew so thirsty that she could stand it no longer, and asked her daughter bring her some water from the river that ran near by.

'I won't go,' said she, 'unless you lend me your bright gold piece.'

'Though I should die you shan't have that,' said the hag.

'Die, then,' said the girl.

'Well, then, take it, you brat,' said the old hag, 'and be off with you, and make haste with the water.'

The girl took the gold and ran out with it, and it was so bright that it shone all over the plain. As soon as she came to the river she lay down to take a drink of the water, but meanwhile the two of them had got down off the roof, and they thrust her, head first, into the river.

The old hag began now to long even more for the water, and said that the girl would be running about with the gold piece all over the plain, so she asked her son to go and get her a drop of water.

'I won't go,' said he, 'unless I get the gold cloak.'

'Though I should die you shan't have that,' said the hag.

'Die, then,' said the son.

'Well, then, take it,' said the old hag, 'and be off with you, but you must make haste with the water.'

He put on the cloak, and when he came outside, it shone so bright that he could see to go with it. On reaching the river he went to take a drink like his sister, but at that moment Ring and Snati sprang upon him, took the cloak from him, and threw him into the river.

The old hag could stand the thirst no longer, and asked her husband to go for a drink for her; the brats, she said, were of course running about and playing thoughtlessly, just as she had expected they would, little wretches that they were.

'I won't go,' said the old troll, 'unless you lend me the gold chessboard.'

'Though I should die you shan't have that,' said the hag.

'I think you may just as well do that,' said he, 'since you won't grant me such a little favour.'

'Take it, then, you utter disgrace!' said the old hag, 'since you are just like those two brats.'

The old troll now went out with the gold chessboard, and down to the river, and was about to take a drink, when Ring and Snati came upon him, took the chessboard from him, and threw him

into the river. Before they had got back again, however, and up on top of the cave, they saw the poor old fellow's ghost come marching up from the river. Snati immediately sprang upon him, and Ring assisted in the attack, and after a hard struggle they mastered him a second time. When they got back again to the window they saw that the old hag was moving towards the door.

'Now we must go in at once,' said Snati, 'and try to master her there, for if she once gets out we shall have no chance with her. She is the worst witch that ever lived, and no iron can cut her. One of us must pour boiling porridge out of the pot on her, and the other punch her with red-hot iron.'

In they went then, and no sooner did the hag see them than she said, 'So you have come, Prince Ring; you must have seen to my husband and children.'

Snati saw that she was about to attack them, and sprang at her with a red-hot iron from the fire, while Ring kept pouring boiling porridge on her without stopping, and in this way they at last got her killed. Then they burned the old troll to ashes, and explored the cave, where they found plenty of gold and treasures. The most valuable of these they carried with them as far as the cliff, and left them there. Then they hastened home to the king with his three treasures, where they arrived late on Christmas night, and Ring handed them over to him.

The king was beside himself with joy, and was astonished at how clever a man Ring was in all kinds of feats, so that he esteemed him still more highly than before, and betrothed his daughter to him; and the feast for this was to last all through Christmastide. Ring thanked the king courteously for this and all his other kindnesses, and as soon as he had finished eating and drinking in the hall went off to sleep in his own room. Snati, however, asked permission to sleep in the prince's bed for that night, while the prince should sleep where the dog usually lay. Ring said he was welcome to do so, and that he deserved more from him than that came to. So Snati went up into the prince's bed, but after a time he came back, and told Ring he could go there himself now, but to take care not to meddle with anything that was in the bed.

Now the story comes back to Red, who came into the hall and showed the king his right arm wanting the hand, and said that now he could see what kind of a man his intended son-in-law was, for he had done this to him without any cause whatever. The king became very angry, and said he would soon find out the truth about it, and if Ring had cut off his hand without good cause he should be hanged; but if it was otherwise, then Red should die. So the king sent for Ring and asked him for what reason he had done this. Snati, however, had just told Ring what had happened during the night, and in reply he asked the king to go with him and he would show him something. The king went with him to his sleeping-room, and saw lying on the bed a man's hand holding a sword.

'This hand,' said Ring, 'came over the partition during the night, and was about to run me through in my bed, if I had not defended myself.'

The king answered that in that case he could not blame him for protecting his own life, and that Red was well worthy of death. So Red was hanged, and Ring married the king's daughter.

The first night that they went to bed together Snati asked Ring to allow him to lie at their feet, and this Ring allowed him to do. During the night he heard a howling and outcry beside them, struck a light in a hurry and saw an ugly dog's skin lying near him, and a beautiful prince at the foot of the bed. Ring instantly took the skin and threw it on the fire in the grate, and then shook the prince, who was lying unconscious, until he woke up. The bridegroom then asked his name; he replied that he was called Ring, and was a king's son. In his youth he had lost his mother, and in her place his father had married a witch, who had laid a spell on him that he should turn into a dog, and never be released from the spell unless a prince of the same name as himself allowed him to sleep at his feet the first night after his marriage. He added further, 'As soon as she knew that you were my namesake she tried to get you destroyed, so that you might not free me from the spell. She was the hind that you and your companions chased; she was the woman that you found in the clearing with the barrel, and the old hag that we just now killed in the cave.'

After the feasting was over the two namesakes, along with other men, went to the cliff and brought all the treasure home to the palace. Then they went to the island and removed all that was valuable from it. Ring gave to his namesake, whom he had freed from the spell, his sister Ingiborg and his father's kingdom to look after, but he himself stayed with his father-in-law the king, and had half the kingdom while he lived and the whole of it after his death.

Princess Belle-Etoile

Once upon a time there were three princesses, named Roussette, Brunette and Blondine, who lived in retirement with their mother, a princess who had lost all her former grandeur. One day an old woman called and asked for a dinner, as this princess was an excellent cook. After the meal was over, the old woman, who was a fairy, promised that their kindness should be rewarded, and immediately disappeared.

Shortly after, the king came that way, with his brother and the lord admiral. They were all so struck with the beauty of the three princesses, that the king married the youngest, Blondine, his brother married Brunette, and the lord admiral married Roussette.

The good fairy, who had brought all this about, also caused the young Queen Blondine to have three lovely children, two boys and a girl, out of whose hair fell fine jewels. Each had a brilliant star on the forehead, and a rich chain of gold around the neck. At the same time Brunette, her sister, gave birth to a handsome boy. Now the young queen and Brunette were much attached to each other, but Roussette was jealous of both, and the old queen, the king's mother, hated them. Brunette died soon after the birth of her son, and the king was absent on a warlike expedition, so Roussette joined the wicked old queen in forming plans to injure Blondine. They ordered Feintise, the old queen's waiting-woman, to strangle the queen's three children and the son of Princess Brunette, and bury them secretly. But as she was about to execute this wicked order, she was so struck by their beauty, and the appearance of the sparkling stars on their foreheads, that she shrank from the deed.

So she had a boat brought round to the beach, and put the four babes, with some strings of jewels, into a cradle, which she placed in the boat, and then set it adrift. The boat was soon far out at sea. The waves rose, the rain poured in torrents, and the thunder roared. Feintise could not doubt that the boat would be swamped, and felt relieved by the thought that the poor little innocents would perish, for she would otherwise always be haunted by the fear that something would occur to betray the share she had had in their preservation.

But the good fairy protected them, and after floating at sea for seven days they were picked up by a corsair. He was so struck by their beauty that he altered his course, and took them home to his wife, who had no children. She was transported with joy when he placed them in her hands. They admired together the wonderful stars, the chains of gold that could not be taken off their necks, and their long ringlets. Much greater was the woman's astonishment when she combed them, for at every instant there rolled out of their hair pearls, rubies, diamonds and emeralds. She told her husband of it, who was not less surprised than herself.

'I am very tired,' said he, 'of a corsair's life, and if the locks of those little children continue to supply us with such treasures, I will give up roaming the seas.' The corsair's wife, whose name was Corsine, was enchanted at this, and loved the four infants so much the more for it. She named the princess, Belle-Etoile, her eldest brother, Petit-Soleil, the second, Heureux, and the son of Brunette, Cheri.

As they grew older, the corsair applied himself seriously to their education, as he felt convinced there was some great mystery attached to their birth.

The corsair and his wife had never told the story of the four children, who passed for their own. They were exceedingly united, but Prince Cheri entertained for Princess Belle-Etoile a greater affection than the other two. The moment she expressed a wish for anything, he would attempt even impossibilities to gratify her.

One day Belle-Etoile overheard the corsair and his wife talking. 'When I fell in with them,' said the corsair, 'I saw nothing that could give me any idea of their birth.' 'I suspect,' said Corsine, 'that Cheri is not their brother, he has neither star nor neck-chain.' Belle-Etoile immediately ran and told this to the three princes, who resolved to speak to the corsair and his wife, and ask them to let them set out to discover the secret of their birth. After some remonstrance they gained their consent. A beautiful vessel was prepared, and the young princess and the three princes set out. They determined to sail to the very spot where the corsair had found them, and made preparations for a grand sacrifice to the fairies, for their protection and guidance. They were about to immolate a turtle-dove, but the princess saved its life, and let it fly. At this moment a syren issued from the water, and said, 'Cease your anxiety, let your vessel go where it will; land where it stops.' The vessel now sailed more quickly. Suddenly they came in sight of a city so beautiful that they were anxious their vessel should enter the port. Their wishes were accomplished; they landed, and the shore in a moment was crowded with people, who had observed the magnificence of their ship. They ran and told the king the news, and as the grand terrace of the palace looked out upon the sea-shore, he speedily repaired thither. The princes, hearing the people say, 'There is the king,' looked up, and made a profound obeisance. He looked earnestly at them, and was as much charmed by the princess's beauty, as by the handsome mien of the young princes. He ordered his equerry to offer them his protection, and everything that they might require.

The king was so intrigued with these four children that he went into the chamber of the queen, his mother, to tell her of the wonderful stars which shone upon their foreheads, and everything that he admired in them. She was thunderstruck at it, and was terribly afraid that Feintise had betrayed her, and sent her secretary to enquire about them. What he told her of their ages confirmed her suspicions. She sent for Feintise, and threatened to kill her. Feintise, half dead with terror, confessed all; but promised, if she spared her, that she would still find means to do away with them. The queen was appeased; and, indeed, old Feintise did all she could for her own sake. Taking a guitar, she went and sat down opposite the princess's window, and sang a song which Belle-Etoile thought so pretty that she invited her into her chamber. 'My fair child,' said Feintise, 'heaven has made you very lovely, but you yet want one thing – the dancing-water. If I had possessed it, you would not have seen a white hair upon my head, nor a wrinkle on my face. Alas! I knew this secret too late; my charms had already faded.' 'But where shall I find this dancing-water?' asked Belle-Etoile. 'It is in the luminous forest,' said Feintise. 'You have three brothers; does not any one of them love you sufficiently to go and fetch some?' 'My brothers all love me,' said the princess, 'but there is one of them who would not refuse me anything.' The perfidious old woman retired, delighted at having been so successful. The princes, returning from the chase, found Belle-Etoile engrossed by the advice of Feintise. Her anxiety about it was so apparent, that Cheri, who thought of nothing but pleasing her, soon found out the cause of it, and, in spite of her entreaties, he mounted his white horse, and set out in search of the dancing-water. When supper-time arrived, and the princess did not see her brother Cheri, she could neither eat nor drink, and desired he might be sought for everywhere, and sent messengers to find him and bring him back.

The wicked Feintise was very anxious to know the result of her advice; and when she heard that Cheri had already set out, she was delighted, and reported to the queen-mother all that had passed. 'I admit, madam,' said she, 'that I can no longer doubt that they are the same four children: but one of the princes is already gone to seek the dancing-water, and will no doubt perish in the attempt, and I shall find similar means to do away with all of them.'

The plan she had adopted with regard to Prince Cheri was one of the most certain, for the dancing-water was not easily to be obtained; it was so notorious from the misfortunes which occurred to all who sought it, that everyone knew the road to it. He was eight days without taking any repose but in the woods. At the end of this period he began to suffer very much from the heat; but it was not the heat of the sun, and he did not know the cause of it, until from the top of a mountain he perceived the luminous forest; all the trees were burning without being consumed, and casting out flames to such a distance that the country around was a dry desert.

Into this terrible scene he descended, and more than once gave himself up for lost. As he approached this great fire he was ready to die with thirst and perceiving a spring falling into a marble basin, he alighted from his horse, approached it, and stooped to take up some water in the little golden vase which he had brought with him, but just then he saw a turtle-dove drowning in the fountain. Cheri took pity on it, and saved it. 'My Lord Cheri,' she said, 'I am not ungrateful; I can guide you to the dancing-water, which, without me, you could never obtain, as it rises in the middle of the forest, and can only be reached by going underground.' The dove then flew away, and summoned a number of foxes, badgers, moles, snails, ants, and all sorts of creatures that burrow in the earth. Cheri got off his horse at the entrance of the subterranean passage they made for him, and groped his way after the kind dove, which safely conducted him to the fountain. The prince filled his golden vase; and returned the same way he came.

He found Belle-Etoile sorrowfully seated under some trees, but when she saw him she was so pleased that she scarcely knew how to welcome him.

Old Feintise learned from her spies that Cheri had returned, and that the princess, having washed her face with the dancing-water, had become more lovely than ever. Finding this, she lost no time in artfully making the princess sigh for the wonderful singing-apple. Prince Cheri again found her unhappy, and again found out the cause, and once more set out on his white horse, leaving a letter for Belle-Etoile.

In the meanwhile, the king did not forget the lovely children, and reproached them for never going to the palace. They excused themselves by saying that their brother's absence prevented them.

Prince Cheri at break of day perceived a handsome young man, from whom he learned where the singing-apple was to be found; but after travelling some time without seeing any sign of it, he saw a poor turtle-dove fall at his feet almost dead. He took pity on it, and restored it, whereupon it said, 'Good-day, handsome Cheri, you are destined to save my life, and I to do you signal service. You are come to seek for the singing-apple but it is guarded by a terrible dragon.' The dove then led him to a place where he found a suit of armour, all of glass, and by her advice he put it on, and boldly went to meet the dragon. The two-headed monster came bounding along, fire issuing from his throat, but when he saw his alarming figure multiplied in the prince's mirrors he was frightened in his turn. He stopped, and looking fiercely at the prince, apparently laden with dragons, he took flight and threw himself into a deep chasm. The prince then found the tree, which was surrounded with human bones, and breaking

off an apple, prepared to return to the princess. She had never slept during his absence, and ran to meet him eagerly.

When the wicked Feintise heard the sweet singing of the apple, her grief was excessive, for instead of doing harm to these lovely children, she only did them good by her perfidious counsels. She allowed some days to pass by without showing herself; and then once more made the princess unhappy by saying that the dancing-water and the singing-apple were useless without the little green bird that tells everything.

Cheri again set out, and after some trouble learnt that this bird was to be found on the top of a frightful rock, in a frozen climate. At length, at dawn of day, he perceived the rock, which was very high and very steep, and upon the summit of it was the bird, speaking like an oracle, telling wonderful things. He thought that with a little dexterity it would be easy to catch it, for it seemed very tame. He got off his horse, and climbed up very quietly. He was so close to the green bird that he thought he could lay hands on it, when suddenly the rock opened and he fell into a spacious hall, and became as motionless as a statue; he could neither stir, nor utter a complaint at his deplorable situation. Three hundred knights, who had made the same attempt, were in the same state. To look at each other was the only thing permitted them.

The time seemed so long to Belle-Etoile, and still no signs of her beloved Cheri, that she fell dangerously ill; and in the hopes of curing her, Petit-Soleil resolved to seek him. But he too was swallowed up by the rock and fell into the great hall. The first person he saw was Cheri, but he could not speak to him; and Prince Heureux, following soon after, met with the same fate as the other two.

When Feintise was aware that the third prince was gone, she was exceedingly delighted at the success of her plan; and when Belle-Etoile, inconsolable at finding not one of her brothers return, reproached herself for their loss, and resolved to follow them, she was quite overjoyed.

The princess was disguised as a cavalier, but had no other armour than her helmet. She was dreadfully cold as she drew near the rock, but seeing a turtle-dove lying on the snow, she took it up, warmed it, and restored it to life: and the dove reviving, gaily said, 'I know you, in spite of your disguise; follow my advice: when you arrive at the rock, remain at the bottom and begin to sing the sweetest song you know; the green bird will listen to you; you must then pretend to go to sleep; when it sees me, it will come down to peck me, and at that moment you will be able to seize it.'

All this fell out as the dove foretold. The green bird begged for liberty. 'First,' said Belle-Etoile, 'I wish that thou wouldst restore my three brothers to me.'

'Under my left wing there is a red feather,' said the bird: 'pull it out, and touch the rock with it.'

The princess hastened to do as she was instructed; the rock split from the top to the bottom and she entered with a victorious air the hall in which stood the three princes with many others; she ran towards Cheri, who did not know her in her helmet and male attire, and could neither speak nor move. The green bird then told

the princess she must rub the eyes and mouths of all those she wished to disenchant with the red feather, which good office she did to all.

The three princes and Belle-Etoile hastened to present themselves to the king; and when Belle-Etoile showed her treasures, the little green bird told him that the Princes Petit-Soleil and Heureux and the Princess Belle-Etoile were his children, and that Prince Cheri was his nephew. Queen Blondine, who had mourned for them all these years, embraced them, and the wicked queen-mother and old Feintise were justly punished. And the king, who thought his nephew Cheri the handsomest man at court, consented to his marriage with Belle-Etoile. And lastly, to make everyone happy, the king sent for the corsair and his wife, who gladly came.

Rapunzel

There were once a man and a woman who had long in vain wished for a child. At length it seemed that God was about to grant their desire.

These people had a little window at the back of their house from which could be seen a splendid garden, which was full of the most beautiful flowers and herbs. It was, however, surrounded by a high wall, and no one dared to go into it because it belonged to an enchantress who had great power and was dreaded by all the world. One day the woman was standing by this window and looking down into the garden, when she saw a bed which was planted with the most beautiful rampion (sometimes called rapunzium), and it looked so fresh and green that she longed for it; she quite pined away, and began to look pale and miserable.

Then her husband was alarmed, and asked: 'What ails you, dear wife?'

'Ah,' she replied, 'if I can't eat some of the rampion which is in the garden behind our house, I shall die.'

The man, who loved her, thought: 'Sooner than let your wife die, bring her some of the rampion yourself, let it cost what it will.'

At twilight, he clambered down over the wall into the garden of the enchantress, hastily clutched a handful of rampion and took it to his wife. She at once made herself a salad of it, and ate it greedily.

He was terribly afraid, for he saw the enchantress standing before him

It tasted so good to her – so very good – that the next day she longed for it three times as much as before. If he was to have any rest, her husband must once more descend into the garden. In the gloom of evening, therefore, he let himself down again; but when he had clambered down the wall he was terribly afraid, for he saw the enchantress standing before him.

'How can you dare,' said she, fixing him with an angry look, 'descend into my garden and steal my rampion like a thief? You shall suffer for it!'

'Ah,' answered he, 'let mercy take the place of justice. I only made up my mind to do it out of necessity. My wife saw your rampion from the window, and felt such a longing for it that she would have died if she had not got some to eat.'

Then the enchantress allowed her anger to be softened, and said to him: 'If the case be as you say, I will allow you to take away with you as much rampion as you will, only I make one condition: you must give me the child which your wife will bring into the world; it shall be well treated, and I will care for it like a mother.'

The man in his terror consented to everything, and when the woman was brought to bed, the enchantress appeared at once, gave the child the name of Rapunzel, and took it away with her.

Rapunzel grew into the most beautiful child under the sun. When she was twelve years old, the enchantress shut her into a tower, which lay in a forest. It had neither stairs nor door, but quite at the top was a little window. When the enchantress wanted to go in, she placed herself beneath it and cried: 'Rapunzel, Rapunzel, let down your hair to me.'

Rapunzel had magnificent long hair, fine as spun gold, and when she heard the voice of the enchantress she unfastened her braided tresses, wound them round one of the hooks of the window above, and let the hair fall twenty metres down, whereupon the enchantress climbed up by it.

After a year or two, it came to pass that the king's son rode through the forest and passed by the tower. Coming from it he heard a song, which was so charming that he stood still and listened. This was Rapunzel, who in her solitude passed her time in letting her sweet voice resound. The king's son wanted to climb up to her, and looked for the door of the tower, but none was to be found. He rode home, but the singing had so deeply touched his heart that every day he went out into the forest and listened to it. Once, when he was thus standing

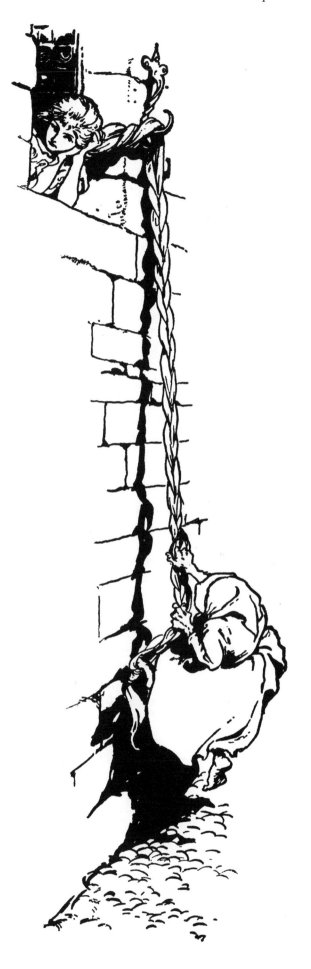

behind a tree, he saw that an enchantress came there, and he heard how she cried: 'Rapunzel, Rapunzel, let down your hair to me.' Then Rapunzel let down the braids of her hair, and the enchantress climbed up to her.

'If that is the ladder by which one mounts, I too will try my fortune,' said he, and the next day when it began to grow dark, he went to the tower and cried: 'Rapunzel, Rapunzel, let down your hair to me.' Immediately the hair fell down and the king's son climbed up.

At first Rapunzel was terribly frightened when a man, such as her eyes had never yet beheld, came to her; but the king's son began to talk to her quite like a friend, and told her that his heart had been so stirred that it had let him have no rest, and he had been determined to see her.

Then Rapunzel lost her fear, and when he asked her if she would take him for her husband, and she saw that he was young and handsome, she did not hesitate; she thought: 'He will love me more than old Dame Gothel does;' and she said yes, and laid her hand in his. She said: 'I will willingly go away with you, but I do not know how to get down. Bring with you a skein of silk every time that you come, and I will weave a ladder with it, and when that is ready I will descend, and you will take me away on your horse.' They agreed that until that time he should come to her every evening, for the old woman came by day.

The enchantress remarked nothing of this, until one day Rapunzel thoughtlessly said to her: 'Tell me, Dame Gothel, how it happens that you are so much heavier for me to draw up than the king's young son – he is with me in a moment.'

'Ah! you wicked child,' cried the enchantress. 'What do I hear you say! I thought I had separated you from all the world, yet you have deceived me!'

In her anger she clutched Rapunzel's beautiful tresses, wrapped them twice round her left hand, seized a pair of scissors with the right, and snip, snap, they were cut off, and the lovely braids lay on the ground. And she was so pitiless that she banished poor Rapunzel to a desert where she had to live in great grief and misery.

On the same day that she cast out Rapunzel, however, the enchantress fastened the braids of hair which she had cut off to the hook of the window, and when the king's son came and cried: 'Rapunzel, Rapunzel, let down your hair to me,' she let the hair down.

The king's son ascended, but instead of finding his dearest Rapunzel, he found the enchantress, who gazed at him with wicked and venomous looks.

'Aha!' she cried mockingly, 'you would fetch your dearest, but the beautiful bird sits no longer singing in the nest; the cat has got it, and will scratch out your eyes as well. Rapunzel is lost to you; you will never see her again.'

The king's son was beside himself with pain, and in his despair he leapt down from the tower. He escaped with his life, but the thorns into which he fell pierced his eyes. Then he wandered quite blind about the forest, ate nothing but roots and berries, and did naught but lament and weep over the loss of his dearest wife. Thus he roamed about in misery for some years, and at length came to the desert where Rapunzel, with the twins to whom she had given birth, a boy and a girl, lived in wretchedness.

He heard a voice, and it seemed so familiar to him that he went towards it, and when he approached, Rapunzel knew him and fell on his neck and wept. Two of her tears wetted his eyes and they grew clear again, and he could see with them as before. He led her to his kingdom, where he was joyfully received, and with their children they lived for a long time afterwards, happy and contented.

The Red Ettin

There was once a widow that lived on a small bit of ground, which she rented from a farmer. And she had two sons; and by and by it was time for the wife to send them away to seek their fortune. So she told her elder son one day to take a can and bring her water from the well, that she might bake a cake for him; and however much or however little water he might bring, the cake would be great or small accordingly, and that cake was to be all that she could give him when he went on his travels.

The lad went away with the can to the well, and filled it with water, and then came away home again; but the can being broken, the most part of the water had run out before he got back. So his cake was very small; yet small as it was, his mother asked him if he was willing to take the half of it with her blessing, telling him that, if he chose rather to take the whole, he would only get it with her curse.

The young man, thinking he might have to travel a far way, and not knowing when or how he might get other provisions, said he would like to have the whole cake, come of his mother's malison what may; so she gave him the whole cake, and her malison along with it. Then he took his brother aside, and gave him a knife to keep till he should come back, desiring him to look at it every morning, and as long as it continued to be clear, then he might be sure that the owner of it was well; but if it grew dim and rusty, then for certain some ill had befallen him.

So the young man went to seek his fortune. And he went all that day, and all the next day; and on the third day, in the afternoon, he came up to where a shepherd was sitting with a flock of sheep. And he went up to the shepherd and asked him who the sheep belonged to; and he answered:

Then he took his brother aside, and gave him a knife to keep till he should come back

'The Red Ettin of Ireland
  Once lived in Ballygan,
And stole King Malcolm's daughter,
  The king of fair Scotland.
He beats her, he binds her,
  He lays her on a band;
And every day he strikes her
  With a bright silver wand.
Like Julian the Roman,
  He's one that fears no man.
It's said there's one predestinate
  To be his mortal foe;
But that man is yet unborn,
  And long may it be so.'

This shepherd also told him to beware of the beasts he should next meet, for they were of a very different kind from any he had yet seen.

So the young man went on, and by and by he saw a multitude of very dreadful beasts, each with two heads, and on every head four horns. And he was sore frightened, and ran away from them as fast as he could; and glad was he when he came to a castle that stood on a hillock, with the door standing wide open to the wall. And he went into the castle for shelter, and there he saw an old wife sitting beside the kitchen fire. He asked the wife if he might stay for the night, as he was tired with a long journey; and the wife said he might, but it was not a good place for him to be in, as it belonged to the Red Ettin, who was a very terrible beast, with three heads, that spared no living man it could get hold of. The young man would have gone away, but he was afraid of the beasts on the outside of the castle; so he beseeched the old woman to hide him as best she could, and not tell the Ettin he was there. He thought, if he could put over the night, he might get away in the morning, without meeting with the beasts, and so escape. But he had not been long in his hiding-hole, before the awful Ettin came in; and no sooner was he in, than he was heard crying:

'Snouk but and snouk ben,
I find the smell of an earthly man,
Be he living, or be he dead,
His heart this night shall kitchen my bread.'

The monster soon found the poor young man, and pulled him from his hole. And when he had got him out, he told him that if he could answer him three questions his life should be spared. So the first head asked: 'A thing without an end, what's that?' But the young man knew not. Then the second head said: 'The smaller, the more dangerous, what's that?' But the young man knew it not. And then the third head asked: 'The dead carrying the living; riddle me that?' But the young man had to give it up. The lad not being able to answer one of these questions, the Red Ettin took a mallet and knocked him on the head, and turned him into a pillar of stone.

On the morning after this happened, the younger brother took out the knife to look at it, and he was grieved to find it all brown with rust. He told his mother that the time was now come for him to go away upon his travels also; so she requested him to take the can to the well for water, that she might make a cake for him. And he went, and as he was bringing home the water, a raven over his head cried to him to look, and he would see that the water was running out. And he was a young man of sense, and seeing the water running out, he took some clay and patched up the holes, so that he brought home enough water to bake a large cake. When his mother put it to him to take the half cake with her blessing, he took it in preference to having the whole with her malison; and yet the half was bigger than what the other lad had got.

So he went away on his journey; and after he had travelled a far way, he met with an old woman that asked him if he would give her a bit of his johnny-cake. And he said: 'I will gladly do that,' and so he gave her a piece of the johnny-cake; and for that she gave him a magical wand, that she might yet be of service to him, if he took care to use it rightly. Then the old woman, who was a fairy, told him a great deal that would happen to him, and what he ought to do in all circumstances; and after that she vanished in an instant out of his sight. He went on a great way farther, and then he came up to the old man herding the sheep; and when he asked whose sheep these were, the answer was:

'The Red Ettin of Ireland
  Once lived in Ballygan,
And stole King Malcolm's daughter,
  The king of fair Scotland.
He beats her, he binds her,
  He lays her on a band;
And every day he strikes her
  With a bright silver wand.
Like Julian the Roman,
  He's one that fears no man.
But now I fear his end is near,
  And destiny at hand;

And you're to be, I plainly see,
The heir of all his land.'

When he came to the place where the monstrous beasts were standing, he did not stop nor run away, but went boldly through among them. One came up roaring with open mouth to devour him, but he struck it with his wand, and laid it in an instant dead at his feet. He soon came to the Ettin's castle, where he knocked, and was admitted. The old woman who sat by the fire warned him of the terrible Ettin, and what had been the fate of his brother; but he was not to be daunted. The monster soon came in, saying:

'Snouk but and snouk ben,
I find the smell of an earthly man;
Be he living, or be he dead,
His heart shall be kitchen to my bread.'

He quickly espied the young man, and bade him come forth on the floor. And then he put the three questions to him; but the young man had been told everything by the good fairy, so he was able to answer all the questions. So when the first head asked, 'What's the thing without an end?' he said: 'A bowl.' And when the second head said:

'The smaller the more dangerous; what's that?' he said at once, 'A bridge.' And last, the third head said: 'When does the dead carry the living, riddle me that?' Then the young man answered up at once and said: 'When a ship sails on the sea with men inside her.' When the Ettin found this, he knew that his power was gone. The young man then took up an axe and hewed off the monster's three heads. He next asked the old woman to show him where the king's daughter lay; and the old woman took him upstairs, and opened a great many doors, and out of every door came a beautiful lady who had been imprisoned there by the Ettin; and one of the ladies was the king's daughter. She also took him down into a low room, and there stood a stone pillar, that he had only to touch with his wand for his brother to start into life. And the whole of the prisoners were overjoyed at their deliverance, for which they thanked the young man. Next day they all set out for the king's court, and a gallant company they made. And the king married his daughter to the young man that had delivered her, and gave a noble's daughter to his brother; and so they all lived happily all the rest of their days.

The Red Shoes

There was once a little girl, very nice and very pretty, but so poor that she had to go barefooted all summer. And in winter she had to wear thick wooden shoes that chafed her ankles until they were red, oh, as red as could be.

In the middle of the village lived Old Mother Shoemaker. She took some old scraps of red cloth and did her best to make them into a little pair of shoes. They were a bit clumsy, but well meant, for she intended to give them to the little girl. Karen was the little girl's name.

The first time Karen wore her new red shoes was on the very day when her mother was buried. Of course, they were not right for mourning, but they were all she had, so she put them on and walked bare-legged after the plain wicker coffin.

Just then a large old carriage came by, with a large old lady inside it. She looked at the little girl and took pity upon her. And she went to the parson and said: 'Give the little girl to me, and I shall take good care of her.'

Karen was sure that this happened because she wore red shoes, but the old lady said the shoes were hideous, and ordered them to be burned. Karen was given proper new clothes. She was taught to read, and she was taught to sew. People said she was pretty, but her mirror told her, 'You are more than pretty. You are beautiful.'

It happened that the queen came travelling through the country with her little daughter, who was a princess. Karen went with all the people who flocked to see them at the castle. The little princess, all dressed in white, came to the window to let them admire her. She didn't wear a train, and she didn't wear a gold crown, but she did wear a pair of splendid red morocco shoes.

Of course, they were much nicer than the ones Old Mother Shoemaker had put together for little Karen, but there's nothing in the world like a pair of red shoes!

When Karen was old enough to be confirmed, new clothes were made for her, and she was to have new shoes. They went to the house of a thriving shoemaker, to have him take the measure of her little feet. In his shop were big glass cases, filled with the prettiest shoes and the shiniest boots. They looked most attractive but, as the old lady did not see very well, they did not attract her. Among the shoes there was a pair of red leather ones which were just like those the princess had worn. How perfect they were! The shoemaker said he had made them for the daughter of a count, but that they did not quite fit her.

'They must be patent leather to shine so,' said the old lady.

'Yes, indeed they shine,' said Karen. As the shoes fitted Karen, the old lady bought them, but she had no idea they were red. If she had known that, she would never have let Karen wear them to her confirmation, which is just what Karen did.

Every eye was turned towards her feet. When she walked up the aisle to the chancel of the church, it seemed to her as if even those portraits of bygone ministers and their wives, in starched ruffs and long black gowns – even they fixed their eyes upon her red shoes. She could think of nothing else, even when the pastor laid his hands upon her head and spoke of her holy baptism, and her covenant with God, and her duty as a Christian. The solemn organ rolled, the children sang sweetly, and

Karen and the old lady took the path through the cornfield to church

the old choir leader sang too, but Karen thought of nothing except her red shoes.

Before the afternoon was over, the old lady had heard from everyone in the parish that the shoes were red. She told Karen it was naughty to wear red shoes to church. Highly improper! In the future she was always to wear black shoes to church, even though they were her old ones.

Next Sunday there was holy communion. Karen looked at her black shoes. She looked at her red ones. She kept looking at her red ones until she put them on.

It was a fair, sunny day. Karen and the old lady took the path through the cornfield, where it was rather dusty. At the church door they met an old soldier, who stood with a crutch and wore a long, curious beard. It was more reddish than white. In fact it was quite red. He bowed down to the ground, and asked the old lady if he might dust her shoes. Karen put out her little foot too.

'Oh, what beautiful shoes for dancing,' the soldier said. 'Never come off when you dance,' he told the shoes, as he tapped the sole of each of them with his hand.

The old lady gave the soldier a penny, and went on into the church with Karen. All the people there stared at Karen's red shoes, and all the portraits stared too. When Karen knelt at the altar rail, and even when the chalice came to her lips, she could think only of her red shoes. It was as if they kept floating around in the chalice, and she forgot to sing the psalm. She forgot to say the lord's prayer.

Then church was over, and the old lady got into her carriage. Karen was lifting her foot to step in after her when the old soldier said, 'Oh, what beautiful shoes for dancing!'

Karen couldn't resist taking a few dancing steps, and once she began her feet kept on dancing. It

was as if the shoes controlled her. She danced round the corner of the church – she simply could not help it. The coachman had to run after her, catch her and lift her into the carriage. But even there her feet went on dancing so that she gave the good old lady a terrible kicking. Only when she took her shoes off did her legs quieten down. When they got home the shoes were put away in a cupboard, but Karen would still go and look at them.

Shortly afterwards the old lady was taken ill, and it was said she could not recover. She required constant care and faithful nursing, and for this she depended on Karen. But a great ball was being given in the town, and Karen was invited. She looked at the old lady, who could not live in any case. She looked at the red shoes, for she thought there was no harm in looking. She put them on, for she thought there was no harm in that either. But

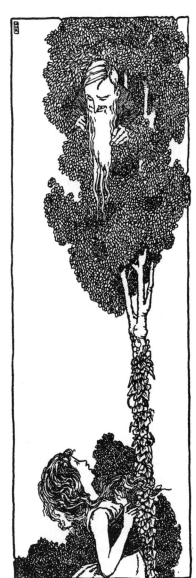

then she went to the ball and began dancing. When she tried to turn to the right, the shoes turned to the left. When she wanted to dance up the ballroom, her shoes danced down. They danced down the stairs, into the street, and out through the gate of the town. Dance she did, and dance she must, straight into the dark woods.

Suddenly something shone through the trees, and she thought it was the moon, but it turned out to be the red-bearded soldier. He nodded and said, 'Oh, what beautiful shoes for dancing.'

She was terribly frightened, and tried to take off her shoes. She tore off her stockings, but the shoes had grown fast to her feet. And dance she did, for dance she must, over fields and valleys, in the rain and in the sun, by day and night. It was most dreadful by night. She danced over an unfenced graveyard, but the dead did not join her dance. They had better things to do. She tried to sit on a pauper's grave, where the bitter fennel grew, but there was no rest or peace for her there. And when she danced towards the open door of the church, she saw it guarded by an angel with long white robes and wings that reached from his shoulders down to the ground. His face was grave and stern, and in his hand he held a broad, shining sword.

'Dance you shall!' he told her. 'Dance in your red shoes until you are pale and cold, and your flesh shrivels down to your skeleton. Dance you shall from door to door, and wherever there are children proud and vain you must knock at the door till they hear you, and are afraid of you. Dance you shall. Dance always.'

'Have mercy upon me!' screamed Karen. But she did not hear the angel answer. Her shoes swept her out through the gate, and across the fields, along highways and byways, forever and always dancing.

One morning she danced by a door she knew well. There was the sound of a hymn, and a coffin was carried out covered with flowers. Then she knew the old lady was dead. She was all alone in the world now, and cursed by the angel of God.

Dance she did and dance she must, through the dark night. Her shoes took her through thorn and briar that scratched her until she bled. She danced across the wastelands until she came to a lonely little house. She knew that this was where the executioner lived, and she tapped with her finger on his window pane.

'Come out!' she called. 'Come out! I can't come in, for I am dancing.'

The executioner said, 'You don't seem to know who I am. I strike off the heads of bad people, and I feel my axe beginning to quiver.'

'Don't strike off my head, for then I could not repent of my sins,' said Karen. 'But strike off my feet with the red shoes on them.'

She confessed her sin, and the executioner struck off her feet with the red shoes on them. The shoes danced away with her little feet, over the fields into the deep forest. But he made wooden feet and a pair of crutches for her. He taught her a hymn that prisoners sing when they are sorry for what they have done. She kissed his hand that held the axe, and went back across the wasteland.

'Now I have suffered enough for those red shoes,' she said. 'I shall go and be seen again in the church.' She hobbled to church as fast as she could, but when she got there the red shoes danced in front of her, and she was frightened and turned back.

All week long she was sorry, and cried many bitter tears. But when Sunday came again she said, 'Now I have suffered and cried enough. I think I must be as good as many who sit in church and hold their heads high.' She started out unafraid, but the moment she came to the church gate she saw her red shoes dancing before her. More frightened than ever, she turned away, and with all her heart she really repented.

She went to the pastor's house, and begged him to give her work as a servant. She promised to work hard, and do all that she could. Wages did not matter, if only she could have a roof over her head and be with good people. The pastor's wife took pity on her, and gave her work at the parsonage. Karen was faithful and serious. She sat quietly in the evening, and listened to every word when the pastor read the Bible aloud. The children were devoted to her, but when they spoke of frills and furbelows, and of being as beautiful as a queen, she would shake her head.

When they went to church next Sunday they asked her to go too, but with tears in her eyes she looked at her crutches, and shook her head. The others went to hear the word of God, but she went to her lonely little room, which was just big enough to hold her bed and one chair. She sat with her hymnal in her hands, and as she read it with a contrite heart she heard the organ roll. The wind carried the sound from the church to her window. Her face was wet with tears as she lifted it up, and said, 'Help me, O Lord!'

Then the sun shone bright, and the white-robed angel stood before her. He was the same angel she had seen that night, at the door of the church. But he no longer held a sharp sword. In his hand was a green branch, covered with roses. He touched the ceiling with it. There was a golden star where it touched and the ceiling rose high. He touched the walls and they opened wide. She saw the deep-toned organ. She saw the portraits of ministers and their wives. She saw the congregation sit in flower-decked pews, and sing from their hymnals. Either

the church had come to the poor girl in her narrow little room or it was she who had been brought to the church. She sat in the pew with the pastor's family. When they had finished the hymn, they looked up and nodded to her.

'It was right for you to come, little Karen,' they said.

'It was God's own mercy,' she told them.

The organ sounded and the children in the choir sang, softly and beautifully. Clear sunlight streamed warm through the window, right down to the pew where Karen sat. She was so filled with the light of it, and with joy and with peace, that her heart broke. Her soul travelled along the shaft of sunlight to heaven, where no one questioned her about the red shoes.

Ricky of the Tuft

Once upon a time there was a queen who bore a son so ugly and misshapen that for some time it was doubtful if he would have human form at all. But a fairy who was present at his birth promised that he should have plenty of brains, and added that by virtue of the gift which she had just bestowed upon him he would be able to impart to the person whom he should love best the same degree of intelligence which he possessed himself.

This somewhat consoled the poor queen, who was greatly disappointed at having brought into the world such a hideous brat. And indeed, no sooner did the child begin to speak than his sayings proved to be full of shrewdness, while all that he did was somehow so clever that he charmed everyone.

I forgot to mention that when he was born he had a little tuft of hair upon his head. For this reason he was called Ricky of the Tuft, Ricky being his family name.

Some seven or eight years later the queen of a neighbouring kingdom gave birth to twin daughters. The first one to come into the world was more beautiful than the dawn, and the queen was so overjoyed that it was feared her great excitement might do her some harm. The same fairy who had assisted at the birth of Ricky of the Tuft was present, and in order to moderate the transports of the queen she declared that this little princess would have no sense at all, and would be as stupid as she was beautiful. The queen was deeply mortified, and a moment or two later her chagrin became greater still, for the second daughter proved to be extremely ugly.

'Do not be distressed, madam,' said the fairy. 'Your daughter shall be recompensed in another way. She shall have so much good sense that her lack of beauty will scarcely be noticed.'

'May heaven grant it!' said the queen. 'But is there no means by which the elder, who is so beautiful, can be endowed with some intelligence?'

'In the matter of brains I can do nothing for her, madam,' said the fairy, 'but as regards beauty I can do a great deal. As there is nothing I would not do to please you, I will bestow upon her the power of making beautiful any person who shall greatly please her.'

As the two princesses grew up their perfections increased, and everywhere the beauty of the elder and the wit of the younger were the subject of common talk.

It is equally true that their defects also increased as they became older. The younger grew uglier every minute, and the elder daily became more stupid. Either she answered nothing at all when spoken to, or replied with some idiotic remark. At the same time she was so awkward that she could not set four china vases on the mantelpiece without breaking one of them, nor drink a glass of water without spilling half of it over her clothes.

Now although the elder girl possessed the great advantage which beauty always confers upon youth, she was nevertheless outshone in almost all company by her younger sister. At first everyone gathered round the beauty to see and admire her, but very soon they were all attracted by the graceful and easy conversation of the clever one. In a very short time the elder girl would be left entirely alone, while everybody clustered round her sister.

The elder princess was not so stupid that she was not aware of this, and she would willingly have surrendered all her beauty for half her sister's cleverness. Sometimes she was ready to die of grief, for the queen, though a sensible woman, could not refrain from occasionally reproaching her for her stupidity.

The princess had retired one day to a wood to bemoan her misfortune, when she saw approaching her an ugly little man, of very disagreeable appearance, but clad in magnificent attire.

This was the young Prince Ricky of the Tuft. He had fallen in love with her portrait, which was everywhere to be seen, and had left his father's kingdom in order to have the pleasure of seeing and talking to her.

Delighted to meet her thus alone, he approached with every mark of respect and politeness. But while he paid her the usual compliments he noticed that she was plunged in melancholy.

'I cannot understand, madam,' he said, 'how anyone with your beauty can be so sad as you appear. I can boast of having seen many fair ladies, and I declare that none of them could compare in beauty with you.'

'It is very kind of you to say so, sir,' answered the princess; and stopped there, at a loss what to say further.

'Beauty,' said Ricky, 'is of such great advantage that everything else can be disregarded; and I do not see that the possessor of it can have anything much to grieve about.'

To this the princess replied, 'I would rather be as plain as you are and have some sense, than be as beautiful as I am and at the same time stupid.'

'Nothing more clearly displays good sense, madam, than a belief that one is not possessed of it. It follows, therefore, that the more one has, the more one fears it to be wanting.'

'I am not sure about that,' said the princess; 'but I know only too well that I am very stupid, and this is the reason of the misery which is nearly killing me.'

'If that is all that troubles you, madam, I can easily put an end to your suffering.'

'How will you manage that?' said the princess.

'I am able, madam,' said Ricky of the Tuft, 'to bestow as much good sense as it is possible to possess on the person whom I love the most. You are that person, and it therefore rests with you to decide whether you will acquire so much intelligence. The only condition is that you shall consent to marry me.'

The princess was dumfounded, and remained silent.

'I can see,' pursued Ricky, 'that this suggestion perplexes you, and I am not surprised. But I will give you a whole year to make up your mind to it.'

The princess had so little sense, and at the same time desired it so ardently, that she persuaded herself the end of this year would never come. So she accepted the offer which had been made to her. No sooner had she given her word to Ricky that she would marry him within one year from that very day, than she felt a complete change come over her. She found herself able to say all that she wished with the greatest ease, and to say it in an elegant, finished and natural manner. She at once engaged Ricky in a brilliant and lengthy conversation, holding her own so well that Ricky feared he had given her a larger share of sense than he had retained for himself.

On her return to the palace amazement reigned throughout the court at such a sudden and extraordinary change. Whereas formerly they had been accustomed to hear her give vent to silly, pert remarks, they now heard her express herself sensibly and very wittily.

The entire court was overjoyed. The only person not too pleased was the younger sister, for now that she had no longer the advantage over the elder in wit, she seemed nothing but a little fright in comparison.

The king himself often took her advice, and several times held his councils in her apartment.

The news of this change spread abroad, and the princes of the neighbouring kingdoms made many attempts to captivate her. Almost all asked her in marriage. But she found none with enough sense, and so she listened to all without promising herself to any.

At last came one who was so powerful, so rich, so witty, and so handsome, that she could not help being somewhat attracted by him. Her father noticed this, and told her she could make her own choice of a husband. She had only to declare herself. Now the more sense one has, the more difficult it is to make up one's mind in an affair of this kind. After thanking her father, therefore, she asked for a little time to think it over. In order to ponder quietly what she had better do she went to walk in a wood – the very one, as it happened, where she had encountered Ricky of the Tuft.

While she walked, deep in thought, she heard beneath her feet a thudding sound, as though many people were running busily to and fro. Listening more attentively she heard voices. 'Bring me that boiler,' said one; then another, 'Put some wood on that fire!'

At that moment the ground opened, and she saw below what appeared to be a large kitchen full of cooks and scullions, and all the train of attendants which the preparation of a great banquet involves. A gang of some twenty or thirty spit-turners emerged and took up their positions round a very long table in a path in the wood. They all wore their cook's caps on one side, and with their basting implements in their hands they kept time together as they worked, to the lilt of a melodious song.

The princess was astonished by this spectacle, and asked for whom their work was being done.

'For Prince Ricky of the Tuft, madam,' said the foreman of the gang. 'His wedding is tomorrow.'

At this the princess was more surprised than ever. In a flash she remembered that it was a year to the very day since she had promised to marry Prince Ricky of the Tuft, and was taken aback by the recollection. The reason she had forgotten was that when she made the promise she was still without sense, and with the acquisition of that intelligence which the prince had bestowed upon her, all memory of her former stupidities had been blotted out.

She had not gone another thirty paces when

They all wore their cook's caps on one side, and with their basting implements in their hands
they kept time together as they worked, to the lilt of a melodious song

Ricky of the Tuft appeared before her, gallant and resplendent, like a prince upon his wedding day.

'As you see, madam,' he said, 'I keep my word to the minute. I do not doubt that you have come to keep yours, and by giving me your hand to make me the happiest of men.'

'I will be frank with you,' replied the princess. 'I have not yet made up my mind on the point, and I am afraid I shall never be able to take the decision you desire.'

'You astonish me, madam,' said Ricky of the Tuft.

'I can well believe it,' said the princess, 'and undoubtedly, if I had to deal with a clown, or a man who lacked good sense, I should feel myself very awkwardly situated. "A princess must keep her word," he would say, "and you must marry me because you promised to!" But I am speaking to a man of the world, of the greatest good sense, and I am sure that he will listen to reason. As you are aware, I could not make up my mind to marry you even when I was entirely without sense; how can you expect that today, possessing the intelligence you bestowed on me, which makes me still more difficult to please than formerly, I should take a decision which I could not take then? If you wished so much to marry me, you were very wrong to relieve me of my stupidity, and to let me see more clearly than I did.'

'If a man who lacked good sense,' replied Ricky of the Tuft, 'would be justified, as you have just said, in reproaching you for breaking your word, why do you expect, madam, that I should act differently where the happiness of my whole life is at stake? Is it reasonable that people who have sense should be treated worse than those who have none? Would you maintain that for a moment – you, who so markedly have sense, and desired so ardently to have it? But, pardon me, let us get to the facts. With the exception of my ugliness, is there anything about me which displeases you? Are you dissatisfied with my breeding, my brains, my disposition, or my manners?'

'In no way,' replied the princess. 'I like exceedingly all that you have displayed of the qualities you mention.'

'In that case,' said Ricky of the Tuft, 'happiness will be mine, for it lies in your power to make me the most attractive of men.'

'How can that be done?' asked the princess.

'It will happen of itself,' replied Ricky of the Tuft, 'if you love me well enough to wish that it be so. To remove your doubts, madam, let me tell you that the same fairy who on the day of my birth bestowed upon me the power of endowing with intelligence the woman of my choice, gave to you also the power of endowing with beauty the man whom you should love, and on whom you should wish to confer this favour.'

'If that is so,' said the princess, 'I wish with all my heart that you may become the handsomest and most attractive prince in the world, and I give you without reserve the boon which it is mine to bestow.'

No sooner had the princess uttered these words than Ricky of the Tuft appeared before her eyes as the handsomest, most graceful and attractive man that she had ever set eyes on.

Some people assert that this was not the work of fairy enchantment, but that love alone brought about the transformation. They say that the princess, as she mused upon her lover's constancy, upon his good sense, and his many admirable qualities of heart and head, grew blind to the deformity of his body and the ugliness of his face; that his humpback seemed no more than was natural in a man who could make the courtliest of bows, and that the dreadful limp which had formerly distressed her now betokened nothing more than a certain diffidence and charming deference of manner. They say further that she found his eyes shine all the brighter for their squint, and that this defect in them was to her but a sign of passionate love; while his great red nose she found naught but martial and heroic.

However that may be, the princess promised to marry him on the spot, provided only that he could obtain the consent of her royal father.

The king knew Ricky of the Tuft to be a prince both wise and witty, and on learning of his daughter's regard for him, he accepted him with pleasure as a son-in-law.

The wedding took place upon the morrow, just as Ricky of the Tuft had foreseen, and in accordance with the arrangements he had long ago put in train.

Moral:
Here's a fairy tale for you,
Which is just as good as true.
What we love is always fair,
Clever, deft and debonair.

Another Moral:
Nature oft, with open arms,
Lavishes a thousand charms;
But it is not these that bring
True love's truest offering.
'Tis some quality that lies
All unseen to other eyes –
Something in the heart or mind.

Rip van Winkle

A Posthumous Writing of Diedrich Knickerbocker

By Woden, God of Saxons,
From whence comes Wednesday, that is Wodensday,
Truth is a thing that ever I will keep
Unto thylke day in which I creep into
My sepulchre.

CARTWRIGHT

The following tale was found among the papers of the late Diedrich Knickerbocker, an old gentleman of New York, who was very curious in the Dutch history of the province and the manners of the descendants from its primitive settlers. His historical researches, however, did not lie so much among books as among men; for the former are lamentably scanty on his favourite topics, whereas he found the old burghers, and still more their wives, rich in that legendary lore so invaluable to true history. Whenever, therefore, he happened upon a genuine Dutch family, snugly shut up in its low-roofed farmhouse under a spreading sycamore, he looked upon it as a little clasped volume of black-letter, and studied it with the zeal of a bookworm.

The result of all these researches was a history of the province during the reign of the Dutch governors, which he published some years since. There have been various opinions as to the literary character of his work, and, to tell the truth, it is not a whit better than it should be. Its chief merit is its scrupulous accuracy, which indeed was a little questioned on its first appearance, but has since been completely established; and it is now admitted into all historical collections as a book of unquestionable authority.

The old gentleman died shortly after the publication of his work, and now that he is dead and gone, it cannot do much harm to his memory to say that his time might have been much better employed in weightier labours. He, however, was apt to ride his hobby his own way; and though it did now and then kick up the dust a little in the eyes of his neighbours, and grieve the spirit of some friends for whom he felt the truest deference and affection, yet his errors and follies are remembered 'more in sorrow than in anger', and it begins to be suspected that he never intended to injure or offend. But, however his memory may be appreciated by critics, it is still held dear by many folk whose good opinion is well worth having; particularly by certain biscuit-bakers, who have gone so far as to imprint his likeness on their new-year cakes, and have thus given him a chance for immortality almost equal to the being stamped on a Waterloo medal or a Queen Anne's farthing.

WHOEVER HAS MADE A VOYAGE UP THE Hudson must remember the Catskill Mountains. They are a dismembered branch of the great Appalachian family, and are seen away to the west of the river, swelling up to a noble height and lording it over the surrounding country. Every change of season, every change of weather, indeed, every hour of the day, produces some change in the magical hues and shapes of these mountains, and they are regarded by all the good wives, far and near, as perfect barometers. When the weather is fair and settled, they are clothed in blue and purple, and print their bold outlines on the clear evening sky; but sometimes, when the rest of the landscape is cloudless, they will gather a hood of grey vapours about their summits, which in the last rays of the setting sun will glow and light up like a crown of glory.

At the foot of these fairy mountains the voyager may have descried the light smoke curling up from a village, whose shingle roofs gleam among the trees just where the blue tints of the upland melt away into the fresh green of the nearer landscape. It is a little village of great antiquity, having been founded by some of the Dutch colonists in the early times of the province, just about the beginning of the government of the good Peter Stuyvesant (may he rest in peace!), and there were some of the houses of the original settlers standing within a few years, built of small yellow bricks brought from Holland, having latticed windows and gable fronts surmounted with weathercocks.

In that same village, and in one of these very houses (which, to tell the precise truth, was sadly timeworn and weather-beaten), there lived many years since, while the country was yet a province of Great Britain, a simple good-natured fellow of the name of Rip van Winkle. He was a descendant of the van Winkles who figured so gallantly in the chivalrous days of Peter Stuyvesant and accompanied him to the siege of Fort Christina. He inherited, however, but little of the martial character of his ancestors. I have observed that he was a simple good-natured man; he was, moreover, a kind neighbour and an obedient henpecked husband. Indeed, to the latter circumstance might be owing that meekness of spirit which gained him such universal popularity; for those men are most apt to be obsequious and conciliating abroad who are under the discipline of shrews at home. Their tempers, doubtless, are rendered pliant and malleable in the fiery furnace of domestic tribulation, and a curtain lecture is worth all the sermons in the world for teaching the virtues of patience and long-suffering. A termagant wife may therefore, in some respects, be considered a tolerable blessing; and if so, Rip van Winkle was thrice blessed.

Certain it is that he was a great favourite among all the good wives of the village, who, as is usual

He made their playthings, taught them to fly kites and shoot marbles

with the amiable sex, took his part in all family squabbles, and never failed, whenever they talked those matters over in their evening gossipings, to lay all the blame on Dame van Winkle. The children of the village, too, would shout with joy whenever he approached. He assisted at their sports, made their playthings, taught them to fly kites and shoot marbles, and told them long stories of ghosts, witches and Indians. Whenever he went dodging about the village he was surrounded by a troop of them, hanging on his skirts, clambering on his back, and playing a thousand tricks on him with impunity; and not a dog would bark at him throughout the neighbourhood.

The great error in Rip's composition was an insuperable aversion to all kinds of profitable labour. It could not be from the want of assiduity or perseverance; for he would sit on a wet rock, with a rod as long and heavy as a Tartar's lance, and fish all day without a murmur, even though he should not be encouraged by a single nibble. He would carry a fowling-piece on his shoulder for hours together, trudging through woods and swamps and up hill and down dale, to shoot a few squirrels or wild pigeons. He would never refuse to assist a neighbour even in the roughest toil, and was a foremost man at all country frolics for husking Indian corn or building stone fences; the women of the village, too, used to employ him to run their errands, and to do such little odd jobs as their less obliging husbands would not do for them. In a word, Rip was ready to attend to anybody's business but his own; but as to doing family duty and keeping his farm in order, he found it impossible.

In fact, he declared it was of no use to work on his farm; it was the most pestilent little piece of ground in the whole country; everything about it went wrong, and would go wrong in spite of him. His fences were continually falling to pieces; his cow would either go astray or get among the cabbages; weeds were sure to grow quicker in his fields than anywhere else; the rain always made a point of setting in just as he had some outdoor work to do; so that, though his patrimonial estate had dwindled away under his management, acre by acre, until there was little more left than a mere patch of Indian corn and potatoes, yet it was the worst conditioned farm in the neighbourhood.

His children, too, were as ragged and wild as if they belonged to nobody. His son Rip, an urchin begotten in his own likeness, promised to inherit the habits with the old clothes of his father. He was generally seen trooping like a colt at his mother's heels, equipped in a pair of his father's cast-off galligaskins, which he had much ado to hold up with one hand, as a fine lady does her train in bad weather.

Rip van Winkle, however, was one of those happy mortals, of foolish, well-oiled dispositions, who take the world easy, eat white bread or brown, whichever can be got with least thought or trouble, and would rather starve on a penny than work for a pound. If left to himself, he would have whistled life away in perfect contentment; but his wife kept continually dinning in his ears about his idleness, his carelessness and the ruin he was bringing on his family. Morning, noon and night her tongue was incessantly going, and everything he said or did was sure to produce a torrent of household eloquence. Rip had but one way of replying to all lectures of the kind, and that, by frequent use, had grown into a habit. He shrugged his shoulders, shook his head, cast up his eyes, but said nothing. This, however, always provoked a fresh volley from his wife; so that he was fain to draw off his forces and take to the outside of the house – the only side which, in truth, belongs to a henpecked husband.

Rip's sole domestic adherent was his dog Wolf, who was as much henpecked as his master; for Dame van Winkle regarded them as companions in idleness, and even looked upon Wolf with an evil eye, as the cause of his master's going so often astray. True it is, in all points of spirit befitting an honourable dog he was as courageous an animal as ever scoured the woods; but what courage can withstand the ever-during and all-besetting terrors of a woman's tongue? The moment Wolf entered the house his crest fell, his tail drooped to the ground or curled between his legs, he sneaked about with a gallows air, casting many a sidelong glance at Dame van Winkle, and at the least flourish of a broomstick or ladle he would fly to the door with yelping precipitation.

Times grew worse and worse with Rip van Winkle as years of matrimony rolled on; a tart temper never mellows with age, and a sharp tongue is the only edged tool that grows keener with constant use. For a long while he used to console himself, when driven from home, by frequenting a kind of perpetual club of the sages, philosophers and other idle personages of the village which held its sessions on a bench before a small inn, designated by a rubicund portrait of His Majesty George III. Here they used to sit in the shade through a long lazy summer's day, talking listlessly over village gossip or telling endless sleepy stories about nothing. But it would have been worth any statesman's money to have heard the profound discussions that sometimes took place when by chance an old newspaper fell into their hands from some passing traveller. How solemnly they would listen to the contents, as drawled out by Derrick van Bummel, the schoolmaster, a dapper learned little man, who was not to be daunted by the most gigantic word in the dictionary, and how sagely they would deliberate upon public events some months after they had taken place!

The opinions of this junto were completely controlled by Nicholas Vedder, a patriarch of the village and landlord of the inn, at the door of which he took his seat from morning till night, just moving sufficiently to avoid the sun and keep in the shade of a large tree; so that the neighbours could tell the hour by his movements as accurately as by a sundial. It is true he was rarely heard to speak, but smoked his pipe incessantly. His adherents, however (for every great man has his adherents), perfectly understood him, and knew how to gather his opinions. When anything that was read or related displeased him, he was observed to smoke his pipe vehemently, and to send forth short, frequent and angry puffs; but when pleased, he would inhale the smoke slowly and tranquilly, and emit it in light and placid clouds; and sometimes, taking the pipe from his mouth and letting the fragrant vapour curl about his nose, would gravely nod his head in token of perfect approbation.

From even this stronghold the unlucky Rip was at length routed by his termagant wife, who would suddenly break in upon the tranquillity of the assemblage and call the members all to naught; nor was that august personage, Nicholas Vedder himself, sacred from the daring tongue of this terrible virago, who charged him outright with encouraging her husband in habits of idleness.

Poor Rip was at last reduced almost to despair, and his only alternative, to escape from the labour of the farm and clamour of his wife, was to take gun in hand and stroll away into the woods. Here he would sometimes seat himself at the foot of a tree, and share the contents of his wallet with Wolf, with whom he sympathised as a fellow-sufferer in persecution. 'Poor Wolf!' he would say, 'thy mistress leads thee a dog's life of it; but never mind, my lad – whilst I live thou shalt never want a friend to stand by thee!' Wolf would wag his tail, look wistfully in his master's face, and, if dogs can feel pity, I verily believe he reciprocated the sentiment with all his heart.

In a long ramble of the kind on a fine autumnal day Rip had unconsciously scrambled to one of the highest parts of the Catskill Mountains. He was after his favourite sport of squirrel-shooting and the still solitudes had echoed and re-echoed with the reports of his gun. Panting and fatigued, he threw himself, late in the afternoon, on a green knoll covered with mountain-herbage that crowned the brow of a precipice. From an opening between the trees he could overlook all the lower country for many a mile of rich woodland. He saw at a distance the lordly Hudson, far, far below him, moving on its silent but majestic course, with the reflection of a purple cloud or the sail of a lagging bark here and there sleeping on its glassy bosom, and at last losing itself in the blue highlands.

On the other side he looked down into a deep mountain-glen, wild, lonely and shagged, the bottom filled with fragments from the impending cliffs, and scarcely lighted by the reflected rays of the setting sun. For some time Rip lay musing on this scene; evening was gradually advancing; the mountains began to throw their long blue shadows over the valleys; he saw that it would be dark long before he could reach the village, and he heaved a heavy sigh when he thought of encountering the terrors of Dame van Winkle.

As he was about to descend he heard a voice from a distance hallooing, 'Rip van Winkle! Rip van Winkle!' He looked round, but could see nothing but a crow winging its solitary flight across the mountain. He thought his fancy must have deceived him, and turned again to descend, when he heard the same cry ring through the still evening air: 'Rip van Winkle! Rip van Winkle!' – at the same time Wolf bristled up his back, and giving a low growl, skulked to his master's side, looking fearfully down into the glen. Rip now felt a vague apprehension stealing over him; he looked anxiously in the same direction, and perceived a strange figure slowly toiling up the rocks and bending under the weight of something he carried on his back. He was surprised to see any human being in this lonely and unfrequented place, but supposing it to be some one of the neighbourhood in need of his assistance, he hastened down to yield it.

On nearer approach he was still more surprised

at the singularity of the stranger's appearance. He was a short, square-built old fellow, with thick bushy hair and a grizzled beard. His dress was of the antique Dutch fashion – a cloth jerkin strapped round the waist – several pairs of breeches, the outer one of ample volume, decorated with rows of buttons down the sides, and bunches at the knees. He bore on his shoulder a stout keg that seemed full of liquor, and made signs for Rip to approach and assist him with the load. Though rather shy and distrustful of this new acquaintance, Rip complied with his usual alacrity; and, mutually relieving each other, they clambered up a narrow gully, apparently the dry bed of a mountain-torrent. As they ascended, Rip every now and then heard long rolling peals, like distant thunder, that seemed to issue out of a deep ravine, or rather cleft, between lofty rocks, towards which their rugged path conducted. He paused for an instant, but supposing it to be the muttering of one of those transient thunder-showers which often take place in mountain-heights, he proceeded. Passing through the ravine, they came to a hollow, like a small amphitheatre, surrounded by perpendicular precipices, over the brinks of which impending trees shot their branches, so that you only caught glimpses of the azure sky and the bright evening cloud. During the whole time Rip and his companion had laboured on in silence; for though the former marvelled greatly what could be the object of carrying a keg of liquor up this wild mountain, yet there was something strange and incomprehensible about the unknown that inspired awe and checked familiarity.

On entering the amphitheatre, new objects of wonder presented themselves. On a level spot in the centre was a company of odd-looking personages playing at ninepins. They were dressed in a quaint outlandish fashion: some wore short doublets, others jerkins, with long knives in their belts, and most of them had enormous breeches, of similar style with that of the guide's. Their visages, too, were peculiar: one had a large head, broad face, and small piggish eyes; the face of another seemed to consist entirely of nose, and was surmounted by a white sugar-loaf hat, set off with a little red cock's tail. They all had beards, of various shapes and colours. There was one who seemed to be the commander. He was a stout old gentleman, with a weather-beaten countenance; he wore a laced doublet, broad belt and hanger, high-crowned hat and feather, red stockings and high-heeled shoes

with roses in them. The whole group reminded Rip of the figures in an old Flemish painting in the parlour of Dominie van Shaick, the village parson, which had been brought over from Holland at the time of the settlement.

What seemed particularly odd to Rip was that though these folks were evidently amusing themselves, yet they maintained the gravest faces, the most mysterious silence, and were, withal, the most melancholy party of pleasure he had ever witnessed. Nothing interrupted the stillness of the scene but the noise of the balls, which, whenever they were rolled, echoed along the mountains like rumbling peals of thunder.

As Rip and his companion approached them they suddenly desisted from their play, and stared at him with such fixed statue-like gaze, and such strange, uncouth, lacklustre countenances, that his heart turned within him and his knees smote together. His companion now emptied the contents of the keg into large flagons, and made signs to him to wait upon the company. He obeyed with fear and trembling; they quaffed the liquor in profound silence, and then returned to their game.

By degrees Rip's awe and apprehension subsided. He even ventured, when no eye was fixed upon him, to taste the beverage, which he found had much of the flavour of excellent Hollands. He was naturally a thirsty soul, and was soon tempted to repeat the draught. One taste provoked another, and he reiterated his visits to the flagon so often that at length his senses were over–powered, his eyes swam in his head, his head gradually declined, and he fell into a deep sleep.

On waking he found himself on the green knoll whence he had first seen the old man of the glen. He rubbed his eyes – it was a bright sunny morning. The birds were hopping and twittering among the bushes, and the eagle was wheeling aloft and breasting the pure mountain-breeze. 'Surely,' thought Rip, 'I have not slept here all night.' He recalled the occurrences before he fell asleep. The strange man with a keg of liquor – the mountain ravine – the wild retreat among the rocks – the woe-begone party at ninepins – the flagon. 'Oh, that flagon! that wicked flagon!' thought Rip – 'what excuse shall I make to Dame van Winkle!'

He looked round for his gun, but in place of the clean, well-oiled fowling-piece, he found an old flintlock lying by him, the barrel encrusted with rust, the lock falling off and the stock worm-eaten.

He even ventured, when no eye was fixed upon him, to taste the beverage,
which he found had much of the flavour of excellent Hollands

He now suspected that the grave roisterers of the mountain had put a trick upon him, and, having dosed him with liquor, had robbed him of his gun. Wolf, too, had disappeared, but he might have strayed away after a squirrel or partridge. He whistled after him and shouted his name, but all in vain; the echoes repeated his whistle and shout, but no dog was to be seen.

He determined to revisit the scene of the last evening's gambol, and if he met with any of the party to demand his dog and gun. As he rose to walk, he found himself stiff in the joints and wanting in his usual activity. 'These mountain-beds do not agree with me,' thought Rip, 'and if this frolic should lay me up with a fit of the rheumatism, I shall have a blessed time with Dame van Winkle.' With some difficulty he got down into the glen: he found the gully up which he and his companion had ascended the preceding evening; but to his astonishment a mountain-stream was now foaming down it, leaping from rock to rock and filling the glen with babbling murmurs. He, however, made shift to scramble up its sides, working his toilsome way through thickets of birch, sassafras, and witch-hazel, and sometimes tripped up or entangled by the wild grape vines that twisted their coils or tendrils from tree to tree and spread a kind of network in his path.

At length he reached to where the ravine had opened through the cliffs to the amphitheatre; but no traces of such opening remained. The rocks presented a high impenetrable wall, over which the torrent came tumbling in a sheet of feathery foam, and fell into a broad, deep basin, black from the shadows of the surrounding forest. Here, then, poor Rip was brought to a stand. He again called and whistled after his dog; he was only answered by the cawing of a flock of idle crows sporting high in the air about a dry tree that overhung a sunny precipice, and who, secure in their elevation, seemed to look down and scoff at the poor man's perplexities. What was to be done? The morning was passing away, and Rip felt famished for want of his breakfast. He grieved to give up his dog and gun; he dreaded to meet his wife; but it would not do to starve among the mountains. He shook his head, shouldered the rusty flintlock, and with a heart full of trouble and anxiety turned his steps homeward.

As he approached the village he met a number of people, none whom he knew, which somewhat surprised him, for he had thought himself acquainted with everyone in the country round. Their dress, too, was of a different fashion from that to which he was accustomed. They all stared at him with equal marks of surprise, and whenever they cast their eyes upon him, invariably stroked their chins. The constant recurrence of this gesture induced Rip, involuntarily, to do the same, when, to his astonishment, he found his beard had grown a foot long!

He had now entered the skirts of the village. A troop of strange children ran at his heels, hooting after him and pointing at his grey beard. The dogs, too, not one of which he recognised for an old acquaintance, barked at him as he passed. The very village was altered; it was larger and more populous. There were rows of houses which he had never seen before, and those which had been his familiar haunts had disappeared. Strange names were over the doors – strange faces at the windows – everything was strange. His mind now misgave him; he began to doubt whether both he and the world around him were not bewitched. Surely this was his native village, which he had left but the day before. There stood the Catskill Mountains – there ran the silver Hudson at a distance – there was every hill and dale precisely as it had always been. Rip was sorely perplexed. 'That flagon last night,' thought he, 'has addled my poor head sadly.'

It was with some difficulty that he found the way to his own house, which he approached with silent awe, expecting every moment to hear the shrill voice of Dame van Winkle. He found the house gone to decay – the roof fallen in, the windows shattered, and the doors off the hinges. A half-starved dog that looked like Wolf was skulking about it. Rip called him by name, but the cur snarled, showed his teeth, and passed on. This was an unkind cut indeed. 'My very dog,' sighed poor Rip, 'has forgotten me!'

He entered the house, which, to tell the truth, Dame van Winkle had always kept in neat order. It was empty, forlorn, and apparently abandoned. This desolateness overcame all his connubial fears and he called loudly for his wife and children; the lonely chambers rang for a moment with his voice, and then all again was silence.

He now hurried forth, and hastened to his old resort, the village inn, but it too was gone. A large rickety wooden building stood in its place, with great gaping windows, some of them broken and mended with old hats and petticoats, and over the door was painted, 'The Union Hotel, by Jonathan

Doolittle'. Instead of the great tree that used to shelter the quiet little Dutch inn of yore, there now was reared a tall, naked pole, with something on the top that looked like a red nightcap, and from it was fluttering a flag, on which was a singular assemblage of stars and stripes. All this was strange and incomprehensible. He recognised on the sign, however, the ruby face of King George, under which he had smoked so many a peaceful pipe; but even this was singularly metamorphosed. The red coat was changed for one of blue and buff, a sword was held in the hand instead of a sceptre, the head was decorated with a cocked hat, and underneath was painted in large characters, General Washington.

There was, as usual, a crowd of folk about the door, but none that Rip recollected. The very character of the people seemed changed. There was a busy, bustling, disputatious tone about it, instead of the accustomed phlegm and drowsy tranquillity. He looked in vain for the sage Nicholas Vedder, with his broad face, double chin, and fair long pipe, uttering clouds of tobacco-smoke instead of idle speeches; or van Bummel, the schoolmaster, doling forth the contents of an ancient newspaper. In place of these, a lean, bilious-looking fellow, with his pockets full of handbills, was haranguing vehemently about rights of citizens – elections – members of Congress – liberty – Bunker's Hill – heroes of 'seventy-six – and other words, which were a perfect Babylonish jargon to the bewildered van Winkle.

The appearance of Rip, with his long, grizzled beard, his rusty fowling-piece, his uncouth dress, and an army of women and children at his heels, soon attracted the attention of the tavern politicians. They crowded round him, eyeing him from head to foot with great curiosity. The orator bustled up to him, and, drawing him partly aside, enquired 'on which side he voted'. Rip stared in vacant stupidity. Another short but busy little fellow pulled him by the arm, and, rising on tiptoe, enquired in his ear, whether he was 'Federal or Democrat'. Rip was equally at a loss to comprehend

A troop of strange children ran at his heels, hooting after him and pointing at his grey beard

the question. Then a knowing, self-important old gentleman, in a sharp cocked hat, made his way through the crowd, putting them to the right and left with his elbows as he passed, and, planting himself before van Winkle, with one arm akimbo, the other resting on his cane, his keen eyes and sharp hat penetrating, as it were, into his very soul, demanded in an austere tone, 'What brought him to the election with a gun on his shoulder and a mob at his heels, and whether he meant to breed a riot in the village?' – 'Alas! gentlemen,' cried Rip, somewhat dismayed, 'I am a poor, quiet man, a native of the place, and a loyal subject of the king, God bless him!'

Here a general shout burst from the bystanders – 'A Tory! a Tory! a spy! a refugee! hustle him! away with him!' It was with great difficulty that the self-important man in the cocked hat restored order; and, having assumed a tenfold austerity of brow demanded again of the unknown culprit what he came there for, and whom he was seeking. The poor man humbly assured him that he meant no harm, but merely came there in search of some of his neighbours, who used to keep about the tavern.

'Well – who are they? – name them.'

Rip bethought himself a moment, and enquired, 'Where's Nicholas Vedder?'

There was a silence for a little while, when an old man replied in a thin piping voice, 'Nicholas Vedder! why, he is dead and gone these eighteen years! There was a wooden tombstone in the churchyard that used to tell all about him, but that's rotten and gone too.'

'Where's Brom Dutcher?'

'Oh, he went off to the army in the beginning of the war; some say he was killed at the storming of Stony Point – others say he was drowned in a squall at the foot of Antony's Nose. I don't know – he never came back again.'

'Where's van Bummel, the schoolmaster?'

'He went off to the wars too, was a great militia general, and is now in Congress.'

Rip's heart died away at hearing of these sad changes in his home and friends and finding himself thus alone in the world. Every answer puzzled him, too, by treating of such enormous lapses of time, and of matters which he could not understand: war – Congress – Stony Point. He had no courage to ask after any more friends, but cried out in despair, 'Does nobody here know Rip van Winkle?'

'Oh, Rip van Winkle!' exclaimed two or three.

'Oh, to be sure! that's Rip van Winkle yonder, leaning against the tree.'

Rip looked and beheld a precise counterpart of himself as he went up the mountain, apparently as lazy and certainly as ragged. The poor fellow was now completely confounded. He doubted his own identity, and whether he was himself or another man. In the midst of his bewilderment the man in the cocked hat demanded who he was and what was his name.

'God knows,' exclaimed he, at his wit's end; 'I'm not myself – I'm somebody else – that's me yonder – no – that's somebody else got into my shoes. I was myself last night, but I fell asleep on the mountain, and they've changed my gun, and everything's changed, and I'm changed, and I can't tell what's my name, or who I am!'

The bystanders began now to look at each other, nod, wink significantly, and tap their fingers against their foreheads. There was a whisper, also, about securing the gun and keeping the old fellow from doing mischief, at the very suggestion of which the self-important man in the cocked hat retired with some precipitation. At this critical moment a fresh comely woman passed through the throng to get a peep at the grey-bearded man. She had a chubby child in her arms, which, frightened at his looks, began to cry. 'Hush, Rip,' cried she, 'hush, you little fool! the old man won't hurt you.' The name of the child, the air of the mother, the tone of her voice, all awakened a train of recollections in his mind. 'What is your name, my good woman?' asked he.

'Judith Gardenier.'

'And your father's name?'

'Ah, poor man! Rip van Winkle was his name, but it's twenty years since he went away from home with his gun, and he never has been heard of since – his dog came home without him; but whether he shot himself, or was carried away by the Indians, nobody can tell. I was then but a little girl.'

Rip had but one question more to ask, but he put it with a faltering voice: 'Where's your mother?'

'Oh, she, too, has died, but a short time since; she broke a blood-vessel in a fit of passion at a New England peddler.'

There was a drop of comfort, at least, in this intelligence. This honest man could contain himself no longer. He caught his daughter and her child in his arms. 'I am your father!' cried he – 'young Rip van Winkle once – old Rip van Winkle now! Does nobody know poor Rip van Winkle?'

All stood amazed, until an old woman, tottering out from among the crowd, put her hand to her brow, and peering under it in his face for a moment, exclaimed, 'Sure enough! it is Rip van Winkle – it is himself! Welcome home again, old neighbour! Why, where have you been these twenty long years?'

Rip's story was soon told, for the whole twenty years had been to him but as one night. The neighbours stared when they heard it; some were seen to wink at each other, and put their tongues in their cheeks; and the self-important man in the cocked hat, who, when the alarm was over, had returned to the field, screwed down the corners of his mouth and shook his head – upon which there was a general shaking of the head throughout the assemblage.

It was determined, however, to take the opinion of old Peter Vanderdonk, who was seen slowly advancing up the road. He was a descendant of the historian of that name, who wrote one of the earliest accounts of the province. Peter was the most ancient inhabitant of the village, and well versed in all the wonderful events and traditions of the neighbourhood. He recollected Rip at once, and corroborated his story in the most satisfactory manner. He assured the company that it was a fact, handed down from his ancestor the historian, that the Catskill Mountains had always been haunted by strange beings. That it was affirmed that the great Hendrick Hudson, the first discoverer of the river and country, kept a kind of vigil there every twenty years, with his crew of the *Half-Moon*, being permitted in this way to revisit the scenes of his enterprise and keep a guardian eye upon the river and the great city called by his name. That his father had once seen them in their old Dutch dresses playing at ninepins in a hollow of the mountain; and that he himself had heard, one summer afternoon, the sound of their balls, like distant peals of thunder.

To make a long story short, the company broke up, and returned to the more important concerns of the election. Rip's daughter took him home to live with her; she had a snug, well-furnished house, and a stout cheery farmer for a husband, whom Rip recollected for one of the urchins that used to climb upon his back. As to Rip's son and heir, who was the ditto of himself, seen leaning against the tree, he was employed to work on the farm, but evinced an hereditary disposition to attend to anything else but his business.

Rip now resumed his old walks and habits; he soon found many of his former cronies, though all rather the worse for the wear and tear of time; and preferred making friends among the rising generation, with whom he soon grew into great favour.

Having nothing to do at home, and being arrived at that happy age when a man can be idle with impunity, he took his place once more on the bench at the inn-door, and was reverenced as one of the patriarchs of the village and a chronicle of the old times 'before the war'. It was some time before he could get into the regular track of gossip, or could be made to comprehend the strange events that had taken place during his torpor. How that there had been a Revolutionary War – that the country had thrown off the yoke of old England – and that, instead of being a subject of His Majesty George III, he was now a free citizen of the United States. Rip, in fact, was no politician; the changes of states and empires made but little impression on him; but there was one species of despotism under which he had long groaned, and that was – petticoat government. Happily, that was at an end; he had got his neck out of the yoke of matrimony, and could go in and out whenever he pleased, without dreading the tyranny of Dame van Winkle. Whenever her name was mentioned, however, he shook his head, shrugged his shoulders, and cast up his eyes; which might pass either for an expression of resignation to his fate or joy at his deliverance.

He used to tell his story to every stranger that arrived at Mr Doolittle's hotel. He was observed, at first, to vary on some points every time he told it, which was, doubtless, owing to his having so recently awaked. It at last settled down precisely to the tale I have related, and not a man, woman or child in the neighbourhood but knew it by heart. Some always pretended to doubt the reality of it, and insisted that Rip had been out of his head, and that this was one point on which he always remained flighty. The old Dutch inhabitants, however, almost universally gave it full credit. Even to this day they never hear a thunderstorm of a summer afternoon about the Catskills but they say Hendrick Hudson and his crew are at their game of ninepins; and it is a common wish of all henpecked husbands in the neighbourhood, when life hangs heavy on their hands, that they might have a quieting draught out of Rip van Winkle's flagon.

Even to this day they never hear a thunderstorm of a summer afternoon about the Catskills but they say Hendrick Hudson and his crew are at their game of ninepins

A Note on Rip van Winkle

The foregoing tale, one would suspect, had been suggested to Mr Knickerbocker by a little German superstition about the Emperor Frederick der Rothbart and the Kypphauser Mountain; the sub-joined note, however, which he had appended to the tale, shows that it is an absolute fact, narrated with his usual fidelity:

> The story of Rip van Winkle may seem incredible to many, but nevertheless I give it my full belief, for I know the vicinity of our old Dutch settlements to have been very subject to marvellous events and appearances. Indeed, I have heard many stranger stories than this in the villages along the Hudson, all of which were too well authenticated to admit of a doubt. I have even talked with Rip van Winkle myself, who, when last I saw him, was a very venerable old man, and so perfectly rational and consistent on every other point that I think no conscientious person could refuse to take this into the bargain; nay, I have seen a certificate on this subject taken before a country justice, and signed with a cross, in the justice's own handwriting. The story, therefore, is beyond the possibility of doubt.

D. K.

A Postscript to Rip van Winkle

taken from the Travelling Notes of a Memorandum book belonging to Mr Knickerbocker

The Kaatsberg, or Catskill, Mountains have always been a region full of fable. The Indians considered them the abode of spirits, who influenced the weather, spreading sunshine or clouds over the landscape and sending good or bad hunting seasons. They were ruled by an old squaw spirit, said to be their mother. She dwelt on the highest peak of the Catskills, and had charge of the doors of day and night to open and shut them at the proper hour. She hung up the new moons in the skies, and cut up the old ones into stars. In times of drought, if properly propitiated, she would spin light summer clouds out of cobwebs and morning dew, and send them off from the crest of the mountain, flake after flake, like flakes of carded cotton, to float in the air; until, dissolved by the heat of the sun, they would fall in gentle showers, causing the grass to spring, the fruits to ripen and the corn to grow an inch an hour. If displeased, however, she would brew up clouds black as ink, sitting in the midst of them like a bottle-bellied spider in the midst of its web; and when these clouds broke, woe betide the valleys!

In old times, say the Indian traditions, there was a kind of manitou or spirit, who kept about the wildest recesses of the Catskill Mountains, and took a mischievous pleasure in wreaking all kinds of evils and vexations upon the red men. Sometimes he would assume the form of a bear, a panther or a deer, lead the bewildered hunter a weary chase through tangled forests and among ragged rocks, and then spring off with a loud ho! ho! leaving him aghast on the brink of a beetling precipice or raging torrent.

The favourite abode of this manitou is still shown. It is a great rock or cliff on the loneliest part of the mountains, which, from the flowering vines which clamber about it and the wild flowers which abound in its neighbourhood, is known by the name of the Garden Rock. Near the foot of it is a small lake, the haunt of the solitary bittern, with water snakes basking in the sun on the leaves of the pond-lilies, which lie on the surface. This place was held in great awe by the Indians, insomuch that the boldest hunter would not pursue his game within its precincts. Once upon a time, however, a hunter who had lost his way penetrated to the Garden Rock, where he beheld a number of gourds placed in the crotches of trees. One of these he seized and made off with it, but in the hurry of his retreat he let it fall among the rocks, when a great stream gushed forth, which washed him away and swept him down precipices, where he was dashed to pieces, and the stream made its way to the Hudson, and continues to flow to the present day, being the identical stream known by the name of the Kaaterskill.

Rosanella

Everybody knows that though the fairies live hundreds of years they do sometimes die, and especially as they are obliged to pass one day in every week under the form of some animal, when of course they are liable to accident. It was in this way that death once overtook the queen of the fairies, and it became necessary to call a general assembly to elect a new sovereign. After much discussion, it appeared that the choice lay between two fairies, one called Surcantine and the other Paridamie; and their claims were so equal that it was impossible without injustice to prefer one to the other. Under these circumstances it was unanimously decided that whichever of the two could show to the world the greatest wonder should be queen; but it was to be a special kind of wonder, no moving of mountains or any such common fairy tricks would do. Surcantine, therefore, resolved that she would bring up a prince whom nothing could make constant. While Paridamie decided to display to admiring mortals a princess so charming that no one could see her without falling in love with her. They were allowed to take their own time, and meanwhile the four oldest fairies were to attend to the affairs of the kingdom.

Now Paridamie had for a long time been very friendly with King Bardondon, who was a most accomplished prince, and whose court was the model of what a court should be. His queen, Balanice, was also charming; indeed it is rare to find a husband and wife so perfectly of one mind about everything. They had one little daughter, whom they had named 'Rosanella', because she had a little pink rose printed upon her white throat. From her earliest infancy she had shown the most astonishing intelligence, and the courtiers knew her smart sayings by heart, and repeated them on all occasions. In the middle of the night following the assembly of fairies, Queen Balanice woke up with a shriek, and when her maids of honour ran to see what was the matter, they found she had had a frightful dream.

'I thought,' said she, 'that my little daughter had changed into a bouquet of roses, and that as I held it in my hand a bird swooped down suddenly and snatched it from me and carried it away. Let some one run and see that all is well with the princess,' she begged.

So they ran; but what was their dismay when they found that the cradle was empty; and though they sought high and low, not a trace of Rosanella could they discover. The queen was inconsolable, and so, indeed, was the king, only being a man he did not say quite so much about his feelings. He presently proposed to Balanice that they should spend a few days at one of their palaces in the country; and to this she willingly agreed, since her grief made the gaiety of the capital distasteful to her. One lovely summer evening, as they sat together on a shady lawn shaped like a star, from which radiated twelve splendid avenues of trees, the queen looked round and saw a charming peasant girl approaching by each path, and what was still more singular was that every one carried something in a basket which appeared to occupy her whole attention. As each drew near she laid her basket at Balanice's feet, saying: 'Beloved queen, may this be some slight consolation to you in your unhappiness!'

The queen hastily opened the baskets, and found in each a lovely baby girl, about the same age as the little princess for whom she sorrowed so deeply. At first the sight of them renewed her grief; but presently their charms so gained upon her that she forgot her melancholy in providing them with nurserymaids, cradle-rockers, and ladies-in-waiting, and in sending hither and thither for swings and dolls and tops, and bushels of the finest sweet-meats.

Oddly enough, every baby had upon its throat a tiny pink rose. The queen found it so difficult to decide on suitable names for all of them that until she could settle the matter she chose a special

colour for every one, by which it was known, when they were all together they looked like nothing so much as a riotous nosegay of flowers. As they grew older it became evident that though they were all remarkably intelligent, and profited equally by the education they received, yet they differed one from another in disposition, so much so that they gradually ceased to be known as 'Pearl' or 'Primrose' or whatever might have been their colour and the queen instead would say: 'Where is my sweet?' or 'my beautiful' or 'my gay'.

Of course, with all these charms they had lovers by the dozen. Not only in their own court, but princes from afar, who were constantly arriving, attracted by the reports which were spread abroad; but these lovely girls, the first maids of honour, were as discreet as they were beautiful, and favoured no one.

But let us return to Surcantine. She had fixed upon the son of a king who was cousin to Bardondon, to bring up as her fickle prince. She

had before, at his christening, given him all the graces of mind and body that a prince could possibly require; but now she redoubled her efforts, and spared no pains in adding every imaginable charm and fascination. So that whether he happened to be cross or amiable, splendidly or simply attired, serious or frivolous, he was always perfectly irresistible! In truth, he was a charming young fellow, since the fairy had given him the best heart in the world as well as the best head, and had left nothing to be desired but – constancy. For it cannot be denied that Prince Mirliflor was a desperate flirt, and as fickle as the wind; so much so, that by the time he arrived at his eighteenth birthday there was not a heart left for him to conquer in his father's kingdom – they were all his own, and he was tired of everyone! Things were in this state when he was invited to visit the court of his father's cousin, King Bardondon.

Imagine his feelings when he arrived and was presented at once to twelve of the loveliest creatures in the world, and his embarrassment was heightened by the fact that they all liked him as much as he liked each one of them, so that things came to such a pass that he was never happy a single instant without them. For could he not whisper soft speeches to Sweet, and laugh with Joy, while he looked at Beauty? And in his more serious moments what could be pleasanter than to talk to Grave upon some shady lawn, while he held the hand of Loving in his own, and all the others lingered near in sympathetic silence? For the first time in his life he really loved, though the object of his devotion was not one person, but twelve, to whom he was equally attached, and even Surcantine was deceived into thinking that this was indeed the height of inconstancy. But Paridamie said not a word.

In vain did Prince Mirliflor's father write commanding him to return, and proposing for him one good match after another. Nothing in the world could tear him from his twelve enchantresses.

One day the queen gave a large garden-party, and just as the guests were all assembled, and Prince Mirliflor was as usual dividing his attentions between the twelve beauties, a humming of bees was heard. The rose-maidens, fearing their stings, uttered little shrieks, and fled all together to a distance from the rest of the company. Immediately, to the horror of all who were looking on, the bees pursued them, and, growing suddenly to an enormous size, pounced each upon a maiden and carried her off into the air, and in an instant they were all lost to view. This amazing occurrence plunged the whole court into the deepest affliction, and Prince Mirliflor, after giving way to the most violent grief at first, fell gradually into a state of such deep dejection that it was feared if nothing could rouse him he would certainly die. Surcantine came in all haste to see what she could do for her darling, but he rejected with scorn all the portraits of lovely princesses which she offered him for his collection. In short, it was evident that he was in a bad way, and the fairy was at her wits' end. One day, as he wandered about absorbed in melancholy reflections, he heard sudden shouts and exclamations of amazement, and if he had taken the trouble to look up he could not have helped being as astonished as everyone else, for through the air a chariot of crystal was slowly approaching which glittered in the sunshine. Six lovely maidens with shining wings drew it by rose-coloured ribbons, while a whole flight of others, equally beautiful, were holding long garlands of roses crossed above

it, so as to form a complete canopy. In it sat the Fairy Paridamie, and by her side a princess whose beauty positively dazzled all who saw her. At the foot of the great staircase they descended, and proceeded to the queen's apartments, though as everyone had run together to see this marvel, it was quite difficult to make a way through the crowd; and exclamations of wonder rose on all sides at the loveliness of the strange princess. 'Great queen,' said Paridamie, 'permit me to restore to you your daughter Rosanella, whom I stole out of her cradle.'

After the first transports of joy were over the queen said to Paridamie: 'But my twelve lovely ones, are they lost to me for ever? Shall I never see them again?'

But Paridamie only said: 'Very soon you will cease to miss them!' in a tone that evidently meant, 'Don't ask me any more questions.' And then mounting again into her chariot she swiftly disappeared.

The news of his beautiful cousin's arrival was soon carried to the prince, but he had hardly the heart to go and see her. However, it became absolutely necessary that he should pay his respects, and he had scarcely been five minutes in her presence before it seemed to him that she combined in her own charming person all the gifts and graces which had so attracted him in the twelve rose-maidens whose loss he had so truly mourned; and after all it is really more satisfactory to make love to one person at a time. So it came to pass that before he knew where he was he was entreating his lovely cousin to marry him, and the moment the words had left his lips, Paridamie appeared, smiling and triumphant, in the chariot of the queen of the fairies, for by that time they had all heard of her success, and declared her to have earned the kingdom. She had to give a full account of how she had stolen Rosanella from her cradle, and divided her character into twelve parts, that each might charm prince Mirliflor, and when once more united might cure him of his inconstancy once and for ever.

And as one more proof of the fascination of the whole Rosanella, I may tell you that even the defeated Surcantine sent her a wedding gift, and was present at the ceremony which took place as soon as the guests could arrive. Prince Mirliflor was constant for the rest of his life. And indeed who would not have been in his place? As for Rosanella, she loved him as much as all the twelve beauties put together, so they reigned in peace and happiness to the end of their long lives.

Rumpelstiltskin

By the side of a wood, in a country a long way off, ran a fine stream of water; and upon the stream there stood a mill. The miller's house was close by, and the miller, you must know, had a very beautiful daughter. She was, moreover, very shrewd and clever; and the miller was so proud of her that he one day told the king of the land, who used to come and hunt in the wood, that his daughter could spin gold out of straw.

Now this king was very fond of money; and when he heard the miller's boast his greediness was aroused, and he sent for the girl to be brought before him. Then he led her to a chamber in his palace where there was a great heap of straw, and gave her a spinning-wheel, and said, 'All this must be spun into gold before morning, if you love your life.' It was in vain that the poor maiden said that it was only a silly boast of her father's, and that she could do no such thing as spin straw into gold; the chamber door was locked, and she was left alone.

She had sat down in one corner of the room and begun to bewail her hard fate, when on a sudden the door opened and a droll-looking little man hobbled in and said, 'Good-morrow to you, my good lass; what are you weeping for?'

'Alas!' said she, 'I must spin this straw into gold, and I know not how.'

'What will you give me,' said the hobgoblin, 'to do it for you?'

'My necklace,' replied the maiden.

He took her at her word, and sat himself down to the wheel, and whistled and sang:

> 'Round about, round about,
> Lo and behold!
> Reel away, reel away,
> Straw into gold!'

And round about the wheel went merrily, the work was quickly done and the straw was all spun into gold.

When the king came and saw this, he was greatly astonished and pleased; but his heart grew still more greedy of gain, and he shut up the poor miller's daughter again with a fresh task. Then she knew not what to do, and sat down once more to weep; but the dwarf soon opened the door, and said, 'What will you give me to do your task?'

'The ring on my finger,' said she. So her little friend took the ring, and began to work at the wheel again, and whistled and sang:

> 'Round about, round about,
> Lo and behold!
> Reel away, reel away,
> Straw into gold!'

till, long before morning, all was done again.

The king was greatly delighted to see all this glittering treasure; but still he had not enough: so he took the miller's daughter to a yet larger heap, and said, 'All this must be spun tonight; and if it is, you shall be my queen.'

As soon as she was alone the dwarf came in and said, 'What will you give me to spin gold for you this third time?'

'I have nothing left,' said she.

'Then say you will give me,' said the little man, 'the first child that you may have when you are queen.'

'Well! That may never be,' thought the miller's daughter; and as she knew no other way to get her task done, she said she would do what he asked.

Round went the wheel again to the old song, and the manikin once more spun the heap into gold. The king came in the morning, and, finding all he wanted, was forced to keep his word; so he married the miller's daughter, and she really became queen.

At the birth of her first little child she was very glad, and forgot the dwarf, and what she had said. But one day he came into her room, where she was sitting playing with her baby, and put her in mind of it. Then she grieved sorely at her misfortune, and said she would give him all the wealth of the kingdom if he would let her off, but in vain; yet at last her tears softened him, and he said, 'I will give you three days' grace, and if during that time you tell me my name, you shall keep your child.'

Now the queen lay awake all night, thinking of all the odd names that she had ever heard; and she sent messengers all over the land to find out new ones. The next day the little man came, and she began with Timothy, Ichabod, Benjamin, Jeremiah, and all the names she could remember; but to all and each of them he said, 'Madam, that is not my name.'

The second day she began with all the comical names she could think of: Bandylegs, Hunchback, Crookshanks, and so on; but the little gentleman still said to every one of them, 'Madam, that is not my name.'

The third day one of the messengers came back, and said, 'I have travelled two days without hearing of any other names; but yesterday, as I was climbing a high hill among the trees of the forest, where the fox and the hare bid each other good-night, I saw a little hut; and before the hut burnt a fire; and round about the fire a funny little dwarf was dancing upon one leg, and singing:

'Merrily the feast I'll make,
Today I'll brew, tomorrow bake;
Merrily I'll dance and sing,
For next day will a stranger bring.
Little does my lady dream
Rumpelstiltskin is my name!'

When the queen heard this she jumped for joy, and as soon as her little friend came she sat down upon her throne, and called all her court round to enjoy the fun; and the nurse stood by her side with the baby in her arms, as if it was quite ready to be given up. Then the little man began to chuckle at the thought of having the poor child to take home with him to his hut in the woods; and he cried out, 'Now, lady, what is my name?'

'Is it John?' asked she.

'No, madam!'

'Is it Tom?'

'No, madam!'

'Is it Jemmy?'

'It is not.'

'Can your name be Rumpelstiltskin?' asked the lady slyly.

'Some witch told you that – some witch told you that!' cried the little man, and dashed his right foot in a rage so deep into the floor that he was forced to lay hold of it with both hands to pull it out.

Then he made off as best he could, while the nurse laughed and the baby crowed; and all the court jeered at him for having had so much trouble for nothing, and said, 'We wish you a very good-morning, and a merry feast, Mr Rumpelstiltskin!'

The Sagacious Monkey and the Boar

Long, long ago, there lived in the province of Shinshin in Japan, a travelling monkey-man, who earned his living by taking round a monkey and showing off the animal's tricks.

One evening the man came home in a very bad temper and told his wife to send for the butcher the next morning.

The wife was very bewildered and asked her husband: 'Why do you wish me to send for the butcher?'

'It's no use taking that monkey round any longer, he's too old and forgets his tricks. I beat him with my stick all I know how, but he won't dance properly. I must now sell him to the butcher and make what money out of him I can. There is nothing else to be done.'

The woman felt very sorry for the poor little animal, and pleaded for her husband to spare the monkey, but her pleading was all in vain, the man was determined to sell him to the butcher.

Now the monkey was in the next room and overheard ever word of the conversation. He soon understood that he was to be killed, and he said to himself: 'Barbarous, indeed, is my master! Here I have served him faithfully for years, and instead of allowing me to end my days comfortably and in peace, he is going to let me be cut up by the butcher, and my poor body is to be roasted and stewed and eaten? Woe is me! What am I to do. Ah! a bright thought has struck me! There is, I know, a wild boar living in the forest near by. I have often heard tell of his wisdom. Perhaps if I go to him and tell him the strait I am in he will give me his counsel. I will go and try.'

There was no time to lose. The monkey slipped out of the house and ran as quickly as he could to the forest to find the boar. The boar was at home, and the monkey began his tale of woe at once.

'Good Mr Boar, I have heard of your excellent wisdom. I am in great trouble and you alone can help me. I have grown old in the service of my master, and because I cannot dance properly now he intends to sell me to the butcher. What do you advise me to do? I know how clever you are!'

The boar was pleased at the flattery and determined to help the monkey. He thought for a little while and then said: 'Hasn't your master a baby?'

'Oh, yes,' said the monkey, 'he has one infant son.'

'Doesn't it lie by the door in the morning when your mistress begins the work of the day? Well, I will come round early and when I see my opportunity I will seize the child and run off with it.'

'What then?' said the monkey.

'Why the mother will be in a tremendous state, and before your master and mistress know what to do, you must run after me and rescue the child and take it home safely to its parents, and you will see that when the butcher comes they won't have the heart to sell you.'

The monkey thanked the boar many times and then went home. He did not sleep much that night, as you may imagine, for thinking of the morrow. His life depended on whether the

512

boar's plan succeeded or not. He was the first up, waiting anxiously for what was to happen. It seemed to him a very long time before his master's wife began to move about and open the shutters to let in the light of day. Then all happened as the boar had planned. The mother placed her child near the porch as usual while she tidied up the house and got her breakfast ready.

The child was crooning happily in the morning sunlight, dabbing on the mats at the play of light and shadow. Suddenly there was a noise in the porch and a loud cry from the child. The mother ran out from the kitchen to the spot, only just in time to see the boar disappearing through the gate with her child in its clutch. She flung out her hands with a loud cry of despair and rushed into the inner room where her husband was still sleeping soundly.

He sat up slowly and rubbed his eyes, and crossly demanded what his wife was making all that noise about. By the time the man was alive to what had happened, and they both got outside the gate, the boar had got well away, but they saw the monkey running after the thief as hard as his legs would carry him.

Both the man and wife were moved to admiration at the plucky conduct of the sagacious monkey, and their gratitude knew no bounds when the faithful monkey brought the child safely back to their arms.

'There!' said the wife. 'This is the animal you want to kill – if the monkey hadn't been here we should have lost our child for ever.'

'You are right, wife, for once,' said the man as he

carried the child into the house. 'You may send the butcher back when he comes, and now give us all a good breakfast and the monkey too.'

When the butcher arrived he was sent away with an order for some boar's meat for the evening dinner, and the monkey was petted and lived the rest of his days in peace, nor did his master ever strike him again.

The Selfish Giant

Every afternoon, as they were coming from school, the children used to go and play in the giant's garden.

It was a large lovely garden, with soft green grass. Here and there over the grass stood beautiful flowers like stars, and there were twelve peach trees that in the springtime broke out into delicate blossoms of pink and pearl, and in the autumn bore rich fruit. The birds sat on the trees and sang so sweetly that the children used to stop their games in order to listen to them. 'How happy we are here!' they cried to each other.

One day the giant came back. He had been to visit his friend the Cornish ogre, and had stayed with him for seven years. After the seven years were over he had said all that he had to say, for his conversation was limited, and he determined to return to his own castle. When he arrived he saw the children playing in the garden.

'What are you doing here?' he cried in a very gruff voice, and the children ran away.

'My own garden is my own garden,' said the giant; 'anyone can understand that, and I will allow nobody to play in it but myself.' So he built a high wall all round it and put up a notice-board:

TRESPASSERS
will be
PROSECUTED

He was a very selfish giant.

The poor children had now nowhere to play. They tried to play on the road, but the road was very dusty and full of hard stones, and they did not like it. They used to wander round the high walls when their lessons were over, and talk about the beautiful garden inside. 'How happy we were there!' they said to each other.

Then the spring came, and all over the country there were little blossoms and little birds. Only in the garden of the selfish giant it was still winter.

The birds did not care to sing in it as there were no children and the trees forgot to blossom. Once a beautiful flower put its head out from the grass, but when it saw the notice-board it was so sorry for the children that it slipped back into the ground again, and went off to sleep. The only people who were pleased were the snow and the frost. 'Spring has forgotten this garden,' they cried, 'so we will live here all the year round.' The snow covered up the grass with her great white cloak, and the frost painted all the trees silver. Then they invited the north wind to stay with them, and he came. He was wrapped in furs, and he roared all day about the garden, and blew the chimney-pots down. 'This is a delightful spot,' he said, 'we must ask the hail on a visit.' So the hail came. Every day for three hours he rattled on the roof of the castle till he broke most of the slates and then he ran round and round the garden as fast as he could go. He was dressed in grey, and his breath was like ice.

'I cannot understand why the spring is so late in coming,' said the selfish giant, as he sat at the window and looked out at his cold, white garden; 'I hope there will be a change in the weather.'

But the spring never came, nor the summer. The autumn gave golden fruit to every garden, but to the giant's garden she gave none. 'He is too selfish,' she said. So it was always winter there, and the north wind and the hail, and the frost and the snow danced about through the trees.

One morning the giant was lying awake in bed when he heard some lovely music. It sounded so sweet to his ears that he thought it must be the king's musicians passing by. It was really only a little linnet singing outside his window, but it was so long since he had heard a bird sing in his garden that it seemed to him to be the most beautiful music in the world. Then the hail stopped dancing over his head, and the north wind ceased roaring, and a delicious perfume came to him through the open casement. 'I believe the spring has come at last,' said the giant; and he jumped out of bed and looked out.

What did he see?

He saw a most wonderful sight. Through a little hole in the wall the children had crept in, and they were sitting in the branches of the trees. In every tree that he could see there was a little child. And the trees were so glad to have the children back again that they had covered themselves with blossoms, and were waving their arms gently above the children's heads. The birds were flying about and twittering with delight, and the flowers were looking up through the green grass and laughing. It was a lovely scene, only in one corner it was still winter. It was the farthest corner of the garden, and in it was standing a little boy. He was so small that he could not reach up to the branches of the tree, and he was wandering all round it, crying bitterly.

The poor tree was still covered with frost and snow and the north wind was blowing and roaring above it. Climb up! little boy,' said the tree, and it bent its branches down as low as it could; but the boy was too tiny.

And the giant's heart melted as he looked out.

'How selfish I have been!' he said; 'now I know why the spring would not come here. I will put that poor little boy on the top of the tree, and then I will knock down the wall, and my garden shall be the children's playground for ever and ever.' He was really very sorry for what he had done.

So he crept downstairs and opened the front door quite softly, and went out into the garden. But when the children saw him they were so frightened that they all ran away, and the garden became winter again. Only the little boy did not run for his eyes were so full of tears that he did not see the

giant coming. And the giant stole up behind him and took him gently in his hand, and put him up into the tree. And the tree broke at once into blossom, and the birds came and sang on it, and the little boy stretched out his two arms and flung them round the giant's neck and kissed him. And the other children when they saw that the giant was not wicked any longer came running back, and with them came the spring. 'It is your garden now, little children,' said the giant, and he took a great axe and knocked down the wall. And when the people were going to market at twelve o'clock they found the giant playing with the children in the most beautiful garden they had ever seen.

All day long they played, and in the evening they came to the giant to bid him goodbye.

'But where is your little companion?' he said: 'the boy I put into the tree.' The giant loved him the best because he had kissed him.

'We don't know,' answered the children, 'he has gone away.'

'You must tell him to be sure and come tomorrow,' said the giant. But the children said that they did not know where he lived and had never seen him before; and the giant felt very sad.

Every afternoon, when school was over, the children came and played with the giant. But the little boy whom the giant loved was never seen again. The giant was very kind to all the children, yet he longed for his first little friend, and often spoke of him. 'How I would like to see him!' he used to say.

Years went over, and the giant grew very old and feeble. He could not play about any more, so he sat in a huge armchair, and watched the children at their games, and admired his garden. 'I have many beautiful flowers,' he said; 'but the children are the most beautiful flowers of all.'

One winter morning he looked out of his window as he was dressing. He did not hate the winter now, for he knew that it was merely the spring asleep, and that the flowers were resting.

Suddenly he rubbed his eyes in wonder and

looked and looked. It certainly was a marvellous sight. In the farthest corner of the garden was a tree quite covered with lovely white blossoms. Its branches were golden and silver fruit hung down from them, and underneath it stood the little boy he had loved.

Downstairs ran the giant in great joy, and out into the garden. He hastened across the grass, and came near to the child. And when he came quite close his face grew red with anger, and he said, 'Who hath dared to wound thee?' For on the palms of the child's hands were the prints of two nails, and the prints of two nails were on the little feet.

'Who hath dared to wound thee?' cried the giant; 'tell me, that I may take my big sword and slay him.'

'Nay!' answered the child, 'but these are the wounds of love.'

'Who art thou?' said the giant, and a strange awe fell on him, and he knelt before the little child.

And the child smiled on the giant, and said to him, 'You let me play once in your garden; today you shall come with me to my garden, which is Paradise.'

And when the children ran in that afternoon, they found the giant lying dead under the tree, all covered with white blossoms.

The Seven-Headed Serpent

Once upon a time there was a king who determined to take a long voyage. He assembled his fleet and all the seamen and set out. They went straight on night and day, until they came to an island which was covered with large trees, and under every tree lay a lion. As soon as the king had landed his men, the lions all rose up together and tried to devour them. After a long battle they managed to overcome the wild beasts, but the greater number of the men were killed. Those who remained alive now went on through the forest and found on the other side of it a beautiful garden, in which all the plants of the world flourished together. There were also in the garden three springs: the first flowed with silver, the second with gold and the third with pearls. The men unbuckled their knapsacks and filled them with these precious things. In the middle of the garden they found a large lake, and when they reached the edge of it the lake began to speak, and said to them, 'What men are you, and what brings you here? Are you come to visit our king?' But they were too much frightened to answer.

Then the lake said, 'You do well to be afraid, for it is at your peril that you are come hither. Our king, who has seven heads, is now asleep, but in a few minutes he will wake up and come to me to take his bath! Woe to anyone who meets him in the garden, for it is impossible to escape from him. This is what you must do if you wish to save your lives. Take off your clothes and spread them on the path which leads from here to the castle. The king will then glide over something soft, which he likes very much, and he will be so pleased with that that he will not devour you. He will give you some punishment, but then he will let you go.'

The men did as the lake advised them, and waited for a time. At noon the earth began to quake, and opened in many places, and out of the openings appeared lions, tigers and other wild beasts, which surrounded the castle, and thousands and thousands of beasts came out of the castle following their king, the seven-headed serpent. The serpent glided over the clothes which were spread for him, came to the lake, and asked it who had strewn those soft things on the path? The lake answered that it had been done by people who had come to do him homage. The king commanded that the men should be brought before him. They came humbly on their knees, and in a few words told him their story. Then he spoke to them with a mighty and terrible voice, and said, 'Because you have dared to come here, I lay upon you the punishment. Every year you must bring me from among your people twelve youths and twelve maidens, that I may devour them. If you do not do this, I will destroy your whole nation.'

Then he desired one of his beasts to show the men the way out of the garden, and dismissed them. They then left the island and went back to their own country, where they related what had happened to them. Soon the time came round when the king of the beasts would expect the youths and maidens to be brought to him. The king therefore issued a proclamation inviting twelve youths and twelve maidens to offer themselves up to save their country; and immediately many young people, far more than enough, hastened to do so. A new ship was built, and set with black sails, and in it the youths and maidens who were appointed for the king of the beasts embarked and set out for his country. When they arrived there they went at once to the lake, and this time the lions did not stir, nor did the springs flow, and neither did the lake speak. So they waited then, and it was not long before the earth quaked even more terribly than the first time. The seven-headed serpent came without his train of beasts, saw his prey waiting for him, and devoured it at one mouthful. Then the ship's crew returned home, and the same thing happened yearly until many years had passed.

Now the king of this unhappy country was growing old, and so was the queen, and they had no children. One day the queen was sitting at the window weeping bitterly because she was childless, and knew that the crown would therefore pass to strangers after the king's death. Suddenly a little old woman appeared before her, holding an apple in her hand, and said, 'Why do you weep, my queen, and what makes you so unhappy?'

'Alas, good mother,' answered the queen, 'I am unhappy because I have no children.'

'Is that what vexes you?' said the old woman. 'Listen to me. I am a nun from the Spinning Convent, and my mother when she died left me this apple. Whoever eats this apple shall have a child.'

The queen gave money to the old woman, and bought the apple from her. Then she peeled it, ate it, and threw the rind out of the window, and it so happened that a mare that was running loose in the court below ate up the rind. After a time the queen had a little boy, and the mare also had a male foal. The boy and the foal grew up together and loved each other like brothers. In course of time the king died, and so did the queen, and their son, who was now nineteen years old, was left alone. One day, when he and his horse were talking together, the horse said to him, 'Listen to me, for I love you and wish for your good and that of the country. If you go on every year sending twelve youths and twelve maidens to the king of the beasts, your country will very soon be ruined. Mount upon my back: I will take you to a woman who can direct you how to kill the seven-headed serpent.'

Then the youth mounted his horse, who carried him far away to a mountain which was hollow, for in its side was a great underground cavern. In the cavern sat an old woman spinning. This was the cloister of the nuns, and the old woman was the abbess. They all spent their time in spinning, and that is why the convent had this name. All round the walls of the cavern there were beds cut out of the solid rock, upon which the nuns slept, and in the middle a light was burning. It was the duty of the nuns to watch the light in turns, that it might never go out, and if any one of them let it go out the others put her to death.

As soon as the king's son saw the old abbess spinning he threw himself at her feet and entreated her to tell him how he could kill the seven-headed serpent.

She made the youth rise, embraced him, and said, 'Know, my son, that it is I who sent the nun to your mother and caused you to be born, and with you the horse, with whose help you will be able to free the world from the monster. I will tell you what you have to do. Load your horse with cotton, and go by a secret passage which I will show you, which is hidden from the wild beasts, to the serpent's palace. You will find the king asleep upon his bed, which is all hung round with bells, and over his bed you will see a sword hanging. With this sword only is it possible to kill the serpent, because even if its blade breaks a new one will grow again for every head the monster has. Thus you will be able to cut off all his seven heads. And this you must also do in order to deceive the king: you must slip into his bedchamber very softly, and stop up all the bells which are round his bed with cotton. Then take down the sword gently, and quickly give the monster a blow on his tail with it. This will make him wake up, and if he catches sight of you he will seize you. But you must quickly cut off his first head, and then wait till the next one comes up. Then strike it off also, and so go on till you have cut off all his seven heads.'

The old abbess then gave the prince her blessing, and he set out upon his enterprise, arrived at the serpent's castle by following the secret passage which she had shown him, and, by carefully attending to all her directions, he happily succeeded in killing the monster. As soon as the wild beasts heard of their king's death, they all hastened to the castle, but the youth had long since mounted his horse and was already far out of their reach. They pursued him as fast as they could, but they found it impossible to overtake him, and he reached home in safety. Thus he freed his country from this terrible oppression.

بِسْمِ اللهِ الرَّحْمٰنِ الرَّحِيمِ

The First Voyage of Sinbad the Sailor

My father left me a considerable estate, the best part of which I spent in riotous living during my youth; but I perceived my error, and reflected that riches were perishable, and quickly consumed by such ill managers as myself. I further considered that by my irregular way of living I had wretchedly misspent my time which is the most valuable thing in the world. Struck with those reflections, I collected the remains of my furniture, and sold all my patrimony by public auction to the highest bidder. Then I entered into a contract with some merchants, who traded by sea: I took the advice of such as I thought most capable to give it me; and resolving to improve what money I had, I went to Balsora and embarked with several merchants on board a ship which we jointly fitted out.

We set sail, and steered our course towards the East Indies, through the Persian Gulf, which is formed by the coasts of Arabia Felix on the right, and by those of Persia on the left, and, according to common opinion, is seventy leagues across at the broadest part. The eastern sea, as well as that of the Indies, is very spacious: it is bounded on one side by the coasts of Abyssinia, and is 4,500 leagues in length to the isles of Vakvak. At first I was troubled with sea-sickness, but speedily recovered my health, and was not afterwards troubled with that disease.

In our voyage we touched at several islands, where we sold or exchanged our goods. One day, whilst under sail, we were becalmed near a little island, almost even with the surface of the water, which resembled a green meadow. The captain ordered his sails to be furled, and permitted such persons as had a mind to do so to land upon the island, amongst whom I was one.

But while we were diverting ourselves with eating and drinking, and recovering ourselves from the fatigue of the sea, the island on a sudden trembled, and shook us terribly.

They perceived the trembling of the island on board the ship, and called us to re-embark speedily, or we should all be lost, for what we took for an island was only the back of a whale. The nimblest got into the sloop, others betook themselves to swimming; but for my part I was still upon the back of the whale when he dived into the sea, and had time only to catch hold of a piece of wood that we had brought out of the ship to make a fire. Meanwhile, the captain, having received those on board who were in the sloop, and taken up some of those that swam, resolved to use the favourable gale that had just risen, and hoisting his sails, pursued his voyage, so that it was impossible for me to regain the ship.

Thus was I exposed to the mercy of the waves, and struggled for my life all the rest of the day and the following night. Next morning I found my strength gone, and despaired of saving my life, when happily a wave threw me against an island. The bank was high and rugged, so that I could scarcely have got up had it not been for some roots of trees, which fortune seemed to have preserved in this place for my safety. Being got up, I lay down upon the ground half dead until the sun appeared;

Then I entered into a contract with some merchants, who traded by sea

then, though I was very feeble, both by reason of my hard labour and want of food, I crept along to look for some herbs fit to eat, and had the good luck not only to find some, but likewise a spring of excellent water, which contributed much to restore me. After this I advanced farther into the island, and came at last into a fine plain, where I perceived a horse feeding at a great distance. I went towards him, between hope and fear, not knowing whether I was going to lose my life or save it. Presently I heard the voice of a man from under ground, who immediately appeared to me, and asked who I was. I gave him an account of my adventure; after which, taking me by the hand, he led me into a cave, where there were several other people, no less amazed to see me than I was to see them.

I ate some victuals which they offered me, and then asked them what they did in such a desert place. They answered that they were grooms belonging to King Mihrage, sovereign of the island, and that every year they brought thither the king's horses. They added that they were to get home tomorrow, and had I been one day later I must have perished, because the inhabited part of the island was at a great distance, and it would have been impossible for me to have got thither without a guide.

Next morning they returned with their horses to

the capital of the island, took me with them, and presented me to King Mihrage. He asked me who I was, and by what adventure I came into his dominions? And, after I had satisfied him he told me he was much concerned for my misfortune, and at the same time ordered that I should want for nothing, which his officers were so generous and careful as to see exactly fulfilled.

Being a merchant, I frequented the society of men of my own profession, and particularly enquired for those who were strangers, if perhaps I might hear any news from Baghdad, or find an opportunity to return thither, for King Mihrage's capital was situated on the edge of the sea, and had a fine harbour, where ships arrived daily from the different quarters of the world. I frequented also the society of the learned Indians, and took delight in hearing them discourse; but withal I took care to make my court regularly to the king, and conversed with the governors and petty kings, his tributaries, that were about him. They asked me a thousand questions about my country, and I, being willing to inform myself as to their laws and customs, asked them everything which I thought worth knowing.

There belonged to this king an island named Cassel. They assured me that every night a noise of drums was heard there, whence the mariners fancied that it was the residence of Degial. I had a great mind to see this wonderful place, and on my way thither saw fishes of one hundred and two hundred cubits long that occasion more fear than hurt, for they are so timid that they will fly at the rattling of two sticks or boards. I saw likewise other fishes, about a cubit in length, that had heads like owls.

As I was one day at the port after my return, a ship arrived, and as soon as she cast anchor, they began to unload her, and the merchants on board ordered their goods to be carried into the warehouse. As I cast my eye upon some bales, and looked at the name, I found my own, and perceived the bales to be the same that I had embarked at Balsora. I also knew the captain; but being persuaded that he believed me to be drowned, I went and asked him whose bales they were. He replied: 'They belonged to a merchant of Baghdad, called Sinbad, who came to sea with us; but one day, being near an island, as we thought, he went ashore with several other passengers upon this supposed island, which was only a monstrous whale that lay asleep upon the surface of the water; but as soon as he felt the heat of the fire they had kindled on his back to dress some victuals he began to move, and

dived under water: most of the persons who were upon him perished, and among them unfortunate Sinbad. Those bales belonged to him, and I am resolved to trade with them until I meet with some of his family, to whom I may return the profit.'

'Captain,' said I, 'I am that Sinbad whom you thought to be dead, and those bales are mine.'

When the captain heard me speak thus, 'O heaven,' said he, 'whom can we ever trust nowadays? There is no faith left among men. I saw Sinbad perish with my own eyes, and the passengers on board saw it as well as I, and yet you tell me you are that Sinbad. What impudence is this! To look at you, one would take you to be a man of honesty, and yet you tell a horrible falsehood, in order to possess yourself of what does not belong to you.'

'Have patience, captain,' replied I; 'do me the favour to hear what I have to say.'

'Very well,' said he, 'speak; I am ready to hear you.' Then I told him how I escaped, and by what adventure I met with the grooms of King Mihrage, who brought me to his court.

He was soon persuaded that I was no cheat, for there came people from his ship who knew me, paid me great compliments, and expressed much joy to see me alive. At last he knew me himself, and embracing me, 'Heaven be praised,' said he, 'for your happy escape; I cannot enough express my joy for it: there are your goods; take and do with them what you will.' I thanked him, acknowledged his honesty, and in return offered him part of my goods as a present, which he generously refused. I took out what was most valuable in my bales, and presented it to King Mihrage, who, knowing my misfortune, asked me how I came by such rarities. I acquainted him with the whole story. He was mightily pleased at my good luck, accepted my present, and gave me one much more considerable in return. Upon this I took leave of him, and went aboard the same ship, after I had exchanged my goods for the commodities of that country. I carried with me wood of aloes, sandal, camphor, nutmegs, cloves, pepper and ginger. We passed by several islands, and at last arrived at Balsora, from whence I came to this city, with the value of one hundred thousand sequins. My family and I received one another with transports of sincere friendship. I bought slaves and fine lands, and built me a great house. And thus I settled myself, resolving to forget the miseries I had suffered, and to enjoy the pleasures of life.

The Second Voyage of Sinbad the Sailor

I designed, after my first voyage, to spend the rest of my days at Baghdad; but it was not long ere I grew weary of a quiet life. My inclination to trade revived. I bought goods suited to the commerce I intended, and put to sea a second time, with merchants of known probity. We embarked on board a good ship, and after recommending ourselves to God, set sail. We traded from island to island, and exchanged commodities with great profit. One day we landed on an island covered with several sorts of fruit trees, but so unpeopled that we could see neither man nor beast upon it. We went to take a little fresh air in the meadows, and along the streams that watered them. Whilst some diverted themselves with gathering flowers, and others with gathering fruits, I took my wine and provisions, and sat down by a stream betwixt two great trees, which formed a curious shape. I made a very good meal, and afterwards fell asleep. I cannot tell how long I slept, but when I awoke the ship was gone.

I was very much surprised to find the ship gone. I got up and looked about everywhere, and could not see one of the merchants who landed with me. At last I perceived the ship under sail, but at such a distance that I lost sight of her in a very little time.

I leave you to guess at my melancholy reflections in this sad condition. I was ready to die with grief: I cried out sadly, beat my head and breast, and threw myself down upon the ground, where I lay some time in a terrible agony. I upbraided myself a hundred times for not being content with the produce of my first voyage, that might well have served me all my life. But all this was in vain, and my repentance out of season.

At last I resigned myself to the will of God; and not knowing what to do, I climbed up to the top of a great tree, from whence I looked about on all sides to see if there was anything that could give me hope. When I looked towards the sea, I could see nothing but sky and water, but looking towards the land I saw something white; and, coming down from the tree, I took up what provisions I had left and went towards it, the distance being so great that I could not distinguish what it was.

When I came nearer, I thought it to be a white bowl of a prodigious height and bigness; and when I came up to it I touched it, and found it to be very smooth. I went round to see if it was open on any side, but saw it was not, and that there was no climbing up to the top of it, it was so smooth. It was at least fifty paces round.

By this time the sun was ready to set, and all of a sudden the sky became as dark as if it had been covered with a thick cloud. I was much astonished at this sudden darkness, but much more when I found it was occasioned by a bird, of a monstrous size, that came flying towards me. I remembered a fowl, called roc, that I had often heard mariners speak of, and conceived that the great bowl, which I so much admired, must needs be its egg. In short, the bird lighted, and sat over the egg to hatch it. As I perceived her coming, I crept close to the egg, so that I had before me one of the legs of the bird, which was as big as the trunk of a tree. I tied myself strongly to it with the cloth that went round my turban, in hopes that when the roc flew away next morning she would carry me with her out of this desert island. And after having passed the night in this condition, the bird flew away next morning, as soon as it was day, and carried me so high that I could not see the earth. Then she descended all of a sudden, with so much rapidity that I lost my senses; but when the roc was settled, and I found myself upon the ground, I speedily untied the knot, and had scarcely done so when the bird, having taken up a serpent of a monstrous length in her bill, flew away.

The place where she left me was a very deep valley, encompassed on all sides with mountains, so high that they seemed to reach above the clouds, and so full of steep rocks that there was no

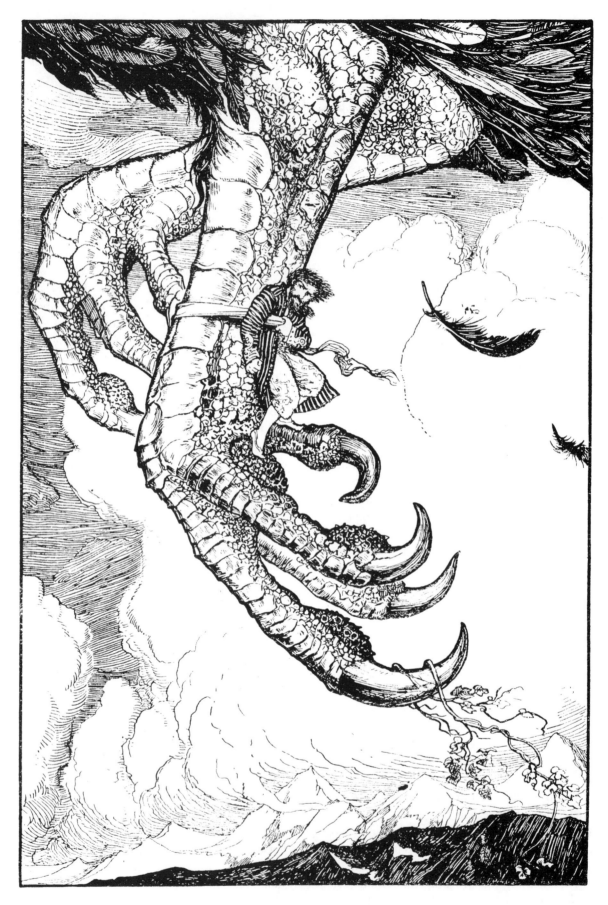

The bird flew away next morning, as soon as it was day, and carried me so high that I could not see the earth

possibility of getting out of the valley. This was a new perplexity, so that when I compared this place with the desert island from which the roc brought me, I found that I had gained nothing by the change.

As I walked through this valley I perceived it was strewn with diamonds, some of which were of surprising bigness. I took a great deal of pleasure in looking at them; but speedily I saw at a distance such objects as very much diminished my satisfaction, and which I could not look upon without terror; they were a great number of serpents, so big and so long that the least of them was capable of swallowing an elephant. They retired in the daytime to their dens, where they hid themselves from the roc, their enemy, and did not come out but in the night-time.

I spent the day in walking about the valley, resting myself at times in such places as I thought most suitable. When night came on I went into a cave, where I thought I might be in safety. I stopped the mouth of it, which was low and straight, with a great stone, to preserve me from the serpents, but not so exactly fitted as to hinder light from coming in. I supped on part of my provisions, but the serpents, which began to appear, hissing about in the meantime, put me into such extreme fear that you may easily imagine I did not sleep. When day appeared the serpents retired, and I came out of the cave trembling. I can justly say that I walked a long time upon diamonds without feeling an inclination to touch any of them. At last I sat down, and notwithstanding my uneasiness, not having shut my eyes during the night, I fell asleep, after having eaten a little more of my provisions; but I had scarcely shut my eyes when something that fell by me with great noise awakened me. This was a great piece of fresh meat, and at the same time I saw several others fall down from the rocks in different places.

I had always looked upon it as a fable when I heard mariners and others discourse of the valley of diamonds, and of the stratagems made use of by some merchants to get jewels from thence; but now I found it to be true. For, in reality, those merchants come to the neighbourhood of this valley when the eagles have young ones and throw great joints of meat into the valley; the diamonds, upon whose points they fall, stick to them; the eagles, which are stronger in this country than anywhere else, pounce with great force upon those pieces of meat, and carry them to their nests upon the top of the

A great number of serpents, so big and so long that the least of them was capable of swallowing an elephant

rocks to feed their young with, at which time the merchants, running to their nests, frighten the eagles by their noise, and take away the diamonds that stick to the meat. And this stratagem they make use of to get the diamonds out of the valley, which is surrounded with such precipices that nobody can enter it.

I believed till then that it was not possible for me to get out of this abyss, which I looked upon as my grave; but now I changed my mind, for the falling in of those pieces of meat put me in hopes of a way of saving my life.

I began to gather together the largest diamonds that I could see, and put them into the leathern bag in which I used to carry my provisions. I afterwards took the largest piece of meat I could find, tied it close round me with the cloth of my turban, and then laid myself upon the ground, with my face downward, the bag of diamonds being tied fast to my girdle, so that it could not possibly drop off.

I had scarcely laid me down before the eagles came. Each of them seized a piece of meat, and one of the strongest having taken me up, with a piece of meat on my back, carried me to his nest on the top of the mountain. The merchants fell straightway to shouting, to frighten the eagles; and when they had obliged them to quit their prey, one of them came to the nest where I was. He was very much afraid when he saw me, but recovering himself, instead of enquiring how I came thither, he began to quarrel with me, and asked why I stole his goods. 'You will treat me,' replied I, 'with more civility when you know me better. Do not trouble yourself; I have diamonds enough for you and myself too, more than all the other merchants together. If they have any, it is by chance; but I chose myself in the bottom of the valley all those which you see in this bag;' and having spoken those words, I showed them to him. I had scarcely done speaking, when the other merchants came trooping about us, much astonished to see me; but they were much more surprised when I told them my story. Yet they did not so much admire my stratagem to save myself as my courage to attempt it.

They took me to the place where they were staying all together, and there, having opened my bag, they were surprised at the largeness of my diamonds, and confessed that in all the courts where they had been they had never seen any that came near them. I prayed the merchant to whom the nest belonged (for every merchant had his own), to take as many for his share as he pleased. He contented himself with one, and that too the least of them; and when I pressed him to take more, without fear of doing me any injury, 'No,' said he, 'I am very well satisfied with this, which is valuable enough to save me the trouble of making any more voyages to raise as great a fortune as I desire.'

I spent the night with those merchants, to whom I told my story a second time, for the satisfaction of those who had not heard it. I could not moderate my joy when I found myself delivered from the danger I have mentioned. I thought I was in a dream, and could scarcely believe myself to be out of danger.

The merchants had thrown their pieces of meat into the valley for several days, and each of them being satisfied with the diamonds that had fallen to his lot, we left the place next morning all together, and travelled near high mountains, where there were serpents of a prodigious length, which we had the good fortune to escape. We took ship at the nearest port and came to the Isle of Roha, where the trees grow that yield camphor. This tree is so large, and its branches so thick, that a hundred men may easily sit under its shade. The juice of which the camphor is made runs out from a hole bored in the upper part of the tree and is received in a vessel, where it grows thick, and becomes what we call camphor; and the juice thus drawn out, the tree withers and dies.

There is in this island the rhinoceros, a creature less than the elephant, but greater than the buffalo; it has a horn upon its nose about a cubit long; this horn is solid, and cleft in the middle from one end to the other, and there are upon it white lines, representing the figure of a man. The rhinoceros fights with the elephant, runs his horn into him, and carries him off upon his head; but the blood of the elephant running into his eyes and making him blind, he falls to the ground, and then, strange to relate, the roc comes and carries them both away in her claws to be food for her young ones.

Here I exchanged some of my diamonds for good merchandise. From thence we went to other isles, and at last, having touched at several trading towns of the mainland, we landed at Balsora, from whence I went to Baghdad. There I immediately gave great alms to the poor, and lived honourably upon the vast riches I had gained with so much fatigue.

The Third Voyage of Sinbad the Sailor

The pleasures of the life which I then led soon made me forget the risks I had run in my two former voyages; but, being then in the flower of my age, I grew weary of living without business; and hardening myself against the thought of any danger I might incur, I went from Baghdad, with the richest commodities of the country, to Balsora: there I embarked again with the merchants. We made a long voyage, and touched at several ports, where we drove a considerable trade. One day, being out in the main ocean, we were attacked by a horrible tempest, which made us lose our course. The tempest continued several days, and brought us before the port of an island, where the captain was very unwilling to enter; but we were obliged to cast anchor there. When we had furled our sails the captain told us that this and some other neighbouring islands were inhabited by hairy savages, who would speedily attack us; and though they were but dwarfs, yet our misfortune was that we must make no resistance, for they were more in number than the locusts; and if we happened to kill one of them they would all fall upon us and destroy us.

This discourse of the captain put the whole company into a great consternation; and we found very soon, to our cost, that what he had told us was but too true; an innumerable multitude of frightful savages, covered all over with red hair, and about two feet high, came swimming towards us, and in a little time encompassed our ship. They spoke to us as they came near, but we understood not their language; they climbed up the sides of the ship with an agility that surprised us. We beheld all this with mortal fear, without daring to offer to defend ourselves, or to speak one word to divert them from their mischievous design. In short, they took down our sails, cut the cable, and, hauling to the shore, made us all get out, and afterwards carried the ship into another island, from whence they had come. All travellers carefully avoided that island where they left us, it being very dangerous to stay

there, for a reason you shall hear anon; but we were forced to bear our affliction with patience.

We went forward into the island, where we found some fruits and herbs to prolong our lives as long as we could; but we expected nothing but death. As we went on we perceived at a distance a great pile of building, and made towards it. We found it to be a palace, well built, and very lofty, with a gate of ebony with double doors, which we thrust open. We entered the court, where we saw before us a vast apartment with a porch, having on one side a heap of men's bones, and on the other a vast number of roasting spits. We trembled at this spectacle, and, being weary with travelling, our legs failed under us: we fell to the ground, seized with deadly fear, and lay a long time motionless.

The sun had set, and whilst we were in the lamentable condition just mentioned, the gate of the apartment opened with a great noise, and there came out the horrible figure of a huge man, as high as a tall palm tree. He had but one eye, and that in the middle of his forehead, where it looked as red as a burning coal. His fore-teeth were very long and sharp, and stood out of his mouth, which was as deep as that of a horse; his lower lip hung down upon his breast; his ears resembled those of an elephant, and covered his shoulders; and his nails were as long and crooked as the talons of the greatest birds. At the sight of so frightful a giant we lost all our senses, and lay like men dead.

At last we came to ourselves, and saw him sitting in the porch, looking at us. When he had considered us well, he advanced towards us, and laying his hand upon me, he took me up by the nape of my neck, and turned me round as a butcher would do a sheep's head. After having viewed me well, and perceiving me to be so lean that I had nothing but skin and bone, he let me go. He took up all the rest, one by one, and viewed them in the same manner; and the captain being the fattest, he held him with one hand, as I might a

There came a huge man, as high as a tall palm tree. He had but one eye, and that in the middle of his forehead, where it looked as red as a burning coal.

sparrow, and thrusting a spit through him, kindled a great fire, roasted, and ate him in his apartment for his supper. This being done, he returned to his porch, where he lay and fell asleep, snoring louder than thunder. He slept thus till morning. For our parts, it was not possible for us to enjoy any rest; so that we passed the night in the most cruel fear that can be imagined. Day being come, the giant awoke, got up, went out, and left us in the palace.

When we thought him at a distance, we broke the melancholy silence we had kept all night, and every one grieving more than another, we made the palace resound with our complaints and groans. Though there were a great many of us, and we had but one enemy, we had not at first the presence of mind to think of delivering ourselves from him by his death.

We thought of several other things, but determined nothing; so that, submitting to what it should please God to order concerning us, we spent the day in running about the island for fruit and herbs to sustain our lives. When evening came, we sought for a place to lie down in, but found none; so that we were forced, whether we would or not, to return to the palace.

The giant failed not to come back, and supped once more upon one of our companions; after which he slept, and snored till day, and then went out and left us as formerly. Our condition was so very terrible that several of my comrades designed to throw themselves into the sea, rather than die so strange a death. Those who were of this mind argued with the rest to follow their example; upon which one of the company answered that we were forbidden to destroy ourselves; but even if it were lawful, it was more reasonable to think of a way to rid ourselves of the barbarous tyrant who designed so cruel a death for us.

Having thought of a project for that end, I communicated the same to my comrades, who approved it. 'Brethren,' said I, 'you know there is a great deal of timber floating upon the coast; if you will be advised by me, let us make several rafts that may carry us, and when they are done, leave them there till we think fit to make use of them. In the meantime we will execute the design to deliver ourselves from the giant, and if it succeed, we may stay here with patience till some ship pass by to carry us out of this fatal island; but if it happen to miscarry, we will speedily get to our rafts, and put to sea. I confess, that by exposing ourselves to the fury of the waves, we run a risk of losing our lives; but if we do, is it not better to be buried in the sea than in the entrails of this monster, who has already devoured two of us?' My advice was relished, and we made rafts capable of carrying three persons each.

We returned to the palace towards evening, and the giant arrived a little while after. We were forced to see another of our comrades roasted. But at last we revenged ourselves on the brutish giant thus. After he had made an end of his cursed supper, he lay down on his back, and fell asleep. As soon as we heard him snore, according to his custom, nine of the boldest among us, and myself, took each of us a spit, and putting the points of them into the fire till they were burning hot, we thrust them into his eye all at once, and blinded him. The pain occasioned him to make a frightful cry, and to get up and stretch out his hands in order to sacrifice some of us to his rage, but we ran to places where he could not find us; and after having sought for us in vain, he groped for the gate, and went out, howling dreadfully.

We went out of the palace after the giant, and came to the shore, where we had left our rafts, and put them immediately into the sea. We waited till day in order to get upon them, in case the giant came towards us with any guide of his own species; but we hoped that if he did not appear by sunrise, and gave over his howling, which we still heard, it might be that he had died; and if that happened to be the case, we resolved to stay in the island, and not to risk our lives upon the rafts. But day had scarcely appeared when we perceived our cruel enemy, accompanied by two others almost of the same size leading him, and a great number more coming before him with a very quick pace.

When we saw this, we made no delay, but got immediately upon our rafts, and rowed off from the shore. The giants, who perceived this, took up great stones, and running to the shore entered the water up to their waists, and threw so exactly that they sank all the rafts but that I was upon, and all my companions, except the two with me, were drowned. We rowed with all our might, and got out of the reach of the giants; but when we got out to sea, we were exposed to the mercy of the waves and winds, and tossed about, sometimes on one side, and sometimes on another, and spent that night and the following day under a cruel uncertainty as to our fate; but next morning we had the good luck to be thrown upon an island, where we landed with much joy. We found excellent fruit there, that gave us great relief, so that we recovered our strength.

In the evening we fell asleep on the bank of the sea, but were awaked by the noise of a serpent as long as a palm tree, whose scales made a rustling as he crept along. He swallowed up one of my comrades, notwithstanding his loud cries and the efforts he made to free himself from the serpent, which shook him several times against the ground, and crushed him; and we could hear him gnaw and tear the poor wretch's bones, when we had fled a great distance from him. Next day we saw the serpent again, to our great terror, and I cried out, 'O heaven, to what dangers are we exposed! We rejoiced yesterday at having escaped from the cruelty of a giant and the rage of the waves, and now are we fallen into another danger altogether as terrible.'

As we walked about we saw a large tall tree, upon which we designed to pass the following night, for our security; and having satisfied our hunger with

We rowed with all our might, and got out of the reach of the giants; but when we got out to sea, we were exposed to the mercy of the waves and winds

fruit, we mounted it accordingly. A little while after, the serpent came hissing to the root of the tree, raised itself up against the trunk of it, and meeting with my comrade, who sat lower than I, swallowed him at once, and went off.

I stayed upon the tree till it was day, and then came down, more like a dead man than one alive, expecting the same fate as my two companions. This filled me with horror, so that I was going to throw myself into the sea; but nature prompting us to a desire to live as long as we can, I withstood this temptation to despair, and submitted myself to the will of God, who disposes of our lives at His pleasure.

In the meantime I gathered together a great quantity of small wood, brambles and dry thorns, and making them up into faggots made a great circle with them round the tree, and also tied some of them to the branches over my head. Having done thus, when the evening came I shut myself up within this circle, with this melancholy piece of satisfaction, that I had neglected nothing which could preserve me from the cruel destiny with which I was threatened. The serpent failed not to come at the usual hour, and went round the tree, seeking for an opportunity to devour me, but was prevented by the rampart I had made, so that he lay till day, like a cat watching in vain for a mouse that has retreated to a place of safety. When day appeared he retired, but I dared not leave my fort until the sun arose.

I was fatigued with the toil he had put me to, and suffered so much from his poisonous breath that, death seeming preferable to me than the horror of such a condition, I came down from the tree, and not thinking on the resignation I had made to the will of God the preceding day, I ran towards the sea, with a design to throw myself into it headlong.

God took compassion on my desperate state, for just as I was going to throw myself into the sea, I perceived a ship at a considerable distance. I called as loud as I could, and taking the linen from my turban, displayed it that they might observe me. This had the desired effect; all the crew perceived me, and the captain sent his boat for me. As soon as I came aboard, the merchants and seamen flocked about me to know how I came to that desert island; and after I had told them of all that befell me, the oldest among them said they had several times heard of the giants that dwelt in that island, that they were cannibals and ate men raw as well as roasted; and as to the serpents, he added, there were abundance in the isle that hid themselves by day and came abroad by night. After having testified their joy at my escaping so many dangers, they brought me the best of what they had to eat; and the captain, seeing that I was all in rags, was so generous as to give me one of his own suits.

We were at sea for some time, touched at several islands, and at last landed at that of Salabat, where there grows sanders, a wood of great use in physic. We entered the port, and came to anchor. The merchants began to unload their goods, in order to sell or exchange them. In the meantime the captain came to me, and said, 'Brother, I have here a parcel of goods that belonged to a merchant who sailed some time on board this ship; and he being dead, I intend to dispose of them for the benefit of his heirs, when I know them.' The bales he spoke of lay on the deck, and showing them to me, he said, 'There are the goods; I hope you will take care to sell them, and you shall have a commission.' I thanked him that he gave me an opportunity to employ myself, because I hated to be idle.

The clerk of the ship took an account of all the bales, with the names of the merchants to whom they belonged; and when he asked the captain in whose name he should enter those he gave me the charge of, 'Enter them,' said the captain, 'in the name of Sinbad the sailor.' I could not hear myself named without some emotion, and looking steadfastly on the captain, I knew him to be the person who, in my second voyage, had left me in the island where I fell asleep by a brook, and set sail without me, and without sending to look for me. But I could not remember him at first, he was so much altered since I saw him.

And as for him, who believed me to be dead, I could not wonder at his not knowing me. 'But, captain,' said I, 'was the merchant's name to whom those goods belonged Sinbad?'

'Yes,' replied he, 'that was his name; he came from Baghdad, and embarked on board my ship at Balsora. One day, when we landed at an island to take in water and other refreshments, I know not by what mistake I set sail without observing that he did not re-embark with us; neither I nor the merchants perceived it till four hours after. We had the wind in our stern and so fresh a gale that it was not then possible for us to tack about for him.'

'You believe him then to be dead?' said I.

'Certainly,' answered he.

'No, captain,' said I; 'look upon me, and you may know that I am Sinbad, whom you left on that desert island. I fell asleep by a brook, and when I awoke I found all the company gone.'

The captain, having considered me attentively, knew me at last, embraced me, and said, 'God be praised that fortune has supplied my defect. There are your goods, which I always took care to preserve and to make the best of at every port where I touched. I restore them to you, with the profit I have made on them.' I took them from him, and at the same time acknowledged how much I owed to him.

From the Isle of Salabat we went to another, where I furnished myself with cloves, cinnamon and other spices. As we sailed from that island we saw a tortoise that was twenty cubits in length and breadth. We observed also a fish which looked like a cow, and gave milk, and its skin is so hard that they usually make bucklers of it. I saw another which had the shape and colour of a camel. In short, after a long voyage, I arrived at Balsora, and from thence returned to this city of Baghdad, with so much riches that I knew not what I had. I gave a great deal to the poor, and bought another great estate in addition to what I had already.

The Fourth Voyage of Sinbad the Sailor

The pleasures I took after my third voyage had not charms enough to divert me from another. I was again prevailed upon by my passion for traffic and curiosity to see new things. I therefore settled my affairs, and having provided a stock of goods fit for the places where I designed to trade, I set out on my journey. I took the way of Persia, of which I travelled over several provinces, and then arrived at a port, where I embarked. We set sail, and having touched at several ports of the mainland and some of the eastern islands, we put out to sea, and were overtaken by a sudden gust of wind that obliged the captain to furl his sails, and to take all other necessary precautions to prevent the danger that threatened us. But all was in vain; our endeavours had no effect, the sails were torn into a thousand pieces, and the ship was stranded; so that a great many of the merchants and seamen were drowned, and the cargo lost.

I had the good fortune, with several of the merchants and mariners, to get a plank, and we were carried by the current to an island which lay before us: there we found fruit and spring water, which preserved our lives. We stayed all night near the place where the sea cast us ashore, without consulting what we should do, our misfortune had dispirited us so much.

Next morning, as soon as the sun was up, we walked from the shore, and advancing into the island, saw some houses, to which we went; and as soon as we came thither we were encompassed by a great number of black men, who seized us, shared us among them, and carried us to their respective habitations.

I and five of my comrades were carried to one place; they made us sit down immediately, and gave us a certain herb, which they made signs to us to eat. My comrades, not taking notice that the black men ate none of it themselves, consulted only the satisfying of their own hunger, and fell to eating with greediness; but I, suspecting some trick, would not so much as taste it, which happened well for me; for in a little time I perceived my companions had lost their senses, and that when they spoke to me they knew not what they said.

The black men fed us afterwards with rice, prepared with oil of coconuts, and my comrades, who had lost their reason, ate of it greedily. I ate of it also, but very sparingly. The black men gave us that herb at first on purpose to deprive us of our senses, that we might not be aware of the sad destiny prepared for us; and they gave us rice on purpose to fatten us, for, being cannibals, their design was to eat us as soon as we grew fat. They did accordingly eat my comrades, who were not aware of their condition; but my senses being entire, you may easily guess that instead of growing fat, as the rest did, I grew leaner every day. The fear of death under which I laboured turned all my food into poison. I fell into a languishing illness which proved my safety, for the black men having killed and eaten up my companions, seeing me to be withered, lean, and sick, deferred my death till another time.

Meanwhile, I had a great deal of liberty, so that there was scarcely any notice taken of what I did, and this gave me an opportunity one day to get at a distance from the houses, and to make my escape. An old man who saw me, and suspected my design, called to me as loud as he could to return, but instead of obeying him, I redoubled my pace, and quickly got out of sight. At that time there was none but the old man about the houses, the rest being away, and not to come home till night, which was pretty usual with them; therefore, being sure that they could not come in time to pursue me, I went on till night, when I stopped to rest a little, and to eat some of the provisions I had taken care to bring; but I speedily set forward again, and travelled seven days, avoiding those places which seemed to be inhabited, and living for the most part upon coconuts, which served me for both meat and drink. On the eighth day I came near the sea, and all of a sudden saw white people like myself, gathering pepper, of which there was great plenty in that place. This I took to be a good omen, and went to them without any scruple.

The people who gathered pepper came to meet me as soon as they saw me, and asked me in Arabic who I was, and whence I came. I was overjoyed to hear them speak in my own language, and satisfied their curiosity by giving them an account of my shipwreck, and how I fell into the hands of the black men. 'Those black men,' replied they, 'are cannibals, and by what miracle did you escape their cruelty?' I told them the same story I now tell you, at which they were wonderfully surprised.

I stayed with them till they had gathered their quantity of pepper, and then sailed with them to the island from whence they came. They presented me to their king, who was a good prince. He had the patience to hear the relation of my adventures, which surprised him, and he afterwards gave me clothes, and commanded care to be taken of me.

The island was very well peopled, plentiful in everything, and the capital was a place of great trade. This agreeable retreat was very comfortable to me after my misfortune, and the kindness of this generous prince towards me completed my satisfaction. In a word, there was not a person more in favour with him than myself; and, in consequence, every man in court and city sought to oblige me, so that in a very little time I was looked upon rather as a native than a stranger.

I observed one thing which to me appeared very extraordinary. All the people, the king himself not excepted, rode their horses without bridle or stirrups. This made me one day take the liberty to ask the king how that came to pass. His majesty answered that I talked to him of things which nobody knew the use of in his dominions. I went immediately to a workman, and gave him a model for making the stock of a saddle. When that was done, I covered it myself with velvet and leather, and embroidered it with gold. I afterwards went to a locksmith, who made me a bridle according to the pattern I showed him, and then he made me also some stirrups. When I had all things completed, I presented them to the king, and put them upon one of his horses. His majesty mounted immediately, and was so pleased with them, that he testified his satisfaction by large presents to me. I could not avoid making several others for his

ministers and the principal officers of his household, who all of them made me presents that enriched me in a little time. I also made some for the people of best quality in the city, which gained me great reputation and regard.

As I paid court very constantly to the king, he said to me one day, 'Sinbad, I love thee; and all my subjects who know thee treat thee according to my example. I have one thing to demand of thee, which thou must grant.'

'Sir,' answered I, 'there is nothing I will not do, as a mark of my obedience to your majesty, whose power over me is absolute.'

'I have a mind thou shouldst marry,' replied he, 'that so thou mayst stay in my dominion, and think no more of thy own country.'

I dared not resist the prince's will, and so he gave me one of the ladies of his court, a noble, beautiful and rich lady. The ceremonies of marriage being over, I went and dwelt with the lady, and for some time we lived together in perfect harmony. I was not, however, very well satisfied with my condition, and therefore designed to make my escape on the first occasion, and to return to Baghdad, which my present settlement, how advantageous soever, could not make me forget.

While I was thinking on this, the wife of one of my neighbours, with whom I had contracted a very close friendship, fell sick and died. I went to see and comfort him in his affliction, and finding him swallowed up with sorrow, I said to him as soon as I saw him, 'God preserve you and grant you a long life.'

'Alas!' replied he, 'how do you think I should obtain that favour you wish me? I have not above an hour to live.'

'Pray,' said I, 'do not entertain such a melancholy thought; I hope it will not be so, but that I shall enjoy your company for many years.'

'I wish you,' said he, 'a long life; but for me my days are at an end, for I must be buried this day with my wife. This is a law which our ancestors established in this island, and always observed inviolably. The living husband is interred with the dead wife, and the living wife with the dead husband. Nothing can save me; everyone must submit to this law.'

While he was entertaining me with an account of this barbarous custom, the very hearing of which frightened me cruelly, his kindred, friends and neighbours came in a body to assist at the funerals. They put on the corpse the woman's richest apparel, as if it had been her wedding day, and dressed her with all her jewels; then they put her into an open coffin, and lifting it up, began their march to the place of burial. The husband walked at the head of the company, and followed the corpse. They went up to a high mountain, and when they came thither, took up a great stone, which covered the mouth of a very deep pit, and let down the corpse, with all its apparel and jewels. Then the husband, embracing his kindred and friends, suffered himself to be put into another open coffin without resistance, with a pot of water, and seven little loaves, and was let down in the same manner as they let down his wife. The mountain was pretty long, and reached to the sea. The ceremony being over, they covered the hole again with the stone, and returned.

It is needless to say that I was the only melancholy spectator of this funeral, whereas the rest were scarcely moved at it, the practice was so customary to them. I could not forbear speaking my thoughts on this matter to the king. 'Sir,' said I, 'I cannot but wonder at the strange custom in this country of burying the living with the dead. I have been a great traveller, and seen many countries, but never heard of so cruel a law.'

'What do you mean, Sinbad?' said the king; 'it is a common law. I shall be interred with the queen, my wife, if she die first.'

'But, sir,' said I, 'may I presume to ask your majesty if strangers be obliged to observe this law?'

'Without doubt,' replied the king, smiling at my question; 'they are not exempted, if they are married in this island.'

I went home very melancholy at this answer, for the fear of my wife dying first, and my being interred alive with her, occasioned me very mortifying reflections. But there was no remedy: I must have patience, and submit to the will of God. I trembled, however, at every little indisposition of my wife; but alas! in a little time my fears came upon me all at once, for she fell ill, and died in a few days.

You may judge of my sorrow; to be interred alive seemed to me as deplorable an end as to be devoured by cannibals. But I must submit; the king and all his court would honour the funeral with their presence, and the most considerable people of the city would do the like. When all was ready for the ceremony, the corpse was put into a coffin, with all her jewels and magnificent apparel. The cavalcade began, and, as second actor in this doleful tragedy, I went next to the corpse, with my eyes full of tears, bewailing my deplorable fate. Before I came to the mountain, I addressed myself to the king, in the first place, and then to all those who were round me, and bowing before them to the earth to kiss the border of their garments, I prayed them to have compassion upon me. 'Consider,' said I, 'that I am a stranger, and ought not to be subject to this rigorous law, and that I have another wife and child in my own country.' It was to no purpose for me to speak thus, no soul was moved at it; on the contrary, they made haste to let down my wife's corpse into the pit, and put me down the next moment in an open coffin, with a vessel full of water and seven loaves. In short, the fatal ceremony being performed, they covered up the mouth of the pit, notwithstanding the excess of my grief and my lamentable cries.

As I came near the bottom, I discovered, by help of the little light that came from above, the nature of this subterranean place; it was a vast long cave, and might be about fifty fathoms deep. I immediately smelt an insufferable stench proceeding from the multitude of corpses which I saw on the right and left; nay, I fancied that I heard some of them sigh out their last. However, when I got down, I immediately left my coffin, and, getting at a distance from the corpses, lay down upon the ground, where I stayed a long time, bathed in tears. Then reflecting on my sad lot, 'It is true,' said I, 'that God disposes all things according to the decrees of His providence; but, poor Sinbad, art not thou thyself the cause of thy being brought to die so strange a death? Would to God thou hadst perished in some of those tempests which thou hast escaped! Then thy death had not been so lingering and terrible in all its circumstances. But thou hast drawn all this upon thyself by thy cursed avarice. Ah! unfortunate wretch, shouldst thou not rather have stayed at home, and quietly enjoyed the fruits of thy labour?'

Such were the vain complaints with which I made the cave echo, beating my head and breast out of rage and despair, and abandoning myself to the most afflicting thoughts. Nevertheless, I must tell you that, instead of calling death to my assistance in that miserable condition, I felt still an inclination to live, and to do all I could to prolong my days. I went groping about, with my nose stopped, for the bread and water that was in my coffin, and took some of it. Though the darkness of the cave was so great that I could not distinguish

They put me down the next moment in an open coffin, with a vessel full of water and seven loaves

day and night, yet I always found my coffin again, and the cave seemed to be more spacious and fuller of corpses than it appeared to me at first. I lived for some days upon my bread and water, which being all used up at last I prepared for death.

As I was thinking of death, I heard something walking, and blowing or panting as it walked. I advanced towards that side from whence I heard the noise, and upon my approach the thing puffed and blew harder, as if it had been running away from me. I followed the noise, and the thing seemed to stop sometimes, but always fled and blew as I approached. I followed it so long and so far that at last I perceived a light resembling a star; I went on towards that light, and sometimes lost sight of it, but always found it again, and at last discovered that it came through a hole in the rock large enough for a man to get out at.

Upon this I stopped some time to rest myself, being much fatigued with pursuing this discovery so fast. Afterwards coming up to the hole I went out at it, and found myself upon the shore of the sea. I leave you to guess the excess of my joy; it was such that I could scarce persuade myself of its being real.

But when I had recovered from my surprise, and was convinced of the truth of the matter, I found that the thing which I had followed and heard puff and blow was a creature which came out of the sea, and was accustomed to enter at that hole to feed upon the dead carcasses.

I examined the mountain, and perceived it to be situated betwixt the sea and the town, but without any passage or way to communicate with the latter, the rocks on the side of the sea were so rugged and steep. I fell down upon the shore to thank God for this mercy, and afterwards entered the cave again and groped about among the biers for all the diamonds, rubies, pearls, gold bracelets and rich stuffs I could find. These I brought to the shore, and, tying them up neatly into bales with the cords that let down the coffins, I laid them together upon the bank to wait till some ship passed by, without fear of rain, for it was not then the season.

After two or three days I perceived a ship that had but just come out of the harbour and passed near the place where I was. I made a sign with the linen of my turban, and called to them as loud as I could. They heard me, and sent a boat to bring me on board, when the mariners asked by what misfortune I came thither. I told them that I had suffered shipwreck two days ago, and made shift to get ashore with the goods they saw. It was happy for me that those people did not consider the place where I was, nor enquire into the probability of what I told them; but without any more ado took me on board with my goods. When I came to the ship, the captain was so well pleased to have saved me, and so much taken up with his own affairs, that he also took the story of my pretended shipwreck upon trust, and generously refused some jewels which I offered him.

We passed with a regular wind by several islands, among others the one called the Isle of Bells, about ten days' sail from Serendib, and six from that of Kela, where we landed. This island produces lead from its mines, Indian canes and excellent camphor.

The king of the Isle of Kela is very rich and potent, and the Isle of Bells, which is about two days' journey in extent, is also subject to him. The inhabitants are so barbarous that they still eat human flesh. After we had finished our commerce in that island we put to sea again, and touched at several other ports. At last I arrived happily at Baghdad with infinite riches, of which it is needless to trouble you with the detail. Out of thankfulness to God for His mercies, I gave great alms for the support of several mosques, and for the subsistence of the poor, and employed myself wholly in enjoying the society of my kindred and friends, and in making merry with them.

The Fifth Voyage of Sinbad the Sailor

The pleasures I enjoyed again had charm enough to make me forget all the troubles and calamities I had undergone, without curing me of my inclination to make new voyages. Therefore I bought goods, ordered them to be packed up and loaded, and set out with them for the best seaport; and there, that I might not be obliged to depend upon a captain, but have a ship at my own command, I waited till one was built on purpose at my own expense. When the ship was ready, I went on board with my goods; but not having enough to load her, I took on board with me several merchants of different nations, with their merchandise.

We sailed with the first fair wind, and after a long voyage, the first place we touched at was a desert island, where we found an egg of a roc, equal in size to that I formerly mentioned. There was a young roc in it just ready to be hatched, and the bill of it began to appear.

The merchants whom I had taken on board my ship, and who landed with me, broke the egg with hatchets, and made a hole in it, from whence they pulled out the young roc piece by piece, and roasted it. I had earnestly entreated them not to meddle with the egg, but they would not listen to me.

Scarcely had they made an end of their feast, when there appeared in the air, at a considerable distance from us, two great clouds. The captain whom I had hired to manage my ship, knowing by experience what it meant, cried that it was the cock and hen roc that belonged to the young one, and pressed us to re-embark with all speed, to prevent the misfortune which he saw would otherwise befall us. We made haste to do so, and set sail with all possible diligence.

In the meantime the two rocs approached with a frightful noise, which they redoubled when they saw the egg broken, and their young one gone. But having a mind to avenge themselves, they flew back towards the place from whence they came, and disappeared for some time, while we made all the sail we could to prevent that which unhappily befell us.

They returned, and we observed that each of them carried between their talons stones, or rather rocks, of a monstrous size. When they came directly over my ship, they hovered, and one of them let fall a stone; but by the dexterity of the steersman, who turned the ship with the rudder, it missed us, and falling by the side of the ship into the sea, divided the water so that we could see almost to the bottom. The other roc, to our misfortune, threw the stone so exactly upon the middle of the ship that it split into a thousand pieces. The mariners and passengers were all killed by the stone, or sunk. I myself had the last fate; but as I came up again I fortunately caught hold of a piece of the wreck, and swimming sometimes with one hand and sometimes with the other, but always holding fast to my board, the wind and the tide favouring me, I came to an island, where the beach was very steep. I overcame that difficulty, however, and got ashore.

I sat down upon the grass, to recover myself a little from my fatigue, after which I got up, and

535

*The other roc, to our misfortune, threw the stone
so exactly upon the middle of the ship that it
split into a thousand pieces*

went into the island to view it. It seemed to be a delicious garden. I found trees everywhere, some of them bearing green and others ripe fruits, and streams of fresh pure water, with pleasant windings and turnings. I ate of the fruits, which I found excellent, and drank of the water, which was very pleasant.

Night being come, I lay down upon the grass in a convenient place enough, but I could not sleep for an hour at a time, my mind was so disturbed with the fear of being alone in so desert a place. Thus I spent the best part of the night in fretting, and reproached myself for my imprudence in not staying at home, rather than undertaking this last voyage. These reflections carried me so far, that I began to form a design against my own life, but daylight dispersed these melancholy thoughts, and I got up, vand walked among the trees, but not without apprehensions of danger.

When I was a little advanced into the island, I saw an old man who appeared very weak and feeble. He sat upon the bank of a stream, and at first I took him to be one who had been shipwrecked like myself. I went towards him and saluted him, but he only bowed his head a little. I asked him what he did there, but instead of answering he made a sign for me to take him upon my back and carry him over the brook, signifying that he wished to gather fruit.

I believed him really to stand in need of my help, so took him upon my back, and having carried him over, bade him get down, and for that end stooped that he might get off with ease: but instead of that (which I laugh at every time I think of it), the old man, who to me had appeared very decrepit, clasped his legs nimbly about my neck, and then I perceived his skin to resemble that of a cow. He sat astride upon my shoulders, and held my throat so tight that I thought he would have strangled me, the fright of which made me faint away and as a consequence fall down.

Notwithstanding my fainting, the ill-natured old fellow kept fast about my neck, but opened his legs a little to give me time to recover my breath. When I had done so, he thrust one of his feet against my stomach, and struck me so rudely on the side with the other that he forced me to rise up against my will. Having got me up, he made me walk under the trees, and forced me now and then to stop, to gather and eat fruit such as we found. He never left me all day, and when I lay down to rest by night, he laid himself down with me, always holding fast about my neck. Every morning he pushed me to make me wake, and afterwards obliged me to get up and walk, and pressed me with his feet. You may judge then what trouble I was in, to be loaded with such a burden, of which I could by no means rid myself.

One day I found in my way several dry calabashes that had fallen from a tree; I took a large one, and, after cleaning it, pressed into it some juice of grapes, which abounded in the island. Having filled the calabash, I set it in a convenient place; and coming hither again some days after, I took up my calabash, and setting it to my mouth found the wine to be so good that it presently made me not only forget my sorrow, but grow vigorous, and so light-hearted that I began to sing and dance as I walked along.

The old man, perceiving the effect which this drink had upon me, and that I carried him with more ease than I did before, made a sign for me to give him some of it. I gave him the calabash, and the liquor pleasing his palate, he drank it all off. He became drunk immediately, and the fumes getting up into his head he began to sing after his manner, and to dance upon my shoulders. His jolting about made him sick, and he loosened his legs from about me by degrees; so finding that he did not press me as before, I threw him upon the ground, where he lay without motion, and then I took up a great stone, with which I crushed his head to pieces.

I was extremely rejoiced to be freed thus for ever from this cursed old fellow, and walked along the shore of the sea, where I met the crew of a ship that had cast anchor to take in water to refresh themselves. They were extremely surprised to see me, and to hear the particulars of my adventures. 'You fell,' said they, 'into the hands of the old man of the sea, and are the first that has ever escaped strangling by him. He never left those he had once

I gave him the calabash, and the liquor pleasing his palate, he drank it all off

made himself master of till he destroyed them, and he has made this island famous for the number of men he has slain; so that the merchants and mariners who landed upon it dared not advance into the island but in numbers together.'

After having informed me of these things they carried me with them to the ship; the captain received me with great satisfaction when they told him what had befallen me. He put out again to sea, and after some days' sail we arrived at the harbour of a great city, where the houses were built of good stone.

One of the merchants of the ship, who had taken me into his friendship, asked me to go along with him, and took me to a place appointed as a retreat for foreign merchants. He gave me a great bag, and having recommended me to some people of the town, who were used to gather coconuts, he desired them to take me with them to do the like: 'Go,' said he, 'follow them, and do as you see them do, and do not separate from them, otherwise you endanger your life.' Having thus spoken, he gave me provisions for the journey, and I went with them.

We came to a great forest of trees, extremely straight and tall, their trunks so smooth that it was not possible for any man to climb up to the branches that bore the fruit. All the trees were coconut trees, and when we entered the forest we saw a great number of apes of all sizes, that fled as soon as they perceived us, and climbed up to the top of the trees with surprising swiftness.

The merchants with whom I was gathered stones, and threw them at the apes on the top of the trees. I did the same, and the apes, out of revenge, threw coconuts at us as fast and with such gestures as sufficiently testified their anger and resentment; we gathered up the coconuts, and from time to time threw stones to provoke the apes; so that by this stratagem we filled our bags with coconuts, which it had been impossible for us to do otherwise.

When we had gathered our number, we returned to the city, where the merchant who sent me to the forest gave me the value of the coconuts I had brought; 'Go on,' said he, 'and do the like every day, until you have money enough to carry you home.' I thanked him for his good advice, and gathered together as many coconuts as amounted to a considerable sum.

The vessel in which I came sailed with merchants who loaded her with coconuts. I expected the arrival of another, whose merchants landed speedily for the like loading. I embarked on board the same all the coconuts that belonged to me, and when she was ready to sail I went and took leave of the merchant who had been so kind to me; but he could not embark with me because he had not finished his business.

We set sail towards the islands where pepper grows in great plenty. From thence we went to the Isle of Comari, where the best sort of wood of aloes grows, and whose inhabitants have made it an inviolable law to drink no wine themselves, nor to suffer any kind of improper conduct. I exchanged my coconuts in those two islands for pepper and wood of aloes, and went with other merchants pearl-fishing. I hired divers, who fetched me up those that were very large and pure. Then I embarked joyfully in a vessel that happily arrived at Balsora; from thence I returned to Baghdad, where I made vast sums by my pepper, wood of aloes and pearls. I gave the tenth of my gains in alms, as I had done upon my return from other voyages, and endeavoured to ease myself from my fatigue by diversions of all sorts.

The Sixth Voyage of Sinbad the Sailor

After being shipwrecked five times, and escaping so many dangers, could I resolve again to try my fortune, and expose myself to new hardships? I am astonished at it myself when I think of it, and must certainly have been induced to it by my stars. But be that as it will, after a year's rest I prepared for a sixth voyage, notwithstanding the entreaties of my kindred and friends, who did all that was possible to prevent me. Instead of taking my way by the Persian Gulf, I travelled once more through several provinces of Persia and the Indies, and arrived at a seaport, where I embarked on board a ship, the captain of which was resolved on a long voyage.

It was very long indeed, but at the same time so unfortunate that the captain and pilot lost their course, and knew not where they were. They found it at last, but we had no reason to rejoice at it. We were all seized with extraordinary fear when we saw the captain quit his post, and cry out. He threw off his turban, pulled his beard, and beat his head like a madman. We asked him the reason, and he answered that he was in the most dangerous place in all the sea. 'A rapid current carries the ship along with it,' he said, 'and we shall all of us perish in less than a quarter of an hour. Pray to God to deliver us from this danger; we cannot escape it if He does not take pity on us.' At these words he ordered the sails to be changed; but all the ropes broke and the ship, without its being possible to help it, was carried by the current to the foot of an inaccessible mountain, where she ran ashore, and was broken to pieces, yet so that we saved our lives, our provisions and the best of our goods.

This being over, the captain said to us, 'God has done what pleased Him; we may every man dig our grave here, and bid the world adieu, for we are all in so fatal a place that none shipwrecked here have ever returned to their homes again.' His discourse afflicted us sorely, and we embraced each other with tears in our eyes, bewailing our deplorable lot.

The mountain at the foot of which we were cast was the coast of a very long and large island. This coast was covered all over with wrecks, and from the vast number of men's bones we saw everywhere, and which filled us with horror, we concluded that abundance of people had died there. It is also impossible to tell what a quantity of goods and riches we found cast ashore there. All these objects served only to augment our grief. Whereas in all other places rivers run from their channels into the sea, here a great river of fresh water runs out of the sea into a dark cave, whose entrance is very high and large. What is most remarkable in this place is that the stones of the mountain are of crystal, rubies or other precious stones. Here is also a sort of fountain of pitch or bitumen, that runs into the sea, which the fishes swallow, and then vomit up again, turned into ambergris; and this the waves throw up on the beach in great quantities. Here also grow trees, most of which are wood of aloes, equal in goodness to those of Comari.

To finish the description of this place – which may well be called a gulf, since nothing ever returns from it – it is not possible for ships to get away again when once they come near it. If they are driven thither by a wind from the sea, the wind and the current ruin them; and if they come into it when a land-wind blows, which might seem to favour their getting out again, the height of the mountain stops the wind, and occasions a calm, so that the force of the current runs them ashore, where they are broken to pieces, as ours was; and that which completes the misfortune is that there is no possibility to get to the top of the mountain, or to get out any manner of way.

We continued upon the shore, like men out of their senses, and expected death every day. At first we divided our provisions as equally as we could, and thus everyone lived a longer or shorter time, according to their temperance, and the use they made of their provisions.

Those who died first were interred by the rest; and, for my part, I paid the last duty to all my companions. Nor are you to wonder at this; for besides that I husbanded the provision that fell to my share better than they, I had provision of my own, which I did not share with my comrades; yet when I buried the last, I had so little remaining that I thought I could not hold out long, so I dug a grave, resolving to lie down in it, because there was none left to inter me. I must confess to you at the same time that while I was thus employed I could not but reflect upon myself as the cause of my own ruin, and repented that I had ever undertaken this last voyage; nor did I stop at reflections only, but had begun to tear my hands with my teeth and well nigh hastened my own death.

But it pleased God once more to take compassion on me, and put it in my mind to go to the bank of the river which ran into the great cave; where, considering the river with great attention, I said to myself, 'This river, which runs thus under ground, must come out somewhere or other. If I make a raft, and leave myself to the current, it will bring me to some inhabited country, or drown me. If I be drowned I lose nothing, but only change one kind of death for another; and if I get out of this fatal place, I shall not only avoid the sad fate of my comrades, but perhaps find some new occasion of enriching myself. Who knows but fortune waits, upon my getting off this dangerous shelf, to compensate my shipwreck with interest?'

I immediately went to work on a raft. I made it of large pieces of timber and cables, for I had choice of them, and tied them together so strongly that I made a very solid little raft. When I had finished it I loaded it with some bales of rubies, emeralds, ambergris, rock-crystal and rich stuffs. Having balanced all my cargo exactly and fastened it well to the raft, I went on board it with two little oars that I had made, and, leaving it to the course of the river, I resigned myself to the will of God.

As soon as I came into the cave I lost all light, and the stream carried me I knew not whither. Thus I floated for some days in perfect darkness, and once found the arch so low that it well nigh broke my head, which made me very cautious afterwards to avoid the like danger. All this while I ate nothing but what was just necessary to support nature; yet, notwithstanding this frugality, all my provisions were spent. Then a pleasing sleep fell upon me. I cannot tell how long it continued; but when I awoke, I was surprised to find myself in the middle of a vast country on the bank of the river, where my raft was tied, amidst a great number of negroes. I got up as soon as I saw them and saluted them. They spoke to me, but I did not understand their language. I was so transported with joy that I knew not whether I was asleep or awake; but being persuaded that I was not asleep, I recited the following words in Arabic aloud: 'Call upon the Almighty, he will help thee; thou needest not perplex thyself about anything else; shut thy eyes, and while thou art asleep, God will change thy bad fortune into good.'

One of the blacks, who understood Arabic, hearing me speak thus, came towards me and said, 'Brother, be not surprised to see us; we are inhabitants of this country, and came hither today to water our fields, by digging little canals from this river, which comes out of the neighbouring mountain. We saw something floating upon the water, went speedily to find out what it was, and perceiving your raft, one of us swam into the river, and brought it hither, where we fastened it, as you see, until you should awake. Pray tell us your history, for it must be extraordinary; how did you venture into this river, and whence did you come?'

I begged of them first to give me something to eat, and then I would satisfy their curiosity. They gave me several sorts of food; and when I had satisfied my hunger, I gave them a true account of all that had befallen me, which they listened to with wonder. As soon as I had finished my discourse, they told me, by the person who spoke Arabic and interpreted to them what I said, that it was one of the most surprising stories they ever heard, and that I must go along with them, and tell it to their king myself; the story was too extraordinary to be told by any other than the person to whom it happened. I told them I was ready to do whatever they pleased.

They immediately sent for a horse, which was brought in a little time; and having made me get upon him, some of them walked before me to show me the way, and the rest took my raft and cargo, and followed me.

We marched thus altogether, till we came to the city of Serendib, for it was in that island I had landed. The blacks presented me to their king; I approached his throne, and saluted him as I used to do the kings of the Indies; that is to say, I prostrated myself at his feet, and kissed the earth. The prince ordered me to rise up, received me with an obliging air, and made me come up, and sit down near him. He first asked me my name, and I answered, 'They call me Sinbad the sailor, because of the many voyages I have undertaken, and I am a citizen of Baghdad.'

'But,' replied he, 'how came you into my dominions, and from whence came you last?'

I concealed nothing from the king; I told him all that I have now told you, and his majesty was so surprised and charmed with it, that he commanded my adventure to be written in letters of gold, and laid up in the archives of his kingdom. At last my raft was brought in, and the bales opened in his presence: he admired the quantity of wood of aloes and ambergris; but, above all, the rubies and emeralds, for he had none in his treasury that came near them.

Observing that he looked on my jewels with pleasure, and viewed the most remarkable among them one after another, I fell prostrate at his feet, and took the liberty to say to him, 'Sir, not only my person is at your majesty's service, but the cargo of the raft, and I would beg of you to dispose of it as your own.'

He answered me with a smile, 'Sinbad, I will take care not to covet anything of yours, nor to take anything from you that God has given you; far from lessening your wealth, I design to augment it, and will not let you go out of my dominions without marks of my liberality.'

All the answer I returned was prayers for the prosperity of this prince, and commendations of his generosity and bounty. He charged one of his officers to take care of me, and ordered people to serve me at his own charge. The officer was very faithful in the execution of his orders, and caused all the goods to be carried to the lodgings provided for me. I went every day at a set hour to pay court to the king, and spent the rest of my time in seeing the city, and what was most worthy of notice.

The Isle of Serendib is situated just under the equinoctial line, so that the days and nights there are always of twelve hours each, and the island is eighty parasangs in length, and as many in breadth.

The capital city stands at the end of a fine valley formed by a mountain in the middle of the island, which is the highest in the world. I made, by way of devotion, a pilgrimage to the place where Adam was confined after his banishment from Paradise, and had the curiosity to go to the top of it.

When I came back to the city, I prayed the king to allow me to return to my country, which he granted me in the most obliging and honourable manner. He would needs force a rich present upon me, and when I went to take my leave of him, he gave me one much more valuable, and at the same time charged me with a letter for the Commander of the Faithful, our sovereign, saying to me, 'I pray you give this present from me and this letter to Caliph Harun-al-Rashid, and assure him of my friendship.' I took the present and letter in a very respectful manner, and promised his majesty punctually to execute the commission with which he was pleased to honour me. Before I embarked, this prince sent for the captain and the merchants who were to go with me, and ordered them to treat me with all possible respect.

The letter from the King of Serendib was written on the skin of a certain animal of great value, because of its being so scarce, and of a yellowish colour. The writing was azure, and the contents as follows:

THE KING OF THE INDIES,
before whom march a hundred elephants, who lives in a palace that shines with a hundred thousand rubies, and who has in his treasury twenty thousand crowns enriched with diamonds, to Caliph Harun-al-Rashid:

Though the present we send you be inconsiderable, receive it as a brother and a friend, in consideration of the hearty friendship which we bear to you, and of which we are willing to give you proof. We desire the same part in your friendship, considering that we believe it to be our merit, being of the same dignity with yourself. We conjure you this in the rank of a brother.

FAREWELL.

The present consisted first, of one single ruby made into a cup, about half a foot high, an inch thick, and filled with round pearls. Secondly, the skin of a serpent, whose scales were as large as an ordinary piece of gold, and had the virtue to preserve from sickness those who lay upon it. Thirdly, fifty thousand drachms of the best wood of aloes, with thirty grains of camphor as big as pistachios. And fourthly, a she-slave of ravishing beauty, whose apparel was covered all over with jewels.

The ship set sail, and after a very long and successful voyage, we landed at Balsora; from thence I went to Baghdad, where the first thing I did was to acquit myself of my commission.

I took the King of Serendib's letter, and went to present myself at the gate of the Commander of the Faithful, followed by the beautiful slave and such of my own family as carried the presents. I gave an account of the reason of my coming, and was immediately conducted to the throne of the caliph. I made my reverence, and after a short speech gave him the letter and present. When he had read what the King of Serendib wrote to him, he asked me if that prince were really so rich and potent as he had said in this letter. I prostrated myself a second time, and in reply, rising again, 'Commander of the Faithful,' said I, 'I can assure your majesty he doth not exceed the truth on that head: I am witness of it. There is nothing more capable of raising a man's admiration than the magnificence of his palace. When the prince appears in public, he has a throne fixed on the back of an elephant, and marches betwixt two ranks of his ministers, favourites, and other people of his court; before him, upon the same elephant, an officer carries a golden lance in his hand, and behind the throne there is another, who stands upright with a column of gold, on the top of which there is an emerald half a foot long and an inch thick; before him march a guard of a thousand men, clad in cloth of gold and silk, and mounted on elephants richly caparisoned.

'While the king is on his march, the officer who is before him on the same elephant cries from time to time, with a loud voice, "Behold the great monarch, the potent and redoubtable Sultan of the Indies, whose palace is covered with a hundred thousand rubies, and who possesses twenty thousand crowns of diamonds." After he has pronounced these words, the officer behind the throne cries in his turn, "This monarch so great and so powerful, must die, must die, must die." And the officer in front replies, "Praise be to Him who lives for ever."

'Further, the King of Serendib is so just that there are no judges in his dominions. His people have no need of them. They understand and observe justice of themselves.'

The caliph was much pleased with my discourse. 'The wisdom of this king,' said he, 'appears in his letter, and after what you tell me, I must confess that his wisdom is beyond price to his people, and his people deserve so wise a prince.' Having spoken thus he dismissed me, and sent me home with a rich present.

The Seventh and Final Voyage of Sinbad the Sailor

Being returned from my sixth voyage, I absolutely laid aside all thoughts of travelling any farther; for, besides that my years now required rest, I was resolved no more to expose myself to such risk as I had run; so that I thought of nothing but to pass the rest of my days in quiet. One day, as I was treating some of my friends, one of my servants came and told me that an officer of the caliph asked for me. I rose from the table, and went to him. 'The caliph,' said he, 'has sent me to tell you that he must speak with you.' I followed the officer to the palace, where, being presented to the caliph, I saluted him by prostrating myself at his feet. 'Sinbad,' said he to me, 'I stand in need of you; you must do me the service to carry my answer and present to the King of Serendib. It is but just I should return his civility.'

This command of the caliph to me was like a clap of thunder. 'Commander of the Faithful,' replied I, 'I am ready to do whatever your majesty shall think fit to command me; but I beseech you most humbly to consider what I have undergone. I have also made a vow never again to go out of Baghdad.' Here I took occasion to give him a large and particular account of all my adventures, which he had the patience to hear out.

As soon as I had finished, 'I confess,' said he, 'that the things you tell me are very extraordinary, yet you must for my sake undertake this voyage which I propose to you. You have nothing to do but to go to the Isle of Serendib, and deliver the commission which I give you. After that you are at liberty to return. But you must go; for you know it would be indecent, and not suitable to my dignity, to remain indebted to the king of that island.' Perceiving that the caliph insisted upon it, I submitted, and told him that I was willing to obey. He was very well pleased at it, and ordered me a thousand sequins for the expense of my journey.

I prepared for my departure in a few days, and as soon as the caliph's letter and present were delivered to me, I went to Balsora, where I embarked, and had a very happy voyage. I arrived at the Isle of Serendib, where I acquainted the king's ministers with my commission, and prayed them to get me speedy audience. They did so, and I was conducted to the palace in an honourable manner, where I saluted the king by prostration, according to custom. That prince knew me immediately, and testified very great joy to see me. 'O Sinbad,' said he, 'you are welcome; I swear to you I have many times thought of you since you went hence; I bless the day upon which we see one another once more.' I made my compliment to him, and after having thanked him for his kindness to me, I delivered the caliph's letter and present, which he received with all imaginable satisfaction.

The caliph's present was a complete set of cloth of gold, valued at one thousand sequins; fifty robes of rich stuff, a hundred others of white cloth, the finest of Cairo, Suez, Cusa and Alexandria; a royal crimson bed, and a second of another fashion; a vessel of agate broader than deep, an inch thick, and half a foot wide, the bottom of which represented in bas-relief a man with one knee on the ground, who held a bow and an arrow, ready to let fly at a lion. He sent him also a rich table, which, according to tradition, belonged to the great Solomon. The caliph's letter was as follows:

> Greeting in the name of the Sovereign
> Guide of the Right Way to
> **THE POTENT AND HAPPY SULTAN**
> from Abdallah Harun-al-Rashid, whom
> God hath set in the place of honour, after
> his ancestors of happy memory:
> We received your letter with joy, and send
> you this from the council of our port, the
> garden of superior wits. We hope, when
> you look upon it, you will find our good
> intention, and be pleased with it.
> FAREWELL.

The King of Serendib was highly pleased that the caliph returned his friendship. A little time after this audience, I solicited leave to depart, and had much difficulty to obtain it. I obtained it, however, at last, and the king, when he dismissed me, made me a very considerable present. I embarked immediately to return to Baghdad, but had not the good fortune to arrive there as I hoped. God ordered it otherwise.

Three or four days after my departure, we were attacked by pirates, who easily seized upon our ship. Some of the crew offered resistance, which cost them their lives. But as for me and the rest, who were not so imprudent, the pirates saved us on purpose to make slaves of us.

We were all stripped, and instead of our own clothes they gave us sorry rags, and carried us into a remote island, where they sold us.

I fell into the hands of a rich merchant, who, as soon as he bought me, carried me to his house, treated me well, and clad me handsomely for a slave. Some days after, not knowing who I was, he asked me if I understood any trade. I answered that I was no mechanic, but a merchant, and that the pirates who sold me had robbed me of all I had.

'But tell me,' replied he, 'can you shoot with a bow?'

I answered that the bow was one of my exercises in my youth, and I had not yet forgotten it. Then he gave me a bow and arrows, and, taking me behind him upon an elephant, carried me to a vast forest some leagues from the town. We went a great way into the forest, and where he thought fit to stop he bade me alight; then showing me a great tree, 'Climb up that tree,' said he, 'and shoot at the elephants as you see them pass by, for there is a prodigious number of them in this forest, and, if any of them fall, come and give me notice of it.' Having spoken thus, he left me victuals, and returned to the town, and I continued upon the tree all night.

I saw no elephant during that time, but next morning, as soon as the sun was up, I saw a great number: I shot several arrows among them, and at last one of the elephants fell; the rest retired immediately, and left me at liberty to go and acquaint my patron with my booty. When I had told him the news, he gave me a good meal, commended my dexterity, and praised me highly. We afterwards went together to the forest, where we dug a hole for the elephant, my patron intending to return when it was rotten, and to take the teeth, etc., to trade with.

I continued this game for two months, and killed an elephant every day, getting sometimes upon one tree, and sometimes upon another. One morning, as I looked for the elephants, I perceived with an extreme amazement that, instead of passing by me across the forest as usual, they stopped, and came to me with a horrible noise, in such a number that the earth was covered with them, and shook under them. They encompassed the tree where I was with their trunks extended and their eyes all fixed upon me. At this frightful spectacle I remained immovable, and was so much frightened that my bow and arrows fell out of my hand.

My fears were not in vain; for after the elephants had stared upon me for some time, one of the largest of them put his trunk round the root of the tree, and pulled so strong that he plucked it up and threw it on the ground; I fell with the tree, and the elephant taking me up with his trunk, laid me on his back, where I sat, more like one dead than alive, with my quiver on my shoulder; then he put himself at the head of the rest, who followed him in troops, and carried me to a place where he laid me down on the ground, and retired with all his companions. Conceive, if you can, the condition I was in: I thought myself to be in a dream; at last, after having lain some time, and seeing the elephants gone, I got up, and found I was upon a long and broad hill, covered all over with the bones and teeth of elephants. I confess to you that this furnished me with abundance of reflections. I admired the instinct of those animals; I doubted not but that this was their burying place, and that they carried me thither on purpose to tell me that I should forbear to persecute them since I did it only for their teeth. I did not stay on the hill, but turned towards the city, and, after having travelled a day and a night, I came to my patron; I met no elephant on my way, which made me think they had retired farther into the forest, to leave me at liberty to come back to the hill without any hindrance.

As soon as my patron saw me: 'Ah, poor Sinbad,' said he, 'I was in great trouble to know what had become of you. I have been at the forest, where I found a tree newly pulled up, and a bow and arrows on the ground, and after having sought for you in vain I despaired of ever seeing you more. Pray tell me what befell you, and by what good hap you are still alive.'

I satisfied his curiosity, and going both of us next morning to the hill, he found to his great joy that what I had told him was true. We loaded the elephant upon which we came with as many teeth

I fell with the tree, and the elephant taking me up with his trunk, laid me down among the bones and teeth of elephants

as he could carry; and when we had returned, 'Brother,' said my patron – 'for I will treat you no more as my slave – after having made such a discovery as will enrich me, may God bless you with all happiness and prosperity. I declare before Him that I give you your liberty. I concealed from you what I am now going to tell you.

'The elephants of our forest have every year killed a great many slaves, whom we sent to seek ivory. Notwithstanding all the cautions we could give them, those crafty animals killed them one time or other. God has delivered you from their fury, and has bestowed that favour upon you only. It is a sign that He loves you, and has use for your service in the world. You have procured me incredible gain. We could not have ivory formerly but by exposing the lives of our slaves, and now our whole city is enriched by your means. Do not think I pretend to have rewarded you by giving you your liberty; I will also give you considerable riches. I could engage all our city to contribute towards making your fortune, but I will have the glory of doing it myself.'

To this obliging discourse I replied, 'Patron, God preserve you. Your giving me my liberty is enough to discharge what you owe me, and I desire no other reward for the service I had the good fortune to do to you and your city than leave to return to my own country.'

'Very well,' said he, 'the monsoon will in a little time bring ships for ivory. I will send you home then, and give you wherewith to pay your expenses.' I thanked him again for my liberty, and his good intentions towards me. I stayed with him until the monsoon; and during that time we made so many journeys to the hill that we filled all our warehouses with ivory. The other merchants who traded in it did the same thing, for it could not be long concealed from them.

The ships arrived at last, and my patron himself having made choice of the ship wherein I was to embark, he loaded half of it with ivory on my account, laid in provisions in abundance for my passage and obliged me besides to accept, as a present, curiosities of the country of great value. After I had returned him a thousand thanks for all his favours, I went on board. We set sail, and as the adventure which procured me this liberty was very extraordinary, I had it continually in my thoughts.

We stopped at some islands to take in fresh provisions. Our vessel being come to a port on the mainland in the Indies, we touched there, and not being willing to venture by sea to Balsora, I landed my proportion of the ivory, resolving to proceed on my journey by land. I made vast sums by my ivory, I bought several rarities, which I intended for presents, and when my equipage was ready, I set out in the company of a large caravan of merchants. I was a long time on the way, and suffered very much, but endured all with patience, when I considered that I had nothing to fear from the seas, from pirates, from serpents, nor from the other perils I had undergone.

All these fatigues ended at last, and I came safe to Baghdad. I went immediately to wait upon the caliph, and gave him an account of my embassy. That prince told me he had been uneasy, by reason that I was so long in returning, but that he always hoped God would preserve me. When I told him the adventure of the elephants, he seemed to be much surprised at it, and would never have given any credit to it had he not known my sincerity. He reckoned this story, and the other narratives I had given him, to be so curious that he ordered one of his secretaries to write them in characters of gold, and lay them up in his treasury. I retired very well satisfied with the honours I received and the presents which he gave me; and after that I gave myself up wholly to my family, kindred and friends.

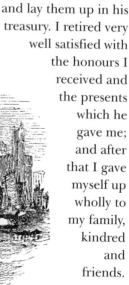

The Six Swans

A king was once hunting in a great wood, and he hunted the game so eagerly that none of his courtiers could follow him. When evening came on he stood still and looked round him, and he saw that he had quite lost himself. He sought a way out, but could find none. Then he saw an old woman with a shaking head coming towards him; but she was a witch.

'Good woman,' he said to her, 'can you not show me the way out of the wood?'

'Oh, certainly, Sir King,' she replied, 'I can quite well do that, but on one condition, which if you do not fulfil you will never get out of the wood, and will die of hunger.'

'What is the condition?' asked the king.

'I have a daughter,' said the old woman, 'who is so beautiful that she has not her equal in the world, and is well fitted to be your wife; if you will make her your lady-queen I will show you the way out of the wood.'

The king in his anguish of mind consented, and the old woman led him to her little house where her daughter was sitting by the fire. She received the king as if she were expecting him, and he saw that she was certainly very beautiful; but she did not please him, and he could not look at her without a secret feeling of horror. As soon as he had lifted the maiden on to his horse the old woman showed him the way, and the king reached his palace, where the wedding was celebrated.

The king had already been married once, and had by his first wife seven children, six boys and one girl, whom he loved more than anything in the world. And now, because he was afraid that their stepmother might not treat them well and might do them harm, he put them in a lonely castle that stood in the middle of a wood. It lay so hidden, and the way to it was so hard to find, that he himself could not have found it out had not a wise-woman given him a reel of thread which possessed a marvellous property: when he threw it before him

it unwound itself and showed him the way. But the king went so often to his dear children that the queen was offended at his absence. She grew curious, and wanted to know what he had to do quite alone in the wood. She gave his servants a great deal of money, and they betrayed the secret to her, and also told her of the reel which alone could point out the way. She had no rest now till she had found out where the king guarded the reel, and then she made some little white shirts, and, as she had learnt from her witch-mother, sewed an enchantment in each of them.

And when the king had ridden off she took the little shirts and went into the wood, and the reel showed her the way. The children, who saw someone coming in the distance, thought it was their dear father coming to them, and sprang to meet him very joyfully. Then she threw over each one a little shirt, which when it had touched their bodies changed them into swans, and they flew away over the forest. The queen went home quite satisfied, and thought she had got rid of her stepchildren; but the girl had not run to meet her with her brothers, and she knew nothing of her.

The next day the king came to visit his children, but he found no one but the girl.

'Where are your brothers?' asked the king.

'Alas! dear father,' she answered, 'they have gone away and left me all alone.' And she told him that looking out of her little window she had seen her brothers flying over the wood in the shape of swans, and she showed him the feathers which they had let fall in the yard, and which she had collected. The king mourned, but he did not think that the queen had done the wicked deed, and as he was afraid the maiden would also be taken from him, he wanted to take her with him. But she was afraid of the stepmother, and begged the king to let her stay just one night more in the castle in the wood. The poor maiden thought, 'My home is no longer here; I will go and seek my brothers.' And when night came she fled away into the forest. She ran all through the night and the next day, till she could go no farther for weariness. Then she saw a little hut, went in, and found a room with six little beds. She was afraid to lie down on one, so she crept under one of them, lay on the hard floor, and was going to spend the night there. But when the sun had set she heard a noise, and saw six swans flying in at the window. They stood on the floor and blew at one another, and blew all their feathers off, and their swan-skin came off like a shirt. Then the maiden recognised her brothers, and overjoyed she crept out from under the bed. Her brothers were not less delighted than she to see their little sister again, but their joy did not last long.

'You cannot stay here,' they said to her. 'This is a den of robbers; if they were to come here and find you they would kill you.'

'Could you not protect me?' asked the little sister.

'No,' they answered, 'for we can only lay aside our swan skins for a quarter of an hour every evening. For this time we regain our human forms, but then we are changed into swans again.'

Then the little sister cried and said, 'Can you not be freed?'

'Oh, no,' they said, 'the conditions are too hard. You must not speak or laugh for six years, and must make in that time six shirts for us out of star-flowers. If a single word comes out of your mouth, all your labour is vain.' And when the brothers had said this the quarter of an hour came to an end, and they flew away out of the window as swans.

But the maiden had determined to free her brothers even if it should cost her her life. She left the hut, went into the forest, climbed a tree, and spent the night there. The next morning she went out, collected star-flowers, and began to sew. She could speak to no one, and she had no wish to laugh, so she sat there, looking only at her work.

When she had lived there some time, it happened that the king of the country was hunting in the forest, and his hunters came to the tree on which the maiden sat. They called to her and said 'Who are you?'

But she gave no answer.

'Come down to us,' they said, 'we will do you no harm.'

But she shook her head silently. As they pressed her further with questions, she threw them the golden chain from her neck. But they did not leave off, and she threw them her girdle, and when this

was no use, her garters, and then her dress. The huntsmen would not leave her alone, but climbed the tree, lifted the maiden down, and led her to the king. The king asked, 'Who are you? What are you doing up that tree?'

But she answered nothing.

He asked her in all the languages he knew, but she remained as dumb as a fish. Because she was so beautiful, however, the king's heart was touched, and he was seized with a great love for her. He wrapped her up in his cloak, placed her before him on his horse and brought her to his castle. There he had her dressed in rich clothes, and her beauty

shone out as bright as day, but not a word could be drawn from her. He set her at table by his side, and her modest ways and behaviour pleased him so much that he said, 'I will marry this maiden and none other in the world,' and after some days he married her. But the king had a wicked mother who was displeased with the marriage, and said wicked things of the young queen. 'Who knows who this girl is?' she said; 'she cannot speak, and is not worthy of a king.'

After a year, when the queen had her first child, the old mother took it away from her. Then she went to the king and said that the queen had killed it. The king would not believe it, and would not allow any harm to be done her. But she sat quietly sewing at the shirts and troubling herself about nothing. The next time she had a child the wicked mother did the same thing, but the king could not make up his mind to believe her. He said, 'She is too sweet and good to do such a thing as that. If she were not dumb and could defend herself, her innocence would be proved.' But when the third child was taken away, and the queen was again accused, and could not utter a word in her own defence, the king was obliged to give her over to the law, which decreed that she must be burnt to death. When the day came on which the sentence was to be executed, it

was the last day of the six years in which she must not speak or laugh, and now she had freed her dear brothers from the power of the enchantment. The six shirts were done; there was only the left sleeve wanting to the last.

When she was led to the stake, she laid the shirts on her arm, and as she stood on the pile and the fire was about to be lighted, she looked around her and saw six swans flying through the air. Then she knew that her release was at hand and her heart danced for joy. The swans fluttered round her, and hovered low so that she could throw the shirts over them. When they had touched them the swan-skins fell off, and her brothers stood before her living, well and beautiful. Only the youngest had a swan's wing instead of his left arm. They embraced and kissed each other, and the queen went to the king, who was standing by in great astonishment, and began to speak to him, saying, 'Dearest husband, now I can speak and tell you openly that I am innocent and have been falsely accused.' She told him of the old woman's deceit, and how she had taken the three children away and hidden them. Then they were fetched, to the great joy of the king, and the wicked mother came to no good end. But the king and the queen with their six brothers lived many years in happiness and peace.

Sleeping Beauty

Once upon a time there was a king and a queen, who were very sorry that they had no children – so sorry that it cannot be told.

At last, however, the queen had a daughter. There was a very fine christening; and the princess had for her godmothers all the fairies they could find in the whole kingdom (there were seven of them), so that every one of them might confer a gift upon her, as was the custom of fairies in those days. By this means the princess had all the perfections imaginable.

After the christening was over, the company returned to the king's palace, where was prepared a great feast for the fairies. There was placed before every one of them a magnificent cover with a case of massive gold, wherein were a spoon and a knife and fork, all of pure gold set with diamonds and rubies. But as they were all sitting down at table they saw a very old fairy come into the hall. She had not been invited, because for more than fifty years she had not been out of a certain tower, and she was believed to be either dead or enchanted.

The king ordered her a cover, but he could not give her a case of gold as the others had, because seven only had been made for the seven fairies. The old fairy fancied she was slighted, and muttered threats between her teeth. One of the young fairies who sat near heard her, and, judging that she might give the little princess some unlucky gift, hid herself behind the curtains as soon as they left the table. She hoped that she might speak last and undo as much as she could the evil which the old fairy might do.

In the meanwhile all the fairies began to give their gifts to the princess. The youngest gave her for her gift that she should be the most beautiful person in the world; the next, that she should have the wit of an angel; the third, that she should be able to do everything she did gracefully; the fourth, that she should dance perfectly; the fifth, that she should sing like a nightingale; and the sixth, that she should play all kinds of musical instruments to the fullest perfection.

The old fairy's turn coming next, her head shaking more with spite than with age, she said that the princess should pierce her hand with a spindle and die of the wound. This terrible gift made the whole company tremble, and everybody fell a-crying.

At this very instant the young fairy came from behind the curtains and said these words in a loud voice: 'Assure yourselves, O king and queen, that your daughter shall not die of this disaster. It is

She said that the princess should pierce her hand
with a spindle and die of the wound

true, I have no power to undo entirely what my elder has done. The princess shall indeed pierce her hand with a spindle; but, instead of dying, she shall only fall into a deep sleep, which shall last a hundred years, at the end of which a king's son shall come and awake her.'

The king, to avoid the misfortune foretold by the old fairy, issued orders forbidding anyone, on pain of death, to spin with a distaff and spindle or to have a spindle in his house. About fifteen or sixteen years after, the king and queen being absent at one of their country villas, the young princess was one day running up and down the palace; she went from room to room, and at last she came into a little garret on the top of the tower, where a good old woman, alone, was spinning with her spindle. This good woman had never heard of the king's orders against spindles.

'What are you doing there, my good woman?' said the princess.

'I am spinning, my pretty child,' said the old woman, who did not know who the princess was.

'Ha!' said the princess, 'this is very pretty; how do you do it? Give it to me. Let me see if I can do it.'

She had no sooner taken it into her hand than, either because she was too quick and heedless, or because the decree of the fairy had so ordained, it ran into her hand, and she fell down in a swoon.

The good old woman, not knowing what to do, cried out for help. People came in from every quarter; they threw water upon the face of the princess, unlaced her, struck her on the palms of her hands, and rubbed her temples with cologne water; but nothing would bring her to herself.

Then the king, who came up at hearing the noise on his return, remembered what the fairies had foretold. He knew very well that this must come to pass, since the fairies had foretold it, and he caused the princess to be carried into the finest room in his palace, and to be laid upon a bed all embroidered with gold and silver. One would have taken her for a little angel, she was so beautiful – for her swooning had not dimmed the brightness of her complexion: her cheeks were carnation and her lips coral. It is true her eyes were shut, but she was heard to breathe softly, which satisfied those about her that she was not dead.

The king gave orders that they should let her sleep quietly till the time came for her to awake. The good fairy who had saved her life by condemning her to sleep a hundred years was in the kingdom of Matakin, twelve thousand leagues

off, when this accident befell the princess; but she was instantly informed of it by a little dwarf, who had seven-league boots, that is, boots with which he could stride over seven leagues of ground at once. The fairy started off at once, and arrived, about an hour later, in a fiery chariot drawn by dragons.

The king handed her out of the chariot, and she approved everything he had done; but as she had very great foresight, she thought that when the princess should awake she might not know what to do with herself, if she was all alone in this old palace. This was what she did: she touched with her wand everything in the palace (except the king and queen), governesses, maids of honour, ladies of the bedchamber, gentlemen, officers, stewards, cooks, undercooks, kitchen maids, guards with their porters, pages and footmen; she likewise touched all the horses which were in the stables, the cart-horses, the hunters and the saddle horses, the grooms, the great dogs in the outward court, and little Mopsey, too, the princess's spaniel, which was lying on the bed.

As soon as she touched them they all fell asleep, not to awake again until their mistress did, that they might be ready to wait upon her when she wanted them. The very spits at the fire, as full as they could hold of partridges and pheasants, fell asleep, and the fire itself as well. All this was done in a moment. Fairies are not long in doing their work.

And now the king and queen, having kissed their dear child without waking her, went out of the palace and sent forth orders that nobody should come near it.

These orders were not necessary; for in a quarter of an hour's time there grew up all round about the park such a vast number of trees, great and small, bushes and brambles, twining one within another, that neither man nor beast could pass through; so that nothing could be seen but the very top of the towers of the palace; and that, too, only from afar off. Everyone knew that this also was the work of the fairy in order that while the princess slept she should have nothing to fear from curious people.

After a hundred years the son of the king then reigning, who was of another family from that of the sleeping princess, was a-hunting on that side of the country, and he asked what those towers were which he saw in the middle of a great thick wood. Everyone answered according as they had heard. Some said that it was an old haunted castle, others that all the witches of the country held their midnight revels there, but the common opinion was that it was an ogre's dwelling, and that he carried to it all the little children he could catch, so as to eat them up at his leisure, without anyone being able to follow him, for he alone had the power to make his way through the wood.

The prince did not know what to believe, and presently a very aged countryman spoke to him thus: 'May it please your royal highness, more than fifty years since I heard from my father that there was then in this castle the most beautiful princess that was ever seen; that she must sleep there a hundred years, and that she should be waked by a king's son, for whom she was reserved.'

The young prince on hearing this was all on fire. He thought, without weighing the matter, that he could put an end to this rare adventure; and, pushed on by love and the desire of glory, resolved at once to look into it.

As soon as he began to get near to the wood, all the great trees, the bushes, and brambles gave way of themselves to let him pass through. He walked up to the castle which he saw at the end of a large avenue; and you can imagine he was a good deal surprised when he saw none of his people following him, because the trees closed again as soon as he had passed through them. However, he did not cease from continuing his way; a young prince in search of glory is ever valiant.

He came into a spacious outer court, and what he saw was enough to freeze him with horror. A frightful silence reigned over all; the image of death was everywhere, and there was nothing to be seen but what seemed to be the outstretched bodies of dead men and animals. He, however, very well knew, by the ruby faces and pimpled noses of the porters, that they were only asleep; and their goblets, wherein still remained some drops of wine, showed plainly that they had fallen asleep while drinking their wine. He then crossed a court paved with marble, went up the stairs, and came into the guard chamber, where guards were standing in their ranks, with their muskets upon their shoulders, and snoring with all their might. He went through several elegant rooms full of gentlemen and ladies, some standing and others sitting, but all were asleep. He came into a gilded chamber, where he saw upon a bed, the curtains of which were all open, the most beautiful sight ever beheld – a princess who appeared to be about fifteen or sixteen years of age, and whose bright and resplendent beauty had something divine in it. He approached with trembling and admiration, and fell down upon his knees before her.

Then, as the end of the enchantment was come, the princess awoke, and looking on him with eyes more tender than could have been expected at first sight, said: 'Is it you, my prince? You have waited a long while.'

The prince, charmed with these words, and much more with the manner in which they were spoken, knew not how to show his joy and gratitude; he assured her that he loved her better than he did himself. Their discourse was not very connected, but they were the better pleased, for where there is much love there is little eloquence. He was more at a loss than she, and we need not wonder at it; she had had time to think of what to say to him; for it is evident (though history says nothing of it) that the good fairy, during so long a sleep, had given her very pleasant dreams. In short, they talked together for four hours, and had not said half they had to say.

In the meanwhile all the palace had woken up

with the princess; everyone thought upon his own business, and as they were not in love, they were ready to die of hunger. The lady of honour, being as sharp set as the other folks, grew very impatient, and told the princess aloud that the meal was served. The prince helped the princess to rise. She was entirely and very magnificently dressed; but his royal highness took care not to tell her that she was dressed like his great-grandmother, and had a high collar. She looked not a bit the less charming and beautiful for all that.

They went into the great mirrored hall, where they supped, and were served by the officers of the princess's household. The violins and hautboys played old tunes, but they were excellent, though they had not been played for a hundred years; and after supper, without losing any time, the lord almoner married them in the chapel of the castle. They had but very little sleep – the princess scarcely needed any; and the prince left her next morning to return into the city, where his father was greatly troubled about him.

The prince told him that he lost his way in the forest as he was hunting, and that he had slept in the cottage of a charcoal-burner, who gave him cheese and brown bread.

The king, his father, who was a good man, believed him; but his mother could not be persuaded that it was true; and seeing that he went almost every day a-hunting, and that he always had some excuse ready for so doing, though he had been out three or four nights together, she began to suspect that he was married; for he lived thus with the princess above two whole years, during which they had two children, the elder, a daughter,

was named Dawn, and the younger, a son, they called Day, because he was a great deal handsomer than his sister.

The queen spoke several times to her son, to learn after what manner he was passing his time, and told him that in this he ought in duty to satisfy her. But he never dared to trust her with his secret; he feared her, though he loved her, for she was of the race of the ogres, and the king married her for her vast riches alone. It was even whispered about the court that she had ogreish inclinations, and that, whenever she saw little children passing by, she had all the difficulty in the world to prevent herself from falling upon them. And so the prince would never tell her one word.

But when the king was dead, which happened about two years afterwards, and he saw himself lord and master, he openly declared his marriage: and he went in great state to conduct his queen to the palace. They made a magnificent entry into the capital city, she riding between her two children.

Soon after, the king made war on Emperor Cantalabutte, his neighbour. He left the government of the kingdom to the queen, his mother, and earnestly commended his wife and children to her care. He was obliged to carry on the war all the summer, and as soon as he left, the queen-mother sent her daughter-in-law and her children to a country house among the woods, that she might with the more ease gratify her horrible longing. Some few days afterwards she went thither herself, and said to her head cook: 'I intend to eat little Dawn for my dinner tomorrow.'

'Oh! madam!' cried the head cook.

'I will have it so,' replied the queen (and this she

spoke in the tone of an ogress who had a strong desire to eat fresh meat), 'and will eat her with a sharp sauce.'

The poor man, knowing very well that he must not play tricks with ogresses, took his great knife and went up into little Dawn's chamber. She was then nearly four years old, and came up to him, jumping and laughing, to put her arms round his neck, and ask him for some sugar-candy. Upon which he began to weep, the great knife fell out of his hand, and he went into the back yard and killed a little lamb, and dressed it with such good sauce that his mistress assured him she had never eaten anything so good in her life. He had at the same time taken up little Dawn and carried her to his wife, to conceal her in his lodging at the end of the courtyard.

Eight days afterwards the wicked queen said to the chief cook, 'I will sup upon little Day.'

He answered not a word, being resolved to cheat her again as he had done before. He went to find little Day, and saw him with a foil in his hand, with which he was fencing with a great monkey: the child was then only three years of age. He took him up in his arms and carried him to his wife, that she might conceal him in her chamber along with his sister, and instead of little Day he served up a young and very tender kid, which the ogress found to be wonderfully good.

All had gone well up to now; but one evening this wicked queen-mother said to her chief cook: 'I will eat the queen with the same sauce I had with her children.'

Now the poor chief cook was in despair and could not imagine how to deceive her again. The young queen was over twenty years old, not reckoning the hundred years she had been asleep: and how to find something to take her place greatly puzzled him. He then decided, to save his own life, to cut the queen's throat; and going up into her chamber, with intent to do it at once, he put himself into as great fury as he possibly could, and came into the young queen's room with his dagger in his hand. He would not, however, deceive her, but told her, with a great deal of respect, the orders he had received from the queen-mother.

'Do it; do it,' she said, stretching out her neck. 'Carry out your orders, and then I shall go and see my children, my poor children, whom I loved so much and so tenderly.' For she thought them dead, since they had been taken away without her knowledge.

'No, no, madam,' cried the poor chief cook, all in tears; 'you shall not die, and you shall see your children again at once. But then you must go home with me to my lodgings, where I have concealed them, and I will deceive the queen once more, by giving her a young hind in your stead.'

Upon this he forthwith conducted her to his room, where, leaving her to embrace her children, and cry along with them, he went and dressed a young hind, which his mistress had for her supper, and devoured with as much appetite as if it had been the young queen. She was now well satisfied with her cruel deeds, and she invented a story to tell the king on his return, of how the queen his wife and her two children had been devoured by mad wolves.

One evening, as she was, according to her custom, rambling round about the courts and yards of the palace to see if she could smell any fresh meat, she heard, in a room on the ground floor, little Day crying, for his mama was going to whip him, because he had been naughty; and she heard, at the same time, little Dawn begging mercy for her brother.

The ogress knew the voice of the queen and her children at once, and being furious at having been thus deceived, she gave orders (in a most horrible voice which made everybody tremble) that, next morning by break of day, they should bring into the middle of the great court a large tub filled with toads, vipers, snakes, and all sorts of serpents, in order to have the queen and her children, the chief cook, his wife and maid, thrown into it, all of whom were to be brought thither with their hands tied behind them.

They were brought out accordingly, and the executioners were just going to throw them into the tub, when the king, who was not so soon expected, entered the court on horseback and asked, with the utmost astonishment, what was the meaning of this horrible spectacle.

No one dared to tell him, but the end came when the ogress, all enraged to see what had happened, threw herself head foremost into the tub, and was instantly devoured by the ugly creatures she had ordered to kill the others. The king was of course very sorry, for she was his mother; but he soon comforted himself with his beautiful wife and his pretty children.

Smallhead and the King's Sons

Long ago there lived in Erin a woman who married a man of high degree and had one daughter. Soon after the birth of the daughter the husband died.

The woman was not long a widow when she married a second time, and had two daughters. These two daughters hated their half-sister, thought she was not so wise as they were, and nicknamed her Smallhead. When the elder of the two sisters was fourteen years old their father died. The mother was in great grief then, and began to pine away. She used to sit at home in the corner and never left the house. Smallhead was kind to her mother, and the mother was fonder of her eldest daughter than of the other two, who were ashamed of her.

At last the two sisters made up in their minds to kill their mother. One day, while their half-sister was gone, they put the mother in a pot, boiled her and threw the bones outside. When Smallhead came home there was no sign of the mother.

'Where is my mother?' asked she of the other two.

'She went out somewhere. How should we know where she is?'

'Oh, wicked girls! You have killed my mother,' said Smallhead.

Smallhead wouldn't leave the house now at all, and the sisters were very angry.

'No man will marry either one of us,' said they, 'if he sees our fool of a sister.'

Since they could not drive Smallhead from the house they made up their minds to go away themselves. One fine morning they left home unknown to their half-sister and travelled for many miles. When Smallhead discovered that her sisters were gone she hurried after them and never stopped till she came up with the two. They had to go home with her that day, but they scolded her bitterly.

The two settled then to kill Smallhead, so one day they took twenty needles and scattered them outside in a pile of straw. 'We are going to that hill beyond,' said they, 'to stay till evening, and if you have not all the needles that are in that straw outside gathered and on the table before us, we'll have your life.'

Away they went to the hill. Smallhead sat down, and was crying bitterly when a short grey cat walked in and spoke to her.

'Why do you cry and lament so?' asked the cat.

'My sisters abuse me and beat me,' answered Smallhead. 'This morning they said they would kill me in the evening unless I had all the needles in the straw outside gathered before them.'

'Sit down here,' said the cat, 'and dry your tears.'

The cat soon found the twenty needles and brought them to Smallhead. 'Stop there now,' said the cat, 'and listen to what I tell you. I am your mother; your sisters killed me and destroyed my body, but don't harm them; do them good, do the best you can for them, save them; obey my words and it will be better for you in the end.'

The cat went away for herself, and the sisters came home in the evening. The needles were on the table before them. Oh, but they were vexed and angry when they saw the twenty needles, and they said someone was helping their sister!

One night when Smallhead was in bed and asleep they started away again, resolved this time never to return. Smallhead slept till morning. When she saw that the sisters were gone she followed, traced them from place to place, enquired here and there day after day, till one evening some person told her that they were in the house of an old hag, a terrible enchantress, who had one son and three daughters; that the house was a bad place to be in, for the old hag had more power of witchcraft than anyone and was very wicked.

Smallhead hurried away to save her sisters, and facing the house knocked at the door, and asked lodgings for God's sake.

'Oh, then,' said the hag, 'it is hard to refuse any-one lodgings, and besides it's such a wild, stormy night. I wonder if you are anything to the young ladies who came this way this evening?'

The two sisters heard this and were angry enough that Smallhead was in it, but they said nothing, not wishing the old hag to know their relationship. After supper the hag told the three strangers to sleep in a room on the right side of the house. When her own daughters were going to bed Smallhead saw her tie a ribbon around the neck of each one of them, and heard her say, 'Do you sleep in the left-hand bed.' Smallhead hurried and said to her sisters, 'Come quickly, or I'll tell the woman who you are.'

They took the bed in the left-hand room and were in it before the hag's daughters came.

'Oh,' said the daughers, 'the other bed is as good.' So they took the bed in the right-hand room. When Smallhead knew that the hag's daughters were asleep she rose, took the ribbons off their necks, and put them on her sisters' necks and on her own. She lay awake and watched them. After a while she heard the hag say to her son, 'Go, now, and kill the three girls; they have the clothes and money.'

'You have killed enough in your life and so let these go,' said the son.

But the old woman would not listen. The boy rose up, fearing his mother, and taking a long knife, went to the right-hand room and cut the throats of the three girls without ribbons. He went to bed then for himself, and when Smallhead found that the old hag was asleep she roused her sisters, told what had happened, made them dress quickly and

follow her. Believe me, they were willing and glad to follow her this time.

The three travelled briskly and came soon to a bridge, called at that time the Bridge of Blood. Whoever had killed a person could not cross the bridge. When the three girls came to the bridge the two sisters stopped: they could not go a step farther. Smallhead ran across and went back again.

'If I did not know that you killed our mother,' said she, 'I might know it now, for this is the Bridge of Blood.'

She carried one sister over the bridge on her back and then the other. Hardly was this done when the hag was at the bridge.

'Bad luck to you, Smallhead!' said she. 'I did not know that it was you that was in it last evening. You have killed my three daughters.'

'It wasn't I that killed them, but yourself,' said Smallhead.

The old hag could not cross the bridge, so she began to curse, and she put every curse on Smallhead that she could remember. The sisters travelled on till they came to a king's castle. They heard that two servants were needed in the castle.

'Go now,' said Smallhead to the two sisters, 'and ask for service. Be faithful and do well. You can never go back by the road you came.'

The two found employment at the king's castle. Smallhead took lodgings in the house of a blacksmith near by.

'I should be glad to find a place as kitchen-maid in the castle,' said Smallhead to the blacksmith's wife.

THE BRIDGE OF BLOOD

'I will go to the castle and find a place for you if I can,' said the woman.

The blacksmith's wife found a place for Smallhead as kitchen-maid in the castle, and she went there next day.

'I must be careful,' thought Smallhead, 'and do my best. I am in a strange place. My two sisters are here in the king's castle. Who knows, we may have great fortune yet.'

She dressed neatly and was cheerful. Everyone liked her, liked her better than her sisters, though they were beautiful. The king had two sons, one at home and the other abroad. Smallhead thought to herself one day, 'It is time for the son who is here in the castle to marry. I will speak to him the first time I can.' One day she saw him alone in the garden, went up to him, and said, 'Why are you not getting married, it is high time for you?'

He only laughed and thought she was too bold, but then, seeing that she was a simple-minded girl who wished to be pleasant, he said, 'I will tell you the reason: My grandfather bound my father by an oath never to let his oldest son marry until he could get the Sword of Light, and I am afraid that I shall be long without marrying.'

'Do you know where the Sword of Light is or who has it?' asked Smallhead.

'I do,' said the king's son. 'An old hag who has great power and enchantment, and she lives a long distance from this, beyond the Bridge of Blood. I cannot go there myself, I cannot cross the bridge, for I have killed men in battle. Even if I could cross the bridge I would not go, for many a king's son has that hag destroyed or enchanted.'

'Suppose some person were to bring you the Sword of Light, and that person a woman, would you marry her?'

'I would, indeed,' said the king's son.

'If you promise to marry not me but my elder sister I will strive to bring the Sword of Light.'

'I will promise most willingly,' said the king's son.

Next morning early, Smallhead set out on her journey. Calling at the first shop she bought a stone weight of salt, and went on her way, never stopping or resting till she reached the hag's house at night-fall. She climbed to the gable, looked down, and saw the son making a great pot of stirabout for his mother, and she hurrying him. 'I am as hungry as a hawk!' cried she.

Whenever the boy looked away, Smallhead dropped salt down, dropped it when he was not looking, dropped it till he had the whole stone of salt in the stirabout. The old hag waited and waited till at last she cried out, 'Bring the stirabout. I am starving! Bring the pot. I will eat from the pot. Give the milk here as well.'

The boy brought the stirabout and the milk, and the old woman began to eat, but the first taste she got she spat out and screamed, 'You put salt in the pot in place of meal!'

'I did not, mother.'

'You did, and it's a mean trick that you played on me. Throw this stirabout to the pig outside and go for water to the well in the field.'

'I cannot go,' said the boy, 'the night is too dark; I might fall into the well.'

'You must go and bring the water; I cannot live till morning without eating.'

'I am as hungry as yourself,' said the boy, 'but how can I go to the well without a light? I will not go unless you give me a light.'

'If I give you the Sword of Light there is no knowing who may follow you; maybe that devil of a Smallhead is outside.'

But sooner than fast till morning the old hag gave the Sword of Light to her son, warning him to take good care of it. He took the Sword of Light and went out. As he saw no one when he came to the well he left the sword on the top of the steps going down to the water, so as to have good light. He had not gone down many steps when Smallhead had the sword, and away she ran over hills, dales and valleys towards the Bridge of Blood.

The boy shouted and screamed with all his might. Out ran the hag. 'Where is the sword?' cried she.

'Someone took it from the step.'

Off rushed the hag, following the light, but she didn't come near Smallhead till she was over the bridge.

'Give me the Sword of Light, or bad luck to you,' cried the hag.

'Indeed, then, I will not; I will keep it, and bad luck to yourself,' answered Smallhead.

On the following morning she walked up to the king's son and said, 'I have the Sword of Light; now will you marry my sister?'

'I will,' said he.

The king's son married Smallhead's sister and got the Sword of Light. Smallhead stayed no longer in the kitchen – the sister didn't care to have her in kitchen or parlour.

The king's second son came home. He was not long in the castle when Smallhead said to herself, 'Maybe he will marry my second sister.'

She saw him one day in the garden and went towards him; he said something, she answered, then asked, 'Is it not time for you to be getting married like your brother?'

'When my grandfather was dying,' said the young man, 'he bound my father not to let his second son marry till he had the Black Book. This book used to shine and give brighter light than ever the Sword of Light did, and I suppose it does yet. The old hag beyond the Bridge of Blood has the book, and no one dares to go near her, for many a king's son has been killed or enchanted by that woman.'

'Would you marry my second sister if you were to get the Black Book?'

'I would, indeed; I would marry any woman if I got the Black Book with her. The Sword of Light and the Black Book were in our family till my grandfather's time, then they were stolen by that cursed old hag.'

'I will have the book,' said Smallhead, 'or die in the trial to get it.'

Knowing that stirabout was the main food of the hag, Smallhead settled in her mind to play another trick. Taking a bag she scraped the chimney, gathered about a stone of soot, and took it with her. The night was dark and rainy. When she reached the hag's house, she climbed up the gable to the chimney and found that the son was making stirabout for his mother. She dropped the soot down

by degrees till at last the whole stone of soot was in the pot; then she scraped around the top of the chimney till a lump of soot fell on the boy's hand.

'Oh, mother,' said he, 'the night is wet and soft, the soot is falling.'

'Cover the pot,' said the hag. 'Be quick with that stirabout, I am starving.'

The boy took the pot to his mother.

'Bad luck to you,' cried the hag the moment she tasted the stirabout, 'this is full of soot; throw it out to the pig.'

'If I throw it out there is no water inside to make more, and I'll not go in the dark and rain to the well.'

'You must go!' screamed she.

'I'll not stir a foot out of this unless I get a light,' said the boy.

'Is it the book you are thinking of, you fool, to take it and lose it as you did the sword? Smallhead is watching you.'

'How could Smallhead, the creature, be outside all the time? If you have no use for the water you can do without it.'

Sooner than remain fasting till morning, the hag gave her son the book, saying, 'Do not put this down or let it from your hand till you come in, or I'll have your life.'

The boy took the book and went to the well. Smallhead followed him carefully. He took the book down into the well with him, and when he was stooping to dip water she snatched the book and pushed him into the well, where he came very near drowning.

Smallhead was far away when the boy recovered, and began to scream and shout to his mother. She came in a hurry, and finding that the book was gone, fell into such a rage that she thrust a knife into her son's heart and ran after Smallhead, who had crossed the bridge before the hag could come up with her.

When the old woman saw Smallhead on the other side of the bridge facing her and dancing with delight, she screamed, 'You took the Sword of Light and the Black Book, and your two sisters are married. Oh, then, bad luck to you. I will put my curse on you wherever you go. You have seen all my children killed, and I a poor, feeble, old woman.'

'Bad luck to yourself,' said Smallhead. 'I am not afraid of a curse from the likes of you. If you had lived an honest life you wouldn't be as you are today.'

'Now, Smallhead,' said the old hag, 'you have me

robbed of everything, and my children destroyed. Your two sisters are well married. Your fortune began with my ruin. Come, now, and take care of me in my old age. I'll take my curse from you, and you will have good luck. I bind myself never to harm a hair of your head.'

Smallhead thought awhile, promised to do this, and said, 'If you harm me, or try to harm me, it will be the worse for yourself.'

The old hag was satisfied and went home. Smallhead went to the castle and was received with great joy. Next morning she found the king's son in the garden, and said, 'If you marry my sister tomorrow, you will have the Black Book.'

'I will marry her gladly,' said the king's son.

Next day the marriage was celebrated and the king's son got the book. Smallhead remained in the castle about a week, then she left good health with her sisters and went to the hag's house. The

old woman was glad to see her and showed the girl her work. All Smallhead had to do was to wait on the hag and feed a large pig that she had.

'I am fatting that pig,' said the hag; 'he is seven years old now, and the longer you keep a pig the harder his meat is: we'll keep this pig a while longer, and then we'll kill and eat him.'

Smallhead did her work; the old hag taught her some things, and Smallhead learned herself far more than the hag dreamt of. The girl fed the pig three times a day, never thinking that he could be anything but a pig. The hag had sent word to a sister that she had in the Eastern World, bidding her come and they would kill the pig and have a great feast. The sister came, and one day when the hag was going to walk with her sister she said to Smallhead, 'Give the pig plenty of meal today; this is the last food he'll have; give him his fill.'

The pig had his own mind and knew what was

coming. He put his nose under the pot and threw it on Smallhead's toes, and she barefoot. With that she ran into the house for a stick, and seeing a rod on the edge of the loft, snatched it and hit the pig.

That moment the pig was a splendid young man. Smallhead was amazed.

'Never fear,' said the young man, 'I am the son of a king that the old hag hated, the King of Munster. She stole me from my father seven years ago and enchanted me – made a pig of me.'

Smallhead told the king's son, then, how the hag had treated her. 'I must make a pig of you again,' said she, 'for the hag is coming. Be patient and I'll save you, if you promise to marry me.'

'I promise you,' said the king's son.

With that she struck him, and he was a pig again. She put the switch in its place and was at her work when the two sisters came. The pig ate his meal now with a good heart, for he felt sure of rescue.

'Who is that girl you have in the house, and where did you find her?' asked the sister.

'All my children died of the plague, and I took this girl to help me. She is a very good servant.'

At night the hag slept in one room, her sister in another, and Smallhead in a third. When the two sisters were sleeping soundly, Smallhead rose, stole the hag's magic book, and then took the rod. She went next to where the pig was, and with one blow of the rod she made a man of him.

With the help of the magic book Smallhead made two doves of herself and the king's son, and they took flight through the air and flew on without stopping. Next morning the hag called Smallhead, but she did not come. She hurried out to see the pig. The pig was gone. She ran to her book. Not a sign of it.

'Oh!' cried she. 'That villain of a Smallhead has robbed me. She has stolen my book, made a man of the pig, and taken him away with her.'

What could she do but tell her whole story to the sister. 'Go you,' said she, 'and follow them. You have more enchantment than Smallhead has.'

'How am I to know them?' asked the sister.

'Bring the first two strange things that you find; they will turn themselves into something wonderful.'

The sister then made a hawk of herself and flew away as swiftly as any March wind.

'Look behind,' said Smallhead to the king's son some hours later; 'see what is coming.'

'I see nothing,' said he, 'but a hawk coming swiftly.'

'That is the hag's sister. She has three times more enchantment than the hag herself. But fly down on the ditch and be picking yourself as doves do in rainy weather, and maybe she'll pass without seeing us.'

The hawk saw the doves, but thinking them nothing wonderful, flew on till evening, and then went back to her sister.

'Did you see anything wonderful?'

'I did not; I saw only two doves, and they picking themselves.'

'You fool, those doves were Smallhead and the king's son. Off with you in the morning and don't let me see you again without the two with you.'

Away went the hawk a second time, and swiftly as Smallhead and the king's son flew, the hawk was gaining on them. Seeing this Smallhead and the king's son dropped down into a large village, and, it being market-day, they made two heather brooms of themselves. The two brooms began to sweep the road without anyone holding them, and swept toward each other. This was a great wonder. Crowds gathered at once around the two brooms.

The old hag flying over in the form of a hawk saw this and thinking that it must be Smallhead and the king's son were in it, came down, turned into a woman, and said to herself, 'I'll have those two brooms.'

She pushed forward so quickly through the crowd that she came near knocking down a man standing before her. The man was vexed.

'You cursed old hag!' cried he. 'Do you want to knock us down?' With that he gave her a blow and drove her against another man, that man gave her a push that sent her spinning against a third man, and so on till between them all they came near putting the life out of her, and pushed her away from the brooms. A woman in the crowd called out then, 'It would be nothing but right to knock the head off that old hag, and she trying to push us away from the mercy of God, for it was God who sent the brooms to sweep the road for us.'

'True for you,' said another woman. With that the people were as angry as angry could be, and were ready to kill the hag. They were going to take the head off the hag when she made a hawk of herself and flew away, vowing never to do another stroke of work for her sister. She might do her own work or let it alone.

When the hawk disappeared the two heather brooms rose and turned into doves. The people felt sure when they saw the doves that the brooms were a blessing from heaven, and it was the old hag that drove them away.

On the following day Smallhead and the king's son saw his father's castle, and the two came down not too far from it in their own forms. Smallhead was a very beautiful woman now, and why not? She had the magic and didn't spare it. She made herself as beautiful as ever she could: the like of her was not to be seen in that kingdom or the next one.

The king's son was in love with her that minute, and did not wish to part with her, but she would not go with him.

'When you are at your father's castle,' said Smallhead, 'all will be overjoyed to see you, and the king will give a great feast in your honour. If you kiss anyone or let any living thing kiss you, you'll forget me for ever.'

'I will not let even my own mother kiss me,' said he.

The king's son went to the castle. All were overjoyed; they had thought him dead, had not seen him for seven years. He would let no one come near to kiss him. 'I am bound by oath to kiss no one,' said he to his mother. At that moment an old greyhound came in, and with one spring was on his shoulder licking his face: all that the king's son had gone through in seven years was forgotten in one moment.

Smallhead went towards a forge near the castle. The smith had a wife far younger than himself, and a stepdaughter. They were no beauties. In the rear of the forge was a well and a tree growing over it. 'I will go up in that tree,' thought Smallhead, 'and spend the night in it.' She went up and sat just over the well. She was not long in the tree when the moon came out high above the hill-tops and shone on the well. The blacksmith's stepdaughter, coming for water, looked down in the well, saw the face

of the woman above in the tree, thought it her own face, and cried, 'Oh, then, to have me bringing water to a smith, and I such a beauty. I'll never bring another drop to him.' With that she cast the pail in the ditch and ran off to find a king's son to marry.

When she was not coming with the water, and the blacksmith waiting to wash after his day's work in the forge, he sent the mother. The mother had nothing but a pot to get the water in, so off she went with that, and coming to the well saw the beautiful face in the water.

'Oh, you black, swarthy villain of a smith,' cried she, 'bad luck to the hour that I met you, and I such a beauty. I'll never draw another drop of water for the life of you!'

She threw the pot down, broke it, and hurried away to find some king's son.

When neither mother nor daughter came back with water the smith himself went to see what was keeping them. He saw the pail in the ditch, and, catching it, went to the well; looking down, he saw the beautiful face of a woman in the water. Being a man, he knew that it was not his own face that was in it, so he looked up, and there in the tree saw a woman. He spoke to her and said, 'I know now why my wife and her daughter did not bring water. They saw your face in the well, and, thinking themselves too good for me, ran away. You must come now and keep the house till I find them.'

'I will help you,' said Smallhead. She came down, went to the smith's house, and showed the road that the women took.

The smith hurried after them, and found the two in a village ten miles away. He explained their own folly to them, and they came home.

The mother and daughter washed fine linen for the castle. Smallhead saw them ironing one day, and said, 'Sit down: I will iron for you.'

560

She caught the iron, and in an hour had the work of the day done.

The women were delighted. In the evening the daughter took the linen to the housekeeper at the castle.

'Who ironed this linen?' asked the housekeeper.

'My mother and I.'

'Indeed, then, you did not. You can't do the like of that work, and tell me who did it.'

The girl was in dread now and answered, 'It is a woman who is stopping with us who did the ironing.'

The housekeeper went to the queen and showed her the linen.

'Send that woman to the castle,' said the queen.

Smallhead went: the queen welcomed her, wondered at her beauty; put her over all the maids in the castle. Smallhead could do anything; everybody was fond of her. The king's son never knew that he had seen her before, and she lived in the castle a year; what the queen told her she did.

The king had made a match for his son with the daughter of the King of Ulster. There was a great feast in the castle in honour of the young couple; the marriage

was to be a week later. The bride's father brought many of his people who were versed in all kinds of tricks and enchantment.

The king knew that Smallhead could do many things, for neither the queen nor himself had asked her to do a thing that she did not do in a twinkle.

'Now,' said the king to the queen, 'I think she can do something that his people cannot do.' He summoned Smallhead and asked, 'Can you amuse the strangers?'

'I can if you wish me to do so.'

When the time came and the Ulster men had shown their best tricks, Smallhead came forward and raised the window, which was forty feet from the ground. She had a small ball of thread in her hand; she tied one end of the thread to the window, threw the ball out and over a wall near the castle; then she passed out of the window, walked on the thread and kept time to music from players that no man could see. She came in; all cheered her and were greatly delighted.

'I can do that,' said the King of Ulster's daughter, and sprang out on the string; but as she did, she fell and broke her neck on the stones below. There were cries, there was lamentation, and, in place of a marriage, a funeral.

The king's son was angry and grieved and wanted to drive Smallhead from the castle in some way. 'She is not to blame,' said the King of Munster, who did nothing but praise her.

Another year passed: the king got the daughter of the King of Connacht for his son. There was a great feast before the wedding day, and as the Connacht people are full of enchantment and witchcraft, the King of Munster called Smallhead and said, 'Now show the best trick of any.'

'I will,' said Smallhead. When the feast was over and the Connacht men had shown their tricks the King of Munster called Smallhead.

She stood before the company, threw two grains of wheat on the

floor, and spoke some magic words. There was a hen and a cock there before her of beautiful plumage; she threw a grain of wheat between them; the hen sprang to eat the wheat, the cock gave her a blow of his bill, the hen drew back, looked at him, and said, 'Bad luck to you, you wouldn't do the like of that when I was serving the old hag and you her pig, and I made a man of you and gave you back your own form.'

The king's son looked at her and thought, 'There must be something in this.'

Smallhead threw a second grain. The cock pecked the hen again. 'Oh,' said the hen, 'you would not do that the day the hag's sister was hunting us, and we two doves.'

The king's son was still more astonished.

She threw a third grain. The cock struck the hen, and she said, 'You would not do that to me the day I made two heather brooms out of you and myself.' She threw a fourth grain. The cock pecked the hen a fourth time. 'You would not do that the day you promised not to let any living thing kiss you or kiss anyone yourself but me – but then you let the hound kiss you and you forgot me.'

The king's son made one bound forward, embraced and kissed Smallhead, and told the king his whole story from beginning to end.

'This is my wife,' said he; 'I'll marry no other woman.'

'Whose wife will my daughter be?' asked the King of Connacht.

'Oh, she will be the wife of the man who will marry her,' said the King of Munster; 'my son gave his word to this woman before he saw your daughter, and he must keep it.'

So Smallhead married the King of Munster's son.

The Snow Queen

There was once a dreadfully wicked hobgoblin. One day he was in capital spirits because he had made a looking-glass which reflected everything that was good and beautiful in such a way that it dwindled almost to nothing, but anything that was bad and ugly stood out very clearly and looked much worse. The most beautiful landscapes looked like boiled spinach, and the best people looked repulsive or seemed to stand on their heads with no bodies; their faces were so changed that they could not be recognised, and if anyone had a freckle you might be sure it would be spread over the nose and mouth.

That was the best part of it, said the hobgoblin.

But one day the looking-glass was dropped, and it broke into a million-billion and more pieces.

And now came the greatest misfortune of all, for each of the pieces was hardly as large as a grain of sand, and they flew about all over the world, and if anyone had a bit in his eye there it stayed, and then he would see everything awry, or else could only see the bad sides of a case. For every tiny splinter of the glass possessed the same power that the whole glass had.

Some people got a splinter in their hearts, and that was dreadful, for then it began to turn into a lump of ice.

The hobgoblin laughed till his sides ached, but still the tiny bits of glass flew about.

And now we will hear all about it.

In a large town, where there were so many people and houses that there was not room enough for everybody to have gardens, lived two poor children. They were not brother and sister, but they loved each other just as much as if they were. Their parents lived opposite

The hobgoblin laughed till his sides ached

one another in two attics, and out on the leads they had put boxes filled with flowers. There were sweet peas, and two rose trees, which grow beautifully, and in summer the two children were allowed to take their little chairs and sit out under the roses. Then they had splendid games.

In the winter they could not do this, but then they put hot pennies against the frozen window panes, and made round holes to look at each other through.

His name was Kay, and hers was Gerda.

Outside it was snowing fast.

'Those are the white bees swarming,' said the old grandmother.

'Have they also a queen bee?' asked the little boy, for he knew that the real bees have one.

'To be sure,' said the grandmother. 'She flies wherever they swarm the thickest. She is larger than any of them, and never stays upon the earth, but flies again up into the black clouds. Often at midnight she flies through the streets, and peeps in at all the windows, and then they freeze in such pretty patterns and look like flowers.'

'Yes, we have seen that,' said both children; they knew that it was true.

'Can the Snow Queen come in here?' asked the little girl.

'Just let her!' cried the boy, 'I would put her on the stove, and melt her!'

But the grandmother stroked his hair, and told some more stories.

In the evening, when little Kay was going to bed, he jumped on the chair by the window, and looked through the little hole. A few snow-flakes were falling outside, and one of them, the largest, lay on the edge of one of the window-boxes. The snowflake grew larger and larger till it took the form of a maiden, dressed in finest white gauze.

She was so beautiful and dainty, but all of ice, hard bright ice.

Still she was alive; her eyes glittered like two clear stars, but there was no rest or peace in them. She nodded at the window, and beckoned with her hand. The little boy was frightened, and sprang down from the chair. It seemed as if a great white bird had flown past the window.

The next day there was a harder frost than before.

Then came the spring, then the summer, when the roses grew and smelt more beautifully than ever.

Kay and Gerda were looking at one of their picture books, and the clock in the great church-tower had just struck five, when Kay exclaimed, 'Oh! something has stung my heart, and I've got something in my eye!'

The little girl threw her arms round his neck; he winked hard with both his eyes; no, she could see nothing in them.

'I think it is gone now,' said he; but it had not gone. It was one of the tiny splinters of the glass of the magic mirror which we have heard about, that turned everything great and good reflected in it small and ugly. And poor Kay had also a splinter in his heart, and it began to change into a lump of ice. It did not hurt him at all, but the splinter was there all the same.

'Why are you crying?' he asked; 'it makes you look so ugly! There's nothing the matter with me. Just look! that rose is all slug-eaten, and this one is stunted! What ugly roses they are!'

And he began to pull them to pieces.

'Kay, what are you doing?' cried the little girl.

And when he saw how frightened she was, he pulled off another rose, and ran in at his window away from dear little Gerda.

When she came later on with the picture book, he said that it was only fit for babies, and when his grandmother told them stories, he was always interrupting with, 'But – ' and then he would get behind her and put on her spectacles, and speak just as she did. This he did very well, and everybody laughed. Very soon he could imitate the way all the people in the street walked and talked.

His games were now quite different. On a winter's day he would take a burning glass and hold it out on his blue coat and let the snowflakes fall on it.

'Look in the glass, Gerda! Just see how regular they are! They are much more interesting than real flowers. Each is perfect; they are all made according to rule. If only they did not melt!'

One morning Kay came out with his warm gloves on, and his little sledge hung over his shoulder. He shouted to Gerda, 'I am going to the marketplace to play with the other boys,' and away he went.

In the marketplace the boldest boys used often to fasten their sledges to the carts of the farmers, and then they got a good ride.

When they were in the middle of their games there drove into the square a large sledge, all white, and in it sat a figure dressed in a rough white fur pelisse with a white fur cap on.

The sledge drove twice round the square, and Kay fastened his little sledge behind it and drove off. It went quicker and quicker into the next street. The driver turned round, and nodded to Kay in a friendly way as if they had known each other before. Every time that Kay tried to unfasten his sledge the driver nodded again, and Kay sat still once more. Then they drove out of the town, and the snow began to fall so thickly that the little boy could not see his hand before him, and on and on they went. He quickly unfastened the cord to get loose from the big sledge, but it was of no use; his little sledge hung on fast, and it went on like the wind.

Then he cried out, but nobody heard him. He was dreadfully frightened.

The snowflakes grew larger and larger till they looked like great white birds. All at once they flew aside, the large sledge stood still, and the figure who was driving stood up. The fur cloak and cap were all of snow. It was a lady, tall and slim, and glittering. It was the Snow Queen.

'We have come at a good rate,' she said; 'but you are almost frozen. Creep in under my cloak.'

And she set him close to her in the big sledge and drew the cloak over him. He felt as though he were sinking into a snowdrift.

'Are you cold now?' she asked, and kissed his forehead. The kiss was cold as ice and reached down to his heart, which was already half a lump of ice.

'My sledge! Don't forget my sledge!' He thought of that first, and it was fastened to one of the great white birds who flew behind with the sledge on its back.

The Snow Queen kissed Kay again, and then he forgot all about little Gerda, his grandmother, and everybody at home.

'Now I must not kiss you any more,' she said, 'or else I should kiss you to death.'

The snowflake grew larger and larger till it took the form of a maiden

Then away they flew, over forests and lakes, over sea and land. Round them whistled the cold wind, the wolves howled, and the snow hissed; over them flew the black shrieking crows. But high up the moon shone large and bright, and thus Kay passed the long winter night. In the day he slept at the Snow Queen's feet.

But what happened to little Gerda when Kay did not come back? What had become of him? Nobody knew. The other boys told how they had seen him fasten his sledge on to a large one which had driven out of the town gate.

Gerda cried a great deal. The winter was long and dark to her.

Then the spring came with warm sunshine. 'I will go and look for Kay,' said Gerda.

So she went down to the river and got into a little boat that was there. Presently the stream began to carry it away.

'Perhaps the river will take me to Kay,' thought Gerda. She glided down, past trees and fields, till she came to a large cherry garden, in which stood a little house with strange red and blue windows and a straw roof. Before the door stood two wooden soldiers, who were shouldering arms.

Gerda called to them, but they naturally did not answer. The river carried the boat on to the land.

Gerda called out still louder, and there came out of the house a very old woman. She leant upon a crutch, and she wore a large sun hat which was painted with the most beautiful flowers.

'You poor little girl!' said the old woman.

Then she stepped into the water, brought the boat in close with her crutch, and lifted little Gerda out.

'And now come and tell me who you are, and how you came here,' she said.

Then Gerda told her everything, and asked her if she had seen Kay. But she said he had not passed that way yet, but he would soon come.

She told Gerda not to be sad, and that she should stay with her and take of the cherry trees and flowers, which were better than any picture-book, as they could each tell a story.

She then took Gerda's hand and led her into the little house and shut the door.

The windows were very high, and the panes were red, blue and yellow, so that the light came through in curious colours. On the table were the most delicious cherries, and the old woman let Gerda eat as many as she liked, while she combed her hair with a gold comb as she ate.

The beautiful sunny hair rippled and shone round the dear little face, which was so soft and sweet. 'I have always longed to have a dear little girl just like you, and you shall see how happy we will be together.'

And as she combed Gerda's hair, Gerda thought less and less about Kay, for the old woman was a witch, but not a wicked witch, for she only enchanted now and then to amuse herself, and she did want to keep little Gerda very much.

So she went into the garden and waved her stick over all the rose bushes and they sank down into the black earth, and no one could see where they had been. The old woman was afraid that if Gerda saw the roses she would begin to think about her own, and then would remember Kay and run away.

Then she led Gerda out into the garden. How glorious it was, and what lovely scents filled the air! All the flowers you can think of blossomed there all the year round.

Gerda jumped for joy and played there till the sun set behind the tall cherry trees, and then she slept in a beautiful bed with red silk pillows filled with violets, and she slept soundly and dreamed as a queen does on her wedding day.

The next day she played again with the flowers in the warm sunshine, and so many days passed by. Gerda knew every flower, but although there were so many, it seemed to her as if one were not there, though she could not remember which.

She was looking one day at the old woman's sun hat which had the painted flowers on it, and there she saw a rose.

The witch had forgotten to make that vanish when she had made the other roses disappear under the earth. It was so difficult to think of everything.

'Why, there are no roses here!' cried Gerda, and she hunted amongst all the flowers, but not one was to be found. Then she sat down and cried, but her tears fell just on the spot where a rose bush had sunk, and when her warm tears watered the earth, the bush came up in full bloom just as it had been before. Gerda kissed the roses and thought of the lovely roses at home, and with them came the thought of little Kay.

'Oh, what have I been doing!' said the little girl. 'I wanted to look for Kay.'

She ran to the end of the garden. The gate was shut, but she pushed against the rusty lock so that it came open.

She ran out with her little bare feet. No one came

And she set him close to her in the sledge and drew the cloak over him

after her. At last she could not run any longer, and she sat down on a large stone. When she looked round she saw that the summer was over; it was late autumn. It had not changed in the beautiful garden, where were sunshine and flowers all the year round.

'Oh, dear, how late I have made myself!' said Gerda. 'It's autumn already! I cannot rest!' And she sprang up to run on.

Oh, how tired and sore her little feet grew, and it became colder and colder.

She had to rest again, and there on the snow in front of her was a large crow.

It had been looking at her for some time, and it nodded its head and said, 'Caw! caw! good day.' Then it asked the little girl why she was alone in the world. She told the crow her story, and asked if he had seen Kay.

The crow nodded very thoughtfully and said, 'It might be! It might be!'

'What! Do you think you have?' cried the little girl, and she almost squeezed the crow to death as she kissed him.

'Gently, gently!' said the crow. 'I think – I know I think – it might be little Kay, but now he has forgotten you for the princess!'

'Does he live with a princess?' asked Gerda.

'Yes, listen,' said the crow.

Then he told her all he knew.

'In the kingdom in which we are now sitting lives a princess who is dreadfully clever. She has read all the newspapers in the world and has forgotten them again. She is as clever as that. The other day she came to the throne, and that is not so pleasant as people think. Then she began to say, "Why should I not marry?" But she wanted a husband who could answer when he was spoken to, not one who would stand up stiffly and look respectable – that would be too dull.

'When she told all the court ladies, they were delighted. You can believe every word I say,' said the crow, 'I have a tame sweetheart in the palace, and she tells me everything.'

Of course his sweetheart was a crow.

'The newspapers came out next morning with a border of hearts round it, and the princess's monogram on it, and inside you could read that every good-looking young man might come into the palace and speak to the princess, and whoever should speak loud enough to be heard would be well fed and looked after, and the one who spoke best should become the princess's husband.

Indeed,' said the crow, 'you can quite believe me. It is as true as that I am sitting here.

'Young men came in streams, and there was such a crowding and a mixing together! But nothing came of it on the first nor on the second day. They could all speak quite well when they were in the street, but as soon as they came inside the palace door, and saw the guards in silver, and upstairs the footmen in gold, and the great hall all lighted up, then their wits left them! And when they stood in front of the throne where the princess was sitting, then they could not think of anything to say except to repeat the last word she had spoken, and she did not much care to hear that again. It seemed as if they were walking in their sleep until they came out into the street again, when they could speak once more. There was a row stretching from the gate of the town up to the castle.

'They were hungry and thirsty, but in the palace they did not even get a glass of water.

'A few of the cleverest had brought some slices of bread and butter with them, but they did not share them with their neighbour, for they thought, "If he looks hungry, the princess will not take him!"'

'But what about Kay?' asked Gerda. 'When did he come? Was he in the crowd?'

'Wait a bit; we are coming to him! On the third day a little figure came without horse or carriage and walked jauntily up to the palace. His eyes shone as yours do; he had lovely curling hair, but quite poor clothes.'

'That was Kay!' cried Gerda with delight. 'Oh, then I have found him!' and she clapped her hands.

'He had a little bundle on his back,' said the crow.

'No, it must have been his skates, for he went away with his skates!'

'Very likely,' said the crow, 'I did not see for certain. But I know this from my sweetheart, that when he came to the palace door and saw the royal guards in silver, and on the stairs the footmen in gold, he was not the least bit put out. He nodded to them, saying, "It must be rather dull standing on the stairs; I would rather go inside!"

'The halls blazed with lights; councillors and ambassadors were walking about in noiseless shoes carrying gold dishes. It was enough to make one nervous! His boots creaked dreadfully loud, but he was not frightened.'

'That must be Kay!' said Gerda. 'I know he had new boots on; I have heard them creaking in his grandmother's room!'

'They did creak, certainly!' said the crow. 'And,

All the ladies-in-waiting were standing round, each with her attendants,
and the lords-in-waiting with their attendants

not one bit afraid, up he went to the princess, who was sitting on a large pearl as round as a spinning wheel. All the ladies-in-waiting were standing round, each with her attendants, and the lords-in-waiting with their attendants. The nearer they stood to the door the prouder they were.'

'It must have been dreadful!' said little Gerda. 'And Kay did win the princess?'

'I heard from my tame sweetheart that he was merry and quick-witted; he had not come to woo, he said, but to listen to the princess's wisdom. And the end of it was that they fell in love with each other.'

'Oh, yes; that was Kay!' said Gerda. 'He was so clever; he could do sums with fractions. Oh, do lead me to the palace!'

'That's easily said!' answered the crow, 'but how are we to manage that? I must talk it over with my tame sweetheart. She may be able to advise us, for I

must tell you that a little girl like you could never get permission to enter it.'

'Yes, I will get it!' said Gerda. 'When Kay hears that I am there he will come out at once and fetch me!'

'Wait for me by the railings,' said the crow, and he nodded his head and flew away.

It was late in the evening when he came back.

'Caw, caw!' he said, 'I am to give you her love, and here is a little roll for you. She took it out of the kitchen; there's plenty there, and you must be hungry. You cannot come into the palace. The guards in silver and the footmen in gold would not allow it. But don't cry! You shall get in all right. My sweetheart knows a little backstairs which leads to the sleeping-room, and she knows where to find the key.'

They went into the garden, and when the lights

in the palace were put out one after the other, the crow led Gerda to a backdoor.

Oh, how Gerda's heart beat with anxiety and longing! It seemed as if she were going to do something wrong, but she only wanted to know if it were little Kay. Yes, it must be he! She remembered so well his clever eyes, his curly hair. She could see him smiling as he did when they were at home under the rose trees! He would be so pleased to see her, and to hear how they all were at home.

Now they were on the stairs; a little lamp was burning, and on the landing stood the tame crow. She put her head on one side and looked at Gerda, who bowed as her grandmother had taught her.

'My betrothed has told me many nice things about you, my dear young lady,' she said. 'Will you take the lamp while I go in front? We go this way so as to meet no one.'

Through beautiful rooms they came to the sleeping-room. In the middle of it, hung on a thick rod of gold, were two beds, shaped like lilies, one all white, in which lay the princess, and the other red, in which Gerda hoped to find Kay. She pushed aside the curtain, and saw a brown neck. Oh, it was Kay! She called his name out loud, holding the lamp towards him.

He woke up, turned his head and – it was not Kay!

It was only his neck that was like Kay's, but he was young and handsome. The princess sat up in her lily-bed and asked who was there.

Then Gerda cried, and told her story and all that the crows had done.

'You poor child!' said the prince and princess, and they praised the crows, and said that they were not angry with them, but that they must not do it again. Now they should have a reward.

'Would you like to fly away free?' said the princess, 'or will you have a permanent place as court crows with what you can get in the kitchen?'

And both crows bowed and asked for a permanent appointment, for they thought of their old age.

And they put Gerda to bed, and she folded her hands, thinking, as she fell asleep, 'How good people and animals are to me!'

The next day she was dressed from head to foot in silk and satin. They wanted her to stay on in the palace, but she begged for a little carriage and a horse and a pair of shoes so that she might go out again into the world to look for Kay.

They gave her a muff as well as some shoes; she was warmly dressed, and when she was ready, there in front of the door stood a coach of pure gold, with a coachman, footmen and postilions with gold crowns on.

The prince and princess helped her into the carriage and wished her good luck.

The wild crow who was now married drove with her for the first three miles; the other crow could not come because she had a bad headache.

'Goodbye, good-bye!' called the prince and princess; and little Gerda cried, and the crow cried.

When he said goodbye, he flew on to a tree and waved with his black wings as long as the carriage, which shone like the sun, was in sight.

They came at last to a dark wood, but the coach lit it up like a torch. When the robbers saw it, they rushed out, exclaiming, 'Gold! gold!'

They seized the horses, killed the coachman, footmen and postilions, and dragged Gerda out of the carriage.

'She is plump and tender! I will eat her!' said the old robber-queen, and she drew her long knife, which glittered horribly.

'You shall not kill her!' cried her little daughter. 'She shall play with me. She shall give me her muff and her beautiful dress, and she shall sleep in my bed.'

The little robber-girl was as big as Gerda, but was stronger, broader, with dark hair and black eyes. She threw her arms round Gerda and said, 'They shall not kill you, so long as you are not naughty. Aren't you a princess?'

'No,' said Gerda, and she told all that had happened to her, and how dearly she loved little Kay.

The robber-girl looked at her very seriously, and nodded her head, saying, 'They shall not kill you, even if you are naughty, for then I will kill you myself!'

And she dried Gerda's eyes, and stuck both her hands in the beautiful warm muff.

The little robber-girl took Gerda to a corner of the robbers' camp where she slept.

All round were more than a hundred wood-pigeons which seemed to be asleep, but they moved a little when the two girls came up.

There was also, near by, a reindeer which the robber-girl teased by tickling it with her long sharp knife.

Gerda lay awake for some time.

'Coo, coo!' said the wood-pigeons. 'We have seen little Kay. A white bird carried his sledge; he was sitting in the Snow Queen's carriage which drove over the forest when our little ones were in the nest. She breathed on them, and all except we two died. Coo, coo!'

'What are you saying over there?' cried Gerda. 'Where was the Snow Queen going to? Do you know at all?'

'She was probably travelling to Lapland, where there is always ice and snow. Ask the reindeer.'

'There is capital ice and snow there!' said the reindeer. 'One can jump about there in the great sparkling valleys. There the Snow Queen has her summer palace, but her best palace is up by the North Pole, on the island called Spitzbergen.'

'Oh Kay, my little Kay!' sobbed Gerda.

'You must lie still,' said the little robber-girl, 'or else I shall stick my knife into you!'

In the morning Gerda told her all that the wood-pigeons had said. She nodded. 'Do you know where Lapland is?' she asked the reindeer.

'Who should know better than I?' said the beast, and his eyes sparkled. 'I was born and bred there on the snow-fields.'

'Listen!' said the robber-girl to Gerda; 'you see that all the robbers have gone; only my mother is left, and she will fall asleep in the afternoon – then I will do something for you!'

When her mother had fallen asleep, the robber-girl went up to the reindeer and said, 'I am going to set you free so that you can run to Lapland. But you must go quickly and carry this little girl to the Snow Queen's palace, where her playfellow is. You must have heard all that she told about it, for she spoke loud enough!'

The reindeer sprang high for joy. The robber-girl lifted little Gerda up, and had the foresight to tie her on firmly, and even gave her a little pillow for a saddle. 'You must have your fur boots,' she said, 'for it will be cold; but I shall keep your muff, for it is so cosy! But, so that you may not freeze, here are my mother's great fur gloves; they will come up to your elbows. Creep into them!'

And Gerda cried for joy.

'Don't make such faces!' said the little robber-girl. 'You must look very happy. And here are two loaves and a sausage; now you won't be hungry!'

They were tied to the reindeer, the little robber-girl opened the door, made all the big dogs come away, cut through the halter with her sharp knife, and said to the reindeer, 'Run now! But take great care of the little girl.'

And Gerda stretched out her hands with the large fur gloves towards the little robber-girl and said, 'Goodbye!'

Then the reindeer flew over the ground, through the great forest, as fast as he could.

The wolves howled, the ravens screamed, the sky seemed on fire.

The robber-girl put little Gerda upon the reindeer

'Those are my dear old northern lights,' said the reindeer; 'see how they shine!'

And then he ran faster still, day and night.

The loaves were eaten, and the sausage also, and then they came to Lapland.

They stopped by a wretched little house; the roof almost touched the ground, and the door was so low that you had to creep in and out.

There was no one in the house except an old Lapland woman who was cooking fish over an oil-lamp. The reindeer told Gerda's whole history, but first he told his own, for that seemed to him much more important, and Gerda was so cold that she could not speak.

'Ah, you poor creatures!' said the Lapland woman; 'you have still farther to go! You must go over a hundred miles into Finland, for there the Snow Queen lives, and every night she burns Bengal lights. I will write some words on a dried stock-fish, for I have no paper, and you must give it to the Finland woman, for she can give you better advice than I can.'

And when Gerda was warmed and had had something to eat and drink, the Lapland woman wrote on a dried stock-fish, and begged Gerda to take care of it, tied Gerda securely on the reindeer's back, and away they went again.

The whole night was ablaze with northern lights, and then they came to Finland and knocked at the Finland woman's chimney, for door she had none.

Inside it was so hot that the Finland woman wore very few clothes; she loosened Gerda's clothes and drew off her fur gloves and boots. She laid a piece of ice on the reindeer's head, and then read what was written on the stock-fish. She read it over three times till she knew it by heart, and then put the fish in the saucepan, for she never wasted anything.

Then the reindeer told his story, and afterwards little Gerda's and the Finland woman blinked her eyes but said nothing.

'You are very clever,' said the reindeer. 'I know. Cannot you give the little girl a drink so that she may have the strength of twelve men and overcome the Snow Queen?'

'The strength of twelve men!' said the Finland woman; 'that would not help much. Little Kay is with the Snow Queen and he likes everything there very much and thinks it the best place in the world. But that is because he has a splinter of glass in his heart and a bit in his eye. If these do not come out, he will never be free, and the Snow Queen will keep her power over him.'

'But cannot you give little Gerda something so that she can have power over her?'

'I can give her no greater power than she has already; don't you see how great it is? Don't you see how men and beasts must help her when she wanders into the wide world with her bare feet? She is powerful already, because she is a dear little innocent child. If she cannot by herself conquer the Snow Queen and take away the glass splinters from little Kay, we cannot help her! The Snow Queen's garden begins two miles from here. You can carry the little maiden so far; put her down by the large bush with red berries growing in the snow. Then you must come back here as fast as you can.'

Then the Finland woman lifted little Gerda on the reindeer and away he sped.

'Oh, I have left my gloves and boots behind!' cried Gerda. She missed them in the piercing cold, but the reindeer did not dare to stop. On he ran till he came to the bush with red berries. Then he set Gerda down and kissed her mouth, and great big tears ran down his cheeks, and then he ran back. There stood poor Gerda, without shoes or gloves in the middle of the bitter cold of Finland.

She ran on as fast as she could. A regiment of gigantic snowflakes came against her, but they melted when they touched her, and she went on with fresh courage.

And now we must see what Kay was doing. He was not thinking of Gerda, and never dreamt that she was standing outside the palace.

The walls of the palace were built of driven snow, and the doors and windows of piercing winds. There were more than a hundred halls in it, all of frozen snow. The largest was several miles long; the bright northern lights lit them up, and very large and empty and cold and glittering they were! In the middle of the great hall was a frozen lake which had cracked in a thousand pieces; each piece was exactly like the others. Here the Snow Queen used to sit when she was at home.

Little Kay was almost blue and black with cold, but he did not feel it, for she had kissed away his feelings and his heart was a lump of ice.

He was pulling about some sharp, flat pieces of ice, and trying to fit one into the other. He thought each was most beautiful, but that was because of the splinter of glass in his eye. He fitted them into a great many shapes, but he wanted to make them spell the word 'Love'. The Snow Queen had said, 'If you can spell out that word you shall be your own master. I will give you the whole world and a new pair of skates.'

But he could not do it.

'Now I must fly to warmer countries,' said the Snow Queen. 'I must go and powder my black kettles!' (This was what she called Mount Etna and Mount Vesuvius.) 'It does the lemons and grapes good.'

And off she flew, and Kay sat alone in the great hall trying to do his puzzle.

He sat so still that you would have thought he was frozen.

Then it happened that little Gerda stepped into the hall. The biting cold winds became quiet as if they had fallen asleep when she appeared in the great, empty, freezing hall.

She caught sight of Kay; she recognised him, and ran and put her arms round his neck, crying, 'Kay! dear little Kay! I have found you at last!'

But he sat quite still and cold. Then Gerda wept hot tears which fell on his neck and thawed his heart and swept away the bit of the looking-glass. He looked at her and then he burst into tears. He cried so much that the glass splinter swam out of his eye; then he knew her, and cried out, 'Gerda! dear little Gerda! Where have you been so long? and where have I been?'

And he looked round him.

'How cold it is here! How wide and empty!' and he threw himself on Gerda, and she laughed and wept for joy. It was such a happy time that the pieces of ice even danced round them for joy, and when they were tired and lay down again they assembled themselves into the letters that the Snow Queen had said he must spell in order to become his own master and have the whole world and a new pair of skates.

And Gerda kissed his cheeks and they grew rosy; she kissed his eyes and they sparkled like hers; she kissed his hands and feet and he became warm and glowing. The Snow Queen might come home now; his release – the word 'Love' – stood written in sparkling ice.

They took each other's hands and wandered out of the great palace; they

talked about the grandmother and the roses on the leads and wherever they came the winds hushed and the sun came out. When they reached the bush with red berries there stood the reindeer waiting for them.

He carried Kay and Gerda first to the Finland woman, who warmed them in her hot room and gave them advice for their journey home.

Then they went to the Lapland woman, who gave them new clothes and mended their sleigh. The reindeer ran with them until they came to the green fields. Here he said goodbye.

They came to the forest, which was bursting into bud, and out of it came a splendid horse which Gerda knew; it was one of those which had drawn the gold coach and was ridden by a young girl with a red cap. It was the little robber-girl who was tired of being at home and wanted to go out into the world. She and Gerda knew each other at once.

'You are a nice fellow!' she said to Kay. 'I should like to know if you deserve to be run after all over the world!'

But Gerda patted her cheeks and asked after the prince and princess.

'They are travelling about,' said the robber-girl.

'And the crow?' asked Gerda.

'Oh, the crow is dead!' answered the robber-girl. 'His tame sweetheart is a widow and hops about with a bit of black crape round her leg. She makes a great fuss, but that's all nonsense. But tell me what happened to you, and how you caught him.'

And Kay and Gerda told her all.

'Dear, dear!' said the robber-girl; she shook both their hands, and promised that if she found herself in their town she would come and see them. Then she rode on. But Gerda and Kay went home hand in hand. There they were reunited with the grandmother and everything was just as it had been, except that when they went through the doorway they found they were grown-up. There were the roses on the leads; it was summer, warm, glorious summer.

Snow White

It was the middle of winter, when the broad flakes of snow were falling around, that the queen of a country many thousand miles off sat working at her window, the frame of which was made of fine black ebony; and as she sat looking out upon the snow, she pricked her finger and three drops of blood fell upon it. Then she gazed thoughtfully upon the red drops that sprinkled the white snow, and said, 'Would that my little daughter may be as white as that snow, as red as that blood and as black as this ebony window frame!' And so it was that the little girl really did grow up – her skin was as white as snow, her cheeks as rosy as the blood and her hair as black as ebony; and she was called Snow White.

But this queen died; and the king soon married another wife, who became queen, and was very beautiful, but so vain that she could not bear to think that anyone could be handsomer than she was. She had a fairy looking-glass, and she would gaze upon herself in it and say:

> 'Tell me, glass, tell me true!
> Of all the ladies in the land,
> Who is fairest, tell me, who?'

And the glass had always answered: 'Thou, queen, art the fairest in all the land.'
But Snow White grew more and more beautiful; and when she was seven years old she was as bright as the day, and fairer than the queen herself. Then the glass one day answered the queen, when she went to look in it as usual:

> 'Thou, queen, art fair, and beauteous to see,
> But Snow White is lovelier far than thee!'

When she heard this she turned pale with rage and envy, and called to one of her servants, and said, 'Take Snow White away into the wide wood, that I may never see her any more.'
Then the servant led her away; but his heart

And the glass had always answered:
'Thou, queen, art the fairest in all the land.'

melted when Snow White begged him to spare her life, and he said, 'I will not hurt you, thou pretty child.' So he left her by herself; and though he

573

thought it most likely that the wild beasts would tear her in pieces, he felt as if a great weight were taken off his heart when he had made up his mind not to kill her but to leave her to her fate, with the chance of someone finding and saving her.

Then poor Snow White wandered along through the wood in great fear; and the wild beasts roared about her, but none did her any harm. In the evening she came to a cottage among the hills, and went in to rest, for her little feet would carry her no farther. Everything was spruce and neat in the cottage: on the table was spread a white cloth, and there were seven little plates, seven little loaves and seven little glasses with wine in them; and seven knives and forks laid in order; and by the wall stood seven little beds. As she was very hungry, she picked a little piece of each loaf and drank a very little wine out of each glass; and after that she thought she would lie down and rest. So she tried all the little beds; but one was too long, and another was too short, and only the seventh suited her: so there she laid herself down and went to sleep.

By and by in came the masters of the cottage. Now they were seven little dwarfs that lived among the mountains and dug and searched for gold. They lit up their seven little lamps, and saw at once that all was not right.

The first said, 'Who has been sitting on my stool?'

The second, 'Who has been eating off my plate?'

The third, 'Who has been picking my bread?'

The fourth, 'Who has been meddling with my spoon?'

The fifth, 'Who has been handling my fork?'

The sixth, 'Who has been cutting with my knife?'

The seventh, 'Who has been drinking my wine?'

Then the first looked round and said, 'Who has been lying on my bed?' And the rest came running to him, and everyone cried out that somebody had been upon his bed. But the seventh saw Snow White, and called all his brethren to come and see her;

and they cried out with wonder and astonishment and brought their lamps to look at her, and said, 'Good heavens! What a lovely child she is!' And they were very glad to see her, and took care not to wake her; and the seventh dwarf slept an hour with each of the other dwarfs in turn, till the night was gone.

In the morning Snow White told them all her story; and they pitied her, and said if she would keep all things in order, and cook and wash and knit and spin for them, she might stay where she was, and they would take good care of her. Then they went out all day long to their work, seeking for gold and silver in the mountains, and Snow White was left at home; but they warned her, and said, 'The queen will soon find out where you are, so take care to let no one in.'

But the queen, now that she thought Snow White was dead, believed that she must be the handsomest lady in the land; and she went to her glass and said:

'Tell me, glass, tell me true!
Of all the ladies in the land,
Who is fairest, tell me, who?'

And the glass answered:

'Thou, queen, art the fairest in all this land:
But over the hills, in the greenwood shade,
Where the seven dwarfs their dwelling
             have made,
There Snow White is hiding her head; and she
Is lovelier far, O queen! than thee.'

Then the queen was very much frightened; for she knew that the glass always spoke the truth, and was sure that the servant had betrayed her. And she could not bear to think that anyone lived who was more beautiful than she was; so she dressed herself up as an old pedlar, and went her way over the hills, to the place where the dwarfs dwelt. Then she knocked at the door, and cried, 'Fine wares to sell!'

Snow White looked out of the window, and said, 'Good-day, good woman! What have you to sell?'

'Good wares, fine wares,' said she; 'laces and bobbins of all colours.'

'I will let the old lady in; she seems to be a very good sort of body,' thought Snow White, as she ran down and unbolted the door.

'Bless me!' said the old woman, 'how badly your stays are laced! Let me lace them up with one of my nice new laces.'

Snow White did not dream of any mischief, so she stood before the old woman; but she set to work so nimbly, and pulled the lace so tight, that Snow White's breath was stopped, and she fell down as if she were dead.

'There's an end to all thy beauty,' said the spiteful queen, and went away home.

In the evening the seven dwarfs came home; and I need not say how grieved they were to see their faithful Snow White stretched out upon the ground, as if she was quite dead. However, they lifted her up, and when they found what ailed her, they cut the lace; and in a little time she began to breathe, and very soon came back to life again. Then they said, 'The old woman was the queen herself; take care another time, and let no one in when we are away.'

When the queen got home, she went straight to her glass and spoke to it as before; but to her great grief it still said:

'Thou, queen, art the fairest in all this land.
But over the hills, in the greenwood shade,
Where the seven dwarfs their dwelling
             have made,
There Snow White is hiding her head; and she
Is lovelier far, O queen! than thee.'

Then the blood ran cold in her heart with spite and malice to see that Snow White still lived; and she dressed herself up again, but in quite another dress from the one she wore before, and took with her a poisoned comb. When she reached the dwarfs' cottage, she knocked at the door, and cried, 'Fine wares to sell!'

But Snow White said, 'I dare not let anyone in.'

Then the queen said, 'Only look at my beautiful combs!' and gave her the poisoned one. And it looked so pretty that she took it up and put it into her hair to try it; but the moment it touched her head, the poison was so powerful that she fell down senseless.

'There you may lie,' said the queen, and went her way.

But by good luck the dwarfs came in very early that evening; and when they saw Snow White lying on the ground, they guessed what had happened, and soon found the poisoned comb. And when they took it away she got well, and told them all that had passed; and they warned her once more not to open the door to anyone.

Meantime the queen went home to her glass, and shook with rage when she read the very same answer as before; and she said, 'Snow White shall die, if it cost me my life.'

So she went by herself into her chamber, and got ready a poisoned apple: the outside looked very rosy and tempting, but whoever tasted it was sure to die. Then she dressed herself up as a peasant's wife, and travelled over the hills to the dwarfs' cottage, and knocked at the door; but Snow White put her head out of the window and said, 'I dare not let anyone in, for the dwarfs have told me not to.'

'Do as you please,' said the old woman, 'but at any rate take this pretty apple; I will give it you.'

'No,' said Snow White, 'I dare not take it.'

'You silly girl!' answered the other, 'what are you afraid of? Do you think it is poisoned? Come! Do you eat one part, and I will eat the other.' Now the apple was made up so that one side was good while the other side was poisoned. Then Snow White was much tempted to taste, for the apple looked so very nice; and when she saw the old woman eat, she could wait no longer. But she had scarcely put the piece into her mouth, when she fell down dead upon the ground.

'This time nothing will save thee,' said the queen; and she went home to her glass, and at last it said: 'Thou, queen, art the fairest of all the fair.'

And then her wicked heart was glad, and as happy as such a heart could be.

When evening came, and the dwarfs arrived home, they found Snow White lying on the ground: no breath came from her lips, and they were afraid that she was quite dead. They lifted her up, and combed her hair, and washed her face with wine and water; but all was in vain, for the little girl seemed quite dead. So they laid her down upon a bier, and all seven watched and bewailed her three whole days; and then they thought they would bury her: but her cheeks were still rosy, and her face looked just as it did while she was alive; so they said, 'We will never bury her in the cold ground.' And they made a coffin of glass, so that they might still look at her, and wrote upon it in golden letters what her name was, and that she was a king's daughter. And the coffin was set beside the cottage among the hills, and one of the dwarfs always sat by it and watched. And the birds of the air came too, and bemoaned Snow White; and first of all came an owl, and then a raven, and at last a dove, and sat by her side.

And thus Snow White lay for a long, long time, and still only looked as though she was asleep; for she was even now as white as snow, and as red as blood, and as black as ebony.

At last a prince came and called at the dwarfs' house; and he saw Snow White, and read what was written in golden letters.

Then he offered the dwarfs money, and prayed and besought them to let him take her away; but they said, 'We will not part with her for all the gold in the world.'

At last, however, they had pity on him, and gave him the coffin; but the moment he lifted it up to carry it home with him, the piece of apple fell from between her lips, and Snow White awoke, and said, 'Where am I?'

And the prince said, 'Thou art quite safe with me.'

Then he told her all that had happened, and said, 'I love you far better than all the world; so come with me to my father's palace, and you shall be my wife.' And Snow White consented, and went home with the prince; and everything was got ready with great pomp and splendour for their wedding.

To the feast was asked, among the rest, Snow White's old enemy the queen; and as she was dressing herself in fine rich clothes, she looked in the glass and said:

> 'Tell me, glass, tell me true!
> Of all the ladies in the land,
> Who is fairest, tell me, who?'

And the glass answered:

> 'Thou, lady, art loveliest here, I ween;
> But lovelier far is the new-made queen.'

When she heard this she started with rage; but her envy and curiosity were so great, that she could not help setting out to see the bride. And when she got there, and saw that it was no other than Snow White, who she thought had been dead a long while, she choked with rage and fell down and died; but Snow White and the prince lived and reigned happily over that land many, many years; and sometimes they went up into the mountains, and paid a visit to the little dwarfs, who had been so kind to Snow White in her time of need.

Snow-White and Rose-Red

A poor widow once lived in a little cottage with a garden in front of it in which grew two rose trees, one bearing white roses and the other red. She had two children, who were just like the two rose trees: one was called Snow-White and the other Rose-Red, and they were the sweetest and best children in the world, always diligent and always cheerful; but Snow-White was quieter and more gentle than Rose-Red. Rose-Red loved to run about the fields and meadows, and to pick flowers and catch butterflies; but Snow-White sat at home with her mother and helped her in the household, or read aloud to her when there was no work to do. The two children loved each other so dearly that they always walked about hand in hand whenever they went out together, and when Snow-White said, 'We will never desert each other,' Rose-Red answered: 'No, not as long as we live'; and the mother added: 'Whatever one gets she shall share with the other.' They often roamed about in the woods gathering berries and no beast offered to hurt them; on the contrary, they came up to them in the most confiding manner; the little hare would eat a cabbage leaf from their hands, the deer grazed beside them, the stag would bound past them merrily, and the birds remained on the branches and sang to them with all their might.

No evil ever befell them; if they tarried late in the wood and night overtook them, they lay down together on the moss and slept till morning, and their mother knew they were quite safe and never felt anxious about them. Once, when they had slept all night in the wood and had been wakened by the morning sun, they perceived a beautiful child in a shining white robe sitting close to their resting place. The figure got up, looked at them kindly, but said nothing, and vanished into the wood. And when they looked round about them they became aware that they had slept quite close to a precipice, over which they would certainly have fallen had they gone on a few steps farther in the darkness.

And when they told their mother of their adventure, she said what they had seen must have been the angel that guards good children.

Snow-White and Rose-Red kept their mother's cottage so beautifully clean and neat that it was a pleasure to go into it. In summer Rose-Red looked after the house, and every morning before her mother awoke she placed a bunch of flowers before her bed with a rose from each tree. In winter Snow-White lit the fire and put on the kettle, which was made of brass, but so beautifully polished that it shone like gold. In the evening when the snowflakes fell, their mother said: 'Snow-White, go and close the shutters,' and they drew round the fire, while the mother put on her spectacles and read aloud from a big book and the two girls listened and sat and span. Beside them on the ground lay a little lamb, and behind them perched a little white dove with its head tucked under its wing.

One evening as they sat thus cosily together someone knocked at the door as though he desired admittance. The mother said: 'Rose-Red, open the door quickly; it must be some traveller seeking shelter.' Rose-Red hastened to unbar the door, and thought she saw a poor man standing in the darkness outside; but it was no such thing, only a bear, who poked his thick black head through the door. Rose-Red screamed aloud and sprang back in terror, the lamb began to bleat, the dove flapped its wings and Snow-White ran and hid behind her mother's bed. But the bear began to speak, and said: 'Don't be afraid: I won't hurt you. I am half frozen, and only wish to warm myself a little.' 'My poor bear,' said the mother, 'lie down by the fire, only take care you don't burn your fur.' Then she called out: 'Snow-White and Rose-Red, come out; the bear will do you no harm; he is a good, honest creature.' So they both came out of their hiding places, and gradually the lamb and dove drew near too, and they all forgot their fear. The bear asked

Snow-White and Rose-Red fetched a brush and scrubbed him till he was dry

the children to beat the snow a little out of his fur, and they fetched a brush and scrubbed him till he was dry. Then the beast stretched himself in front of the fire, and growled happily and comfortably. The children soon grew quite at their ease with him, and led their helpless guest a fearful life. They tugged his fur with their hands, put their small feet on his back and rolled him about here and there or took a hazel wand and beat him with it; and if he growled they only laughed. The bear submitted to everything with the best possible good nature, only when they went too far he cried: 'Oh! children, spare my life!

> Snow-White and Rose-Red,
> Don't beat your lover dead.'

When it was time to retire for the night, and the others went to bed, the mother said to the bear: 'You can lie there on the hearth, in heaven's name; it will be shelter for you from the cold and wet.' As soon as day dawned the children led him out, and he trotted over the snow into the wood. From this time on the bear came every evening at the same hour, and lay down by the hearth and let the children play what pranks they liked with him; and

they got so accustomed to him that the door was never shut till their black friend had made his appearance.

When spring came, and all outside was green, the bear said one morning to Snow-White: 'Now I must go away, and not return again the whole summer.'

'Where are you going to, dear bear?' asked Snow-White.

'I must go to the wood and protect my treasure from the wicked dwarfs. In winter, when the earth is frozen hard, they are obliged to remain underground, for they can't work their way through; but now, when the sun has thawed and warmed the ground, they break through and come up above to spy out the land and steal what they can; what once falls into their hands and into their caves is not easily brought back to light.'

Snow-White was quite sad over their friend's departure, and when she unbarred the door for him, the bear, stepping out, caught a piece of his fur in the door knocker, and Snow-White thought she glimpsed glittering gold beneath it, but she couldn't be certain of it; and the bear ran hastily away, and soon disappeared behind the trees.

A short time after this the mother sent the

children into the wood to collect faggots. They came in their wanderings upon a big tree which lay felled on the ground, and on the trunk among the long grass they noticed something jumping up and down, but what it was they couldn't distinguish. When they approached nearer they perceived a dwarf with a wizened face and a beard a yard long. The end of the beard was jammed into a cleft of the tree, and the little man sprang about like a dog on a chain, and didn't seem to know what he was to do. He glared at the girls with his fiery red eyes, and screamed out: 'What are you standing there for? Can't you come and help me?'

'What were you doing, little man?' asked Rose-Red.

'You stupid, inquisitive goose!' replied the dwarf; 'I wanted to split the tree, in order to get little chips of wood for our kitchen fire; those thick logs that serve to make fires for coarse, greedy people like yourselves quite burn up all the little fuel we need. I had successfully driven in the wedge, and all was going well, but the cursed wood was so slippery that it suddenly sprang out, and the tree closed up so rapidly that I had no time to take my beautiful white beard out; so here I am stuck fast, and I can't get away; and you silly, smooth-faced, milk-and-water girls just stand and laugh! Ugh! what wretches you are!'

The children did all in their power, but they couldn't get the beard out; it was wedged in far too firmly. 'I will run and fetch somebody,' said Rose-Red.

'Crazy blockheads!' snapped the dwarf; 'what's the good of calling anyone else? You're already two

Snow-White took her scissors out of her pocket and cut off the end of his beard

too many for me. Does nothing better occur to you than that?'

'Don't be so impatient,' said Snow-White, 'I'll see you get help;' and taking her scissors out of her pocket she cut off the end of his beard.

As soon as the dwarf felt himself free he seized a bag full of gold which was hidden among the roots of the tree, lifted it up, and muttered aloud: 'Curse these rude wretches, cutting off a piece of my splendid beard!' With these words he swung the bag over his back, and disappeared without as much as looking at the children again.

Shortly after this Snow-White and Rose-Red went out to get a dish of fish. As they approached the stream they saw something which looked like an enormous grasshopper springing towards the water as if it were going to jump in. They ran forward and recognised their old friend the dwarf.

'Where are you going to?' asked Rose-Red; 'you're surely not going to jump into the water?'

'I'm not such a fool,' screamed the dwarf. 'Don't you see that cursed fish is trying to drag me in?' The little man had been sitting on the bank fishing, when unfortunately the wind had entangled his beard in the line; and when immediately afterwards a big fish bit, the feeble little creature had no strength to pull it out; the fish had the upper fin, and dragged the dwarf towards him. He clung on with all his might to every rush and blade of grass, but it didn't help him much; he had to follow every movement of the fish, and was in great danger of being drawn into the water. The girls came up just at the right moment, held him firm, and did all they could to disentangle his beard from the line; but in vain, beard and line were in a hopeless muddle. Nothing remained but to produce the scissors and cut the beard, so that another small part of it was sacrificed.

When the dwarf perceived what they were about he yelled at them: 'Do you call that manners, you toadstools! to disfigure a fellow's face? It wasn't enough that you shortened my beard before, but you must now needs cut off the best bit of it. I can't appear like this before my own people. I wish you'd been in Jericho first.' Then he fetched a sack of pearls that lay among the rushes, and without saying another word he dragged it away and disappeared behind a stone.

It happened that soon after this the mother sent the two girls to the town to buy needles, thread, laces and ribbons. Their road led over a heath where huge boulders of rock lay scattered here and there. While trudging along they saw a big bird hovering in the air, circling slowly above them, but always descending lower, till at last it settled on a rock not far from them. Immediately afterwards they heard a sharp, piercing cry. They ran forward, and saw with horror that the eagle had pounced on their old friend the dwarf, and was about to carry him off. The tender-hearted children seized hold of the little man, and struggled so long with the bird that at last he let go his prey. When the dwarf had recovered from the first shock he screamed in his screeching voice: 'Couldn't you have treated me more carefully? You have torn my thin little coat all to shreds, useless, awkward hussies that you are!' Then he took a bag of precious stones and vanished under the rocks into his cave.

The girls were accustomed to his ingratitude, and went on their way and did their business in town. On their way home, as they were again passing the heath, they surprised the dwarf pouring out his precious stones on an open space, for he had thought no one would pass by at so late an hour. The evening sun shone on the glittering stones, and they glanced and gleamed so beautifully that the children stood still and gazed on them. 'What are you standing there gaping for?' screamed the dwarf, and his ashen-grey face became scarlet with rage.

He was about to go off with these angry words when a sudden growl was heard, and a black bear trotted out of the wood.

The dwarf jumped back in great fright, but

he hadn't time to reach his place of retreat, for the bear was already close to him. Then he cried in terror: 'Dear Mr Bear, spare me! I'll give you all my treasure. Look at those beautiful precious stones lying there. Spare my life! what pleasure would you get from a poor feeble little fellow like me? You won't feel me between your teeth. There, lay hold of these two wicked girls, they will be a tender morsel for you, as fat as young quails; eat them up, for heaven's sake.' But the bear, paying no attention to his words, gave the evil little creature one blow with his paw, and he never moved again.

The girls had run away, but the bear called after them: 'Snow-White and Rose-Red, don't be afraid; wait, and I'll come with you.' Then they recognised his voice and stood still, and when the bear was quite close to them his skin suddenly fell off, and a beautiful man stood beside them, all dressed in gold. 'I am a king's son,' he said, 'and have been doomed by that unholy little dwarf, who had stolen my treasure, to roam about the woods as a wild bear till his death should set me free. Now he has got his well-merited punishment.'

Snow-White married him, and Rose-Red his brother, and they divided the great treasure the dwarf had collected in his cave between them. The old mother lived for many years peacefully with her children; and she carried the two rose trees with her, and they stood in front of her window, and every year they bore the finest red and white roses.

The Snowman

'How astonishingly cold it is! My body is cracking all over!' said the snowman. 'The wind is really cutting out one's very life! And how that fiery thing up there glares!' He meant the sun, which was just setting. 'It shan't make me blink, though, and I shall keep quite cool and collected.'

Instead of eyes he had two large three-cornered pieces of slate in his head; his mouth consisted of an old rake, so that he had teeth as well.

He was born amidst the shouts and laughter of the boys, and greeted by the jingling bells and cracking whips of the sledges.

The sun went down, the full moon rose, large, round, clear and beautiful, in the dark blue sky.

'There it is again on the other side!' said the snowman, by which he meant the sun was appearing again. 'I have become quite accustomed to its glaring. I hope it will hang there and shine, so that I may be able to see myself. I wish I knew, though, how one ought to see about changing one's position. I should very much like to move about. If I only could, I would glide up and down the ice there, as I saw the boys doing; but somehow or other, I don't know how to run.'

'Bow-wow!' barked the old yard-dog; he was rather hoarse and couldn't bark very well. His hoarseness came on when he was a house-dog and used to lie in front of the stove. 'The sun will soon teach you to run! I saw that last winter with your predecessor, and further back still with his predecessors! They have all run away!'

'I don't understand you, my friend,' said the snowman. 'That thing up there is to teach me to run?' He meant the moon. 'Well, it certainly did run just now, for I saw it quite plainly over there, and now here it is on this side.'

'You know nothing at all about it,' said the yard-dog. 'Why, you have only just been made. The thing you see there is the moon; the other thing you saw going down the other side was the sun. He

will come up again tomorrow morning, and will soon teach you how to run away down the gutter. The weather is going to change; I feel it already by the pain in my left hind-leg; the weather is certainly going to change.'

'I can't understand him,' said the snowman; 'but I have an idea that he is speaking of something unpleasant. That thing that glares so, and then disappears, the sun, as he calls it, is not my friend. I know that by instinct.'

'Bow-wow!' barked the yard-dog, and walked three times round himself, and then crept into his kennel to sleep. The weather really did change. Towards morning a dense damp fog lay over the whole neighbourhood; later on came an icy wind, which sent the frost packing. But when the sun rose, it was a glorious sight. The trees and shrubs were covered with rime, and looked like a wood of coral, and every branch was thick with long white blossoms. The most delicate twigs, which are lost among the foliage in summertime, came now into prominence, and it was like a spider's web of glistening white. The lady-birches waved in the wind; and when the sun shone, everything glittered and sparkled as if it were sprinkled with diamond dust, and great diamonds were lying on the snowy carpet.

'Isn't it wonderful?' exclaimed a girl who was walking with a young man in the garden. They stopped near the snowman, and looked at the glistening trees. 'Summer cannot show a more beautiful sight,' she said, with her eyes shining.

'And one can't get a fellow like this in summer either,' said the young man, pointing to the snowman. 'He's a beauty!'

The girl laughed, and nodded to the snowman, and then they both danced away over the snow.

'Who were those two?' asked the snowman of the yard-dog. 'You have been in this yard longer than I have. Do you know who they are?'

'The sun will soon teach you to run!' said the yard-dog

'Do I know them indeed?' answered the yard-dog. 'She has often stroked me, and he has given me bones. I don't bite either of them!'

'But what are they?' asked the snowman.

'Lovers!' replied the yard-dog. 'They will go into one kennel and gnaw the same bone!'

'Are they the same kind of beings that we are?' asked the snowman.

'They are our masters,' answered the yard-dog. 'Really people who have only been in the world one day know very little.' That's the conclusion I have come to. Now I have age and wisdom; I know everyone in the house, and I can remember a time when I was not lying here in a cold kennel. Bow-wow!'

'The cold is splendid,' said the snowman. 'Tell me some more. But don't rattle your chain so, it makes me crack!'

'Bow-wow!' barked the yard-dog. 'They used to say I was a pretty little fellow; then I lay in a velvet-covered chair in my master's house. My mistress used to nurse me, and kiss and fondle me, and call me her dear, sweet little puppy! But by and by I grew too big, and I was given to the housekeeper, and I went into the kitchen. You can see into it from where you are standing; you can look at the room in which I was master, for so I was when I was with the housekeeper. Of course it was a smaller place than upstairs, but it was more comfortable, for I wasn't chased about and teased by the children as I had been before. My food was just as good, or even better. I had my own pillow, and there was a stove there, which at this time of year is the most beautiful thing in the world. I used to creep right under that stove. Ah me! I often dream of that stove still! Bow-wow!'

'Is a stove so beautiful?' asked the snowman. 'Is it anything like me?'

'It is just the opposite of you! It is coal-black, and has a long neck with a brass pipe. It eats firewood, so that fire spouts out of its mouth. One has to keep close beside it – quite underneath is the nicest of all. You can see it through the window from where you are standing.'

And the snowman looked in that direction, and saw a smooth polished object with a brass pipe. The flicker from the fire reached him across the snow. The snowman felt wonderfully happy, and a feeling came over him which he could not express; but all those who are not snowmen know about it.

'Why did you leave her?' asked the snowman. He had a feeling that such a being must be a lady. 'How could you leave such a place?'

'I had to!' said the yard-dog. 'They turned me out of doors, and chained me up here. I had bitten the youngest boy in the leg, because he took away the bone I was gnawing; a bone for a bone, I thought! But they were very angry, and from that time I have been chained here, and I have lost my voice. Don't you hear how hoarse I am? Bow-wow! I can't speak like other dogs. Bow-wow! That was the end of happiness!'

The snowman, however, was not listening to him any more; he was looking into the room where the housekeeper lived, where the stove stood on its four iron legs, and seemed to be just the same size as the snowman.

'How something is cracking inside me!' he said. 'Shall I never be able to get in there? It is certainly a very innocent wish, and our innocent wishes ought to be fulfilled. I must get there, and lean against the stove, if I have to break the window first!'

'You will never get inside there!' said the yard-dog; 'and if you were to reach the stove you would disappear. Bow-wow!'

'I'm as good as gone already!' answered the snowman. 'I believe I'm breaking up!'

The whole day the snowman looked through the window; towards dusk the room grew still more inviting; the stove gave out a mild light, not at all like the moon or even the sun; no, as only a stove can shine, when it has something to feed upon. When the door of the room was open, it flared up – this was one of its peculiarities; it flickered quite red upon the snowman's white face.

'I can't stand it any longer!' he said. 'How beautiful it looks with its tongue stretched out like that!'

It was a long night, but the snowman did not find it so; there he stood, wrapped in his pleasant thoughts, and they froze, so that he cracked.

Next morning the panes of the kitchen window were covered with ice, and the most beautiful ice-flowers that even a snowman could desire, only they blotted out the stove. The window would not open; he couldn't see the stove which he thought was such a lovely lady. There was a cracking and cracking inside him and all around; there was just such a frost as a snowman would delight in. But this snowman was different: how could he feel happy?

'Yours is a bad illness for a snowman!' said the yard-dog. 'I also suffered from it, but I have got over it. Bow-wow!' he barked. 'The weather is going to change!' he added.

The weather did change. There came a thaw.

When this set in the snowman set off. He did not say anything, and he did not complain, and those are bad signs.

One morning he broke up altogether. And lo! where he had stood there remained a broomstick standing upright, round which the boys had built him!

'Ah! now I understand why he loved the stove,' said the yard-dog. 'That is the raker they use to clean out the stove! The snowman had a stove-raker in his body! That's what was the matter with him! And now it's all over with him! Bow-wow!'

And before long it was all over with the winter too! 'Bow-wow!' barked the hoarse yard-dog.

But the young girl sang:

> 'Woods, your bright green garments don!
> Willows, your woolly gloves put on!
> Lark and cuckoo, daily sing –
> February has brought the spring!
> My heart joins in your song so sweet;
> Come out, dear sun, the world to greet!'

And no one thought of the snowman.

The Steadfast Tin-Soldier

There were once upon a time five-and-twenty tin-soldiers – all brothers, as they were made out of the same old tin spoon. Their uniform was red and blue, and they shouldered their guns and looked straight in front of them. The first words that they heard in this world, when the lid of the box in which they lay was taken off, were: 'Hurrah, tin-soldiers!' This was exclaimed by a little boy, clapping his hands; they had been given to him because it was his birthday, and now he began setting them out on the table. Each soldier was exactly like the other in shape, except just one, who had been made last when the tin had run short; but there he stood as firmly on his one leg as the others did on two, and he is the one that became famous.

There were many other playthings on the table on which they were being set out, but the nicest of all was a pretty little castle made of cardboard, with windows through which you could see into the rooms. In front of the castle stood some little trees surrounding a tiny mirror which looked like a lake. Wax swans were floating about and reflecting themselves in it. That was all very pretty; but the most beautiful thing was a little lady, who stood in the open doorway. She was cut out of paper, but she had on a dress of the finest muslin, with a scarf of narrow blue ribbon round her shoulders, fastened in the middle with a glittering rose made of gold paper, which was as large as her head. The little lady was stretching out both her arms, for she was a dancer, and was lifting up one leg so high in the air that the tin-soldier couldn't find it anywhere, and thought that she, too, had only one leg.

'That's the wife for me!' he thought; 'but she is so grand, and lives in a castle, whilst I have only a box with four-and-twenty others. This is no place for her! But I must make her acquaintance.' Then he stretched himself out behind a snuffbox that lay on the table; from thence he could watch the dainty little lady, who continued to stand on one leg without losing her balance.

When the night came all the other tin-soldiers went into their box, and the people of the house went to bed. Then the toys began to play at visiting, dancing and fighting. The tin-soldiers rattled in their box, for they wanted to be out too, but they could not raise the lid. The nutcrackers played at leapfrog, and the slate-pencil ran about the slate; there was such a noise that the canary woke up and began to talk to them, in poetry too! The only two who did not stir from their places were the tin-soldier and the little dancer. She remained on tiptoe, with both arms outstretched; he stood steadfastly on his one leg, never moving his eyes from her face.

The clock struck twelve, and crack! off flew the lid of the snuff- box; but there was no snuff inside, only a little black imp – that was the beauty of it.

'Hullo, tin-soldier!' said the imp. 'Don't look at things that aren't intended for the likes of you!'

But the tin-soldier took no notice, and seemed not to hear.

'Very well, wait till tomorrow!' said the imp.

When it was morning, and the children had got up, the tin-soldier was put in the window; and whether it was the wind or the little black imp, I don't know, but all at once the window flew open and out fell the little tin-soldier, head over heels, from the third-storey window! That was a terrible fall, I can tell you! He landed on his head with his leg in the air, his gun being wedged between two paving-stones.

The nurserymaid and the little boy came down at once to look for him, but, though they were so near him that they almost trod on him, they did not notice him. If the tin-soldier had only called out, 'Here I am!' they must have found him; but he did not think it fitting for him to cry out, because he had on his uniform.

Soon it began to drizzle; then the drops came faster, and there was a regular downpour. When it was over, two little street boys came along.

'Just look!' cried one. 'Here is a tin-soldier! He shall sail up and down in a boat!'

So they made a little boat out of newspaper, put the tin-soldier in it, and made him sail up and down the gutter; both the boys ran along beside him, clapping their hands. What great waves there were in the gutter, and what a swift current! The paper-boat tossed up and down, and in the middle of the stream it went so quick that the tin-soldier trembled; but he remained steadfast, showed no emotion, looked straight in front of him, shouldering his gun. All at once the boat passed under a long tunnel that was as dark as his box had been.

'Where can I be coming now?' he wondered. 'Oh, dear! This is the black imp's fault! Ah, if only the little lady were sitting beside me in the boat, it might be twice as dark for all I should care!'

Suddenly there came along a great water-rat that lived in the tunnel.

'Have you a passport?' asked the rat. 'Out with your passport!'

But the tin-soldier was silent, and grasped his gun more firmly.

The boat sped on, and the rat behind it. Ugh! how he showed his teeth, as he cried to the chips of wood and straw: 'Hold him, hold him! he has not paid the toll! He has not shown his passport!'

But the current became swifter and stronger. The tin-soldier could already see daylight where the tunnel ended; but in his ears there sounded a roaring enough to frighten any brave man. Only think! at the end of the tunnel the gutter discharged itself into a great canal; that would be just as dangerous for him as it would be for us to go down a waterfall.

Now he was so near to it that he could not hold on any longer. On went the boat, the poor tin-soldier keeping himself as stiff as he could: no one should say of him afterwards that he had flinched. The boat whirled three, four times round, and became filled to the brim with water; it began to sink! The tin-soldier was standing up to his neck in water, and deeper and deeper sank the boat, and softer and softer grew the paper; now the water was over his head. He was thinking of the pretty little dancer, whose face he should never see again, and there sounded in his ears, over and over again: 'Forward, forward, soldier bold! Death's before thee, grim and cold!'

The paper came in two, and the soldier fell – but at that moment he was swallowed by a great fish.

Oh! how dark it was inside, even darker than in the tunnel, and it was really very close quarters! But there the steadfast little tin-soldier lay full length, shouldering his gun.

Up and down swam the fish, then he made the most dreadful contortions, and became suddenly quite still. Then it was as if a flash of lightning had passed through him; the daylight streamed in, and a voice exclaimed, 'Why, here is the little tin-soldier!' The fish had been caught, taken to market, sold, and brought into the kitchen, where the cook had cut it open with a great knife. She took up the soldier between her finger and thumb, and carried him into the room, where everyone wanted to see the hero who had been found inside a fish; but the tin-soldier was not at all proud. They put him on the table, and – no, but what strange things do happen in this world! – the tin-soldier was in the same room in which he had been before! He saw the same children, and the same toys on the table; and there was the same grand castle with the pretty little dancer. She was still standing on one leg with the other high in the air; she too was steadfast. That so touched the tin-soldier, he was nearly going to shed tin-tears; but that would not have been fitting for a soldier. He looked at her, but she said nothing.

All at once one of the little boys took up the tin-soldier, and threw him into the stove, giving no reasons; but doubtless the little black imp in the snuffbox was at the bottom of this too.

There the tin-soldier lay, and felt a heat that was truly terrible; but whether he was suffering from actual fire, or from the ardour of his passion, he did not know. All his colour had disappeared; whether this had happened on his travels or whether it was the result of trouble, who can say? He looked at the little lady, she looked at him, and he felt that he was melting; but he remained steadfast, with his gun at his shoulder. Suddenly a door opened, the draught caught up the little dancer, and off she flew like a sylph to the tin-soldier in the stove and burst into flames – and that was the end of her! Then the tin-soldier melted down into a little lump, and when next morning the maid was taking out the ashes, she found him in the shape of a heart. There was nothing left of the little dancer but her gilt rose, burnt as black as a cinder.

The Storyteller at Fault

At the time when the Tuatha De Dannan held the sovereignty of Ireland, there reigned in Leinster a king, who was remarkably fond of hearing stories. Like the other princes and chieftains of the island, he had a favourite storyteller, who held a large estate from his majesty, on condition of telling him a new story every night of his life, before he went to sleep. Many indeed were the stories he knew, so that he had already reached a good old age without failing even for a single night in his task; and such was the skill he displayed that whatever cares of state or other annoyances might prey upon the monarch's mind, his storyteller was sure to send him to sleep.

One morning the storyteller arose early, and as his custom was, strolled out into his garden turning over in his mind incidents which he might weave into a story for the king at night. But this morning he found himself quite at fault; after pacing his whole demesne, he returned to his house without being able to think of anything new or strange, He found no difficulty in 'there was once a king who had three sons' or 'one day the king of all Ireland', but further than that he could not get. At length he went into breakfast, and found his wife much perplexed at his delay.

'Why don't you come to breakfast, my dear?' said she.

'I have no mind to eat anything,' replied the storyteller; 'long as I have been in the service of the king of Leinster, I never sat down to breakfast without having a new story ready for the evening, but this morning my mind is quite shut up, and I don't know what to do. I might as well lie down and die at once. I'll be disgraced for ever this evening, when the king calls for his storyteller.'

Just at this moment the lady looked out of the window.

'Do you see that black thing at the end of the field?' said she.

'I do,' replied her husband.

They drew nigh, and saw a miserable looking old man lying on the ground with a wooden leg placed beside him.

'Who are you, my good man?' asked the storyteller.

'Oh, then 'tis little matter who I am. I'm a poor, old, lame, decrepit, miserable creature, sitting down here to rest awhile.'

'An' what are you doing with that box and dice I see in your hand?'

'I am waiting here to see if anyone will play a game with me,' replied the beggar-man.

'Play with you! Why what has a poor old man like you to play for?'

'I have one hundred pieces of gold in this leathern purse,' replied the old man.

'You may as well play with him,' said the storyteller's wife; 'and perhaps you'll have something to tell the king in the evening.'

A smooth stone was placed between them, and upon it they cast their throws.

It was but a little while and the storyteller lost every penny of his money.

'Much good may it do you, friend,' said he. 'What better hap could I look for, fool that I am!'

'Will you play again?' asked the old man.

'Don't be talking, man; you have all my money.'

'Haven't you chariot and horses and hounds?'

'Well, what of them!'

'I'll stake all the money I have against thine.'

'Nonsense, man! Do you think for all the money in Ireland, I'd run the risk of seeing my lady tramp home on foot?'

'Maybe you'd win,' said the bocough.

'Maybe I wouldn't,' said the storyteller.

'Play with him, husband,' said his wife. 'I don't mind walking, if you do, love.'

'I never refused you before,' said the storyteller, 'and I won't do so now.'

Down he sat again, and in one throw lost houses, hounds and chariot.

'Will you play again?' asked the beggar.

'Are you making game of me, man; what else have I to stake?'

'I'll stake all my winnings against your wife,' said the old man.

The storyteller turned away in silence, but his wife stopped him.

'Accept his offer,' said she. 'This is the third time, and who knows what luck you may have? You'll surely win now.'

They played again, and the storyteller lost. No sooner had he done so, than to his sorrow and surprise, his wife went and sat down near the ugly old beggar.

'Is that the way you're leaving me?' said the storyteller.

'Sure I was won,' said she. 'You would not cheat the poor man, would you?'

'Have you any more to stake?' asked the old man.

'You know very well I have not,' replied the storyteller.

'I'll stake the whole now, wife and all, against your own self,' said the old man.

Again they played, and again the storyteller lost.

'Well! Here I am, and what do you want with me?'

'I'll soon let you know,' said the old man, and he took from his pocket a long cord and a wand.

'Now,' said he to the storyteller, 'what kind of animal would you rather be, a deer, a fox or a hare? You have your choice now, but you may not have it later.'

To make a long story short, the storyteller made his choice of a hare; the old man threw the cord round him, struck him with the wand, and lo! A long-eared, frisking hare was skipping and jumping on the green.

But it wasn't for long; who but his wife called the hounds, and set them on him. The hare fled, the dogs followed. Round the field ran a high wall, so that run as he might, he couldn't get out, and mightily diverted were beggar and lady to see him twist and double.

In vain did he take refuge with his wife, she kicked him back again to the hounds, until at length the beggar stopped the hounds, and with a stroke of the wand, panting and breathless, the storyteller stood before them again.

'And how did you like the sport?' said the beggar.

'It might be sport to others,' replied the storyteller, looking at his wife, 'for my part I could well put up with the loss of it.'

'Would it be asking too much,' he went on to the beggar, 'to know who you are at all, or where you come from, or why you take a pleasure in plaguing a poor old man like me?'

'Oh!' replied the stranger, 'I'm an odd kind of good-for-little fellow, one day poor, another day rich, but if you wish to know more about me or my habits, come with me and perhaps I may show you more than you would make out if you went alone.'

'I'm not my own master to go or stay,' said the storyteller, with a sigh.

The stranger put one hand into his wallet and drew out of it before their eyes a well-looking middle-aged man, to whom he spoke as follows, 'By all you heard and saw since I put you into my wallet, take charge of this lady and of the carriage and horses, and have them ready for me whenever I want them.'

Scarcely had he said these words when all vanished, and the storyteller found himself at the Foxes' Ford, near the castle of Red Hugh O'Donnell. He could see all but none could see him.

O'Donnell was in his hall, and heaviness of flesh and weariness of spirit were upon him.

'Go out,' said he to his doorkeeper, 'and see who or what may be coming.'

The doorkeeper went, and what he saw was a lank, grey beggar-man; half his sword bared behind his haunch, his two shoes full of cold road-a-wayish water sousing about him, the tips of his two ears

out through his old hat, his two shoulders out through his scant tattered cloak, and in his hand a green wand of holly.

'Save you, O'Donnell,' said the lank grey beggar-man.

'And you likewise,' said O'Donnell. 'Whence come you, and what is your craft?'

> 'I come from the outmost stream of earth,
> From the glens where the white swans glide,
> A night in Islay, a night in Man,
> A night on the cold hillside.'

'It's the great traveller you are,' said O'Donnell. 'Maybe you've learnt something on the road.'

'I am a juggler,' said the lank grey beggar-man, 'and for five pieces of silver you shall see a trick of mine.'

'You shall have them,' said O'Donnell; and the lank grey beggar-man took three small straws and placed them in his hand.

'The middle one,' said he, 'I'll blow away; the other two I'll leave.'

'Thou canst not do it,' said one and all.

But the lank grey beggar-man put a finger on either outside straw and, whiff, away he blew the middle one.

' 'Tis a good trick,' said O'Donnell; and he paid him his five pieces of silver.

'For half the money,' said one of the chief's lads, 'I'll do the same trick.'

'Take him at his word, O'Donnell.'

The lad put the three straws on his hand, and a finger on either outside straw and he blew; and what happened was that the fist was blown away with the straw.

'Thou art sore, and thou wilt be sorer,' said O'Donnell.

'Six more pieces, O'Donnell, and I'll do another trick for thee,' said the lank grey beggar-man.

'Six shalt thou have.'

'Seest thou my two ears! One I'll move but not t'other.'

' 'Tis easy to see them, they're big enough, but thou canst never move one ear and not the two together.'

The lank grey beggar-man put his hand to his ear, and he gave it a pull.

O'Donnell laughed and paid him the six pieces.

'Call that a trick,' said the fistless lad, 'anyone can do that,' and so saying, he put up his hand, pulled his ear, and what happened was that he pulled away ear and head.

'Sore thou art, and sorer thou'lt be,' said O'Donnell.

'Well, O'Donnell,' said the lank grey beggar-man, 'stranger are the tricks I've shown thee, but I'll show thee a stranger one yet for the same money.'

'Thou hast my word for it,' said O'Donnell.

With that the lank grey beggar-man took a bag from under his armpit, and from out the bag a ball of silk, and he unwound the ball and he flung it slantwise up into the clear blue heavens, and it became a ladder; then he took a hare and placed it upon the thread, and up it ran; again he took out a red-eared hound, and it swiftly ran up after the hare.

'Now,' said the lank grey beggar-man. 'Has anyone a mind to run after the dog and on the course?'

'I will,' said a lad of O'Donnell's.

'Up with you then,' said the juggler; 'but I warn you if you let my hare be killed I'll cut off your head when you come down.'

The lad ran up the thread and all three soon disappeared. After looking up for a long time, the lank grey beggar-man said, 'I'm afraid the hound is eating the hare, and that our friend has fallen asleep.'

Saying this he began to wind the thread, and down came the lad fast asleep; and down came the red-eared hound and in his mouth the last morsel of the hare.

He struck the lad a stroke with the edge of his sword, and so cast his head off. As for the hound, if he used it no worse, he used it no better.

'It's little I'm pleased, and sore I'm angered,' said O'Donnell, 'that a hound and a lad should be killed at my court.'

'Five pieces of silver twice over for each of them,' said the juggler, 'and their heads shall be on them as before.'

'Thou shalt get that,' said O'Donnell.

Five pieces, and again five were paid him, and lo! The lad had his head and the hound his. And though they lived to the uttermost end of time, the hound would never touch a hare again, and the lad took good care to keep his eyes open.

Scarcely had the lank grey beggar-man done this when he vanished from out their sight, and no one present could say if he had flown through the

air or if the earth had swallowed him up.

> He moved as wave tumbling o'er wave,
> As whirlwind following whirlwind,
> As a furious wintry blast,
> So swiftly, sprucely, cheerily,
> Right proudly,
> And no stop made
> Until he came
> To the court of Leinster's king,
> He gave a cheery light leap
> O'er top of turret,
> Of court and city
> Of Leinster's king.

Heavy was the flesh and weary the spirit of Leinster's king. 'Twas the hour he was wont to hear a story, but send he might right and left, not a jot of tidings about the storyteller could he get.

'Go to the door,' said he to his doorkeeper, 'and see if a soul is in sight who may tell me something about my storyteller.'

The doorkeeper went, and what he saw was a lank grey beggar-man, half his sword bared behind his haunch, his two old shoes full of cold road-a-wayish water sousing about him, the tips of his two ears out through his old hat, his two shoulders out through his scant tattered cloak, and in his hand a three-stringed harp.

'What canst thou do?' said the doorkeeper.

'I can play,' said the lank grey beggar-man. 'Never fear,' added he to the storyteller, 'thou shalt see all, and not a man shall see thee.'

When the king heard a harper was outside, he bade him in.

'It is I that have the best harpers in the five-fifths of Ireland,' said he, and he signed them to play. They did so, and as they played, the lank grey beggar-man listened.

'Heardst thou ever the like?' said the king.

'Did you ever, O king, hear a cat purring over a bowl of broth, or the buzzing of beetles in the twilight, or a shrill-tongued old woman scolding your head off?'

'That I have often,' said the king.

'More melodious to me,' said the lank grey beggar-man, 'were the worst of these sounds than the sweetest harping of thy harpers.'

When the harpers heard this, they drew their swords and rushed at him, but instead of striking him, their blows fell on each other, and soon not a man but was cracking his neighbour's skull and getting his own cracked in turn.

When the king saw this, he thought it hard the harpers weren't content with murdering their music, but must needs murder each other.

'Hang the fellow who began it all,' said he; 'and if I can't have a story, let me have peace.'

Up came the guards, seized the lank grey beggar-man, marched him to the gallows and hanged him high and dry. Back they marched to the hall, and who should they see but the lank grey beggar-man seated on a bench with his mouth to a flagon of ale.

'Never welcome you in!' cried the captain of the guard, 'didn't we hang you this minute, and what brings you here?'

'Is it me myself, you mean?'

'Who else?' said the captain.

'May your hand turn into a pig's foot with you when you think of tying the rope; why should you speak of hanging me?'

Back they scurried to the gallows, and there hung the king's favourite brother.

Back they hurried to the king who had fallen fast asleep.

'Please, your majesty,' said the captain, 'we hanged that strolling vagabond, but here he is back again as well as ever.'

'Hang him again,' said the king, and off he went to sleep once more.

They did as they were told, but what happened was that they found the king's chief harper hanging where the lank grey beggar-man should have been.

The captain of the guard was sorely puzzled.

'Are you wishful to hang me a third time?' said the lank grey beggar-man.

'Go where you will,' said the captain, 'and as fast as you please if you'll only go far enough. It's trouble enough you've given us already.'

'Now you're reasonable,' said the beggar-man; 'and since you've given up trying to hang a stranger because he finds fault with your music, I don't mind telling you that if you go back to the gallows you'll find your friends sitting on the sward none the worse for what has happened.'

As he said these words he vanished; and the storyteller found himself on the spot where they first met, and where his wife still was with the carriage and horses.

'Now,' said the lank grey beggar-man, 'I'll torment you no longer. There's your carriage and your horses, and your money and your wife; do what you please with them.'

'For my carriage and my horses and my hounds,'

said the storyteller, 'I thank you; but my wife and my money you may keep.'

'No,' said the other. 'I want neither, and as for your wife, don't think ill of her for what she did, she couldn't help it.'

'Not help it! Not help kicking me into the mouth of my own hounds! Not help casting me off for the sake of a beggarly old – '

'I'm not as beggarly or as old as ye think. I am Angus of the Bruff; many a good turn you've done me with the King of Leinster. This morning my magic told me the difficulty you were in, and I made up my mind to get you out of it. As for your wife there, the power that changed your body changed her mind. Forget and forgive as man and wife should do, and now you have a story for the King of Leinster when he calls for one;' and with that he disappeared.

It's true enough he now had a story fit for a king. From first to last he told all that had befallen him; so long and loud laughed the king that he couldn't go to sleep at all. And he told the storyteller never to trouble for fresh stories, but every night as long as he lived he listened again and he laughed afresh at the tale of the lank grey beggarman.

The Strange Visitor

A woman was sitting at her reel one night; and still she sat, and still she reeled, and still she wished for company.

In came a pair of broad broad feet, and sat down at the fireside; and still she sat, and still she reeled, and still she wished for company.

In came a pair of small small legs, and sat down on the broad broad feet; and still she sat, and still she reeled, and still she wished for company.

In came a pair of thick thick knees, and sat down on the small small legs; and still she sat, and still she reeled, and still she wished for company.

In came a pair of thin thin thighs, and sat down on the thick thick knees; and still she sat, and still she reeled, and still she wished for company.

In came a pair of huge huge hips, and sat down on the thin thin thighs; and still she sat, and still she reeled, and still she wished for company.

In came a wee wee waist, and sat down on the huge huge hips; and still she sat, and still she reeled, and still she wished for company.

In came a pair of broad broad shoulders, and sat down on the wee wee waist; and still she sat, and still she reeled, and still she wished for company.

In came a pair of small small arms, and sat down on the broad broad shoulders; and still she sat, and still she reeled, and still she wished for company.

In came a pair of huge huge hands, and sat down on the small small arms; and still she sat, and still she reeled, and still she wished for company.

In came a small small neck, and sat down on the broad broad shoulders; and still she sat, and still she reeled, and still she wished for company.

In came a huge huge head, and sat down on the small small neck.

'How did you get such broad broad feet?' quoth the woman.

'Much tramping, much tramping' (*gruffly*).

'How did you get such small small legs?'

'Aih–h–h! – late – and wee–e–e – moul' (*whiningly*).

'How did you get such thick thick knees?'

'Much praying, much praying' (*piously*).

'How did you get such thin thin thighs?'

'Aih–h–h! – late – and wee–e–e – moul' (*whiningly*).

'How did you get such big big hips?'

'Much sitting, much sitting' (*gruffly*).

'How did you get such a wee wee waist?'

'Aih–h–h! – late – and wee–e–e–moul' (*whiningly*).

J.D.B.

'How did you get such broad broad shoulders?'

'With carrying broom, with carrying broom' (*gruffly*).

'How did you get such small small arms?'

'Aih–h–h! – late – and wee–e–e – moul' (*whiningly*.)

'How did you get such huge huge hands?'

'Threshing with an iron flail, threshing with an iron flail' (*gruffly*).

'How did you get such a small small neck?'

'Aih–h–h! – late – wee–e–e – moul' (*pitifully*).

'How did you get such a huge huge head?'

'Much knowledge, much knowledge' (*keenly*).

'What do you come for?'

'For you!' (*At the top of the voice, with a wave of the arm and a stamp of the feet.*)

Struwwelpeter

Merry Stories and Funny Pictures

When the children have been good,
That is, be it understood,
Good at meal-times, good at play,
Good all night and good all day –
They shall have the pretty things
Merry Christmas always brings.
Naughty, romping girls and boys
Tear their clothes and make a noise,
Spoil their pinafores and frocks,
And deserve no Christmas-box.
Such as these shall never look
At this pretty picture-book.

Shock-Headed Peter

Just look at him! there he stands,
With his nasty hair and hands.
See! his nails are never cut;
They are grimed as black as soot;
And the sloven, I declare,
Never once has combed his hair;
Anything to me is sweeter
Than to see Shock-Headed Peter.

Cruel Frederick

Here is cruel Frederick, see!
A horrid wicked boy was he;
He caught the flies, poor little things,
And then tore off their tiny wings,
He killed the birds, and broke the chairs,
And threw the kitten down the stairs;
And oh! far worse than all beside,
He whipped his Mary, till she cried.

The trough was full, and faithful Tray
Came out to drink one sultry day;
He wagged his tail, and wet his lip,
When cruel Fred snatched up a whip,
And whipped poor Tray till he was sore,
And kicked and whipped him more and more;
At this, good Tray grew very red,
And growled, and bit him till he bled;
Then you should only have been by,
To see how Fred did scream and cry!

So Frederick had to go to bed:
His leg was very sore and red!
The doctor came, and shook his head,
And made a very great to-do,
And gave him nasty physic too.

But good dog Tray is happy now;
He has no time to say: 'Bow-wow!'
He seats himself in Frederick's chair
And laughs to see the nice things there:
The soup he swallows, sup by sup –
And eats the pies and puddings up.

Dreadful Story of Harriet and the Matches

It almost makes me cry to tell
What foolish Harriet befell.
Mama and Nurse went out one day
And left her all alone at play.
Now, on the table close at hand,
A box of matches chanced to stand;
And kind Mama and Nurse had told her
That if she touched them they would scold her.
But Harriet said: 'Oh, what a pity!
For, when they burn, it is so pretty;
They crackle so, and spit, and flame:
Mama, too, often does the same.'

The pussy-cats heard this,
And they began to hiss,
And stretch their claws,
And raise their paws;
'Me–ow,' they said, 'me–ow, me–o,
You'll burn to death, if you do so.'

But Harriet would not take advice:
She lit a match, it was so nice!
It crackled so, it burned so clear –
Exactly like the picture here.
She jumped for joy and ran about
And was too pleased to put it out.

The pussy-cats saw this
And said: 'Oh, naughty, naughty miss!'
And stretched their claws,
And raised their paws:
' 'Tis very, very wrong, you know,
Me–ow, me–o, me–ow, me–o,
You will be burnt, if you do so.'

And see! oh, what dreadful thing!
The fire has caught her apron-string;
Her apron burns, her arms, her hair –
She burns all over everywhere.

Then how the pussy-cats did mew –
What else, poor pussies, could they do?
They screamed for help, 'twas all in vain!
So then they said: 'We'll scream again;
Make haste, make haste, me-ow, me-o,
She'll burn to death; we told her so.'

So she was burnt, with all her clothes,
And arms, and hands, and eyes, and nose;
Till she had nothing more to lose
Except her little scarlet shoes;
And nothing else but these was found
Among her ashes on the ground.

And when the good cats sat beside
The smoking ashes, how they cried!
'Me–ow, me–oo, me–ow, me–oo,
What will Mama and Nursey do?'
Their tears ran down their cheeks so fast,
They made a little pond at last.

The Story of the Man that went out Shooting

This is the man that shoots the hares;
This is the coat he always wears:
With game-bag, powder-horn and gun,
He's going out to have some fun.

He finds it hard without a pair
Of spectacles to shoot the hare.
The hare sits snug in leaves and grass,
And laughs to see the green man pass.

Now, as the sun grew very hot,
And he a heavy gun had got,
He lay down underneath a tree
And went to sleep, as you may see.
And, while he slept like any top,
The little hare came, hop, hop, hop,
Took gun and spectacles and then
On her hind legs went off again.

The green man wakes and sees her place
The spectacles upon her face;
And now she's trying all she can
To shoot the sleepy, green-coat man.
He cries and screams and runs away;
The hare runs after him all day
And hears him call out everywhere:
'Help! Fire! Help! The Hare! The Hare!'

At last he stumbled at the well,
Head over ears, and in he fell.
The hare stopped short, took aim and, hark!
Bang went the gun – she missed her mark!

The poor man's wife was drinking up
Her coffee in her coffee-cup;
The gun shot cup and saucer through;
'Oh dear!' cried she; 'what shall I do?'
There lived close by the cottage there
The hare's own child, the little hare;
And while she stood upon her toes,
The coffee fell and burned her nose.
'Oh dear!' she cried, with spoon in hand,
'Such fun I do not understand.'

The Story of Little Suck-a-Thumb

One day Mama said 'Conrad dear,
I must go out and leave you here.
But mind now, Conrad, what I say,
Don't suck your thumb while I'm away.
The great tall tailor always comes
To little boys who suck their thumbs;
And ere they dream what he's about,
He takes his great sharp scissors out,
And cuts their thumbs clean off – and then,
You know, they never grow again.'

Mama had scarcely turned her back,
The thumb was in. Alack! Alack!

The door flew open, in he ran,
The great, long, red-legged scissor-man.
Oh! children, see! the tailor's come
And caught out little Suck-a-Thumb.
Snip! Snap! Snip! the scissors go,
And Conrad cries out: 'Oh! Oh! Oh!'
Snip! Snap! Snip! They go so fast,
That both his thumbs are off at last.

Mama comes home: there Conrad stands,
And looks quite sad, and shows his hands;
'Ah!' said Mama, 'I knew he'd come
To naughty little Suck-a-Thumb.'

The Story of Augustus who would not
have any Soup

Augustus was a chubby lad:
Fat ruddy cheeks Augustus had,
And everybody saw with joy
The plump and hearty, healthy boy.
He ate and drank as he was told,
And never let his soup get cold.
But one day, one cold winter's day,
He screamed out: 'Take the soup away!
Oh take the nasty soup away!
I won't have any soup today.'

Next day, now look, the picture shows
How lank and lean Augustus grows!
Yet, though he feels so weak and ill,
The naughty fellow cries out still:
'Not any soup for me, I say;
Oh take the nasty soup away!
I *won't* have any soup today.'

The third day comes: Oh what a sin!
To make himself so pale and thin.
Yet, when the soup is put on table,
He screams, as loud as he is able:
'Not any soup for me, I say;
Oh take the nasty soup away!
I WON'T have any soup today.'

Look at him, now the fourth day's come!
He scarcely weighs a sugarplum;
He's like a little bit of thread,
And, on the fifth day, he was – dead!

The Swineherd

There was once a poor prince. He possessed a kingdom which, though small, was yet large enough for him to marry on, and married he wished to be.

Now it was certainly a little audacious of him to venture to say to the emperor's daughter, 'Will you marry me?' But he did venture to say so, for his name was known far and wide. There were hundreds of princesses who would gladly have said 'Yes,' but would she say the same?

Well, we shall see.

On the grave of the prince's father grew a rose-tree, a very beautiful rose-tree. It only bloomed every five years, and then bore but a single rose, but oh, such a rose! Its scent was so sweet that when you smelt it you forgot all your cares and troubles. And he had also a nightingale which could sing as if all the beautiful melodies in the world were shut up in its little throat. This rose and this nightingale the princess was to have, and so they were both put into silver caskets and sent to her.

The emperor had them brought to him in the great hall, where the princess was playing 'Here comes a duke a-riding' with her ladies-in-waiting. And when she caught sight of the big caskets which contained the presents, she clapped her hands for joy.

'If only it were a little pussy cat!' she said. But the rose-tree with the beautiful rose came out.

'But how prettily it is made!' said all the ladies-in-waiting.

'It is more than pretty,' said the emperor, 'it is charming!'

But the princess felt it, and then she almost began to cry.

'Ugh! papa,' she said, 'it is not artificial, it is *real*!'

'Ugh!' said all the ladies-in-waiting, 'it is real!'

'Let us see first what is in the other casket before we begin to be angry,' thought the emperor, and there came out the nightingale.

It sang so beautifully that one could scarcely utter a cross word against it.

'*Superbe! charmante!*' said the ladies-in-waiting, for they all chattered French, each one worse than the other.

'How much the bird reminds me of the musical snuffbox of the late empress!' said an old courtier. 'Ah, yes, it is the same tone, the same execution!'

'Yes,' said the emperor; and then he wept like a little child.

'I hope that this, at least, is not real?' asked the princess.

'Yes, it is a real bird,' said those who had brought it.

'Then let the bird fly away,' said the princess; and she would not on any account allow the prince to come.

But he was nothing daunted. He painted his face brown and black, drew his cap well down, and knocked at the door. 'Good-day, emperor,' he said. 'Can I get a place here as a servant in the castle?'

'Yes,' said the emperor, 'but there are so many who ask for a place that I don't know whether there will be one for you; but, still, I will think of you. Stay, it has just occurred to me that I want someone to look after the swine, for I have so very many of them.'

And the prince got the situation of imperial swineherd. He had a wretched little room close to the pigsties; here he had to stay, but the whole day he sat working, and when evening was come he had made a pretty little pot. All round it were little bells, and when the pot boiled they jingled most beautifully and played the old tune:

'Where is Augustus dear?
Alas! he's not here, here, here!'

But the most wonderful thing was that when one held one's finger in the steam of the pot, then at once one could smell what dinner was ready in any fireplace in the town. That was indeed something quite different from the rose.

Now the princess came walking past with all her ladies-in-waiting, and when she heard the tune she stood still and her face beamed with joy, for she also could play 'Where is Augustus dear?'

It was the only tune she knew, and she could play it with one finger.

'Why, that is what I play!' she said. 'He must be a most accomplished swineherd! Listen! Go down and ask him what the instrument costs.'

And one of the ladies-in-waiting had to go down; but she put on wooden clogs. 'What will you take for the pot?' asked the lady-in-waiting.

'I will have ten kisses from the princess,' answered the swineherd.

'Heaven forbid!' said the lady-in-waiting.

'Yes, I will sell it for nothing less,' replied the swineherd.

'Well, what does he say?' asked the princess.

'I really hardly like to tell you,' answered the lady-in-waiting.

'Oh, then you can whisper it to me.'

'He is disobliging!' said the princess, and went

The swineherd got his ten kisses, and the princess got the pot

away. But she had only gone a few steps when the bells rang out so prettily:

> 'Where is Augustus dear?
> Alas! he's not here, here, here.'

'Listen!' said the princess. 'Ask him whether he will take ten kisses from my ladies-in-waiting.'

'No, thank you,' said the swineherd. 'Ten kisses from the princess, or else I keep my pot.'

'That is very tiresome!' said the princess. 'But you must put yourselves in front of me, so that no one can see.'

And the ladies-in-waiting placed themselves in front and then spread out their dresses; so the swineherd got his ten kisses, and she got the pot.

What happiness that was! The whole night and the whole day the pot was made to boil; there was not a fireplace in the whole town where they did not know what was being cooked, whether it was at the chancellor's or at the shoemaker's.

The ladies-in-waiting danced and clapped their hands.

'We know who is going to have soup and pancakes; we know who is going to have porridge and sausages – isn't it interesting?'

'Yes, very interesting!' said the first lady-in-waiting.

'But don't say anything about it, for I am the emperor's daughter.'

'Oh, no, of course we won't!' said everyone.

The swineherd – that is to say, the prince (though they did not know he was anything but a true swineherd) – let no day pass without making something, and one day he made a rattle which, when it was turned round, played all the waltzes, gallops and polkas which had ever been known since the world began.

'But that is *superbe*!' said the princess as she passed by. 'I have never heard a more beautiful composition. Listen! Go down and ask him what this instrument costs; but I won't kiss him again.'

'He wants a hundred kisses from the princess,' said the lady-in-waiting who had gone down to ask him.

'I believe he is mad!' said the princess, and then she went on; but she had only gone a few steps when she stopped. 'One ought to encourage art,' she said. 'I am the emperor's daughter! Tell him he shall have, as before, ten kisses; the rest he can take from my ladies-in-waiting.'

'But we won't at all like being kissed by him,' said the ladies-in-waiting.

'That's nonsense,' said the princess; 'and if I can kiss him, you can too. Besides, remember that I give you board and lodging.'

So the ladies-in-waiting had to go down to him again.

'A hundred kisses from the princess,' said he, 'or each keeps his own.'

'Put yourselves in front of us,' she said then; and so all the ladies-in-waiting put themselves in front, and he began to kiss the princess.

'What can that commotion be by the pigsties?' asked the emperor, who was standing on the balcony. He rubbed his eyes and put on his spectacles. 'Why those are the ladies-in-waiting playing their games; I must go down to them.'

So he took off his shoes, which were shoes though he had trodden them down into slippers. What a hurry he was in, to be sure!

As soon as he came into the yard he walked very softly, and the ladies-in-waiting were so busy counting the kisses and seeing fair play that they never noticed the emperor. He stood on tiptoe.

'What is that?' he said, when he saw the kissing; and then he threw one of his slippers at their heads just as the swineherd was taking his eighty-sixth kiss.

'Be off with you!' said the emperor, for he was very angry. And the princess and the swineherd were driven out of the empire.

Then she stood still and wept; the swineherd was scolding, and the rain was streaming down.

'Alas, what an unhappy creature I am!' sobbed the princess.

'If only I had taken the beautiful prince! Alas, how unfortunate I am!'

And the swineherd went behind a tree, washed the black and brown off his face, threw away his old clothes, and then stepped forward in his splendid dress, looking so beautiful that the princess was obliged to courtesy.

'I now come to this. I despise you!' he said. 'You would have nothing to do with a noble prince; you did not understand the rose or the nightingale, but you could kiss the swineherd for the sake of a toy. This is what you get for it!' And he went into his kingdom and shut the door in her face, and she had to stay outside singing:

> 'Where's my Augustus dear?
> Alas! he's not here, here, here.'

Tattercoats

In a great palace by the sea there once dwelt a very rich old lord, who had neither wife nor children living, only one little granddaughter, whose face he had never seen in all her life. He hated her bitterly, because at her birth his favourite daughter died; and when the old nurse brought him the baby he swore that it might live or die as it liked, but he would never look on its face as long as it lived.

So he turned his back, and sat by his window looking out over the sea, and weeping great tears for his lost daughter, till his white hair and beard grew down over his shoulders and twined round his chair and crept into the chinks of the floor, and his tears, dropping on to the window-ledge wore a channel through the stone, and ran away in a little river to the great sea. Meanwhile, his grand-daughter grew up with no one to care for her, or clothe her; only the old nurse, when no one was by, would sometimes give her a dish of scraps from the kitchen, or a torn petticoat from the rag-bag; while the other servants of the palace would drive her from the house with blows and mocking words, calling her 'Tattercoats', and pointing to her bare feet and shoulders, till she ran away, crying, to hide among the bushes.

So she grew up, with little to eat or to wear, spending her days out of doors, her only com-panion a crippled gooseherd, who fed his flock of geese on the common. And this gooseherd was a queer, merry little chap and, when she was hungry, or cold, or tired, he would play to her so gaily on his little pipe, that she forgot all her troubles, and would fall to dancing with his flock of noisy geese for partners.

Now one day people told each other that the king was travelling through the land, and was to give a great ball to all the lords and ladies of the country in the town near by, and that the prince, his only son, was to choose a wife from among the maidens in the company. In due time one of the royal invitations to the ball was brought to the palace by the sea, and the servants carried it up to the old lord, who still sat by his window, wrapped in his long white hair and weeping into the little river that was fed by his tears.

But when he heard the king's command, he dried his eyes and bade them bring shears to cut him loose, for his hair had bound him a fast prisoner, and he could not move. And then he sent them for rich clothes, and jewels, which he put on; and he ordered them to saddle the white horse, with gold and silk, that he might ride to meet the king; but he quite forgot he had a granddaughter to take to the ball.

Meanwhile Tattercoats sat by the kitchen-door weeping, because she could not go to see the grand doings. And when the old nurse heard her crying she went to the lord of the palace, and begged him to take his granddaughter with him to the king's ball.

But he only frowned and told her to be silent; while the servants laughed and said, 'Tattercoats is happy in her rags, playing with the gooseherd! Let her be – it is all she is fit for.'

A second, and then a third time, the old nurse begged him to let the girl go with him; but she was answered only by black looks and fierce words, till she was driven from the room by the leering servants, with blows and mocking words.

Weeping over her ill-success, the old nurse went to look for Tattercoats; but the girl had been turned from the door by the cook, and had run away to tell her friend the gooseherd how unhappy she was because she could not go to the king's ball.

Now when the gooseherd had listened to her story, he bade her cheer up, and proposed that they should go together into the town to see the king, and all the fine things; and when she looked sorrowfully down at her rags and bare feet he played a note or two upon his pipe, so gay and merry, that she forgot all about her tears and her troubles, and before she well knew, the gooseherd had taken her by the hand, and she, and he, and the geese before them, were dancing down the road towards the town.

'Even cripples can dance when they choose,' said the gooseherd.

Before they had gone very far a handsome young man, splendidly dressed, riding up, stopped to ask the way to the castle where the king was staying, and when he found that they too were going thither, he got off his horse and walked beside them along the road.

'You seem merry folk,' he said, 'and will be good company.'

'Good company, indeed,' said the gooseherd, and played a new tune that was not a dance.

It was a curious tune, and it made the strange young man stare and stare and stare at Tattercoats till he couldn't see her rags. Till he couldn't, to tell the truth, see anything but her beautiful face.

Then he said, 'You are the most beautiful maiden in the world. Will you marry me?'

Then the gooseherd smiled to himself, and played sweeter than ever.

But Tattercoats laughed. 'Not I,' said she, 'you would be finely put to shame, and so would I be, if you took a goose-girl for your wife! Go and ask one of the great ladies you will see tonight at the king's ball and do not flout poor Tattercoats.'

But the more she refused him the sweeter the pipe played, and the deeper the young man fell in love; till at last he begged her to come that night at twelve to the king's ball, just as she was, with the gooseherd and his geese, in her torn petticoat and bare feet, and see if he wouldn't dance with her before the king, and the lords and ladies, and present her to them all, as his dear and honoured bride.

Now at first Tattercoats said she would not; but the gooseherd said, 'Take fortune when it comes, little one.'

So when night came, and the hall in the castle was full of light and music, and the lords and ladies were dancing before the king, just as the clock struck twelve, Tattercoats and the gooseherd, followed by his flock of noisy geese, hissing and swaying their heads, entered at the great doors, and walked straight up the ballroom, while on either side the ladies whispered, the lords laughed, and the king seated at the far end stared in amazement.

But as they came in front of the throne, 'Tattercoats' lover rose from beside the king, and came to meet her. Taking her by the hand, he kissed her thrice before them all, and turned to the king.

'Father!' he said – for it was the prince himself – 'I have made my choice, and here is my bride, the loveliest girl in all the land, and the sweetest as well!'

Before he had finished speaking the gooseherd had put his pipe to his lips and played a few notes that sounded like a bird singing far off in the woods; and as he played Tattercoats' rags were changed to shining robes sewn with glittering jewels, a golden crown lay upon her golden hair, and the flock of geese behind her became a crowd of dainty pages, bearing her long train.

And as the king rose to greet her as his daughter the trumpets sounded loudly in honour of the new princess, and the people outside in the street said to each other: 'Ah! now the prince has chosen for his wife the loveliest girl in all the land!'

But the gooseherd was never seen again, and no one knew what became of him; while the old lord went home once more to his palace by the sea, for he could not stay at court when he had sworn never to look on his granddaughter's face.

So there he still sits by his window – if you could only see him, as you may someday – weeping more bitterly than ever. And his white hair has bound him to the stones, and the river of his tears runs away to the great sea.

'Father!' he said – for it was the prince himself – 'I have made my choice, and here is my bride.'

Teeny-Tiny

Once upon a time there was a teeny-tiny woman lived in a teeny-tiny house in a teeny-tiny village. Now, one day this teeny-tiny woman put on her teeny-tiny bonnet, and went out of her teeny-tiny house to take a teeny-tiny walk. And when this teeny-tiny woman had gone a teeny-tiny way she came to a teeny-tiny gate; so the teeny-tiny woman opened the teeny-tiny gate, and went into a teeny-tiny churchyard. And when this teeny-tiny woman had got into the teeny-tiny churchyard, she saw a teeny-tiny bone on a teeny-tiny grave, and the teeny-tiny woman said to her teeny-tiny self, 'This teeny-tiny bone will make me some teeny-tiny soup for my teeny-tiny supper.' So the teeny-tiny woman put the teeny-tiny bone into her teeny-tiny pocket, and went home to her teeny-tiny house.

Now when the teeny-tiny woman got home to her teeny-tiny house she was a teeny-tiny bit tired; so she went up her teeny-tiny stairs to her teeny-tiny bed, and put the teeny-tiny bone into a teeny-tiny cupboard. And when this teeny-tiny woman had been to sleep a teeny-tiny time, she was awakened by a teeny-tiny voice from the teeny-tiny cupboard, which said: 'Give me my bone!'

And this teeny-tiny woman was a teeny-tiny bit frightened, so she hid her teeny-tiny head under the teeny-tiny clothes and went to sleep again. And when she had been to sleep again a teeny-tiny time, the teeny-tiny voice again cried out from the teeny-tiny cupboard a teeny-tiny bit louder, 'Give me my bone!'

This made the teeny-tiny woman a teeny-tiny bit more frightened, so she hid her teeny-tiny head a teeny-tiny bit farther under the teeny-tiny clothes. And when the teeny-tiny woman had been to sleep again a teeny-tiny time, the teeny-tiny voice from the teeny-tiny cupboard said again a teeny-tiny bit louder, 'Give me my bone!'

And this teeny-tiny woman was a teeny-tiny bit more frightened, but she put her teeny-tiny head out of the teeny-tiny clothes, and said in her loudest teeny-tiny voice, 'Take it!'

The Three Billy Goats Gruff

Once upon a time there were three billy goats, who were to go up to the hillside to make themselves fat, and the name of all three was 'Gruff'.

On the way up was a bridge over a cascading stream they had to cross; and under the bridge lived a great ugly troll, with eyes as big as saucers, and a nose as long as a poker.

So first of all came the youngest Billy Goat Gruff to cross the bridge.

Trip, trap, trip, trap, went the bridge.

'Who's that tripping over my bridge?' roared the troll.

'Oh, it is only I, the tiniest Billy Goat Gruff, and I'm going up to the hillside to make myself fat,' said the billy goat, with such a small voice.

'I'm coming to gobble you up,' said the troll.

'Oh, no! pray don't take me. I'm too little, that I am,' said the billy goat. 'Wait a bit till the second Billy Goat Gruff comes. He's much bigger.'

'Well, be off with you,' said the troll.

A little while after came the second Billy Goat Gruff to cross the bridge.

Trip, trap, trip, trap, trip, trap, went the bridge.

'Who's that tripping over my bridge?' roared the troll.

'Oh, it's the second Billy Goat Gruff, and I'm going up to the hillside to make myself fat,' said the billy goat, who hadn't such a small voice.

'I'm coming to gobble you up,' said the troll.

'Oh, no! Don't take me. Wait a little till the big Billy Goat Gruff comes. He's much bigger.'

'Very well! Be off with you,' said the troll.

But just then up came the big Billy Goat Gruff.

Trip, trap, trip, trap, trip, trap! went the bridge, for the billy goat was so heavy that the bridge creaked and groaned under him.

'Who's that tramping over my bridge?' roared the troll.

'It's I! The big Billy Goat Gruff,' said the billy goat, who had an ugly hoarse voice of his own.

'I'm coming to gobble you up,' roared the troll.

'Well, come along! I've got two spears,
And I'll poke your eyeballs out at your ears;
I've got besides two curling-stones,
And I'll crush you to bits, body and bones.'

That was what the big billy goat said. And then he flew at the troll, and poked his eyes out with his horns, and crushed him to bits, body and bones, and tossed him out into the cascade, and after that he went up to the hillside. There the billy goats got so fat they were scarcely able to walk home again. And if the fat hasn't fallen off them, why, they're still fat; and so,

Snip, snap, snout.
This tale's told out.

606

Three Feathers

Once upon a time there was a girl who was married to a husband whom she never saw. And the way this was, was that he was only at home at night, and would never have any light in the house. The girl thought this was funny, and all her friends told her there must be something wrong with her husband, some great deformity that made him want not to be seen.

Well, one night when he came home she suddenly lit a candle and saw him. He was handsome enough to make all the women of the world fall in love with him. But scarcely had she seen him when he began to change into a bird, and then he said: 'Now you have seen me, you shall see me no more, unless you are willing to serve seven years and a day for me, so that I may become a man once more.' Then he told her to take three feathers from under his side, and whatever she wished through them would come to pass. Then he left her at a great house to be laundry-maid for seven years and a day.

And the girl used to take the feathers and say: 'By virtue of my three feathers may the copper be lit, and the clothes washed, and mangled, and folded, and put away to the missus's satisfaction.'

And then she had no more care about it. The feathers did the rest, and the lady set great store by her, for a better laundress she had never had. Well, one day the butler, who had a notion to have the pretty laundry-maid for his wife, said to her that he should have spoken before but he did not want to vex her. 'Why should it when I am but a fellow-servant?' the girl said. And then he felt free to go on, and explain he had seventy pounds laid by with the master, and how would she like him for a husband?

And the girl told him to fetch her the money, and he asked his master for it, and brought it to her. But as they were going upstairs, she cried, 'Oh John, I must go back, sure I've left my shutters undone, and they'll be slashing and banging all night.'

The butler said, 'Never you trouble, I'll put them right,' and he ran back, while she took her feathers, and said: 'By virtue of my three feathers may the shutters slash and bang till morning, and John not be able to fasten them nor yet to get his fingers free from them.'

And so it was. Try as he might the butler could not leave hold, nor yet keep the shutters from blowing open as he closed them. And he was angry, but could not help himself, and he did not care to tell of it and get the laugh on him, so no one knew.

Then after a bit the coachman began to notice her, and she found he had some forty pounds with the master, and he said she might have it if she would take him with it.

So, after the laundry-maid had his money in her apron, as they went merrily along, she stopped, exclaiming: 'My clothes are left outside, I must run back and bring them in.'

'Stop for me while I go; it is a cold frosty night,' said William, 'you'd be catching your death.'

So the girl waited long enough to take her feathers out and say, 'By virtue of my three feathers may the clothes slash and blow about till morning,

and may William not be able to take his hand from them nor yet to gather them up.' And then she was away to bed and to sleep. The coachman did not want to be everyone's jest, and he said nothing.

So after a bit, the footman comes to her and said he: 'I have been with my master for years and have saved up a good bit, and you have been three years here, and must have saved up as well. Let us put it together, and make us a home or else stay on at service as pleases you.' Well, she got him to bring the savings to her as the others had, and then she pretended she was faint, and said to him: 'James, I feel so queer, run down to the cellar for me, that's a dear, and fetch me up a drop of brandy.' Now no sooner had he started than she said: 'By virtue of my three feathers may there be slashing and spilling, and James not be able to pour the brandy straight nor yet to take his hand from it until morning.'

And so it was. Try as he might James could not get his glass filled, and there was slashing and spilling, and right on it all, down came the master to know what it meant! So James told him he could not make it out, but he could not get the drop of brandy the laundry-maid had asked for, and his hand would shake and spill everything, and yet come away he could not.

This got him in for a regular scrape, and the master when he got back to his wife said: 'What has come over the men, they were all right until that laundry-maid of yours came. Something is up now, though. They have all drawn out their pay, and yet they don't leave, and what can it be anyway?'

But his wife said she could not hear of the laundry-maid being blamed, for she was the best servant she had and worth all the rest put together.

So it went on until one day as the girl stood in the hall door, the coachman happened to say to the footman: 'Do you know how that girl served me, James?' And then William told about the clothes. The butler put in, 'That was nothing to how she served me,' and he told of the shutters clapping all night.

Just then the master came through the hall, and the girl said: 'By virtue of my three feathers may there be slashing and striving between master and men, and may all get splashed in the pond.'

And so it was: the men fell to disputing which had suffered the most by her, and when the master came up all would be heard at once and none listened to him, and it came to blows all round, and the first they knew they had shoved one another into the pond.

When the girl thought they had had enough she took the spell off, and the master asked her what had begun the row, for he had not heard in the confusion.

And the girl said: 'They were ready to fall on anyone; they'd have beat me if you had not come by.'

So it blew over for that time, and through her feathers she made the best laundress ever known. But to make a long story short, when the seven years and a day were up, the bird-husband, who had known her doings all along, came after her, restored to his own shape again. And he told her mistress he had come to take her from being a servant, and that she should have servants under her. But he did not tell of the feathers.

And then he bade her give the men back their savings. 'That was a rare game you had with them,' said he, 'but now you are going where there is plenty, leave them each their own.' So she did; and they drove off to their castle, where they lived happy ever after.

The Three Heads in the Well

Long before Arthur and the Knights of the Round Table, there reigned in the eastern part of England a king who kept his court at Colchester. In the midst of all his glory, his queen died, leaving behind her an only daughter, about fifteen years of age, who for her beauty and kindness was the wonder of all that knew her. But the king, hearing of a lady who had likewise an only daughter, had a mind to marry her for the sake of her riches, though she was old, ugly, hook-nosed and hump-backed. Her daughter was a yellow dowdy, full of envy and ill nature; and, in short, was much of the same mould as her mother. But in a few weeks the king, attended by the nobility and gentry, brought his deformed bride to the palace, where the marriage rites were performed.

They had not been long in the court before they set the king against his own beautiful daughter by false reports. The young princess having lost her father's love, grew weary of the court, and one day, meeting with her father in the garden, she begged him, with tears in her eyes, to let her go and seek her fortune; to which the king consented, and ordered her stepmother to give her what she pleased. She went to the queen, who gave her a canvas bag of brown bread and hard cheese, with a bottle of beer; though this was but a pitiful dowry for a king's daughter. She took it, with thanks, and proceeded on her journey, passing through groves, woods and valleys, till at length she saw an old man sitting on a stone at the mouth of a cave, who said: 'Good-morrow, fair maiden, whither away so fast?'

'Aged father,' says she, 'I am going to seek my fortune.'

'What have you got in your bag and bottle?'

'In my bag I have got bread and cheese, and in my bottle good small beer. Would you like to have some?'

'Yes,' said he, 'with all my heart.'

With that the lady pulled out her provisions, and bade him eat and welcome. He did so, and gave her many thanks, and said: 'There is a thick thorny hedge before you, which you cannot get through, but take this wand in your hand, strike it three times, and say, "Pray, hedge, let me come through," and it will open immediately; then, a little farther, you will find a well; sit down on the brink of it, and there will come up three golden heads, which will speak; and whatever they require, that do.'

Promising she would, she took her leave of him. Coming to the hedge and using the old man's wand, she found it divided and let her through; then, coming to the well, she had no sooner sat down than a golden head came up singing:

'Wash me, and comb me,
And lay me down softly,
And lay me on a bank to dry,
That I may look pretty,
When somebody passes by.'

'Yes,' said she, and taking it in her lap combed it with a silver comb and then placed it upon a prim-rose bank. Then up came a second and a third head, saying the same as the first. So she did the same for them, and then, pulling out her pro-visions, sat down to eat her dinner.

Then said the heads one to another: 'What shall we weird for this damsel who has used us so kindly?'

The first said: 'I weird her to be so beautiful that she shall charm the most powerful prince in the world.'

The second said: 'I weird her such a sweet voice as shall far exceed the nightingale.'

The third said: 'My gift shall be not inconsider-able, as she is a king's daughter; I'll weird her so fortunate that she shall become queen to the greatest prince that reigns.'

She then let them down into the well again, and so went on her journey. She had not travelled long before she saw a king hunting in the park with his nobles. She would have avoided him, but the king,

having caught a sight of her, approached, and, what with her beauty and sweet voice, fell desperately in love with her and soon induced her to marry him.

This king, finding that she was the King of Colchester's daughter, ordered some chariots to be got ready, that he might pay the king, his father-in-law, a visit. The chariot in which the king and queen rode was adorned with rich gems of gold. The king, her father, was at first astonished that his daughter had been so fortunate, till the young king let him know of all that had happened. Great was the joy at court amongst all, with the exception of the queen and her club-footed daughter, who were ready to burst with envy. The rejoicings, with feasting and dancing, continued many days. Then at length they returned home with the dowry her father gave her.

The hump-backed princess, perceiving that her sister had been so lucky in seeking her fortune, wanted to do the same; so she told her mother, and all preparations were made, and she was furnished with rich dresses, and with sugar, almonds and sweetmeats, in great quantities, and a large bottle of Malaga sack. With these she went the same road as her sister; and when she came near the cave, the old man said: 'Young woman, whither so fast?'

'What's that to you?' said she.

'Then,' said he, 'what have you in your bag and bottle?'

She answered: 'Good things, which you shall not be troubled with.'

'Won't you give me some?' said he.

'No, not a bit, nor a drop, unless it would choke you.'

The old man frowned, saying: 'Evil fortune attend ye!'

Going on, she came to the hedge, through which she espied a gap, and thought to pass through it; but the hedge closed, and the thorns ran into her flesh, so that it was with great difficulty that she got through. Being now all over blood, she searched for water to wash herself, and, looking round, she saw the well. She sat down on the brink of it, and one of the heads came up, saying: 'Wash me, comb me, and lay me down softly,' as before, but she banged it with her bottle, saying, 'Take that for your washing.' So the second and third heads came up, and met with no better treatment than the first. Whereupon the heads consulted among themselves what evils to plague her with for such usage.

The first said: 'Let her be struck with leprosy in her face.'

The second: 'Let her voice be as harsh as a corncrake's.'

The third said: 'Let her have for husband but a poor country cobbler.'

Well, she went on till she came to a town, and it being market-day, the people looked at her, and, seeing such a mangy face and hearing such a squeaky voice, all fled but a poor country cobbler. Now he not long before had mended the shoes of an old hermit, who, having no money, gave him a box of ointment for the cure of the leprosy and a bottle of spirits for a harsh voice. So the cobbler, having a mind to do an act of charity, was induced to go up to her and ask her who she was.

'I am,' said she, 'the King of Colchester's stepdaughter.'

'Well,' said the cobbler, 'if I restore you to your natural complexion, and make a sound cure both in face and voice, will you in reward take me for a husband?'

'Yes, friend,' replied she, 'with all my heart!'

With this the cobbler applied the remedies, and they made her well in a few weeks; after which they were married, and so set forward for the court at Colchester. When the queen found that her daughter had married nothing but a poor cobbler, she hanged herself in wrath. The death of the queen so pleased the king, who was glad to get rid of her so soon, that he gave the cobbler a hundred pounds to quit the court with his lady, and take her to a remote part of the kingdom, where he lived many years mending shoes, his wife spinning the thread for him.

The Three Little Pigs

There was once upon a time a pig who lived with her three children on a large, comfortable, old-fashioned farmyard. The eldest of the little pigs was called Browny, the second Whitey, and the youngest and best looking Blacky. Now Browny was a very dirty little pig, and I am sorry to say spent most of his time rolling and wallowing about in the mud. He was never so happy as on a wet day, when the mud in the farmyard got soft, and thick, and slab. Then he would steal away from his mother's side, and finding the muddiest place in the yard, would roll about in it and thoroughly enjoy himself. His mother often found fault with him for this, and would shake her head sadly and say: 'Ah, Browny! some day you will be sorry that you did not obey your old mother.' But no words of advice or warning could cure Browny of his bad habits.

Whitey was quite a clever little pig, but she was greedy. She was always thinking of her food, and looking forward to her dinner; and when the farm girl was seen carrying the pails across the yard, she would rise up on her hind legs and dance and caper with excitement. As soon as the food was poured into the trough she jostled Blacky and Browny out of the way in her eagerness to get the best and biggest bits for herself. Her mother often scolded her for her selfishness, and told her that someday she would suffer for being so greedy and grabbing.

Blacky was a good, nice little pig, neither dirty nor greedy. He had nice dainty ways (for a pig), and his skin was always as smooth and shining as black satin. He was much cleverer than Browny and Whitey, and his mother's heart used to swell with pride when she heard the farmer's friends say to each other that someday the little black fellow would be a prize pig.

Now the time came when the mother pig felt old and feeble and near her end. One day she called the three little pigs round her and said: 'My children, I feel that I am growing odd and weak, and that I shall not live long. Before I die I should like to build a house for each of you, as this dear old sty in which we have lived so happily will be given to a new family of pigs, and you will have to turn out. Now, Browny, what sort of a house would you like to have?'

'A house of mud,' replied Browny, looking with longing at a wet puddle in the corner of the yard.

'And you, Whitey?' said the mother pig in rather a sad voice, for she was disappointed that Browny had made so foolish a choice.

'A house of cabbage,' answered Whitey, with a mouth full, and scarcely raising her snout out of the trough in which she was grubbing for some potato-parings.

'Foolish, foolish child!' said the mother pig, looking quite distressed.

'And you, Blacky?' turning to her youngest son, 'what sort of a house shall I order for you?'

'A house of brick, please mother, as it will be warm in winter, and cool in summer, and safe all the year round.'

'That is a sensible little pig,' replied his mother, looking fondly at him. 'I will see that the three houses are got ready at once. And now one last piece of advice. You have heard me talk of our old enemy the fox. When he hears that I am dead, he is sure to try and get hold of you, to carry you off to his den. He is very sly and will no doubt disguise himself, and pretend to be a friend, but you must promise me not to let him enter your houses on any pretext whatever.'

And the little pigs readily promised, for they had always had a great fear of the fox, of whom they had heard many terrible tales. A short time afterwards the old pig died, and the little pigs went to live in their own houses.

Browny was quite delighted with his soft mud walls and with the clay floor, which soon looked like nothing but a big mud pie. But that was what Browny enjoyed, and he was as happy as possible, rolling about all day and getting himself in such a mess. One day, as he was lying half asleep in the mud, he heard a soft knock at his door, and a gentle voice said: 'May I come in, Master Browny? I want to see your beautiful new house.'

'Who are you?' said Browny, starting up in great fright, for though the voice sounded gentle, he felt sure it was a feigned voice, and he feared it was the fox.

'I am a friend come to call on you,' answered the voice.

'No, no,' replied Browny, 'I don't believe you are a friend. You are the wicked fox, against whom our mother warned us. I won't let you in.'

'Oho! is that the way you answer me?' said the fox, speaking very roughly in his natural voice. 'We shall soon see who is master here,' and with his paws he set to work and scraped a large hole in the soft mud walls. A moment later he had jumped through it, and catching Browny by the neck, flung him on his shoulders and trotted off with him to his den.

The next day, as Whitey was munching a few leaves of cabbage out of the corner of her house, the fox stole up to her door, determined to carry her off to join her brother in his den. He began speaking to her in the same feigned gentle voice in which he had spoken to Browny; but it frightened her very much when he said: 'I am a friend come to visit you, and to have some of your good cabbage for my dinner.'

'Please don't touch it,' cried Whitey in great distress. 'The cabbages are the walls of my house, and if you eat them you will make a hole, and the wind and rain will come in and give me a cold. Do go away; I am sure you are not a friend, but our wicked enemy the fox.' And poor Whitey began to whine and to whimper, and to wish that she had not been such a greedy little pig, and had chosen a more solid material than cabbages for her house. But it was too late now, and in another minute the fox had eaten his way through the cabbage walls, and had caught the trembling, shivering Whitey, and carried her off to his den.

The next day the fox started off for Blacky's house, because he had made up his mind that he would get the three little pigs together in his den, and then kill them, and invite all his friends to a feast. But when he reached the brick house, he found that the door was bolted and barred, so in his sly manner he began, 'Do let me in, dear Blacky. I have brought you a present of some eggs that I picked up in a farmyard on my way here.'

'No, no, Mr Fox,' replied Blacky, 'I am not going to open my door to you. I know your cunning ways. You have carried off poor Browny and Whitey, but you are not going to get me.'

At this the fox was so angry that he dashed with all his force against the wall, and tried to knock it down. But it was too strong and well-built; and though the fox scraped and tore at the bricks with his paws he only hurt himself, and at last he had to give it up, and limp away with his forepaws all bleeding and sore.

'Never mind!' he cried angrily as he went off, 'I'll catch you another day, see if I don't, and won't I grind your bones to powder when I have got you in my den!' and he snarled fiercely and showed his teeth.

Next day Blacky had to go into the neighbouring town to do some marketing and to buy a big kettle. As he was walking home with it slung over his shoulder, he heard a sound of steps stealthily creeping after him. For a moment his heart stood still with fear, and then a happy thought came to him. He had just reached the top of a hill, and could see his own little house nestling at the foot of it among the trees. In a moment he had snatched the lid off the kettle and had jumped in himself. Coiling himself round he lay quite snug in the bottom of the kettle, while with his foreleg he managed to put the lid on, so that he was entirely hidden. With a little kick from the inside he started the kettle off, and down the hill it rolled full tilt; and when

the fox came up, all that he saw was a large black kettle spinning over the ground at a great pace. Very much disappointed, he was just going to turn away, when he saw the kettle stop close to the little brick house, and a moment later Blacky jumped out of it and escaped with the kettle into the house; then he barred and bolted the door, and put the shutter up over the window.

'Oho!' exclaimed the fox to himself, 'you think you will escape me that way, do you? We shall soon see about that, my friend,' and very quietly and stealthily he prowled round the house looking for some way to climb on to the roof.

In the meantime Blacky had filled the kettle with water, and having put it on the fire, sat down quietly waiting for it to boil. Just as the kettle was beginning to sing, and steam to come out of the spout, he heard a sound like a soft, muffled step going patter, patter, patter overhead, and the next moment the fox's head and forepaws were seen coming down the chimney. But Blacky very wisely had not put the lid on the kettle, and, with a yelp of pain, the fox fell into the boiling water; before he could escape, Blacky popped the lid on, and the fox was scalded to death.

As soon as he was sure that their wicked enemy was really dead, and could do them no further harm, Blacky started off to rescue Browny and Whitey. As he approached the den he heard piteous grunts and squeals from his poor little brother and sister, who lived in constant terror of the fox killing and eating them. But when they saw Blacky appear at the entrance to the den their joy knew no bounds. He quickly found a sharp stone and cut the cords by which they were tied to a stake in the ground, and then all three started off together for Blacky's house, where they lived happily ever after; and Browny quite gave up rolling in the mud, and Whitey ceased to be greedy, for they never forgot how nearly these faults had brought them to an untimely end.

The Three Sillies

Once upon a time there was a farmer and his wife who had one daughter, and she was courted by a gentleman. Every evening he used to come and see her, and stop to supper at the farmhouse, and the daughter used to be sent down into the cellar to draw the beer for supper. So one evening she had gone down to draw the beer, and she happened to look up at the ceiling while she was drawing, and she saw a mallet stuck in one of the beams. It must have been there a long, long time, but somehow or other she had never noticed it before, and she began a-thinking. And she thought it was very dangerous to have that mallet there, for she said to herself: 'Suppose him and me was to be married, and we was to have a son, and he was to grow up to be a man, and come down into the cellar to draw the beer, like as I'm doing now, and the mallet was to fall on his head and kill him, what a dreadful thing it would be!' And she put down the candle and the jug, and sat herself down and began a-crying.

Well, they began to wonder upstairs how it was that she was so long drawing the beer, and her mother went down to see after her, and she found her sitting on the settle crying, and the beer running over the floor. 'Why, whatever is the matter?' said her mother. 'Oh, mother!' says she, 'look at that horrid mallet! Suppose we was to be married, and was to have a son, and he was to grow up, and was to come down to the cellar to draw the beer, and the mallet was to fall on his head and kill him, what a dreadful thing it would be!'

'Dear, dear! what a dreadful thing it would be!' said the mother, and she sat her down aside of the daughter and started a-crying too.

Then after a bit the father began to wonder that they didn't come back, and he went down into the cellar to look after them himself, and there they two sat a-crying, and the beer running all over the floor. 'Whatever is the matter?' says he. 'Why,' says the mother, 'look at that horrid mallet. Just suppose, if

our daughter and her sweetheart was to be married, and was to have a son, and he was to grow up, and was to come down into the cellar to draw the beer, and the mallet was to fall on his head and kill him, what a dreadful thing it would be!'

'Dear, dear, dear! so it would!' said the father, and he sat himself down aside of the other two, and started a-crying.

Now the gentleman got tired of stopping up in the kitchen by himself, and at last he went down into the cellar too, to see what they were after; and there they three sat a-crying side by side, and the beer running all over the floor. And he ran straight and turned off the tap. Then he said: 'Whatever are you three doing, sitting there crying, and letting the beer run all over the floor?'

'Oh!' says the father, 'look at that horrid mallet! Suppose you and our daughter was to be married, and was to have a son, and he was to grow up, and was to come down into the cellar to draw the beer, and the mallet was to fall on his head and kill him!' And then they all started a-crying worse than before.

But the gentleman burst out a-laughing, and reached up and pulled out the mallet, and then he said: 'I've travelled many miles, but I never met three such big sillies as you three before; and now I shall start out on my travels again, and when I can find three bigger sillies than you three, then I'll come back and marry your daughter.' So he wished them goodbye, and started off on his travels, and left them all crying because the girl had lost her sweetheart.

Well, he set out, and he travelled a long way, and at last he came to a woman's cottage that had some grass growing on the roof. And the woman was trying to get her cow to go up a ladder to the grass, and the poor thing durst not go. So the gentleman asked the woman what she was doing. 'Why, look-ye,' she said, 'look at all that beautiful grass. I'm going to get the cow on to the roof to eat it. She'll be quite safe, for I shall tie a string round her neck, and pass it down the chimney, and tie it to my wrist as I go about the house, so she can't fall off without my knowing it.'

'Oh, you poor silly!' said the gentleman, 'you should cut the grass and throw it down to the cow!' But the woman thought it was easier to get the cow up the ladder than to get the grass down, so she pushed her and coaxed her and got her up, and tied a string round her neck, and passed it down the chimney, and fastened it to her own wrist. And the gentleman went on his way, but he hadn't gone far when the cow tumbled off the roof, and hung by the string tied round her neck, and it strangled her. And the weight of the cow tied to her wrist pulled the woman up the chimney, and she stuck fast halfway and was smothered in the soot.

Well, that was one big silly.

And the gentleman went on and on, and he went to an inn to stop the night, and they were so full at the inn that they had to put him in a double-bedded room, and another traveller was to sleep in the other bed. The other man was a very pleasant fellow, and they got very friendly together; but in the morning, when they were both getting up, the gentleman was surprised to see the other hang his trousers on the knobs of the chest of drawers and run across the room and try to jump into them, and he tried over and over again, and couldn't manage it; and the gentleman wondered whatever he was

doing it for. At last he stopped and wiped his face with his handkerchief. 'Oh dear,' he says, 'I do think trousers are the most awkwardest kind of clothes that ever were. I can't think who could have invented such things. It takes me the best part of an hour to get into mine every morning, and I get so hot! How do you manage yours?' So the gentleman burst out a-laughing, and showed him how to put them on; and he was very much obliged to him, and said he never should have thought of doing it that way.

So that was another big silly.

Then the gentleman went on his travels again; and he came to a village, and outside the village there was a pond, and round the pond was a crowd of people. And they had got rakes, and brooms, and pitchforks, reaching into the pond; and the gentleman asked what was the matter. 'Why,' they say, 'matter enough! Moon's tumbled into the pond, and we can't rake her out anyhow!' So the gentleman burst out a-laughing, and told them to look up into the sky, and that it was only the reflection in the water. But they wouldn't listen to him, and abused him shamefully, and he got away as quick as he could.

So there was a whole lot of sillies bigger than them three sillies at home. So the gentleman turned back home again and married the farmer's daughter, and if they didn't live happy for ever after, that's nothing to do with you or me.

Thumbelina

There was once a woman who wanted to have quite a tiny little child, but she did not know where to get one from. So one day she went to an old witch and said to her: 'I should so much like to have a tiny little child; can you tell me where I can get one?'

'Oh, we have just got one ready!' said the witch. 'Here is a barleycorn for you, but it's not the kind the farmer sows in his field or feeds the cocks and hens with, I can tell you. Put it in a flowerpot, and then you will see something happen.'

'Oh, thank you!' said the woman, and gave the witch a shilling, for that was what it cost. Then she went home and planted the barleycorn; immediately there grew out of it a large and beautiful flower, which looked like a tulip, but the petals were tightly closed as if it were still only a bud.

'What a beautiful flower!' exclaimed the woman, and she kissed the red and yellow petals; but as she kissed them the flower burst open. It was a real tulip, such as one can see any day; but in the middle of the blossom, on the green velvety petals, sat a little girl, quite tiny, trim and pretty. She was scarcely half a thumb in height; so they called her Thumbelina. An elegant polished walnut shell served Thumbelina as a cradle, the blue petals of a violet were her mattress and a rose leaf her coverlet. There she lay at night, but in the daytime she used to play about on the table; here the woman had put a bowl, surrounded by a ring of flowers, with their stalks in water, in the middle of which floated a great tulip pedal, and on this Thumbelina sat, and sailed from one side of the bowl to the other, rowing herself with two white horse hairs for oars. It was such a pretty sight! She could sing, too, with a voice more soft and sweet than had ever been heard before.

One night, when she was lying in her pretty little bed, an old toad crept in through a broken pane in the window. She was very ugly, clumsy and clammy; she hopped on to the table where Thumbelina lay asleep under the red rose leaf.

'This would make a beautiful wife for my son,' said the toad, taking up the walnut shell, with Thumbelina inside, and hopping with it through the window into the garden.

There flowed a great wide stream, with slippery and marshy banks; here the toad lived with her son. Ugh! how ugly and clammy he was, just like his mother! 'Croak, croak, croak!' was all he could say when he saw the pretty little girl in the walnut shell.

'Croak, croak, croak!' was all he could say when he saw the pretty little girl in the walnut shell

'Don't talk so loud, or you'll wake her,' said the old toad. 'She might escape us even now; she is as light as a feather. We will put her at once on a broad water-lily leaf in the stream. That will be quite an island for her, she is so small and light. She can't run away from us there, while we are preparing the guest chamber under the marsh where she shall live.'

Outside in the brook grew many water lilies, with broad green leaves, which looked as if they were swimming about on the water.

The leaf farthest away was the largest, and to this

the old toad swam with Thumbelina in her walnut shell.

The tiny Thumbelina woke up very early in the morning, and when she saw where she was she began to cry bitterly; for on every side of the great green leaf was water, and she could not get to the land.

The old toad was down under the marsh, decorating her room with rushes and yellow marigold leaves, to make it very grand for her new daughter-in-law; then she swam out with her ugly son to the leaf where Thumbelina lay. She wanted to fetch the pretty cradle to put it into her room before Thumbelina herself came there. The old toad bowed low in the water before her, and said: 'Here is my son; you shall marry him, and live in great magnificence down under the marsh.'

'Croak, croak, croak!' was all that the son could say. Then they took the neat little cradle and swam away with it; but Thumbelina sat alone on the great green leaf and wept, for she did not want to live with the clammy toad, or marry her ugly son. The little fishes swimming about under the water had seen the toad quite plainly, and heard what she had said; so they put up their heads to see the little girl. When they saw her, they thought her so pretty that they were very sorry she should go down with the ugly toad to live. No; that must not happen. They assembled in the water round the green stalk which supported the leaf on which she was sitting, and nibbled the stem in two. Away floated the leaf down the stream, bearing Thumbelina far beyond the reach of the toad.

On she sailed past several towns, and the little birds sitting in the bushes saw her, and sang, 'What a pretty little girl!' The leaf floated farther and farther away; thus Thumbelina left her native land.

Away floated the leaf down the stream, bearing
Thumbelina far beyond the reach of the toad

A beautiful little white butterfly fluttered above her, and at last settled on the leaf. Thumbelina pleased him, and she, too, was delighted, for now the toads could not reach her, and it was so beautiful where she was travelling; the sun shone on the water and made it sparkle like the brightest silver. She took off her sash, and tied one end round the butterfly; the other end she fastened to the leaf, so that now it glided along with her faster than ever.

A great cockchafer came flying past; he caught sight of Thumbelina, and in a moment had put his arms round her slender waist, and had flown off with her to a tree. The green leaf floated away down the stream, and the butterfly with it, for he was fastened to the leaf and could not get loose from it. Oh, dear! how terrified poor little Thumbelina was when the cockchafer flew off with her to the tree! But she was especially distressed on the beautiful white butterfly's account, as she had tied him fast, so that if he could not get away he must starve to death. But the cockchafer did not trouble himself about that; he sat down with her on a large green leaf, gave her the honey out of the flowers to eat, and told her that she was very pretty, although she wasn't in the least like a cockchafer. Later on, all the other cockchafers who lived in the same tree came to pay calls; they examined Thumbelina closely, and remarked, 'Why, she has only two legs! How very miserable!'

'She has no feelers!' cried another.

'How ugly she is!' said all the lady chafers – and yet Thumbelina was really very pretty.

The cockchafer who had stolen her knew this very well; but when he heard all the ladies saying she was ugly, he began to think so too, and would not keep her; she might go wherever she liked. So he flew down from the tree with her and put her on a daisy. There she sat and wept, because she was so ugly that the cockchafer would have nothing to do with her; and yet she was the most beautiful creature imaginable, so soft and delicate, like the loveliest rose leaf.

The whole summer poor little Thumbelina lived alone in the great wood. She plaited a bed for herself of blades of grass, and hung it up under a clover leaf, so that she was protected from the rain; she gathered honey from the flowers for food, and drank the dew on the leaves every morning. Thus the summer and autumn passed, but then came winter – the long, cold winter. All the birds who had sung so sweetly about her had flown away; the trees shed their leaves, the flowers died; the great clover leaf under which she had lived curled up, and nothing remained of it but the withered stalk. She was terribly cold, for her clothes were ragged, and she herself was so small and thin. Poor little Thumbelina! she would surely be frozen to death. It began to snow, and every snowflake that fell on her was to her as a whole shovelful thrown on one of us, for we are so big, and she was only an inch high. She wrapped herself round in a dead leaf, but it was torn in the middle and gave her no warmth; she was trembling with cold.

Just outside the wood where she was now living lay a great cornfield. But the corn had been gone a long time; only the dry, bare stubble was left standing in the frozen ground. This made a forest for her to wander about in. All at once she came across the door of a fieldmouse, who had a little hole under a cornstalk. There the mouse lived warm and snug, with a storeroom full of corn, a splendid kitchen and dining-room. Poor little Thumbelina went up to the door and begged for a little piece of barley, for she had not had anything to eat for the last two days.

'Poor little creature!' said the fieldmouse, for she was a kind-hearted old thing at the bottom. 'Come into my warm room and have some dinner with me.'

As Thumbelina pleased her, she said: 'As far as I am concerned you may spend the winter with me; but you must keep my room clean and tidy, and tell me stories, for I like that very much.'

And Thumbelina did all that the kind old fieldmouse asked, and did it remarkably well too.

'Now I am expecting a visitor,' said the fieldmouse; 'my neighbour comes to call on me once a week. He is in better circumstances than I am, has great big rooms, and wears a fine black velvet coat. If you could only marry him, you would be well provided for. But he is blind. You must tell him all the prettiest stories you know.'

But Thumbelina did not trouble her head about him, for he was only a mole. He came and paid them a visit in his black velvet coat.

'He is so rich and so accomplished,' the fieldmouse told her. 'His house is twenty times larger than mine; he possesses great knowledge, but he cannot bear the sun and the beautiful flowers, and speaks slightingly of them, for he has never seen them.'

Thumbelina had to sing to him, so she sang 'Ladybird, ladybird, fly away home!' and other songs so prettily that the mole fell in love with her;

but he did not say anything as he was a very cautious man. A short time before he had dug a long passage through the ground from his own house to that of his neighbour; in this he gave the fieldmouse and Thumbelina permission to walk as often as they liked. But he begged them not to be afraid of the dead bird that lay in the passage: it was a real bird with beak and feathers, and must have died a little time ago, and now laid buried just where he had made his tunnel. The mole took a piece of rotten wood in his mouth, for that glows like fire in the dark, and went in front, lighting them through the long dark passage. When they came to the place where the dead bird lay, the mole put his broad nose against the ceiling and pushed a hole through, so that the daylight could shine down. In the middle of the path lay a dead swallow, his pretty wings pressed close to his sides, his claws and head drawn under his feathers; the poor bird had evidently died of cold. Thumbelina was very sorry, for she was very fond of all little birds; they had sung and twittered so beautifully to her all through the summer. But the mole kicked him with his bandy legs and said: 'Now he can't sing any more! It must be very miserable to be a little bird! I'm thankful that none of my children are; birds always starve in winter.'

'Yes, you speak like a sensible man,' said the fieldmouse. 'What has a bird, in spite of all his singing, in the wintertime? He must starve and freeze, and that must be very pleasant for him, I must say!'

Thumbelina did not say anything; but when the other two had passed on she bent down to the bird, brushed aside the feathers from his head, and kissed his closed eyes gently. 'Perhaps it was he that sang to me so prettily in the summer,' she thought. 'How much pleasure he did give me, dear little bird!'

The mole closed up the hole again which let in the light, and then escorted the ladies home. But Thumbelina could not sleep that night; so she got out of bed, and plaited a great big blanket of straw, and carried it off, and spread it over the dead bird, and piled upon it thistledown, as soft as cotton wool, which she had found in the fieldmouse's room, so that the poor little thing should lie warmly buried.

'Farewell, pretty little bird!' she said. 'Farewell, and thank you for your beautiful songs in the summer, when the trees were green and the sun shone down warmly on us!' Then she laid her head against the bird's heart. But the bird was not dead:

*Thumbelina piled thistledown, as soft as cotton wool,
on to the straw blanket*

he had been frozen, but now that she had warmed him, he was coming to life again.

In autumn the swallows fly away to foreign lands; but there are some who are late in starting, and then they get so cold that they drop down as if dead, and the snow comes and covers them over.

Thumbelina trembled, she was so frightened; for the bird was very large in comparison with herself – only an inch high. But she took courage, piled up the down more closely over the poor swallow and fetched her own coverlet and laid it over his head.

Next night she crept out again to him. There he was – alive, but very weak; he could only open his eyes for a moment and look at Thumbelina, who was standing in front of him with a piece of rotten wood in her hand, for she had no other lantern.

'Thank you, pretty little child!' said the swallow to her. 'I am so beautifully warm! Soon I shall regain my strength, and then I shall be able to fly out again into the warm sunshine.'

'Oh!' she said, 'it is very cold outside; it is snowing and freezing! Stay in your warm bed; I will take care of you!'

Then she brought him water in a petal, which he drank, after which he related to her how he had torn one of his wings on a bramble, so that he could not fly as fast as the other swallows, who had flown far away to warmer lands. So at last he had dropped down exhausted, and then he could remember no more. The whole winter he remained down there, and Thumbelina looked after him and nursed him tenderly. Neither the mole nor the fieldmouse learnt anything of this, for they could not bear the poor swallow.

When the spring came, and the sun warmed the earth again, the swallow said farewell to Thumbelina, who opened the hole in the roof for

him which the mole had made. The sun shone brightly down upon her, and the swallow asked her if she would go with him; she could sit upon his back. Thumbelina wanted very much to fly far away into the greenwood, but she knew that the old fieldmouse would be sad if she ran away. 'No, I mustn't come!' she said.

'Farewell, dear good little girl!' said the swallow, and flew off into the sunshine. Thumbelina gazed after him with the tears standing in her eyes, for she was very fond of the swallow.

'Tweet, tweet!' sang the bird, and flew into the greenwood. Thumbelina was very unhappy. She was not allowed to go out into the warm sunshine. The corn which had been sown in the field over the fieldmouse's home grew up high into the air, and made a thick forest for the poor little girl, who was only an inch high.

'Now you are to be a bride, Thumbelina!' said the fieldmouse, 'for our neighbour has proposed for you! What a piece of fortune for a poor child like you! Now you must set to work at your linen for your dowry, for nothing must be lacking if you are to become the wife of our neighbour, the mole!'

Thumbelina had to spin all day long, and every evening the mole visited her, and told her that when the summer was over the sun would not shine so hotly; now it was burning the earth as hard as a stone. Yes, when the summer had passed, they would hold the wedding.

But she was not at all pleased about it, for she did not like the stupid mole. Every morning when the sun was rising, and every evening when it was setting, she would steal out of the house door, and

Thumbelina had to spin all day long

when the breeze parted the ears of corn so that she could see the blue sky through them, she thought how bright and beautiful it must be outside, and longed to see her dear swallow again. But he never came; no doubt he had flown away far into the great greenwood.

By the autumn Thumbelina had finished the dowry.

'In four weeks you will be married!' said the fieldmouse; 'don't be obstinate, or I shall bite you with my sharp white teeth! You will get a fine husband! The king himself has not such a velvet coat. His storeroom and cellar are full, and you should be thankful for that.'

Well, the wedding day arrived. The mole had come to fetch Thumbelina to live with him deep down under the ground, never to come out into the warm sun again, for that was what he didn't like. The poor little girl was very sad, for now she must say goodbye to the beautiful sun.

'Farewell, bright sun!' she cried, stretching out her arms towards it, and taking another step outside the house; for now the corn had been reaped, and only the dry stubble was left standing. 'Farewell, farewell!' she said, and put her arms round a little red flower that grew there. 'Give my love to the dear swallow when you see him!'

'Tweet, tweet!' sounded in her ear all at once. She looked up. There was the swallow flying past! As soon as he saw Thumbelina, he was very glad. She told him how unwilling she was to marry the ugly mole, as then she would have to live underground where the sun never shone, and she could not help bursting into tears.

'The cold winter is coming now,' said the swallow. 'I must fly away to warmer lands: will you come with me? You can sit on my back, and we will fly far away from the ugly mole and his dark house, over the mountains, to the warm countries where the sun shines more brightly than here, where it is always summer, and there are always beautiful flowers. Do come with me, dear little Thumbelina, who saved my life when I lay frozen in the dark tunnel!'

'Yes, I will go with you,' said Thumbelina, and got on the swallow's back, with her feet on one of his outstretched wings. Up he flew into the air, over woods and seas, over the great mountains where the snow is always lying. And if she was cold she crept under his warm feathers, only keeping her little head out to admire all the beautiful things in the world beneath. At last they came to warm lands; there the sun was brighter, the sky seemed twice as high, and in the hedges hung the finest green and purple grapes; in the woods grew oranges and lemons; the air was scented with myrtle and mint, and on the roads were pretty little children running about and playing with great gorgeous butterflies. But the swallow flew on farther, and it became more and more beautiful. Under the most splendid green trees beside a blue lake stood a glittering white marble castle. Vines hung about the high pillars; there were many swallows' nests, and in one of these lived the swallow who was carrying Thumbelina.

'Here is my house!' said he. 'But it won't do for you to live with me; I am not tidy enough to please you. Find a home for yourself in one of the lovely flowers that grow down there; now I will set you down, and you can do whatever you like.'

'That will be splendid!' said she, clapping her little hands.

There lay a great white marble column which had fallen to the ground and broken into three pieces, but between these grew the most beautiful white flowers. The swallow flew down with Thumbelina, and set her upon one of the broad leaves. But there, to her astonishment, she found a tiny little man sitting in the middle of the flower, as white and transparent as if he were made of glass; he had the prettiest golden crown on his head, and the most beautiful wings on his shoulders; he himself was no bigger than Thumbelina. He was the spirit of the flower. In each blossom there dwelt a tiny man or woman; but this one was the king over the others.

'How handsome he is!' whispered Thumbelina to the swallow.

The little prince was very much frightened at the swallow, for in comparison with one so tiny as himself he seemed a giant. But when he saw Thumbelina, he was delighted, for she was the most beautiful girl he had ever seen. So he took his golden crown from off his head and put it on hers, asking her her name, and if she would be his wife, and then she would be queen of all the flowers. Yes! he was a different kind of husband from the son of the toad and the mole with the black velvet coat. So she said, 'Yes,' to the noble prince. And out of each flower came a lady and gentleman, each so tiny and pretty that it was a pleasure to see them. Each brought Thumbelina a present, but the best of all was a beautiful pair of wings which were fastened on to her back, and now she too could fly from flower to flower. They all wished her joy, and the swallow sat above in his nest and sang the wedding march, and that he did as well as he could; but he was sad, because he was very fond of Thumbelina and did not want to be separated from her.

'You shall not be called Thumbelina!' said the spirit of the flower to her; 'that is an ugly name, and you are much too pretty for that. We will call you May Blossom.'

'Farewell, farewell!' said the little swallow with a heavy heart, and flew away to farther lands, far, far away, right back to Denmark. There he had a little nest above a window, where his wife lived, who can tell fairy stories. 'Tweet, tweet!' he sang to her. And that is the way we learnt the whole story.

The Tiger, the Brahman and the Jackal

Once upon a time, a tiger was caught in a trap. He tried in vain to get out through the bars, and rolled and bit with rage and grief when he failed.

By chance a poor Brahman came by. 'Let me out of this cage, oh pious one!' cried the tiger.

'Nay, my friend,' replied the Brahman mildly, 'you would probably eat me if I did.'

'Not at all!' swore the tiger with many oaths; 'on the contrary, I should be for ever grateful, and serve you as a slave!'

Now when the tiger sobbed and sighed and wept and swore, the pious Brahman's heart softened, and at last he consented to open the door of the cage. Out popped the tiger, and, seizing the poor man, cried, 'What a fool you are! What is to prevent my eating you now, for after being cooped up so long I am just terribly hungry!'

In vain the Brahman pleaded for his life; the most he could gain was a promise to abide by the decision of the first three things he chose to question as to the justice of the tiger's action.

So the Brahman first asked a pipal tree what it thought of the matter, but the pipal tree replied coldly, 'What have you to complain about? Don't I give shade and shelter to everyone who passes by, and don't they in return tear down my branches to feed their cattle? Don't whimper – be a man!'

Then the Brahman, sad at heart, went farther afield till he saw a buffalo turning a well-wheel; but he fared no better from it, for it answered, 'You are a fool to expect gratitude! Look at me! While I gave milk they fed me on cotton-seed and oil-cake, but now I am dry they yoke me here, and give me refuse as fodder!'

The Brahman, still more sad, asked the road to give him its opinion.

'My dear sir,' said the road, 'how foolish you are to expect anything else! Here am I, useful to everybody, yet all, rich and poor, great and small, trample on me as they go past, giving me nothing but the ashes of their pipes and the husks of their grain!'

On this the Brahman turned back sorrowfully, and on the way he met a jackal, who called out, 'Why, what's the matter, Mr Brahman? You look as miserable as a fish out of water!'

The Brahman told him all that had occurred. 'How very confusing!' said the jackal, when the recital was ended; 'would you mind telling me over again, for everything has got so mixed up?'

The Brahman told it all over again, but the jackal shook his head in a distracted sort of way, and still could not understand.

'It's very odd,' said he, sadly, 'but it all seems to go in at one ear and out at the other! I will go to the place where it all happened, and then perhaps I shall be able to give a judgement.'

So they returned to the cage, by which the tiger

was waiting for the Brahman, and sharpening his teeth and claws.

'You've been away a long time!' growled the savage beast, 'but now let us begin our dinner.'

'*Our* dinner!' thought the wretched Brahman, as his knees knocked together with fright; 'what a remarkably delicate way of putting it!'

'Give me five minutes, my lord!' he pleaded, 'in order that I may explain matters to the jackal here, who is somewhat slow in his wits.'

The tiger consented, and the Brahman began the whole story over again, not missing a single detail, and spinning as long a yarn as possible.

'Oh, my poor brain! oh, my poor brain!' cried the jackal, wringing its paws. 'Let me see! how did it all begin? You were in the cage, and the tiger came walking by – '

'Pooh!' interrupted the tiger, 'what a fool you are! *I* was in the cage.'

'Of course!' cried the jackal, pretending to tremble with fright; 'yes! I was in the cage – no I wasn't – dear! dear! where are my wits? Let me see – the tiger was in the Brahman, and the cage came walking by – no, that's not it, either! Well, don't mind me, but begin your dinner, for I shall never understand!'

'Yes, you shall!' returned the tiger, in a rage at the jackal's stupidity; 'I'll *make* you understand! Look here – I am the tiger – '

'Yes, my lord!'

'And that is the Brahman – '

'Yes, my lord!'

'And that is the cage – '

'Yes, my lord!'

'And I was in the cage – do you understand?'

'Yes – no – Please, my lord – '

'Well?' cried the tiger impatiently.

'Please, my lord! – how did you get in?'

'How! – why in the usual way, of course!'

'Oh, dear me! – my head is beginning to whirl again! Please don't be angry, my lord, but what is the usual way?'

At this the tiger lost patience, and, jumping into the cage, cried, 'This way! Now do you understand how it was?'

'Perfectly!' grinned the jackal, as he dexterously shut the door, 'and if you will permit me to say so, I think matters should remain as they were!'

The Tinderbox

A soldier came marching along the high road – left, right! left, right! He had his knapsack on his back and a sword by his side, for he had been to the wars and was now returning home.

An old witch met him on the road. She was very ugly to look at: her underlip hung down to her breast.

'Good-evening, soldier!' she said. 'What a fine sword and knapsack you have! You are something like a soldier! You ought to have as much money as you would like to carry!'

'Thank you, old witch,' said the soldier.

'Do you see that great tree there?' said the witch, pointing to a tree beside them. 'It is hollow within. You must climb up to the top, and then you will see a hole through which you can let yourself down into the tree. I will tie a rope round your waist, so that I may be able to pull you up again when you call.'

'What shall I do down there?' asked the soldier.

'Get money!' answered the witch. 'Listen! When you reach the bottom of the tree you will find yourself in a large hall; it is light there, for there are more than three hundred lamps burning. Then you will see three doors, which you can open – the keys are in the locks. If you go into the first room, you will see a

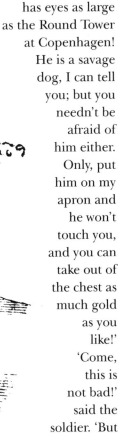

great chest in the middle of the floor with a dog sitting upon it; he has eyes as large as saucers, but you needn't trouble about him. I will give you my blue-check apron, which you must spread out on the floor, and then go back quickly and fetch the dog and set him upon it; open the chest and take as much money as you like. It is copper there. If you would rather have silver, you must go into the next room, where there is a dog with eyes as large as mill-wheels. But don't take any notice of him; just set him upon my apron, and help yourself to the money. If you prefer gold, you can get that too, if you go into the third room, and as much as you like to carry. But the dog that guards the chest there has eyes as large as the Round Tower at Copenhagen! He is a savage dog, I can tell you; but you needn't be afraid of him either. Only, put him on my apron and he won't touch you, and you can take out of the chest as much gold as you like!'

'Come, this is not bad!' said the soldier. 'But what am I to give you, old witch; for surely you are not going to do this for nothing?'

'Yes, I am!' replied the witch. 'Not a single farthing will I take! For me you shall bring nothing but an old tinderbox which my grandmother forgot last time she was down there.'

'Well, tie the rope round my waist!' said the soldier.

'Here it is,' said the witch, 'and here is my blue-check apron.'

Then the soldier climbed up the tree, let himself down through the hole, and found himself standing, as the witch had said, underground in the large hall, where the three hundred lamps were burning.

Well, he opened the first door. Ugh! there sat the dog with eyes as big as saucers glaring at him.

'You are a fine fellow!' said the soldier, and put him on the witch's apron, took as much copper as his pockets could hold; then he shut the chest, put the dog on it again, and went into the second room. Sure enough there sat the dog with eyes as large as mill-wheels.

'You had better not look at me so hard!' said the soldier. 'Your eyes will come out of their sockets!'

And then he set the dog on the apron. When he saw all the silver in the chest, he threw away the copper he had taken, and filled his pockets and knapsack with nothing but silver.

Then he went into the third room. Horrors! the dog there had two eyes, each as large as the Round Tower at Copenhagen, spinning round in his head like wheels.

'Good-evening!' said the soldier and saluted, for he had never seen a dog like this before. But when he had examined him more closely, he thought to himself: 'Now then, I've had enough of this!' and put him down on the floor, and opened the chest. Heavens! what a heap of gold there was! With all that he could buy up the whole town, and all the sugar pigs, all the tin soldiers, whips and rocking-horses in the whole world. Now he threw away all the silver with which he had filled his pockets and knapsack, and filled them with gold instead – yes, all his pockets, his knapsack, cap and boots even, so that he could hardly walk. Now he was rich indeed. He put the dog back upon the chest, shut the door, and then called up through the tree: 'Now pull me up again, old witch!'

'Have you got the tinderbox also?' asked the witch.

'Botheration!' said the soldier, 'I had clean forgotten it!' And then he went back and fetched it.

The witch pulled him up, and there he stood again on the high road, with pockets, knapsack, cap and boots filled with gold.

'What do you want to do with the tinderbox?' asked the soldier.

'That doesn't matter to you,' replied the witch. 'You have got your money, give me my tinderbox.'

'We'll see!' said the soldier. 'Tell me at once what you want to do with it, or I will draw my sword, and cut off your head!'

'No!' screamed the witch.

The soldier immediately cut off her head. That was the end of her! But he tied up all his gold in her apron, slung it like a bundle over his shoulder, put the tinderbox in his pocket, and set out towards the town.

It was a splendid town! He turned into the finest inn, ordered the best chamber and his favourite dinner; for now that he had so much money he was really rich.

It certainly occurred to the servant who had to clean his boots that they were astonishingly old boots for such a rich lord. But that was because he had not yet bought new ones; next day he appeared in respectable boots and fine clothes. Now, instead of a common soldier he had become a noble lord, and the people told him about all the grand doings of the town and the king, and what a beautiful princess his daughter was.

'How can one get to see her?' asked the soldier.

'She is never to be seen at all!' they told him; 'she lives in a great copper castle, surrounded by many walls and towers! No one except the king may go in or out, for it is prophesied that she will marry a common soldier, and the king cannot submit to that.'

'I should very much like to see her,' thought the soldier; but he could not get permission.

Now he lived very gaily, went to the theatre, drove in the king's garden, and gave the poor a great deal of money, which was very nice of him; he had experienced in former times how hard it is not to have a farthing in the world. Now he was rich, wore fine clothes, and made many friends, who all said that he was an excellent man, a real nobleman. And the soldier liked that. But as he was always spending money, and never made any more, at last the day came when he had nothing left but two shillings, and he had to leave the beautiful rooms in which he had been living, and go into a little attic under the roof, and clean his own boots, and mend them with a darning-needle. None of his friends came to visit him there, for there were too many stairs to climb.

It was a dark evening, and he could not even buy a light. But all at once it flashed across him that there was a little end of tinder in the tinderbox, which he had taken from the hollow tree into which the witch had helped him down. He found the box with the tinder in it; but just as he was kindling a light, and had struck a spark out of the tinderbox, the door burst open, and the dog with eyes as large as saucers, which he had seen down in the tree, stood before him and said: 'What does my lord command?'

'What's the meaning of this?' exclaimed the soldier. 'This is a pretty kind of tinderbox, if I can get whatever I want like this. Get me money!' he cried to the dog, and hey, presto! he was off and back again, holding a great purse full of money in his mouth.

Now the soldier knew what a capital tinderbox this was. If he rubbed once, the dog that sat on the chest of copper appeared; if he rubbed twice, there came the dog that watched over the silver chest; and if he rubbed three times, the one that guarded the gold appeared. Now, the soldier went down again to his beautiful rooms, and appeared once more in splendid clothes. All his friends immediately recognised him again, and paid him great court.

One day he thought to himself: 'It is very strange that no one can get to see the princess. They all say she is very pretty, but what's the use of that if she has to sit for ever in the great copper castle with all the towers? Can I not manage to see her somehow? Where is my tinderbox?' and so he struck a spark, and, presto! there came the dog with eyes as large as saucers.

'It is the middle of the night, I know,' said the soldier; 'but I should very much like to see the princess for a moment.'

The dog was already outside the door, and before the soldier could look round, in he came with the princess. She was lying asleep on the dog's back, and was so beautiful that anyone could see she was a real princess. The soldier really could not refrain from kissing her – he was such a thorough soldier. Then the dog ran back with the princess. But when it was morning, and the king and queen were drinking tea, the princess said that the night before she had had such a strange dream about a dog and a soldier: she had ridden on the dog's back, and the soldier had kissed her.

'That is certainly a fine story,' said the queen. But the next night one of the ladies-in-waiting was to watch at the princess's bed, to see if it was only a dream, or if it had actually happened.

The soldier had an overpowering longing to see the princess again, and so the dog came in the middle of the night and fetched her, running as fast as he could. But the lady-in-waiting slipped on india-rubber shoes and followed them. When she saw them disappear into a large house, she thought to herself: 'Now I know where it is;' and made a great cross on the door with a piece of chalk. Then she went home and lay down, and the dog came back also, with the princess. But when he saw that a cross had been made on the door of the house where the soldier lived, he took a piece of chalk also, and made crosses on all the doors in the town; and that was very clever, for now the lady-in-waiting could not find the right house, as there were crosses on all the doors.

Early next morning the king, queen, ladies-in-waiting and officers came out to see where the princess had been.

'There it is!' said the king, when he saw the first door with a cross on it.

'No, there it is, my dear!' said the queen, when she likewise saw a door with a cross.

'But here is one, and there is another!' they all exclaimed; wherever they looked there was a cross on the door. Then they realised that the sign would not help them at all.

But the queen was an extremely clever woman, who could do a great deal more than just drive in a coach. She took her great golden scissors, cut up a piece of silk, and made a pretty little bag of it. This she filled with the finest buckwheat grains, and tied it round the princess's neck; this done, she cut a little hole in the bag, so that the grains would strew the whole road wherever the princess went.

In the night the dog came again, took the princess on his back and ran away with her to the soldier, who was very much in love with her, and would have liked to have been a prince, so that he might have had her for his wife.

The dog did not notice how the grains were strewn right from the castle to the soldier's window, to reach which he ran up the wall with the princess.

In the morning the king and the queen saw plainly where their daughter had been, and they took the soldier and put him in prison.

There he sat. Oh, how dark and dull it was there! And they told him: 'Tomorrow you are to be hanged.' Hearing that did not exactly cheer him, and he had left his tinderbox in the inn.

Next morning he could see through the iron grating in front of his little window how the people were hurrying out of the town to see him hanged. He heard the drums and saw the soldiers marching; all the people were running to and fro. Just below his window was a shoemaker's apprentice, with leather apron and shoes; he was skipping along so merrily that one of his shoes flew off and fell against the wall, just where the soldier was sitting peeping through the iron grating.

'Oh, shoemaker's boy, you needn't be in such a hurry!' said the soldier to him. 'There's nothing going on till I arrive. But if you will run back to the house where I lived, and fetch me my tinderbox, I will give you four shillings. But you must put your best foot foremost.'

The shoemaker's boy was very willing to earn four shillings, and fetched the tinderbox, gave it to the soldier, and – yes – now you shall hear.

Outside the town a great scaffold had been erected, and all round were standing the soldiers, and hundreds of thousands of people. The king and queen were sitting on a magnificent throne opposite the judges and the whole council.

The soldier was already standing on the top of the ladder; but when they wanted to put the rope round his neck, he said that the fulfilment of one innocent request was always granted to a poor criminal before he underwent his punishment. He would so much like to smoke a small pipe of tobacco; it would be his last pipe in this world.

The king could not refuse him this, and so he took out his tinderbox, and rubbed it once, twice, three times. And lo, and behold! there stood all three dogs – the one with eyes as large as saucers, the second with eyes as large as mill-wheels, and the third with eyes each as large as the Round Tower of Copenhagen.

'Help me now, so that I may not be hanged!' cried the soldier. And thereupon the dogs fell upon the judges and the whole council, seized some by the legs, others by the nose, and threw them so high into the air that they fell and were smashed into pieces.

'I won't stand this!' said the king; but the largest dog seized him too, and the queen as well, and threw them up after the others. This frightened the soldiers, and all the people cried: 'Good soldier, you shall be our king, and marry the beautiful princess!'

Then they put the soldier into the king's coach, and the three dogs danced in front, crying 'Hurrah!' And the boys whistled and the soldiers presented arms.

The princess came out of the copper castle, and became queen; and that pleased her very much.

The wedding festivities lasted for eight days, and the dogs sat at table and made eyes at everyone.

Titty Mouse and Tatty Mouse

Titty Mouse and Tatty Mouse both lived in a house,

Titty Mouse went a-leasing and Tatty Mouse went a-leasing,

So they both went a-leasing.

Titty Mouse leased an ear of corn, and Tatty Mouse leased an ear of corn,

So they both leased an ear of corn.

Titty Mouse made a pudding, and Tatty Mouse made a pudding,

So they both made a pudding.

And Tatty Mouse put her pudding into the pot to boil, but when Titty went to put hers in, the pot tumbled over and scalded her to death.

Then Tatty sat down and wept; then a three-legged stool said: 'Tatty, why do you weep?' 'Titty's dead,' said Tatty, 'and so I weep.' 'Then,' said the stool, 'I'll hop,' so the stool hopped.

Then a broom in the corner of the room said, 'Stool, why do you hop?' 'Oh!' said the stool, 'Titty's dead, and Tatty weeps, and so I hop.' 'Then,' said the broom, 'I'll sweep,' so the broom began to sweep.

'Then,' said the door, 'Broom, why do you sweep?' 'Oh!' said the broom, 'Titty's dead, and Tatty weeps, and the stool hops, and so I sweep.' 'Then,' said the door, 'I'll jar,' so the door jarred.

'Then,' said the window, 'Door, why do you jar?' 'Oh!' said the door, 'Titty's dead, and Tatty weeps, and the stool hops, and the broom sweeps, and so I jar.' 'Then,' said the window, 'I'll creak,' so the window creaked.

Now there was an old form outside the house, and when the window creaked, the form said: 'Window, why do you creak?' 'Oh!' said the window, 'Titty's dead, and Tatty weeps, and the stool hops, and the broom sweeps, the door

jars, and so I creak.' 'Then,' said the old form, 'I'll run round the house,' then the old form ran round the house.

Now there was a fine large walnut tree growing by the cottage, and the tree said to the form: 'Form, why do you run round the house?' 'Oh!' said the form, 'Titty's dead, and Tatty weeps, and the stool hops, and the broom sweeps, the door jars, and the window creaks, and so I run round the house.' 'Then,' said the walnut tree, 'I'll shed my leaves,' so the walnut tree shed all its beautiful green leaves.

Now there was a little bird perched on one of the boughs of the tree, and when all the leaves fell, it said: 'Walnut tree, why do you shed your leaves?' 'Oh!' said the tree, 'Titty's dead, and Tatty weeps, the stool hops, and the broom sweeps, the door jars, and the window creaks, the old form runs round the house, and so I shed my leaves.' 'Then,' said the little bird, 'I'll moult all my feathers,' so he moulted all his pretty feathers.

Now there was a little girl walking below, carrying a jug of milk for her brothers and sisters' supper, and when she saw the poor little bird moult all its feathers, she said: 'Little bird, why do you moult all your feathers?' 'Oh!' said the little bird, 'Titty's dead, and Tatty weeps, the stool hops, and the broom sweeps, the door jars, and the window creaks, the old form runs round the house, the walnut tree sheds its leaves, and so I moult all my feathers.' 'Then,' said the little girl, 'I'll spill the milk,' so she dropped the pitcher and spilt the milk.

Now there was an old man just by on the top of a ladder thatching a rick, and when he saw the little girl spill the milk, he said: 'Little girl, what do you mean by spilling the milk? Your little brothers and sisters must go without their supper!' Then said the little girl: 'Titty's dead, and Tatty weeps, the stool hops, and the broom sweeps, the door jars, and the window creaks, the old form runs round the house, the walnut tree sheds all its leaves, the little bird moults all its feathers, and so I spill the milk.'

'Oh!' said the old man, 'then I'll tumble off the ladder and break my neck,' so he tumbled off the ladder and broke his neck; and when the old man broke his neck, the great walnut tree fell down with a crash, and upset the old form and knocked down the house, and the house falling knocked the window out, and the window knocked the door down, and the door upset the broom, and the broom upset the stool, and poor little Tatty Mouse was buried beneath the ruins.

The History of Tom Thumb

In the days of the great Prince Arthur, there lived a mighty magician, called Merlin, the most learned and skilful enchanter the world has ever seen.

This famous magician, who could take any form he pleased, was travelling about as a poor beggar, and, being very tired, he stopped at the cottage of a ploughman to rest himself, and asked for some food.

The countryman bade him welcome, and his wife, who was a very good-hearted woman, soon brought him some milk in a wooden bowl, and some coarse brown bread on a platter.

Merlin was much pleased with the kindness of the ploughman and his wife; but he could not help noticing that though everything was neat and comfortable in the cottage, they seemed both to be very unhappy. He therefore asked them why they were so melancholy, and learned that they were miserable because they had no children.

The poor woman said, with tears in her eyes: 'I should be the happiest creature in the world if I had a son; although he was no bigger than my husband's thumb, I would be satisfied.'

Merlin was so much amused with the idea of a boy no bigger than a man's thumb, that he determined to grant the poor woman's wish. Accordingly, in a short time after, the ploughman's wife had a son, who, wonderful to relate! was not a bit bigger than his father's thumb.

The queen of the fairies, wishing to see the little fellow, came in at the window while the mother was sitting up in the bed admiring him. The queen kissed the child, and, giving it the name of Tom Thumb, sent for some of the fairies, who dressed her little godson according to her orders:

> An oak-leaf hat he had for his crown;
> His shirt of web by spiders spun;
> With jacket wove of thistle's down;
> His trousers were of feathers done.

> His stockings, of apple-rind, they tie
> With eyelash from his mother's eye
> His shoes were made of mouse's skin,
> Tann'd with the downy hair within.

Tom never grew any larger than his father's thumb, which was only of ordinary size; but as he got older he became very cunning and full of tricks. When he was old enough to play with the boys, and had lost all his own cherry-stones, he used to creep into the bags of his playfellows, fill his pockets, and, getting out without their noticing him, would again join in the game.

One day, however, as he was coming out of a bag of cherry-stones, where he had been stealing as usual, the boy to whom it belonged chanced to see him. 'Ah, ah! my little Tommy,' said the boy, 'so I have caught you stealing my cherry-stones at last, and you shall be rewarded for your thievish tricks.' On saying this, he drew the string tight round his neck, and gave the bag such a hearty shake, that poor little Tom's legs, thighs, and body were sadly bruised. He roared out with pain, and begged to be let out, promising never to steal again.

A short time afterwards his mother was making a batter-pudding, and Tom, being very anxious to see how it was made, climbed up to the edge of the bowl; but his foot slipped, and he plumped over head and ears into the batter, without his mother noticing him, so that she stirred him into the pudding-bag and put him in the pot to boil.

The batter filled Tom's mouth, and prevented him from crying out; but, on feeling the hot water, he kicked and struggled so much in the pot that his mother thought that the pudding was bewitched, and, pulling it out of the pot, she threw it outside the door. A poor tinker, who was passing by, lifted up the pudding, and, putting it into his budget, he then walked off. As Tom had now got his mouth cleared of the batter, he began to cry aloud, which so frightened the tinker that he flung down the pudding and ran away. The pudding being broke to pieces by the fall, Tom crept out covered all over with the batter, and walked home. His mother, who was very sorry to see her darling in such a woeful state, put him into a teacup, and soon washed off the batter; after which she kissed him, and laid him in bed.

Soon after the adventure of the pudding, Tom's mother went to milk her cow in the meadow, and she took him along with her. As the wind was very high, for fear of his being blown away, she tied him to a thistle with a piece of fine thread. The cow soon observed Tom's oak-leaf hat, and liking the appearance of it, took poor Tom and the thistle at one mouthful. While the cow was chewing the thistle Tom was afraid of her great teeth, which threatened to crush him in pieces, and he roared out as loud as he could: 'Mother, mother!'

'Where are you, Tommy, my dear Tommy?' said his mother.

'Here, mother,' replied he, 'in the red cow's mouth.'

His mother began to cry and wring her hands; but the cow, surprised at the odd noise in her throat, opened her mouth and let Tom drop out. Fortunately his mother caught him in her apron as he was falling to the ground, or he would have been dreadfully hurt. She then put Tom in her bosom and ran home with him.

Tom's father made him a whip of a barley straw to drive the cattle with, and having one day gone into the fields, he lost his footing and rolled into a furrow. A raven, which was flying over, picked him up, and flew with him over the sea, and there dropped him.

A large fish swallowed Tom the moment he fell into the sea, but was soon after caught, and bought for the table of King Arthur. When they opened the fish in order to cook it, everyone

was astonished at finding such a little boy, and Tom was quite delighted at being free again. They carried him to the king, who made Tom his dwarf, and he soon grew a great favourite at court; for by his tricks and gambols he not only amused the king and queen, but also all the Knights of the Round Table.

It is said that when the king rode out on horseback, he often took Tom along with him, and if a shower came on, he used to creep into his majesty's waistcoat-pocket, where he slept till the rain was over.

King Arthur one day asked Tom about his parents, wishing to know if they were as small as he was, and whether they were well off. Tom told the king that his father and mother were as tall as anybody about the court, but in rather poor circumstances. On hearing this, the king carried Tom to his treasury, the place where he kept all his money, and told him to take as much money as he could carry home to his parents, which made the poor little fellow caper with joy. Tom went immediately to procure a purse, which was made of a waterbubble, and then returned to the treasury, where be received a silver threepenny-piece to put into it.

Our little hero had some difficulty in lifting the burden upon his back; but he at last succeeded in getting it placed to his liking, and set forward on his journey. Eventually, without meeting with any accident, and after resting himself more than a hundred times by the way, in two days and two nights he reached his father's house in safety.

Tom had travelled forty-eight hours with a huge silver-piece on his back, and was almost tired to death when his mother ran out to meet him, and carried him into the house. But he soon returned to court. As Tom's clothes had suffered much in the batter-pudding, and the inside of the fish, his majesty ordered him a new suit of clothes, and had him mounted as a knight on a mouse.

Of butterfly's wings his shirt was made,
His boots of chicken's hide;
And by a nimble fairy blade,
Well learned in the tailoring trade,
His clothing was supplied.
A needle dangled by his side;
A dapper mouse he used to ride,
Thus strutted Tom in stately pride!

It was certainly very diverting to see Tom in this dress and mounted on the mouse, as he rode out a-hunting with the king and nobility, who were all ready to expire with laughter at Tom and his fine prancing charger.

The king was so charmed with his protégé that he ordered a little chair to be made, in order that Tom might sit upon his table, and also a palace of gold, a span high, with a door an inch wide, to live in. He also gave him a coach, drawn by six small mice.

The queen was so enraged at the honours conferred on Sir Thomas that she resolved to ruin him, and told the king that the little knight had been saucy to her.

The king sent for Tom in great haste, but being fully aware of the danger of royal anger, he crept into an empty snail-shell, where he lay for a long time until he was almost starved with hunger; but at last he ventured to peep out, and seeing a fine large butterfly on the ground, near the place of his concealment, he got close to it and, jumping astride on it, was carried up into the air. The butterfly flew with him from tree to tree and from field to field, and at last returned to the court, where the king and nobility all strove to catch him; but at last poor Tom fell from his seat into a watering-pot, in which he was almost drowned.

When the queen saw him she was in a rage, and said he should be beheaded; and he was put into a mousetrap until the time of his execution.

However a cat, observing something alive in the trap, patted it about till the wires broke, and set Thomas at liberty.

The king received Tom again into favour, which he did not live to enjoy, for a large spider one day attacked him; and although he drew his sword and fought well, yet the spider's poisonous breath at last overcame him.

He fell dead on the ground where he stood, And the spider suck'd every drop of his blood.

King Arthur and his whole court were so sorry at the loss of their little favourite that they went into mourning and raised a fine white marble monument over his grave with the following epitaph:

Here lies
TOM THUMB,
King Arthur's knight,
Who died by a spider's cruel bite.
He was well known in Arthur's court,
Where he afforded gallant sport;
He rode at tilt and tournament,
And on a mouse a-hunting went.
Alive he filled the court with mirth;
His death to sorrow soon gave birth.
Wipe, wipe your eyes, and shake your head
And cry – Alas! Tom Thumb is dead!

Tom Tit Tot

Once upon a time there was a woman, and she baked five pies. And when they came out of the oven, they were that overbaked the crusts were too hard to eat. So she says to her daughter: 'Darter,' says she, 'put you them there pies on the shelf, and leave 'em there a little, and they'll come again.' She meant, you know, the crust would get soft.

But the girl, she says to herself: 'Well, if they'll come again, I'll eat 'em now.' And she set to work and ate 'em all, first and last.

Well, come suppertime the woman said: 'Go you, and get one o' them there pies. I dare say they've come again now.'

The girl went and she looked, and there was nothing but the dishes. So back she came and says she: 'Noo, they ain't come again.'

'Not one of 'em?' says the mother.

'Not one of 'em,' says she.

'Well, come again, or not come again,' said the woman 'I'll have one for supper.'

'But you can't, if they ain't come,' said the girl.

'But I can,' says she. 'Go you, and bring the best of 'em.'

'Best or worst,' says the girl, 'I've ate 'em all, and you can't have one till that's come again.'

Well, the woman she was done, and she took her spinning to the door to spin, and as she span she sang:

> My darter ha' ate five, five pies today.
> My darter ha' ate five, five pies today.

The king was coming down the street, and he heard her sing, but what she sang he couldn't hear, so he stopped and said: 'What was that you were singing, my good woman?'

The woman was ashamed to let him hear what her daughter had been doing, so she sang, instead of that:

My darter ha' spun five, five skeins today.
My darter ha' spun five, five skeins today.

'Stars o' mine!' said the king, 'I never heard tell of anyone that could do that.'

Then he said: 'Look you here, I want a wife, and I'll marry your daughter. But look you here,' says he, 'eleven months out of the year she shall have all she likes to eat, and all the gowns she likes to get, and all the company she likes to keep; but the last month of the year she'll have to spin five skeins every day, and if she don't I shall kill her.'

'All right,' says the woman; for she thought what a grand marriage that was. And as for the five skeins, when the time came, there'd be plenty of ways of getting out of it, and likeliest, he'd have forgotten all about it.

Well, so they were married. And for eleven months the girl had all she liked to eat, and all the gowns she liked to get, and all the company she liked to keep.

But when the time was getting over, she began to think about the skeins and to wonder if he had 'em in mind. But not one word did he say about 'em, and she thought he'd wholly forgotten 'em.

However, the last day of the last month he takes her to a room she'd never set eyes on before. There was nothing in it but a spinning-wheel and a stool. And says he: 'Now, my dear, here you'll be shut in tomorrow with some victuals and some flax, and if you haven't spun five skeins by the night, your head'll go off.'

And away he went about his business.

Well, she was that frightened, she'd always been such a gatless girl, that she didn't so much as know how to spin, and what was she to do tomorrow with no one to come nigh her to help her? She sat down on a stool in the kitchen, and law! how she did cry!

However, all of a sudden she heard a sort of a knocking low down on the door. She upped and oped it, and what should she see but a small little black thing with a long tail. That looked up at her right curious, and that said: 'What are you a-crying for?'

'What's that to you?' says she.

'Never you mind,' that said, 'but tell me what you're a-crying for.'

'That won't do me no good if I do,' says she.

'You don't know that,' that said, and twirled that's tail round.

'Well,' says she, 'that won't do no harm, if that don't do no good,' and she upped and told about the pies, and the skeins, and everything.

'This is what I'll do,' says the little black thing, 'I'll come to your window every morning and take the flax and bring it spun at night.'

'What's your pay?' says she.

That looked out of the corner of that's eyes, and that said: 'I'll give you three guesses every night to guess my name, and if you haven't guessed it before the month's up you shall be mine.'

Well, she thought she'd be sure to guess that's name before the month was up. 'All right,' says she, 'I agree.'

'All right,' that says, and law! how that twirled that's tail.

Well, the next day, her husband took her into the room, and there was the flax and the day's food.

'Now there's the flax,' says he, 'and if that ain't spun up this night, off goes your head.' And then he went out and locked the door.

He'd hardly gone, when there was a knocking against the window.

She upped and she oped it, and there sure enough was the little old thing sitting on the ledge.

'Where's the flax?' says he.

'Here it be,' says she. And she gave it to him.

Well, come the evening a knocking came again to the window. She upped and she oped it, and there was the little old thing with five skeins of flax on his arm.

'Here it be,' says he, and he gave it to her.

'Now, what's my name?' says he.

'What, is that Bill?' says she.

'Noo, that ain't,' says he, and he twirled his tail.

'Is that Ned?' says she.

'Noo, that ain't,' says he, and he twirled his tail.

'Well, is that Mark?' says she.

'Noo, that ain't,' says he, and he twirled his tail harder, and away he flew.

Well, when her husband came in, there were the five skeins ready for him. 'I see I shan't have to kill you tonight, my dear,' says he; 'you'll have your food and your flax in the morning,' says he, and away he goes.

Well, every day the flax and the food were brought, and every day that there little black impet used to come mornings and evenings. And all the day the girl sat trying to think of names to say to it when it came at night. But she never hit on the right one. And as it got towards the end of the month, the impet began to look so maliceful, and that twirled that's tail faster and faster each time she gave a guess.

At last it came to the last day but one. The impet came at night along with the five skeins, and that said, 'What, ain't you got my name yet?'

'Is that Nicodemus?' says she.

'Noo, t'ain't,' that says.

'Is that Sammle?' says she.

'Noo, t'ain't,' that says.

'A-well, is that Methusalem?' says she.

'Noo, t'ain't that neither,' that says.

Then that looks at her with that's eyes like coals o' fire, and that says: 'Woman, there's only tomorrow night, and then you'll be mine!' And away it flew.

Well, she felt that horrid. However, she heard the king coming along the passage. In he came, and when he sees the five skeins, he says, says he,

'Well, my dear,' says he, 'I don't see but what you'll have your skeins ready tomorrow night as well, and as I reckon I shan't have to kill you, I'll have supper in here tonight.' So they brought supper, and another stool for him, and down the two sat.

Well, he hadn't eaten but a mouthful or so, when he stops and begins to laugh.

'What is it?' says she.

'A-why,' says he, 'I was out a-hunting today, and I got away to a place in the wood I'd never seen before And there was an old chalk-pit. And I heard a kind of a sort of a humming. So I got off my hobby, and I went right quiet to the pit, and I looked down. Well, what should there be but the funniest little black thing you ever set eyes on. And what was that doing, but that had a little spinning-wheel, and that was spinning wonderful fast, and twirling that's tail. And as that span that sang:

> 'Nimmy nimmy not,
> My name's Tom Tit Tot.'

Well, when the girl heard this, she felt as if she could have jumped out of her skin for joy, but she didn't say a word.

Next day that there little thing looked so maliceful when he came for the flax. And when night came, she heard that knocking against the window panes. She oped the window, and that come right in on the ledge. That was grinning from ear to ear, and Oo! that's tail was twirling round so fast.

'What's my name?' that says, as that gave her the skeins.

'Is that Solomon?' she says, pretending to be afeard.

'Noo, t'ain't,' that says, and that came farther into the room.

'Well, is that Zebedee?' says she again.

'Noo, t'ain't,' says the impet. And then that laughed and twirled that's tail till you couldn't hardly see it.

'Take time, woman,' that says; 'next guess, and you're mine.' And that stretched out that's black hands at her.

Well, she backed a step or two, and she looked at it, and then she laughed out, and says she, pointing her finger at it:

> 'Ninny, Ninny not,
> Your name's TOM TIT TOT.'

Well, when that heard her, that gave an awful shriek and away that flew into the dark, and she never saw it any more.

636

The Travelling Musicians

An honest farmer had once an ass that had been a faithful servant to him a great many years, but was now growing old and every day more and more unfit for work. His master therefore was tired of keeping him and began to think of putting an end to him; but the ass, who saw that some mischief was in the wind, took himself slyly off, and began his journey towards the great city, 'For there,' thought he, 'I may turn musician.'

After he had travelled a little way, he spied a dog lying by the roadside and panting as if he were tired. 'What makes you pant so, my friend?' said the ass.

'Alas!' said the dog, 'my master was going to knock me on the head, because I am old and weak, and can no longer make myself useful to him in hunting; so I ran away; but what can I do to earn my livelihood?'

'Hark ye!' said the ass, 'I am going to the great city to turn musician: suppose you come with me, and see what you can do in the same way?' The dog said he was willing, and they jogged on together.

They had not gone far before they saw a cat sitting in the middle of the road and making a most rueful face.

'Pray, my good lady,' said the ass, 'what's the matter with you? You look quite out of spirits!'

'Ah, me!' said the cat, 'how can one be in good spirits when one's life is in danger? Because I am beginning to grow old, and had rather lie at my ease by the fire than run about the house after the mice, my mistress laid hold of me, and was going to drown me; and though I have been lucky enough to get away from her, I do not know what I am to live upon.'

'Oh,' said the ass, 'by all means come with us to the great city; you are a good night singer, and may make your fortune as a musician.' The cat was pleased with the thought, and joined the party.

Soon afterwards, as they were passing by a farm-yard, they saw a cock perched upon a gate, and screaming out with all his might and main. 'Bravo!' said the ass; 'upon my word, you make a famous noise; pray what is all this about?'

'Why,' said the cock, 'I was just now saying that we should have fine weather for our washing-day, and yet my mistress and the cook don't thank me for my pains, but threaten to cut off my head tomorrow, and make broth of me for the guests that are coming on Sunday!'

'Heaven forbid!' said the ass, 'come with us Master Chanticleer; it will be better, at any rate, than staying here to have your head cut off! Besides, who knows? If we care to sing in tune, we may get up some kind of a concert; so come along with us.'

'With all my heart,' said the cock; so they all four went on jollily together.

They could not, however, reach the great city the first day; so when night came on, they went into a wood to sleep. The ass and the dog laid themselves down under a great tree, and the cat climbed up into the branches; while the cock, thinking that the higher he sat the safer he should be, flew up to the very top of the tree, and then, according to his custom, before he went to sleep, looked out on all sides of him to see that everything was well. In doing this, he saw afar off something bright and shining, and calling to his companions said, 'There must be a house no great way off, for I see a light.'

'If that be the case,' said the ass, 'we had better change our quarters, for our lodging is not the best in the world!'

'Besides,' added the dog, 'I should not be the worse for a bone or two, or a bit of meat.' So they walked off together towards the spot where Chanticleer had seen the light, and as they drew near it became larger and brighter, till they at last came close to a house in which a gang of robbers lived.

The ass, being the tallest of the company, marched up to the window and peeped in. 'Well, donkey,' said Chanticleer, 'what do you see?'

'What do I see?' replied the ass. 'Why, I see a table spread with all kinds of good things, and robbers sitting round it making merry.'

'That would be a noble lodging for us,' said the cock. 'Yes,' said the ass, 'if we could only get in;' so they consulted together how they should contrive to get the robbers out; and at last they hit upon a plan. The ass placed himself upright on his hind legs, with his forefeet resting against the window; the dog got upon his back; the cat scrambled up to the dog's shoulders; and the cock flew up and sat upon the cat's head. When all was ready a signal was given, and they began their music. The ass brayed, the dog barked, the cat mewed and the cock screamed; and then they all broke through the window at once, and came tumbling into the room, among the broken glass, with a most hideous clatter! The robbers, who had been not a little frightened by the opening concert, had now no doubt that some frightful hobgoblin had broken in upon them, and scampered away as fast as they could.

The coast once clear, our travellers soon sat down and dispatched what the robbers had left, with as much eagerness as if they had not expected to eat again for a month. As soon as they had satisfied themselves, they put out the lights, and each once more sought out a resting-place to his own liking. The donkey laid himself down upon a heap of straw in the yard, the dog stretched himself upon a mat behind the door, the cat rolled herself up on the hearth before the warm ashes, and the cock perched upon a beam on the top of the house; and, as they were all rather tired with their journey, they soon fell asleep.

But about midnight, when the robbers saw from afar that the lights were out and that all seemed quiet, they began to think that they had been in too great a hurry to run away; and one of them, who was bolder than the rest, went to see what was going on. Finding everything still, he marched into the kitchen, and groped about till he found a match in order to light a candle; and then, espying the glittering fiery eyes of the cat, he mistook them for live coals, and held the match to them to light it. But the cat, not understanding this joke, sprang at his face, and spat, and scratched at him. This frightened him dreadfully, and away he ran to the back door; but there the dog jumped up and bit him in the leg; and as he was crossing over the yard the ass kicked him; and the cock, who had been awakened by the noise, crowed with all his might.

At this the robber ran back as fast as he could to his comrades, and told the captain how a horrid witch had got into the house, and had spat at him and scratched his face with her long bony fingers; how a man with a knife in his hand had hidden himself behind the door, and stabbed him in the leg; how a black monster stood in the yard and struck him with a club, and how the devil had sat upon the top of the house and cried out, 'Throw the rascal up here!' After this the robbers never dared to go back to the house; but the musicians were so pleased with their quarters that they took up their abode there; and there they are, I dare say, at this very day.

The Twelve Brothers

Once upon a time there lived a king and queen very peacefully together; they had twelve children, all boys. Now the king said to the queen one day, 'If our thirteenth child should be a girl the twelve boys shall die, so that her riches may be the greater, and the kingdom fall to her alone.'

Then he caused twelve coffins to be made; and they were filled with shavings, and a little pillow laid in each, and they were brought and put in a locked-up room; and the king gave the key to the queen, and told her to say nothing about it to anyone.

But the mother sat the whole day sorrowing, so that her youngest son, who never left her, and to whom she had given the Bible name Benjamin, said to her, 'Dear mother, why are you so sad?'

'Dearest child,' answered she, 'I dare not tell you.'

But he let her have no peace until she went and unlocked the room, and showed him the twelve coffins with the shavings and the little pillows. Then she said, 'My dear Benjamin, your father has caused these coffins to be made for you and your eleven brothers, and if I bring a little girl into the world you are all to be put to death together and buried therein.'

And she wept as she spoke, and her little son comforted her and said, 'Weep not, dear mother, we will save ourselves and go far away.'

Then she answered, 'Yes, go with your eleven brothers out into the world, and let one of you always sit on the top of the highest tree that can be found, and keep watch upon the tower of this castle. If a little son is born I will put out a white flag, and then you may safely venture back again; but if it is a little daughter I will put out a red flag, and then flee away as fast as you can, and the dear God watch over you. Every night will I arise and pray for you – in winter that you may have a fire to warm yourselves by, and in summer that you may not languish in the heat.'

After that, when she had given her sons her blessing, they went away out into the wood. One after another kept watch, sitting on the highest oak tree, looking towards the tower. When eleven days had passed, and Benjamin's turn came, he saw a flag put out, but it was not white, but blood red, to warn them that they were to die.

When the brothers knew this they became angry, saying, 'Shall we suffer death because of a girl! We swear to be revenged; wherever we find a girl we will shed her blood.'

Then they went deeper into the wood and in the middle, where it was darkest, they found a little enchanted house, standing empty. Then they said, 'Here will we dwell; and you, Benjamin, the youngest and weakest, shall stay at home and keep house; we others will go abroad and purvey food.'

Then they went into the wood and caught hares, wild roes, birds, and pigeons, and whatever else is

639

good to eat, and brought them to Benjamin for him to cook and make ready to satisfy their hunger. So they lived together in the little house for ten years, and the time did not seem long.

By this time the queen's little daughter was growing up, she had a kind heart and a beautiful face, and a golden star on her forehead. Once when there was a great wash she saw among the clothes twelve shirts, and she asked her mother, 'Whose are these twelve shirts? they are too small to be my father's.'

Then the mother answered with a sore heart, 'Dear child, they belong to your twelve brothers.'

The little girl said, 'Where are my twelve brothers? I have never heard of them.'

And her mother answered, 'God only knows where they are wandering about in the world.' Then she led the little girl to the secret room and unlocked it, and showed her the twelve coffins with the shavings and the little pillows.

'These coffins,' said she, 'were intended for your twelve brothers, but they went away far from home when you were born,' and she related how everything had come to pass.

Then said the little girl, 'Dear mother, do not weep, I will go and seek my brothers.'

So she took the twelve shirts and went far and wide in the great forest. The day sped on, and in the evening she came to the enchanted house.

She went in and found a youth, who asked, 'Whence do you come, and what do you want?' and he marvelled at her beauty, her royal garments, and the star on her forehead.

Then she answered, 'I am a king's daughter, and I seek my twelve brothers, and I will go everywhere under the blue sky until I find them.' And she showed him the twelve shirts which belonged to them.

Then Benjamin saw that it must be his sister, and said, 'I am Benjamin, your youngest brother.'

And she began weeping for joy, and Benjamin also, and they kissed and cheered each other with great love.

After a while he said, 'Dear sister, there is still a hindrance; we have sworn that any maiden that we meet must die, as it was because of a maiden that we had to leave our kingdom.'

Then she said, 'I will willingly die, if so I may benefit my twelve brothers.'

'No,' answered he, 'you shall not die; sit down under this tub until the eleven brothers come, and I agree with them about it.'

She did so; and as night came on they returned from hunting, and supper was ready. And as they were sitting at table and eating, they asked, 'What news?'

And Benjamin said, 'Don't you know any?'

'No,' answered they.

So he said, 'You have been in the wood, and I have stayed at home, and yet I know more than you.'

'Tell us!' cried they.

He answered, 'Promise me that the first maiden we see shall not be put to death.'

'Yes, we promise,' cried they all, 'she shall have mercy; tell us now.'

Then he said, 'Our sister is here,' and lifted up the tub, and the king's daughter came forth in her royal garments with her golden star on her forehead, and she seemed so beautiful, delicate and sweet that they all rejoiced, and fell on her neck and kissed her, and loved her with all their hearts.

After this she remained with Benjamin in the house and helped him with the work. The others went forth into the woods to catch wild animals, does, birds and pigeons for food for them all, and their sister and Benjamin took care that all was made ready for them. She fetched the wood for cooking, and the vegetables, and watched the pots on the fire, so that supper was always ready when the others came in. She kept also great order in the house, and the beds were always beautifully white and clean and the brothers were contented, and lived in unity.

One day the two got ready a fine feast, and when they were all assembled they sat down and ate and drank, and were full of joy. Now there was a little garden belonging to the enchanted house, in which grew twelve lilies; the maiden, thinking to please her brothers, went out to gather the twelve flowers, meaning to give one to each as they sat at meat. But as she broke off the flowers, in the same moment the brothers were changed into twelve ravens and flew over the wood far away, and the house with the garden also disappeared.

So the poor maiden stood alone in the wild wood, and as she was looking around her she saw an old woman standing by her, who said, 'My child, what hast thou done! why couldst thou not leave the twelve flowers standing? they were thy twelve brothers, who are now changed to ravens for ever.'

The maiden said, weeping, 'Is there no means of setting them free?'

'No,' said the old woman, 'there is in the whole world no way but one, and that is difficult; thou canst not release them but by being dumb for seven years; thou must neither speak nor laugh; and wert thou to speak one single word, and it wanted but one hour of the seven years, all would be in vain, and thy brothers would perish because of that one word.'

Then the maiden said in her heart, 'I am quite sure that I can set my brothers free,' and went and sought a tall tree, climbed up, and sat there spinning, and never spoke or laughed. Now it happened that a king, who was hunting in the wood, had with him a large greyhound, who ran to the tree where the maiden was, sprang up at it and barked loudly. Up came the king and saw the beautiful princess with the golden star on her forehead, and he was so charmed with her beauty that he prayed her to become his wife. She gave no answer, only a little nod of her head. Then he himself climbed the tree and brought her down, set her on his horse and took her home. The wedding was held with great splendour and rejoicing, but the bride neither spoke nor laughed. After they had lived pleasantly together for a few years, the king's mother, who was a wicked woman, began to slander the young queen, and said to the king, 'She is only a low beggar-maid that you have taken to yourself; who knows what mean tricks she is playing? Even if she is really dumb and cannot speak she might at least laugh; not to laugh is the sign of a bad conscience.'

At first the king would believe nothing of it, but

the old woman talked so long, and suggested so many bad things, that he at last let himself be persuaded, and condemned the queen to death.

Now a great fire was kindled in the courtyard, and she was to be burned in it; and the king stood above at the window, and watched it all with weeping eyes, for he had held her very dear. And when she was already fast bound to the stake, and the fire was licking her garments with red tongues, the last moment of the seven years came to an end. Then a rushing sound was heard in the air, and twelve ravens came flying and sank downwards; and as they touched the earth they became her twelve brothers that she had lost. They rushed through the fire and quenched the flames, and set their dear sister free, kissing and consoling her. And now that her mouth was opened and that she might venture to speak, she told the king the reason of her dumbness, and why she had never laughed. The king rejoiced when he heard of her innocence, and they all lived together in happiness until their death.

But the wicked mother-in-law was very unhappy, and died miserably.

The Twelve Dancing Princesses

There was a king who had twelve beautiful daughters. They slept in twelve beds all in one room; and when they went to bed, the doors were shut and locked up; but every morning their shoes were found to be quite worn through as if they had been danced in all night; and yet nobody could find out how it happened, or where they had been.

Then the king made it known to all the land that if any man could discover the secret, and find out where it was that the princesses danced in the night, he should have the one he liked best for his wife, and should be king after his death; but whoever tried and did not succeed, after three days and nights should be put to death.

A king's son soon came. He was well entertained, and in the evening was taken to the chamber next to the one where the princesses lay in their twelve beds. There he was to sit and watch where they went to dance; and, in order that nothing might pass without his hearing it, the door of his chamber was left open. But the king's son soon fell asleep;

and when he awoke in the morning he found that the princesses had all been dancing, for the soles of their shoes were full of holes. The same thing happened the second and third night, so the king ordered his head to be cut off. After him came several others; but they had all the same luck, and all lost their lives in the same manner.

Now it chanced that an old soldier, who had been wounded in battle and could fight no longer, passed through the country where this king reigned, and as he was travelling through a wood, he met an old woman, who asked him where he was going. 'I hardly know where I am going, or what I had better do,' said the soldier; 'but I think I should like very well to find out where it is that the princesses dance, and then in time I might be a king.'

'Well,' said the old dame, 'that is no very hard task, only take care not to drink any of the wine which one of the princesses will bring to you in the evening; and as soon as she leaves you pretend to

be fast asleep.' Then she gave him a cloak, and said, 'As soon as you put that on you will become invisible, and you will then be able to follow the princesses wherever they go.'

When the soldier heard all this good counsel, he determined to try his luck: so he went to the king, and said he was willing to undertake the task. He was as well received as the others had been, and the king ordered fine royal robes to be given him; and when the evening came he was led to the outer chamber. Just as he was going to lie down, the eldest of the princesses brought him a cup of wine; but the soldier threw it all away secretly, taking care not to drink a drop. Then he laid himself down on his bed, and in a little while began to snore very loud as if he was fast asleep.

When the twelve princesses heard this they laughed heartily; and the eldest said, 'This fellow too might have done a wiser thing than lose his life in this way!'

Then they rose up and opened their drawers and boxes, and took out all their fine clothes, and dressed themselves at the glass, and skipped about as if they were eager to begin dancing. But the youngest said, 'I don't know why it is, but while you are all so happy I feel very uneasy; I am sure some mischance will befall us.'

'You simpleton,' said the eldest, 'you are always afraid; have you forgotten how many kings' sons have already watched in vain? And as for this soldier, even if I had not given him his sleeping draught, he would have slept soundly enough.'

When they were all ready, they went and looked at the soldier; but he snored on, and did not stir hand or foot, so they thought they were quite safe; and the eldest went up to her own bed and clapped her hands, and the bed sank into the floor and a trap-door flew open. The soldier saw them going down through the trap-door one after another, the eldest leading the way; and thinking he had no time to lose, he jumped up, put on the cloak which the old woman had given him, and followed them; but in the middle of the stairs he trod on the gown of the youngest princess, and she cried out to her sisters, 'All is not right; someone took hold of my gown.'

'You silly creature!' said the eldest, 'it is nothing but a nail in the wall.'

Then down they all went, and at the bottom they found themselves in a most delightful grove of trees; and the leaves were all of silver, and glittered and sparkled beautifully. The soldier wished to take away some token of the place; so he broke off a little branch, and there came a loud noise from the tree. Then the youngest daughter said again, 'I am sure all is not right – did not you hear that noise? That never happened before.'

But the eldest said, 'It is only our princes, who are shouting for joy at our approach.'

Then they came to another grove of trees, where all the leaves were of gold; and afterwards to a third, where the leaves were all glittering diamonds. And the soldier broke a branch from each; and every time there was a loud noise, which made the youngest sister tremble with fear; but the eldest still said, it was only the princes, who were crying for joy. So they went on till they came to a great lake; and at the side of the lake there lay twelve little boats with twelve handsome princes in them, who seemed to be waiting there for the princesses.

One of the princesses went into each boat, and the soldier stepped into the same boat as the youngest. As they were rowing over the lake, the prince who was in the boat with the youngest princess and the soldier said, 'I do not know why it is, but though I am rowing with all my might we do not get on so fast as usual, and I am quite tired: the boat seems very heavy today.'

'It is only the heat of the weather,' said the princess. 'I feel very warm too.'

On the other side of the lake stood a fine illuminated castle, from which came the merry music of horns and trumpets. There they all landed, and went into the castle, and each prince danced with his princess; and the soldier, who was all the time invisible, danced with them too; and when any of the princesses had a cup of wine set by her, he drank it all up, so that when she put the cup to her mouth it was empty. At this, too, the youngest sister was terribly frightened, but the eldest always silenced her. They danced on till three o'clock in the morning, and then all their shoes were worn out, so that they were obliged to leave off. The princes rowed them back again over the lake (but this time the soldier placed himself in the boat with the eldest princess); and on the opposite shore they took leave of each other, the princesses promising to come again the next night.

When they came to the stairs, the soldier ran on before the princesses, and laid himself down; and as the twelve sisters slowly came up, very much tired, they heard him snoring in his bed; so they said, 'Now all is quite safe;' then they undressed themselves, put away their fine clothes, pulled off their shoes, and went to bed. In the morning the soldier said nothing about what had happened, but determined to see more of this strange adventure, and went again the second and third night; and everything happened just as before; the princesses danced each time till their shoes were worn to pieces, and then returned home.

However, on the third night the soldier carried away one of the golden cups as a token of where he had been.

As soon as the time came when he was to declare the secret, he was taken before the king with the three branches and the golden cup; and the twelve princesses stood listening behind the door to hear what he would say. And when the king asked him,

'Where do my twelve daughters dance at night?' he answered, 'With twelve princes in a castle underground.' And then he told the king all that had happened, and showed him the three branches and the golden cup which he had brought with him. Then the king called for the princesses, and asked them whether what the soldier said was true; and when they saw that they were discovered, and that it was of no use to deny what had happened, they confessed it all. And the king asked the soldier which of them he would choose for his wife; and he answered, 'I am not very young, so I will have the eldest.' And they were married that very day, and the soldier was chosen to be the king's heir.

The Story of the Two Jealous Sisters

Once upon a time there reigned over Persia a sultan named Kosroushah, who from his boyhood had been fond of putting on a disguise and seeking adventures in all parts of the city, accompanied by one of his officers, disguised like himself. And no sooner was his father buried and the ceremonies over that marked his accession to the throne, than the young man hastened to throw off his robes of state, and calling to his grand-vizier to make ready likewise, stole out in the simple dress of a private citizen into the less known streets of the capital.

Passing down a lonely street, the sultan heard women's voices in loud discussion; and peeping through a crack in the door, he saw three sisters, sitting on a sofa in a large hall, talking in a very lively and earnest manner. Judging from the few words that reached his ear, they were each explaining what sort of man they wished to marry.

'I ask nothing better,' cried the eldest, 'than to have the sultan's baker for a husband. Think of being able to eat as much as one wanted of that delicious bread that is baked for his highness alone! Let us see if your wishes are as good as mine.'

'I,' replied the second sister, 'should be quite content with the sultan's head cook. What delicate stews I should feast upon! And, as I am persuaded that the sultan's bread is used all through the palace, I should have that into the bargain. You see, my dear sister, my taste is as good as yours.'

It was now the turn of the youngest sister, who was by far the most beautiful of the three, and had, besides, more sense than the other two. 'As for me,' she said, 'I should take a higher flight; and if we are to wish for husbands, nothing less than the sultan himself will do for me.'

The sultan was so much amused by the conversation he had overheard that he made up his mind

to gratify their wishes, and turning to the grand-vizier, he bade him note the house, and on the following morning to bring the ladies into his presence.

The grand-vizier fulfilled his commission, and hardly giving them time to change their dresses, desired the three sisters to follow him to the palace. Here they were presented one by one, and when they had bowed before the sultan, the sovereign abruptly put the question to them: 'Tell me, do you remember what you wished for last night, when you were making merry? Fear nothing, but answer me the truth.'

These words, which were so unexpected, threw the sisters into great confusion, their eyes fell, and the blushes of the youngest did not fail to make an impression on the heart of the sultan. All three remained silent, and he hastened to continue: 'Do not be afraid, I have not the slightest intention of giving you pain, and let me tell you at once that I know the wishes formed by each one. You,' he said, turning to the youngest, 'who desired to have me for a husband, shall be satisfied this very day. And you,' he added, addressing himself to the other two, 'shall be married at the same moment to my baker and to my chief cook.'

When the sultan had finished speaking the three sisters flung themselves at his feet, and the youngest faltered out, 'Oh, sire, since you know my foolish words, believe, I pray you, that they were only said in joke. I am unworthy of the honour you propose to do me, and I can only ask pardon for my boldness.'

The other sisters also tried to excuse themselves, but the sultan would hear nothing.

'No, no,' he said, 'my mind is made up. Your wishes shall be accomplished.'

So the three weddings were celebrated that same day, but with a great difference. That of the youngest was marked by all the magnificence that was customary at the marriage of the Shah of Persia, while the festivities attending the nuptials of the sultan's baker and his chief cook were only such as were suitable to their conditions.

This, though quite natural, was highly displeasing to the elder sisters, who fell into a passion of jealousy, which in the end caused a great deal of trouble and pain to several people. And the first time that they had the opportunity of speaking to each other, which was not till several days later at a public bath, they did not attempt to disguise their feelings.

'Can you possibly understand what the sultan saw in that little cat,' said one to the other, 'for him to be so fascinated by her?'

'He must be quite blind,' returned the wife of the chief cook. 'As for her looking a little younger than we do, what does that matter? You would have made a far better sultana than she.'

'Oh, I say nothing of myself,' replied the elder, 'and if the sultan had chosen you it would have been all very well; but it really grieves me that he should have selected a wretched little creature like that. However, I will be revenged on her somehow, and I beg you will give me your help in the matter, and to tell me anything that you can think of that is likely to mortify her.'

In order to carry out their wicked scheme the two sisters met constantly to talk over their ideas, though all the while they pretended to be as friendly as ever towards the sultana, who, on her part, invariably treated them with kindness. For a long time no plan occurred to the two plotters that seemed in the least likely to meet with success, but at length the expected birth of an heir gave them the chance for which they had been hoping.

They obtained permission of the sultan to take up their abode in the palace for some weeks, and never left their sister night or day. When at last a little boy, beautiful as the sun, was born, they laid him in his cradle and carried it down to a canal which passed through the grounds of the palace. Then, leaving it to its fate, they informed the sultan that instead of the son he had so fondly desired the sultana had given birth to a puppy. At

When at last a little boy, beautiful as the sun, was born, they laid
him in his cradle and carried it down to a canal

this dreadful news the sultan was so overcome with rage and grief that it was with great difficulty that the grand-vizier managed to save the sultana from his wrath.

Meanwhile the cradle continued to float peacefully along the canal till, on the outskirts of the royal gardens, it was suddenly perceived by the attendant, one of the highest and most respected officials in the kingdom.

'Go,' he said to a gardener who was working near, 'and get that cradle out for me.'

The gardener did as he was bid, and soon placed the cradle in the hands of the attendant.

The official was much astonished to see that the cradle, which he had supposed to be empty, contained a baby, which, young though it was, already gave promise of great beauty. Having no children himself, although he had been married some years, it at once occurred to him that here was a child which he could take and bring up as his own. And, bidding the man pick up the cradle and follow him, he turned towards home.

'My wife,' he exclaimed as he entered the room, 'heaven has denied us any children, but here is one that has been sent in their place. Send for a nurse, and I will do what is needful publicly to recognise it as my son.'

The wife accepted the baby with joy, and though the attendant saw quite well that it must have come from the royal palace, he did not think it was his business to enquire further into the mystery.

The following year another prince was born and set adrift, but happily for the baby, the attendant of the gardens again was walking by the canal, and carried it home as before.

The sultan, naturally enough, was still more furious the second time than the first, but when the same curious accident was repeated in the third year he could control himself no longer, and, to the great joy of the jealous sisters, commanded that the sultana should be executed. But the poor lady was so much beloved at court that not even the dread of sharing her fate could prevent the grand-vizier and the courtiers from throwing themselves at the sultan's feet and imploring him not to inflict so cruel a punishment for what, after all, was not her fault.

'Let her live,' entreated the grand-vizier, 'and banish her from your presence for the rest of her days. That in itself will be punishment enough.'

His first passion spent, the sultan had regained his self-command. 'Let her live then,' he said,

'since you have it so much at heart. But if I grant her life it shall only be on one condition, which shall make her daily pray for death. Let a box be built for her at the door of the principal mosque, and let the window of the box be always open. There she shall sit, in the coarsest clothes, and every Mussulman who enters the mosque shall spit in her face in passing. Anyone that refuses to obey shall be exposed to the same punishment himself. You, vizier, will see that my orders are carried out.'

The grand-vizier saw that it was useless to say more, and, full of triumph, the sisters watched the building of the box, and then listened to the jeers of the people at the helpless sultana sitting inside. But the poor lady bore herself with so much dignity and meekness that it was not long before she had won the sympathy of those that were best among the crowd.

But it is now time to return to the fate of the third baby, this time a princess. Like its brothers, it was found by the attendant of the gardens, and adopted by him and his wife, and all three were brought up with the greatest care and tenderness.

As the children grew older their beauty and air of distinction became more and more marked, and their manners had all the grace and ease that is proper to people of high birth. The princes had been named by their foster-father Bahman and Perviz, after two of the ancient kings of Persia, while the princess was called Parizade, or the child of the genii.

The attendant was careful to bring them up as befitted their real rank, and soon appointed a tutor to teach the young princes how to read and write. And the princess, determined not to be left behind, showed herself so anxious to learn with her brothers, that the attendant consented to her joining in their lessons, and it was not long before she knew as much as they did.

From that time all their studies were done in common. They had the best masters for the fine arts, geography, poetry, history and science, and even for sciences which are learned by few, and every branch seemed so easy to them that their teachers were astonished at the progress they made. The princess had a passion for music, and could sing and play upon all sorts of instruments; she could also ride and drive as well as her brothers, shoot with a bow and arrow, and throw a javelin with the same skill as they, and sometimes even better.

In order to set off these accomplishments, the attendant resolved that his foster-children should not be pent up any longer in the narrow borders of the palace gardens, where he had always lived, so he bought a splendid country house a few miles from the capital, surrounded by an immense park. This park he filled with wild beasts of various sorts, so that the princes and princess might hunt as much as they pleased.

When everything was ready, the attendant threw himself at the sultan's feet, and after referring to his age and his long service, begged his highness's permission to resign his post. This was granted by the sultan in a few gracious words, and he then enquired what reward he could give to his faithful servant. But the attendant declared that he wished for nothing except the continuance of his highness's favour, and prostrating himself once more, he retired from the sultan's presence.

Five or six months passed away in the pleasures of the country, when death attacked the attendant so suddenly that he had no time to reveal the secret of their birth to his adopted children, and as his wife had long been dead also, it seemed as if the princes and the princess would never know that they had been born to a higher station than the one they filled. Their sorrow for their father was very deep, and they lived quietly on in their new home, without feeling any desire to leave it for court gaieties or intrigues.

One day the princes as usual went out to hunt, but their sister remained alone in her apartments. While they were gone an old Mussulman devotee appeared at the door, and asked leave to enter, as it was the hour of prayer. The princess sent orders at once that the old woman was to be taken to the private oratory in the grounds, and when she had finished her prayers was to be shown the house and gardens, and then to be brought before her.

Although the old woman was very pious, she was not at all indifferent to the magnificence of all around her, which she seemed to understand as well as to admire, and when she had seen it all she was led by the servants before the princess, who was seated in a room which surpassed in splendour all the rest.

'My good woman,' said the princess pointing to a sofa, 'come and sit beside me. I am delighted at the opportunity of speaking for a few moments with so holy a person.' The old woman made some objections to so much honour being done her, but the princess refused to listen, and insisted that her guest should take the best seat, and as she thought she must be tired, ordered refreshments.

While the old woman was eating, the princess put several questions to her as to her mode of life, and the pious exercises she practised, and then enquired what she thought of the house now that she had seen it.

'Madam,' replied the pilgrim, 'one must be hard indeed to please to find any fault. It is beautiful, comfortable and well ordered, and it is impossible to imagine anything more lovely than the garden. But since you ask me, I must confess that it lacks three things to make it absolutely perfect.'

'And what can they be?' cried the princess. 'Only tell me, and I will lose no time in getting them.'

'The three things, madam,' replied the old woman, 'are, first, the Talking Bird, whose voice draws all other singing birds to it, to join in chorus. And second, the Singing Tree, where every leaf is a song that is never silent. And lastly the Golden Water, of which it is only needful to pour a single drop into a basin for it to shoot up into a fountain, which will never be exhausted, nor will the basin ever overflow.'

'Oh, how can I thank you,' cried the princess, 'for telling me of such treasures! But add, I pray you, to your goodness by further informing me where I can find them.'

'Madam,' replied the pilgrim, 'I should ill repay the hospitality you have shown me if I refused to answer your question. The three things of which I have spoken are all to be found in one place, on the borders of this kingdom, towards India. Your messenger has only to follow the road that passes by your house, for twenty days, and at the end of that time, he is to ask the first person he meets for the Talking Bird, the Singing Tree and the Golden Water.' She then rose, and bidding farewell to the princess, went her way.

The old woman had taken her departure so abruptly that the Princess Parizade did not perceive till she was really gone that the directions were hardly clear enough to enable the search to be successful. And she was still thinking of the subject, and how delightful it would be to possess such rarities, when the princes, her brothers, returned from the chase.

'What is the matter, my sister?' asked Prince Bahman; 'why are you so grave? Are you ill? Or has anything happened?'

Princess Parizade did not answer directly, but at length she raised her eyes, and replied that there was nothing wrong.

'But there must be something,' persisted Prince

Bahman, 'for you to have changed so much during the short time we have been absent. Hide nothing from us, I beseech you, unless you wish us to believe that the confidence we have always had in one another is now to cease.'

'When I said that it was nothing,' said the princess, moved by his words, 'I meant that it was nothing that affected you, although I admit that it is certainly of some importance to me. Like myself, you have always thought this house that our father built for us was perfect in every respect, but only today I have learned that three things are still lacking to complete it. These are the Talking Bird, the Singing Tree and the Golden Water.' After explaining the peculiar qualities of each, the princess continued: 'It was a Mussulman devotee who told me all this, and where they might all be found. Perhaps you will think that the house is beautiful enough as it is, and that we can do quite well without them; but in this I cannot agree with you, and I shall never be content until I have got them. So counsel me, I pray, whom to send on the undertaking.'

'My dear sister,' replied Prince Bahman, 'that you should care about the matter is quite enough, even if we took no interest in it ourselves. But we both feel with you, and I claim, as the elder, the right to make the first attempt, if you will tell me where I am to go, and what steps I am to take.'

Prince Perviz at first objected that, being the head of the family, his brother ought not to be allowed to expose himself to danger; but Prince Bahman would hear nothing, and retired to make the needful preparations for his journey.

The next morning Prince Bahman got up very early, and after bidding farewell to his brother and sister, mounted his horse. But just as he was about to touch it with his whip, he was stopped by a cry from the princess.

'Oh, perhaps after all you may never come back; one never can tell what accidents may happen. Give it up, I implore you, for I would a thousand times rather lose the Talking Bird and the Singing Tree and the Golden Water than that you should run into danger.'

'My dear sister,' answered the prince, 'accidents only happen to unlucky people, and I hope that I am not one of them. But as everything is uncertain, I promise you to be very careful. Take this knife,' he continued, handing her one that hung sheathed from his belt, 'and every now and then draw it out and look at it. As long as it keeps bright and clean

as it is today, you will know that I am living; but if the blade is spotted with blood, it will be a sign that I am dead, and you shall weep for me.'

So saying, Prince Bahman bade them farewell once more, and started on the high road, well mounted and fully armed. For twenty days he rode straight on, turning neither to the right hand nor to the left, till he found himself drawing near the frontiers of Persia. Seated under a tree by the wayside he noticed a hideous old man, with a long white moustache, and beard that almost fell to his feet. His nails had grown to an enormous length, and on his head he wore a huge hat, which served him for an umbrella.

Prince Bahman, who, remembering the directions of the old woman, had been since sunrise on the lookout for someone, recognised the old man at once to be a dervish. He dismounted from his horse, and bowed low before the holy man, saying by way of greeting, 'My father, may your days be long in the land, and may all your wishes be fulfilled!'

The dervish did his best to reply, but his moustache was so thick that his words were hardly intelligible, and the prince, perceiving what was the matter, took a pair of scissors from his saddle pockets, and requested permission to cut off some of the moustache, as he had a question of great importance to ask the dervish. The dervish made a sign that he might do as he liked, and when a few inches of his hair and beard had been pruned all round the prince assured the holy man that he would hardly believe how much younger he

The prince assured the holy man that he would hardly believe how much younger he looked

looked. The dervish smiled at his compliments, and thanked him for what he had done.

'Let me,' he said, 'show you my gratitude for making me more comfortable by telling me what I can do for you.'

'Gentle dervish,' replied Prince Bahman, 'I come from afar, and I seek the Talking Bird, the Singing Tree and the Golden Water. I know that they are to be found somewhere in these parts, but I am ignorant of the exact spot. Tell me, I pray you, if you can, so that I may not have travelled on a useless quest.' While he was speaking, the prince observed a change in the countenance of the dervish, who waited for some time before he made reply.

'My lord,' he said at last, 'I do know the road for which you ask, but your kindness and the friendship I have conceived for you make me loath to point it out.'

'But why?' enquired the prince. 'What danger can there be?'

'The very greatest danger,' answered the dervish. 'Other men, as brave as you, have ridden down this road, and have put to me that question. I did my best to turn them also from their purpose, but it was of no use. Not one of them would listen to my words, and not one of them came back. Be warned in time, and seek to go no farther.'

'I am grateful to you for your interest in me,' said Prince Bahman, 'and for the advice you have given, though I cannot follow it. But what dangers can there be in the adventure which courage and a good sword cannot meet?'

'And suppose,' answered the dervish, 'that your enemies are invisible, how then?'

'Nothing will make me give it up,' replied the prince, 'and for the last time I ask you to tell me where I am to go.'

When the dervish saw that the prince's mind was made up, he drew a ball from a bag that lay near him, and held it out. 'If it must be so,' he said, with a sigh, 'take this, and when you have mounted your horse throw the ball in front of you. It will roll on till it reaches the foot of a mountain, and when it stops you will stop also. You will then throw the bridle on your horse's neck without any fear of his straying, and will dismount. On each side you will see vast heaps of big black stones, and will hear a multitude of insulting voices, but pay no heed to them, and, above all, beware of ever turning your head. If you do, you will instantly become a black stone like the rest. For those stones are in reality

men like yourself, who have been on the same quest, and have failed, as I fear that you may fail also. If you manage to avoid this pitfall, and to reach the top of the mountain, you will find there the Talking Bird in a splendid cage, and you can ask of him where you are to seek the Singing Tree and the Golden Water. That is all I have to say. You know what you have to do, and what to avoid, but if you are wise you will think of it no more, but return whence you have come.'

The prince smilingly shook his head, and thanking the dervish once more, he sprang on his horse and threw the ball before him.

The ball rolled along the road so fast that Prince Bahman had much difficulty in keeping up with it, and it never relaxed its speed till the foot of the mountain was reached. Then it came to a sudden halt, and the prince at once got down and flung the bridle on his horse's neck. He paused for a moment and looked round him at the masses of black stones with which the sides of the mountain were covered, and then began resolutely to ascend. He had hardly gone four steps when he heard the sound of voices around him, although not another creature was in sight.

'Who is this imbecile?' cried some, 'stop him at once.' 'Kill him,' shrieked others. 'Help! robbers! murderers! help! help!' 'Oh, let him alone,' sneered another, and this was the most trying of all, 'he is such a beautiful young man; I am sure the bird and the cage must have been kept for him.'

At first the prince took no heed of all this clamour, but continued to press forward on his way. Unfortunately this conduct, instead of silencing the voices, only seemed to irritate them the more, and they arose with redoubled fury, in front as well as behind. After some time he grew bewildered, his knees began to tremble, and finding himself in the act of falling, he forgot altogether the advice of the dervish. He turned to fly down the mountain, and in one moment became a black stone.

As may be imagined, Prince Perviz and his sister were all this time in the greatest anxiety, and consulted the magic knife, not once but many times a day. Hitherto the blade had remained bright and spotless, but at the fatal hour on which Prince Bahman and his horse were changed into black stones, large drops of blood appeared on the surface. 'Ah! my beloved brother,' cried the princess in horror, throwing the knife from her, 'I shall never see you again, and it is I who have killed you. Fool that I was to listen to the voice of that temptress, who probably was not speaking the truth. What are the Talking Bird and the Singing Tree to me in comparison with you, passionately though I long for them!'

Prince Perviz's grief at his brother's loss was not less than that of Princess Parizade, but he did not waste his time on useless lamentations.

'My sister,' he said, 'why should you think the old woman was deceiving you about these treasures, and what would have been her object in doing so! No, no, our brother must have met his death by some accident, or want of precaution, and tomorrow I will start on the same quest.'

Terrified at the thought that she might lose her only remaining brother, the princess entreated him to give up his project, but he remained firm. Before setting out, however, he gave her a chaplet of a hundred pearls, and said, 'When I am absent, tell this over daily for me. But if you should find that the beads stick, so that they will not slip one after the other, you will know that my brother's fate has befallen me. Still, we must hope for better luck.'

Then he departed, and on the twentieth day of his journey fell in with the dervish on the same spot as Prince Bahman had met him, and began to question him as to the place where the Talking Bird, the Singing Tree and the Golden Water were to be found. As in the case of his brother, the dervish tried to make him give up his project, and even told him that only a few weeks since a young man, bearing a strong resemblance to himself, had passed that way, but had never come back again.

'That, holy dervish,' replied Prince Perviz, 'was my elder brother, who is now dead, though how he died I cannot say.'

'He is changed into a black stone,' answered the dervish, 'like all the rest who have gone on the same errand, and you will become one likewise if you are not more careful in following my directions.' Then he charged the prince, as he valued his life, to take no heed of the clamour of voices that would pursue him up the mountain, and handing him a ball from the bag, which still seemed to be half full, he sent him on his way.

When Prince Perviz reached the foot of the mountain he jumped from his horse, and paused for a moment to recall the instructions the dervish had given him. Then he strode boldly on, but had scarcely gone five or six paces when he was startled by a man's voice that seemed close to his ear, exclaiming: 'Stop, rash fellow, and let me punish your audacity.' This outrage entirely put the dervish's advice out of the prince's head. He drew his sword, and turned to avenge himself, but almost before he had realised that there was nobody there, he and his horse were two black stones.

Not a morning had passed since Prince Perviz had ridden away without Princess Parizade telling her beads, and at night she even hung them round her neck, so that if she woke she could assure herself at once of her brother's safety. She was in the very act of moving them through her fingers at the moment that the prince fell a victim to his impatience, and her heart sank when the first pearl remained fixed in its place. However she had long made up her mind what she would do in such a case, and the following morning the princess, disguised as a man, set out for the mountain.

As she had been accustomed to riding from her childhood, she managed to travel as many miles daily as her brothers had done, and it was, as before, on the twentieth day that she arrived at the place where the dervish was sitting. 'Good dervish,' she said politely, 'will you allow me to rest by you for a few moments, and perhaps you will be so kind as to tell me if you have ever heard of a Talking Bird, a Singing Tree and some Golden Water that are to be found somewhere near this?'

'Madam,' replied the dervish, 'for in spite of your manly dress your voice betrays you, I shall be proud to serve you in any way I can. But may I ask the purpose of your question?'

'Good dervish,' answered the princess, 'I have heard such glowing descriptions of these three things, that I cannot rest till I possess them.'

'Madam,' said the dervish, 'they are far more beautiful than any description, but you seem ignorant of all the difficulties that stand in your way, or you would hardly have undertaken such an adventure. Give it up, I pray you, and return home, and do not ask me to help you to a cruel death.'

'Holy father,' answered the princess, 'I come from afar, and I should be in despair if I turned back without having attained my object. You have spoken of difficulties; tell me, I entreat you, what they are, so that I may know if I can overcome them, or see if they are beyond my strength.'

So the dervish repeated his tale, and dwelt more firmly than before on the clamour of the voices, the horrors of the black stones, which were once living men, and the difficulties of climbing the mountain; and pointed out that the chief means of success was never to look behind till you had the cage in your grasp.

'As far as I can see,' said the princess, 'the first thing is not to mind the tumult of the voices that follow you till you reach the cage, and then never to look behind. As to this, I think I have enough self-control to look straight before me; but as it is quite possible that I might be frightened by the voices, as even the boldest men have been, I will stop up my ears with cotton, so that, let them make as much noise as they like, I shall hear nothing.'

'Madam,' cried the dervish, 'out of all the number who have asked me the way to the mountain, you are the first who has ever suggested such a means of escaping the danger! It is possible that you may succeed, but all the same, the risk is great.'

'Good dervish,' answered the princess, 'I feel in my heart that I shall succeed, and it only remains for me to ask you the way I am to go.'

Then the dervish said that it was useless to say more, and he gave her a ball, which she flung before her.

The first thing the princess did on arriving at the mountain was to stop her ears with cotton, and then, making up her mind which was the best way to go, she began her ascent. In spite of the cotton, some echoes of the voices reached her ears, but not so as to trouble her. Indeed, though they grew

The princess began her ascent

louder and more insulting the higher she climbed, the princess only laughed, and said to herself that she certainly would not let a few rough words stand between her and the goal. At last she perceived in the distance the cage and the bird, whose voice joined itself in tones of thunder to those of the rest: 'Return, return! never dare to come near me.'

At the sight of the bird, the princess hastened her steps, and without vexing herself at the noise which by this time had grown deafening, she walked straight up to the cage, and seizing it, she said: 'Now, my bird, I have got you, and I shall take good care that you do not escape.' As she spoke she took the cotton from her ears, for it was needed no longer.

'Brave lady,' answered the bird, 'do not blame me for having joined my voice to those who did their best to preserve my freedom. Although confined in a cage, I was content with my lot, but if I must become a slave, I could not wish for a nobler mistress than one who has shown so much constancy, and from this moment I swear to serve you faithfully. Someday you will put me to the proof, for I know who you are better than you do yourself. Meanwhile, tell me what I can do, and I will obey you.'

'Bird,' replied the princess, who was filled with a joy that seemed strange to herself when she thought that the bird had cost her the lives of both her brothers, 'bird, let me first thank you for your goodwill, and then let me ask you where the Golden Water is to be found.'

The bird described the place, which was not far distant, and the princess filled a small silver flask that she had brought with her for the purpose. She then returned to the cage, and said: 'Bird, there is still something else; where shall I find the Singing Tree?'

'Behind you, in that wood,' replied the bird, and the princess wandered through the wood, till a sound of the sweetest voices told her she had found what she sought. But the tree was tall and strong, and it was hopeless to think of uprooting it.

'You need not do that,' said the bird, when she had returned to ask counsel. 'Break off a twig, and plant it in your garden, and it will take root, and grow into a magnificent tree.'

When the Princess Parizade held in her hands the three wonders promised her by the old woman, she said to the bird: 'All that is not enough. It was owing to you that my brothers became black stones. I cannot tell them from the mass of others, but you must know, and point them out to me, I beg you, for I wish to carry them away.'

For some reason that the princess could not guess these words seemed to displease the bird, and he did not answer. The princess waited a moment, and then continued in severe tones, 'Have you forgotten that you yourself said that you are my slave to do my bidding, and also that your life is in my power?'

'No, I have not forgotten,' replied the bird, 'but what you ask is very difficult. However, I will do my best. If you look round,' he went on, 'you will see a pitcher standing near. Take it, and, as you go down the mountain, scatter a little of the water it contains over every black stone and you will soon find your two brothers.'

Princess Parizade took the pitcher, and, carrying with her besides the cage the twig and the flask, returned down the mountainside. At every black stone she stopped and sprinkled it with water, and as the water touched it the stone instantly became a man. When she suddenly saw her brothers before her her delight was mixed with astonishment.

'Why, what are you doing here?' she cried.

'We have been asleep,' they said.

'Yes,' returned the princess, 'but without me your sleep would probably have lasted till the day of judgment. Have you forgotten that you came here in search of the Talking Bird, the Singing Tree and the Golden Water, and had to pass the black stones that were heaped up along the road? Look round and see if there is one left. These gentlemen and yourselves and all your horses were changed into these stones, and I have delivered you by sprinkling you with the water from this pitcher. As I could not return home without you, even though I had gained the prizes on which I had set my heart, I forced the Talking Bird to tell me how to break the spell.'

On hearing these words Prince Bahman and Prince Perviz understood all they owed their sister, and the knights who stood by declared themselves her slaves and ready to carry out her wishes. But the princess, while thanking them for their politeness, explained that she wished for no company but that of her brothers, and that the rest were free to go where they would.

So saying the princess mounted her horse, and, declining to allow even Prince Bahman to carry the cage with the Talking Bird, she entrusted him with the branch of the Singing Tree, while Prince Perviz took care of the flask containing the Golden Water.

Then they rode away, followed by the knights and gentlemen, who begged to be permitted to escort them.

It had been the intention of the party to stop and tell their adventures to the dervish, but they found to their sorrow that he was dead, whether from old age, or whether from the feeling that his task was done, they never knew.

As they continued their road their numbers grew daily smaller, for the knights turned off one by one to their own homes, and only the brothers and sister finally drew up at the gate of the palace.

The princess carried the cage straight into the garden, and, as soon as the bird began to sing, nightingales, larks, thrushes, finches and all sorts of other birds mingled their voices in chorus. The branch she planted in a corner near the house, and in a few days it had grown into a great tree. As for the Golden Water, it was poured into a great marble basin specially prepared for it, and it swelled and bubbled and then shot up into the air in a fountain twenty feet high.

The fame of these wonders soon spread abroad, and people came from far and near to see and admire.

After a few days Prince Bahman and Prince Perviz fell back into their ordinary way of life, and passed most of their time hunting. One day it happened that the Sultan of Persia was also hunting in the same direction, and, not wishing to interfere with his sport, the young men, on hearing the noise of the hunt approaching, prepared to retire, but, as luck would have it, they turned into the very path down which the sultan was coming. They threw themselves from their horses and prostrated themselves to the earth, but the sultan was curious to see their faces, and commanded them to rise.

The princes stood up respectfully, but quite at their ease, and the sultan looked at them for a few moments without speaking, then he asked who they were and where they lived.

'Sire,' replied Prince Bahman, 'we are sons of your highness's late attendant of the gardens, and we live in a house that he built a short time before his death, waiting till an occasion should offer itself to serve your highness.'

'You seem fond of hunting,' answered the sultan.

'Sire,' replied Prince Bahman, 'it is our usual exercise, and one that should be neglected by no man who expects to comply with the ancient customs of the kingdom and bear arms.'

The sultan was delighted with this remark, and said at once, 'In that case I shall take great pleasure in watching you. Come, choose what sort of beasts you would like to hunt.'

The princes jumped on their horses and followed the sultan at a little distance. They had not gone very far before they saw a number of wild animals appear at once, and Prince Bahman started to give chase to a lion and Prince Perviz to a bear. Both used their javelins with such skill that, directly they arrived within striking range, the lion and the bear fell, pierced through and through. Then Prince Perviz pursued a lion and Prince Bahman a bear, and in a very few minutes they, too, lay dead. As they were making ready for a third assault the sultan interfered, and, sending one of his officials to summon them, he said smiling, 'If I let you go on, there will soon be no beasts left to hunt. Besides, your courage and manners have so won my heart that I will not have you expose yourselves to further danger. I am convinced that some day or other I shall find you useful as well as agreeable.'

He then gave them a warm invitation to stay with him altogether, but with many thanks for the honour done them, they begged to be excused, and to be suffered to remain at home.

The sultan, who was not accustomed to see his offers rejected, enquired their reasons, and Prince Bahman explained that they did not wish to leave their sister, and were accustomed to do nothing without consulting all three together.

'Ask her advice, then,' replied the sultan, 'and tomorrow come and hunt with me, and give me your answer.'

The two princes returned home, but their adventure made so little impression on them that they quite forgot to speak to their sister on the subject. The next morning when they went to hunt they met the sultan in the same place, and he enquired what advice their sister had given. The young men looked at each other and blushed. At last Prince Bahman said, 'Sire, we must throw ourselves on your highness's mercy. Neither my brother nor myself remembered anything about it.'

'Then be sure you do not forget today,' answered the sultan, 'and bring me back your reply tomorrow.'

When, however, the same thing happened a second time, they feared that the sultan might be angry with them for their carelessness. But he took it in good part, and, drawing three little golden balls from his purse, he held them out to Prince Bahman, saying, 'Put these in your bosom and you will not forget a third time, for when you remove your girdle tonight the noise they will make in falling will remind you of my wishes.'

It all happened as the sultan had foreseen, and the two brothers appeared in their sister's apartments just as she was in the act of stepping into bed, and told their tale.

The Princess Parizade was much disturbed at the news, and did not conceal her feelings. 'Your meeting with the sultan is very honourable to you,' she said, 'and will, I dare say, be of service to you, but it places me in a very awkward position. It is on my account, I know, that you have resisted the sultan's wishes, and I am very grateful to you for it. But kings do not like to have their offers refused, and in time he would bear a grudge against you, which would render me very unhappy. Consult the Talking Bird, who is wise and far-seeing, and let me hear what he says.'

So the bird was sent for and the case laid before him.

'The princes must on no account refuse the sultan's proposal,' said he, 'and they must even invite him to come and see your house.'

'But, bird,' objected the princess, 'you know how dearly we love each other; will not all this spoil our friendship?'

'Not at all,' replied the bird, 'it will make it all the closer.'

'Then the sultan will have to see me,' said the princess.

The bird answered that it was necessary that he should see her, and everything would turn out for the best.

The following morning, when the sultan enquired if they had spoken to their sister and what advice she had given them, Prince Bahman replied that they were ready to agree to his highness's wishes, and that their sister had reproved them for their hesitation about the matter. The sultan received their excuses with great kindness, and told them that he was sure they would be equally faithful to him, and kept them by his side for the rest of the day, to the vexation of the grand-vizier and the rest of the court.

When the procession entered in this order the gates of the capital, the eyes of the people who crowded the streets were fixed on the two young men, strangers to everyone.

'Oh, if only the sultan had had sons like that!' they murmured, 'they look so distinguished and are about the same age that his sons would have been!'

The sultan commanded that splendid apartments should be prepared for the two brothers, and even insisted that they should sit at table with him. During dinner he led the conversation to various scientific subjects, and also to history, of which he was especially fond, but whatever topic they might be discussing he found that the views of the young men were always worth listening to. 'If they were my own sons,' he said to himself, 'they could not be better educated!' and aloud he complimented them on their learning and taste for knowledge.

At the end of the evening the princes once more prostrated themselves before the throne and asked leave to return home; and then, encouraged by the gracious words of farewell uttered by the sultan, Prince Bahman said: 'Sire, may we dare to take the liberty of asking whether you would do us and our sister the honour of resting for a few minutes at our house the first time the hunt passes that way?'

'With the utmost pleasure,' replied the sultan; 'and as I am all impatience to see the sister of such accomplished young men, you may expect me the day after tomorrow.'

The princess was of course most anxious to entertain the sultan in a fitting way, but as she had no experience in court customs she ran to the Talking Bird, and begged he would advise her as to what dishes should be served.

'My dear mistress,' replied the bird, 'your cooks are very good and you can safely leave all to them, except that you must be careful to have a dish of cucumbers, stuffed with pearl sauce, served with the first course.'

'Cucumbers stuffed with pearls!' exclaimed the princess. 'Why, bird, whoever heard of such a dish? The sultan will expect a dinner he can eat, and not one he can only admire! Besides, if I were to use all the pearls I possess, they would not be half enough.'

'Mistress,' replied the bird, 'do what I tell you and nothing but good will come of it. And as to the pearls, if you go at dawn tomorrow and dig at the foot of the first tree in the park, on the right hand, you will find as many as you want.'

The princess had faith in the bird, who generally proved to be right, and taking the gardener with her early next morning followed out his directions carefully. After digging for some time they came upon a golden box fastened with little clasps.

These were easily undone, and the box was found to be full of pearls, not very large ones, but well shaped and of a good colour. So leaving the gardener to fill up the hole he had made under the tree, the princess took up the box and returned to the house.

The two princes had seen her go out, and had wondered what could have made her rise so early. Full of curiosity they got up and dressed, and met their sister as she was returning with the box under her arm.

'What have you been doing?' they asked. 'Did the gardener come to tell you he had found a treasure?'

'On the contrary,' replied the princess, 'it is I who have found one,' and opening the box she showed her astonished brothers the pearls inside. Then, on the way back to the palace, she told them of her consultation with the bird, and the advice it had given her. All three tried to guess the meaning of the singular counsel, but they were forced at last to admit the explanation was beyond them, and they must be content blindly to obey.

The first thing the princess did on entering the palace was to send for the head cook and to order the repast for the sultan. When she had finished she suddenly added, 'Besides the dishes I have mentioned there is one that you must prepare expressly for the sultan, and that no one must touch but yourself. It consists of a stuffed cucumber, and the stuffing is to be made of these pearls.'

The head cook, who had never in all his experience heard of such a dish, stepped back in amazement.

'You think I am mad,' answered the princess, who perceived what was in his mind. 'But I know quite well what I am doing. Go, and do your best, and take the pearls with you.'

The next morning the princes started for the forest, and were soon joined by the sultan. The hunt began and continued till midday, when the heat became so great that they were obliged to leave off. Then, as arranged, they turned their horses' heads towards the palace, and while Prince Bahman remained by the side of the sultan, Prince Perviz rode on to warn his sister of their approach.

The moment his highness entered the courtyard, the princess flung herself at his feet, but he bent and raised her, and gazed at her for some time, struck with her grace and beauty, and also with the indefinable air of courts that seemed to hang round this country girl. 'They are all worthy one of the other,' he said to himself, 'and I am not surprised that they think so much of her opinions. I must know more of them.'

By this time the princess had recovered from the first embarrassment of meeting, and proceeded to make her speech of welcome.

'This is only a simple country house, sire,' she said, 'suitable to people like ourselves, who live a quiet life. It cannot compare with the great city mansions, much less, of course, with the smallest of the sultan's palaces.'

'I cannot quite agree with you,' he replied; 'even the little that I have seen I admire greatly, and I will reserve my judgement until you have shown me the whole.'

The princess then led the way from room to room, and the sultan examined everything carefully. 'Do you call this a simple country house?' he said at last. 'Why, if every country house was like this, the towns would soon be deserted. I am no longer astonished that you do not wish to leave it. Let us go into the gardens, which I am sure are no less beautiful than the rooms.'

A small door opened straight into the garden, and the first object that met the sultan's eyes was the Golden Water.

'What lovely coloured water!' he exclaimed; 'where is the spring, and how do you make the fountain rise so high? I do not believe there is anything like it in the world.' He went forward to examine it, and when he had satisfied his curiosity, the princess conducted him towards the Singing Tree.

As they drew near, the sultan was startled by the sound of strange voices, but could see nothing. 'Where have you hidden your musicians?' he asked the princess; 'are they up in the air, or under the earth? Surely the owners of such charming voices ought not to conceal themselves!'

'Sire,' answered the princess, 'the voices all come from the tree which is straight in front of us; and if you will deign to advance a few steps, you will see that they become clearer.'

The sultan did as he was told, and was so wrapped in delight at what he heard that he stood some time in silence.

'Tell me, madam, I pray you,' he said at last, 'how this marvellous tree came into your garden? It must have been brought from a great distance, or else, fond as I am of all curiosities, I could not have missed hearing of it! What is its name?'

'The only name it has, sire,' replied she, 'is the Singing Tree, and it is not a native of this country. Its history is mixed up with those of the Golden Water and the Talking Bird, which you have not yet seen. If your highness wishes I will tell you the whole story, when you have recovered from your fatigue.'

'Indeed, madam,' returned he, 'you show me so many wonders that it is impossible to feel any fatigue. Let us go once more and look at the Golden Water; and I am dying to see the Talking Bird.'

The sultan could hardly tear himself away from the Golden Water, which puzzled him more and more. 'You say,' he observed to the princess, 'that this water does not come from any spring, neither is brought by pipes. All I understand is that neither it nor the Singing Tree is a native of this country.'

'It is as you say, sire,' answered the princess, 'and if you examine the basin, you will see that it is all in one piece, and therefore the water could not have been brought through it. What is more astonishing is, that I only emptied a small flaskful into the basin and it increased to the quantity you now see.'

'Well, I will look at it no more today,' said the sultan. 'Take me to the Talking Bird.'

On approaching the house, the sultan noticed a vast quantity of birds, whose voices filled the air, and he enquired why they were so much more

'Tell me, madam, I pray you,' he said at last, 'how this marvellous tree came into your garden?'

numerous here than in any other part of the garden.

'Sire,' answered the princess, 'do you see that cage hanging in one of the windows of the saloon? That is the Talking Bird, whose voice you can hear above them all, even above that of the nightingale. And the birds crowd to this spot, to add their songs to his.'

The sultan stepped through the window, but the bird took no notice, continuing his song as before.

'My slave,' said the princess, 'this is the sultan; make him a pretty speech.'

The bird stopped singing at once, and all the other birds stopped too.

'The sultan is welcome,' he said. 'I wish him long life and all prosperity.'

'I thank you, good bird,' answered the sultan, seating himself before the repast, which was spread at a table near the window, 'and I am enchanted to see in you the sultan and king of the birds.'

The sultan, noticing that his favourite dish of cucumber was placed before him, proceeded to help himself to it, and was amazed to find that the stuffing was of pearls. 'A novelty, indeed!' cried he, 'but I do not understand the reason of it; one cannot eat pearls!'

'Sire,' replied the bird, before either the princes or the princess could speak, 'surely your highness cannot be so surprised at beholding a cucumber stuffed with pearls, when you believed without any difficulty that the sultana had presented you, instead of children, with a dog, a cat and a log of wood.'

'I believed it,' answered the sultan, 'because the women attending on her told me so.'

'The women, sire,' said the bird, 'were the sisters of the sultana, who were devoured with jealousy at the honour you had done her, and in order to revenge themselves invented this story. Have them examined, and they will confess their crime. These are your children, who were saved from death by the attendant of your gardens, and brought up by him as if they were his own.'

Like a flash the truth came to the mind of the sultan. 'Bird,' he cried, 'my heart tells me that what you say is true. My children,' he added, 'let me embrace you, and embrace each other, not only as brothers and sister, but as having in you the blood royal of Persia which could flow in no nobler veins.'

When the first moments of emotion were over, the sultan hastened to finish his repast, and then turning to his children he exclaimed: 'Today you have made acquaintance with your father. Tomorrow I will bring you the sultana your mother. Be ready to receive her.'

The sultan then mounted his horse and rode quickly back to the capital. Without an instant's delay he sent for the grand-vizier, and ordered him to seize and question the sultana's sisters that very day. This was done. They were confronted with each other and proved guilty, and were executed in less than an hour.

But the sultan did not wait to hear that his orders had been carried out before going on foot, followed by his whole court, to the door of the great mosque, and drawing the sultana with his own hand out of the narrow prison where she had spent so many years, 'Madam,' he cried, embracing her with tears in his eyes, 'I have come to ask your pardon for the injustice I have done you, and to repair it as far as I may. I have already begun by punishing the authors of this abominable crime, and I hope you will forgive me when I introduce you to our children, who are the most charming and accomplished creatures in the whole world. Come with me, and take back your position and all the honour that is due to you.'

This speech was delivered in the presence of a vast multitude of people, who had gathered from all parts on the first hint of what was happening, and the news was passed from mouth to mouth in a few seconds.

Early next day the sultan and sultana, dressed in robes of state and followed by all the court, set out for the country house of their children. Here the sultan presented them to the sultana one by one, and for some time there was nothing but embraces and tears and tender words. Then they ate of the magnificent dinner which had been prepared for them, and after they were all refreshed they went into the garden, where the sultan pointed out to his wife the Golden Water and the Singing Tree. As to the Talking Bird, she had already made acquaintance with him.

In the evening they rode together back to the capital, the princes on each side of their father, and the princess with her mother. Long before they reached the gates the way was lined with people, and the air filled with shouts of welcome, with which were mingled the songs of the Talking Bird, sitting in its cage on the lap of the princess, and of the birds who followed it.

And in this manner they came back to their father's palace.

The Ugly Duckling

The country was lovely just then; it was summer. The heat was golden and the oats still green; the hay was stacked in the rich low-lying meadows, where the stork was marching about on his long red legs, chattering Egyptian, the language his mother had taught him.

Round about field and meadow lay great woods, in the midst of which were deep lakes. Yes, the country certainly was delicious. In the sunniest spot stood an old mansion surrounded by a deep moat, and great dock leaves grew from the walls of the house right down to the water's edge; some of them were so tall that a small child could stand upright under them. In amongst the leaves it was as secluded as in the depths of a forest, and there a duck was sitting on her nest. Her little ducklings were just about to be hatched, but she was nearly tired of sitting, for it had lasted such a long time. Moreover, she had very few visitors, as the other ducks liked swimming about in the moat better than waddling up to sit under the dock leaves and gossip with her.

At last one egg after another began to crack. 'Cheep cheep!' they said. All the chicks had come to life, and were poking their heads out.

'Quack! quack!' said the duck; and then they all quacked their hardest, and looked about them on all sides among the green leaves; their mother allowed them to look as much as they liked, for green is good for the eyes.

'How big the world is to be sure!' said all the young ones; for they certainly had ever so much more room to move about now than when they were inside the eggshell.

'Do you imagine this is the whole world?' said the mother. 'It stretches a long way on the other side of the garden, right into the parson's field: but I have never been as far as that! I suppose you are all here now?' and she got up. 'No! I declare I have not got you all yet! The biggest egg is still there; how long is it going to last?' and then she settled herself on the nest again.

'Well, how are you getting on?' said an old duck who had come to pay her a visit

'This one egg is taking such a long time,' answered the sitting duck, 'the shell will not crack; but now you must look at the others; they are the finest ducklings I have ever seen! they are all exactly like their father, the rascal! he never comes to see me.'

'Let me look at the egg which won't crack,' said the old duck. 'You may be sure that it is a turkey's egg! I was cheated like that once, and I had no end of trouble and worry with the creatures, for I may tell you that they are afraid of the water. I could not get them into it. I quacked and snapped at them, but it was no good. Let me see the egg! Yes, it is a turkey's egg! You just leave it alone and teach the other children to swim.'

'I will sit on it a little longer. I have sat so long already, that I may as well go on till the Midsummer Fair comes round.'

'Please yourself,' said the old duck, and she went away.

At last the big egg cracked. 'Cheep, cheep!' said the young one and tumbled out; how big and ugly he was! The duck looked at him.

'That is a monstrous big duckling,' she said; 'none of the others looked like that; can he be a turkey chick? well we shall soon find that out; into the water he shall go, if I have to kick him in myself.'

Next day was gloriously fine, and the sun shone on all the green dock leaves. The mother duck with her

660

whole family went down to the moat. Splash, into the water she sprang. 'Quack, quack!' she said, and one duckling plumped in after the other. The water dashed over their heads, but they came up again and floated beautifully; their legs went of themselves, and they were all there; even the big ugly grey one swam about with them.

'No, that is no turkey,' she said; 'see how beautifully he uses his legs and how erect he holds himself: he is my own chick! after all, he is not so bad when you come to look at him properly. Quack, quack! Now come with me and I will take you into the world, and introduce you to the duckyard; but keep close to me all the time, so that no one may tread upon you, and beware of the cat!'

Then they went into the duckyard. There was a fearful uproar going on, for two broods were fighting for the head of an eel, and in the end the cat captured it.

'That's how things go in this world,' said the mother duck, and she licked her bill for she had wanted the eel's head herself.

'Use your legs,' said she; 'mind you quack properly, and bend your necks to the old duck over there! She is the grandest of them all; she has Spanish blood in her veins and that accounts for her size; and, do you see? she has a red rag round her leg; that is a wonderfully fine thing, the most extraordinary mark of distinction any duck can have. It shows clearly that she is not to be parted with, and that she is worthy of recognition both by beasts and men! Quack now! don't turn your toes in, a well-brought-up duckling keeps his legs wide apart just like father and mother; that's it, now bend your necks, and say quack!'

They did as they were bid, but the other ducks round about looked at them and said, quite loud: 'Just look there! now we are to have that tribe! just as if there were not enough of us already, and, oh dear! how ugly that duckling is, we won't stand

him!' and a duck flew at him at once and bit him in the neck.

'Let him be,' said the mother; 'he is doing no harm.'

'Very likely not, but he is so ungainly and queer,' said the biter; 'he must be whacked.'

'They are handsome children mother has,' said the old duck with the rag round her leg; 'all good-looking except this one, and he is not a good specimen; it's a pity you can't make him over again.'

'That can't be done, your grace,' said the mother duck; 'he is not handsome, but he is a thorough good creature, and he swims as beautifully as any of the others; nay, I think I might venture even to add that I think he will improve as he goes on, or perhaps in time he may grow smaller! He was too long in the egg, and so he has not come out with a very good figure.' And then she patted his neck and stroked his down. 'Besides he is a drake,' said she; 'so it does not matter so much. I believe he will be very strong, and I don't doubt but he will make his way in the world.'

'The other ducklings are very pretty,' said the old duck. 'Now make yourselves quite at home, and if you find the head of an eel you may bring it to me!'

After that they felt quite at home. But the poor duckling who had been the last to come out of the shell, and who was so ugly, was bitten, pushed about, and made fun of both by the ducks and the hens. 'He is too big,' they all said; and the turkey-cock, who was born with his spurs on, and therefore thought himself quite an emperor, puffed himself up like a vessel in full sail, made for him, and gobbled and gobbled till he became quite red in the face. The poor duckling was at his wit's end, and did not know which way to turn; he was in despair because he was so ugly, and the butt of the whole duckyard.

So the first day passed, and afterwards matters grew worse and worse. The poor duckling was chased and hustled by all of them; even his brothers and sisters ill-used him and they were always saying, 'If only the cat would get hold of you, you hideous object!' Even his mother said, 'I wish to goodness you were miles away.' The ducks bit him, the hens pecked him and the girl who fed them kicked him aside.

Then he ran off and flew right over the hedge, where the little birds flew up into the air in a fright.

'That is because I am so ugly,' thought the poor duckling, shutting his eyes, but he ran on all the same. Then he came to a great marsh where the

wild ducks lived; he was so tired and miserable that he stayed there the whole night.

In the morning the wild ducks flew up to inspect their new comrade.

'What sort of a creature are you?' they enquired, as the duckling turned from side to side and greeted them as well as he could. 'You are frightfully ugly,' said the wild ducks; 'but that does not matter to us, so long as you do not marry into our family!' Poor fellow! he had no thought of marriage, all he wanted was permission to lie among the rushes, and to drink a little of the marsh water.

He stayed there two whole days, then two wild geese came, or rather two wild ganders; they were not long out of the shell, and therefore rather pert.

'I say, comrade,' they said, 'you are so ugly that we have taken quite a fancy to you; will you join us and be a bird of passage? There is another marsh close by, and there are some charming wild geese there; all sweet young ladies, who can say quack! You are ugly enough to make your fortune among them.' Just at that moment, bang! bang! was heard up above, and both the wild geese fell dead among the reeds, and the water turned blood red. Bang! bang! went the guns, and whole flocks of wild geese flew up from the rushes and the shot peppered among them again.

There was a grand shooting party, and the sports-men lay hidden round the marsh; some even sat on the branches of the trees which overhung the water; the blue smoke rose like clouds among the dark trees and swept over the pool.

The water-dogs wandered about in the swamp, splash! splash! The rushes and reeds bent beneath their tread on all sides. It was terribly alarming to the poor duckling. He twisted his head round to get it under his wing and just at that moment a frightful big dog appeared close beside him; his tongue hung right out of his mouth and his eyes glared wickedly. He opened his great chasm of a mouth close to the duckling, showed his sharp teeth – and – splash – went on without touching him.

'Oh, thank heaven!' sighed the duckling. 'I am so ugly that even the dog won't bite me!'

Then he lay quite still while the shot whistled among the bushes, and bang after bang rent the air. It only became quiet late in the day, but even then the poor duckling did not dare to get up; he waited several hours more before he looked about and then he hurried away from the marsh as fast as he could. He ran across fields and meadows, and there was such a wind that he had hard work to make his way.

Towards night he reached a poor little cottage; it was such a miserable hovel that it could not make up its mind which way to fall even, and so it remained standing. The wind whistled so fiercely round the duckling that he had to sit on his tail to resist it, and it blew harder and harder; then he saw that the door had fallen off one hinge and hung so crookedly that he could creep into the house through the crack and by this means he made his way into the room. An old woman lived there with her cat and her hen. The cat, which she called Sonnie, could arch his back, purr, and give off electric sparks, that is to say if you stroked his fur the wrong way. The hen had quite tiny short legs and so she was called Chuckie-Low-Legs. She laid good eggs, and the old woman was as fond of her as if she had been her own child.

In the morning the strange duckling was dis-covered immediately, and the cat began to purr and the hen to cluck.

'What on earth is that!' said the old woman looking round, but her sight was not good and she thought the duckling was a fat duck which had escaped. 'This is a capital find,' said she; 'now I shall have duck's eggs if only it is not a drake! we must find out about that!'

So she took the duckling on trial for three weeks, but no eggs made their appearance. The cat was the master of the house and the hen the mistress, and they always spoke of 'we and the world', for they thought that they represented the half of the world, and that quite the better half.

The duckling thought there might be two opinions on the subject, but the cat would not hear of it.

'Can you lay eggs?' she asked.

'No!'

'Will you have the goodness to hold your tongue then!'

And the cat said, 'Can you arch your back, purr or give off sparks?'

'No.'

'Then you had better keep your opinions to yourself when people of sense are speaking!'

The duckling sat in the corner nursing his ill-humour; then he began to think of the fresh air and the sunshine, an uncontrollable longing seized him to float on the water, and at last he could not help telling the hen about it.

'What on earth possesses you?' she asked; 'you have nothing to do, that is why you get these freakish ideas into your head. Lay some eggs or take to purring, and you will get over it.'

'But it is so delicious to float on the water,' said the duckling; 'so delicious to feel it rushing over your head when you dive to the bottom.'

'That would be a fine amusement,' said the hen. 'I think you have gone mad. Ask the cat about it, he is the wisest creature I know; ask him if he is fond of floating on the water or diving under it. I say nothing about myself. Ask our mistress yourself, the old woman, there is no one in the world cleverer than she is. Do you suppose she has any desire to float on the water, or to dive underneath it?'

'You do not understand me,' said the duckling.

'Well, if we don't understand you, who should? I suppose you don't consider yourself cleverer than the cat or the old woman, not to mention me. Don't make a fool of yourself, child, and thank your stars for all the good we have done you! Have you not lived in this warm room, and in such society that you might have learnt something? But you are an idiot, and there is no pleasure in associating with you. You may believe me – I mean you well, I tell you home truths, and there is no surer way than that of knowing who are one's friends. You just see about laying some eggs, or learn to purr or to emit sparks.'

'I think I will go out into the wide world,' said the duckling.

'Oh, do so by all means,' said the hen.

So away went the duckling; he floated on the water and ducked underneath it, but he was looked at askance by every living creature for his ugliness. Now the autumn came on, the leaves in the woods turned yellow and brown; the wind took hold of them, and they danced about. The sky looked very cold, and the clouds hung heavy with snow and hail. A raven stood on the fence and croaked Caw! Caw! from sheer cold; it made one shiver only to think of it; the poor duckling certainly was in a bad case.

One evening, the sun was just setting in wintry splendour, when a flock of beautiful large birds appeared out of the bushes; the duckling had never seen anything so beautiful. They were dazzlingly white with long waving necks; they were swans, and uttering a peculiar cry they spread out their magnificent broad wings and flew away from the cold regions to warmer lands and open seas. They mounted so high, so very high, and the ugly little duckling became strangely uneasy; he circled round and round in the water like a wheel, craning his neck up into the air after them. Then he uttered a shriek so piercing and so strange, that he was quite frightened by it himself. Oh, he could not forget those beautiful birds, those happy birds, and as soon as they were out of sight he ducked right down to the bottom, and when he came up again he was quite beside himself. He did not know what the birds were, or whither they flew, but all the same he was more drawn towards them than he had ever been by any creatures before. He did not envy them in the least; how could it occur to him even to wish to be such a marvel of beauty? He would have been thankful if only the ducks would have tolerated him among them – the poor ugly creature!

The winter was so bitterly cold that the duckling was obliged to swim about in the water to keep it from freezing, but every night the hole in which he swam got smaller and smaller. Then it froze so hard that the surface ice cracked, and the duckling had to use his legs all the time, so that the ice should not close in round him; at last he was so weary that he could move no more, and he was frozen fast into the ice.

Early in the morning a peasant came along and saw him; he went out on to the ice and hammered a hole in it with his heavy wooden shoe, and carried the duckling home to his wife. There it soon revived. The children wanted to play with it, but the duckling thought they were going to ill-use him, and rushed in his fright into the milk pan, and the milk spurted out all over the room. The woman shrieked and threw up her hands, and in its confusion it flew into the butter cask, and down into the meal tub and out again. Just imagine what it looked like by this time! The woman screamed and tried to hit it with the tongs, and the children tumbled over one another in trying to catch it, and they screamed with laughter; by good luck the door stood open, and the duckling flew out among the bushes and the new-fallen snow – and it lay there thoroughly exhausted.

It would be too sad to mention all the privation and misery it had to go through during that hard winter. When the sun began to shine warmly again, the duckling was in the marsh, lying among the rushes; the larks were singing and the beautiful spring had come.

Then all at once it raised its wings and they flapped with much greater strength than before, and bore him off vigorously. Before he knew where he was, he found himself in a large garden where the apple trees were in full blossom, and the air was scented with lilacs, the long branches of which overhung the indented shores of the lake! Oh! the spring freshness was so delicious!

Just in front of him he saw three beautiful white swans advancing towards him from a thicket; with rustling feathers they swam lightly over the water. The duckling recognised the majestic birds, and he was overcome by a strange melancholy.

'I will fly to them, the royal birds, and they will hack me to pieces, because I, who am so ugly, venture to approach them! But it won't matter; better be killed by them than be snapped at by the ducks, pecked by the hens or spurned by the henwife, or suffer so much misery in the winter.'

So he flew into the water and swam towards the stately swans; they saw him and darted towards him with ruffled feathers.

'Kill me, oh, kill me!' said the poor creature, and

bowing his head towards the water, he awaited his death. But what did he see reflected in the transparent water?

He saw below him his own image, but he was no longer a clumsy dark grey bird, ugly and ungainly, he was himself a swan! It does not matter in the least having been born in a duckyard, if only you come out of a swan's egg!

He felt quite glad of all the misery and tribulation he had gone through; he was the better able to appreciate his good fortune now, and all the beauty which greeted him. The big swans swam round and round him, and stroked him with their bills.

Some little children came into the garden with corn and pieces of bread, which they threw into the water; and the smallest one cried out: 'There is a new one!' The other children shouted with joy, 'Yes, a new one has come!' And they clapped their hands and danced about, running after their father and mother. They threw the bread into the water, and one and all said that 'the new one was the prettiest; he was so young and handsome'. And the old swans bent their heads and did homage before him.

He felt quite shy, and hid his head under his wing; he did not know what to think; he was so very happy, but not at all proud; a good heart never becomes proud. He thought of how he had been pursued and scorned, and now he heard them all say that he was the most beautiful of all beautiful birds. The lilacs bent their boughs right down into the water before him, and the bright sun was warm and cheering, and he rustled his feathers and raised his slender neck aloft, saying with exultation in his heart: 'I never dreamt of so much happiness when I was that ugly duckling!'

Urashima Taro, the Fisher Lad

Long, long ago in the province of Tango there lived on the shore of Japan in the little fishing village of Mizu-no-ye a young fisherman named Urashima Taro. His father had been a fisherman before him, and his skill had more than doubly descended to his son, for Urashima was the most skilful fisher in all that countryside, and could catch more bonito and tai in a day than his comrades could in a week.

But in the little fishing village, more than for being a clever fisher of the sea was he known for his kind heart. In his whole life he had never hurt anything, either great or small, and when a boy, his companions had always laughed at him, for he would never join with them in teasing animals, but always tried to keep them from this cruel sport.

One soft summer twilight he was going home at the end of a day's fishing when he came upon a group of children. They were all screaming and talking at the tops of their voices, and seemed to be in a state of great excitement about something, and on his going up to them to see what was the matter he found that they were tormenting a tortoise. First one boy pulled it this way, then another boy pulled it that way, while a third child beat it with a stick, and the fourth hammered its shell with a stone.

Now Urashima felt very sorry for the poor tortoise and made up his mind to rescue it. He spoke to the boys: 'Look here, boys, you are treating that poor tortoise so badly that it will soon die!'

The boys, who were all of an age when children seem to delight in being cruel to animals, took no notice of Urashima's gentle reproof, but went on teasing it as before. One of the older boys answered: 'Who cares whether it lives or dies? We do not. Here, boys, go on, go on!'

And they began to treat the poor tortoise more cruelly than ever. Urashima waited a moment, turning over in his mind what would be the best way to deal with the boys. He would try to persuade them to give the tortoise up to him, so he smiled at them and said: 'I am sure you are all good, kind boys! Now won't you give me the tortoise? I should like to have it so much!'

'No, we won't give you the tortoise,' said one of the boys. 'Why should we? We caught it ourselves.'

'What you say is true,' said Urashima, 'but I do not ask you to give it to me for nothing. I will give you some money for it – in other words, Ojisan (Uncle) will buy it of you. Won't that do for you, my boys?' He held up the money to them, strung on a piece of string through a hole in the center of each coin. 'Look, boys, you can buy anything you like with this money. You can do much more with this money than you can with that poor tortoise. See what good boys you are to listen to me'

The boys were not bad boys at all, they were only mischievous, and as Urashima spoke they were won by his kind smile and gentle words and began 'to be of his spirit', as they say in Japan. Gradually they all came up to him, the ringleader of the little band holding out the tortoise to him.

'Very well, Ojisan, we will give you the tortoise if you will give us the money!' And Urashima took the tortoise and gave the money to the boys, who, calling to each other, scampered away and were soon out of sight.

Then Urashima stroked the tortoise's back, saying as he did so: 'Oh, you poor thing! Poor thing! – there, there! you are safe now! They say that a stork lives for a thousand years, but the tortoise for ten thousand years. You have the longest life of any creature in this world, and you were in great danger of having that precious life cut short by those cruel boys. Luckily I was passing by and saved you, and so life is still yours. Now I am going to take you back to your home, the sea, at once. Do not let yourself be caught again, for there might be no one to save you next time!'

All the time that the kind fisherman was speaking he was walking quickly to the shore and out upon the rocks; then putting the tortoise into the water he watched the animal disappear, and turned homewards himself, for he was tired and the sun had set.

The next morning Urashima went out as usual in his boat. The weather was fine and the sea and sky were both blue and soft in the tender haze of the summer morning. Urashima got into his boat and dreamily pushed out to sea, throwing his line as he did so. He soon passed the other fishing boats and left them behind him till they were lost to sight in the distance, and his boat drifted farther and farther out upon the blue waters. Somehow, he knew not why, he felt unusually happy that morning; and he could not help wishing that, like the tortoise he set free the day before, he had thousands of years to live instead of his own short span of human life.

He was suddenly startled from his reverie by hearing his own name called: 'Urashima, Urashima!'

Clear as a bell and soft as the summer wind the name floated over the sea.

He stood up and looked in every direction, thinking that one of the other boats had overtaken him, but gaze as he might over the wide expanse of water, near or far there was no sign of a boat, so the voice could not have come from any human being.

Startled, and wondering who or what it was that had called him so clearly, he looked in all directions round about him and saw that without his knowing it a tortoise had come to the side of the boat. Urashima saw with surprise that it was the very tortoise he had rescued the day before.

'Well, Mr Tortoise,' said Urashima, 'was it you who called my name just now?'

The tortoise nodded its head several times and said: 'Yes, it was I. Yesterday in your honorable shadow my life was saved, and I have come to offer you my thanks and to tell you how grateful I am for your kindness to me.'

'Indeed,' said Urashima, 'that is very polite of you. Come up into the boat. I would offer you a smoke, but as you are a tortoise doubtless you do not smoke,' and the fisherman laughed at the joke.

'He–he–he–he!' laughed the tortoise; 'rice wine is my favorite refreshment, but I do not care for tobacco.'

'Indeed,' said Urashima, 'I regret very much that I have no sake in my boat to offer you, but come up and dry your back in the sun – tortoises always love to do that.'

So, with the aid of the fisherman, the tortoise climbed into the boat, and after an exchange of complimentary speeches the tortoise said: 'Have you ever seen Rin Gin, the palace of the Dragon King of the Sea, Urashima?'

The fisherman shook his head and replied; 'No; year after year the sea has been my home, but though I have often heard of the Dragon King's realm under the sea I have never yet set eyes on that wonderful place. It must be very far away, if it exists at all!'

'Is that really so? You have never seen the Sea King's palace? Then you have missed seeing one of the most wonderful sights in the whole universe. It is far away at the bottom of the sea, but if I take you there we shall soon reach the place. If you would like to see the Sea King's land I will be your guide.'

'I should like to go there, certainly, and you are very kind to think of taking me, but you must remember that I am only a poor mortal and have not the power of swimming like a sea creature such as you are – '

Before the fisherman could say more the tortoise stopped him, saying: 'What? You need not swim yourself. If you will ride on my back I will take you without any trouble on your part.'

'But,' said Urashima, 'how is it possible for me to ride on your small back?'

'It may seem absurd to you. but I assure you that you can do so. Try at once! Just come and get on my back, and see if it is as impossible as you think!'

As the tortoise finished speaking, Urashima looked at its shell, and strange to say be saw that the creature had suddenly grown so big that a man could easily sit on its back.

'This is strange indeed!' said Urashima; 'then. Mr Tortoise, with your kind permission I will get on your back. Dokoisho!' he exclaimed as he jumped on.

The tortoise, with an unmoved face, as if this strange proceeding were quite an ordinary event, said: 'Now we will set out at our leisure,' and with these words he leapt into the sea with Urashima on his back. Down through the water the tortoise dived and for a long time these two strange companions rode through the sea. Urashima never grew tired, nor his clothes moist with the water. At last, far away in the distance a magnificent gate appeared, and behind the gate, the long, sloping roofs of a palace on the horizon.

'Ya,' exclaimed Urashima. 'that looks like the gate of some large palace just appearing! Mr Tortoise, can you tell what that place is we can now see?'

'That is the great gate of the Rin Gin Palace, the

large roof that you see behind the gate is the Sea King's palace itself.'

'Then we have at last come to the realm of the Sea King and to his palace,' said Urashima.

'Yes, indeed,' answered the tortoise, 'and don't you think we have come very quickly?' And while he was speaking the tortoise reached the side of the gate. 'And here we are, and you must please walk from here.'

The tortoise now went in front, and speaking to the gatekeeper, said: 'This is Urashima Taro, from the country of Japan. I have had the honour of bringing him as a visitor to this kingdom. Please show him the way.'

Then the gatekeeper, who was a fish, at once led the way through the gate before them.

The red bream, the flounder, the sole, the cuttle-fish and all the chief vassals of the Dragon King of the Sea now came out with courtly bows to welcome the stranger.

'Urashima Sama, Urashima Sama! welcome to the Sea Palace, the home of the Dragon King of the Sea. Thrice welcome are you, having come from such a distant country. And you, Mr Tortoise, we are greatly indebted to you for all your trouble in bringing Urashima here.' Then, turning again to Urashima, they said, 'Please follow us this way,' and from here the whole band of fishes became his guides.

Urashima, being only a poor fisher lad, did not know how to behave in a palace; but, strange though it all was to him, he did not feel ashamed or embarrassed, but followed his kind guides quite calmly where they led to the inner palace. When he reached the portals a beautiful princess with her attendant maidens came out to welcome him. She was more beautiful than any human being, and was robed in flowing garments of red and soft green like the under side of a wave, and golden threads glimmered through the folds of her gown. Her lovely black hair streamed over her shoulders in the fashion of a king's daughter many hundreds of years ago, and when she spoke her voice sounded like music over the water. Urashima was lost in wonder while he looked upon her, and he could not speak. Then he remembered that he ought to bow, but before he could make a low obeisance the princess took him by the hand and led him to a beautiful hall, and to the seat of honour at the upper end, and bade him be seated.

'Urashima Taro, it gives me the highest pleasure to welcome you to my father's kingdom,' said the princess. 'Yesterday you set free a tortoise, and I have sent for you to thank you for saving my life, for I was that tortoise. Now if you like you shall live here for ever in the land of eternal youth, where summer never dies and where sorrow never comes, and I will be your bride if you will, and we will live together happily for ever afterwards!'

And as Urashima listened to her sweet words and gazed upon her lovely face his heart was filled with a great wonder and joy, and he answered her, wondering if it was not all a dream: 'Thank you a thousand times for your kind speech. There is nothing I could wish for more than to be permitted to stay here with you in this beautiful land, of which I have often heard, but have never seen to this day. Beyond all words, this is the most wonderful place I have ever seen.'

While he was speaking a train of fishes appeared, all dressed in ceremonial, trailing garments. One by one, silently and with stately steps, they entered the hall, bearing on coral trays delicacies of fish and seaweed, such as no one can dream of, and this wondrous feast was set before the bride and bridegroom. The bridal was celebrated with dazzling splendour, and in the Sea King's realm there was great rejoicing. As soon as the young pair had pledged themselves in the wedding cup of wine, three times three, music was played, and

songs were sung, and fishes with silver scales and golden tails stepped in from the waves and danced. Urashima enjoyed himself with all his heart. Never in his whole life had he sat down to such a marvelous feast.

When the feast was over the princes asked the bridegroom if he would like to walk through the palace and see all there was to be seen. Then the happy fisherman, following his bride, the Sea King's daughter, was shown all the wonders of that enchanted land where youth and joy go hand in hand and neither time nor age can touch them. The palace was built of coral and adorned with pearls, and the beauties and wonders of the place were so great that the tongue fails to describe them.

But, to Urashima, more wonderful than the palace was the garden that surrounded it. Here was to be seen at one time the scenery of the four different seasons: the beauties of summer and winter, spring and autumn, were displayed to the wondering visitor all at once.

First, when he looked to the east, the plum and cherry trees were seen in full bloom, the nightingales sang in the pink avenues, and butterflies flitted from flower to flower.

Looking to the south all the trees were green in the fullness of summer, and the day cicala and the night cricket chirruped loudly.

Looking to the west the autumn maples were ablaze like a sunset sky, and the chrysanthemums were in perfection.

Looking to the north the change made Urashima start, for the ground was silver white with snow, and trees and bamboos were also covered with snow and the pond was thick with ice.

And each day there were new joys and new wonders for Urashima, and so great was his happiness that he forgot everything, even the home he had left behind and his parents and his own country, and three days passed without his even thinking of all he had left behind. Then his mind came back to him and he remembered who he was, and that he did not belong to this wonderful land or the Sea King's palace, and he said to himself: 'O dear! I must not stay on here, for I have an old father and mother at home. What can have happened to them all this time? How anxious they must have been these days when I did not return as usual. I must go back at once without letting one more day pass.' And he began to prepare for the journey in great haste.

Then he went to his beautiful wife, the princess, and bowing low before her he said: 'Indeed, I have been very happy with you for a long time, Otohime Sama' (for that was her name), 'and you have been kinder to me than any words can tell. But now I must say goodbye. I must go back to my old parents.'

Then Otohime Sama began to weep, and said softly and sadly: 'Is it not well with you here, Urashima, that you wish to leave me so soon? Where is the haste? Stay with me yet another day only!'

But Urashima had remembered his old parents, and in Japan the duty to parents is stronger than everything else, stronger even than pleasure or love, and he would not be persuaded, but answered: 'Indeed, I must go. Do not think that I wish to leave you. It is not that. I must go and see my old parents. Let me go for one day and I will come back to you.'

'Then,' said the Princess sorrowfully, 'there is nothing to be done. I will send you back today to your father and mother, and instead of trying to keep you with me one more day, I shall give you this as a token of our love – please take it back with you;' and she brought him a beautiful lacquer box tied about with a silken cord and tassels of red silk.

Urashima had received so much from the princess already that he felt some compunction in taking the gift, and said: 'It does not seem right for me to take yet another gift from you after all the many favours I have received at your hands, but because it is your wish I will do so,' and then he added: 'Tell me what is this box?'

'That,' answered the princess 'is the tamate-bako (box of the jewelled hand), and it contains something very precious. You must not open this box, whatever happens! If you open it something dreadful will happen to you! Now promise me that you will never open this box!'

And Urashima promised that he would never, never open the box whatever happened.

Then bidding goodbye to Otohime Sama he went down to the seashore, the princess and her attendants following him, and there he found a large tortoise waiting for him.

He quickly mounted the creature's back and was carried away over the shining sea into the east. He looked back to wave his hand to Otohime Sama till at last he could see her no more, and the land of the Sea King and the roofs of the wonderful palace were lost in the far, far distance. Then, with his face turned eagerly towards his own land, he looked for the blue hills on the horizon before him.

At last the tortoise carried him into the bay he

knew so well, and to the shore whence he had set out. He stepped on to the shore and looked about him while the tortoise rode away back to the Sea King's realm.

But what is the strange fear that seizes Urashima as he stands and looks about him? Why does he gaze so fixedly at the people that pass him by, and why do they in turn stand and look at him? The shore is the same and the hills are the same, but the people that he sees walking past him have very different faces from those he had known so well.

Wondering what it can mean he walks quickly towards his old home. Even that looks different, but a house stands on the spot, and he calls out: 'Father, I have just returned!' and he was about to enter, when he saw a strange man coming out.

'Perhaps my parents have moved while I have been away, and have gone somewhere else,' was the fisherman's thought. Somehow he began to feel strangely anxious, he could not tell why.

'Excuse me,' said he to the man who was staring at him, 'but till within the last few days I have lived in this house. My name is Urashima Taro. Where have my parents gone whom I left here?'

A very bewildered expression came over the face of the man, and, still gazing intently on Urashima's face, he said: 'What? Are you Urashima Taro?'

'Yes,' said the fisherman, 'I am Urashima Taro!'

'Ha, ha!' laughed the man, 'you must not make such jokes. It is true that once upon a time a man called Urashima Taro did live in this village, but that is a story three hundred years old. He could not possibly be alive now!'

When Urashima heard these strange words he was frightened, and said: 'Please, please, you must not joke with me, I am greatly perplexed. I am really Urashima Taro, and I certainly have not lived three hundred years. Till four or five days ago I lived on this spot. Tell me what I want to know without more joking, please.'

But the man's face grew more and more grave, and he answered: 'You may or may not be Urashima Taro, I don't know. But the Urashima Taro of whom I have heard is a man who lived three hundred years ago. Perhaps you are his spirit come to revisit your old home?'

'Why do you mock me?' said Urashima. 'I am no spirit! I am a living man – do you not see my feet;' and he stamped on the ground, first with one foot and then with the other, to show the man. (Japanese ghosts have no feet.)

'But Urashima Taro lived three hundred years ago, that is all I know; it is written in the village chronicles,' persisted the man, who could not believe what the fisherman said.

Urashima was lost in bewilderment and trouble. He stood looking all around him, terribly puzzled, and, indeed, something in the appearance of everything was different to what he remembered before he went away, and the awful feeling came over him that what the man said was perhaps true. He seemed to be in a strange dream. The few days he had spent in the Sea King's palace beyond the sea had not been days at all: they had been hundreds of years, and in that time his parents had died and all the people he had ever known, and the village had written down his story. There was no use in staying here any longer. He must get back to his beautiful wife beyond the sea.

He made his way back to the beach, carrying in his hand the box which the princess had given him. But which was the way? He could not find it alone! Suddenly he remembered the box, the tamate-bako.

'The princess told me when she gave me the box never to open it – that it contained a very precious thing. But now that I have no home, now that I have lost everything that was dear to me here, and my heart grows thin with sadness, at such a time, if I open the box, surely I shall find something that will help me, something that will show me the way back to my beautiful princess over the sea. There is nothing else for me to do now. Yes, yes, I will open the box and look in!'

And so his heart consented to this act of disobedience, and he tried to persuade himself that he was doing the right thing in breaking his promise.

Slowly, very slowly, he untied the red silk cord, slowly and wonderingly he lifted the lid of the precious box. And what did he find? Strange to say only a beautiful little purple cloud rose out of the box in three soft wisps. For an instant it covered his face and wavered over him as if loath to go, and then it floated away like vapour over the sea.

Urashima, who had been till that moment like a strong and handsome youth of twenty-four, suddenly became very, very old. His back doubled up with age, his hair turned snowy white, his face wrinkled and he fell down dead on the beach.

Poor Urashima! because of his disobedience he could never return to the Sea King's realm or the lovely princess beyond the sea.

Little children, never be disobedient to those who are wiser than you, for disobedience was the beginning of all the miseries and sorrows of life.

The Valiant Little Tailor

One summer's morning a little tailor was sitting on his table by the window; he was in good spirits, and sewed with all his might.

Then came a peasant woman down the street crying: 'Good jams, cheap! Good jams, cheap!'

This rang pleasantly in the tailor's ears; he stretched his delicate head out of the window, and called: 'Come up here, dear woman; here you will get rid of your goods.'

The woman came up the three steps to the tailor with her heavy basket, and he made her unpack all the pots for him.

He inspected each one, lifted it up, put his nose to it, and at length said: 'The jam seems to me to be good, so weigh out four ounces, dear woman, and if it is a quarter of a pound that is of no consequence.'

The woman who had hoped to find a good sale, gave him what he desired, but went away quite angry and grumbling.

'Now, this jam shall be blessed by God,' cried the little tailor, 'and give me health and strength;' so he brought the bread out of the cupboard, cut himself a piece right across the loaf and spread the jam over it. 'This won't taste bitter,' said he, 'but I will just finish the jacket before I take a bite.'

He laid the bread near him and sewed on, in his joy making bigger and bigger stitches. In the meantime the smell of the sweet jam rose to where the flies were sitting in great numbers, and they were attracted and descended on it in hosts.

'Hi! Who invited you?' said the little tailor, and drove the unbidden guests away.

The flies, however, who understood not a word, would not be turned away, but came back again in ever-increasing companies. The little tailor at last lost all patience, and drew a piece of cloth from the hole under his work-table, and, saying: 'Wait, and I will give it to you,' struck it mercilessly on them.

When he drew it away and counted, there lay before him no fewer than seven dead and with legs stretched out.

'Are you a fellow of that sort?' said he, and could not help admiring his own bravery. 'The whole town shall know of this!' And the little tailor hastened to cut himself a girdle, stitched it, and embroidered on it in large letters: 'Seven at one stroke'.

'Why stop at the town?' he continued. 'The whole world shall hear of it!' and his heart wagged with joy like a lamb's tail.

The tailor put on the girdle, and resolved to go forth into the world, because he thought his workshop was too small for his valour. Before he went away, he sought about in the house to see if there was anything which he could take with him; however, he found nothing but an old cheese, and that he put in his pocket. In front of the door he observed a bird which had caught itself in the thicket. It had to go into his pocket with the cheese. Now he took to the road boldly, and as he was light and nimble, he felt no fatigue. The road led him up a mountain, and when he had reached the highest point of it, there sat a powerful giant looking peacefully about him.

The little tailor went bravely up, spoke to him and said: 'Good-day, comrade, so you are sitting there overlooking the widespread world! I am just on my way thither, and want to try my luck. Have you any inclination to go with me?'

The giant looked contemptuously at the tailor, and said: 'You ragamuffin! You miserable creature!'

'Oh, indeed?' answered the little tailor and, unbuttoning his coat, showed the giant the girdle. 'There may you read what kind of a man I am!'

The giant read: 'Seven at one stroke', and thought that they had been men whom the tailor had killed, and began to feel a little respect for the tiny fellow. Nevertheless, he wished to try him first, and took a stone in his hand and squeezed it together so that water dropped out of it. 'Do that likewise,' said the giant, 'if you have strength.'

'Is that all?' said the tailor; 'that is child's play with us!' and put his hand into his pocket, brought out the soft cheese, and pressed it until the liquid ran out of it. 'Faith,' said he, 'that was a little better, wasn't it?'

The giant did not know what to say, and could not believe it of the little man. Then the giant picked up a stone and threw it so high that the eye could scarcely follow it. 'Now, little mite of a man, do that likewise.'

'Well thrown,' said the tailor; 'but after all the stone came down to earth again; I will throw you one which shall never come back at all,' and he put his hand into his pocket, took out the bird, and threw it into the air. The bird, delighted with its liberty, rose, flew away and did not come back. 'How does that shot please you, comrade?' asked the tailor.

'You can certainly throw,' said the giant; 'but now we will see if you are able to carry anything properly.'

He took the little tailor to a mighty oak tree which lay there felled on the ground, and said: 'If you are strong enough, help me to carry the tree out of the forest.'

'Readily,' answered the little man; 'take you the trunk on your shoulders, and I will raise up the branches and twigs; after all, they are the heaviest.' The giant took the trunk on his shoulder, but the tailor seated himself on a branch, and the giant, who could not look round, had to carry away the whole tree, and the little tailor into the bargain; he, behind, was quite merry and happy, and whistled the song 'Three tailors rode forth from the gate', as if carrying the tree were child's play.

The giant, after he had dragged the heavy burden part of the way, could go no farther, and cried: 'Hark you, I shall have to let the tree fall!'

The tailor sprang nimbly down, seized the tree with both arms as if he had been carrying it, and said to the giant: 'You are such a great fellow, and yet cannot even carry the tree!'

They went on together, and as they passed a cherry tree, the giant laid hold of the top of the tree where the ripest fruit was hanging, bent it down, gave it into the tailor's hand, and bade him eat. But the little tailor was much too weak to hold the tree, and when the giant let it go, it sprang back again, and the tailor was tossed into the air with it.

When he had fallen down again without injury, the giant said: 'What is this? Have you not strength enough to hold a weak twig?'

'There is no lack of strength,' answered the little tailor. 'Do you think that could be anything to a man who has struck down seven at one blow? I leapt over the tree because the huntsmen are shooting down there in the thicket. Jump, as I did, if you can do it.'

The giant made the attempt but he could not get over the tree, and remained hanging in the branches, so that in this also the tailor kept the upper hand.

The giant said: 'If you are such a valiant fellow, come with me into our cavern and spend the night with us.'

The little tailor was willing, and followed him. When they went into the cave, other giants were sitting there by the fire, and each of them had a roasted sheep in his hand and was eating it. The little tailor looked round and thought: 'It is much more spacious here than in my workshop.' The giant showed him a bed, and said he was to lie down in it and sleep. The bed, however, was too big for the little tailor; he did not lie down in it, but crept into a corner.

When it was midnight, and the giant thought that the little tailor was lying in a sound sleep, he got up, took a great iron bar, cut through the bed with one blow, and thought he had finished off the grasshopper for good.

With the earliest dawn the giants went into the forest, and had quite forgotten the little tailor, when all at once he walked up to them quite merrily and boldly. The giants were terrified, they were afraid that he would strike them all dead, and ran away in a great hurry.

The little tailor went onwards, always following his own pointed nose. After he had walked for a long time, he came to the courtyard of a royal palace, and as he felt weary, he lay down on the grass and fell asleep.

While he lay there, the people came and inspected him on all sides, and read on his girdle: 'Seven at one stroke'.

'Ah!' said they, 'what does the great warrior want here in the midst of peace? He must be a mighty lord.' They went and announced him to the king, and gave it as their opinion that if war should break out, this would be a weighty and useful man who ought on no account to be allowed to depart. The counsel pleased the king, and he sent one of his courtiers to the little tailor to offer him military service when he awoke. The ambassador remained standing by the sleeper, waited until he stretched his limbs and opened his eyes, and then conveyed to him this proposal.

'For this very reason have I come here,' the tailor replied. 'I am ready to enter the king's service.'

He was therefore honourably received, and a special dwelling was assigned him.

The soldiers, however, were set against the little tailor, and wished him a thousand miles away.

'What is to be the end of this?' they said among themselves. 'If we quarrel with him, and he strikes about him, seven of us will fall at every blow; not one of us can stand against him.'

They came therefore to a decision, betook themselves in a body to the king, and begged for their dismissal. 'We are not prepared,' said they, 'to stay with a man who kills seven at one stroke.'

The king was sorry that for the sake of one he should lose all his faithful servants, wished that he had never set eyes on the tailor, and would willingly have been rid of him again. But he did not venture to give him his dismissal, for he dreaded lest he should strike him and all his people dead and place himself on the royal throne. He thought about it for a long time, and at last found good counsel. He sent to the little tailor and caused him to be informed that, as he was a great warrior, he had one request to make to him.

In a forest of his country lived two giants, who caused great mischief with their robbing, murdering, ravaging and burning, and no one could approach them without putting himself in danger of death. If the tailor conquered and killed these two giants, he would give him his only daughter to wife, and half of his kingdom as a dowry, likewise one hundred horsemen should go with him to assist him. 'That would indeed be a fine thing for a man like me!' thought the little tailor. 'One is not offered a beautiful princess and half a kingdom every day of one's life!'

'Oh, yes,' he replied, 'I will soon subdue the giants, and do not require the help of the hundred horsemen to do it; he who can hit seven with one blow has no need to be afraid of two.'

The little tailor went forth, and the hundred horsemen followed him. When he came to the outskirts of the forest, he said to his followers: 'Just stay waiting here, I alone will soon finish off the giants.' Then he bounded into the forest and looked about right and left.

After a while he perceived both giants. They lay sleeping under a tree, and snored so that the branches waved up and down. The little tailor, not idle, gathered two pocketfuls of stones, and with these climbed up the tree. When he was halfway up, he slipped down by a branch until he sat just above the sleepers, and then let one stone after another fall on the breast of one of the giants. For a long time the giant felt nothing, but at last he awoke, pushed his comrade, and said: 'Why are you knocking me?'

'You must be dreaming,' said the other. 'I am not knocking you.'

They laid themselves down to sleep again, and then the tailor threw a stone down on to the second. 'What is the meaning of this?' cried the other. 'Why are you pelting me?'

'I am not pelting you,' answered the first, growling. They disputed about it for a time, but as they were weary they let the matter rest, and their eyes closed once more.

The little tailor began his game again, picked out the biggest stone, and threw it with all his might on the breast of the first giant.

'That is too bad!' cried he, and springing up like a madman, he pushed his companion against the tree until it shook. The other paid him back in the same coin, and they got into such a rage that they tore up trees and belaboured each other so long that at last they both fell down dead on the ground at the same time.

Then the little tailor leapt down. 'It is a lucky thing,' said he, 'that they did not tear up the tree on which I was sitting, or I should have had to sprint on to another like a squirrel; but we tailors are nimble.'

He drew out his sword and gave each of them a couple of thrusts in the breast, and then went out to the horsemen and said: 'The job is done; I have finished both of them off, but it was hard work! They tore up trees in their sore need, and defended themselves with them, but all that is to no purpose against a man like myself, who can kill seven at one blow.'

'But are you not wounded?' asked the horsemen.

'You need not concern yourself about that,' answered the tailor, 'they have not bent one hair of mine.' The horsemen would not believe him, and rode into the forest; there they found the giants swimming in their blood, and all round about lay the torn-up trees.

The little tailor demanded of the king the promised reward; he, however, repented of his promise, and again bethought himself how he could get rid of the hero. 'Before you receive my daughter, and half of my kingdom,' said he, 'you must perform one more heroic deed. In the forest

roams a unicorn which does great harm, and you must catch it first.'

'I fear one unicorn still less than two giants. Seven at one blow is my kind of affair.'

He took a rope and an axe with him, went forth into the forest, and again bade those who were sent with him to wait outside. He had not long to seek. The unicorn soon came towards him, and rushed directly on the tailor, as if it would gore him with its horn without more ado. 'Softly, softly; it can't be done as quickly as that,' said he, and stood still and waited until the animal was quite close, and then sprang nimbly behind the tree.

The unicorn ran against the tree with all its force and stuck its horn so fast in the trunk that it had not strength enough to draw it out again, and thus it was caught. 'Now, I have got the bird,' said the tailor, and came out from behind the tree and put the rope round its neck, and then with his axe he hewed the horn out of the tree, and when all was ready he led the beast away and took it to the king.

The king still would not give him the promised reward, and made a third demand. Before the wedding the tailor was to catch him a wild boar that made great havoc in the forest, and the huntsmen should give him their help.

'Willingly,' said the tailor, 'that is child's play!' He did not take the huntsmen with him into the forest, and they were well pleased that he did not, for the wild boar had several times received them in such a manner that they had no inclination to lie in wait for him.

When the boar perceived the tailor, it ran on him with foaming mouth and whetted tusks, and was about to throw him to the ground, but the hero fled into a chapel which was near and in one bound sprang out again by the window. The boar ran after him, but the tailor ran round outside and shut the door behind it, and then the raging beast, which was much too heavy and awkward to leap out of the window, was caught.

The little tailor called the huntsmen thither that they might see the prisoner with their own eyes.

The hero, however, went to the king, who was now, whether he liked it or not, obliged to keep his promise and give him his daughter and half his kingdom. Had he known that it was no warlike hero but a little tailor who was standing before him, it would have grieved him still more than it did. The wedding was held with great magnificence and small joy, and out of a tailor a king was made.

After some time the young queen heard her husband say in his dreams at night: 'Boy, make me the doublet, and patch the pantaloons, or else I will rap the yard-measure over your ears.' Then she discovered in what state of life the young lord had been born, and next morning complained of her wrongs to her father, and begged him to help her to get rid of her husband, who was nothing else but a tailor.

The king comforted her and said: 'Leave your bedroom door open this night, and my servants shall stand outside, and when he has fallen asleep shall go in, bind him, and take him on board a ship which shall carry him into the wide world.' The woman was satisfied with this; but the king's armour-bearer, who had heard all, was friendly with the young lord, and informed him of the whole plot. 'I'll put a screw into that business,' said the little tailor.

At night he went to bed with his wife at the usual time, and when she thought that he had fallen asleep, she got up, opened the door, and then lay down again. The little tailor, who was only pretending to be asleep, began to cry out in a clear voice: 'Boy, make me the doublet and patch me the pantaloons, or I will rap the yard-measure over your ears. I smote seven at one blow. I killed two giants, I brought away one unicorn and caught a wild boar, and am I to fear those who are standing outside the room?' When these men heard the tailor speaking thus, they were overcome by a great dread, and ran as if the wild huntsman were behind them, and none of them would venture anything further against him. So the little tailor was and remained a king to the end of his life.

The Well at the World's End

Once upon a time, and a very good time it was, though it wasn't in my time, nor in your time, nor anyone else's time, there was a girl whose mother had died, and her father married again. And her stepmother hated her because she was more beautiful than herself, and she was very cruel to her. She used to make her do all the servant's work, and never let her have any peace. At last, one day, the stepmother thought to get rid of her altogether; so she handed her a sieve and said to her: 'Go, fill it at the Well of the World's End and bring it home to me full, or woe betide you.' For she thought she would never be able to find the Well of the World's End, and, if she did, how could she bring home a sieve full of water?

Well, the girl started off, and asked everyone she met to tell her where was the Well of the World's End. But nobody knew, and she didn't know what to do, when a queer little old woman, all bent double, told her where it was, and how she could get to it. So she did what the old woman told her, and at last arrived at the Well of the World's End. But when she dipped the sieve in the cold, cold water, it all ran out again. She tried and tried again, but every time it was the same; and at last she sat down and cried as if her heart would break.

Suddenly she heard a croaking voice, and she looked up and saw a great frog with goggle eyes looking at her and speaking to her.

'What's the matter, dearie?' it said.

'Oh, dear, oh dear,' she said, 'my stepmother has sent me all this long way to fill this sieve with water from the Well of the World's End, and I can't fill it no how at all.'

'Well,' said the frog, 'if you promise me to do whatever I bid you for a whole night long, I'll tell you how to fill it.'

So the girl agreed, and the frog said:

'Stop it with moss and daub it with clay,
And then it will carry the water away';

and then it gave a hop, skip and jump, and went flop into the Well of the World's End.

So the girl looked about for some moss, and lined the bottom of the sieve with it, and over that she put some clay, and then she dipped it once again into the Well of the World's End; and this time, the water didn't run out, and she turned to go away.

Just then the frog popped up its head out of the Well of the World's End, and said: 'Remember your promise.'

'All right,' said the girl; for thought she, 'What harm can a frog do me?'

So she went back to her stepmother, and brought the sieve full of water from the Well of the World's End. The stepmother was angry as angry, but she said nothing at all.

That very evening they heard something tap-tapping at the door low down, and a voice cried out:

Open the door, my hinny, my heart,
　Open the door, my own darling;
Mind you the words that you and I spoke,
　Down in the meadow, at the World's End Well.

'Whatever can that be?' cried out the stepmother, and the girl had to tell her about it, and what she had promised the frog.

'Girls must keep their promises,' said the step-mother. 'Go and open the door this instant.' For she was glad the girl would have to obey a nasty frog.

So the girl went and opened the door, and there was the frog from the Well of the World's End. And it hopped, and it hopped and it jumped, till it reached the girl, and then it said:

Lift me to your knee, my hinny, my heart;
　Lift me to your knee, my own darling;
Remember the words you and I spoke,
　Down in the meadow, by the World's End Well.

But the girl didn't like to, till her stepmother said: 'Lift it up this instant, you hussy! Girls must keep their promises!'

So at last she lifted the frog up on to her lap, and it lay there for a time, till at last it said:

Give me some supper, my hinny, my heart,
　Give me some supper, my darling;
Remember the words you and I spoke,
　In the meadow, by the Well of the World's End.

Well, she didn't mind doing that, so she got it a

bowl of milk and bread, and fed it well. And when the frog had finished, it said:

Go with me to bed, my hinny, my heart,
　Go with me to bed, my own darling;
Mind you the words you spoke to me,
　Down by the cold well, so weary.

But that the girl wouldn't do, till her stepmother said: 'Do what you promised, girl; girls must keep their promises. Do what you're bid, or out you go, you and your froggie.'

So the girl took the frog with her to bed, and kept it as far away from her as she could. Well, just as the day was beginning to break what should the frog say but:

Chop off my head, my hinny, my heart,
　Chop off my head, my own darling;
Remember the promise you made to me,
　Down by the cold well, so weary.

At first the girl wouldn't, for she thought of what the frog had done for her at the Well of the World's End. But when the frog said the words over again she went and took an axe and chopped off its head, and lo! and behold, there stood before her a hand-some young prince, who told her that he had been enchanted by a wicked magician, and he could never be unspelled till some girl would do his bidding for a whole night, and chop off his head at the end of it.

The stepmother was surprised indeed when she found the young prince instead of the nasty frog, and she wasn't best pleased, you may be sure, when the prince told her that he was going to marry her stepdaughter because she had unspelled him. But married they were, and went away to live in the castle of the king, his father, and all the stepmother had to console her was that it was all through her that her stepdaughter was married to a prince.

The White Cat

Once upon a time there was a king who had three sons, who were all so clever and brave that he began to be afraid that they would want to reign over the kingdom before he was dead. Now the king, though he felt that he was growing old, did not at all wish to give up the government of his kingdom while he could still manage it very well, so he thought the best way to live in peace would be to divert the minds of his sons by promises which he could always get out of when the time came for keeping them.

So he sent for them all, and, after speaking to them kindly, he added: 'You will quite agree with me, my dear children, that my great age makes it impossible for me to look after my affairs of state as carefully as I once did. I begin to fear that this may affect the welfare of my subjects, therefore I wish that one of you should succeed to my crown; but in return for such a gift as this it is only right that you should do something for me. Now, as I think of retiring into the country, it seems to me that a pretty, lively, faithful little dog would be very good company for me; so, without any regard for your ages, I promise that the one who brings me the most beautiful little dog shall succeed me at once.'

The three princes were greatly surprised by their father's sudden fancy for a little dog, but as it gave the two younger ones a chance they would not otherwise have had of being king, and as the eldest was too polite to make any objection, they accepted the commission with pleasure. They bade farewell to the king, who gave them presents of silver and precious stones, and appointed to meet them at the same hour, in the same place, after a year had passed, to see the little dogs they had brought for him.

Then they went together to a castle which was about a league from the city, accompanied by all their particular friends, to whom they gave a grand banquet, and the three brothers promised to be friends always, to share whatever good fortune befell them, and not to be parted by any envy or jealousy; and so they set out, agreeing to meet at the same castle at the appointed time, to present themselves before the king together. Each one took a different road, and the two eldest met with many adventures; but it is about the youngest that you are going to hear. He was young, and dark, and handsome, and knew everything that a prince ought to know; and as for his courage, there was simply no end to it.

Hardly a day passed without his buying several dogs – big and little, greyhounds, mastiffs, spaniels and lapdogs. As soon as he had bought a pretty one he was sure to see a still prettier, and then he had to get rid of all the others and buy that one, as, being alone, he found it impossible to take thirty or forty thousand dogs about with him. He journeyed from day to day, not knowing where he was going, until at last, just at nightfall, he reached a great, gloomy forest. He did not know his way, and, to make matters worse, it began to thunder, and the rain poured down. He took the first path he could find, and after walking for a long time he fancied he saw a faint light, and began to hope that he was coming to some cottage where he might find shelter for the night. At length, guided by the light, he reached the door of the most splendid castle he could have imagined. This door was of gold covered with carbuncles, and it was the pure red light which shone from them that had shown him the way through the forest. The walls were of the finest porcelain in all the most delicate colours, and the prince saw that all the stories he had ever read were pictured upon them; but as he was terribly wet, and the rain still fell in torrents, he could not stay to look about any more, but came back to the golden door. There he saw a deer's foot hanging by a chain of diamonds, and he began to wonder who could live in this magnificent castle.

'They must feel very secure against robbers,' he said to himself. 'What is to hinder anyone from cutting off that chain and digging out those carbuncles, and making himself rich for life?'

He pulled the deer's foot, and immediately a silver bell sounded and the door flew open, but the prince could see nothing but numbers of hands in the air, each holding a torch. He was so much surprised that he stood quite still, until he felt himself pushed forward by other hands, so that, though he was somewhat uneasy, he could not help going on. With his hand on his sword, to be prepared for whatever might happen, he entered a hall paved with lapis lazuli, while two lovely voices sang:

> 'The hands you see floating above
>   Will swiftly your bidding obey;
> If your heart dreads not conquering Love,
>   In this place you may fearlessly stay.'

The prince could not believe that any danger threatened him when he was welcomed in this way, so, guided by the mysterious hands, he went towards a door of coral, which opened of its own accord, and he found himself in a vast hall of mother-of-pearl, out of which opened a number of other rooms, glittering with thousands of lights, and full of such beautiful pictures and precious things that the prince felt quite bewildered. After passing through sixty rooms the hands that conducted him stopped, and the prince saw a most comfortable-looking armchair drawn up close to the chimney-corner; at the same moment the fire lighted itself, and the pretty, soft, clever hands took off the prince's wet, muddy clothes, and presented him with fresh ones made of the richest stuffs, all embroidered with gold and emeralds. He could not help admiring everything he saw, and the deft

way in which the hands waited on him, though they sometimes appeared so suddenly that they made him jump.

When he was quite ready – and I can assure you that he looked very different from the wet and weary prince who had stood outside in the rain, and pulled the deer's foot – the hands led him to a splendid room, upon the walls of which were painted the histories of Puss in Boots and a number of other famous cats. The table was laid for supper with two golden plates, and golden spoons and forks, and the sideboard was covered with dishes and glasses of crystal set with precious stones. The prince was wondering who the second place could be for, when suddenly in came about a dozen cats carrying guitars and rolls of music, who took their places at one end of the room, and under the direction of a cat who beat time with a roll of paper began to mew in every imaginable key, and to draw their claws across the strings of the guitars, making the strangest kind of music that could be heard. The prince hastily stopped up his ears, but even then the sight of these comical musicians sent him into fits of laughter.

'What funny thing shall I see next?' he said to himself, and instantly the door opened, and in came a tiny figure covered by a long black veil. It was conducted by two cats wearing black mantles and carrying swords, and a large party of cats followed, who brought in cages full of rats and mice.

The prince was so much astonished that he thought he must be dreaming, but the little figure came up to him and threw back its veil, and he saw that it was the loveliest little white cat it is possible to imagine. She looked very young and very sad, and in a sweet little voice that went straight to his heart she said to the prince: 'King's son, you are welcome; the Queen of the Cats is glad to see you.'

'Lady Cat,' replied the prince, 'I thank you for receiving me so kindly, but surely you are no ordinary pussy-cat? Indeed, the way you speak and the magnificence of your castle prove it plainly.'

'King's son,' said the White Cat, 'I beg you to spare me these compliments, for I am not used to them. But now,' she added, 'let supper be served, and let the musicians be silent, as the prince does not understand what they are saying.'

So the mysterious hands began to bring in the supper, and first they put on the table two dishes, one containing stewed pigeons and the other a fricassee of fat mice. The sight of the latter made the Prince feel as if he could not enjoy his supper at all; but the White Cat, seeing this, assured him that the dishes intended for him were prepared in a separate kitchen, and he might be quite certain that they contained neither rats nor mice; and the prince felt so sure that she would not deceive him that he had no more hesitation in beginning. Presently he noticed that on the little paw that was next him the White Cat wore a bracelet containing a portrait, and he begged to be allowed to look at it. To his great surprise he found it represented an extremely handsome young man, who was so like himself that it might have been his own portrait! The White Cat sighed as he looked at it, and seemed sadder than ever, and the prince dared not ask any questions for fear of displeasing her; so he began to talk about other things, and found that she was interested in all the subjects he cared for himself, and seemed to know quite well what was going on in the world. After supper they went into another room, which was fitted up as a theatre, and the cats acted and danced for their amusement, and then the White Cat said good-night to him, and the hands conducted him into a room he had not seen before, hung with tapestry worked with butterflies' wings of every colour; there were mirrors that reached from the ceiling to the floor, and a little white bed with curtains of gauze tied up with ribbons. The prince went to bed in silence, as he did not quite know how to begin a conversation with the hands that waited on him, and in the morning he was awakened by a noise and confusion outside of his window, and the hands came and quickly dressed him in hunting costume. When he looked out all the cats were assembled in the courtyard, some leading greyhounds, some blowing horns, for the White Cat was going out hunting. The hands led a wooden horse up to the prince, and seemed to expect him to mount it, at which he was very indignant; but it was no use for him to object, for he speedily found himself upon its back, and it pranced gaily off with him.

The White Cat herself was riding a monkey, which climbed even up to the eagles' nests when she had a fancy for the young eaglets. Never was there a pleasanter hunting party, and when they returned to the castle the prince and the White Cat supped together as before, but when they had finished she offered him a crystal goblet, which must have contained a magic draught, for as soon as he had swallowed its contents, he forgot everything, even the little dog that he was seeking for

the king, and only thought how happy he was to be with the White Cat! And so the days passed, in every kind of amusement, until the year was nearly gone. The prince had forgotten all about meeting his brothers: he did not even know what country he belonged to; but the White Cat knew when he ought to go back, and one day she said to him: 'Do you know that you have only three days left to look for the little dog for your father, and your brothers have found lovely ones?'

Then the prince suddenly recovered his memory, and cried: 'What can have made me forget such an important thing? My whole fortune depends upon it; and even if I could in such a short time find a dog pretty enough to gain me a kingdom, where should I find a horse that would carry me all that way in three days?' And he began to be very vexed. But the White Cat said to him: 'King's son, do not trouble yourself; I am your friend, and will make everything easy for you. You can still stay here for a day, as the good wooden horse can take you to your country in twelve hours.'

'I thank you, beautiful Cat,' said the prince; 'but what good will it do me to get back if I have not a dog to take to my father?'

'See here,' answered the White Cat, holding up an acorn; 'there is a prettier one in this than in the Dogstar!'

'Oh! White Cat dear,' said the prince, 'how unkind you are to laugh at me now!'

'Only listen,' she said, holding the acorn to his ear.

And inside it he distinctly heard a tiny voice say: 'Bow-wow!'

The prince was delighted, for a dog that can be shut up in an acorn must be very small indeed. He wanted to take it out and look at it, but the White Cat said it would be better not to open the acorn till he was before the king, in case the tiny dog should be cold on the journey. He thanked her a thousand times, and said goodbye quite sadly when the time came for him to set out.

'The days have passed so quickly with you,' he said, 'I only wish I could take you with me now.'

But the White Cat shook her head and sighed deeply in answer.

After all, the prince was the first to arrive at the castle where he had agreed to meet his brothers, but they came soon after, and stared in amazement when they saw the wooden horse in the courtyard jumping like a hunter.

The prince met them joyfully, and they began to

tell him all their adventures; but he managed to hide from them what he had been doing, and even led them to think that a turnspit dog which he had with him was the one he was bringing for the king. Fond as they all were of one another, the two eldest could not help being glad to think that their dogs certainly had a better chance. The next morning they started in the same chariot. The elder brothers carried in baskets two such tiny, fragile dogs that they hardly dared to touch them. As for the turnspit, he ran after the chariot, and got so covered with mud that one could hardly see what he was like at all. When they reached the palace everyone crowded round to welcome them as they went into the king's great hall; and when the two brothers presented their little dogs nobody could decide which was the prettier. They were already arranging between themselves to share the kingdom equally, when the youngest stepped forward, drawing from his pocket the acorn the White Cat had given him. He opened it quickly, and there upon a white cushion they saw a dog so small that it could easily have been put through a ring. The prince laid it upon the ground, and it got up at once and began to dance. The king did not know what to say, for it was impossible that anything could be prettier than this little creature.

Nevertheless, as he was in no hurry to part with his crown, he told his sons that, as they had been so successful the first time, he would ask them to go once again, and seek by land and sea for a piece of muslin so fine that it could be drawn through the eye of a needle. The brothers were not very willing to set out again, but the two eldest consented because it gave them another chance, and they started as before. The youngest again mounted the wooden horse, and rode back at full speed to his beloved White Cat. Every door of the castle stood wide open, and every window and turret was illuminated, so it looked more wonderful than before. The hands hastened to meet him, and led the wooden horse off to the stable, while he hurried in to find the White Cat. She was asleep in a little basket on a white satin cushion, but she very soon started up when she heard the prince, and was overjoyed at seeing him once more.

'How could I hope that you would come back to me, king's son?' she said. And then he stroked and petted her, and told her of his successful journey, and how he had come back to ask her help, as he believed that it was impossible to find what the king demanded. The White Cat looked serious, and said she must think what was to be done, but that, luckily, there were some cats in the castle who

The king did not know what to say, for it was impossible that anything could be prettier than this little creature

could spin very well, and if anybody could manage it they could, and she would set them the task herself.

And then the hands appeared carrying torches, and conducted the prince and the White Cat to a long gallery which overlooked the river, from the windows of which they saw a magnificent display of fireworks of all sorts; after which they had supper, which the prince liked even better than the fireworks, for it was very late, and he was hungry after his long ride. And so the days passed quickly as before; it was impossible to feel dull with the White Cat, and she had quite a talent for inventing new amusements – indeed, she was cleverer than a cat has any right to be. But when the Prince asked her how it was that she was so wise, she only said: 'King's son, do not ask me; guess what you please. I may not tell you anything.'

The prince was so happy that he did not trouble himself at all about the time, but presently the White Cat told him that the year was gone, and that he need not be at all anxious about the piece of muslin, as they had made it very well.

'This time,' she added, 'I can give you a suitable escort'; and on looking out into the courtyard the Prince saw a superb chariot of burnished gold, enamelled in flame colour with a thousand different devices. It was drawn by twelve snow-white horses, harnessed four abreast; their trappings were flame-coloured velvet, embroidered with diamonds. A hundred chariots followed, each drawn by eight horses, and filled with officers in splendid uniforms, and a thousand guards surrounded the procession. 'Go!' said the White Cat, 'and when you appear before the king in such state he surely will not refuse you the crown which you deserve. Take this walnut, but do not open it until you are before him, then you will find in it the piece of stuff you asked me for.'

'Lovely Blanchette,' said the Prince, 'how can I thank you properly for all your kindness to me? Only tell me that you wish it, and I will give up for ever all thought of being king, and will stay here with you always.'

'King's son,' she replied, 'it shows the goodness of your heart that you should care so much for a little white cat, who is good for nothing but to catch mice; but you must not stay.'

So the prince kissed her little paw and set out. You can imagine how fast he travelled when I tell you that they reached the king's palace in just half the time it had taken the wooden horse to get

So the Prince kissed her little paw and set out

there. This time the prince was so late that he did not try to meet his brothers at their castle, so they thought he could not be coming, and were rather glad of it, and displayed their pieces of muslin to the king proudly, feeling sure of success. And indeed the stuff was very fine, and would go through the eye of a very large needle; but the king, who was only too glad to make a difficulty, sent for a particular needle, which was kept among the crown jewels and had such a small eye that everybody saw at once that it was impossible that the muslin should pass through it. The princes were angry, and were beginning to complain that it was a trick, when suddenly the trumpets sounded and the youngest prince came in. His father and brothers were quite astonished at his magnificence, and after he had greeted them he took the walnut from his pocket and opened it, fully expecting to find the piece of muslin, but instead there was only a hazelnut. He cracked it, and there lay a cherry-stone. Everybody was looking on, and the king was chuckling to himself at the idea of finding the piece of muslin in a nutshell.

However, the prince cracked the cherry-stone, but everyone laughed when they saw it contained only its own kernel. He opened that and found a grain of wheat, and in that was a millet seed. Then he himself began to wonder, and muttered softly: 'White Cat, White Cat, are you making fun of me?'

In an instant he felt a cat's claw give his hand quite a sharp scratch, and hoping that it was meant as an encouragement he opened the millet seed, and drew out of it a piece of muslin four hundred ells long, woven with the loveliest colours and most wonderful patterns; and when the needle was brought it went through the eye six times with the greatest ease! The king turned pale, and the other princes stood silent and sorrowful, for nobody could deny that this was the most marvellous piece of muslin that was to be found in the world.

Presently the king turned to his sons, and said, with a deep sigh: 'Nothing could console me more in my old age than to realise your willingness to gratify my wishes. Go then once more, and whoever at the end of a year can bring back the loveliest princess shall be married to her, and shall, without further delay, receive the crown, for my successor must certainly be married.' The prince considered that he had earned the kingdom fairly twice over but still he was too well bred to argue about it, so he just went back to his gorgeous chariot, and, surrounded by his escort, returned to the White Cat faster than he had come. This time she was expecting him, the path was strewn with flowers, and a thousand braziers were burning scented woods which perfumed the air. Seated in a gallery from which she could see his arrival, the White Cat waited for him. 'Well, king's son,' she said, 'here you are once more, without a crown.' 'Madam,' said he, 'thanks to your generosity I have earned one twice over; but the fact is that my father is so loth to part with it that it would be no pleasure to me to take it.'

'Never mind,' she answered, 'it's just as well to try and deserve it. As you must take back a lovely princess with you next time I will be on the look-out for one for you. In the meantime let us enjoy ourselves; tonight I have ordered a battle between my cats and the river rats on purpose to amuse you.'

So this year slipped away even more pleasantly than the preceding ones. Sometimes the prince could not help asking the White Cat how it was she could talk. 'Perhaps you are a fairy,' he said. 'Or has some enchanter changed you into a cat?'

But she only gave him answers that told him nothing. Days go by so quickly when one is very happy that it is certain the prince would never have thought of its being time to go back, but one evening as they sat together the White Cat said to him that if he wanted to take a lovely princess home with him the next day he must be prepared to do what she told him.

'Take this sword,' she said, 'and cut off my head!'

'I!' cried the prince, 'I cut off your head! Blanchette darling, how could I do it?'

'I entreat you to do as I tell you, king's son,' she replied.

The tears came into the prince's eyes as he begged her to ask him anything but that – to set him any task she pleased as a proof of his devotion, but to spare him the grief of killing his dear pussy. But nothing he could say altered her determination, and at last he drew his sword, and desperately, with a trembling hand, cut off the little white head. But imagine his astonishment and delight when suddenly a lovely princess stood before him, and, while he was still speechless with amazement, the door opened and a goodly company of knights and ladies entered, each carrying a cat's skin! They hastened with every sign of joy to the princess, kissing her hand and congratulating her on being once more restored to her natural shape.

She received them graciously, but after a few minutes begged that they would leave her alone with the prince, to whom she said: 'You see, prince, that you were right in supposing me to be no ordinary cat. My father reigned over six kingdoms. The queen, my mother, whom he loved dearly, had a passion for travelling and exploring, and when I was only a few weeks old she obtained his permission to visit a certain mountain of which she had heard many marvellous tales, and set out, taking with her a number of her attendants. On the way they had to pass near an old castle belonging to the fairies. Nobody had ever been into it, but it was reported to be full of the most wonderful things, and my mother remembered to have heard that the fairies had in their garden such fruits as were to be seen and tasted nowhere else. She began to wish to try them for herself, and turned her steps in the direction of the garden. On arriving at the door, which blazed with gold and jewels, she ordered her servants to knock loudly, but it was useless; it seemed as if all the inhabitants of the castle must be asleep or dead. Now the more difficult it became to obtain the fruit, the more the pueen was determined that have it she would. So she ordered that they should bring ladders, and get over the wall into the garden; but though the wall did not look very high, and they tied the ladders together to make them very long, it was quite impossible to get to the top.

'The queen was in despair, but as night was coming on she ordered that they should encamp just where they were, and went to bed herself, feeling quite ill, she was so disappointed. In the middle of the night she was suddenly awakened, and saw to her surprise a tiny, ugly old woman seated by her bedside, who said to her: ' "I must say that we consider it somewhat troublesome of your majesty to insist upon tasting our fruit; but to save you annoyance, my sisters and I will consent to give you as much as you can carry away, on one condition – that is, that you shall give us your little daughter to bring up as our own."

' "Ah! my dear madam," cried the Queen, "is there nothing else that you will take for the fruit? I will give you my kingdoms willingly."

' "No," replied the old fairy, "we will have nothing but your little daughter. She shall be as happy as the day is long, and we will give her everything that is worth having in fairyland, but you must not see her again until she is married."

' "Though it is a hard condition," said the Queen, "I consent, for I shall certainly die if I do not taste the fruit, and so I should lose my little daughter either way."

'So the old fairy led her into the castle, and, though it was still the middle of the night, the queen could see plainly that it was far more beautiful than she had been told, which you can easily believe, prince,' said the White Cat, 'when I tell you that it was this castle that we are now in. "Will you gather the fruit yourself, queen?" said the old fairy, "or shall I call it to come to you?"

' "I beg you to let me see it come when it is called," cried the queen; "that will be something quite new." The old fairy whistled twice, then she cried: ' "Apricots, peaches, nectarines, cherries, plums, pears, melons, grapes, apples, oranges, lemons, gooseberries, strawberries, raspberries, come!"

'And in an instant they came tumbling in, one over another, and yet they were neither dusty nor spoilt, and the queen found them quite as good as she had fancied them. You see they grew upon fairy trees.

'The old fairy gave her golden baskets in which to take the fruit away, and it was as much as four hundred mules could carry. Then she reminded the queen of her agreement, and led her back to the camp, and next morning she went back to her kingdom, but before she had gone very far she began to repent of her bargain, and when the king came out to meet her she looked so sad that he guessed that something had happened, and asked what was the matter. At first the queen was afraid to tell him, but when, as soon as they reached the palace, five frightful little dwarfs were sent by the fairies to fetch me, she was obliged to confess what she had promised. The king was very angry, and had the queen and myself shut up in a great tower and safely guarded, and drove the little dwarfs out

of his kingdom; but the fairies sent a great dragon who ate up all the people he met, and whose breath burnt up everything as he passed through the country; and at last, after trying in vain to rid himself of this monster, the king, to save his subjects, was obliged to consent that I should be given up to the fairies. This time they came themselves to fetch me, in a chariot of pearl drawn by sea-horses, followed by the dragon, who was led with chains of diamonds. My cradle was placed between the old fairies, who loaded me with caresses, and away we whirled through the air to a tower which they had built on purpose for me. There I grew up surrounded with everything that was beautiful and rare, and learning everything that is ever taught to a princess, but without any companions but a parrot and a little dog, who could both talk; and receiving every day a visit from one of the old fairies, who came mounted upon the dragon. One day, however, as I sat at my window, I saw a handsome young prince, who seemed to have been hunting in the forest which surrounded my prison, and who was standing and looking up at me. When he saw that I observed him he saluted me with great deference. You can imagine that I was delighted to have someone new to talk to, and in spite of the height of my window our conversation was prolonged till night fell, when my prince reluctantly bade me farewell. But after that he came again many times and at last I consented to marry him, but the question was how was I to escape from my tower. The fairies always supplied me with flax for my spinning, and by great diligence I made enough cord for a ladder that would reach to the foot of the tower; but, alas! just as my prince was helping me to descend it, the crossest and ugliest of the old fairies flew in. Before he had time to defend himself my unhappy lover was swallowed up by the dragon. As for me, the fairies, furious at having their plans defeated (for they intended me to marry the king of the dwarfs, and I utterly refused), changed me into a white cat. When they brought me here I found all the lords and ladies of my father's court awaiting me under the same enchantment, while the people of lesser rank had been made invisible, all but their hands.

'As they laid me under the enchantment the fairies told me all my history, for until then I had quite believed that I was their child, and warned me that my only chance of regaining my natural form was to win the love of a prince who resembled in every way my unfortunate lover.'

'And you have won it, lovely princess,' interrupted the prince.

'You are indeed wonderfully like him,' resumed the princess – 'in voice, in features, and everything; and if you really love me all my troubles will be at an end.'

'And mine too,' cried the prince, throwing himself at her feet, 'if you will consent to marry me.'

'I love you already better than anyone in the world,' she said; 'but now it is time to go back to your father, and we shall hear what he says about it.'

So the prince gave her his hand and led her out, and they mounted the chariot together; it was even more splendid than before, and so was the whole company. Even the horses' shoes were of rubies with diamond nails, and I suppose that is the first time such a thing was ever seen.

As the princess was as kind and clever as she was beautiful, you may imagine what a delightful journey the prince found it, for everything the princess said seemed to him quite charming.

When they came near the castle where the brothers were to meet, the princess got into a chair carried by four of the guards; it was hewn out of one splendid crystal, and had silken curtains, which she drew round her that she might not be seen. The prince saw his brothers walking upon the terrace, each with a lovely princess, and they came to meet him, asking if he had also found a wife. He said that he had found something much rarer – a white cat! At which they laughed very much, and asked him if he was afraid of being eaten up by mice in the palace. And then they set out together for the town. Each prince and princess rode in a splendid carriage; the horses were decked with plumes of feathers, and glittered with gold. After them came the

youngest prince, and last of all the crystal chair, at which everybody looked with admiration and curiosity. When the courtiers saw them coming they hastened to tell the king.

'Are the ladies beautiful?' he asked anxiously.

And when they answered that nobody had ever before seen such lovely princesses he seemed quite annoyed.

However, he received them graciously, but found it impossible to choose between them.

Then turning to his youngest son he said: 'Have you come back alone, after all?'

'Your majesty,' replied the prince, 'will find in that crystal chair a little white cat, which has such soft paws, and mews so prettily, that I am sure you will be charmed with it.'

The king smiled, and went to draw back the curtains himself, but at a touch from the princess the crystal shivered into a thousand splinters, and there she stood in all her beauty; her fair hair floated over her shoulders and was crowned with flowers, and her softly falling robe was of the purest white. She saluted the king gracefully, while a murmur of admiration rose from all around.

'Sire,' she said, 'I am not come to deprive you of the throne you fill so worthily. I have already six kingdoms; permit me to bestow one upon you, and one upon each of your older sons. I ask nothing but your friendship, and your gracious consent to my marriage with your youngest son; we shall still have three kingdoms left for ourselves.' The king and all the courtiers could not conceal their joy and astonishment, and the marriages of the three princes were celebrated at once. The festivities lasted several months, and then each king and queen departed to their own kingdom and lived happily ever after.

The White Dove

A king had two sons. They were a pair of reckless fellows, who always had something foolish to do. One day they rowed out alone on the sea in a little boat. It was beautiful weather when they set out, but as soon as they had got some distance from the shore there arose a terrific storm. The oars went overboard at once, and the little boat was tossed about on the rolling billows like a nutshell. The princes had to hold fast by the seats to keep from being thrown out of the boat.

In the midst of all this they met a wonderful vessel – it was a dough-trough, in which there sat an old woman. She called to them, and said that they could still get to shore alive if they would promise her the son that was next to come to their mother the queen.

'We can't do that,' shouted the princes; 'he doesn't belong to us so we can't give him away.'

'Then you can rot at the bottom of the sea, both of you,' said the old woman; 'but perhaps it may be the case that your mother would rather keep the two sons she has than the one she hasn't got yet.'

Then she rowed away in her dough-trough, while the storm howled still louder than before, and the water dashed over their boat until it was almost sinking. Then the princes thought that there was something in what the old woman had said about their mother, and being, of course, eager to save their lives, they shouted to her, and promised that she should have their brother if she would deliver them from this danger. As soon as they had done so the storm ceased and the waves fell. The boat drove ashore below their father's castle, and both princes were received with open arms by their father and mother, who had suffered great anxiety for them.

The two brothers said nothing about what they had promised, neither at that time nor later on when the queen's third son came, a beautiful boy, whom she loved more than anything else in the world. He was brought up and educated in his father's house until he was full grown, and still his brothers had never seen or heard anything about the witch to whom they had promised him before he was born.

It happened one evening that there arose a raging storm, with mist and darkness. It howled and roared around the king's palace, and in the midst of it there came a loud knock on the door of the hall where the youngest prince was. He went to the door and found there an old woman with a dough-trough on her back, who said to him that he must go with her at once; his brothers had promised him to her if she would save their lives.

'Yes,' said he; 'if you saved my brothers' lives, and they promised me to you, then I will go with you.'

They therefore went down to the beach together, where he had to take his seat in the trough, along with the witch, who sailed away with him, over the sea, home to her dwelling.

The prince was now in the witch's power, and in her service. The first thing she set him to was to pick feathers. 'The heap of feathers that you see here,' said she, 'you must get finished before I come home in the evening, otherwise you shall be set to harder work.' He started to the feathers, and picked and picked until there was only a single feather left that had not passed through his hands. But then there came a whirlwind and sent all the feathers flying, and swept them along the floor into a heap, where they lay as if they were trampled together. He had now to begin all his work over again, but by this time it only wanted an hour to evening, when the witch was to be expected home, and he easily saw that it was impossible for him to be finished by that time.

Then he heard something tapping at the window pane, and a thin voice said, 'Let me in, and I will help you.' It was a white dove, which sat outside the window, and was pecking at it with its beak. He opened the window, and the dove came in and set to work at once, and picked all the feathers out of the heap with its beak. Before the hour was past the feathers were all nicely arranged; the dove flew out at the window, and, at the same moment, the witch came in at the door.

'Well, well,' said she, 'it was more than I would have expected of you to get all the feathers put in order so nicely. However, such a prince might be expected to have neat fingers.'

Next morning the witch said to the prince, 'Today you shall have some easy work to do. Outside the door I have some firewood lying; you must split that for me into little bits that I can kindle the fire with. That will soon be done, but you must be finished before I come home.'

The prince got a little axe and set to work at once. He split and clove away, and thought that he was getting on fast; but the day wore on until it was long past midday, and he was still very far from having finished. He thought, in fact, that the pile of wood rather grew bigger than smaller, in spite of

The Witch comes home

what he took off it; so he let his hand fall by his side, and dried the sweat from his forehead, and was ill at ease, for he knew that it would be bad for him if he was not finished with the work before the witch came home.

Then the white dove came flying and settled down on the pile of wood, and cooed and said, 'Shall I help you?'

'Yes,' said the prince, 'many thanks for your help yesterday, and for what you offer today.' Thereupon the little dove seized one piece of wood after another and split it with its beak. The prince could not take away the wood as quickly as the dove could split it, and in a short time it was all cleft into little sticks.

The dove then flew up on his shoulder and sat there and the prince thanked it, and stroked and caressed its white feathers, and kissed its little red beak. With that it was a dove no longer, but a beautiful young maiden, who stood by his side. She told him then that she was a princess whom the witch had stolen, and had changed to this shape, but with his kiss she had got her human form again; and if he would be faithful to her, and take her to wife, she could free them both from the witch's power.

The prince was quite captivated by the beautiful princess, and was quite willing to do anything whatsoever to get her for himself.

She then said to him, 'When the witch comes home you must ask her to grant you a wish, when you have accomplished so well all that she has demanded of you. When she agrees to this you must ask her straight out for the princess that she has flying about as a white dove. But just now you must take a red silk thread and tie it round my little finger, so that you may be able to recognise me again, into whatever shape she turns me.'

The prince made haste to get the silk thread tied round her little white finger; at the same moment the princess became a dove again and flew away, and immediately after that the old witch came home with her dough-trough on he back.

'Well,' said she, 'I must say that you are clever at your work, and it is something, too, that such princely hands are not accustomed to.'

'Since you are so well pleased with my work,' said the prince, 'you will, no doubt, be willing to give me a little pleasure too, and give me something that I have taken a fancy to.'

'Oh yes, indeed,' said the old woman; 'what is it that you want?'

'I want the princess here who is in the shape of a white dove,' said the prince.

'What nonsense!' said the witch. 'Why should you imagine that there are princesses here flying about in the shape of white doves? But if you will have a princess, you can get one such as we have them.' She then came to him, dragging a shaggy little grey ass with long ears. 'Will you have this?' said she; 'you can't get any other princess!'

The prince used his eyes and saw the red silk thread on one of the ass's hoofs, so he said, 'Yes, just let me have it.'

'What will you do with it?' asked the witch.

'I will ride on it,' said the prince; but with that the witch dragged it away again, and came back with an old, wrinkled, toothless hag, whose hands trembled with age. 'You can have no other princess,' said she. 'Will you have her?'

'Yes, I will,' said the prince, for he saw the red silk thread on the old woman's finger.

At this the witch became so furious that she danced about and knocked everything to pieces that she could lay her hands upon, so that the splinters flew about the ears of the prince and princess, who now stood there in her own beautiful shape.

Then their marriage had to be celebrated, for the witch had to stick to what she had promised, and he must get the princess whatever might happen afterwards.

The princess now said to him, 'At the marriage feast you may eat what you please, but you must not drink anything whatever, for if you do that you will forget me.'

This, however, the prince forgot on the wedding day, and stretched out his hand and took a cup of wine; but the princess was keeping watch over him, and gave him a push with her elbow, so that the wine flew over the tablecloth.

Then the witch got up and laid about her among the plates and dishes, so that the pieces flew about their ears, just as she had done when she was cheated the first time.

They were then taken to the bridal chamber, and the door was shut. Then the princess said, 'Now the witch has kept her promise, but she will do no more if she can help it, so we must fly immediately. I shall lay two pieces of wood in the bed to answer for us when the witch speaks to us. You can take the flowerpot and the glass of water that stands in the window, and we must slip out by that and get away.'

No sooner said than done. They hurried off out into the dark night, the princess leading, because she knew the way, having spied it out while she flew about as a dove.

At midnight the witch came to the door of the room and called in to them, and the two pieces of wood answered her, so that she believed they were there, and went away again. Before daybreak she was at the door again and called to them, and again the pieces of wood answered for them. She thus thought that she had them, and when the sun rose the bridal night was past: she had then kept her promise, and could vent her anger and revenge on both of them. With the first sunbeam she broke into the room, but there she found no prince and no princess – nothing but the two pieces of firewood, which lay in the bed, and stared, and spoke not a word. These she threw on the floor, so that they were splintered into a thousand pieces, and off she hastened after the fugitives.

With the first sunbeam the princess said to the prince, 'Look round; do you see anything behind us?'

'Yes, I see a dark cloud, far away,' said he.

'Then throw the flowerpot over your head,' said she. When this was done there was a large thick forest behind them.

When the witch came to the forest she could not get through it until she went home and brought her axe to cut a path.

A little after this the princess said again to the prince, 'Look round; do you see anything behind us?'

'Yes,' said the prince, 'the big black cloud is there again.'

'Then throw the glass of water over your head,' said she.

When he had done this there was a great lake behind them, and this the witch could not cross until she ran home again and brought her dough-trough.

Meanwhile the fugitives had reached the castle which was the prince's home. They climbed over the garden wall, ran across the garden, and crept in at an open window. By this time the witch was just at their heels, but the princess stood in the window and blew upon the witch; hundreds of white doves flew out of her mouth, fluttered and flapped around the witch's head until she grew so angry that she turned into flint, and there she stands to this day, in the shape of a large flint stone, outside the window.

Within the castle there was great rejoicing over the prince and his bride. His two elder brothers came and knelt before him and confessed what they had done, and said that he alone should inherit the kingdom, and they would always be his faithful subjects.

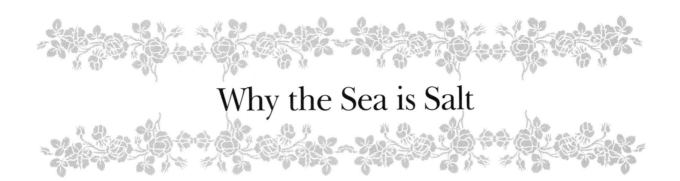

Why the Sea is Salt

Once upon a time, long, long ago, there were two brothers, the one rich and the other poor. When Christmas Eve came, the poor one had not a bite in the house, either of meat or bread; so he went to his brother, and begged him, in God's name, to give him something for Christmas Day. It was by no means the first time that the brother had been forced to give something to him, and he was not better pleased at being asked now than he generally was.

'If you will do what I ask you, you shall have a whole ham,' said he. The poor one immediately thanked him, and promised this.

'Well, here is the ham, and now you must go straight to Dead Man's Hall,' said the rich brother, throwing the ham to him.

'Well, I will do what I have promised,' said the other, and he took the ham and set off. He went on and on for the livelong day, and at nightfall he came to a place where there was a bright light.

'I have no doubt this is the place,' thought the man with the ham.

An old man with a long white beard was standing in the outhouse, chopping yule logs.

'Good-evening,' said the man with the ham.

'Good-evening to you. Where are you going at this late hour?' said the man.

'I am going to Dead Man's Hall, if only I am on the right track,' answered the poor man.

'Oh! yes, you are right enough, for it is here,' said the old man. 'When you get inside they will all want to buy your ham, for they don't get much meat to eat there; but you must not sell it unless you can get the hand-mill which stands behind the door for it. When you come out I will teach you how to stop the hand-mill, which is useful for almost everything.'

So the man with the ham thanked the other for his good advice, and rapped at the door.

When he got in, everything happened just as the old man had said it would: all the people, great and small, came round him like ants on an ant-hill, and each tried to outbid the other for the ham.

'By rights my old woman and I ought to have it for our Christmas dinner, but, since you have set your hearts upon it, I must just give it up to you,' said the man. 'But, if I sell it, I will have the hand-mill which is standing there behind the door.'

At first they would not hear to this, and haggled and bargained with the man, but he stuck to what he had said, and the people were forced to give him the hand-mill. When the man came out again into the yard, he asked the old woodcutter how he was to stop the hand-mill, and when he had learned that, he thanked him and set off home with all the speed he could; but did not get there until after the clock had struck twelve on Christmas Eve.

'Where in the world have you been?' said the old woman. 'Here I have sat waiting hour after hour, and have not even two sticks to lay across each other under the Christmas porridge-pot.'

'Oh! I could not come before; I had something of importance to see about, and a long way to go, too; but now you shall just see!' said the man, and then he set the hand-mill on the table, and bade it first grind light, then a tablecloth, and then meat, and beer, and everything else that was good for a Christmas Eve's supper; and the mill ground all that he ordered. 'Bless me!' said the old woman as one thing after another appeared; and she wanted to know where her husband had got the mill from, but he would not tell her that.

'Never mind where I got it; you can see that it is a good one, and the water that turns it will never freeze,' said the man. So he ground meat and drink, and all kinds of good things, to last all Christmas-tide, and on the third day he invited all his friends to come to a feast.

Now when the rich brother saw all that there was at the banquet and in the house, he was both vexed and angry, for he grudged everything his brother had. 'On Christmas Eve he was so poor that he came to me and begged for a trifle, for God's sake, and now he gives a feast as if he were both a count and a king!' thought he. 'But, for heaven's sake, tell me where you got your riches from,' said he to his brother.

'From behind the door,' said he who owned the mill, for he did not choose to satisfy his brother on that point; but later in the evening, when he had taken a drop too much, he could not refrain from telling how he had come by the hand-mill. 'There you see what has brought me all my wealth!' said he, and brought out the mill, and made it grind first one thing and then another. When the brother saw that, he insisted on having the mill, and after a great deal of persuasion got it; but he had to give three hundred sovereigns for it, and the poor brother was to keep it till the haymaking was over, for he thought: 'If I keep it as long as that, I can make it grind meat and drink that will last many a long year.' During that time you may imagine that the mill did not grow rusty, and when hay-harvest came the rich brother got it, but the other had taken good care not to teach him how to stop it. It was evening when the rich man got the mill home, and in the morning he bade the old woman go out and spread the hay after the mowers, and he would attend to the house himself that day, he said.

So, when dinner-time drew near, he set the mill on the kitchen-table, and said: 'Grind herrings and milk pottage, and do it both quickly and well.'

So the mill began to grind herrings and milk pottage, and first all the dishes and tubs were filled, and then it came out all over the kitchen-floor. The man twisted and turned it, and did all he could to make the mill stop, but, howsoever he turned it and screwed it, the mill went on grinding, and in a short time the pottage rose so high that the man was like to be drowned. So he threw open the parlour door, but it was not long before the mill had ground the parlour full too, and it was with difficulty and danger that the man could go through the stream of pottage and get hold of the door-latch. When he got the door open, he did not stay long in the room, but ran out, and the herrings and pottage came after him, and it streamed out over both farm and field. Now the old woman, who was out spreading the hay, began to think dinner was long in coming, and said to the women and the mowers: 'Though the master does not call us home, we may as well go. It may be that he finds he is not good at making pottage and I should do well to help him.' So they began to straggle homeward, but when they had got a little

way up the hill they met the herrings and pottage and bread, all pouring forth and winding about one over the other, and the man himself in front of the flood. 'Would to heaven that each of you had a hundred stomachs! Take care that you are not drowned in the pottage!' he cried as he went by them as if Mischief were at his heels, down to where his brother dwelt. Then he begged him, for God's sake, to take the mill back again, and that in an instant, for, said he: 'If it grind one hour more the whole district will be destroyed by herrings and pottage.' But the brother would not take it until the other paid him the three hundred sovereigns, and that he was obliged to do. Now the poor brother had both the money and the mill again. So it was not long before he had a farmhouse much finer than that in which his brother lived, but the mill ground him so much money that he covered it with plates of gold; and the farmhouse lay close by the seashore, so it shone and glittered far out to sea. Everyone who sailed by there now had to put in to visit the rich man in the gold farmhouse, and everyone wanted to see the wonderful mill, for the report of it spread far and wide, and there was no one who had not heard tell of it.

After a long, long time came also a skipper, who wished to see the mill. He asked if it could make salt. 'Yes, it could make salt,' said he who owned it, and when the skipper heard that, he wished with all his might and main to have the mill, let it cost what it might, for, he thought, if he had it, he would get off having to sail far away over the perilous sea for freights of salt. At first the man would not hear of parting with it, but the skipper begged and prayed, and at last the man sold it to him, and got many, many thousand sovereigns for it. When the skipper had got the mill on his back he did not stay there long, for he was so afraid that the man would change his mind, and he had no time to ask how he was to stop it grinding, but got on board his ship as fast as he could.

When he had gone a little way out to sea he took the mill on deck. 'Grind salt, and grind both quickly and well,' said the skipper. So the mill began to grind salt, till it spouted out like water, and when the skipper had got the ship filled he wanted to stop the mill, but whichsoever way he turned it, and how much soever he tried, it went on grinding, and the heap of salt grew higher and higher, until at last the ship sank. There lies the mill at the bottom of the sea, and still, day by day, it grinds on; and that is why the sea is salt.

The Wise Men of Gotham

Of Buying of Sheep

There were two men of Gotham, and one of them was going to market to Nottingham to buy sheep, and the other came from the market, and they both met together upon Nottingham bridge.

'Where are you going?' said the one who came from Nottingham.

'Marry,' said he that was going to Nottingham, 'I am going to buy sheep.'

'Buy sheep?' said the other, 'and which way will you bring them home?'

'Marry,' said the other, 'I will bring them over this bridge.'

'By Robin Hood,' said he that came from Nottingham, 'but thou shalt not.'

'By Maid Marion,' said he that was going thither, 'but I will.'

'You will not,' said the one.

'I will.'

Then they beat their staves against the ground one against the other, as if there had been a hundred sheep between them.

'Hold in,' said one; 'beware lest my sheep leap over the bridge.'

'I care not,' said the other; 'they shall not come this way.'

'But they shall,' said the other.

Then the other said: 'If that thou make much to do, I will put my fingers in thy mouth.'

'Will you?' said the other.

Now, as they were at their contention, another man of Gotham came from the market with a sack of meal upon a horse, and seeing and hearing his neighbours at strife about sheep, though there were none between them, said: 'Ah, fools! will you ever learn wisdom? Help me, and lay my sack upon my shoulders.'

They did so, and he went to the side of the bridge, unloosened the mouth of the sack, and shook all his meal out into the river.

'Now, neighbours,' he said, 'how much meal is there in my sack?'

'Marry,' said they, 'there is none at all.'

'Now, by my faith,' said he, 'even as much wit as is in your two heads to stir up strife about a thing you have not.'

Which was the wisest of these three persons, judge yourself.

Of Hedging a Cuckoo

Once upon a time the men of Gotham would have kept the cuckoo so that she might sing all the year, and in the midst of their town they made a hedge round in compass and they got a Cuckoo, and put her into it, and said, 'Sing there all through the year, or thou shalt have neither meat nor water.' The cuckoo, as soon as she perceived herself within the hedge, flew away. 'A vengeance on her!' said they. 'We did not make our hedge high enough.'

Of Sending Cheeses

There was a man of Gotham who went to the market at Nottingham to sell cheese, and as he was going down the hill to Nottingham bridge, one of his cheeses fell out of his wallet and rolled down the hill. 'Ah, gaffer,' said the fellow, 'can you run to market alone? I will send one after another after you.'

Then he laid down his wallet and took out the cheeses, and rolled them down the hill. Some went into one bush; and some went into another.

'I charge you all to meet me near the market-place,' he said, and when the fellow came to the market to meet his cheeses, he stayed there till the

691

market was nearly done. Then he went about to enquire of his friends and neighbours, and other men, if they had seen his cheeses come to the market.

'Who should bring them?' said one of the market men.

'Marry, themselves,' said the fellow; 'they know the way well enough.' But after reflection, he said, 'A vengeance on them all. I did fear, to see them run so fast, that they would run beyond the market. I am now fully persuaded that they must be almost at York.'

Whereupon he forthwith hired a horse to ride to York, to seek his cheeses where they were not, but to this day no man can tell him of his cheeses.

Of Drowning Eels

When Good Friday came, the men of Gotham cast their heads together what to do with their white herrings, their red herrings, their sprats and other salt fish. One consulted with the other, and agreed that such fish should be cast into their pond (which was in the middle of the town), that they might breed against the next year, and every man that had salt fish left cast them into the pool.

'I have many white herrings,' said one.

'I have many sprats,' said another.

'I have many red herrings,' said the other.

'I have much salt fish. Let all go into the pond or pool, and we shall fare like lords next year.'

At the beginning of next year following the men drew near the pond to have their fish, and there was nothing but a great eel. 'Ah,' said they all, 'a mischief on this eel, for he has eaten up all our fish.'

'What shall we do to him?' said one to the others.

'Kill him,' said one.

'Chop him into pieces,' said another.

'Not so,' said another; 'let us drown him.'

'Be it so,' said all. And they went to another pond, and cast the eel into the pond. 'Lie there and shift for yourself, for no help thou shalt have from us;' and they left the eel to drown.

Of Sending Rent

Once on a time the men of Gotham had forgotten to pay their landlord. One said to the other, 'Tomorrow is our payday, and what shall we find to send our money to our landlord?'

The one said, 'This day I have caught a hare, and he shall carry it, for he is light of foot.'

'Be it so,' said all; 'he shall have a letter and a purse to put our money in, and we shall direct him the right way.' So when the letter was written and the money put in a purse, they tied it round the hare's neck, saying, 'First you go to Lancaster, then you must go to Loughborough, and Newarke is our landlord, and commend us to him and there are his dues.'

The hare, as soon as he was out of their hands, ran on along the country way. Some cried, 'You must go to Lancaster first.'

'Let the hare alone,' said another; 'he can tell a nearer way than the best of us all. Let him go.'

Another said, 'It is a subtle hare, let him alone; he will not keep the highway for fear of dogs.'

Of Counting

On a certain time there were twelve men of Gotham who went fishing, and some went into the water and some stayed on dry ground; and, as they were coming back, one of them said, 'We have ventured much this day wading; I pray God that none of us that did come from home be drowned.'

'Marry,' said one, 'let us see about that. Twelve of us came out;' and every man did count eleven, and the twelfth man did never count himself.

'Alas!' said one to another, 'one of us is drowned.' They went back to the brook where they had been fishing, and looked up and down for him that was drowned, and made great lamentation. A courtier came riding by, and he did ask what they were seeking, and why they were so sorrowful. 'Oh,' said they, 'this day we came to fish in this brook, and there were twelve of us, and one is drowned.'

'Why,' said the courtier, 'count me how many of you there be,' and one counted eleven and did not count himself. 'Well,' said the courtier, 'what will you give me if I find the twelfth man?'

'Sir,' said they, 'all the money we have.'

'Give me the money,' said the courtier; and he began with the first, and gave him such a whack over the shoulders that he groaned, and he said, 'There is one;' and he served all of them that they groaned; but when he came to the last he gave him a good blow, saying, 'Here is the twelfth man.'

'God bless you on your heart,' said all the company; 'you have found our neighbour.'

The Yellow Dwarf

Once upon a time there lived a queen who had been the mother of a great many children, and of them all only one daughter was left. But then *she* was worth at least a thousand.

Her mother, who, since the death of the king, her father, had nothing in the world she cared for so much as this little princess, was so terribly afraid of losing her that she quite spoiled her, and never tried to correct any of her faults. The consequence was that this little person, who was as pretty as possible, and was one day to wear a crown, grew up so proud and so much in love with her own beauty that she despised everyone else in the world.

The queen, her mother, by her caresses and flatteries, helped to make her believe that there was nothing too good for her. She was dressed almost always in the prettiest frocks, as a fairy, or as a queen going out to hunt, and the ladies of the court followed her dressed as forest fairies.

And to make her more vain than ever the queen caused her portrait to be taken by the cleverest painters and sent it to several neighbouring kings with whom she was very friendly.

When they saw this portrait they fell in love with the princess – every one of them, but upon each it had a different effect. One fell ill, one went quite crazy, and a few of the luckiest set off to see her as soon as possible, and these poor princes became her slaves the moment they set eyes on her.

Never has there been a gayer court. Twenty delightful kings did everything they could think of to make themselves agreeable, and after having spent ever so much money in giving a single entertainment, thought themselves very lucky if the princess said, 'That's pretty.'

All this admiration vastly pleased the queen. Not a day passed but her daughter received seven or eight thousand sonnets, and as many elegies, madrigals and songs, which were sent her by all the poets in the world. All the prose and the poetry that was written just then was about Bellissima – for that was the princess's name – and all the bonfires that they had were made of these verses, which crackled and sparkled better than any other sort of fuel.

Bellissima was already fifteen years old, and every one of the princes wished to marry her, but not one dared to say so. How could they when they knew that any of them might have cut off his head five or six times a day just to please her, and she would have thought it a mere trifle, so little did she care? You may imagine how hard-hearted her lovers thought her; and the queen, who wished to see her married, did not know how to persuade her to think of it seriously.

'Bellissima,' she said, 'I do wish you would not be so proud. What makes you despise all these nice kings? I wish you to marry one of them, and you do not try to please me.'

'I am so happy,' Bellissima answered: 'do leave me in peace, madam. I don't want to care for anyone.'

'But you would be very happy with any of these princes,' said the queen, 'and I shall be very angry if you fall in love with anyone who is not worthy of you.'

But the princess thought so much of herself that she did not consider any one of her lovers clever or handsome enough for her; and her mother, who was getting really angry at her determination not to be married, began to wish that she had not allowed her to have her own way so much.

At last, not knowing what else to do, she resolved to consult a certain witch who was called the Fairy of the Desert. Now this was very difficult to do, as she was guarded by some terrible lions; but happily the queen had heard a long time before that whoever wanted to pass these lions safely must throw to them a cake made of millet flour, sugar-candy and crocodile's eggs. This cake she prepared with her own hands, and putting it in a little basket, she set out to seek the fairy. But as she was not used to walking far, she soon felt very tired and sat down at the foot of a tree to rest, and presently fell fast asleep. When she awoke she was dismayed to find her basket empty. The cake was all gone! and, to make matters worse, at that moment she heard the roaring of the great lions, who had found out that she was near and were coming to look for her.

'What shall I do?' she cried; 'I shall be eaten up!' and being too frightened to run a single step, she began to cry, and leaned against the tree under which she had been asleep.

Just then she heard someone say: 'H'm, h'm!'

She looked all round her, and then up the tree, and there she saw a little tiny man, who was eating oranges.

'Oh! queen,' said he, 'I know you very well, and I know how much afraid you are of the lions; and you are quite right too, for they have eaten many other people: and what can you expect, as you have not any cake to give them?'

'I must make up my mind to die,' said the poor queen. 'Alas! I should not care so much if only my dear daughter were married.'

'Oh! you have a daughter?' cried the Yellow Dwarf (who was so called because he *was* a dwarf and had such a yellow face, and lived in the orange

There she saw a little tiny man, who was eating oranges

694

tree). 'I'm really glad to hear that, for I've been looking for a wife all over the world. Now, if you will promise that she shall marry me, not one of the lions, tigers or bears shall touch you.'

The queen looked at him and was almost as much afraid of his ugly little face as she had been of the lions before, so that she could not speak a word.

'What! you hesitate, madam,' cried the dwarf. 'You must be very fond of being eaten up alive.'

And, as he spoke, the queen saw the lions, which were running down a hill towards them. Each one had two heads, eight feet and four rows of teeth, and their skins were bright red and as hard as turtle shells.

At this dreadful sight, the poor queen, who was trembling like a dove when it sees a hawk, cried out as loud as she could, 'Oh! dear Mr Dwarf, Bellissima shall marry you.'

'Oh, indeed!' said he disdainfully. 'Bellissima is pretty enough, but I don't particularly want to marry her – you can keep her.'

'Oh! noble sir,' said the queen in great distress, 'do not refuse her. She is the most charming princess in the world.'

'Oh! well,' he replied, 'out of charity I will take her; but be sure and don't forget that she is mine.'

As he spoke a little door opened in the trunk of the orange tree, in rushed the queen, only just in time, and the door shut with a bang in the faces of the lions.

The queen was so confused that at first she did not notice another little door in the orange tree, but presently it opened and she found herself in a field of thistles and nettles. It was encircled by a muddy ditch, and a little farther on was a tiny thatched cottage, out of which came the Yellow Dwarf with a very jaunty air. He wore wooden shoes and a little yellow coat, and as he had no hair and very long ears he looked altogether a shocking little object.

'I am delighted,' said he to the queen, 'that, as you are to be my mother-in-law, you should see the little house in which your Bellissima will live with me. With these thistles and nettles she can feed a donkey which she can ride whenever she likes; under this humble roof no weather can hurt her; she will drink the water of this brook and eat frogs – which grow very fat about here; and then she will have me always with her, handsome, agreeable and amusing, as you see me now. For if her shadow stays by her more closely than I do, I shall be surprised.'

The unhappy queen, seeing all at once what a

miserable life her daughter would have with this dwarf could not bear the idea, and fell down insensible without saying a word.

When she revived she found to her great surprise that she was lying in her own bed at home, and, what was more, that she had on the loveliest lace night cap that she had ever seen in her life. At first she thought that all her adventures, the terrible lions, and her promise to the Yellow Dwarf that he should marry Bellissima, must have been a dream, but there was the new cap with its beautiful ribbon and lace to remind her that it was all true, which made her so unhappy that she could neither eat, drink nor sleep for thinking of it.

The princess, who, in spite of her wilfulness, really loved her mother with all her heart, was much grieved when she saw her looking so sad, and often asked her what was the matter; but the queen, who didn't want her to find out the truth, only said that she was ill, or that one of her neighbours was threatening to make war against her. Bellissima knew quite well that something was being hidden from her – and that neither of these was the real reason of the queen's uneasiness. So she made up her mind that she would go and consult the Fairy of the Desert about it, especially as she had often heard how wise she was, and she thought that at the same time she might ask her advice as to whether it would be as well to be married, or not.

So, with great care, she made some of the proper cake to pacify the lions, and one night went up to her room very early, pretending that she was going to bed; but instead of that, she wrapped herself in a long white veil, and went down a secret staircase, and set off all by herself to find the witch.

But when she got as far as the same fatal

The princess went down a secret staircase

orange tree, and saw it covered with flowers and fruit, she stopped and began to gather some of the oranges – and then, putting down her basket, she sat down to eat them. But when it was time to go on again the basket had disappeared and, though she looked everywhere, not a trace of it could she find. The more she hunted for it, the more frightened she got, and at last she began to cry. Then all at once she saw before her the Yellow Dwarf.

'What's the matter with you, my pretty one?' said he. 'What are you crying about?'

'Alas!' she answered; 'no wonder that I am crying, seeing that I have lost the basket of cake that was to help me to get safely to the cave of the Fairy of the Desert.'

'And what do you want with her, pretty one?' said the little monster, 'for I am a friend of hers, and, for the matter of that, I am quite as clever as she is.'

'The queen, my mother,' replied the princess, 'has lately fallen into such deep sadness that I fear that she will die; and I am afraid that perhaps I am the cause of it, for she very much wishes me to be married, and I must tell you truly that as yet I have not found anyone I consider worthy to be my husband. So for all these reasons I wished to talk to the fairy.'

'Do not give yourself any further trouble, princess,' answered the dwarf. 'I can tell you all you want to know better than she could. The queen, your mother, has promised you in marriage – '

'Has promised *me*!' interrupted the princess. 'Oh! no. I'm sure she has not. She would have told me if she had. I am too much interested in the matter for her to promise anything without my consent – you must be mistaken.'

'Beautiful princess,' cried the dwarf suddenly, throwing himself on his knees before her, 'I flatter myself that you will not be displeased at her choice when I tell you that it is to *me* she has promised the happiness of marrying you.'

'You!' cried Bellissima, starting back. 'My mother wishes me to marry you! How can you be so silly as to think of such a thing?'

'Oh! it isn't that I care much to have that honour,' cried the dwarf angrily; 'but here are the lions coming; they'll eat you up in three mouthfuls, and there will be an end of you and your pride.'

And, indeed, at that moment the poor princess heard their dreadful howls coming nearer and nearer.

'What shall I do?' she cried. 'Must all my happy days come to an end like this?'

The malicious dwarf looked at her and began to laugh spitefully. 'At least,' said he, 'you have the satisfaction of dying unmarried. A lovely princess like you must surely prefer to die rather than be the wife of a poor little dwarf like myself.'

'Oh, don't be angry with me,' cried the princess, clasping her hands. 'I'd rather marry all the dwarfs in the world than die in this horrible way.'

'Look at me well, princess, before you give me your word,' said he. 'I don't want you to promise me in a hurry.'

'Oh!' cried she, 'the lions are coming. I have looked at you enough. I am so frightened. Save me this minute, or I shall die of terror.'

Indeed, as she spoke she fell down insensible, and when she recovered she found herself in her own little bed at home; how she got there she could not tell, but she was dressed in the most beautiful lace and ribbons, and on her finger was a little ring, made of a single red hair, which fitted so tightly that, try as she might, she could not get it off.

When the princess saw all these things, and remembered what had happened, she, too, fell into the deepest sadness, which surprised and alarmed the whole court, and the queen more than anyone else. A hundred times she asked Bellissima if anything was the matter with her; but she always said that there was nothing.

At last the chief men of the kingdom, anxious to see their princess married, sent to the queen to beg her to choose a husband for her as soon as possible. She replied that nothing would please her better, but that her daughter seemed so unwilling to marry; she recommended them to go and talk to the princess about it themselves so this they at once did. Now Bellissima was much less proud since her adventure with the Yellow Dwarf, and she could not think of a better way of getting rid of the little monster than by marrying some powerful king, therefore she replied to their request much more favourably than they had hoped, saying that, though she was very happy as she was, still, to please them, she would consent to marry the King of the Gold Mines. Now he was a very handsome and powerful prince, who had been in love with the princess for years, but had not thought that she would ever care about him at all. You can easily imagine how delighted he was when he heard the news, and how angry it made all the other kings to lose for ever the hope of marrying the princess; but, after all, Bellissima could not have married

twenty kings – indeed, she had found it quite difficult enough to choose one, for her vanity made her believe that there was nobody in the world who was worthy of her.

Preparations were begun at once for the grandest wedding that had ever been held at the palace. The King of the Gold Mines sent such immense sums of money that the whole sea was covered with the ships that brought it. Messengers were sent to all the gayest and most refined courts, particularly to the Court of France, to seek out everything rare and precious to adorn the princess, although her beauty was so perfect that nothing she wore could make her look prettier. At least that is what the King of the Gold Mines thought, and he was never happy unless he was with her.

As for the princess, the more she saw of the king the more she liked him; he was so generous, so handsome and clever, that at last she was almost as much in love with him as he was with her. How happy they were as they wandered about in the beautiful gardens together, sometimes listening to sweet music! And the king used to write songs for Bellissima. This is one that she liked very much:

> In the forest all is gay
> When my princess walks that way.
> All the blossoms then are found
> Downward fluttering to the ground,
> Hoping she may tread on them.
> And bright flowers on slender stem
> Gaze up at her as she passes
> Brushing lightly through the grasses.
> Oh! my princess, birds above
> Echo back our songs of love,
> As through this enchanted land
> Blithe we wander, hand in hand.

They really were as happy as the day was long. All the king's unsuccessful rivals had gone home in despair. They said goodbye to the princess so sadly that she could not help being sorry for them.

'Ah! madam,' the King of the Gold Mines said to her 'how is this? Why do you waste your pity on these princes, who love you so much that all their trouble would be well repaid by a single smile from you?'

'I should be sorry,' answered Bellissima, 'if you had not noticed how much I pitied these princes who were leaving me for ever; but for you, sire, it is very different: you have every reason to be pleased with me, but they are going sorrowfully away, so you must not grudge them my compassion.'

How happy they were as they wandered about in the beautiful gardens together, sometimes listening to sweet music! And the king used to write songs for Bellissima.

The King of the Gold Mines was quite overcome by the princess's good-natured way of taking his interference, and, throwing himself at her feet, he kissed her hand a thousand times and begged her to forgive him.

At last the happy day came. Everything was ready for Bellissima's wedding. The trumpets sounded, all the streets of the town were hung with flags and strewn with flowers, and the people ran in crowds to the great square before the palace. The queen was so overjoyed that she had hardly been able to sleep at all, and she got up before it was light to give the necessary orders and to choose the jewels that the princess was to wear. These were nothing less than diamonds, even to her shoes, which were

covered with them, and her dress of silver brocade was embroidered with a dozen of the sun's rays. You may imagine how much these had cost; but then nothing could have been more brilliant, except the beauty of the princess! Upon her head she wore a splendid crown, her lovely hair waved nearly to her feet, and her stately figure could easily be distinguished among all the ladies who attended her.

The King of the Gold Mines was not less noble and splendid; it was easy to see by his face how happy he was, and everyone who went near him returned loaded with presents, for all round the great banqueting hall had been arranged a thousand barrels full of gold, and numberless bags made of velvet embroidered with pearls and filled with money, each one containing at least a hundred thousand gold pieces, which were given away to everyone who liked to hold out his hand, which numbers of people hastened to do, you may be sure – indeed, some found this by far the most amusing part of the wedding festivities.

The queen and the princess were just ready to set out with the king when they saw, advancing towards them from the end of the long gallery, two great basilisks, dragging after them a very badly made box; behind them came a tall old woman, whose ugliness was even more surprising than her extreme old age. She wore a ruff of black taffeta, a red velvet hood, and a farthingale all in rags, and she leaned heavily upon a crutch. This strange old woman, without saying a single word, hobbled three times round the gallery, followed by the basilisks, then stopping in the middle, and brandishing her crutch threateningly, she cried: 'Ho, ho, queen! Ho, ho, princess! Do you think you are going to break with impunity the promise that you made to my friend the Yellow Dwarf? I am the Fairy of the Desert; without the Yellow Dwarf and his orange tree my great lions would soon have eaten you up, I can tell you, and in Fairyland we do not suffer ourselves to be insulted like this. Make up your minds at once what you will do, for I vow that you shall marry the Yellow Dwarf. If you don't, may I burn my crutch!'

'Ah! princess,' said the queen, weeping, 'what is this that I hear? What have you promised?'

'Ah! my mother,' replied Bellissima sadly, 'what did *you* promise, yourself?'

The King of the Gold Mines, indignant at being kept from his happiness by this wicked old woman, went up to her, and threatening her with his sword, said: 'Get away out of my country at once, and for ever, miserable creature, lest I take your life, and so rid myself of your malice.'

He had hardly spoken these words when the lid of the box fell back on the floor with a terrible noise, and to their horror out sprang the Yellow Dwarf, mounted upon a great Spanish cat. 'Rash youth!' he cried, rushing between the Fairy of the Desert and the king. 'Dare to lay a finger upon this illustrious fairy! Your quarrel is with me only. I am your enemy and your rival. That faithless princess who would have married you is promised to me. See if she has not upon her finger a ring made of one of my hairs. Just try to take it off, and you will soon find out that I am more powerful than you are!'

'Wretched little monster!' said the king; 'do you dare to call yourself the princess's lover, and to lay claim to such a treasure? Do you know that you are a dwarf – that you are so ugly that one cannot bear to look at you – and that I should have killed you myself long before this if you had been worthy of such a glorious death?'

The Yellow Dwarf, deeply enraged at these words, set spurs to his cat, which yelled horribly, and leaped hither and thither – terrifying everybody except the brave king, who pursued the dwarf closely, till he, drawing a great knife with which he was armed, challenged the king to meet him in single combat, and rushed down into the courtyard of the palace with a terrible clatter. The king, quite provoked, followed him hastily, but they had hardly taken their places facing one another, and the whole court had only just had time to rush out upon the balconies to watch what was going on, when suddenly the sun became as red as blood, and it was so dark that they could scarcely see at all. The thunder crashed, and the lightning seemed as if it must burn up everything; the two basilisks appeared, one on each side of the bad dwarf, like giants, mountains high, and fire flew from their mouths and ears, until they looked like flaming furnaces. None of these things could terrify the noble young king, and the boldness of his looks and actions reassured those who were looking on, and perhaps even embarrassed the Yellow Dwarf himself; but even *his* courage gave way when he saw what was happening to his beloved princess. For the Fairy of the Desert, looking more terrible than before, mounted upon a winged griffin, and with long snakes coiled round her neck, had given her such a blow with the lance she carried that Bellissima fell into the queen's arms bleeding and senseless. Her fond mother, feeling as much hurt by the blow as the princess herself, uttered such piercing cries and lamentations that the king, hearing them, entirely lost his courage and presence of mind. Giving up the combat, he flew towards the princess, to rescue or to die with her; but the Yellow Dwarf was too quick for him. Leaping with his Spanish cat upon the balcony, he snatched Bellissima from the queen's arms, and before any of the ladies of the court could stop him he had sprung upon the roof of the palace and disappeared with his prize.

The king, motionless with horror, looked on despairingly at this dreadful occurrence, which he was quite powerless to prevent, and to make matters worse his sight failed him, everything became dark, and he felt himself carried along through the air by a strong hand.

This new misfortune was the work of the wicked Fairy of the Desert, who had come with the Yellow Dwarf to help him carry off the princess, and had fallen in love with the handsome young King of the Gold Mines directly she saw him. She thought that if she carried him off to some frightful cavern and chained him to a rock, then the fear of death would make him forget Bellissima and become her slave. So, as soon as they reached the place, she gave him back his sight, but without releasing him from his chains, and by her magic power she appeared before him as a young and beautiful fairy, and pretended to have come there quite by chance.

'What do I see?' she cried. 'Is it *you*, dear prince? What misfortune has brought you to this dismal place?'

The king, who was quite deceived by her altered appearance, replied: 'Alas! beautiful fairy, the fairy who brought me here first took away my sight, but by her voice I recognised her as the Fairy of the Desert, though what she should have carried me off for I cannot tell you.'

'Ah!' cried the pretended fairy, 'if you have fallen into *her* hands, you won't get away until you have married her. She has carried off more than one prince like this, and she will certainly have anything she takes a fancy to.' While she was thus pretending to be sorry for the king, he suddenly noticed her feet, which were like those of a griffin, and knew in a moment that this must be the Fairy of the Desert, for her feet were the one thing she could not change, however pretty she might make her face.

Without seeming to have noticed anything, he

said, in a confidential way: 'Not that I have any dislike of the Fairy of the Desert, but I really cannot endure the way in which she protects the Yellow Dwarf and keeps me chained here like a criminal. It is true that I love a charming princess, but if the fairy should set me free my gratitude would oblige me to love her only.'

'Do you really mean what you say, sire?' said the fairy, quite deceived.

'Surely,' replied the king; 'how could I deceive you? You see it is so much more flattering to my vanity to be loved by a fairy than by a simple princess. But, even if I am dying of love for her, I shall pretend to hate her until I am set free.'

The Fairy of the Desert, quite taken in by these words, resolved at once to transport the king to a pleasanter place. So, making him mount her chariot, to which she had harnessed swans instead of the bats which generally drew it, away she flew with him. But imagine the distress of the king when, from the giddy height at which they were rushing through the air, he saw his beloved princess in a castle built of polished steel, the walls of which reflected the sun's rays so hotly that no one could approach it without being burnt to a cinder! Bellissima was sitting near by in a little thicket by a brook, leaning her head upon her hand and weeping bitterly, but just as they passed she looked up and saw the king and the Fairy of the Desert. Now, the fairy was so clever that she could not only seem beautiful to the king, but even the poor princess thought her the most lovely being she had ever seen.

'What!' she cried; 'was I not unhappy enough in this lonely castle to which that frightful Yellow Dwarf brought me? Must I also be made to know that the King of the Gold Mines ceased to love me as soon as he lost sight of me? But who can my rival be, whose fatal beauty is greater than mine?'

While she was saying this, the king, who really loved her as much as ever, was feeling terribly sad at being so rapidly torn away from his beloved princess, but he knew too well how powerful the fairy was to have any hope of escaping from her except by great patience and cunning.

The Fairy of the Desert had also seen Bellissima, and she tried to read in the king's eyes the effect that this unexpected sight had had upon him.

'No one can tell you what you wish to know better than I can,' said he. 'This chance meeting with an unhappy princess for whom I once had a passing fancy, before I was lucky enough to meet you, has affected me a little, I admit, but you are so much more to me than she is that I would rather die than leave you.'

'Ah, sire,' she said, 'can I believe that you really love me so much?'

'Time will show, madam,' replied the king; 'but if you wish to convince me that you have some regard for me, do not, I beg of you, refuse to aid Bellissima.'

'Do you know what you are asking?' said the Fairy of the Desert, frowning, and looking at him suspiciously. 'Do you want me to employ my art against the Yellow Dwarf, who is my best friend, and take away from him a proud princess whom I cannot but look upon as my rival?'

The king sighed, but made no answer – indeed, what was there to be said to such a clear-sighted person? At last they reached a vast meadow, gay with all sorts of flowers; a deep river surrounded it, and many little brooks murmured softly under the shady trees, where it was always cool and fresh. A little way off stood a splendid palace, the walls of which were of transparent emeralds. As soon as the swans which drew the fairy's chariot had alighted under a porch, which was paved with diamonds and had arches of rubies, they were greeted on all sides by thousands of beautiful beings, who came to meet them joyfully, singing these words:

'When Love within a heart would reign,
Useless to strive against him 'tis.
The proud but feel a sharper pain,
And make a greater triumph his.'

The Fairy of the Desert was delighted to hear them sing of her triumphs; she led the king into the most splendid room that can be imagined, and left him alone for a little while, just that he might not feel that he was a prisoner; but he felt sure that she had not really gone quite away, but was watching him from some hiding-place. So walking up to a great mirror, he said to it, 'Trusty counsellor, let me see what I can do to make myself agreeable to the charming Fairy of the Desert; for I can think of nothing but how to please her.'

And he at once set to work to curl his hair, and, seeing upon a table a grander coat than his own, he put it on carefully. The fairy came back so delighted that she could not conceal her joy.

'I am quite aware of the trouble you have taken to please me,' said she, 'and I must tell you that you have succeeded perfectly already. You see it is not difficult to do if you really care for me.'

The king, who had his own reasons for wishing to keep the old fairy in a good humour, did not spare pretty speeches, and after a time he was allowed to walk by himself upon the seashore. The Fairy of the Desert had by her enchantments raised such a terrible storm that the boldest pilot would not venture out in it, so she was not afraid of her prisoner's being able to escape; and he found it some relief to think sadly over his terrible situation without being interrupted by his cruel captor.

Presently, after walking wildly up and down, he wrote these verses upon the sand with his stick:

At last may I upon this shore
Lighten my sorrow with soft tears.
Alas! alas! I see no more
My love, who yet my sadness cheers.

'And thou, O raging, stormy sea,
Stirred by wild winds, from depth to height,
Thou hold'st my loved one far from me,
And I am captive to thy might.

'My heart is still more wild than thine,
For fate is cruel unto me.
Why must I thus in exile pine?
Why is my princess snatched from me?

'O! lovely nymphs, from ocean caves,
Who know how sweet true love may be,
Come up and calm the furious waves
And set a desperate lover free!

While he was still writing he heard a voice which attracted his attention in spite of himself. Seeing that the waves were rolling in higher than ever, he looked all round, and presently saw a lovely lady floating gently towards him upon the crest of a huge billow, her long hair spread all about her; in one hand she held a mirror, and in the other a comb, and instead of feet she had a beautiful tail like a fish, with which she swam.

The king was struck dumb with astonishment at this unexpected sight; but as soon as she came within speaking distance, she said to him, 'I know how sad you are at losing your princess and being kept a prisoner by the Fairy of the Desert; if you like I will help you to escape from this fatal place, where you may otherwise have to drag on a weary existence for thirty years or more.'

The King of the Gold Mines hardly knew what answer to make to this proposal. Not because he did not wish very much to escape, but he was afraid that this might be only another device by which the Fairy of the Desert was trying to deceive him. As he hesitated the mermaid, who guessed his thoughts, said to him: 'You may trust me: I am not trying to entrap you. I am so angry with the Yellow Dwarf and the Fairy of the Desert that I am not likely to wish to help them, especially since I constantly see your poor princess, whose beauty and goodness make me pity her so much; and I tell you that if you will have confidence in me I will help you to escape.'

'I trust you absolutely,' cried the king, 'and I will do whatever you tell me; but if you have seen my princess I beg of you to tell me how she is and what is happening to her.'

'We must not waste time in talking,' said she. 'Come with me and I will carry you to the Castle of Steel, and we will leave upon this shore a figure so like you that even the fairy herself will be deceived.'

So saying, she quickly collected a bundle of seaweed, and, blowing it three times, she said: 'My friendly seaweed, I order you to stay here stretched upon the sand until the Fairy of the Desert comes to take you away.' And at once the seaweed became like the king, who stood looking in great astonishment, for it was even dressed in a coat like his, and lay there pale and still as the king himself might have lain if one of the great waves had overtaken him and thrown him senseless upon the shore. And then the mermaid caught up the king, and away they swam joyfully together.

'Now,' said she, 'I have time to tell you about the princess. In spite of the blow which the Fairy of the Desert gave her, the Yellow Dwarf compelled her to mount behind him upon his terrible Spanish cat; but she soon fainted away with pain and terror, and did not recover till they were within the walls of his frightful Castle of Steel. Here she was received by the prettiest girls it was possible to find, who had been carried there by the Yellow Dwarf, who hastened to wait upon her and showed her every possible attention. She was laid upon a couch covered with cloth of gold, embroidered with pearls as big as nuts.'

'Ah!' interrupted the King of the Gold Mines, 'if Bellissima forgets me, and consents to marry him, I shall break my heart.'

'You need not be afraid of that,' answered the mermaid, 'the princess thinks of no one but you, and the frightful dwarf cannot persuade her to look at him.'

'Pray go on with your story,' said the king.

'What more is there to tell you?' replied the

mermaid. 'Bellissima was sitting in the wood when you passed, and saw you with the Fairy of the Desert, who was so cleverly disguised that the princess took her to be prettier than herself; you may imagine her despair, for she thought that you had fallen in love with her.'

'She believes that I love her!' cried the king. 'What a fatal mistake! What is to be done to undeceive her?'

'You know best,' answered the mermaid, smiling kindly at him. 'When people are as much in love with one another as you two are, they don't need advice from anyone else.'

As she spoke they reached the Castle of Steel, the side next the sea being the only one which the Yellow Dwarf had left unprotected by the dreadful burning walls.

'I know quite well,' said the mermaid, 'that the princess is sitting by the brookside, just where you saw her as you passed, but as you will have many enemies to fight with before you can reach her, take this sword; armed with it you may dare any danger, and overcome the greatest difficulties, only beware of one thing – that is, never to let it fall from your hand. Farewell; now I will wait by that rock, and if you need my help in carrying off your beloved princess I will not fail you, for the queen, her mother, is my best friend, and it was for her sake that I went to rescue you.'

So saying, she gave to the king a sword made from a single diamond, which was more brilliant than the sun. He could not find words to express his gratitude, but he begged her to believe that he fully appreciated the importance of her gift, and would never forget her help and kindness.

We must now go back to the Fairy of the Desert. When she found that the king did not return, she hastened out to look for him, and reached the shore, with a hundred of the ladies of her train, loaded with splendid presents for him. Some carried baskets full of diamonds, others golden cups of wonderful workmanship, and amber, coral and pearls; others, again, balanced upon their heads bales of the richest and most beautiful stuffs, while the rest brought fruit and flowers, and even birds. But what was the horror of the fairy, who followed this gay troop, when she saw, stretched upon the sands, the image of the king which the mermaid had made with the seaweed. Struck with astonishment and sorrow, she uttered a terrible cry, and threw herself down beside the pretended king, weeping, and howling, and

calling upon her eleven sisters, who were also fairies, and who came to her assistance. But they were all taken in by the image of the king, for, clever as they were, the mermaid was still cleverer, and all they could do was to help the Fairy of the Desert to make a wonderful monument over what they thought was the grave of the King of the Gold Mines. But while they were collecting jasper and porphyry, agate and marble, gold and bronze, statues and devices, to immortalise the king's memory, he was thanking the good mermaid and begging her still to help him, which she graciously promised to do as she disappeared; and then he set out for the Castle of Steel. He walked fast, looking anxiously round him, and longing once more to see his darling Bellissima, but he had not gone far before he was surrounded by four terrible sphinxes who would very soon have torn him to pieces with their sharp talons if it had not been for the mermaid's diamond sword. For, no sooner had he flashed it before their eyes than down they fell at his feet quite helpless, and he killed them with one blow. But he had hardly turned to continue his search when he met six dragons covered with scales that were harder than iron. Frightful as this encounter was the king's courage was unshaken, and by the aid of his wonderful sword he cut them in pieces one after the other. Now he hoped his difficulties were over, but at the next turning he was met by one which he did not know how to overcome. Four-and-twenty pretty and graceful nymphs advanced towards him, holding garlands of flowers, with which they barred the way.

'Where are you going, sire?' they said; 'it is our duty to guard this place, and if we let you pass great misfortunes will happen to you and to us. We beg you not to insist upon going on. Do you want to kill four-and-twenty girls who have never displeased you in any way?'

The king did not know what to do or to say. It went against all his ideas as a knight to do anything a lady begged him not to do; but, as he hesitated, a voice in his ear said: 'Strike! strike! and do not spare, or your princess is lost for ever!'

So, without reply to the nymphs, he rushed forward instantly, breaking their garlands, and scattering them in all directions; and then went on without further hindrance to the little wood where he had seen Bellissima. She was seated by the brook looking pale and weary when he reached her, and he would have thrown himself down at

Four-and-twenty pretty and graceful nymphs advanced towards him, holding garlands of flowers,
with which they barred the way

her feet, but she drew herself away from him with as much indignation as if he had been the Yellow Dwarf.

'Ah! princess,' he cried, 'do not be angry with me. Let me explain everything. I am not faithless or to blame for what has happened. I am a miserable wretch who has displeased you without being able to help himself.'

'Ah!' cried Bellissima, 'did I not see you flying through the air with the loveliest being imaginable? Was that against your will?'

'Indeed it was, princess,' he answered; 'the wicked Fairy of the Desert, not content with chaining me to a rock, carried me off in her chariot to the other end of the earth, where I should even now be a captive but for the unexpected help of a friendly mermaid, who brought me here to rescue you, my princess, from the unworthy hands that hold you. Do not refuse the aid of your most faithful lover.' So saying, he threw himself at her feet and held her by her robe. But, alas! in so doing he let fall the magic sword, and the Yellow Dwarf, who was crouching behind a lettuce, no sooner saw it than he sprang out and seized it, well knowing its wonderful power.

The princess gave a cry of terror on seeing the dwarf, but this only irritated the little monster; muttering a few magical words he summoned two giants, who bound the king with great chains of iron.

'Now,' said the dwarf, 'I am master of my rival's fate, but I will give him his life and permission to depart unharmed if you, princess, will consent to marry me.'

'Let me die a thousand times rather,' cried the unhappy king.

'Alas!' cried the princess, 'must you die? Could anything be more terrible?'

'That you should marry that little wretch would be far more terrible,' answered the king.

'At least,' continued she, 'let us die together.'

'Let me have the satisfaction of dying for you, my princess,' said he.

'Oh, no, no!' she cried, turning to the dwarf; 'rather than that I will do as you wish.'

'Cruel princess!' said the king, 'would you make my life horrible to me by marrying another before my eyes?'

'Not so,' replied the Yellow Dwarf; 'you are a rival of whom I am too much afraid; you shall not see our marriage.' So saying, in spite of Bellissima's tears and cries, he stabbed the king to the heart with the diamond sword.

The poor princess, seeing her lover lying dead at her feet, could no longer live without him; she sank down by him and died of a broken heart.

So ended these unfortunate lovers, whom not even the mermaid could help, because all the magic power had been lost with the diamond sword.

As to the wicked dwarf, he preferred to see the princess dead rather than married to the King of the Gold Mines; and the Fairy of the Desert, when she heard of the king's adventures, pulled down the grand monument which she had built, and was so angry at the trick that had been played on her that she hated him as much as she had loved him before.

The kind mermaid, grieved at the sad fate of the lovers, caused them to be changed into two tall palm trees, which stand always side by side, whispering together of their faithful love and caressing one another with their interlacing branches.

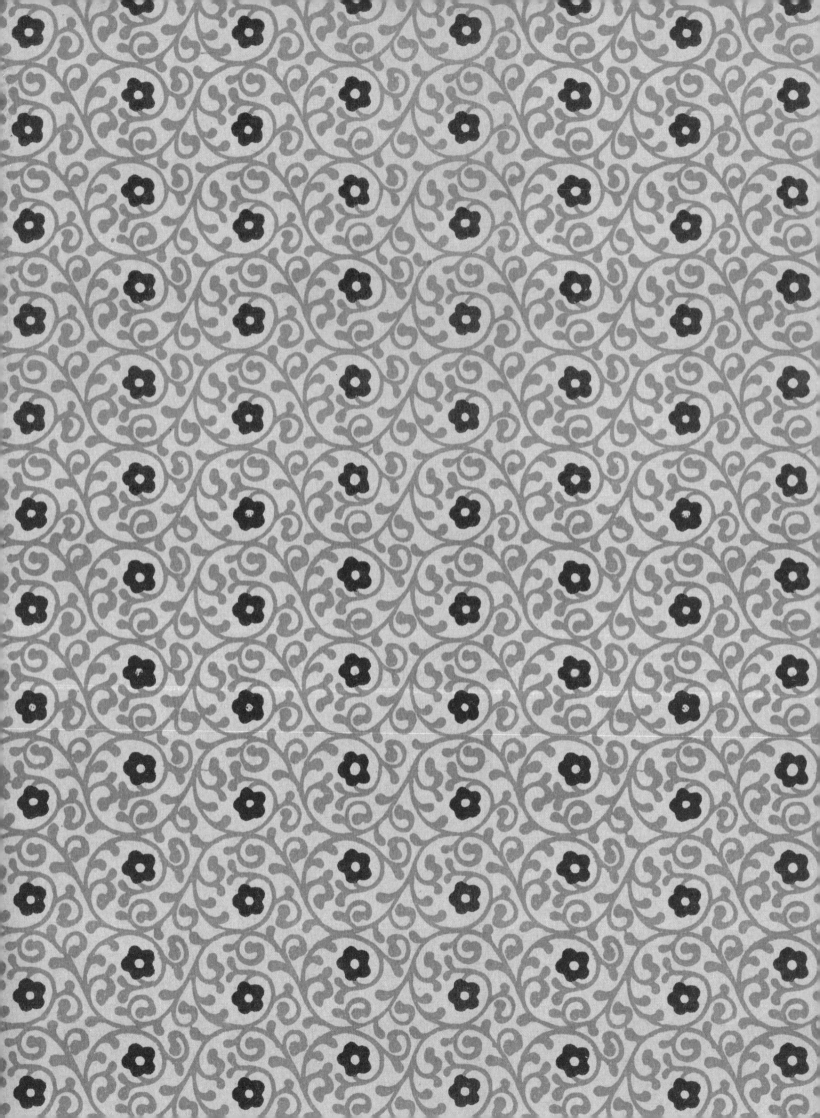